Complete Works of Baruch Spinoza

Baruch Spinoza;
Original Thinkers Institute

GRAPEVINE INDIA

Published by

GRAPEVINE INDIA PUBLISHERS PVT LTD

www.grapevineindia.com

Delhi | Mumbai

email: grapevineindiapublishers@gmail.com

Ordering Information:

Quantity sales: Special discounts are available on quantity

purchases by corporations, associations, and others.

For details, reach out to the publisher.

First published by Grapevine India 2024

Copyright © Grapevine 2024

CONTENTS

A SHORT TREATISE ON GOD, MAN AND HIS WELL-BEING

PREVIOUSLY WRITTEN IN the Latin tongue by B.D.S. for the use of his disciples who wanted to devote themselves to the study of Ethics and true Philosophy. And now translated into the Dutch language for the use of the Lovers of Truth and Virtue: so that they who spout so much about it, and put their dirt and filth into the hands of simpletons as though it were ambergris, may just have their mouths stopped, and cease to profane what they do not understand: God, themselves, and how to help people to have regard for each others well-being, and how to heal those whose mind is sick, in a spirit of tenderness and tolerance, after the example of the Lord Christ, our best Teacher

ETHICA OR MORAL SCIENCE

COMPOSED IN TWO PARTS

WHICH TREAT

I. Of Gods Existence, and Attributes II. Of Man, with reference to the character and origin of his Passions, the use of his reason in this respect, and the means whereby he is educated to his Happiness and supreme freedom

Also an Appendix, containing a brief account of the nature of Substance — as well as that of the human Soul, and its union with the Body

COMPOSED BY

BENEDICTUS DE SPINOZA

FIRST PART. ON GOD

CHAPTER I.
THAT GOD EXISTS

AS REGARDS THE first, namely, whether there is a God, this, we say, can be proved.

I. In the first place, a priori thus:

1. Whatever we clearly and distinctly know to belong to the nature of a thing, we can also truly affirm of that thing. Now we can know clearly and distinctly that existence belongs to the nature of God; (Understand the definite nature through which a thing is what it is, and which can by no means be removed from it without at the same time destroying that thing: thus, for instance, it belongs to the essence of a mountain that it should have a valley, or the essence of a mountain is that it has a valley; this is truly eternal and immutable, and must always be included in the concept of a mountain, even if it never existed, or did not exist now.)

Therefore...

Otherwise also thus:

2. The essence of things are from all eternity, and unto all eternity shall remain immutable; The existence of God is essence; Therefore...

II. A posteriori, thus:

If man has an idea of God, then God must exist formaliter; (From the definition which follows in chapter 2, namely, that God has infinite attributes, we can prove his existence thus: Whatever we clearly and distinctly see to belong to the nature of a thing, that we can also with truth affirm of that thing; now to the nature of a being that has infinite attributes belongs existence, which is an attribute; therefore... To assert that this may well be affirmed of the idea, but not of the thing itself, is false: for the Idea does not really consist of the attribute which belongs to this being, so that that which is affirmed is [affirmed] neither of the thing, nor of that which is affirmed of the thing; so that there is a great difference between the Idea and the Ideaturn therefore what is affirmed of the thing is not affirmed of the Idea, and vice versa Now, man has an idea of God; Therefore...

The first we prove thus:

If there is an idea of God, then the cause thereof must exist formaliter, and contain in itself all that the idea has objective; Now there is an idea of God; Therefore...

In order to prove the first part of this argument we state the following principles, namely:

1. That the number of knowable things is infinite;

2. That a finite understanding cannot apprehend the infinite;

3. That a finite understanding, unless it is determined by something external, cannot through itself know anything; because, just as it has no power to know all things equally, so little also has it the power to begin or to commence to know this, for instance, sooner than that, or that sooner than this. Since, then, it can do neither the one nor the other it can know nothing.

The first (or the major premiss) is proved thus:

If the imagination of man were the sole cause of his ideas, then it would be impossible that he should be able to apprehend anything, but he can apprehend something; Therefore...

The first is proved by the first principle, namely, that the knowable things are infinitely numerous. Also, following the second principle, man cannot know all, because the human understanding is finite, and if not determined by external things to know this sooner than that, and that sooner than this, then according to the third principle it should be impossible for it to know anything.

(Further, to say that this idea is a fiction, this also is false: for it is impossible to have this [idea] if it [the ideatum] does not exist; this is shown on pages 37-8, and we also add the following:

It is quite true that when an idea has first come to us from a particular thing, and we have generalised it in abstracto, then our understanding may fancy various things about it, and we can add to it many other attributes abstracted from other things. But it is impossible to do this without a prior knowledge of the things themselves from which these abstractions have been made. Once, however, it is assumed that this idea [of God] is a fiction, then all other ideas that we have must be fictions no less. If this is so, whence comes it that we find such a great difference among them? For as regards some we see that it is impossible they should exist; e g., all monsters supposed to be composed of two natures, such as an animal that should be both a bird and a horse, and the like, for which it is impossible to have a place in Nature, which we find differently constituted; other ideas may, but need not, exist; whether, however, they exist or do not exist, their essence is always necessary, such is the idea of a triangle, and that of the love in the soul apart from the body, etc, so that even if I at first thought that I had imagined these, I am nevertheless compelled afterwards to say that they are, and would be, the same no less even if neither I nor anybody had ever thought about them. They are, consequently, not merely imagined by me, and must also have outside me a subjectum other than myself, without which subjectum they cannot be In addition to these there is yet a third idea, and it is an only one; this one carries with it necessary existence, and not, like the foregoing, the mere possibility of existence for, in the case of those, their essence was indeed necessary, but not their existence, while in its case, both its existence and its essence are necessary, and it is nothing without them. I therefore see now that the truth, essence, or existence of anything never depends on me: for, as was shown with reference to the second kind of ideas, they are what they are independently of me, whether as regards their essence alone, or as regards both essence and existence. 1 find this to be true also, indeed much more so, of this third unique idea; not only does it not depend on me, but on the contrary, he alone must be the subjectum of that which I affirm of him. Consequently, if he did not exist, I should not be able to assert anything at all about him, although this can be done in the case of other things, even when they do not exist He must also be, indeed, the subjectum of all other things.

From what has been said so far it is clearly manifest that the idea of infinite attributes in the perfect being is no fiction; we shall, however, still add the following. According to the foregoing consideration of Nature, we have so far not been able to discover more than two attributes only which belong to this all-perfect being. And these give us nothing adequate to satisfy us that this is all of which this perfect being consists, quite the contrary, we find in us a something which openly tells us not only of more, but of infinite perfect attributes, which must belong to this perfect being before he can be said to be perfect And whence comes this idea of perfection? This something cannot be the outcome of these two [attributes]: for two can only yield two, and not an infinity. Whence then? From myself, never; else I must be able to give what I did not possess. Whence, then, but from the infinite attributes themselves which tell us that they are, without however telling us, at the same time, what they are; for only of two do we know what they are.)

From all this the second point is proved, namely, that the cause of a marts ideas is not his imagination but some external cause, which compels him to apprehend one thing sooner than another, and it is no other than this, that the things whose essentia objectiva is in his understanding exist formaliter, and are nearer to him than other things. If, then, man has the idea of God, it is clear that God must exist formaliter, though not eminenter, as there is nothing more real or more excellent beside or outside him. Now, that man has the idea of God, this is clear, because he knows his attributes, which attributes cannot be derived from [man] himself, because he is imperfect. And that he knows these attributes is evident from this, namely, that he knows that the infinite cannot be obtained by putting together divers finite parts; that there cannot be two infinites, but only one; that it is perfect and immutable, for we know that nothing seeks, of itself, its own annihilation, and also that it cannot change into anything better, because it is perfect, which it would not be in that case, or also that such a being cannot be subjected to anything outside it, since it is omnipotent, and so forth.

From all this, then, it follows clearly that we can prove both a priori and a posteriori that God exists. Better, indeed, a priori. For things which are proved in the latter way [a posteriori] must be proved through their external causes, which is a manifest imperfection in them, inasmuch as they cannot make themselves known through themselves, but only through external causes. God, however, who is the first cause of all things, and also the cause of himself [causa sui], makes himself known through himself. Hence one need not attach much importance to the saying of Thomas Aquinas, namely, that God could not be proved a priori because he, forsooth, has no cause.

CHAPTER II.
WHAT GOD IS

NOW THAT WE have proved above that God is, it is time to show what he is. Namely, we say that he is a being of whom all or infinite attributes are predicated of which attributes every one is infinitely perfect in its kind. Now, in order to express our views clearly, we shall premise the four following propositions:

(The reason is this, since Nothing can have no attributes, the All must have all attributes, and just as Nothing has no attribute because it is Nothing, so that which is Something has attributes because it is Something. Hence, the more it is Something, the more attributes it must have, and consequently God being the most perfect, and all that is Anything, he must also have infinite, perfect, and all attributes)

1. That there is no finite substance, but that every substance must be infinitely perfect in its kind, that is to say, that in the infinite understanding of God no substance can be more perfect than that which already exists in Nature.

(Once we can prove that there can be no Finite Substance, then all substance must without limitation belong to the divine being. We do it thus: 1. It must either have limited itself or some other must have limited it. It could not have done so itself, because having been infinite it would have had to change its whole essence. Nor can it be limited by another, for this again must be either finite or infinite, the former is impossible, therefore the latter, therefore it [i.e.., the other thing] is God. He must, then, have made it finite because he lacked either the power or the will [to make it infinite], but the first [supposition] is contrary to his omnipotence, the second is contrary to his goodness. 2. That there can be no finite substance is clear from this, namely, that, if so, it would necessarily have something which it would have from Nothing, which is impossible. For whence can it derive that wherein it differs from God Certainly not from God, for he has nothing imperfect or finite, etc. So, whence then but from Nothing? Therefore there is no substance other than infinite. Whence it follows, that there cannot be two like infinite substances, for to posit such necessitates limitation. And from this, again, it follows that one substance cannot produce another; thus)

2. That there are not two like substances.

3. That one substance cannot produce another.

4. That in the infinite understanding of God there is no other substance than that which is formaliter in Nature.

As regards the first, namely, that there is no finite substance, etc., should any one want to maintain the opposite, we would ask the following question, namely, whether this substance is finite through itself, whether it has made itself thus finite and did not want to make itself less finite; or whether it is thus finite through its cause, which cause either could not or would not give more? The first [alternative] is not true, because it is impossible that a substance should have wanted to make itself finite, especially a substance which had come into existence through itself. Therefore, I say, it is made finite by its cause, which is necessarily God. Further, if it is finite through its cause, this must be so either because its cause could not give more, or because it would not give more. That he should not have been able to give more would contradict his omnipotence; that he should not have been willing to give more, when he could well do so, savours of ill-will, which is nowise in God, who is all goodness and perfection.

As regards the second, that there are not two like substances, we prove this on the ground that each substance is perfect in its kind; for if there were two alike they would necessarily limit one another, and would consequently not be infinite, as we have already shown before.

As to the third, namely, that one substance cannot produce another: should any one again maintain the opposite, we ask whether the cause, which is supposed to produce this substance, has or has not the same attributes as the produced [substance], The latter is impossible, because something cannot come from nothing; therefore the former. And then we ask whether in the attribute which is presumed to be the cause of this produced [substance], there is just as much perfection as in the produced substance, or less, or more. Less, we say, there cannot be, for the reasons given above. More, also not, we say, because in that case this second one would be finite, which is opposed to what has already been proved by us. Just as much, then; they are therefore alike, and are two like substances, which clearly conflicts with our previous demonstration. Further, that which is created is by no means produced from Nothing, but must necessarily have been produced from something existing. But that something should have come forth from this, and that it should nonetheless have this something even after it has issued from it, that we cannot grasp with our understanding. Lastly, if we would seek the cause of the substance which is the origin of the things which issue from its attribute, then it behoves us to seek also the cause of that cause, and then again the cause of that cause, et sic in infinitum; so that if we must necessarily stop and halt somewhere, as indeed we must, it is necessary to stop at this only substance.

As regards the fourth, that there is no substance or attribute in the infinite understanding of God other than what exists "formaliter' in Nature, this can be, and is, proved by us: (1) from the infinite power of God, since in him there can be no cause by which he might have been induced to create one sooner or more than another; (2) from the simplicity of his will; (3) because he cannot omit to do what is good, as we shall show afterwards; (4) because it would be impossible for that which does not now exist to come into existence, since one substance cannot produce another. And, what is more, in that case there would be more infinite substances not in existence than there are in existence, which is absurd. From all this it follows then: that of Nature all in all is predicated, and that consequently Nature consists of infinite attributes, each of which is perfect in its kind. And this is just equivalent to the definition usually given of God.

Against what we have just said, namely, that there is no thing in the infinite understanding of God but what exists formaliter in Nature, some want to argue in this way: If God has created all, then he can create nothing more; but that he should be able to create nothing more conflicts with his omnipotence; therefore...

Concerning the first, we admit that God can create nothing more. And with regard to the second, we say that we own, if God were not able to create all that could be created, then it would conflict with his omnipotence; but that is by no means the case if he cannot create what is self-contradictory; as it is, to say that he has created all, and also that he should be able to create still more. Assuredly it is a far greater perfection in God that he has created all that was in his infinite understanding than if he had not created it, or, as they say, if he had never been able to create it. But why say so much about it? Do they not themselves argue thus or must they not argue thus from God's omniscience: If God is omniscient then he can know nothing more; but that God can know nothing more is incompatible with his perfection; therefore...? But if God has all in his understanding, and, owing to his infinite perfection, can know nothing more, well then, why can we not say that he has also created all that he had in his understanding, and has made it so that it exists or should exist formaliter in Nature?

Since, then, we know that all alike is in the infinite understanding of God, and that there is no cause why he should have created this sooner and more than that, and that he could have produced all things in a moment, so let us see, for once, whether we cannot use against them the same weapons which they take up against us; namely, thus:

If God can never create so much that he cannot create more, then he can never create what he can create; but that he cannot create what he can create is self-contradictory. Therefore...

Now the reasons why we said that all these attributes, which are in Nature, are but one single being, and by no means different things (although we can know them clearly and distinctly the one without the other, and the other without another), are these:

1. Because we have found already before that there must be an infinite and perfect being, by which nothing else can be meant than such a being of which all in all must be predicated. Why? [Because] to a being which has any essence attributes must be referred, and the more essence one ascribes to it, the more attributes also must one ascribe to it, and consequently if a being is infinite then its attributes also must be infinite, and this is just what we call a perfect being.

2. Because of the unity which we see everywhere in Nature. If there were different beings in it then it would be impossible for them to unite with one another.

3. Because although, as we have already seen, one substance cannot produce another, and if a substance does not exist it is impossible for it to begin to exist, we see, nevertheless, that in no substance (which we nonetheless know to exist in Nature), when considered separately, is there any necessity to be real, since existence does not pertain to its separate essence. So it must necessarily follow that Nature, which results from no causes, and which we nevertheless know to exist, must necessarily be a perfect being to which existence belongs.

From all that we have so far said it is evident, then, that we posit extension as an attribute of God; and this seems not at all appropriate to a perfect being: for since extension is divisible, the perfect being would have to consist of parts, and this is altogether inapplicable to God, because he is a simple being. Moreover, when extension is divided it is passive, and with God (who is never passive, and cannot be affected by any other being, because he is the first efficient cause of all) this can by no means be the case.

To this we reply: (1) that "part" and "whole" are not true or real entities, but only "things of reason," and consequently there are in Nature neither whole nor parts. (2) A thing composed of different parts must be such that the parts thereof, taken separately, can be conceived and understood one without another. Take, for instance, a clock which is composed of many different wheels, cords, and other things; in it, I say, each wheel, cord, etc., can be conceived and understood separately, without the composite whole being necessary thereto. Similarly also in the case of water, which consists of straight oblong particles, each part thereof can be conceived and understood, and can exist without the whole; but extension, being a substance, one cannot say of it that it has parts, since it can neither diminish nor increase, and no parts thereof can be understood apart, because by its nature it must be infinite. And that it must be such, follows from this, namely, because if it were not such, but consisted of parts, then it would not be infinite by its nature, as it is said to be; and it is impossible to conceive parts in an infinite nature, since by their nature all parts are finite.' Add to this still: if it consisted of different parts then it should be intelligible that supposing some parts thereof to be annihilated, extension might remain all the same, and not be annihilated together with the annihilation of some of its parts; this is clearly contradictory in what is infinite by its own nature and can never be, or be conceived, as limited or finite. Further, as regards the parts in Nature, we maintain that division, as has also been said already before, never takes place in substance, but always and only in the mode of substance. Thus, if I want to divide water, I only divide the mode of substance, and not substance itself. And whether this mode is that of water or something else it is always the same.

Division, then, or passivity, always takes place in the mode; thus when we say that man passes away or is annihilated, then this is understood to apply to man only insofar as he is such a composite being, and a mode of substance, and not the substance on which he depends.

Moreover, we have already stated, and we shall repeat it later, that outside God there is nothing at all, and that he is an Immanent Cause. Now, passivity, whenever the agent and the patient are different entities, is a palpable imperfection, because the patient must necessarily be dependent on that which has caused the passivity from outside; it has, therefore, no place in God, who is perfect. Furthermore, of such an agent who acts in himself it can never be said that he has the imperfection of a patient, because he is not affected by another; such, for instance, is the case with the understanding, which, as the philosophers also assert, is the cause of its ideas, since, however, it is an immanent cause, what right has one to say that it is imperfect, howsoever frequently it is affected by itself? Lastly, since substance is [the cause] and the origin of all its modes, it may with far greater right be called an agent than a patient. And with these remarks we consider all adequately answered.

It is further objected, that there must necessarily be a first cause which sets body in motion, because when at rest it is impossible for it to set itself in motion. And since it is clearly manifest that rest and motion exist in Nature, these must, they think, necessarily result from an external cause. But it is easy for us to reply to this; for we concede that, if body were a thing existing through itself, and had no other attributes than length, breadth, and depth, then, if it really rested there would be in it no cause whereby to begin to move itself; but we have already stated before that Nature is a being of which all attributes are predicated, and this being so, it can be lacking in nothing wherewith to produce all that there is to be produced.

Having so far discussed what God is, we shall say but a word, as it were, about his attributes: that those which are known to us consist of two only, namely, Thought and Extension; for here we speak only of attributes which might be called the proper attributes of God, through which we come to know him [as he is] in himself, and not [merely] as he acts [towards things] outside himself. All else, then, that men ascribe to God beyond these two attributes, all that (if it otherwise pertains to him) must be either an "extraneous denomination," such as that he exists through himself, is Eternal, One, Immutable, etc., or, I say, has reference to his activity, such as that he is a cause, predestines, and rules all things: all which are properties of God, but give us no information as to what he is. But how and in what manner these attributes can nevertheless have a place in God we shall explain in the following chapters. But, for the better understanding of this and in further exposition thereof, we have thought it well and have decided to add the following arguments consisting of a [Dialogue].

FIRST DIALOGUE. BETWEEN THE UNDERSTANDING, LOVE, REASON, AND DESIRE

LOVE: I SEE, Brother, that both my essence and perfection depend on your perfection; and since the perfection of the object which you have conceived is your perfection, while from yours again mine proceeds, so tell me now, I pray you, whether you have conceived such a being as is supremely perfect, not capable of being limited by any other, and in which I also am comprehended.

UNDERSTANDING: I for my part consider Nature only in its totality as infinite, and supremely perfect, but you, if you have any doubts about it, ask Reason, she will tell you.

REASON: TO me the truth of the matter is indubitable, for if we would limit Nature then we should, absurdly enough, have to limit it with a mere Nothing we avoid this absurdity by stating that it is One Eternal Unity, infinite, omnipotent, etc., that is, that Nature is infinite and that all is contained therein; and the negative of this we call Nothing.

DESIRE: Ah indeed! It is wondrously congruous to suppose that Unity is in keeping with the Difference which I observe everywhere in Nature. But how? I see that thinking substance has nothing in common with extended substance, and that the one limits [not] the other; and if, in addition to these substances, you want to posit yet a third one which is perfect in all respects, then look how you involve yourself in manifest contradictions; for if this third one is placed outside the first two, then it is wanting in all the attributes which belong to those two, but this can never be the case with a whole outside of which there is nothing. Moreover if this being is omnipotent and perfect, then it must be such because it has made itself, and not because another has made it; that, however, which could produce both itself and yet another besides would be even more omnipotent. And lastly, if you call it omniscient then it is necessary that it should know itself; and, at the same time, you must know that the knowledge of oneself alone is less than the knowledge of oneself together with the knowledge of other substances. All these are manifest contradictions. I would, therefore, have advised Love to rest content with what I show her, and to look about for no other things.

LOVE: What now, O dishonourable one, have you shown me but what would result in my immediate ruin. For, if I had ever united myself with what you have shown me, then from that moment I should have been persecuted by the two archenemies of the human race, namely, Hatred and Remorse, and sometimes also by

Oblivion; and therefore I turn again to Reason only to proceed and stop the mouths of these foes.

REASON: What you say, O Desire, that there are different substances, that, I tell you, is false; for I see clearly that there is but One, which exists through itself, and is a support to all other attributes. And if you will refer to the material and the mental as substances, in relation to the modes which are dependent on them, why then, you must also call them modes in relation to the substance on which they depend: for they are not conceived by you as existing through themselves. And in the same way that willing, feeling, understanding, loving, etc., are different modes of that which you call a thinking substance, in which you bring together and unite all these in one, so I also conclude, from your own proofs, that Both Infinite Extension and Thought together with all other infinite attributes (or, according to your usage, other substances) are only modes of the One, Eternal, Infinite Being, who exists through himself; and from all these we posit, as stated, An Only One or a Unity outside which nothing can be imagined to be.°

DESIRE: Methinks I see a very great confusion in this argument of yours; for, it seems you will have it that the whole must be something outside of or apart from its parts, which is truly absurd. For all philosophers are unanimous in saying that "whole" is a second notion, and that it is nothing in Nature apart from human thought. Moreover, as I gather from your example, you confuse whole with cause: for, as I say, the whole only consists of and [exists] through its parts, and so it comes that you represent the thinking power as a thing on which the Understanding, Love, etc., depend. But you cannot call it a Whole, only a Cause of the Effects just named by you.

REASON: I see decidedly how you muster all your friends against me, and that, after the method usually adopted by those who oppose the truth, you are designing to achieve by quibbling what you have not been able to accomplish with your fallacious reasoning. But you will not succeed in winning Love to your side by such means. Your assertion, then, is, that the cause (since it is the Originator of the effects) must therefore be outside these. But you say this because you only know of the transeunt and not of the immanent cause, which by no means produces anything outside itself, as is exemplified by the Understanding, which is the cause of its ideas. And that is why I called the understanding (insofar as, or because, its ideas depend on it) a cause; and on the other hand, since it consists of its ideas, a whole: so also God is both an Immanent Cause with reference to his works or creatures, and also a whole, considered from the second point of view.

SECOND DIALOGUE. BETWEEN ERASMUS AND THEOPHILUS RELATING PARTLY TO THE PRECEDING, PARTLY TO THE FOLLOWING SECOND PART

ERASMUS: I HAVE heard you say, Theophilus, that God is a cause of all things, and, at the same time, that he can be no other than an Immanent cause. Now, if he is an immanent cause of all things, how then can you call him a remote cause? For, that is impossible in the case of an Immanent cause.

THEOPHILUS: When I said that God is a remote cause, I only said it with reference to the things [which God has produced mediately, and not with reference to those] which God (without any other conditions beyond his mere existence) has produced immediately; but on no account did I mean to call him a remote cause absolutely: as you might also have clearly gathered from my remarks. For, I also said that in some respects we can call him a remote cause.

ERASMUS: I understand now adequately what you want to say; but I note also that you have said, that the effect of the immanent cause remains united with its cause in such a way that together they constitute a whole. Now, if this is so, then, methinks, God cannot be an immanent cause. For, if he and that which is produced by him together form a whole, then you ascribe to God at one time more essence than at another time. I pray you, remove these doubts for me.

THEOPHILUS: If, Erasmus, you want to extricate yourself from this confusion, then mark well what I am going to tell you now. The essence of a thing does not increase through its union with another thing with which it constitutes a whole; on the contrary, the first remains unchanged. I will give you an illustration, so that you may understand me the better. An image-carver has made from wood various forms after the likeness of the parts of the human body; he takes one of these, which has the form of a human breast, joins it to another, which has the form of a human head, and of these two he makes a whole, which represents the upper part of a human body; would you therefore say that the essence of the head has increased because it has been joined to the breast? That would be erroneous, because it is the same that it was before. For the sake of greater clearness let me give you another illustration, namely, an idea that I have of a triangle, and another resulting from an extension of one of the angles, which extended or extending angle is necessarily equal to the two interior opposite angles, and so forth. These, I say, have produced a new idea, namely, that the three angles of the triangle are equal to two right angles. This idea is so connected with the first, that it can neither be, nor be conceived without the same. Mark well now that although the new idea is joined to the preceding one, the essence of the preceding idea does not undergo any change in consequence; on the contrary, it remains without the slightest change. The same you may also observe in every idea which produces love in itself: this love in no way adds to the essence of the idea. But why multiply illustrations? since you can see it clearly in the subject which I have been illustrating and which we are discussing now. I have distinctly stated that all attributes, which depend on no other cause, and whose definition requires no genus pertain to the essence of God; and since the created things are not competent to establish an attribute, they do not increase the essence of God, however intimately they become united to him. Add to this, that "whole" is but a thing of Reason, and does not differ from the general except in this alone that the general results from various Disconnected individuals, the Whole, from various United individuals; also in this, that the General only comprises parts of the same kind, but the Whole, parts both the same and different in kind.

ERASMUS: SO far as this is concerned you have satisfied me. But, in addition to this, you have also said, that the effect of the inner cause cannot perish so long as its cause lasts; this, I well see, is certainly true, but if this is so, then how can God be an inner cause of all things, seeing that many things perish? After your previous distinction you will say, that God is really a cause of the effects which he has produced immediately, without any other conditions except his attributes alone; and that these cannot perish so long as their cause endures; but that you do not call God an inner cause of the effects whose existence does not depend on him immediately, but which have come into being through some other thing, except insofar as their causes do not operate, and cannot operate, without God, nor also outside him, and that for this reason also, since they are not produced immediately by God, they can perish. But this does not satisfy me. For I see that you conclude, that the human understanding is immortal, because it is a product which God has produced in himself. Now it is impossible that more than the attributes of God should have been necessary in order to produce such an understanding; for, in order to be a being of such supreme perfection, it must have been created from eternity, just like all other things which depend immediately on God. And I have heard you say so, if I am not mistaken. And this being so, how will you reconcile this without leaving over any difficulties?

THEOPHILUS: It is true, Erasmus, that the things (for the existence of which no other thing is required, except the attributes of God) which have been created immediately by him have been created from eternity. It is to be remarked, however, that although in order that a thing may exist there is required a special modification and a thing beside the attributes of God, for all that, God does not cease to be able to produce a thing immediately. For, of the necessary things which are required to bring things into existence, some are there in order that they should produce the thing, and others in order that the thing should be capable of being produced. For example, I want to have light in a certain room; I kindle a light, and this lights up the room through itself; or I open a window [shutter], now this act of opening does not itself give light, but still it brings it about that the light can enter the room. Likewise in order to set a body in motion another body is required that shall have all the motion that is to pass from it to the other. But in order to produce in us an idea of God there is no need for another special thing that shall have what is to be produced in us, but only such a body in Nature whose idea is necessary in order to represent God immediately. This you could also have gathered from my remarks: for I said that God is only known through himself, and not through something else. However, I tell you this, that so long as we have not such a clear idea of God as shall unite us with him in such a way that it will not let us love anything beside him, we cannot truly say that we are united with God, so as to depend immediately on him. If there is still anything that you may have to ask, leave it for another time; just now circumstances require me to attend to other matters. Farewell.

ERASMUS: Nothing at present, but I shall ponder what you have just told me till the next opportunity. God be with you.

CHAPTER III.
THAT GOD IS A CAUSE OF ALL THINGS

WE SHALL NOW begin to consider those attributes [of God] which we called Propia. And, first of all, how God is a cause of all things.

Now, we have already said above that one substance cannot produce another; and that God is a being of whom all attributes are predicated; whence it clearly follows that all other things can by no means be, or be understood, apart from or outside him. Wherefore we may say with all reason that God is a cause of all things.

As it is usual to divide the efficient cause in eight divisions, let me, then, inquire how and in what sense God is a cause.

First, then, we say that he is an emanative or productive cause of his works; and, insofar as there is activity, an active or operating cause, which we regard as one and the same, because they involve each other.

Secondly, he is an immanent, and not a transeunt cause, since all that he produces is within himself, and not outside him, because there is nothing outside him.

Thirdly, God is a free cause, and not a natural cause, as we shall make clear and manifest when we come to consider whether God can omit to do what he does, and then it will also be explained wherein true freedom consists.

Fourthly, God is a cause through himself, and not by accident; this will become more evident from the discussion on Predestination.

Fifthly, God is a principal cause of his works which he has created immediately, such as movement in matter, etc.; in which there is no place for a subsidiary [instrumental] cause, since this is confined to particular things; as when he dries the sea by means of a strong wind, and so forth in the case of all particular things in Nature.

The subsidiary provoking cause is not [found] in God, because there is nothing outside him to incite him. The predisposing cause, on the other hand, is his perfection itself; through it he is a cause of himself, and, consequently, of all other things.

Sixthly, God alone is the first or Initial cause, as is evident from our foregoing proof.

Seventhly, God is also a Universal cause, but only insofar as he produces various things; otherwise this can never be predicated of him, as he needs no one in order to produce any results.

Eighthly, God is the proximate cause of the things that are infinite, and immutable, and which we assert to have been created immediately by him, but, in one sense, he is the remote cause of all particular things.

CHAPTER IV.

ON GOD'S NECESSARY ACTIVITY

WE DENY THAT God can omit to do what he does, and we shall also prove it when we treat of Predestination; when we will show that all things necessarily depend on their causes. But, in the second place, this conclusion also follows from the perfection of God; for it is true, beyond a doubt, that God can make everything just as perfect as it is conceived in his Idea; and just as things that are conceived by him cannot be conceived by him more perfectly than he conceives them, so all things can be made by him so perfect that they cannot come from him in a more perfect condition. Again, when we conclude that God could not have omitted to do what he has done, we deduce this from his perfection; because, in God, it would be an imperfection to be able to omit to do what he does; we do not, however, suppose that there is a subsidiary provoking cause in God that might have moved him to action, for then he were no God.

But now, again, there is the controversy whether, namely, of all that is in his Idea, and which he can realise so perfectly, whether, I say, he could omit to realise anything, and whether such an omission would be a perfection in him. Now, we maintain that, since all that happens is done by God, it must therefore necessarily be predetermined by him, otherwise he would be mutable, which would be a great imperfection in him. And as this predetermination by him must be from eternity, in which eternity there is no before or after, it follows irresistibly that God could never have predetermined things in any other way than that in which they are determined now, and have been from eternity, and that God could not have been either before or without these determinations. Further, if God should omit to do anything, then he must either have some cause for it, or not; if he has, then it is necessary that he should omit doing it; if he has not, then it is necessary that he should not omit to do it; this is self-evident. Moreover, in a created thing it is a perfection to exist and to have been produced by God, for, of all imperfection, nonexistence is the greatest imperfection; and since God desires the welfare and perfection of all things, it would follow that if God desired that a certain thing should not exist, then the welfare and perfection of this thing must be supposed to consist in its nonexistence, which is self-contradictory. That is why we deny that God can omit to do what he does. Some regard this as blasphemy, and as a belittling of God; but such an assertion results from a misapprehension of what constitutes true freedom; this is by no means what they think it is, namely, the ability to do or to omit to do something good or evil; but true freedom is only, or no other than [the status of being] the first cause, which is in no way constrained or coerced by anything else, and which through its perfection alone is the cause of all perfection; consequently, if God could omit to do this, he would not be perfect: for the ability to omit doing some good, or accomplishing some perfection in what he does, can have no place in him, except through defect.

That God alone is the only free cause is, therefore, clear not only from what has just been said, but also from this, namely, that there is no external cause outside him to force or constrain him; all this is not the case with created things.

Against this it is argued thus: The good is only good because God wills it, and this being so, he can always bring it about that evil should be good. But such reasoning is about as conclusive as if I said: It is because God wills to be God that he is God; therefore it is in his power not to be God, which is absurdity itself. Furthermore, when people do anything, and they are asked why they do it, their answer is, because it is what justice demands. If the question is then put, why justice, or rather the first cause of all that is just, makes such a demand, then the answer must be, because justice wills it so. But, dear me, I think to myself, could Justice really be other than just? By no means, for then it could not be Justice. Those, however, who say that God does all that he does because it is good in itself, these, I say, may possibly think that they do not differ from us. But that is far from being the case, since they suppose that there is something before God to which he has duties or obligations, namely, a cause [through] which [God] desires that this shall be good, and, again, that that shall be just.

Then comes the further controversy, namely, whether God, supposing all things had been created by him in some other way from eternity, or had been ordered and predetermined to be otherwise than they now are, whether, I say, he would then be just as perfect as he is now. To this it may serve as an answer, that if Nature had, from all eternity, been made different from what it is now, then, from the standpoint of those who ascribe to God will and understanding, it would necessarily follow that God had a different will and a different understanding then, in consequence of which he would have made it different; and so we should be compelled to think that God has a different character now from what he had then, and had a different character then from what he has now; so that, if we assume he is most perfect now, we are compelled to say that he would not have been so had he created all things differently. All these things, involving as they do palpable absurdities, can in no way be attributed to God, who now, in the past, and unto all eternity, is, has been, and will remain immutable. We prove this also from the definition that we have given of a free cause, which is not one that can do or omit to do anything, but is only such as is not dependent on anything else, so that whatever God does is done and carried into effect by him as the freest cause. If, therefore, he had formerly made things different from what they are now, it would needs follow that he was at one time imperfect, which is false. For, since God is the first cause of all things, there must be something in him, through which he does what he does, and omits not to do it. Since we say that Freedom does not consist in [having the choice of] doing or not doing something, and since we have also shown that that which makes him [God] do anything can be nothing else than his own perfection, we conclude that, had it not been that his perfection made him do all this, then the things would not exist, and could not come into existence, in order to be what they are now. This is just like saying: if God were imperfect then things would be different from what they are now.

So much as regards the first [attribute]; we shall now pass on to the second attribute, which we call a proprium of God, and see what we have to say about it, and so on to the end.

CHAPTER V.

ON DIVINE PROVIDENCE

THE SECOND ATTRIBUTE, which we call a proprium [of God] is his Providence, which to us is nothing else than the striving which we find in the whole of Nature and in individual things to maintain and preserve their own existence. For it is manifest that no thing could, through its own nature, seek its own annihilation, but, on the contrary, that every thing has in itself a striving to preserve its condition, and to improve itself. Following these definitions of ours we, therefore, posit a general and a special providence. The general [providence] is that through which all things are produced and sustained insofar as they are parts of the whole of Nature. The special providence is the striving of each thing separately to preserve its existence [each thing, that is to say], considered not as a part of Nature, but as a whole [by itself]. This is explained by the following example: All the limbs of man are provided for, and cared for, insofar as they are parts of man, this is general providence; while special [providence] is the striving of each separate limb (as a whole in itself, and not as a part of man) to preserve and maintain its own well-being.

CHAPTER VI.

ON DIVINE PREDESTINATION

THE THIRD ATTRIBUTE, we say, is divine predestination.

1. We proved before that God cannot omit to do what he does; that he has, namely, made everything so perfect that it cannot be more perfect.

2. And, at the same time, that without him nothing can be, or be conceived.

It remains to be seen now whether there are in Nature any accidental things, that is to say, whether there are any things which may happen and may also not happen. Secondly, whether there is any thing concerning which we cannot ask why it is.

Now that there are no accidental things we prove thus: That which has no cause to exist cannot possibly exist; that which is accidental has no cause: therefore..

The first is beyond all dispute; the second we prove thus: If any thing that is accidental has a definite and certain cause why it should exist, then it must necessarily exist; but that it should be both accidental and necessary at the same time, is self-contradictory; Therefore...

Perhaps some one will say, that an accidental thing has indeed no definite and certain cause, but an accidental one. If this should be so, it must be so either in sensu diviso or in sensu composito, that is to say, either the existence of the cause is accidental, and not its being a cause; or it is accidental that a certain thing (which indeed must necessarily exist in Nature) should be the cause of the occurrence of that accidental thing. However, both the one and the other are false.

For, as regards the first, if the accidental something is accidental because [the existence of] its cause is accidental, then that cause must also be accidental, because the cause which has produced it is also accidental, et sic in infinitum.

And since it has already been proved, that all things depend on one single cause, this cause would therefore also have to be accidental: which is manifestly false.

As regards the second: if the cause were no more compelled to produce one thing than another, that is, [if the cause were no more compelled] to produce this something than not to produce it, then it would be impossible at once both that it should produce it and that it should not produce it, which is quite contradictory.

Concerning the second [question raised] above, whether there is no thing in Nature about which one cannot ask why it is, this remark of ours shows that we have to inquire through what cause a thing is real; for if this [cause] did not exist it were impossible that the thing should exist. Now, we must look for this cause either in the thing or outside the thing. If, however, any one should ask for a rule whereby to conduct this inquiry, we say that none whatever seems necessary. For if existence pertains to the nature of a thing, then it is certain that we must not look outside it for its cause; but if such is not the case, then we must always look outside the thing for its cause. Since, however, the first pertains to God alone, it is thereby proved (as we have already also proved before) that God alone is the first cause of all things. From this it is also evident that this or that will of man (since the existence of the will does not pertain to its essence) must also have an external cause, by which it is necessarily caused; that this is so is also evident from all that we have said in this chapter; and it will be still more evident when, in the second part, we come to consider and discuss the freedom of man.

Against all this others object: how is it possible that God, who is said to be supremely perfect, and the sole cause, disposer, and provider of all, nevertheless permits such confusion to be seen everywhere in Nature? Also, why has he not made man so as not to be able to sin?

Now, in the first place, it cannot be rightly said that there is confusion in Nature, since nobody knows all the causes of things so as to be able to judge accordingly. This objection, however, originates in this kind of ignorance, namely, that they have set up general Ideas, with which, they think, particular things must agree if they are to be perfect. These Ideas, they state, are in the understanding of God, as many of Plato's followers have said, namely, that these general Ideas (such as Rational, Animal, and the like) have been created by God; and although those who follow Aristotle say, indeed, that these things are not real things, only things of Reason, they nevertheless regard them frequently as [real] things, since they have clearly said that his providence does not extend to particular things, but only to kinds; for example, God has never exercised his providence over Bucephalus, etc., but only over the whole genus Horse. They say also that God has no knowledge of particular and transient things, but only of the general, which, in their opinion, are imperishable. We have, however, rightly considered this to be due to their ignorance. For it is precisely the particular things, and they alone, that have a cause, and not the general, because they are nothing.

God then is the cause of, and providence over, particular things only. If particular things had to conform to some other Nature, then they could not conform to their own, and consequently could not be what they truly are. For example, if God had made all human beings like Adam before the fall, then indeed he would only have created Adam, and no Paul nor Peter; but no, it is just perfection in God, that he gives to all things, from the greatest to the least, their essence, or, to express it better, that he has all things perfectly in himself.

As regards the other [objection], why God has not made mankind so that they should not sin, to this it may serve [as an answer], that whatever is said about sin is only said with reference to us, that is, as when we compare two things with each other, or [consider one thing] from different points of view. For instance, if someone has made a clock precisely in order to strike and to show the hours, and the mechanism quite fulfils the aims of its maker, then we say that it is good, but if it does not do so, then we say that it is bad, notwithstanding that even then it might still be good if only it had been his intention to make it irregular and to strike at wrong times.

We say then, in conclusion, that Peter must, as is necessary, conform to the Idea of Peter, and not to the Idea of Man; good and evil, or sin, these are only modes of thought, and by no means things, or anything that has reality, as we shall very likely show yet more fully in what follows. For all things and works which are in Nature are perfect.

CHAPTER VII.

ON THE ATTRIBUTES

WHICH DO NOT Pertain to God Here we shall take up the consideration of those attributes which are commonly attributed to God, but which, nevertheless, do not pertain to him; as also of those through which it is sought to prove the existence of God, though in vain; and also of the rules of accurate definition.

For this purpose, we shall not trouble ourselves very much about the ideas that people commonly have of God, but we shall only inquire briefly into what the Philosophers can tell us about it. Now these have defined God as a being existing through or of himself, cause of all things, Omniscient, Almighty, eternal, simple, infinite, the highest good, of infinite compassion, etc. But before we approach this inquiry, let us just see what admissions they make to us.

In the first place, they say that it is impossible to give a true or right definition of God, because, according to their opinion, there can be no definition except per genus et differentiam, and as God is not a species of any genus, he cannot be defined rightly, or according to the rules.

In the second place, they say that God cannot be defined, because the definition must describe the thing itself and also positively; while, according to their standpoint, our knowledge of God cannot be of a positive, but only of a negative kind; therefore no proper definition can be given of God.

They also say, besides, that God can never be proved a priori, because he has no cause, but only by way of probability, or from his effects.

Since by these assertions of theirs they admit sufficiently that their knowledge of God is very little and slight, let us now proceed to examine their definition.

In the first place, we do not see that they give us in it any attribute or attributes through which it can be known what the thing (God) is, but only some propria or properties which do, indeed, belong to a thing, but never explain what the thing is. For although self-subsisting, being the cause of all things, highest good, eternal and immutable, etc., are peculiar to God alone, nevertheless, from those properties we cannot know what that being, to whom these properties pertain, is, and what attributes he has.

It is now also time for us to consider the things which they ascribe to God, and which do not, however, pertain to him, such as omniscient, merciful, wise, and so forth, which things, since they are only certain modes of the thinking thing, and can by no means be, or be understood without the substances whose modes they are, can, consequently, also not be attributed to him, who is a Being subsisting without the aid of anything, and solely through himself Lastly, they call him the highest good; but if they understand by it something different from what they have already said, namely, that God is immutable, and a cause of all things, then they have become entangled in their own thought, or are unable to understand themselves. This is the outcome of their misconception of good and evil, for they believe that man himself, and not God, is the cause of his sins and wickedness — which, according to what we have already proved, cannot be the case, else we should be compelled to assert that man is also the cause of himself. However, this will appear yet more evident when we come to consider the will of man.

It is necessary that we should now unravel their specious arguments wherewith they seek to excuse their ignorance in Theology.

First of all, then, they say that a correct definition must consist of a "genus" and "differentia." Now, although all the Logicians admit this, I do not know where they get it from. And, to be sure, if this must be true, then we can know nothing whatever. For if it is through a definition consisting of genus and differentia that we can first get to know a thing perfectly, then we can never know perfectly the highest genus, which has no genus above it. Now then: If the highest genus, which is the cause of our knowledge of all other things, is not known, much less, then, can the other things be understood or known which are explained by that genus. However, since we are free, and do not consider ourselves in any way tied to their assertions, we shall, in accordance with true logic, propose other rules of definition, namely, on the lines of our division of Nature.

Now we have already seen that the attributes (or, as others call them, substances) are things, or, to express ourselves better and more aptly, [constitute] a being which subsists through itself, and therefore makes itself known and reveals itself through itself.

As to the other things, we see that they are but modes of the attributes, without which also they can neither be, nor be understood. Consequently definitions must be of two kinds (or sorts):

1. The first, namely, are those of attributes, which pertain to a self-subsisting being, these need no genus, or anything, through which they might be better understood or explained: for, since they exist as attributes of a self-subsisting being, they also become known through themselves.

2. The second [kind of definitions] are those [of things] which do not exist through themselves, but only through the attributes whose modes they are, and through which, as their genus, they must be understood.

And this is [all that need be said] concerning their statement about definitions. As regards the other [assertion], namely, that God can [not] be known by us adequately, this has been sufficiently answered by D. des Cartes in his answers to the objections relating to these things, page 39.

And the third [assertion], namely, that God cannot be proved a priori, has also already been answered by us. Since God is the cause of himself, it is enough that we prove him through himself, and such a proof is also much more conclusive than the a posteriori proof, which generally rests only on external causes.

CHAPTER VIII .

ON NATURA NATURANS

HERE, BEFORE WE proceed to something else, we shall briefly divide the whole of Nature — namely, into Natura naturans and Natura naturata. By Natura naturans we understand a being that we conceive clearly and distinctly through itself, and without needing anything beside itself (like all the attributes which we have so far described), that is, God. The Thomists likewise understand God by it, but their Natura naturans was a being (so they called it) beyond all substances.

The Natura naturata we shall divide into two, a general, and a particular. The general consists of all the modes which depend immediately on God, of which we shall treat in the following chapter; the particular consists of all the particular things which are produced by the general mode. So that the Natura naturata requires some substance in order to be well understood.

CHAPTER IX.

ON NATURA NATURATA

NOW, AS REGARDS the general Natura naturata, or the modes, or creations which depend on, or have been created by, God immediately, of these we know no more than two, namely, motion in matter, and the understanding in the thinking thing.

(Note. — What is here said about motion in matter is not said seriously. For the Author still intends to discover the cause thereof, as he has already done to some extent a posteriori. But it can stand just as it is, because nothing is based upon it, or dependent thereon [B omits this note])

These, then, we say, have been from all eternity, and to all eternity will remain immutable. A work truly as great as becomes the greatness of the work-master.

All that specially concerns Motion, such as that it has been from all eternity, and to all eternity will remain immutable; that it is infinite in its kind; that it can neither be, nor be understood through itself, but only by means of Extension, — all this, I say, since it [Motion] more properly belongs to a treatise on Natural Science rather than here, we shall not consider in this place, but we shall only say this about it, that it is a Son, Product, or Effect created immediately by God.

As regards the Understanding in the thinking thing, this, like the first, is also a Son, Product, or immediate Creation of God, also created by him from all eternity, and remaining immutable to all eternity. It has but one function, namely, to understand clearly and distinctly all things at all times; which produces invariably an infinite or most perfect satisfaction, which cannot omit to do what it does. Although what we have just said is sufficiently self-evident, still, we shall prove it more clearly afterwards in our account of the Affects of the Soul, and shall therefore say no more about it here.

CHAPTER X.

WHAT GOOD AND EVIL

ARE IN ORDER to explain briefly what good and evil are in themselves, we shall begin thus: Some things are in our understanding and not in Nature, and so they are also only our own creation, and their purpose is to understand things distinctly: among these we include all relations, which have reference to different things, and these we call Entia Rationis [things of reason]. Now the question is, whether good and evil belong to the Entia Rationis or to the Entia Realia [real things]. But since good and evil are only relations, it is beyond doubt that they must be placed among the Entia Rationis; for we never say that something is good except with reference to something else which is not so good, or is not so useful to us as some other thing. Thus we say that a man is bad, only in comparison with one who is better, or also that an apple is bad, in comparison with another which is good or better.

All this could not possibly be said, if that which is better or good, in comparison with which it [the bad] is so called, did not exist.

Therefore, when we say that something is good, we only mean that it conforms well to the general Idea which we have of such things. But, as we have already said before, the things must agree with their particular Ideas, whose essence must be a perfect essence, and not with the general [Ideas], since in that case they would not exist.

As to confirming what we have just said, the thing is clear to us; but still, to conclude our remarks, we will add yet the following proofs:

All things which are in Nature, are either things or actions. Now good and evil are neither things nor actions. Therefore good and evil do not exist in Nature.

For, if good and evil are things or actions, then they must have their definitions. But good and evil (as, for example, the goodness of Peter and the wickedness of Judas) have no definitions apart from the essence of Judas or Peter, because this alone exists in Nature, and they cannot be defined without their essence. Therefore, as above — it follows that good and evil are not things or actions which exist in Nature.

SECOND PART.

ON MAN AND WHAT PERTAINS TO HIM

PREFACE

HAVING, IN THE first part, discoursed on God, and on the universal and infinite things, we shall proceed now, in the second part, to the treatment of particular and finite things; though not of all, since they are innumerable, but we shall only treat of those which concern man; and, in the first place, we shall consider here what man is, insofar as he consists of certain modes (contained in the two attributes which we have remarked in God). I say of certain modes, for I by no means think that man, insofar as he consists of spirit, soul, or body, is a substance. Because, already at the beginning of this book, we proved (1) that no substance can have a beginning; (2) that one substance cannot produce another; and lastly (3), that there cannot be two like substances.

As man has not been in existence from eternity, is finite, and is like many men, he can be no substance; so that all that he has of thought are only modes of the attribute thought which we have attributed to God. And, again, all that he has of form, motion, and other things, are likewise [modes] of the other attribute which is attributed by us to God.

And although from this, [namely,] that the nature of man can neither be, nor be understood without the attributes which we ourselves admit to constitute substance, some try to prove that man is a substance, yet this has no other ground than false suppositions. For, since the nature of matter or body existed before the form of this human body existed, that nature cannot be peculiar to the human body, because it is clear that during the time when man was not, it could never belong to the nature of man.

And what they set up as a fundamental principle, [namely,] that that pertains to the nature of a thing, without which the thing can neither be, nor be understood, we deny. For we have already shown that without God no thing can be or be understood. That is, God must first be and be understood before these particular things can be and be understood. We have also shown that genera do not belong to the nature of definition, but that only such things as cannot exist without others, can also not be understood without these. This being so, what kind of a rule shall we, then, state, whereby it shall be known what belongs to the nature of a thing?

Well, the rule is this: That belongs to the nature of a thing, without which the thing can neither be, nor be understood; not merely so, however, but in such wise that the judgment must be convertible, that is, that the predicate can neither be, nor be understood without the thing. Of these modes, then, of which man consists, we shall begin to treat at the commencement of the following first chapter.

CHAPTER I.

ON OPINION, BELIEF, AND KNOWLEDGE

TO BEGIN OUR consideration of the modes of which man consists, we shall state, (1) what they are, (2) their effects, and (3) their cause.

As regards the first, let us begin with those that are first known to us: namely, certain ideas or the consciousness of the knowledge of ourselves, and of the things which are outside us.

Now we get these ideas (1) either merely through belief (which belief arises either from experience, or from hearsay), (2) or, in the second place, we acquire them by way of a true belief, (3) or, thirdly, we have them as the result of clear and distinct conception.

The first is commonly subject to error.

The second and third, however, although they differ from one another, cannot err.

To make all this somewhat clearer and more intelligible, we shall give the following illustration taken from the Rule of Three.

Some one has just heard it said that if, in the Rule of Three, the second number is multiplied by the third, and then divided by the first, a fourth number will then be obtained which has the same relation to the third as the second has to the first. And notwithstanding the possibility that he who put this before him might have been lying, he still made his calculations accordingly, and he did so without having acquired any more knowledge of the Rule of Three than a blind man has of colour, so that whatever he may have said about it, he simply repeated as a parrot repeats what it has been taught.

Another, having a more active intelligence, is not so easily satisfied with mere hearsay, but tests it by some actual calculations, and when he finds that they agree with it, then he gives credence to it. But we have rightly said that this one also is subject to error; for how can he possibly be sure that his experience of a few particulars can serve him as a rule for all?

A third, who is not satisfied with hearsay, because it may deceive, nor with experience of a few particulars, because this cannot possibly serve as a rule, examines it in the light of true Reason, which, when properly applied, has never deceived. This then tells him that on account of the nature of the proportion in these numbers it had to be so, and could not happen otherwise.

A fourth, however, having the clearest knowledge of all, has no need of hearsay, or experience, or the art of reasoning, because by his penetration he sees the proportion in all such calculations immediately.

CHAPTER II.

WHAT OPINION, BELIEF, AND CLEAR KNOWLEDGE ARE

WE COME NOW to the consideration of the effects of the different grades of knowledge, of which we spoke in the preceding chapter, and, in passing as it were, we shall explain what Opinion, Belief, and clear Knowledge are.

The first [kind of knowledge], then, we call Opinion, the second Belief, but the third is what we call clear Knowledge.

We call it Opinion because it is subject to error, and has no place when we are sure of anything, but only in those cases when we are said to guess and to surmise. The second we call Belief, because the things we apprehend only with our reason are not seen by us, but are only known to us through the conviction of our understanding that it must be so and not otherwise. But we call that clear Knowledge which comes, not from our being convinced by reasons, but from our feeling and enjoying the thing itself, and it surpasses the others by far.

After these preliminary remarks let us now turn to their effects. Of these we say this, namely, that from the first proceed all the "passions" which are opposed to good reason; from the second, the good desires; and from the third, true and sincere Love, with all its offshoots.

We thus maintain that Knowledge is the proximate cause of all the "passions" in the soul. For we consider it once for all impossible that any one, who neither thinks nor knows in any of the preceding ways and modes, should be capable of being incited to Love or Desire or any other mode of Will.

CHAPTER III.

THE ORIGIN OF PASSION.
PASSION DUE TO OPINION

HERE, THEN, LET us see how, as we have said, the passions derive their origin from opinion. To do this well and intelligently we shall take some special ones, and prove what we say by using these as illustrations.

Let Surprise, then, be the first. This is found in one who knows a thing after the first manner [of Knowledge]; for, since from a few particulars he draws a conclusion which is general, he stands surprised whenever he sees anything that goes against his conclusion; like one who, having never seen any sheep except with short tails, is surprised at the sheep from Morocco which have long ones. So it is related of a peasant that he had persuaded himself that beyond his fields there were no others, but when he happened to miss a cow, and was compelled to go and look for her far away, he was surprised at the great number of fields that there were beyond his few acres. And, to be sure, this must also be the case with many Philosophers who have persuaded themselves that beyond this field or little globe, on which they are, there are no more [worlds] (because they have seen no others). But surprise is never felt by him who draws true inferences. This is the first.

The second is Love. Since this arises either from true ideas, or from opinion, or, lastly, from hearsay only, we shall see first how [it arises] from opinion, then how [it arises] from [true] ideas; for the first tends to our ruin, and the second to our supreme happiness; and then [we shall see how it arises] from the last.

As regards the first, it is certain that whenever any one sees, or thinks he sees, something good, he is always inclined to unite himself with it, and, for the sake of the good which he discerns therein, he chooses it as the best, outside which he then knows nothing better or more agreeable. Yet if ever it happens (as it mostly does happen in these things) that he gets to know something better than this good at present known to him, then his love changes immediately from the one (first) to the other (second). All this we shall show more clearly when we treat of the freedom of man.

As to love from true ideas, since this is not the place to speak of it, we shall pass it over now, and speak of the third, and last, namely, the Love that comes from hearsay only. This we generally observe in the attitude of children to their father: because their father tells them that this or that is good they incline towards it, without knowing anything more about it. We see it also in those who from Love give their lives for the Fatherland, and also in those who from hearsay about something fall in love with it.

Next, Hatred, the exact opposite of love, arises from error which is the outcome of opinion. For when some one has come to the conclusion that a certain thing is good, and another happens to do something to the detriment of the same thing, then there arises in him a hatred against the one who did it, and this, as we shall explain afterwards, could never happen if the true good were known. For, in comparison with the true good, all indeed that is, or is conceived, is naught but wretchedness itself; and is not such a lover of what is wretched much more deserving of pity than of hatred?

Hatred, lastly, comes also from mere hearsay, as we see it in the Turks against Jews and Christians, in the Jews against the Turks and Christians, in the Christians against the Jews and Turks, etc. For, among all these, how ignorant is the one multitude of the religion and morals of the others!

Desire. Whether (as some will have it) it consists only in a longing or inclination to obtain what is wanting, or (as others will have it) to retain the things which we already enjoy, it is certain that it cannot be found to have come upon any one except for an apparent good [sub specie boni]. It is therefore clear that Desire, as also Love which we have already discussed, is the outcome of the first kind of knowledge. For if any one has heard that a certain thing is good, he feels a longing and inclination for the same, as may be seen in the case of an invalid who, through hearing the doctor say that such or such a remedy is good for his ailment, at once longs for the same, and feels a desire for it.

Desire arises also from experience, as may be seen in the practice of doctors, who when they have found a certain remedy good several times are wont to regard it as something unfailing.

All that we have just said of these, the same we can say of all other passions, as is clear to everyone. And as, in what follows, we shall begin to inquire which of them are rational, and which of them are irrational, we shall leave the subject now, and say no more about it.

What has now been said of these few though most important [passions] can also be said of all others; and with this we conclude the subject of the Passions which arise from Opinion.

CHAPTER IV.

WHAT COMES FROM BELIEF; AND ON THE GOOD AND EVIL OF MAN

SINCE WE HAVE shown in the preceding chapter how the Passions arise from the error of Opinion, let us now see here the effects of the two other modes of Knowing. And first of all, [the effect] of what we have called True Belief.

This shows us, indeed, what a thing ought to be, but not what it really is. And this is the reason why it can never unite us with the object of our belief. I say, then, that it only teaches us what the thing ought to be, and not what it is; between these two there is a great difference. For, as we remarked à propos of the example taken from the rule of three, when any one can, by the aid of proportion, find a fourth number that shall be related to the third as the second is to the first, then (having used division and multiplication) he can say that the four numbers must be proportional; and although that is so, he speaks of it nonetheless as of a thing that is beyond him. But when he comes to see the proportion in the way which we have shown in the fourth example, then he says with truth that the thing is so, because then it is in him and not beyond him. Let this suffice as regards the first [effect].

The second effect of true belief is that it brings us to a clearer understanding, through which we love God, and thus it makes us intellectually aware of the things which are not in us, but outside us.

The third effect is, that it gives us the knowledge of good and evil, and shows us all the passions which should be suppressed. And as we have already said that the passions which come from opinion are liable to great evil, it is worth the pains to see how these also are sifted out by this second kind of knowledge, so that we may see what is good and what is bad in them.

To do so conveniently, let us, using the same method as before, look at them closely, so that we may know through it which of them should be chosen and which rejected. But, before proceeding to this, let us first state briefly what is the good and evil of man.

We have already said before that all things are necessarily what they are, and that in Nature there is no good and no evil. So that whatever we want man to be [in this respect] must refer to his kind, which is nothing else than a thing of Reason. And when we have conceived in our mind an Idea of a perfect man, it should make us look (when we examine ourselves) to see whether we have any means of attaining to such perfection.

Hence, then, whatever advances us towards perfection, we call good, and, on the contrary, what hinders, or also what does not advance us towards it, bad.

I must therefore, I say, conceive a perfect man, if I want to assert anything concerning the good and evil of man, because if I were to consider the good and evil of some individual man, say, e g., of Adam, I should be confusing a real thing (ens reale) with a thing of Reason (ens Rationis), which must be most scrupulously avoided by an upright Philosopher, for reasons which we shall state in the sequel, or on another occasion. Furthermore, since the destiny of Adam, or of any other individual creature, is not known to us except through the result, so it follows that what we can say even of the destiny of man must be based on the idea which our understanding forms of a perfect man, which destiny, since it is a thing of Reason, we may well know; so also, as already remarked, are good and evil, which are only modes of thinking.

To come gradually to the point: We have already pointed out before how the movement, passions, and activities of the soul arise from ideas, and these ideas we have divided into four kinds, namely, [according as they are based on] mere hearsay, experience, belief, clear knowledge. And from what we have now seen of the effects of all these, it is evident that the fourth, namely, clear knowledge, is the most perfect of all. For opinion often leads us into error. True belief is good only because it is the way to true knowledge, and awakens us to things which are really lovable. So that the final end that we seek, and the highest that we know, is true knowledge. But even this true knowledge varies with the objects that come before it: the better the object is with which it happens to unite itself, so much the better also is this knowledge. And, for this reason, he is the most perfect man who is united with God (who is the most perfect being of all), and so enjoys him.

Now, in order to find out what is good and bad in the affects or passions, let us, as suggested, take them one by one. And first of all, Surprise. This, since it arises either from ignorance or prejudice, is an imperfection in the man who is subject to this perturbance. I say an imperfection, because, through itself, surprise does not lead to any evil.

CHAPTER V.

ON LOVE

LOVE, WHICH IS nothing else than the enjoyment of a thing and union therewith, we shall divide according to the qualities of its object; the object, that is, which man seeks to enjoy, and to unite himself with.

Now some objects are in themselves transient; others, indeed, are not transient by virtue of their cause. There is yet a third that is eternal and imperishable through its own power and might.

The transient are all the particular things which did not exist from all time, or have had a beginning.

The others are all those modes, which we have stated to be the cause of the particular modes.

But the third is God, or, what we regard as one and the same, Truth.

Love, then, arises from the idea and knowledge that we have of a thing; and according as the thing shows itself greater and more glorious, so also is our love greater.

In two ways it is possible to free ourselves from love: either by getting to know something better, or by discovering that the loved object, which is held by us to be something great and glorious, brings in its train much woe and disaster.

It is also characteristic of love that we never think of emancipating ourselves from it (as from surprise and other passions); and this for the following two reasons: (1) because it is impossible, (2) because it is necessary that we should not be released from the same.

It is impossible because it does not depend on us, but only on the good and useful which we discern in the object; it is necessary that these should never have become known to us, if we would not or should not love it; and this is not a matter of our free choice, or dependent on us, for if we knew nothing, it is certain that we should also be nothing.

It is necessary that we should not be released from it, because, owing to the weakness of our nature, we could not exist without enjoying something with which we become united, and from which we draw strength.

Now which of these three kinds of objects are we to choose or to reject?

As regards the transient (since, as remarked, we must, owing to the weakness of our nature, necessarily love something and become united with it in order to exist), it is certain that our nature becomes nowise strengthened through our loving, and becoming united with, these, for they are weak themselves, and the one cripple cannot carry the other. And not only do they not advance us, but they are even harmful to us. For we have said that love is a union with the object which our understanding judges to be good and glorious; and by this we mean such a union whereby both the lover and what is loved become one and the same thing, or together constitute one whole. He, therefore, is indeed always wretched who is united to transient things. For, since these are beyond his power, and subject to many accidents, it is impossible that, when they are affected, he should be free from these affects. And, consequently, we conclude: If those who love transient things that have some measure of reality are so wretched, how wretched must they be who love honour, riches, and pleasures, which have no reality whatever!

Let this suffice to show us how Reason teaches us to keep away from things so fleeting. For what we have just said shows us clearly the poison and the evil which lurk concealed in the love of these things. But we see this yet incomparably clearer when we observe from what glorious and excellent a good we are kept away through the enjoyment of this.

We said before that the things which are transient are beyond our power. But let us be well understood; we do not mean to say that we are a free cause depending upon nothing else; only when we say that some things are in, others beyond our power, we mean by those that are in our power such as we can produce through the order of or together with Nature, of which we are a part; by those which are not in our power, such as, being outside us, are not liable to suffer any change through us, because they are very far removed from our real essence as thus fashioned by Nature.

To proceed, we come now to the second kind of objects, which though eternal and imperishable, are not such through their own power. However, if we institute a brief inquiry here, we become immediately aware that these are only mere modes which depend immediately on God. And since the nature of these is such, they cannot be conceived by us unless we, at the same time, have a conception of God. In this, since he is perfect, our Love must necessarily rest. And, to express it in a word, if we use our understanding aright it will be impossible for us not to love God.

The Reasons why, are clear. First of all, because we find that God alone has essence only, and all other things are not essences but modes. And since the modes cannot be rightly understood without the entity on which they immediately depend; and [as] we have already shown before that if, when loving something, we get to know a better thing than that which we then love, we always prefer it immediately, and forsake the first; it follows, therefore, incontrovertibly that when we get to know God, who has all perfection in himself, we must necessarily love him.

Secondly, if we use our understanding well in acquiring a knowledge of things, then we must know them in [relation to] their causes. Now then, since God is a first cause of all other things, therefore, from the nature of the case (ex rerum natura), the knowledge of God is, and remains, before the knowledge of all other things: because the knowledge of all other things must follow from the knowledge of the first cause. And true love results always from the knowledge that the thing is glorious and good. What else, then, can follow but that it can be lavished upon no one more ardently than upon the Lord our God? For he alone is glorious, and a perfect good.

So we see now, how we can make love strong, and also how it must rest only in God.

What more we had still to say about love, we shall bear in mind to say it when we consider the last kind of knowledge. In what follows here we shall inquire, as we promised before, as to which of the passions we are to entertain, which we are to reject.

CHAPTER VI.

ON HATRED

HATRED IS AN inclination to ward off from us that which has caused us some harm. Now it is to be remarked that we perform our actions in two ways, namely, either with or without passion. With passion, as is commonly seen in the [conduct of] masters towards their servants who have done something amiss. Without passion, as is related of Socrates, who, when he was compelled to chastise his slave for [the latter's own] good, never did so when he felt that he was enraged against his slave.

Now that we see that our actions are performed by us either with, or without passion, we think that it is clear that those things which hinder or have hindered us can be removed, when necessary, without any perturbation on our part. And so, which is better: that we should flee from the things with aversion and hatred, or that, with the strength of reason, we should (for we think it possible) endure them without loss of temper? First of all, it is certain that when we do what we have to do without passion, then no evil can result therefrom. And, since there is no mean between good and evil, we see that, as it is bad to do anything in a passion, so it must be good to act without it.

But let us examine whether there is any harm in fleeing from things with hatred and aversion.

As regards the hatred which comes from opinion, it is certain that it should have no place in us, because we know that one and the same thing is good for us at one time, bad for us at another time, as is always the case with medicinal herbs.

It therefore depends, in the end, on whether the hatred arises in us only through opinion, and not also through true reasoning. But to ascertain this properly we deem it right to explain distinctly what hatred is, and to distinguish it from aversion.

Now I say that Hatred is a perturbation of the soul against some one who has done some ill to us willingly and knowingly. But aversion is the perturbation which arises in us against a thing on account of some infirmity or injury which we either know or think is in it by nature. I say, by nature; for when we do not suppose or think that it is so, then, even if we have suffered some hindrance or injury from it, we have no aversion for it, because we may, on the contrary, expect something useful from it. Thus, when someone is hurt by a stone or a knife, he does not on that account feel any aversion for the same.

After these observations let us now briefly consider the consequences of both of them. From hatred there ensues sorrow; and when the hatred is great, it produces anger, which not only, like hatred, seeks to flee from what is hated, but also to annihilate it, when that is practicable: from this great hatred comes also envy. But from aversion there comes a certain sorrow, because we consider ourselves to be deprived of something which, since it is real, must always have its essence and perfection.

From what has just been said it may be easily understood that, if we use our Reason aright, we can feel no hatred or aversion for anything, because, if we do, we deprive ourselves of that perfection which is to be found in everything. We see likewise with our Reason that we can never [reasonably] feel any hatred whatever against anybody, because whatsoever exists in Nature, if we entertain any wish about it, then we must always improve it, whether for our sake or for the sake of the thing itself. And since a perfect man is the best thing for us that we know of all that we have around us or before our eyes, it is by far the best both for us and for all people individually that we should at all times seek to educate them to this perfect state. For only then can we reap the greatest benefit from them, and they from us. The means thereto is, to give regard to them always in the manner in which we are constantly taught and exhorted to do by our good Conscience; for this never prompts us to our undoing, but always to our happiness and well-being.

In conclusion, we say that Hatred and Aversion have in them as many imperfections as Love, on the contrary, has perfections. For this always produces improvement, invigoration, and enlargement, which constitute perfection; while Hatred, on the contrary, always makes for desolation, enervation, and annihilation, which constitute imperfection itself.

CHAPTER VII.

ON JOY AND SORROW

HAVING SEEN THAT Hatred and Surprise are such that we may freely say, that they can have no place in those who use their understanding as they should, we shall now proceed in the same manner to speak of the other passions. To begin with, Desire and Joy shall come first. Since these arise from the same causes from which love ensues, we shall only say concerning them that we must remember and call to mind what we then said; and with this we leave the subject.

We turn next to Sorrow, of which we may say that it arises only from opinion and imagination which follows therefrom: for it comes from the loss of some good.

Now we have already remarked above, that whatsoever we do should tend towards progress and amelioration. But it is certain that so long as we are sorrowing we render ourselves unfit to act thus; on this account it is necessary that we should free ourselves from it. This we can do by thinking of the means whereby we may recover what we have lost, if it is in our power to do so. If not, [we must reflect] that it is just as necessary to make an end of it, lest we fall a prey to all the miseries and disasters which sorrow necessarily brings in its train. And either course must be adopted with joy; for it is foolish to try to restore and make good a lost good by means of a self-sought and provoked evil.

Lastly, he who uses his understanding aright must necessarily know God first. Now God, as we have shown, is the highest good and all that is good. Hence it follows incontrovertibly, that one who uses his understanding aright can fall a prey to no sorrow. How should he? Since he finds repose in that good which is all that is good, and in which there is the fulness of all joy and contentment.

Sorrow, then, comes from opinion or want of understanding, as explained.

CHAPTER VIII.

ON ESTEEM AND CONTEMPT, ETC.

WE SHALL NOW proceed to speak of Esteem and Contempt, of Self-respect and Humility, of Conceit and Culpable Humility. We shall take them in the above order, and try to distinguish accurately what is good and what is bad in them.

Esteem and Contemptare felt insofar as we know a thing to be something great or small, be this great or little thing in us or outside us.

Self-respect does not extend [to anything] outside us, and is only attributed to one who knows the real worth of his perfection, dispassionately and without seeking esteem for himself.

Humility is felt when anyone knows his own imperfection, without regard to the contempt [of others] for himself; so that Humility does not refer to anything outside the humble man.

Conceit is this, when someone attributes to himself a perfection which is not to be found in him.

Culpable humility is this, when some one attributes to himself an imperfection which he has not. I am not speaking of those hypocrites who, without meaning it, humble themselves in order to deceive others; but only of those who really think they have the imperfections which they attribute to themselves.

From these observations it is sufficiently evident what good and evil there is in each of these passions. For, as regards Self-respect and Humility, these show their excellence through themselves. For we say that the possessor thereof knows his perfection and imperfection for what it is. And this, according to what Reason teaches us, is the most important thing for the attainment of our perfection. Because if we know exactly our powers and perfection, we see thereby clearly what it is we have to do in order to attain our good end. And, on the other hand, if we know our fault and frailty, then we know what we have to avoid.

As regards Conceit and Culpable Humility, the definition of them already shows sufficiently that they arise from a certain opinion; for we said that it [conceit] is attributed to one who ascribes to himself a certain perfection, although he does not possess it, and culpable humility is the precise opposite.

From what has just been said it is evident, then, that just as Self-respect and True Humility are good and salutary, so, on the contrary, Conceit and Culpable Humility are bad and pernicious. For those [Self-respect and True Humility] not only put their possessor into a very good attitude, but are also, besides, the right ladder by which we may rise to supreme bliss. But these [Conceit and Culpable Humility] not only prevent us from attaining to our perfection, but also lead us to utter ruin. Culpable Humility is what prevents us from doing that which we should otherwise have to do in order to become perfect; we see this, for instance, in the case of the Sceptics, who, just because they deny that man can attain to any truth, deprive themselves thereof through this very denial. Conceit on the other hand is what makes us undertake things which tend straight to our ruin; as is seen in the case of all those who had the conceit, and have the conceit, that they stood, and stand, wondrously well in the opinion of God, and consequently brave fire and water, and thus, avoiding no danger, and facing every risk, they die most miserably.

As regards Esteem and Contempt, there is no more to be said about them, we have only to recall to memory what we said before about Love.

CHAPTER IX.

ON HOPE AND FEAR, ETC.

WE SHALL NOW begin to speak of Hope and Fear, of Confidence, Despair, and Vacillation, of Courage, Boldness and Emulation, of Pusillanimity and Timidity, and lastly of Jealousy, and, as is our wont, we shall take them one by one, and then indicate which of these can hinder us, and which can profit us. We shall be able to do all this very easily, if only we attend closely to the thoughts that we can have about a thing that is yet to come, be it good, be it bad.

The ideas which we have about things have reference either

1. To the things themselves; or,

2. To the person who has the ideas.

The ideas that we have as regards the thing itself are these, either the thing is regarded by us as accidental, that is as something which may come or may not come, or [we think] that it necessarily must come. So much as regards the thing itself.

Next, as regards him who thinks about the thing, the case is this: he must do something either in order to advance the thing, or in order to prevent it. Now from these thoughts all these passions result as follows: when we think that a certain thing which is yet to come is good and that it can happen, the soul assumes, in consequence of this, that form which we call hope, which is nothing else than a certain kind of joy, though mingled with some sorrow.

And, on the other hand, if we judge that that which may be coming is bad, then that form enters into our soul which we call fear.

If, however, the thing is regarded by us as good, and, at the same time, as something that necessarily must come, then there comes into the soul that repose which we call confidence; which is a certain joy not mingled with sorrow, as hope is.

But when we think that the thing is bad, and that it necessarily must come, then despair enters into the soul; which is nothing else than a certain kind of sorrow.

So far we have spoken of the passions considered in this chapter, and given positive definitions of the same, and have thus stated what each of them is; we may now proceed in a converse manner, and define them negatively. We hope that the evil may not come, we fear lest the good should not come, we are confident that the evil will not come, we despair because the good will not come.

Having said this much about the passions insofar as they arise from our thoughts concerning the thing itself, we have now to speak of those which arise from the thoughts relating to him who thinks about the thing; namely:

If something must be done in order to bring the thing about, and we come to no decision concerning it, then the soul receives that form which we call vacillation. But when it makes a manly resolve to produce the thing, and this can be brought about, then that is called courage; and if the thing is difficult to effect, then that is called intrepidity or bravery.

When, however, some one decides to do a thing because another (who had done it first) has met with success, then we call it emulation. Lastly, if any one knows what he must decide to do in order to advance a good thing, and to hinder a bad one, and yet does not do so, then we call it pusillanimity; and when the same is very great, we call it timidity. Lastly, jealousness or jalousie is the anxiety which we feel that we may have the sole enjoyment and possession of something already acquired.

Since we know now whence these passions originate, it will be very easy for us to show which of them are good, and which are bad.

As regards Hope, Fear, Confidence, Despair, and Jealousy, it is certain that they arise from a wrong opinion. For, as we have already shown above, all things have their necessary causes, and must necessarily happen just as they do happen. And although Confidence and Despair seem to have a place in the inviolable order and sequence of causes or to confirm the same, yet (when the truth of the matter is rightly looked into) that is far from being the case. For Confidence and Despair never arise, unless Hope and Fear (from which they derive their being) have preceded them. For example, if any one thinks that something, for which he still has to wait, is good, then he receives that form in his soul which we call Hope; and when he is confident about the acquisition of the supposed good, his soul gains that repose which we call Confidence. What we are now saying about Confidence, the same must also be said about Despair. But, according to that which we have said about Love, this also can have no place in a perfect man: because they presuppose things which, owing to the mutability to which they are subject (as remarked in our account of Love), we must not become attached to; nor (as shown in our account of Hatred) may we even have an aversion to them. The man, however, who persists in these passions is at all times subject to such attachment and aversion.

As regards Vacillation, Pusillanimity, and Timidity, these betray their imperfection through their very character and nature: for whatsoever they do to our advantage comes only negatively from the effects of their nature. For example, some one hopes for something which he thinks is good, although it is not good, yet, owing to his Vacillation or Pusillanimity, he happens to lack the courage necessary for its realisation, and so it comes about that he is negatively or by accident saved from the evil which he thought was good. These Passions, therefore, can also have no place whatever in the man who is guided by true Reason.

Lastly, as regards Courage, Boldness, and Emulation, about these there is nothing else to be said than that which we have already said about Love and Hatred.

CHAPTER X.

ON REMORSE AND REPENTANCE

ON THE PRESENT occasion we shall speak, though briefly, about remorse and repentance. These never arise except as the result of rashness; because remorse comes only from this, that we do something about which we are then in doubt whether it is good, or whether it is bad; and repentance, from this, that we have done something which is bad.

And since many people (who use their understanding aright) sometimes (because they lack that habitual readiness which is required in order that the understanding may at all times be used aright) go astray, it might perchance be thought that such Remorse and Repentance might soon set them right again, and thence it might be inferred, as the whole world does infer, that they are good. If, however, we will get a proper insight into them, we shall find that they are not only not good, but that they are, on the contrary, pernicious, and that they are consequently bad. For it is obvious that we always succeed better through Reason and the love of truth than through remorse and sorrow. They are, therefore, pernicious and bad, because they are a certain kind of sorrow, which [sorrow] we have already shown above to be injurious, and which, for that reason, we must try to avert as an evil, and consequently we must likewise shun and flee from these also, which are like it.

CHAPTER XI.

ON DERISION AND JESTING

DERISION AND JESTING rest on a false opinion, and betray an imperfection in him who derides and jests.

The opinion on which they rest is false, because it is supposed that he who is derided is the first cause of the effects which he produces, and that they do not necessarily (like the other things in Nature) depend on God. They betray an imperfection in the Derider; because either that which is derided is such that it is derisible, or it is not such. If it is not such, then it shows bad manners, to deride that which is not to be derided; if it is such, then they [who deride it] show thereby that they recognise some imperfection in that which they deride, which they ought to remedy, not by derision, but much rather by good reasoning.

Laughter does not refer to another, but only to the man who observes some good in himself; and since it is a certain kind of Joy, there is nothing else to be said about it than what has already been said about Joy. I speak of such laughter as is caused by a certain Idea which provokes one to it, and not at all of such laughter as is caused by the movement of the [vital] spirits; as to this (since it has no reference to good or to evil) we had no intention to speak of it here.

As to Envy, Anger, Indignation, we shall say nothing about them here, but only just refer back to what we have already said above concerning hatred.

CHAPTER XII.

ON GLORY, SHAME, AND SHAMELESSNESS

WE SHALL NOW also briefly consider glory, shame, and shamelessness. The first is a certain kind of Joy which every one feels in himself whenever he becomes aware that his conduct is esteemed and praised by others, without regard to any other advantage or profit which they may have in view.

Shame is a certain kind of sorrow which arises in one when he happens to see that his conduct is despised by others, without regard to any other disadvantage or injury that they may have in view.

Shamelessness is nothing else than a want, or shaking off, of shame, not through Reason, but either from innocence of shame, as is the case with children, savage people, etc., or because, having been held in great contempt, one goes now to any length without regard for anything.

Now that we know these passions, we also know, at the same time, the vanity and imperfection which they have in them. For Glory and Shame are not only of no advantage, because of what we have observed in their definitions, but also (inasmuch as they are based on self-love, and on the opinion that man is the first cause of his action, and therefore deserving of praise and blame) they are pernicious and must be rejected.

I will not, however, say that one ought to live among men in the same way that one would live away from them, where Glory and Shame have no place; quite the contrary, I admit that we are not only free to utilise them, when we apply them in the service of mankind and for their amelioration, but that we may even do so at the price of curtailing our own (otherwise perfect and legitimate) freedom. For example: if any one wears costly clothes in order to be respected, he seeks a Glory which results from his self-love without any consideration for his fellow-men; but when some one observes that his wisdom (wherewith he can be of service to his neighbours) is despised and trampled under foot simply because he is dressed in shabby clothes, then he will do well if (from the motive to help them) he provides himself with clothes to which they cannot take exception, thereby becoming like his fellow-man in order that he may win over his fellow-man.

Further, as regards Shamelessness, this shows itself to be such that in order to see its deformity all that we need is merely its definition, and that will be enough for us.

CHAPTER XIII.

ON FAVOUR, GRATITUDE, AND INGRATITUDE

NOW FOLLOWS [THE consideration] of favour, gratitude, and ingratitude. As regards the first two, they are the inclinations which the soul has to wish and to do some good to one's neighbour. I say, to wish, [this happens] when good is returned to one who has done some good; I say, to do, [this is the case] when we ourselves have obtained or received some good.

I am well aware that almost all people consider these affects to be good; but, notwithstanding this, I venture to say that they can have no place in a perfect man. For a perfect man is moved to help his fellow-man by sheer necessity only, and by no other cause, and therefore he feels it all the more to be his duty to help the most godless, seeing that his misery and need are so much greater.

Ingratitude is a disregard or shaking off of Gratitude, as Shamelessness is of Shame, and that without any rational ground, but solely as the result either of greed or of immoderate self-love; and that is why it can have no place in a perfect man.

CHAPTER XIV.

ON GRIEF

GRIEF SHALL BE the last of which we shall speak in our treatment of the passions, and with it we will conclude. Now grief is a certain kind of sorrow arising from the contemplation of some good which we have lost, and [lost] in such a way that there is no hope of recovering the same. It makes its imperfection so manifest that as soon as we only examine it we think it bad. For we have already shown above that it is bad to bind and link ourselves to things which may easily, or at some time, fail us, and which we cannot have when we want them. And since it is a certain kind of sorrow, we have to shun it, as we have already remarked above, when we were treating of sorrow.

I think, now, that I have already shown and proved sufficiently that it is only True Belief or Reason that leads us to the knowledge of good and evil. And so when we come to prove that Knowledge is the first and principal cause of all these passions, it will be clearly manifest that if we use our understanding and Reason aright, it should be impossible for us ever to fall a prey to one of these passions which we ought to reject. I say our Understanding, because I do not think that Reason alone is competent to free us from all these: as we shall afterwards show in its proper place.

We must, however, note here as an excellent thing about the passions, that we see and find that all the passions which are good are of such kind and nature that we cannot be or exist without them, and that they belong, as it were, to our essence; such is the case with Love, Desire, and all that pertains to love.

But the case is altogether different with those which are bad and must be rejected by us; seeing that we cannot only exist very well without these, but even that only then, when we have freed ourselves from them, are we really what we ought to be.

To give still greater clearness to all this, it is useful to note that the foundation of all good and evil is Love bestowed on a certain object: for if we do not love that object which (nota bene) alone is worthy of being loved, namely, God, as we have said before, but things which through their very character and nature are transient, then (since the object is liable to so many accidents, ay, even to annihilation) there necessarily results hatred, sorrow, etc., according to the changes in the object loved. Hatred, when any one deprives him of what he loves. Sorrow, when he happens to lose it. Glory, when he leans on self-love. Favour and Gratitude, when he does not love his fellow-man for the sake of God.

But, in contrast with all these, when man comes to love God who always is and remains immutable, then it is impossible for him to fall into this welter of passions. And for this reason we state it as a fixed and immovable principle that God is the first and only cause of all our good and delivers us from all our evil.

Hence it is also to be noted lastly, that only Love, etc., are limitless: namely, that as it increases more and more, so also it grows more excellent, because it is bestowed on an object which is infinite, and can therefore always go on increasing, which can happen in the case of no other thing except this alone. And, maybe, this will afterwards give us the material from which we shall prove the immortality of the soul, and how or in what way this is possible.

Having so far considered all that the third kind of effect of true belief makes known we shall now proceed to speak, in what follows, of the fourth, and last, effect which was not stated by us on page 67.

CHAPTER XV.

ON THE TRUE AND THE FALSE

LET US NOW examine the true and the false, which indicate to us the fourth, and last, consequence of true belief. Now, in order to do this, we shall first state the definitions of Truth and Falsity. Truth is an affirmation (or a denial) made about a certain thing, which agrees with that same thing; and Falsity is an affirmation (or a denial) about a thing, which does not agree with the thing itself. But this being so, it may appear that there is no difference between the false and the true Idea, or, since the [affirmation or] denial of this or that are mere modes of thought, and [the true and the false Idea] differ in no other way except that the one agrees with the thing, and the other does not, that they are therefore, not really, but only logically different; and if this should be so, one may justly ask, what advantage has the one from his Truth, and what harm does the other incur through his falsity? And how shall the one know that his conception or Idea agrees with the thing more than the other does? Lastly, whence does it come that the one errs, and the other does not?

To this it may, in the first place, serve as an answer that the clearest things of all make known both themselves and also what is false, in such a manner that it would be a great folly to ask how we are to become aware of them: for, since they are said to be the clearest of all, there can never be any other clearness through which they might be made clear; it follows, therefore, that truth at once reveals itself and also what is false, because truth is made clear through truth, that is through itself, and through it also is falsity made clear; but falsity is never revealed and made manifest through itself. So that any one who is in possession of the truth cannot doubt that he possesses it, while one who is sunk in falsity or in error can well suppose that he has got at the truth; just as someone who is dreaming can well think that he is awake, but one who is actually awake can never think that he is dreaming.

These remarks also explain to some extent what we said about God being the Truth, or that the Truth is God himself.

Now the reason why the one is more conscious of his truth than the other is, is because the Idea of [his] affirmation (or denial) entirely agrees with the nature of the thing, and consequently has more essence. It may help some to grasp this better if it be observed that Understanding (although the word does not sound like it) is a mere or pure passivity; that is, that our soul is changed in such a way that it receives other modes of thought, which it did not have before. Now when someone, in consequence of the whole object having acted upon him, receives corresponding forms or modes of thought, then it is clear that he receives a totally different feeling of the form or character of the object than does another who has not had so many causes [acting upon him], and is therefore moved to make an affirmation or denial about that thing by a different and slighter action (because he becomes aware of it only through a few, or the less important, of its attributes). From this, then, we see the perfection of one who takes his stand upon Truth, as contrasted with one who does not take his stand upon it. Since the one changes easily, while the other does not change easily, it follows therefrom that the one has more stability and essence than the other has: likewise, since the modes of thought which agree with the thing have had more causes [to produce them] they have also more stability and essence in them: and, since they entirely agree with the thing, it is impossible that they should after a time be made different or undergo some change, all the less so because we have already seen before that the essence of a thing is unchangeable. Such is not the case with falsity. And with these remarks all the above questions will be sufficiently answered.

CHAPTER XVI.

ON THE WILL

NOW THAT WE know the nature of Good and Evil, Truth and Falsity, and also wherein the well-being of a perfect man consists, it is time to begin to examine ourselves, and to see whether we attain to such well-being voluntarily or of necessity.

To this end it is necessary to inquire what the Will is, according to those who posit a Will, and wherein it is different from Desire. Desire, we have said, is the inclination which the soul has towards something which it chooses as a good; whence it follows that before our desire inclines towards something outside, we have already inwardly decided that such a thing is good, and this affirmation, or, stated more generally, the power to affirm and to deny, is called the Will.

It thus turns on the question whether our Affirmations are made voluntarily or necessarily, that is, whether we can make any affirmation or denial about a thing without some external cause compelling us to do so. Now we have already shown that a thing which is not explained through itself, or whose existence does not pertain to its essence, must necessarily have an external cause; and that a cause which is to produce something must produce it necessarily; it must therefore also follow that each separate act of willing this or that, each separate act of affirming or denying this or that of a thing, these, I say, must also result from some external cause: so also the definition which we have given of a cause is, that it cannot be free.

Possibly this will not satisfy some who are accustomed to keep their understanding busy with things of Reason more than with Particular things which really exist in Nature; and, through doing so, they come to regard a thing of Reason not as such, but as a real thing. For, because man has now this, now that volition, he forms in his soul a general mode which he calls Will, just as from this man and that man he also forms the Idea of man; and because he does not adequately distinguish the real things from the things of Reason, he comes to regard the things of Reason as things which really exist in Nature, and so he regards himself as a cause of some things. This happens not infrequently in the treatment of the subject about which we are speaking. For if any one is asked why people want this or that, the answer usually given is, because they have a will. But, since the Will, as we have said, is only an Idea of our willing this or that, and therefore only a mode of thought, a thing of Reason, and nota real thing, nothing can be caused by it; for out of nothing, nothing comes. And so, as we have shown that the will is not a thing in Nature, but only in fancy, I also think it unnecessary to ask whether the will is free or not free.

I say this not [only] of will in general, which we have shown to be a mode of thought, but also of the particular act of willing this or that, which act of willing some have identified with affirmation and denial. Now this should be clearly evident to every one who only attends to what we have already said. For we have said that the understanding is purely passive; it is an awareness, in the soul, of the essence and existence of things; so that it is never we who affirm or deny something of a thing, but it is the thing itself that affirms or denies, in us, something of itself.

Possibly some will not admit this, because it seems to them that they are well able to affirm or to deny of the thing something different from what they know about the thing. But this is only because they have no idea of the conception which the soul has of the thing apart from or without the words [in which it is expressed]. It is quite true that (when there are reasons which prompt us to do so) we can, in words or by some other means, represent the thing to others differently from what we know it to be; but we can never bring it so far, either by words or by any other means, that we should feel about the things differently from what we feel about them; that is impossible, and clearly so to all who have for once attended to their understanding itself apart from the use of words or other significant signs.

Against this, however, some perchance may say: If it is not we, but the thing itself, that makes the affirmation and denial about itself in us, then nothing can be affirmed or denied except what is in agreement with the thing; and consequently there is no falsity. For we have said that falsity consists in affirming (or denying) aught of a thing which does not accord with that thing; that is, what the thing does not affirm or deny about itself. I think, however, that if only we consider well what we have already said about Truth and Falsity, then we shall see at once that these objections have already been sufficiently answered. For we have said that the object is the cause of what is affirmed or denied thereof, be it true or false: falsity arising thus, namely, because, when we happen to know something or a part of an object, we imagine that the object (although we only know very little of it) nevertheless affirms or denies that of itself as a whole; this takes place mostly in feeble souls, which receive very easily a mode or an idea through a slight action of the object, and make no further affirmation or denial apart from this.

Lastly, it might also be objected that there are many things which we sometimes want and [sometimes also] do not want, as, for example, to assert something about a thing or not to assert it, to speak the truth, and not to speak it, and so forth. But this results from the fact that Desire is not adequately distinguished from Will. For the Will, according to those who maintain that there is a Will, is only the activity of the understanding whereby we affirm or deny something about a thing, with regard to good or evil. Desire, however, is the disposition of the soul to obtain or to do something for the sake of the good or evil that is discerned therein; so that even after we have made an affirmation or denial about the thing, Desire still remains, namely, when we have ascertained or affirmed that the thing is good; such is the Will, according to their statements, while desire is the inclination, which we only subsequently feel, to advance it — so that, even according to their own statements, the Will may well exist without the Desire, but not the Desire without the Will, which must have preceded it.

All the activities, therefore, which we have discussed above (since they are carried out through Reason under the appearance of good, or are hindered by Reason under the appearance of evil) can only be subsumed under that inclination which is called Desire, and by no means under the designation of Will, which is altogether inappropriate.

CHAPTER XVII.

ON THE DISTINCTION BETWEEN WILL AND DESIRE

NOW THAT IT is known that we have no free will to make an affirmation or a denial, let us just see what is the correct and true distinction between will and desire, or what may the Will be which was called by the Latins voluntas.

According to Aristotle's definition, Desire appears to be a genus containing two species. For he says that the Will is the longing or inclination which one feels towards that which is or seems good. Whence it appears to me that by Desire (or cupiditas) he means any inclination, be it towards good, be it towards evil; but when the inclination is only towards what is or appears to be good, or when the man who has such inclination, has it under the appearance of good, then he calls it voluntas or good will; while, if it is bad, that is, when we observe in another an inclination towards something which is bad, he calls that voluptas or bad will. So that the inclination of the soul is not something whereby affirmations or denials are made, but only an inclination to obtain something which appears to be good, and to flee from what appears to be bad.

It, therefore, remains to inquire now whether the Desire is free or not free. In addition to what we have already said, namely, that Desire depends on the idea of its objects, and that this understanding must have an external cause, and in addition also to what we have said about the will, it still remains to prove that Desire is not free. Many people, although they see quite well that the knowledge which man has of various things is a medium through which his longing or inclination passes over from one thing to another, yet fail to observe what that may be which thus lures the inclination from the one to the other.

However, to show that this inclination of ours is not of our own free will (and in order to present vividly before our eyes what it is to pass over, and to be drawn, from one thing to another), we shall imagine a child becoming aware of something for the first time. For example, I hold before him a little Bell, which produces a pleasant sound for his ears, so that he conceives a longing for it; consider now whether he could really help feeling this longing or desire. If you say, Yes, then I ask, how, through what cause is this to happen? Certainly not through something which he knows to be better, because this is all that he knows; nor, again, through its appearing to be bad to him, for he knows nothing else, and this pleasure is the very best that has ever come to him. But perchance he has the freedom to banish from him the longing which he feels; whence it would follow that this longing may well arise in us without our free will, but that all the same we have in us the freedom to banish it from us. This freedom, however, will not bear examination; for what, indeed, might it be that shall be able to annihilate the longing? The longing itself? Surely no, for there is nothing that through its own nature seeks its own undoing. What then might it ultimately be that shall be able to wean him from his longing? Nothing else, forsooth, except that in the natural order and course of things he is affected by something which he finds more pleasant than the first. And, therefore, just as, when we were considering the Will, we said that the human Will is nothing but this and that Volition, so also man has no other than this and that Desire which is caused by this and that idea; Desire [in the abstract] is not anything actually existing in Nature, but is only an abstraction from the particular acts of desiring this or that. Desire, then, as it is not really anything, can also not really cause anything. So that when we say that Desire is free, it is just as much as if we said that this or that Desire is its own cause — that is, that before it existed it had already arranged that it should exist; which is absurdity itself, and cannot be.

CHAPTER XVIII.
ON THE USES OF THE FOREGOING

THUS WE SEE now that man, being a part of the whole of Nature, on which he depends, and by which also he is governed, cannot of himself do anything for his happiness and well-being; let us, then, just see what Uses we can derive from these propositions of ours. And this [is] all the more [necessary] because we have no doubt that they will appear not a little offensive to some.

In the first place, it follows therefrom that we are truly servants, aye, slaves, of God, and that it is our greatest perfection to be such necessarily. For, if we were thrown back upon ourselves, and thus not dependent on God, we should be able to accomplish very little, or nothing, and that would justly give us cause to lament our lot; especially so in contrast with what we now see, namely, that we are dependent on that which is the most perfect of all, in such a way that we exist also as a part of the whole, that is, of him; and we contribute, so to say, also our share to the realisation of so many skilfully ordered and perfect works, which depend on him.

Secondly, this knowledge brings it about that we do not grow proud when we have accomplished something excellent (which pride causes us to come to a standstill, because we think that we are already great, and that we need do nothing further; thereby militating precisely against our own perfection, which consists in this — that we must at all times endeavour to advance further and further); but that, on the contrary, we attribute all that we do to God, who is the first and only cause of all that we accomplish and succeed in effecting.

Thirdly, in addition to the fact that this knowledge inspires us with a real love of our neighbour, it shapes us so that we never hate him, nor are we angry with him, but love to help him, and to improve his condition. All these are the actions of such men as have great perfection or essence.

Fourthly, this knowledge also serves to promote the greatest Common Good, because through it a judge can never side with one party more than with the other, and when compelled to punish the one, and to reward the other, he will do it with a view to help and to improve the one as much as the other.

Fifthly, this knowledge frees us from Sorrow, from Despair, from Envy, from Terror, and other evil passions, which, as we shall presently say, constitute the real hell itself.

Sixthly, this knowledge brings us so far that we cease to stand in awe of God, as others do of the Devil (whom they imagine), lest he should do them harm. For why indeed should we fear God, who is the highest good itself, through whom all things are what they are, and also we who live in him?

Seventhly, this knowledge also brings us so far that we attribute all to God, love him alone because he is the most glorious and the most perfect, and thus offer ourselves up entirely to him; for these really constitute both the true service of God and our own eternal happiness and bliss. For the sole perfection and the final end of a slave and of a tool is this, that they duly fulfil the task imposed on them. For example, if a carpenter, while doing some work, finds his Hatchet of excellent service, then this Hatchet has thereby attained its end and perfection; but if he should think: this Hatchet has rendered me such good service now, therefore I shall let it rest, and exact no further service from it, then precisely this Hatchet would fail of its end, and be a Hatchet no more. Thus also is it with man, so long as he is a part of Nature he must follow the laws of Nature, and this is divine service; and so long as he does this, it is well with him. But if God should (so to say) will that man should serve him no more, that would be equivalent to depriving him of his well-being and annihilating him; because all that he is consists in this, that he serves God.

CHAPTER XIX.

ON OUR HAPPINESS

NOW THAT WE have seen the advantages of this True Belief, we shall endeavour to fulfil the promise we have made, namely, to inquire whether through the knowledge which we already have (as to what is good, what is evil, what truth is, and what falsity is, and what, in general, the uses of all these are), whether, I say, we can thereby attain to our well-being, namely, the LOVE of God (which we have remarked to be our supreme happiness), and also in what way we can free ourselves from the passions which we have judged to be bad.

To begin with the consideration of the last, namely, of the liberation from the passions, I say that, if we suppose that they have no other causes than those which we have assigned to them, then, provided only we use our understanding aright, as we can do very easily (now that we have a criterion of truth and falsity), we shall never fall into them.

But what we have now to prove is that they have no other causes; for this, methinks, it is required that we should study ourselves in our entirety, having regard to the body as well as to the spirit.

And first [we have] to show that in Nature there is a body through whose form and activities we are affected, and thus become aware of it. And the reason why we do this is, because when we get an insight into the activities of the body and the effects which they produce, then we shall also discover the first and foremost cause of all those passions; and, at the same time, also that through which all those passions might be annihilated. From this we shall then also be able to see whether it is possible to do such a thing by the aid of Reason. And then we shall also proceed to speak about our Love of God.

Now to prove that there is a body in Nature, can be no difficult task for us, now that we already know that God is, and what God is; whom we have defined as a being of infinite attributes, each of which is infinite and perfect. And since extension is an attribute which we have shown to be infinite in its kind, it must therefore also necessarily be an attribute of that infinite being. And as we have also already demonstrated that this infinite being exists, it follows at once that this attribute also exists.

Moreover, since we have also proved that outside Nature, which is infinite, there is, and can be, no being, it is clearly manifest that this effect of body through which we become aware [of it] can proceed from nothing else than from extension itself, and by no means from something else which (as some will have it) has extension in an eminent degree [eminenter]-, for (as we have already shown in the first chapter) there is no such thing.

We have to remark, therefore, that all the effects which are seen to depend necessarily on extension must be attributed to this attribute; such as Motion and Rest. For if the power to produce these did not exist in Nature, then (even though it [Nature] might have many other attributes) it would be impossible that these should exist. For if a thing is to produce something then there must be that in it through which it, rather than another, can produce that something.

What we have just said here about extension, the same we also wish to be regarded as though it had been said about thought, and further about all that is.

It is to be observed further, that there is nothing whatever in us, but we have the power to become aware of it: so that if we find that there is nothing else in us except the effects of the thinking thing and those of extension, then we may say with certainty that there is nothing else in us.

In order that the workings of both these may be clearly understood, we shall take them up first each by itself only, and afterwards both together; as also the effects of both the one and the other.

Now when we consider extension alone, then we become aware of nothing else in it except Motion and Rest, from which we then discover all the effects that result therefrom. And these two modes of body are such that it is impossible for any other thing to change them, except only themselves. Thus, for example, when a stone lies still, then it is impossible that it should be moved by the power of thought or anything else, but [it may] well [be moved] by motion, as when another stone, having greater motion than this has rest, makes it move. Likewise also the moving stone will not be made to rest except through something else which has less motion. It follows, accordingly, that no mode of thought can bring motion or rest into a body. In accordance, however, with what we observe in ourselves, it may well happen that a body which is moving now in one direction may nevertheless turn aside in another direction; as when I stretch out my arm and thereby bring it about that the [vital] spirits which were already moving in a different direction, nevertheless move now in this direction, though not always, but according to the disposition of the [vital] spirits, as will be stated presently.

The cause of this can be none other than that the soul, being an Idea of this body, is united with it in such a way that it and this body, thus constituted, together form a whole.

The most important effect of the other or thinking attribute is an Idea of things, which is such that, according to the manner in which it apprehends them, there arises either Love or Hatred, etc. This effect, then, as it implies no extension, can also not be attributed to the same, but only to thought; so that, whatever the changes which happen to arise in this mode, their cause must on no account be sought for in extension, but only in the thinking thing. We can see this, for instance, in the case of Love, which, whether it is to be suppressed or whether it is to be awakened, can only be thus affected through the idea itself, and this happens, as we have already remarked, either because something bad is perceived to be in the object, or because something better comes to be known. Now whenever these attributes happen to act the one on the other, there results a passivity which one suffers from the other; namely [in the case of extension], through the determination of movements which we have the power to direct in whatever direction we please. The process, then, whereby the one comes to be passively affected by the other, is this: namely, the soul in the body, as has already been remarked, can well bring it about that the [vital] spirits, which would otherwise move in the one direction, should nevertheless move in the other direction; and since these [vital] spirits can also be made to move, and therefore directed, by the body, it may frequently happen that, when the body directs their movements towards one place, while the soul directs them towards another place, they bring about and occasion in us those peculiar fits of depression which we sometimes feel without knowing the reasons why we have them. For otherwise the reasons are generally well known to us.

Furthermore, the power which the soul has to move the [vital] spirits may well be hindered also either because the motion of the [vital] spirits is much diminished, or because it is much increased. Diminished, as when, having run much, we bring it about that the [vital] spirits, owing to this running, impart to the body much more than the usual amount of motion," and by losing this [motion] they are necessarily that much weakened; this may also happen through taking all too little food. Increased, as when, by drinking too much wine or other strong drink, we thereby become either merry or drunk, and bring it about that the soul has no power to control the body.

Having said thus much about the influences which the soul exercises on the body, let us now consider the influences of the body on the soul. The most important of these, we maintain, is that it causes the soul to become aware of it, and through it also of other bodies. This is effected by Motion and Rest conjointly, and by nothing else: for the body has nothing else than these wherewith to operate; so that whatever else comes to the soul, besides this awareness, cannot be caused through the body. And as the first thing which the soul gets to know is the body, the result is that the soul loves it so, and becomes united with it. But since, as we have already said before, the cause of Love, Hatred, and Sorrow must not be sought for in the body but only in the soul (because all the activities of the body must proceed from motion and rest), and since we see clearly and distinctly that one love comes to an end as soon as we come to know something else that is better, it follows clearly from all this that, If once we get to know God, at least with a knowledge as clear as that with which we also know our body, then we must become united with him even more closely than we are with our body, and be, as it were, released from the body. I say more closely, because we have already proved before that without him we can neither be, nor be known; and this is so because we know and must know him, not through something else, as is the case with all other things, but only through himself, as we have already said before. Indeed, we know him better even than we know ourselves, because without him we could not know ourselves at all.

From what we have said so far it is easily gathered which are the chief causes of the passions. For, as regards the Body with its effects, Motion and Rest, these cannot affect the soul otherwise except so as to make themselves known to it as objects; and according to the appearances which they present to it, that is according as they appear good or bad, so also is the soul affected by them, and that [happens] not inasmuch as it is a body (for then the body would be the principal cause of the passions), but inasmuch as it is an object like all other things, which would also act in the same way if they happened to reveal themselves to the soul in the same way. (By this, however, I do not mean to say that the Love, Hatred, and Sorrow which proceed from the contemplation of incorporeal things produce the same effects as those which arise from the contemplation of corporeal things; for, as we shall presently say, these have yet other effects according to the nature of the thing through the apprehension of which Love, Hatred, and Sorrow, etc., are awakened in the soul which contemplates the incorporeal things.) So that, to return to our previous subject, if something else should appear to the soul to be more glorious than the body really is, it is certain that the body would then have no power to produce such effects as it certainly does now. Whence it follows,? not alone that the body is not the principal cause of the passions, but also that even if there were in us something else besides what we have just stated to be capable, in our opinion, of producing the passions, such a thing, even if there were such, could likewise affect the soul neither more nor differently than the body does in fact now. For it could never be anything else than such an object as would once for all be different from the soul, and would consequently show itself to be such and no other, as we have likewise stated also of the body. So that we may, with truth, conclude that Love, Hatred, Sorrow, and other passions are produced in the soul in various forms according to the kind of knowledge which, from time to time, it happens to have of the thing; and consequently, if once it can come to know the most glorious of all, it should be impossible for any of these passions to succeed in causing it the least perturbation.

CHAPTER XX.

CONFIRMATION OF THE FOREGOING

NOW, AS REGARDS what we have said in the preceding chapter, the following difficulties might be raised by way of objection.

First, if motion is not the cause of the passions then why is it possible, nevertheless, to banish sorrow by the aid of certain means, as is often done by means of wine? To this it serves [as an answer] that a distinction must be made between the soul's awareness, when it first becomes aware of the body, and the judgment which it presently comes to form as to whether it is good or bad for it.

Now the soul, being such as just stated, has, as we have already shown before, the power to move the [vital] spirits whithersoever it pleases; but this power may, nevertheless, be taken away from it, as when, owing to other causes [arising out] of the body generally, their form, constituted by certain proportions [of motion and rest], disappears or is changed; and when it becomes aware of this [change] in it, there arises sorrow, which varies with the change which the [vital] spirits undergo. This sorrow results from its love for, and union with, the body.

That this is so may be easily deduced from the fact that this sorrow can be alleviated in one of these two ways; either by restoring the [vital] spirits to their original form that is by relieving him of the pain, or by being persuaded by good reasons to make no ado about this body. The first is temporary, and [the sorrow] is liable to return; but the second is eternal, permanent, and unchangeable.

The second objection may be this: as we see that the soul, although it has nothing in common with the body, can yet bring it about that the [vital] spirits, although they were about to move in one direction, nevertheless move now in the other direction, why should it not also be able to effect that a body which is perfectly still and at rest should begin to move itself? Likewise, why should it not also be able to move in whatever direction it pleases all other bodies which are already in motion?

But if we recall what we have already said before concerning the thinking thing, it can remove this difficulty for us quite easily. Namely, we then said that although Nature has various attributes, it is, all the same, but one only Being, of which all these attributes are predicated. Besides this we have also said that the thinking thing, too, was but one only thing in Nature, and is expressed in infinite Ideas, in accordance with the infinite things which exist in Nature; for if the body receives such a mode as, for example, the body of Peter, and again another such as is the body of Paul, the result of this is that there are in the thinking thing two different Ideas: namely, one idea of the body of Peter, which constitutes the Soul of Peter, and another of [the body of] Paul, which constitutes the Soul of Paul. Now the thinking thing can well move the body of Peter by means of the Idea of the body of Peter, but not by means of the Idea of the body of Paul; so that the soul of Paul can well move its own body, but by no means that of another, such as that of Peter. And for this reason also it cannot move a stone which rests or lies still: because the stone, again, makes another Idea in the Soul. Hence also it is no less clear that it is impossible that a stone, which is perfectly at rest and still, should be made to move by any mode of thought, for the same reasons as above.

The third objection may be this: We seem to be able to see clearly that we can, nevertheless, produce a certain stillness in the body. For, after we have kept moving our [vital] spirits for a long time, we find that we are tired; which, assuredly, is nothing else than a certain stillness in the [vital] spirits brought about by ourselves. We answer, however, that it is quite true that the soul is a cause of this stillness, but only indirectly; for it puts a stop to the movement not directly, but only through other bodies which it has moved, and which must then necessarily have lost as much as they had imparted to the [vital] spirits. It is therefore clear on all sides that in Nature there is only one and the same kind of motion.

CHAPTER XXI.

ON REASON

AT PRESENT WE have to inquire why it happens that sometimes, although we see that a certain thing is good or bad, we nevertheless do not find in us the power either to do the good or to abstain from the bad, and sometimes, however, we do indeed [find this power in us]. This we can easily understand if we consider the causes that we assigned to opinions, which we stated to be the causes of all affects. These, we then said, [arise] either from hearsay, or from experience. And since all that we find in ourselves has greater power over us than that which comes to us from outside, it certainly follows that Reason can be the cause of the extinction of opinions which we have got from hearsay only (and this is so because reason has not like these come to us from outside), but by no means of those which we have got from experience. For the power which the thing itself gives us is always greater than that which we obtain by way of consequence through a second thing; we noted this difference when speaking of reasoning and of clear understanding, page 62, and we did so with the rule of three as an illustration. For more power comes to us from the understanding of proportion itself, than from the understanding of the rule of proportion. And it is for this reason that we have said so often that one love may be extinguished by another which is greater, because in saying this we did not, by any means, intend to refer to desire which does not, like love, come from true knowledge, but comes from reasoning.

CHAPTER XXII.

ON TRUE KNOWLEDGE, REGENERATION, ETC.

SINCE, THEN, REASON has no power to lead us to the attainment of our well-being, it remains for us to inquire whether we can attain it through the fourth, and last, kind of knowledge. Now we have said that this kind of knowledge does not result from something else, but from a direct revelation of the object itself to the understanding. And if that object is glorious and good, then the soul becomes necessarily united with it, as we have also remarked with reference to our body. Hence it follows incontrovertibly that it is this knowledge which evokes love. So that when we get to know God after this manner then (as he cannot reveal himself, nor become known to us otherwise than as the most glorious and best of all) we must necessarily become united with him. And only in this union, as we have already remarked, does our blessedness consist.

I do not say that we must know him just as he is, or adequately, for it is sufficient for us to know him to some extent, in order to be united with him. For even the knowledge that we have of the body is not such that we know it just as it is, or perfectly; and yet, what a union! What a love!

That this fourth [kind of] knowledge, which is the knowledge of God, is not the consequence of something else, but immediate, is evident from what we have proved before, [namely,] that he is the cause of all knowledge that is acquired through itself alone, and through no other thing; moreover, also from this, that we are so united with him by nature that without him we can neither be, nor be known. And for this reason, since there is such a close union between God and us, it is evident that we cannot know him except directly.

We shall endeavour to explain, next, this union of ours with him through nature and love.

We said before that in Nature there can be nothing of which there should not be an Idea in the soul of that same thing. And according as the thing is either more or less perfect, so also is the union and the influence of the Idea with the thing, or with God himself, less or more perfect. For as the whole of Nature is but one only substance, and one whose essence is infinite, all things are united through Nature, and they are united into one [being], namely, God. And now, as the body is the very first thing of which our soul becomes aware (because as already remarked, nothing can exist in Nature, the Idea of which is not in the thinking thing, this Idea being the soul of that thing) so that thing must necessarily be the first cause of the Idea.

But, as this Idea can by no means find rest in the knowledge of the body without passing on to the knowledge of that without which the body and Idea could neither be, nor be understood, so (after knowing it first) it becomes united with it immediately through love. This union is better understood, and one may gather what it must be like, from its action with the body, in which we see how through knowledge of, and feelings towards corporeal things, there arise in us all the effects which we are constantly becoming aware of in the body, through the movements of the [vital] spirits; and therefore (if once our knowledge and love come to embrace that without which we can neither be, nor be understood, and which is in no way corporeal) how incomparably greater and more glorious will and must be the kind of effects resulting from this union; for these must necessarily be commensurate with the thing with which it is united. And when we become aware of these excellent effects, then we may say with truth, that we have been born again. For our first birth took place when we were united with the body, through which the activities and movements of the [vital] spirits have arisen; but this our other or second birth will take place when we become aware in us of entirely different effects of love, commensurate with the knowledge of this incorporeal object, and as different from the first as the corporeal is different from the incorporeal, spirit from flesh. And this may, therefore, all the more justly and truly be called Regeneration, inasmuch as only from this love and union does Eternal and unchangeable existence ensue, as we shall prove.

CHAPTER XXIII.

ON THE IMMORTALITY OF THE SOUL

IF ONLY WE consider attentively what the Soul is, and whence its change and duration originate, then we shall easily see whether it is mortal or immortal.

Now we have said that the Soul is an Idea which is in the thinking thing, arising from the reality of a thing which exists in Nature. Whence it follows that according to the duration and change of the thing, so must also be the duration and change of the Soul. We remarked, at the same time, that the Soul can become united either with the body of which it is the Idea, or with God, without whom it can neither be, nor be known.

From this, then, it can easily be seen, (1) that, if it is united with the body alone, and that body happens to perish, then it must perish also; for when it is deprived of the body, which is the foundation of its love, it must perish with it. But (2) if it becomes united with some other thing which is and remains unchangeable, then, on the contrary, it must also remain unchangeable and lasting. For, in that case, through what shall it be possible for it to perish? Not through itself; for as little as it could begin to exist through itself when it did not yet exist, so little also can it change or perish through itself, now that it does exist.

Consequently, that thing which alone is the cause of its existence, must also (when it is about to perish) be the cause of its nonexistence, because it happens to change itself or to perish.

CHAPTER XXIV.

ON GOD'S LOVE OF MAN

THUS FAR WE have shown sufficiently, we think, what our love of God is, also its consequences, namely, our eternal duration. So we do not think it necessary here to say anything about other things, such as joy in God, peace of mind, etc., as from what has been said it may easily be seen what there is to or should be said about them. Thus (as we have, so far, only considered our love of God) it still remains to be seen whether there is also a divine love of us, that is, whether God also loves mankind, namely, when they love him. Now, in the first place, we have said that to God no modes of thought can be ascribed except those which are in his creatures; therefore, it cannot be said that God loves mankind, much less [can it be said] that he should love them because they love him, or hate them because they hate him. For in that case we should have to suppose that people do so of their own free will, and that they do not depend on a first cause; which we have already before proved to be false. Besides, this would necessarily involve nothing less than a great mutability on the part of God, who, though he neither loved nor hated before, would now have to begin to love and to hate, and would be induced or made to do so by something supposed to be outside him; but this is absurdity itself.

Still, when we say that God does not love man, this must not be taken to mean that he (so to say) leaves man to pursue his course all alone, but only that because man together with all that is, are in God in such a way, and God consists of all these in such a way, therefore, properly speaking, there can be in him no love for something else: since all form only one thing, which is God himself.

From this it follows also that God gives no laws to mankind so as to reward them when they fulfil them [and to punish them when they transgress them,] or, to state it more clearly, that God's laws are not of such a nature that they could be transgressed. For the regulations imposed by God on Nature, according to which all things come into existence and continue to exist, these, if we will call them laws, are such that they can never be transgressed; such, for instance, is [the law] that the weakest must yield to the strongest, that no cause can produce more than it contains in itself, and the like, which are of such a kind that they never change, and never had a beginning, but all things are subjected and subordinated to them. And, to say briefly something about them: all laws that cannot be transgressed, are divine laws; the reason [is this], because whatsoever happens, is not contrary to, but in accordance with, his own decision. All laws that can be transgressed are human laws; the reason [is this], because all that people decide upon for their own wellbeing does not necessarily, on that account, tend also to the well-being of the whole of Nature, but may, on the contrary, tend to the annihilation of many other things.

When the laws of Nature are stronger, the laws of men are made null; the divine laws are the final end for the sake of which they exist, and not subordinate; human [laws] are not. Still, notwithstanding the fact that men make laws for their own well-being, and have no other end in view except to promote their own well-being by them, this end of theirs may yet (insofar as it is subordinate to other ends which another has in view, who is above them, and lets them act thus as parts of Nature) serve that end [which] coincides with the eternal laws established by God from eternity, and so, together with all others, help to accomplish everything. For example, although the Bees, in all their work and the orderly discipline which they maintain among themselves, have no other end in view than to make certain provisions for themselves for the winter, still, man who is above them, has an entirely different end in view when he maintains and tends them, namely, to obtain honey for himself. So also [is it with] man, insofar as he is an individual thing and looks no further than his finite character can reach; but, insofar as he is also a part and tool of the whole of Nature, this end of man cannot be the final end of Nature, because she is infinite, and must make use of him, together also with all other things, as an instrument.

Thus far [we have been speaking] of the law imposed by God; it is now to be remarked also that man is aware of two kinds of law even in himself; 1 mean such a man who uses his understanding aright, and attains to the knowledge of God; and these [two kinds of law] result from his fellowship with God, and from his fellowship with the modes of Nature. Of these the one is necessary, and the other is not. For, as regards the law which results from his fellowship with God, since he can never be otherwise but must always necessarily be united with him, therefore he has, and always must have before his eyes the laws by which he must live for and with God. But as regards the law which results from his fellowship with the modes, since he can separate himself from men, this is not so necessary.

Now, since we posit such a fellowship between God and men, it might justly be asked, how God can make himself known to men, and whether this happens, or could have happened, by means of spoken words, or directly through himself, without using any other thing to do it with.

We answer, not by means of words, in any case; for in that case man must have known the signification of the words before they were spoken to him. For example, if God had said to the Israelites, I am Jehovah your God, then they would have had to know first, apart from these words, that God existed, before they could be assured thereby that it was he [who was speaking to them]. For they already knew quite well then that the voice, thunder and lightning were not God, although the voice proclaimed that it was God. And the same that we say here about words, we also mean to hold good of all external signs.

We consider it, therefore, impossible that God should make himself known to men by means of external signs.

And we consider it to be unnecessary that it should happen through any other thing than the mere essence of God and the understanding of man; for, as the Understanding is that in us which must know God, and as it stands in such immediate union with him that it can neither be, nor be understood without him, it is incontrovertibly evident from this that nothing can ever come into such close touch with the Understanding as God himself can. It is also impossible to get to know God through something else. 1. Because, in that case, such a thing would have to be better known to us than God himself, which is in open conflict with all that we have hitherto clearly shown, namely, that God is a cause both of our knowledge and of all essence, and that without him all individual things not only cannot exist, but cannot even be understood. 2. Because we can never attain to the knowledge of God through any other thing, the nature of which is necessarily finite, even if it were far better known to us; for how is it possible that we should infer an infinite and limitless thing from a finite and limited thing? For even if we did observe some effects or work in Nature the cause of which was unknown to us, still it would be impossible for us to conclude from this that there must be in Nature an infinite and limitless thing in order to produce this result. For how can we know whether many causes have concurred in order to produce this, or whether there was only one? Who is to tell us?

We therefore conclude, finally, that, in order to make himself known to men, God can and need use neither words, nor miracles, nor any other created thing, but only himself.

CHAPTER XXV.

ON DEVILS

WE SHALL NOW briefly say something about devils, whether they exist or do not exist, and it is this:

If the Devil is a thing that is once for all opposed to God, and has absolutely nothing from God, then he is precisely identical with Nothing, which we have already discussed before.

If, with some, we represent him as a thinking thing that absolutely neither wills nor does any good, and so sets himself, once for all, in opposition to God, then surely he is very wretched, and, if prayers could help, then one ought to pray for his conversion.

But let us just see whether such a wretched thing could even exist for a single moment. And, if we do so, we shall immediately find out that it cannot; for whatever duration a thing has results entirely from the perfection of the thing, and the more essence and godliness things possess, the more lasting are they: therefore, as the Devil has not the least perfection in him, how should he then, I think to myself, be able to exist? Add to this, that the persistence or duration of a mode of the thinking thing only results from the union in which such a mode is, through love, joined to God. As the precise opposite of this union is supposed in the case of the Devils, they cannot possibly exist.

As, however, there is no necessity whatever why we should posit the existence of Devils, why then should they be posited? For we need not, like others, posit Devils in order to find [in them] the cause of Hatred, Envy, Wrath, and such-like passions, since we have found this sufficiently, without such fictions.

CHAPTER XXVI.

ON TRUE FREEDOM

BY THE ASSERTION of what precedes we not only wanted to make known that there are no Devils, but also, indeed, that the causes (or, to express it better, what we call Sins) which hinder us in the attainment of our perfection are in ourselves. We have also shown already, in what precedes, how and in what manner, through reason as also through the fourth kind of knowledge, we must attain to our blessedness, and how the passions which are bad and should be banished must be done away with: not as is commonly urged, namely, that these [passions] must first be subdued before we can attain to the knowledge, and consequently to the love, of God. That would be just like insisting that some one who is ignorant must first forsake his ignorance before he can attain to knowledge. But [the truth is] this, that only knowledge can cause the disappearance thereof — as is evident from all that we have said. Similarly, it may also be clearly gathered from the above that without Virtue, or (to express it better) without the guidance of the Understanding, all tends to ruin, so that we can enjoy no rest, and we live, as it were, outside our element. So that even if from the power of knowledge and divine love there accrued to the understanding not an eternal rest, such as we have shown, but only a temporary one, it is our duty to seek even this, since this also is such that if once we taste it we would exchange it for nothing else in the world.

This being so, we may, with reason, regard as a great absurdity what many, who are otherwise esteemed as great theologians, assert, namely, that if no eternal life resulted from the love of God, then they would seek what is best for themselves: as though they could discover anything better than God! This is just as silly as if a fish (for which, of course, it is impossible to live out of the water) were to say: if no eternal life is to follow this life in the water, then I will leave the water for the land; what else, indeed, can they say to us who do not know God?

Thus we see, therefore, that in order to arrive at the truth of what we assert for sure concerning our happiness and repose, we require no other principles except only this, namely, to take to heart our own interest, which is very natural in all things. And since we find that, when we pursue sensuousness, pleasures, and worldly things, we do not find our happiness in them, but, on the contrary, our ruin, we therefore choose the guidance of our understanding. As, however, this can make no progress, unless it has first attained to the knowledge and love of God, therefore it was highly necessary to seek this (God); and as (after the foregoing reflections and considerations) we have discovered that he is the best good of all that is good, we are compelled to stop and to rest here. For we have seen that, outside him, there is nothing that can give us any happiness. And it is a true freedom to be, and to remain, bound with the loving chains of his love.

Lastly, we see also that reasoning is not the principal thing in us, but only like a staircase by which we can climb up to the desired place, or like a good genius which, without any falsity or deception, brings us tidings of the highest good in order thereby to stimulate us to pursue it, and to become united with it; which union is our supreme happiness and bliss.

So, to bring this work to a conclusion, it remains to indicate briefly what human freedom is, and wherein it consists. For this purpose I shall make use of these following propositions, as things which are certain and demonstrated.

1. The more essence a thing has, so much more has it also of activity, and so much less of passivity. For it is certain that what is active acts through what it has, and that the thing which is passive is affected through what it has not.

2. All passivity that passes from non-being to being, or from being to non-being, must result from some external agent, and not from an inner one: because nothing, considered by itself, contains in itself the conditions that will enable it to annihilate itself when it exists, or to create itself when it does not exist.

3. Whatever is not produced by external causes can have nothing in common with them, and can, consequently, be neither changed nor transformed by them.

And from these last two [propositions] I infer the following fourth proposition:

4. The effect of an immanent or inner cause (which is all one to me) cannot possibly pass away or change so long as this cause of it remains. For such an effect, just as it is not produced by external causes, so also it cannot be changed [by them]; following the third proposition. And since nothing whatever can come to naught except through external causes, it is not possible that this effect should be liable to perish so long as its cause endures; following the second proposition.

5. The freest cause of all, and that which is most appropriate to God, is the immanent: for the effect of this cause depends on it in such a way that it can neither be, nor be understood without it, nor is it subjected to any other cause; it is, moreover, united with it in such a way that together they form one whole.

Now let us just see what we must conclude from the above propositions. In the first place, then:

1. Since the essence of God is infinite, therefore it has an infinite activity, and an infinite negation of passivity, following the first proposition; and, in consequence of this, the more that, through their greater essence, things are united with God, so much the more also do they have of activity, and the less of passivity: and so much the more also are they free from change and corruption.

2. The true Understanding can never perish; for in itself it can have no cause to destroy itself, following the second proposition. And as it did not emanate from external causes, but from God, so it is not susceptible to any change through them, following the third proposition. And since God has produced it immediately and he is only an inner cause, it follows necessarily that it cannot perish so long as this cause of it remains, following the fourth proposition. Now this cause of it is eternal, therefore it is too.

3. All the effects of the true understanding, which are united with it, are the most excellent, and must be valued above all the others; for as they are inner effects, they must be the most excellent; following the fifth proposition; and, besides this, they are also necessarily eternal, because their cause is such.

4. All the effects which we produce outside ourselves are the more perfect, the more they are capable of becoming united with us, so as to constitute one and the same nature with us; for in this way they come nearest to inner effects. For example, if I teach my neighbours to love pleasure, glory, avarice, then whether I myself also love these or do not love them, whatever the case may be, I deserve to be punished, this is clear. Not so, however, when the only end that I endeavour to

attain is, to be able to taste of union with God, and to bring forth true ideas, and to make these things known also to my neighbours; for we can all participate equally in this happiness, as happens when it creates in them the same desire that I have, thus causing their will and mine to be one and the same, constituting one and the same nature, agreeing always in all things.

From all that has been said it may now be very easily conceived what is human freedom, which I define to be this: it is, namely, a firm reality which our understanding acquires through direct union with God, so that it can bring forth ideas in itself, and effects outside itself, in complete harmony with its nature; without, however, its effects being subjected to any external causes, so as to be capable of being changed or transformed by them. Thus it is, at the same time, evident from what has been said, what things there are that are in our power, and are not subjected to any external causes; we have likewise also proved here, and that in a different way from before, the eternal and lasting duration of our understanding; and, lastly, which effects it is that we have to value above all others.

So, to make an end of all this, it only remains for me still to say to my friends to whom I write this: Be not astonished at these novelties; for it is very well known to you that a thing does not therefore cease to be true because it is not accepted by many. And also, as the character of the age in which we live is not unknown to you, I would beg of you most earnestly to be very careful about the communication of these things to others. I do not want to say that you should absolutely keep them to yourselves, but only that if ever you begin to communicate them to anybody, then let no other aim prompt you except only the happiness of your neighbour, being at the same time clearly assured by him that the reward will not disappoint your labour. Lastly, if, on reading this through, you should meet with some difficulty about what I state as certain, I beseech you that you should not therefore hasten at once to refute it, before you have pondered it long enough and thoughtfully enough, and if you do this I feel sure that you will attain to the enjoyment of the fruits of this tree which you promise yourselves.

APPENDICES

APPENDIX I. ON GOD

Axioms

1. SUBSTANCE IS, by its nature, prior to all its modifications.

2. Things which are different are distinguished either realiter or modaliter.

3. Things which are distinguished realiter either have different attributes, such as Thought and Extension, or are referred to different attributes, as in the case of Understanding and Motion; one of which belongs to Thought, and the other to Extension.

4. Things which have different attributes, as also the things which belong to different attributes, do not have anything the one of the other.

5. That which has not in itself something of another thing, can also not be a cause of the existence of such another thing.

6. It is impossible that that which is a cause of itself should have limited itself.

7. That by which the things are sustained is by its nature prior to such things.

PROPOSITION I

To no substance that exists can one and the same attribute be ascribed that is ascribed to another substance; or (which is the same) in Nature there cannot be two substances, unless they are distinguished realiter.

Proof If there are two substances, then they are distinct; and consequently (Axiom 2) they are distinguished either realiter or modaliter; not modaliter, for in that case the modes would by their nature be prior to the substance, which is contrary to the first axiom; therefore, realiter; and consequently, what is predicated of the one cannot be predicated of the other, which is what we intended to prove.

PROPOSITION II

One substance cannot be the cause of the existence of another substance.

Proof Such a cause cannot contain in itself anything of such an effect (Prop. 1); because the difference between them is real, and therefore it cannot (Axiom 5) produce it.

PROPOSITION III

Every attribute or substance is by nature infinite, and supremely perfect in its kind.

Proof No substance is produced by another (Prop. 2) and consequently, if it exists, it is either an attribute of God, or it has been its own cause outside God. If the first, then it is necessarily infinite, and supremely perfect in its kind, such as are all other attributes of God. If the second, then it is also necessarily such because (Axiom 6) it could not have limited itself.

PROPOSITION IV

To such an extent does existence pertain by nature to the essence of every substance, that it is impossible to posit in an infinite understanding the Idea of the essence of a substance that does not exist in Nature.

Proof The true essence of an object is something which is realiter different from the Idea of the same object; and this something exists (Axiom 3) either realiter, or is contained in some other thing which exists realiter; from which other thing this essence cannot be distinguished realiter, but only modaliter; such are all the essences of the things which we see, which before they yet existed were already contained in extension, motion, and rest, and when they do exist are not distinguished from extension realiter, but only modaliter. Moreover, it would involve self-contradiction to suppose that the essence of a substance is contained thus in some other thing; because in that case it could not be distinguished from this realiter, contrary to the first proposition; also, it could in that case be produced by the subject which contains it, contrary to the second proposition; and lastly, it could not by its nature be infinite and supremely perfect in its kind, contrary to the third proposition. Therefore, as its essence is not contained in any other thing, it must be a thing that exists through itself.

Corollary Nature is known through itself, and not through any other thing. It consists of infinite attributes every one of them infinite and perfect in its kind; to its essence pertains existence, so that outside it there is no other essence or existence, and it thus coincides exactly with the essence of God who alone is glorious and blessed.

APPENDIX II. ON THE HUMAN SOUL

AS MAN IS a created finite thing, etc., it necessarily follows that what he has of Thought, and what we call the Soul, is a mode of the attribute which we call Thought, and that nothing else except this mode belongs to his essence: so much so that when this mode comes to naught, the soul perishes also, although the above attribute remains unchanged. Similarly as regards what he has of Extension; what we call Body is nothing else than a mode of the other attribute which we call Extension; when this is destroyed, the human body also ceases to be, although the attribute Extension remains unchanged.

Now in order to understand what this mode is, which we call Soul, and how it derives its origin from the body, and also how its change (only) depends on the body (which to me constitutes the union of soul and body), it must be observed:

1. That the most immediate mode of the attribute which we call thought contains objective the formal essence of all things; so much so, that if one could posit a real thing whose essence was not objective in the above-named attribute, then this would not be infinite, nor supremely perfect in its kind; contrary to what has already been proved in the third proposition. And since, as a matter of fact, Nature or God is one being of which infinite attributes are predicated, and which contains in itself all the essences of created things, it necessarily follows that of all this there is produced in Thought an infinite Idea, which comprehends objective the whole of Nature just as it is realiter.

2. It is to be observed that all the remaining modes, such as Love, Desire, Joy, etc., derive their origin from this first immediate mode; and that, too, in such wise, that if it did not precede, then there could be no love, desire, nor joy, etc. Whence it clearly follows that the natural love which prompts everything to preserve its body (I mean the mode) cannot have any other origin than in the Idea or the "objective" essence of such body which is in the thinking attribute. Further, since for the real existence of an Idea (or "objective" essence) no other thing is required than the thinking attribute and the object (or "formal" essence), it is certain, as we have said, that the Idea, or the "objective" essence, is the most immediate mode of the thinking attribute. And, consequently, there can be in the thinking attribute no other mode, that should belong to the essence of the soul of every thing, except only the Idea, which must be in the thinking attribute when its object exists: for such an idea brings with it the remaining modes of Love, Desire, Joy, etc. Now as the Idea comes from the existence of the object, therefore according as the object changes or perishes, so its Idea must change or perish, and such being the case, it is that which is united with the object.

Lastly, if we should want to proceed and ascribe to the essence of the soul that through which it can be real, we shall be able to find nothing else than the attribute [Thought] and the object of which we have just been speaking; and neither of these can belong to the essence of the Soul, as the object has nothing of Thought, and is realiter different from the Soul. And with regard to the attribute, we have also proved already that it cannot pertain to the above-mentioned essence, as appears even more clearly from what we said subsequently; for the attribute as attribute is not united with the object, since it neither changes nor perishes, although the object changes or perishes.

Therefore the essence of the soul consists in this alone, namely, in the existence of an Idea or "objective" essence in the thinking attribute, arising from the essence of an object which in fact exists in Nature. I say, of an object which in fact exists, etc., without more particulars, so as to include under this not only the modes of extension, but also the modes of all the infinite attributes, which have also each its soul, just as in the case of extension. And in order that this definition may be somewhat more fully understood, it should be borne in mind what I have already said when speaking about the attributes, which, I said, are not different as regards their existence, for they are themselves the "subjects" of their essences; also that the essence of every one of the modes is contained in the above-named attributes, and, lastly, that all the attributes are attributes of One infinite Being. Wherefore also, in the ninth chapter of the First Part, I called this Idea a creation created immediately by God; since it contains objective the "formal" essence of all things, without omission or addition. And this is necessarily but one, considering that all the essences of the attributes, and the essences of the modes comprehended in these attributes, are the essence of one only infinite being. But it has still to be remarked that these modes, now under consideration, [even when] none of them exists, are nevertheless equally comprehended in their attributes; and as there is no inequality whatever in the attributes, nor yet in the essences of the modes, there can be no particularity in the idea when there is none in Nature. But as soon as ever some of these modes take on their particular existence, and thereby become in some way different from their attributes (because then their particular existence, which they have in the attribute, as the "subject" of their essence), then there shows itself a particularity in the essences of the modes, and consequently in the "objective" essences of these which are necessarily comprehended in the Idea. And this is the reason why we said, in the definition, that the Idea arises from an object, which really exists in Nature. And with this we think we have sufficiently explained what kind of a thing the soul is in general, understanding by this expression not only the Ideas which arise from the existence of corporeal modes, but also those which arise from the existence of every mode of the remaining attributes.

But, since we have no such knowledge of the remaining attributes as we have of extension, let us just see whether, having regard to the modes of extension, we can discover a more special definition, and one that shall be more appropriate to express the essence of our souls, for this is the real task before us. Now we shall presuppose here, as something already demonstrated, that extension contains no other modes than motion and rest, and that every particular material thing is nothing else than a certain proportion of motion and rest, so much so indeed that, even if extension contained nothing else except motion only or rest only, then no particular thing could be shown or exist in the whole of extension; the human body, therefore, is nothing else than a certain proportion of motion and rest. Now the "objective essence" of this actual ratio of motion and rest which is in the thinking attribute, this (we say) is the soul of the body; so that whenever one of these two modes changes into more or less (motion or rest) the Idea or the soul also changes accordingly. For example, when the [amount of] rest happens to increase, while the [quantity of] motion is diminished, then there is produced thereby that pain or sorrow which we call cold; but if, on the contrary, this [increase] takes place in the [amount of] motion, then there is produced thereby that pain which we call heat. And so when it happens that the degrees of motion and rest are not equal in all the parts of our body, but that some have more motion and rest than others, there arises therefrom a difference of feeling (and thence arises the different kind of pain which we feel when we are struck in the eyes or on the hands with a cane). And when it happens that the external causes, which bring about these changes, are different from one another, and have not all the same effect, then there results from this a difference of feeling in one and the same part (and from this results the difference of feeling according as one and the same hand is struck with a piece of wood or of iron). And, again, if the change which occurs in a part restores it to its first proportion of motion and rest, there arises from this that joy which we call repose, pleasurable activity, and cheerfulness. Lastly, now that we have explained what feeling is, we can easily see how this gives rise to an Idea reflexiva, or the knowledge of oneself, Experience and Reasoning. And from all this (as also because our soul is united with God, and is a part of the infinite Idea, arising immediately from God) there can also be clearly seen the origin of clear knowledge, and the immortality of the soul. But, for the present, what we have said must be enough.

TREATISE ON THE EMENDATION OF THE INTELLECT

NOTICE TO THE READER.

THIS TREATISE ON the Emendation of the Intellect etc., which we give you here, kind reader, in its unfinished [that is, defective] state, was written by the author many years ago now. He always intended to finish it. But hindered by other occupations, and finally snatched away by death, he was unable to bring it to the desired conclusion. But since it contains many excellent and useful things, which — we have no doubt — will be of great benefit to anyone sincerely seeking the truth, we did not wish to deprive you of them. And so that you would be aware of, and find less difficult to excuse, the many things that are still obscure, rough, and unpolished, we wished to warn you of them. Farewell.

This notice to the reader was written by the editors of the Opera Postuma in 1677.

INTRODUCTION

On the Improvement of the Understanding

AFTER EXPERIENCE HAD taught me that all the usual surroundings of social life are vain and futile; seeing that none of the objects of my fears contained in themselves anything either good or bad, except in so far as the mind is affected by them, I finally resolved to inquire whether there might be some real good having power to communicate itself, which would affect the mind singly, to the exclusion of all else: whether, in fact, there might be anything of which the discovery and attainment would enable me to enjoy continuous, supreme, and unending happiness.

I say "I finally resolved," for at first sight it seemed unwise willingly to lose hold on what was sure for the sake of something then uncertain. I could see the benefits which are acquired through fame and riches, and that I should be obliged to abandon the quest of such objects, if I seriously devoted myself to the search for something different and new. I perceived that if true happiness chanced to be placed in the former I should necessarily miss it; while if, on the other hand, it were not so placed, and I gave them my whole attention, I should equally fail.

OF THE ORDINARY OBJECTS
OF MEN'S DESIRES

I THEREFORE DEBATED whether it would not be possible to arrive at the new principle, or at any rate at a certainty concerning its existence, without changing the conduct and usual plan of my life; with this end in view I made many efforts, in vain. For the ordinary surroundings of life which are esteemed by men (as their actions testify) to be the highest good, may be classed under the three heads — Riches, Fame, and the Pleasures of Sense: with these three the mind is so absorbed that it has little power to reflect on any different good.

By sensual pleasure the mind is enthralled to the extent of quiescence, as if the supreme good were actually attained, so that it is quite incapable of thinking of any other object; when such pleasure has been gratified it is followed by extreme melancholy, whereby the mind, though not enthralled, is disturbed and dulled. The pursuit of honors and riches is likewise very absorbing, especially if such objects be sought simply for their own sake, 1 inasmuch as they are then supposed to constitute the highest good.

In the case of fame the mind is still more absorbed, for fame is conceived as always good for its own sake, and as the ultimate end to which all actions are directed. Further, the attainment of riches and fame is not followed as in the case of sensual pleasures by repentance, but, the more we acquire, the greater is our delight, and, consequently, the more are we incited to increase both the one and the other; on the other hand, if our hopes happen to be frustrated we are plunged into the deepest sadness. Fame has the further drawback that it compels its votaries to order their lives according to the opinions of their fellow-men, shunning what they usually shun, and seeking what they usually seek.

When I saw that all these ordinary objects of desire would be obstacles in the way of a search for something different and new — nay, that they were so opposed thereto, that either they or it would have to be abandoned, I was forced to inquire which would prove the most useful to me: for, as I say, I seemed to be willingly losing hold on a sure good for the sake of something uncertain. However, after I had reflected on the matter, I came in the first place to the conclusion that by abandoning the ordinary objects of pursuit, and betaking myself to a new quest, I should be leaving a good, uncertain by reason of its own nature, as may be gathered from what has been said, for the sake of a good not uncertain in its nature (for I sought for a fixed good), but only in the possibility of its attainment.

Further reflection convinced me that if I could really get to the root of the matter I should be leaving certain evils for a certain good. I thus perceived that I was in a state of great peril, and I compelled myself to seek with all my strength for a remedy, however uncertain it might be; as a sick man struggling with a deadly disease, when he sees that death will surely be upon him unless a remedy be found, is compelled to seek a remedy with all his strength, inasmuch as his whole hope lies therein. All the objects pursued by the multitude not only bring no remedy that tends to preserve our being, but even act as hindrances, causing the death not seldom of those who possess them 2 and always of those who are possessed by them.

There are many examples of men who have suffered persecution even to death for the sake of their riches, and of men who in pursuit of wealth have exposed themselves to so many dangers, that they have paid away their life as a penalty for their folly. Examples are no less numerous of men, who have endured the utmost wretchedness for the sake of gaining or preserving their reputation. Lastly, are innumerable cases of men, who have hastened their death through over-indulgence in sensual pleasure.

All these evils seem to have arisen from the fact, that happiness or unhappiness is made wholly dependent on the quality of the object which we love. When a thing is not loved, no quarrels will arise concerning it — no sadness be felt if it hatred, in short no disturbances of the mind. All these arise from the love of what is perishable, such as the objects already mentioned.

But love towards a thing eternal and infinite feeds the mind wholly with joy, and is itself unmingled with any sadness, wherefore it is greatly to be desired and sought for with all our strength. Yet it was not at random that I used the words, "If I could go to the root of the matter," for, though what I have urged was perfectly clear to my mind, I could not forthwith lay aside all love of riches, sensual enjoyment, and fame.

One thing was evident, namely, that while my mind was employed with these thoughts it turned away from its former objects of desire, and seriously considered the search for a new principle; this state of things was a great comfort to me, for I perceived that the evils were not such as to resist all remedies. Although these intervals were at first rare, and of very short duration, yet afterwards, as the true good became more and more discernible to me, they became more frequent and more lasting; especially after I had recognized that the acquisition of wealth, sensual pleasure, or fame, is only a hindrance, so long as they are sought as ends not as means; if they be sought as means, they will be under restraint, and, far from being hindrances, will further not a little the end for which they are sought, as I will show in due time.

1 This might be explained more at large and more clearly: I mean by distinguishing riches according as they are pursued for their own sake, in or furtherance of fame, or sensual pleasure, or the advancement of science and art. But this subject is reserved to its own place, for it is not here proper to investigate the matter more accurately.

2 These considerations should be set forth more precisely.

OF THE TRUE AND FINAL GOOD

I WILL HERE only briefly state what I mean by true good, and also what is the nature of the highest good. In order that this may be rightly understood, we must bear in mind that the terms good and evil are only applied relatively, so that the same thing may be called both good and bad according to the relations in view, in the same way as it may be called perfect or imperfect. Nothing regarded in its own nature can be called perfect or imperfect; especially when we are aware that all things which come to pass, come to pass according to the eternal order and fixed laws of nature.

However, human weakness cannot attain to this order in its own thoughts, but meanwhile man conceives a human character much more stable than his own, and sees that there is no reason why he should not himself acquire such a character. Thus he is led to seek for means which will bring him to this pitch of perfection, and calls everything which will serve as such means a true good. The chief good is that he should arrive, together with other individuals if possible, at the possession of the aforesaid character. What that character is we shall show in due time, namely, that it is the knowledge of the union existing being the mind and the whole of nature. 3

This, then, is the end for which I strive, to attain to such a character myself, and to endeavor that many should attain to it with me. In other words, it is part of my happiness to lend a helping hand, that many others may understand even as I do, so that their understanding and desire may entirely agree with my own. In order to bring this about, it is necessary to understand as much of nature as will enable us to attain to the aforesaid character, and also to form a social order such as is most conducive to the attainment of this character by the greatest number with the least difficulty and danger.

We must seek the assistance of Moral Philosophy 4 and the Theory of Education; further, as health is no insignificant means for attaining our end, we must also include the whole science of Medicine, and, as many difficult things are by contrivance rendered easy, and we can in this way gain much time and convenience, the science of Mechanics must in no way be despised.

But before all things, a means must be devised for improving the understanding and purifying it, as far as may be at the outset, so that it may apprehend things without error, and in the best possible way. Thus it is apparent to everyone that I wish to direct all science to one end 5 and aim, so that we may attain to the supreme human perfection which we have named; and, therefore, whatsoever in the sciences does not serve to promote our object will have to be rejected as useless. To sum up the matter in a word, all our actions and thoughts must be directed to this one end.

3 These matters are explained more at length elsewhere.

4 N.B. I do no more here than enumerate the sciences necessary for our purpose; I lay no stress on their order.

5 There is for the sciences but one end, to which they should all be directed.

CERTAIN RULES OF LIFE

YET, AS IT is necessary that while we are endeavoring to attain our purpose, and bring the understanding into the right path we should carry on our life, we are compelled first of all to lay down certain rules of life as provisionally good, to wit the following: —

I. To speak in a manner intelligible to the multitude, and to comply with every general custom that does not hinder the attainment of our purpose. For we can gain from the multitude no small advantages, provided that we strive to accommodate ourselves to its understanding as far as possible: moreover, we shall in this way gain a friendly audience for the reception of the truth.

II. To indulge ourselves with pleasures only in so far as they are necessary for preserving health.

III. Lastly, to endeavor to obtain only sufficient money or other commodities to enable us to preserve our life and health, and to follow such general customs as are consistent with our purpose.

Having laid down these preliminary rules, I will betake myself to the first and most important task, namely, the amendment of the understanding, and the rendering it capable of understanding things in the manner necessary for attaining our end. In order to bring this about, the natural order demands that I should here recapitulate all the modes of perception, which I have hitherto employed for affirming or denying anything with certainty, so that I may choose the best, and at the same time begin to know my own powers and the nature which I wish to perfect.

OF THE FOUR MODES OF PERCEPTION

REFLECTION SHOWS THAT all modes of perception or knowledge may be reduced to four: —

I. Perception arising from hearsay or from some sign which everyone may name as he please.

II. Perception arising from mere experience — that is, form experience not yet classified by the intellect, and only so called because the given event has happened to take place, and we have no contradictory fact to set against it, so that it therefore remains unassailed in our minds.

III. Perception arising when the essence of one thing is inferred from another thing, but not adequately; this comes when 6 from some effect we gather its cause, or when it is inferred from some general proposition that some property is always present.

IV. Lastly, there is the perception arising when a thing is perceived solely through its essence, or through the knowledge of its proximate cause.

All these kinds of perception I will illustrate by examples. By hearsay I know the day of my birth, my parentage, and other matters about which I have never felt any doubt. By mere experience I know that I shall die, for this I can affirm from having seen that others like myself have died, though all did not live for the same period, or die by the same disease. I know by mere experience that oil has the property of feeding fire, and water of extinguishing it. In the same way I know that a dog is a barking animal, man a rational animal, and in fact nearly all the practical knowledge of life.

We deduce one thing from another as follows: when we clearly perceive that we feel a certain body and no other, we thence clearly infer that the mind is united 7 to the body, and that their union is the cause of the given sensation; but we cannot thence absolutely understand 8 the nature of the sensation and the union. Or, after I have become acquainted with the nature of vision, and know that it has the property of making one and the same thing appear smaller when far off than when near, I can infer that the sun is larger than it appears, and can draw other conclusions of the same kind.

Lastly, a thing may be perceived solely through its essence; when, from the fact of knowing something, I know what it is to know that thing, or when, from knowing the essence of the mind, I know that it is united to the body. By the same kind of knowledge we know that two and three make five, or that two lines each parallel to a third, are parallel to one another, &c. The things which I have been able to know by this kind of knowledge are as yet very few.

In order that the whole matter may be put in a clearer light, I will make use of a single illustration as follows. Three numbers are given — it is required to find a fourth, which shall be to the third as the second is to the first. Tradesmen will at once tell us that they know what is required to find the fourth number, for they have not yet forgotten the rule which was given to them arbitrarily without proof by their masters; others construct a universal axiom from their experience with simple numbers, where the fourth number is self-evident, as in the case of 2, 4, 3, 6; here it is evident that if the second number be multiplied by the third, and the product divided by the first, the quotient is 6; when they see that by this process the number is produced which they knew beforehand to be the proportional, they infer that the process always holds good for finding a fourth number proportional.

Mathematicians, however, know by the proof of the nineteenth proposition of the seventh book of Euclid, what numbers are proportionals, namely, from the nature and property of proportion it follows that the product of the first and fourth will be equal to the product of the second and third: still they do not see the adequate proportionality of the given numbers, or, if they do see it, they see it not by virtue of Euclid's proposition, but intuitively, without going through any process.

6 In this case we do not understand anything of the cause from the consideration of it in the effect. This is sufficiently evident from the fact that the cause is only spoken of in very general terms, such as — there exists then something; there exists then some power, &c.; or from the that we only express it in a negative manner — it is not or that, &c. In the second case something is ascribed to the cause because of the effect, as we shall show in an example, but only a property, never an essence.

7 From this example may be clearly seen what I have just drawn attention to. For through this union we understand nothing beyond the sensation, the effect, to wit, from which we inferred the cause of which we understand nothing.

8 A conclusion of this sort, though it be certain, is yet not to be relied on without great caution; for unless we are exceedingly careful we shall forthwith fall into error. When things are conceived thus abstractedly, and not through their true essence, they are apt to be confused by the imagination. For that which is in itself one, men imagine to be multiplex. To those things which are conceived abstractedly, apart, and confusedly, terms are applied which are apt to become wrested from their strict meaning, and bestowed on things more familiar; whence it results that these latter are imagined in the same way as the former to which the terms were originally given.

OF THE BEST MODE OF PERCEPTION

IN ORDER THAT from these modes of perception the best may be selected, it is well that we should briefly enumerate the means necessary for attaining our end.

I. To have an exact knowledge of our nature which we desire to perfect, and to know as much as is needful of nature in general. II. To collect in this way the differences, the agreements, and the oppositions of things. III. To learn thus exactly how far they can or cannot be modified. IV. To compare this result with the nature and power of man. We shall thus discern the highest degree of perfection to which man is capable of attaining.

We shall then be in a position to see which mode of perception we ought to choose. As to the first mode, it is evident that from hearsay our knowledge must always be uncertain, and, moreover, can give us no insight into the essence of a thing, as is manifest in our illustration; now one can only arrive at knowledge of a thing through knowledge of its essence, as will hereafter appear. We may, therefore clearly conclude that the certainty arising from hearsay cannot be scientific in its character. For simple hearsay cannot affect anyone whose understanding does not, so to speak, meet it half way.

The second mode of perception 9 cannot be said to give us the idea of the proportion of which we are in search. Moreover its results are very uncertain and indefinite, for we shall never discover anything in natural phenomena by its means, except accidental properties, which are never clearly understood, unless the essence of the things in question be known first. Wherefore this mode also must be rejected.

Of the third mode of perception we may say in a manner that it gives us the idea of the thing sought, and that it us to draw conclusions without risk of error; yet it is not by itself sufficient to put us in possession of the perfection we aim at.

The fourth mode alone apprehends the adequate essence of a thing without danger of error. This mode, therefore, must be the one which we chiefly employ. How, then, should we avail ourselves of it so as to gain the fourth kind of knowledge with the least delay concerning things previously unknown? I will proceed to explain.

Now that we know what kind of knowledge is necessary for us, we must indicate the way and the method whereby we may gain the said knowledge concerning the things needful to be known. In order to accomplish this, we must first take care not to commit ourselves to a search, going back to infinity — that is, in order to discover the best method of finding truth, there is no need of another method to discover such method; nor of a third method for discovering the second, and so on to infinity. By such proceedings, we should never arrive at the knowledge of the truth, or, indeed, at any knowledge at all. The matter stands on the same footing as the making of material tools, which might be argued about in a similar way. For, in order to work iron, a hammer is needed, and the hammer cannot be forthcoming unless it has been made; but, in order to make it, there was need of another hammer and other tools, and so on to infinity. We might thus vainly endeavor to prove that men have no power of working iron.

But as men at first made use of the instruments supplied by nature to accomplish very easy pieces of workmanship, laboriously and imperfectly, and then, when these were finished, wrought other things more difficult with less labour and greater perfection; and so gradually mounted from the simplest operations to the making of tools, and from the making of tools to the making of more complex tools, and fresh feats of workmanship, till they arrived at making, complicated mechanisms which they now possess. So, in like manner, the intellect, by its native strength 10, makes for itself intellectual instruments, whereby it acquires strength for performing other intellectual operations 11, and from these operations again fresh instruments, or the power of pushing its investigations further, and thus gradually proceeds till it reaches the summit of wisdom.

That this is the path pursued by the understanding may be readily seen, when we understand the nature of the method for finding out the truth, and of the natural instruments so necessary complex instruments, and for the progress of investigation. I thus proceed with my demonstration.

9 I shall here treat a little more in detail of experience, and shall examine the method adopted by the Empirics, and by recent philosophers.

10 By native strength, I mean that not bestowed on us by external causes, as I shall afterwards explain in my philosophy.

11 Here I term them operations: I shall explain their nature in my philosophy.

OF THE INSTRUMENTS OF THE INTELLECT, OR TRUE IDEAS

A TRUE IDEA 12, (for we possess a true idea) is something different from its correlate (ideatum); thus a circle is different from the idea of a circle. The idea of a circle is not something having a circumference and a center, as a circle has; nor is the idea of a body that body itself. Now, as it is something different from its correlate, it is capable of being understood through itself; in other words, the idea, in so far as its actual essence (essentia formalis) is concerned, may be the subject of another subjective essence (essentia objectiva). 12a And, again, this second subjective essence will, regarded in itself, be something real, capable of being understood; and so on, indefinitely.

For instance, the man Peter is something real; the true idea of Peter is the reality of Peter represented subjectively, and is in itself something real, and quite distinct from the actual Peter. Now, as this true idea of Peter is in itself something real, and has its own individual existence, it will also be capable of being understood — that is, of being the subject of another idea, which will contain by representation (objective) all that the idea of Peter contains actually (formaliter). And, again, this idea of the idea of Peter has its own individuality, which may become the subject of yet another idea; and so on, indefinitely. This everyone may make trial of for himself, by reflecting that he knows what Peter is, and also knows that he knows, and further knows that he knows that he knows, &c. Hence it is plain that, in order to understand the actual Peter, it is not necessary first to understand the idea of Peter, and still less the idea of the idea of Peter. This is the same as saying that, in order to know, there is no need to know that we know, much less to know that we know that we know. This is no more necessary than to know the nature of a circle before knowing the nature of a triangle. 13. But, with these ideas, the contrary is the case: for, in order to know that I know, I must first know.

Hence it is clear that certainty is nothing else than the subjective essence of a thing: in other words, the mode in which we perceive an actual reality is certainty. Further, it is also evident that, for the certitude of truth, no further sign is necessary beyond the possession of a true idea: for, as I have shown, it is not necessary to know that we know that we know. Hence, again, it is clear that no one can know the nature of the highest certainty, unless he possesses an adequate idea, or the subjective essence of a thing: certainty is identical with such subjective essence.

Thus, as the truth needs no sign — it being to possess the subjective essence of things, or, in other words, the ideas of them, in order that all doubts may be removed — it follows that the true method does not consist in seeking for the signs of truth after the acquisition of the idea, but that the true method teaches us the order in which we should seek for truth itself 14 or the subjective essences of things, or ideas, for all these expressions are synonymous.

Again, method must necessarily be concerned with reasoning or understanding — I mean, method is not identical with reasoning in the search for causes, still less is it the comprehension of the causes of things: it is the discernment of a true idea, by distinguishing it from other perceptions, and by investigating its nature, in order that we may so train our mind that it may, by a given standard, comprehend whatsoever is intelligible, by laying down certain rules as aids, and by avoiding useless mental exertion.

Whence we may gather that method is nothing else than reflective knowledge, or the idea of an idea; and that as there can be no idea of an idea — unless an idea exists previously, — there can be no method without a pre-existent idea. Therefore, that will be a good method which shows us how the mind should be directed, according to the standard of the given true idea. Again, seeing that the ratio existing between two ideas is the same as the ratio between the actual realities corresponding to those ideas, it follows that the reflective knowledge which has for its object the most perfect being is more excellent than reflective knowledge concerning other objects — in other words, that method will be most perfect which affords the standard of the given idea of the most perfect being whereby we may direct our mind.

We thus easily understand how, in proportion as it acquires new ideas, the mind simultaneously acquires fresh instruments for pursuing its inquiries further. For we may gather from what has been said, that a true idea must necessarily first of all exist in us as a natural instrument; and that when this idea is apprehended by the mind, it enables us to understand the difference existing between itself and all other perceptions. In this, one part of the method consists. Now it is clear that the mind apprehends itself better in proportion as it understands a greater number of natural objects; it follows, therefore, that this portion of the method will be more perfect in proportion as the mind attains to the comprehension of a greater number of objects, and that it will be absolutely perfect when the mind gains a knowledge of the absolutely perfect being, or becomes conscious thereof.

Again, the more things the mind knows, the better does it understand its own strength and the order of nature; by increased self-knowledge, it can direct itself more easily, and lay down rules for its own guidance; and, by increased knowledge of nature, it can more easily avoid what is useless. And this is the sum total of method, as we have already stated.

We may add that the idea in the world of thought is in the same case as its correlate in the world of reality. If, therefore, there be anything in nature which is without connection with any other thing, and if we assign to it a subjective essence, which would in every way correspond to the objective reality, the subjective essence would have no connection 15 with any other ideas — in other words, we could not draw any conclusions with regard to it. On the other hand, those things which are connected with others — as all things that exist in nature — will be understood by the mind, and their subjective essences will maintain the same mutual relations as their objective realities — that is to say, we shall infer from these ideas other ideas, which will in turn be connected with others, and thus our instruments for proceeding with our investigation will increase. This is what we were endeavoring to prove.

Further, from what has just been said — namely, that an idea must, in all respects, correspond to its correlate in the world of reality, — it is evident that, in order to reproduce in every respect the faithful image of nature, our mind must deduce all its ideas from the idea which represents the origin and source of the whole of nature, so that it may itself become the source of other ideas.

12 I shall take care not only to demonstrate what I have just advanced, but also that we have hitherto proceeded rightly, and other things needful to be known.

12a In modern language, "the idea may become the subject of another presentation." Objectivus generally corresponds to the modern "subjective," formalis to the modern "objective." [Trans. — Note 1]

13 Observe that we are not here inquiring how the first subjective essence is innate in us. This belongs to an investigation into nature, where all these matters are amply explained, and it is shown that without ideas neither affirmation, nor negation, nor volition are possible.

14 The nature of mental search is explained in my philosophy.

15 To be connected with other things is to be produced by them, or to produce them.

ANSWERS TO OBJECTIONS

IT MAY, PERHAPS, provoke astonishment that, after having said that the good method is that which teaches us to direct our mind according to the standard of the given true idea, we should prove our point by reasoning, which would seem to indicate that it is not self-evident. We may, therefore, be questioned as to the validity of our reasoning. If our reasoning be sound, we must take as a starting-point a true idea. Now, to be certain that our starting-point is really a true idea, we need proof. This first course of reasoning must be supported by a second, the second by a third, and so on to infinity.

To this I make answer that, if by some happy chance anyone had adopted this method in his investigations of nature — that is, if he had acquired new ideas in the proper order, according to the standard of the original true idea, he would never have doubted 16 of the truth of his knowledge, inasmuch as truth, as we have shown, makes itself manifest, and all things would flow, as it were, spontaneously towards him. But as this never, or rarely, happens, I have been forced so to arrange my proceedings, that we may acquire by reflection and forethought what we cannot acquire by chance, and that it may at the same time appear that, for proving the truth, and for valid reasoning, we need no other means than the truth and valid reasoning themselves: for by valid reasoning I have established valid reasoning, and, in like measure, I seek still to establish it.

Moreover, this is the order of thinking adopted by men in their inward meditations. The reasons for its rare employment in investigations of nature are to be found in current misconceptions, whereof we shall examine the causes hereafter in our philosophy. Moreover, it demands, as we shall show, a keen and accurate discernment. Lastly, it is hindered by the conditions of human life, which are, as we have already pointed out, extremely changeable. There are also other obstacles, which we will not here inquire into.

If anyone asks why I have not at the starting-point set forth all the truths of nature in their due order, inasmuch as truth is self-evident, I reply by warning him not to reject as false any paradoxes he may find here, but to take the trouble to reflect on the chain of reasoning by which they are supported; he will then be no longer in doubt that we have attained to the truth. This is why I have as above.

If there yet remains some sceptic, who doubts of our primary truth, and of all deductions we make, taking such truth as our standard, he must either be arguing in bad faith, or we must confess that there are men in complete mental blindness either innate or due to misconceptions — that is, to some external influence. Such persons are not conscious of themselves. If they affirm or doubt anything, they know not that they affirm or doubt: they say that they know nothing, and they say that they are ignorant of the very fact of their knowing nothing. Even this they do not affirm absolutely, they are afraid of confessing that they exist, so long as they know nothing; in fact, they ought to remain dumb, for fear of haply supposing which should smack of truth.

Lastly, with such persons, one should not speak of sciences: for, in what relates to life and conduct, they are compelled by necessity to suppose that they exist, and seek their own advantage, and often affirm and deny, even with an oath. If they deny, grant, or gainsay, they know not that they deny, grant, or gainsay, so that they ought to be regarded as automata, utterly devoid of intelligence.

Let us now return to our proposition. Up to the present, we have, first, defined the end to which we desire to direct all our thoughts; secondly, we have determined the mode of perception best adapted to aid us in attaining our perfection; thirdly, we have discovered the way which our mind should take, in order to make a good beginning — namely, that it should use every true idea as a standard in pursuing its inquiries according to fixed rules. Now, in order that it may thus proceed, our method must furnish us, first, with a means of distinguishing a true idea from all other perceptions, and enabling the mind to avoid the latter; secondly, with rules for perceiving unknown things according to the standard of the true idea; thirdly, with an order which enables us to avoid useless labor. When we became acquainted with this method, we saw that, fourthly, it would be perfect when we had attained to the idea of the absolutely perfect Being. This is an observation which should be made at the outset, in order that we may arrive at the knowledge of such a being more quickly.

16 In the same way as we have here no doubt of the truth of our knowledge.

FIRST PART OF METHOD

Distinction of true ideas from fictitious ideas

LET US THEN make a beginning with the first part of the method, which is, as we have said, to distinguish and separate the true idea from other perceptions, and to keep the mind from confusing with true ideas those which are false, fictitious, and doubtful. I intend to dwell on this point at length, partly to keep a distinction so necessary before the reader's mind, and also because there are some who doubt of true ideas, through not having attended to the distinction between a true perception and all others. Such persons are like men who, while they are awake, doubt not that they are awake, but afterwards in a dream, as often happens, thinking that they are surely awake, and then finding that they were in error, become doubtful even of being awake. This state of mind arises through neglect of the distinction between sleeping and waking.

Meanwhile, I give warning that I shall not here give essence of every perception, and explain it through its proximate cause. Such work lies in the province of philosophy. I shall confine myself to what concerns method — that is, to the character of fictitious, false and doubtful perceptions, and the means of freeing ourselves therefrom. Let us then first inquire into the nature of a fictitious idea.

Every perception has for its object either a thing considered as existing, or solely the essence of a thing. Now "fiction" is chiefly occupied with things considered as existing. I will, therefore, consider these first — I mean cases where only the existence of an object is feigned, and the thing thus feigned is understood, or assumed to be understood. For instance, I feign that Peter, whom I know to have gone home, is gone to see me 17 or something of that kind. With what is such an idea concerned? It is concerned with things possible, and not with things necessary or impossible.

I call a thing impossible when its existence would imply a contradiction; necessary, when its non-existence would imply a contradiction; possible, when neither its existence nor its non-existence imply a contradiction, but when the necessity or impossibility of its nature depends on causes unknown to us, while we feign that it exists. If the necessity or impossibility of its existence depending on external causes were known to us, we could not form any fictitious hypotheses about it;

Whence it follows that if there be a God, or omniscient Being, such an one cannot form fictitious hypotheses. For, as regards ourselves, when I know that I exist 18 I cannot hypothesize that I exist or do not exist, any more than I can hypothesize an elephant that can go through the eye of a needle; nor when I know the nature of God, can I hypothesize that He or does not exist. 19 The same thing must be said of the Chimaera, whereof the nature implies a contradiction. From these considerations, it is plain, as I have already stated, that fiction cannot be concerned with eternal truths. 20

But before proceeding further, I must remark, in passing, that the difference between the essence of one thing and the essence of another thing is the same as that which exists between the reality or existence of one thing and the reality or existence of another; therefore, if we wished to conceive the existence, for example, of Adam, simply by means of existence in general, it would be the same as if, in order to conceive his existence, we went back to the nature of being, so as to define Adam as a being. Thus, the more existence is conceived generally, the more is it conceived confusedly and the more easily can it be ascribed to a given object. Contrariwise, the more it is conceived particularly, the more is it understood clearly, and the less liable is it to be ascribed, through negligence of Nature's order, to anything save its proper object. This is worthy of remark.

We now proceed to consider those cases which are commonly called fictions, though we clearly understood that the thing is not as we imagine it. For instance, I know that the earth is round, but nothing prevents my telling people that it is a hemisphere, and that it is like a half apple carved in relief on a dish; or, that the sun moves round the earth, and so on. However, examination will show us that there is nothing here inconsistent with what has been said, provided we first admit that we may have made mistakes, and be now conscious of them; and, further, that we can hypothesize, or at least suppose, that others are under the same mistake as ourselves, or can, like us, fall under it. We can, I repeat, thus hypothesize so long as we see no impossibility. Thus, when I tell anyone that the earth is not round, &c., I merely recall the error which I perhaps made myself, or which I might have fallen into, and afterwards I hypothesize that the person to whom I tell it, is still, or may still fall under the same mistake. This I say, I can feign so long as I do not perceive any impossibility or necessity; if I truly understood either one or the other I should not be able to feign, and I should be reduced to saying that I had made the attempt.

It remains for us to consider hypotheses made in problems, which sometimes involve impossibilities. For instance, when we say — let us assume that this burning candle is not burning, or, let us assume that it burns in some imaginary space, or where there are no physical objects. Such assumptions are freely made, though the last is clearly seen to be impossible. But, though this be so, there is no fiction in the case. For, in the first case, I have merely recalled to memory 21 another candle not burning, or conceived the candle before me as without a flame, and then I understand as applying to the latter, leaving its flame out of the question, all that I think of the former. In the second case, I have merely to abstract my thoughts from the objects surrounding the candle, for the mind to devote itself to the contemplation of the candle singly looked at in itself only; I can then draw the conclusion that the candle contains in itself no causes for its own destruction, so that if there were no physical objects the candle, and even the flame, would remain unchangeable, and so on. Thus there is here no fiction, but 22 true and bare assertions.

Let us now pass on to the fictions concerned with essences only, or with some reality or existence simultaneously. Of these we must specially observe that in proportion as the mind's understanding is smaller, and its experience multiplex, so will its power of coining fictions be larger, whereas as its understanding increases, its capacity for entertaining fictitious ideas becomes less. For instance, in the same way as we are unable, while we are thinking, to feign that we are thinking or not thinking, so, also, when we know the nature of body we cannot imagine an infinite fly; or, when we know the nature of the soul 23 we cannot imagine it as square, though anything may be expressed verbally. But, as we said above, the less men know of nature the more easily can they coin fictitious ideas, such as trees speaking, men instantly changed into stones, or into fountains, ghosts appearing in mirrors, something issuing from nothing, even gods changed into beasts and men and infinite other absurdities of the same kind.

Some persons think, perhaps, that fiction is limited by fiction, and not by understanding; in other words, after I have formed some fictitious idea, and have affirmed of my own free will that it exists under a certain form in nature, I am thereby precluded from thinking of it under any other form. For instance, when I have feigned (to repeat their argument) that the nature of body is of a certain kind, and have of my own free will desired to convince myself that it actually exists under this form, I am no longer able to hypothesize that a fly, for example, is infinite; so, when I have hypothesized the essence of the soul, I am not able to think of it as square, &c.

But these arguments demand further inquiry. First, their upholders must either grant or deny that we can understand anything. If they grant it, then necessarily the same must be said of understanding, as is said of fiction. If they deny it, let us, who know that we do know something, see what they mean. They assert that the soul can be conscious of, and perceive in a variety of ways, not itself nor things which exist, but only things which are neither in itself nor anywhere else, in other words, that the soul can, by its unaided power, create sensations or ideas unconnected with things. In fact, they regard the soul as a sort of god. Further, they assert that we or our soul have such freedom that we can constrain ourselves, or our soul, or even our soul's freedom. For, after it has formed a fictitious idea, and has given its assent thereto, it cannot think or feign it in any other manner, but is constrained by the first fictitious idea to keep all its other thoughts in harmony therewith. Our opponents are thus driven to admit, in support of their fiction, the absurdities which I have just enumerated; and which are not worthy of rational refutation.

While leaving such persons in their error, we will take care to derive from our argument with them a truth serviceable for our purpose, namely 24 that the mind, in paying attention to a thing hypothetical or false, so as to meditate upon it and understand it, and derive the proper conclusions in due order therefrom, will readily discover its falsity; and if the thing hypothetical be in its nature true, and the mind pays attention to it, so as to understand it, and deduce the truths which are derivable from it, the mind will proceed with an uninterrupted series of apt conclusions; in the same way as it would at once discover (as we showed just now) the absurdity of a false hypothesis, and of the conclusions drawn from it.

We need, therefore, be in no fear of forming hypotheses, so long as we have a clear and distinct perception of what is involved. For, if we were to assert, haply, that men are suddenly turned into beasts, the statement would be extremely general, so general that there would be no conception, that is, no idea or connection of subject and predicate, in our mind. If there were such a conception we should at the same time be aware of the means and the causes whereby the event took place. Moreover, we pay no attention to the nature of the subject and the predicate.

Now, if the first idea be not fictitious, and if all the other ideas be deduced therefrom, our hurry to form fictitious ideas will gradually subside. Further, as a fictitious idea cannot be clear and distinct, but is necessarily confused, and as all confusion arises from the fact that the mind has only partial knowledge of a thing either simple or complex, and does not distinguish between the known and the unknown, and, again, that it directs its attention promiscuously to all parts of an object at once without making distinctions, it follows, first, that if the idea be of something very simple, it must necessarily be clear and distinct. For a very simple object cannot be known in part, it must either be known altogether or not at all.

17 See below the note on hypotheses, whereof we have a clear understanding; the fiction consists in saying that such hypotheses exist in heavenly bodies.

18 As a thing, when once it is understood, manifests itself, we have need only of an example without further proof. In the same way the contrary has only to be presented to our minds to be recognized as false, as will forthwith appear when we come to discuss fiction concerning essences.

19 Observe, that although many assert that they doubt whether God exists, they have nought but his name in their minds, or else some fiction which they call God: this fiction is not in harmony with God's real nature, as we will duly show.

20 I shall presently show that no fiction can concern eternal truths. By an eternal truth, I mean that which being positive could never become negative. Thus it is a primary and eternal truth that God exists, but it is not an eternal truth that Adam thinks. That the Chimaera does not exist is an eternal truth, that Adam does not think is not so.

21 Afterwards, when we come to speak of fiction that is concerned with essences, it will be evident that fiction never creates or furnishes the mind with anything new; only such things as are already in the brain or imagination are recalled to the memory, when the attention is directed to them confusedly and all at once. For instance, we have remembrance of spoken words and of a tree; when the mind directs itself to them confusedly, it forms the notion of a tree speaking. The same may be said of existence, especially when it is conceived quite generally as an entity; it is then readily applied to all things together in the memory. This is specially worthy of remark.

22 We must understand as much in the case of hypotheses put forward to explain certain movements accompanying celestial phenomena; but from these, when applied to the celestial motions, we any draw conclusions as to the nature of the heavens, whereas this last may be quite different, especially as many other causes are conceivable which would account for such motions.

23 It often happens that a man recalls to mind this word soul, and forms at the same time some corporeal image: as the two representations are simultaneous, he easily thinks that he imagines and feigns a corporeal soul: thus confusing the name with the thing itself. I here beg that my readers will not be in a hurry to refute this proposition; they will, I hope, have no mind to do so, if they pay close attention to the examples given and to what follows.

24 Though I seem to deduce this from experience, some may deny its cogency because I have given no formal proof. I therefore append the following for those who may desire it. As there can be nothing in nature contrary to nature's laws, since all things come to pass by fixed laws, so that each thing must irrefragably produce its own proper effect, it follows that the soul, as soon as it possesses the true conception of a thing, proceeds to reproduce in thought that thing's effects. See below, where I speak of the false idea.

AND FROM FALSE IDEAS

SECONDLY, IT FOLLOWS that if a complex object be divided by thought into a number of simple component parts, and if each be regarded separately, all confusion will disappear. Thirdly, it follows that fiction cannot be simple, but is made up of the blending of several confused ideas of diverse objects or actions existent in nature, or rather is composed of attention directed to all such ideas at once 25 and unaccompanied by any mental assent. Now a fiction that was simple would be clear and distinct, and therefore true, also a fiction composed only of distinct ideas would be clear and distinct, and therefore true. For instance, when we know the nature of the circle and the square, it is impossible for us to blend together these two figures, and to hypothesize a square circle, any more than a square soul, or things of that kind.

Let us shortly come to our conclusion, and again repeat that we need have no fear of confusing with true ideas that which is only a fiction. As for the first sort of fiction of which we have already spoken, when a thing is clearly conceived, we saw that if the existence of a that thing is in itself an eternal trut fiction can have no part in it; but if the existence of the conceived be not an eternal truth, we have only to be careful such existence be compared to the thing's essence, and to consider the order of nature. As for the second sort of fiction, which we stated to be the result of simultaneously directing the attention, without the assent of the intellect, to different confused ideas representing different things and actions existing in nature, we have seen that an absolutely simple thing cannot be feigned, but must be understood, and that a complex thing is in the same case if we regard separately the simple parts whereof it is composed; we shall not even be able to hypothesize any untrue action concerning such objects, for we shall be obliged to consider at the same time the causes and manner of such action.

These matters being thus understood, let us pass on to consider the false idea, observing the objects with which it is concerned, and the means of guarding ourselves from falling into false perceptions. Neither of these tasks will present much difficulty, after our inquiry concerning fictitious ideas. The false idea only differs from the fictitious idea in the fact of implying a mental assent — that is, as we have already remarked, while the representations are occurring, there are no causes present to us, wherefrom, as in fiction, we can conclude that such representations do not arise from external objects: in fact, it is much the same as dreaming with our eyes open, or while awake. Thus, a false idea is concerned with, or (to speak more correctly) is attributable to, the existence of a thing whereof the essence is known, or the essence itself, in the same way as a fictitious idea.

If attributable to the existence of the thing, it is corrected in the same way as a fictitious idea under similar circumstances. If attributable to the essence, it is likewise corrected in the same way as a fictitious idea. For if the nature of the thing known implies necessary existence, we cannot possible be in error with regard to its existence; but if the nature of the thing be not an eternal truth, like its essence, but contrariwise the necessity or impossibility of its existence depends on external causes, then we must follow the same course as we adopted in the of fiction, for it is corrected in the same manner.

As for false ideas concerned with essences, or even with actions, such perceptions are necessarily always confused, being compounded of different confused perceptions of things existing in nature, as, for instance, when men are persuaded that deities are present in woods, in statues, in brute beasts, and the like; that there are bodies which, by their composition alone, give rise to intellect; that corpses reason, walk about, and speak; that God is deceived, and so on. But ideas which are clear and distinct can never be false: for ideas of things clearly and distinctly conceived are either very simple themselves, or are compounded from very simple ideas, that is, are deduced therefrom. The impossibility of a very simple idea being false is evident to everyone who understands the nature of truth or understanding and of falsehood.

As regards that which constitutes the reality of truth, it is certain that a true idea is distinguished from a false one, not so much by its extrinsic object as by its intrinsic nature. If an architect conceives a building properly constructed, though such a building may never have existed, and amy never exist, nevertheless the idea is true; and the idea remains the same, whether it be put into execution or not. On the other hand, if anyone asserts, for instance, that Peter exists, without knowing whether Peter really exists or not, the assertion, as far as its asserter is concerned, is false, or not true, even though Peter actually does exist. The assertion that Peter exists is true only with regard to him who knows for certain that Peter does exist.

Whence it follows that there is in ideas something real, whereby the true are distinguished from the false. This reality must be inquired into, if we are to find the best standard of truth (we have said that we ought to determine our thoughts by the given standard of a true idea, and that method is reflective knowledge), and to know the properties of our understanding. Neither must we say that the difference between true and false arises from the fact, that true knowledge consists in knowing things through their primary causes, wherein it is totally different from false knowledge, as I have just explained it: for thought is said to be true, if it involves subjectively the essence of any principle which has no cause, and is known through itself and in itself.

Wherefore the reality (forma) of true thought must exist in the thought itself, without reference to other thoughts; it does not acknowledge the object as its cause, but must depend on the actual power and nature of the understanding. For, if we suppose that the understanding has perceived some new entity which has never existed, as some conceive the understanding of God before He created thing (a perception which certainly could not arise any object), and has legitimately deduced other thoughts from said perception, all such thoughts would be true, without being determined by any external object; they would depend solely on the power and nature of the understanding. Thus, that which constitutes the reality of a true thought must be sought in the thought itself, and deduced from the nature of the understanding.

In order to pursue our investigation, let us confront ourselves with some true idea, whose object we know for certain to be dependent on our power of thinking, and to have nothing corresponding to it in nature. With an idea of this kind before us, we shall, as appears from what has just been said, be more easily able to carry on the research we have in view. For instance, in order to form the conception of a sphere, I invent a cause at my pleasure — namely, a semicircle revolving round its center, and thus producing a sphere. This is indisputably a true idea; and, although we know that no sphere in nature has ever actually been so formed, the perception remains true, and is the easiest manner of conceiving a sphere. We must observe that this perception asserts the rotation of a semicircle — which assertion would be false, if it were not associated with the conception of a sphere, or of a cause determining a motion of the kind, or absolutely, if the assertion were isolated. The mind would then only tend to the affirmation of the sole motion of a semicircle, which is not contained in the conception of a semicircle, and does not arise from the conception of any cause capable of producing such motion. Thus falsity consists only in this, that something is affirmed of a thing, which is not contained in the conception we have formed of that thing, as motion or rest of a semicircle. Whence it follows that simple ideas cannot be other than true — e.g., the simple idea of a semicircle, of motion, of rest, of quantity, &c. Whatsoever affirmation such ideas contain is equal to the concept formed, and does not extend further. Wherefore we form as many simple ideas as we please, without any fear of error.

It only remains for us to inquire by what power our mind can form true ideas, and how far such power extends. It is certain that such power cannot extend itself infinitely. For when we affirm somewhat of a thing, which is not contained in the concept we have formed of that thing, such an affirmation shows a defect of our perception, or that we have formed fragmentary or mutilated ideas. Thus we have seen that the notion of a semicircle is false when it is isolated in the mind, but true when it is associated with the concept of a sphere, or of some cause determining such a motion. But if it be the nature of a thinking being, as seems, prima facie, to be the case, to form true or adequate thoughts, it is plain that inadequate ideas arise in us only because we are parts of a thinking being, whose thoughts — some in their entirety, others in fragments only — constitute our mind.

But there is another point to be considered, which was not worth raising in the case of fiction, but which give rise to complete deception — namely, that certain things presented to the imagination also exist in the understanding — in other words, are conceived clearly and distinctly. Hence, so long as we do not separate that which is distinct from that which is confused, certainty, or the true idea, becomes mixed with indistinct ideas. For instance, certain Stoics heard, perhaps, the term "soul," and also that the soul is immortal, yet imagined it only confusedly; they imaged, also, and understood that very subtle bodies penetrate all others, and are penetrated by none. By combining these ideas, and being at the same time certain of the truth of the axiom, they forthwith became convinced that the mind consists of very subtle bodies; that these very subtle bodies cannot be divided &c.

But we are freed from mistakes of this kind, so long as we endeavor to examine all our perceptions by the standard of the given true idea. We must take care, as has been said, to separate such perceptions from all those which arise from hearsay or unclassified experience. Moreover, such mistakes arise from things being conceived too much in the abstract; for it is sufficiently self-evident that what I conceive as in its true object I cannot apply to anything else. Lastly, they arise from a want of understanding of the primary elements of nature as a whole; whence we proceed without due order, and confound nature with abstract rules, which, although they be true enough in their sphere, yet, when misapplied, confound themselves, and pervert the order of nature. However, if we proceed with as little abstraction as possible, and begin from primary elements — that is, from the source and origin of nature, as far back as we can reach, — we need not fear any deceptions of this kind.

As far as the knowledge of the origin of nature is concerned, there is no danger of our confounding it with abstractions. For when a thing is conceived in the abstract, as are all universal notions, the said universal notions are always more extensive in the mind than the number of individuals forming their contents really existing in nature. Again, there are many things in nature, the difference between which is so slight as to be hardly perceptible to the understanding; so that it may readily happen that such things are confounded together, if they be conceived abstractedly. But since the first principle of nature cannot (as we shall see hereafter) be conceived abstractedly or universally, and cannot extend further in the understanding than it does in reality, and has no likeness to mutable things, no confusion need be feared in respect to the idea of it, provided (as before shown) that we possess a standard of truth. This is, in fact, a being single and infinite 26; in other words, it is the sum total of being, beyond which there is no being found. 27

25 Observe that fiction regarded in itself, only differs from dreams in that in the latter we do not perceive the external causes which we perceive through the senses while awake. It has hence been inferred that representations occurring in sleep have no connection with objects external to us. We shall presently see that error is the dreaming of a waking man: if it reaches a certain pitch it becomes delirium.

26 These are not attributes of God displaying His essence, as I will show in my philosophy.

27 This has been shown already. For if such a being did not exist it would never be produced; therefore the mind would be able to understand more than nature could furnish; and this has been shown above to be false.

OF DOUBT

THUS FAR WE have treated of the false idea. We have now to investigate the doubtful idea — that is, to inquire what can cause us to doubt, and how doubt may be removed. I speak of real doubt existing in the mind, not of such doubt as we see exemplified when a man says that he doubts, though his mind does not really hesitate. The cure of the latter does not fall within the province of method, it belongs rather to inquiries concerning obstinacy and its cure.

Real doubt is never produced in the mind by the thing doubted of. In other words, if there were only one idea in the mind, whether that idea were true or false, there would be no doubt or certainty present, only a certain sensation. For an idea is in itself nothing else than a certain sensation. But doubt will arise through another idea, not clear and distinct enough for us to be able to draw any certain conclusions with regard to the matter under consideration; that is, the idea which causes us to doubt is not clear and distinct. To take an example. Supposing that a man has never reflected, taught by experience or by any other means, that our senses sometimes deceive us, he will never doubt whether the sun be greater or less than it appears. Thus rustics are generally astonished when they hear that the sun is much larger than the earth. But from reflection on the deceitfulness of the senses 28 doubt arises, and if, after doubting, we acquire a true knowledge of the senses, and how things at a distance are represented through their instrumentality, doubt is again removed.

Hence we cannot cast doubt on true ideas by the supposition that there is a deceitful Deity, who leads us astray even in what is most certain. We can only hold such an hypothesis so long as we have no clear and distinct idea — in other words, until we reflect the knowledge which we have of the first principle of all things, and find that which teaches us that God is not a deceiver, and until we know this with the same certainty as we know from reflecting on the are equal to two right angles. But if we have a knowledge of God equal to that which we have of a triangle, all doubt is removed. In the same way as we can arrive at the said knowledge of a triangle, though not absolutely sure that there is not some arch-deceiver leading us astray, so can we come to a like knowledge of God under the like condition, and when we have attained to it, it is sufficient, as I said before, to remove every doubt which we can possess concerning clear and distinct ideas.

Thus, if a man proceeded with our investigations in due order, inquiring first into those things which should first be inquired into, never passing over a link in the chain of association, and with knowledge how to define his questions before seeking to answer them, he will never have any ideas save such as are very certain, or, in other words, clear and distinct; for doubt is only a suspension of the spirit concerning some affirmation or negation which it would pronounce upon unhesitatingly if it were not in ignorance of something, without which the knowledge of the matter in hand must needs be imperfect. We may, therefore, conclude that doubt always proceeds from want of due order in investigation.

28 That is, it is known that the senses sometimes deceive us. But it is only known confusedly, for it is not known how they deceive us.

OF MEMORY AND FORGETFULNESS

THESE ARE THE points I promised to discuss in the first part of my treatise on method. However, in order not to omit anything which can conduce to the knowledge of the understanding and its faculties, I will add a few words on the subject of memory and forgetfulness. The point most worthy of attention is, that memory is strengthened both with and without the aid of the understanding. For the more intelligible a thing is, the more easily is it remembered, and the less intelligible it is, the more easily do we forget it. For instance, a number of unconnected words is much more difficult to remember than the same number in the form of a narration.

The memory is also strengthened without the aid of the understanding by means of the power wherewith the imagination or the sense called common, is affected by some particular physical object. I say particular, for the imagination is only affected by particular objects. If we read, for instance, a single romantic comedy, we shall remember it very well, so long as we do not read many others of the same kind, for it will reign alone in the memory If, however, we read several others of the same kind, we shall think of them altogether, and easily confuse one with another. I say also, physical. For the imagination is only affected by physical objects. As, then, the memory is strengthened both with and without the aid of the understanding, we may conclude that it is different from the understanding, and that in the latter considered in itself there is neither memory nor forgetfulness.

What, then, is memory? It is nothing else than the actual sensation of impressions on the brain, accompanied with the thought of a definite duration 29 of the sensation. This is also shown by reminiscence. For then we think of the sensation, but without the notion of continuous duration; thus the idea of that sensation is not the actual duration of the sensation or actual memory. Whether ideas are or are not subject to corruption will be seen in philosophy. If this seems too absurd to anyone, it will be sufficient for our purpose, if he reflect on the fact that a thing is more easily remembered in proportion to its singularity, as appears from the example of the comedy just cited. Further, a thing is remembered more easily in proportion to its intelligibility; therefore we cannot help remember that which is extremely singular and sufficiently intelligible. Thus, then, we have distinguished between a true idea and other perceptions, and shown that ideas fictitious, false, and the rest, originate in the imagination — that is, in certain sensations fortuitous (so to speak) and disconnected, arising not from the power of the mind, but from external causes, according as the body, sleeping or waking, receives various motions. But one may take any view one likes of the imagination so long as one acknowledges that it is different from the understanding, and that the soul is passive with regard to it. The view taken is immaterial, if we know that the imagination is something indefinite, with regard to which the soul is passive, and that we can by some means or other free ourselves therefrom with the help of the understanding. Let no one then be astonished that before proving the existence of body, and other necessary things, I speak of imagination of body, and of its composition. The view taken is, I repeat, immaterial, so long as we know that imagination is something indefinite, &c.

As regards as a true idea, we have shown that it is simple or compounded of simple ideas; that it shows how and why something is or has been made; and that its subjective effects in the soul correspond to the actual reality of its object. This conclusion is identical with the saying of the ancients, that true proceeds from cause to effect; though the ancients, so far as I know, never formed the conception put forward here that the soul acts according to fixed laws, and is as it were an immaterial automaton.

29 If the duration be indefinite, the recollection is imperfect; this everyone seems to have learnt from nature. For we often ask, to strengthen our belief in something we hear of, when and where it happened; though ideas themselves have their own duration in the mind, yet, as we are wont to determine duration by the aid of some measure of motion which, again, takes place by aid of imagination, we preserve no memory connected with pure intellect.

MENTAL HINDRANCES FROM WORDS — AND FROM THE POPULAR CONFUSION OF READY IMAGINATION WITH DISTINCT UNDERSTANDING.

HENCE, AS FAR as is possible at the outset, we have acquired a knowledge of our understanding, and such a standard of a true idea that we need no longer fear confounding truth with falsehood and fiction. Neither shall we wonder why we understand some things which in nowise fall within the scope of the imagination, while other things are in the imagination but wholly opposed to the understanding, or others, again, which agree therewith. We now know that the operations, whereby the effects of imagination are produced, take place under other laws quite different from the laws of the understanding, and that the mind is entirely passive with regard to them.

Whence we may also see how easily men may fall into grave errors through not distinguishing accurately between the imagination and the understanding; such as believing that extension must be localized, that it must be finite, that its parts are really distinct one from the other, that it is the primary and single foundation of all things, that it occupies more space at one time than at another and other similar doctrines, all entirely opposed to truth, as we shall duly show.

Again, since words are a part of the imagination — that is, since we form many conceptions in accordance with confused arrangements of words in the memory, dependent on particular bodily conditions, — there is no doubt that words may, equally with the imagination, be the cause of many and great errors, unless we strictly on our guard.

Moreover, words are formed according to popular fancy and intelligence, and are, therefore, signs of things as existing in the imagination, not as existing in the understanding. This is evident from the fact that to all such things as exist only in the understanding, not in the imagination, negative names are often given, such as incorporeal, infinite, &c. So, also, many conceptions really affirmative are expressed negatively, and vice versa, such as uncreate, independent, infinite, immortal, &c., inasmuch as their contraries are much more easily imagined, and, therefore, occurred first to men, and usurped positive names. Many things we affirm and deny, because the nature of words allows us to do so, though the nature of things does not. While we remain unaware of this fact, we may easily mistake falsehood for truth.

Let us also beware of another great cause of confusion, which prevents the understanding from reflecting on itself. Sometimes, while making no distinction between the imagination and the intellect, we think that what we more readily imagine is clearer to us; and also we think that what we imagine we understand. Thus, we put first that which should be last: the true order of progression is reversed, and no legitimate conclusion is drawn.

SECOND PART OF METHOD. 30

ITS OBJECT, THE ACQUISITION OF CLEAR AND DISTINCT IDEAS

NOW, IN ORDER at length to pass on to the second part of this method, I shall first set forth the object aimed at, and next the means for its attainment. The object aimed at is the acquisition of clear and distinct ideas, such as are produced by the pure intellect, and not by chance physical motions. In order that all ideas may be reduced to unity, we shall endeavor so to associate and arrange them that our mind may, as far as possible, reflect subjectively the reality of nature, both as a whole and as parts.

As for the first point, it is necessary (as we have said) for our purpose that everything should be conceived, either solely through its essence, or through its proximate cause. If the thing be self-existent, or, as is commonly said, the cause of itself, it must be understood through its essence only; if it be not self-existent, but requires a cause for its existence, it must be understood through its proximate cause. For, in reality, the knowledge 31 of an effect is nothing else than the acquisition of more perfect knowledge of its cause.

Therefore, we may never, while we are concerned with inquiries into actual things, draw any conclusion from abstractions; we shall be extremely careful not to confound that which is only in the understanding with that which is in the thing itself. The best basis for drawing a conclusion will be either some particular affirmative essence, or a true and legitimate definition. For the understanding cannot descend from universal axioms by themselves to particular things, since axioms are of infinite extent, and do not determine the understanding to contemplate one particular thing more than another.

30 The chief rule of this part is, as appears from the first part, to review all the ideas coming to us through pure intellect, so as to distinguish them from such as we imagine: the distinction will be shown through the properties of each, namely, of the imagination and of the understanding.

31 Observe that it is thereby manifest that we cannot understand anything of nature without at the same time increasing our knowledge of the first cause, or God.

ITS MEANS, GOOD DEFINITIONS
CONDITIONS OF DEFINITION

THUS THE TRUE method of discovery is to form thoughts from some given definition. This process will be the more fruitful and easy in proportion as the thing given be better defined. Wherefore, the cardinal point of all this second part of method consists in the knowledge of the conditions of good definition, and the means of finding them. I will first treat of the conditions of definition.

A definition, if it is to be called perfect, must explain the inmost essence of a thing, and must take care not to substitute for this any of its properties. In order to illustrate my meaning, without taking an example which would seem to show a desire to expose other people's errors, I will choose the case of something abstract, the definition of which is of little moment. Such is a circle. If a circle be defined as a figure, such that all straight lines drawn from the center to the circumference are equal, every one can see that such a definition does not in the least explain the essence of a circle, but solely one of its properties. Though, as I have said, this is of no importance in the case of figures and other abstractions, it is of great importance in the case of physical beings and realities: for the properties of things are not understood so long as their essences are unknown. If the latter be passed over, there is necessarily a perversion of the succession of ideas which should reflect the succession of nature, and we go far astray from our object.

In order to be free from this fault, the following rules should be observed in definition: —

I. If the thing in question be created, the definition must (as we have said) comprehend the proximate cause. For instance, a circle should, according to this rule, be defined as follows: the figure described by any line whereof one end is fixed and the other free. This definition clearly comprehends the proximate cause.

II. A conception or definition of a thing should be such that all the properties of that thing, in so far as it is considered by itself, and not in conjunction with other things, can be deduced from it, as may be seen in the definition given of a circle: for from that it clearly follows that all straight lines drawn from the center to the circumference are equal. That this is a necessary characteristic of a definition is so clear to anyone, who reflects on the matter, that there is no need to spend time in proving it, or in showing that, owing to this second condition, every definition should be affirmative. I speak of intellectual affirmation, giving little thought to verbal affirmations which, owing to the poverty of language, must sometimes, perhaps, be expressed negatively, though the idea contained is affirmative.

The rules for the definition of an uncreated thing are as follows: —

I. The exclusion of all idea of cause — that is, the thing must not need explanation by Anything outside itself.

II. When the definition of the thing has been given, there must be no room for doubt as to whether the thing exists or not.

III. It must contain, as far as the mind is concerned, no substantives which could be put into an adjectival form; in other words, the object defined must not be explained through abstractions.

IV. Lastly, though this is not absolutely necessary, it should be possible to deduce from the definition all the properties of the thing defined.

All these rules become obvious to anyone giving strict attention to the matter.

I have also stated that the best basis for drawing a conclusion is a particular affirmative essence. The more specialized the idea is, the more it is distinct, and therefore clear. Wherefore a knowledge of particular things should be sought for as diligently as possible.

As regards the order of our perceptions, and the manner in which they should be arranged and united, it is necessary that, as soon as is possible and rational, we should inquire whether there be any being (and, if so, what being), that is the cause of all things, so that its essence, represented in thought, may be the cause of all our ideas, and then our mind will to the utmost possible extent reflect nature. For it will possess, subjectively, nature's essence, order, and union. Thus we can see that it is before all things necessary for us to deduce all our ideas from physical things — that is, from real entities, proceeding, as far as may be, according to the series of causes, from one real entity to another real entity, never passing to universals and abstractions, either for the purpose of deducing some real entity from them, or deducing them from some real entity. Either of these processes interrupts the true progress of the understanding.

But it must be observed that, by the series of causes and real entities, I do not here mean the series of particular and mutable things, but only the series of fixed and eternal things. It would be impossible for human infirmity to follow up the series of particular mutable things, both on account their multitude, surpassing all calculation, and on account of the infinitely diverse circumstances surrounding one and the same thing, any one of which may be the cause of its existence or non-existence. Indeed, their existence has no connection with their essence, or (as we have said already) is not an eternal truth.

Neither is there any need that we should understand their series, for the essences of particular mutable things are not to be gathered from their series or order of existence, which would furnish us with nothing beyond their extrinsic denominations, their relations, or, at most, their circumstances, all of which are very different from their inmost essence. This inmost essence must be sought solely from fixed and eternal things, and from the laws, inscribed (so to speak) in those things as in their true codes, according to which all particular things take place and are arranged; nay, these mutable particular things depend so intimately and essentially (so to phrase it) upon the fixed things, that they cannot either be conceived without them.

But, though this be so, there seems to be no small difficulty in arriving at the knowledge of these particular things, for to conceive them all at once would far surpass the powers of the human understanding. The arrangement whereby one thing is understood, before another, as we have stated, should not be sought from their series of existence, nor from eternal things. For the latter are all by nature simultaneous. Other aids are therefore needed besides those employed for understanding eternal things and their laws. However, this is not the place to recount such aids, nor is there any need to do so, until we have acquired a sufficient knowledge of eternal things and their infallible laws, and until the nature of our senses has become plain to us.

Before betaking ourselves to seek knowledge of particular things, it will be seasonable to speak of such aids, as all tend to teach us the mode of employing our senses, and to make certain experiments under fixed rules and arrangements which may suffice to determine the object of our inquiry, so that we may therefrom infer what laws of eternal things it has been produced under, and may gain an insight into its inmost nature, as I will duly show. Here, to return to my purpose, I will only endeavor to set forth what seems necessary for enabling us to attain to knowledge of eternal things, and to define them under the conditions laid down above.

With this end, we must bear in mind what has already been stated, namely, that when the mind devotes itself to any thought, so as to examine it, and to deduce therefrom in due order all the legitimate conclusions possible, any falsehood which may lurk in the thought will be detected; but if the thought be true, the mind will readily proceed without interruption to deduce truths from it. This, I say, is necessary for our purpose, for our thoughts may be brought to a close by the absence of a foundation.

If, therefore, we wish to investigate the first thing of all, it will be necessary to supply some foundation which may direct our thoughts thither. Further, since method is reflective knowledge, the foundation which must direct our thoughts can be nothing else than the knowledge of that which constitutes the reality of truth, and the knowledge of the understanding, its properties, and powers. When this has been acquired we shall possess a foundation wherefrom we can deduce our thoughts, and a path whereby the intellect, according to its capacity, may attain the knowledge of eternal things, allowance being made for the extent of the intellectual powers.

If, as I stated in the first part, it belongs to the nature of thought to form true ideas, we must here inquire what is meant by the faculties and power of the understanding. The chief part of our method is to understand as well as possible the powers of the intellect, and its nature; we are, therefore, compelled (by the considerations advanced in the second part of the method) necessarily to draw these conclusions from the definition itself of thought and understanding.

HOW TO DEFINE UNDERSTANDING

BUT, SO FAR as we have not got any rules for finding definitions, and, as we cannot set forth such rules without a previous knowledge of nature, that is without a definition of the understanding and its power, it follows either that the definition of the understanding must be clear in itself, or that we can understand nothing. Nevertheless this definition is not absolutely clear in itself; however, since its properties, like all things that we possess through the understanding, cannot be known clearly and distinctly, unless its nature be known previously, understanding makes itself manifest, if we pay attention to its properties, which we know clearly and distinctly. Let us, then, enumerate here the properties of the understanding, let us examine them, and begin by discussing the instruments for research which we find innate in us. See [para. 31]

The properties of the understanding which I have chiefly remarked, and which I clearly understand, are the following: —

I. It involves certainty — in other words, it knows that a thing exists in reality as it is reflected subjectively.

II. That it perceives certain things, or forms some ideas absolutely, some ideas from others. Thus it forms the idea of quantity absolutely, without reference to any other thoughts; but ideas of motion it only forms after taking into consideration the idea of quantity.

III. Those ideas which the understanding forms absolutely express infinity; determinate ideas are derived from other ideas. Thus in the idea of quantity, perceived by means of a cause, the quantity is determined, as when a body is perceived to be formed by the motion of a plane, a plane by the motion of a line, or, again, a line by the motion of a point. All these are perceptions which do not serve towards understanding quantity, but only towards determining it. This is proved by the fact that we conceive them as formed as it were by motion, yet this motion is not perceived unless the quantity be perceived also; we can even prolong the motion to form an infinite line, which we certainly could not do unless we had an idea of infinite quantity.

IV. The understanding forms positive ideas before forming negative ideas.

V. It perceives things not so much under the condition of duration as under a certain form of eternity, and in an infinite number; or rather in perceiving things it does not consider either their number or duration, whereas, in imagining them, it perceives them in a determinate number, duration, and quantity.

VI. The ideas which we form as clear and distinct, seem to follow from the sole necessity of our nature, that they appear to depend absolutely on our sole power; with confused ideas the contrary is the case. They are often formed against our will.

VII. The mind can determine in many ways the ideas of things, which the understanding forms from other ideas: thus, for instance, in order to define the plane of an ellipse, it supposes a point adhering to a cord to be moved around two centers, or, again, it conceives an infinity of points, always in the same fixed relation to a given straight line, angle of the vertex of the cone, or in an infinity of other ways.

VIII. The more ideas express perfection of any object, the more perfect are they themselves; for we do not admire the architect who has planned a chapel so much as the architect who has planned a splendid temple.

I do not stop to consider the rest of what is referred to thought, such as love, joy, &c. They are nothing to our present purpose, and cannot even be conceived unless the understanding be perceived previously. When perception is removed, all these go with it.

False and fictitious ideas have nothing positive about them (as we have abundantly shown), which causes them to be called false or fictitious; they are only considered as such through the defectiveness of knowledge. Therefore, false and fictitious ideas as such can teach us nothing concerning the essence of thought; this must be sought from the positive properties just enumerated; in other words, we must lay down some common basis from which these properties necessarily follow, so that when this is given, the properties are necessarily given also, and when it is removed, they too vanish with it.

The rest of the treatise is wanting.

I. DE BONIS QUAE HOMINES PLERUMQUE APPETUNT.

1. POSTQUAM ME experientia docuit, omnia, quae in communi vita frequenter occurrunt, vana et futilia esse ; cum viderem omnia, a quibus et quae timebam, nihil neque boni neque mali in se habere, nisi quatenus ab iis animus movebatur ; constitui tandem inquirere, an aliquid daretur, quod verum bonum et sui communicabile esset, et a quo solo reiectis ceteris omnibus animus afficeretur ; imo an aliquid daretur, quo invento et acquisito continua ac summa in aeternum fruerer laetitia.

2. Dico me tandem constituisse. Primo enim intuitu inconsultum videbatur, propter rem tunc incertam certam amittere velle. Videbam nimirum commoda, quae ex honore ac divitiis acquiruntur, et quod ab iis quaerendis cogebar abstinere, si seriam rei alii novae operam dare vellem, et si forte summa felicitas in iis esset sita, perspiciebam me ea debere carere ; si vero in iis non esset sita eisque tantum darem operam, tum etiam summa carerem felicitate.

3. Volvebam igitur animo, an forte esset possibile ad novum institutum, aut saltem ad ipsius certitudinem pervenire, licet ordo et commune vitae meae institutum non mutaretur, quod saepe frustra tentavi. Nam quae plerumque in vita occurrunt, et apud homines, ut ex eorum operibus colligere licet, tamquam summum bonum aestimantur, ad haec tria rediguntur : divitias scilicet, honorem atque libidinem. His tribus adeo distrahitur mens, ut minime possit de alio aliquo bono cogitare.

4. Nam quod ad libidinem attinet, ea adeo suspenditur animus, ac si in aliquo bono quiesceret ; quo maxime impeditur, ne de alio cogitet. Sed post illius fruitionem summa sequitur tristitia, quae si non suspendit mentem, tamen perturbat et hebetat. Honores ac divitias prosequendo non parum etiam distrahitur mens, praesertim ubi hae non nisi propter se quaeruntur , quia tum supponuntur summum esse bonum.

5. Honore vero multo adhuc magis mens distrahitur ; supponitur enim semper bonum esse per se et tamquam finis ultimus, ad quem omnia diriguntur. Deinde in his non datur, sicut in libidine, poenitentia, sed quo plus utriusque possidetur, eo magis augetur laetitia, et consequenter magis ac magis incitamur ad utrumque augendum ; si autem spe in aliquo casu frustremur, tum summa oritur tristitia. Est denique honor magno impedimento eo, quod, ut ipsum assequamur, vita necessario ad captum hominum est dirigenda, fugiendo scilicet quod vulgo fugiunt, et quaerendo quod vulgo quaerunt homines.

6. Cum itaque viderem, haec omnia adeo obstare, quominus operam novo alicui instituto darem, imo adeo esse opposita, ut ab uno aut altero necessario esset abstinendum, cogebar inquirere, quid mihi esset utilius ; nempe, ut dixi, videbar bonum certum pro incerto amittere velle. Sed postquam aliquantulum huic rei incubueram, inveni primo, si hisce omissis ad novum institutum accingerer, me bonum sua natura incertum, ut clare ex dictis possumus colligere, omissurum pro incerto, non quidem sua natura (fixum enim bonum quaerebam), sed tantum quoad ipsius consecutionem.

7. Assidua autem meditatione eo perveni, ut viderem, quod tum, modo possem penitus deliberare, mala certa pro bono certo omitterem. Videbam enim me in summo versari periculo, et me cogi, remedium, quamvis incertum, summis viribus quaerere ; veluti aeger letali morbo laborans, qui ubi mortem certam praevidet,

ni adhibeatur remedium, illud ipsum, quamvis incertum, summis viribus cogitur quaerere ; nempe in eo tota eius spes est sita ; illa autem omnia, quae vulgus sequitur, non tantum nullum conferunt remedium ad nostrum esse conservandum, sed etiam id impediunt, et frequenter sunt causa interitus eorum, qui ea possident, et semper causa interitus eorum, qui ab iis possidentur.

8. Permulta enim exstant exempla eorum, qui persecutionem ad necem usque passi sunt propter ipsorum divitias, et etiam eorum, qui, ut opes compararent, tot periculis sese exposuerunt, ut tandem vita poenam luerent suae stultitiae. Neque eorum pauciora sunt exempla, qui, ut honorem assequerentur aut defenderent, miserrime passi sunt. Innumeranda denique exstant exempla eorum, qui prae nimia libidine mortem sibi acceleraverunt.

9. Videbantur porro ex eo haec orta esse mala, quod tota felicitas aut infelicitas in hoc solo sita est ; videlicet in qualitate obiecti, cui adhaeremus amore. Nam propter illud, quod non amatur, nunquam orientur lites, nulla erit tristitia, si pereat, nulla invidia, si ab alio possideatur, nullus timor, nullum odium, et, ut verbo dicam, nullae commotiones animi ; quae quidem omnia contingunt in amore eorum, quae perire possunt, uti haec omnia, de quibus modo locuti sumus.

10. Sed amor erga rem aeternam et infinitam sola laetitia pascit animum, ipsaque omnis tristitiae est expers ; quod valde est desiderandum totisque viribus quaerendum. Verum non absque ratione usus sum his verbis : modo possem serio deliberare. Nam quamvis haec mente adeo clare perciperem, non poteram tamen ideo omnem avaritiam, libidinem, atque gloriam deponere.

II. DE BONO VERO ET SUMMO.

11. HOC UNUM videbam, quod, quamdiu mens circa has cogitationes versabatur, tamdiu illa aversabatur, et serio de novo cogitabat instituto ; quod magno mihi fuit solatio. Nam videbam illa mala non esse talis conditionis, ut remediis nollent cedere. Et quamvis in initio haec intervalla essent rara et per admodum exiguum temporis spatium durarent, postquam tamen verum bonum magis ac magis mihi innotuit, intervalla ista frequentiora et longiora fuerunt ; praesertim postquam vidi nummorum acquisitionem aut libidinem et gloriam tamdiu obesse, quamdiu propter se, et non tamquam media ad alia quaeruntur. Si vero tamquam media quaeruntur, modum tunc habebunt, et minime oberunt, sed contra ad finem, propter quem quaeruntur, multum conducent, ut suo loco ostendemus.

12. Hic tantum breviter dicam, quid per verum bonum intelligam, et simul quid sit summum bonum. Quod ut recte intelligatur, notandum est, quod bonum et malum non nisi respective dicantur ; adeo ut una, eademque res possit dici bona et mala secundum diversos respectus, eodem modo ac perfectum, et imperfectum. Nihil enim in sua natura spectatum perfectum dicetur vel imperfectum ; praesertim postquam noverimus, omnia, quae fiunt, secundum aeternum ordinem et secundum certas naturae leges fieri.

13. Cum autem humana imbecillitas illum ordinem cogitatione sua non assequatur, et interim homo concipiat naturam aliquam humanam sua multo firmiorem, et simul nihil obstare videat, quominus talem naturam acquirat, incitatur ad media quaerendum, quae ipsum ad talem ducant perfectionem : et omne illud, quod potest esse medium, ut eo perveniat, vocatur verum bonum. Summum autem bonum est eo pervenire, ut ille cum aliis individuis, si fieri potest, tali natura fruatur. Quaenam autem illa sit natura, ostendemus suo loco, nimirum esse cognitionem unionis, quam mens cum tota natura habet .

14. Hic est itaque finis, ad quem tendo, talem scilicet naturam acquirere, et ut multi mecum eam acquirant conari, hoc est, de mea felicitate etiam est operam dare, ut alii multi idem atque ego intelligant, ut eorum intellectus et cupiditas prorsus cum meo intellectu et cupiditate conveniant ; utque hoc fiat, necesse est tantum de natura intelligere, quantum sufficit ad talem naturam acquirendam ; deinde formare talem societatem, qualis est desideranda, ut quamplurimi quam facillime, et secure eo perveniant.

15. Porro danda est opera morali philosophiae, ut et doctrinae de puerorum educatione ; et quia valetudo non parvum est medium ad hunc finem assequendum, concinnanda est integra medicina ; et quia arte multa, quae difficilia sunt, facilia redduntur, multumque temporis et commoditatis in vita ea lucrari possumus, ideo mechanica nullo modo est contemnenda.

16. Sed ante omnia excogitandus est modus medendi intellectus, ipsumque, quantum initio licet, expurgandi, ut feliciter res absque errore, et quam optime intelligat. Unde quisque iam poterit videre, me omnes scientias ad unum finem et scopum velle dirigere, scilicet ut ad summam humanam, quam diximus, perfectionem perveniatur ; et sic omne illud, quod in scientiis nihil ad finem nostrum nos promovet, tamquam inutile erit reiiciendum, hoc est, ut uno verbo dicam, omnes nostrae operationes simul et cogitationes ad hunc sunt dirigendae finem.

III. QUAEDAM VIVENDI REGULAE.

17. SED QUIA, dum curamus eum consequi, et operam damus, ut intellectum in rectam viam redigamus, necesse est vivere, propterea ante omnia cogimur quasdam vivendi regulas, tanquam bonas, supponere, has scilicet.

I. Ad captum vulgi loqui, et illa omnia operari, quae nihil impedimenti adferunt, quominus nostrum scopum attingamus. Nam non parum emolumenti ab eo possumus acquirere, modo ipsius captui, quantum fieri potest, concedamus ; adde, quod tali modo amicas praebebunt aures ad veritatem audiendam.

II. Deliciis in tantum frui, in quantum ad tuendam valetudinem sufficit.

III. Denique tantum nummorum, aut cuiuscumque alterius rei quaerere, quantum sufficit ad vitam, et valetudinem sustentandam, et ad mores civitatis, qui nostrum scopum non oppugnant, imitandos.

IV. DE DIVERSIS PERCIPIENDI MODIS.

18. HISCE SIC positis, ad primum, quod ante omnia faciendum est, me accingam, ad emendandum scilicet intellectum, eumque aptum reddendum ad res tali modo intelligendas, quo opus est, ut nostrum finem assequamur. Quod ut fiat, exigit ordo, quem naturaliter habemus, ut hic resumam omnes modos percipiendi, quos hucusque habui ad aliquid indubie affirmandum vel negandum, quo omnium optimum eligam, et simul meas vires et naturam, quam perficere cupio, noscere incipiam.

19. Si accurate attendo, possunt omnes ad quatuor potissimum reduci.

I. Est perceptio, quam ex auditu aut ex aliquo signo, quod vocant ad placitum, habemus.

II. Est perceptio, quam habemus ab experientia vaga, hoc est, ab experientia, quae non determinatur ab intellectu, sed tantum ita dicitur, quia casu sic occurrit, et nullum aliud habemus experimentum, quod hoc oppugnat, et ideo tanquam inconcussum apud nos manet.

III. Est perceptio, ubi essentia rei ex alia re concluditur, sed non adaequate ; quod fit, cum vel ab aliquo effectu causam colligimus, vel cum concluditur ab aliquo universali, quod semper aliqua proprietas concomitatur .

IV. Denique perceptio est, ubi res percipitur per solam suam essentiam, vel per cognitionem suae proximae causae.

20. Quae omnia exemplis illustrabo. Ex auditu tantum scio meum natalem diem, et quod tales parentes habui, et similia ; de quibus nunquam dubitavi. Per experientiam vagam scio me moriturum ; hoc enim ideo affirmo, quia vidi alios mei similes obiisse mortem, quamvis neque omnes per idem temporis spatium vixerint, neque ex eodem morbo obierint. Deinde per experientiam vagam etiam scio, quod oleum sit aptum alimentum ad nutriendam flammam, quodque aqua ad eam extinguendam apta sit ; scio etiam, quod canis sit animal latrans, et homo animal rationale, et sic fere omnia novi, quae ad usum vitae faciunt.

21. Ex alia vero re hoc modo concludimus : postquam clare percipimus, nos tale corpus sentire et nullum aliud, inde, inquam, clare concludimus animam unitam esse corpori, quae unio est causa talis sensationis ; sed quaenam sit illa sensatio et unio, non absolute inde possumus intelligere . Vel postquam novi naturam visus, et simul, eum habere talem proprietatem, ut unam eandemque rem ad magnam distantiam minorem videamus, quam si eam cominus intueamur ; inde concludimus solem maiorem esse, quam apparet, et alia his similia.

22. Per solam denique rei essentiam res percipitur, quando ex eo, quod aliquid novi, scio, quid hoc sit aliquid nosse, vel ex eo, quod novi essentiam animae, scio eam corpori esse unitam. Eadem cognitione novimus duo et tria esse quinque, et si dentur duae lineae uni tertiae parallelae, eas etiam inter sese parallelas etc. Ea tamen, quae hucusque tali cognitione potui intelligere, perpauca fuerunt.

23. Ut autem haec omnia melius intelligantur, unico tantum utar exemplo, hoc scilicet. Dantur tres numeri ; quaerit quis quartum, qui sit ad tertium, ut secundus ad primum. Dicunt hic passim mercatores, se scire, quid sit agendum, ut quartus inveniatur, quia nempe eam operationem nondum oblivioni tradiderunt, quam

nudam sine demonstratione a suis magistris audiverunt. Alii vero ab experientia simplicium faciunt axioma universale, scilicet ubi quartus numerus per se patet, ut in his 2, 4, 3, 6, ubi experiuntur, quod ducto secundo in tertium, et producto deinde per primum diviso fiat quotiens 6 ; et cum vident eundem numerum produci, quem sine hac operatione noverant esse proportionalem, inde concludunt operationem esse bonam ad quartum numerum proportionalem semper inveniendum.

24. Sed mathematici vi demonstrationis pro. lib. 7. element. Euclidis sciunt, quales numeri inter se sint proportionales, scilicet ex natura proportionis eiusque proprietate, quod nempe numerus, qui fit ex primo et quarto aequalis sit numero, qui fit ex secundo et tertio. Attamen adaequatam proportionalitatem datorum numerorum non vident ; et si videant, non vident eam vi illius propositionis, sed intuitive, nullam operationem facientes.

V. DE OPTIMO MODO PERCIPIENDI.

25. UT AUTEM ex his optimus eligatur modus percipiendi, requiritur, ut breviter enumeremus, quae sint necessaria media, ut nostrum finem assequamur ; haec scilicet :

I. Nostram naturam, quam cupimus perficere, exacte nosse, et simul tantum de rerum natura, quantum sit necesse.

II. Ut inde rerum differentias, convenientias et oppugnantias recte colligamus.

III. Ut recte concipiatur, quid possint pati, quid non.

IV. Ut hoc conferatur cum natura et potentia hominis. Et ex istis facile apparebit summa, ad quam homo potest pervenire, perfectio.

26. His sic consideratis videamus, quis modus percipiendi nobis sit eligendus.

Quod ad primum attinet, per se patet, quod ex auditu, praeterquam quod sit res admodum incerta, nullam percipiamus essentiam rei, sicuti ex nostro exemplo apparet ; et cum singularis existentia alicuius rei non noscatur nisi cognita essentia (uti postea videbitur), hinc clare concludimus omnem certitudinem, quam ex auditu habemus, a scientiis esse secludendam. Nam a simplici auditu, ubi non praecessit proprius intellectus, nunquam quis poterit affici.

27. Quoad secundum ; nullus etiam dicendus est, quod habeat ideam illius proportionis, quam quaerit . Praeterquam quod sit res admodum incerta et sine fine, nihil tamen unquam tali modo quis in rebus naturalibus percipiet praeter accidentia, quae nunquam clare intelliguntur, nisi praecognitis essentiis. Unde etiam et ille secludendus est.

28. De tertio autem aliquo modo dicendum, quod habeamus ideam rei, deinde quod etiam absque periculo erroris concludamus ; sed tamen per se non erit medium, ut nostram perfectionem acquiramus.

29. Solus quartus modus comprehendit essentiam rei adaequatam, et absque erroris periculo ; ideoque maxime erit usurpandus. Quomodo ergo sit adhibendus, ut res incognitae tali cognitione a nobis intelligantur, simulque ut hoc quam compendiose fiat, curabimus explicare.

VI. DE INTELLECTUS
INSTRUMENT IS, IDEIS VERIS.

30. POSTQUAM NOVIMUS, quaenam cognitio nobis sit necessaria, tradenda est via et methodus, qua res, quae sunt cognoscendae, tali cognitione cognoscamus. Quod ut fiat, venit prius considerandum, quod hic non dabitur inquisitio in infinitum ; scilicet ut inveniatur optima methodus verum investigandi, non opus est alia methodo, ut methodus veri investigandi investigetur ; et ut secunda methodus investigetur, non opus est alia tertia, et sic in infinitum. Tali enim modo nunquam ad veri cognitionem, imo ad nullam cognitionem perveniretur. Hoc vero eodem modo se habet, ac se habent instrumenta corporea, ubi eodem modo liceret argumentari. Nam ut ferrum cudatur, malleo opus est, et ut malleus habeatur, eum fieri necessum est ; ad quod alio malleo, aliisque instrumentis opus est, quae etiam ut habeantur, aliis opus erit instrumentis, et sic in infinitum ; et hoc modo frustra aliquis probare conaretur, homines nullam habere potestatem ferrum cudendi.

31. Sed quemadmodum homines initio innatis instrumentis quaedam facillima, quamvis laboriose et imperfecte, facere quiverunt, iisque confectis alia difficiliora minori labore, et perfectius confecerunt, et sic gradatim ab operibus simplicissimis ad instrumenta, et ab instrumentis ad alia opera, et instrumenta pergendo eo pervenerunt, ut tot et tam difficilia parvo labore perficiant, sic etiam intellectus vi sua nativa facit sibi instrumenta intellectualia, quibus alias vires acquirit ad alia opera intellectualia, et ex iis operibus alia instrumenta seu potestatem ulterius investigandi ; et sic gradatim pergit, donec sapientiae culmen attingat.

32. Quod autem intellectus ita sese habeat, facile erit videre, modo intelligatur, quid sit methodus verum investigandi, et quaenam sint illa innata instrumenta, quibus tantum eget ad alia ex iis instrumenta conficienda, ut ulterius procedat. Ad quod ostendendum sic procedo .

33. Idea vera (habemus enim ideam veram) est diversum quid a suo ideato. Nam aliud est circulus, aliud idea circuli ; idea enim circuli non est aliquid, habens peripheriam et centrum, uti circulus, nec idea corporis est ipsum corpus. Et cum sit quid diversum a suo ideato, erit etiam per se aliquid intelligibile, hoc est, idea quoad suam essentiam formalem potest esse obiectum alterius essentiae obiectivae, et rursus haec altera essentia obiectiva erit etiam in se spectata quid reale et intelligibile, et sic indefinite.

34. Petrus ex. gr. est quid reale ; vera autem idea Petri est essentia Petri obiectiva, et in se quid reale, et omnino diversum ab ipso Petro. Cum itaque idea Petri sit quid reale habens suam essentiam peculiarem, erit etiam quid intelligibile, id est, obiectum alterius ideae, quae idea habebit in se obiective omne id, quod idea Petri habet formaliter, et rursus idea, quae est ideae Petri, habet iterum suam essentiam, quae etiam potest esse obiectum alterius ideae, et sic indefinite. Quod quisque potest experiri, dum videt se scire, quid sit Petrus, et etiam scire se scire, et rursus scit se scire, quod scit etc. Unde constat, quod, ut intelligatur essentia Petri, non sit necesse, ipsam ideam Petri intelligere, et multo minus ideam ideae Petri ; quod idem est, ac si dicerem, non esse opus, ut sciam, quod sciam me scire, et multo minus esse opus scire, quod sciam me scire ; non magis, quam ad intelligendam essentiam trianguli opus sit essentiam circuli intelligere . Sed contrarium datur in his ideis. Nam ut sciam me scire, necessario debeo prius scire.

35. Hinc patet, quod certitudo nihil sit praeter ipsam essentiam obiectivam ; id

est, modus, quo sentimus essentiam formalem, est ipsa certitudo. Unde iterum patet, quod ad certitudinem veritatis nullo alio signo sit opus, quam veram habere ideam ; nam, uti ostendimus, non opus est, ut sciam, quod sciam me scire. Ex quibus rursum patet, neminem posse scire, quid sit summa certitudo, nisi qui habet adaequatam ideam aut essentiam obiectivam alicuius rei ; nimirum, quia idem est certitudo et essentia obiectiva.

VII. DE RECTA METHODO COGNOSCENDI.

36. CUM ITAQUE veritas nullo egeat signo, sed sufficiat habere essentias rerum obiectivas, aut, quod idem est, ideas, ut omne tollatur dubium ; hinc sequitur, quod vera non est methodus signum veritatis quaerere post acquisitionem idearum, sed quod vera methodus est via, ut ipsa veritas, aut essentiae obiectivae rerum aut ideae (omnia illa idem significant) debito ordine quaerantur .

37. Rursus methodus necessario debet loqui de ratiocinatione aut de intellectione ; id est, methodus non est ipsum ratiocinari ad intelligendum causas rerum, et multo minus est τo intelligere causas rerum ; sed est intelligere, quid sit vera idea, eam a ceteris perceptionibus distinguendo eiusque naturam investigando, ut inde nostram intelligendi potentiam noscamus, et mentem ita cohibeamus, ut ad illam normam omnia intelligat, quae sunt intelligenda, tradendo tamquam auxilia certas regulas, et etiam faciendo, ne mens inutilibus defatigetur.

38. Unde colligitur, methodum nihil aliud esse, nisi cognitionem reflexivam aut ideam ideae ; et quia non datur idea ideae, nisi prius detur idea, ergo methodus non dabitur, nisi prius detur idea. Unde illa bona erit methodus, quae ostendit, quomodo mens dirigenda sit ad datae verae ideae normam. Porro cum ratio, quae est inter duas ideas, sit eadem cum ratione, quae est inter essentias formales idearum illarum, inde sequitur, quod cognitio reflexiva, quae est ideae entis perfectissimi, praestantior erit cognitione reflexiva ceterarum idearum ; hoc est, perfectissima ea erit methodus, quae ad datae ideae entis perfectissimi normam ostendit, quomodo mens sit dirigenda.

39. Ex his facile intelligitur, quomodo mens plura intelligendo alia simul acquirat instrumenta, quibus facilius pergat intelligere. Nam, ut ex dictis licet colligere, debet ante omnia in nobis existere vera idea tamquam innatum instrumentum, qua intellecta intelligatur simul differentia, quae est inter talem perceptionem, et ceteras omnes. Qua in re consistit una methodi pars. Et cum per se clarum sit, mentem eo melius se intelligere, quo plura de natura intelligit, inde constat, hanc methodi partem eo perfectiorem fore, quo mens plura intelligit, et tum fore perfectissimam, cum mens ad cognitionem entis perfectissimi attendit sive reflectit.

40. Deinde, quo plura mens novit, eo melius et suas vires et ordinem naturae intelligit : quo autem melius suas vires intelligit, eo facilius potest se ipsam dirigere et regulas sibi proponere ; et quo melius ordinem naturae intelligit, eo facilius potest se ab inutilibus cohibere ; in quibus tota consistit methodus, uti diximus.

41. Adde quod idea eodem modo se habet obiective, ac ipsius ideatum se habet realiter. Si ergo daretur aliquid in natura, nihil commercii habens cum aliis rebus, eius etiam si daretur essentia obiectiva, quae convenire omnino deberet cum formali, nihil etiam commercii haberet cum aliis ideis , id est, nihil de ipsa poterimus concludere ; et contra, quae habent commercium cum aliis rebus, uti sunt omnia quae in natura existunt, intelligentur et ipsorum etiam essentiae obiectivae idem habebunt commercium, id est, aliae ideae ex eis deducentur, quae iterum habebunt commercium cum aliis, et sic instrumenta ad procedendum ulterius crescent. Quod conabamur demonstrare.

42. Porro ex hoc ultimo, quod diximus, scilicet quod idea omnino cum sua essentia formali debeat convenire, patet iterum quod, ut mens nostra omnino referat

naturae exemplar, debeat omnes suas ideas producere ab ea, quae refert originem et fontem totius naturae, ut ipsa etiam sit fons ceterarum idearum.

43. Hic forte aliquis mirabitur, quod nos, ubi diximus, bonam methodum eam esse, quae ostendit, quomodo mens sit dirigenda ad datae verae ideae normam, hoc ratiocinando probemus ; id quod ostendere videtur, hoc per se non esse notum ; atque adeo quaeri potest, utrum nos bene ratiocinemur. Si bene ratiocinamur, debemus incipere a data idea, et cum incipere a data idea egeat demonstratione, deberemus iterum nostrum ratiocinium probare, et tum iterum illud alterum, et sic in infinitum.

44. Sed ad hoc respondeo : quod si quis fato quodam sic processisset naturam investigando, scilicet ad datae verae ideae normam alias acquirendo ideas debito ordine, nunquam de sua veritate dubitasset , eo quod veritas, uti ostendimus, se ipsam patefacit, et etiam sponte omnia ipsi affluxissent. Sed quia hoc nunquam aut raro contingit, ideo coactus fui illa sic ponere, ut illud, quod non possumus fato, praemeditato tamen consilio acquiramus, et simul ut appareret, ad probandam veritatem et bonum ratiocinium nullis nos egere instrumentis, nisi ipsa veritate et bono ratiocinio. Nam bonum ratiocinium bene ratiocinando comprobavi, et adhuc probare conor.

45. Adde, quod etiam hoc modo homines assuefiant meditationibus suis internis. Ratio autem, cur in naturae inquisitione raro contingat, ut debito ordine ea investigetur, est propter praeiudicia, quorum causas postea in nostra philosophia explicabimus ; deinde quia opus est magna et accurata distinctione, sicut postea ostendemus (id quod valde est laboriosum) ; denique propter statum rerum humanarum, qui, ut iam ostensum est, prorsus est mutabilis. Sunt adhuc aliae rationes, quas non inquirimus.

46. Si quis forte quaerat, cur ipse statim ante omnia veritates naturae isto ordine ostenderim (nam veritas se ipsam patefacit), ei respondeo simulque moneo, ne propter paradoxa, quae forte passim occurrent, ea velit tamquam falsa reiicere, sed prius dignetur ordinem considerare, quo ea probemus, et tum certus evadet, nos verum assequutos fuisse. Et haec fuit causa, cur haec praemiserim.

47. Si postea forte quis scepticus et de ipsa prima veritate et de omnibus, quas ad normam primae deducemus, dubius adhuc maneret, ille profecto aut contra conscientiam loquetur, aut nos fatebimur, dari homines penitus etiam animo obcaecatos a nativitate aut a praeiudiciorum causa, id est, aliquo externo casu. Nam neque se ipsos sentiunt. Si aliquid affirmant,vel dubitant, nesciunt se dubitare aut affirmare ; dicunt se nihil scire, et hoc ipsum, quod nihil sciunt, dicunt se ignorare ; neque hoc absolute dicunt ; nam metuunt fateri, se existere, quamdiu nihil sciunt, adeo ut tandem debeant obmutescere, ne forte aliquid supponant, quod veritatem redoleat.

48. Denique cum ipsis non est loquendum de scientiis ; nam quod ad vitae et societatis usum attinet, necessitas eos coegit, ut supponerent se esse, et ut suum utile quaererent, et iureiurando multa affirmarent et negarent. Nam, si aliquid ipsis probetur, nesciunt, an probet aut deficiat argumentatio. Si negant, concedunt aut opponunt, nesciunt se negare, concedere aut opponere ; adeoque habendi sunt tanquam automata, quae mente omnino carent.

49. Resumamus iam nostrum propositum. Habuimus hucusque primo finem, ad quem omnes nostras cogitationes dirigere studemus. Cognovimus secundo,

quaenam sit optima perceptio, cuius ope ad nostram perfectionem pervenire possimus. Cognovimus tertio, quaenam sit prima via, cui mens insistere debeat, ut bene incipiat ; quae est, ut ad normam datae cuiuscumque verae ideae pergat certis legibus inquirere. Quod ut recte fiat, haec debet methodus praestare : primo veram ideam a ceteris omnibus perceptionibus distinguere, et mentem a ceteris perceptionibus cohibere ; secundo tradere regulas, ut res incognitae ad talem normam percipiantur ; tertio ordinem constituere, ne inutilibus defatigemur. Postquam hanc methodum novimus, vidimus quarto hanc methodum perfectissimam futuram, ubi habuerimus ideam entis perfectissimi. Unde initio illud erit maxime observandum, ut quanto ocius ad cognitionem talis entis perveniamus.

VIII. METHODI PARS PRIMA.
DE IDEA FICTA.

50. INCIPIAMUS ITAQUE a prima parte methodi, quae est, uti diximus, distinguere et separare ideam veram a ceteris perceptionibus, et cohibere mentem, ne falsas, fictas et dubias cum veris confundat. Quod utcumque fuse hic explicare animus est, ut lectores detineam in cogitatione rei adeo necessariae, et etiam quia multi sunt, qui vel de veris dubitant ex eo, quod non attenderunt ad distinctionem, quae est inter veram perceptionem et alias omnes ; adeo ut sint veluti homines, qui cum vigilarent, non dubitabant se vigilare ; sed postquam semel in somniis, ut saepe fit, putarunt se certo vigilare, quod postea falsum esse reperiebant, etiam de suis vigiliis dubitarunt ; quod contingit, quia nunquam distinxerunt inter somnum et vigiliam.

51. Interim moneo, me hic essentiam uniuscuiusque perceptionis, eamque per proximam suam causam non explicaturum, quia hoc ad philosophiam pertinet ; sed tantum traditurum id, quod methodus postulat, id est, circa quae perceptio ficta, falsa et dubia versetur, et quomodo ab unaquaque liberabimur. Sit itaque prima inquisitio circa ideam fictam.

52. Cum omnis perceptio sit vel rei tamquam existentis consideratae, vel solius essentiae, et frequentiores fictiones contingant circa res tamquam existentes consideratas, ideo prius de hac loquar ; scilicet ubi sola existentia fingitur, et res, quae in tali actu fingitur, intelligitur sive supponitur intelligi. Ex. gr. fingo Petrum, quem novi ire domum, eum me invisere, et similia . Hic quaero, circa quae talis idea versetur ? Video eam tantum versari circa possibilia, non vero circa necessaria, neque circa impossibilia.

53. Rem impossibilem voco, cuius natura in existendo implicat contradictionem, ut ea existat ; necessariam, cuius natura implicat contradictionem, ut ea non existat ; possibilem, cuius quidem existentia ipsa sua natura non implicat contradictionem, ut existat aut non existat, sed cuius existentiae necessitas aut impossibilitas pendet a causis nobis ignotis, quamdiu ipsius existentiam fingimus ; ideoque si ipsius necessitas aut impossibilitas, quae a causis externis pendet, nobis esset nota, nihil etiam de ea potuissemus fingere.

54. Unde sequitur, si detur aliquis Deus aut omniscium quid, nihil prorsus eum posse fingere. Nam quod ad nos attinet, postquam novi me existere, non possum fingere me existere aut non existere ; nec etiam possum fingere elephantem, qui transeat per acus foramen ; nec possum, postquam naturam Dei novi, fingere eum existentem aut non existentem . Idem intelligendum est de chimaera, cuius natura existere implicat. Ex quibus patet id, quod dixi, scilicet quod fictio, de qua hic loquimur, non contingit circa aeternas veritates .

55. Sed antequam ulterius pergam, hic obiter notandum est, quod illa differentia, quae est inter essentiam unius rei et essentiam alterius, ea ipsa sit inter actualitatem aut existentiam eiusdem rei, et inter actualitatem aut existentiam alterius rei ; adeo ut si existentiam ex. gr. Adami tantum per generalem existentiam concipere velimus, idem futurum sit, ac si ad concipiendam ipsius essentiam, ad naturam entis attendamus, ut tandem definiamus, Adamum esse ens. Itaque quo existentia generalius concipitur, eo etiam confusius concipitur faciliusque unicuique rei potest affingi ; e contra, ubi particularius concipitur, clarius tum intelligitur, et difficilius alicui, nisi rei ipsi, ubi non attendimus ad naturae ordinem, affingitur. Quod notatu dignum est.

56. Veniunt iam hic ea consideranda, quae vulgo dicuntur fingi, quamvis clare intelligamus, rem ita sese non habere, uti eam fingimus. Ex. gr. quamvis sciam terram esse rotundam, nihil tamen vetat, quominus alicui dicam terram medium globum esse et tamquam medium pomum auriacum in scutella, aut solem circum terram moveri, et similia. Ad haec si attendamus, nihil videbimus, quod non cohaereat cum iam dictis, modo prius advertamus, nos aliquando potuisse errare, et iam errorum nostrorum esse conscios ; deinde quod possumus fingere, aut ad minimum putare, alios homines in eodem esse errore, aut in eum, ut nos antehac, posse incidere. Hoc, inquam, fingere possumus, quamdiu nullam videmus impossibilitatem nullamque necessitatem. Quando itaque alicui dico, terram non esse rotundam etc., nihil aliud ago, quam in memoriam revoco errorem, quem forte habui aut in quem labi potui, et postea fingo aut puto eum, cui hoc dico, adhuc esse aut posse labi in eundem errorem. Quod, ut dixi, fingo, quamdiu nullam video impossibilitatem nullamque necessitatem ; hanc vero si intellexissem, nihil prorsus fingere potuissem, et tantum dicendum fuisset, me aliquid operatum esse.

57. Superest iam, ut ea etiam notemus, quae in quaestionibus supponuntur ; id quod passim etiam contingit circa impossibilia. Ex. gr. cum dicimus : supponamus hanc candelam ardentem iam non ardere, aut supponamus eam ardere in aliquo spatio imaginario, sive ubi nulla dantur corpora. Quorum similia passim supponuntur, quamvis hoc ultimum clare intelligatur impossibile esse. Sed quando hoc fit, nil prorsus fingitur. Nam primo nihil aliud egi, quam quod in memoriam revocavi aliam candelam non ardentem (aut hanc eandem concepi sine flamma), et quod cogito de ea candela, id ipsum de hac intelligo, quamdiu ad flammam non attendo. In secundo nihil aliud fit, quam abstrahere cogitationes a corporibus circumiacentibus, ut mens se convertat ad solam candelae in se sola spectatae contemplationem ; ut postea concludat candelam nullam habere causam ad sui ipsius destructionem, adeo ut si nulla essent corpora circumiacentia, candela haec ac etiam flamma manerent immutabiles, aut similia. Nulla igitur datur hic fictio, sed verae ac merae assertiones .

58. Transeamus iam ad fictiones, quae versantur circa essentias solas, vel cum aliqua actualitate sive existentia simul. Circa quas hoc maxime venit considerandum, quod, quo mens minus intelligit, et tamen plura percipit, eo maiorem habeat potentiam fingendi, et quo plura intelligit, eo magis illa potentia diminuatur. Eodem ex. gr. modo, quo supra vidimus, nos non posse fingere, quamdiu cogitamus, nos cogitare et non cogitare, sic etiam, postquam novimus naturam corporis, non possumus fingere muscam infinitam ; sive postquam novimus naturam animae , non possumus fingere eam esse quadratam, quamvis omnia verbis possimus effari. Sed, uti diximus, quominus homines norunt naturam, eo facilius multa possunt fingere ; veluti, arbores loqui, homines in momento mutari in lapides, in fontes, apparere in speculis spectra, nihil fieri aliquid, etiam deos in bestias et homines mutari, ac infinita eius generis alia.

59. Aliquis forte putabit, quod fictio fictionem terminat, sed non intellectio ; hoc est, postquam finxi aliquid, et quadam libertate volui assentiri, id sic in rerum natura existere, hoc efficit, ut postea non possimus id alio modo cogitare. Ex. gr. postquam finxi (ut cum iis loquar) naturam corporis talem, mihique ex mea libertate persuadere volui, eam sic realiter existere, non amplius licet muscam v. g. infinitam fingere ; et postquam finxi essentiam animae, eam quadrare non possum etc.

60. Sed hoc examinandum. Primo vel negant vel concedunt nos aliquid posse intelligere. Si concedunt, necessario id ipsum, quod de fictione dicunt, etiam de

intellectione dicendum erit. Si vero hoc negant, videamus nos, qui scimus, nos aliquid scire, quid dicant. Hoc scilicet dicunt, animam posse sentire et multis modis percipere non se ipsam, neque res quae existunt, sed tantum ea, quae nec in se, nec ullibi sunt, hoc est, animam posse sola sua vi creare sensationes aut ideas, quae non sunt rerum ; adeo ut ex parte eam tamquam Deum considerent. Porro dicunt, nos aut animam nostram talem habere libertatem, ut nosmet, aut se, imo suam ipsam libertatem cogat. Nam postquam ea aliquid finxit, et assensum ei praebuit, non potest id alio modo cogitare aut fingere, et etiam ea fictione cogitur, ut etiam alia tali modo cogitentur, ut prima fictio non oppugnetur ; sicut hic etiam coguntur absurda, quae hic recenseo, admittere propter suam fictionem ; ad quae explodenda non defatigabimur ullis demonstrationibus .

61. Sed eos in suis deliriis linquendo, curabimus, ut ex verbis, quae cum ipsis fecimus, aliquid veri ad nostram rem hauriamus, nempe hoc. Mens cum ad rem fictam et sua natura falsam attendit, ut eam pensitet et ntelligat, bonoque ordine ex ea deducat quae sunt deducenda, facile falsitatem patefaciet ; et si res ficta sua natura sit vera, cum mens ad eam attendit, ut eam intelligat, et ex ea bono ordine incipit deducere, quae inde sequuntur, feliciter perget sine ulla interruptione, sicut vidimus, quod ex falsa fictione modo allata statim ad ostendendam eius absurditatem et alias inde deductas praebuit se intellectus.

62. Nullo ergo modo timendum erit, nos aliquid fingere, si modo clare et distincte rem percipiamus. Nam si forte dicamus, homines in momento mutari in bestias, id valde generaliter dicitur, adeo ut nullus detur conceptus, id est, idea sive cohaerentia subiecti et praedicati in mente ; si enim daretur, simul videret medium et causas, quo et cur tale quid factum sit. Deinde nec ad naturam subiecti et praedicati attenditur.

63. Porro, modo prima idea non sit ficta et ex ea ceterae omnes ideae deducantur, paulatim praecipitantia fingendi evanescet. Deinde cum idea ficta non possit esse clara et distincta, sed solummodo confusa, et omnis confusio inde procedat, quod mens rem integram aut ex multis compositam tantum ex parte noscat, et notum ab ignoto non distinguat ; praeterea quod ad multa, quae continentur in unaquaque re, simul attendat sine ulla distinctione ; inde sequitur primo, quod si idea sit alicuius rei simplicissimae, ea non nisi clara et distincta poterit esse. Nam res illa non ex parte, sed tota aut nihil eius innotescere debebit.

64. Sequitur secundo, quod si res, quae componitur ex multis, in partes omnes simplicissimas cogitatione dividatur, et ad unamquamque seorsim attendatur, omnis tum confusio evanescet. Sequitur tertio, quod fictio non possit esse simplex, sed quod fiat ex compositione diversarum idearum confusarum, quae sunt diversarum rerum atque actionum in natura existentium, vel melius ex attentione simul sine assensu ad tales diversas ideas . Nam si esset simplex, esset clara et distincta, et per consequens vera. Si ex compositione idearum distinctarum, esset etiam earum compositio clara et distincta, ac proinde vera. Ex. gr. postquam novimus naturam circuli ac etiam naturam quadrati, iam non possumus ea duo componere, et circulum facere quadratum, aut animam quadratam, et similia.

65. Concludamus iterum breviter, et videamus, quomodo fictio nullo modo sit timenda, ut ea cum veris ideis confundatur. Nam quoad primam, de qua prius locuti sumus, ubi scilicet res clare concipitur, vidimus, quod si ea res, quae clare concipitur, et etiam ipsius existentia sit per se aeterna veritas, nihil circa talem rem poterimus fingere ; sed si existentia rei conceptae non sit aeterna veritas, tantum est curandum, ut existentia rei cum eius essentia conferatur, et simul ad

ordinem naturae attendatur. Quoad secundam fictionem, quam diximus esse simul attentionem sine assensu ad diversas ideas confusas, quae sunt diversarum rerum atque actionum in natura existentium, vidimus etiam rem simplicissimam non posse fingi, sed intelligi, et etiam rem compositam, modo ad partes simplicissimas, ex quibus componitur, attendamus ; imo nec ex ipsis ullas actiones, quae verae non sunt, nos posse fingere. Nam simul cogemur contemplari, quomodo et cur tale quid fiat.

IX. DE IDEA FALSA.

66. HIS SIC intellectis, transeamus iam ad inquisitionem ideae falsae, ut videamus, circa quae versetur, et quomodo nobis possimus cavere, ne in falsas perceptiones incidamus. Quod utrumque non erit nobis iam difficile post inquisitionem ideae fictae. Nam inter ipsas nulla alia datur differentia, nisi quod haec supponat assensum, hoc est (uti iam notavimus) quod nullae offeruntur causae, dum repraesentamina ipsi offeruntur, quibus, sicut fingens, possit colligere, ea non oriri a rebus extra se, et quod fere nihil aliud sit, quam oculis apertis, sive dum vigilamus, somniare. Versatur itaque idea falsa, vel (ut melius loquar) refertur ad existentiam rei, cuius essentia cognoscitur, sive circa essentiam eodem modo ac idea ficta.

67. Quae ad existentiam refertur, emendatur eodem modo ac fictio. Nam si natura rei notae supponat existentiam necessariam, impossibile est, ut circa existentiam illius rei fallamur ; sed si existentia rei non sit aeterna veritas, uti est eius essentia, sed quod necessitas aut impossibilitas existendi pendeat a causis externis, tum cape omnia eodem modo, quo diximus, cum de fictione sermo esset ; nam eodem modo emendatur.

68. Quod attinet ad alteram, quae ad essentias refertur, vel etiam ad actiones, tales perceptiones necessario semper sunt confusae, compositae ex diversis confusis perceptionibus rerum in natura existentium, ut cum hominibus persuadetur, in silvis, in imaginibus, in brutis et ceteris adesse numina ; dari corpora, ex quorum sola compositione fiat intellectus ; cadavera ratiocinari, ambulare, loqui ; Deum decipi, et similia. Sed ideae, quae sunt clarae et distinctae, nunquam possunt esse falsae : Nam ideae rerum, quae clare et distincte concipiuntur, sunt vel simplicissimae, vel compositae ex ideis simplicissimis, id est, a simplicissimis ideis deductae. Quod vero idea simplicissima non queat esse falsa, poterit unusquisque videre, modo sciat, quid sit verum sive intellectus, et simul quid falsum.

69. Nam quod id spectat, quod formam veri constituit, certum est, cogitationem veram a falsa non tantum per denominationem extrinsecam, sed maxime per intrinsecam distingui. Nam si quis faber ordine concepit fabricam aliquam, quamvis talis fabrica nunquam exstiterit, nec etiam unquam exstitura sit, eius nihilominus cogitatio vera est, et cogitatio eadem est, sive fabrica existat, sive minus ; et contra si aliquis dicit, Petrum ex. gr. existere, nec tamen scit, Petrum existere, illa cogitatio respectu illius falsa est, vel si mavis, non est vera ; quamvis Petrus revera existat. Nec haec enunciatio, Petrus existit, vera est, nisi respectu illius, qui certo scit, Petrum existere.

70. Unde sequitur in ideis dari aliquid reale, per quod verae a falsis distinguuntur ; quod quidem iam investigandum erit, ut optimam veritatis normam habeamus (ex data enim verae ideae norma nos nostras cogitationes debere determinare diximus, methodumque cognitionem esse reflexivam), et proprietates intellectus noscamus ; nec dicendum hanc differentiam ex eo oriri, quod cogitatio vera est res cognoscere per primas suas causas, in quo quidem a falsa valde differret, prout eandem supra explicui. Cogitatio enim vera etiam dicitur, quae essentiam alicuius principii obiective involvit, quod causam non habet, et per se et in se cognoscitur.

71. Quare forma verae cogitationis in eadem ipsa cogitatione sine relatione ad alias debet esse sita ; nec obiectum tamquam causam agnoscit, sed ab ipsa intellectus potentia, et natura pendere debet. Nam si supponamus, intellectum ens aliquod novum percepisse, quod nunquam exstitit, sicut aliqui Dei intellectum concipiunt,

antequam res crearet (quae sane perceptio a nullo obiecto oriri potuit), et ex tali perceptione alias legitime deduceret, omnes illae cogitationes verae essent, et a nullo obiecto externo determinatae, sed a sola intellectus potentia et natura dependerent. Quare id, quod formam verae cogitationis constituit, in ipsa eadem cogitatione est quaerendum, et ab intellectus natura deducendum.

72. Hoc igitur ut investigetur, ideam aliquam veram ob oculos ponamus, cuius obiectum maxime certo scimus a vi nostra cogitandi pendere, nec obiectum aliquod in natura habere ; in tali enim idea, ut ex iam dictis patet, facilius id, quod volumus, investigare poterimus. Ex. gr. ad formandum conceptum globi fingo ad libitum causam, nempe semicirculum circa centrum rotari, et ex rotatione globum quasi oriri. Haec sane idea vera est, et quamvis sciamus nullum in natura globum sic unquam ortum fuisse, est haec tamen vera perceptio et facillimus modus formandi globi conceptum. Iam notandum hanc perceptionem affirmare semicirculum rotari, quae affirmatio falsa esset, si non esset iuncta conceptui globi vel causae talem motum determinantis, sive absolute, si haec affirmatio nuda esset. Nam tum mens tantum tenderet ad affirmandum solum semicirculi motum, qui nec in semicirculi conceptu continetur, nec ex conceptu causae motum determinantis oritur. Quare falsitas in hoc solo consistit, quod aliquid de aliqua re affirmetur, quod in ipsius quem formavimus conceptu non continetur ; ut motus vel quies de semicirculo. Unde sequitur simplices cogitationes non posse non esse veras, ut simplex semicirculi, motus, quantitatis etc. idea. Quicquid hae affirmationis continent, earum adaequat conceptum, nec ultra se extendit. Quare nobis licet ad libitum sine ullo erroris scrupulo ideas simplices formare.

73. Superest igitur tantum quaerere, qua potentia mens nostra eas formare possit, et quousque ea potentia se extendat ; hoc enim invento facile videbimus summam, ad quam possumus pervenire, cognitionem. Certum enim est, hanc eius potentiam se non extendere in infinitum : Nam cum aliquid de aliqua re affirmamus, quod in conceptu, quem de ea formamus, non continetur, id defectum nostrae perceptionis indicat, sive quod mutilatas quasi et truncatas habemus cogitationes sive ideas. Motum enim semicirculi falsum esse vidimus, ubi nudus in mente est, eum ipsum autem verum, si conceptui globi iungatur, vel conceptui alicuius causae talem motum determinantis. Quod si de natura entis cogitantis sit, uti prima fronte videtur, cogitationes veras sive adaequatas formare, certum est, ideas inadaequatas ex eo tantum in nobis oriri, quod pars sumus alicuius entis cogitantis, cuius quaedam cogitationes ex toto, quaedam ex parte tantum nostram mentem constituunt.

74. Sed quod adhuc venit considerandum, et quod circa fictionem non fuit operae pretium notare, et ubi maxima datur deceptio, est, quando contingit, ut quaedam, quae in imaginatione offeruntur, sint etiam in intellectu, hoc est, quod clare et distincte concipiantur, quod tum, quamdiu distinctum a confuso non distinguitur, certitudo, hoc est, idea vera cum non distinctis commiscetur. Ex. gr. quidam Stoicorum forte audiverunt nomen animae, et etiam quod sit immortalis, quae tantum confuse imaginabantur ; imaginabantur etiam, et simul intelligebant corpora subtilissima cetera omnia penetrare, et a nullis penetrari. Cum haec omnia simul imaginabantur, concomitante certudine huius axiomatis, statim certi reddebantur, mentem esse subtilissima illa corpora, et subtilissima illa corpora non dividi etc.

75. Sed ab hoc etiam liberamur, dum conamur ad normam datae verae ideae omnes nostras perceptiones examinare cavendo, uti initio diximus, ab iis, quas ex auditu aut ab experientia vaga habemus. Adde quod talis deceptio ex eo oritur, quod res nimis abstracte concipiunt ; nam per se satis clarum est, me illud, quod in suo vero obiecto concipio, alteri non posse applicare. Oritur denique etiam

ex eo, quod prima elementa totius naturae non intelligunt ; unde sine ordine procedendo, et naturam cum abstractis, quamvis sint vera axiomata, confundendo, se ipsos confundunt ordinemque naturae pervertunt. Nobis autem, si quam minime abstracte procedamus, et a primis elementis, hoc est, a fonte et origine naturae, quam primum fieri potest, incipiamus, nullo modo talis deceptio erit metuenda.

76. Quod autem attinet ad cognitionem originis naturae, minime est timendum, ne eam cum abstractis confundamus. Nam cum aliquid abstracte concipitur, uti sunt omnia universalia, semper latius comprehenduntur in intellectu, quam revera in natura existere possunt eorum particularia. Deinde cum in natura dentur multa, quorum differentia adeo est exigua, ut fere intellectum effugiat, tum facile (si abstracte concipiantur) potest contingere, ut confundantur. At cum origo naturae, ut postea videbimus, nec abstracte sive universaliter concipi possit, nec latius possit extendi in intellectu, quam revera est, nec ullam habeat similitudinem cum mutabilibus, nulla circa eius ideam metuenda est confusio, modo normam veritatis (quam iam ostendimus) habeamus. Est nimirum hoc ens unicum, infinitum , hoc est, est omne esse, et praeter quod nullum datur esse .

X. DE IDEA DUBIA.

77. HUCUSQUE DE idea falsa. Superest, ut de idea dubia inquiramus, hoc est, ut inquiramus, quaenam sint ea, quae nos possunt in dubium pertrahere, et simul quomodo dubitatio tollatur. Loquor de vera dubitatione in mente, et non de ea, quam passim videmus contingere, ubi scilicet verbis, quamvis animus non dubitet, dicit quis se dubitare. Non est enim methodi hoc emendare, sed potius pertinet ad inquisitionem pertinaciae et eius emendationem.

78. Dubitatio itaque in anima nulla datur per rem ipsam, de qua dubitatur, hoc est, si tantum unica sit idea in anima, sive ea sit vera sive falsa, nulla dabitur dubitatio, neque etiam certitudo, sed tantum talis sensatio. Est enim in se nihil aliud nisi talis sensatio ; sed dabitur per aliam ideam, quae non adeo clara ac distincta est, ut possimus ex ea aliquid certi circa rem, de qua dubitatur, concludere, hoc est, idea, quae nos in dubium coniicit, non est clara et distincta. Ex. gr. si quis nunquam cogitaverit de sensuum fallacia, sive experientia sive quomodocumque sit, nunquam dubitabit, an sol maior aut minor sit, quam apparet. Inde rustici passim mirantur, cum audiunt solem multo maiorem esse, quam globum terrae. Sed cogitando de fallacia sensuum oritur dubitatio , et si quis post dubitationem acquisiverit veram cognitionem sensuum, et quomodo per eorum instrumenta res ad distantiam repraesententur, tum dubitatio iterum tollitur.

79. Unde sequitur, nos non posse veras ideas in dubium vocare ex eo, quod forte aliquis Deus deceptor existat, qui vel in maxime certis nos fallit, nisi quamdiu nullam habemus claram et distinctam Dei ideam, hoc est, si attendamus ad cognitionem, quam de origine omnium rerum habemus, et nihil inveniamus, quod nos doceat, eum non esse deceptorem eadem illa cognitione, qua, cum attendimus ad naturam trianguli, invenimus eius tres angulos aequales esse duobus rectis. Sed si talem cognitionem Dei habemus, qualem habemus trianguli, tum omnis dubitatio tollitur. Et eodem modo, quo possumus pervenire ad talem cognitionem trianguli, quamvis non certo sciamus, an aliquis summus deceptor nos fallat, eodem etiam modo possumus pervenire ad talem Dei cognitionem, quamvis non certo sciamus, an detur quis summus deceptor, et, modo eam habeamus, sufficiet ad tollendam, uti dixi, omnem dubitationem, quam de ideis claris et distinctis habere possumus.

80. Porro si quis recte procedat investigando quae prius sunt investiganda, nulla interrupta concatenatione rerum, et sciat, quomodo quaestiones sint determinandae, antequam ad earum cognitionem accingamur, nunquam nisi certissimas ideas, id est, claras et distinctas habebit. Nam dubitatio nihil aliud est, quam suspensio animi circa aliquam affirmationem aut negationem, quam affirmaret aut negaret, nisi occurreret aliquid, quo ignoto cognitio eius rei debet esse imperfecta. Unde colligitur, quod dubitatio semper oritur ex eo, quod res absque ordine investigentur.

I. DE MEMORIA ET OBLIVIONE. CONCLUSIO.

81. HAEC SUNT, quae promisi tradere in hac prima parte methodi. Sed ut nihil omittam eorum, quae ad cognitionem intellectus et eius vires possunt conducere, tradam etiam pauca de memoria et oblivione ; ubi hoc maxime venit considerandum, quod memoria corroboretur ope intellectus, et etiam absque ope intellectus. Nam quoad primum, quo res magis est intelligibilis, eo facilius retinetur, et contra, quo minus, eo facilius eam obliviscimur. Ex. gr. si tradam alicui copiam verborum solutorum, ea multo difficilius retinebit, quam si eadem verba in forma narrationis tradam.

82. Corroboratur etiam absque ope intellectus, scilicet a vi, qua imaginatio aut sensus, quem vocant communem, afficitur ab aliqua re singulari corporea. Dico singularem ; imaginatio enim tantum a singularibus afficitur. Nam si quis legerit ex. gr. unam tantum Fabulam amatoriam, eam optime retinebit, quamdiu non legerit plures alias eius generis, quia tum sola viget in imaginatione. Sed si plures sint eiusdem generis, simul omnes imaginamur, et facile confunduntur. Dico etiam corpoream ; nam a solis corporibus afficitur imaginatio. Cum itaque memoria ab intellectu corroboretur, et etiam sine intellectu, inde concluditur, eam quid diversum esse ab intellectu, et circa intellectum in se spectatum nullam dari memoriam, neque oblivionem.

83. Quid ergo erit memoria ? Nihil aliud, quam sensatio impressionum cerebri simul cum cogitatione ad determinatam durationem sensationis ; quod etiam ostendit reminiscentia. Nam ibi anima cogitat de illa sensatione ; sed non sub continua duratione ; et sic idea istius sensationis non est ipsa duratio sensationis, id est, ipsa memoria. An vero ideae ipsae aliquam patiantur corruptionem, videbimus in philosophia. Et si hoc alicui valde absurdum videatur, sufficiet ad nostrum propositum, ut cogitet, quod, quo res est singularior, eo facilius retineatur, sicut ex exemplo comoediae modo allato patet. Porro quo res intelligibilior, eo etiam facilius retinetur. Unde maxime singularem et tantummodo intelligibilem non poterimus non retinere.

84. Sic itaque distinximus inter ideam veram et ceteras perceptiones, ostendimusque, quod ideae fictae, falsae et ceterae habeant suam originem ab imaginatione, hoc est, a quibusdam sensationibus fortuitis (ut sic loquar) atque solutis, quae non oriuntur ab ipsa mentis potentia, sed a causis externis, prout corpus sive somniando sive vigilando varios accipit motus. Vel si placet, hic per imaginationem quicquid velis cape, modo sit quid diversum ab intellectu, et unde anima habeat rationem patientis. Perinde enim est quicquid capias, postquam novimus eandem quid vagum esse, et a quo anima patitur, et simul etiam novimus, quomodo ope intellectus ab eadem liberamur. Quare etiam nemo miretur, me hic nondum probare, dari corpus et alia necessaria, et tamen loqui de imaginatione, de corpore et eius constitutione. Nempe, ut dixi, est perinde quid capiam, postquam novi, esse quid vagum etc.

85. At ideam veram simplicem esse ostendimus aut ex simplicibus compositam, et quae ostendit, quomodo et cur aliquid sit aut factum sit, et quod ipsius effectus obiectivi in anima procedunt ad rationem formalitatis ipsius obiecti ; id quod idem est, quod veteres dixerunt, nempe veram scientiam procedere a causa ad effectus ; nisi quod nunquam, quod sciam, conceperunt, uti nos hic, animam secundum certas leges agentem et quasi aliquod automatum spirituale.

86. Unde, quantum in initio licuit, acquisivimus notitiam nostri intellectus, et talem normam verae ideae, ut iam non vereamur, ne vera cum falsis aut fictis confundamus ; nec etiam mirabimur, cur quaedam intelligamus, quae nullo modo sub imaginationem cadunt, et alia sint in imaginatione, quae prorsus oppugnant intellectum ; alia denique cum intellectu conveniant. Quandoquidem novimus operationes illas, a quibus imaginationes producuntur, fieri secundum alias leges prorsus diversas a legibus intellectus, et animam circa imaginationem tantum habere rationem patientis.

87. Ex quo etiam constat, quam facile ii in magnos errores possunt delabi, qui non accurate distinxerunt inter imaginationem et intellectionem. In hos ex. gr. quod extensio debeat esse in loco, debeat esse finita, cuius partes ab invicem distinguuntur realiter, quod sit primum et unicum fundamentum omnium rerum, et uno tempore maius spatium occupet, quam alio, multaque eiusmodi alia, quae omnia prorsus oppugnant veritatem, ut suo loco ostendemus.

88. Deinde cum verba sint pars imaginationis, hoc est, quod, prout vage ex aliqua dispositione corporis componuntur in memoria, multos conceptus fingamus, ideo non dubitandum, quin etiam verba, aeque ac imaginatio, possint esse causa multorum magnorumque errorum, nisi magnopere ab ipsis caveamus.

89. Adde quod sint constituta ad libitum et ad captum vulgi, adeo ut non sint nisi signa rerum, prout sunt in imaginatione, non autem prout sunt in intellectu ; quod clare patet ex eo, quod omnibus iis, quae tantum sunt in intellectu, et non in imaginatione, nomina imposuerunt saepe negativa, uti sunt, incorporeum, infinitum etc. ; et etiam multa, quae sunt revera affirmativa, negative exprimunt, et contra, uti sunt increatum, independens, infinitum, immortale etc., quia nimirum horum contraria multo facilius imaginamur ; ideoque prius primis hominibus occurrerunt et nomina positiva usurparunt. Multa affirmamus et negamus, quia natura verborum id affirmare et negare patitur, non vero rerum natura ; adeoque hac ignorata facile aliquid falsum pro vero sumeremus.

90. Vitamus praeterea aliam magnam causam confusionis, et quae facit, quominus intellectus ad se reflectat. Nempe cum non distinguimus inter imaginationem et intellectionem, putamus ea, quae facilius imaginamur, nobis esse clariora, et id, quod imaginamur, putamus intelligere. Unde quae sunt postponenda, anteponimus, et sic verus ordo progrediendi pervertitur, nec aliquid legitime concluditur.

XII. METHODI PARS SECUNDA.
DE DUPLICI PERCEPTIONE.

91. PORRO, UT tandem ad secundam partem huius methodi perveniamus, proponam primo nostrum scopum in hac methodo, ac deinde media, ut eum attingamus. Scopus itaque est claras et distinctas habere ideas, tales videlicet, quae ex pura mente, et non ex fortuitis motibus corporis factae sint. Deinde omnes ideae ad unam ut redigantur, conabimur eas tali modo concatenare et ordinare, ut mens nostra, quoad eius fieri potest, referat obiective formalitatem naturae, quoad totam et quoad eius partes.

92. Quoad primum, ut iam tradidimus, requiritur ad nostrum ultimum finem, ut res concipiatur vel per solam suam essentiam vel per proximam suam causam. Scilicet si res sit in se, sive, ut vulgo dicitur, causa sui, tum per solam suam essentiam debebit intelligi ; si vero res non sit in se, sed requirat causam, ut existat, tum per proximam suam causam debet intelligi. Nam revera cognitio effectus nihil aliud est, quam perfectiorem causae cognitionem acquirere .

93. Unde nunquam nobis licebit, quamdiu de inquisitione rerum agimus, ex abstractis aliquid concludere, et magnopere cavebimus, ne misceamus ea, quae tantum sunt in intellectu, cum iis, quae sunt in re. Sed optima conclusio erit depromenda ab essentia aliqua particulari affirmativa, sive a vera et legitima definitione. Nam ab axiomatibus solis universalibus non potest intellectus ad singularia descendere, quandoquidem axiomata ad infinita se extendunt, nec intellectum magis ad unum, quam ad aliud singulare contemplandum, determinant.

94. Quare recta inveniendi via est ex data aliqua definitione cogitationes formare : quod eo felicius et facilius procedet, quo rem aliquam melius definiverimus. Quare cardo totius huius secundae Methodi partis in hoc solo versatur, nempe in conditionibus bonae definitionis cognoscendis, et deinde in modo eas inveniendi. Primo itaque de conditionibus definitionis agam.

XIII. DE CONDITIONIBUS DEFINITIONIS.

95. DEFINITIO UT dicatur perfecta, debebit intimam essentiam rei explicare, et cavere, ne eius loco propria quaedam usurpemus. Ad quod explicandum, ut alia exempla omittam, ne videar aliorum errores velle detegere, adferam tantum exemplum alicuius rei abstractae, quae perinde est, quomodocumque definiatur, circuli scilicet ; quod si definiatur, esse figuram aliquam, cuius lineae, a centro ad circumferentiam ductae, sunt aequales, nemo non videt talem definitionem minime explicare essentiam circuli, sed tantum eius aliquam proprietatem. Et quamvis, ut dixi, circa figuras et cetera entia rationis hoc parum referat, multum tamen refert circa entia physica et realia ; nimirum, quia proprietates rerum non intelliguntur, quamdiu earum essentiae ignorantur ; si autem has praetermittimus, necessario concatenationem intellectus, quae naturae concatenationem referre debet, pervertemus, et a nostro scopo prorsus aberrabimus.

96. Ut itaque hoc vitio liberemur, erunt haec observanda in definitione.

I. Si res sit creata, definitio debebit, uti diximus, comprehendere causam proximam. Ex. gr. circulus secundum hanc legem sic esset definiendus : eum esse figuram, quae describitur a linea quacunque, cuius alia extremitas est fixa, alia mobilis, quae definitio clare comprehendit causam proximam.

II. Talis requiritur conceptus rei sive definitio, ut omnes proprietates rei, dum sola, non autem cum aliis coniuncta, spectatur, ex ea concludi possint, uti in hac definitione circuli videre est. Nam ex ea clare concluditur omnes lineas a centro ad circumferentiam ductas aequales esse ; quodque hoc sit necessarium requisitum definitionis, adeo per se est attendenti manifestum, ut non videatur operae pretium in ipsius demonstratione morari, nec etiam ostendere ex hoc secundo requisito omnem definitionem debere esse affirmativam. Loquor de affirmatione intellectiva, parum curando verbalem, quae propter verborum penuriam poterit fortasse aliquando negative exprimi, quamvis affirmative intelligatur.

97. Definitionis vero rei increatae haec sunt requisita.

I. Ut omnem causam secludat, hoc est, obiectum nullo alio praeter suum esse egeat ad sui explicationem.

II. Ut data eius rei definitione nullus maneat locus quaestioni, an sit.

III. Ut nulla quoad mentem habeat substantiva, quae possint adiectivari, hoc est, ne per aliqua abstracta explicetur.

IV. Et ultimo (quamvis hoc notare non sit valde necessarium) requiritur, ut ab eius definitione omnes eius proprietates concludantur. Quae etiam omnia attendenti accurate fiunt manifesta.

98. Dixi etiam, quod optima conclusio erit depromenda ab essentia aliqua particulari affirmativa. Quo enim specialior est idea, eo distinctior, ac proinde clarior est. Unde cognitio particularium quam maxime nobis quaerenda est.

XIV. DE MEDIIS QUIBUS RES AETERNAS COGNOSCUNTUR.

99. QUOAD ORDINEM vero, et ut omnes nostrae perceptiones ordinentur, et uniantur, requiritur, ut, quamprimum fieri potest et ratio postulat, inquiramus, an detur quoddam ens, et simul quale, quod sit omnium rerum causa, ut eius essentia obiectiva sit etiam causa omnium nostrarum idearum, et tum mens nostra, uti diximus, quam maxime referet naturam. Nam et ipsius essentiam et ordinem et unionem habebit obiective. Unde possumus videre, apprime nobis esse necessarium, ut semper a rebus physicis sive ab entibus realibus omnes nostras ideas deducamus, progrediendo, quoad eius fieri potest, secundum seriem causarum ab uno ente reali ad aliud ens reale, et ita quidem, ut ad abstracta et universalia non transeamus, sive ut ab iis aliquid reale non concludamus, sive ut ea ab aliquo reali non concludantur. Utrumque enim verum progressum intellectus interrumpit.

100. Sed notandum, me hic per seriem causarum et realium entium non intelligere seriem rerum singularium mutabilium, sed tantummodo seriem rerum fixarum aeternarumque. Seriem enim rerum singularium mutabilium impossibile foret humanae imbecillitati assequi, cum propter earum omnem numerum superantem multitudinem, tum propter infinitas circumstantias in una et eadem re, quarum unaquaeque potest esse causa, ut res existat, aut non existat. Quandoquidem earum existentia nullam habet connexionem cum earundem essentia, sive (ut iam diximus) non est aeterna veritas.

101. Verumenimvero neque etiam opus est, ut earum seriem intelligamus ; siquidem rerum singularium mutabilium essentiae non sunt depromendae ab earum serie sive ordine existendim, cum hic nihil aliud nobis praebeat praeter denominationes extrinsecas, relationes, aut ad summum circumstantias ; quae omnia longe absunt ab intima essentia rerum. Haec vero tantum est petenda a fixis atque aeternis rebus, et simul a legibus in iis rebus, tamquam in suis veris codicibus inscriptis, secundum quas omnia singularia et fiunt et ordinantur ; imo haec mutabilia singularia adeo intime atque essentialiter (ut sic dicam) ab iis fixis pendent, ut sine iis nec esse, nec concipi possint. Unde haec fixa et aeterna, quamvis sint singularia, tamen ob eorum ubique praesentiam ac latissimam potentiam erunt nobis tamquam universalia sive genera definitionum rerum singularium mutabilium, et causae proximae omnium rerum.

102. Sed cum hoc ita sit, non parum difficultatis videtur subesse, ut ad horum singularium cognitionem pervenire possimus ; nam omnia simul concipere res est longe supra humani intellectus vires. Ordo autem, ut unum ante aliud intelligatur, uti diximus, non est petendus ab eorum existendi serie, neque etiam a rebus aeternis. Ibi enim omnia haec sunt simul natura. Unde alia auxilia necessario sunt quaerenda praeter illa, quibus utimur ad res aeternas earumque leges intelligendum ; attamen non est huius loci ea tradere, neque etiam opus est, nisi postquam rerum aeternarum earumque infallibilium legum sufficientem acquisiverimus cognitionem, sensuumque nostrorum natura nobis innotuerit.

103. Antequam ad rerum singularium cognitionem accingamur, tempus erit, ut ea auxilia tradamus, quae omnia eo tendent, ut nostris sensibus sciamus uti, et experimenta certis legibus et ordine facere, quae sufficient ad rem, quae inquiritur, determinandam, ut tandem ex iis concludamus, secundum quasnam rerum aeternarum leges facta sit, et intima eius natura nobis innotescat, ut suo loco

ostendam. Hic, ut ad propositum revertar, tantum enitar tradere, quae videntur necessaria, ut ad cognitionem rerum aeternarum pervenire possimus, earumque definitiones formemus conditionibus supra traditis.

104. Quod ut fiat, revocandum in memoriam id, quod supra diximus, nempe quod, ubi mens ad aliquam cogitationem attendit, ut ipsam perpendat, bonoque ordine ex ea deducat quae legitime sunt deducenda, si ea falsa fuerit, falsitatem deteget ; sin autem vera, tum feliciter perget sine ulla interruptione res veras inde deducere ; hoc, inquam, ad nostram rem requiritur. Nam ex nullo alio fundamento cogitationes nostrae determinari queunt.

105. Si igitur rem omnium primam investigare velimus, necesse est dari aliquod fundamentum, quod nostras cogitationes eo dirigat. Deinde quia methodus est ipsa cognitio reflexiva, hoc fundamentum, quod nostras cogitationes dirigere debet, nullum aliud potest esse, quam cognitio eius, quod formam veritatis constituit, et cognitio intellectus eiusque proprietatum et virium. Hac enim acquisita fundamentum habebimus, a quo nostras cogitationes deducemus, et viam, qua intellectus, prout eius fert capacitas, pervenire poterit ad rerum aeternarum cognitionem, habita nimirum ratione virium intellectus.

XV. DE VIRIBUS INTELLECTUS EIUSQUE PROPRIETATIBUS.

106. QUOD SI vero ad naturam cogitationis pertineat veras formare ideas, ut in prima parte ostensum, hic iam inquirendum, quid per vires et potentiam intellectus intelligamus. Quoniam vero praecipua nostrae methodi pars est, vires intellectus eiusque naturam optime intelligere, cogimur necessario (per ea, quae in hac secunda parte methodi tradidi), haec deducere ex ipsa cogitationis, et intellectus definitione.

107. Sed hucusque nullas regulas inveniendi definitiones habuimus, et quia eas tradere non possumus, nisi cognita natura sive definitione intellectus eiusque potentia, hinc sequitur, quod vel definitio intellectus per se debet esse clara, vel nihil intelligere possumus. Illa tamen per se absolute clara non est. Attamen quia eius proprietates, ut omnia, quae ex intellectu habemus, clare et distincte percipi nequeunt, nisi cognita earum natura ; ergo definitio intellectus per se innotescet, si ad eius proprietates, quas clare et distincte intelligimus, attendamus. Intellectus igitur proprietates hic enumeremus easque perpendamus, deque nostris innatis instrumentis agere incipiamus.

108. Intellectus proprietates, quas praecipue notavi et clare intelligo, hae sunt.

I. Quod certitudinem involvat, hoc est, quod sciat res ita esse formaliter, ut in ipso obiective continentur.

II. Quod quaedam percipiat, sive quasdam formet ideas absolute, quasdam ex aliis. Nempe quantitatis ideam format absolute, nec ad alias attendit cogitationes ; motus vero ideas non, nisi attendendo ad ideam quantitatis.

III. Quas absolute format, infinitatem exprimunt ; at determinatas ex aliis format. Ideam enim quantitatis, si eam per causam percipit, tum per quantitatem determinat, ut cum ex motu alicuius plani corpus, ex motu lineae vero planum, ex motu denique puncti lineam oriri percipit ; quae quidem perceptiones non inserviunt ad intelligendam, sed tantum ad determinandam quantitatem. Quod inde apparet, quia eas quasi ex motu oriri concipimus, cum tamen motus non percipiatur nisi percepta quantitate, et motum etiam ad formandam lineam in infinitum continuare possumus, quod minime possemus facere, si non haberemus ideam infinitae quantitatis.

IV. Ideas positivas prius format, quam negativas.

V. Res non tam sub duratione, quam sub quadam specie aeternitatis percipit et numero infinito ; vel potius ad res percipiendas, nec ad numerum, nec ad durationem attendit. Cum autem res imaginatur, eas sub certo numero, determinata duratione et quantitate percipit.

VI. Ideae, quas claras et distinctas formamus, ita ex sola necessitate nostrae naturae sequi videntur, ut absolute a sola nostra potentia pendere videantur ; confusae autem contra. Nobis enim invitis saepe formantur.

VII. Ideas rerum, quas intellectus ex aliis format, multis modis mens determinare potest ; ut ad determinandum ex. gr. planum ellipseos, fingit stylum chordae adhaerentem circa duo centra moveri, vel concipit infinita puncta eandem semper et certam rationem ad datam aliquam rectam lineam habentia, vel conum plano aliquo obliquo sectum, ita ut angulus inclinationis maior sit angulo verticis coni, vel aliis infinitis modis.

VIII. Ideae quo plus perfectionis alicuius obiecti exprimunt, eo perfectiores sunt. Nam fabrum, qui fanum aliquod excogitavit, non ita admiramur, ac illum, qui templum aliquod insigne excogitavit.

109. Reliqua, quae ad cogitationem referuntur, ut amor, laetitia etc. nihil moror ; nam nec ad nostrum institutum praesens faciunt, nec etiam possunt concipi, nisi percepto intellectu. Nam perceptione omnino sublata ea omnia tolluntur.

110. Ideae falsae et fictae nihil positivum habent (ut abunde ostendimus), per quod falsae aut fictae dicuntur ; sed ex solo defectu cognitionis ut tales considerantur. Ideae ergo falsae et fictae, quatenus tales, nihil nos de essentia cogitationis docere possunt ; sed haec petenda ex modo recensitis proprietatibus positivis, hoc est, iam aliquid commune statuendum est, ex quo hae proprietates necessario sequantur, sive quo dato hae necessario dentur, et quo sublato haec omnia tollantur.

Reliqua desiderantur.

ON THE IMPROVEMENT OF THE UNDERSTANDING

NOTICE TO THE READER.

THIS TREATISE ON the Emendation of the Intellect etc., which we give you here, kind reader, in its unfinished [that is, defective] state, was written by the author many years ago now. He always intended to finish it. But hindered by other occupations, and finally snatched away by death, he was unable to bring it to the desired conclusion. But since it contains many excellent and useful things, which — we have no doubt — will be of great benefit to anyone sincerely seeking the truth, we did not wish to deprive you of them. And so that you would be aware of, and find less difficult to excuse, the many things that are still obscure, rough, and unpolished, we wished to warn you of them. Farewell.

This notice to the reader was written by the editors of the Opera Postuma in 1677.

INTRODUCTION

On the Improvement of the Understanding

AFTER EXPERIENCE HAD taught me that all the usual surroundings of social life are vain and futile; seeing that none of the objects of my fears contained in themselves anything either good or bad, except in so far as the mind is affected by them, I finally resolved to inquire whether there might be some real good having power to communicate itself, which would affect the mind singly, to the exclusion of all else: whether, in fact, there might be anything of which the discovery and attainment would enable me to enjoy continuous, supreme, and unending happiness.

I say "I finally resolved," for at first sight it seemed unwise willingly to lose hold on what was sure for the sake of something then uncertain. I could see the benefits which are acquired through fame and riches, and that I should be obliged to abandon the quest of such objects, if I seriously devoted myself to the search for something different and new. I perceived that if true happiness chanced to be placed in the former I should necessarily miss it; while if, on the other hand, it were not so placed, and I gave them my whole attention, I should equally fail.

OF THE ORDINARY OBJECTS
OF MEN'S DESIRES

I THEREFORE DEBATED whether it would not be possible to arrive at the new principle, or at any rate at a certainty concerning its existence, without changing the conduct and usual plan of my life; with this end in view I made many efforts, in vain. For the ordinary surroundings of life which are esteemed by men (as their actions testify) to be the highest good, may be classed under the three heads — Riches, Fame, and the Pleasures of Sense: with these three the mind is so absorbed that it has little power to reflect on any different good.

By sensual pleasure the mind is enthralled to the extent of quiescence, as if the supreme good were actually attained, so that it is quite incapable of thinking of any other object; when such pleasure has been gratified it is followed by extreme melancholy, whereby the mind, though not enthralled, is disturbed and dulled. The pursuit of honors and riches is likewise very absorbing, especially if such objects be sought simply for their own sake, 1 inasmuch as they are then supposed to constitute the highest good.

In the case of fame the mind is still more absorbed, for fame is conceived as always good for its own sake, and as the ultimate end to which all actions are directed. Further, the attainment of riches and fame is not followed as in the case of sensual pleasures by repentance, but, the more we acquire, the greater is our delight, and, consequently, the more are we incited to increase both the one and the other; on the other hand, if our hopes happen to be frustrated we are plunged into the deepest sadness. Fame has the further drawback that it compels its votaries to order their lives according to the opinions of their fellow-men, shunning what they usually shun, and seeking what they usually seek.

When I saw that all these ordinary objects of desire would be obstacles in the way of a search for something different and new — nay, that they were so opposed thereto, that either they or it would have to be abandoned, I was forced to inquire which would prove the most useful to me: for, as I say, I seemed to be willingly losing hold on a sure good for the sake of something uncertain. However, after I had reflected on the matter, I came in the first place to the conclusion that by abandoning the ordinary objects of pursuit, and betaking myself to a new quest, I should be leaving a good, uncertain by reason of its own nature, as may be gathered from what has been said, for the sake of a good not uncertain in its nature (for I sought for a fixed good), but only in the possibility of its attainment.

Further reflection convinced me that if I could really get to the root of the matter I should be leaving certain evils for a certain good. I thus perceived that I was in a state of great peril, and I compelled myself to seek with all my strength for a remedy, however uncertain it might be; as a sick man struggling with a deadly disease, when he sees that death will surely be upon him unless a remedy be found, is compelled to seek a remedy with all his strength, inasmuch as his whole hope lies therein. All the objects pursued by the multitude not only bring no remedy that tends to preserve our being, but even act as hindrances, causing the death not seldom of those who possess them 2 and always of those who are possessed by them.

There are many examples of men who have suffered persecution even to death for the sake of their riches, and of men who in pursuit of wealth have exposed themselves to so many dangers, that they have paid away their life as a penalty for their folly. Examples are no less numerous of men, who have endured the utmost wretchedness for the sake of gaining or preserving their reputation. Lastly, are innumerable cases of men, who have hastened their death through over-indulgence in sensual pleasure.

All these evils seem to have arisen from the fact, that happiness or unhappiness is made wholly dependent on the quality of the object which we love. When a thing is not loved, no quarrels will arise concerning it — no sadness be felt if it hatred, in short no disturbances of the mind. All these arise from the love of what is perishable, such as the objects already mentioned.

But love towards a thing eternal and infinite feeds the mind wholly with joy, and is itself unmingled with any sadness, wherefore it is greatly to be desired and sought for with all our strength. Yet it was not at random that I used the words, "If I could go to the root of the matter," for, though what I have urged was perfectly clear to my mind, I could not forthwith lay aside all love of riches, sensual enjoyment, and fame.

One thing was evident, namely, that while my mind was employed with these thoughts it turned away from its former objects of desire, and seriously considered the search for a new principle; this state of things was a great comfort to me, for I perceived that the evils were not such as to resist all remedies. Although these intervals were at first rare, and of very short duration, yet afterwards, as the true good became more and more discernible to me, they became more frequent and more lasting; especially after I had recognized that the acquisition of wealth, sensual pleasure, or fame, is only a hindrance, so long as they are sought as ends not as means; if they be sought as means, they will be under restraint, and, far from being hindrances, will further not a little the end for which they are sought, as I will show in due time.

1 This might be explained more at large and more clearly: I mean by distinguishing riches according as they are pursued for their own sake, in or furtherance of fame, or sensual pleasure, or the advancement of science and art. But this subject is reserved to its own place, for it is not here proper to investigate the matter more accurately.

2 These considerations should be set forth more precisely.

OF THE TRUE AND FINAL GOOD

I WILL HERE only briefly state what I mean by true good, and also what is the nature of the highest good. In order that this may be rightly understood, we must bear in mind that the terms good and evil are only applied relatively, so that the same thing may be called both good and bad according to the relations in view, in the same way as it may be called perfect or imperfect. Nothing regarded in its own nature can be called perfect or imperfect; especially when we are aware that all things which come to pass, come to pass according to the eternal order and fixed laws of nature.

However, human weakness cannot attain to this order in its own thoughts, but meanwhile man conceives a human character much more stable than his own, and sees that there is no reason why he should not himself acquire such a character. Thus he is led to seek for means which will bring him to this pitch of perfection, and calls everything which will serve as such means a true good. The chief good is that he should arrive, together with other individuals if possible, at the possession of the aforesaid character. What that character is we shall show in due time, namely, that it is the knowledge of the union existing being the mind and the whole of nature. 3

This, then, is the end for which I strive, to attain to such a character myself, and to endeavor that many should attain to it with me. In other words, it is part of my happiness to lend a helping hand, that many others may understand even as I do, so that their understanding and desire may entirely agree with my own. In order to bring this about, it is necessary to understand as much of nature as will enable us to attain to the aforesaid character, and also to form a social order such as is most conducive to the attainment of this character by the greatest number with the least difficulty and danger.

We must seek the assistance of Moral Philosophy 4 and the Theory of Education; further, as health is no insignificant means for attaining our end, we must also include the whole science of Medicine, and, as many difficult things are by contrivance rendered easy, and we can in this way gain much time and convenience, the science of Mechanics must in no way be despised.

But before all things, a means must be devised for improving the understanding and purifying it, as far as may be at the outset, so that it may apprehend things without error, and in the best possible way. Thus it is apparent to everyone that I wish to direct all science to one end 5 and aim, so that we may attain to the supreme human perfection which we have named; and, therefore, whatsoever in the sciences does not serve to promote our object will have to be rejected as useless. To sum up the matter in a word, all our actions and thoughts must be directed to this one end.

3 These matters are explained more at length elsewhere.

4 N.B. I do no more here than enumerate the sciences necessary for our purpose; I lay no stress on their order.

5 There is for the sciences but one end, to which they should all be directed.

CERTAIN RULES OF LIFE

YET, AS IT is necessary that while we are endeavoring to attain our purpose, and bring the understanding into the right path we should carry on our life, we are compelled first of all to lay down certain rules of life as provisionally good, to wit the following: —

I. To speak in a manner intelligible to the multitude, and to comply with every general custom that does not hinder the attainment of our purpose. For we can gain from the multitude no small advantages, provided that we strive to accommodate ourselves to its understanding as far as possible: moreover, we shall in this way gain a friendly audience for the reception of the truth.

II. To indulge ourselves with pleasures only in so far as they are necessary for preserving health.

III. Lastly, to endeavor to obtain only sufficient money or other commodities to enable us to preserve our life and health, and to follow such general customs as are consistent with our purpose.

Having laid down these preliminary rules, I will betake myself to the first and most important task, namely, the amendment of the understanding, and the rendering it capable of understanding things in the manner necessary for attaining our end. In order to bring this about, the natural order demands that I should here recapitulate all the modes of perception, which I have hitherto employed for affirming or denying anything with certainty, so that I may choose the best, and at the same time begin to know my own powers and the nature which I wish to perfect.

OF THE FOUR MODES OF PERCEPTION

REFLECTION SHOWS THAT all modes of perception or knowledge may be reduced to four: —

I. Perception arising from hearsay or from some sign which everyone may name as he please.

II. Perception arising from mere experience — that is, form experience not yet classified by the intellect, and only so called because the given event has happened to take place, and we have no contradictory fact to set against it, so that it therefore remains unassailed in our minds.

III. Perception arising when the essence of one thing is inferred from another thing, but not adequately; this comes when 6 from some effect we gather its cause, or when it is inferred from some general proposition that some property is always present.

IV. Lastly, there is the perception arising when a thing is perceived solely through its essence, or through the knowledge of its proximate cause.

All these kinds of perception I will illustrate by examples. By hearsay I know the day of my birth, my parentage, and other matters about which I have never felt any doubt. By mere experience I know that I shall die, for this I can affirm from having seen that others like myself have died, though all did not live for the same period, or die by the same disease. I know by mere experience that oil has the property of feeding fire, and water of extinguishing it. In the same way I know that a dog is a barking animal, man a rational animal, and in fact nearly all the practical knowledge of life.

We deduce one thing from another as follows: when we clearly perceive that we feel a certain body and no other, we thence clearly infer that the mind is united 7 to the body, and that their union is the cause of the given sensation; but we cannot thence absolutely understand 8 the nature of the sensation and the union. Or, after I have become acquainted with the nature of vision, and know that it has the property of making one and the same thing appear smaller when far off than when near, I can infer that the sun is larger than it appears, and can draw other conclusions of the same kind.

Lastly, a thing may be perceived solely through its essence; when, from the fact of knowing something, I know what it is to know that thing, or when, from knowing the essence of the mind, I know that it is united to the body. By the same kind of knowledge we know that two and three make five, or that two lines each parallel to a third, are parallel to one another, &c. The things which I have been able to know by this kind of knowledge are as yet very few.

In order that the whole matter may be put in a clearer light, I will make use of a single illustration as follows. Three numbers are given — it is required to find a fourth, which shall be to the third as the second is to the first. Tradesmen will at once tell us that they know what is required to find the fourth number, for they have not yet forgotten the rule which was given to them arbitrarily without proof by their masters; others construct a universal axiom from their experience with simple numbers, where the fourth number is self-evident, as in the case of 2, 4, 3, 6; here it is evident that if the second number be multiplied by the third, and the product divided by the first, the quotient is 6; when they see that by this process the number is produced which they knew beforehand to be the proportional, they infer that the process always holds good for finding a fourth number proportional.

Mathematicians, however, know by the proof of the nineteenth proposition of the seventh book of Euclid, what numbers are proportionals, namely, from the nature and property of proportion it follows that the product of the first and fourth will be equal to the product of the second and third: still they do not see the adequate proportionality of the given numbers, or, if they do see it, they see it not by virtue of Euclid's proposition, but intuitively, without going through any process.

6 In this case we do not understand anything of the cause from the consideration of it in the effect. This is sufficiently evident from the fact that the cause is only spoken of in very general terms, such as — there exists then something; there exists then some power, &c.; or from the that we only express it in a negative manner — it is not or that, &c. In the second case something is ascribed to the cause because of the effect, as we shall show in an example, but only a property, never an essence.

7 From this example may be clearly seen what I have just drawn attention to. For through this union we understand nothing beyond the sensation, the effect, to wit, from which we inferred the cause of which we understand nothing.

8 A conclusion of this sort, though it be certain, is yet not to be relied on without great caution; for unless we are exceedingly careful we shall forthwith fall into error. When things are conceived thus abstractedly, and not through their true essence, they are apt to be confused by the imagination. For that which is in itself one, men imagine to be multiplex. To those things which are conceived abstractedly, apart, and confusedly, terms are applied which are apt to become wrested from their strict meaning, and bestowed on things more familiar; whence it results that these latter are imagined in the same way as the former to which the terms were originally given.

OF THE BEST MODE OF PERCEPTION

IN ORDER THAT from these modes of perception the best may be selected, it is well that we should briefly enumerate the means necessary for attaining our end.

I. To have an exact knowledge of our nature which we desire to perfect, and to know as much as is needful of nature in general. II. To collect in this way the differences, the agreements, and the oppositions of things. III. To learn thus exactly how far they can or cannot be modified. IV. To compare this result with the nature and power of man. We shall thus discern the highest degree of perfection to which man is capable of attaining.

We shall then be in a position to see which mode of perception we ought to choose. As to the first mode, it is evident that from hearsay our knowledge must always be uncertain, and, moreover, can give us no insight into the essence of a thing, as is manifest in our illustration; now one can only arrive at knowledge of a thing through knowledge of its essence, as will hereafter appear. We may, therefore clearly conclude that the certainty arising from hearsay cannot be scientific in its character. For simple hearsay cannot affect anyone whose understanding does not, so to speak, meet it half way.

The second mode of perception 9 cannot be said to give us the idea of the proportion of which we are in search. Moreover its results are very uncertain and indefinite, for we shall never discover anything in natural phenomena by its means, except accidental properties, which are never clearly understood, unless the essence of the things in question be known first. Wherefore this mode also must be rejected.

Of the third mode of perception we may say in a manner that it gives us the idea of the thing sought, and that it us to draw conclusions without risk of error; yet it is not by itself sufficient to put us in possession of the perfection we aim at.

The fourth mode alone apprehends the adequate essence of a thing without danger of error. This mode, therefore, must be the one which we chiefly employ. How, then, should we avail ourselves of it so as to gain the fourth kind of knowledge with the least delay concerning things previously unknown? I will proceed to explain.

Now that we know what kind of knowledge is necessary for us, we must indicate the way and the method whereby we may gain the said knowledge concerning the things needful to be known. In order to accomplish this, we must first take care not to commit ourselves to a search, going back to infinity — that is, in order to discover the best method of finding truth, there is no need of another method to discover such method; nor of a third method for discovering the second, and so on to infinity. By such proceedings, we should never arrive at the knowledge of the truth, or, indeed, at any knowledge at all. The matter stands on the same footing as the making of material tools, which might be argued about in a similar way. For, in order to work iron, a hammer is needed, and the hammer cannot be forthcoming unless it has been made; but, in order to make it, there was need of another hammer and other tools, and so on to infinity. We might thus vainly endeavor to prove that men have no power of working iron.

But as men at first made use of the instruments supplied by nature to accomplish very easy pieces of workmanship, laboriously and imperfectly, and then, when these were finished, wrought other things more difficult with less labour and greater perfection; and so gradually mounted from the simplest operations to the making of tools, and from the making of tools to the making of more complex tools, and fresh feats of workmanship, till they arrived at making, complicated mechanisms which they now possess. So, in like manner, the intellect, by its native strength 10, makes for itself intellectual instruments, whereby it acquires strength for performing other intellectual operations 11, and from these operations again fresh instruments, or the power of pushing its investigations further, and thus gradually proceeds till it reaches the summit of wisdom.

That this is the path pursued by the understanding may be readily seen, when we understand the nature of the method for finding out the truth, and of the natural instruments so necessary complex instruments, and for the progress of investigation. I thus proceed with my demonstration.

9 I shall here treat a little more in detail of experience, and shall examine the method adopted by the Empirics, and by recent philosophers.

10 By native strength, I mean that not bestowed on us by external causes, as I shall afterwards explain in my philosophy.

11 Here I term them operations: I shall explain their nature in my philosophy.

OF THE INSTRUMENTS OF THE INTELLECT, OR TRUE IDEAS

A TRUE IDEA 12, (for we possess a true idea) is something different from its correlate (ideatum); thus a circle is different from the idea of a circle. The idea of a circle is not something having a circumference and a center, as a circle has; nor is the idea of a body that body itself. Now, as it is something different from its correlate, it is capable of being understood through itself; in other words, the idea, in so far as its actual essence (essentia formalis) is concerned, may be the subject of another subjective essence (essentia objectiva). 12a And, again, this second subjective essence will, regarded in itself, be something real, capable of being understood; and so on, indefinitely.

For instance, the man Peter is something real; the true idea of Peter is the reality of Peter represented subjectively, and is in itself something real, and quite distinct from the actual Peter. Now, as this true idea of Peter is in itself something real, and has its own individual existence, it will also be capable of being understood — that is, of being the subject of another idea, which will contain by representation (objective) all that the idea of Peter contains actually (formaliter). And, again, this idea of the idea of Peter has its own individuality, which may become the subject of yet another idea; and so on, indefinitely. This everyone may make trial of for himself, by reflecting that he knows what Peter is, and also knows that he knows, and further knows that he knows that he knows, &c. Hence it is plain that, in order to understand the actual Peter, it is not necessary first to understand the idea of Peter, and still less the idea of the idea of Peter. This is the same as saying that, in order to know, there is no need to know that we know, much less to know that we know that we know. This is no more necessary than to know the nature of a circle before knowing the nature of a triangle. 13. But, with these ideas, the contrary is the case: for, in order to know that I know, I must first know.

Hence it is clear that certainty is nothing else than the subjective essence of a thing: in other words, the mode in which we perceive an actual reality is certainty. Further, it is also evident that, for the certitude of truth, no further sign is necessary beyond the possession of a true idea: for, as I have shown, it is not necessary to know that we know that we know. Hence, again, it is clear that no one can know the nature of the highest certainty, unless he possesses an adequate idea, or the subjective essence of a thing: certainty is identical with such subjective essence.

Thus, as the truth needs no sign — it being to possess the subjective essence of things, or, in other words, the ideas of them, in order that all doubts may be removed — it follows that the true method does not consist in seeking for the signs of truth after the acquisition of the idea, but that the true method teaches us the order in which we should seek for truth itself 14 or the subjective essences of things, or ideas, for all these expressions are synonymous.

Again, method must necessarily be concerned with reasoning or understanding — I mean, method is not identical with reasoning in the search for causes, still less is it the comprehension of the causes of things: it is the discernment of a true idea, by distinguishing it from other perceptions, and by investigating its nature, in order that we may so train our mind that it may, by a given standard, comprehend whatsoever is intelligible, by laying down certain rules as aids, and by avoiding useless mental exertion.

Whence we may gather that method is nothing else than reflective knowledge, or the idea of an idea; and that as there can be no idea of an idea — unless an idea exists previously, — there can be no method without a pre-existent idea. Therefore, that will be a good method which shows us how the mind should be directed, according to the standard of the given true idea. Again, seeing that the ratio existing between two ideas is the same as the ratio between the actual realities corresponding to those ideas, it follows that the reflective knowledge which has for its object the most perfect being is more excellent than reflective knowledge concerning other objects — in other words, that method will be most perfect which affords the standard of the given idea of the most perfect being whereby we may direct our mind.

We thus easily understand how, in proportion as it acquires new ideas, the mind simultaneously acquires fresh instruments for pursuing its inquiries further. For we may gather from what has been said, that a true idea must necessarily first of all exist in us as a natural instrument; and that when this idea is apprehended by the mind, it enables us to understand the difference existing between itself and all other perceptions. In this, one part of the method consists. Now it is clear that the mind apprehends itself better in proportion as it understands a greater number of natural objects; it follows, therefore, that this portion of the method will be more perfect in proportion as the mind attains to the comprehension of a greater number of objects, and that it will be absolutely perfect when the mind gains a knowledge of the absolutely perfect being, or becomes conscious thereof.

Again, the more things the mind knows, the better does it understand its own strength and the order of nature; by increased self-knowledge, it can direct itself more easily, and lay down rules for its own guidance; and, by increased knowledge of nature, it can more easily avoid what is useless. And this is the sum total of method, as we have already stated.

We may add that the idea in the world of thought is in the same case as its correlate in the world of reality. If, therefore, there be anything in nature which is without connection with any other thing, and if we assign to it a subjective essence, which would in every way correspond to the objective reality, the subjective essence would have no connection 15 with any other ideas — in other words, we could not draw any conclusions with regard to it. On the other hand, those things which are connected with others — as all things that exist in nature — will be understood by the mind, and their subjective essences will maintain the same mutual relations as their objective realities — that is to say, we shall infer from these ideas other ideas, which will in turn be connected with others, and thus our instruments for proceeding with our investigation will increase. This is what we were endeavoring to prove.

Further, from what has just been said — namely, that an idea must, in all respects, correspond to its correlate in the world of reality, — it is evident that, in order to reproduce in every respect the faithful image of nature, our mind must deduce all its ideas from the idea which represents the origin and source of the whole of nature, so that it may itself become the source of other ideas.

12 I shall take care not only to demonstrate what I have just advanced, but also that we have hitherto proceeded rightly, and other things needful to be known.

12a In modern language, "the idea may become the subject of another presentation." Objectivus generally corresponds to the modern "subjective," formalis to the modern "objective." [Trans. — Note 1]

13 Observe that we are not here inquiring how the first subjective essence is innate in us. This belongs to an investigation into nature, where all these matters are amply explained, and it is shown that without ideas neither affirmation, nor negation, nor volition are possible.

14 The nature of mental search is explained in my philosophy.

15 To be connected with other things is to be produced by them, or to produce them.

ANSWERS TO OBJECTIONS

IT MAY, PERHAPS, provoke astonishment that, after having said that the good method is that which teaches us to direct our mind according to the standard of the given true idea, we should prove our point by reasoning, which would seem to indicate that it is not self-evident. We may, therefore, be questioned as to the validity of our reasoning. If our reasoning be sound, we must take as a starting-point a true idea. Now, to be certain that our starting-point is really a true idea, we need proof. This first course of reasoning must be supported by a second, the second by a third, and so on to infinity.

To this I make answer that, if by some happy chance anyone had adopted this method in his investigations of nature — that is, if he had acquired new ideas in the proper order, according to the standard of the original true idea, he would never have doubted 16 of the truth of his knowledge, inasmuch as truth, as we have shown, makes itself manifest, and all things would flow, as it were, spontaneously towards him. But as this never, or rarely, happens, I have been forced so to arrange my proceedings, that we may acquire by reflection and forethought what we cannot acquire by chance, and that it may at the same time appear that, for proving the truth, and for valid reasoning, we need no other means than the truth and valid reasoning themselves: for by valid reasoning I have established valid reasoning, and, in like measure, I seek still to establish it.

Moreover, this is the order of thinking adopted by men in their inward meditations. The reasons for its rare employment in investigations of nature are to be found in current misconceptions, whereof we shall examine the causes hereafter in our philosophy. Moreover, it demands, as we shall show, a keen and accurate discernment. Lastly, it is hindered by the conditions of human life, which are, as we have already pointed out, extremely changeable. There are also other obstacles, which we will not here inquire into.

If anyone asks why I have not at the starting-point set forth all the truths of nature in their due order, inasmuch as truth is self-evident, I reply by warning him not to reject as false any paradoxes he may find here, but to take the trouble to reflect on the chain of reasoning by which they are supported; he will then be no longer in doubt that we have attained to the truth. This is why I have as above.

If there yet remains some sceptic, who doubts of our primary truth, and of all deductions we make, taking such truth as our standard, he must either be arguing in bad faith, or we must confess that there are men in complete mental blindness either innate or due to misconceptions — that is, to some external influence. Such persons are not conscious of themselves. If they affirm or doubt anything, they know not that they affirm or doubt: they say that they know nothing, and they say that they are ignorant of the very fact of their knowing nothing. Even this they do not affirm absolutely, they are afraid of confessing that they exist, so long as they know nothing; in fact, they ought to remain dumb, for fear of haply supposing which should smack of truth.

Lastly, with such persons, one should not speak of sciences: for, in what relates to life and conduct, they are compelled by necessity to suppose that they exist, and seek their own advantage, and often affirm and deny, even with an oath. If they deny, grant, or gainsay, they know not that they deny, grant, or gainsay, so that they ought to be regarded as automata, utterly devoid of intelligence.

Let us now return to our proposition. Up to the present, we have, first, defined the end to which we desire to direct all our thoughts; secondly, we have determined the mode of perception best adapted to aid us in attaining our perfection; thirdly, we have discovered the way which our mind should take, in order to make a good beginning — namely, that it should use every true idea as a standard in pursuing its inquiries according to fixed rules. Now, in order that it may thus proceed, our method must furnish us, first, with a means of distinguishing a true idea from all other perceptions, and enabling the mind to avoid the latter; secondly, with rules for perceiving unknown things according to the standard of the true idea; thirdly, with an order which enables us to avoid useless labor. When we became acquainted with this method, we saw that, fourthly, it would be perfect when we had attained to the idea of the absolutely perfect Being. This is an observation which should be made at the outset, in order that we may arrive at the knowledge of such a being more quickly.

16 In the same way as we have here no doubt of the truth of our knowledge.

FIRST PART OF METHOD

Distinction of true ideas from fictitious ideas

LET US THEN make a beginning with the first part of the method, which is, as we have said, to distinguish and separate the true idea from other perceptions, and to keep the mind from confusing with true ideas those which are false, fictitious, and doubtful. I intend to dwell on this point at length, partly to keep a distinction so necessary before the reader's mind, and also because there are some who doubt of true ideas, through not having attended to the distinction between a true perception and all others. Such persons are like men who, while they are awake, doubt not that they are awake, but afterwards in a dream, as often happens, thinking that they are surely awake, and then finding that they were in error, become doubtful even of being awake. This state of mind arises through neglect of the distinction between sleeping and waking.

Meanwhile, I give warning that I shall not here give essence of every perception, and explain it through its proximate cause. Such work lies in the province of philosophy. I shall confine myself to what concerns method — that is, to the character of fictitious, false and doubtful perceptions, and the means of freeing ourselves therefrom. Let us then first inquire into the nature of a fictitious idea.

Every perception has for its object either a thing considered as existing, or solely the essence of a thing. Now "fiction" is chiefly occupied with things considered as existing. I will, therefore, consider these first — I mean cases where only the existence of an object is feigned, and the thing thus feigned is understood, or assumed to be understood. For instance, I feign that Peter, whom I know to have gone home, is gone to see me 17 or something of that kind. With what is such an idea concerned? It is concerned with things possible, and not with things necessary or impossible.

I call a thing impossible when its existence would imply a contradiction; necessary, when its non-existence would imply a contradiction; possible, when neither its existence nor its non-existence imply a contradiction, but when the necessity or impossibility of its nature depends on causes unknown to us, while we feign that it exists. If the necessity or impossibility of its existence depending on external causes were known to us, we could not form any fictitious hypotheses about it;

Whence it follows that if there be a God, or omniscient Being, such an one cannot form fictitious hypotheses. For, as regards ourselves, when I know that I exist 18 I cannot hypothesize that I exist or do not exist, any more than I can hypothesize an elephant that can go through the eye of a needle; nor when I know the nature of God, can I hypothesize that He or does not exist. 19 The same thing must be said of the Chimaera, whereof the nature implies a contradiction. From these considerations, it is plain, as I have already stated, that fiction cannot be concerned with eternal truths. 20

But before proceeding further, I must remark, in passing, that the difference between the essence of one thing and the essence of another thing is the same as that which exists between the reality or existence of one thing and the reality or existence of another; therefore, if we wished to conceive the existence, for example, of Adam, simply by means of existence in general, it would be the same as if, in order to conceive his existence, we went back to the nature of being, so as to define Adam as a being. Thus, the more existence is conceived generally, the more is it conceived confusedly and the more easily can it be ascribed to a given object. Contrariwise, the more it is conceived particularly, the more is it understood clearly, and the less liable is it to be ascribed, through negligence of Nature's order, to anything save its proper object. This is worthy of remark.

We now proceed to consider those cases which are commonly called fictions, though we clearly understood that the thing is not as we imagine it. For instance, I know that the earth is round, but nothing prevents my telling people that it is a hemisphere, and that it is like a half apple carved in relief on a dish; or, that the sun moves round the earth, and so on. However, examination will show us that there is nothing here inconsistent with what has been said, provided we first admit that we may have made mistakes, and be now conscious of them; and, further, that we can hypothesize, or at least suppose, that others are under the same mistake as ourselves, or can, like us, fall under it. We can, I repeat, thus hypothesize so long as we see no impossibility. Thus, when I tell anyone that the earth is not round, &c., I merely recall the error which I perhaps made myself, or which I might have fallen into, and afterwards I hypothesize that the person to whom I tell it, is still, or may still fall under the same mistake. This I say, I can feign so long as I do not perceive any impossibility or necessity; if I truly understood either one or the other I should not be able to feign, and I should be reduced to saying that I had made the attempt.

It remains for us to consider hypotheses made in problems, which sometimes involve impossibilities. For instance, when we say — let us assume that this burning candle is not burning, or, let us assume that it burns in some imaginary space, or where there are no physical objects. Such assumptions are freely made, though the last is clearly seen to be impossible. But, though this be so, there is no fiction in the case. For, in the first case, I have merely recalled to memory 21 another candle not burning, or conceived the candle before me as without a flame, and then I understand as applying to the latter, leaving its flame out of the question, all that I think of the former. In the second case, I have merely to abstract my thoughts from the objects surrounding the candle, for the mind to devote itself to the contemplation of the candle singly looked at in itself only; I can then draw the conclusion that the candle contains in itself no causes for its own destruction, so that if there were no physical objects the candle, and even the flame, would remain unchangeable, and so on. Thus there is here no fiction, but 22 true and bare assertions.

Let us now pass on to the fictions concerned with essences only, or with some reality or existence simultaneously. Of these we must specially observe that in proportion as the mind's understanding is smaller, and its experience multiplex, so will its power of coining fictions be larger, whereas as its understanding increases, its capacity for entertaining fictitious ideas becomes less. For instance, in the same way as we are unable, while we are thinking, to feign that we are thinking or not thinking, so, also, when we know the nature of body we cannot imagine an infinite fly; or, when we know the nature of the soul 23 we cannot imagine it as square, though anything may be expressed verbally. But, as we said above, the less men know of nature the more easily can they coin fictitious ideas, such as trees speaking, men instantly changed into stones, or into fountains, ghosts appearing in mirrors, something issuing from nothing, even gods changed into beasts and men and infinite other absurdities of the same kind.

Some persons think, perhaps, that fiction is limited by fiction, and not by understanding; in other words, after I have formed some fictitious idea, and have affirmed of my own free will that it exists under a certain form in nature, I am thereby precluded from thinking of it under any other form. For instance, when I have feigned (to repeat their argument) that the nature of body is of a certain kind, and have of my own free will desired to convince myself that it actually exists under this form, I am no longer able to hypothesize that a fly, for example, is infinite; so, when I have hypothesized the essence of the soul, I am not able to think of it as square, &c.

But these arguments demand further inquiry. First, their upholders must either grant or deny that we can understand anything. If they grant it, then necessarily the same must be said of understanding, as is said of fiction. If they deny it, let us, who know that we do know something, see what they mean. They assert that the soul can be conscious of, and perceive in a variety of ways, not itself nor things which exist, but only things which are neither in itself nor anywhere else, in other words, that the soul can, by its unaided power, create sensations or ideas unconnected with things. In fact, they regard the soul as a sort of god. Further, they assert that we or our soul have such freedom that we can constrain ourselves, or our soul, or even our soul's freedom. For, after it has formed a fictitious idea, and has given its assent thereto, it cannot think or feign it in any other manner, but is constrained by the first fictitious idea to keep all its other thoughts in harmony therewith. Our opponents are thus driven to admit, in support of their fiction, the absurdities which I have just enumerated; and which are not worthy of rational refutation.

While leaving such persons in their error, we will take care to derive from our argument with them a truth serviceable for our purpose, namely 24 that the mind, in paying attention to a thing hypothetical or false, so as to meditate upon it and understand it, and derive the proper conclusions in due order therefrom, will readily discover its falsity; and if the thing hypothetical be in its nature true, and the mind pays attention to it, so as to understand it, and deduce the truths which are derivable from it, the mind will proceed with an uninterrupted series of apt conclusions; in the same way as it would at once discover (as we showed just now) the absurdity of a false hypothesis, and of the conclusions drawn from it.

We need, therefore, be in no fear of forming hypotheses, so long as we have a clear and distinct perception of what is involved. For, if we were to assert, haply, that men are suddenly turned into beasts, the statement would be extremely general, so general that there would be no conception, that is, no idea or connection of subject and predicate, in our mind. If there were such a conception we should at the same time be aware of the means and the causes whereby the event took place. Moreover, we pay no attention to the nature of the subject and the predicate.

Now, if the first idea be not fictitious, and if all the other ideas be deduced therefrom, our hurry to form fictitious ideas will gradually subside. Further, as a fictitious idea cannot be clear and distinct, but is necessarily confused, and as all confusion arises from the fact that the mind has only partial knowledge of a thing either simple or complex, and does not distinguish between the known and the unknown, and, again, that it directs its attention promiscuously to all parts of an object at once without making distinctions, it follows, first, that if the idea be of something very simple, it must necessarily be clear and distinct. For a very simple object cannot be known in part, it must either be known altogether or not at all.

17 See below the note on hypotheses, whereof we have a clear understanding; the fiction consists in saying that such hypotheses exist in heavenly bodies.

18 As a thing, when once it is understood, manifests itself, we have need only of an example without further proof. In the same way the contrary has only to be presented to our minds to be recognized as false, as will forthwith appear when we come to discuss fiction concerning essences.

19 Observe, that although many assert that they doubt whether God exists, they have nought but his name in their minds, or else some fiction which they call God: this fiction is not in harmony with God's real nature, as we will duly show.

20 I shall presently show that no fiction can concern eternal truths. By an eternal truth, I mean that which being positive could never become negative. Thus it is a primary and eternal truth that God exists, but it is not an eternal truth that Adam thinks. That the Chimaera does not exist is an eternal truth, that Adam does not think is not so.

21 Afterwards, when we come to speak of fiction that is concerned with essences, it will be evident that fiction never creates or furnishes the mind with anything new; only such things as are already in the brain or imagination are recalled to the memory, when the attention is directed to them confusedly and all at once. For instance, we have remembrance of spoken words and of a tree; when the mind directs itself to them confusedly, it forms the notion of a tree speaking. The same may be said of existence, especially when it is conceived quite generally as an entity; it is then readily applied to all things together in the memory. This is specially worthy of remark.

22 We must understand as much in the case of hypotheses put forward to explain certain movements accompanying celestial phenomena; but from these, when applied to the celestial motions, we any draw conclusions as to the nature of the heavens, whereas this last may be quite different, especially as many other causes are conceivable which would account for such motions.

23 It often happens that a man recalls to mind this word soul, and forms at the same time some corporeal image: as the two representations are simultaneous, he easily thinks that he imagines and feigns a corporeal soul: thus confusing the name with the thing itself. I here beg that my readers will not be in a hurry to refute this proposition; they will, I hope, have no mind to do so, if they pay close attention to the examples given and to what follows.

24 Though I seem to deduce this from experience, some may deny its cogency because I have given no formal proof. I therefore append the following for those who may desire it. As there can be nothing in nature contrary to nature's laws, since all things come to pass by fixed laws, so that each thing must irrefragably produce its own proper effect, it follows that the soul, as soon as it possesses the true conception of a thing, proceeds to reproduce in thought that thing's effects. See below, where I speak of the false idea.

AND FROM FALSE IDEAS

SECONDLY, IT FOLLOWS that if a complex object be divided by thought into a number of simple component parts, and if each be regarded separately, all confusion will disappear. Thirdly, it follows that fiction cannot be simple, but is made up of the blending of several confused ideas of diverse objects or actions existent in nature, or rather is composed of attention directed to all such ideas at once 25 and unaccompanied by any mental assent. Now a fiction that was simple would be clear and distinct, and therefore true, also a fiction composed only of distinct ideas would be clear and distinct, and therefore true. For instance, when we know the nature of the circle and the square, it is impossible for us to blend together these two figures, and to hypothesize a square circle, any more than a square soul, or things of that kind.

Let us shortly come to our conclusion, and again repeat that we need have no fear of confusing with true ideas that which is only a fiction. As for the first sort of fiction of which we have already spoken, when a thing is clearly conceived, we saw that if the existence of a that thing is in itself an eternal trut fiction can have no part in it; but if the existence of the conceived be not an eternal truth, we have only to be careful such existence be compared to the thing's essence, and to consider the order of nature. As for the second sort of fiction, which we stated to be the result of simultaneously directing the attention, without the assent of the intellect, to different confused ideas representing different things and actions existing in nature, we have seen that an absolutely simple thing cannot be feigned, but must be understood, and that a complex thing is in the same case if we regard separately the simple parts whereof it is composed; we shall not even be able to hypothesize any untrue action concerning such objects, for we shall be obliged to consider at the same time the causes and manner of such action.

These matters being thus understood, let us pass on to consider the false idea, observing the objects with which it is concerned, and the means of guarding ourselves from falling into false perceptions. Neither of these tasks will present much difficulty, after our inquiry concerning fictitious ideas. The false idea only differs from the fictitious idea in the fact of implying a mental assent — that is, as we have already remarked, while the representations are occurring, there are no causes present to us, wherefrom, as in fiction, we can conclude that such representations do not arise from external objects: in fact, it is much the same as dreaming with our eyes open, or while awake. Thus, a false idea is concerned with, or (to speak more correctly) is attributable to, the existence of a thing whereof the essence is known, or the essence itself, in the same way as a fictitious idea.

If attributable to the existence of the thing, it is corrected in the same way as a fictitious idea under similar circumstances. If attributable to the essence, it is likewise corrected in the same way as a fictitious idea. For if the nature of the thing known implies necessary existence, we cannot possible be in error with regard to its existence; but if the nature of the thing be not an eternal truth, like its essence, but contrariwise the necessity or impossibility of its existence depends on external causes, then we must follow the same course as we adopted in the of fiction, for it is corrected in the same manner.

As for false ideas concerned with essences, or even with actions, such perceptions are necessarily always confused, being compounded of different confused perceptions of things existing in nature, as, for instance, when men are persuaded that deities are present in woods, in statues, in brute beasts, and the like; that there are bodies which, by their composition alone, give rise to intellect; that corpses reason, walk about, and speak; that God is deceived, and so on. But ideas which are clear and distinct can never be false: for ideas of things clearly and distinctly conceived are either very simple themselves, or are compounded from very simple ideas, that is, are deduced therefrom. The impossibility of a very simple idea being false is evident to everyone who understands the nature of truth or understanding and of falsehood.

As regards that which constitutes the reality of truth, it is certain that a true idea is distinguished from a false one, not so much by its extrinsic object as by its intrinsic nature. If an architect conceives a building properly constructed, though such a building may never have existed, and amy never exist, nevertheless the idea is true; and the idea remains the same, whether it be put into execution or not. On the other hand, if anyone asserts, for instance, that Peter exists, without knowing whether Peter really exists or not, the assertion, as far as its asserter is concerned, is false, or not true, even though Peter actually does exist. The assertion that Peter exists is true only with regard to him who knows for certain that Peter does exist.

Whence it follows that there is in ideas something real, whereby the true are distinguished from the false. This reality must be inquired into, if we are to find the best standard of truth (we have said that we ought to determine our thoughts by the given standard of a true idea, and that method is reflective knowledge), and to know the properties of our understanding. Neither must we say that the difference between true and false arises from the fact, that true knowledge consists in knowing things through their primary causes, wherein it is totally different from false knowledge, as I have just explained it: for thought is said to be true, if it involves subjectively the essence of any principle which has no cause, and is known through itself and in itself.

Wherefore the reality (forma) of true thought must exist in the thought itself, without reference to other thoughts; it does not acknowledge the object as its cause, but must depend on the actual power and nature of the understanding. For, if we suppose that the understanding has perceived some new entity which has never existed, as some conceive the understanding of God before He created thing (a perception which certainly could not arise any object), and has legitimately deduced other thoughts from said perception, all such thoughts would be true, without being determined by any external object; they would depend solely on the power and nature of the understanding. Thus, that which constitutes the reality of a true thought must be sought in the thought itself, and deduced from the nature of the understanding.

In order to pursue our investigation, let us confront ourselves with some true idea, whose object we know for certain to be dependent on our power of thinking, and to have nothing corresponding to it in nature. With an idea of this kind before us, we shall, as appears from what has just been said, be more easily able to carry on the research we have in view. For instance, in order to form the conception of a sphere, I invent a cause at my pleasure — namely, a semicircle revolving round its center, and thus producing a sphere; and, although we know that no sphere in nature has ever actually been so formed, the perception remains true, and is the easiest manner of conceiving a sphere. We must observe that this perception asserts the rotation of a semicircle — which assertion would be false, if it were not associated with the conception of a sphere, or of a cause determining a motion of the kind, or absolutely, if the assertion were isolated. The mind would then only tend to the affirmation of the sole motion of a semicircle, which is not contained in the conception of a semicircle, and does not arise from the conception of any cause capable of producing such motion. Thus falsity consists only in this, that something is affirmed of a thing, which is not contained in the conception we have formed of that thing, as motion or rest of a semicircle. Whence it follows that simple ideas cannot be other than true — e.g., the simple idea of a semicircle, of motion, of rest, of quantity, &c. Whatsoever affirmation such ideas contain is equal to the concept formed, and does not extend further. Wherefore we form as many simple ideas as we please, without any fear of error.

It only remains for us to inquire by what power our mind can form true ideas, and how far such power extends. It is certain that such power cannot extend itself infinitely. For when we affirm somewhat of a thing, which is not contained in the concept we have formed of that thing, such an affirmation shows a defect of our perception, or that we have formed fragmentary or mutilated ideas. Thus we have seen that the notion of a semicircle is false when it is isolated in the mind, but true when it is associated with the concept of a sphere, or of some cause determining such a motion. But if it be the nature of a thinking being, as seems, prima facie, to be the case, to form true or adequate thoughts, it is plain that inadequate ideas arise in us only because we are parts of a thinking being, whose thoughts — some in their entirety, others in fragments only — constitute our mind.

But there is another point to be considered, which was not worth raising in the case of fiction, but which give rise to complete deception — namely, that certain things presented to the imagination also exist in the understanding — in other words, are conceived clearly and distinctly. Hence, so long as we do not separate that which is distinct from that which is confused, certainty, or the true idea, becomes mixed with indistinct ideas. For instance, certain Stoics heard, perhaps, the term "soul," and also that the soul is immortal, yet imagined it only confusedly; they imaged, also, and understood that very subtle bodies penetrate all others, and are penetrated by none. By combining these ideas, and being at the same time certain of the truth of the axiom, they forthwith became convinced that the mind consists of very subtle bodies; that these very subtle bodies cannot be divided &c.

But we are freed from mistakes of this kind, so long as we endeavor to examine all our perceptions by the standard of the given true idea. We must take care, as has been said, to separate such perceptions from all those which arise from hearsay or unclassified experience. Moreover, such mistakes arise from things being conceived too much in the abstract; for it is sufficiently self-evident that what I conceive as in its true object I cannot apply to anything else. Lastly, they arise from a want of understanding of the primary elements of nature as a whole; whence we proceed without due order, and confound nature with abstract rules, which, although they be true enough in their sphere, yet, when misapplied, confound themselves, and pervert the order of nature. However, if we proceed with as little abstraction as possible, and begin from primary elements — that is, from the source and origin of nature, as far back as we can reach, — we need not fear any deceptions of this kind.

As far as the knowledge of the origin of nature is concerned, there is no danger of our confounding it with abstractions. For when a thing is conceived in the abstract, as are all universal notions, the said universal notions are always more extensive in the mind than the number of individuals forming their contents really existing in nature. Again, there are many things in nature, the difference between which is so slight as to be hardly perceptible to the understanding; so that it may readily happen that such things are confounded together, if they be conceived abstractedly. But since the first principle of nature cannot (as we shall see hereafter) be conceived abstractedly or universally, and cannot extend further in the understanding than it does in reality, and has no likeness to mutable things, no confusion need be feared in respect to the idea of it, provided (as before shown) that we possess a standard of truth. This is, in fact, a being single and infinite 26; in other words, it is the sum total of being, beyond which there is no being found. 27

25 Observe that fiction regarded in itself, only differs from dreams in that in the latter we do not perceive the external causes which we perceive through the senses while awake. It has hence been inferred that representations occurring in sleep have no connection with objects external to us. We shall presently see that error is the dreaming of a waking man: if it reaches a certain pitch it becomes delirium.

26 These are not attributes of God displaying His essence, as I will show in my philosophy.

27 This has been shown already. For if such a being did not exist it would never be produced; therefore the mind would be able to understand more than nature could furnish; and this has been shown above to be false.

OF DOUBT

THUS FAR WE have treated of the false idea. We have now to investigate the doubtful idea — that is, to inquire what can cause us to doubt, and how doubt may be removed. I speak of real doubt existing in the mind, not of such doubt as we see exemplified when a man says that he doubts, though his mind does not really hesitate. The cure of the latter does not fall within the province of method, it belongs rather to inquiries concerning obstinacy and its cure.

Real doubt is never produced in the mind by the thing doubted of. In other words, if there were only one idea in the mind, whether that idea were true or false, there would be no doubt or certainty present, only a certain sensation. For an idea is in itself nothing else than a certain sensation. But doubt will arise through another idea, not clear and distinct enough for us to be able to draw any certain conclusions with regard to the matter under consideration; that is, the idea which causes us to doubt is not clear and distinct. To take an example. Supposing that a man has never reflected, taught by experience or by any other means, that our senses sometimes deceive us, he will never doubt whether the sun be greater or less than it appears. Thus rustics are generally astonished when they hear that the sun is much larger than the earth. But from reflection on the deceitfulness of the senses 28 doubt arises, and if, after doubting, we acquire a true knowledge of the senses, and how things at a distance are represented through their instrumentality, doubt is again removed.

Hence we cannot cast doubt on true ideas by the supposition that there is a deceitful Deity, who leads us astray even in what is most certain. We can only hold such an hypothesis so long as we have no clear and distinct idea — in other words, until we reflect the knowledge which we have of the first principle of all things, and find that which teaches us that God is not a deceiver, and until we know this with the same certainty as we know from reflecting on the are equal to two right angles. But if we have a knowledge of God equal to that which we have of a triangle, all doubt is removed. In the same way as we can arrive at the said knowledge of a triangle, though not absolutely sure that there is not some arch-deceiver leading us astray, so can we come to a like knowledge of God under the like condition, and when we have attained to it, it is sufficient, as I said before, to remove every doubt which we can possess concerning clear and distinct ideas.

Thus, if a man proceeded with our investigations in due order, inquiring first into those things which should first be inquired into, never passing over a link in the chain of association, and with knowledge how to define his questions before seeking to answer them, he will never have any ideas save such as are very certain, or, in other words, clear and distinct; for doubt is only a suspension of the spirit concerning some affirmation or negation which it would pronounce upon unhesitatingly if it were not in ignorance of something, without which the knowledge of the matter in hand must needs be imperfect. We may, therefore, conclude that doubt always proceeds from want of due order in investigation.

28 That is, it is known that the senses sometimes deceive us. But it is only known confusedly, for it is not known how they deceive us.

F MEMORY AND FORGETFULNESS

THESE ARE THE points I promised to discuss in the first part of my treatise on method. However, in order not to omit anything which can conduce to the knowledge of the understanding and its faculties, I will add a few words on the subject of memory and forgetfulness. The point most worthy of attention is, that memory is strengthened both with and without the aid of the understanding. For the more intelligible a thing is, the more easily is it remembered, and the less intelligible it is, the more easily do we forget it. For instance, a number of unconnected words is much more difficult to remember than the same number in the form of a narration.

The memory is also strengthened without the aid of the understanding by means of the power wherewith the imagination or the sense called common, is affected by some particular physical object. I say particular, for the imagination is only affected by particular objects. If we read, for instance, a single romantic comedy, we shall remember it very well, so long as we do not read many others of the same kind, for it will reign alone in the memory If, however, we read several others of the same kind, we shall think of them altogether, and easily confuse one with another. I say also, physical. For the imagination is only affected by physical objects. As, then, the memory is strengthened both with and without the aid of the understanding, we may conclude that it is different from the understanding, and that in the latter considered in itself there is neither memory nor forgetfulness.

What, then, is memory? It is nothing else than the actual sensation of impressions on the brain, accompanied with the thought of a definite duration 29 of the sensation. This is also shown by reminiscence. For then we think of the sensation, but without the notion of continuous duration; thus the idea of that sensation is not the actual duration of the sensation or actual memory. Whether ideas are or are not subject to corruption will be seen in philosophy. If this seems too absurd to anyone, it will be sufficient for our purpose, if he reflect on the fact that a thing is more easily remembered in proportion to its singularity, as appears from the example of the comedy just cited. Further, a thing is remembered more easily in proportion to its intelligibility; therefore we cannot help remember that which is extremely singular and sufficiently intelligible. Thus, then, we have distinguished between a true idea and other perceptions, and shown that ideas fictitious, false, and the rest, originate in the imagination — that is, in certain sensations fortuitous (so to speak) and disconnected, arising not from the power of the mind, but from external causes, according as the body, sleeping or waking, receives various motions. But one may take any view one likes of the imagination so long as one acknowledges that it is different from the understanding, and that the soul is passive with regard to it. The view taken is immaterial, if we know that the imagination is something indefinite, with regard to which the soul is passive, and that we can by some means or other free ourselves therefrom with the help of the understanding. Let no one then be astonished that before proving the existence of body, and other necessary things, I speak of imagination of body, and of its composition. The view taken is, I repeat, immaterial, so long as we know that imagination is something indefinite, &c.

As regards as a true idea, we have shown that it is simple or compounded of simple ideas; that it shows how and why something is or has been made; and that its subjective effects in the soul correspond to the actual reality of its object. This conclusion is identical with the saying of the ancients, that true proceeds from cause to effect; though the ancients, so far as I know, never formed the conception put forward here that the soul acts according to fixed laws, and is as it were an immaterial automaton.

29 If the duration be indefinite, the recollection is imperfect; this everyone seems to have learnt from nature. For we often ask, to strengthen our belief in something we hear of, when and where it happened; though ideas themselves have their own duration in the mind, yet, as we are wont to determine duration by the aid of some measure of motion which, again, takes place by aid of imagination, we preserve no memory connected with pure intellect.

MENTAL HINDRANCES FROM WORDS — AND FROM THE POPULAR CONFUSION OF READY IMAGINATION WITH DISTINCT UNDERSTANDING.

HENCE, AS FAR as is possible at the outset, we have acquired a knowledge of our understanding, and such a standard of a true idea that we need no longer fear confounding truth with falsehood and fiction. Neither shall we wonder why we understand some things which in nowise fall within the scope of the imagination, while other things are in the imagination but wholly opposed to the understanding, or others, again, which agree therewith. We now know that the operations, whereby the effects of imagination are produced, take place under other laws quite different from the laws of the understanding, and that the mind is entirely passive with regard to them.

Whence we may also see how easily men may fall into grave errors through not distinguishing accurately between the imagination and the understanding; such as believing that extension must be localized, that it must be finite, that its parts are really distinct one from the other, that it is the primary and single foundation of all things, that it occupies more space at one time than at another and other similar doctrines, all entirely opposed to truth, as we shall duly show.

Again, since words are a part of the imagination — that is, since we form many conceptions in accordance with confused arrangements of words in the memory, dependent on particular bodily conditions, — there is no doubt that words may, equally with the imagination, be the cause of many and great errors, unless we strictly on our guard.

Moreover, words are formed according to popular fancy and intelligence, and are, therefore, signs of things as existing in the imagination, not as existing in the understanding. This is evident from the fact that to all such things as exist only in the understanding, not in the imagination, negative names are often given, such as incorporeal, infinite, &c. So, also, many conceptions really affirmative are expressed negatively, and vice versa, such as uncreate, independent, infinite, immortal, &c., inasmuch as their contraries are much more easily imagined, and, therefore, occurred first to men, and usurped positive names. Many things we affirm and deny, because the nature of words allows us to do so, though the nature of things does not. While we remain unaware of this fact, we may easily mistake falsehood for truth.

Let us also beware of another great cause of confusion, which prevents the understanding from reflecting on itself. Sometimes, while making no distinction between the imagination and the intellect, we think that what we more readily imagine is clearer to us; and also we think that what we imagine we understand. Thus, we put first that which should be last: the true order of progression is reversed, and no legitimate conclusion is drawn.

SECOND PART OF METHOD.

Its object, the acquisition of clear and distinct ideas

NOW, IN ORDER at length to pass on to the second part of this method, I shall first set forth the object aimed at, and next the means for its attainment. The object aimed at is the acquisition of clear and distinct ideas, such as are produced by the pure intellect, and not by chance physical motions. In order that all ideas may be reduced to unity, we shall endeavor so to associate and arrange them that our mind may, as far as possible, reflect subjectively the reality of nature, both as a whole and as parts.

As for the first point, it is necessary (as we have said) for our purpose that everything should be conceived, either solely through its essence, or through its proximate cause. If the thing be self-existent, or, as is commonly said, the cause of itself, it must be understood through its essence only; if it be not self-existent, but requires a cause for its existence, it must be understood through its proximate cause. For, in reality, the knowledge 31 of an effect is nothing else than the acquisition of more perfect knowledge of its cause.

Therefore, we may never, while we are concerned with inquiries into actual things, draw any conclusion from abstractions; we shall be extremely careful not to confound that which is only in the understanding with that which is in the thing itself. The best basis for drawing a conclusion will be either some particular affirmative essence, or a true and legitimate definition. For the understanding cannot descend from universal axioms by themselves to particular things, since axioms are of infinite extent, and do not determine the understanding to contemplate one particular thing more than another.

30 The chief rule of this part is, as appears from the first part, to review all the ideas coming to us through pure intellect, so as to distinguish them from such as we imagine: the distinction will be shown through the properties of each, namely, of the imagination and of the understanding.

31 Observe that it is thereby manifest that we cannot understand anything of nature without at the same time increasing our knowledge of the first cause, or God.

THUS THE TRUE method of discovery is to form thoughts from some given definition. This process will be the more fruitful and easy in proportion as the thing given be better defined. Wherefore, the cardinal point of all this second part of method consists in the knowledge of the conditions of good definition, and the means of finding them. I will first treat of the conditions of definition.

A definition, if it is to be called perfect, must explain the inmost essence of a thing, and must take care not to substitute for this any of its properties. In order to illustrate my meaning, without taking an example which would seem to show a desire to expose other people's errors, I will choose the case of something abstract, the definition of which is of little moment. Such is a circle. If a circle be defined as a figure, such that all straight lines drawn from the center to the circumference are equal, every one can see that such a definition does not in the least explain the essence of a circle, but solely one of its properties. Though, as I have said, this is of no importance in the case of figures and other abstractions, it is of great importance in the case of physical beings and realities: for the properties of things are not understood so long as their essences are unknown. If the latter be passed over, there is necessarily a perversion of the succession of ideas which should reflect the succession of nature, and we go far astray from our object.

In order to be free from this fault, the following rules should be observed in definition: —

I. If the thing in question be created, the definition must (as we have said) comprehend the proximate cause. For instance, a circle should, according to this rule, be defined as follows: the figure described by any line whereof one end is fixed and the other free. This definition clearly comprehends the proximate cause.

II. A conception or definition of a thing should be such that all the properties of that thing, in so far as it is considered by itself, and not in conjunction with other things, can be deduced from it, as may be seen in the definition given of a circle: for from that it clearly follows that all straight lines drawn from the center to the circumference are equal. That this is a necessary characteristic of a definition is so clear to anyone, who reflects on the matter, that there is no need to spend time in proving it, or in showing that, owing to this second condition, every definition should be affirmative. I speak of intellectual affirmation, giving little thought to verbal affirmations which, owing to the poverty of language, must sometimes, perhaps, be expressed negatively, though the idea contained is affirmative.

The rules for the definition of an uncreated thing are as follows: —

I. The exclusion of all idea of cause — that is, the thing must not need explanation by Anything outside itself.

II. When the definition of the thing has been given, there must be no room for doubt as to whether the thing exists or not.

III. It must contain, as far as the mind is concerned, no substantives which could be put into an adjectival form; in other words, the object defined must not be explained through abstractions.

IV. Lastly, though this is not absolutely necessary, it should be possible to deduce from the definition all the properties of the thing defined.

All these rules become obvious to anyone giving strict attention to the matter.

I have also stated that the best basis for drawing a conclusion is a particular affirmative essence. The more specialized the idea is, the more it is distinct, and therefore clear. Wherefore a knowledge of particular things should be sought for as diligently as possible.

As regards the order of our perceptions, and the manner in which they should be arranged and united, it is necessary that, as soon as is possible and rational, we should inquire whether there be any being (and, if so, what being), that is the cause of all things, so that its essence, represented in thought, may be the cause of all our ideas, and then our mind will to the utmost possible extent reflect nature. For it will possess, subjectively, nature's essence, order, and union. Thus we can see that it is before all things necessary for us to deduce all our ideas from physical things — that is, from real entities, proceeding, as far as may be, according to the series of causes, from one real entity to another real entity, never passing to universals and abstractions, either for the purpose of deducing some real entity from them, or deducing them from some real entity. Either of these processes interrupts the true progress of the understanding.

But it must be observed that, by the series of causes and real entities, I do not here mean the series of particular and mutable things, but only the series of fixed and eternal things. It would be impossible for human infirmity to follow up the series of particular mutable things, both on account their multitude, surpassing all calculation, and on account of the infinitely diverse circumstances surrounding one and the same thing, any one of which may be the cause of its existence or non-existence. Indeed, their existence has no connection with their essence, or (as we have said already) is not an eternal truth.

Neither is there any need that we should understand their series, for the essences of particular mutable things are not to be gathered from their series or order of existence, which would furnish us with nothing beyond their extrinsic denominations, their relations, or, at most, their circumstances, all of which are very different from their inmost essence. This inmost essence must be sought solely from fixed and eternal things, and from the laws, inscribed (so to speak) in those things as in their true codes, according to which all particular things take place and are arranged; nay, these mutable particular things depend so intimately and essentially (so to phrase it) upon the fixed things, that they cannot either be conceived without them.

But, though this be so, there seems to be no small difficulty in arriving at the knowledge of these particular things, for to conceive them all at once would far surpass the powers of the human understanding. The arrangement whereby one thing is understood, before another, as we have stated, should not be sought from their series of existence, nor from eternal things. For the latter are all by nature simultaneous. Other aids are therefore needed besides those employed for understanding eternal things and their laws. However, this is not the place to recount such aids, nor is there any need to do so, until we have acquired a sufficient knowledge of eternal things and their infallible laws, and until the nature of our senses has become plain to us.

Before betaking ourselves to seek knowledge of particular things, it will be seasonable to speak of such aids, as all tend to teach us the mode of employing our senses, and to make certain experiments under fixed rules and arrangements which may suffice to determine the object of our inquiry, so that we may therefrom infer what laws of eternal things it has been produced under, and may gain an insight into its inmost nature, as I will duly show. Here, to return to my purpose, I will only endeavor to set forth what seems necessary for enabling us to attain to knowledge of eternal things, and to define them under the conditions laid down above.

With this end, we must bear in mind what has already been stated, namely, that when the mind devotes itself to any thought, so as to examine it, and to deduce therefrom in due order all the legitimate conclusions possible, any falsehood which may lurk in the thought will be detected; but if the thought be true, the mind will readily proceed without interruption to deduce truths from it. This, I say, is necessary for our purpose, for our thoughts may be brought to a close by the absence of a foundation.

If, therefore, we wish to investigate the first thing of all, it will be necessary to supply some foundation which may direct our thoughts thither. Further, since method is reflective knowledge, the foundation which must direct our thoughts can be nothing else than the knowledge of that which constitutes the reality of truth, and the knowledge of the understanding, its properties, and powers. When this has been acquired we shall possess a foundation wherefrom we can deduce our thoughts, and a path whereby the intellect, according to its capacity, may attain the knowledge of eternal things, allowance being made for the extent of the intellectual powers.

If, as I stated in the first part, it belongs to the nature of thought to form true ideas, we must here inquire what is meant by the faculties and power of the understanding. The chief part of our method is to understand as well as possible the powers of the intellect, and its nature; we are, therefore, compelled (by the considerations advanced in the second part of the method) necessarily to draw these conclusions from the definition itself of thought and understanding.

HOW TO DEFINE UNDERSTANDING

BUT, SO FAR as we have not got any rules for finding definitions, and, as we cannot set forth such rules without a previous knowledge of nature, that is without a definition of the understanding and its power, it follows either that the definition of the understanding must be clear in itself, or that we can understand nothing. Nevertheless this definition is not absolutely clear in itself; however, since its properties, like all things that we possess through the understanding, cannot be known clearly and distinctly, unless its nature be known previously, understanding makes itself manifest, if we pay attention to its properties, which we know clearly and distinctly. Let us, then, enumerate here the properties of the understanding, let us examine them, and begin by discussing the instruments for research which we find innate in us. See [para. 31]

The properties of the understanding which I have chiefly remarked, and which I clearly understand, are the following: —

I. It involves certainty — in other words, it knows that a thing exists in reality as it is reflected subjectively.

II. That it perceives certain things, or forms some ideas absolutely, some ideas from others. Thus it forms the idea of quantity absolutely, without reference to any other thoughts; but ideas of motion it only forms after taking into consideration the idea of quantity.

III. Those ideas which the understanding forms absolutely express infinity; determinate ideas are derived from other ideas. Thus in the idea of quantity, perceived by means of a cause, the quantity is determined, as when a body is perceived to be formed by the motion of a plane, a plane by the motion of a line, or, again, a line by the motion of a point. All these are perceptions which do not serve towards understanding quantity, but only towards determining it. This is proved by the fact that we conceive them as formed as it were by motion, yet this motion is not perceived unless the quantity be perceived also; we can even prolong the motion to form an infinite line, which we certainly could not do unless we had an idea of infinite quantity.

IV. The understanding forms positive ideas before forming negative ideas.

V. It perceives things not so much under the condition of duration as under a certain form of eternity, and in an infinite number; or rather in perceiving things it does not consider either their number or duration, whereas, in imagining them, it perceives them in a determinate number, duration, and quantity.

VI. The ideas which we form as clear and distinct, seem to follow from the sole necessity of our nature, that they appear to depend absolutely on our sole power; with confused ideas the contrary is the case. They are often formed against our will.

VII. The mind can determine in many ways the ideas of things, which the understanding forms from other ideas: thus, for instance, in order to define the plane of an ellipse, it supposes a point adhering to a cord to be moved around two centers, or, again, it conceives an infinity of points, always in the same fixed relation to a given straight line, angle of the vertex of the cone, or in an infinity of other ways.

VIII. The more ideas express perfection of any object, the more perfect are they themselves; for we do not admire the architect who has planned a chapel so much as the architect who has planned a splendid temple.

I do not stop to consider the rest of what is referred to thought, such as love, joy, &c. They are nothing to our present purpose, and cannot even be conceived unless the understanding be perceived previously. When perception is removed, all these go with it.

False and fictitious ideas have nothing positive about them (as we have abundantly shown), which causes them to be called false or fictitious; they are only considered as such through the defectiveness of knowledge. Therefore, false and fictitious ideas as such can teach us nothing concerning the essence of thought; this must be sought from the positive properties just enumerated; in other words, we must lay down some common basis from which these properties necessarily follow, so that when this is given, the properties are necessarily given also, and when it is removed, they too vanish with it.

The rest of the treatise is wanting.

THE ORIGINAL LATIN TEXT
I. DE BONIS QUAE HOMINES PLERUMQUE APPETUNT.

1. POSTQUAM ME experientia docuit, omnia, quae in communi vita frequenter occurrunt, vana et futilia esse ; cum viderem omnia, a quibus et quae timebam, nihil neque boni neque mali in se habere, nisi quatenus ab iis animus movebatur ; constitui tandem inquirere, an aliquid daretur, quod verum bonum et sui communicabile esset, et a quo solo reiectis ceteris omnibus animus afficeretur ; imo an aliquid daretur, quo invento et acquisito continua ac summa in aeternum fruerer laetitia.

2. Dico me tandem constituisse. Primo enim intuitu inconsultum videbatur, propter rem tunc incertam certam amittere velle. Videbam nimirum commoda, quae ex honore ac divitiis acquiruntur, et quod ab iis quaerendis cogebar abstinere, si seriam rei alii novae operam dare vellem, et si forte summa felicitas in iis esset sita, perspiciebam me ea debere carere ; si vero in iis non esset sita eisque tantum darem operam, tum etiam summa carerem felicitate.

3. Volvebam igitur animo, an forte esset possibile ad novum institutum, aut saltem ad ipsius certitudinem pervenire, licet ordo et commune vitae meae institutum non mutaretur, quod saepe frustra tentavi. Nam quae plerumque in vita occurrunt, et apud homines, ut ex eorum operibus colligere licet, tamquam summum bonum aestimantur, ad haec tria rediguntur : divitias scilicet, honorem atque libidinem. His tribus adeo distrahitur mens, ut minime possit de alio aliquo bono cogitare.

4. Nam quod ad libidinem attinet, ea adeo suspenditur animus, ac si in aliquo bono quiesceret ; quo maxime impeditur, ne de alio cogitet. Sed post illius fruitionem summa sequitur tristitia, quae si non suspendit mentem, tamen perturbat et hebetat. Honores ac divitias prosequendo non parum etiam distrahitur mens, praesertim ubi hae non nisi propter se quaeruntur , quia tum supponuntur summum esse bonum.

5. Honore vero multo adhuc magis mens distrahitur ; supponitur enim semper bonum esse per se et tamquam finis ultimus, ad quem omnia diriguntur. Deinde in his non datur, sicut in libidine, poenitentia, sed quo plus utriusque possidetur, eo magis augetur laetitia, et consequenter magis ac magis incitamur ad utrumque augendum ; si autem spe in aliquo casu frustremur, tum summa oritur tristitia. Est denique honor magno impedimento eo, quod, ut ipsum assequamur, vita necessario ad captum hominum est dirigenda, fugiendo scilicet quod vulgo fugiunt, et quaerendo quod vulgo quaerunt homines.

6. Cum itaque viderem, haec omnia adeo obstare, quominus operam novo alicui instituto darem, imo adeo esse opposita, ut ab uno aut altero necessario esset abstinendum, cogebar inquirere, quid mihi esset utilius ; nempe, ut dixi, videbar bonum certum pro incerto amittere velle. Sed postquam aliquantulum huic rei incubueram, inveni primo, si hisce omissis ad novum institutum accingerer, me bonum sua natura incertum, ut clare ex dictis possumus colligere, omissurum pro incerto, non quidem sua natura (fixum enim bonum quaerebam), sed tantum quoad ipsius consecutionem.

7. Assidua autem meditatione eo perveni, ut viderem, quod tum, modo possem

penitus deliberare, mala certa pro bono certo omitterem. Videbam enim me in summo versari periculo, et me cogi, remedium, quamvis incertum, summis viribus quaerere ; veluti aeger letali morbo laborans, qui ubi mortem certam praevidet, ni adhibeatur remedium, illud ipsum, quamvis incertum, summis viribus cogitur quaerere ; nempe in eo tota eius spes est sita ; illa autem omnia, quae vulgus sequitur, non tantum nullum conferunt remedium ad nostrum esse conservandum, sed etiam id impediunt, et frequenter sunt causa interitus eorum, qui ea possident, et semper causa interitus eorum, qui ab iis possidentur.

8. Permulta enim exstant exempla eorum, qui persecutionem ad necem usque passi sunt propter ipsorum divitias, et etiam eorum, qui, ut opes compararent, tot periculis sese exposuerunt, ut tandem vita poenam luerent suae stultitiae. Neque eorum pauciora sunt exempla, qui, ut honorem assequerentur aut defenderent, miserrime passi sunt. Innumeranda denique exstant exempla eorum, qui prae nimia libidine mortem sibi acceleraverunt.

9. Videbantur porro ex eo haec orta esse mala, quod tota felicitas aut infelicitas in hoc solo sita est ; videlicet in qualitate obiecti, cui adhaeremus amore. Nam propter illud, quod non amatur, nunquam orientur lites, nulla erit tristitia, si pereat, nulla invidia, si ab alio possideatur, nullus timor, nullum odium, et, ut verbo dicam, nullae commotiones animi ; quae quidem omnia contingunt in amore eorum, quae perire possunt, uti haec omnia, de quibus modo locuti sumus.

10. Sed amor erga rem aeternam et infinitam sola laetitia pascit animum, ipsaque omnis tristitiae est expers ; quod valde est desiderandum totisque viribus quaerendum. Verum non absque ratione usus sum his verbis : modo possem serio deliberare. Nam quamvis haec mente adeo clare perciperem, non poteram tamen ideo omnem avaritiam, libidinem, atque gloriam deponere.

II. DE BONO VERO ET SUMMO.

11. HOC UNUM videbam, quod, quamdiu mens circa has cogitationes versabatur, tamdiu illa aversabatur, et serio de novo cogitabat instituto ; quod magno mihi fuit solatio. Nam videbam illa mala non esse talis conditionis, ut remediis nollent cedere. Et quamvis in initio haec intervalla essent rara et per admodum exiguum temporis spatium durarent, postquam tamen verum bonum magis ac magis mihi innotuit, intervalla ista frequentiora et longiora fuerunt ; praesertim postquam vidi nummorum acquisitionem aut libidinem et gloriam tamdiu obesse, quamdiu propter se, et non tamquam media ad alia quaeruntur. Si vero tamquam media quaeruntur, modum tunc habebunt, et minime oberunt, sed contra ad finem, propter quem quaeruntur, multum conducent, ut suo loco ostendemus.

12. Hic tantum breviter dicam, quid per verum bonum intelligam, et simul quid sit summum bonum. Quod ut recte intelligatur, notandum est, quod bonum et malum non nisi respective dicantur ; adeo ut una, eademque res possit dici bona et mala secundum diversos respectus, eodem modo ac perfectum, et imperfectum. Nihil enim in sua natura spectatum perfectum dicetur vel imperfectum ; praesertim postquam noverimus, omnia, quae fiunt, secundum aeternum ordinem et secundum certas naturae leges fieri.

13. Cum autem humana imbecillitas illum ordinem cogitatione sua non assequatur, et interim homo concipiat naturam aliquam humanam sua multo firmiorem, et simul nihil obstare videat, quominus talem naturam acquirat, incitatur ad media quaerendum, quae ipsum ad talem ducant perfectionem : et omne illud, quod potest esse medium, ut eo perveniat, vocatur verum bonum. Summum autem bonum est eo pervenire, ut ille cum aliis individuis, si fieri potest, tali natura fruatur. Quaenam autem illa sit natura, ostendemus suo loco, nimirum esse cognitionem unionis, quam mens cum tota natura habet .

14. Hic est itaque finis, ad quem tendo, talem scilicet naturam acquirere, et ut multi mecum eam acquirant conari, hoc est, de mea felicitate etiam est operam dare, ut alii multi idem atque ego intelligant, ut eorum intellectus et cupiditas prorsus cum meo intellectu et cupiditate conveniant ; utque hoc fiat, necesse est tantum de natura intelligere, quantum sufficit ad talem naturam acquirendam ; deinde formare talem societatem, qualis est desideranda, ut quamplurimi quam facillime, et secure eo perveniant.

15. Porro danda est opera morali philosophiae, ut et doctrinae de puerorum educatione ; et quia valetudo non parvum est medium ad hunc finem assequendum, concinnanda est integra medicina ; et quia arte multa, quae difficilia sunt, facilia redduntur, multumque temporis et commoditatis in vita ea lucrari possumus, ideo mechanica nullo modo est contemnenda.

16. Sed ante omnia excogitandus est modus medendi intellectus, ipsumque, quantum initio licet, expurgandi, ut feliciter res absque errore, et quam optime intelligat. Unde quisque iam poterit videre, me omnes scientias ad unum finem et scopum velle dirigere, scilicet ut ad summam humanam, quam diximus, perfectionem perveniatur ; et sic omne illud, quod in scientiis nihil ad finem nostrum nos promovet, tamquam inutile erit reiiciendum, hoc est, ut uno verbo dicam, omnes nostrae operationes simul et cogitationes ad hunc sunt dirigendae finem.

III. QUAEDAM VIVENDI REGULAE.

17. SED QUIA, dum curamus eum consequi, et operam damus, ut intellectum in rectam viam redigamus, necesse est vivere, propterea ante omnia cogimur quasdam vivendi regulas, tanquam bonas, supponere, has scilicet.

I. Ad captum vulgi loqui, et illa omnia operari, quae nihil impedimenti adferunt, quominus nostrum scopum attingamus. Nam non parum emolumenti ab eo possumus acquirere, modo ipsius captui, quantum fieri potest, concedamus ; adde, quod tali modo amicas praebebunt aures ad veritatem audiendam.

II. Deliciis in tantum frui, in quantum ad tuendam valetudinem sufficit.

III. Denique tantum nummorum, aut cuiuscumque alterius rei quaerere, quantum sufficit ad vitam, et valetudinem sustentandam, et ad mores civitatis, qui nostrum scopum non oppugnant, imitandos.

IV. DE DIVERSIS PERCIPIENDI MODIS.

18. HISCE SIC positis, ad primum, quod ante omnia faciendum est, me accingam, ad emendandum scilicet intellectum, eumque aptum reddendum ad res tali modo intelligendas, quo opus est, ut nostrum finem assequamur. Quod ut fiat, exigit ordo, quem naturaliter habemus, ut hic resumam omnes modos percipiendi, quos hucusque habui ad aliquid indubie affirmandum vel negandum, quo omnium optimum eligam, et simul meas vires et naturam, quam perficere cupio, noscere incipiam.

19. Si accurate attendo, possunt omnes ad quatuor potissimum reduci.

I. Est perceptio, quam ex auditu aut ex aliquo signo, quod vocant ad placitum, habemus.

II. Est perceptio, quam habemus ab experientia vaga, hoc est, ab experientia, quae non determinatur ab intellectu, sed tantum ita dicitur, quia casu sic occurrit, et nullum aliud habemus experimentum, quod hoc oppugnat, et ideo tanquam inconcussum apud nos manet.

III. Est perceptio, ubi essentia rei ex alia re concluditur, sed non adaequate ; quod fit, cum vel ab aliquo effectu causam colligimus, vel cum concluditur ab aliquo universali, quod semper aliqua proprietas concomitatur .

IV. Denique perceptio est, ubi res percipitur per solam suam essentiam, vel per cognitionem suae proximae causae.

20. Quae omnia exemplis illustrabo. Ex auditu tantum scio meum natalem diem, et quod tales parentes habui, et similia ; de quibus nunquam dubitavi. Per experientiam vagam scio me moriturum ; hoc enim ideo affirmo, quia vidi alios mei similes obiisse mortem, quamvis neque omnes per idem temporis spatium vixerint, neque ex eodem morbo obierint. Deinde per experientiam vagam etiam scio, quod oleum sit aptum alimentum ad nutriendam flammam, quodque aqua ad eam extinguendam apta sit ; scio etiam, quod canis sit animal latrans, et homo animal rationale, et sic fere omnia novi, quae ad usum vitae faciunt.

21. Ex alia vero re hoc modo concludimus : postquam clare percipimus, nos tale corpus sentire et nullum aliud, inde, inquam, clare concludimus animam unitam esse corpori, quae unio est causa talis sensationis ; sed quaenam sit illa sensatio et unio, non absolute inde possumus intelligere . Vel postquam novi naturam visus, et simul, eum habere talem proprietatem, ut unam eandemque rem ad magnam distantiam minorem videamus, quam si eam cominus intueamur ; inde concludimus solem maiorem esse, quam apparet, et alia his similia.

22. Per solam denique rei essentiam res percipitur, quando ex eo, quod aliquid novi, scio, quid hoc sit aliquid nosse, vel ex eo, quod novi essentiam animae, scio eam corpori esse unitam. Eadem cognitione novimus duo et tria esse quinque, et si dentur duae lineae uni tertiae parallelae, eas etiam inter sese parallelas etc. Ea tamen, quae hucusque tali cognitione potui intelligere, perpauca fuerunt.

23. Ut autem haec omnia melius intelligantur, unico tantum utar exemplo, hoc scilicet. Dantur tres numeri ; quaerit quis quartum, qui sit ad tertium, ut secundus ad primum. Dicunt hic passim mercatores, se scire, quid sit agendum, ut quartus inveniatur, quia nempe eam operationem nondum oblivioni tradiderunt, quam

nudam sine demonstratione a suis magistris audiverunt. Alii vero ab experientia simplicium faciunt axioma universale, scilicet ubi quartus numerus per se patet, ut in his 2, 4, 3, 6, ubi experiuntur, quod ducto secundo in tertium, et producto deinde per primum diviso fiat quotiens 6 ; et cum vident eundem numerum produci, quem sine hac operatione noverant esse proportionalem, inde concludunt operationem esse bonam ad quartum numerum proportionalem semper inveniendum.

24. Sed mathematici vi demonstrationis pro. lib. 7. element. Euclidis sciunt, quales numeri inter se sint proportionales, scilicet ex natura proportionis eiusque proprietate, quod nempe numerus, qui fit ex primo et quarto aequalis sit numero, qui fit ex secundo et tertio. Attamen adaequatam proportionalitatem datorum numerorum non vident ; et si videant, non vident eam vi illius propositionis, sed intuitive, nullam operationem facientes.

V. DE OPTIMO MODO PERCIPIENDI.

25. UT AUTEM ex his optimus eligatur modus percipiendi, requiritur, ut breviter enumeremus, quae sint necessaria media, ut nostrum finem assequamur ; haec scilicet :

I. Nostram naturam, quam cupimus perficere, exacte nosse, et simul tantum de rerum natura, quantum sit necesse.

II. Ut inde rerum differentias, convenientias et oppugnantias recte colligamus.

III. Ut recte concipiatur, quid possint pati, quid non.

IV. Ut hoc conferatur cum natura et potentia hominis. Et ex istis facile apparebit summa, ad quam homo potest pervenire, perfectio.

26. His sic consideratis videamus, quis modus percipiendi nobis sit eligendus.

Quod ad primum attinet, per se patet, quod ex auditu, praeterquam quod sit res admodum incerta, nullam percipiamus essentiam rei, sicuti ex nostro exemplo apparet ; et cum singularis existentia alicuius rei non noscatur nisi cognita essentia (uti postea videbitur), hinc clare concludimus omnem certitudinem, quam ex auditu habemus, a scientiis esse secludendam. Nam a simplici auditu, ubi non praecessit proprius intellectus, nunquam quis poterit affici.

27. Quoad secundum ; nullus etiam dicendus est, quod habeat ideam illius proportionis, quam quaerit . Praeterquam quod sit res admodum incerta et sine fine, nihil tamen unquam tali modo quis in rebus naturalibus percipiet praeter accidentia, quae nunquam clare intelliguntur, nisi praecognitis essentiis. Unde etiam et ille secludendus est.

28. De tertio autem aliquo modo dicendum, quod habeamus ideam rei, deinde quod etiam absque periculo erroris concludamus ; sed tamen per se non erit medium, ut nostram perfectionem acquiramus.

29. Solus quartus modus comprehendit essentiam rei adaequatam, et absque erroris periculo ; ideoque maxime erit usurpandus. Quomodo ergo sit adhibendus, ut res incognitae tali cognitione a nobis intelligantur, simulque ut hoc quam compendiose fiat, curabimus explicare.

VI. DE INTELLECTUS INSTRUMENTIS, IDEIS VERIS.

30. POSTQUAM NOVIMUS, quaenam cognitio nobis sit necessaria, tradenda est via et methodus, qua res, quae sunt cognoscendae, tali cognitione cognoscamus. Quod ut fiat, venit prius considerandum, quod hic non dabitur inquisitio in infinitum ; scilicet ut inveniatur optima methodus verum investigandi, non opus est alia methodo, ut methodus veri investigandi investigetur ; et ut secunda methodus investigetur, non opus est alia tertia, et sic in infinitum. Tali enim modo nunquam ad veri cognitionem, imo ad nullam cognitionem perveniretur. Hoc vero eodem modo se habet, ac se habent instrumenta corporea, ubi eodem modo liceret argumentari. Nam ut ferrum cudatur, malleo opus est, et ut malleus habeatur, eum fieri necessum est ; ad quod alio malleo, aliisque instrumentis opus est, quae etiam ut habeantur, aliis opus erit instrumentis, et sic in infinitum ; et hoc modo frustra aliquis probare conaretur, homines nullam habere potestatem ferrum cudendi.

31. Sed quemadmodum homines initio innatis instrumentis quaedam facillima, quamvis laboriose et imperfecte, facere quiverunt, iisque confectis alia difficiliora minori labore, et perfectius confecerunt, et sic gradatim ab operibus simplicissimis ad instrumenta, et ab instrumentis ad alia opera, et instrumenta pergendo eo pervenerunt, ut tot et tam difficilia parvo labore perficiant, sic etiam intellectus vi sua nativa facit sibi instrumenta intellectualia, quibus alias vires acquirit ad alia opera intellectualia, et ex iis operibus alia instrumenta seu potestatem ulterius investigandi ; et sic gradatim pergit, donec sapientiae culmen attingat.

32. Quod autem intellectus ita sese habeat, facile erit videre, modo intelligatur, quid sit methodus verum investigandi, et quaenam sint illa innata instrumenta, quibus tantum eget ad alia ex iis instrumenta conficienda, ut ulterius procedat. Ad quod ostendendum sic procedo .

33. Idea vera (habemus enim ideam veram) est diversum quid a suo ideato. Nam aliud est circulus, aliud idea circuli ; idea enim circuli non est aliquid, habens peripheriam et centrum, uti circulus, nec idea corporis est ipsum corpus. Et cum sit quid diversum a suo ideato, erit etiam per se aliquid intelligibile, hoc est, idea quoad suam essentiam formalem potest esse obiectum alterius essentiae obiectivae, et rursus haec altera essentia obiectiva erit etiam in se spectata quid reale et intelligibile, et sic indefinite.

34. Petrus ex. gr. est quid reale ; vera autem idea Petri est essentia Petri obiectiva, et in se quid reale, et omnino diversum ab ipso Petro. Cum itaque idea Petri sit quid reale habens suam essentiam peculiarem, erit etiam quid intelligibile, id est, obiectum alterius ideae, quae idea habebit in se obiective omne id, quod idea Petri habet formaliter, et rursus idea, quae est ideae Petri, habet iterum suam essentiam, quae etiam potest esse obiectum alterius ideae, et sic indefinite. Quod quisque potest experiri, dum videt se scire, quid sit Petrus, et etiam scire se scire, et rursus scit se scire, quod scit etc. Unde constat, quod, ut intelligatur essentia Petri, non sit necesse, ipsam ideam Petri intelligere, et multo minus ideam ideae Petri ; quod idem est, ac si dicerem, non esse opus, ut sciam, quod sciam me scire, et multo minus esse opus scire, quod sciam me scire ; non magis, quam ad intelligendam essentiam trianguli opus sit essentiam circuli intelligere . Sed contrarium datur in his ideis. Nam ut sciam me scire, necessario debeo prius scire.

35. Hinc patet, quod certitudo nihil sit praeter ipsam essentiam obiectivam ; id

est, modus, quo sentimus essentiam formalem, est ipsa certitudo. Unde iterum patet, quod ad certitudinem veritatis nullo alio signo sit opus, quam veram habere ideam ; nam, uti ostendimus, non opus est, ut sciam, quod sciam me scire. Ex quibus rursum patet, neminem posse scire, quid sit summa certitudo, nisi qui habet adaequatam ideam aut essentiam obiectivam alicuius rei ; nimirum, quia idem est certitudo et essentia obiectiva.

II. DE RECTA METHODO
COGNOSCENDI.

36. CUM ITAQUE veritas nullo egeat signo, sed sufficiat habere essentias rerum obiectivas, aut, quod idem est, ideas, ut omne tollatur dubium ; hinc sequitur, quod vera non est methodus signum veritatis quaerere post acquisitionem idearum, sed quod vera methodus est via, ut ipsa veritas, aut essentiae obiectivae rerum aut ideae (omnia illa idem significant) debito ordine quaerantur .

37. Rursus methodus necessario debet loqui de ratiocinatione aut de intellectione ; id est, methodus non est ipsum ratiocinari ad intelligendum causas rerum, et multo minus est τo intelligere causas rerum ; sed est intelligere, quid sit vera idea, eam a ceteris perceptionibus distinguendo eiusque naturam investigando, ut inde nostram intelligendi potentiam noscamus, et mentem ita cohibeamus, ut ad illam normam omnia intelligat, quae sunt intelligenda, tradendo tamquam auxilia certas regulas, et etiam faciendo, ne mens inutilibus defatigetur.

38. Unde colligitur, methodum nihil aliud esse, nisi cognitionem reflexivam aut ideam ideae ; et quia non datur idea ideae, nisi prius detur idea, ergo methodus non dabitur, nisi prius detur idea. Unde illa bona erit methodus, quae ostendit, quomodo mens dirigenda sit ad datae verae ideae normam. Porro cum ratio, quae est inter duas ideas, sit eadem cum ratione, quae est inter essentias formales idearum illarum, inde sequitur, quod cognitio reflexiva, quae est ideae entis perfectissimi, praestantior erit cognitione reflexiva ceterarum idearum ; hoc est, perfectissima ea erit methodus, quae ad datae ideae entis perfectissimi normam ostendit, quomodo mens sit dirigenda.

39. Ex his facile intelligitur, quomodo mens plura intelligendo alia simul acquirat instrumenta, quibus facilius pergat intelligere. Nam, ut ex dictis licet colligere, debet ante omnia in nobis existere vera idea tamquam innatum instrumentum, qua intellecta intelligatur simul differentia, quae est inter talem perceptionem, et ceteras omnes. Qua in re consistit una methodi pars. Et cum per se clarum sit, mentem eo melius se intelligere, quo plura de natura intelligit, inde constat, hanc methodi partem eo perfectiorem fore, quo mens plura intelligit, et tum fore perfectissimam, cum mens ad cognitionem entis perfectissimi attendit sive reflectit.

40. Deinde, quo plura mens novit, eo melius et suas vires et ordinem naturae intelligit : quo autem melius suas vires intelligit, eo facilius potest se ipsam dirigere et regulas sibi proponere ; et quo melius ordinem naturae intelligit, eo facilius potest se ab inutilibus cohibere ; in quibus tota consistit methodus, uti diximus.

41. Adde quod idea eodem modo se habet obiective, ac ipsius ideatum se habet realiter. Si ergo daretur aliquid in natura, nihil commercii habens cum aliis rebus, eius etiam si daretur essentia obiectiva, quae convenire omnino deberet cum formali, nihil etiam commercii haberet cum aliis ideis , id est, nihil de ipsa poterimus concludere ; et contra, quae habent commercium cum aliis rebus, uti sunt omnia quae in natura existunt, intelligentur et ipsorum etiam essentiae obiectivae idem habebunt commercium, id est, aliae ideae ex eis deducentur, quae iterum habebunt commercium cum aliis, et sic instrumenta ad procedendum ulterius crescent. Quod conabamur demonstrare.

42. Porro ex hoc ultimo, quod diximus, scilicet quod idea omnino cum sua essentia formali debeat convenire, patet iterum quod, ut mens nostra omnino referat

naturae exemplar, debeat omnes suas ideas producere ab ea, quae refert originem et fontem totius naturae, ut ipsa etiam sit fons ceterarum idearum.

43. Hic forte aliquis mirabitur, quod nos, ubi diximus, bonam methodum eam esse, quae ostendit, quomodo mens sit dirigenda ad datae verae ideae normam, hoc ratiocinando probemus ; id quod ostendere videtur, hoc per se non esse notum ; atque adeo quaeri potest, utrum nos bene ratiocinemur. Si bene ratiocinamur, debemus incipere a data idea, et cum incipere a data idea egeat demonstratione, deberemus iterum nostrum ratiocinium probare, et tum iterum illud alterum, et sic in infinitum.

44. Sed ad hoc respondeo : quod si quis fato quodam sic processisset naturam investigando, scilicet ad datae verae ideae normam alias acquirendo ideas debito ordine, nunquam de sua veritate dubitasset , eo quod veritas, uti ostendimus, se ipsam patefacit, et etiam sponte omnia ipsi affluxissent. Sed quia hoc nunquam aut raro contingit, ideo coactus fui illa sic ponere, ut illud, quod non possumus fato, praemeditato tamen consilio acquiramus, et simul ut appareret, ad probandam veritatem et bonum ratiocinium nullis nos egere instrumentis, nisi ipsa veritate et bono ratiocinio. Nam bonum ratiocinium bene ratiocinando comprobavi, et adhuc probare conor.

45. Adde, quod etiam hoc modo homines assuefiant meditationibus suis internis. Ratio autem, cur in naturae inquisitione raro contingat, ut debito ordine ea investigetur, est propter praeiudicia, quorum causas postea in nostra philosophia explicabimus ; deinde quia opus est magna et accurata distinctione, sicut postea ostendemus (id quod valde est laboriosum) ; denique propter statum rerum humanarum, qui, ut iam ostensum est, prorsus est mutabilis. Sunt adhuc aliae rationes, quas non inquirimus.

46. Si quis forte quaerat, cur ipse statim ante omnia veritates naturae isto ordine ostenderim (nam veritas se ipsam patefacit), ei respondeo simulque moneo, ne propter paradoxa, quae forte passim occurrent, ea velit tamquam falsa reiicere, sed prius dignetur ordinem considerare, quo ea probemus, et tum certus evadet, nos verum assequutos fuisse. Et haec fuit causa, cur haec praemiserim.

47. Si postea forte quis scepticus et de ipsa prima veritate et de omnibus, quas ad normam primae deducemus, dubius adhuc maneret, ille profecto aut contra conscientiam loquetur, aut nos fatebimur, dari homines penitus etiam animo obcaecatos a nativitate aut a praeiudiciorum causa, id est, aliquo externo casu. Nam neque se ipsos sentiunt. Si aliquid affirmant,vel dubitant, nesciunt se dubitare aut affirmare ; dicunt se nihil scire, et hoc ipsum, quod nihil sciunt, dicunt se ignorare ; neque hoc absolute dicunt ; nam metuunt fateri, se existere, quamdiu nihil sciunt, adeo ut tandem debeant obmutescere, ne forte aliquid supponant, quod veritatem redoleat.

48. Denique cum ipsis non est loquendum de scientiis ; nam quod ad vitae et societatis usum attinet, necessitas eos coegit, ut supponerent se esse, et ut suum utile quaererent, et iureiurando multa affirmarent et negarent. Nam, si aliquid ipsis probetur, nesciunt, an probet aut deficiat argumentatio. Si negant, concedunt aut opponunt, nesciunt se negare, concedere aut opponere ; adeoque habendi sunt tanquam automata, quae mente omnino carent.

49. Resumamus iam nostrum propositum. Habuimus hucusque primo finem, ad quem omnes nostras cogitationes dirigere studemus. Cognovimus secundo,

quaenam sit optima perceptio, cuius ope ad nostram perfectionem pervenire possimus. Cognovimus tertio, quaenam sit prima via, cui mens insistere debeat, ut bene incipiat ; quae est, ut ad normam datae cuiuscumque verae ideae pergat certis legibus inquirere. Quod ut recte fiat, haec debet methodus praestare : primo veram ideam a ceteris omnibus perceptionibus distinguere, et mentem a ceteris perceptionibus cohibere ; secundo tradere regulas, ut res incognitae ad talem normam percipiantur ; tertio ordinem constituere, ne inutilibus defatigemur. Postquam hanc methodum novimus, vidimus quarto hanc methodum perfectissimam futuram, ubi habuerimus ideam entis perfectissimi. Unde initio illud erit maxime observandum, ut quanto ocius ad cognitionem talis entis perveniamus.

VIII. METHODI PARS PRIMA.
DE IDEA FICTA.

50. INCIPIAMUS ITAQUE a prima parte methodi, quae est, uti diximus, distinguere et separare ideam veram a ceteris perceptionibus, et cohibere mentem, ne falsas, fictas et dubias cum veris confundat. Quod utcumque fuse hic explicare animus est, ut lectores detineam in cogitatione rei adeo necessariae, et etiam quia multi sunt, qui vel de veris dubitant ex eo, quod non attenderunt ad distinctionem, quae est inter veram perceptionem et alias omnes ; adeo ut sint veluti homines, qui cum vigilarent, non dubitabant se vigilare ; sed postquam semel in somniis, ut saepe fit, putarunt se certo vigilare, quod postea falsum esse reperiebant, etiam de suis vigiliis dubitarunt ; quod contingit, quia nunquam distinxerunt inter somnum et vigiliam.

51. Interim moneo, me hic essentiam uniuscuiusque perceptionis, eamque per proximam suam causam non explicaturum, quia hoc ad philosophiam pertinet ; sed tantum traditurum id, quod methodus postulat, id est, circa quae perceptio ficta, falsa et dubia versetur, et quomodo ab unaquaque liberabimur. Sit itaque prima inquisitio circa ideam fictam.

52. Cum omnis perceptio sit vel rei tamquam existentis consideratae, vel solius essentiae, et frequentiores fictiones contingant circa res tamquam existentes consideratas, ideo prius de hac loquar ; scilicet ubi sola existentia fingitur, et res, quae in tali actu fingitur, intelligitur sive supponitur intelligi. Ex. gr. fingo Petrum, quem novi ire domum, eum me invisere, et similia . Hic quaero, circa quae talis idea versetur ? Video eam tantum versari circa possibilia, non vero circa necessaria, neque circa impossibilia.

53. Rem impossibilem voco, cuius natura in existendo implicat contradictionem, ut ea existat ; necessariam, cuius natura implicat contradictionem, ut ea non existat ; possibilem, cuius quidem existentia ipsa sua natura non implicat contradictionem, ut existat aut non existat, sed cuius existentiae necessitas aut impossibilitas pendet a causis nobis ignotis, quamdiu ipsius existentiam fingimus ; ideoque si ipsius necessitas aut impossibilitas, quae a causis externis pendet, nobis esset nota, nihil etiam de ea potuissemus fingere.

54. Unde sequitur, si detur aliquis Deus aut omniscium quid, nihil prorsus eum posse fingere. Nam quod ad nos attinet, postquam novi me existere, non possum fingere me existere aut non existere ; nec etiam possum fingere elephantem, qui transeat per acus foramen ; nec possum, postquam naturam Dei novi, fingere eum existentem aut non existentem . Idem intelligendum est de chimaera, cuius natura existere implicat. Ex quibus patet id, quod dixi, scilicet quod fictio, de qua hic loquimur, non contingit circa aeternas veritates .

55. Sed antequam ulterius pergam, hic obiter notandum est, quod illa differentia, quae est inter essentiam unius rei et essentiam alterius, ea ipsa sit inter actualitatem aut existentiam eiusdem rei, et inter actualitatem aut existentiam alterius rei ; adeo ut si existentiam ex. gr. Adami tantum per generalem existentiam concipere velimus, idem futurum sit, ac si ad concipiendam ipsius essentiam, ad naturam entis attendamus, ut tandem definiamus, Adamum esse ens. Itaque quo existentia generalius concipitur, eo etiam confusius concipitur faciliusque unicuique rei potest affingi ; e contra, ubi particularius concipitur, clarius tum intelligitur, et difficilius alicui, nisi rei ipsi, ubi non attendimus ad naturae ordinem, affingitur. Quod notatu dignum est.

56. Veniunt iam hic ea consideranda, quae vulgo dicuntur fingi, quamvis clare intelligamus, rem ita sese non habere, uti eam fingimus. Ex. gr. quamvis sciam terram esse rotundam, nihil tamen vetat, quominus alicui dicam terram medium globum esse et tamquam medium pomum auriacum in scutella, aut solem circum terram moveri, et similia. Ad haec si attendamus, nihil videbimus, quod non cohaereat cum iam dictis, modo prius advertamus, nos aliquando potuisse errare, et iam errorum nostrorum esse conscios ; deinde quod possumus fingere, aut ad minimum putare, alios homines in eodem esse errore, aut in eum, ut nos antehac, posse incidere. Hoc, inquam, fingere possumus, quamdiu nullam videmus impossibilitatem nullamque necessitatem. Quando itaque alicui dico, terram non esse rotundam etc., nihil aliud ago, quam in memoriam revoco errorem, quem forte habui aut in quem labi potui, et postea fingo aut puto eum, cui hoc dico, adhuc esse aut posse labi in eundem errorem. Quod, ut dixi, fingo, quamdiu nullam video impossibilitatem nullamque necessitatem ; hanc vero si intellexissem, nihil prorsus fingere potuissem, et tantum dicendum fuisset, me aliquid operatum esse.

57. Superest iam, ut ea etiam notemus, quae in quaestionibus supponuntur ; id quod passim etiam contingit circa impossibilia. Ex. gr. cum dicimus : supponamus hanc candelam ardentem iam non ardere, aut supponamus eam ardere in aliquo spatio imaginario, sive ubi nulla dantur corpora. Quorum similia passim supponuntur, quamvis hoc ultimum clare intelligatur impossibile esse. Sed quando hoc fit, nil prorsus fingitur. Nam primo nihil aliud egi, quam quod in memoriam revocavi aliam candelam non ardentem (aut hanc eandem concepi sine flamma), et quod cogito de ea candela, id ipsum de hac intelligo, quamdiu ad flammam non attendo. In secundo nihil aliud fit, quam abstrahere cogitationes a corporibus circumiacentibus, ut mens se convertat ad solam candelae in se sola spectatae contemplationem ; ut postea concludat candelam nullam habere causam ad sui ipsius destructionem, adeo ut si nulla essent corpora circumiacentia, candela haec ac etiam flamma manerent immutabiles, aut similia. Nulla igitur datur hic fictio, sed verae ac merae assertiones .

58. Transeamus iam ad fictiones, quae versantur circa essentias solas, vel cum aliqua actualitate sive existentia simul. Circa quas hoc maxime venit considerandum, quod, quo mens minus intelligit, et tamen plura percipit, eo maiorem habeat potentiam fingendi, et quo plura intelligit, eo magis illa potentia diminuatur. Eodem ex. gr. modo, quo supra vidimus, nos non posse fingere, quamdiu cogitamus, nos cogitare et non cogitare, sic etiam, postquam novimus naturam corporis, non possumus fingere muscam infinitam ; sive postquam novimus naturam animae , non possumus fingere eam esse quadratam, quamvis omnia verbis possimus effari. Sed, uti diximus, quominus homines norunt naturam, eo facilius multa possunt fingere ; veluti, arbores loqui, homines in momento mutari in lapides, in fontes, apparere in speculis spectra, nihil fieri aliquid, etiam deos in bestias et homines mutari, ac infinita eius generis alia.

59. Aliquis forte putabit, quod fictio fictionem terminat, sed non intellectio ; hoc est, postquam finxi aliquid, et quadam libertate volui assentiri, id sic in rerum natura existere, hoc efficit, ut postea non possimus id alio modo cogitare. Ex. gr. postquam finxi (ut cum iis loquar) naturam corporis talem, mihique ex mea libertate persuadere volui, eam sic realiter existere, non amplius licet muscam v. g. infinitam fingere ; et postquam finxi essentiam animae, eam quadrare non possum etc.

60. Sed hoc examinandum. Primo vel negant vel concedunt nos aliquid posse intelligere. Si concedunt, necessario id ipsum, quod de fictione dicunt, etiam de

intellectione dicendum erit. Si vero hoc negant, videamus nos, qui scimus, nos aliquid scire, quid dicant. Hoc scilicet dicunt, animam posse sentire et multis modis percipere non se ipsam, neque res quae existunt, sed tantum ea, quae nec in se, nec ullibi sunt, hoc est, animam posse sola sua vi creare sensationes aut ideas, quae non sunt rerum ; adeo ut ex parte eam tamquam Deum considerent. Porro dicunt, nos aut animam nostram talem habere libertatem, ut nosmet, aut se, imo suam ipsam libertatem cogat. Nam postquam ea aliquid finxit, et assensum ei praebuit, non potest id alio modo cogitare aut fingere, et etiam ea fictione cogitur, ut etiam alia tali modo cogitentur, ut prima fictio non oppugnetur ; sicut hic etiam coguntur absurda, quae hic recenseo, admittere propter suam fictionem ; ad quae explodenda non defatigabimur ullis demonstrationibus .

61. Sed eos in suis deliriis linquendo, curabimus, ut ex verbis, quae cum ipsis fecimus, aliquid veri ad nostram rem hauriamus, nempe hoc. Mens cum ad rem fictam et sua natura falsam attendit, ut eam pensitet et ntelligat, bonoque ordine ex ea deducat quae sunt deducenda, facile falsitatem patefaciet ; et si res ficta sua natura sit vera, cum mens ad eam attendit, ut eam intelligat, et ex ea bono ordine incipit deducere, quae inde sequuntur, feliciter perget sine ulla interruptione, sicut vidimus, quod ex falsa fictione modo allata statim ad ostendendam eius absurditatem et alias inde deductas praebuit se intellectus.

62. Nullo ergo modo timendum erit, nos aliquid fingere, si modo clare et distincte rem percipiamus. Nam si forte dicamus, homines in momento mutari in bestias, id valde generaliter dicitur, adeo ut nullus detur conceptus, id est, idea sive cohaerentia subiecti et praedicati in mente ; si enim daretur, simul videret medium et causas, quo et cur tale quid factum sit. Deinde nec ad naturam subiecti et praedicati attenditur.

63. Porro, modo prima idea non sit ficta et ex ea ceterae omnes ideae deducantur, paulatim praecipitantia fingendi evanescet. Deinde cum idea ficta non possit esse clara et distincta, sed solummodo confusa, et omnis confusio inde procedat, quod mens rem integram aut ex multis compositam tantum ex parte noscat, et notum ab ignoto non distinguat ; praeterea quod ad multa, quae continentur in unaquaque re, simul attendat sine ulla distinctione ; inde sequitur primo, quod si idea sit alicuius rei simplicissimae, ea non nisi clara et distincta poterit esse. Nam res illa non ex parte, sed tota aut nihil eius innotescere debebit.

64. Sequitur secundo, quod si res, quae componitur ex multis, in partes omnes simplicissimas cogitatione dividatur, et ad unamquamque seorsim attendatur, omnis tum confusio evanescet. Sequitur tertio, quod fictio non possit esse simplex, sed quod fiat ex compositione diversarum idearum confusarum, quae sunt diversarum rerum atque actionum in natura existentium, vel melius ex attentione simul sine assensu ad tales diversas ideas . Nam si esset simplex, esset clara et distincta, et per consequens vera. Si ex compositione idearum distinctarum, esset etiam earum compositio clara et distincta, ac proinde vera. Ex. gr. postquam novimus naturam circuli ac etiam naturam quadrati, iam non possumus ea duo componere, et circulum facere quadratum, aut animam quadratam, et similia.

65. Concludamus iterum breviter, et videamus, quomodo fictio nullo modo sit timenda, ut ea cum veris ideis confundatur. Nam quoad primam, de qua prius locuti sumus, ubi scilicet res clare concipitur, vidimus, quod si ea res, quae clare concipitur, et etiam ipsius existentia sit per se aeterna veritas, nihil circa talem rem poterimus fingere ; sed si existentia rei conceptae non sit aeterna veritas, tantum est curandum, ut existentia rei cum eius essentia conferatur, et simul ad

ordinem naturae attendatur. Quoad secundam fictionem, quam diximus esse simul attentionem sine assensu ad diversas ideas confusas, quae sunt diversarum rerum atque actionum in natura existentium, vidimus etiam rem simplicissimam non posse fingi, sed intelligi, et etiam rem compositam, modo ad partes simplicissimas, ex quibus componitur, attendamus ; imo nec ex ipsis ullas actiones, quae verae non sunt, nos posse fingere. Nam simul cogemur contemplari, quomodo et cur tale quid fiat.

IX. DE IDEA FALSA.

66. HIS SIC intellectis, transeamus iam ad inquisitionem ideae falsae, ut videamus, circa quae versetur, et quomodo nobis possimus cavere, ne in falsas perceptiones incidamus. Quod utrumque non erit nobis iam difficile post inquisitionem ideae fictae. Nam inter ipsas nulla alia datur differentia, nisi quod haec supponat assensum, hoc est (uti iam notavimus) quod nullae offeruntur causae, dum repraesentamina ipsi offeruntur, quibus, sicut fingens, possit colligere, ea non oriri a rebus extra se, et quod fere nihil aliud sit, quam oculis apertis, sive dum vigilamus, somniare. Versatur itaque idea falsa, vel (ut melius loquar) refertur ad existentiam rei, cuius essentia cognoscitur, sive circa essentiam eodem modo ac idea ficta.

67. Quae ad existentiam refertur, emendatur eodem modo ac fictio. Nam si natura rei notae supponat existentiam necessariam, impossibile est, ut circa existentiam illius rei fallamur ; sed si existentia rei non sit aeterna veritas, uti est eius essentia, sed quod necessitas aut impossibilitas existendi pendeat a causis externis, tum cape omnia eodem modo, quo diximus, cum de fictione sermo esset ; nam eodem modo emendatur.

68. Quod attinet ad alteram, quae ad essentias refertur, vel etiam ad actiones, tales perceptiones necessario semper sunt confusae, compositae ex diversis confusis perceptionibus rerum in natura existentium, ut cum hominibus persuadetur, in silvis, in imaginibus, in brutis et ceteris adesse numina ; dari corpora, ex quorum sola compositione fiat intellectus ; cadavera ratiocinari, ambulare, loqui ; Deum decipi, et similia. Sed ideae, quae sunt clarae et distinctae, nunquam possunt esse falsae : Nam ideae rerum, quae clare et distincte concipiuntur, sunt vel simplicissimae, vel compositae ex ideis simplicissimis, id est, a simplicissimis ideis deductae. Quod vero idea simplicissima non queat esse falsa, poterit unusquisque videre, modo sciat, quid sit verum sive intellectus, et simul quid falsum.

69. Nam quod id spectat, quod formam veri constituit, certum est, cogitationem veram a falsa non tantum per denominationem extrinsecam, sed maxime per intrinsecam distingui. Nam si quis faber ordine concepit fabricam aliquam, quamvis talis fabrica nunquam exstiterit, nec etiam unquam exstitura sit, eius nihilominus cogitatio vera est, et cogitatio eadem est, sive fabrica existat, sive minus ; et contra si aliquis dicit, Petrum ex. gr. existere, nec tamen scit, Petrum existere, illa cogitatio respectu illius falsa est, vel si mavis, non est vera ; quamvis Petrus revera existat. Nec haec enunciatio, Petrus existit, vera est, nisi respectu illius, qui certo scit, Petrum existere.

70. Unde sequitur in ideis dari aliquid reale, per quod verae a falsis distinguuntur ; quod quidem iam investigandum erit, ut optimam veritatis normam habeamus (ex data enim verae ideae norma nos nostras cogitationes debere determinare diximus, methodumque cognitionem esse reflexivam), et proprietates intellectus noscamus ; nec dicendum hanc differentiam ex eo oriri, quod cogitatio vera est res cognoscere per primas suas causas, in quo quidem a falsa valde differret, prout eandem supra explicui. Cogitatio enim vera etiam dicitur, quae essentiam alicuius principii obiective involvit, quod causam non habet, et per se et in se cognoscitur.

71. Quare forma verae cogitationis in eadem ipsa cogitatione sine relatione ad alias debet esse sita ; nec obiectum tamquam causam agnoscit, sed ab ipsa intellectus potentia, et natura pendere debet. Nam si supponamus, intellectum ens aliquod novum percepisse, quod nunquam exstitit, sicut aliqui Dei intellectum concipiunt, antequam res crearet (quae sane perceptio a nullo obiecto oriri potuit), et ex tali perceptione alias legitime deduceret, omnes illae cogitationes verae essent, et a nullo obiecto externo determinatae, sed a sola intellectus potentia et natura dependerent. Quare id, quod formam verae cogitationis constituit, in ipsa eadem cogitatione est quaerendum, et ab intellectus natura deducendum.

72. Hoc igitur ut investigetur, ideam aliquam veram ob oculos ponamus, cuius obiectum maxime certo scimus a vi nostra cogitandi pendere, nec obiectum aliquod in natura habere ; in tali enim idea, ut ex iam dictis patet, facilius id, quod volumus, investigare poterimus. Ex. gr. ad formandum conceptum globi fingo ad libitum causam, nempe semicirculum circa centrum rotari, et ex rotatione globum quasi oriri. Haec sane idea vera est, et quamvis sciamus nullum in natura globum sic unquam ortum fuisse, est haec tamen vera perceptio et facillimus modus formandi globi conceptum. Iam notandum hanc perceptionem affirmare semicirculum rotari, quae affirmatio falsa esset, si non esset iuncta conceptui globi vel causae talem motum determinantis, sive absolute, si haec affirmatio nuda esset. Nam tum mens tantum tenderet ad affirmandum solum semicirculi motum, qui nec in semicirculi conceptu continetur, nec ex conceptu causae motum determinantis oritur. Quare falsitas in hoc solo consistit, quod aliquid de aliqua re affirmetur, quod in ipsius quem formavimus conceptu non continetur ; ut motus vel quies de semicirculo. Unde sequitur simplices cogitationes non posse non esse veras, ut simplex semicirculi, motus, quantitatis etc. idea. Quicquid hae affirmationis continent, earum adaequat conceptum, nec ultra se extendit. Quare nobis licet ad libitum sine ullo erroris scrupulo ideas simplices formare.

73. Superest igitur tantum quaerere, qua potentia mens nostra eas formare possit, et quousque ea potentia se extendat ; hoc enim invento facile videbimus summam, ad quam possumus pervenire, cognitionem. Certum enim est, hanc eius potentiam se non extendere in infinitum : Nam cum aliquid de aliqua re affirmamus, quod in conceptu, quem de ea formamus, non continetur, id defectum nostrae perceptionis indicat, sive quod mutilatas quasi et truncatas habemus cogitationes sive ideas. Motum enim semicirculi falsum esse vidimus, ubi nudus in mente est, eum ipsum autem verum, si conceptui globi iungatur, vel conceptui alicuius causae talem motum determinantis. Quod si de natura entis cogitantis sit, uti prima fronte videtur, cogitationes veras sive adaequatas formare, certum est, ideas inadaequatas ex eo tantum in nobis oriri, quod pars sumus alicuius entis cogitantis, cuius quaedam cogitationes ex toto, quaedam ex parte tantum nostram mentem constituunt.

74. Sed quod adhuc venit considerandum, et quod circa fictionem non fuit operae pretium notare, et ubi maxima datur deceptio, est, quando contingit, ut quaedam, quae in imaginatione offeruntur, sint etiam in intellectu, hoc est, quod clare et distincte concipiantur, quod tum, quamdiu distinctum a confuso non distinguitur, certitudo, hoc est, idea vera cum non distinctis commiscetur. Ex. gr. quidam Stoicorum forte audiverunt nomen animae, et etiam quod sit immortalis, quae tantum confuse imaginabantur ; imaginabantur etiam, et simul intelligebant corpora subtilissima cetera omnia penetrare, et a nullis penetrari. Cum haec omnia simul imaginabantur, concomitante certudine huius axiomatis, statim certi reddebantur, mentem esse subtilissima illa corpora, et subtilissima illa corpora non dividi etc.

75. Sed ab hoc etiam liberamur, dum conamur ad normam datae verae ideae omnes nostras perceptiones examinare cavendo, uti initio diximus, ab iis, quas ex auditu aut ab experientia vaga habemus. Adde quod talis deceptio ex eo oritur, quod res nimis abstracte concipiunt ; nam per se satis clarum est, me illud, quod in suo vero obiecto concipio, alteri non posse applicare. Oritur denique etiam

ex eo, quod prima elementa totius naturae non intelligunt ; unde sine ordine procedendo, et naturam cum abstractis, quamvis sint vera axiomata, confundendo, se ipsos confundunt ordinemque naturae pervertunt. Nobis autem, si quam minime abstracte procedamus, et a primis elementis, hoc est, a fonte et origine naturae, quam primum fieri potest, incipiamus, nullo modo talis deceptio erit metuenda.

76. Quod autem attinet ad cognitionem originis naturae, minime est timendum, ne eam cum abstractis confundamus. Nam cum aliquid abstracte concipitur, uti sunt omnia universalia, semper latius comprehenduntur in intellectu, quam revera in natura existere possunt eorum particularia. Deinde cum in natura dentur multa, quorum differentia adeo est exigua, ut fere intellectum effugiat, tum facile (si abstracte concipiantur) potest contingere, ut confundantur. At cum origo naturae, ut postea videbimus, nec abstracte sive universaliter concipi possit, nec latius possit extendi in intellectu, quam revera est, nec ullam habeat similitudinem cum mutabilibus, nulla circa eius ideam metuenda est confusio, modo normam veritatis (quam iam ostendimus) habeamus. Est nimirum hoc ens unicum, infinitum , hoc est, est omne esse, et praeter quod nullum datur esse .

X. DE IDEA DUBIA.

77. HUCUSQUE DE idea falsa. Superest, ut de idea dubia inquiramus, hoc est, ut inquiramus, quaenam sint ea, quae nos possunt in dubium pertrahere, et simul quomodo dubitatio tollatur. Loquor de vera dubitatione in mente, et non de ea, quam passim videmus contingere, ubi scilicet verbis, quamvis animus non dubitet, dicit quis se dubitare. Non est enim methodi hoc emendare, sed potius pertinet ad inquisitionem pertinaciae et eius emendationem.

78. Dubitatio itaque in anima nulla datur per rem ipsam, de qua dubitatur, hoc est, si tantum unica sit idea in anima, sive ea sit vera sive falsa, nulla dabitur dubitatio, neque etiam certitudo, sed tantum talis sensatio. Est enim in se nihil aliud nisi talis sensatio ; sed dabitur per aliam ideam, quae non adeo clara ac distincta est, ut possimus ex ea aliquid certi circa rem, de qua dubitatur, concludere, hoc est, idea, quae nos in dubium coniicit, non est clara et distincta. Ex. gr. si quis nunquam cogitaverit de sensuum fallacia, sive experientia sive quomodocumque sit, nunquam dubitabit, an sol maior aut minor sit, quam apparet. Inde rustici passim mirantur, cum audiunt solem multo maiorem esse, quam globum terrae. Sed cogitando de fallacia sensuum oritur dubitatio , et si quis post dubitationem acquisiverit veram cognitionem sensuum, et quomodo per eorum instrumenta res ad distantiam repraesententur, tum dubitatio iterum tollitur.

79. Unde sequitur, nos non posse veras ideas in dubium vocare ex eo, quod forte aliquis Deus deceptor existat, qui vel in maxime certis nos fallit, nisi quamdiu nullam habemus claram et distinctam Dei ideam, hoc est, si attendamus ad cognitionem, quam de origine omnium rerum habemus, et nihil inveniamus, quod nos doceat, eum non esse deceptorem eadem illa cognitione, qua, cum attendimus ad naturam trianguli, invenimus eius tres angulos aequales esse duobus rectis. Sed si talem cognitionem Dei habemus, qualem habemus trianguli, tum omnis dubitatio tollitur. Et eodem modo, quo possumus pervenire ad talem cognitionem trianguli, quamvis non certo sciamus, an aliquis summus deceptor nos fallat, eodem etiam modo possumus pervenire ad talem Dei cognitionem, quamvis non certo sciamus, an detur quis summus deceptor, et, modo eam habeamus, sufficiet ad tollendam, uti dixi, omnem dubitationem, quam de ideis claris et distinctis habere possumus.

80. Porro si quis recte procedat investigando quae prius sunt investiganda, nulla interrupta concatenatione rerum, et sciat, quomodo quaestiones sint determinandae, antequam ad earum cognitionem accingamur, nunquam nisi certissimas ideas, id est, claras et distinctas habebit. Nam dubitatio nihil aliud est, quam suspensio animi circa aliquam affirmationem aut negationem, quam affirmaret aut negaret, nisi occurreret aliquid, quo ignoto cognitio eius rei debet esse imperfecta. Unde colligitur, quod dubitatio semper oritur ex eo, quod res absque ordine investigentur.

XI. DE MEMORIA ET OBLIVIONE. CONCLUSIO.

81. HAEC SUNT, quae promisi tradere in hac prima parte methodi. Sed ut nihil omittam eorum, quae ad cognitionem intellectus et eius vires possunt conducere, tradam etiam pauca de memoria et oblivione ; ubi hoc maxime venit considerandum, quod memoria corroboretur ope intellectus, et etiam absque ope intellectus. Nam quoad primum, quo res magis est intelligibilis, eo facilius retinetur, et contra, quo minus, eo facilius eam obliviscimur. Ex. gr. si tradam alicui copiam verborum solutorum, ea multo difficilius retinebit, quam si eadem verba in forma narrationis tradam.

82. Corroboratur etiam absque ope intellectus, scilicet a vi, qua imaginatio aut sensus, quem vocant communem, afficitur ab aliqua re singulari corporea. Dico singularem ; imaginatio enim tantum a singularibus afficitur. Nam si quis legerit ex. gr. unam tantum Fabulam amatoriam, eam optime retinebit, quamdiu non legerit plures alias eius generis, quia tum sola viget in imaginatione. Sed si plures sint eiusdem generis, simul omnes imaginamur, et facile confunduntur. Dico etiam corpoream ; nam a solis corporibus afficitur imaginatio. Cum itaque memoria ab intellectu corroboretur, et etiam sine intellectu, inde concluditur, eam quid diversum esse ab intellectu, et circa intellectum in se spectatum nullam dari memoriam, neque oblivionem.

83. Quid ergo erit memoria ? Nihil aliud, quam sensatio impressionum cerebri simul cum cogitatione ad determinatam durationem sensationis ; quod etiam ostendit reminiscentia. Nam ibi anima cogitat de illa sensatione ; sed non sub continua duratione ; et sic idea istius sensationis non est ipsa duratio sensationis, id est, ipsa memoria. An vero ideae ipsae aliquam patiantur corruptionem, videbimus in philosophia. Et si hoc alicui valde absurdum videatur, sufficiet ad nostrum propositum, ut cogitet, quod, quo res est singularior, eo facilius retineatur, sicut ex exemplo comoediae modo allato patet. Porro quo res intelligibilior, eo etiam facilius retinetur. Unde maxime singularem et tantummodo intelligibilem non poterimus non retinere.

84. Sic itaque distinximus inter ideam veram et ceteras perceptiones, ostendimusque, quod ideae fictae, falsae et ceterae habeant suam originem ab imaginatione, hoc est, a quibusdam sensationibus fortuitis (ut sic loquar) atque solutis, quae non oriuntur ab ipsa mentis potentia, sed a causis externis, prout corpus sive somniando sive vigilando varios accipit motus. Vel si placet, hic per imaginationem quicquid velis cape, modo sit quid diversum ab intellectu, et unde anima habeat rationem patientis. Perinde enim est quicquid capias, postquam novimus eandem quid vagum esse, et a quo anima patitur, et simul etiam novimus, quomodo ope intellectus ab eadem liberamur. Quare etiam nemo miretur, me hic nondum probare, dari corpus et alia necessaria, et tamen loqui de imaginatione, de corpore et eius constitutione. Nempe, ut dixi, est perinde quid capiam, postquam novi, esse quid vagum etc.

85. At ideam veram simplicem esse ostendimus aut ex simplicibus compositam, et quae ostendit, quomodo et cur aliquid sit aut factum sit, et quod ipsius effectus obiectivi in anima procedunt ad rationem formalitatis ipsius obiecti ; id quod idem est, quod veteres dixerunt, nempe veram scientiam procedere a causa ad effectus ; nisi quod nunquam, quod sciam, conceperunt, uti nos hic, animam secundum certas leges agentem et quasi aliquod automatum spirituale.

86. Unde, quantum in initio licuit, acquisivimus notitiam nostri intellectus, et talem normam verae ideae, ut iam non vereamur, ne vera cum falsis aut fictis confundamus ; nec etiam mirabimur, cur quaedam intelligamus, quae nullo modo sub imaginationem cadunt, et alia sint in imaginatione, quae prorsus oppugnant intellectum ; alia denique cum intellectu conveniant. Quandoquidem novimus operationes illas, a quibus imaginationes producuntur, fieri secundum alias leges prorsus diversas a legibus intellectus, et animam circa imaginationem tantum habere rationem patientis.

87. Ex quo etiam constat, quam facile ii in magnos errores possunt delabi, qui non accurate distinxerunt inter imaginationem et intellectionem. In hos ex. gr. quod extensio debeat esse in loco, debeat esse finita, cuius partes ab invicem distinguuntur realiter, quod sit primum et unicum fundamentum omnium rerum, et uno tempore maius spatium occupet, quam alio, multaque eiusmodi alia, quae omnia prorsus oppugnant veritatem, ut suo loco ostendemus.

88. Deinde cum verba sint pars imaginationis, hoc est, quod, prout vage ex aliqua dispositione corporis componuntur in memoria, multos conceptus fingamus, ideo non dubitandum, quin etiam verba, aeque ac imaginatio, possint esse causa multorum magnorumque errorum, nisi magnopere ab ipsis caveamus.

89. Adde quod sint constituta ad libitum et ad captum vulgi, adeo ut non sint nisi signa rerum, prout sunt in imaginatione, non autem prout sunt in intellectu ; quod clare patet ex eo, quod omnibus iis, quae tantum sunt in intellectu, et non in imaginatione, nomina imposuerunt saepe negativa, uti sunt, incorporeum, infinitum etc. ; et etiam multa, quae sunt revera affirmativa, negative exprimunt, et contra, uti sunt increatum, independens, infinitum, immortale etc., quia nimirum horum contraria multo facilius imaginamur ; ideoque prius primis hominibus occurrerunt et nomina positiva usurparunt. Multa affirmamus et negamus, quia natura verborum id affirmare et negare patitur, non vero rerum natura ; adeoque hac ignorata facile aliquid falsum pro vero sumeremus.

90. Vitamus praeterea aliam magnam causam confusionis, et quae facit, quominus intellectus ad se reflectat. Nempe cum non distinguimus inter imaginationem et intellectionem, putamus ea, quae facilius imaginamur, nobis esse clariora, et id, quod imaginamur, putamus intelligere. Unde quae sunt postponenda, anteponimus, et sic verus ordo progrediendi pervertitur, nec aliquid legitime concluditur.

XII. METHODI PARS SECUNDA. DE DUPLICI PERCEPTIONE.

91. PORRO, UT tandem ad secundam partem huius methodi perveniamus, proponam primo nostrum scopum in hac methodo, ac deinde media, ut eum attingamus. Scopus itaque est claras et distinctas habere ideas, tales videlicet, quae ex pura mente, et non ex fortuitis motibus corporis factae sint. Deinde omnes ideae ad unam ut redigantur, conabimur eas tali modo concatenare et ordinare, ut mens nostra, quoad eius fieri potest, referat obiective formalitatem naturae, quoad totam et quoad eius partes.

92. Quoad primum, ut iam tradidimus, requiritur ad nostrum ultimum finem, ut res concipiatur vel per solam suam essentiam vel per proximam suam causam. Scilicet si res sit in se, sive, ut vulgo dicitur, causa sui, tum per solam suam essentiam debebit intelligi ; si vero res non sit in se, sed requirat causam, ut existat, tum per proximam suam causam debet intelligi. Nam revera cognitio effectus nihil aliud est, quam perfectiorem causae cognitionem acquirere .

93. Unde nunquam nobis licebit, quamdiu de inquisitione rerum agimus, ex abstractis aliquid concludere, et magnopere cavebimus, ne misceamus ea, quae tantum sunt in intellectu, cum iis, quae sunt in re. Sed optima conclusio erit depromenda ab essentia aliqua particulari affirmativa, sive a vera et legitima definitione. Nam ab axiomatibus solis universalibus non potest intellectus ad singularia descendere, quandoquidem axiomata ad infinita se extendunt, nec intellectum magis ad unum, quam ad aliud singulare contemplandum, determinant.

94. Quare recta inveniendi via est ex data aliqua definitione cogitationes formare : quod eo felicius et facilius procedet, quo rem aliquam melius definiverimus. Quare cardo totius huius secundae Methodi partis in hoc solo versatur, nempe in conditionibus bonae definitionis cognoscendis, et deinde in modo eas inveniendi. Primo itaque de conditionibus definitionis agam.

XIII. DE CONDITIONIBUS DEFINITIONIS.

95. DEFINITIO UT dicatur perfecta, debebit intimam essentiam rei explicare, et cavere, ne eius loco propria quaedam usurpemus. Ad quod explicandum, ut alia exempla omittam, ne videar aliorum errores velle detegere, adferam tantum exemplum alicuius rei abstractae, quae perinde est, quomodocumque definiatur, circuli scilicet ; quod si definiatur, esse figuram aliquam, cuius lineae, a centro ad circumferentiam ductae, sunt aequales, nemo non videt talem definitionem minime explicare essentiam circuli, sed tantum eius aliquam proprietatem. Et quamvis, ut dixi, circa figuras et cetera entia rationis hoc parum referat, multum tamen refert circa entia physica et realia ; nimirum, quia proprietates rerum non intelliguntur, quamdiu earum essentiae ignorantur ; si autem has praetermittimus, necessario concatenationem intellectus, quae naturae concatenationem referre debet, pervertemus, et a nostro scopo prorsus aberrabimus.

96. Ut itaque hoc vitio liberemur, erunt haec observanda in definitione.

I. Si res sit creata, definitio debebit, uti diximus, comprehendere causam proximam. Ex. gr. circulus secundum hanc legem sic esset definiendus : eum esse figuram, quae describitur a linea quacunque, cuius alia extremitas est fixa, alia mobilis, quae definitio clare comprehendit causam proximam.

II. Talis requiritur conceptus rei sive definitio, ut omnes proprietates rei, dum sola, non autem cum aliis coniuncta, spectatur, ex ea concludi possint, uti in hac definitione circuli videre est. Nam ex ea clare concluditur omnes lineas a centro ad circumferentiam ductas aequales esse ; quodque hoc sit necessarium requisitum definitionis, adeo per se est attendenti manifestum, ut non videatur operae pretium in ipsius demonstratione morari, nec etiam ostendere ex hoc secundo requisito omnem definitionem debere esse affirmativam. Loquor de affirmatione intellectiva, parum curando verbalem, quae propter verborum penuriam poterit fortasse aliquando negative exprimi, quamvis affirmative intelligatur.

97. Definitionis vero rei increatae haec sunt requisita.

I. Ut omnem causam secludat, hoc est, obiectum nullo alio praeter suum esse egeat ad sui explicationem.

II. Ut data eius rei definitione nullus maneat locus quaestioni, an sit.

III. Ut nulla quoad mentem habeat substantiva, quae possint adiectivari, hoc est, ne per aliqua abstracta explicetur.

IV. Et ultimo (quamvis hoc notare non sit valde necessarium) requiritur, ut ab eius definitione omnes eius proprietates concludantur. Quae etiam omnia attendenti accurate fiunt manifesta.

98. Dixi etiam, quod optima conclusio erit depromenda ab essentia aliqua particulari affirmativa. Quo enim specialior est idea, eo distinctior, ac proinde clarior est. Unde cognitio particularium quam maxime nobis quaerenda est.

XIV. DE MEDIIS QUIBUS RES AETERNAS COGNOSCUNTUR.

99. QUOAD ORDINEM vero, et ut omnes nostrae perceptiones ordinentur, et uniantur, requiritur, ut, quamprimum fieri potest et ratio postulat, inquiramus, an detur quoddam ens, et simul quale, quod sit omnium rerum causa, ut eius essentia obiectiva sit etiam causa omnium nostrarum idearum, et tum mens nostra, uti diximus, quam maxime referet naturam. Nam et ipsius essentiam et ordinem et unionem habebit obiective. Unde possumus videre, apprime nobis esse necessarium, ut semper a rebus physicis sive ab entibus realibus omnes nostras ideas deducamus, progrediendo, quoad eius fieri potest, secundum seriem causarum ab uno ente reali ad aliud ens reale, et ita quidem, ut ad abstracta et universalia non transeamus, sive ut ab iis aliquid reale non concludamus, sive ut ea ab aliquo reali non concludantur. Utrumque enim verum progressum intellectus interrumpit.

100. Sed notandum, me hic per seriem causarum et realium entium non intelligere seriem rerum singularium mutabilium, sed tantummodo seriem rerum fixarum aeternarumque. Seriem enim rerum singularium mutabilium impossibile foret humanae imbecillitati assequi, cum propter earum omnem numerum superantem multitudinem, tum propter infinitas circumstantias in una et eadem re, quarum unaquaeque potest esse causa, ut res existat, aut non existat. Quandoquidem earum existentia nullam habet connexionem cum earundem essentia, sive (ut iam diximus) non est aeterna veritas.

101. Verumenimvero neque etiam opus est, ut earum seriem intelligamus ; siquidem rerum singularium mutabilium essentiae non sunt depromendae ab earum serie sive ordine existendim, cum hic nihil aliud nobis praebeat praeter denominationes extrinsecas, relationes, aut ad summum circumstantias ; quae omnia longe absunt ab intima essentia rerum. Haec vero tantum est petenda a fixis atque aeternis rebus, et simul a legibus in iis rebus, tamquam in suis veris codicibus inscriptis, secundum quas omnia singularia et fiunt et ordinantur ; imo haec mutabilia singularia adeo intime atque essentialiter (ut sic dicam) ab iis fixis pendent, ut sine iis nec esse, nec concipi possint. Unde haec fixa et aeterna, quamvis sint singularia, tamen ob eorum ubique praesentiam ac latissimam potentiam erunt nobis tamquam universalia sive genera definitionum rerum singularium mutabilium, et causae proximae omnium rerum.

102. Sed cum hoc ita sit, non parum difficultatis videtur subesse, ut ad horum singularium cognitionem pervenire possimus ; nam omnia simul concipere res est longe supra humani intellectus vires. Ordo autem, ut unum ante aliud intelligatur, uti diximus, non est petendus ab eorum existendi serie, neque etiam a rebus aeternis. Ibi enim omnia haec sunt simul natura. Unde alia auxilia necessario sunt quaerenda praeter illa, quibus utimur ad res aeternas earumque leges intelligendum ; attamen non est huius loci ea tradere, neque etiam opus est, nisi postquam rerum aeternarum earumque infallibilium legum sufficientem acquisiverimus cognitionem, sensuumque nostrorum natura nobis innotuerit.

103. Antequam ad rerum singularium cognitionem accingamur, tempus erit, ut ea auxilia tradamus, quae omnia eo tendent, ut nostris sensibus sciamus uti, et experimenta certis legibus et ordine facere, quae sufficient ad rem, quae inquiritur, determinandam, ut tandem ex iis concludamus, secundum quasnam rerum aeternarum leges facta sit, et intima eius natura nobis innotescat, ut suo loco

ostendam. Hic, ut ad propositum revertar, tantum enitar tradere, quae videntur necessaria, ut ad cognitionem rerum aeternarum pervenire possimus, earumque definitiones formemus conditionibus supra traditis.

104. Quod ut fiat, revocandum in memoriam id, quod supra diximus, nempe quod, ubi mens ad aliquam cogitationem attendit, ut ipsam perpendat, bonoque ordine ex ea deducat quae legitime sunt deducenda, si ea falsa fuerit, falsitatem deteget ; sin autem vera, tum feliciter perget sine ulla interruptione res veras inde deducere ; hoc, inquam, ad nostram rem requiritur. Nam ex nullo alio fundamento cogitationes nostrae determinari queunt.

105. Si igitur rem omnium primam investigare velimus, necesse est dari aliquod fundamentum, quod nostras cogitationes eo dirigat. Deinde quia methodus est ipsa cognitio reflexiva, hoc fundamentum, quod nostras cogitationes dirigere debet, nullum aliud potest esse, quam cognitio eius, quod formam veritatis constituit, et cognitio intellectus eiusque proprietatum et virium. Hac enim acquisita fundamentum habebimus, a quo nostras cogitationes deducemus, et viam, qua intellectus, prout eius fert capacitas, pervenire poterit ad rerum aeternarum cognitionem, habita nimirum ratione virium intellectus.

XV. DE VIRIBUS INTELLECTUS EIUSQUE PROPRIETATIBUS.

106. QUOD SI vero ad naturam cogitationis pertineat veras formare ideas, ut in prima parte ostensum, hic iam inquirendum, quid per vires et potentiam intellectus intelligamus. Quoniam vero praecipua nostrae methodi pars est, vires intellectus eiusque naturam optime intelligere, cogimur necessario (per ea, quae in hac secunda parte methodi tradidi), haec deducere ex ipsa cogitationis, et intellectus definitione.

107. Sed hucusque nullas regulas inveniendi definitiones habuimus, et quia eas tradere non possumus, nisi cognita natura sive definitione intellectus eiusque potentia, hinc sequitur, quod vel definitio intellectus per se debet esse clara, vel nihil intelligere possumus. Illa tamen per se absolute clara non est. Attamen quia eius proprietates, ut omnia, quae ex intellectu habemus, clare et distincte percipi nequeunt, nisi cognita earum natura ; ergo definitio intellectus per se innotescet, si ad eius proprietates, quas clare et distincte intelligimus, attendamus. Intellectus igitur proprietates hic enumeremus easque perpendamus, deque nostris innatis instrumentis agere incipiamus.

108. Intellectus proprietates, quas praecipue notavi et clare intelligo, hae sunt.

I. Quod certitudinem involvat, hoc est, quod sciat res ita esse formaliter, ut in ipso obiective continentur.

II. Quod quaedam percipiat, sive quasdam formet ideas absolute, quasdam ex aliis. Nempe quantitatis ideam format absolute, nec ad alias attendit cogitationes ; motus vero ideas non, nisi attendendo ad ideam quantitatis.

III. Quas absolute format, infinitatem exprimunt ; at determinatas ex aliis format. Ideam enim quantitatis, si eam per causam percipit, tum per quantitatem determinat, ut cum ex motu alicuius plani corpus, ex motu lineae vero planum, ex motu denique puncti lineam oriri percipit ; quae quidem perceptiones non inserviunt ad intelligendam, sed tantum ad determinandam quantitatem. Quod inde apparet, quia eas quasi ex motu oriri concipimus, cum tamen motus non percipiatur nisi percepta quantitate, et motum etiam ad formandam lineam in infinitum continuare possumus, quod minime possemus facere, si non haberemus ideam infinitae quantitatis.

IV. Ideas positivas prius format, quam negativas.

V. Res non tam sub duratione, quam sub quadam specie aeternitatis percipit et numero infinito ; vel potius ad res percipiendas, nec ad numerum, nec ad durationem attendit. Cum autem res imaginatur, eas sub certo numero, determinata duratione et quantitate percipit.

VI. Ideae, quas claras et distinctas formamus, ita ex sola necessitate nostrae naturae sequi videntur, ut absolute a sola nostra potentia pendere videantur ; confusae autem contra. Nobis enim invitis saepe formantur.

VII. Ideas rerum, quas intellectus ex aliis format, multis modis mens determinare potest ; ut ad determinandum ex. gr. planum ellipseos, fingit stylum chordae adhaerentem circa duo centra moveri, vel concipit infinita puncta eandem semper et certam rationem ad datam aliquam rectam lineam habentia, vel conum plano aliquo obliquo sectum, ita ut angulus inclinationis maior sit angulo verticis coni, vel aliis infinitis modis.

VIII. Ideae quo plus perfectionis alicuius obiecti exprimunt, eo perfectiores sunt. Nam fabrum, qui fanum aliquod excogitavit, non ita admiramur, ac illum, qui templum aliquod insigne excogitavit.

109. Reliqua, quae ad cogitationem referuntur, ut amor, laetitia etc. nihil moror ; nam nec ad nostrum institutum praesens faciunt, nec etiam possunt concipi, nisi percepto intellectu. Nam perceptione omnino sublata ea omnia tolluntur.

110. Ideae falsae et fictae nihil positivum habent (ut abunde ostendimus), per quod falsae aut fictae dicuntur ; sed ex solo defectu cognitionis ut tales considerantur. Ideae ergo falsae et fictae, quatenus tales, nihil nos de essentia cogitationis docere possunt ; sed haec petenda ex modo recensitis proprietatibus positivis, hoc est, iam aliquid commune statuendum est, ex quo hae proprietates necessario sequantur, sive quo dato hae necessario dentur, et quo sublato haec omnia tollantur.

Reliqua desiderantur.

THE PRINCIPLES OF
CARTESIAN PHILOSOPHY

PREFACE

Baruch Spinoza, the Dutch rabbi without congregation, was often referred to as the thinker of finalities. He did not hesitate to step where Descartes had hesitated and where his religious teachers turned back.

Spinoza declared when others hinted, and raised his voice to a clamor when others dared little more than whisper. He thus drew the brunt of orthodoxy in attack upon himself and became the anti-Christ of seventeenth-century Europe, that grand epoch which marked the end of Scholasticism and the dawn of the Enlightenment. He walked the crimson path of martyrdom, bevenomed by Christians, denounced by his kinsmen and denied even by his early admirers, who, though sparked by his brilliance, fled in fear of its inherent danger.

The flame of Spinozism shone across the lands of Europe, cold and cutting to the bigots, an inspiration to those spiritually yearning in the chains of traditional circumspection.

For a hundred years Spinoza slept the slumber of oblivion following the nightmare of persecution. Then in the years of the American and the French Revolutions the tortured spirit of the lonely rabbi was lifted from its darkness to the summit of philosophical esteem by the hands of such men as Goethe, Herder, Shelley, Lessing and others.

Baruch Spinoza was born in 1632, a small merchant's son, in Amsterdam, the "New Jerusalem" of that day. His father, a crypto-Jew, had fled the latter-day Inquisition of Portugal to found a new home in Holland. Hundreds of his kinsmen had taken sail to the same protective harbor in order to renew the practice of their ancient faith, which they had denied under threat and terror.

For some, life as pseudo-Catholics had lasted too long and even such zealots as Rabbi Isaak Uziel (died 1622) could not completely eradicate its traces. Uziel's successors, Rabbis Saul Levi Morteira, Isaak Aboab da Fonseca, and the tireless Menasseh ben Israel—whose work of talmudic "reconciliation" dominated the Amsterdam rabbinical school which sent a formidable new generation of Jewish teachers and scholars into the world—were deeply grounded in Torah, Talmud and Kabalah, the three fountainheads of Israel.

In this rabbinical school the young Spinoza received his training. In early years he was informed of the many attempts by Jews and Protestants alike to demythologize the Torah, to discredit the Talmud and to disparage the Kabalah.

Spinoza was an eager student and, as visitors to his home reported, a respected one, but in adolescence he seems already to have been inclined towards skepticism. He was not satisfied with Rabbi ben Israel's efforts to "even out" discrepancies and contradictions within the Bible and the Talmud and he rejected vehemently the numerology, word play and miracle lore of the Kabalah. He attached himself strongly, however, to the profound spirituality of the Kabalah, its cardinal concept of God being the Ain Soph—the Endless One—Whose Eternal Being (Elohim) lives in the soul of man (Shekinah). The Kabalistic mystic teaching that man's love of God and man's love to man are one and the same thing is found time and again in Spinoza's profound "Man can be a God to Man."

The Kabalistic concept of the Zaddik, the Sage, who lives a life of perfection guided only by reason, justice and generosity, is close to Spinoza's "Free Man" who like a tower in the wind is not subject to the great avarices, greed, lust and glory, but lives rather in equanimity and security, forever conscious of the idea of God or Creative Nature (Tikkun).

As his library and correspondence indicate, Spinoza was well acquainted with the Hebrew philosophies of Ibn Ezra, Maimonides, Gersonides, Chasdai Crescas, Leo Abravanel and others. His statements on seeing the world sub specie aeternitatis can be traced directly to the medieval Hebraists.

While Spinoza's father was alive, the young theologian seemed to have constrained his rising opposition to traditionalism. In 1654 Michael Spinoza died. In 1656 Baruch Spinoza was expelled from the Amsterdam synagogue, largely because of the pressure of the Christian community.

Looking for a way to earn his living, Spinoza became a tutor in Hebrew at the Latin College of Franciscus Affinius van den Enden, a runaway Jesuit, natural scientist and dedicated Cartesian. Spinoza's friendship with van den Enden was of decisive influence upon his career. Rapidly the young tutor acquired Latin, history and mathematics; he became so proficient in the latter that he commenced a textbook on algebra.

We have a number of books and projects from this period in Spinoza's life, set down for his students: an Apologia in Spanish concerning his faith (this manuscript, as well as the pages on algebra, are still undiscovered); an essay on the improvement of the mind; a Hebrew grammar (fragmentary); a book on God; and the present presentation of Descartes's philosophical principles and metaphysics.

Spinoza eagerly absorbed the philosophy of Descartes. Here he found a man after his own mind, a doubter, a searcher, a breaker of tradition. He became one of the many bright young followers of the grandiose Frenchman, who also had fled to Holland for sanctuary.

But contrary to Descartes, Spinoza had no room in his universe for a Church God besides God the Substance, nor for the concept of sin based on the premise of what he considered nonexistent, "free will." To Spinoza there was no good nor evil except in man's mind; no free will, only awareness of an act.

Virtue to him was its own reward; God, or natura naturans, not a punishing Lord but ens perfectissimum, the Ever-Being, acting according to timeless laws. To Spinoza the sinner was only a fool and the virtuous and free man a sage, since the greatest good leads also to the greatest happiness. Therefore the most ethical deed is to be most selfish in realizing one's inner self. Self-preservation is the Way to Virtue, and happiness a guide to self-improvement. Supreme Egoism is Egoism Supreme. To live by desire is the highest form of ethical conduct, but desire that springs from reason and not from confusion or affectations.

Spinoza did not come to Descartes empty-handed. He came with a mind full of ancient Hebrew wisdom and a strong wish to break with the morbid past and the presence of a Scholastic Europe. Descartes became his teacher and leader, but he went beyond the earth-shaking Frenchman deep into the finalities of One God and One Soul experiencing its essence in union with Him, dedicated to a life of reason, kindness and devotion.

Only in a few instances did Spinoza cite exact quotations from the writings of Descartes. He added brief explanations to the latter's axioms strongly supporting the point of view that in his mind not all was axiomatic with the Cartesian axioms, indicating that Spinoza would rather have seen some of them presented as propositions.

There is no doubt that in the given era of seventeenth-century Europe the mathematical investigation of philosophical themata by means of axioms, definitions and postulates seemed to hold the key to certainty. However, Spinoza did not concur in Descartes' limitation of knowledge by the confines of its procedure, nor did he accede to Descartes' hidden postulates of Divine Providence beyond the finite substances of mind and matter with man acting out in free will within them.

Rather, Spinoza admitted to only one substance, natura naturans or Creative Nature, which man in his limitations conceives under two infinite attributes— namely, mind and matter—but which in reality does perexist (substantia) in innumerable attributes of which only these two are within man's vision.

Consequently, this Infinite Substance is not a creation of God but God Himself in His creative process, and man's so-called free will is no more than awareness of being driven in a certain direction among the oceanic motions of existence. In the words of Goethe, "One thinks he is pushing whilst being pushed."

I personally think that the illustrious Frenchman was not unaware of his self-imposed dualism but that he decided in view of the distressing cultural scene of his time to let caution be his guide.

Descartes paid homage to the Church and even managed to reach the protecting hand of Cardinal Mazarin. Learning of Galileo's predicament, the philosopher offered to the pyre his Du Monde, based on Copernican theories. Descartes was not the man to go the way of Giordano Bruno, who was burned alive in Rome in 1600 for saying what Descartes avoided.

Spinoza too was hesitant about writing the present work, lest his intimate personal views penetrate the cautious Cartesian structure and betray what his later works propounded. I am almost sure that these final thoughts were not unknown to Descartes, though hidden in the depths of his heart.

The dichotomy of Cartesian Catholicism was so deep that his contemporaries, Catholics and Protestants alike, with a few important exceptions, rejected, derided and persecuted him.

After a youth spent in a Jesuit college and dedicated mainly to mathematics, he refused to submit to the burdensome academic discipline of the world of Scholasticism and took up a career as mercenary soldier in various armies. After a brief return to Paris, he left for a freer Holland, where, like Spinoza, he led a life dedicated to philosophy and its liberation from the Scholastic yoke.

Even there he was subject to Church harassment, both Catholic and Protestant, and moved his domicile almost twenty times. In fact, he once had to appeal to the Prince of Orange for protection. The leader of a large Calvinist group in Holland, the Rector of the University of Utrecht, Gisbertus Voetius, had his writing banned and urged book burning and severe punishment.

In 1663, only thirteen years after Descartes's death, his books were placed on the Papal Index and in 1671 the teaching of his philosophy was prohibited at the University of Paris.

It is interesting to note that in the following centuries this very system of Cartesian reasoning was employed by Catholic critics to attack the theories of Spinoza, who in his later years threw off the saving discretion of his much admired teacher and spelled out the secret dreams of Descartes.

With his unresolved "dualism," his gentle obeisance to Rome and his indulgence of a bit of illogical voluntarism, Descartes, the dedicated mathematician and founder of analytical geometry, managed to head a gigantic wave of rationalism that finally broke the Scholastic bastions of Europe.

No man has done so much to free the mind of modern man as this René Descartes. His influence can be compared only with the impact of Charles Darwin in the nineteenth century.

In his lifetime and during the following centuries school after school closed its doors to the thoughts of this ungainly little bearded man, but man's yearning for truth, once detected or even envisioned, was touched by the greatness of Cartesianism, its elevation of reason to competence and of doubt as the sole gate to knowledge.

And what held good for Cartesianism was relevant equally to Spinozism, its final consequence. The pillorying of Descartes and of Spinoza placed their teaching in the focus of studious attention and the impies novateurs became the advance guard of a new world.

The casual reader may perhaps wonder how such remote essays as those before us here could have had the great and liberating effects they did. Let him be reminded of the primitiveness of ancient weapons such as wooden catapults and battering rams with which whole cities and civilizations were conquered.

Descartes and Spinoza represent the best in intellectual leadership in critical times when a minor deviation from Scholastic Aristotelianism could and did lead to a kind of Church inquisitiveness that was a deterrent to all but a few.

The work before us appeared in Latin in 1663 carrying Spinoza's name as author, the only book published during his lifetime under his name. It was almost immediately translated into Dutch, indicating the wide popularity Descartes and Spinoza enjoyed, even in nonacademic circles.

Spinoza was assisted in its preparation by his tutor and later teaching associate, Franciscus Affinius van den Enden, and his friend Lodewijk Meyer, a physician and poet.

DAGOBERT D. RUNES

PART I

INTRODUCTION

Before entering upon the propositions themselves and their proofs, it seemed fitting to offer a succinct explanation why Descartes questioned everything, in what manner he discovered the firm foundations of knowledge, and finally by what means he freed himself from all his doubts. All this matter we should certainly have reduced to a mathematical orderliness, had we not considered the prolixity necessary for its presentation a hindrance for a proper understanding of the entire subject that ought to be viewed, as in the case of a picture, by a comprehensive survey.

Descartes, then, proceeding with the utmost caution in the investigation of nature, attempted:

1. to reject all pre-conceived notions;

2. to find the bases for all necessary superstructures;

3. to discover the cause of error;

4. to understand everything clearly and distinctly.

In order to attain the first, second, and third objectives, he proceeds to question everything; not indeed as a skeptic, for whom the final end is nothing but doubt, but with a view to freeing his mind from all pre-conceptions and hence to discover ultimately the solid and irrefutable bases of knowledge that he could not fail to discover, if such exist. For the true principles of knowledge must be so lucid and convincing that they require no proof, exclude all risk of doubt, and make any proof impossible without them. After prolonged doubt, Descartes discovered such principles. Upon their discovery, it was not difficult for him to distinguish truth from falsity, to discover the cause of error, and furthermore to take precautions not to assume what is false and doubtful as truth and certainty.

To reach the fourth and last objective, that is, to understand clearly and distinctly, his principal rule was to review all the simple ideas, of which all the others are composed, and to examine them severally. For if he could perceive simple ideas clearly and distinctly, he would doubtless understand all the other ideas composed of these simple ones, with the same clarity and perspicuity. With these preliminary remarks, we shall briefly explain how Descartes called everything into question, found the true principles of knowledge, and liberated himself from the difficulties of doubt.

Universal Doubt

First of all he considers all things perceived by the senses, namely: heaven, earth, and such notions, and even his own person; all these things he had until then believed to exist in the scheme of Nature. And he doubts their certainty, because his own senses had sometimes deceived him and in his dreams had often convinced him that many things really had an objective existence that he had afterward discovered to be illusory; and finally because he had heard others, even in waking moments, assert that they felt pain in limbs that they had long since lost.

Therefore it was not without reason that he was able to doubt the existence even of his own body.

From all these circumstances he was able to deduce rightly that the senses were not a very strong foundation on which to build the superstructure of all knowledge—for they can be called in question—but that certainty depends on other, more convincing principles. To pursue such speculations further, he next considers all the universals, such as material nature in general and its extent, likewise shape, quantity, and so on, and also all the mathematical truths. Although these ideas seemed to him more convincing than all those that he had experienced by the sense, he still found a reason for doubting them; since others too had been mistaken about them, and particularly since a certain old notion had been implanted in his mind that a God existed, all-powerful, by whom he had been created just as he was, and who had perhaps made it possible for him to be deceived about those ideas that seemed very clear to him. By this means he questioned everything.

Discovery of the Basis of All Knowledge

To discover the true principles of knowledge, he investigated next whether he had called into question everything that could come within his thought: thus he would examine whether there was not something left perhaps that he had not yet doubted. If indeed he found anything, by such a method of doubting, that could not be called in question for any of the preceding reasons, or for any other reason, he rightly considered that he could accept it as a basis on which to build the superstructure of all his knowledge. And although he now appeared to doubt everything—for he had doubted equally both the notions that he had received through the senses, and those that he perceived through comprehension only—still there was something left to be examined, namely, himself who doubted thus; not in so far as he was composed of a head, hands, and other members of the body, all matters of doubt; but only in so far as he doubted, thought, and so on.

After a careful examination, he realized that he could entertain doubt on this point for none of the previously mentioned reasons. For, whether the thinking process persists in sleep or in wakefulness, he still thinks and is; whether others were in error about other subjects, or even himself, none the less they existed, since they were in error. Nor could he imagine any author of his own nature, however cunning, who could deceive him in this regard; for it must be granted that he himself existed as long as he supposed himself to be deceived. Finally, whatever other cause for doubt might be conceived, none could be adduced that did not at the same time make him overwhelmingly certain of his own existence. Furthermore, adducing more reasons for doubt meant adducing also more proofs to convince him of his own existence. So much so, that wherever he turned to doubt, he was none the less constrained to exclaim: I doubt, I think, therefore I am.

With the discovery of this truth he likewise found the basis of all the sciences; and even a standard and rule for all the other truths, namely: Whatever is perceived as clearly and distinctly as this truth is true.

That no other basis for knowledge than this is possible is abundantly and more than sufficiently clear from what has preceded, since all the other notions can most readily be called in question, but this one cannot be questioned in any manner whatever. However, in regard to this principle, it must first of all be observed that the statement I doubt, I think, therefore I am is not a syllogism, whose major premise has been omitted. For, if it were a syllogism, the premises ought to have been clearer and better known than the conclusion itself, therefore I am: and so I am would not be the first basis of all knowledge; besides, it would not be a certain conclusion, for its truth would depend on universal premises that the author had long since called in question. So I think, therefore I am is a single proposition, equivalent to this one: I am a thinking being.

Furthermore, to avoid confusion in what follows (for the matter must be perceived clearly and distinctly), we must understand what we are. For, once this is clearly and distinctly understood, our being will not be confused with others. To deduce this therefore from what precedes, our author thus continues.

He recalls in memory all the thoughts that he once had regarding himself: that his soul was a subtle body similar to wind, fire, or air, pervading the thicker parts of the body; that his body was more familiar to him than his soul, and that he had a clearer and more distinct perception of it. He found that all this was manifestly at variance with what he had until then understood. For it was possible for him to doubt his body, but not his existence in so far as he could think. Moreover, not perceiving this clearly or distinctly, he consequently had to reject it as false, according to the method that he had proposed for himself. Hence, since he could not, considering what he already knew of himself, recognize the relation of these questions to himself, he proceeded to investigate further what properly belonged to his being, what he had been unable to doubt, and on account of which he was forced to affirm his existence.

Such are the following notions: He must beware of self-deception; he wanted to comprehend many concepts; he questioned everything that he could not comprehend; up to this time he had posited one truth only; he denied everything else, rejecting it as false; even in spite of himself he imagined many things; finally, he observed many things that appeared to come from the senses. Since, equally evidently, his existence rested on each one of these assertions and since he was unable to view any one of them as among the ideas that he had questioned, and finally since they could all be conceived under the same attribute, it followed that they were all truths and belonged to his nature. And so, in saying I think, he understood all these modes of thought: doubt, understanding, affirmation, denial, wishing, not wishing, imagination, and feeling.

It must first of all be observed—and this will be very useful in what follows, where the distinction between mind and matter is discussed:

1st. These modes of thought are clearly and distinctly comprehended without other questions that are still in doubt.

2nd. The clear and distinct concept that we have of these modes of thought is rendered obscure and confused, if we wish to add to them something that still remains in doubt.

Release from All Doubts

Finally, to reach assurance on what he had questioned and to remove all doubt, he proceeded to inquire into the nature of the most perfect Being and on its existence. For, upon discovering the existence of a most perfect Being, by whose power all things are produced and conserved, and whose nature refutes the possibility of his being an impostor, the reason for doubt, that he entertained through his ignorance of his true cause, will be eliminated. For he will know that the faculty of distinguishing the true from the false was not given to him by a God supremely good and veracious to produce deception. And so the mathematical truths and all those things that appear very evident to him will not admit of any suspicion whatever. Then he advances a step forward to eliminate the other causes of doubt and inquiries: How does it happen that we are sometimes mistaken? When he discovered that this arises from our own use of free will in giving assent even to what we perceived only confusedly, he was at once able to conclude that he could avoid error in the future, provided he gave assent to clear and distinctive perceptions only. Each one may easily achieve this of his own accord, since he has the power of restraining his will and confining it within the limits of the understanding. But as, in early youth, we acquire many preconceptions from which we are not easily liberated, he proceeds, in order to free us so that we accept nothing that we do not clearly and distinctly perceive, to review all the simple notions and ideas, of which all our thoughts are composed; to examine each one separately, in order to discover whatever is obscure in each of them. Thus he will be in a position to make an easy distinction between what is clear and what is obscure, and from clear and distinct thoughts, and so to discover easily the real distinction between the soul and the body: what is clear and what is obscure in the perceptions that we experience by the senses; and lastly, the difference between sleep and wakefulness. Thereupon, he could no longer doubt his wakeful periods or be deceived by the sense; and thus he emancipated himself from all the doubts previously considered.

But, before I stop at this point, I must, it appears, give a satisfactory reply to those who argue as follows: Since the existence of God is not known to us by itself, it does not seem that we can ever be certain of anything: nor will the existence of God ever be known to us. For from uncertain premises (and we saw that everything is uncertain as long as we are unaware of our origin) no certainty can be reached.

To resolve this difficulty, Descartes replies thus: From the fact that we do not yet know whether perhaps the author of our origin has treated us such as to be deceived, even in what appears to us most evident, we cannot in the slightest degree doubt what we know clearly and distinctly by itself, or by reasoning, so long as we give our attention to it; we can doubt only what we previously proved to be true, the memory of which can recur, when we no longer regard the reasons that led to these conclusions and which we have forgotten. Therefore, although the existence of God can be known not by itself but only by some other thing, we shall still be able to attain positive knowledge of God's existence, provided we pay the most careful attention to all the premises from which we draw this conclusion. See Principles, Part I, article 13, and the Response to the Two Objections, No. 3 and the end of the Fifth Meditation.

But, since this reply does not satisfy certain questioners, I shall offer another one. We have seen in the preceding arguments, when we spoke of the certainty and the evidence of our existence, that we reached this conclusion from the fact that, in whatever direction we turned our mental gaze, we encountered no reason for doubt that did not assure us, by that very fact, of our existence; whether we considered our own nature, or whether we imagined the author of our nature as a cunning impostor, or finally whether we appealed to any other reason for doubt outside ourselves; a condition that we never hitherto found present in any other matter. For, although, if we consider the nature of, for example, the Triangle, we are forced to conclude that its three angles are equal to two right angles, we cannot however draw the same conclusion from the fact that perhaps we are deceived by the author of our nature: whereas we thus reached the most certain conclusion of our existence. Therefore we are not forced to conclude, wherever we turn our mental gaze, that the three angles of a Triangle are equal to two right angles, but on the contrary we find a reason for doubt, because we have no idea of God such as to make us think it is impossible for God to be an impostor. For it is just as easy for one who does not have a true idea of God, that we now suppose we do not have, to conceive his author as an impostor or as not an impostor: just as, for the person who has no idea of a Triangle, it is as easy to conceive its three angles as equal or as not equal to two right angles.

Hence we grant that, apart from our existence, we cannot be absolutely certain of anything, however carefully we consider its demonstration, so long as we have no clear and distinct conception of God that obliges us to declare that God is supremely veracious, just as the idea that we have of the Triangle forces us to conclude that its three angles are equal to two right angles; but we deny that we cannot on that account attain a knowledge of anything. For, as is clear from all that has just been said, the crux of the entire question rests on this point only: that we can form a concept of God that does not induce us to conceive him, equally well, as being an impostor, but that forces us to affirm that he is supremely veracious. For as soon as we form such an idea, the reason for doubting the mathematical truths is removed. For, wherever we turn our mental gaze, to question any of these truths, we shall encounter nothing from which we ought not to conclude that this truth is quite certain, as in the case of our existence. For example, if, after attaining the idea of God, we carefully consider the nature of the Triangle, this idea will compel us to assert that its three angles are equal to two right angles; but if we consider the idea of God, it will force us to assert that he is supremely veracious, the author and the continuous preserver of our nature and hence does not deceive us in regard to this truth respecting the Triangle.

It will be no less impossible for us to think, on considering the idea of God (that we assume we have now discovered), that he is an impostor than, on considering the idea of the Triangle, to think that its three angles are not equal to two right angles. And, just as we can form such an idea of a Triangle, although we do not know whether the author of our nature is deceiving us, so we can also make the idea of God clear to us and set it before our gaze, although doubtful at the same time whether the author of our nature deceives us in all respects. And, provided we have this idea, however we may have acquired it, it will be sufficient, as has now been shown, to remove all doubt. Having predicated what has just been said, I now answer the difficulty that has been raised: we cannot be certain about anything—not indeed, so long as we are ignorant of the existence of God (for I have not spoken of this)—but so long as we have no clear and distinct idea of him. Therefore, if anyone wishes to dispute with me, his argument will have to be as follows: We can be certain of nothing until we have a clear and distinct idea of God. But we cannot have a clear and distinct idea of God, so long as we do not know whether the author of our nature deceives us. Therefore we cannot be certain about anything so long as we do not know whether the author of our nature deceives us, and so on. To this I reply by granting the major premise, and denying the minor premise. For we have a clear and distinct idea of the Triangle, although we do not know whether the author of our nature deceives us; and, providing we have such an idea of God as I have just shown at great length, we shall be capable of doubting neither his existence, nor any mathematical truth. With these preliminary remarks, we now approach the exposition itself.

DEFINITIONS

I. By the term thought I comprehend all that is in us and of which we are immediately conscious.

Thus all the operations of the will, understanding, imagination, and of the senses are thoughts. But I have added immediately, to exclude those things that are the consequences of thoughts; thus voluntary motion has thought as a principle, but is not itself a thought.

II. By the term idea I understand that form of any thought whatever by the immediate perception of which I am conscious of the thought itself.

Thus I can explain nothing in words, when I understand what I say, without its being certain thereby that there is in me the idea of what is signified by these words. And so I do not call ideas those images only depicted in imagination; rather, I do not call them ideas at all, in as much as they are in the corporeal imagination, that is, depicted in some part of the brain, but only in so far as they inform the mind itself that is directed to that part of the brain.

III. By the objective1 reality of an idea I understand the entity of the thing represented by the idea, in so far as this entity is in the idea.

In the same way me may say objective perfection, objective artifice, and so on. For whatever we perceive in the objects of the ideas is objectively in the ideas themselves.

IV. The same things are said to be formally1 in the objects of the ideas, when they are in them such as we perceived them; and eminently, when they are not indeed such, but so great that they can take the place of such as are.

Note, when I say that the cause eminently contains the perfections of its effect, then I want to signify that the cause contains the perfections of the effect more excellently than the effect itself contains them. See also Axiom 8.

V. Everything in which there dwells immediately, as in a subject, or by which something exists that we perceive, that is, some property or quality or attribute, whose real idea is in us, is called Substance.

We have no other idea of the Substance itself, precisely considered, except that it is a thing in which exists formally 1 and eminently this something that we perceive or which is objectively1 in one of our ideas.

VI. The substance in which thought exists immediately is called Mind.

I speak here of Mind rather than of Soul, since the term Soul is ambiguous and is often used for a corporeal object.

VII. The substance that is the immediate subject of extension and of the accidents that presuppose extension, as shape, position, spatial motion, and so on, is called Body.

There will have to be a later investigation whether the substance that is called Mind and Body is one and the same substance, or whether they are two different substances.

VIII. The substance which we understand to be supremely perfect in itself, and in which we conceive absolutely nothing that involves some defect or a limitation of perfection, is called God.

IX. When we say that some attribute is contained in the nature or concept of a thing, it is the same as if we said that this attribute is true of this being, or can be truly affirmed of it.

X. Two substances are said to be really distinguished when each one can exist without the other.

We have omitted here the postulates of Descartes, because we draw no conclusions from them in what follows; however, we seriously ask our readers to read them and carefully meditate on them.

AXIOMS

I. We attain knowledge and certainty of an unknown thing only through knowledge and certainty of another thing that is itself anterior in certainty and knowledge.

II. Reasons are postulated that make us doubt the existence of our bodies.

This has been forcefully established in the Introduction, and for this reason is presented here as an axiom.

III. If we have anything beyond Mind and Body, it is less known to us than Mind and Body.

Note that these axioms affirm nothing about things exterior to us, but only what we find in ourselves, in so far as we are thinking beings.

PROPOSITION I

We can be absolutely certain of nothing so long as we do not know that we exist.

PROOF

This proposition is self-evident. For a person who does not know absolutely that he exists does not know either that he is an affirming or denying being, that is, that he affirms or denies with certainty.

At this point it must be observed that, although we affirm and deny many things with great certainty without regard to the fact of our existence, nevertheless, everything could be called in question, unless this were first posited as an indubitable fact.

PROPOSITION II

"I am" must be known by itself.

PROOF

If it is denied, it will then not become known except by another thing, the knowledge (by Axiom 1) and the certainty of which will be anterior in us to this affirmation: I am. But that is absurd (by the preceding proposition) ; therefore I am must be known by itself.

Q.E.D.

PROPOSITION III

I am is not the first truth and is not known by itself, in so far as I am a thing consisting of a body.

PROOF

There are certain reasons that make us doubt the existence of our body (by Axiom 2), therefore (by Axiom 1) we shall not reach certainty in regard to it, except through the knowledge and certainty of something else, that is itself anterior in knowledge and certainty. Therefore this affirmation I am is not the first truth and is not known by itself in so far as I am a thing formed of a body. Q.E.D.

PROPOSITION IV

I am cannot be the first truth known, except in so far as we think.

PROOF

This affirmation I am a corporeal thing or formed of a body is not the first known truth (by the preceding proposition) ; nor am I certain even of my own existence, in as much as I am composed of some thing other than mind and body: for if we are formed of some other thing, different from mind and body, this thing is less known to us than the body (by Axiom 3): therefore I am cannot be the first known truth, except in so far as we think.

Q.E.D.

COROLLARY

Hence it is evident that the mind or the thinking thing is more known than the body.

But for a fuller explanation read the Principles, Part I, articles 11 and 12.

SCHOLIUM

Each person perceives with the greatest certainty that he affirms, denies, doubts, understands, imagines, and so on; or, that he exists as doubting, understanding, affirming, and so on; or, in a word, as thinking; nor can he call this in question. Therefore this affirmation, I think, or I am a thinking being is the sole and most certain basis of all philosophy (by Proposition I), and since in the sciences, to acquire most certainty about things, the only thing to be sought and desired is to deduce everything as clear and distinct as the principles from which they were deduced, it manifestly follows that everything that is as evident to us and all that we perceive as clearly and distinctly as this principle of ours that has already been established, and all that coincides with this principle and depends on it so that, if we wanted to doubt it, it would be necessary to doubt this principle also, must be accepted as an ultimate truth. But, to proceed with the utmost caution possible in enumerating these things, I shall first of all admit as equally evident and perceived by us as clearly and distinctly only those things that each person observes in himself or in so far as he is a thinking being. As, for example, that he wishes this or that, that he has such and such assured ideas, and that one idea contains in itself more reality and perfection than another idea; thus the idea that objectively the entity and the perfection of the substance are far more perfect than the idea that contains only the objective perfection of some accident; that idea finally is the most perfect of all that is the idea of the supremely perfect being. We perceive these things, I assert, not only with equal evidence and equal clarity, but perhaps even more distinctly. For not only do they affirm that we think but also the manner of our thinking.

Furthermore, we shall also say that those things agree with this principle that cannot be called in question, unless at the same time this unshakable basis is also called in question. As for example, if anyone wants to doubt whether something can be produced from nothing, he will at the same time be able to doubt whether we exist as long as we think. For if I can affirm something from nothing, namely, that it can be the cause of something, I shall be able, with equal justification, to affirm thought from nothing and say that I am nothing while I think. Since this is impossible for me, it will also be impossible for me to think that something comes from nothing.

After these considerations, I have decided to set forth here in the proper order those principles that now seem to us necessary, so that we may advance further and add them to the number of axioms, since they are proposed as Axioms by Descartes, at the end of the Responses to the Second Objections, and I do not want to be more rigorous than myself. However, in order not to diverge from the order already begun, I shall try to clarify them as far as possible and to show how they depend on each other, and how they all depend on this principle I am a thinking being or agree with it through evidence and reason.

AXIOMS

Taken from Descartes

IV. There are different degrees of reality or entity: for the substance has more reality than the accident or the mode; and the infinite substance more than the finite; and so there is more objective reality in the idea of the substance than in that of the accident, and in the idea of the infinite substance than in the idea of the finite substance.

This axiom is known from contemplation alone of our ideas, of whose existence we are certain, since they are modes of thought: for we know how much reality or perfection the idea of the substance affirms of the substance, and how much the idea of the mode affirms of the mode. Since this is so, we also find necessarily that the idea of the substance contains more objective reality than the idea of any accident, and so on. See Proposition 4, Scholium.

V. A thinking thing, if it knows some perfections that it lacks, will immediately attach them to itself, if they are in its power.

Each person observes this in himself, in as much as he is a thinking being; therefore (by Proposition 4, Scholium) we are quite certain of it and for the same reason we are not less certain of the following axiom, namely:

VI. In the idea or the concept of every thing is contained existence, either possible or necessary (See Descartes' Axiom 10).

Existence is necessary in the concept of God, that is, of the supremely perfect being; for otherwise he would be conceived as an imperfect thing, contrary to the supposed conception: existence contingent or possible in the concept of a limited thing.

VII. Nothing, and no perfection of anything actually existing can have nothing, that is, a non-existent thing, as the cause of its existence.

This axiom is as evident to us as I am a thinking being, as I have shown in Proposition 4, Scholium.

VIII. Whatever reality or perfection there is in a thing is, either formally or eminently, in its primary and adequate cause.

By eminently I understand that the cause contains all the reality of the effect more perfectly than the effect itself; by formally, that it contains it with equal perfection.

This axiom depends on the preceding one: for, if it were assumed that there is nothing or less in the cause than in the effect the nothing in the cause would be the cause of the effect. But this is absurd (by the preceding axiom) ; therefore no thing whatever can be the cause of some effect, but precisely that thing in which there is eminently, or at least formally, every perfection that is in the effect.

IX. The objective reality of our ideas requires a cause, in which the same reality is contained, not only objectively, but formally and eminently.

This axiom is accepted by all, although many have misused it. For when anyone conceives anything new, there is no one who does not seek the cause of that concept or idea. When one can assign some cause in which formally or eminently as much reality is contained as there is objectively in that concept, one is satisfied. This is explained by the example of the machine given by Descartes in the Principles, Part I, article 17. So also, if one asks whence man has the ideas of his thinking and of his body, everyone sees that he has them from himself, in as much as he contains formally all that the ideas contain objectively. Therefore, if a man had any idea that contained more objective reality than he himself has formal reality, then, directed by the natural light of reason, we should necessarily seek, outside man himself, another cause that would contain all that perfection formally or eminently. No one has ever assigned a cause other than this one, that he conceived with equal clarity and distinction. Furthermore, in regard to the truth of this axiom, it depends on the preceding. There are (by Axiom 4) different degrees of reality or entity in the ideas; and accordingly, (by Axiom 4), in proportion to their degree of perfection they require a more perfect, cause. But since the degrees of reality,2 that we observe in the ideas, are not in the ideas in so far as they are considered as modes of thought, but in so far as one represents a substance, and the other only a mode of the substance, or, in a word, in so far as they are considered images of things, it clearly follows that no other first cause of the ideas can be assumed except that which, as we have just shown, all know clearly and distinctly by the natural light of reason, namely, that in which the same reality itself, that they have objectively, is contained formally and eminently. To make it more clearly understood, I shall explain this conclusion by one or two examples. If a person sees books written by one and the same hand (say one is by a famous philosopher and another by some trifler) and he pays attention not to the meaning of the words (that is, in so far as they are images) , but only to the characters traced and the order of the letters, he will discern no inequality that compels him to seek different causes for the books, but they will seem to have resulted from the same cause and in the same manner.

But, if he considers the meaning of the words and the contents, he will find a great inequality in the books, and will accordingly conclude that the first cause of one book was quite different from the first cause of the other and that one was really more perfect than the other in so far as he found a difference in the meaning of the contents of each book or in the words, in so far as they are considered images.

I now speak of the first cause of the books that must necessarily exist, although I grant and even assume that one book can be copied from another, as is self-evident. Similarly, too, it may be clearly explained by the example of a portrait, let us say of a prince. For if we consider only the material aspect of the portrait, we shall find no inequality between it and other portraits that would force us to seek different causes; nothing in fact will prevent us from thinking that this portrait has been copied from another portrait, and that one in turn from still another, and so on to infinity. For we shall recognize sufficiently that no other cause is required for the delineation of the portrait. But if we regard the picture in so far as it is a picture, we shall immediately be obliged to seek a first cause that contains formally or eminently that which this picture contains representatively. And I do not see anything more to ask in order to establish and clarify this axiom.

X. To conserve a thing, no lesser cause is required than for producing that thing originally.

From the fact that we think at this moment, it does not necessarily follow that we shall think afterward. For the concept that we have of our thought does not involve or contain the necessary existence of thought; for I can clearly and distinctly conceive a thought,3 although assuming that it does not exist.

Now since the nature of every cause must contain in itself or involve the perfection of its own effect (by Axiom 8), it clearly follows that something in us, or outside us, that we do not yet know, necessarily still exists, the concept or nature of which involves existence, and that is the cause why our thought begins to exist and also that it continues to exist. For, although our thought has begun to exist, its nature and essence do not thereby involve necessary existence more than before its existence and therefore, to continue its existence needs the same power that it needs to begin its existence. And what we say of thought must also be said of every thing whose essence does not involve necessary existence.

XI. Nothing exists of which it cannot be asked what is the cause (or the reason) for its existence. See Descartes' Axiom 1.

Since existence is something positive, we cannot say that it has nothing as a cause (by Axiom 7) : we must therefore assign some positive cause or reason for a thing's existence, (and that) namely, either an external cause, that is, outside the thing itself, or an internal cause, that is, such as is contained in the nature of the existing thing itself.

The following four Propositions are taken from Descartes.

PROPOSITION V

The existence of God is known (solely) from a consideration of his nature.

PROOF

To say that something is contained in the nature or concept of a thing is the same as saying that this something itself is true of this thing (by Definition 9) . But necessary existence is contained in the concept of God (by Axiom 6). Therefore it is true to say of God that necessary existence is in him or that he exists.

SCHOLIUM

From this proposition many important results follow; from this fact alone, indeed, that existence belongs to God's nature, or that the concept of God involves necessary existence, as the concept of a triangle that its three angles equal two right angles; or that its existence, no less than its entity, is an eternal truth, almost all the knowledge of God's attributes, that leads us to the love of God or supreme happiness, depends. Therefore it is greatly to be desired that mankind comprehend these matters with us. I admit indeed that certain prejudices exist4 that prevent each person from understanding them as easily. If however anyone with good intention and impelled only by love of truth and its true use would examine the matter and weigh in his mind what is said in the Fifth Meditation and at the end of the Responses to the First Objections, and also what we expound about eternity in Part 2, chapter 1 of the Appendix, he will unquestionably understand the matter as clearly as possible, and no one will be able to doubt whether he has any idea of God (which is certainly the first basis of human happiness) . For he will also see clearly that the idea of God is far different from the ideas of other things; when he understands that God, in so far as regards essences and existence, is completely different from other things. Therefore there is no need to detain the reader any longer on this point.

PROPOSITION VI

The existence of God is proved a posteriori by the fact alone that the idea of him is in us.

PROOF

The objective reality of any of our ideas requires a cause in which this same reality is contained not only objectively but formally or eminently (by Axiom 9). Now we have the idea of God (by Definitions 2 and 8) and the objective reality of this idea is contained in us neither formally nor eminently (by Axiom 4) and cannot be contained in anything else but God himself (by Definition 8). Hence this idea of God that is in us requires God as a cause, and accordingly God exists (by Axiom 7).

SCHOLIUM

There are certain men who deny that they have any idea of God and who still, as they say, worship and love him. And although you set before their eyes the definition and the attributes of God, it will be of no avail; no more in fact than if one tried to teach a man, blind from birth, the distinction of colors as we see them. But, unless we wish to consider them as a new kind of animal, intermediary between man and beast, we ought to have little regard for their words. How, I ask, can we demonstrate the idea of a thing otherwise than by stating its definition and by explaining its attributes? Since we expound this in regard to the idea of God, there is no reason for our lingering over the words of men who deny the idea of God only because they cannot form any image of him in their brain.

It must be observed next that, when Descartes cites Axiom 4 to show that the objective reality of the idea of God is contained neither formally nor eminently in us, he assumes that everyone knows that he is not an infinite substance, that is, supremely knowing, supremely powerful, and so on. He can assume this; for who knows that he thinks also knows that he doubts many things and that he does not know everything clearly and distinctly.

It must be observed finally that according to Definition 8 it also follows clearly that there cannot be several Gods, but one only, as we show clearly in Proposition 11 and in our Appendix, Part 2, chapter 2.

PROPOSITION VII

The existence of God is proved also from the fact that we ourselves, who have an idea of him, exist.

SCHOLIUM

To prove this proposition, Descartes assumes these two Axioms, namely:

1. What can produce what is greater or more difficult can also produce what is smaller.

2. It is a greater thing to create or (by Axiom 10) to conserve a substance than to create or conserve the attributes or properties of a substance.

What he means by this I do not know. What does he call easy, or difficult? Nothing is called easy or difficult absolutely5 but only in respect of its cause. So that one and the same thing, at the same time, in respect of different causes, can be called easy and difficult. But if Descartes calls difficult what can be produced with great labor, and easy what can be produced with less labor by the same cause; as, for example, a force that can raise fifty pounds can raise twenty-five pounds twice as easily; then the axiom will clearly not be absolutely true and he will not be able to prove by it what he proposes. For when he says, If I had the power to conserve myself, I would also have the power of giving myself all the perfections that are lacking in me (because they do not require such a great power); I would grant Descartes that the powers that I expend for my conservation could produce many other things far more easily, if I did not need them for my conservation: but, as long as I use them for my conservation, I deny that I can expend them to produce other, though easier, things, as is clearly seen in our example. Nor is the difficulty removed by saying that, being a thinking thing, I ought necessarily to know whether I am expending all my powers for my conservation and also whether that is the cause for my not giving myself the other perfections.

For (apart from the fact that this point is not now under dispute, but only how from this axiom the necessity of this proposition follows) if I knew I would be greater and perhaps I would require, to conserve myself in this greater perfection, greater power than I have, then I do not know if it is a greater task to create a substance than to create (or conserve) attributes; that is, to speak more clearly and more philosophically, I do not know whether a substance does not need all its virtue and essence, by which it perhaps conserves itself, for conserving its attributes.

But let us leave this and let us examine further what the distinguished author means here; that is, what he understands by easy and difficult. I do not think and I can in no way convince myself that by difficult he understands that which is impossible (and hence no one can conceive in any way how that may be), and by easy that which implies no contradiction (and hence one easily conceives how that may be); although in the Third Meditation he seems at first glance to mean this, when he says I must not believe that things that are lacking in me can perhaps be acquired with more difficulty than those that are already in me. For, on the contrary, it is evident that it was far more difficult for me, that is, a thing or a substance that thinks, to spring from nothing than, and so on. That would neither be in accordance with the author's words nor would it even suggest his genius. For, to omit the first point, between the possible and the impossible, or between that which is comprehensible and that which is not comprehensible, there is no relationship, just as there is none between something and nothing. A power can no more apply to impossible things than creation and generation to what is non-existent: and on that account no comparison is possible between the possible and the impossible. In addition, I can compare things with each other and find their relationship to each other only when I have a clear and distinct concept of them all. I therefore deny that it follows that he who can do the impossible can also do what is possible. For I ask what kind of reasoning this would be: If a person can square the circle, he can also make a circle in which all the radii that can be drawn from the center to the circumference are equal; or, if anyone can make nothingness react and use it as matter from which to produce something, he will likewise have the power to make something out of something?

For, as I have said, between the possible and the impossible and in similar cases, there is no agreement nor analogy, nor comparison, nor any other relationship whatever. And everyone can see this, however slightly he considers the question. I think therefore that this view is altogether at variance with Descartes' genius. But, if I consider the second of the axioms just quoted, it appears that by greater and more difficult he means that which is more perfect, by smaller and easier that which is more imperfect. But this too seems very obscure. For there is the same difficulty here as before: for I deny, as before, that he who can make a thing greater can, at the same time and by the same operation, as must be assumed in the Proposition, make what is smaller. Then, when he says that it is a greater thing to create (or conserve) a substance than attributes, he surely cannot mean by attributes that which is formally contained in the substance and is distinguished from the substance itself only by Reason.

For then to create a substance is the same thing as to create attributes. Nor, by the same reasoning, can he mean the properties of the substance that necessarily follow from its essence and definition. Still less can he mean, although he seems to do so, the properties and the attributes of another substance; as, for example, if I say that I have the power to conserve myself, a finite thinking substance, I cannot on that account say that I have also the power of giving myself the perfections of the infinite substance, that differs in all its essence from mine. For the force or the essence by which I conserve6 myself in my being is completely different from the force or essence by which an absolutely infinite substance conserves itself, from which its strength and properties are distinguished only by Reason. And so (although I were to suppose that I conserved myself), if I wanted to conceive that I can give myself the perfections of the absolutely infinite substance, I would be merely supposing that I could reduce to nothing all my essence and then create an infinite substance. That would certainly be far greater than to suppose only that I could conserve myself as a finite substance.

And so, since by attributes or properties he can mean none of these things, nothing else could be meant but the qualities that the substance itself eminently contains (as such and such a thought in the mind, that I clearly perceive to be lacking in me), not those that another substance eminently contains (as such and such a motion in extension: for such perfections are not perfections to me, as a thinking being, and so are not lacking in me). But then what Descartes wants to prove can in no wise be concluded from this axiom: namely, that, if I conserve myself, I also have the power of giving myself all the perfections that I clearly find belonging to the supremely perfect being, as is clearly established by what has been said. But, not to leave the matter unproved and to avoid all confusion, it seemed best to prove first the following Lemmata and then to build upon them the proof of Proposition 7.

LEMMA I

The more perfect a thing is by its own nature, the greater and more necessary is the existence that it involves; and inversely, the more necessary the existence that a thing involves by its own nature, the more perfect it is.

PROOF

In the idea or concept of everything is contained existence (by Axiom 6). Let A then be a thing assumed to have ten degrees of perfection. I say that its concept involves more existence than if it were assumed to contain only five degrees of perfection. For since we can affirm no existence of nothingness (See Scholium of Proposition 4), whatever we take away from A's perfection by thought and accordingly more and more conceive it as participating in nothingness, so much possibility of existence too do we deny it. And hence, if we conceive the degrees of its perfection diminished to infinity, to zero or a cipher, A will contain no existence or an absolutely impossible existence. If, on the contrary, we increase its degrees to infinity, we shall conceive it as involving supreme existence, and hence supremely necessary. This is the first part. Then, since necessity and perfection can in no sense be separated (as is sufficiently established from Axiom 6 and the entire first part of this Proof); it clearly follows what was proposed for proof in the second place.

Observation 1: Although many things are said to exist necessarily from the fact alone that a determined cause exists to produce them, it is not of these things that we shall speak here, but only of that necessity and possibility that follow from the sole consideration of the nature or the essence of a thing, without regard to any cause.

Observation 2: We are not speaking here of beauty and the other perfections that men have wanted to call perfections through superstition and ignorance. But I understand by perfection only reality or being; as, for example, I perceive that more reality is contained in the substance than in the modes or accidents; and consequently I know clearly that it contains more necessary and more perfect existence than the accidents, as is sufficiently established from Axioms 4 and 6.

COROLLARY

It follows hence that whatever involves necessary existence is a being supremely perfect, that is, God.

LEMMA II

Whoever has the power to conserve himself, has a nature involving necessary existence.

PROOF

Whoever has the power of self-conservation also has the power of self-creation (by Axiom 10), that is (as all will readily grant), needs no external cause in order to exist, his nature alone being a sufficient cause for his existence, either possibly or necessarily. But not possibly; for (by what I have proved about Axiom 10) then it would not follow that, from the fact that he already existed, he would exist afterward (which is contrary to the hypothesis). Therefore, necessarily; that is, his nature involves necessary existence.

Q.E.D.

PROOF of Proposition VII

If I had the power of self-conservation, I would have such a nature that I would involve necessary existence (by Lemma 2); therefore (by the Corollary of Lemma 1) my nature would contain all the perfections. But I find in me, in as much as I am a thinking thing, many imperfections, as doubting, desiring, and so on of which I am certain (by the Scholium of Proposition 4); therefore I have no power of self-conservation. Nor can I say that I now lack these perfections because I now want to deny myself of them; for that would clearly refute the first Lemma and what I find clearly in myself (by Axiom 5).

Next I cannot exist now without being conserved, so long as I exist, either by myself, if I have such power, or by another who has that power (by Axioms 10 and 11). But I exist (by the Scholium of Proposition 4), and yet I do not have the power of self-conservation, as has just been proved; therefore I am conserved by another. But not by another who does not have the power of self-conservation (for the same reason by which I have just shown that I am myself incapable of self-conservation); therefore, by another who has the power of self-conservation, that is (by Lemma 2), whose nature involves necessary existence, that is (by the Corollary of Lemma 1), who contains all the perfections which I clearly know belong to the being supremely perfect, that is (by Definition 8), God, exists.

Q.E.D.

COROLLARY

God can create all the things that we clearly perceive, according as we perceive them.

PROOF

All these things follow clearly from the preceding Proposition. For in it the existence of God is proved from the fact that someone must exist in whom there are all the perfections of which some idea is in us. Now there is in us the idea of some power so great that by him alone, in whom this power resides, heaven, earth, and also all other things that are comprehended by me as possible, can be created. Therefore along with the existence of God all these things as well have been proved by him.

PROPOSITION VIII

The mind and the body are really distinct.

PROOF

Whatever we perceive clearly, that can be created by God in the manner we perceive it (by the preceding corollary). But we clearly perceive the mind, that is (by Definition 6), a thinking substance, without body (by Definition 7), without any extended substance (by Propositions 3 and 4) and, inversely, the body without mind (as all readily agree). Therefore, at least by the divine power, the mind can exist without the body and the body without the mind.

Furthermore, the substances that can be one without the other are really distinct (by Definition 10); now the mind and the body are substances (by Definitions 5, 6, 7) that can exist one without the other (as has just been proved); therefore the mind and the body are really distinct.

See Proposition 4 at the end of Descartes' Responses to the Second Objections; and Part I of the Principles from article 22 to article 29. For I do not consider it knowing.

Q.E.D.

SCHOLIUM

If this is denied, then God either knows nothing, or not everything, or only certain things. But to know certain things only and not to know other things assumes a limited and imperfect understanding, which it is absurd to ascribe to God (by Definition 8). As for God knowing nothing, that indicates either a lack of understanding in God, as in the case of men who know nothing, and it involves imperfection that cannot happen to God (by the same Definition); or it indicates that for him to know anything is contrary to the perfection of God. But, since understanding is altogether denied to him, he will not be able to create any understanding (by Axiom 8). Now, since understanding is clearly and distinctly perceived by us, God can be the cause of this (by the Corollary to Proposition 7). Therefore for him to know something is far from being contrary to the perfection of God. Therefore he will be supremely worth while to transcribe them here.

PROPOSITION IX

God is supremely knowing.

PROOF

Although it must be granted that God is incorporeal, as is proved by Proposition 16, this however must not be considered as if all the perfections of extensions should be withdrawn from him, but only in so far as the nature of the extension and the properties involve some imperfection. The same statement also must be made about the intelligence of God, as all admit who want to acquire wisdom beyond the crowd of philosophers, as will be explained at length in our Appendix, Part 2, chapter 7.

PROPOSITION X

Whatever perfection is found in God comes from God.

PROOF

If it is denied, let it be assumed that there is in God some perfection that is not from God. This perfection will be in God, or by itself, or by some being different from God. If it is by itself, it will then have necessary existence or at least possible existence (by Lemma 2, Proposition 7) and so it will be something supremely perfect (by Corollary, Lemma 1 of the same Proposition), and hence (by Definition 8) God. If then it is said that there is something in God that is by itself, it is like saying that it is from God.

Q.E.D.

If however it is in God from a being different from God, God cannot be conceived as supremely perfect by himself, which is contrary to Definition 8. Therefore whatever perfection is found in God is from God.

Q.E.D.

PROPOSITION XI

Several Gods cannot exist.

PROOF

If it is denied, conceive, if it is possible, several Gods, for example, A and B. Then necessarily (by Proposition 9) both A and B will be supremely intelligent, that is, A will know everything, that is, it will know itself and B, and inversely B will know itself and A. But, since A and B exist necessarily (by Proposition 5), the cause of truth and of the necessity of the idea of B, which is in A, is B itself; and, on the other hand, the cause of truth and of the necessity of the idea of A, which is in B, is A itself. Therefore there will be some perfection in A that is not from A, and in B some perfection that is not from B; and hence (by the preceding Proposition) neither A nor B will be Gods; and so there cannot be several Gods.

Q.E.D.

It must here be observed that from this fact alone, that some thing involves from itself necessary existence, as God, it necessarily follows that it is unique; as every one will be able to recognize by deep meditation within himself, and as I could have shown here, but not in a manner as perceptible to all as was done in this Proposition.

PROPOSITION XII

All that exists is conserved by the power of God alone.

PROOF

If it is denied, let it be assumed that something conserves itself; therefore (by Lemma 2, Proposition 7) its nature involves necessary existence; and hence (by the Corollary of Lemma 1 of Proposition 7) it would be God, and there would be several Gods, which is absurd (by the preceding Proposition). Therefore nothing exists that is not conserved by the power of God alone.

Q.E.D.

COROLLARY I

God is the Creator of all things.

PROOF

God (by the preceding Proposition) conserves, that is (by Axiom 10), all that exists he created and still continues to create.

COROLLARY II

A thing has no essence in itself that is the cause of cognition of God; but on the contrary God is the cause of things in relation also to their essence.

PROOF

Since no perfection is found in God that is not from God (by Proposition 10), things will have no essence in themselves that can be the cause of cognition of God. But on the contrary, since God has created nothing from another thing but has created directly (by Proposition 12 and Corollary) and the act of creation recognizes no other cause except the efficient cause (for that is how I define creation) which is God, it follows that things before creation were absolutely nothing and accordingly that God too was the cause of their essence.

Q.E.D.

It should be noted that this Corollary is also evident from the fact that God is the cause or creator of all things (by Corollary 1) and that the cause must contain in itself all the perfections of the effect (by Axiom 8), as everyone can easily perceive.

COROLLARY III

Hence it follows clearly that God does not feel and properly speaking does not perceive; for his understanding is not determined by anything outside himself, but everything flows from him

COROLLARY IV

God is by his causality anterior to the essence and existence of things, as clearly follows from Corollaries 1 and 2 of the preceding Proposition.

PROPOSITION XIII

God is supremely veracious and in no sense deceptive.

PROOF

We can imaginatively attribute to God nothing (by Definition 8) in which we recognize any imperfection. And since all deceit (as is self-evident7) or the will to deceive originates solely from malice or fear—fear assuming a diminution of power and malice a deprivation of goodness—no deceit or will to deceive can be attributed to God, that is, to a being supremely powerful and supremely good, but on the contrary he must be considered supremely veracious and in no sense deceitful.

Q.E.D.

See the Response to the Second Objections, number 4.

PROPOSITION XIV

Whatever we perceive clearly and distinctly is true.

PROOF

The faculty of distinguishing between truth and falsehood which is in us (as everyone discovers in himself and as it is possible to see from all that has already been proved) was created by God and is continuously conserved by him (by Proposition 12 and Corollaries); that is (by the preceding Proposition), by a being supremely veracious and in no sense whatever deceitful; and he has not given us any power (as everyone discovers in himself) of withholding belief in those things that we perceive clearly and distinctly, or of not assenting to them. Therefore, if we were deceived in regard to them, we would be completely deceived by God and he would be deceitful, which is absurd (by the preceding Proposition).

Whatever therefore we perceive clearly and distinctly is true.

Q.E.D.

SCHOLIUM

Since those things to which we necessarily assent when they are perceived by us clearly and distinctly are necessarily true; and since we have the faculty (as everyone discovers in himself) of not assenting to those things that are obscure and doubtful, that is, those things that are not deduced from the most convincing principles; it clearly follows that we can always take care not to fall into error and never to be deceived (this will be understood still more clearly from what follows); provided we seriously decide for ourselves to affirm nothing that we do not perceive clearly and distinctly, that is, that has not been deduced from clear and certain principles.

PROPOSITION XV

Error is not something positive.

PROOF

If error were something positive, it would have only God as a cause, by whom it would have to be created continuously (by Proposition 12). But that is absurd (by Proposition 13). Therefore error is not something positive.

Q.E.D.

SCHOLIUM

Since error is not something positive in man, it cannot be anything else but the negation of the proper use of freedom (by the Scholium of Proposition 14); and so only in the sense in which we say that the absence of the sun is the cause of darkness, or in which God is said to be the cause of blindness, because he created a child like others except for sight, can God be said to be the cause of error: because he has given us an understanding that extends only to a few things. To understand this clearly, and at the same time how error comes solely from the abuse of our will, and finally how we can avoid error; let us recall to our memory all the modes of thought that we have, that is, all the modes of perceiving (as feeling, imagining, and purely knowing) and of wishing (as desiring, shunning, affirming, denying, and doubting); for all of them can be reduced to these two.

In regard to them it must now be noted: 1), that the mind, in so far as it understands things clearly and distinctly, and gives assent to them, cannot be deceived (by Proposition 14): not in so far as it only perceives things without giving its assent to them. For, although I should now perceive a winged horse, it is certain that this perception contains nothing false as long as I do not assent that it is true that a winged horse exists and even as long as I doubt whether a winged horse exists. And since to assent is merely to determine one's will, it follows that error depends solely on the use of the will.

To clarify this still further, it must be noted: 2), that we have the power not only of giving assent to those things that we perceive clearly and distinctly, but also to those things that we perceive in any other manner whatever.

For our will is not determined by any limits. This everyone can see clearly, provided he considers that, if God wanted to make our faculty of understanding infinite, he would not require to give us a greater faculty of assent than the faculty that we now have for us to be able to assent to everything understood by us. But this same faculty, that we now have, would suffice for affirming an infinite number of things. And we also experience really that we assent to many things that we have not deduced from established principles. Furthermore, it is clearly evident from this that, if the understanding extended as far as the faculty of the will, or if the faculty of the will could not extend beyond the understanding, or if, lastly, we could restrain the faculty of the will within the limits of the understanding, we should never fall into error (by Proposition 14).

But we have no power to make the understanding extend as far as the faculty of the will, or the will not extend beyond the understanding: for that implies that the will is not infinite and that the understanding is not created finite. It remains therefore to consider the third question: whether we have the power to contain our faculty of the will within the limits of the understanding. Now since the will is free to determine itself, it follows that we have the power of containing the faculty of assent within the limits of the understanding and hence of avoiding falling into error; hence it is very clearly evident that our never being deceived depends solely on the use of the freedom of the will. That our will is free is proved in Article 39, Part I of the Principles and in the Fourth Meditation, and by us too in great detail in our Appendix, last chapter. And, although, when we perceive a thing clearly and distinctly, we cannot refuse assent to it, that necessary assent does not depend on the weakness, but solely on the freedom and perfection of our will.

For to assent is in us perfection (as is sufficiently well known by itself) nor is the will ever more perfect or more free than when it is entirely self-determining. As this can occur when the mind understands something clearly and distinctly, of necessity it will at once assume that perfection for itself (by Axiom 5). Therefore it is far from being the case that, when we are least indifferent in comprehending the truth, we should consider ourselves as less free. For on the contrary we hold it certain that, the more we are indifferent, the less free we are.

It only remains therefore to explain here how error in respect to man is nothing but privation, and in respect to God mere negation. We shall see this easily, if we observe first that, from the fact that we perceive many things apart from those that we clearly understand, we are more perfect than if we did not perceive them: as is quite evident from the fact that, if it were assumed that we could perceive nothing clearly and distinctly, but only confusedly, we should have no greater perfection than the confused perception of things and no other thing would be desired for our nature. Further, to assent to things, however confused, is perfection, in so far as it is an act. This will be clear to everyone if, as before, it is assumed that clear and distinct perception is contrary to man's nature; for then it will be evident that it is far better for man to assent to things though confused and to exercise freedom than to remain always indifferent, that is (as we have just shown) in the lowest degree of freedom. And if we also consider the use and the interest of human life, we shall find it absolutely necessary, and daily experience is a good teacher for everyone.

Since therefore all the modes of thought that we have, in so far as they are considered in themselves alone, are perfect, that which constitutes the form of error cannot exist in them as such. But if we consider the modes of the will, in so far as they differ from each other, we shall find some more perfect than others, in so far as some make the will less indifferent, that is, more free, than others. Then we shall also see that, as long as we assent to confused things, we make the mind less apt to distinguish true and false, and accordingly we lack freedom in the best sense. Therefore to assent to confused things, in so far as that is something positive, contains no imperfection or form of error; but only in so far as we thus deprive ourselves of the best form of freedom that belongs to our nature and is in our power. All the imperfection of error then will consist solely of the privation of the best form of freedom; this is called error. It is called privation because we are deprived of some perfection demanded by our nature. Error, because we lack this perfection through our own fault, in as much as we do not contain the will, as far as we can, within the limits of the understanding.

Since therefore error is nothing, in respect to man, but the privation of the perfect or right use of freedom, it follows that it does not reside in any faculty that it has from God, nor in any operation of the faculties in so far as it depends on God. Nor can we say that God has deprived us of a greater understanding than he could have given us and hence made us capable of falling into error. For the nature of no thing can demand anything of God nor does anything belong to anything apart from that which the will of God has wished to bestow on it; for nothing exists and can even be conceived before the will of God; (as is fully explained in our Appendix, chapters 7 and 8). Therefore God has not deprived us of greater understanding, or of a more perfect faculty of understanding, any more than he has deprived the circle of the properties of the sphere, or the circumference of the properties of the sphere.

Since therefore none of our faculties, however considered, can show any imperfection in God, it clearly follows that the imperfection of which the form of error consists is only, in respect to man, a privation: but related to God, as to its cause, it cannot be called a privation, but only a negation.

PROPOSITION XVI

God is incorporeal.

PROOF

The body is the immediate subject of spatial motion (by Definition 7); therefore, if God were corporeal, he would be divided into parts: since this clearly involves an imperfection, it is absurd to affirm it of God (by Definition 8).

ANOTHER PROOF

If God were corporeal, he could be divided into parts (by Definition 7). Now each part could either subsist by itself, or could not so subsist: if it could not, it would be like the other things that have been created by God, and hence, like everything created, it would be continuously created by God by the same power (by Proposition 10 and Axiom 11), and would not belong to God's nature any more than the other created things, which is absurd (by Proposition 5). But if each part subsists by itself, each part must also involve necessary existence (by Lemma 2 of Proposition 7), and consequently each part would be a supremely perfect being (by Corollary to Lemma 2, Proposition 7). But this too is absurd (by Proposition 11): therefore God is incorporeal.

Q.E.D.

PROPOSITION XVII

God is a very simple being.

PROOF

If God were composed of parts, these parts would have to be, at least by their nature, anterior to God (as all will readily admit), which is absurd (by Corollary 4 of Proposition 12). Therefore he is a very simple being.

Q.E.D.

COROLLARY

It follows from this that the intelligence of God, his will, or his Decree and his Power are not distinct from his essence except in our thinking.

PROPOSITION XVIII

God is immutable.

PROOF

If God were changeable, he could not change partially, but would have to change according to his entire essence (by Proposition 7). But the essence of God exists necessarily (by Propositions 5, 6, and 7); therefore God is immutable.

Q.E.D.

PROPOSITION XIX

God is eternal.

PROOF

God is a being supremely perfect (by Definition 8); hence it follows (by Proposition 5) that he exists necessarily. Now if we attribute to him a limited existence, the limits of that existence must necessarily be known if not to us, at least to God himself (by Proposition 9), because he is supremely intelligent; therefore God will know himself beyond those limits, that is (by Definition 8, will know a supremely perfect being as non-existent, which is absurd (by Proposition 5). Therefore God has an infinite, not a limited existence, that we call eternity. (See chapter 1, Part 2 of our Appendix.) Therefore God is eternal.

Q.E.D

PROPOSITION XX

God has preordained everything from eternity.

PROOF

Since God is eternal (by the preceding Proposition), his intelligence is eternal, because it belongs to his eternal essence (by the Corollary to Proposition 17). But his understanding does not differ in fact from his will or decree (by the Corollary to Proposition 17); therefore, when we say that God has known things from eternity, we are likewise saying that he has thus willed or decreed things from eternity.

Q.E.D.

COROLLARY

From this Proposition it follows that God is supremely consistent in his operations.

PROPOSITION XXI

A substance extended in length, width, and depth really exists; and we are united to one of its parts.

PROOF

An extended thing, according to our clear and distinct perception of it, does not belong to the Nature of God (by Proposition 10). But it can be created by God (by Corollary to Proposition 7 and by Proposition 8). Now we perceive clearly and distinctly (as everyone discovers in himself, in so far as he thinks) that the extended substance is a cause sufficient to produce in us pleasure, grief, and similar ideas or sensations that are continuously produced in us against our will. But, if we want to imagine a cause of our sensations other than the extended substance, say God or an Angel, we at once destroy the clear and distinct concept that we have. Therefore,8 as long as we pay strict attention to our perceptions without admitting anything, except what is perceived clearly and distinctly, we shall be quite inclined, or least indifferent, to the affirmation that the extended substance is the sole cause of our sensations; and accordingly to the affirmation that an extended thing created by God exists. And in this respect we cannot be deceived (by Proposition 14, with Scholium). Therefore it is truthfully affirmed that a substance extended in length, width, and depth exists: which was the first point to prove.

Further, we observe a great difference among our sensations, which (as we have just proved) must be produced in us from an extended substance; as when we say that I feel or I see a tree, or when I say I am thirsty or that I suffer, and so on. Now I see that I cannot perceive clearly the cause of the difference, unless I first know that I am closely united to one part of matter and not likewise to the other parts. Since I know this clearly and distinctly, and that this cannot be perceived by me in any other way, it is true (by Proposition 14, with Scholium) that I am united to one part of matter. This was the second point. We have therefore proved it.

Q.E.D

Note: Unless the reader here considers himself only as a thinking being, without body, and rejects as preconceptions all the reasons that he had previously had for believing that the body exists, his attempt to understand this proof will be useless.

PART II

Here it is asked only that everyone consider his perceptions with the greatest possible care in order to be able to distinguish what is clear and obscure.

DEFINITIONS

I. Extension is that which consists of three dimensions; but we do not understand by extension the act of extending or anything different from quantity.

II. By Substance we understand that which needs, in order to exist, only the co-operation of God.

III. An Atom is a part of matter indivisible by its nature.

IV. Indefinite is that whose limits (if it has any) cannot be investigated by human understanding.

V. Void is extension without corporeal substance.

VI. Between Space and extension we make no distinction except in our thinking, that is, there is no real difference. Read Article 10, Part 2 of the Principles.

VII. That which we know can be divided mentally, that is, is divisible, at least potentially.

VIII. Spatial Motion is a transference of one part of matter, or of a body, from the vicinity of those bodies that touch it immediately and are considered as motionless, to the vicinity of other bodies.

Descartes uses this definition to explain spatial motion. To understand it properly, it must be considered:

1. That by a part of matter he understands all that is transferred at the same time, although that itself may in turn be composed of many parts.

2. That, to avoid confusion in this definition, he speaks only of that which is always in the movable thing, that is, transference, which is not to be confused, as has occasionally been done by others, with the force or the action that transfers. It is commonly thought that this force or action is required for motion only, not for rest: this is a total misconception. For, as is self-evident, the same force is required for certain degrees of motion to be exerted at the same time on anybody in respose as for those certain degrees of motion to be withdrawn in turn from the same body, so that it comes to rest. This is even proved by experience: for we use almost the same force to move a ship at rest in stagnant water as to halt it suddenly when it moves; and certainly the force would be the same if we were not helped in holding back the ship by the weight and inertia of the water displaced by the ship.

3. That he says that transference occurs from the vicinity of contiguous bodies to the vicinity of other bodies, but not from one place to another. For a place (as he himself has explained in Article 13, Part 2) is not something real but depends only on our thought, so that the same body may be said to change place and yet not to

change; but not that it is transferred from the vicinity of a contiguous body and at the same time not transferred; for only certain bodies can at the same moment be contiguous to the same mobile body.

4. That he does not say that transference can occur absolutely from the vicinity of contiguous bodies, but only of those that are considered as being at rest. For, to transfer a body A from a body B at rest, the same force and action are required from one direction as from the other; this is quite apparent from the example of a boat clinging to the mud or the sand at the bottom of the water; for in order to dislodge it, equal force will necessarily have to be applied to the bottom of the water as to the boat. Therefore the force, by which the bodies must be moved, is exerted equally on the moving body and on the body at rest. Transference therefore is reciprocal; for, if the boat is removed from the sand, the sand too is removed from the boat. So, if, in an absolute sense, we wanted to attribute equal motions in different directions to one and the other of two bodies that are separated from each other and to consider one of them not at rest, and that only because there is the same action in one as in the other; then we should be forced to attribute just as much motion to the bodies considered by all as at rest, for example, to the sand from which the boat is separated, as to the moving bodies; for, as we have shown, the same action is required from one direction as from the other, and the transference is reciprocal. But this would be too much at variance with the common manner of speaking. However, although those bodies, from which others are separated, are considered at rest, and are even so called, yet we shall recall that all that is in a moving body, on account of which it is said to move, is also in the body at rest.

5. Finally, it also appears clearly from the Definition that every body has only one motion peculiar to itself, since it is understood to withdraw from certain bodies only that are contiguous to it and motionless. However, if the moving body is a part of other bodies, having other motions, we know clearly that it can also participates in numberless other motions; but, as so many motions cannot easily be conceived at the same time and cannot even all be recognized, it will be sufficient to consider in each body only the motion that is peculiar to that body.

Read Article 31, Part 2 of the Principles.

IX. By a Circle of Moving Bodies we understand only what occurs, when the last body, moving by the impulsion of another body, immediately touches the first of the moving bodies; although the line described by all the bodies by the impulsion of one motion at the same time is very distorted.AXIOMS

I. Nothingness has no properties.

II. Whatever can be taken away from something, without affecting its integrity, does not constitute its essence; but that which, if it is taken away, destroys the thing, constitutes its essence.

III. In hardness, sense tells us nothing else, nor do we know anything else about it clearly and distinctly, except that the parts of hard bodies resist the motion of our hands.

IV. If two bodies approach each other, or recede from each other, they will not on that account occupy a larger or smaller space.

V. A part of matter, whether it yields or resists, does not on that account lose the nature of its body.

VI. Motion, rest, shape, and similar ideas cannot be conceived without extension.

VII. Apart from the sensory qualities nothing remains in a body except extension and its affections, mentioned in Part I of the Principles.

VIII. A space, or an extension, cannot be greater at one time than at another.

IX. Every extension can be divided, at least in thought.

No one who has learned the elements of mathematics can doubt the truth of this Axiom. For the given space between the tangent and the circle can always be divided by an infinite number of other greater circles. The same thing is also evident from the asymptotes of a hyperbole.

X. No one can conceive the limits of any extension or space unless he also conceives beyond these limits themselves other spaces immediately following the first space.

XI. If matter is multiple and one matter does not immediately touch another, each is necessarily composed under the limits beyond which matter does not exist.

XII. The most minute bodies yield easily to the motion of our hands.

XIII. A space does not penetrate another space, and is not greater at one time more than at another time.

XIV. If pipe A is of the same length as C and C twice as large as A, and if some fluid passes twice as quickly through pipe A as that which passes through pipe C, as much matter will pass through pipe A in the same space of time as through pipe C. And if as much matter passes through pipe A as through C, the matter passing through pipe A will move twice as quickly.

XV. Things that agree with a third, agree with each other. And things that are double the same third are equal to each other.

XVI. Matter that moves in different ways has at least as many parts actually divided as the various degrees of speed that are observed at the same time in the matter.

XVII. The shortest line between two points is a straight line.

XVIII. The body A that moves from C to B, if repelled by a contrary impulsion, will move through the same line toward C.

XIX. Bodies that have contrary motions, when they meet together, are both forced to experience some change, or at least one of the two bodies.

XX. Change in a thing proceeds from a greater force.

XXI. If, when body 1 moves toward body 2, and impels it, and body 8 moves by this impulsion toward 1, bodies 1, 2, 3, etc. cannot be in a straight line: but all, including 1, form a complete circle: see Definition 9.

LEMMA I

Where there is Extension or Space, a Substance is necessarily there.

PROOF

Extension or space (by Axiom 1) cannot be absolute nothingness; it is therefore an attribute, which must necessarily be assigned to something. Not to God (by Proposition 16, Part I): then to a thing that, in order to exist, needs only the co-operation of God (by Proposition 12, Part I), that is, to a substance (by Definition 2 of Part II).

Q.E.D.

LEMMA II

Rarefaction and Condensation are conceived clearly and distinctly by us although we do not admit that bodies occupy in rarefaction more space than in condensation.

PROOF

They can be conceived clearly and distinctly by the mere fact that the parts of any body withdraw from each other and approach each other. Therefore (by Axiom 4) they will occupy neither a larger nor a smaller space. For, if the parts of a body, say a sponge, from the mere fact that they approach each other, expel the bodies with which the intervals are filled; by that very fact alone this body will become more dense, but its parts will not on that account occupy less space than before (by Axiom 4). And if they again withdraw from each other, and the interstices are filled by other bodies, rarefaction will take place, yet the parts will not occupy a greater space. And what, with the aid of the senses we clearly perceive in the sponge, we can perceive by the understanding alone for all bodies, although the intervals of the parts elude entirely the human sense. Therefore Rarefaction and Condensation are clearly and distinctly conceived by us, and so on.

Q.E.D.

It seemed fitting to preface here the above remarks so as to clarify the understanding of its preconceptions of space, rarefaction, and so on, and to make it fit to understand what follows.

PROPOSITION I

Although hardness, weight, and other sensory qualities are taken away from a body, the nature of the body will nevertheless remain unaffected.

PROOF

In the case of hardness, say of a stone, sense tells us nothing more, nor do we know clearly and distinctly anything more than that the parts of hard bodies resist the motion of our hands (by Axiom 3). Therefore (by Proposition 14, Part I) hardness too will be nothing else. If the body is reduced to as minute particles of powder as possible, its parts will yield (by Axiom 12) easily and yet will not lose the nature of the body (by Axiom 5).

Q.E.D.

In regard to weight and other sensory qualities, the proof proceeds in the same manner.

PROPOSITION II

The nature of a body or matter consists solely of extension.

PROOF

The nature of a body is not destroyed by the withdrawal of the sensory qualities (by Proposition I, Part II); therefore they do not constitute its essence (by Axiom 2). Therefore nothing remains except extension and its affections (by Axiom 7). Therefore, if extension is withdrawn, nothing will be left that belongs to the nature of the body, but it will be completely destroyed; therefore (by Axiom 2) the nature of the body consists solely of extension.

Q.E.D

COROLLARY

Space and body are not really different.

PROOF

Body and extension are not really different (by the preceding Proposition); space also and extension are not really different (by Definition 6); therefore (by Axiom 15) space and body are not really different.

Q.E.D.

SCHOLIUM

Although we say9 that God is ubiquitous, it is not admitted on that account that God is extended, that is (by the preceding Proposition), corporeal; for his ubiquity refers solely to the power of God and his cooperation by means of which he conserves all things; so that the ubiquity of God refers not to extension or body any more than to angels or human souls. But it must be observed that, when we say that his power is ubiquitous, we do not exclude his essence; for, wherever his power is, there also is his essence (Corollary to Proposition 17, Part I); but only that we exclude his corporeality, that is, that God is not ubiquitous by some corporeal power, but by a divine power or essence, that equally conserves extension and thinking things (Proposition 17, Part I); this he certainly could not have conserved, if his power, that is, his essence, were corporeal.

PROPOSITION III

It is a contradiction for a void to exist.

PROOF

By void is understood extension without corporeal substance (by Definition 5), that is (by Proposition 2, Part II), a body without a body, which is absurd.

For a fuller explanation and for correcting a preconception about void, read Articles 17 and 18, Part II of the Principles, where it is specially noted that bodies between which nothing is interposed necessarily touch each other and also that nothingness has no properties.

PROPOSITION IV

The same part of a body does not occupy more space at one time than at another time and inversely the same space does not contain more body at one time than at another.

PROOF

Space and body are not really different (by Corollary to Proposition 2, Part II). Therefore, when we say that a space is not greater at one time than at another (by Axiom 13), we are also saying that a body cannot be greater, that is, occupy more space, at one time than at another. This was the first point. Further, from the fact that space and body do not really differ, it follows that, when we say that a body cannot occupy a greater space at one time than at another, we are simply saying that the same space cannot contain more body at one time than at another.

Q.E.D.

COROLLARY

Bodies that occupy the same space, say gold and air, have an equal amount of matter or corporeal substance.

PROOF

A corporeal substance consists not of hardness, for example gold, nor of softness, for example air, nor of any of the sensory qualities (by Proposition I, Part II), but solely of extension (by Proposition II, Part II). Now since (by hypothesis) there is as much space, that is, extension, in the one as in the other, there is therefore as much corporeal substance.

Q.E.D.

PROPOSITION V

Atoms do not exist.

PROOF

Atoms are parts of matter indivisible by their nature (by Definition 3). But, since the nature of matter consists of extension (by Proposition 2, Part II) which, however small, is divisible by its nature (by Axiom 9 and Definition 7), a part of matter, however small, is therefore divisible by its nature; that is, there are no Atoms or parts of matter indivisible by their nature.

Q.E.D.

SCHOLIUM

The questions of Atoms has always been important and complicated. Some affirm the existence of Atoms from the fact that an infinity cannot be greater than another infinity: and, if two quantities, say A and a quantity double the amount of A, are divisible to infinity, they will also, by the power of God who knows their infinite parts at a glance, be able to be actually divided into infinite parts. Therefore, since, as has been said, one infinity cannot be greater than another infinity, the quantity A will be equal to double the quantity of A, which is absurd. They also ask whether half of an infinite number is also infinite; and whether it is equal or unequal, and other questions of a like tenor. To all this Descartes replies that we ought not to reject those things that come within our understanding and are accordingly perceived clearly and distinctly, on account of other things that pass our understanding or comprehension and hence are perceived by us only very inadequately. Now infinity and its properties transcend human understanding, which is finite by nature; and so it would be inept to reject as false what we conceive clearly and distinctly about space, or to doubt it because of our inability to comprehend infinity. And for this reason Descartes considers infinite the things in which we observe no limits, such as the extension of the universe, the divisibility of the parts of matter, and so forth. Read Article 26, Part I of the Principles.

PROPOSITION VI

Matter is indefinitely extended, and the matter of heaven and of earth is one and the same.

PROOF

1. Proof of the first part.

We can imagine no limits to extension, that is (by Proposition 2, Part II), to matter, without conceiving beyond these limits themselves other spaces following immediately (by Axiom 10), that is (by Definition 6), extension or matter, and that to infinity. This was the first point.

2. Proof of the second part.

The essence of matter consists of extension (by Proposition 2, Part II) and it is infinite (by the first part of this proof), that is (by Definition 4), it cannot be perceived under any limits by human understanding: therefore (by Axiom 11) it is not multiple, but everywhere one and the same. This was the second point.

SCHOLIUM

Up to this point we have discussed the nature or essence of extension. That it exists, created by God, such as we conceive it, we have proved in the last Proposition of Part I; and from Proposition 12, Part I it follows that it is now conserved by the same power that created it. Further, in the same last Proposition, Part I, we have proved that we, in so far as thinking things, are united to some part of that matter by whose aid we perceived that all those variations actually exist of which, from the mere contemplation of matter, we know it is capable: as divisibility, spatial motion, or the movement of one part from one place to another, that we perceive clearly and distinctly, provided that we know that other parts of matter take the place of the transferred parts. And this division and this motion are conceived by us in an infinite number of ways, and hence infinite variations too of matter are conceived by us. I say that they are clearly and distinctly conceived by us, as long as we conceive them as modes of extension, not as things really distinct from extension, as has been fully explained in Part I of the Principles. And although philosophers have imagined a great many other motions, we however, who admit nothing that we do not conceive clearly and distinctly, must admit no motion except spatial motion, because we know clearly and distinctly that extension is capable of no other motion except spatial and that we can imagine no other motion.

But Zeno, it is said, denied spatial motion, and that for various reasons Diogenes the Cynic refuted in his own peculiar way, marching into the School where Zeno was expounding these principles and disturbing the audience by walking around. When he realized that he was being stopped by one of the listeners, to prevent him from walking about, he rebuked him thus: 'Why have you thus dared to refute your Master's reasoning?' However, to prevent anyone who is deceived by Zeno's reasoning from thinking that the senses show us something, namely motion, that is utterly in conflict with the understanding, so that the mind is deceived even in regard to those things that it clearly and distinctly perceived with the aid of the understanding, I shall here repeat the principal arguments of the master and I shall likewise prove that they are based on nothing else but false preconceptions: because he had no true conception of matter.

First of all, it is said, he declared that, if spatial motion existed, the motion of a body moving with the utmost speed in a circular sense would not be different from rest: but this is absurd; therefore the supposition too is absurd. He also proves the conclusion. A body is at rest when all its points continuously remain in the same place: but all the points of a body moving with the utmost speed in a circular sense remain constantly in the same place; therefore, and so on. And this too, it is said, he explained by the example of a wheel, say ABC. If it moves around its center at a certain speed, point A will describe a circle through B and C more quickly than if the wheel moved more slowly. Let it be assumed then, for example, when it slowly begins to move, that at the end of an hour it is in the same place from which it began. If it is assumed that it moves at double the speed, it will be in the place from which it began to move after the lapse of half an hour, and if the speed is quadrupled, after the lapse of a quarter of an hour: and, if we conceive this speed increased to infinity, and the time reduced to instantaneity, then point A, at the greatest speed, will be at every instant, that is, constantly in the place from which it began to move, and so always remains in the same place; and what we know about point A must also be understood of all points of this wheel; and so all the points at this greatest speed constantly remain in the same place.

In reply, it must be observed that this argument is against the utmost speed of motion rather than against motion itself: however, we shall not examine here the correctness of Zeno's argument but we shall rather expose the misconceptions on which this entire argument is based, in so far as it proposes to refute motion. In the first place, then, he assumes that bodies can be conceived as moving with such speed that they cannot move faster. In the second place, that time is composed of instants, just as others have conceived that quantity is composed of indivisible points. Both assumptions are false. For we can never conceive a motion so swift that we cannot at the same time conceive a swifter one.

For it is contrary to our understanding to conceive a motion, describing a line however small, so swift that there cannot be a swifter one. And it is the same with slowness: for it implies the conception of a motion so slow that there cannot be a slower one.

We make the same assertion about time also, which is the measure of motion, that is, it is clearly contrary to our understanding to conceive such a time that there cannot be a shorter one. To prove all this, let us follow Zeno's procedure. Let us suppose then, as he did, a wheel ABC moving around its center with such speed that point A is at every moment at the place A from which it moves. I say that I clearly conceive a speed infinitely greater than this one and consequently smaller instants to infinity. For let it be assumed that, while the wheel ABC moves around its center, with the help of chord H, another wheel too, DEF (which I assume to be twice as small) moves around its own center. Now as wheel DEF is assumed to be twice as small as ABC, it is clear that wheel DEF moves twice as fast as wheel ABC; and consequently point D is, at instants twice as small, in the same place from which it began to move. Then, if we assign to wheel ABC the motion of wheel DEF, DEF will move four times faster than before (ABC); and if again we assign this speed of DEF to wheel ABC, then DEF will move eight times faster; and so on to infinity. But this seems quite clear from the mere conception of matter. For the essence of matter consists of extension or space always divisible, as we have proved; and there is no motion without space. We have also proved that one part of matter cannot at the same time occupy two spaces; for that would be tantamount to saying that one part of matter is equal to double the amount; as is evident from what has been proved above; therefore, if a part of matter moves, it moves through some space, and this space, however small it may be imagined to be, and consequently also the time through which that space is measured, will still be divisible, and consequently the duration or time of that motion will likewise be divisible, and that to infinity.

Q.E.D.

Let us now proceed to another sophism, which is said to have been advanced by the same Zeno, as follows: If a body moves, it either moves in the place where it is, or where it is not. But not in the place where it is: for, if it is somewhere, it necessarily is at rest. Nor in the place where it is not. Therefore the body does not move. But this argument is just like the previous one; for it assumes that there is a time than which there is no shorter one; for if we answer Zeno that a body moves not in a place, but from the place where it is to the place where it is not; he will ask whether the body has not been in intermediate places. If we reply with this distinction: If by has been he means has been at rest, we deny that it was somewhere as long as it moved; but if by has been he means has existed, we say that as long as it moved, it necessarily existed; he will again ask: where did it exist, while it moved? If, finally, we answer: If by this where it existed he means what place it occupied while it moved, we say that it occupied no place; but if he asks what place it left we say that it left all the places that he wants to assign in the space through which it moved; he will continue to ask whether at the same instant it could occupy a place and change it. To which we finally reply with this distinction: If by an instant of time he means such a time that there cannot be a shorter one, he is asking an unintelligible question, as has been fully proved, and for that reason undeserving of a reply. But if he assumes time in the sense that I have explained above, that is, in its true sense, he can never assign a time so small in which, however infinitely shorter it may be imagined, a body cannot occupy and change a place: a fact that is evident to one who is sufficiently observant. Hence it is quite clear, as we said above, that Zeno assumes a time so short that there cannot be a shorter one, and accordingly he proves nothing.

Apart from these two arguments, another argument still is attributed to Zeno, that may be read simultaneously along with the refutation in Descartes' Letters, the penultimate letter in volume I.

I should however like my readers to observe here that I have confronted Zeno's reasoning with my own reasoning; and so I have refuted him by Reason, not by the senses, as Diogenes did. For the senses cannot suggest to the searcher after truth anything but the Phenomena of Nature by which he is limited in the investigation of their causes; nor can they ever show the falsity of whatever the understanding comprehends clearly and distinctly as true. For that is how we judge and so this is our Method: to prove the things that we propose by reasons perceived clearly and distinctly by the understanding; considering as supererogatory whatever the senses tell us that seems contrary to them; as we have said, they can determine the understanding only in investigating one thing rather than another, but cannot convict it of falsity when it has perceived anything clearly and distinctly.

PROPOSITION VII

No body takes the place of another, unless at the same time this other body takes the place of some other body.

PROOF 10

If it is denied, let it be assumed, if possible, that a body A takes the place of a body B, that I assume equal to A itself, and that does not leave its own place. Then the space that contained only B now contains (by hypothesis) A and B: and so double the corporeal substance that it previously contained, which (by Proposition 4, Part II) is absurd. Therefore no body takes the place of another body, and so on.

Q.E.D.

PROPOSITION VIII

When some body takes the place of another, at the same instant the place left by it is occupied by another body that touches it immediately.

PROOF

If the body B moves toward D the bodies A and C at the same instant will approach each other and touch each other, or not. If they approach and touch each other, the proposition is granted. But if they do not approach each other, and the entire space left by B separates A and C, then a body equal to B (by the Corollary to Proposition 2 and the Corollary to Proposition 4, Part II) lies between them. But this body is not B (by hypothesis); therefore it is another body that at the same instant takes the place of B and, since it takes that place at the same instant, it cannot be anything else but a body that touches B immediately (by the Scholium of Proposition 6, Part II); for we have proved there that there is no motion from one place to another that does not require a time than which there can always be a shorter one. Hence it follows that the space of body B cannot be occupied at the same instant by another body which has to move through some space before occupying it. Therefore only the body that touches B immediately takes its place at the same instant.

Q.E.D.

SCHOLIUM

Since the parts of matter are really distant from each other (by Article 61, Part I of the Principles), one can be without the other (by the Corollary to Proposition

7, Part I) and they do not depend on each other. Therefore all these imaginative figments about Sympathy and Antipathy must be rejected as false. Furthermore, since the cause of any effect must always be positive (by Axiom 8, Part I), it must never be said that a body moves to prevent the existence of a void, but only from the impulsion of another body.

COROLLARY

In every motion there is a complete circle of bodies moving simultaneously.

PROOF

In the time that body 1 occupies the place of body 2, this body 2 must occupy the place of another, say 3, and so forth (by Proposition 7, Part II). Then at the same instant that body 1 occupied the place of body 2, the place left by body 1 must be occupied by another body (by Proposition 8, Part II), say 8, or another that touches 1 itself immediately; since this occurs solely from the impulsion of another body (by the Scholium of the preceding Proposition), that is here assumed to be 1, all these bodies cannot move in the same straight line (by Axiom 21) but (by Definition 9) describe a complete circle.

Q.E.D.

PROPOSITION IX

If a circular pipe ABC is full of water, and if A is four times wider than B, in the time that the water (or any other fluid body) that is in A begins to move toward B, the water that is in B will move four times as fast.

PROOF

Since all the water that is in A moves toward B, as much water from C, which touches A immediately, must take its place (by Proposition 8, Part II); and from B an equal quantity of water must take the place of C (by the same Proposition); therefore (by Axiom 14) it will move four times as fast.

Q.E.D.

What we say about a circular pipe must also be understood of all unequal spaces through which bodies that move simultaneously are forced to pass: the proof will be the same in the other cases.

LEMMA

If two semicircles are described from the same center, as A and B, the space between the perimeters will be everywhere equal. But if they are described from different centers, as C and D, the space between the perimeters will be everywhere unequal. The proof is evident solely from the definition of a circle.

PROPOSITION X

A fluid body that moves through pipe ABC receives limitless degrees of speed.

PROOF

(See the figure of the preceding Proposition).

The space between A and B is everywhere unequal (by the preceding Lemma); therefore (by Proposition 9, Part II) the speed with which the fluid body moves through pipe ABC will be everywhere unequal. Further, since between A and B we conceive by thought infinite spaces always smaller and smaller (by Proposition 5, Part II), we also conceive, in infinite numbers, the inequalities that are everywhere, and hence (by Proposition 9, Part II), there will be infinite degrees of speed.

Q.E.D.

PROPOSITION XI

In a matter that flows through pipe ABC, there is a division into particles infinite in number.

PROOF

(See figure in Proposition 9).

The matter that flows through pipe ABC acquires at the same time infinite degrees of speed (by Proposition 10, Part II); therefore (by Axiom 16) it has infinite parts truly divided.

Read Articles 34 and 35, Part II of the Principles.

Q.E.D.

SCHOLIUM

Hitherto we have discussed the nature of motion; it is now necessary for us to investigate its cause, which is two-fold: namely, a first and general cause, that is the cause of all motions that there are in the universe, and a particular cause, by means of which it happens that the individual parts of matter acquire motions that they did not have previously. In regard to the general cause, since nothing must be admitted (by Proposition 14, Part I and the Scholium of Proposition 17, Part I) except what we perceive clearly and distinctly, and since we know clearly and distinctly no other cause except God (that is, the creator of matter), it is quite evident that no other general cause must be admitted except God. What we say here about motion, moreover, must also be understood of rest.

PROPOSITION XII

God is the principal cause of motion.

PROOF

See the Scholium immediately preceding.

PROPOSITION XIII

God still conserves by his co-operation the same quantity of motion and rest that he once implanted in matter.

PROOF

Since God is the cause of motion and rest (by Proposition 12, Part II); he conserves them still by the same power by which he created them (by Axiom 10, Part II); and in the same quantity as he first created them (by Corollary to Proposition 20, Part I).

Q.E.D.

SCHOLIUM

I. Although Theology declares that God accomplishes many acts through his good pleasure and in order to display his power to many, however, since those things that depend solely on his good pleasure are not known except by divine revelation, they must not be admitted in the Philosophy where only what Reason dictates is investigated, to avoid confusion between Philosophy and Theology.

II. Although motion is nothing else, in moving matter, but its mode, it still has a certain determined quantity: it will be clear from what follows how this quantity should be understood. Read Article 36, Part II of the Principles.

PROPOSITION XIV

Every thing, in as much as it is simple and undivided, and considered in itself alone, always persists in the same state, as much as it is in itself.

This Proposition is treated by many as an axiom: however, we shall prove it.

PROOF

Since nothing is in a particular state except through the co-operation of God alone (by Proposition 12, Part I); and since God is supremely consistent in his operations (by Corollary to Proposition 20, Part I); if we consider no external causes, that is, particular causes, but we view a thing only in itself, it will have to be asserted that, as far as it is in itself, it always persists in the state in which it is.

Q.E.D.

COROLLARY

A body that moves once always continues to move unless it is slowed down by external causes.

PROOF

This is evident from the preceding Proposition; however, to correct a misconception on motion, read Articles 37 and 38, Part II of the Principles.

PROPOSITION XV

Every moving body tends from itself to move continuously along a straight and not a curved line.

Although this Proposition might be classed among the Axioms, nevertheless I shall prove it from the preceding ones.

PROOF

Motion, having God only as cause (by Proposition 12, Part II), never has by itself any power to exist (by Axiom 10, Part I), but it is as it were procreated by God at every instant (by what is proved of the Axiom just mentioned). Therefore, as long as we consider solely the nature of motion, we shall never be able to assign to it duration, as belonging to its nature, one duration being able to be conceived greater than another. But if it is said that it is a property of the nature of a moving body to describe a curved line by its own motion, a greater duration would be assigned to the nature of motion than if it were assumed that it is in the nature of a moving body to tend to move continuously along a straight line (by Axiom 17). Now, since (as we have already proved) we cannot assign such duration to the nature of motion, we therefore cannot either postulate that it is in the nature of a moving body to move continuously along any curved line, but only along a straight line.

Q.E.D.

SCHOLIUM

This proof will perhaps appear to many to show that it is no more in the nature of motion not to describe a curved line than a straight line; and that because no straight line can be assigned than which there cannot be a shorter one, either straight or curved, nor any curved line, than which too there cannot be another shorter curved line. However, although I take account of this, I consider that my proof is none the less correct: since it concludes from the universal essence alone, that is, from the essential difference of lines (not from the quantity of each one, that is, from an accidental difference) what was proposed for proof. But, not to make a point that is sufficiently clear by itself more obscure by demonstration, I refer Readers to the definition alone of motion, that affirms nothing more of motion than the transference of a part of matter from the vicinity, and so on, to the vicinity of other bodies, and so on. And so, unless we conceive this transference as the simplest possible, that it occurs along a straight line, we are assigning by a fiction something to motion that is not contained in its definition or essence and hence does not belong to its nature.

COROLLARY

From this Proposition it follows that every body, that moves along a curved line continuously, deflects from the line along which it would continue to move; and that by the force of some external cause (by Proposition 14, Part II).

PROPOSITION XVI

Every body that moves in a circular direction, as a stone, for example, in a sling, is continuously determined to move along the tangent.

PROOF

A body that moves in a circular direction is continuously prevented by an external force from moving in a straight line (by the preceding Corollary); if the force ceases, the body will of itself continue to move in a straight line (by Proposition 15). I say, in addition, that a body that moves in a circular direction is determined by an external cause to move along the tangent. For, if it is denied, let it be assumed, for example, that a stone in B, determined by a sling, moves not along tangent BD, but along another line from the same point and conceived outside or within the circle, as BF, when the sling is assumed to come from direction L toward B; or along BG (which I understand to make with line BH that is drawn from the center through the circumference and dissects it at point B, an angle equal to angle FBH), if on the contrary the sling is assumed to come from direction C toward B. But, if the stone at point B is assumed to be determined by the sling that moves in a circular direction from L toward B, proceeding to move toward F; necessarily (by Axiom 18) when the sling moves by a contrary determination from C toward K, the stone will be determined to move along the same line BF by a contrary determination and accordingly will tend toward K, not toward G: which is contrary to the hypothesis. And since 11 no line that can be drawn through point B, except the tangent, can be considered to make with line BH equal angles in the same direction, as DBH and ABH, there can be no line except the tangent that can validate the same hypothesis, whether the sling moves from L toward B or from C toward B; and consequently no line can be assumed except the tangent along which the stone tends to move.

Q.E.D.

ANOTHER PROOF

Instead of a circle, let a hexagon ABH be assumed, inscribed in a circle and a body C at rest on one side AB. Then suppose a ruler DBE (one end of which I assume fixed in center D and the other movable) moving around center D and continuously cutting line AB. It is clear that, if the ruler DBE, while it is conceived to be moving, meets body C at the moment when it cuts line AB at right angles, the ruler itself will by its impulsion determine body C to continue to move along line FBAG toward G, that is, along the side AB extended to infinity. But since we have taken a hexagon arbitrarily, the same affirmation will have to be made of any other figure whatever that can, as we conceive, be inscribed in this circle; because, when C, at rest on one side of the figure, is impelled by the ruler DBE at the moment when it cuts that side at right angles, it will be determined by the ruler to move along that side extended to infinity. Let us therefore conceive, in place of the hexagon, a rectilinear figure with an infinite number of sides (that is, a circle, by Archimedes' definition); it is clear that the ruler DBE, when it meets body C, always meets it at the moment when it cuts at right angles some side of that figure; and so it will never meet body C without at the same time determining it to move along that side extended to infinity. And as any side extended in either direction must always fall outside the figure, this side extended to infinity will be tangent to the figure with an infinite number of sides, that is, a circle. And so if, in place of a ruler, we conceive a sling moving in a circular direction, it will continuously determine a stone to move steadily along a tangent.

Q.E.D.

It should here be noted that both proofs can apply to any curvilinear figure.

PROPOSITION XVII

Every body that moves in a circular direction tends to recede from the center of the circle that it describes.

PROOF

As long as any body moves in a circular direction, so long is it under compulsion of some external cause: at whose cessation it at once proceeds to move along a tangent (by the preceding Proposition), all whose points, except that which touches the circle, fall outside the circle (by Proposition 16, Book 3 of the Elements), and hence are further from the center. Therefore, when a stone, that moves in a circular direction in sling EA, is at point A, it tends to proceed along a line whose points are further from center E than all the points of the circumference LAB; which is nothing but a tendency to recede from the center of the circle that it describes. Q.E.D.

PROPOSITION XVIII

If any body, say A, moves toward another body B at rest, and B does not lose any of its rest through the force of body A; then neither will A lose any of its motion, but will retain entirely the same amount of motion that it had previously.

PROOF

If it is denied, suppose body A loses its motion and yet does not transfer what it has lost into another body, say B; there will be in Nature, when that occurs, an amount of motion less than before, which is absurd (by Proposition 13, Part II). The proof proceeds in like manner in respect of rest in body B; therefore, if one body does not transfer it to the other, B will retain all its rest and A all its motion. Q.E.D.

PROPOSITION XIX

Motion, considered in itself, differs from its direction, impelling it toward one side or another; and it is not necessary for a moving body to be at rest for any length of time in order to be carried or repelled in an opposite direction.

PROOF

Suppose, as in the preceding Proposition, that a body A moves in a direct line toward B, and is prevented by body B from proceeding further; therefore (by the preceding Proposition) A will retain its motion intact, and will not be at rest for even the smallest space of time; however, when it proceeds to move, it will not move in the same direction toward which it moved previously, for it is assumed that it is prevented by B; therefore, its motion remaining intact, and its previous direction being lost, it will move in an opposite direction (by what is said in Chapter 2 of the Dioptrics); and so (by Axiom 2) direction does not belong to the essence of motion, but differs from it, and the moving body, when repelled, is at no time at rest. Q.E.D.

COROLLARY

Hence it follows that motion is not contrary to motion.

PROPOSITION XX

If body A meets body B, and carries it along with it, A loses from its motion as much motion as B acquires from A on account of its encounter with A.

PROOF

If it is denied, suppose that B acquires more or less motion from A than A loses; all that difference will have to be added or subtracted from the amount of motion of all Nature, which is absurd (by Proposition 13, Part II).

Therefore, since body B can acquire neither more nor less motion, it will acquire just as much as A loses.

Q.E.D.

PROPOSITION XXI

If body A is twice as large as B, and moves with equal speed, A will have a motion twice as great as B, that is, a power to retain equal speed with B. (See the figure of the preceding Proposition.)

PROOF

Let us assume, for example, in place of A, twice B, that is (by hypothesis) A alone divided into two equal parts; each B has the power to remain in the position in which it is (by Proposition 14 Part II), and this power is equal in each one (by hypothesis). If now these two B's are joined, each retaining its own speed, there will be one A, whose power and amount will equal two B's, that is, double one B.

Q.E.D.

Note that this follows also from the definition of motion alone; for the greater a moving body is, the greater the matter that is separated from another matter; and therefore the separation is greater, that is (by Definition 8), the motion is greater. See our fourth Observation on the definition of motion.

PROPOSITION XXII

If body A equals body B, and A moves twice as fast as B, the power and motion in A will be double that of B. (See the figure in Proposition 20.)

PROOF

Suppose B, as soon as it has acquired a certain power of motion, has acquired four degrees of speed. If nothing approaches, it will proceed to move (by Proposition 14, Part II) and to persist in its position. Suppose now that it acquires from some new impulsion another new power equal to the first; it will therefore then acquire four new degrees of speed, in addition to the four previous ones, that it will also conserve (by the same Proposition), that is, it will move twice as fast, that is, with a speed equal to A's and at the same time it will have double the power equal to A itself; therefore the motion in A is double that in B.

Q.E.D.

Note that we here understand by power in moving bodies the amount of motion: an amount that in equal bodies must be greater in proportion to the speed of the motion, in so far as by that speed equal bodies are separated from bodies immediately tangential more than they would be at the same instant if they moved more slowly: and so (by Definition 8) they have also more motion. In bodies at rest by power of resistance is understood the amount of rest. Hence it follows:

COROLLARY I

The more slowly bodies move, the more they participate in rest; for they show more resistance to bodies moving more rapidly that meet them and have less power than they have, and they are also less separated from bodies that touch them immediately.

COROLLARY II

If body A moves twice as fast as body B, and body B is twice as big as A, there is as much motion in B, the greater, as in A, the smaller, and consequently also equal power.

PROOF

Let B be twice as big as A, and let A move twice as quickly as B, and further let C be twice as small as B and let it move twice as slowly as A; than B (by Proposition 21, Part II) will have a motion twice as great as C, and A (by Proposition 22, Part II) will have a motion twice as great as C; therefore (by Axiom 15) B and A have an equal motion: for the motion of each of them is twice the same third C.

Q.E.D.

COROLLARY III

From this it follows that motion is distinct from velocity. For we conceive that one of two bodies that have equal velocity can have more motion than the other (by Propositions 21, Part II); and inversely that bodies that have unequal speeds can have equal motion (by the preceding Corollary). This same corollary is also deduced from the definition of motion itself; for it is nothing but the transference of a body from the vicinity, and so on.

But it must here be noted that this third Corollary does not contradict the first. For velocity is conceived by us in two ways: either in so far as a body is separated more or less at the same time from bodies immediately touching it, and as such participates more or less in the motion or rest; or in so far as it describes a greater or smaller line at the same time and in this respect is distinct from motion.

I could have added here other Propositions in order to develop more fully Proposition 14, Part II and to explain the powers of things in any state whatever, as we have here done in the case of motion; but it wll be sufficient to read Article 43, Part II of the Principles, and add only one Proposition that is necessary for the comprehension of what follows.

PROPOSITION XXIII

When the modes of a body are forced to undergo a change, that change will always be the smallest possible.

PROOF

This Proposition follows clearly enough from Proposition 14, Part II.

PROPOSITION XXIV

Rule 1

If two bodies, say A and B (see the figure in Proposition 20), were quite equal and moved with the same speed in a straight line toward each other, when they meet, each will be deflected in the opposite direction without losing any part of its speed.

In this hypothesis it is quite clear that, to remove the opposition of these two bodies, either both must be deflected in opposite directions, or one must carry the other along with it; for they are opposed only in direction, but not in power of motion.

PROOF

When A and B meet, they must undergo some change (by Axiom 19); as moreover one motion is not opposed to the other motion (by the Corollary to Proposition 19, Part II), they must lose none of their motion (by Axiom 19). Therefore the change will occur in direction only; but we cannot conceive that the direction of one body only, say B, is changed, unless we assume (by Axiom 20) that A, by which it must be changed, is the stronger body. But this would be contrary to the hypothesis; therefore, since a change of direction cannot take place in one body only, it will take place in both, that is, A and B will be deflected in opposite directions (by what is said in Chapter 2 of the Dioptrics), and will retain their motion intact.

Q.E.D.

PROPOSITION XXV

Rule 2

If the bodies were unequal in volume, that is, B is greater than A, (see the figure in Proposition 20), other conditions being the same as before, then A only would be deflected, and both bodies would proceed to move with the same speed.

PROOF

Since A is assumed to be smaller than B, it will also have (by Proposition 21, Part II) less power than B; now, since in this hypothesis, as in the preceding one, there is opposition in the direction only, and so, as we have proved in the preceding Proposition, change must occur in direction only, it will occur only in A and not in B (by Axiom 20); therefore only A will be deflected in an opposite direction by B, which is stronger, while retaining its own speed intact.

Q.E.D.

PROPOSITION XXVI

If bodies are unequal in volume and speed, that is, B twice as large as A (see figure in Proposition 20), but the motion in A twice as fast as in B, other conditions being assumed as before, both bodies will be deflected in opposite directions, each one retaining the speed that it had.

PROOF

Since A and B move toward each other, according to the hypothesis, there is as much motion in one as in the other (by Corollary to Proposition 22, Part II); therefore the motion of one is not contrary to the motion of the other (by Corollary to Proposition 19, Part II), and the powers are equal in each (by Corollary 2 to Proposition 22, Part II). Therefore this hypothesis is altogether similar to the hypothesis of Proposition 24, Part II; and so by the same proof A and B will be deflected in opposite directions, while maintaining their own motion intact.

Q.E.D.

COROLLARY

From these three preceding Propositions it appears clear that the direction of a body requires, in order to change, the same power as the motion; hence it follows that a body that loses more than half of its direction and more than half of its motion undergoes more change than the body that loses all its direction.

PROPOSITION XXVII

Rule 3

If bodies are equal in volume, but B moves a little faster than A, not only will A be deflected in the opposite direction, but B also will transfer half of its speed, in which it exceeds A, to A and both will proceed to move in the same direction with equal speed.

PROOF

A (by hypothesis) is opposed to B not only by its direction, but also by its slowness, in so far as this slowness participates in rest (by the Corollary to Proposition 22, Part II). Hence, although it is deflected in the opposite direction and only its direction changes, all opposition of those bodies is not on that account removed; therefore (by Axiom 19) there must occur a change both in direction and in motion. But, since B by hypothesis moves faster than A, B (by Proposition 22, Part II) will be stronger than A; therefore (by Axiom 20), a change will arise in A from B, by which A is deflected in the opposite direction. This was the first point.

Then, as long as A moves more slowly than B, it is opposed to B (by Corollary 1 to Proposition 22, Part II); therefore the change must proceed (by Axiom 19) until A does not move more slowly than B. But in this hypothesis no cause is so strong as to force A to move faster than B; therefore since it can move neither more slowly than B, since it is impelled by B, nor more quickly than B, it will proceed to move with the same speed as B. Furthermore, if B transfers less than half of its excess speed to A, then A will proceed to move more slowly than B; but if B transfers more than half of its excess speed, then A will proceed to move more quickly than B; both are absurdities, as we have already proved. Therefore the change will continue to the point where B transfers to A half of its excess speed, that B (by Proposition 20, Part II) must lose; and so both will continue to move at equal speed, without any opposition, in the same direction.

Q.E.D.

COROLLARY

Hence it follows that the faster a body moves, the more momentum it has to continue moving along the line that it traverses; and on the other hand, the more slowly it moves, the less momentum it has.

SCHOLIUM

To prevent confusion among readers between the power of direction and the power of motion, it seemed fitting to add a few remarks explaining the distinction between the power of direction and the power of motion. If then equal bodies A and C are conceived, moving with equal speed in a direct line toward each other, these two bodies (by Proposition 24, Part II) will be deflected in opposite directions, while retaining their own motion intact. But if body C is in B, and moves obliquely toward A, it is clear that it is now less determined to move along line BD, or CA. Therefore, although it has motion equal

to A, still the force of direction A, is greater than the force of direction of C itself, moving from B toward A, and is as much greater as line BA is greater than line CA: for the greater line BA is than line CA, so much more time also (when B and A move with equal speed, as is here assumed) does B require to be able to move along line BD or CA, through which it is opposed to the direction of body A. And so, when C meets A obliquely from B, it will be directed, as though proceeding to move along line AB' toward B' (that I assume, when it is at the point where line AB' cuts BC extended, is equidistant from C as C is from B). A, however, maintaining its motion and direction intact, will proceed to move toward C and will draw body B along with it, since B, as long as it is determined to move along diagonal AB' and moves with the same speed as A, requires more time than A to describe a part of line AC by its motion, and to that extent is opposed to the direction of body A, that is stronger. But, in order that the force of direction of C itself moving from B toward A, in so far as it participates in line CA, may equal the force of direction of C itself moving directly toward A (by hypothesis, a power equal to A itself), necessarily B will have to have as many degrees of motion more than A as line BA is longer in extent than line CA and then, when it meets body A obliquely, A will be deflected in the opposite direction toward A' and B toward B', each of them maintaining its own motion intact. But if the excess of B over A is greater than the excess of line BA over line CA, then B will drive A toward A' and will transmit to it so much of its own motion until the motion of B is in the same relation to the motion of A as line BA is to line CA while losing as much motion as it transferred to A, and it will proceed to move in the direction in which it previously moved. For example, if line AC is to line AB as 1 to 2, and the motion of body A to the motion of body B as 1 to 5, then B will transfer to A one degree of its motion, and will repel it in the opposite direction, and B with the remaining four degrees of motion will continue to move in the same direction in which it previously moved.

PROPOSITION XXVIII

Rule 4

If a body A (see figure in Proposition 27) is completely at rest and is a little larger than B, with whatever speed B moves toward A, B will never move A, but will be repelled by it in the opposite direction, while maintaining its own motion intact.

Observe that the opposition of these bodies is removed in three ways: either when one of them draws the other with it, and afterward they proceed to move in the same direction with the same speed; or when one is deflected in the opposite direction and the other retains its rest intact; or when one is deflected in the opposite direction and transfers some of its motion to the other body at rest; there is no fourth possibility (by virtue of Proposition 13, Part II). Therefore it will have to be proved now (on account of Proposition 23, Part II) that according to our hypothesis the change in these bodies is minimal.

PROOF

If B moved A until they both continued to move with the same speed, B (by Proposition 20, Part II) would have to transfer as much of its power to A as A required, and (by Proposition 21, Part II) it would have to lose more than half of its motion, and consequently (by the Corollary to Proposition 27, Part II) more than half of its direction; and so (by the Corollary to Proposition 26, Part II) it would undergo more change than if it lost only its own direction. And if A loses some of its rest, but not so much as to continue finally to move with the same speed as B, then the opposition of these two bodies is not removed; for A will be opposed to the speed of B by its slowness, in so far as it participates in rest (by the Corollary to Proposition 22, Part II), and so B will have to be deflected in the opposite direction, and will lose all its direction and part of its motion, that it transferred to A; which is an even greater change than if it lost only its direction. The change therefore, following this hypothesis, will be, since it is in direction alone, the smallest that is possible in these bodies, and accordingly (by Proposition 23, Part II) no other will occur.

Q.E.D.

It must be observed in the proof of this Proposition that the same thing takes place in other cases: we have not in fact cited Proposition 19, Part II, in which it is proved that direction can be completely changed, while the motion itself remains nevertheless intact; care however must be taken that the power of direction is properly conceived. For in Proposition 23, Part II we did not say that the change will always be absolutely minimal, but the least possible. That a change, consisting solely in direction, can occur such as we have assumed in this proof, is clear from Propositions 18 and 19, Part II, with the Corollary.

PROPOSITION XXIX

Rule 5

If a body A at rest (see figure in Proposition 30) is smaller than B, however slowly B moves toward A, B will move it along with itself, transferring to it a part of its motion such that both then move with equal speed (Read Article 50, Part II of the Principles).

In this Rule also, as in the preceding one, only three cases can be conceived in which this opposition is removed; we shall prove by our hypothesis that the change in these bodies is minimal; and so (by Proposition 23, Part II) they must change in such a way.

PROOF

According to our hypothesis B transfers to A (by Proposition 21, Part II) less than half of its motion and (by the Corollary to Proposition 27, Part II) less than half of its direction. Now if B did not carry A along with it but was deflected in the opposite direction, it would lose its entire direction and a great change would occur (by the Corollary to Proposition 26, Part II); and much greater, if it loses all its direction, and at the same time a part of its motion, as is assumed in the third case; therefore according to our hypothesis the change is minimal.

Q.E.D.

PROPOSITION XXX

Rule 6

If a body A at rest were scrupulously equal to a body B moving toward it, it would partly be impelled by it, and partly repelled in the opposite direction.

Here too, as in the preceding Proposition, only three cases can be conceived: and so it will have to be proved that we are here assuming the smallest possible change.

PROOF

If a body B carries a body A along with it, until both continue to move with the same speed, there will then be as much motion in the one as in the other (by Proposition 22, Part II), and (by the Corollary to Proposition 27, Part II) B will have to lose half of its direction and also (by Proposition 20, Part II) half of its motion. But if B is repelled by A in the opposite direction, then it will lose its entire direction, and will retain all its motion (by Proposition 18, Part II); a change that is equal to the previous one (by the Corollary to Proposition 26, Part II). But neither of these situations can occur; for, if A retained its state and could change B's direction, it would necessarily (by Axiom 20) be stronger than B, which would be contrary to the hypothesis. And if B carried A along with it until both moved with the same speed, B would be stronger than A, which is also contrary to the hypothesis. Since therefore neither of these two cases takes place, the third case therefore will occur, namely that B will impel A slightly and will be repelled by A.

Q.E.D.

Read Article 51, Part II of the Principles.

PROPOSITION XXXI

Rule 7

If B and A (see figure in the preceding Proposition) moved in the same direction, A more slowly than B, so that B finally reached A, and if A were greater than B, but the excess speed in B were greater than the excess size in A; then B would transfer to A so much of the motion that both would then advance with the same speed and in the same direction. But if on the other hand the excess size in A were greater than the excess speed in B, B would be deflected by it in the opposite direction, while maintaining all its motion intact.

Read Article 52, Part II of the Principles. Here again, as before, only three cases can be conceived.

PROOF

Part 1. B cannot be deflected in the opposite direction by A (by Axiom 20), for it is assumed (by Propositions 21 and 22, Part II) to be stronger than A; therefore, since B is stronger, it will move A along with it, and in such a way that both continue to move with the same speed. For a minimal change will occur, as is easily clear from what precedes.

Part 2. B cannot impel A (by Axiom 20) for it is assumed to be less strong than A (by Propositions 21 and 22, therefore (by the Corollary to Proposition 14, Part II) B will retain all its motion; not in the same direction, for it is assumed to be prevented by A; therefore (by what has been said in Chapter 2 of the Dioptrics) it will be deflected in the opposite direction, while maintaining its motion intact (by Proposition 18, Part II).

Q.E.D.

Observe that here and in the preceding Propositions we have assumed as proved that every body meeting another body directly is prevented absolutely by it from advancing further in the same direction and not in any other direction; to comprehend this, read Chapter 2 of the Dioptrics.

SCHOLIUM

So far, to explain the changes in bodies as a result of reciprocal impact, we have considered the two bodies as if separated from all bodies, without taking any account of those bodies that surround them on all sides. Now we shall consider the state and the changes in these bodies with respect to the bodies by which they are surrounded on all sides.

PROPOSITION XXXII

If a body B is surrounded on all sides by small moving bodies, impelling it at the same time with the same power in all directions, so long as no other cause intervenes, it will remain motionless in the same place.

PROOF

This Proposition is self-evident: for if it moved in any direction, by the impulsion of small bodies coming from one direction, these small bodies that move it would drive it with greater force than the other bodies that drive it at the same time in the opposite direction, and they cannot achieve their effect (by Axiom 20): which would be contrary to the hypothesis.

PROPOSITION XXXIII

A body B, under the same conditions as before, can, by the intervention of however small a force, move in any direction whatever.

PROOF

All bodies touching B immediately, because (by hypothesis) they are in motion and B (by the preceding Proposition) remains motionless, as soon as they touch B, will be deflected in the opposite direction, while maintaining their motion intact (by Proposition 28, Part II); and so body B is continuously and readily abandoned by the bodies touching it immediately; however great therefore B is conceived to be, no action is required to separate it from the bodies immediately touching it (by our fourth Observation on Definition 8). Therefore no external force, however small it may be, can impinge on B without being greater than the force that B has to remain in the same place (for we have already proved that it has no power itself to cling to bodies touching it immediately), and also, added to the impulsion of the small bodies driving B in the same direction as itself by an external force, without being greater than the force of the small bodies driving B in the opposite direction (for it was assumed equal to the contrary impulsion without external force); therefore (by Axiom 20) body B will move in any direction whatever by this external force, however small it may be.

Q.E.D.

PROPOSITION XXXIV

A body B, under the same conditions as before, cannot move faster than it is impelled by an external force, although the particles by which it is surrounded are agitated far more quickly.

PROOF

The small bodies that at the same time as the external force drive B toward the same direction, although agitated much faster than the external force can move B, have not however (by hypothesis) a greater force than the bodies that drive B in the opposite direction, and will expend all their forces of direction only in resisting them, and will not transfer any speed to B (by Proposition 32, Part II). Therefore, since no other circumstances or causes are assumed, B will not receive any speed from any other cause except external force, and accordingly (by Axiom 8, Part I) will not be able to move faster than the impulsion of an external force.

Q.E.D.

PROPOSITION XXXV

When a body B is so moved by an external impulsion, it receives most of its motion from the bodies by which it is continuously surrounded, not by an external force.

PROOF

B, however great it may be conceived to be, must move by an impulsion, however small (by Proposition 33, Part II). Let us conceive therefore that B is four times as great as the external body by whose force it is impelled; then, since (by the preceding Proposition) both must move with equal speed, there will be four times as much motion in B as in the external body by which it is impelled (by Proposition 21, Part II); therefore (by Axiom 8, Part I) it does not have the principal part of its motion from the external force. And since no other causes are assumed except the bodies by which it is continuously surrounded (for B is assumed to be motionless by itself); it receives therefore (by Axiom 7, Part I) only from the bodies by which it is surrounded the principal part of its motion, not from an external force.

Q.E.D.

Observe that we cannot say here, as before, that the motion of the particles coming from one direction is required to resist the motion of particles coming from the opposite direction; for the bodies, moving with equal motion (as the assumption is) toward each other, are opposed by direction alone,12 not by motion (by the Corollary to Proposition 19, Part II) and so give up only their direction, not their motion, in resisting each other; and for this reason B can receive no direction, and consequently (by the Corollary to Proposition 27, Part II) no speed, in so far as distinct from motion, from the bodies that surround it. But it receives motion; in fact, at the intervention of an external force it must necessarily be moved by them, as we have proved in this Proposition and as is clearly evident from the manner in which we have proved Proposition 33.

PROPOSITION XXXVI

If any body, for example our hand, can move in any direction whatever with equal motion so that it can in no way resist any bodies and no other bodies can resist it in any way, necessarily, in the space through which it thus moves, as many bodies will move in one direction as in any other direction whatever, with a force of speed equal to that of the hand.

PROOF

A body cannot move through any space that is not full of bodies (by Proposition 3, Part II). I say therefore that the space through which our hand can move thus is filled with bodies that will move under the same conditions that I have stated. For if that is denied, let it be assumed that they are at rest or that they move in some other way. If they are at rest, necessarily they will resist the motion of the hand (by Proposition 14, Part II) until its motion is communicated to them so that finally they move along with it in the same direction with equal speed (by Proposition 20, Part II). But in the hypothesis they are assumed not to resist; therefore these bodies move; which is the first point.

Furthermore, they must move in all directions. For if that is denied, let it be assumed that they do not move in some direction, say from A toward B. If therefore the hand moves from A toward B, necessarily it will encounter moving bodies (by the first part of this proof) and by our hypothesis with another direction different from that of the hand; therefore they will resist it (by Proposition 14, Part II) until they move along with the hand itself in the same direction (by Proposition 24 and the Scholium of Proposition 27, Part II). But they do not resist the hand (by hypothesis); therefore they will move in any direction whatever; which was the second point.

Again, these bodies will move in all directions with the same force of speed. For if it were assumed that they do not move with the same force of speed, and that the bodies moving from A toward B do not move with as much force of speed as the bodies moving from A toward C: then, if the hand moved from A toward B with the same speed as the bodies move from A toward C (for it is assumed to be able to move with equal motion in all directions without resistance), the bodies moving from A toward B will resist the hand (by Proposition 14, Part II) until they move with the same force of speed as the hand (by Proposition 31, Part II). But this is contrary to the hypothesis; therefore the bodies will move with the same force of speed in all directions; which was the third point.

Finally, if the bodies moved with a force of speed unequal to that of the hand, either the hand will move more slowly or with less force of speed, or more quickly, with a greater force of speed, than the bodies. In the first case, the hand will resist the bodies following it in the same direction (by Proposition 31, Part II). In the latter case, the bodies that the hand follows and with which it moves in the same direction will resist it (by the same Proposition). Both alternatives are contrary to the hypothesis. Therefore, since the hand can move neither more quickly nor more slowly, it will move with the same speed as the bodies.

Q.E.D.

If it is asked, why I say with the same force of speed, not absolutely with the same speed, read the Scholium of the Corollary to Proposition 27, Part II. If it is then asked whether, while moving for example from A toward B, the hand does not resist the bodies moving at the same time from B toward A with the same speed, read Proposition 33, Part II, from which it will be understood that their force is compensated by the force of the bodies (for this force, by Part 3 of this Proof, is equal to the other) that move at the same time with the hand from A toward B.

PROPOSITION XXXVII

If any body, say A, can be moved by however small a force in any direction whatever, it is necessarily surrounded by bodies that move with the same speed for all of them.

PROOF

The body A must be surrounded on all sides by bodies (by Proposition 6, Part II), and those bodies move with speed in any direction. For if they were at rest, A could not be moved by however small a force in any direction (as assumed) but only by such a force as could at least move with it the bodies touching A immediately (by Axiom 20, Part II). Then, if the bodies by which A is surrounded were moved by a force greater in one direction than in another, say from B toward C rather than from C toward B, as it is surrounded on all sides by moving bodies (as we have already proved); necessarily (by what we have proved in Proposition 33) the bodies moving from B toward C would draw A along with them in the same direction. And so no force, however small, will be sufficient to move A toward B, but precisely a force so great as to compensate the excess motion of the bodies coming from B toward C (by Axiom 20); therefore they must move with the same force in all directions.

Q.E.D.

SCHOLIUM

Since these conditions occur in regard to bodies called Fluids, it follows that fluid bodies are those that are divided into many small particles moving with the same force in all directions. And, although those particles cannot be perceived even by the lynx-eyed, what we have just clearly proved cannot nevertheless be denied. For from what has been said in Propositions 10 and 11 such a subtle refinement of Nature is established as cannot be determined or reached by any thought (not to mention the senses). Furthermore, since it is also quite certain from what has been said that bodies resist other bodies solely by their being at rest and that in hardness, as the senses tell us, we perceive nothing else except that the parts of hard bodies resist the motion of our hands; we clearly deduce that those bodies, all whose particles are mutually at rest, are hard. Read Articles 54, 55, 56, Part II of the Principles.

PART III

Now that the most universal principles of the natural sciences have thus been expounded, we must now proceed to the exposition of the Principles. And from Article 20 to Article 43 the hypothesis is proposed that Descartes considers most suitable not only for the comprehension of the heavenly Phenomena, but also for the investigation of the natural causes.

Furthermore, since the best way to understand the nature of plants and man is to consider how they gradually arise and are generated from seeds, such principles will have to be thought out as are very simple and very easy to understand; and from which we may prove that the stars, the earth, and in short all that we find in this visible world could have arisen as though from certain seeds; although we know quite well that they never arose thus. For in this way we shall explain their nature far better than if we described them only as they are now.

I say that we are searching for simple principles, easy to understand; for unless they are such, we shall not require them; because we shall assume seeds in things for the sole reason that their nature may become known to us and in the manner of Mathematicians we may rise from the clearest things to more obscure one and from the most simple to the more complex.

Next we say that we are searching for such principles from which to prove that the stars, the earth, and so on could have arisen. For we are not seeking such causes, as is generally the case with Astronomers, as are only sufficient to explain the Phenomena of the heavens; but such as lead us also to a knowledge of those things that are on the earth (because all things that we observe occurring on earth we judge should be included among the Phenomena of Nature). To find these principles, the following points must be observed in a good Hypothesis:

I. That it implies no contradiction (considered only in itself).

II. That it is as simple as possible.

III. That it is very easy to understand; which follows from the second condition.

IV. That everything that is observed in all Nature can be deduced from it.

We say finally that it is permissible for us to assume a Hypothesis from which as the cause we can deduce the Phenomena of Nature, although we know quite well that they did not arise thus. To make this clear, we shall use this example. If one finds traced on a paper the curved line called a Parabola, and one wants to investigate its nature, it is the same thing whether he assumes that the line was first a section of some Cone and then imprinted on the paper, or that it was traced by the movement of two straight lines, or produced in some other manner; provided that he deduces all the properties of the Parabola from what is assumed. Further, although he knows that the Parabola came from the impression of the section of the Cone on the paper, he will none the less be able to imagine at will another cause that seems most suitable to him to explain all the properties of the Parabola. So too, to explain the lines of Nature, it is permissible to assume a hypothesis at will, provided that we deduce therefrom by mathematical consequences all the Phenomena of Nature. And, what is more noteworthy, we shall scarcely be able to assume any hypothesis from which the same effects cannot be deduced, although more laboriously perhaps, by the Laws of Nature previously explained. For since by the aid of these Laws matter successively assumes all the forms of which it is capable; if we consider these forms in order, we shall finally be able to reach the form that is the form of this world; so that there is no error to be feared from a false hypothesis.

POSTULATE

It is asked that it be conceded that all this matter, of which this visible world is composed, was divided in the beginning by God into particles as equal as possible among themselves; not indeed into spherical particles, because many globules joined together do not fill a continuous space, but into parts shaped in another way, and of average size, that is, intermediary between all those of which heaven and the stars are composed; and that those particles had in themselves as much motion as is now found in the world, and that they moved equally: either individually around their own particular center, and mutually separated from each other, so as to constitute a fluid body, such as we conceive heaven to be: or several certain other points, equally distant from each other, and distributed in the same way as the centers of the fixed stars are now: and even around other somewhat greater centers that equal the number of the Planets; and so they would compose as many different vortices as there are now stars in the world. See the figure in Article 47, Part 3 of the Principles.

This hypothesis considered in itself implies no contradiction: for it confers on matter nothing but divisibility and moton; and these modifications we have already previously proved exist really in matter; and, because we have shown that matter is infinite and that the matter of heaven and earth is one and the same, we can suppose without any risk of contradiction that the modifications have existed in all matter.

This hypothesis too is most simple, because it supposes no inequality or dissimilarity in the particles into which matter was divided in the beginning, nor even in their motion: whence it follows that this hypothesis is also very easy to understand. This is also clear from the fact that, by this hypothesis, nothing is assumed to have been in matter except of matter, namely divisibility and spatial motion.

That from this hypothesis itself all that is observed in Nature can be really deduced, we shall try to show, as far as possible, and that in the following order. First of all, we shall deduce the fluidity of the Heavens from this hypothesis, and we shall explain how it is the cause of light. Then we shall proceed to the nature of the Sun, and at the same time to what is observed in the fixed stars. After which we shall speak of the Comets, and lastly of the Planets and their Phenomena.

DEFINITIONS

I. By Ecliptic we understand that part of a vortex that, while revolving on its axis, describes the largest circle.

II. By Poles we understand the parts of a vortex that are most distant from the Ecliptic, that is, that describe the smallest circles.

III. By Tendency to Motion we understand not some thought but only that a part of matter is so situated and impelled to motion that it would really go in some direction if it were not prevented by any cause.

IV. By Angle we understand whatever in a body projects beyond the spherical shape.

AXIOMS

I. Many globules joined together cannot occupy a continuous space.

II. A portion of matter divided into angular parts, if its parts move round their own centers, requires a greater space than if all its parts were at rest and all their sides touched each other immediately.

III. The smaller a part of matter is, the more easily is it divided by the same force.

IV. Parts of matter that are in motion in the same direction, and in that motion do not recede from each other, are not actually divided.

PROPOSITION I

Parts of matter into which it was first divided were not round but angular.

PROOF

All matter was divided into equal and similar parts from the beginning (by the Postulate); therefore (by Axiom 1 and Proposition 2, Part II) they were not round; and therefore they were angular (by Definition 4).

Q.E.D.

PROPOSITION II

A force that made the particles of matter move around their own centers, at the same time made the angles of the particles rub together on their meeting.

PROOF

All matter in the beginning was divided into equal (by the Postulate) and angular (by Proposition 1, Part III). If therefore, as soon as they began to move round their own centers, their angles had not been rubbed away, necessarily (by Axiom 2) all matter would have had to occupy a greater space than when it was at rest; but this is absurd (by Proposition 4, Part II); therefore their angles were rubbed away as soon as they began to move.

Q.E.D.

THOUGHTS ON METAPHYSICS
APPENDIX: PART I
CONTAINING
METAPHYSICAL SPECULATIONS

Wherein are briefly explained the principal questions that commonly arise in the general field of Metaphysics concerning Being and its affections.

CHAPTER 1

True Being, False Being, and Being deduced by Reason

I say nothing about the definitions of this science nor even about the matter of which it treats. My intention is solely to explain here the points that are rather obscure and are discussed by authors in their metaphysical writings.

Definition of Being

Let us begin therefore with Being, by which I understand: All that, when perceived clearly and distinctly, we find necessarily existing or at least potentially existing.

A Chimera, an Imaginary Being, and a Being deduced by Reason are not Beings

From this definition, or if it is preferred, from this description, it follows that a Chimera, an Imaginary Being, and a Being deduced by Reason can in no sense be accepted among beings. For a Chimera13 by its very nature cannot exist. As for an Imaginary Being, it excludes clear and distinct perception; because man, from the mere use of freedom alone, and not unwittingly, as in the case of error, but purposely and knowingly, joins together what he wishes to join and disunites what it pleases him to disunite. Finally, a Being deduced by Reason is nothing but a way of thinking, that serves to retain, explain, and imagine more easily things that are known. It should be observed now that by a way of thinking we understand what we have already explained in the Scholium to proposition 4, Part I; namely, all the affections of thought, such as understanding, joy, imagination, and so on.

In What Ways of Thinking We Retain Things

That there are certain ways of thinking that serve to retain things more firmly and more easily, and to recall them to mind whenever we so desire, or to retain them in our mind, is sufficiently well established for those who use that well known rule of memory; to remember a totally new item and to imprint it on the memory, we resort to another item that is familiar to us, and that has identity with this one either in name only or in reality. In a similar manner the Philosophers have arranged all natural things in certain categories to which they have recourse to them, that they call genus, species, and so on.

In What Ways of Thinking We Explain Things

To explain a thing, we have also ways of thinking; we determine it by comparison with something else. The ways of thinking that we use for this purpose are called time, number, measurement, and whatever others there may be. Of those mentioned, time serves to explain duration; number, the separation of quantity; measurement, the continuity of quantity.

In What Ways of Thinking We Imagine Things

Lastly, as we are accustomed, every time we know things, to represent them also by some image in our imagination, it happens that we imagine positively non-beings as beings. For the mind, considered solely in itself, in so far as a thinking thing, does not have a greater power to affirm than to deny; but since imagination is nothing but sensation of those traces found in the brain as a result of the movement of spirits, a movement that is aroused in the senses by objects, such sensation cannot be other than a confused affirmation. Hence it happens that we imagine as beings all the modes that the mind uses for denial; such as blindness, extremity or finality, terminus, darkness, etc.

Why The Beings Deduced by Reason Are Not Ideas of Things and Yet Are so Considered

Hence it is clearly evident that these ways of thinking are not ideas of things and cannot in any sense be classed as ideas; and so too they have no idea that necessarily exists or can exist. But the reason why these ways of thinking are considered as ideas of things is that they spring and arise from ideas of things so immediately as to be confused very readily with them by those who are not scrupulously alert. That is why also names have been assigned to them as if to signify beings that exist outside our own mind and why these beings, or rather these non-beings, have been called Beings deduced by Reason.

False Distinction Between Real Being And Being Deduced by Reason

From what precedes it is easy to see how inept is the division that separates Being into Real Being and Being deduced by Reason. For Being is thus divided into Being and Non-Being, or into Being and Mode of Thinking. However I am not surprised that Philosophers who are concerned with words or grammar fall into such errors: for they judge things by names, not names by things.

How Being Deduced by Reason can be Termed Mere Nothingness and How it can be Termed Real Being

No less unreasonable is the man who asserts that Being deduced by Reason is not mere Nothingness. For if he seeks for the significance of these terms beyond his understanding, he will find that it is mere Nothingness. If on the contrary he understands the ways of thinking themselves, they are Real Beings. For when I ask what a species is, I am merely asking the nature of this way of thinking that is really a Being and is distinct from any other way of thinking. But these ways of thinking cannot be called ideas and cannot be called either true or false, just as love cannot be called true or false, but good or bad. So when Plato said that man is a biped animal without feathers he did not commit a greater error than those who said that man is a rational animal. For Plato knew, as well as others know, that man is a rational animal. But he classified man in a particular category so that, whenever he wanted to think of man, he would instantly encounter the thought of man by referring to the category that he could remember easily. Moreover Aristotle was very gravely mistaken if he thought that he had adequately explained the essence of man by his own definition. Whether Plato acted properly might be questioned. But this is not the place for such a discussion.

In an Investigation of Things, Real Beings are not to be Confused with Beings Deduced by Reason

From all that has been said before, it is evident that there is no agreement between a Real Being and the objects represented by the Beings deduced by Reason. Hence it is easy to see how carefully we must guard, in the investigation of things, against confusing Real Beings with Beings deduced by Reason. For there is a difference between inquiring into the nature of things and inquiring into the ways in which we perceive them. If these two processes are confused, we shall be able to understand neither the ways of perception nor the nature itself; besides, and this is a very serious matter, we shall fall into grave errors, as has hitherto been the case with many.

How to Distinguish Between the Being Deduced by Reason and the Imaginary Being

It should also be observed that many have confused Being deduced by Reason with Imaginary Being. They believe that Imaginary Being is also Being deduced by Reason, because it has no existence outside the mind. But if one carefully considers the definitions just proposed of Being deduced by Reason and Imaginary Being, a great difference between them will be discovered, not only in respect of their cause, but also as a result of their nature, without respect to their cause. For we saw that Imaginary Being is nothing but two termini conjoined solely by the will without any guidance by Reason. Hence Imaginary Being may by accident be true. But Being deduced by Reason neither depends on the will alone, nor is it composed of any termini mutually conjoined, as is sufficiently evident from the definition. If anyone then asks whether Imaginary Being is Real Being, or Being deduced by Reason, we must repeat and assert only that we have already said, that the division of Being into Real Being and Being deduced by Reason is bad. For that reason the question whether Imaginary Being is Real Being or Being deduced by Reason is founded on no valid basis; for it is assumed that all Beings are divided into Real Beings and Beings deduced by Reason.

Division of Being

But let us return to our proposed topic, from which we seem to have digressed to some extent. From the definition of Being, or, if one prefers, from the definition already given, it is easy to see that a Being must be divided into a being that exists necessarily by its own nature, that is, whose essence involves existence, and into a being whose essence involves only a possible existence. This latter being is divided into Substance and Mode, whose definitions are given in Part I of the Principles of Philosophy, articles 51, 52 and 56; it is therefore not necessary to repeat them here. I only want this to be observed in regard to this division, that we expressly state: A Being is divided into Substance and Mode, but not into Substance and Accident; for the Accident is nothing more than a way of thinking, since it denotes only a respect. For example, when I say that a triangle moves, the motion is not a mode of the triangle but of the body that moves. Hence in respect of the triangle the motion is called an Accident, but in respect of the body the motion is a real being, or a mode. For the motion cannot be conceived without the body but it can be so conceived without the triangle.

Moreover, to clarify the comprehension of what has already been said and also of what follows, we shall attempt to explain what must be understood by the being of essence, the being of existence, and lastly the being of power. Our motive is the ignorance of certain persons, who recognize no distinction between essence and existence or, if they do so, confuse the being of essence with the being of the idea or the being of power. To satisfy them and to elucidate the question itself we shall explain the problem as distinctly as we can in the following chapter.

CHAPTER 2

The Nature of the Being of Essence, of the Being of Existence, of the Being of Idea, of the Being of Power

To obtain a clear perception of the meaning of these four beings, it is only necessary to set before us what we have said about the uncreated substance, that is God, namely:

Creatures are Eminently in God

1. God contains eminently what is found formally in created things, that is, God has such attributes that all created things are contained therein in a more eminent way; see Part I, Axiom 8 and Corollary I to Proposition

12. For example, we clearly conceive extension without any existence and so, since it has by itself no power to exist, we proved that it was created by God (Last Proposition, Part I). And, because there must be in the cause as much perfection at least as in the effect, it follows that all the perfections of extension are in God, since we afterward saw that the extended thing was by its nature divisible, that is, contains an imperfection, we could not consequently attribute extension to God (Part I, Proposition 16), and so we were compelled to admit that there is in God some attitute that contains all the imperfections of matter in a more excellent form (Scholium to Proposition 9, Part I), and that can take the place of matter.

2. God knows Himself and all other things; that is, He has also in Himself all things objectively (Part I, Proposition 9).

3. God is the cause of all things, and He operates through the absolute fredom of His will.

The Nature of the Being of Essence, of Existence, of Idea, and of Power

So it is clearly to be seen from this what we mean by these four beings.

First of all, the being of essence is nothing more than the manner in which created things are comprehended in the attributes of God. Secondly, the being of idea is so called in so far as all things are contained in the idea of God. Then the being of power is so called with regard to the power of God, by which He had been able to create by the absolute freedom of His will all that did not exist until then. Lastly, the being of existence is the essence itself of things outside God and considered in itself, and it is attributed to things after their creation by God.

These Four Beings are not Distinguished from each other except in Created Things

From this it is quite clear that these four beings are distinguished from each other only in created things, but in no respect in God. For we do not conceive that God was in power in another being and His existence and His understanding are not distinguished from His essence.

Reply to Certain Questions on Essence

From these conclusions we can easily reply to the questions that are frequently raised on the subject of essence. These questions are as follows: Is essence distinct from existence? If it is distinct, is it something different from idea? If it is something different from idea, does it have some existence beyond the understanding?

This last point must necessarily be admitted. Now to the first question on the distinction we reply that in God the essence is not distinct from the existence, since without existence essence cannot be conceived; in the other beings the essence differs from existence, for the former can be conceived without the latter. To the second question we reply that a thing that is perceived beyond the understanding clearly and distinctly, that is, truly, is something different from an idea. But a final question is posed: Is the being beyond the understanding something by itself or is it created by God?

Our answer is that formal essence is not by itself, nor is it created; for these two assertions would imply that a thing exists in action, but that it depends solely on the divine essence, in which all things are contained. And so in this sense we concur with those who say that the essences of things are eternal. It might still be asked: How do we know the essence of things before knowing the nature of God?; since those essences, as we have just said, depend solely on the nature of God. To this I reply that this arises from the fact that things are already created; for if they were not created, I would wholeheartedly agree that this knowledge would be impossible without a previous adequate knowledge of the nature of God. Likewise it would be impossible, even more impossible, to know the nature of the ordinates without knowing the nature of the Parabola.

Why the Author in his Definition of Essence Resorts to the Attributes of God

It must further be observed that, although the essences of the non-existing modes are comprehended in their substances, and their being of essence is in their substances, we have nevertheless wished to resort to God in order to explain in a general sense the essence of the modes and substance, and also because the essence of the modes was not in their substance until these substances were created and until we sought the eternal being of the essences.

Why the Author has not Examined the Definitions Proposed by Others

I do not think it worthwhile to refute here the authors whose opinions differ from ours, or to examine their definitions or descriptions of essence and existence; for in this way we should be making more obscure what is now clear. For what is clearer than understanding what essence and existence are? Since we cannot attach any definition to a thing without at the same time explaining its essence.

How to Learn Easily the Distinction between Essence and Existence

Finally, if any Philosopher still doubts whether essence is distinct from existence in created things, he has no reason to exert himself much to banish this doubt about the definitions of essence and existence. For if he merely approaches any sculptor or wood carver, they will show him how they conceive in a certain orderliness a statue that does not yet exist and afterward they will present it to him as existing.

CHAPTER 3

The Meaning of Necessary, Impossible, Possible, and Contingent

What we must here Understand by Affections

Having thus explained the nature of being in so far as it is being, we pass on to the explanation of some affections of being; where it is to be observed that by affections we understand here what Descartes has elsewhere designated as attributes in Part I, Philosophical Principles, article 52. For Being, in so far as it is a being, does not affect us by itself, as a substance. It must therefore be explained by some attribute, from which however it differs only by the distinction of Reason.

I cannot therefore be sufficiently surprised at the excessively subtle ingenuities of those who have sought, not without great detriment to the truth, an intermediary between Being and Nothingness. But I shall not stop to refute their error, since they themselves, when they try to give definitions of such affections, dissipate themselves completely in their own vain subtleties.

Definitions of Affections

We shall therefore pursue our subject and state that the affections of Being are certain attributes, under which we know the essence or the existence of every being, from which however they are not distinct except by a distinction of Reason. Certain of these affections I shall try to explain here (for I am not understanding to treat all of them) and to distinguish them from the denominations that are not the affections of any being. And first of all I shall discuss the meaning of necessary and impossible.

In How Many Ways a Thing is Said to be Necessary and Impossible

A thing is said to be necessary and impossible in two ways; either in respect of its essence, or in respect of its cause. In respect of the essence, we know that God exists necessarily; for His essence cannot be conceived without existence. But a Chimera in respect of the contradiction contained in its essence exists. In respect of the cause, things, for example material things, are said to be impossible or necessary; for if we consider only their essence, we can conceive it clearly and distinctly without existence. For this reason they can never exist by the force and necessity of their essence, but only by the force of their cause, that is, God, the creator of all things. Therefore, if it is the divine decree that a thing exist, it will exist necessarily; if not, it will be impossible for it to exist. For it is self-evident that a thing that has no cause, either internal or external, for existence, cannot possibly exist. But in this second hypothesis a thing is considered of such a nature that neither by the force of its essence, which is what I understand by internal cause, nor by the force of the divine decree, the eternal and sole cause of all things, can it exist. Hence it follows that it is impossible for things such as we have assumed in the second hypothesis to exist.

How the Chimera can be Called a verbal Being

It must here be observed:

1. That a Chimera, being neither in the understanding nor in the imagination, can properly be called a Verbal Being; for it cannot be expressed except by words. For

example, we express in words a squared circle, but we cannot in any way imagine it and still less can we understand it. Therefore a Chimera is nothing but a word, and so Impossibility cannot be numbered among its affections of being, for it is a simple negation.

Created Things, in as much as Essence and Existence, Depend on God

2. It must be observed that not only the existence of created beings, but also, as we shall prove later in the second part with the most convincing evidence, their essence and nature depend solely on the decree of God. Hence it clearly follows that created things have not of themselves any necessity, since they have no essence by themselves and do not exist by themselves.

The Necessity that is in Created Things by a Cause is Related to their Essence or their Existence, but in God these two Things are not Distinct

3. It must be observed that the necessity such as is in created things by the power of the cause is said to be so in respect of their essence or in respect of their existence: for these two are distinct from each other in created things. For essence depends on the eternal laws of nature, while existence depends on the succession and order of causes. But in God, whose essence is not distinct from His existence, the necessity of the essence also is not distinct from the necessity of existence. Hence it follows that, if we conceived the entire order of Nature, we should find that many things, whose nature we perceive clearly and distinctly, that is, whose essence is necessarily such and such, could in no manner exist; for we should find that it is as impossible for such things to exist in Nature as we know it at present as it is impossible for a huge elephant to be able to pass through the eye of a needle; although we clearly perceive the nature of both. Hence the existence of those things would be merely a Chimera, that we could neither imagine nor understand.

Possibility and Contingency are not Affections of Things

4. To these observations on necessity and impossibility it has seemed fitting to add a few words on possibility and contingency; for these two concepts are considered by some as affections of things, although they are really nothing but defects in our understanding. This I shall show clearly after explaining the meaning of these two terms.

The Meaning of Possible and of Contingent

A thing is said to be possible when we know its efficient cause and yet are unaware whether it is a determined cause. Hence we can consider it as possible, but not as necessary or impossible. If however we consider the essence of a thing simply, but not its cause, we shall call it contingent; that is, we shall consider it, so to speak, as intermediary between God and a Chimera; because we do not find in it, considered from the viewpoint of essence, any necessity for existence, as in the divine essence, or any contradiction or impossibility, as in a Chimera. But if anyone wants to call contingent what I term possible and on the other hand possible what I call contingent, I shall not contradict him; for I am not accustomed to dispute about names. It will be sufficient to grant that these two terms are nothing but defects in our perception and not something real.

Possibility and Contingency are only Defects of our Understanding

If anyone should want to deny this, his error can be proved without any difficulty. For if he considers Nature, and how it depends on God, he will find nothing contingent in things, that is, nothing that, considered as a thing, can exist or not exist, or, to use the popular idiom, that is really contingent. This is readily evident from what we have explained in Axiom 10, Part I: As much force is required to create a thing as to conserve it. Therefore no created thing does anything by its own power, just as no created thing begins to exist by its own power. From which it follows that nothing happens except by the power of the all-creating cause, that is, God, who by his intervention procreates all things every moment. Since nothing happens except by the divine power alone, it is easy to see that those things that happen occur by the power of God's decree and by His will.

But, since there is no inconsistency or change in God (by Proposition 18 and Corollary to Proposition 20, Part I), He must have decreed from all eternity that He would produce those things that He now produces; and, since nothing is more necessary than the existence of what God has decreed should exist, it follows that the necessity of existence has been since all eternity in all created things. Nor can we say that those things are contingent, because God could have decreed otherwise. For since in eternity when does not exist, nor before, nor after, or any temporal affection, it follows that God did not exist before those decrees so as to be able to decree otherwise.

Reconciliation of Freedom of our Will with the Predestination of God Transcends Human Comprehension

In regard to the freedom of the human will, that we have asserted is free (Scholium to Proposition 15, Part I), it too is conserved by God's intervention, and no man wishes anything or does anything except what God has since eternity decreed that he should wish or do How that is possible, with the maintenance of human freedom, transcends our comprehension. Nor should we for that reason reject on account of our ignorance what we clearly perceive. For we know clearly and distinctly, if we consider our own nature, that we are free in our actions and that we deliberate on many of them for the sole reason that we want these actions. If we also consider the nature of God, as we have just shown, we clearly and distinctly perceive that everything depends on Him and that nothing exists except that of which the existence has been decreed by God since eternity. How the human will is procreated by God every single moment in such a fashion as to remain free, that we know not. For there are many things that transcend our understanding and yet we know that they were performed by God; for example, that real division of matter into infinite particles was proved by us with sufficient evidence (in Part 2, Proposition II), although we do not know how that division arose. Observe that we assume here as a known fact that these two notions, possibility and contingency, signify only a defect in our knowledge of the existence of a thing.

CHAPTER 4

Duration of Time

From the division of Being that we made above into being whose essence involves existence and into being whose essence involves only possible existence, arises the distinction between eternity and duration.

What Eternity is

Of eternity we shall speak at greater length later on. At this point we shall say only that it is the attribute under which we conceive the infinite existence of God.

What Duration is

Duration is the attribute under which we conceive the existence of created things, in so far as they persist in their actuality. From this it clearly follows that between duration and the entire existence of anything there is no distinction except that of Reason.

For whatever you withdraw from the duration of a thing must necessarily be withdrawn from its existence. To determine duration, we compare it with the duration of those things that have an unvarying and determined motion and this comparison is called time.

What Time is

Time therefore is not an affection of things, but only a simple way of thinking, or, as we have already stated, a being deduced by Reason: it is a way of thinking that serves to explain duration. Here it must be observed, in regard to duration,– and this will later on be serviceable when we discuss eternity—that duration is conceived as greater and smaller, as though composed of parts, and finally that it is an attribute of existence only, not of essence.

CHAPTER 5

Opposition, Order, etc.

From the fact that we compare things with each other, certain notions arise that, however, are nothing, outside the things themselves, but ways of thinking. This is evident because, if we wish to consider them as things placed outside thought, we instantly confuse a clear concept that we have of them elsewhere. Such are the notions of Opposition, Order, Agreement, Diversity, Subject, Complement and whatever other notions similar to these there may be.

What are Opposition, Order, Agreement, Diversity, Subject, Complement, etc.

These things, I assert, are perceived clearly enough by us, as long as we conceive them, not as something distinct from the essences of things opposed, classified, etc., but only as modes of thinking by which we retain or imagine more easily the things themselves. Therefore I do not consider it necessary to discuss them at greater length at this point, but I proceed to the terms commonly called transcendental.

CHAPTER 6

One, the True, the Good

These terms are considered by almost all Metaphysicians as the most general Affections of Being. For they say that all Being is One, True, and Good, although nobody thinks it. But we shall see what they mean by these terms when we have examined each of them separately.

What Oneness is

Let us begin therefore with the first, namely, One. They say that this term signifies something real beyond the understanding; but they cannot explain what this adds to being. This clearly shows that they confuse beings deduced by Reason with Real Being; hence they create confusion out of what they understand clearly. Now we assert that Oneness is in no sense distinct from the thing, or adds nothing to being, but is only a mode of thinking, by means of which we separate one thing from other things that are similar to it or agree with it in some manner.

What Plurality is and in what Respect God can be Said to be One and in what Respect Unique

To Oneness is opposed Plurality, which certainly adds nothing to things, and is nothing but another mode of thinking, as we know clearly and distinctly. Nor do I see what remains to be said further about a subject that is clear. Only this should be observed here, that God, in so far as we distinguish Him from other beings, can be said to be One; but, in so far as we conceive that there cannot be several with the same nature, He is called unique. But, if we wanted to examine the question more carefully, we could perhaps show that God is not called one and unique except incorrectly. But it is not such an important matter; in fact, it is actually of no importance, to those who are concerned with them, not with names. Therefore, leaving this question, we pass on to the next one and we shall explain in the same way what false is.

What False is, What True is, both to the People and to the Philosopher

To acquire a proper conception of these two notions, true and false, we shall begin with the significance of the words; from which it will be apparent that they are nothing but the external denominations of things, and cannot be assigned to them except in a rhetorical sense. But since the people first discovered words, that are afterward used by Philosophers, it seems to be the province of the person who searches for the first significance of a word to ask what it first meant to the people; especially in the absence of other causes that could be drawn from the nature of language for such an investigation. The first meaning therefore of true and false seems to have originated from stories; and a story was said to be true that described an incident that had actually occurred; false, that described an incident that had not occurred anywhere at all. Afterward Philosophers used this term to denote agreement or non-agreement of an idea with its object. Therefore an idea is called True when it shows us a thing as it is in itself. False when it shows us a thing otherwise than it is in reality. Ideas are, in fact, nothing but stories or mental histories of nature. And hence there was later on a metaphorical transference to inert things; as when we say that gold is true or false, as if the gold presented to us told us something about itself that is in it, or not.

True is not a Transcendental Term

Those persons therefore are quite deceived who have considered true a transcendental term or an affection of Being. For it cannot be applied to things themselves except incorrectly, or, if you prefer, rhetorically.

The Difference Between Truth and a True Idea

If one asks further what truth is apart from a true idea, one may also ask what whiteness is apart from a white body: for these things are related to each other in the same way.

The cause of True and the cause of False we have already discussed previously: therefore nothing remains to be observed here nor would it have been worth while to observe what we have said, if writers had not been so involved in similar fatuities as not to be able to extricate themselves afterward in their search everywhere for trouble where there is none.

What are the Properties of Truth? Certainty is not in Things

The properties of truth or of an idea are true.

1. Because it is clear and distinct.

2. Because it banishes all doubt, by a single word, as to its certainty. Those who seek certainty in things themselves are deceived in the same way as when they seek Truth in them. And although we say A thing is uncertain, we take the object for the idea, as orators do, just as when we say that A thing is doubtful: unless perhaps we understand by uncertainty either the thing that induces uncertainty or the doubt in us. Nor is there any need to dwell any longer on these questions. Therefore we shall proceed to the third term, and at the same time we shall explain what its contrary means.

Good and Bad are so Called Only Relatively

A thing considered by itself is said to be neither good nor bad, but only in relation to another thing, to which it is useful or harmful in securing what it likes. And so every single thing may be said to be good and bad in different respects and at the same time. Thus, for example, Ahitophel's advice to Absalom is called good in the Holy Scriptures: yet it was bad for David, whose death it presaged. But many other things are good that are not good for all: thus, salvation is good for men, but it is neither good nor bad for animals or plants with which it has no relation. God is called supremely good, because He is beneficial to all: by His intervention He conserves the being of everyone, than which nothing is more beloved. Nothing can be absolutely bad, as is self-evident.

Why Some Have Granted a Metaphysical Good

Those who are in quest of a metaphysical good that lacks every relation labor under a false preconception: because they confuse a distinction of Reason with a Real or Modal distinction. For they distinguish between a thing itself and the tendency that is in everything to conserve its being, although they do not know what they mean by tendency. For between these two concepts, although they are distinguished by Reason or rather by words,–a fact that has especially led to error—there is really no distinction whatever.

How to Distinguish Things and the Tendency by Virtue of which they tend to Persist in their own State

To make it clearly understood, we shall present an example of something very simple. Motion has the power of persisting in its state. This power is certainly nothing but the motion itself, that is, the nature of motion is such.

For if I say that in this body A there is nothing else but a certain amount of motion, it clearly follows from this, so long as I consider this body A, that I must always say that this body moves. For if I said that this body has lost by itself its power of motion, I should necessarily atttribute to it something more than what we assumed in the hypothesis, and thus it would lose its nature.

But if this reasoning seems rather obscure, let us agree then that this tendency to move is something beyond the laws themselves and the nature of motion: since therefore it is assumed that this tendency is a metaphysical good, this tendency will also necessarily have in itself a tendency to persist in itself and this tendency in turn will have another and so on to infinity. Which is the greatest absurdity imaginable.

Now the Reason why some distinguish the tendency from the thing itself is that they find in themselves a desire to conserve themselves and imagine such a desire in everything.

Whether God may be Called Good before the Creation of Things

The question however is asked whether God can be called good before He created things. From our definition it seems to follow that God did not have such an attribute, because we say that a thing, considered in itself, can be called neither good nor bad. Now this will appear absurd to many: but on what grounds, I do not know. For we affirm of God many attributes of this kind that, before the creation of things, did not apply to Him, except in regard to power: as when He is called creator, judge, all-merciful, etc. Therefore such arguments ought not to delay us.

How Perfect Can be so Called Relatively and how it can be Called Absolutely

Furthermore, just as good and bad can be predicated only relatively, so too with perfection, except when we take perfection for the essence itself of a thing, in which sense, as we said previously, God has infinite perfection, that is, infinite essence, or infinite being.

It is not my intention to add anything more to this: for I think that the rest of what relates to the general field of Metaphysics is well enough known: and hence it is not worthwhile to pursue it any further.

PART II

Wherein are Briefly Explained the Principal Questions that Commonly Arise in the Special Field of Metaphysics on God and His Attributes and on the Human Mind

CHAPTER 1

THE ETERNITY OF GOD

Division of Substances

We have already explained that in the nature of things nothing exists except substances and their modes. It will therefore not be expected for us to say anything here about substantial forms and real accidents. For these concepts, and others of the same kind, are totally inept. We have then divided substances into two principal classes, namely Extension and Thought, and Thought into created thought, or the human mind, and uncreated thought, that is, God. Now we have previously proved adequately the existence of God both a posteriori, that is, from the idea that we have of Him, and a priori, that is, from His essence as the cause of God's existence. But, since we have treated some of His attributes more cursorily than the importance of the subject demands, we have decided to resume them here, and to explain them at greater length, and at the same time to resolve certain problems.

No Duration Belongs to God

The principal attribute that must be considered before all others is the Eternity of God, whereby we explain His duration: or rather, to attribute no duration to God, we say that He is eternal. For, as we have noted in Part I, duration is an affection of existence, not of the essence of things. Thus we cannot affirm any duration of God, whose existence is of His own essence. For to attribute duration to God is to distinguish His existence from His essence. There are however some who ask whether God has now not existed longer than since he created Adam. And as this seems quite clear to them, they conclude for that reason that Duration should in no sense be withdrawn from God. But they beg the question. For they assume that the essence of God is distinct from His existence. For they ask whether God, who existed as far back as the creation of Adam, did not add to His existence the time since the creation of Adam to our time. Thus they assign to God a longer duration every single day, and assume that He is continuously as it were self-created. For if they did not distinguish God's existence from His essence, they would in no sense attribute duration to God, since duration can in no manner whatever belong to the essence of things. For no one will ever say that the essence of a circle or a triangle, in so far as it is an eternal truth, has lasted longer now than in the time of Adam.

Furthermore, since duration is conceived as greater or smaller, that is, composed of parts, it manifestly follows that no duration can be attributed to God. For, since His Being is eternal, that is, since nothing before or after can be predicated of Him, we can never affirm duration of Him without at the same time destroying the true concept that we have of God: that is, by attributing duration to Him, we should be dividing into parts what is infinite by its nature and what can never be conceived except as infinite.

Reasons Why Authors Attributed Duration to God

The reasons for the errors made by authors are:

1. That they have attempted to explain eternity without regard to God, as if eternity could be understood without contemplation of the divine essence or as if it were anything other than the divine essence: and that again arises from our having become accustomed, on account of an insufficiency of vocabulary, to attribute eternity to things too whose essence is distinct from their existence: as when we say that there is no contradiction in the world having existed since eternity: and also to the essences of things, while we do not conceive the things as existing: for we then call the essences eternal.

2. Because they did not attribute duration to things except in so far as they considered them to be subjected to a continuous variation, not, as we do, in as much as their essence is distinct from their existence.

3. Finally, because they distinguished the essence of God, as the essence of created things, from His existence.

These errors, I assert, have been for them an opportunity for new errors. For the first mistake was the reason for their not understanding what eternity was, and for considering it as though it were some aspect of duration.

The second error was their inability to discover readily the difference between the duration of things created and the eternity of God.

Finally, the last error was, since duration is merely an affection of existence, to distinguish the existence of God Himself from His essence and, as we have already said, to attribute duration to God.

What Eternity is

But, to understand more clearly what Eternity is and how it cannot be conceived without the divine essence, what we have already asserted must be considered, namely: that created things, that is, all things except God, always exist solely by the power or essences of God, not by their own power. Hence it follows that the present existence of things is not the cause of their future existence, but only the immutability of God, on account of which we are compelled to say: From the moment that God has created a thing, He will conserve it afterward, that is, He will continue the same action of creation.

Whence we conclude:

1. That a created thing can be said to enjoy existence, because the existence is not of its own essence. But God cannot be said to enjoy existence, for the existence of God is God Himself. So too with His essence.

Whence it follows:

That created things enjoy duration, but God does not do so in any manner whatever.

2. That all created things, while enjoying their present duration and existence, completely lack a future duration, because it must continuously be attributed to them: but in regard to their essence nothing similar can be predicated. But as

for God, since His existence is His essence, we cannot attribute to Him a future existence: for this same existence that He would then have must be attributed to Him in action from this present moment: or, to speak more correctly, infinite existence in action belongs to God in the same way as infinite understanding belongs to Him in action. This infinite existence I term Eternity, which is to be attributed to God only, although the duration of these things is unlimited in either direction.

So much for eternity. Of God's necessity I say nothing, because there is no need, since we have proved His existence from His essence. Let us therefore proceed to Unity.

CHAPTER 2

THE UNITY OF GOD

We have very often been amazed at the futile arguments with which authors try to establish the Unity of God, such as: If one God could create the world, other gods would be useless. If all things tend to the same end, they have been produced by a single constructor: and other arguments of a like nature, drawn from external relationships and denominations. Disregarding therefore all these superfluities, we shall here propose our proof as lucidly and briefly as we can, and that in the following manner.

God is Unique

Among the attributes we listed supreme intelligence and we added that He has all His perfection from Himself and not from another. If one now says that there are many gods or many supremely perfect beings, they will all necessarily have to be supremely intelligent. In such a case, it is not sufficient for each one to know only himself. For since each god must know all things, he must know both himself and the other gods. Hence it would follow that the perfection of knowledge of each would depend partly on himself and partly on another god. No god then will be able to be a supremely perfect being: that is, as we have just observed, a being that has all his perfection from himself, not from another. Yet we have already proved that God is a supremely perfect being and that He exists. We can therefore now conclude that He is the unique God in existence. For if many existed it would follow that the most perfect being has an imperfection, which is absurd. So much for the Unity of God.

CHAPTER 3

THE IMMENSITY OF GOD

How God can be Said to be Infinite and How, Immense

We have previously explained that no being can be conceived finite and imperfect, that is, participating in Nothing, unless we first consider the perfect and infinite being, that is, God. That is why God alone can be said to be absolutely infinite, since we find that He is composed in reality of infinite perfection. But He can also be called immense or interminable, in so far as we are mindful that no other being exists by whom the perfection of God can be terminated. Hence it follows that the Infinity of God, despite the term, is something supremely positive. For we say that He is infinite in so far as we consider His essence or His supreme perfection. But Immensity is ascribed to God only in a relative sense: for it does not belong to God in so far as He is considered absolutely as a supremely perfect being, but in so far as He is considered the first cause. And even if this first cause were not perfect in a supreme degree, but only so in relation to secondary beings, none the less it would be immense. For there would be no being, and consequently no being could be conceived, more perfect than Himself by whom He could be limited or measured. (See more fully on these points Axiom 9, Part I).

What is Commonly Understood by the Immensity of God

Often however authors, when discussing the Immensity of God, seem to ascribe quantity to God.

For they wish to conclude from this attribute that God must necessarily be present everywhere. As if they wished to say that, if God were not in a certain place, His quantity was limited. This view appears still more clearly from another argument that they adduce to prove that God is infinite or immense (for these two attributes are confused) and also that He is ubiquitous. If God, they declare, is a pure act, as He really is, He is necessarily ubiquitous and infinite. For if He were not ubiquitous, or could not be wherever He wanted to be or had necessarily to move (Note this), it is clearly evident that they attribute Immensity to God in so far as they consider Him as a Quantity. For they adduce these arguments of theirs from the properties of extension in order to affirm the Immensity of God, which is the greatest absurdity possible.

It is Proved that God is Ubiquitous

If one were to ask now how we shall prove God is ubiquitous, I reply that this has already been proved and more than adequately by us, when we showed that nothing can exist for even an instant without being re-created by God every single instant.

The Omniscience of Good cannot be Explained

Furthermore, to understand duly the Ubiquity or Presence of God in every single thing, it would be necessary to be able to penetrate into the intimate nature of the divine will by means of which He created things and continually re-creates them. Since this transcends human understanding, it is impossible to explain how God is ubiquitous.

Some Consider the Immensity of God Triple, but Wrongly so

Some assert that the Immensity of God is triple, namely: immensity of essence, immensity of power, and lastly immensity of presence.

But they are talking nonsense, for they seem to make a distinction between God's essence and His power.

God's Power is not Distinct from His Essence

Others have expressed the same view more openly, declaring that God is ubiquitous by His power, not by His essence. As if the power of God were distinct from all His attributes, or His infinite essence, whereas it can be nothing else.

For if it were anything else, it would be either a creature, or some accident of the divine essence, without which this essence could be conceived. Both conclusions are absurd. For if it were a creature, it would need God's power for its conservation; and so there would be a succession to infinity.

If it were something accidental, God would not be a being supremely simple, contrary to what has been proved previously.

The Omnipresence of God is Not Distinct either from His Essence

Finally, by Immensity of the presence they also seem to mean something other than God's essence, by which things are created and conserved continuously. Which is certainly a great absurdity into which they have fallen because they have confused God's understanding with human understanding, often comparing His power with that of kings.

CHAPTER 4

THE IMMUTABILITY OF GOD

What Change is and What Transformation is

By change we understand in this place the variation that can exist in any subject whatever, with the essence itself of the subject remaining unimpaired; although the term is commonly taken in a wider sense to signify the corruption of things, not indeed an absolute corruption, but one that at the same time involves a subsequent generation: as when we say turf changes into ashes, or that men change into animals. But Philosophers use a different expression to denote this change, namely Transformation. But we are here speaking only of the change in which there is no transformation of the subject, as when we say: Peter has changed color, character, etc.

In God Transformation Does not take Place

We must now see whether such changes take place in God: for there is no need to say anything of transformation, since we have shown that God necessarily exists, that is, that God cannot cease being, or transform Himself into another god: for in that case He would cease to be and there would be many gods at the same time; which we have shown to be two absurdities.

What are the Causes of Change

To understand more clearly what remains to be said here, we must consider that every change proceeds either from external causes, with or without the will of the subject, or from an internal cause, and by the choice of the subject itself. For example, being dark, or sickness, or growing, and such like notions proceed in man from external causes: against the will of the subect or according to his wish: but the desire to walk, to display anger, etc. proceed from internal causes.

God is not Changed by Another Being

The first changes that proceed from external causes, do not take place in God. For He alone is the cause of all things, and does not suffer anyone else. In addition, no created thing has in itself any power to exist: and hence much less has it the power of action outside itself or on its own cause. And although we often find in the Holy Scriptures that God was angry or saddened on account of the sins of man, and similar things, the effect is taken in these cases as the cause: as when we say that the Sun is stronger and higher in summer than in winter, although it has neither changed place, nor acquired strength. And that such notions are often taught even in the Holy Scriptures may easily be seen in Isaiah: for he says, chapter 59, verse 2, in rebuking the people: Your iniquities have separated between you and your God.

Nor is God Changed by Himself

Let us proceed then and ask whether there can exist in God any change coming from God. This we cannot grant in the case of God; or rather we deny it utterly. For all change that depends on the will of the subject occurs for the purpose of changing his condition for the better: which cannot take place in the supremely perfect being.

Then also a change of this kind does not occur except to avoid some disadvantage with a view to the acquisition of some benefit that is lacking: either of these two suppositions can have no place in God. Hence we conclude that God is an immutable being.

Observe that I have here purposely omitted the ordinary divisions of change, although we have also included them in some way. For there was no need to show each one singly as having no place in God, since we have proved in Proposition 16, Part I that God is incorporeal and that these ordinary divisions comprise only changes of matter.

CHAPTER 5

THE SIMPLICITY OF GOD

Three Kinds of Distinction among Things: Real, Modal, Distinction of Reason

Let us proceed to the simplicity of God. To understand rightly this attribute of God, we must recall to mind what Descartes said in his Principles of Philosophy, Part I, articles 48 and 49: That there is nothing in the nature of things beyond substances and their modes, from which is deduced the triple distinction (articles 60, 61, and 62), namely: The Real, the Modal, and the Distinction of Reason. Real distinction is so called when two substances are distinguished from each other, whether they have a different attribute or the same attribute: as, for example, thought and extension, or the parts of matter. The distinction is identifiable from the fact that each substance can be conceived and consequently can exist without the help of the other. Modal distinction is shown to be double, namely: that which exists between the mode of a substance and the substance itself: and that which exists between two modes of one and the same substance. And we know this distinction from the fact that, although each mode is conceived without the help of the other, yet neither one is conceived without the help of the substance whose modes they are. This we recognize from the fact that, although the substance can be conceived without its mode, the mode cannot be conceived without the substance. Lastly, a distinction of Reason is so called, when it exists between a substance and its attribute: as when duration is distinguished from extension. This distinction is recognized when such a substance cannot be conceived without such an attribute.

The Origin of all Combinations and How Many Kinds of Combination there are

From these three distinctions arises every combination. The first combination is that of two or more substances of the same attribute: as every combination that unites two or more bodies, or of different attribute, as man. The second combination is formed by the union of different modes. Lastly, the third combination is not formed, but is only conceived by Reason as if being formed to produce a readier comprehension of a thing. Things that are not combined in these first two modes must be called simple.

God is Being Supremely Simple

It must therefore be shown that God is not something combined: whence we shall be able to conclude that he is a supremely simple being. And this will be easy to do. For since it is self-evident that the component parts are anterior at least by nature to the combined thing, the substances, by the assemblage and union of which God is composed, will necessarily be by nature anterior to God

Himself and each one will be able to be conceived by itself, without being attributed to God. Then, as these substances are necessarily distinguished from each other in reality, each one of them will also necessarily be able to exist by itself and without the help of the others: and so, as we have just said, there could be as many gods as there are substances, of which God is assumed to be composed. For each, being able to exist by itself, will have to exist of itself: and accordingly will also have the power of assigning to itself all the perfections that we have shown to be in God, and so on: as we have already explained fully in Proposition 7, Part I, where we proved the existence of God. Now since nothing more absurd than this can be uttered, we conclude that God is not composed of an assemblage and union of substances. That in God too there exists no combination of different modes is sufficiently demonstrated from the fact that in God there are no modes. For modes arise from an alteration of the substance (see Principles, Part I, article 56). Finally, if anyone wishes to form another combination from the essence of things and their existence, we in no sense contradict him. But let it be remembered that we have now sufficiently proved that these two notions are not distinct in God.

The Attributes of God are Distinguished only by Reason

And hence we can now clearly conclude that all the distinctions that we make among God's attributes are only distinctions of Reason, and that they are not really distinct from each other: by which is understood distinctions of Reason such as I have just mentioned; that are recognized from the fact that such and such a substance cannot exist without such and such an attribute. Hence we conclude that God is a supremely simple being.

With the hodge-podge of distinctions of the Peripatetics we are not concerned: let us therefore pass on to to the life of God.

CHAPTER 6

THE LIFE OF GOD

What Philosophers Commonly Understand by Life

To understand rightly this attribute of God, namely Life, it is necessary for us to explain in a general manner what is denoted in everything by its life. And in the first place we shall examine the opinion of the Peripatetics. These philosophers understand by life the persistence of the nourishing soul with heat (see Aristotle, Treatise on Respiration, Book I, chapter 8). And, since they have imagined three souls, namely: the vegetative, the sensitive, and the intellectual souls, that they attribute only to plants, animals, and men, it follows, as they themselves admit, that other beings are lacking in life.

But yet they did not dare to say that minds and God lack life. Perhaps they were afraid of falling into what is the contrary view of life: If minds and Gods lacked life, they were dead. That is why Aristotle, in his Metaphysics, Book II, chapter 7, gives still another definition of life, peculiar only to minds, namely: Life is the act of understanding. And in this sense he ascribes life to God, who understands and is pure action. But we shall not exhaust ourselves in refuting these views: for as far as the three souls that they attribute to plants, animals, and men are concerned, we have adequately proved that they are nothing but figments; since we have shown that in matter there are only mechanical assemblages and operations. As for the life of God, I do not know why in Aristotle God is called an act of understanding rather than an act of will and such like. But, expecting no reply to this, I proceed to the explanation of life, as I promised.

To What Things Life may be Attributed

Although this term is often taken metaphorically to signify the character of a man, we shall briefly explain mainly what it denotes philosophically.

It must be observed that, if life is to be attributed to corporeal things too, nothing will be without life. If it is attributed to those beings only in which a soul is united to the body, it will have to be ascribed only to men, or perhaps to animals too; but not to minds or to God. Since however the expression life has generally a wider denotation, there is no doubt that it must be attributed to corporeal things too and to minds separated from bodies.

What Life is and What it is in God

We therefore understand by life the power through which things persist in their being. And, since that power is different from the things themselves, we rightly say that these things have life. But the power by which God persists in His being is merely His essence. Hence they make a very acceptable assertion when they say that God is life. There are not a few Theologians who believe that for this reason God is life and is not distinct from life. The Jews, when they took an oath, said: by the living Jehovah, and not by the life of Jehovah: as Joseph, swearing by the life of Pharaoh, said: By the life of Pharaoh.

CHAPTER 7
THE UNDERSTANDING OF GOD

God is Omniscient

Among God's attributes we previously enumerated Omniscience, which, it is sufficiently established, belongs to God: because knowledge contains a perfection in itself, and God, a being supremely perfect, must lack no perfection. Therefore knowledge must be attributed to God in the highest degree, such as presupposes or implies no ignorance or deprivation of knowledge.

For then there would be an imperfection in the attribute itself, that is, in God. Hence it follows that God never had understanding by power, nor draws any conclusion by reasoning.

Things Exterior to God are not the Objects of God's Knowledge

Furthermore, from the perfection of God it follows that His ideas are not limited, as ours are, by objects situated outside God. But, on the contrary, the things created by God are determined by God's understanding:14 for otherwise objects would have by themselves their own nature and essence and would be anterior, at least by nature, to the divine understanding: which is absurd. And certain others, who have not observed this carefully enough, have fallen into grave errors. For some have asserted in fact that there exists a matter outside God, co-eternal with Him, existing by itself, that, according to some, God in his intelligence arranged only in a certain order; while according to others, He imposed certain forms on them besides. Still others have admitted that there are things that, from their nature, are either necessary, or impossible, or contingent, and that for this reason God too knows these things as contingent, and is totally ignorant of whether they are or not. Finally, others have said that God knows contingent things from the circumstances, perhaps because He has had long experience, apart from these I could still mention here other errors of the same kind, did I not consider it superfluous: since the falsity of these opinions becomes self-evident from what has previously been said.

God Himself is the Object of God's Knowledge

Let us therefore return to our proposition, that outside God there is no object of His knowledge, but that He Himself is the object of His knowledge, and that He is even His own knowledge. Those who think that the world is also the object of God's knowledge are far less intelligent than those who propose that an edifice, constructed by some famous architect, be considered as the object of his knowledge. For the architect is compelled to seek suitable matter outside himself: but God has sought no matter outside Himself, but things, as far as their essence and their existence are concerned, have been produced by His understanding, that is, His will.

How God Knows Sin, and Beings of Reason, etc.

The question is now asked whether God knows evil and sin, and beings of Reason, and other similar things. We reply that God must necessarily know those things of which He is the cause: especially as they could not exist even for an instant without the aid of the divine cooperation. Since therefore evil and sin are not in things, but only in the human mind that makes comparisons between one thing and another, it follows that God does not know them outside human minds. We have said that Beings of Reason are modes of thinking, and they must be understood by God in this manner, that is, in so far as we perceive that He conserves and re-creates the human mind as it has been constituted: not that God has in Himself such modes of thinking in order to retain more easily what He knows. And provided attention is paid to the few things that we have said, no question will be able to be proposed in regard to God's understanding that cannot be resolved with the greatest ease.

How God Knows Particular Things and How He Knows Universals

But meanwhile an error must not be passed over in silence that some make who assert that God knows nothing except the eternal things, such as angels and skies, that they have imagined as being by their nature not engendered or corruptible: and, in this world, He knows nothing except species, in as much as they too are non-engendered or corruptible. Those philosophers in fact seem to want to show as it were a particular eagerness in their errors and in imagining the greatest absurdities. For what is more absurd than to take away from God the knowledge of particular things that cannot exist even for an instant without the intervention of God. Then, while asserting that God does not know things that really exist, they attribute to Him in their imagination the knowledge of the universal things that are not and have no essence outside the particular things. We, on the contrary, attribute to God the knowledge of particular things, and deny Him that of the universal things, except in so far as He knows the minds of men.

In God there is only One Idea and a Simple One

Lastly, before we conclude this argument, it seems that a reply should be made to the question whether there are in God many ideas, or only one and that a very simple one. To this I reply that the idea of God, by reason of which He is called omniscient, is unique and very simple. For in reality God is not called omniscient for any other reason except that He has the idea of Himself: this idea or knowledge has always existed at the same time as God, for outside His essence nothing exists, nor could that idea too exist in any other way.

What God's Knowledge is in Regard to Created Things

But God's knowledge in regard to created things cannot properly be related to God's knowledge. For if God had so willed, created things would have had another essence, and this has no place in the knowledge that God has of Himself. It will however be asked whether this knowledge of created things, properly or improperly so called, is multiple or unique. But we reply, this question is in no way different from those that ask whether God's decrees and volitions are many or one: and whether God's ubiquity or cooperation by means of which He conserves every single thing, is the same in all of them: of all which, as we have already said, we can have no distinct knowledge. Still, we know very evidently that, just as God's cooperation, if related to His omnipotence, must be unique, although it is revealed in its effects in different modes, so too God's volitions and decrees (for so it is fitting to call His knowledge in regard to created things), considered in God, are not plural, although they are expressed in different modes through or rather in created things. Lastly, if we consider the analogy of all Nature, we can view it as one Being and consequently the idea or the decree of God in regard to the creation of Nature will be only one.

CHAPTER 8

GOD'S WILL

We do not Know how God's Essence and Understanding, by Means of Which He Knows Himself, and His Will, by Means of which He loves Himself, Are Distinguished

God's Will, through which He wills to love Himself, necessarily follows from His infinite understanding, by means of which He knows Himself. But how these three notions are distinguished from each other, namely His essence, His understanding, by which He knows Himself, and His will, through which He wills to love Himself, this we set in the sphere of knowledge that we lack. Nor are we unaware of the term (namely personality) that Theologians occasionally use to explain the point: but, although we are aware of the term, we still are not aware of its meaning, and we cannot form any clear and distinct concept of it: although we firmly believe that in the most blessed vision of God, promised to the faithful, God will reveal this to His own.

The Will and Power of God, in their External Action, are not Distinct from His Understanding

God's Will and Power in their external action are not distinct from His understanding, as is sufficiently established from what precedes. For we have shown that God has not only decreed that things should be, but also that they should be of a particular nature, that is, that their essence and their existence must have depended on God's will and power: from which we clearly and distinctly perceive that God's understanding, and His power and will , by which He has created, known, and conserves or loves created things, are in no sense distinguished from each other, but only relatively to our thought.

It is Incorrectly said that God Hates Certain Things and Loves Certain Things

When we say that God hates certain things, and loves certain things, these statements are made in the same sense in which the Scriptures say that the earth will vomit forth men, and other things of this kind. That God has no anger against anyone and does not love things in the way that the common people believe is a conclusion readily drawn from the Scriptures themselves. For Isaiah says so, and more clearly the Apostle in the Epistle to the Romans, chapter 9:

For the children (that is, the sons of Isaac) being not yet born, neither having done any good or evil, that the purpose of God according to election might stand, not of works, but of him that calleth:

It was said unto her, The elder shall serve the younger.

And, somewhat further on:

There hath he mercy on whom he will have mercy, and whom he will he hardeneth.

Thou wilt say then unto me, What, doth he yet find fault? For who hath resisted his will?

Nay but, O man, who art thou that repliest against God? Shall the thing formed say to him that formed it, Why hast thou made me thus?

Hath not the potter power over the clay, of the same lump to make one vessel unto honor, and another unto dishonor? etc.

Why God Warns Men. Why He does not Save them without Warning: and why the Wicked are Punished

If it is now asked: Why does God warn men? it will be easy to reply that God decreed since eternity to warn men at such and such a time so that those whom He wanted to save could be converted.

If it is still asked: Could God not have saved them without warning? we reply: He could have.

Why then does He not save them? one may perhaps persist in asking.

To this I shall reply when I have said why God did not make the Red Sea passable without a violent east wind and why He does not accomplish every single motion without others: and an infinite number of other actions that God accomplishes by means of causes.

It will again be asked: Why then are the wicked punished? For they act according to their own nature and the divine decree.

I reply that it is also in accordance with the divine decree that they should be punished: and if only those whom we imagine as sinning by virtue of their own freedom were to be punished, why do men try to exterminate poisonous serpents? For they sin only in accordance with their own nature, and cannot do otherwise.

Scripture Teaches Nothing that Contradicts the Light of Natural Reason

Lastly, if other things encountered in the Holy Scriptures induce a doubt in us, this is not the place to explain them: for here we are inquiring only into those questions that we can resolve with the greatest certainty by natural Reason, and it is sufficient to demonstrate these with proof in order to know that the Holy Scriptures must teach the same things. For truth does not contradict truth, nor can the Scriptures teach such nonsense as is commonly imagined.

For if we found something in it that was contrary to the light of Natural Reason, we could refute it with the same freedom as we refute the Koran and the Talmud. But far be it from us to think that in the Holy Scriptures anything can be found that contradicts the Light of Natural Reason.

CHAPTER 9

THE POWER OF GOD

How the Omnipotence of God is to be Understood

It has already been adequately proved that God is omnipotent. Here we shall only try to explain briefly how this attribute is to be understood. For many speak about it without sufficient piety nor in accordance with the truth. For they say that certain things are possible by their own nature and not in accordance with God's decree; that certain things are impossible, and lastly that certain things are necessary, and that the omnipotence of God takes place only in regard to the possible things. We, however, who have already shown that all things depend absolutely on God's decree, say that God is omnipotent: but perceiving that He has decreed certain things from the mere freedom of His will and secondly that He is immutable we say then that nothing can act contrary to His decree and that this is impossible for the sole reason that it contradicts God's perfection.

All Things are Necessary by Virtue of God's Decree: and Not Some Things in Themselves, and Some Things by Virtue of His Decree

But perhaps some one will object that we find certain things necessary only in regard to God's decree, and others on the contrary without regard to God's decree. For example: Josias burned the bones of the idolaters on the altar of Jerobeam. If we consider only Josias' will, we shall judge the thing as being possible and we shall not say that it must necessarily be so, except that the Prophet had predicted it in accordance with God's decree. But that the three angles of a triangle must be equal to two right angles, the thing itself demonstrates this. But those men imagine distinctions in things through their ignorance. For, if men clearly knew the entire order of Nature, they would find everything as necessary as all those things that are treated in mathematics. But, as this is beyond human understanding, certain things are for this reason judged possible by us, but not necessary. Hence it must be asserted either that God can do nothing since all things are really necessary: or that God can do everything, and that the necessity that we find in things came solely from God's decree.

That if God had Created Differently the Nature of Things, He should also Have given us a Different Understanding

If it is now asked: What if God had decreed things otherwise and had made the things that are now true false, should we not recognize them still as quite true?

Assuredly, if God had left us the nature that He gave us: but if, as He has already done, He had wished to give us such a nature that we should know the nature of things and their laws as they are established by God, that too He would have been able to do: in fact, if we consider His veracity, He ought to have given it. This is also evident from what we have previously said, that all Creative Nature is nothing but a unique being. Hence it follows that man is a part of Nature that must be coherent with the rest.

Therefore it would also follow from the simplicity of God's decree that, if God had created things in another way, He would thereby also have constituted our nature such that we should understand things as they were created by God. For this reason, although we wish to retain the same distinction of God's power that is commonly taught by the Philosophers, we are however obliged to explain it otherwise.

Of How Many Kinds is the Power of God

We therefore divide the power of God into regulated and absolute power.

What is Absolute Power, What is Regulated Power, What is Ordinary, What is Extraordinary

We say that the power of God is absolute, when we consider His omnipotence without reference to His decrees; regulated, when we consider His decrees.

There is furthermore an ordinary power and an extraordinary power of God. Ordinary power is that whereby He conserves the world in a certain order: extraordinary is what He uses when He does something outside the order of Nature: as, for example, all the miracles, such as speech given to a she-ass, the apparition of angels, and in similar phenomena. Although there could be grave doubt about this last example, not without reason: for the miracle would seem greater, if God always governed the world in one and the same determined and immutable order than if He abrogated, on account of the stupidity of men, the laws that He Himself excellently established in Nature and by his mere freedom (which cannot be denied by anyone except a person wholly blind). But we leave this decision to the Theologians.

Finally we omit other questions that are customarily raised regarding God's power, namely: Whether God's power extends to the past: Whether He can do things better than He does: Whether He can do many more things than He has done.

For these questions can be very easily answered from what has previously been said.

CHAPTER 10

CREATION

We have already established previously that God is the creator of all things. Here we shall now attempt to explain what is to be understood by creation: then we shall clarify as far as we can those assertions about creation that are commonly made. Let us begin therefore with the first point.

What Creation is

We say then that Creation is the operation involving no other causes except the efficient cause, that is, a created thing is one that for its existence presupposes nothing before it except God.

The Common Definition of Creation is Rejected

It must be observed:

1. That we omit the words from nothing that Philosophers commonly use, as if nothing were a matter from which things were produced.

If they express themselves thus, it is due to the fact that, being accustomed, when it is a question of the generation of things, to suppose before these things something from which they are made, they have been unable to omit, in creation, the little word from. It is the same with them in regard to matter. Seeing that all bodies are in some place and surrounded by other bodies, they have asked themselves where matter was totally contained, and have replied: In some imaginary space.

There is no doubt therefore that, far from considering this nothing as a negation of all reality, they have invented or imagined it as something real.

Explanation of the Proposed Definition

2. That I say that in creation no other causes are involved except the efficient cause. I could have said that creation denies or excludes all causes except the efficient cause. I preferred however to say that no causes are involved, to prevent my being compelled to reply to those who ask whether God did not set an end for Himself in creation, in view of which He created things. Moreover, to offer a better explanation, I have added a second definition, namely: A created thing presupposes nothing except God: for, if God set some end of Himself, that end was certainly not exterior to God: for nothing exists outside God by which He is urged to action.

Accidents and Modes are not Created

3. From this definition it follows sufficiently that there is no creation of accidents and modes: for they assume a substance created apart from God.

There was no Time or Duration before Creation

4. Finally, before creation we cannot imagine any time or duration, but time and duration began with things. For time is the measurement of duration, or rather it is nothing but a mode of thinking. Therefore it presupposes not only whatever

thing has been created, but especially thinking men. Now duration ceases when created things cease to be and it begins when created things begin to exist. I say created things: for no duration applies to God but only eternity, as we have shown previously with sufficient evidence.

Therefore duration supposes things created before it or at least implies created things. Those who imagine duration and time before created things labor under the same misconception as those who imagine a space beyond matter, as is sufficiently self-evident. So much for the definition of creation.

God's Operation of Creating the World and of Conserving it is the same

Furthermore, there is no need to repeat here once again what we have proved in Axiom 10, Part I, namely: That as much power is required to create a thing as to conserve it: that is, God's operation of creating the world is the same as the operation of conserving it.

After these observations, we shall now proceed to what we promised in the second place.

1. We must therefore inquire what was created, what was uncreated.

2. Whether what was created could be created from eternity.

What Things are Created?

To the first question therefore we reply briefly that all that was created, of which the essence is clearly conceived without any existence, although it is conceived by itself: as, for example, matter, of which we have a clear and distinct concept when we conceive it under the attribute of extension and conceive it with equal clarity and distinctness, whether it exists or does not exist.

How God's Thought Differs from Ours

But someone will perhaps say that we perceive thought clearly and distinctly without existence and still ascribe it to God. But to this we reply that we do not ascribe to God such thought as ours is, that is capable of being affected by things and determined by the nature of things; but thought that is pure act and hence involving existence, as we have proved previously at sufficient length. For we showed that God's understanding and His will are not distinguished from His power and His essence, that involves existence.

Outside God Nothing Exists Co-eternal with God

Since therefore all that of which the essence involves no existence must necessarily be created by God in order to exist, and, we have previously frequently expounded, must be continuously conserved by its creator Himself, we shall not linger to refute the opinion of those who have established a world, or chaos, or matter without any form, co-eternal with God, and so independent. We must therefore proceed to the second question and ask: Whether that which was created could have been created from eternity.

The Meaning Here of These Words: from eternity

To understand this properly, we must consider this mode of speaking: from eternity: for by this expression we wish to signify at this point quite a different thing from that which we hitherto explained when we spoke of God's eternity. For here we understand nothing more than duration without the beginning of duration, or such a duration that, although we should like to multiply it through many years or myriads of years and this product in turn through other myriads, we should never however be able to express it by any number, however great.

It is Proved that a Thing Could not have been Created From all Eternity

Now it is clearly proved that such duration cannot exist. For, if the world retrogressed from this present moment, it would never be able to have such a duration: therefore the world too could not have appeared since such a beginning up to this present moment.

You will perhaps say that for God nothing is impossible: for He is omnipotent and so will be able to produce the greatest possible duration. We reply that God, because He is omnipotent, will never create duration without the possibility of a greater duration being created. For such is the nature of creation that a greater and smaller duration can always be conceived than a given duration, as in the case of a number.

You will perhaps insist that God has been since eternity, and so has endured to this moment, and so there is a duration such that a greater one cannot be conceived. But in this way duration is ascribed to God consisting of parts, an error that has sufficiently and more than sufficiently been refuted by us, when we proved that eternity, not duration, applies to God. And it would have been good for men to consider this carefully: for they would have been able to extricate themselves very easily from many arguments and absurdities, and, to their great delight, they would have dwelt in the greatest happiest contemplation of this being.

Let us proceed however to answer the arguments adduced by some philosophers, namely by those who try to show the possibility of such infinite duration from the duration that has already passed.

From the Eternity of God it does not Follow that His Effects too can be since Eternity

First of all they assert that a produced thing can exist at the same time with its cause: now since God has been since eternity, His effects could have been produced since eternity.

And they support this assertion further by the example of the son of God, who has been produced since eternity by the father.

But it is clear to see from what has been said before that they confuse eternity with duration, and that they attribute only to God duration since eternity. This is also evident from the example that they adduce. For they assert that this same eternity that they ascribe to the son of God is possible for created things. Moreover, they imagine time and duration before the creation of the world, and propose a duration independent of created things, just as others propose an eternity outside God. It is now evident that both views are as far removed from the truth as possible. We therefore reply that it is utterly false that God can communicate His eternity to creatures: and that the son of God is not a creature but, like the father, is eternal. Thus when we say that the father produced the son since eternity, we mean nothing else than that He always communicated His eternity to the son.

If God Acted from Necessity, He would not Have Infinite Virtue

Their second argument is that God, when acting freely, has no less a power than when He acts by necessity. But if God acted by necessity, since He has infinite virtue, He would have had to create the world from eternity.

But this argument too can be very easily answered, if consideration is given to its basis. For these good folk suppose that they can have different ideas of a being of infinite virtue: for they conceive God as having infinite virtue, both when He acts by the necessity of nature, and when He acts freely. We however deny that God has infinite virtue, if He acts by the necessity of nature. This we may now deny: in fact it must be necessarily conceded even by them, after we have proved that a supremely perfect being acts freely, and that only one such can be conceived.

But if they object that it can however be assumed, although it is impossible, that a God acting by the necessity of nature has infinite virtue, we shall reply that it is no more permissible to assume this than a squared circle implying the conclusions that all lines drawn from the centre to the circumference are not equal. And, not to repeat what has been said some time ago, this is quite clear from what precedes. For we have just proved that there is no duration of which the double cannot be conceived, or a duration than which a greater or smaller cannot be conceived: and hence a greater or a smaller duration than a given duration can always be created by God, who acts freely through His infinite virtue. But if God acted through a necessity of nature, this would not follow at all. For only the duration resulting from His nature could be produced by Him and not an infinity of others greater than the given duration. We therefore argue briefly thus: If God created the greatest duration, of such a nature that He could not create a greater one, He would necessarily diminish His power.

But this latter consequence is false, for His power does not differ from His essence. Therefore, and so on. Furthermore, if God acted from the necessity of nature, He would have to create such a duration that He could not create a greater one. But a God creating a duration has not infinite virtue: for we can always conceive a greater duration than the given one. Therefore, if God acted from the necessity of nature, He would not have infinite virtue.

From What we Derive the Concept of a Duration Greater than that of this World

A doubt might here arise in some mind as to how, since the world was created 5000 years ago and more, if the calculation of the Chronologists is correct, we can still conceive a greater duration, that we asserted could not be comprehended without created things.

Such a person can very easily be enlightened, if he takes notice that we know duration not only from the contemplation of created things, but also from the contemplation of God's infinite power to create. For created things cannot be conceived as existing or enduring by themselves, but only by God's infinite power in virtue of which alone they have all their duration. See Proposition 12, Part I, and its Corollary.

CHAPTER 11

THE INTERVENTION OF GOD

Little or nothing remains to be said on the subject of this attribute after we have shown that God continuously creates a thing afresh as it were every single moment. From this we have proved that things never have any power by themselves to perform any act nor to determine themselves for any act: and this takes place in things exterior to man, but also in the human will itself.

Then we also answered certain arguments bearing on this point: and, although many others are usually adduced, still, since they concern Theology particularly, it is my intention here to pass them over. However, as there are many men who admit the intervention of God and take it in a sense altogether different from the one that we have indicated, it must here be observed, with a view to discovering their error very easily, what we proved before, namely: That the present time has no connection with the future (see Axiom 10, Part I), and that this is clearly and distinctly perceived by us. And if only this is carefully considered, it will be possible to answer without any difficulty all their arguments that can be drawn from Philosophy.

Wherein Consists the Conserving Power of God in the Things that Must be Determined for Action

But, not to touch upon this question idly, we shall answer it in passing. The question is: Is something added to God's act of conservation when He determines to perform an action?

When we spoke of motion we already gave an answer to some extent. For we said that God conserves the same amount of motion in Nature. If we therefore consider all material Nature, nothing new is added to the act of conservation: but it may be said in a way that something new is added in respect of particular things. Whether this takes place in spiritual things as well, is not clear: for it does not seem that there is mutual dependence among them. Lastly, as the parts of duration have no connection with each other, we may say that God does not, properly speaking, conserve things so much as He re-creates them. Therefore if a man now has the Fredom determined to perform some act, we must say that God created him thus at that moment. And this is not contradicted by the fact that the human will is often determined by things placed exterior to itself, and that all the things that are in Nature mutually determined to some act: for these things also are thus determined by God.

Nothing can determine a will, and inversely no will can be determined except by the sole power of God. But as for how this does not conflct with human freedom, or how God can achieve this without impairing human freedom, that is something of which we confess ourselves ignorant. On this matter we have already spoken frequently.

The Common Division of God's Attributes is Nominal rather than Real

This is what I had decided to say about God's attributes, among which I have so far established no division. The division that is often described by Authors, who divide God's attributes into incommunicable and communicable, seems to me, to tell the truth, a nominal rather than a real division.

For God's knowledge does not coincide with human knowledge any more than the dog, the heavenly sign, coincides with the dog that is a barking animal, and perhaps God's knowledge resembles human knowledge still less.

The Author's own Division

Now we propose this division. Some attributes of God explain His active essence: others expose nothing of His action, but they do expose His mode of existence.

In this latter category belong unity, eternity, necessity, etc. In the former category belong knowledge, will, life, omnipotence, etc. This division is sufficiently clear and precise, and embraces all the attributes of God.

CHAPTER 12

THE HUMAN MIND

We must now pass on to the created substance, that we have divided into extended substance and thinking substance. By extended substance we understood matter or corporal substance. By thinking substance, we understood only human minds.

Angels are not a Matter of Metaphysical but of Theological Consideration

Although Angels too were created, however, not being recognized by the Light of Natural Reason, they do not concern Metaphysics.

For their essence and existence are not known except through Revelation, and so they apply solely to Theology: and the knowledge of Theology, being far different from natural knowledge and totally distinct from it, must not in any way be confused with natural knowledge.

Let no one therefore expect us to say anything about angels.

The Human Mind does not Come from an Intermediary, but is Created by God: but we do not know at what Moment it is so Created

Let us return therefore to human minds, about which only a few things now remain to be said. Only, a warning must be given that we have said nothing about the time of the creation of the human mind, because it is not quite certain at what time God creates it, since it can exist without the body. What is certain is that the human mind does not stem from an intermediary: for that takes place only in things that are generated, as in the modes of a substance: while the substance itself cannot be generated, but only created solely by the Omnipontent Being, as we have adequately proved in what precedes.

In What Sense The Human Soul is Mortal

To add something about its immortality, it is quite certain that we cannot say of any created thing that it conflicts with its nature to be destroyed by God's power.

For one who had the power of creating a thing also has the power of destroying it. Furthermore, as we have proved sufficiently, nothing created can exist by its nature even for an instant but is continuously re-created by God.

In What Sense it is Immortal

But, although this is the case, we still see clearly and distinctly that we have no idea by means of which to conceive the destruction of a substance in the way that we have ideas of corruption and the generation of modes. For we conceive clearly, when we consider the structure of the human body, that such and such a structure can be destroyed: but if we consider the corporeal substance, we do not similarly conceive that it can be annihilated. Lastly, the Philosopher does not inquire what the supreme power of God can perform: he judges the Nature of things according to the laws that God has imposed on them: he judges therefore that what is deduced to be fixed and constant according to these laws, is fixed and constant, although he does not deny that God can change these laws and all the rest. For this reason, when we speak of the soul, we do not inquire what God can perform, but only what follows from the laws of Nature.

Proof of the Immortality of the Soul

Since it follows clearly from these laws that a substance cannot be destroyed either by itself or by another created substance, as we have already previously proved abundantly, unless I am mistaken, we are compelled by the laws of Nature to consider the soul as immortal.

And if we want to investigate the subject still more thoroughly we shall be able to prove with the most convincing evidence that the soul is immortal.

For, as we have just shown, it clearly follows from the laws of Nature that the soul is immortal. Now the laws of Nature are the decrees of God revealed by the Light of Natural Reason, as is very manifestly certain from what preceded. Moreover, we have already proved that the decrees of God are immutable. From all these assertions we clearly conclude that God has revealed to men His immutable will regarding the duration of souls, not only by revelation, but also by the Light of Natural Reason.

God does not Act against Nature but above it. What this Act is, according to the Author

We are not refuted by the possible objection that God destroys at any moment these natural laws in order to produce miracles: for most of the wiser Theologians grant that God does nothing against Nature, but acts above it, that is, as I explain, that God has many laws of action that He has not communicated to the human understanding and that, if they had been communicated to the human understanding, would be as natural as the others.

Hence it is most perfectly clear that souls are immortal, and I do not see what remains to be said at this point about the human soul in general.

And there would be nothing further to say especially about its functions, but for the arguments of certain authors, by means of which they try to take it upon themselves not to see and feel what they do see and feel, and which induce me to answer them.

Why Some Think That the Will is not Free

Some believe that they can show that the will is not free, but is always determined by something else. And this belief arises from their understanding by will something distinct from the soul, that they consider as a substance whose nature consists solely in its being indifferent. To remove all confusion, we shall first of all explain the problem and after that we shall very easily discover the fallacies in their arguments.

We have said that the human mind is a thinking thing: whence it follows that solely by its own nature, and considered in itself alone, it can perform any act, namely think; that is, affirm and deny. But these thoughts are either determined by things placed outside the mind, or solely by the mind: since it is itself a substance from whose thinking essence many acts of thought can and must follow. Now it is those acts of thought that have no other cause than the human mind, that are called volitions. As for the human mind, in so far as it is conceived as a sufficient cause for producing such acts, it is called the will.

Will Exists

That the soul has such a power, although it is not determined by any external things, can be most aptly explained by the example of Buridan's ass. For if we suppose a man instead of an ass in such an equilibrium, the man will have to be considered not as a thinking thing, but as a very stupid ass, if he dies through hunger or thirst. This also follows clearly from the fact that, as we previously stated, we wanted to doubt all things, and not only consider as doubtful those things that can be questioned, but reject them as false. See the Principles of Cartesian Philosophy, Part I, article 39.

The Will is Free

It must further be observed that, although the soul is determined to affirm or deny something by external things, it is not however so determined as if it were compelled by external things, but always remains free. For nothing has the power to destroy the essence of the soul: therefore, whatever it affirms and denies, it always affirms and denies freely, as has been adequately explained in the Fourth Meditation.

Hence, if it is asked why the soul wishes this or that, or does not wish this or that, we shall reply:

Because the soul is a thinking thing, that is, a thing that from its nature has the power of willing and not willing, affirming and denying: for it is in this that a thinking thing consists.

Will Must not be Confused With Appetite

After these explanations, let us now examine the arguments of our opponents.

1. The first argument is this: If the will can will something against the decision of the understanding, if it can desire something contrary to the good prescribed by the last decision of the understanding, it will be able to desire evil by reason of evil. But this conclusion is absurd. Therefore the principle also is absurd.

From this argument it is clear that they do not understand what the will is: for they confuse it with the appetite that the soul has, after it has affirmed or denied something. This they have learned from their Master, who defined the will as an appetite by reason of the good. But we say that the will consists of affirming or denying that such and such a thing is good, as we have already previously explained adequately in regard to the cause of error, which we have shown to arise from the fact that the will displays itself more expansively than the understanding.

But if the soul, being free, had not affirmed that a particular thing was good, there would be no appetite. We therefore answer the argument by granting that the soul can will nothing contrary to the last decision of the understanding, that is, cannot will anything in so far as it it supposed not to will: as is the case here, when it is said that it judged something to be bad, that is, it did not will something.

We deny, however, that it could not absolutely have willed what is bad, that is, judge it to be bad: for that would be contrary to experience itself. For we consider good many things that are bad and, on the other hand, we consider bad many things that are good.

The Will is Nothing But Mind Itself

2. The second argument (or, if one prefers, the first, since there has been no argument so far) is as follows:

If the will is not determined to wish by the last decision of the practical understanding, it will determine itself. But the will is not self-determined, because it is by its nature undetermined.

Hence they proceed to argue thus:

If the will is of itself and by its nature indifferent to willing and not willing, it cannot be determined by itself to will: for what determines must be as determined as what must be determined is undetermined.

But the will, considered as self-determining, is as undetermined as when it is considered determined. For our opponents assume nothing in the determining will that is not also in the will to be determined or that has been determined; nor is it possible to suppose anything here. The will therefore cannot by itself be determined to will. If it is not determined by itself, it is then determined from another source.

These are the exact words of Professor Heereboord of Leyden I, by which he shows clearly that he understands by will not the mind itself, but something else, outside or inside the mind, something like a tabula rasa cleaned of all thought and capable of receiving any impression whatever: or rather like a weight in equilibrium that is propelled by another weight in one direction or another, according as this added weight is itself determined: or, lastly, something that neither himself nor any other mortal can grasp by any thought.

We have just said, we have even shown clearly, that the will is nothing but the mind itself, that we call a thinking thing, that is, affirming and denying. Hence we clearly deduce that, if we consider solely the nature of the mind, it has an equal power to affirm and deny. For that, I assert, is what thinking is.15

If therefore we consider, from the fact that the mind thinks, that it has the power to affirm and deny, why then do we look for adventitious causes for producing what follows by its own nature? But, you will say, the mind itself is not more determined to affirm than to deny: and so you will conclude that we necessarily ought to seek for a cause by which it is determined. But to this I reply with this argument:

If the mind by itself and by its own nature were only determined to affirm (however impossible it might be to conceive this as long as we think of the mind as a thinking being), then by its nature alone it could affirm only, but never deny, however many causes were adduced. But if it is determined neither to affirm nor to deny, it will be capable of doing neither. If, finally, it has either power, as we have just shown to be the case, it will be able solely by its own nature and without any other cause to help it, to do both. This will be clear and certain to all those who consider the thinking thing as a thinking thing: that is, who do not make any distinction whatever, except a distinction of Reason, between the attribute of thought and the thinking thing itself, as our opponents do, who strip the thinking thing of all thought and picture it imaginatively as the first matter of the Peripatetics. This is the manner in which I reply to the argument, and, first, to the major argument: If by will is understood a thing deprived of all thought, we grant that the will by its own nature is undetermined. But we deny that the will is something deprived of all thought and on the contrary we assert that it is thought, that is, power in either sense, to affirm and to deny: by which nothing else can certainly be understood except a cause sufficient for both purposes. Then we also deny that, if the will were undetermined, that is, deprived of all thought, some adventitious cause, other than God by his infinite power to create, could determine it. For to conceive a thinking thing, without any thought, is the same as wanting to conceive an extended thing without extension.

Why Philosophers Have Confused the Mind with Corporeal Things

Lastly, to avoid the need to review here any more arguments, I give this warning only, that our opponents, not having understood the will, and not having any clear and distinct conception of the mind, have confused the mind with corporeal things. This springs from the use that they have made of words commonly applied to corporeal things, to express spiritual things that they did not understand. For they were accustomed to call undetermined, because they are in equilibrium, those bodies that are propelled in opposite directions by external causes equally powerful and exactly contrary.

Admitting therefore the determination of the will, they seem to conceive it as a body placed in equilibrium: and, as those bodies have nothing except what they received from external causes (whence it follows that they must always be determined by an external cause), they believe that the same thing occurs in the will. But since we have already explained sufficiently what the situation is, we shall stop at this point.

Of extended substance we have previously spoken at sufficient length, and apart from these two substances we know no others. As for real accidents and the other qualities, these are things sufficiently explored, and there is no need to spend time in refuting them. We therefore lay aside our pen here.

NOTES

1

Spinoza's use of "objective" corresponds to our use of "subjective." In IV, "formally" corresponds to our use of "objectively." Translator's note.

2

We are also certain of this because we find it in us in so far as we are thinking beings. See the previous Scholium.

3

Each person finds this in himself, in as much as he is a thinking thing.

4

Read the Principles, Part I, article 16.

5

Not to seek other examples, take the example of a spider that easily spins a web that men could not spin except with the greatest difficulty; on the other hand, men do very easily a very great number of things that are perhaps impossible for angels.

6

Note that the force by which a substance is conserved is nothing outside its essence and differs from it only in name; this question will have its place especially when we treat the power of God, in the Appendix.

7

I have not listed this axiom among the axioms, because there was no need to do so. I did not require it, except to prove this proposition only, and also because, as long as I did not know the existence of God, I was unwilling to accept the truth of anything except what I could deduce from the first thing known: I am, as I have indicated in the Scholium, Proposition 4. Furthermore, I did not list the definitions of fear and malice among the definitions, because no one is unaware of them, and I did not require them except for this proposition alone.

8

See the proof of Proposition 14, and Proposition 15, Scholium.

9

See on these points more explicit details in the Appendix, Part II, chapter 3 and 9.

10

See the figure in the following Proposition.

11

This is evident by Propositions 18 and 19 of Book 3 of the Elements.

12

See Proposition 24, Part II: for there it is proved that two bodies, by mutual resistance, give up their direction, not their motion.

13

Observe that by the expression Chimera here and in what follows is understood that of which the nature involves an apparent contradiction, as is fully explained in Chapter 3.

14

Hence is clearly follows that God's understanding through which He knows created things, and His will and His power, by which He has determined them, are one and the same thing.

15

See his Melemata Philosophica, second edition, Leyden, 1659.

A THEOLOGICO-POLITICAL TREATISE

PREFACE.

MEN WOULD NEVER be superstitious, if they could govern all their circumstances by set rules, or if they were always favoured by fortune: but being frequently driven into straits where rules are useless, and being often kept fluctuating pitiably between hope and fear by the uncertainty of fortune's greedily coveted favours, they are consequently, for the most part, very prone to credulity. The human mind is readily swayed this way or that in times of doubt, especially when hope and fear are struggling for the mastery, though usually it is boastful, over — confident, and vain.

This as a general fact I suppose everyone knows, though few, I believe, know their own nature; no one can have lived in the world without observing that most people, when in prosperity, are so over-brimming with wisdom (however inexperienced they may be), that they take every offer of advice as a personal insult, whereas in adversity they know not where to turn, but beg and pray for counsel from every passer-by. No plan is then too futile, too absurd, or too fatuous for their adoption; the most frivolous causes will raise them to hope, or plunge them into despair — if anything happens during their fright which reminds them of some past good or ill, they think it portends a happy or unhappy issue, and therefore (though it may have proved abortive a hundred times before) style it a lucky or unlucky omen. Anything which excites their astonishment they believe to be a portent signifying the anger of the gods or of the Supreme Being, and, mistaking superstition for religion, account it impious not to avert the evil with prayer and sacrifice. Signs and wonders of this sort they conjure up perpetually, till one might think Nature as mad as themselves, they interpret her so fantastically.

Thus it is brought prominently before us, that superstition's chief victims are those persons who greedily covet temporal advantages; they it is, who (especially when they are in danger, and cannot help themselves) are wont with Prayers and womanish tears to implore help from God: upbraiding Reason as blind, because she cannot show a sure path to the shadows they pursue, and rejecting human wisdom as vain; but believing the phantoms of imagination, dreams, and other childish absurdities, to be the very oracles of Heaven. As though God had turned away from the wise, and written His decrees, not in the mind of man but in the entrails of beasts, or left them to be proclaimed by the inspiration and instinct of fools, madmen, and birds. Such is the unreason to which terror can drive mankind!

Superstition, then, is engendered, preserved, and fostered by fear. If anyone desire an example, let him take Alexander, who only began superstitiously to seek guidance from seers, when he first learnt to fear fortune in the passes of Sysis (Curtius, v. 4); whereas after he had conquered Darius he consulted prophets no more, till a second time frightened by reverses. When the Scythians were provoking a battle, the Bactrians had deserted, and he himself was lying sick of his wounds, "he once more turned to superstition, the mockery of human wisdom, and bade Aristander, to whom he confided his credulity, inquire the issue of affairs with sacrificed victims." Very numerous examples of a like nature might be cited, clearly showing the fact, that only while under the dominion of fear do men fall a prey to superstition; that all the portents ever invested with the reverence of misguided religion are mere phantoms of dejected and fearful minds; and lastly, that prophets have most power among the people, and are most formidable to rulers, precisely at those times when the state is in most peril. I think this is sufficiently plain to all, and will therefore say no more on the subject.

The origin of superstition above given affords us a clear reason for the fact, that it comes to all men naturally, though some refer its rise to a dim notion of God, universal to mankind, and also tends to show, that it is no less inconsistent and variable than other mental hallucinations and emotional impulses, and further that it can only be maintained by hope, hatred, anger, and deceit; since it springs, not from reason, but solely from the more powerful phases of emotion. Furthermore, we may readily understand how difficult it is, to maintain in the same course men prone to every form of credulity. For, as the mass of mankind remains always at about the same pitch of misery, it never assents long to any one remedy, but is always best pleased by a novelty which has not yet proved illusive.

This element of inconsistency has been the cause of many terrible wars and revolutions; for, as Curtius well says (lib. iv. chap. 10): "The mob has no ruler more potent than superstition," and is easily led, on the plea of religion, at one moment to adore its kings as gods, and anon to execrate and abjure them as humanity's common bane. Immense pains have therefore been taken to counteract this evil by investing religion, whether true or false, with such pomp and ceremony, that it may, rise superior to every shock, and be always observed with studious reverence by the whole people — a system which has been brought to great perfection by the Turks, for they consider even controversy impious, and so clog men's minds with dogmatic formulas, that they leave no room for sound reason, not even enough to doubt with.

But if, in despotic statecraft, the supreme and essential mystery be to hoodwink the subjects, and to mask the fear, which keeps them clown, with the specious garb of religion, so that men may fight as bravely for slavery as for safety, and count it not shame but highest honour to risk their blood and their lives for the vainglory of a tyrant; yet in a free state no more mischievous expedient could be planned or attempted. Wholly repugnant to the general freedom are such devices as enthralling men's minds with prejudices, forcing their judgment, or employing any of the weapons of quasi-religious sedition; indeed, such seditions only spring up, when law enters the domain of speculative thought, and opinions are put on trial and condemned on the same footing as crimes, while those who defend and follow them are sacrificed, not to public safety, but to their opponents' hatred and cruelty. If deeds only could be made the grounds of criminal charges, and words were always allowed to pass free, such seditions would be divested of every semblance of justification, and would be separated from mere controversies by a hard and fast line.

Now, seeing that we have the rare happiness of living in a republic, where everyone's judgment is free and unshackled, where each may worship God as his conscience dictates, and where freedom is esteemed before all things dear and precious, I have believed that I should be undertaking no ungrateful or unprofitable task, in demonstrating that not only can such freedom be granted without prejudice to the public peace, but also, that without such freedom, piety cannot flourish nor the public peace be secure.

Such is the chief conclusion I seek to establish in this treatise; but, in order to reach it, I must first point out the misconceptions which, like scars of our former bondage, still disfigure our notion of religion, and must expose the false views about the civil authority which many have most impudently advocated, endeavouring to turn the mind of the people, still prone to heathen superstition, away from its legitimate rulers, and so bring us again into slavery. As to the order of my treatise I will speak presently, but first I will recount the causes which led me to write.

I have often wondered, that persons who make a boast of professing the Christian religion, namely, love, joy, peace, temperance, and charity to all men, should quarrel with such rancorous animosity, and display daily towards one another such bitter hatred, that this, rather than the virtues they claim, is the readiest criterion of their faith. Matters have long since come to such a pass, that one can only pronounce a man Christian, Turk, Jew, or Heathen, by his general appearance and attire, by his frequenting this or that place of worship, or employing the phraseology of a particular sect — as for manner of life, it is in all cases the same. Inquiry into the cause of this anomaly leads me unhesitatingly to ascribe it to the fact, that the ministries of the Church are regarded by the masses merely as dignities, her offices as posts of emolument — in short, popular religion may be summed up as respect for ecclesiastics. The spread of this misconception inflamed every worthless fellow with an intense desire to enter holy orders, and thus the love of diffusing God's religion degenerated into sordid avarice and ambition. Every church became a theatre, where orators, instead of church teachers, harangued, caring not to instruct the people, but striving to attract admiration, to bring opponents to public scorn, and to preach only novelties and paradoxes, such as would tickle the ears of their congregation. This state of things necessarily stirred up an amount of controversy, envy, and hatred, which no lapse of time could appease; so that we can scarcely wonder that of the old religion nothing survives but its outward forms (even these, in the mouth of the multitude, seem rather adulation than adoration of the Deity), and that faith has become a mere compound of credulity and prejudices — aye, prejudices too, which degrade man from rational being to beast, which completely stifle the power of judgment between true and false, which seem, in fact, carefully fostered for the purpose of extinguishing the last spark of reason! Piety, great God! and religion are become a tissue of ridiculous mysteries; men, who flatly despise reason, who reject and turn away from understanding as naturally corrupt, these, I say, these of all men, are thought, 0 lie most horrible! to possess light from on High. Verily, if they had but one spark of light from on High, they would not insolently rave, but would learn to worship God more wisely, and would be as marked among their fellows for mercy as they now are for malice; if they were concerned for their opponents' souls, instead of for their own reputations, they would no longer fiercely persecute, but rather be filled with pity and compassion.

Furthermore, if any Divine light were in them, it would appear from their doctrine. I grant that they are never tired of professing their wonder at the profound mysteries of Holy Writ; still I cannot discover that they teach anything but speculations of Platonists and Aristotelians, to which (in order to save their credit for Christianity) they have made Holy Writ conform; not content to rave with the Greeks themselves, they want to make the prophets rave also; showing conclusively, that never even in sleep have they caught a glimpse of Scripture's Divine nature. The very vehemence of their admiration for the mysteries plainly attests, that their belief in the Bible is a formal assent rather than a living faith: and the fact is made still more apparent by their laying down beforehand, as a foundation for the study and true interpretation of Scripture, the principle that it is in every passage true and divine. Such a doctrine should be reached only after strict scrutiny and thorough comprehension of the Sacred Books (which would teach it much better, for they stand in need no human factions), and not be set up on the threshold, as it were, of inquiry.

As I pondered over the facts that the light of reason is not only despised, but by many even execrated as a source of impiety, that human commentaries are accepted as divine records, and that credulity is extolled as faith; as I marked the fierce controversies of philosophers raging in Church and State, the source of bitter hatred and dissension, the ready instruments of sedition and other ills innumerable, I determined to examine the Bible afresh in a careful, impartial, and unfettered spirit, making no assumptions concerning it, and attributing to it no doctrines, which I do not find clearly therein set down. With these precautions I constructed a method of Scriptural interpretation, and thus equipped proceeded to inquire — what is prophecy? In what sense did God reveal himself to the prophets, and why were these particular men — chosen by him? Was it on account of the sublimity of their thoughts about the Deity and nature, or was it solely on account of their piety? These questions being answered, I was easily able to conclude, that the authority of the prophets has weight only in matters of morality, and that their speculative doctrines affect us little.

Next I inquired, why the Hebrews were called God's chosen people, and discovering that it was only because God had chosen for them a certain strip of territory, where they might live peaceably and at ease, I learnt that the Law revealed by God to Moses was merely the law of the individual Hebrew state, therefore that it was binding on none but Hebrews, and not even on Hebrews after the downfall of their nation. Further, in order to ascertain, whether it could be concluded from Scripture, that the human understanding standing is naturally corrupt, I inquired whether the Universal Religion, the Divine Law revealed through the Prophets and Apostles to the whole human race, differs from that which is taught by the light of natural reason, whether miracles can take place in violation of the laws of nature, and if so, whether they imply the existence of God more surely and clearly than events, which we understand plainly and distinctly through their immediate natural causes.

Now, as in the whole course of my investigation I found nothing taught expressly by Scripture, which does not agree with our understanding, or which is repugnant thereto, and as I saw that the prophets taught nothing, which is not very simple and easily to be grasped by all, and further, that they clothed their leaching in the style, and confirmed it with the reasons, which would most deeply move the mind of the masses to devotion towards God, I became thoroughly convinced, that the Bible leaves reason absolutely free, that it has nothing in common with philosophy, in fact, that Revelation and Philosophy stand on different footings. In order to set this forth categorically and exhaust the whole question, I point out the way in which the Bible should be interpreted, and show that all of spiritual questions should be sought from it alone, and not from the objects of ordinary knowledge. Thence I pass on to indicate the false notions, which have from the fact that the multitude — ever prone to superstition, and caring more for the shreds of antiquity for eternal truths — pays homage to the Books of the Bible, rather than to the Word of God. I show that the Word of God has not been revealed as a certain number of books, was displayed to the prophets as a simple idea of the mind, namely, obedience to God in singleness of heart, and in the practice of justice and charity; and I further point out, that this doctrine is set forth in Scripture in accordance with the opinions and understandings of those, among whom the Apostles and Prophets preached, to the end that men might receive it willingly, and with their whole heart.

Having thus laid bare the bases of belief, I draw the conclusion that Revelation has obedience for its sole object, therefore, in purpose no less than in foundation and method, stands entirely aloof from ordinary knowledge; each has its separate province, neither can be called the handmaid of the other.

Furthermore, as men's habits of mind differ, so that some more readily embrace one form of faith, some another, for what moves one to pray may move another only to scoff, I conclude, in accordance with what has gone before, that everyone should be free to choose for himself the foundations of his creed, and that faith should be judged only by its fruits; each would then obey God freely with his whole heart, while nothing would be publicly honoured save justice and charity.

Having thus drawn attention to the liberty conceded to everyone by the revealed law of God, I pass on to another part of my subject, and prove that this same liberty can and should be accorded with safety to the state and the magisterial authority — in fact, that it cannot be withheld without great danger to peace and detriment to the community.

In order to establish my point, I start from the natural rights of the individual, which are co-extensive with his desires and power, and from the fact that no one is bound to live as another pleases, but is the guardian of his own liberty. I show that these rights can only be transferred to those whom we depute to defend us, who acquire with the duties of defence the power of ordering our lives, and I thence infer that rulers possess rights only limited by their power, that they are the sole guardians of justice and liberty, and that their subjects should act in all things as they dictate: nevertheless, since no one can so utterly abdicate his own power of self-defence as to cease to be a man, I conclude that no one can be deprived of his natural rights absolutely, but that subjects, either by tacit agreement, or by social contract, retain a certain number, which cannot be taken from them without great danger to the state.

From these considerations I pass on to the Hebrew State, which I describe at some length, in order to trace the manner in which Religion acquired the force of law, and to touch on other noteworthy points. I then prove, that the holders of sovereign power are the depositories and interpreters of religious no less than of civil ordinances, and that they alone have the right to decide what is just or unjust, pious or impious; lastly, I conclude by showing, that they best retain this right and secure safety to their state by allowing every man to think what he likes, and say what he thinks.

Such, Philosophical Reader, are the questions I submit to your notice, counting on your approval, for the subject matter of the whole book and of the several chapters is important and profitable. I would say more, but I do not want my preface to extend to a volume, especially as I know that its leading propositions are to Philosophers but common places. To the rest of mankind I care not to commend my treatise, for I cannot expect that it contains anything to please them: I know how deeply rooted are the prejudices embraced under the name of religion; I am aware that in the mind of the masses superstition is no less deeply rooted than fear; I recognize that their constancy is mere obstinacy, and that they are led to praise or blame by impulse rather than reason. Therefore the multitude, and those of like passions with the multitude, I ask not to read my book; nay, I would rather that they should utterly neglect it, than that they should misinterpret it after their wont. They would gain no good themselves, and might prove a stumbling-block to others, whose philosophy is hampered by the belief that Reason is a mere handmaid to Theology, and whom I seek in this work especially to benefit. But as there will be many who have neither the leisure, nor, perhaps, the inclination to read through all I have written, I feel bound here, as at the end of my treatise, to declare that I have written nothing, which I do not most willingly submit to the examination and judgment of my country's rulers, and that I am ready to retract anything, which they shall decide to be repugnant to the laws or prejudicial to the public good. I know that I am a man and, as a man, liable to error, but against error I have taken scrupulous care, and striven to keep in entire accordance with the laws of my country, with loyalty, and with morality.

CHAPTER I.

Of Prophecy

PROPHECY, OR REVELATION is sure knowledge revealed by God to man. A prophet is one who interprets the revelations of God {insights} to those who are unable to attain to sure knowledge of the matters revealed, and therefore can only apprehend them by simple faith.

The Hebrew word for prophet is "nabi", 1 i.e. speaker or interpreter, but in Scripture its meaning is restricted to interpreter of God, as we may learn from Exodus vii:1, where God says to Moses, "See, I have made thee a god to Pharaoh, and Aaron thy brother shall be thy prophet;" implying that, since in interpreting Moses' words to Pharaoh, Aaron acted the part of a prophet, Moses would be to Pharaoh as a god, or in the attitude of a god.

Prophets I will treat of in the next chapter, and at present consider prophecy.

Now it is evident, from the definition above given, that prophecy really includes ordinary knowledge; for the knowledge which we acquire by our natural faculties depends on knowledge of God and His eternal laws; but ordinary knowledge is common to all men as men, and rests on foundations which all share, whereas the multitude always strains after rarities and exceptions, and thinks little of the gifts of nature; so that, when prophecy is talked of, ordinary knowledge is not supposed to be included. Nevertheless it has as much right as any other to be called Divine, for God's nature, in so far as we share therein, and God's laws, dictate it to us; nor does it suffer from that to which we give the preeminence, except in so far as the latter transcends its limits and cannot be accounted for by natural laws taken in themselves. In respect to the certainty it involves, and the source from which it is derived, i.e. God, ordinary, knowledge is no whit inferior to prophetic, unless indeed we believe, or rather dream, that the prophets had human bodies but superhuman minds, and therefore that their sensations and consciousness were entirely different from our own.

But, although ordinary knowledge is Divine, its professors cannot be called prophets 2, for they teach what the rest of mankind could perceive and apprehend, not merely by simple faith, but as surely and honourably as themselves.

Seeing then that our mind subjectively contains in itself and partakes of the nature of God, and solely from this cause is enabled to form notions explaining natural phenomena and inculcating morality, it follows that we may rightly assert the nature of the human mind (in so far as it is thus conceived) to be a primary cause of Divine revelation. All that we clearly and distinctly understand is dictated to us, as I have just pointed out, by the idea and nature of God; not indeed through words, but in a way far more excellent and agreeing perfectly with the nature of the mind, as all who have enjoyed intellectual certainty will doubtless attest. Here, however, my chief purpose is to speak of matters having reference to Scripture, so these few words on the light of reason will suffice.

I will now pass on to, and treat more fully, the other ways and means by which God makes revelations to mankind, both of that which transcends ordinary knowledge, and of that within its scope; for there is no reason why God should not employ other means to communicate what we know already by the power of reason.

Our conclusions on the subject must be drawn solely from Scripture; for what can we affirm about matters transcending our knowledge except what is told us by the words or writings of prophets? And since there are, so far as I know, no prophets now alive, we have no alternative but to read the books of prophets departed, taking care the while not to reason from metaphor or to ascribe anything to our authors which they do not themselves distinctly state. I must further premise that the Jews never make any mention or account of secondary, or particular causes, but in a spirit of religion, piety, and what is commonly called godliness, refer all things directly to the Deity. For instance if they make money by a transaction, they say God gave it to them; if they desire anything, they say God has disposed their hearts towards it; if they think anything, they say God told them. Hence we must not suppose that everything is prophecy or revelation which is described in Scripture as told by God to anyone, but only such things as are expressly announced as prophecy or revelation, or are plainly pointed to as such by the context.

A perusal of the sacred books will show us that all God's revelations to the prophets were made through words or appearances, or a combination of the two. These words and appearances were of two kinds; 1. — real when external to the mind of the prophet who heard or saw them, 2. — imaginary when the imagination of the prophet was in a state which led him distinctly to suppose that he heard or saw them.

With a real voice God revealed to Moses the laws which He wished to be transmitted to the Hebrews, as we may see from Exodus xxv:22, where God says, "And there I will meet with thee and I will commune with thee from the mercy seat which is between the Cherubim." Some sort of real voice must necessarily have been employed, for Moses found God ready to commune with him at any time. This, as I shall shortly show, is the only instance of a real voice.

We might, perhaps, suppose that the voice with which God called Samuel was real, for in 1 Sam. iii:21, we read, "And the Lord appeared again in Shiloh, for the Lord revealed Himself to Samuel in Shiloh by the word of the Lord;" implying that the appearance of the Lord consisted in His making Himself known to Samuel through a voice; in other words, that Samuel heard the Lord speaking. But we are compelled to distinguish between the prophecies of Moses and those of other prophets, and therefore must decide that this voice was imaginary, a conclusion further supported by the voice's resemblance to the voice of Eli, which Samuel was in the habit of hearing, and therefore might easily imagine; when thrice called by the Lord, Samuel supposed it to have been Eli.

The voice which Abimelech heard was imaginary, for it is written, Gen. xx:6, "And God said unto him in a dream." So that the will of God was manifest to him, not in waking, but only, in sleep, that is, when the imagination is most active and uncontrolled. Some of the Jews believe that the actual words of the Decalogue were not spoken by God, but that the Israelites heard a noise only, without any distinct words, and during its continuance apprehended the Ten Commandments by pure intuition; to this opinion I myself once inclined, seeing that the words of the Decalogue in Exodus are different from the words of the Decalogue in Deuteronomy, for the discrepancy seemed to imply (since God only spoke once) that the Ten Commandments were not intended to convey the actual words of the Lord, but only His meaning. However, unless we would do violence to Scripture, we must certainly admit that the Israelites heard a real voice, for Scripture expressly says, Deut. v:4," God spake with you face to face," i.e. as two men ordinarily interchange ideas through the instrumentality of their two bodies; and therefore it seems more consonant with Holy Writ to suppose that God really did create a voice of some kind with which the Decalogue was revealed. The discrepancy of the two versions is treated of in Chap. VIII.

Yet not even thus is all difficulty removed, for it seems scarcely reasonable to affirm that a created thing, depending on God in the same manner as other created things, would be able to express or explain the nature of God either verbally or really by means of its individual organism: for instance, by declaring in the first person, "I am the Lord your God."

Certainly when anyone says with his mouth, "I understand," we do not attribute the understanding to the mouth, but to the mind of the speaker; yet this is because the mouth is the natural organ of a man speaking, and the hearer, knowing what understanding is, easily comprehends, by a comparison with himself, that the speaker's mind is meant; but if we knew nothing of God beyond the mere name and wished to commune with Him, and be assured of His existence, I fail to see how our wish would be satisfied by the declaration of a created thing (depending on God neither more nor less than ourselves), "I am the Lord." If God contorted the lips of Moses, or, I will not say Moses, but some beast, till they pronounced the words, "I am the Lord," should we apprehend the Lord's existence therefrom?

Scripture seems clearly to point to the belief that God spoke Himself, having descended from heaven to Mount Sinai for the purpose — and not only that the Israelites heard Him speaking, but that their chief men beheld Him (Ex:xxiv.) Further the law of Moses, which might neither be added to nor curtailed, and which was set up as a national standard of right, nowhere prescribed the belief that God is without body, or even without form or figure, but only ordained that the Jews should believe in His existence and worship Him alone: it forbade them to invent or fashion any likeness of the Deity, but this was to insure purity of service; because, never having seen God, they could not by means of images recall the likeness of God, but only the likeness of some created thing which might thus gradually take the place of God as the object of their adoration. Nevertheless, the Bible clearly implies that God has a form, and that Moses when he heard God speaking was permitted to behold it, or at least its hinder parts.

Doubtless some mystery lurks in this question which we will discuss more fully below. For the present I will call attention to the passages in Scripture indicating the means by which God has revealed His laws to man.

Revelation may be through figures only, as in I Chron:xxii., where God displays his anger to David by means of an angel bearing a sword, and also in the story of Balaam.

Maimonides and others do indeed maintain that these and every other instance of angelic apparitions (e.g. to Manoah and to Abraham offering up Isaac) occurred during sleep, for that no one with his eyes open ever could see an angel, but this is mere nonsense. The sole object of such commentators seems to be to extort from Scripture confirmations of Aristotelian quibbles and their own inventions, a proceeding which I regard as the acme of absurdity.

In figures, not real but existing only in the prophet's imagination, God revealed to Joseph his future lordship, and in words and figures He revealed to Joshua that He would fight for the Hebrews, causing to appear an angel, as it were the Captain of the Lord's host, bearing a sword, and by this means communicating verbally. The forsaking of Israel by Providence was portrayed to Isaiah by a vision of the Lord, the thrice Holy, sitting on a very lofty throne, and the Hebrews, stained with the mire of their sins, sunk as it were in uncleanness, and thus as far as possible distant from God. The wretchedness of the people at the time was thus revealed, while future calamities were foretold in words. I could cite from Holy Writ many similar examples, but I think they are sufficiently well known already.

However, we get a still more clear confirmation of our position in Num xii:6,7, as follows: "If there be any prophet among you, I the Lord will make myself known unto him in a vision" (i.e. by appearances and signs, for God says of the prophecy of Moses that it was a vision without signs), "and will speak unto him in a dream " (i.e. not with actual words and an actual voice). "My servant Moses is not so; with him will I speak mouth to mouth, even apparently, and not in dark speeches, and the similitude of the Lord he shall behold," i.e. looking on me as a friend and not afraid, he speaks with me (cf. Ex xxxiii:17).

This makes it indisputable that the other prophets did not hear a real voice, and we gather as much from Deut. xxiv:10: "And there arose not a prophet since in Israel like unto Moses whom the Lord knew face to face," which must mean that the Lord spoke with none other; for not even Moses saw the Lord's face. These are the only media of communication between God and man which I find mentioned in Scripture, and therefore the only ones which may be supposed or invented. We may be able quite to comprehend that God can communicate immediately with man, for without the intervention of bodily means He communicates to our minds His essence; still, a man who can by pure intuition comprehend ideas which are neither contained in nor deducible from the foundations of our natural knowledge, must necessarily possess a mind far superior to those of his fellow men, nor do I believe that any have been so endowed save Christ. To Him the ordinances of God leading men to salvation were revealed directly without words or visions, so that God manifested Himself to the Apostles through the mind of Christ as He formerly did to Moses through the supernatural voice. In this sense the voice of Christ, like the voice which Moses heard, may be called the voice of God, and it may be said that the wisdom of God (,i.e. wisdom more than human) took upon itself in Christ human nature, and that Christ was the way of salvation. I must at this juncture declare that those doctrines which certain churches put forward concerning Christ, I neither affirm nor deny, for I freely confess that I do not understand them. What I have just stated I gather from Scripture, where I never read that God appeared to Christ, or spoke to Christ, but that God was revealed to the Apostles through Christ; that Christ was the Way of Life, and that the old law was given through an angel, and not immediately by God; whence it follows that if Moses spoke with God face to face as a man speaks with his friend (i.e. by means of their two bodies) Christ communed with God mind to mind.

Thus we may conclude that no one except Christ received the revelations of God without the aid of imagination, whether in words or vision. Therefore the power of prophecy implies not a peculiarly perfect mind, but a peculiarly vivid imagination, as I will show more clearly in the next chapter. We will now inquire what is meant in the Bible by the Spirit of God breathed into the prophets, or by the prophets speaking with the Spirit of God; to that end we must determine the exact signification of the Hebrew word ruagh, commonly translated spirit.

The word ruagh literally means a wind, e..q. the south wind, but it is frequently employed in other derivative significations.

It is used as equivalent to,

(1.) Breath: "Neither is there any spirit in his mouth," Ps. cxxxv:17.

(2.) Life, or breathing: "And his spirit returned to him" 1 Sam. xxx:12; i.e. he breathed again.

(3.) Courage and strength: "Neither did there remain any more spirit in any man," Josh. ii:11; "And the spirit entered into me, and made me stand on my feet," Ezek. ii:2.

(4.) Virtue and fitness: "Days should speak, and multitudes of years should teach wisdom; but there is a spirit in man,"Job xxxii:7; i.e. wisdom is not always found among old men for I now discover that it depends on individual virtue and capacity. So, "A man in whom is the Spirit," Numbers xxvii:18.

(5.) Habit of mind: "Because he had another spirit with him," Numbers xiv:24; i.e. another habit of mind. "Behold I will pour out My Spirit unto you," Prov. i:23.

(6.) Will, purpose, desire, impulse: "Whither the spirit was to go, they went," Ezek. 1:12; "That cover with a covering, but not of My Spirit," Is. xxx:1; "For the Lord hath poured out on you the spirit of deep sleep," Is. xxix:10; "Then was their spirit softened," Judges viii:3; "He that ruleth his spirit, is better than he that taketh a city," Prov. xvi:32; "He that hath no ru over his own spirit," Prov. xxv:28; "Your spirit as fire shall devour you," Isaiah xxxiii:l.

From the meaning of disposition we get —

(7.) Passions and faculties. A lofty spirit means pride, a lowly spirit humility, an evil spirit hatred and melancholy. So, too, the expressions spirits of jealousy, fornication, wisdom, counsel, bravery, stand for a jealous, lascivious, wise, prudent, or brave mind (for we Hebrews use substantives in preference to adjectives), or these various qualities.

(8.) The mind itself, or the life: "Yea, they have all one spirit," Eccles. iii:19 "The spirit shall return to God Who gave it."

(9.) The quarters of the world (from the winds which blow thence), or even the side of anything turned towards a particular quarter — Ezek. xxxvii:9; xlii:16, 17, 18, 19, &c.

I have already alluded to the way in which things are referred to God, and said to be of God.

(1.) As belonging to His nature, and being, as it were, part of Him; e.g the power of God, the eyes of God.

(2.) As under His dominion, and depending on His pleasure; thus the heavens are called the heavens of the Lord, as being His chariot and habitation. So Nebuchadnezzar is called the servant of God, Assyria the scourge of God, &c.

(3.) As dedicated to Him, e.g. the Temple of God, a Nazarene of God, the Bread of God.

(4.) As revealed through the prophets and not through our natural faculties. In this sense the Mosaic law is called the law of God.

(5.) As being in the superlative degree. Very high mountains are styled the mountains of God, a very deep sleep, the sleep of God, &c. In this sense we must explain Amos iv:11: "I have overthrown you as the overthrow of the Lord came upon Sodom and Gomorrah," i.e. that memorable overthrow, for since God Himself is the Speaker, the passage cannot well be taken otherwise. The wisdom of Solomon is called the wisdom of God, or extraordinary. The size of the cedars of Lebanon is alluded to in the Psalmist's expression, "the cedars of the Lord."

Similarly, if the Jews were at a loss to understand any phenomenon, or were ignorant of its cause, they referred it to God. Thus a storm was termed the chiding of God, thunder and lightning the arrows of God, for it was thought that God kept the winds confined in caves, His treasuries; thus differing merely in name from the Greek wind-god Eolus. In like manner miracles were called works of God, as being especially marvellous; though in reality, of course, all natural events are the works of God, and take place solely by His power. The Psalmist calls the miracles in Egypt the works of God, because the Hebrews found in them a way of safety which they had not looked for, and therefore especially marvelled at.

As, then, unusual natural phenomena are called works of God, and trees of unusual size are called trees of God, we cannot wonder that very strong and tall men, though impious robbers and whoremongers, are in Genesis called sons of God.

This reference of things wonderful to God was not peculiar to the Jews. Pharaoh, on hearing the interpretation of his dream, exclaimed that the mind of the gods was in Joseph. Nebuchadnezzar told Daniel that he possessed the mind of the holy gods; so also in Latin anything well made is often said to be wrought with Divine hands, which is equivalent to the Hebrew phrase, wrought with the hand of God.

We can now very easily understand and explain those passages of Scripture which speak of the Spirit of God. In some places the expression merely means a very strong, dry, and deadly wind, as in Isaiah xl:7, "The grass withereth, the flower fadeth, because the Spirit of the Lord bloweth upon it." Similarly in Gen. i:2: "The Spirit of the Lord moved over the face of the waters." At other times it is used as equivalent to a high courage, thus the spirit of Gideon and of Samson is called the Spirit of the Lord, as being very bold, and prepared for any emergency. Any unusual virtue or power is called the Spirit or Virtue of the Lord, Ex. xxxi:3: "I will fill him (Bezaleel) with the Spirit of the Lord," i.e., as the Bible itself explains, with talent above man's usual endowment. So Isa. xi:2: "And the Spirit of the Lord shall rest upon him," is explained afterwards in the text to mean the spirit of wisdom and understanding, of counsel and might.

The melancholy of Saul is called the melancholy of the Lord, or a very deep melancholy, the persons who applied the term showing that they understood by it nothing supernatural, in that they sent for a musician to assuage it by harp-playing. Again, the "Spirit of the Lord" is used as equivalent to the mind of man, for instance, Job xxvii:3: "And the Spirit of the Lord in my nostrils," the allusion being to Gen. ii:7: "And God breathed into man's nostrils the breath of life." Ezekiel also, prophesying to the dead, says (xxvii:14), "And I will give to you My Spirit, and ye shall live;" i.e. I will restore you to life. In Job xxxiv:14, we read: "If He gather unto Himself His Spirit and breath;" in Gen. vi:3: "My Spirit shall not always strive with man, for that he also is flesh," i.e. since man acts on the dictates of his body, and not the spirit which I gave him to discern the good, I will let him alone. So, too, Ps. li:12: "Create in me a clean heart, 0 God, and renew a right spirit within me; cast me not away from Thy presence, and take not Thy Holy Spirit from me." It was supposed that sin originated only from the body, and that good impulses come from the mind; therefore the Psalmist invokes the aid of God against the bodily appetites, but prays that the spirit which the Lord, the Holy One, had given him might be renewed. Again, inasmuch as the Bible, in concession to popular ignorance, describes God as having a mind, a heart, emotions — nay, even a body and breath — the expression Spirit of the Lord is used for God's mind, disposition, emotion, strength, or breath. Thus, Isa. xl:13: "Who hath disposed the Spirit of the Lord?" i.e. who, save Himself, hath caused the mind of the Lord to will anything,? and Isa. lxiii:10: "But they rebelled, and vexed the Holy Spirit."

The phrase comes to be used of the law of Moses, which in a sense expounds God's will, Is. lxii. 11, "Where is He that put His Holy Spirit within him?" meaning, as we clearly gather from the context, the law of Moses. Nehemiah, speaking of the giving of the law, says, i:20, "Thou gavest also thy good Spirit to instruct them." This is referred to in Deut. iv:6, "This is your wisdom and understanding," and in Ps. cxliii:10, "Thy good Spirit will lead me into the land of uprightness." The Spirit of the Lord may mean the breath of the Lord, for breath, no less than a mind, a heart, and a body are attributed to God in Scripture, as in Ps. xxxiii:6. Hence it gets to mean the power, strength, or faculty of God, as in Job xxxiii:4, "The Spirit of the Lord made me," i.e. the power, or, if you prefer, the decree of the Lord. So the Psalmist in poetic language declares, xxxiii:6, "By the word of the Lord were the heavens made, and all the host of them by the breath of His mouth," i.e. by a mandate issued, as it were, in one breath. Also Ps. cxxxix:7, "Wither shall I go from Thy Spirit, or whither shall I flee from Thy presence?" i.e. whither shall I go so as to be beyond Thy power and Thy presence?

Lastly, the Spirit of the Lord is used in Scripture to express the emotions of God, e.g. His kindness and mercy, Micah ii:7, "Is the Spirit [i.e. the mercy] of the Lord straitened? Are these cruelties His doings?" Zech. iv:6, "Not by might or by power, but My Spirit [i.e. mercy], saith the Lord of hosts." The twelfth verse of the seventh chapter of the same prophet must, I think, be interpreted in like manner: "Yea, they made their hearts as an adamant stone, lest they should hear the law, and the words which the Lord of hosts hath sent in His Spirit [i.e. in His mercy] by the former prophets." So also Haggai ii:5: "So My Spirit remaineth among you: fear not."

The passage in Isaiah xlviii:16, "And now the Lord and His Spirit hath sent me," may be taken to refer to God's mercy or His revealed law; for the prophet says, "From the beginning" (i.e. from the time when I first came to you, to preach God's anger and His sentence forth against you) "I spoke not in secret; from the time that it was, there am I," and now I am sent by the mercy of God as a joyful messenger to preach your restoration. Or we may understand him to mean by the revealed law that he had before come to warn them by the command of the law (Levit. xix:17) in the same manner under the same conditions as Moses had warned them, that now, like Moses, he ends by preaching their restoration. But the first explanation seems to me the best.

Returning, then, to the main object of our discussion, we find that the Scriptural phrases, "The Spirit of the Lord was upon a prophet," "The Lord breathed His Spirit into men," "Men were filled with the Spirit of God, with the Holy Spirit," &c., are quite clear to us, and mean that prophets were endowed with a peculiar and extraordinary power, and devoted themselves to piety with especial constancy 3; that thus they perceived the mind or the thought of God, for we have shown that God's Spirit signifies in Hebrew God's mind or thought, and that the law which shows His mind and thought is called His Spirit; hence that the imagination of the prophets, inasmuch as through it were revealed the decrees of God, may equally be called the mind of God, and the prophets be said to have possessed the mind of God. On our minds also the mind of God and His eternal thoughts are impressed; but this being the same for all men is less taken into account, especially by the Hebrews, who claimed a pre-eminence, and despised other men and other men's knowledge.

Lastly, the prophets were said to possess the Spirit of God because men knew not the cause of prophetic knowledge, and in their wonder referred it with other marvels directly to the Deity, styling it Divine knowledge.

We need no longer scruple to affirm that the prophets only perceived God's revelation by the aid of imagination, that is, by words and figures either real or imaginary. We find no other means mentioned in Scripture, and therefore must not invent any. As to the particular law of Nature by which the communications took place, I confess my ignorance. I might, indeed, say as others do, that they took place by the power of God; but this would be mere trifling, and no better than explaining some unique specimen by a transcendental term. Everything takes place by the power of God. Nature herself is the power of God under another name, and our ignorance of the power of God is co-extensive with our ignorance of Nature. It is absolute folly, therefore, to ascribe an event to the power of God when we know not its natural cause, which is the power of God.

However, we are not now inquiring into the causes of prophetic knowledge. We are only attempting, as I have said, to examine the Scriptural documents, and to draw our conclusions from them as from ultimate natural facts; the causes of the documents do not concern us.

As the prophets perceived the revelations of God by the aid of imagination, they could indisputably perceive much that is beyond the boundary of the intellect, for many more ideas can be constructed from words and figures than from the principles and notions on which the whole fabric of reasoned knowledge is reared.

Thus we have a clue to the fact that the prophets perceived nearly everything in parables and allegories, and clothed spiritual truths in bodily forms, for such is the usual method of imagination. We need no longer wonder that Scripture and the prophets speak so strangely and obscurely of God's Spirit or Mind (cf. Numbers xi:17, 1 Kings xxii:21, &c.), that the Lord was seen by Micah as sitting, by Daniel as an old man clothed in white, by Ezekiel as a fire, that the Holy Spirit appeared to those with Christ as a descending dove, to the apostles as fiery tongues, to Paul on his conversion as a great light. All these expressions are plainly in harmony with the current ideas of God and spirits.

Inasmuch as imagination is fleeting and inconstant, we find that the power of prophecy did not remain with a prophet for long, nor manifest itself frequently, but was very rare; manifesting itself only in a few men, and in them not often.

We must necessarily inquire how the prophets became assured of the truth of what they perceived by imagination, and not by sure mental laws; but our investigation must be confined to Scripture, for the subject is one on which we cannot acquire certain knowledge, and which we cannot explain by the immediate causes. Scripture teaching about the assurance of prophets I will treat of in the next chapter.

1 The word nabi is rightly interpreted by Rabbi Salomon Jarchi, but the sense is hardly caught by Aben Ezra, who was not so good a Hebraist. We must also remark that this Hebrew word for prophecy has a universal meaning and embraces all kinds of prophecy. Other terms are more special, and denote this or that sort of prophecy, as I believe is well known to the learned.

2 "Although, ordinary knowledge is Divine, its professors cannot be called prophets." That is, interpreters of God. For he alone is an interpreter of God, who interprets the decrees which God has revealed to him, to others who have not received such revelation, and whose belief, therefore, rests merely on the prophet's authority and the confidence reposed in him. If it were otherwise, and all who listen to prophets became prophets themselves, as all who listen to philosophers become philosophers, a prophet would no longer be the interpreter of Divine decrees, inasmuch as his hearers would know the truth, not on the, authority of the prophet, but by means of actual Divine revelation and inward testimony. Thus the sovereign powers are the interpreters of their own rights of sway, because these are defended only by their authority and supported by their testimony.

3 "Prophets were endowed with a peculiar and extraordinary power." Though some men enjoy gifts which nature has not bestowed on their fellows, they are not said to surpass the bounds of human nature, unless their special qualities are such as cannot be said to be deducible from the definition of human nature. For instance, a giant is a rarity, but still human. The gift of composing poetry extempore is given to very few, yet it is human. The same may, therefore, be said of the faculty possessed by some of imagining things as vividly as though they saw them before them, and this not while asleep, but while awake. But if anyone could be found who possessed other means and other foundations for knowledge, he might be said to transcend the limits of human nature.

CHAPTER II.

Of Prophets.

IT FOLLOWS FROM the last chapter that, as I have said, the prophets were endowed with unusually vivid imaginations, and not with unusually, perfect minds. This conclusion is amply sustained by Scripture, for we are told that Solomon was the wisest of men, but had no special faculty of prophecy. Heman, Calcol, and Dara, though men of great talent, were not prophets, whereas uneducated countrymen, nay, even women, such as Hagar, Abraham's handmaid, were thus gifted. Nor is this contrary to ordinary experience and reason. Men of great imaginative power are less fitted for abstract reasoning, whereas those who excel in intellect and its use keep their imagination more restrained and controlled, holding it in subjection, so to speak, lest it should usurp the place of reason.

Thus to suppose that knowledge of natural and spiritual phenomena can be gained from the prophetic books, is an utter mistake, which I shall endeavour to expose, as I think philosophy, the age, and the question itself demand. I care not for the girdings of superstition, for superstition is the bitter enemy, of all true knowledge and true morality. Yes; it has come to this! Men who openly confess that they can form no idea of God, and only know Him through created things, of which they know not the causes, can unblushingly, accuse philosophers of Atheism. Treating the question methodically, I will show that prophecies varied, not only according to the imagination and physical temperament of the prophet, but also according to his particular opinions; and further that prophecy never rendered the prophet wiser than he was before. But I will first discuss the assurance of truth which the prophets received, for this is akin to the subject-matter of the chapter, and will serve to elucidate somewhat our present point.

Imagination does not, in its own nature, involve any certainty of truth, such as is implied in every clear and distinct idea, but requires some extrinsic reason to assure us of its objective reality: hence prophecy cannot afford certainty, and the prophets were assured of God's revelation by some sign, and not by the fact of revelation, as we may see from Abraham, who, when he had heard the promise of God, demanded a sign, not because he did not believe in God, but because he wished to be sure that it was God Who made the promise. The fact is still more evident in the case of Gideon: "Show me," he says to God, "show me a sign, that I may know that it is Thou that talkest with me." God also says to Moses: "And let this be a sign that I have sent thee." Hezekiah, though he had long known Isaiah to be a prophet, none the less demanded a sign of the cure which he predicted. It is thus quite evident that the prophets always received some sign to certify them of their prophetic imaginings; and for this reason Moses bids the Jews (Deut. xviii.) ask of the prophets a sign, namely, the prediction of some coming event. In this respect, prophetic knowledge is inferior to natural knowledge, which needs no sign, and in itself implies certitude. Moreover, Scripture warrants the statement that the certitude of the prophets was not mathematical, but moral. Moses lays down the punishment of death for the prophet who preaches new gods, even though he confirm his doctrine by signs and wonders (Deut. xiii.); "For," he says, "the Lord also worketh signs and wonders to try His people." And Jesus Christ warns His disciples of the same thing (Matt. xxiv:24). Furthermore, Ezekiel (xiv:9) plainly states that God sometimes deceives men with false revelations; and Micaiah bears like witness in the case of the prophets of Ahab.

Although these instances go to prove that revelation is open to doubt, it nevertheless contains, as we have said, a considerable element of certainty, for God never deceives the good, nor His chosen, but (according to the ancient proverb, and as appears in the history of Abigail and her speech), God uses the good as instruments of goodness, and the wicked as means to execute His wrath. This may be seen from the case of Micaiah above quoted; for although God had determined to deceive Ahab, through prophets, He made use of lying prophets; to the good prophet He revealed the truth, and did not forbid his proclaiming it.

Still the certitude of prophecy, remains, as I have said, merely, moral; for no one can justify himself before God, nor boast that he is an instrument for God's goodness. Scripture itself teaches and shows that God led away David to number the people, though it bears ample witness to David's piety.

The whole question of the certitude of prophecy, was based on these three considerations:

1. That the things revealed were imagined very vividly, affecting the prophets in the same way as things seen when awake;

2. The presence of a sign;

3. Lastly, and chiefly, that the mind of the prophet was given wholly, to what was right and good.

Although Scripture does not always make mention of a sign, we must nevertheless suppose that a sign was always vouchsafed; for Scripture does not always relate every, condition and circumstance (as many, have remarked), but rather takes them for granted. We may, however, admit that no sign was needed when the prophecy declared nothing that was not already contained in the law of Moses, because it was confirmed by that law. For instance, Jeremiah's prophecy, of the destruction of Jerusalem was confirmed by the prophecies of other prophets, and by the threats in the law, and, therefore, it needed no sign; whereas Hananiah, who, contrary to all the prophets, foretold the speedy restoration of the state, stood in need of a sign, or he would have been in doubt as to the truth of his prophecy, until it was confirmed by facts. "The prophet which prophesieth of peace, when the word of the prophet shall come to pass, then shall the prophet be known that the Lord hath truly sent him."

As, then, the certitude afforded to the prophet by signs was not mathematical (i.e. did not necessarily follow from the perception of the thing perceived or seen), but only moral, and as the signs were only given to convince the prophet, it follows that such signs were given according to the opinions and capacity of each prophet, so that a sign which convince one prophet would fall far short of convincing another who was imbued with different opinions. Therefore the signs varied according to the individual prophet.

So also did the revelation vary, as we have stated, according to individual disposition and temperament, and according to the opinions previously held.

It varied according to disposition, in this way: if a prophet was cheerful, victories, peace, and events which make men glad, were revealed to him; in that he was naturally more likely to imagine such things. If, on the contrary, he was melancholy, wars, massacres, and calamities were revealed; and so, according as a prophet was merciful, gentle, quick to anger, or severe, he was more fitted for one kind of revelation than another. It varied according to the temper of imagination in this way: if a prophet was cultivated he perceived the mind of God in a cultivated way, if he was confused he perceived it confusedly. And so with revelations perceived through visions. If a prophet was a countryman he saw visions of oxen, cows, and the like; if he was a soldier, he saw generals and armies; if a courtier, a royal throne, and so on.

Lastly, prophecy varied according to the opinions held by the prophets; for instance, to the Magi, who believed in the follies of astrology, the birth of Christ was revealed through the vision of a star in the East. To the augurs of Nebuchadnezzar the destruction of Jerusalem was revealed through entrails, whereas the king himself inferred it from oracles and the direction of arrows which he shot into the air. To prophets who believed that man acts from free choice and by his own power, God was revealed as standing apart from and ignorant of future human actions. All of which we will illustrate from Scripture.

The first point is proved from the case of Elisha, who, in order to prophecy to Jehoram, asked for a harp, and was unable to perceive the Divine purpose till he had been recreated by its music; then, indeed, he prophesied to Jehoram and to his allies glad tidings, which previously he had been unable to attain to because he was angry with the king, and these who are angry with anyone can imagine evil of him, but not good. The theory that God does not reveal Himself to the angry or the sad, is a mere dream: for God revealed to Moses while angry, the terrible slaughter of the firstborn, and did so without the intervention of a harp. To Cain in his rage, God was revealed, and to Ezekiel, impatient with anger, was revealed the contumacy and wretchedness of the Jews. Jeremiah, miserable and weary of life, prophesied the disasters of the Hebrews, so that Josiah would not consult him, but inquired of a woman, inasmuch as it was more in accordance with womanly nature that God should reveal His mercy thereto. So, Micaiah never prophesied good to Ahab, though other true prophets had done so, but invariably evil. Thus we see that individual prophets were by temperament more fitted for one sort of revelation than another.

The style of the prophecy also varied according to the eloquence of the individual prophet. The prophecies of Ezekiel and Amos are not written in a cultivated style like those of Isaiah and Nahum, but more rudely. Any Hebrew scholar who wishes to inquire into this point more closely, and compares chapters of the different prophets treating of the same subject, will find great dissimilarity of style. Compare, for instance, chap. i. of the courtly Isaiah, verse 11 to verse 20, with chap. v. of the countryman Amos, verses 21-24. Compare also the order and reasoning of the prophecies of Jeremiah, written in Idumaea (chap. xhx.), with the order and reasoning of Obadiah. Compare, lastly, Isa. xl:19, 20, and xliv:8, with Hosea viii:6, and xiii:2. And so on.

A due consideration of these passage will clearly show us that God has no particular style in speaking, but, according to the learning and capacity of the prophet, is cultivated, compressed, severe, untutored, prolix, or obscure.

There was, moreover, a certain variation in the visions vouchsafed to the prophets, and in the symbols by which they expressed them, for Isaiah saw the glory of the Lord departing from the Temple in a different form from that presented to Ezekiel. The Rabbis, indeed, maintain that both visions were really the same, but that Ezekiel, being a countryman, was above measure impressed by it, and therefore set it forth in full detail; but unless there is a trustworthy tradition on the subject, which I do not for a moment believe, this theory is plainly an invention. Isaiah saw seraphim with six wings, Ezekiel beasts with four wings; Isaiah saw God clothed and sitting on a royal throne, Ezekiel saw Him in the likeness of a fire; each doubtless saw God under the form in which he usually imagined Him.

Further, the visions varied in clearness as well as in details; for the revelations of Zechariah were too obscure to be understood by the prophet without explanation, as appears from his narration of them; the visions of Daniel could not be understood by him even after they had been explained, and this obscurity did not arise from the difficulty of the matter revealed (for being merely human affairs, these only transcended human capacity in being future), but solely in the fact that Daniel's imagination was not so capable for prophecy while he was awake as while he was asleep; and this is further evident from the fact that at the very beginning of the vision he was so terrified that he almost despaired of his strength. Thus, on account of the inadequacy of his imagination and his strength, the things revealed were so obscure to him that he could not understand them even after they had been explained. Here we may note that the words heard by Daniel, were, as we have shown above, simply imaginary, so that it is hardly wonderful that in his frightened state he imagined them so confusedly and obscurely that afterwards he could make nothing of them. Those who say that God did not wish to make a clear revelation, do not seem to have read the words of the angel, who expressly says that he came to make the prophet understand what should befall his people in the latter days (Dan. x:14).

The revelation remained obscure because no one was found, at that time, with imagination sufficiently strong to conceive it more clearly. Lastly, the prophets, to whom it was revealed that God would take away Elijah, wished to persuade Elisha that he had been taken somewhere where they would find him; showing sufficiently clearly that they had not understood God's revelation aright.

There is no need to set this out more amply, for nothing is more plain in the Bible than that God endowed some prophets with far greater gifts of prophecy than others. But I will show in greater detail and length, for I consider the point more important, that the prophecies varied according to the opinions previously embraced by the prophets, and that the prophets held diverse and even contrary opinions and prejudices. (I speak, be it understood, solely of matters speculative, for in regard to uprightness and morality the case is widely different.) From thence I shall conclude that prophecy never rendered the prophets more learned, but left them with their former opinions, and that we are, therefore, not at all bound to trust them in matters of intellect.

Everyone has been strangely hasty in affirming that the prophets knew everything within the scope of human intellect; and, although certain passages of Scripture plainly affirm that the prophets were in certain respects ignorant, such persons would rather say that they do not understand the passages than admit that there was anything which the prophets did not know; or else they try to wrest the Scriptural words away from their evident meaning.

If either of these proceedings is allowable we may as well shut our Bibles, for vainly shall we attempt to prove anything from them if their plainest passages may be classed among obscure and impenetrable mysteries, or if we may put any interpretation on them which we fancy. For instance, nothing is more clear in the Bible than that Joshua, and perhaps also the author who wrote his history, thought that the sun revolves round the earth, and that the earth is fixed, and further that the sun for a certain period remained still. Many, who will not admit any movement in the heavenly bodies, explain away the passage till it seems to mean something quite different; others, who have learned to philosophize more correctly, and understand that the earth moves while the sun is still, or at any rate does not revolve round the earth, try with all their might to wrest this meaning from Scripture, though plainly nothing of the sort is intended. Such quibblers excite my wonder! Are we, forsooth, bound to believe that Joshua the Soldier was a learned astronomer? or that a miracle could not be revealed to him, or that the light of the sun could not remain longer than usual above the horizon, without his knowing the cause? To me both alternatives appear ridiculous, and therefore I would rather say, that Joshua was ignorant of the true cause of the lengthened day, and that he and the whole host with him thought that the sun moved round the earth every day, and that on that particular occasion it stood still for a time, thus causing the light to remain longer; and I would say, that they did not conjecture that, from the amount of snow in the air (see Josh. x:11), the refraction may have been greater than usual, or that there may have been some other cause which we will not now inquire into.

So also the sign of the shadow going back was revealed to Isaiah according to his understanding; that is, as proceeding from a going backwards of the sun; for he, too, thought that the sun moves and that the earth is still; of parhelia he perhaps never even dreamed. We may arrive at this conclusion without any, scruple, for the sign could really have come to pass, and have been predicted by Isaiah to the king, without the prophet being aware of the real cause.

With regard to the building of the Temple by Solomon, if it was really dictate by God we must maintain the same doctrine: namely, that all the measurements were revealed according to the opinions and understanding of the king; for as we are not bound to believe that Solomon was a mathematician, we may affirm that he was ignorant of the true ratio between the circumference and the diameter of a circle, and that, like the generality of workmen, he thought that it was as three to one. But if it is allowable to declare that we do not understand the passage, in good sooth I know nothing in the Bible that we can understand; for the process of building is there narrated simply and as a mere matter of history. If, again, it is permitted to pretend that the passage has another meaning, and was written as it is from some reason unknown to us, this is no less than a complete subversal of the Bible; for every absurd and evil invention of human perversity could thus, without detriment to Scriptural authority, be defended and fostered. Our conclusion is in no wise impious, for though Solomon, Isaiah, Joshua, &c. were prophets, they were none the less men, and as such not exempt from human shortcomings.

According to the understanding of Noah it was revealed to him that God as about to destroy the whole human race, for Noah thought that beyond the limits of Palestine the world was not inhabited.

Not only in matters of this kind, but in others more important, the about the Divine attributes, but held quite ordinary notions about God, and to these notions their revelations were adapted, as I will demonstrate by ample Scriptural testimony; from all which one may easily see that they were praised and commended, not so much for the sublimity and eminence of their intellect as for their piety and faithfulness.

Adam, the first man to whom God was revealed, did not know that He is omnipotent and omniscient; for he hid himself from Him, and attempted to make excuses for his fault before God, as though he had had to do with a man; therefore to him also was God revealed according to his understanding — that is, as being unaware of his situation or his sin, for Adam heard, or seemed to hear, the Lord walling, in the garden, calling him and asking him where he was; and then, on seeing his shamefacedness, asking him whether he had eaten of the forbidden fruit. Adam evidently only knew the Deity as the Creator of all things. To Cain also God was revealed, according to his understanding, as ignorant of human affairs, nor was a higher conception of the Deity required for repentance of his sin.

To Laban the Lord revealed Himself as the God of Abraham, because Laban believed that each nation had its own special divinity (see Gen. xxxi:29). Abraham also knew not that God is omnipresent, and has foreknowledge of all things; for when he heard the sentence against the inhabitants of Sodom, he prayed that the Lord should not execute it till He had ascertained whether they all merited such punishment; for he said (see Gen. xviii:24), "Peradventure there be fifty righteous within the city," and in accordance with this belief God was revealed to him; as Abraham imagined, He spake thus: "I will go down now, and see whether they have done altogether according to the cry of it which is come unto Me; and, if not, I will know." Further, the Divine testimony concerning Abraham asserts nothing but that he was obedient, and that he "commanded his household after him that they should keep the way of the Lord" (Gen. xviii:19); it does not state that he held sublime conceptions of the Deity.

Moses, also, was not sufficiently aware that God is omniscient, and directs human actions by His sole decree, for although God Himself says that the Israelites should hearken to Him, Moses still considered the matter doubtful and repeated, "But if they will not believe me, nor hearken unto my voice." To him in like manner God was revealed as taking no part in, and as being ignorant of, future human actions: the Lord gave him two signs and said, "And it shall come to pass that if they will not believe thee, neither hearken to the voice of the first sign, that they will believe the voice of the latter sign; but if not, thou shalt take of the water of the river," &c. Indeed, if any one considers without prejudice the recorded opinions of Moses, he will plainly see that Moses conceived the Deity as a Being Who has always existed, does exist, and always will exist, and for this cause he calls Him by the name Jehovah, which in Hebrew signifies these three phases of existence: as to His nature, Moses only taught that He is merciful, gracious, and exceeding jealous, as appears from many passages in the Pentateuch. Lastly, he believed and taught that this Being was so different from all other beings, that He could not be expressed by the image of any visible thing; also, that He could not be looked upon, and that not so much from inherent impossibility as from human infirmity; further, that by reason of His power He was without equal and unique. Moses admitted, indeed, that there were beings (doubtless by the plan and command of the Lord) who acted as God's vicegerents — that is, beings to whom God had given the right, authority, and power to direct nations, and to provide and care for them; but he taught that this Being Whom they were bound to obey was the highest and Supreme God, or (to use the Hebrew phrase) God of gods, and thus in the song (Exod. xv:11) he exclaims, "Who is like unto Thee, 0 Lord, among the gods?" and Jethro says (Exod. xviii:11), "Now I know that the Lord is greater than all gods." That is to say, "I am at length compelled to admit to Moses that Jehovah is greater than all gods, and that His power is unrivalled." We must remain in doubt whether Moses thought that these beings who acted as God's vicegerents were created by Him, for he has stated nothing, so far as we know, about their creation and origin. He further taught that this Being had brought the visible world into order from Chaos, and had given Nature her germs, and therefore that He possesses supreme right and power over all things; further, that by reason of this supreme right and power He had chosen for Himself alone the Hebrew nation and a certain strip of territory, and had handed over to the care of other gods substituted by Himself the rest of the nations and territories, and that therefore He was called the God of Israel and the God of Jerusalem, whereas the other gods were called the gods of the Gentiles. For this reason the Jews believed that the strip of territory which God had chosen for Himself, demanded a Divine worship quite apart and different from the worship which obtained elsewhere, and that the Lord would not suffer the worship of other gods adapted to other countries. Thus they thought that the people whom the king of Assyria had brought into Judaea were torn in pieces by lions because they knew not the worship of the National Divinity (2 Kings xvii:25).

Jacob, according to Aben Ezra's opinion, therefore admonished his sons when he wished them to seek out a new country, that they should prepare themselves for a new worship, and lay aside the worship of strange, gods — that is, of the gods of the land where they were (Gen. xxxv:2, 3).

David, in telling Saul that he was compelled by the king's persecution to live away from his country, said that he was driven out from the heritage of the Lord, and sent to worship other gods (1 Sam. xxvi:19). Lastly, he believed that this Being or Deity had His habitation in the heavens (Deut. xxxiii:27), an opinion very common among the Gentiles.

If we now examine the revelations to Moses, we shall find that they were accommodated to these opinions; as he believed that the Divine Nature was subject to the conditions of mercy, graciousness, &c., so God was revealed to him in accordance with his idea and under these attributes (see Exodus xxxiv:6, 7, and the second commandment). Further it is related (Ex. xxxiii:18) that Moses asked of God that he might behold Him, but as Moses (as we have said) had formed no mental image of God, and God (as I have shown) only revealed Himself to the prophets in accordance with the disposition of their imagination, He did not reveal Himself in any form. This, I repeat, was because the imagination of Moses was unsuitable, for other prophets bear witness that they saw the Lord; for instance, Isaiah, Ezekiel, Daniel, &c. For this reason God answered Moses, "Thou canst not see My face;" and inasmuch as Moses believed that God can be looked upon — that is, that no contradiction of the Divine nature is therein involved (for otherwise he would never have preferred his request) — it is added, "For no one shall look on Me and live," thus giving a reason in accordance with Moses' idea, for it is not stated that a contradiction of the Divine nature would be involved, as was really the case, but that the thing would not come to pass because of human infirmity.

When God would reveal to Moses that the Israelites, because they worshipped the calf, were to be placed in the same category as other nations, He said (ch. xxxiii:2, 3), that He would send an angel (that is, a being who should have charge of the Israelites, instead of the Supreme Being), and that He Himself would no longer remain among them; thus leaving Moses no ground for supposing that the Israelites were more beloved by God than the other nations whose guardianship He had entrusted to other beings or angels (vide verse 16).

Lastly, as Moses believed that God dwelt in the heavens, God was revealed to him as coming down from heaven on to a mountain, and in order to talk with the Lord Moses went up the mountain, which he certainly need not have done if he could have conceived of God as omnipresent.

The Israelites knew scarcely anything of God, although He was revealed to them; and this is abundantly evident from their transferring, a few days afterwards, the honour and worship due to Him to a calf, which they believed to be the god who had brought them out of Egypt. In truth, it is hardly likely that men accustomed to the superstitions of Egypt, uncultivated and sunk in most abject slavery, should have held any sound notions about the Deity, or that Moses should have taught them anything beyond a rule of right living; inculcating it not like a philosopher, as the result of freedom, but like a lawgiver compelling them to be moral by legal authority. Thus the rule of right living, the worship and love of God, was to them rather a bondage than the true liberty, the gift and grace of the Deity. Moses bid them love God and keep His law, because they had in the past received benefits from Him (such as the deliverance from slavery in Egypt), and further terrified them with threats if they transgressed His commands, holding out many promises of good if they should observe them; thus treating them as parents treat irrational children. It is, therefore, certain that they knew not the excellence of virtue and the true happiness.

Jonah thought that he was fleeing from the sight of God, which seems to show that he too held that God had entrusted the care of the nations outside Judaea to other substituted powers. No one in the whole of the Old Testament speaks more rationally of God than Solomon, who in fact surpassed all the men of his time in natural ability. Yet he considered himself above the law (esteeming it only to have been given for men without reasonable and intellectual grounds for their actions), and made small account of the laws concerning kings, which are mainly three: nay, he openly violated them (in this he did wrong, and acted in a manner unworthy of a philosopher, by indulging in sensual pleasure), and taught that all Fortune's favours to mankind are vanity, that humanity has no nobler gift than wisdom, and no greater punishment than folly. See Proverbs xvi:22, 23.

But let us return to the prophets whose conflicting opinions we have undertaken to note. The expressed ideas of Ezekiel seemed so diverse from those of Moses to the Rabbis who have left us the extant prophetic books (as is told in the treatise of Sabbathus, i:13, 2), that they had serious thoughts of omitting his prophecy from the canon, and would doubtless have thus excluded it if a certain Hananiah had not undertaken to explain it; a task which (as is there narrated) he with great zeal and labour accomplished. How he did so does not sufficiently appear, whether it was by writing a commentary which has now perished, or by altering Ezekiel's words and audaciously — striking out phrases according to his fancy. However this may be, chapter xviii. certainly does not seem to agree with Exodus xxxiv:7, Jeremiah xxxii:18, &c.

Samuel believed that the Lord never repented of anything He had decreed (1 Sam. xv:29), for when Saul was sorry for his sin, and wished to worship God and ask for forgiveness, Samuel said that the Lord would not go back from his decree.

To Jeremiah, on the other hand, it was revealed that, "If that nation against whom I (the Lord) have pronounced, turn from their evil, I will repent of the evil that I thought to do unto them. If it do evil in my sight, that it obey not my voice, then I will repent of the good wherewith I said I would benefit them" (Jer. xviii:8-10). Joel (ii:13) taught that the Lord repented Him only of evil. Lastly, it is clear from Gen iv: 7 that a man can overcome the temptations of sin, and act righteously; for this doctrine is told to Cain, though, as we learn from Josephus and the Scriptures, he never did so overcome them. And this agrees with the chapter of Jeremiah just cited, for it is there said that the Lord repents of the good or the evil pronounced, if the men in question change their ways and manner of life. But, on the other hand, Paul (Rom.ix:10) teaches as plainly as possible that men have no control over the temptations of the flesh save by the special vocation and grace of God. And when (Rom. iii:5 and vi:19) he attributes righteousness to man, he corrects himself as speaking merely humanly and through the infirmity of the flesh.

We have now more than sufficiently proved our point, that God adapted revelations to the understanding and opinions of the prophets, and that in matters of theory without bearing on charity or morality the prophets could be, and, in fact, were, ignorant, and held conflicting opinions. It therefore follows that we must by no means go to the prophets for knowledge, either of natural or of spiritual phenomena.

We have determined, then, that we are only bound to believe in the prophetic writings, the object and substance of the revelation; with regard to the details, every one may believe or not, as he likes.

For instance, the revelation to Cain only teaches us that God admonished him to lead the true life, for such alone is the object and substance of the revelation, not doctrines concerning free will and philosophy. Hence, though the freedom of the will is clearly implied in the words of the admonition, we are at liberty to hold a contrary opinion, since the words and reasons were adapted to the understanding of Cain.

So, too, the revelation to Micaiah would only teach that God revealed to him the true issue of the battle between Ahab and Aram; and this is all we are bound to believe. Whatever else is contained in the revelation concerning the true and the false Spirit of God, the army of heaven standing on the right hand and on the left, and all the other details, does not affect us at all. Everyone may believe as much of it as his reason allows.

The reasonings by which the Lord displayed His power to Job (if they really were a revelation, and the author of the history is narrating, and not merely, as some suppose, rhetorically adorning his own conceptions), would come under the same category — that is, they were adapted to Job's understanding, for the purpose of convincing him, and are not universal, or for the convincing of all men.

We can come to no different conclusion with respect to the reasonings of Christ, by which He convicted the Pharisees of pride and ignorance, and exhorted His disciples to lead the true life. He adapted them to each man's opinions and principles. For instance, when He said to the Pharisees (Matt. xii:26), "And if Satan cast out devils, his house is divided against itself, how then shall his kingdom stand? "He only wished to convince the Pharisees according, to their own principles, not to teach that there are devils, or any kingdom of devils. So, too, when He said to His disciples (Matt. viii:10), "See that ye despise not one of these little ones, for I say unto you that their angels," &c., He merely desired to warn them against pride and despising any of their fellows, not to insist on the actual reason given, which was simply adopted in order to persuade them more easily.

Lastly, we should say, exactly the same of the apostolic signs and reasonings, but there is no need to go further into the subject. If I were to enumerate all the passages of Scripture addressed only to individuals, or to a particular man's understanding, and which cannot, without great danger to philosophy, be defended as Divine doctrines, I should go far beyond the brevity at which I aim. Let it suffice, then, to have indicated a few instances of general application, and let the curious reader consider others by himself. Although the points we have just raised concerning prophets and prophecy are the only ones which have any direct bearing on the end in view, namely, the separation of Philosophy from Theology, still, as I have touched on the general question, I may here inquire whether the gift of prophecy was peculiar to the Hebrews, or whether it was common to all nations. I must then come to a conclusion about the vocation of the Hebrews, all of which I shall do in the ensuing chapter.

CHAPTER III.

Of the Vocation of the Hebrews, and
Whether the Gift of Prophecy was Peculiar to Them.

EVERY MAN'S TRUE happiness and blessedness consist solely in the enjoyment of what is good, not in the pride that he alone is enjoying it, to the exclusion of others. He who thinks himself the more blessed because he is enjoying benefits which others are not, or because he is more blessed or more fortunate than his fellows, is ignorant of true happiness and blessedness, and the joy which he feels is either childish or envious and malicious. For instance, a man's true happiness consists only in wisdom, and the knowledge of the truth, not at all in the fact that he is wiser than others, or that others lack such knowledge: such considerations do not increase his wisdom or true happiness.

Whoever, therefore, rejoices for such reasons, rejoices in another's misfortune, and is, so far, malicious and bad, knowing neither true happiness nor the peace of the true life.

When Scripture, therefore, in exhorting the Hebrews to obey the law, says that the Lord has chosen them for Himself before other nations (Deut. x:15); that He is near them, but not near others (Deut. iv:7); that to them alone He has given just laws (Deut. iv:8); and, lastly, that He has marked them out before others (Deut. iv:32); it speaks only according to the understanding of its hearers, who, as we have shown in the last chapter, and as Moses also testifies (Deut. ix:6, 7), knew not true blessedness. For in good sooth they would have been no less blessed if God had called all men equally to salvation, nor would God have been less present to them for being equally present to others; their laws, would have been no less just if they had been ordained for all, and they themselves would have been no less wise. The miracles would have shown God's power no less by being wrought for other nations also; lastly, the Hebrews would have been just as much bound to worship God if He had bestowed all these gifts equally on all men.

When God tells Solomon (1 Kings iii:12) that no one shall be as wise as he in time to come, it seems to be only a manner of expressing surpassing wisdom; it is little to be believed that God would have promised Solomon, for his greater happiness, that He would never endow anyone with so much wisdom in time to come; this would in no wise have increased Solomon's intellect, and the wise king would have given equal thanks to the Lord if everyone had been gifted with the same faculties.

Still, though we assert that Moses, in the passages of the Pentateuch just cited, spoke only according to the understanding of the Hebrews, we have no wish to deny that God ordained the Mosaic law for them alone, nor that He spoke to them alone, nor that they witnessed marvels beyond those which happened to any other nation; but we wish to emphasize that Moses desired to admonish the Hebrews in such a manner, and with such reasonings as would appeal most forcibly to their childish understanding, and constrain them to worship the Deity. Further, we wished to show that the Hebrews did not surpass other nations in knowledge, or in piety, but evidently in some attribute different from these; or (to speak like the Scriptures, according to their understanding), that the Hebrews were not chosen by God before others for the sake of the true life and sublime ideas, though they were often thereto admonished, but with some other object. What that object was,

I will duly show.

But before I begin, I wish in a few words to explain what I mean by the guidance of God, by the help of God, external and inward, and, lastly, what I understand by fortune.

By the help of God, I mean the fixed and unchangeable order of nature or the chain of natural events: for I have said before and shown elsewhere that the universal laws of nature, according to which all things exist and are determined, are only another name for the eternal decrees of God, which always involve eternal truth and necessity.

So that to say that everything happens according to natural laws, and to say that everything is ordained by the decree and ordinance of God, is the same thing. Now since the power in nature is identical with the power of God, by which alone all things happen and are determined, it follows that whatsoever man, as a part of nature, provides himself with to aid and preserve his existence, or whatsoever nature affords him without his help, is given to him solely by the Divine power, acting either through human nature or through external circumstance. So whatever human nature can furnish itself with by its own efforts to preserve its existence, may be fitly called the inward aid of God, whereas whatever else accrues to man's profit from outward causes may be called the external aid of God.

We can now easily understand what is meant by the election of God. For since no one can do anything save by the predetermined order of nature, that is by God's eternal ordinance and decree, it follows that no one can choose a plan of life for himself, or accomplish any work save by God's vocation choosing him for the work or the plan of life in question, rather than any other. Lastly, by fortune, I mean the ordinance of God in so far as it directs human life through external and unexpected means. With these preliminaries I return to my purpose of discovering the reason why the Hebrews were said to be elected by God before other nations, and with the demonstration I thus proceed.

All objects of legitimate desire fall, generally speaking, under one of these three categories:

1. The knowledge of things through their primary causes. 2. The government of the passions, or the acquirement of the habit of virtue. 3. Secure and healthy life.

The means which most directly conduce towards the first two of these ends, and which may be considered their proximate and efficient causes are contained in human nature itself, so that their acquisition hinges only on our own power, and on the laws of human nature. It may be concluded that these gifts are not peculiar to any nation, but have always been shared by the whole human race, unless, indeed, we would indulge the dream that nature formerly created men of different kinds. But the means which conduce to security and health are chiefly in external circumstance, and are called the gifts of fortune because they depend chiefly on objective causes of which we are ignorant; for a fool may be almost as liable to happiness or unhappiness as a wise man. Nevertheless, human management and watchfulness can greatly assist towards living in security and warding off the injuries of our fellow-men, and even of beasts. Reason and experience show no more certain means of attaining this object than the formation of a society with fixed laws, the occupation of a strip of territory and the concentration of all forces, as it were, into one body, that is the social body. Now for forming and preserving a society, no ordinary ability and care is required: that society will be most secure, most stable, and least liable to reverses, which is founded and directed by far-seeing and careful men; while, on the other hand, a society constituted by men without trained skill, depends in a great measure on fortune, and is less constant. If, in spite of all, such a society lasts a long time, it is owing to some other directing influence than its own; if it overcomes great perils and its affairs prosper, it will perforce marvel at and adore the guiding Spirit of God (in so far, that is, as God works through hidden means, and not through the nature and mind of man), for everything happens to it unexpectedly and contrary to anticipation, it may even be said and thought to be by miracle. Nations, then, are distinguished from one another in respect to the social organization and the laws under which they live and are governed; the Hebrew nation was not chosen by God in respect to its wisdom nor its tranquillity of mind, but in respect to its social organization and the good fortune with which it obtained supremacy and kept it so many years. This is abundantly clear from Scripture. Even a cursory perusal will show us that the only respects in which the Hebrews surpassed other nations, are in their successful conduct of matters relating to government, and in their surmounting great perils solely by God's external aid; in other ways they were on a par with their fellows, and God was equally gracious to all. For in respect to intellect (as we have shown in the last chapter) they held very ordinary ideas about God and nature, so that they cannot have been God's chosen in this respect; nor were they so chosen in respect of virtue and the true life, for here again they, with the exception of a very few elect, were on an equality with other nations: therefore their choice and vocation consisted only in the temporal happiness and advantages of independent rule. In fact, we do not see that God promised anything beyond this to the patriarchs 4 or their successors; in the law no other reward is offered for obedience than the continual happiness of an independent commonwealth and other goods of this life; while, on the other hand, against contumacy and the breaking of the covenant is threatened the downfall of the commonwealth and great hardships. Nor is this to be wondered at; for the ends of every social organization and commonwealth are (as appears from what we have said, and as we will explain more at length hereafter) security and comfort; a commonwealth can only exist by the laws being binding on all. If all the members of a state wish to disregard the law, by that very fact they dissolve the state and destroy the commonwealth. Thus, the only reward which could be promised to the Hebrews for continued obedience to the law was security 5 and its attendant advantages, while no surer punishment could be threatened for disobedience, than the ruin of the state and the evils which generally follow therefrom, in addition to such further consequences as might accrue to the Jews in particular from the ruin of their especial state. But there is no need here to go into this point at more length. I will only add that the laws of the Old Testament were revealed and ordained to the Jews only, for as God chose them in respect to the special constitution of their society and government, they must, of course, have had special laws. Whether God ordained special laws for other nations also, and revealed Himself to their lawgivers prophetically, that is, under the attributes by which the latter were accustomed to imagine Him, I cannot sufficiently determine. It is evident from Scripture itself that other nations acquired supremacy and particular laws by the external aid of God; witness only the two following passages:

In Genesis xiv:18, 19, 20, it is related that Melchisedek was king of Jerusalem and priest of the Most High God, that in exercise of his priestly functions he blessed Abraham, and that Abraham the beloved of the Lord gave to this priest of God a tithe of all his spoils. This sufficiently shows that before He founded the Israelitish nation God constituted kings and priests in Jerusalem, and ordained for them rites and laws. Whether He did so prophetically is, as I have said, not sufficiently clear; but I am sure of this, that Abraham, whilst he sojourned in the city, lived scrupulously according to these laws, for Abraham had received no special rites from God; and yet it is stated (Gen. xxvi:5), that he observed the worship, the precepts, the statutes, and the laws of God, which must be interpreted to mean the worship, the statutes, the precepts, and the laws of king Melchisedek. Malachi chides the Jews as follows (i:10-11.): "Who is there among you that will shut the doors? [of the Temple]; neither do ye kindle fire on mine altar for nought. I have no pleasure in you, saith the Lord of Hosts. For from the rising of the sun, even until the going down of the same My Name shall be great among the Gentiles; and in every place incense shall be offered in My Name, and a pure offering; for My Name is great among the heathen, saith the Lord of Hosts." These words, which, unless we do violence to them, could only refer to the current period, abundantly testify that the Jews of that time were not more beloved by God than other nations, that God then favoured other nations with more miracles than He vouchsafed to the Jews, who had then partly recovered their empire without miraculous aid; and, lastly, that the Gentiles possessed rites and ceremonies acceptable to God. But I pass over these points lightly: it is enough for my purpose to have shown that the election of the Jews had regard to nothing but temporal physical happiness and freedom, in other words, autonomous government, and to the manner and means by which they obtained it; consequently to the laws in so far as they were necessary to the preservation of that special government; and, lastly, to the manner in which they were revealed. In regard to other matters, wherein man's true happiness consists, they were on a par with the rest of the nations.

When, therefore, it is said in Scripture (Deut. iv:7) that the Lord is not so nigh to any other nation as He is to the Jews, reference is only made to their government, and to the period when so many miracles happened to them, for in respect of intellect and virtue — that is, in respect of blessedness — God was, as we have said already, and are now demonstrating, equally gracious to all. Scripture itself bears testimony to this fact, for the Psalmist says (cxlv:18), "The Lord is near unto all them that call upon Him, to all that call upon Him in truth." So in the same Psalm, verse 9, "The Lord is good to all, and His tender mercies are over all His works." In Ps. xxxiii:16, it is clearly stated that God has granted to all men the same intellect, in these words, He fashioneth their hearts alike." The heart was considered by the Hebrews, as I suppose everyone knows, to be the seat of the soul and the intellect.

Lastly, from Job xxxviii:28, it is plain that God had ordained for the whole human race the law to reverence God, to keep from evil doing, or to do well, and that Job, although a Gentile, was of all men most acceptable to God, because he exceeded all in piety and religion. Lastly, from Jonah iv:2, it is very evident that, not only to the Jews but to all men, God was gracious, merciful, long — suffering, and of great goodness, and repented Him of the evil, for Jonah says: "Therefore I determined to flee before unto Tarshish, for I know that Thou art a gracious God, and merciful, slow to anger, and of great kindness," &c., and that, therefore, God would pardon the Ninevites. We conclude, therefore (inasmuch as God is to all men equally gracious, and the Hebrews were only, chosen by him in respect to their social organization and government), that the individual Jew, taken apart from his social organization and government, possessed no gift of God above other men, and that there was no difference between Jew and Gentile. As it is a fact that God is equally gracious, merciful, and the rest, to all men; and as the function of the prophet was to teach men not so much the laws of their country, as true virtue, and to exhort them thereto, it is not to be doubted that all nations possessed prophets, and that the prophetic gift was not peculiar to the Jews. Indeed, history, both profane and sacred, bears witness to the fact. Although, from the sacred histories of the Old Testament, it is not evident that the other nations had as many prophets as the Hebrews, or that any Gentile prophet was expressly sent by God to the nations, this does not affect the question, for the Hebrews were careful to record their own affairs, not those of other nations. It suffices, then, that we find in the Old Testament Gentiles, and uncircumcised, as Noah, Enoch, Abimelech, Balaam, &c., exercising prophetic gifts; further, that Hebrew prophets were sent by God, not only to their own nation but to many others also. Ezekiel prophesied to all the nations then known; Obadiah to none, that we are aware of, save the Idumeans; and Jonah was chiefly the prophet to the Ninevites. Isaiah bewails and predicts the calamities, and hails the restoration not only of the Jews but also of other nations, for he says (chap. xvi:9), "Therefore I will bewail Jazer with weeping;" and in chap. xix. he foretells first the calamities and then the restoration of the Egyptians (see verses 19, 20, 21, 25), saying that God shall send them a Saviour to free them, that the Lord shall be known in Egypt, and, further, that the Egyptians shall worship God with sacrifice and oblation; and, at last, he calls that nation the blessed Egyptian people of God; all of which particulars are specially noteworthy.

Jeremiah is called, not the prophet of the Hebrew nation, but simply the prophet of the nations (see Jer:i.5). He also mournfully foretells the calamities of the nations, and predicts their restoration, for he says (xlviii:31) of the Moabites, "Therefore will I howl for Moab, and I will cryout for all Moab" (verse 36), "and therefore mine heart shall sound for Moab like pipes;" in the end he prophesies their restoration, as also the restoration of the Egyptians, Ammonites, and Elamites. Wherefore it is beyond doubt that other nations also, like the Jews, had their prophets, who prophesied to them.

Although Scripture only, makes mention of one man, Balaam, to whom the future of the Jews and the other nations was revealed, we must not suppose that Balaam prophesied only once, for from the narrative itself it is abundantly clear that he had long previously been famous for prophesy and other Divine gifts. For when Balak bade him to come to him, he said (Num. xxii:6), "For I know that he whom thou blessest is blessed, and he whom thou cursest is cursed." Thus we see that he possessed the gift which God had bestowed on Abraham. Further, as accustomed to prophesy, Balaam bade the messengers wait for him till the will of the Lord was revealed to him. When he prophesied, that is, when he interpreted the true mind of God, he was wont to say this of himself: "He hath said, which heard the words of God and knew the knowledge of the Most High, which saw the vision of the Almighty falling into a trance, but having his eyes open." Further, after he had blessed the Hebrews by the command of God, he began (as was his custom) to prophesy to other nations, and to predict their future; all of which abundantly shows that he had always been a prophet, or had often prophesied, and (as we may also remark here) possessed that which afforded the chief certainty to prophets of the truth of their prophecy, namely, a mind turned wholly to what is right and good, for he did not bless those whom he wished to bless, nor curse those whom he wished to curse, as Balak supposed, but only those whom God wished to be blessed or cursed. Thus he answered Balak: "If Balak should give me his house full of silver and gold, I cannot go beyond the commandment of the Lord to do either good or bad of my own mind; but what the Lord saith, that will I speak." As for God being angry with him in the way, the same happened to Moses when he set out to Egypt by the command of the Lord; and as to his receiving money for prophesying, Samuel did the same (1 Sam. ix:7, 8); if in anyway he sinned, "there is not a just man upon earth that doeth good and sinneth not," Eccles. vii:20. (Vide 2 Epist. Peter ii:15, 16, and Jude 5:11.)

His speeches must certainly have had much weight with God, and His power for cursing must assuredly have been very great from the number of times that we find stated in Scripture, in proof of God's great mercy to the Jews, that God would not hear Balaam, and that He changed the cursing to blessing (see Deut. xxiii:6, Josh. xxiv:10, Neh. xiii:2). Wherefore he was without doubt most acceptable to God, for the speeches and cursings of the wicked move God not at all. As then he was a true prophet, and nevertheless Joshua calls him a soothsayer or augur, it is certain that this title had an honourable signification, and that those whom the Gentiles called augurs and soothsayers were true prophets, while those whom Scripture often accuses and condemns were false soothsayers, who deceived the Gentiles as false prophets deceived the Jews; indeed, this is made evident from other passages in the Bible, whence we conclude that the gift of prophecy was not peculiar to the Jews, but common to all nations. The Pharisees, however, vehemently contend that this Divine gift was peculiar to their nation, and that the other nations foretold the future (what will superstition invent next?) by some unexplained diabolical faculty. The principal passage of Scripture which they cite, by way of confirming their theory with its authority, is Exodus xxxiii:16, where Moses says to God, "For wherein shall it be known here that I and Thy people have found grace in Thy sight? is it not in that Thou goest with us? so shall we be separated, I and Thy people, from all the people that are upon the face of the earth." From this they would infer that Moses asked of God that He should be present to the Jews, and should reveal Himself to them prophetically; further, that He should grant this favour to no other nation. It is surely absurd that Moses should have been jealous of God's presence among the Gentiles, or that he should have dared to ask any such thing. The act is, as Moses knew that the disposition and spirit of his nation was rebellious, he clearly saw that they could not carry out what they had begun without very great miracles and special external aid from God; nay, that without such aid they must necessarily perish: as it was evident that God wished them to be preserved, he asked for this special external aid. Thus he says (Ex. xxxiv:9), "If now I have found grace in Thy sight, 0 Lord, let my Lord, I pray Thee, go among us; for it is a stiffnecked people." The reason, therefore, for his seeking special external aid from God was the stiffneckedness of the people, and it is made still more plain, that he asked for nothing beyond this special external aid by God's answer — for God answered at once (verse 10 of the same chapter)— "Behold, I make a covenant: before all Thy people I will do marvels, such as have not been done in all the earth, nor in any nation." Therefore Moses had in view nothing beyond the special election of the Jews, as I have explained it, and made no other request to God. I confess that in Paul's Epistle to the Romans, I find another text which carries more weight, namely, where Paul seems to teach a different doctrine from that here set down, for he there says (Rom. iii:1): "What advantage then hath the Jew? or what profit is there of circumcision? Much every way: chiefly, because that unto them were committed the oracles of God."

But if we look to the doctrine which Paul especially desired to teach, we shall find nothing repugnant to our present contention; on the contrary, his doctrine is the same as ours, for he says (Rom. iii:29) "that God is the God of the Jews and of the Gentiles, and" (ch. ii:25, 26) "But, if thou be a breaker of the law, thy circumcision is made uncircumcision. Therefore if the uncircumcision keep the righteousness of the law, shall not his uncircumcision be counted for circumcision?" Further, in chap. iv:verse 9, he says that all alike, Jew and Gentile, were under sin, and that without commandment and law there is no sin. Wherefore it is most evident that to all men absolutely was revealed the law under which all lived — namely, the law which has regard only to true virtue, not the law established in respect to, and in the formation of a particular state and adapted to the disposition of a particular people. Lastly, Paul concludes that since God is the God of all nations, that is, is equally gracious to all, and since all men equally live under the law and under sin, so also to all nations did God send His Christ, to free all men equally from the bondage of the law, that they should no more do right by the command of the law, but by the constant determination of their hearts. So that Paul teaches exactly the same as ourselves. When, therefore, he says "To the Jews only were entrusted the oracles of God," we must either understand that to them only were the laws entrusted in writing, while they were given to other nations merely in revelation and conception, or else (as none but Jews would object to the doctrine he desired to advance) that Paul was answering only in accordance with the understanding and current ideas of the Jews, for in respect to teaching things which he had partly seen, partly heard, he was to the Greeks a Greek, and to the Jews a Jew.

It now only remains to us to answer the arguments of those who would persuade themselves that the election of the Jews was not temporal, and merely in respect of their commonwealth, but eternal; for, they say, we see the Jews after the loss of their commonwealth, and after being scattered so many years and separated from all other nations, still surviving, which is without parallel among other peoples, and further the Scriptures seem to teach that God has chosen for Himself the Jews for ever, so that though they have lost their commonwealth, they still nevertheless remain God's elect.

The passages which they think teach most clearly this eternal election, are chiefly:

(1.) Jer. xxxi:36, where the prophet testifies that the seed of Israel shall for ever remain the nation of God, comparing them with the stability of the heavens and nature;

(2.) Ezek. xx:32, where the prophet seems to intend that though the Jews wanted after the help afforded them to turn their backs on the worship of the Lord, that God would nevertheless gather them together again from all the lands in which they were dispersed, and lead them to the wilderness of the peoples — as He had led their fathers to the wilderness of the land of Egypt — and would at length, after purging out from among them the rebels and transgressors, bring them thence to his Holy mountain, where the whole house of Israel should worship Him. Other passages are also cited, especially by the Pharisees, but I think I shall satisfy everyone if I answer these two, and this I shall easily accomplish after showing from Scripture itself that God chose not the Hebrews for ever, but only on the condition under which He had formerly chosen the Canaanites, for these last, as we have shown, had priests who religiously worshipped God, and whom God at length rejected because of their luxury, pride, and corrupt worship.

Moses (Lev. xviii:27) warned the Israelites that they be not polluted with whoredoms, lest the land spue them out as it had spued out the nations who had dwelt there before, and in Deut. viii:19, 20, in the plainest terms He threatens their total ruin, for He says, "I testify against you that ye shall surely perish. As the nations which the Lord destroyeth before your face, so shall ye perish." In like manner many other passages are found in the law which expressly show that God chose the Hebrews neither absolutely nor for ever. If, then, the prophets foretold for them a new covenant of the knowledge of God, love, and grace, such a promise is easily proved to be only made to the elect, for Ezekiel in the chapter which we have just quoted expressly says that God will separate from them the rebellious and transgressors, and Zephaniah (iii:12, 13), says that "God will take away the proud from the midst of them, and leave the poor." Now, inasmuch as their election has regard to true virtue, it is not to be thought that it was promised to the Jews alone to the exclusion of others, but we must evidently believe that the true Gentile prophets (and every nation, as we have shown, possessed such) promised the same to the faithful of their own people, who were thereby comforted. Wherefore this eternal covenant of the knowledge of God and love is universal, as is clear, moreover, from Zeph. iii:10, 11: no difference in this respect can be admitted between Jew and Gentile, nor did the former enjoy any special election beyond that which we have pointed out.

When the prophets, in speaking of this election which regards only true virtue, mixed up much concerning sacrifices and ceremonies, and the rebuilding of the temple and city, they wished by such figurative expressions, after the manner and nature of prophecy, to expound matters spiritual, so as at the same time to show to the Jews, whose prophets they were, the true restoration of the state and of the temple to be expected about the time of Cyrus.

At the present time, therefore, there is absolutely nothing which the Jews can arrogate to themselves beyond other people.

As to their continuance so long after dispersion and the loss of empire, there is nothing marvellous in it, for they so separated themselves from every other nation as to draw down upon themselves universal hate, not only by their outward rites, rites conflicting with those of other nations, but also by the sign of circumcision which they most scrupulously observe.

That they have been preserved in great measure by Gentile hatred, experience demonstrates. When the king of Spain formerly compelled the Jews to embrace the State religion or to go into exile, a large number of Jews accepted Catholicism. Now, as these renegades were admitted to all the native privileges of Spaniards, and deemed worthy of filling all honourable offices, it came to pass that they straightway became so intermingled with the Spaniards as to leave of themselves no relic or remembrance. But exactly the opposite happened to those whom the king of Portugal compelled to become Christians, for they always, though converted, lived apart, inasmuch as they were considered unworthy of any civic honours.

The sign of circumcision is, as I think, so important, that I could persuade myself that it alone would preserve the nation for ever. Nay, I would go so far as to believe that if the foundations of their religion have not emasculated their minds they may even, if occasion offers, so changeable are human affairs, raise up their empire afresh, and that God may a second time elect them.

Of such a possibility we have a very famous example in the Chinese. They, too, have some distinctive mark on their heads which they most scrupulously observe, and by which they keep themselves apart from everyone else, and have thus kept themselves during so many thousand years that they far surpass all other nations in antiquity. They have not always retained empire, but they have recovered it when lost, and doubtless will do so again after the spirit of the Tartars becomes relaxed through the luxury of riches and pride.

Lastly, if any one wishes to maintain that the Jews, from this or from any other cause, have been chosen by God for ever, I will not gainsay him if he will admit that this choice, whether temporary or eternal, has no regard, in so far as it is peculiar to the Jews, to aught but dominion and physical advantages (for by such alone can one nation be distinguished from another), whereas in regard to intellect and true virtue, every nation is on a par with the rest, and God has not in these respects chosen one people rather than another.

4 In Gen. xv. it is written that God promised Abraham to protect him, and to grant him ample rewards. Abraham answered that he could expect nothing which could be of any value to him, as he was childless and well stricken in years.

5 That a keeping of the commandments of the old Testament is not sufficient for eternal life, appears from Mark x:21.

CHAPTER IV.

Of the Divine Law.

THE WORD LAW, taken in the abstract, means that by which an individual, or all things, or as many things as belong to a particular species, act in one and the same fixed and definite manner, which manner depends either on natural necessity or on human decree. A law which depends on natural necessity is one which necessarily follows from the nature, or from the definition of the thing in question; a law which depends on human decree, and which is more correctly called an ordinance, is one which men have laid down for themselves and others in order to live more safely or conveniently, or from some similar reason.

For example, the law that all bodies impinging on lesser bodies, lose as much of their own motion as they communicate to the latter is a universal law of all bodies, and depends on natural necessity. So, too, the law that a man in remembering one thing, straightway remembers another either like it, or which he had perceived simultaneously with it, is a law which necessarily follows from the nature of man. But the law that men must yield, or be compelled to yield, somewhat of their natural right, and that they bind themselves to live in a certain way, depends on human decree. Now, though I freely admit that all things are predetermined by universal natural laws to exist and operate in a given, fixed, and definite manner, I still assert that the laws I have just mentioned depend on human decree.

(1.) Because man, in so far as he is a part of nature, constitutes a part of the power of nature. Whatever, therefore, follows necessarily from the necessity of human nature (that is, from nature herself, in so far as we conceive of her as acting through man) follows, even though it be necessarily, from human power. Hence the sanction of such laws may very well be said to depend on man's decree, for it principally depends on the power of the human mind; so that the human mind in respect to its perception of things as true and false, can readily be conceived as without such laws, but not without necessary law as we have just defined it.

(2.) I have stated that these laws depend on human decree because it is well to define and explain things by their proximate causes. The general consideration of fate and the concatenation of causes would aid us very little in forming and arranging our ideas concerning particular questions. Let us add that as to the actual coordination and concatenation of things, that is how things are ordained and linked together, we are obviously ignorant; therefore, it is more profitable for right living, nay, it is necessary for us to consider things as contingent. So much about law in the abstract.

Now the word law seems to be only applied to natural phenomena by analogy, and is commonly taken to signify a command which men can either obey or neglect, inasmuch as it restrains human nature within certain originally exceeded limits, and therefore lays down no rule beyond human strength. Thus it is expedient to define law more particularly as a plan of life laid down by man for himself or others with a certain object.

However, as the true object of legislation is only perceived by a few, and most men are almost incapable of grasping it, though they live under its conditions, legislators, with a view to exacting general obedience, have wisely put forward another object, very different from that which necessarily follows from the nature of law: they promise to the observers of the law that which the masses chiefly desire, and threaten its violators with that which they chiefly fear: thus endeavouring to restrain the masses, as far as may be, like a horse with a curb; whence it follows that the word law is chiefly applied to the modes of life enjoined on men by the sway of others; hence those who obey the law are said to live under it and to be under compulsion. In truth, a man who renders everyone their due because he fears the gallows, acts under the sway and compulsion of others, and cannot be called just. But a man who does the same from a knowledge of the true reason for laws and their necessity, acts from a firm purpose and of his own accord, and is therefore properly called just. This, I take it, is Paul's meaning when he says, that those who live under the law cannot be justified through the law, for justice, as commonly defined, is the constant and perpetual will to render every man his due. Thus Solomon says (Prov. xxi:15), "It is a joy to the just to do judgment," but the wicked fear.

Law, then, being a plan of living which men have for a certain object laid down for themselves or others, may, as it seems, be divided into human law and Divine law. {But both are opposite sides of the same coin}

By human law I mean a plan of living which serves only to render life and the state secure. By Divine law I mean that which only regards the highest good, in other words, the true knowledge of God and love.

I call this law Divine because of the nature of the highest good, which I will here shortly explain as clearly as I can.

Inasmuch as the intellect is the best part of our being, it is evident that we should make every effort to perfect it as far as possible if we desire to search for what is really profitable to us. For in intellectual perfection the highest good should consist. Now, since all our knowledge, and the certainty which removes every doubt, depend solely on the knowledge of God; — firstly, because without God nothing can exist or be conceived; secondly, because so long as we have no clear and distinct idea of God we may remain in universal doubt — it follows that our highest good and perfection also depend solely on the knowledge of God. Further, since without God nothing can exist or be conceived, it is evident that all natural phenomena involve and express the conception of God as far as their essence and perfection extend, so that we have greater and more perfect knowledge of God in proportion to our knowledge of natural phenomena: conversely (since the knowledge of an effect through its cause is the same thing as the knowledge of a particular property of a cause) the greater our knowledge of natural phenomena, the more perfect is our knowledge of the essence of God (which is the cause of all things). So, then, our highest good not only depends on the knowledge of God, but wholly consists therein; and it further follows that man is perfect or the reverse in proportion to the nature and perfection of the object of his special desire; hence the most perfect and the chief sharer in the highest blessedness is he who prizes above all else, and takes especial delight in, the intellectual knowledge of God, the most perfect Being.

Hither, then, our highest good and our highest blessedness aim — namely, to the knowledge and love of God; therefore the means demanded by this aim of all human actions, that is, by God in so far as the idea of him is in us, may be called the commands of God, because they proceed, as it were, from God Himself, inasmuch as He exists in our minds, and the plan of life which has regard to this aim may be fitly called the law of God.

The nature of the means, and the plan of life which this aim demands, how the foundations of the best states follow its lines, and how men's life is conducted, are questions pertaining to general ethics. Here I only proceed to treat of the Divine law in a particular application.

As the love of God is man's highest happiness and blessedness, and the ultimate end and aim of all human actions, it follows that he alone lives by the Divine law who loves God not from fear of punishment, or from love of any other object, such as sensual pleasure, fame, or the like; but solely because he has knowledge of God, or is convinced that the knowledge and love of God is the highest good. The sum and chief precept, then, of the Divine law is to love God as the highest good, namely, as we have said, not from fear of any pains and penalties, or from the love of any other object in which we desire to take pleasure. The idea of God lays down the rule that God is our highest good — in other words, that the knowledge and love of God is the ultimate aim to which all our actions should be directed. The worldling cannot understand these things, they appear foolishness to him. because he has too meager a knowledge of God, and also because in this highest good he can discover nothing which he can handle or eat, or which affects the fleshly appetites wherein he chiefly delights, for it consists solely in thought and the pure reason. They, on the other hand, who know that they possess no greater gift than intellect and sound reason, will doubtless accept what I have said without question.

We have now explained that wherein the Divine law chiefly consists, and what are human laws, namely, all those which have a different aim unless they have been ratified by revelation, for in this respect also things are referred to God (as we have shown above) and in this sense the law of Moses, although it was not universal, but entirely adapted to the disposition and particular preservation of a single people, may yet be called a law of God or Divine law, inasmuch as we believe that it was ratified by prophetic insight. If we consider the nature of natural Divine law as we have just explained it, we shall see:

I. — That it is universal or common to all men, for we have deduced it from universal human nature.

II. That it does not depend on the truth of any historical narrative whatsoever, for inasmuch as this natural Divine law is comprehended solely by the consideration of human nature, it is plain that we can conceive it as existing as well in Adam as in any other man, as well in a man living among his fellows, as in a man who lives by himself.

The truth of a historical narrative, however assured, cannot give us the knowledge nor consequently the love of God, for love of God springs from knowledge of Him, and knowledge of Him should be derived from general ideas, in themselves certain and known, so that the truth of a historical narrative is very far from being a necessary requisite for our attaining our highest good.

Still, though the truth of histories cannot give us the knowledge and love of God, I do not deny that reading them is very useful with a view to life in the world, for the more we have observed and known of men's customs and circumstances, which are best revealed by their actions, the more warily we shall be able to order our lives among them, and so far as reason dictates to adapt our actions to their dispositions.

III. We see that this natural Divine law does not demand the performance of ceremonies — that is, actions in themselves indifferent, which are called good from the fact of their institution, or actions symbolizing something profitable for salvation, or (if one prefers this definition) actions of which the meaning surpasses human understanding. The natural light of reason does not demand anything which it is itself unable to supply, but only such as it can very clearly show to be good, or a means to our blessedness. Such things as are good simply because they have been commanded or instituted, or as being symbols of something good, are mere shadows which cannot be reckoned among actions that are the offsprings as it were, or fruit of a sound mind and of intellect. There is no need for me to go into this now in more detail.

IV. Lastly, we see that the highest reward of the Divine law is the law itself, namely, to know God and to love Him of our free choice, and with an undivided and fruitful spirit; while its penalty is the absence of these things, and being in bondage to the flesh — that is, having an inconstant and wavering spirit.

These points being noted, I must now inquire:

I. Whether by the natural light of reason we can conceive of God as a law-giver or potentate ordaining laws for men?

II. What is the teaching of Holy Writ concerning this natural light of reason and natural law?

III. With what objects were ceremonies formerly instituted?

IV. Lastly, what is the good gained by knowing the sacred histories and believing them?

Of the first two I will treat in this chapter, of the remaining two in the following one.

Our conclusion about the first is easily deduced from the nature of God's will, which is only distinguished from His understanding in relation to our intellect — that is, the will and the understanding of God are in reality one and the same, and are only distinguished in relation to our thoughts which we form concerning God's understanding. For instance, if we are only looking to the fact that the nature of a triangle is from eternity contained in the Divine nature as an eternal verity, we say that God possesses the idea of a triangle, or that He understands the nature of a triangle; but if afterwards we look to the fact that the nature of a triangle is thus contained in the Divine nature, solely by the necessity of the Divine nature, and not by the necessity of the nature and essence of a triangle — in fact, that the necessity of a triangle's essence and nature, in so far as they are conceived of as eternal verities, depends solely on the necessity of the Divine nature and intellect, we then style God's will or decree, that which before we styled His intellect. Wherefore we make one and the same affirmation concerning God when we say that He has from eternity decreed that three angles of a triangle are equal to two right angles, as when we say that He has understood it.

Hence the affirmations and the negations of God always involve necessity or truth; so that, for example, if God said to Adam that He did not wish him to eat of the tree of knowledge of good and evil, it would have involved a contradiction that Adam should have been able to eat of it, and would therefore have been impossible that he should have so eaten, for the Divine command would have involved an eternal necessity and truth. But since Scripture nevertheless narrates that God did give this command to Adam, and yet that none the less Adam ate of the tree, we must perforce say that God revealed to Adam the evil which would surely follow if he should eat of the tree, but did not disclose that such evil would of necessity come to pass. Thus it was that Adam took the revelation to be not an eternal and necessary truth, but a law — that is, an ordinance followed by gain or loss, not depending necessarily on the nature of the act performed, but solely on the will and absolute power of some potentate, so that the revelation in question was solely in relation to Adam, and solely through his lack of knowledge a law, and God was, as it were, a lawgiver and potentate. From the same cause, namely, from lack of knowledge, the Decalogue in relation to the Hebrews was a law, for since they knew not the existence of God as an eternal truth, they must have taken as a law that which was revealed to them in the Decalogue, namely, that God exists, and that God only should be worshipped. But if God had spoken to them without the intervention of any bodily means, immediately they would have perceived it not as a law, but as an eternal truth.

What we have said about the Israelites and Adam, applies also to all the prophets who wrote laws in God's name — they did not adequately conceive God's decrees as eternal truths. For instance, we must say of Moses that from revelation, from the basis of what was revealed to him, he perceived the method by which the Israelitish nation could best be united in a particular territory, and could form a body politic or state, and further that he perceived the method by which that nation could best be constrained to obedience; but he did not perceive, nor was it revealed to him, that this method was absolutely the best, nor that the obedience of the people in a certain strip of territory would necessarily imply the end he had in view. Wherefore he perceived these things not as eternal truths, but as precepts and ordinances, and he ordained them as laws of God, and thus it came to be that he conceived God as a ruler, a legislator, a king, as merciful, just, &c., whereas such qualities are simply attributes of human nature, and utterly alien from the nature of the Deity. Thus much we may affirm of the prophets who wrote laws in the name of God; but we must not affirm it of Christ, for Christ, although He too seems to have written laws in the name of God, must be taken to have had a clear and adequate perception, for Christ was not so much a prophet as the mouthpiece of God. For God made revelations to mankind through Christ as He had before done through angels — that is, a created voice, visions, &c. It would be as unreasonable to say that God had accommodated his revelations to the opinions of Christ as that He had before accommodated them to the opinions of angels (that is, of a created voice or visions) as matters to be revealed to the prophets, a wholly absurd hypothesis. Moreover, Christ was sent to teach not only the Jews but the whole human race, and therefore it was not enough that His mind should be accommodated to the opinions the Jews alone, but also to the opinion and fundamental teaching common to the whole human race — in other words, to ideas universal and true. Inasmuch as God revealed Himself to Christ, or to Christ's mind immediately, and not as to the prophets through words and symbols, we must needs suppose that Christ perceived truly what was revealed, in other words, He understood it, for a, matter is understood when it is perceived simply by the mind without words or symbols.

Christ, then, perceived (truly and adequately) what was revealed, and if He ever proclaimed such revelations as laws, He did so because of the ignorance and obstinacy of the people, acting in this respect the part of God; inasmuch as He accommodated Himself to the comprehension of the people, and though He spoke somewhat more clearly than the other prophets, yet He taught what was revealed obscurely, and generally through parables, especially when He was speaking to those to whom it was not yet given to understand the kingdom of heaven. (See Matt. xiii:10, &c.) To those to whom it was given to understand the mysteries of heaven, He doubtless taught His doctrines as eternal truths, and did not lay them down as laws, thus freeing the minds of His hearers from the bondage of that law which He further confirmed and established. Paul apparently points to this more than once (e.g. Rom. vii:6, and iii:28), though he never himself seems to wish to speak openly, but, to quote his own words (Rom. iii:6, and vi:19), "merely humanly." This he expressly states when he calls God just, and it was doubtless in concession to human weakness that he attributes mercy, grace, anger, and similar qualities to God, adapting his language to the popular mind, or, as he puts it (1 Cor. iii:1, 2), to carnal men. In Rom. ix:18, he teaches undisguisedly that God's auger and mercy depend not on the actions of men, but on God's own nature or will; further, that no one is justified by the works of the law, but only by faith, which he seems to identify with the full assent of the soul; lastly, that no one is blessed unless he have in him the mind of Christ (Rom. viii:9), whereby he perceives the laws of God as eternal truths. We conclude, therefore, that God is described as a lawgiver or prince, and styled just, merciful, &c., merely in concession to popular understanding, and the imperfection of popular knowledge; that in reality God acts and directs all things simply by the necessity of His nature and perfection, and that His decrees and volitions are eternal truths, and always involve necessity. So much for the first point which I wished to explain and demonstrate.

Passing on to the second point, let us search the sacred pages for their teaching concerning the light of nature and this Divine law. The first doctrine we find in the history of the first man, where it is narrated that God commanded Adam not to eat of the fruit of the tree of the knowledge of good and evil; this seems to mean that God commanded Adam to do and to seek after righteousness because it was good, not because the contrary was evil: that is, to seek the good for its own sake, not from fear of evil. We have seen that he who acts rightly from the true knowledge and love of right, acts with freedom and constancy, whereas he who acts from fear of evil, is under the constraint of evil, and acts in bondage under external control. So that this commandment of God to Adam comprehends the whole Divine natural law, and absolutely agrees with the dictates of the light of nature; nay, it would be easy to explain on this basis the whole history or allegory of the first man. But I prefer to pass over the subject in silence, because, in the first place, I cannot be absolutely certain that my explanation would be in accordance with the intention of the sacred writer; and, secondly, because many do not admit that this history is an allegory, maintaining it to be a simple narrative of facts. It will be better, therefore, to adduce other passages of Scripture, especially such as were written by him, who speaks with all the strength of his natural understanding, in which he surpassed all his contemporaries, and whose sayings are accepted by the people as of equal weight with those of the prophets. I mean Solomon, whose prudence and wisdom are commended in Scripture rather than his piety and gift of prophecy. Life being taken to mean the true life (as is evident from Deut. xxx:19), the fruit of the understanding consists only in the true life, and its absence constitutes punishment. All this absolutely agrees with what was set out in our fourth point concerning natural law. Moreover our position that it is the well-spring of life, and that the intellect alone lays down laws for the wise, is plainly taught by, the sage, for he says (Prov. xiii14): "The law of the wise is a fountain of life " — that is, as we gather from the preceding text, the understanding. In chap. iii:13, he expressly teaches that the understanding renders man blessed and happy, and gives him true peace of mind. "Happy is the man that findeth wisdom, and the man that getteth understanding," for "Wisdom gives length of days, and riches and honour; her ways are ways of pleasantness, and all her paths peace" (xiiii6, 17). According to Solomon, therefore, it is only, the wise who live in peace and equanimity, not like the wicked whose minds drift hither and thither, and (as Isaiah says, chap. Ivii:20) "are like the troubled sea, for them there is no peace."

Lastly, we should especially note the passage in chap. ii. of Solomon's proverbs which most clearly confirms our contention: "If thou criest after knowledge, and liftest up thy voice for understanding . . . then shalt thou understand the fear of the Lord, and find the knowledge of God; for the Lord giveth wisdom; out of His mouth cometh knowledge and understanding." These words clearly enunciate, that wisdom or intellect alone teaches us to fear God wisely — that is, to worship Him truly;, that wisdom and knowledge flow from God's mouth, and that God bestows on us this gift; this we have already shown in proving that our understanding and our knowledge depend on, spring from, and are perfected by the idea or knowledge of God, and nothing else. Solomon goes on to say in so many words that this knowledge contains and involves the true principles of ethics and politics: "When wisdom entereth into thy heart, and knowledge is pleasant to thy soul, discretion shall preserve thee, understanding shall keep thee, then shalt thou understand righteousness, and judgment, and equity, yea every good path." All of which is in obvious agreement with natural knowledge: for after we have come to the understanding of things, and have tasted the excellence of knowledge, she teaches us ethics and true virtue.

Thus the happiness and the peace of him who cultivates his natural understanding lies, according to Solomon also, not so much under the dominion of fortune (or God's external aid) as in inward personal virtue (or God's internal aid), for the latter can to a great extent be preserved by vigilance, right action, and thought.

Lastly, we must by no means pass over the passage in Paul's Epistle to the Romans, i:20, in which he says: "For the invisible things of God from the creation of the world are clearly seen, being understood by the things that are made, even His eternal power and Godhead; so that they are without excuse, because, when they knew God, they glorified Him not as God, neither were they thankful." These words clearly show that everyone can by the light of nature clearly understand the goodness and the eternal divinity of God, and can thence know and deduce what they should seek for and what avoid; wherefore the Apostle says that they are without excuse and cannot plead ignorance, as they certainly might if it were a question of supernatural light and the incarnation, passion, and resurrection of Christ. "Wherefore," he goes on to say (ib. 24), "God gave them up to uncleanness through the lusts of their own hearts;" and so on, through the rest of the chapter, he describes the vices of ignorance, and sets them forth as the punishment of ignorance. This obviously agrees with the verse of Solomon, already quoted, "The instruction of fools is folly," so that it is easy to understand why Paul says that the wicked are without excuse. As every man sows so shall he reap: out of evil, evils necessarily spring, unless they be wisely counteracted.

Thus we see that Scripture literally approves of the light of natural reason and the natural Divine law, and I have fulfilled the promises made at the beginning of this chapter.

CHAPTER V.

Of the Ceremonial Law.

IN THE FOREGOING chapter we have shown that the Divine law, which renders men truly blessed, and teaches them the true life, is universal to all men; nay, we have so intimately deduced it from human nature that it must be esteemed innate, and, as it were, ingrained in the human mind.

But with regard to the ceremonial observances which were ordained in the Old Testament for the Hebrews only, and were so adapted to their state that they could for the most part only be observed by the society as a whole and not by each individual, it is evident that they formed no part of the Divine law, and had nothing to do with blessedness and virtue, but had reference only to the election of the Hebrews, that is (as I have shown in Chap. II.), to their temporal bodily happiness and the tranquillity of their kingdom, and that therefore they were only valid while that kingdom lasted. If in the Old Testament they are spoken of as the law of God, it is only because they were founded on revelation, or a basis of revelation. Still as reason, however sound, has little weight with ordinary theologians, I will adduce the authority of Scripture for what I here assert, and will further show, for the sake of greater clearness, why and how these ceremonials served to establish and preserve the Jewish kingdom. Isaiah teaches most plainly that the Divine law in its strict sense signifies that universal law which consists in a true manner of life, and does not signify ceremonial observances. In chapter i:10, the prophet calls on his countrymen to hearken to the Divine law as he delivers it, and first excluding all kinds of sacrifices and all feasts, he at length sums up the law in these few words, "Cease to do evil, learn to do well: seek judgment, relieve the oppressed." Not less striking testimony is given in Psalm xl:7 — 9, where the Psalmist addresses God: "Sacrifice and offering Thou didst not desire; mine ears hast Thou opened; burnt offering and sin-offering hast Thou not required; I delight to do Thy will, 0 my God; yea, Thy law is within my heart." Here the Psalmist reckons as the law of God only that which is inscribed in his heart, and excludes ceremonies therefrom, for the latter are good and inscribed on the heart only from the fact of their institution, and not because of their intrinsic value.

Other passages of Scripture testify to the same truth, but these two will suffice. We may also learn from the Bible that ceremonies are no aid to blessedness, but only have reference to the temporal prosperity of the kingdom; for the rewards promised for their observance are merely temporal advantages and delights, blessedness being reserved for the universal Divine law. In all the five books commonly attributed to Moses nothing is promised, as I have said, beyond temporal benefits, such as honours, fame, victories, riches, enjoyments, and health. Though many moral precepts besides ceremonies are contained in these five books, they appear not as moral doctrines universal to all men, but as commands especially adapted to the understanding and character of the Hebrew people, and as having reference only to the welfare of the kingdom. For instance, Moses does not teach the Jews as a prophet not to kill or to steal, but gives these commandments solely as a lawgiver and judge; he does not reason out the doctrine, but affixes for its non-observance a penalty which may and very properly does vary in different nations. So, too, the command not to commit adultery is given merely with reference to the welfare of the state; for if the moral doctrine had been intended, with reference not only to the welfare of the state, but also to the tranquillity and blessedness of the individual, Moses would have condemned not merely the outward act, but also the mental acquiescence, as is done by Christ, Who taught only universal moral precepts, and for this cause promises a spiritual instead of a temporal reward. Christ, as I have said, was sent into the world, not to preserve the state nor to lay down laws, but solely to teach the universal moral law, so we can easily understand that He wished in nowise to do away with the law of Moses, inasmuch as He introduced no new laws of His own — His sole care was to teach moral doctrines, and distinguish them from the laws of the state; for the Pharisees, in their ignorance, thought that the observance of the state law and the Mosaic law was the sum total of morality; whereas such laws merely had reference to the public welfare, and aimed not so much at instructing the Jews as at keeping them under constraint. But let us return to our subject, and cite other passages of Scripture which set forth temporal benefits as rewards for observing the ceremonial law, and blessedness as reward for the universal law.

None of the prophets puts the point more clearly than Isaiah. (18.) After condemning hypocrisy he commends liberty and charity towards one's self and one's neighbours, and promises as a reward: "Then shall thy light break forth as the morning, and thy health shall spring forth speedily, thy righteousness shall go before thee, and the glory of the Lord shall be thy reward" (chap. lviii:8). Shortly afterwards he commends the Sabbath, and for a due observance of it, promises: "Then shalt thou delight thyself in the Lord, and I will cause thee to ride upon the high places of the earth, and feed thee with the heritage of Jacob thy father: for the mouth of the Lord has spoken it." Thus the prophet for liberty bestowed, and charitable works, promises a healthy mind in a healthy body, and the glory of the Lord even after death; whereas, for ceremonial exactitude, he only promises security of rule, prosperity, and temporal happiness.

In Psalms xv. and xxiv. no mention is made of ceremonies, but only of moral doctrines, inasmuch as there is no question of anything but blessedness, and blessedness is symbolically promised: it is quite certain that the expressions, "the hill of God," and "His tents and the dwellers therein," refer to blessedness and security of soul, not to the actual mount of Jerusalem and the tabernacle of Moses, for these latter were not dwelt in by anyone, and only the sons of Levi ministered there. Further, all those sentences of Solomon to which I referred in the last chapter, for the cultivation of the intellect and wisdom, promise true blessedness, for by wisdom is the fear of God at length understood, and the knowledge of God found.

That the Jews themselves were not bound to practise their ceremonial observances after the destruction of their kingdom is evident from Jeremiah. For when the prophet saw and foretold that the desolation of the city was at hand, he said that God only delights in those who know and understand that He exercises loving-kindness, judgment, and righteousness in the earth, and that such persons only are worthy of praise. (Jer. ix:23.) As though God had said that, after the desolation of the city, He would require nothing special from the Jews beyond the natural law by which all men are bound.

The New Testament also confirms this view, for only moral doctrines are therein taught, and the kingdom of heaven is promised as a reward, whereas ceremonial observances are not touched on by the Apostles, after they began to preach the Gospel to the Gentiles. The Pharisees certainly continued to practise these rites after the destruction of the kingdom, but more with a view of opposing the Christians than of pleasing God: for after the first destruction of the city, when they were led captive to Babylon, not being then, so far as I am aware, split up into sects, they straightway neglected their rites, bid farewell to the Mosaic law, buried their national customs in oblivion as being plainly superfluous, and began to mingle with other nations, as we may abundantly learn from Ezra and Nehemiah. We cannot, therefore, doubt that they were no more bound by the law of Moses, after the destruction of their kingdom, than they had been before it had been begun, while they were still living among other peoples before the exodus from Egypt, and were subject to no special law beyond the natural law, and also, doubtless, the law of the state in which they were living, in so far as it was consonant with the Divine natural law.

As to the fact that the patriarchs offered sacrifices, I think they did so for the purpose of stimulating their piety, for their minds had been accustomed from childhood to the idea of sacrifice, which we know had been universal from the time of Enoch; and thus they found in sacrifice their most powerful incentive. The patriarchs, then, did not sacrifice to God at the bidding of a Divine right, or as taught by the basis of the Divine law, but simply in accordance with the custom of the time; and, if in so doing they followed any ordinance, it was simply the ordinance of the country they were living in, by which (as we have seen before in the case of Melchisedek) they were bound.

I think that I have now given Scriptural authority for my view: it remains to show why and how the ceremonial observances tended to preserve and confirm the Hebrew kingdom; and this I can very briefly do on grounds universally accepted.

The formation of society serves not only for defensive purposes, but is also very useful, and, indeed, absolutely necessary, as rendering possible the division of labour. If men did not render mutual assistance to each other, no one would have either the skill or the time to provide for his own sustenance and preservation: for all men are not equally apt for all work, and no one would be capable of preparing all that he individually stood in need of. Strength and time, I repeat, would fail, if every one had in person to plough, to sow, to reap, to grind corn, to cook, to weave, to stitch, and perform the other numerous functions required to keep life going; to say nothing of the arts and sciences which are also entirely necessary to the perfection and blessedness of human nature. We see that peoples living, in uncivilized barbarism lead a wretched and almost animal life, and even they would not be able to acquire their few rude necessaries without assisting one another to a certain extent.

Now if men were so constituted by nature that they desired nothing but what is designated by true reason, society would obviously have no need of laws: it would be sufficient to inculcate true moral doctrines; and men would freely, without hesitation, act in accordance with their true interests. But human nature is framed in a different fashion: every one, indeed, seeks his own interest, but does not do so in accordance with the dictates of sound reason, for most men's ideas of desirability and usefulness are guided by their fleshly instincts and emotions, which take no thought beyond the present and the immediate object. Therefore, no society can exist without government, and force, and laws to restrain and repress men's desires and immoderate impulses. Still human nature will not submit to absolute repression. Violent governments, as Seneca says, never last long; the moderate governments endure. So long as men act simply from fear they act contrary to their inclinations, taking no thought for the advantages or necessity of their actions, but simply endeavouring to escape punishment or loss of life. They must needs rejoice in any evil which befalls their ruler, even if it should involve themselves; and must long for and bring about such evil by every means in their power. Again, men are especially intolerant of serving and being ruled by their equals. Lastly, it is exceedingly difficult to revoke liberties once granted.

From these considerations it follows, firstly, that authority should either be vested in the hands of the whole state in common, so that everyone should be bound to serve, and yet not be in subjection to his equals; or else, if power be in the hands of a few, or one man, that one man should be something above average humanity, or should strive to get himself accepted as such. Secondly, laws should in every government be so arranged that people should be kept in bounds by the hope of some greatly desired good, rather than by fear, for then everyone will do his duty willingly.

Lastly, as obedience consists in acting at the bidding of external authority, it would have no place in a state where the government is vested in the whole people, and where laws are made by common consent. In such a society the people would remain free, whether the laws were added to or diminished, inasmuch as it would not be done on external authority, but their own free consent. The reverse happens when the sovereign power is vested in one man, for all act at his bidding; and, therefore, unless they had been trained from the first to depend on the words of their ruler, the latter would find it difficult, in case of need, to abrogate liberties once conceded, and impose new laws.

From these universal considerations, let us pass on to the kingdom of the Jews. The Jews when they first came out of Egypt were not bound by any national laws, and were therefore free to ratify any laws they liked, or to make new ones, and were at liberty to set up a government and occupy a territory wherever they chose. However, they, were entirely unfit to frame a wise code of laws and to keep the sovereign power vested in the community; they were all uncultivated and sunk in a wretched slavery, therefore the sovereignty was bound to remain vested in the hands of one man who would rule the rest and keep them under constraint, make laws and interpret them. This sovereignty was easily retained by Moses, because he surpassed the rest in virtue and persuaded the people of the fact, proving it by many testimonies (see Exod. chap. xiv., last verse, and chap. xix:9). He then, by the Divine virtue he possessed, made laws and ordained them for the people, taking the greatest care that they should be obeyed willingly and not through fear, being specially induced to adopt this course by the obstinate nature of the Jews, who would not have submitted to be ruled solely by constraint; and also by the imminence of war, for it is always better to inspire soldiers with a thirst for glory than to terrify them with threats; each man will then strive to distinguish himself by valour and courage, instead of merely trying to escape punishment. Moses, therefore, by his virtue and the Divine command, introduced a religion, so that the people might do their duty from devotion rather than fear. Further, he bound them over by benefits, and prophesied many advantages in the future; nor were his laws very severe, as anyone may see for himself, especially if he remarks the number of circumstances necessary in order to procure the conviction of an accused person.

Lastly, in order that the people which could not govern itself should be entirely dependent on its ruler, he left nothing to the free choice of individuals (who had hitherto been slaves); the people could do nothing but remember the law, and follow the ordinances laid down at the good pleasure of their ruler; they were not allowed to plough, to sow, to reap, nor even to eat; to clothe themselves, to shave, to rejoice, or in fact to do anything whatever as they liked, but were bound to follow the directions given in the law; and not only this, but they were obliged to have marks on their door-posts, on their hands, and between their eyes to admonish them to perpetual obedience.

This, then, was the object of the ceremonial law, that men should do nothing of their own free will, but should always act under external authority, and should continually confess by their actions and thoughts that they were not their own masters, but were entirely under the control of others.

From all these considerations it is clearer than day that ceremonies have nothing to do with a state of blessedness, and that those mentioned in the Old Testament, i.e. the whole Mosaic Law, had reference merely to the government of the Jews, and merely temporal advantages.

As for the Christian rites, such as baptism, the Lord's Supper, festivals, public prayers, and any other observances which are, and always have been, common to all Christendom, if they were instituted by Christ or His Apostles (which is open to doubt), they were instituted as external signs of the universal church, and not as having anything to do with blessedness, or possessing any sanctity in themselves. Therefore, though such ceremonies were not ordained for the sake of upholding a government, they were ordained for the preservation of a society, and accordingly he who lives alone is not bound by them: nay, those who live in a country where the Christian religion is forbidden, are bound to abstain from such rites, and can none the less live in a state of blessedness. We have an example of this in Japan, where the Christian religion is forbidden, and the Dutch who live there are enjoined by their East India Company not to practise any outward rites of religion. I need not cite other examples, though it would be easy to prove my point from the fundamental principles of the New Testament, and to adduce many confirmatory instances; but I pass on the more willingly, as I am anxious to proceed to my next proposition. I will now, therefore, pass on to what I proposed to treat of in the second part of this chapter, namely, what persons are bound to believe in the narratives contained in Scripture, and how far they are so bound. Examining this question by the aid of natural reason, I will proceed as follows.

If anyone wishes to persuade his fellows for or against anything which is not self-evident 6, he must deduce his contention from their admissions, and convince them either by experience or by ratiocination; either by appealing to facts of natural experience, or to self-evident intellectual axioms. Now unless the experience be of such a kind as to be clearly and distinctly understood, though it may convince a man, it will not have the same effect on his mind and disperse the clouds of his doubt so completely as when the doctrine taught is deduced entirely from intellectual axioms — that is, by the mere power of the understanding and logical order, and this is especially the case in spiritual matters which have nothing to do with the senses.

But the deduction of conclusions from general truths . priori, usually requires a long chain of arguments, and, moreover, very great caution, acuteness, and self-restraint — qualities which are not often met with; therefore people prefer to be taught by experience rather than deduce their conclusion from a few axioms, and set them out in logical order. Whence it follows, that if anyone wishes to teach a doctrine to a whole nation (not to speak of the whole human race), and to be understood by all men in every particular, he will seek to support his teaching with experience, and will endeavour to suit his reasonings and the definitions of his doctrines as far as possible to the understanding of the common people, who form the majority of mankind, and he will not set them forth in logical sequence nor adduce the definitions which serve to establish them. Otherwise he writes only for the learned — that is, he will be understood by only a small proportion of the human race.

All Scripture was written primarily for an entire people, and secondarily for the whole human race; therefore its contents must necessarily be adapted as far as possible to the understanding of the masses, and proved only by examples drawn from experience. We will explain ourselves more clearly. The chief speculative doctrines taught in Scripture are the existence of God, or a Being Who made all things, and Who directs and sustains the world with consummate wisdom; furthermore, that God takes the greatest thought for men, or such of them as live piously and honourably, while He punishes, with various penalties, those who do evil, separating them from the good. All this is proved in Scripture entirely through experience-that is, through the narratives there related. No definitions of doctrine are given, but all the sayings and reasonings are adapted to the understanding of the masses. Although experience can give no clear knowledge of these things, nor explain the nature of God, nor how He directs and sustains all things, it can nevertheless teach and enlighten men sufficiently to impress obedience and devotion on their minds.

It is now, I think, sufficiently clear what persons are bound to believe in the Scripture narratives, and in what degree they are so bound, for it evidently follows from what has been said that the knowledge of and belief in them is particularly necessary to the masses whose intellect is not capable of perceiving things clearly and distinctly. Further, he who denies them because he does not believe that God exists or takes thought for men and the world, may be accounted impious; but a man who is ignorant of them, and nevertheless knows by natural reason that God exists, as we have said, and has a true plan of life, is altogether blessed — yes, more blessed than the common herd of believers, because besides true opinions he possesses also a true and distinct conception. Lastly, he who is ignorant of the Scriptures and knows nothing by the light of reason, though he may not be impious or rebellious, is yet less than human and almost brutal, having none of God's gifts.

We must here remark that when we say that the knowledge of the sacred narrative is particularly necessary to the masses, we do not mean the knowledge of absolutely all the narratives in the Bible, but only of the principal ones, those which, taken by themselves, plainly display the doctrine we have just stated, and have most effect over men's minds.

If all the narratives in Scripture were necessary for the proof of this doctrine, and if no conclusion could be drawn without the general consideration of every one of the histories contained in the sacred writings, truly the conclusion and demonstration of such doctrine would overtask the understanding and strength not only of the masses, but of humanity; who is there who could give attention to all the narratives at once, and to all the circumstances, and all the scraps of doctrine to be elicited from such a host of diverse histories? I cannot believe that the men who have left us the Bible as we have it were so abounding in talent that they attempted setting about such a method of demonstration, still less can I suppose that we cannot understand Scriptural doctrine till we have given heed to the quarrels of Isaac, the advice of Achitophel to Absalom, the civil war between Jews and Israelites, and other similar chronicles; nor can I think that it was more difficult to teach such doctrine by means of history to the Jews of early times, the contemporaries of Moses, than it was to the contemporaries of Esdras. But more will be said on this point hereafter, we may now only note that the masses are only bound to know those histories which can most powerfully dispose their mind to obedience and devotion. However, the masses are not sufficiently skilled to draw conclusions from what they read, they take more delight in the actual stories, and in the strange and unlooked-for issues of events than in the doctrines implied; therefore, besides reading these narratives, they are always in need of pastors or church ministers to explain them to their feeble intelligence.

But not to wander from our point, let us conclude with what has been our principal object — namely, that the truth of narratives, be they what they may, has nothing to do with the Divine law, and serves for nothing except in respect of doctrine, the sole element which makes one history better than another. The narratives in the Old and New Testaments surpass profane history, and differ among themselves in merit simply by reason of the salutary doctrines which they inculcate. Therefore, if a man were to read the Scripture narratives believing the whole of them, but were to give no heed to the doctrines they contain, and make no amendment in his life, he might employ himself just as profitably in reading the Koran or the poetic drama, or ordinary chronicles, with the attention usually given to such writings; on the other hand, if a man is absolutely ignorant of the Scriptures, and none the less has right opinions and a true plan of life, he is absolutely blessed and truly possesses in himself the spirit of Christ.

The Jews are of a directly contrary way of thinking, for they hold that true opinions and a true plan of life are of no service in attaining blessedness, if their possessors have arrived at them by the light of reason only, and not like the documents prophetically revealed to Moses. Maimonides ventures openly to make this assertion: "Every man who takes to heart the seven precepts and diligently follows them, is counted with the pious among the nation, and an heir of the world to come; that is to say, if he takes to heart and follows them because God ordained them in the law, and revealed them to us by Moses, because they were of aforetime precepts to the sons of Noah: but he who follows them as led thereto by reason, is not counted as a dweller among the pious or among the wise of the nations." Such are the words Of Maimonides, to which R. Joseph, the son of Shem Job, adds in his book which he calls "Kebod Elohim, or God's Glory," that although Aristotle (whom he considers to have written the best ethics and to be above everyone else) has not omitted anything that concerns true ethics, and which he has adopted in his own book, carefully following the lines laid down, yet this was not able to suffice for his salvation, inasmuch as he embraced his doctrines in accordance with the dictates of reason and not as Divine documents prophetically revealed.

However, that these are mere figments, and are not supported by Scriptural authority will, I think, be sufficiently evident to the attentive reader, so that an examination of the theory will be sufficient for its refutation. It is not my purpose here to refute the assertions of those who assert that the natural light of reason can teach nothing, of any value concerning the true way of salvation. People who lay no claims to reason for themselves, are not able to prove by reason this their assertion; and if they hawk about something superior to reason, it is a mere figment, and far below reason, as their general method of life sufficiently shows. But there is no need to dwell upon such persons. I will merely add that we can only judge of a man by his works. If a man abounds in the fruits of the Spirit, charity, joy, peace, long-suffering, kindness, goodness, faith, gentleness, chastity, against which, as Paul says (Gal. v:22), there is no law, such an one, whether he be taught by reason only or by the Scripture only, has been in very truth taught by God, and is altogether blessed. Thus have I said all that I undertook to say concerning Divine law.

6 We doubt of the existence of God, and consequently of all else, so long as we have no clear and distinct idea of God, but only a confused one. For as he who knows not rightly the nature of a triangle, knows not that its three angles are equal to two right angles, so he who conceives the Divine nature confusedly, does not see that it pertains to the nature of God to exist. Now, to conceive the nature of God clearly and distinctly, it is necessary to pay attention to a certain number of very simple notions, called general notions, and by their help to associate the conceptions which we form of the attributes of the Divine nature. It then, for the first time, becomes clear to us, that God exists necessarily, that He is omnipresent, and that all our conceptions involve in themselves the nature of God and are conceived through it. Lastly, we see that all our adequate ideas are true. Compare on this point the prolegomena to book, "Principles of Descartes's philosophy set forth geometrically."

CHAPTER VI.

Of Miracles.

AS MEN ARE accustomed to call Divine the knowledge which transcends human understanding, so also do they style Divine, or the work of God, anything of which the cause is not generally known: for the masses think that the power and providence of God are most clearly displayed by events that are extraordinary and contrary to the conception they have formed of nature, especially if such events bring them any profit or convenience: they think that the clearest possible proof of God's existence is afforded when nature, as they suppose, breaks her accustomed order, and consequently they believe that those who explain or endeavour to understand phenomena or miracles through their natural causes are doing away with God and His providence. They suppose, forsooth, that God is inactive so long as nature works in her accustomed order, and vice versa, that the power of nature and natural causes are idle so long as God is acting: thus they imagine two powers distinct one from the other, the power of God and the power of nature, though the latter is in a sense determined by God, or (as most people believe now) created by Him. What they mean by either, and what they understand by God and nature they do not know, except that they imagine the power of God to be like that of some royal potentate, and nature's power to consist in force and energy.

The masses then style unusual phenomena, "miracles," and partly from piety, partly for the sake of opposing the students of science, prefer to remain in ignorance of natural causes, and only to hear of those things which they know least, and consequently admire most. In fact, the common people can only adore God, and refer all things to His power by removing natural causes, and conceiving things happening out of their due course, and only admires the power of God when the power of nature is conceived of as in subjection to it.

This idea seems to have taken its rise among the early Jews who saw the Gentiles round them worshipping visible gods such as the sun, the moon, the earth, water, air, &c., and in order to inspire the conviction that such divinities were weak and inconstant, or changeable, told how they themselves were under the sway of an invisible God, and narrated their miracles, trying further to show that the God whom they worshipped arranged the whole of nature for their sole benefit: this idea was so pleasing to humanity that men go on to this day imagining miracles, so that they may believe themselves God's favourites, and the final cause for which God created and directs all things.

What pretension will not people in their folly advance! They have no single sound idea concerning either God or nature, they confound God's decrees with human decrees, they conceive nature as so limited that they believe man to be its chief part! I have spent enough space in setting forth these common ideas and prejudices concerning nature and miracles, but in order to afford a regular demonstration I will show —

I. That nature cannot be contravened, but that she preserves a fixed and immutable order, and at the same time I will explain what is meant by a miracle.

II. That God's nature and existence, and consequently His providence cannot be known from miracles, but that they can all be much better perceived from the fixed and immutable order of nature.

III. That by the decrees and volitions, and consequently the providence of God, Scripture (as I will prove by Scriptural examples) means nothing but nature's order following necessarily from her eternal laws.

IV. Lastly, I will treat of the method of interpreting Scriptural miracles, and the chief points to be noted concerning the narratives of them.

Such are the principal subjects which will be discussed in this chapter, and which will serve, I think, not a little to further the object of this treatise.

Our first point is easily proved from what we showed in Chap. IV. about Divine law — namely, that all that God wishes or determines involves eternal necessity, and truth, for we demonstrated that God's understanding is identical with His will, and that it is the same thing to say that God wills a thing, as to say, that He understands it; hence, as it follows necessarily, from the Divine nature and perfection that God understands a thing as it is, it follows no less necessarily that He wills it as it is. Now, as nothing is necessarily true save only by, Divine decree, it is plain that the universal laws of nature are decrees of God following from the necessity and perfection of the Divine nature. Hence, any event happening in nature which contravened nature's universal laws, would necessarily also contravene the Divine decree, nature, and understanding; or if anyone asserted that God acts in contravention to the laws of nature, he, ipso facto, would be compelled to assert that God acted against His own nature — an evident absurdity. One might easily show from the same premises that the power and efficiency, of nature are in themselves the Divine power and efficiency, and that the Divine power is the very essence of God, but this I gladly pass over for the present.

Nothing, then, comes to pass in nature (N.B. I do not mean here by "nature," merely matter and its modifications, but infinite other things besides matter.) in contravention to her universal laws, nay, everything agrees with them and follows from them, for whatsoever comes to pass, comes to pass by the will and eternal decree of God; that is, as we have just pointed out, whatever comes to pass, comes to pass according to laws and rules which involve eternal necessity and truth; nature, therefore, always observes laws and rules which involve eternal necessity, and truth, although they may not all be known to us, and therefore she keeps a fixed and mutable order. Nor is there any sound reason for limiting the power and efficacy of nature, and asserting that her laws are fit for certain purposes, but not for all; for as the efficacy, and power of nature, are the very, efficacy and power of God, and as the laws and rules of nature are the decrees of God, it is in every way to be believed that the power of nature is infinite, and that her laws are broad enough to embrace everything conceived by, the Divine intellect; the only alternative is to assert that God has created nature so weak, and has ordained for her laws so barren, that He is repeatedly compelled to come afresh to her aid if He wishes that she should be preserved, and that things should happen as He desires: a conclusion, in My opinion, very far removed from reason. Further, as nothing happens in nature which does not follow from her laws, and as her laws embrace everything conceived by the Divine intellect, and lastly, as nature preserves a fixed and immutable order; it most clearly follows that miracles are only intelligible as in relation to human opinions, and merely mean events of which the natural cause cannot be explained by a reference to any ordinary occurrence, either by us, or at any rate, by the writer and narrator of the miracle.

We may, in fact, say that a miracle is an event of which the causes annot be explained by the natural reason through a reference to ascertained workings of nature; but since miracles were wrought according to the understanding of the masses, who are wholly ignorant of the workings of nature, it is certain that the ancients took for a miracle whatever they could not explain by the method adopted by the unlearned in such cases, namely, an appeal to the memory, a recalling of something similar, which is ordinarily regarded without wonder; for most people think they sufficiently understand a thing when they have ceased to wonder at it. The ancients, then, and indeed most men up to the present day, had no other criterion for a miracle; hence we cannot doubt that many things are narrated in Scripture as miracles of which the causes could easily be explained by reference to ascertained workings of nature. We have hinted as much in Chap. II., in speaking of the sun standing still in the time of Joshua, and to say on the subject when we come to treat of the interpretation of miracles later on in this chapter.

It is now time to pass on to the second point, and show that we cannot gain an understanding of God's essence, existence, or providence by means of miracles, but that these truths are much better perceived through the fixed and immutable order of nature. I thus proceed with the demonstration. As God's existence is not self-evident it must necessarily be inferred from ideas so firmly and incontrovertibly true, that no power can be postulated or conceived sufficient to impugn them. They ought certainly so to appear to us when we infer from them God's existence, if we wish to place our conclusion beyond the reach of doubt; for if we could conceive that such ideas could be impugned by any power whatsoever, we should doubt of their truth, we should doubt of our conclusion, namely, of God's existence, and should never be able to be certain of anything. Further, we know that nothing either agrees with or is contrary to nature, unless it agrees with or is contrary to these primary ideas; wherefore if we would conceive that anything could be done in nature by any power whatsoever which would be contrary to the laws of nature, it would also be contrary to our primary ideas, and we should have either to reject it as absurd, or else to cast doubt (as just shown) on our primary ideas, and consequently on the existence of God, and on everything howsoever perceived. Therefore miracles, in the sense of events contrary to the laws of nature, so far from demonstrating to us the existence of God, would, on the contrary, lead us to doubt it, where, otherwise, we might have been absolutely certain of it, as knowing that nature follows a fixed and immutable order.

Let us take miracle as meaning that which cannot be explained through natural causes. This may be interpreted in two senses: either as that which has natural causes, but cannot be examined by the human intellect; or as that which has no cause save God and God's will. But as all things which come to pass through natural causes, come to pass also solely through the will and power of God, it comes to this, that a miracle, whether it has natural causes or not, is a result which cannot be explained by its cause, that is a phenomenon which surpasses human understanding; but from such a phenomenon, and certainly from a result surpassing our understanding, we can gain no knowledge. For whatsoever we understand clearly and distinctly should be plain to us either in itself or by means of something else clearly and distinctly understood; wherefore from a miracle or a phenomenon which we cannot understand, we can gain no knowledge of God's essence, or existence, or indeed anything about God or nature; whereas when we know that all things are ordained and ratified by God, that the operations of nature follow from the essence of God, and that the laws of nature are eternal decrees and volitions of God, we must perforce conclude that our knowledge of God, and of God's will increases in proportion to our knowledge and clear understanding of nature, as we see how she depends on her primal cause, and how she works according to eternal law. Wherefore so far as our understanding goes, those phenomena which we clearly and distinctly understand have much better right to be called works of God, and to be referred to the will of God than those about which we are entirely ignorant, although they appeal powerfully to the imagination, and compel men's admiration.

It is only phenomena that we clearly and distinctly understand, which heighten our knowledge of God, and most clearly indicate His will and decrees. Plainly, they are but triflers who, when they cannot explain a thing, run back to the will of God; this is, truly, a ridiculous way of expressing ignorance. Again, even supposing that some conclusion could be drawn from miracles, we could not possibly infer from them the existence of God: for a miracle being an event under limitations is the expression of a fixed and limited power; therefore we could not possibly infer from an effect of this kind the existence of a cause whose power is infinite, but at the utmost only of a cause whose power is greater than that of the said effect. I say at the utmost, for a phenomenon may be the result of many concurrent causes, and its power may be less than the power of the sum of such causes, but far greater than that of any one of them taken individually. On the other hand, the laws of nature, as we have shown, extend over infinity, and are conceived by us as, after a fashion, eternal, and nature works in accordance with them in a fixed and immutable order; therefore, such laws indicate to us in a certain degree the infinity, the eternity, and the immutability of God.

We may conclude, then, that we cannot gain knowledge of the existence and providence of God by means of miracles, but that we can far better infer them from the fixed and immutable order of nature. By miracle, I here mean an event which surpasses, or is thought to surpass, human comprehension: for in so far as it is supposed to destroy or interrupt the order of nature or her laws, it not only can give us no knowledge of God, but, contrariwise, takes away that which we naturally have, and makes us doubt of God and everything else.

Neither do I recognize any difference between an event against the laws of nature and an event beyond the laws of nature (that is, according to some, an event which does not contravene nature, though she is inadequate to produce or effect it) — for a miracle is wrought in, and not beyond nature, though it may be said in itself to be above nature, and, therefore, must necessarily interrupt the order of nature, which otherwise we conceive of as fixed and unchangeable, according to God's decrees. If, therefore, anything should come to pass in nature which does not follow from her laws, it would also be in contravention to the order which God has established in nature for ever through universal natural laws: it would, therefore, be in contravention to God's nature and laws, and, consequently, belief in it would throw doubt upon everything, and lead to Atheism.

I think I have now sufficiently established my second point, so that we can again conclude that a miracle, whether in contravention to, or beyond, nature, is a mere absurdity; and, therefore, that what is meant in Scripture by a miracle can only be a work of nature, which surpasses, or is believed to surpass, human comprehension. Before passing on to my third point, I will adduce Scriptural authority for my assertion that God cannot be known from miracles. Scripture nowhere states the doctrine openly, but it can readily be inferred from several passages. Firstly, that in which Moses commands (Deut. xiii.) that a false prophet should be put to death, even though he work miracles: "If there arise a prophet among you, and giveth thee a sign or wonder, and the sign or wonder come to pass, saying, Let us go after other gods . . . thou shalt not hearken unto the voice of that prophet; for the Lord your God proveth you, and that prophet shall be put to death." From this it clearly follows that miracles could be wrought even by false prophets; and that, unless men are honestly endowed with the true knowledge and love of God, they may be as easily led by miracles to follow false gods as to follow the true God; for these words are added: "For the Lord your God tempts you, that He may know whether you love Him with all your heart and with all your mind."

Further, the Israelites, from all their miracles, were unable to form a sound conception of God, as their experience testified: for when they had persuaded themselves that Moses had departed from among them, they petitioned Aaron to give them visible gods; and the idea of God they had formed as the result of all their miracles was — a calf!

Asaph, though he had heard of so many miracles, yet doubted of the providence of God, and would have turned himself from the true way, if he had not at last come to understand true blessedness. (See Ps. lxxxiii.) Solomon, too, at a time when the Jewish nation was at the height of its prosperity, suspects that all things happen by chance. (See Eccles. iii:19, 20, 21; and chap. ix:2, 3, &c.)

Lastly, nearly all the prophets found it very hard to reconcile the order of nature and human affairs with the conception they had formed of God's providence, whereas philosophers who endeavour to understand things by clear conceptions of them, rather than by miracles, have always found the task extremely easy — at least, such of them as place true happiness solely in virtue and peace of mind, and who aim at obeying nature, rather than being obeyed by her. Such persons rest assured that God directs nature according to the requirements of universal laws, not according to the requirements of the particular laws of human nature, and trial, therefore, God's scheme comprehends, not only the human race, but the whole of nature.

It is plain, then, from Scripture itself, that miracles can give no knowledge of God, nor clearly teach us the providence of God. As to the frequent statements in Scripture, that God wrought miracles to make Himself plain to man — as in Exodus x:2, where He deceived the Egyptians, and gave signs of Himself, that the Israelites might know that He was God — it does not, therefore, follow that miracles really taught this truth, but only that the Jews held opinions which laid them easily open to conviction by miracles. We have shown in Chap. II. that the reasons assigned by the prophets, or those which are formed from revelation, are not assigned in accordance with ideas universal and common to all, but in accordance with the accepted doctrines, however absurd, and with the opinions of those to whom the revelation was given, or those whom the Holy Spirit wished to convince.

This we have illustrated by many Scriptural instances, and can further cite Paul, who to the Greeks was a Greek, and to the Jews a Jew. But although these miracles could convince the Egyptians and Jews from their standpoint, they could not give a true idea and knowledge of God, but only cause them to admit that there was a Deity more powerful than anything known to them, and that this Deity took special care of the Jews, who had just then an unexpectedly happy issue of all their affairs. They could not teach them that God cares equally for all, for this can be taught only by philosophy: the Jews, and all who took their knowledge of God's providence from the dissimilarity of human conditions of life and the inequalities of fortune, persuaded themselves that God loved the Jews above all men, though they did not surpass their fellows in true human perfection.

I now go on to my third point, and show from Scripture that the decrees and mandates of God, and consequently His providence, are merely the order of nature — that is, when Scripture describes an event as accomplished by God or God's will, we must understand merely that it was in accordance with the law and order of nature, not, as most people believe, that nature had for a season ceased to act, or that her order was temporarily interrupted. But Scripture does not directly teach matters unconnected with its doctrine, wherefore it has no care to explain things by their natural causes, nor to expound matters merely speculative. Wherefore our conclusion must be gathered by inference from those Scriptural narratives which happen to be written more at length and circumstantially than usual. Of these I will cite a few.

In the first book of Samuel, ix:15, 16, it is related that God revealed to Samuel that He would send Saul to him, yet God did not send Saul to Samuel as people are wont to send one man to another. His "sending" was merely the ordinary course of nature. Saul was looking for the asses he had lost, and was meditating a return home without them, when, at the suggestion of his servant, he went to the prophet Samuel, to learn from him where he might find them. From no part of the narrative does it appear that Saul had any command from God to visit Samuel beyond this natural motive.

In Psalm cv. 24 it is said that God changed the hearts of the Egyptians, so that they hated the Israelites. This was evidently a natural change, as appears from Exodus, chap.i., where we find no slight reason for the Egyptians reducing the Israelites to slavery.

In Genesis ix:13, God tells Noah that He will set His bow in the cloud; this action of God's is but another way of expressing the refraction and reflection which the rays of the sun are subjected to in drops of water.

In Psalm cxlvii:18, the natural action and warmth of the wind, by which hoar frost and snow are melted, are styled the word of the Lord, and in verse 15 wind and cold are called the commandment and word of God.

In Psalm civ:4, wind and fire are called the angels and ministers of God, and various other passages of the same sort are found in Scripture, clearly showing that the decree, commandment, fiat, and word of God are merely expressions for the action and order of nature.

Thus it is plain that all the events narrated in Scripture came to pass naturally, and are referred directly to God because Scripture, as we have shown, does not aim at explaining things by their natural causes, but only at narrating what appeals to the popular imagination, and doing so in the manner best calculated to excite wonder, and consequently to impress the minds of the masses with devotion. If, therefore, events are found in the Bible which we cannot refer to their causes, nay, which seem entirely to contradict the order of nature, we must not come to a stand, but assuredly believe that whatever did really happen happened naturally. This view is confirmed by the fact that in the case of every miracle there were many attendant circumstances, though these were not always related, especially where the narrative was of a poetic character.

The circumstances of the miracles clearly show, I maintain, that natural causes were needed. For instance, in order to infect the Egyptians with blains, it was necessary that Moses should scatter ashes in the air (Exod. ix: 10); the locusts also came upon the land of Egypt by a command of God in accordance with nature, namely, by an east wind blowing for a whole day and night; and they departed by a very strong west wind (Exod. x:14, 19). By a similar Divine mandate the sea opened a way for the Jews (Exo. xiv:21), namely, by an east wind which blew very strongly all night.

So, too, when Elisha would revive the boy who was believed to be dead, he was obliged to bend over him several times until the flesh of the child waxed warm, and at last he opened his eyes (2 Kings iv:34, 35).

Again, in John's Gospel (chap. ix.) certain acts are mentioned as performed by Christ preparatory to healing the blind man, and there are numerous other instances showing that something further than the absolute fiat of God is required for working a miracle.

Wherefore we may believe that, although the circumstances attending miracles are not related always or in full detail, yet a miracle was never performed without them.

This is confirmed by Exodus xiv:27, where it is simply stated that "Moses stretched forth his hand, and the waters of the sea returned to their strength in the morning," no mention being made of a wind; but in the song of Moses (Exod. xv:10) we read, "Thou didst blow with Thy wind (i.e. with a very strong wind), and the sea covered them." Thus the attendant circumstance is omitted in the history, and the miracle is thereby enhanced.

But perhaps someone will insist that we find many things in Scripture which seem in nowise explicable by natural causes, as for instance, that the sins of men and their prayers can be the cause of rain and of the earth's fertility, or that faith can heal the blind, and so on. But I think I have already made sufficient answer: I have shown that Scripture does not explain things by their secondary causes, but only narrates them in the order and the style which has most power to move men, and especially uneducated men, to devotion; and therefore it speaks inaccurately of God and of events, seeing that its object is not to convince the reason, but to attract and lay hold of the imagination. If the Bible were to describe the destruction of an empire in the style of political historians, the masses would remain unstirred, whereas the contrary is the case when it adopts the method of poetic description, and refers all things immediately to God. When, therefore, the Bible says that the earth is barren because of men's sins, or that the blind were healed by faith, we ought to take no more notice than when it says that God is angry at men's sins, that He is sad, that He repents of the good He has promised and done; or that on seeing a sign he remembers something He had promised, and other similar expressions, which are either thrown out poetically or related according to the opinion and prejudices of the writer.

We may, then, be absolutely certain that every event which is truly described in Scripture necessarily happened, like everything else, according to natural laws; and if anything is there set down which can be proved in set terms to contravene the order of nature, or not to be deducible therefrom, we must believe it to have been foisted into the sacred writings by irreligious hands; for whatsoever is contrary to nature is also contrary to reason, and whatsoever is contrary to reason is absurd, and, ipso facto, to be rejected.

There remain some points concerning the interpretation of miracles to be noted, or rather to be recapitulated, for most of them have been already stated. These I proceed to discuss in the fourth division of my subject, and I am led to do so lest anyone should, by wrongly interpreting a miracle, rashly suspect that he has found something in Scripture contrary to human reason.

It is very rare for men to relate an event simply as it happened, without adding any element of their own judgment. When they see or hear anything new, they are, unless strictly on their guard, so occupied with their own preconceived opinions that they perceive something quite different from the plain facts seen or heard, especially if such facts surpass the comprehension of the beholder or hearer, and, most of all, if he is interested in their happening in a given way.

Thus men relate in chronicles and histories their own opinions rather than actual events, so that one and the same event is so differently related by two men of different opinions, that it seems like two separate occurrences; and, further, it is very easy from historical chronicles to gather the personal opinions of the historian.

I could cite many instances in proof of this from the writings both of natural philosophers and historians, but I will content myself with one only from Scripture, and leave the reader to judge of the rest.

In the time of Joshua the Hebrews held the ordinary opinion that the sun moves with a daily motion, and that the earth remains at rest; to this preconceived opinion they adapted the miracle which occurred during their battle with the five kings. They did not simply relate that that day was longer than usual, but asserted that the sun and moon stood still, or ceased from their motion — a statement which would be of great service to them at that time in convincing and proving by experience to the Gentiles, who worshipped the sun, that the sun was under the control of another deity who could compel it to change its daily course. Thus, partly through religious motives, partly through preconceived opinions, they conceived of and related the occurrence as something quite different from what really happened.

Thus in order to interpret the Scriptural miracles and understand from the narration of them how they really happened, it is necessary to know the opinions of those who first related them, and have recorded them for us in writing, and to distinguish such opinions from the actual impression made upon their senses, otherwise we shall confound opinions and judgments with the actual miracle as it really occurred: nay, further, we shall confound actual events with symbolical and imaginary ones. For many things are narrated in Scripture as real, and were believed to be real, which were in fact only symbolical and imaginary. As, for instance, that God came down from heaven (Exod. xix:28, Deut. v:28), and that Mount Sinai smoked because God descended upon it surrounded with fire; or, again that Elijah ascended into heaven in a chariot of fire, with horses of fire; all these things were assuredly merely symbols adapted to the opinions of those who have handed them down to us as they were represented to them, namely, as real. All who have any education know that God has no right hand nor left; that He is not moved nor at rest, nor in a particular place, but that He is absolutely infinite and contains in Himself all perfections.

These things, I repeat, are known to whoever judges of things by the perception of pure reason, and not according as his imagination is affected by his outward senses. Following the example of the masses who imagine a bodily Deity, holding a royal court with a throne on the convexity of heaven, above the stars, which are believed to be not very, far off from the earth.

To these and similar opinions very many narrations in Scripture are adapted, and should not, therefore, be mistaken by philosophers for realities.

Lastly, in order to understand, in the case of miracles, what actually took place, we ought to be familiar with Jewish phrases and metaphors; anyone who did not make sufficient allowance for these, would be continually seeing miracles in Scripture where nothing of the kind is intended by the writer; he would thus miss the knowledge not only of what actually happened, but also of the mind of the writers of the sacred text. For instance, Zechariah speaking of some future war says (chap. xiv;7): "It shall be one day which shall be known to the Lord, not day, nor night; but at even time it shall be light." In these words he seems to predict a great miracle, yet he only means that the battle will be doubtful the whole day, that the issue will be known only to God, but that in the evening they will gain the victory: the prophets frequently used to predict victories and defeats of the nations in similar phrases. Thus Isaiah, describing the destruction of Babylon, says (chap. xiii.): "The stars of heaven, and the constellations thereof, shall not give their light; the sun shall be darkened in his going forth, and the moon shall not cause her light to shine." Now I suppose no one imagines that at the destruction of Babylon these phenomena actually occurred any more than that which the prophet adds, "For I will make the heavens to tremble, and remove the earth out of her place."

So, too, Isaiah in foretelling to the Jews that they would return from Babylon to Jerusalem in safety, and would not suffer from thirst on their journey, says: "And they thirsted not when He led them through the deserts; He caused the waters to flow out of the rocks for them; He clave the rocks, and the waters gushed out." These words merely mean that the Jews, like other people, found springs in the desert, at which they quenched their thirst; for when the Jews returned to Jerusalem with the consent of Cyrus, it is admitted that no similar miracles befell them.

In this way many occurrences in the Bible are to be regarded merely as Jewish expressions. There is no need for me to go through them in detail; but I will call attention generally to the fact that the Jews employed such phrases not only rhetorically, but also, and indeed chiefly, from devotional motives. Such is the reason for the substitution of "bless God" for "curse God" in 1 Kings xxi:10, and Job ii:9, and for all things being referred to God, whence it appears that the Bible seems to relate nothing but miracles, even when speaking of the most ordinary occurrences, as in the examples given above.

Hence we must believe that when the Bible says that the Lord hardened Pharaoh's heart, it only means that Pharaoh was obstinate; when it says that God opened the windows of heaven, it only means that it rained very hard, and so on. When we reflect on these peculiarities, and also on the fact that most things are related very shortly, with very little details and almost in abridgments, we shall see that there is hardly anything in Scripture which can be proved contrary to natural reason, while, on the other hand, many things which before seemed obscure, will after a little consideration be understood and easily explained.

I think I have now very clearly explained all that I proposed to explain, but before I finish this chapter I would call attention to the fact that I have adopted a different method in speaking of miracles to that which I employed in treating of prophecy. Of prophecy I have asserted nothing which could not be inferred from promises revealed in Scripture, whereas in this chapter I have deduced my conclusions solely from the principles ascertained by the natural light of reason. I have proceeded in this way advisedly, for prophecy, in that it surpasses human knowledge, is a purely theological question; therefore, I knew that I could not make any assertions about it, nor learn wherein it consists, except through deductions from premises that have been revealed; therefore I was compelled to collate the history of prophecy, and to draw therefrom certain conclusions which would teach me, in so far as such teaching is possible, the nature and properties of the gift. But in the case of miracles, as our inquiry is a question purely philosophical (namely, whether anything can happen which contravenes or does not follow from the laws of nature), I was not under any such necessity: I therefore thought it wiser to unravel the difficulty through premises ascertained and thoroughly known by could also easily have solved the problem merely from the doctrines and fundamental principles of Scripture: in order that everyone may acknowledge this, I will briefly show how it could be done.

Scripture makes the general assertion in several passages that nature's course is fixed and unchangeable. In Ps. cxlviii:6, for instance, and Jer. xxxi:35. The wise man also, in Eccles. i:10, distinctly teaches that "there is nothing new under the sun," and in verses 11, 12, illustrating the same idea, he adds that although something occasionally happens which seems new, it is not really new, but "hath been already of old time, which was before us, whereof there is no remembrance, neither shall there be any remembrance of things that are to come with those that come after." Again in chap. iii:11, he says, "God hath made everything beautiful in his time," and immediately afterwards adds, "I know that whatsoever God doeth, it shall be for ever; nothing can be put to it, nor anything taken from it."

Now all these texts teach most distinctly that nature preserves a fixed and unchangeable order, and that God in all ages, known and unknown, has been the same; further, that the laws of nature are so perfect, that nothing can be added thereto nor taken therefrom; and, lastly, that miracles only appear as something new because of man's ignorance.

Such is the express teaching of Scripture: nowhere does Scripture assert that anything happens which contradicts, or cannot follow from the laws of nature; and, therefore, we should not attribute to it such a doctrine.

To these considerations we must add, that miracles require causes and attendant circumstances, and that they follow, not from some mysterious royal power which the masses attribute to God, but from the Divine rule and decree, that is (as we have shown from Scripture itself) from the laws and order of nature; lastly, that miracles can be wrought even by false prophets, as is proved from Deut. xiii. and Matt. xxiv:24.

The conclusion, then, that is most plainly put before us is, that miracles were natural occurrences, and must therefore be so explained as to appear neither new (in the words of Solomon) nor contrary to nature, but, as far as possible, in complete agreement with ordinary events. This can easily be done by anyone, now that I have set forth the rules drawn from Scripture. Nevertheless, though I maintain that Scripture teaches this doctrine, I do not assert that it teaches it as a truth necessary to salvation, but only that the prophets were in agreement with ourselves on the point; therefore everyone is free to think on the subject as he likes, according as he thinks it best for himself, and most likely to conduce to the worship of God and to singlehearted religion.

This is also the opinion of Josephus, for at the conclusion of the second book of his "Antiquities," he writes: Let no man think this story incredible of the sea's dividing to save these people, for we find it in ancient records that this hath been seen before, whether by God's extraordinary will or by the course of nature it is indifferent. The same thing happened one time to the Macedonians, under the command of Alexander, when for want of another passage the Pamphylian Sea divided to make them way; God's Providence making use of Alexander at that time as His instrument for destroying the Persian Empire. This is attested by all the historians who have pretended to write the Life of that Prince. But people are at liberty to think what they please."

Such are the words of Josephus, and such is his opinion on faith in miracles.

CHAPTER VII.

Of the Interpretation
of Scripture

WHEN PEOPLE DECLARE, as all are ready, to do, that the Bible is the Word of God teaching man true blessedness and the way of salvation, they evidently do not mean what they, say; for the masses take no pains at all to live according to Scripture, and we see most people endeavouring to hawk about their own commentaries as the word of God, and giving their best efforts, under the guise of religion, to compelling others to think as they do: we generally see, I say, theologians anxious to learn how to wring their inventions and sayings out of the sacred text, and to fortify, them with Divine authority. Such persons never display, less scruple or more zeal than when they, are interpreting Scripture or the mind of the Holy Ghost; if we ever see them perturbed, it is not that they fear to attribute some error to the Holy Spirit, and to stray from the right path, but that they are afraid to be convicted of error by, others, and thus to overthrow and bring into contempt their own authority. But if men really believed what they verbally testify of Scripture, they would adopt quite a different plan of life: their minds would not be agitated by so many contentions, nor so many hatreds, and they would cease to be excited by such a blind and rash passion for interpreting the sacred writings, and excogitating novelties in religion. On the contrary, they would not dare to adopt, as the teaching of Scripture, anything which they could not plainly deduce therefrom: lastly, those sacrilegious persons who have dared, in several passages, to interpolate the Bible, would have shrunk from so great a crime, and would have stayed their sacrilegious hands.

Ambition and unscrupulousness have waxed so powerful, that religion is thought to consist, not so much in respecting the writings of the Holy Ghost, as in defending human commentaries, so that religion is no longer identified with charity, but with spreading discord and propagating insensate hatred disguised under the name of zeal for the Lord, and eager ardour.

To these evils we must add superstition, which teaches men to despise reason and nature, and only to admire and venerate that which is repugnant to both: whence it is not wonderful that for the sake of increasing the admiration and veneration felt for Scripture, men strive to explain it so as to make it appear to contradict, as far as possible, both one and the other: thus they dream that most profound mysteries lie hid in the Bible, and weary themselves out in the investigation of these absurdities, to the neglect of what is useful. Every result of their diseased imagination they attribute to the Holy Ghost, and strive to defend with the utmost zeal and passion; for it is an observed fact that men employ their reason to defend conclusions arrived at by reason, but conclusions arrived at by the passions are defended by the passions.

If we would separate ourselves from the crowd and escape from theological prejudices, instead of rashly accepting human commentaries for Divine documents, we must consider the true method of interpreting Scripture and dwell upon it at some length: for if we remain in ignorance of this we cannot know, certainly, what the Bible and the Holy Spirit wish to teach.

I may sum up the matter by saying that the method of interpreting Scripture does not widely differ from the method of interpreting nature — in fact, it is almost the same. For as the interpretation of nature consists in the examination of the history of nature, and therefrom deducing definitions of natural phenomena on certain fixed axioms, so Scriptural interpretation proceeds by the examination of Scripture, and inferring the intention of its authors as a legitimate conclusion from its fundamental principles. By working in this manner everyone will always advance without danger of error — that is, if they admit no principles for interpreting Scripture, and discussing its contents save such as they find in Scripture itself — and will be able with equal security to discuss what surpasses our understanding, and what is known by the natural light of reason.

In order to make clear that such a method is not only correct, but is also the only one advisable, and that it agrees with that employed in interpreting nature, I must remark that Scripture very often treats of matters which cannot be deduced from principles known to reason: for it is chiefly made up of narratives and revelation: the narratives generally contain miracles — that is, as we have shown in the last chapter, relations of extraordinary natural occurrences adapted to the opinions and judgment of the historians who recorded them: the revelations also were adapted to the opinions of the prophets, as we showed in Chap. II., and in themselves surpassed human comprehension. Therefore the knowledge of all these — that is, of nearly the whole contents of Scripture, must be sought from Scripture alone, even as the knowledge of nature is sought from nature. As for the moral doctrines which are also contained in the Bible, they may be demonstrated from received axioms, but we cannot prove in the same manner that Scripture intended to teach them, this can only be learned from Scripture itself.

If we would bear unprejudiced witness to the Divine origin of Scripture, we must prove solely on its own authority that it teaches true moral doctrines, for by such means alone can its Divine origin be demonstrated: we have shown that the certitude of the prophets depended chiefly on their having minds turned towards what is just and good, therefore we ought to have proof of their possessing this quality before we repose faith in them. From miracles God's divinity cannot be proved, as I have already shown, and need not now repeat, for miracles could be wrought by false prophets. Wherefore the Divine origin of Scripture must consist solely in its teaching true virtue. But we must come to our conclusion simply on Scriptural grounds, for if we were unable to do so we could not, unless strongly prejudiced accept the Bible and bear witness to its Divine origin.

Our knowledge of Scripture must then be looked for in Scripture only.

Lastly, Scripture does not give us definition of things any more than nature does: therefore, such definitions must be sought in the latter case from the diverse workings of nature; in the former case, from the various narratives about the given subject which occur in the Bible.

The universal rule, then, in interpreting Scripture is to accept nothing as an authoritative Scriptural statement which we do not perceive very clearly when we examine it in the light of its history. What I mean by its history, and what should be the chief points elucidated, I will now explain.

The history of a Scriptural statement comprises —

I. The nature and properties of the language in which the books of the Bible were written, and in which their authors were, accustomed to speak. We shall thus be able to investigate every expression by comparison with common conversational usages.

Now all the writers both of the Old Testament and the New were Hebrews: therefore, a knowledge of the Hebrew language is before all things necessary, not only for the comprehension of the Old Testament, which was written in that tongue, but also of the New: for although the latter was published in other languages, yet its characteristics are Hebrew.

II. An analysis of each book and arrangement of its contents under heads; so that we may have at hand the various texts which treat of a given subject. Lastly, a note of all the passages which are ambiguous or obscure, or which seem mutually contradictory.

I call passages clear or obscure according as their meaning is inferred easily or with difficulty in relation to the context, not according as their truth is perceived easily or the reverse by reason. We are at work not on the truth of passages, but solely on their meaning. We must take especial care, when we are in search of the meaning of a text, not to be led away by our reason in so far as it is founded on principles of natural knowledge (to say nothing of prejudices): in order not to confound the meaning of a passage with its truth, we must examine it solely by means of the signification of the words, or by a reason acknowledging no foundation but Scripture.

I will illustrate my meaning by an example. The words of Moses, "God is a fire" and "God is jealous," are perfectly clear so long as we regard merely the signification of the words, and I therefore reckon them

among the clear passages, though in relation to reason and truth they are most obscure: still, although the literal meaning is repugnant to the natural light of reason, nevertheless, if it cannot be clearly overruled on grounds and principles derived from its Scriptural "history," it, that is, the literal meaning, must be the one retained: and contrariwise if these passages literally interpreted are found to clash with principles derived from Scripture, though such literal interpretation were in absolute harmony with reason, they must be interpreted in a different manner, i.e. metaphorically.

If we would know whether Moses believed God to be a fire or not, we must on no account decide the question on grounds of the reasonableness or the reverse of such an opinion, but must judge solely by the other opinions of Moses which are on record.

In the present instance, as Moses says in several other passages that God has no likeness to any visible thing, whether in heaven or in earth, or in the water, either all such passages must be taken metaphorically, or else the one before us must be so explained. However, as we should depart as little as possible from the literal sense, we must first ask whether this text, God is a fire, admits of any but the literal meaning — that is, whether the word fire ever means anything besides ordinary natural fire. If no such second meaning can be found, the text must be taken literally, however repugnant to reason it may be: and all the other passages, though in complete accordance with reason, must be brought into harmony with it. If the verbal expressions would not admit of being thus harmonized, we should have to set them down as irreconcilable, and suspend our judgment concerning them. However, as we find the name fire applied to anger and jealousy (see Job xxxi:12) we can thus easily reconcile the words of Moses, and legitimately conclude that the two propositions God is a fire, and God is jealous, are in meaning identical.

Further, as Moses clearly teaches that God is jealous, and nowhere states that God is without passions or emotions, we must evidently infer that Moses held this doctrine himself, or at any rate, that he wished to teach it, nor must we refrain because such a belief seems contrary to reason: for as we have shown, we cannot wrest the meaning of texts to suit the dictates of our reason, or our preconceived opinions. The whole knowledge of the Bible must be sought solely from itself.

III. Lastly, such a history should relate the environment of all the prophetic books extant; that is, the life, the conduct, and the studies of the author of each book, who he was, what was the occasion, and the epoch of his writing, whom did he write for, and in what language. Further, it should inquire into the fate of each book: how it was first received, into whose hands it fell, how many different versions there were of it, by whose advice was it received into the Bible, and, lastly, how all the books now universally accepted as sacred, were united into a single whole.

All such information should, as I have said, be contained in the "history" of Scripture. For, in order to know what statements are set forth as laws, and what as moral precepts, it is important to be acquainted with the life, the conduct, and the pursuits of their author: moreover, it becomes easier to explain a man's writings in proportion as we have more intimate knowledge of his genius and temperament.

Further, that we may not confound precepts which are eternal with those which served only a temporary purpose, or were only meant for a few, we should know what was the occasion, the time, the age, in which each book was written, and to what nation it was addressed.Lastly, we should have knowledge on the other points I have mentioned, in order to be sure, in addition to the authenticity of the work, that it has not been tampered with by sacrilegious hands, or whether errors can have crept in, and, if so, whether they have been corrected by men sufficiently skilled and worthy of credence. All these things should be known, that we may not be led away by blind impulse to accept whatever is thrust on our notice, instead of only that which is sure and indisputable.

Now when we are in possession of this history of Scripture, and have finally decided that we assert nothing as prophetic doctrine which does not directly follow from such history, or which is not clearly deducible from it, then, I say, it will be time to gird ourselves for the task of investigating the mind of the prophets and of the Holy Spirit. But in this further arguing, also, we shall require a method very like that employed in interpreting nature from her history. As in the examination of natural phenomena we try first to investigate what is most universal and common to all nature — such, for instance, as motion and rest, and their laws and rules, which nature always observes, and through which she continually works — and then we proceed to what is less universal; so, too, in the history of Scripture, we seek first for that which is most universal, and serves for the basis and foundation of all Scripture, a doctrine, in fact, that is commended by all the prophets as eternal and most profitable to all men. For example, that God is one, and that He is omnipotent, that He alone should be worshipped, that He has a care for all men, and that He especially loves those who adore Him and love their neighbour as themselves, &c. These and similar doctrines, I repeat, Scripture everywhere so clearly and expressly teaches, that no one was ever in doubt of its meaning concerning them.

The nature of God, His manner of regarding and providing for things, and similar doctrines, Scripture nowhere teaches professedly, and as eternal doctrine; on the contrary, we have shown that the prophets themselves did not agree on the subject; therefore, we must not lay down any doctrine as Scriptural on such subjects, though it may appear perfectly clear on rational grounds.

From a proper knowledge of this universal doctrine of Scripture, we must then proceed to other doctrines less universal, but which, nevertheless, have regard to the general conduct of life, and flow from the universal doctrine like rivulets from a source; such are all particular external manifestations of true virtue, which need a given occasion for their exercise; whatever is obscure or ambiguous on such points in Scripture must be explained and defined by its universal doctrine; with regard to contradictory instances, we must observe the occasion and the time in which they were written. For instance, when Christ says, "Blessed are they that mourn, for they shall be comforted" we do not know, from the actual passage, what sort of mourners are meant; as, however, Christ afterwards teaches that we should have care for nothing, save only for the kingdom of God and His righteousness, which is commended as the highest good (see Matt. vi;33), it follows that by mourners He only meant those who mourn for the kingdom of God and righteousness neglected by man: for this would be the only cause of mourning to those who love nothing but the Divine kingdom and justice, and who evidently despise the gifts of fortune. So, too, when Christ says: "But if a man strike you on the right cheek, turn to him the left also," and the words which follow.

If He had given such a command, as a lawgiver, to judges, He would thereby have abrogated the law of Moses, but this He expressly says He did not do (Matt. v:17). Wherefore we must consider who was the speaker, what was the occasion, and to whom were the words addressed. Now Christ said that He did not ordain laws as a legislator, but inculcated precepts as a teacher: inasmuch as He did not aim at correcting outward actions so much as the frame of mind. Further, these words were spoken to men who were oppressed, who lived in a corrupt commonwealth on the brink of ruin, where justice was utterly neglected. The very doctrine inculcated here by Christ just before the destruction of the city was also taught by Jeremiah before the first destruction of Jerusalem, that is, in similar circumstances, as we see from Lamentations iii:25-30.

Now as such teaching was only set forth by the prophets in times of oppression, and was even then never laid down as a law; and as, on the other hand, Moses (who did not write in times of oppression, but — mark this — strove to found a well-ordered commonwealth), while condemning envy and hatred of one's neighbour, yet ordained that an eye should be given for an eye, it follows most clearly from these purely Scriptural grounds that this precept of Christ and Jeremiah concerning submission to injuries was only valid in places where justice is neglected, and in a time of oppression, but does not hold good in a well-ordered state.

In a well-ordered state where justice is administered every one is bound, if he would be accounted just, to demand penalties before the judge (see Lev:1), not for the sake of vengeance (Lev. xix:17, 18), but in order to defend justice and his country's laws, and to prevent the wicked rejoicing in their wickedness. All this is plainly in accordance with reason. I might cite many other examples in the same manner, but I think the foregoing are sufficient to explain my meaning and the utility of this method, and this is all my present purpose. Hitherto we have only shown how to investigate those passages of Scripture which treat of practical conduct, and which, therefore, are more easily examined, for on such subjects there was never really any controversy among the writers of the Bible.

The purely speculative passages cannot be so easily, traced to their real meaning: the way becomes narrower, for as the prophets differed in matters speculative among themselves, and the narratives are in great measure adapted to the prejudices of each age, we must not, on any, account infer the intention of one prophet from clearer passages in the writings of another; nor must we so explain his meaning, unless it is perfectly plain that the two prophets were at one in the matter.

How we are to arrive at the intention of the prophets in such cases I will briefly explain. Here, too, we must begin from the most universal proposition, inquiring first from the most clear Scriptural statements what is the nature of prophecy or revelation, and wherein does it consist; then we must proceed to miracles, and so on to whatever is most general till we come to the opinions of a particular prophet, and, at last, to the meaning of a particular revelation, prophecy, history, or miracle. We have already pointed out that great caution is necessary not to confound the mind of a prophet or historian with the mind of the Holy Spirit and the truth of the matter; therefore I need not dwell further on the subject. I would, however, here remark concerning the meaning of revelation, that the present method only teaches us what the prophets really saw or heard, not what they desired to signify or represent by symbols. The latter may be guessed at but cannot be inferred with certainty from Scriptural premises.

We have thus shown the plan for interpreting Scripture, and have, at the same time, demonstrated that it is the one and surest way of investigating its true meaning. I am willing indeed to admit that those persons (if any such there be) would be more absolutely certainly right, who have received either a trustworthy tradition or an assurance from the prophets themselves, such as is claimed by the Pharisees; or who have a pontiff gifted with infallibility in the interpretation of Scripture, such as the Roman Catholics boast. But as we can never be perfectly sure, either of such a tradition or of the authority of the pontiff, we cannot found any certain conclusion on either: the one is denied by the oldest sect of Christians, the other by the oldest sect of Jews. Indeed, if we consider the series of years (to mention no other point) accepted by the Pharisees from their Rabbis, during which time they say they have handed down the tradition from Moses, we shall find that it is not correct, as I show elsewhere. Therefore such a tradition should be received with extreme suspicion; and although, according to our method, we are bound to consider as uncorrupted the tradition of the Jews, namely, the meaning of the Hebrew words which we received from them, we may accept the latter while retaining our doubts about the former.

No one has ever been able to change the meaning of a word in ordinary use, though many have changed the meaning of a particular sentence. Such a proceeding would be most difficult; for whoever attempted to change the meaning of a word, would be compelled, at the same time, to explain all the authors who employed it, each according to his temperament and intention, or else, with consummate cunning, to falsify them.

Further, the masses and the learned alike preserve language, but it is only the learned who preserve the meaning of particular sentences and books: thus, we may easily imagine that the learned having a very rare book in their power, might change or corrupt the meaning of a sentence in it, but they could not alter the signification of the words; moreover, if anyone wanted to change the meaning of a common word he would not be able to keep up the change among posterity, or in common parlance or writing.

For these and such-like reasons we may readily conclude that it would never enter into the mind of anyone to corrupt a language, though the intention of a writer may often have been falsified by changing his phrases or interpreting them amiss. As then our method (based on the principle that the knowledge of Scripture must be sought from itself alone) is the sole true one, we must evidently renounce any knowledge which it cannot furnish for the complete understanding of Scripture. I will now point out its difficulties and shortcomings, which prevent our gaining a complete and assured knowledge of the Sacred Text.

Its first great difficulty consists in its requiring a thorough knowledge of the Hebrew language. Where is such knowledge to be obtained? The men of old who employed the Hebrew tongue have left none of the principles and bases of their language to posterity; we have from them absolutely nothing in the way of dictionary, grammar, or rhetoric.

Now the Hebrew nation has lost all its grace and beauty (as one would expect after the defeats and persecutions it has gone through), and has only retained certain fragments of its language and of a few books. Nearly all the names of fruits, birds, and fishes, and many other words have perished in the wear and tear of time. Further, the meaning of many nouns and verbs which occur in the Bible are either utterly lost, or are subjects of dispute. And not only are these gone, but we are lacking in a knowledge of Hebrew phraseology. The devouring tooth of time has destroyed turns of expression peculiar to the Hebrews, so that we know them no more.

Therefore we cannot investigate as we would all the meanings of a sentence by the uses of the language; and there are many phrases of which the meaning is most obscure or altogether inexplicable, though the component words are perfectly plain.

To this impossibility of tracing the history of the Hebrew language must be added its particular nature and composition: these give rise to so many ambiguities that it is impossible to find a method which would enable us to gain a certain knowledge of all the statements in Scripture 7. In addition to the sources of ambiguities common to all languages, there are many peculiar to Hebrew. These, I think, it worth while to mention.

Firstly, an ambiguity often arises in the Bible from our mistaking one letter for another similar one. The Hebrews divide the letters of the alphabet into five classes, according to the five organs of the month employed in pronouncing them, namely, the lips, the tongue, the teeth, the palate, and the throat. For instance, Alpha, Ghet, Hgain, He, are called gutturals, and are barely distinguishable, by any sign that we know, one from the other. El, which signifies to, is often taken for hgal, which signifies above, and vice versa. Hence sentences are often rendered rather ambiguous or meaningless.

A second difficulty arises from the multiplied meaning of conjunctions and adverbs. For instance, vau serves promiscuously for a particle of union or of separation, meaning, and, but, because, however, then: ki, has seven or eight meanings, namely, wherefore, although, if, when, inasmuch as, because, a burning, &c., and so on with almost all particles.

The third very fertile source of doubt is the fact that Hebrew verbs in the indicative mood lack the present, the past imperfect, the pluperfect, the future perfect, and other tenses most frequently employed in other languages; in the imperative and infinitive moods they are wanting in all except the present, and a subjunctive mood does not exist. Now, although all these defects in moods and tenses may be supplied by certain fundamental rules of the language with ease and even elegance, the ancient writers evidently neglected such rules altogether, and employed indifferently future for present and past, and vice versa past for future, and also indicative for imperative and subjunctive, with the result of considerable confusion.

Besides these sources of ambiguity there are two others, one very important. Firstly, there are in Hebrew no vowels; secondly, the sentences are not separated by any marks elucidating the meaning or separating the clauses. Though the want of these two has generally been supplied by points and accents, such substitutes cannot be accepted by us, inasmuch as they were invented and designed by men of an after age whose authority should carry no weight. The ancients wrote without points (that is, without vowels and accents), as is abundantly testified; their descendants added what was lacking, according to their own ideas of Scriptural interpretation; wherefore the existing accents and points are simply current interpretations, and are no more authoritative than any other commentaries.

Those who are ignorant of this fact cannot justify the author of the Epistle to the Hebrews for interpreting (chap. xi;21) Genesis (xlvii:31) very differently from the version given in our Hebrew text as at present pointed, as though the Apostle had been obliged to learn the meaning of Scripture from those who added the points. In my opinion the latter are clearly wrong. In order that everyone may judge for himself, and also see how the discrepancy arose simply from the want of vowels, I will give both interpretations. Those who pointed our version read, "And Israel bent himself over, or (changing Hqain into Aleph, a similar letter) towards, the head of the bed." The author of the Epistle reads, "And Israel bent himself over the head of his staff," substituting mate for mita, from which it only differs in respect of vowels. Now as in this narrative it is Jacob's age only that is in question, and not his illness, which is not touched on till the next chapter, it seems more likely that the historian intended to say that Jacob bent over the head of his staff (a thing commonly used by men of advanced age for their support) than that he bowed himself at the head of his bed, especially as for the former reading no substitution of letters is required. In this example I have desired not only to reconcile the passage in the Epistle with the passage in Genesis, but also and chiefly to illustrate how little trust should be placed in the points and accents which are found in our present Bible, and so to prove that he who would be without bias in interpreting Scripture should hesitate about accepting them, and inquire afresh for himself. Such being the nature and structure of the Hebrew language, one may easily understand that many difficulties are likely to arise, and that no possible method could solve all of them. It is useless to hope for a way out of our difficulties in the comparison of various parallel passages (we have shown that the only method of discovering the true sense of a passage out of many alternative ones is to see what are the usages of the language), for this comparison of parallel passages can only accidentally throw light on a difficult point, seeing that the prophets never wrote with the express object of explaining their own phrases or those of other people, and also because we cannot infer the meaning of one prophet or apostle by the meaning of another, unless on a purely practical question, not when the matter is speculative, or if a miracle, or history is being narrated. I might illustrate my point with instances, for there are many inexplicable phrases in Scripture, but I would rather pass on to consider the difficulties and imperfections of the method under discussion.

A further difficulty attends the method, from the fact that it requires the history of all that has happened to every book in the Bible; such a history we are often quite unable to furnish. Of the authors, or (if the expression be preferred), the writers of many of the books, we are either in complete ignorance, or at any rate in doubt, as I will point out at length. Further, we do not know either the occasions or the epochs when these books of unknown authorship were written; we cannot say into what hands they fell, nor how the numerous varying versions originated; nor, lastly, whether there were not other versions, now lost. I have briefly shown that such knowledge is necessary, but I passed over certain considerations which I will now draw attention to.

If we read a book which contains incredible or impossible narratives, or is written in a very obscure style, and if we know nothing of its author, nor of the time or occasion of its being written, we shall vainly endeavour to gain any certain knowledge of its true meaning. For being in ignorance on these points we cannot possibly know the aim or intended aim of the author; if we are fully informed, we so order our thoughts as not to be in any way prejudiced either in ascribing to the author or him for whom the author wrote either more or less than his meaning, and we only take into consideration what the author may have had in his mind, or what the time and occasion demanded. I think this must be tolerably evident to all.

It often happens that in different books we read histories in themselves similar, but which we judge very differently, according to the opinions we have formed of the authors. I remember once to have read in some book that a man named Orlando Furioso used to drive a kind of winged monster through the air, fly over any countries he liked, kill unaided vast numbers of men and giants, and such like fancies, which from the point of view of reason are obviously absurd. A very similar story I read in Ovid of Perseus, and also in the books of Judges and Kings of Samson, who alone and unarmed killed thousands of men, and of Elijah, who flew through the air, said at last went up to heaven in a chariot of fire, with horses of fire. All these stories are obviously alike, but we judge them very differently. The first only sought to amuse, the second had a political object, the third a religious object. We gather this simply from the opinions we had previously formed of the authors. Thus it is evidently necessary to know something of the authors of writings which are obscure or unintelligible, if we would interpret their meaning; and for the same reason, in order to choose the proper reading from among a great variety, we ought to have information as to the versions in which the differences are found, and as to the possibility of other readings having been discovered by persons of greater authority.

A further difficulty attends this method in the case of some of the books of Scripture, namely, that they are no longer extant in their original language. The Gospel according to Matthew, and certainly the Epistle to the Hebrews, were written, it is thought, in Hebrew, though they no longer exist in that form. Aben Ezra affirms in his commentaries that the book of Job was translated into Hebrew out of another language, and that its obscurity arises from this fact. I say nothing of the apocryphal books, for their authority stands on very inferior ground.

The foregoing difficulties in this method of interpreting Scripture from its own history, I conceive to be so great that I do not hesitate to say that the true meaning of Scripture is in many places inexplicable, or at best mere subject for guesswork; but I must again point out, on the other hand, that such difficulties only arise when we endeavour to follow the meaning of a prophet in matters which cannot be perceived, but only imagined, not in things, whereof the understanding can give a clear idea, and which are conceivable through themselves:, 8, matters which by their nature are easily perceived cannot be expressed so obscurely as to be unintelligible; as the proverb says, "a word is enough to the wise." Euclid, who only wrote of matters very simple and easily understood, can easily be comprehended by anyone in any language; we can follow his intention perfectly, and be certain of his true meaning, without having a thorough knowledge of the language in which he wrote; in fact, a quite rudimentary acquaintance is sufficient. We need make no researches concerning the life, the pursuits, or the habits of the author; nor need we inquire in what language, nor when he wrote, nor the vicissitudes of his book, nor its various readings, nor how, nor by whose advice it has been received.

What we here say of Euclid might equally be said of any book which treats of things by their nature perceptible: thus we conclude that we can easily follow the intention of Scripture in moral questions, from the history we possess of it, and we can be sure of its true meaning.

The precepts of true piety are expressed in very ordinary language, and are equally simple and easily understood. Further, as true salvation and blessedness consist in a true assent of the soul — and we truly assent only to what we clearly understand — it is most plain that we can follow with certainty the intention of Scripture in matters relating to salvation and necessary to blessedness; therefore, we need not be much troubled about what remains: such matters, inasmuch as we generally cannot grasp them with our reason and understanding, are more curious than profitable.

I think I have now set forth the true method of Scriptural interpretation, and have sufficiently explained my own opinion thereon. Besides, I do not doubt that everyone will see that such a method only requires the aid of natural reason. The nature and efficacy of the natural reason consists in deducing and proving the unknown from the known, or in carrying premises to their legitimate conclusions; and these are the very processes which our method desiderates. Though we must admit that it does not suffice to explain everything in the Bible, such imperfection does not spring from its own nature, but from the fact that the path which it teaches us, as the true one, has never been tended or trodden by men, and has thus, by the lapse of time, become very difficult, and almost impassable, as, indeed, I have shown in the difficulties I draw attention to.

There only remains to examine the opinions of those who differ from me. The first which comes under our notice is, that the light of nature has no power to interpret Scripture, but that a supernatural faculty is required for the task. What is meant by this supernatural faculty I will leave to its propounders to explain. Personally, I can only suppose that they have adopted a very obscure way of stating their complete uncertainty about the true meaning of Scripture. If we look at their interpretations, they contain nothing supernatural, at least nothing but the merest conjectures.

Let them be placed side by side with the interpretations of those who frankly confess that they have no faculty beyond their natural ones; we shall see that the two are just alike — both human, both long pondered over, both laboriously invented. To say that the natural reason is insufficient for such results is plainly untrue, firstly, for the reasons above stated, namely, that the difficulty of interpreting Scripture arises from no defect in human reason, but simply from the carelessness (not to say malice) of men who neglected the history of the Bible while there were still materials for inquiry; secondly, from the fact (admitted, I think, by all) that the supernatural faculty is a Divine gift granted only to the faithful. But the prophets and apostles did not preach to the faithful only, but chiefly to the unfaithful and wicked. Such persons, therefore, were able to understand the intention of the prophets and apostles, otherwise the prophets and apostles would have seemed to be preaching to little boys and infants, not to men endowed with reason. Moses, too, would have given his laws in vain, if they could only be comprehended by the faithful, who need no law. Indeed, those who demand supernatural faculties for comprehending the meaning of the prophets and apostles seem truly lacking in natural faculties, so that we should hardly suppose such persons the possessors of a Divine supernatural gift.

The opinion of Maimonides was widely different. He asserted that each passage in Scripture admits of various, nay, contrary, meanings; but that we could never be certain of any particular one till we knew that the passage, as we interpreted it, contained nothing contrary or repugnant to reason. If the literal meaning clashes with reason, though the passage seems in itself perfectly clear, it must be interpreted in some metaphorical sense. This doctrine he lays down very plainly in chap. xxv. part ii. of his book, "More Nebuchim," for he says: "Know that we shrink not from affirming that the world hath existed from eternity, because of what Scripture saith concerning the world's creation. For the texts which teach that the world was created are not more in number than those which teach that God hath a body; neither are the approaches in this matter of the world's creation closed, or even made hard to us: so that we should not be able to explain what is written, as we did when we showed that God hath no body, nay, peradventure, we could explain and make fast the doctrine of the world's eternity more easily than we did away with the doctrines that God hath a beatified body. Yet two things hinder me from doing as I have said, and believing that the world is eternal. As it hath been clearly shown that God hath not a body, we must perforce explain all those passages whereof the literal sense agreeth not with the demonstration, for sure it is that they can be so explained. But the eternity of the world hath not been so demonstrated, therefore it is not necessary to do violence to Scripture in support of some common opinion, whereof we might, at the bidding of reason, embrace the contrary."

Such are the words of Maimonides, and they are evidently sufficient to establish our point: for if he had been convinced by reason that the world is eternal, he would not have hesitated to twist and explain away the words of Scripture till he made them appear to teach this doctrine. He would have felt quite sure that Scripture, though everywhere plainly denying the eternity of the world, really intends to teach it. So that, however clear the meaning of Scripture may be, he would not feel certain of having grasped it, so long as he remained doubtful of the truth of what, was written. For we are in doubt whether a thing is in conformity with reason, or contrary thereto, so long as we are uncertain of its truth, and, consequently, we cannot be sure whether the literal meaning of a passage be true or false.

If such a theory as this were sound, I would certainly grant that some faculty beyond the natural reason is required for interpreting Scripture. For nearly all things that we find in Scripture cannot be inferred from known principles of the natural reason, and, therefore, we should be unable to come to any conclusion about their truth, or about the real meaning and intention of Scripture, but should stand in need of some further assistance.

Further, the truth of this theory would involve that the masses, having generally no comprehension of, nor leisure for, detailed proofs, would be reduced to receiving all their knowledge of Scripture on the authority and testimony of philosophers, and, consequently, would be compelled to suppose that the interpretations given by philosophers were infallible.

Truly this would be a new form of ecclesiastical authority, and a new sort of priests or pontiffs, more likely to excite men's ridicule than their veneration. Certainly our method demands a knowledge of Hebrew for which the masses have no leisure; but no such objection as the foregoing can be brought against us. For the ordinary Jews or Gentiles, to whom the prophets and apostles preached and wrote, understood the language, and, consequently, the intention of the prophet or apostle addressing them; but they did not grasp the intrinsic reason of what was preached, which, according to Maimonides, would be necessary for an understanding of it.

There is nothing, then, in our method which renders it necessary that the masses should follow the testimony of commentators, for I point to a set of unlearned people who understood the language of the prophets and apostles; whereas Maimonides could not point to any such who could arrive at the prophetic or apostolic meaning through their knowledge of the causes of things.

As to the multitude of our own time, we have shown that whatsoever is necessary to salvation, though its reasons may be unknown, can easily be understood in any language, because it is thoroughly ordinary and usual; it is in such understanding as this that the masses acquiesce, not in the testimony of commentators; with regard to other questions, the ignorant and the learned fare alike.

But let us return to the opinion of Maimonides, and examine it more closely. In the first place, he supposes that the prophets were in entire agreement one with another, and that they were consummate philosophers and theologians; for he would have them to have based their conclusions on the absolute truth. Further, he supposes that the sense of Scripture cannot be made plain from Scripture itself, for the truth of things is not made plain therein (in that it does not prove any thing, nor teach the matters of which it speaks through their definitions and first causes), therefore, according to Maimonides, the true sense of Scripture cannot be made plain from itself, and must not be there sought.

The falsity of such a doctrine is shown in this very chapter, for we have shown both by reason and examples that the meaning of Scripture is only made plain through Scripture itself, and even in questions deducible from ordinary knowledge should be looked for from no other source.

Lastly, such a theory supposes that we may explain the words of Scripture according to our preconceived opinions, twisting them about, and reversing or completely changing the literal sense, however plain it may be. Such licence is utterly opposed to the teaching of this and the preceding chapters, and, moreover, will be evident to everyone as rash and excessive.

But if we grant all this licence, what can it effect after all? Absolutely nothing. Those things which cannot be demonstrated, and which make up the greater part of Scripture, cannot be examined by reason, and cannot therefore be explained or interpreted by this rule; whereas, on the contrary, by following our own method, we can explain many questions of this nature, and discuss them on a sure basis, as we have already shown, by reason and example. Those matters which are by their nature comprehensible we can easily explain, as has been pointed out, simply by means of the context.

Therefore, the method of Maimonides is clearly useless: to which we may add, that it does away with all the certainty which the masses acquire by candid reading, or which is gained by any other persons in any other way. In conclusion, then, we dismiss Maimonides' theory as harmful, useless, and absurd.

As to the tradition of the Pharisees, we have already shown that it is not consistent, while the authority of the popes of Rome stands in need of more credible evidence; the latter, indeed, I reject simply on this ground, for if the popes could point out to us the meaning of Scripture as surely as did the high priests of the Jews, I should not be deterred by the fact that there have been heretic and impious Roman pontiffs; for among the Hebrew high-priests of old there were also heretics and impious men who gained the high — priesthood by improper means, but who, nevertheless, had Scriptural sanction for their supreme power of interpreting the law. (See Deut. xvii:11, 12, and xxxiii:10, also Malachi ii:8.)

However, as the popes can show no such sanction, their authority remains open to very grave doubt, nor should anyone be deceived by the example of the Jewish high-priests and think that the Catholic religion also stands in need of a pontiff; he should bear in mind that the laws of Moses being also the ordinary laws of the country, necessarily required some public authority to insure their observance; for, if everyone were free to interpret the laws of his country as he pleased, no state could stand, but would for that very reason be dissolved at once, and public rights would become private rights.

With religion the case is widely different. Inasmuch as it consists not so much in outward actions as in simplicity and truth of character, it stands outside the sphere of law and public authority. Simplicity and truth of character are not produced by the constraint of laws, nor by the authority of the state, no one the whole world over can be forced or legislated into a state of blessedness; the means required for such a consummation are faithful and brotherly admonition, sound education, and, above all, free use of the individual judgment.

Therefore, as the supreme right of free thinking, even on religion, is in every man's power, and as it is inconceivable that such power could be alienated, it is also in every man's power to wield the supreme right and authority of free judgment in this behalf, and to explain and interpret religion for himself. The only reason for vesting the supreme authority in the interpretation of law, and judgment on public affairs in the hands of the magistrates, is that it concerns questions of public right. Similarly the supreme authority in explaining religion, and in passing judgment thereon, is lodged with the individual because it concerns questions of individual right. So far, then, from the authority of the Hebrew high-priests telling in confirmation of the authority of the Roman pontiffs to interpret religion, it would rather tend to establish individual freedom of judgment. Thus in this way also, we have shown that our method of interpreting Scripture is the best. For as the highest power of Scriptural interpretation belongs to every man, the rule for such interpretation should be nothing but the natural light of reason which is common to all — not any supernatural light nor any external authority; moreover, such a rule ought not to be so difficult that it can only be applied by very skilful philosophers, but should be adapted to the natural and ordinary faculties and capacity of mankind. And such I have shown our method to be, for such difficulties as it has arise from men's carelessness, and are no part of its nature.

7 "It is impossible to find a method which would enable us to gain a certain knowledge of all the statements in Scripture." I mean impossible for us who have not the habitual use of the language, and have lost the precise meaning of its phraseology.

8 "Not in things whereof the understanding can gain a clear and distinct idea, and which are conceivable through themselves." By things conceivable I mean not only those which are rigidly proved, but also those whereof we are morally certain, and are wont to hear without wonder, though they are incapable of proof. Everyone can see the truth of Euclid's propositions before they are proved. So also the histories of things both future and past which do not surpass human credence, laws, institutions, manners, I call conceivable and clear, though they cannot be proved mathematically. But hieroglyphics and histories which seem to pass the bounds of belief I call inconceivable; yet even among these last there are many which our method enables us to investigate, and to discover the meaning of their narrator.

CHAPTER VIII.

Of the Authorship of the Pentateuch and the
Other Historical Books of the Old Testament

IN THE FORMER chapter we treated of the foundations and principles of Scriptural knowledge, and showed that it consists solely in a trustworthy history of the sacred writings; such a history, in spite of its indispensability, the ancients neglected, or at any rate, whatever they may have written or handed down has perished in the lapse of time, consequently the groundwork for such an investigation is to a great extent, cut from under us. This might be put up with if succeeding generations had confined themselves within the limits of truth, and had handed down conscientiously what few particulars they had received or discovered without any additions from their own brains: as it is, the history of the Bible is not so much imperfect as untrustworthy: the foundations are not only too scanty for building upon, but are also unsound. It is part of my purpose to remedy these defects, and to remove common theological prejudices. But I fear that I am attempting my task too late, for men have arrived at the pitch of not suffering contradiction, but defending obstinately whatever they have adopted under the name of religion. So widely have these prejudices taken possession of men's minds, that very few, comparatively speaking, will listen to reason. However, I will make the attempt, and spare no efforts, for there is no positive reason for despairing of success.

In order to treat the subject methodically, I will begin with the received opinions concerning the true authors of the sacred books, and in the first place, speak of the author of the Pentateuch, who is almost universally supposed to have been Moses. The Pharisees are so firmly convinced of his identity, that they account as a heretic anyone who differs from them on the subject. Wherefore, Aben Ezra, a man of enlightened intelligence, and no small learning, who was the first, so far as I know, to treat of this opinion, dared not express his meaning openly, but confined himself to dark hints which I shall not scruple to elucidate, thus throwing, full light on the subject.

The words of Aben Ezra which occur in his commentary on Deuteronomy are as follows: "Beyond Jordan, &c . . . If so be that thou understandest the mystery of the twelve . . . moreover Moses wrote the law . . . The Canaanite was then in the land . . . . it shall be revealed on the mount of God . . . . then also behold his bed, his iron bed, then shalt thou know the truth." In these few words he hints, and also shows that it was not Moses who wrote the Pentateuch, but someone who lived long after him, and further, that the book which Moses wrote was something different from any now extant.

To prove this, I say, he draws attention to the facts:

I. That the preface to Deuteronomy could not have been written by Moses, inasmuch as he ad never crossed the Jordan.

II. That the whole book of Moses was written at full length on the circumference of a single altar (Deut. xxvii, and Josh. viii:37), which altar, according to the Rabbis, consisted of only twelve stones: therefore the book of Moses must have been of far less extent than the Pentateuch. This is what our author means, I think, by the mystery of the twelve, unless he is referring to the twelve curses contained in the chapter of Deuteronomy above cited, which he thought could not have been contained in the law, because Moses bade the Levites read them after the recital of the law, and so bind the people to its observance. Or again, he may have had in his mind the last chapter of Deuteronomy which treats of the death of Moses, and which contains twelve verses. But there is no need to dwell further on these and similar conjectures.

III. That in Deut. xxxi:9, the expression occurs, "and Moses wrote the law:" words that cannot be ascribed to Moses, but must be those of some other writer narrating the deeds and writings of Moses.

IV. That in Genesis xii:6, the historian, after narrating that Abraham journeyed through the and of Canaan, adds, "and the Canaanite was then in the land," thus clearly excluding the time at which he wrote. So that this passage must have been written after the death of Moses, when the Canaanites had been driven out, and no longer possessed the land.

Aben Ezra, in his commentary on the passage, alludes to the difficulty as follows:— "And the Canaanite was then in the land: it appears that Canaan, the grandson of Noah, took from another the land which bears his name; if this be not the true meaning, there lurks some mystery in the passage, and let him who understands it keep silence." That is, if Canaan invaded those regions, the sense will be, the Canaanite was then in the land, in contradistinction to the time when it had been held by another: but if, as follows from Gen. chap. x. Canaan was the first to inhabit the land, the text must mean to exclude the time present, that is the time at which it was written; therefore it cannot be the work of Moses, in whose time the Canaanites still possessed those territories: this is the mystery concerning which silence is recommended.

V. That in Genesis xxii:14 Mount Moriah is called the mount of God, 9, a name which it did not acquire till after the building of the Temple; the choice of the mountain was not made in the time of Moses, for Moses does not point out any spot as chosen by God; on the contrary, he foretells that God will at some future time choose a spot to which this name will be given.

VI. Lastly, that in Deut. chap. iii., in the passage relating to Og, king of Bashan, these words are inserted: "For only Og king of Bashan remained of the remnant of giants: behold, his bedstead was a bedstead of iron: is it not in Rabbath of the children of Ammon? nine cubits was the length thereof, and four cubits the breadth of it, after the cubit of a man." This parenthesis most plainly shows that its writer lived long after Moses; for this mode of speaking is only employed by one treating of things long past, and pointing to relics for the sake of gaining credence: moreover, this bed was almost certainly first discovered by David, who conquered the city of Rabbath (2 Sam. xii:30.) Again, the historian a little further on inserts after the words of Moses, "Jair, the son of Manasseh, took all the country of Argob unto the coasts of Geshuri and Maachathi; and called them after his own name, Bashan-havoth-jair, unto this day." This passage, I say, is inserted to explain the words of Moses which precede it. "And the rest of Gilead, and all Bashan, being the kingdom of Og, gave I unto the half tribe of Manasseh; all the region of Argob, with all Bashan, which is called the land of the giants." The Hebrews in the time of the writer indisputably knew what territories belonged to the tribe of Judah, but did not know them under the name of the jurisdiction of Argob, or the land of the giants. Therefore the writer is compelled to explain what these places were which were anciently so styled, and at the same time to point out why they were at the time of his writing known by the name of Jair, who was of the tribe of Manasseh, not of Judah. We have thus made clear the meaning of Aben Ezra and also the passages of the Pentateuch which he cites in proof of his contention. However, Aben Ezra does not call attention to every instance, or even the chief ones; there remain many of greater importance, which may be cited. Namely (I.), that the writer of the books in question not only speaks of Moses in the third person, but also bears witness to many details concerning him; for instance, "Moses talked with God;" "The Lord spoke with Moses face to face; " "Moses was the meekest of men" (Numb. xii:3); "Moses was wrath with the captains of the host; "Moses, the man of God, "Moses, the servant of the Lord, died;" "There was never a prophet in Israel like unto Moses," &c. On the other hand, in Deuteronomy, where the law which Moses had expounded to the people and written is set forth, Moses speaks and declares what he has done in the first person: "God spake with me " (Deut. ii:1, 17, &c.), "I prayed to the Lord," &c. Except at the end of the book, when the historian, after relating the words of Moses, begins again to speak in the third person, and to tell how Moses handed over the law which he had expounded to the people in writing, again admonishing them, and further, how Moses ended his life. All these details, the manner of narration, the testimony, and the context of the whole story lead to the plain conclusion that these books were written by another, and not by Moses in person.

III. We must also remark that the history relates not only the manner of Moses' death and burial, and the thirty days' mourning of the Hebrews, but further compares him with all the prophets who came after him, and states that he surpassed them all. "There was never a prophet in Israel like unto Moses, whom the Lord knew face to face." Such testimony cannot have been given of Moses by, himself, nor by any who immediately succeeded him, but it must come from someone who lived centuries afterwards, especially, as the historian speaks of past times. "There was never a prophet," &c. And of the place of burial, "No one knows it to this day."

III. We must note that some places are not styled by the names they bore during Moses' lifetime, but by others which they obtained subsequently. For instance, Abraham is said to have pursued his enemies even unto Dan, a name not bestowed on the city till long after the death of Joshua (Gen. xiv;14, Judges xviii;29).

IV. The narrative is prolonged after the death of Moses, for in Exodus xvi:34 we read that "the children of Israel did eat manna forty years until they came to a land inhabited, until they came unto the borders of the land of Canaan." In other words, until the time alluded to in Joshua vi:12.

So, too, in Genesis xxxvi:31 it is stated, "These are the kings that reigned in Edom before there reigned any king over the children of Israel." The historian, doubtless, here relates the kings of Idumaea before that territory was conquered by David 10 and garrisoned, as we read in 2 Sam. viii:14. From what has been said, it is thus clearer than the sun at noonday that the Pentateuch was not written by Moses, but by someone who lived long after Moses. Let us now turn our attention to the books which Moses actually did write, and which are cited in the Pentateuch; thus, also, shall we see that they were different from the Pentateuch. Firstly, it appears from Exodus xvii:14 that Moses, by the command of God, wrote an account of the war against Amalek. The book in which he did so is not named in the chapter just quoted, but in Numb. xxi:12 a book is referred to under the title of the wars of God, and doubtless this war against Amalek and the castrametations said in Numb. xxxiii:2 to have been written by Moses are therein described. We hear also in Exod. xxiv:4 of another book called the Book of the Covenant, which Moses read before the Israelites when they first made a covenant with God. But this book or this writing contained very little, namely, the laws or commandments of God which we find in Exodus xx:22 to the end of chap. xxiv., and this no one will deny who reads the aforesaid chapter rationally and impartially. It is there stated that as soon as Moses had learnt the feeling of the people on the subject of making a covenant with God, he immediately wrote down God's laws and utterances, and in the morning, after some ceremonies had been performed, read out the conditions of the covenant to an assembly of the whole people. When these had been gone through, and doubtless understood by all, the whole people gave their assent.

Now from the shortness of the time taken in its perusal and also from its nature as a compact, this document evidently contained nothing more than that which we have just described. Further, it is clear that Moses explained all the laws which he had received in the fortieth year after the exodus from Egypt; also that he bound over the people a second time to observe them, and that finally he committed them to writing (Deut. i:5; xxix:14; xxxi:9), in a book which contained these laws explained, and the new covenant, and this book was therefore called the book of the law of God: the same which was afterwards added to by Joshua when he set forth the fresh covenant with which he bound over the people and which he entered into with God (Josh. xxiv:25, 26).

Now, as we have extent no book containing this covenant of Moses and also the covenant of Joshua, we must perforce conclude that it has perished, unless, indeed, we adopt the wild conjecture of the Chaldean paraphrast Jonathan, and twist about the words of Scripture to our heart's content. This commentator, in the face of our present difficulty, preferred corrupting the sacred text to confessing his own ignorance. The passage in the book of Joshua which runs, "and Joshua wrote these words in the book of the law of God," he changes into "and Joshua wrote these words and kept them with the book of the law of God." What is to be done with persons who will only see what pleases them? What is such a proceeding if it is not denying Scripture, and inventing another Bible out of our own heads? We may therefore conclude that the book of the law of God which Moses wrote was not the Pentateuch, but something quite different, which the author of the Pentateuch duly inserted into his book. So much is abundantly plain both from what I have said and from what I am about to add. For in the passage of Deuteronomy above quoted, where it is related that Moses wrote the book of the law, the historian adds that he handed it over to the priests and bade them read it out at a stated time to the whole people. This shows that the work was of much less length than the Pentateuch, inasmuch as it could be read through at one sitting so as to be understood by all; further, we must not omit to notice that out of all the books which Moses wrote, this one book of the second covenant and the song (which latter he wrote afterwards so that all the people might learn it), was the only one which he caused to be religiously guarded and preserved. In the first covenant he had only bound over those who were present, but in the second covenant he bound over all their descendants also (Dent. xxix:14), and therefore ordered this covenant with future ages to be religiously preserved, together with the Song, which was especially addressed to posterity: as, then, we have no proof that Moses wrote any book save this of the covenant, and as he committed no other to the care of posterity; and, lastly, as there are many passages in the Pentateuch which Moses could not have written, it follows that the belief that Moses was the author of the Pentateuch is ungrounded and even irrational. Someone will perhaps ask whether Moses did not also write down other laws when they were first revealed to him — in other words, whether, during the course of forty years, he did not write down any of the laws which he promulgated, save only those few which I have stated to be contained in the book of the first covenant. To this I would answer, that although it seems reasonable to suppose that Moses wrote down the laws at the time when he wished to communicate them to the people, yet we are not warranted to take it as proved, for I have shown above that we must make no assertions in such matters which we do not gather from Scripture, or which do not flow as legitimate consequences from its fundamental principles. We must not accept whatever is reasonably probable. However even reason in this case would not force such a conclusion upon us: for it may be that the assembly of elders wrote down the decrees of Moses and communicated them to the people, and the historian collected them, and duly set them forth in his narrative of the life of Moses. So much for the five books of Moses: it is now time for us to turn to the other sacred writings.

The book of Joshua may be proved not to be an autograph by reasons similar to those we have just employed: for it must be some other than Joshua who testifies that the fame of Joshua was spread over the whole world; that he omitted nothing of what Moses had taught (Josh. vi:27; viii. last verse; xi:15); that he grew old and summoned an assembly of the whole people, and finally that he departed this life. Furthermore, events are related which took place after Joshua's death. For instance, that the Israelites worshipped God, after his death, so long as there were any old men alive who remembered him; and in chap. xvi:10, we read that "Ephraim and Manasseh did not drive out the Canaanites which dwelt in Gezer, but the Canaanite dwelt in the land of Ephraim unto this day, and was tributary to him." This is the same statement as that in Judges, chap. i., and the phrase "unto this day" shows that the writer was speaking of ancient times. With these texts we may compare the last verse of chap. xv., concerning the sons of Judah, and also the history of Caleb in the same chap. v:14. Further, the building of an altar beyond Jordan by the two tribes and a half, chap. xxii:10, sqq., seems to have taken place after the death of Joshua, for in the whole narrative his name is never mentioned, but the people alone held council as to waging war, sent out legates, waited for their return, and finally approved of their answer.

Lastly, from chap. x:14, it is clear that the book was written many generations after the death of Joshua, for it bears witness, there was never any, day like unto, that day, either before or after, that the Lord hearkened to the voice of a man," &c. If, therefore, Joshua wrote any book at all, it was that which is quoted in the work now before us, chap. x:13.

With regard to the book of Judges, I suppose no rational person persuades himself that it was written by the actual Judges. For the conclusion of the whole history contained in chap. ii. clearly shows that it is all the work — of a single historian. Further, inasmuch as the writer frequently tells us that there was then no king in Israel, it is evident that the book was written after the establishment of the monarchy.

The books of Samuel need not detain us long, inasmuch as the narrative in them is continued long after Samuel's death; but I should like to draw attention to the fact that it was written many generations after Samuel's death. For in book i. chap. ix:9, the historian remarks in a, parenthesis, "Beforetime, in Israel, when a man went to inquire of God, thus he spake: Come, and let us go to the seer; for he that is now called a prophet was beforetime called a seer."

Lastly, the books of Kings, as we gather from internal evidence, were compiled from the books of King Solomon (I Kings xi:41), from the chronicles of the kings of Judah (1 Kings xiv:19, 29), and the chronicles of the kings of Israel.

We may, therefore, conclude that all the books we have considered hitherto are compilations, and that the events therein are recorded as having happened in old time. Now, if we turn our attention to the connection and argument of all these books, we shall easily see that they were all written by a single historian, who wished to relate the antiquities of the Jews from their first beginning down to the first destruction of the city. The way in which the several books are connected one with the other is alone enough to show us that they form the narrative of one and the same writer. For as soon as he has related the life of Moses, the historian thus passes on to the story of Joshua: "And it came to pass after that Moses the servant of the Lord was dead, that God spake unto Joshua," &c., so in the same way, after the death of Joshua was concluded, he passes with identically the same transition and connection to the history of the Judges: "And it came to pass after that Joshua was dead, that the children of Israel sought from God," &c. To the book of Judges he adds the story of Ruth, as a sort of appendix, in these words: "Now it came to pass in the days that the judges ruled, that there was a famine in the land."

The first book of Samuel is introduced with a similar phrase; and so is the second book of Samuel. Then, before the history of David is concluded, the historian passes in the same way to the first book of Kings, and, after David's death, to the Second book of Kings.

The putting together, and the order of the narratives, show that they are all the work of one man, writing with a create aim; for the historian begins with relating the first origin of the Hebrew nation, and then sets forth in order the times and the occasions in which Moses put forth his laws, and made his predictions. He then proceeds to relate how the Israelites invaded the promised land in accordance with Moses' prophecy (Deut. vii.); and how, when the land was subdued, they turned their backs on their laws, and thereby incurred many misfortunes (Deut. xxxi:16, 17). He tells how they wished to elect rulers, and how, according as these rulers observed the law, the people flourished or suffered (Deut. xxviii:36); finally, how destruction came upon the nation, even as Moses had foretold. In regard to other matters, which do not serve to confirm the law, the writer either passes over them in silence, or refers the reader to other books for information. All that is set down in the books we have conduces to the sole object of setting forth the words and laws of Moses, and proving them by subsequent events.When we put together these three considerations, namely, the unity of the subject of all the books, the connection between them, and the fact that they are compilations made many generations after the events they relate had taken place, we come to the conclusion, as I have just stated, that they are all the work of a single historian. Who this historian was, it is not so easy to show; but I suspect that he was Ezra, and there are several strong reasons for adopting this hypothesis.

The historian whom we already know to be but one individual brings his history down to the liberation of Jehoiakim, and adds that he himself sat at the king's table all his life — that is, at the table either of Jehoiakim, or of the son of Nebuchadnezzar, for the sense of the passage is ambiguous: hence it follows that he did not live before the time of Ezra. But Scripture does not testify of any except of Ezra (Ezra vii:10), that he "prepared his heart to seek the law of the Lord, and to set it forth, and further that he was a ready scribe in the law of Moses." Therefore, I can not find anyone, save Ezra, to whom to attribute the sacred books.

Further, from this testimony concerning Ezra, we see that he prepared his heart, not only to seek the law of the Lord, but also to set it forth; and, in Nehemiah viii:8, we read that "they read in the book of the law of God distinctly, and gave the sense, and caused them to understand the reading."

As, then, in Deuteronomy, we find not only the book of the law of Moses, or the greater part of it, but also many things inserted for its better explanation, I conjecture that this Deuteronomy is the book of the law of God, written, set forth, and explained by Ezra, which is referred to in the text above quoted. Two examples of the way matters were inserted parenthetically in the text of Deuteronomy, with a view to its fuller explanation, we have already given, in speaking of Aben Ezra's opinion. Many others are found in the course of the work: for instance, in chap. ii:12: "The Horims dwelt also in Seir beforetime; but the children of Esau succeeded them, when they had destroyed them from before them, and dwelt in their stead; as Israel did unto the land of his possession, which the Lord gave unto them." This explains verses 3 and 4 of the same chapter, where it is stated that Mount Seir, which had come to the children of Esau for a possession, did not fall into their hands uninhabited; but that they invaded it, and turned out and destroyed the Horims, who formerly dwelt therein, even as the children of Israel had done unto the Canaanites after the death of Moses.

So, also, verses 6, 7, 8, 9, of the tenth chapter are inserted parenthetically among the words of Moses. Everyone must see that verse 8, which begins, "At that time the Lord separated the tribe of Levi," necessarily refers to verse 5, and not to the death of Aaron, which is only mentioned here by Ezra because Moses, in telling of the golden calf worshipped by the people, stated that he had prayed for Aaron.

He then explains that at the time at which Moses spoke, God had chosen for Himself the tribe of Levi in order that He may point out the reason for their election, and for the fact of their not sharing in the inheritance; after this digression, he resumes the thread of Moses' speech. To these parentheses we must add the preface to the book, and all the passages in which Moses is spoken of in the third person, besides many which we cannot now distinguish, though, doubtless, they would have been plainly recognized by the writer's contemporaries.

If, I say, we were in possession of the book of the law as Moses wrote it, I do not doubt that we should find a great difference in the words of the precepts, the order in which they are given, and the reasons by which they are supported.

A comparison of the decalogue in Deuteronomy with the decalogue in Exodus, where its history is explicitly set forth, will be sufficient to show us a wide discrepancy in all these three particulars, for the fourth commandment is given not only in a different form, but at much greater length, while the reason for its observance differs wholly from that stated in Exodus. Again, the order in which the tenth commandment is explained differs in the two versions. I think that the differences here as elsewhere are the work of Ezra, who explained the law of God to his contemporaries, and who wrote this book of the law of God, before anything else; this I gather from the fact that it contains the laws of the country, of which the people stood in most need, and also because it is not joined to the book which precedes it by any connecting phrase, but begins with the independent statement, "these are the words of Moses." After this task was completed, I think Ezra set himself to give a complete account of the history of the Hebrew nation from the creation of the world to the entire destruction of the city, and in this account he inserted the book of Deuteronomy, and, possibly, he called the first five books by the name of Moses, because his life is chiefly contained therein, and forms their principal subject; for the same reason he called the sixth Joshua, the seventh Judges, the eighth Ruth, the ninth, and perhaps the tenth, Samuel, and, lastly, the eleventh and twelfth Kings. Whether Ezra put the finishing touches to this work and finished it as he intended, we will discuss in the next chapter.

9 "Mount Moriah is called the mount of God." That is by the historian, not by Abraham, for he says that the place now called "In the mount of the Lord it shall be revealed," was called by Abraham, "the Lord shall provide."

10 "Before that territory [Idumoea] was conquered by David." From this time to the reign of Jehoram when they again separated from the Jewish kingdom (2 Kings viii:20), the Idumaeans had no king, princes appointed by the Jews supplied the place of kings (1 Kings xxii:48), in fact the prince of Idumaea is called a king (2 Kings iii:9).

It may be doubted whether the last of the Idumaean kings had begun to reign before the accession of Saul, or whether Scripture in this chapter of Genesis wished to enumerate only such kings as were independent. It is evidently mere trifling to wish to enrol among Hebrew kings the name of Moses, who set up a dominion entirely different from a monarchy.

CHAPTER IX.

Other questions concerning the same Books: namely, whether they were
completely finished by Ezra, and, further, whether the Marginal notes which are
found in the Hebrew texts were various readings.

HOW GREATLY THE inquiry we have just made concerning the real writer of the
twelve books aids us in attaining a complete understanding of them, may be easily
gathered solely from the passages which we have adduced in confirmation of our
opinion, and which would be most obscure without it. But besides the question of
the writer, there are other points to notice which common superstition forbids the
multitude to apprehend. Of these the chief is, that Ezra (whom I will take to be the
author of the aforesaid books until some more likely person be suggested) did not
put the finishing touches to the narrative contained therein, but merely collected
the histories from various writers, and sometimes simply set them down, leaving
their examination and arrangement to posterity.

The cause (if it were not untimely death) which prevented him from completing
his work in all its portions, I cannot conjecture, but the fact remains most clear,
although we have lost the writings of the ancient Hebrew historians, and can only
judge from the few fragments which are still extant. For the history of Hezekiah
(2 Kings xviii:17), as written in the vision of Isaiah, is related as it is found in the
chronicles of the kings of Judah. We read the same story, told with few exceptions,
11, in the same words, in the book of Isaiah which was contained in the chronicles
of the kings of Judah (2 Chron. xxxii:32). From this we must conclude that there
were various versions of this narrative of Isaiah's, unless, indeed, anyone would
dream that in this, too, there lurks a mystery. Further, the last chapter of 2 Kings
27-30 is repeated in the last chapter of Jeremiah, v.31-34.

Again, we find 2 Sam. vii. repeated in I Chron. xvii., but the expressions in the
two passages are so curiously varied 12, that we can very easily see that these two
chapters were taken from two different versions of the history of Nathan.

Lastly, the genealogy of the kings of Idumaea contained in Genesis xxxvi:31, is
repeated in the same words in 1 Chron. i., though we know that the author of the
latter work took his materials from other historians, not from the twelve books
we have ascribed to Ezra. We may therefore be sure that if we still possessed the
writings of the historians, the matter would be made clear; however, as we have
lost them, we can only examine the writings still extant, and from their order and
connection, their various repetitions, and, lastly, the contradictions in dates which
they contain, judge of the rest.

These, then, or the chief of them, we will now go through. First, in the story of
Judah and Tamar (Gen. xxxviii.) the historian thus begins: "And it came to pass at
that time that Judah went down from his brethren." This time cannot refer to what
immediately precedes 13, but must necessarily refer to something else, for from
the time when Joseph was sold into Egypt to the time when the patriarch Jacob,
with all his family, set out thither, cannot be reckoned as more than twenty-two
years, for Joseph, when he was sold by his brethren, was seventeen years old, and
when he was summoned by Pharaoh from prison was thirty; if to this we add the
seven years of plenty and two of famine, the total amounts to twenty-two years.
Now, in so short a period, no one can suppose that so many things happened as are
described; that Judah had three children, one after the other, from one wife, whom

he married at the beginning of the period; that the eldest of these, when he was old enough, married Tamar, and that after he died his next brother succeeded to her; that, after all this, Judah, without knowing it, had intercourse with his daughter-inlaw, and that she bore him twins, and, finally, that the eldest of these twins became a father within the aforesaid period. As all these events cannot have taken place within the period mentioned in Genesis, the reference must necessarily be to something treated of in another book: and Ezra in this instance simply related the story, and inserted it without examination among his other writings.

However, not only this chapter but the whole narrative of Joseph and Jacob is collected and set forth from various histories, inasmuch as it is quite inconsistent with itself. For in Gen. xlvii. we are told that Jacob, when he came at Joseph's bidding to salute Pharaoh, was 130 years old. If from this we deduct the twenty-two years which he passed sorrowing for the absence of Joseph and the seventeen years forming Joseph's age when he was sold, and, lastly, the seven years for which Jacob served for Rachel, we find that he was very advanced in life, namely, eighty four, when he took Leah to wife, whereas Dinah was scarcely seven years old when she was violated by Shechem, 14. Simeon and Levi were aged respectively eleven and twelve when they spoiled the city and slew all the males therein with the sword.

There is no need that I should go through the whole Pentateuch. If anyone pays attention to the way in which all the histories and precepts in these five books are set down promiscuously and without order, with no regard for dates; and further, how the same story is often repeated, sometimes in a different version, he will easily, I say, discern that all the materials were promiscuously collected and heaped together, in order that they might at some subsequent time be more readily examined and reduced to order. Not only these five books, but also the narratives contained in the remaining seven, going down to the destruction of the city, are compiled in the same way. For who does not see that in Judges ii:6 a new historian is being quoted, who had also written of the deeds of Joshua, and that his words are simply copied? For after our historian has stated in the last chapter of the book of Joshua that Joshua died and was buried, and has promised, in the first chapter of Judges, to relate what happened after his death, in what way, if he wished to continue the thread of his history, could he connect the statement here made about Joshua with what had gone before?

So, too, 1 Sam. 17, 18, are taken from another historian, who assigns a cause for David's first frequenting Saul's court very different from that given in chap. xvi. of the same book. For he did not think that David came to Saul in consequence of the advice of Saul's servants, as is narrated in chap. xvi., but that being sent by chance to the camp by his father on a message to his brothers, he was for the first time remarked by Saul on the occasion of his victory, over Goliath the Philistine, and was retained at his court.

I suspect the same thing has taken place in chap. xxvi. of the same book, for the historian there seems to repeat the narrative given in chap. xxiv. according to another man's version. But I pass over this, and go on to the computation of dates.

In I Kings, chap. vi., it is said that Solomon built the Temple in the four hundred and eightieth year after the exodus from Egypt; but from the historians themselves we get a much longer period, for:

	Years
Moses governed the people in the desert	40
Joshua, who lived 110 years, did not, according to Josephus and others' opinion rule more than	26
Cusban Rishathaim held the people in subjection	8
Othniel, son of Kenag, was judge for 15	40
Eglon, King of Moab, governed the people	18
Ehucl and Shamgar were judges	80
Jachin, King of Canaan, held the people in subjection	20
The people was at peace subsequently for	40
It was under subjection to Median	7
It obtained f r e e d o m under Gideon for	40

It fell under the rule of Abimelech	3
Tola, son of Puah, was judge	23
Jair was judge	22
The people was in subjection to the Philistines a n d Ammonites	18
Jephthah was judge	6
Ibzan, the Bethlehemite, was judge	7
Elon, the Zabulonite	10
Abclon, the Pirathonite	8
The people was again subject to the Philistines	40
Samson was judge 16	20
Eli was judge	40
The people again fell into s u b j e c t i o n to the Philistines, till they were delivered by Samuel	20
David reigned	40
S o l o m o n r e i g n e d before he built the temple	4

All these periods added together make a total of 580 years. But to these must be added the years during which the Hebrew republic flourished after the death of Joshua, until it was conquered by Cushan Rishathaim, which I take to be very numerous, for I cannot bring myself to believe that immediately after the death of Joshua all those who had witnessed his miracles died simultaneously, nor that their successors at one stroke bid farewell to their laws, and plunged from the highest virtue into the depth of wickedness and obstinacy.

Nor, lastly, that Cushan Rishathaim subdued them on the instant; each one of these circumstances requires almost a generation, and there is no doubt that Judges ii:7, 9, 10, comprehends a great many years which it passes over in silence. We must also add the years during which Samuel was judge, the number of which is not stated in Scripture, and also the years during which Saul reigned, which are not clearly shown from his history. It is, indeed, stated in 1 Sam. xiii:1, that he reigned two years, but the text in that passage is mutilated, and the records of his reign lead us to suppose a longer period. That the text is mutilated I suppose no one will doubt who has ever advanced so far as the threshold of the Hebrew language, for it runs as follows: "Saul was in his — year, when he began to reign, and he reigned two years over Israel." Who, I say, does not see that the number of the years of Saul's age when he began to reign has been omitted? That the record of the reign presupposes a greater number of years is equally beyond doubt, for in the same book, chap. xxvii:7, it is stated that David sojourned among the Philistines, to whom he had fled on account of Saul, a year and four months; thus the rest of the reign must have been comprised in a space of eight months, which I think no one will credit. Josephus, at the end of the sixth book of his antiquities, thus corrects the text: Saul reigned eighteen years while Samuel was alive, and two years after his death. However, all the narrative in chap. Xiii. is in complete disagreement with what goes before. At the end of chap. vii. it is narrated that the Philistines were so crushed by the Hebrews that they did not venture, during Samuel's life, to invade the borders of Israel; but in chap. xiii. we are told that the Hebrews were invaded during the life of Samuel by the Philistines, and reduced by them to such a state of wretchedness and poverty that they were deprived not only of weapons with which to defend themselves, but also of the means of making more. I should be at pains enough if I were to try and harmonize all the narratives contained in this first book of Samuel so that they should seem to be all written and arranged by a single historian. But I return to my object. The years, then, during which Saul reigned must be added to the above computation; and, lastly, I have not counted the years of the Hebrew anarchy, for I cannot from Scripture gather their number. I cannot, I say, be certain as to the period occupied by the events related in Judges chap. xvii. on till the end of the book.

It is thus abundantly evident that we cannot arrive at a true computation of years from the histories, and, further, that the histories are inconsistent themselves on the subject. We are compelled to confess that these histories were compiled from various writers without previous arrangement and examination. Not less discrepancy is found between the dates given in the Chronicles of the Kings of Judah, and those in the Chronicles of the Kings of Israel; in the latter, it is stated that Jehoram, the son of Ahab, began to reign in the second year of the reign of Jehoram, the son of Jehoshaphat (2 Kings i:17), but in the former we read that Jehoram, the son of Jehoshaphat, began to reign in the fifth year of Jehoram, the son of Ahab (2 Kings viii:16). Anyone who compares the narratives in Chronicles with the narratives in the books of Kings, will find many similar discrepancies. These there is no need for me to examine here, and still less am I called upon to treat of the commentaries of those who endeavour to harmonize them. The Rabbis evidently let their fancy run wild. Such commentators as I have, read, dream, invent, and as a last resort, play fast and loose with the language. For instance, when it is said in 2 Chronicles, that Ahab was forty-two years old when he began to reign, they pretend that these years are computed from the reign of Omri, not from the birth of Ahab. If this can be shown to be the real meaning of the writer of the book of Chronicles, all I can say is, that he did not know how to state a fact. The commentators make many other assertions of this kind, which if true, would prove that the ancient Hebrews were ignorant both of their own language, and of the way to relate a plain narrative. I should in such case recognize no rule or reason in interpreting Scripture, but it would be permissible to hypothesize to one's heart's content.

If anyone thinks that I am speaking too generally, and without sufficient warrant, I would ask him to set himself to showing us some fixed plan in these histories which might be followed without blame by other writers of chronicles, and in his efforts at harmonizing and interpretation, so strictly to observe and explain the phrases and expressions, the order and the connections, that we may be able to imitate these also in our writings 17. If he succeeds, I will at once give him my hand, and he shall be to me as great Apollo; for I confess that after long endeavours I have been unable to discover anything of the kind. I may add that I set down nothing here which I have not long reflected upon, and that, though I was imbued from my boyhood up with the ordinary opinions about the Scriptures, I have been unable to withstand the force of what I have urged.

However, there is no need to detain the reader with this question, and drive him to attempt an impossible task; I merely mentioned the fact in order to throw light on my intention.

I now pass on to other points concerning the treatment of these books. For we must remark, in addition to what has been shown, that these books were not guarded by posterity with such care that no faults crept in. The ancient scribes draw attention to many doubtful readings, and some mutilated passages, but not to all that exist: whether the faults are of sufficient importance to greatly embarrass the reader I will not now discuss. I am inclined to think that they are of minor moment to those, at any rate, who read the Scriptures with enlightenment: and I can positively, affirm that I have not noticed any fault or various reading in doctrinal passages sufficient to render them obscure or doubtful.

There are some people, however, who will not admit that there is any corruption, even in other passages, but maintain that by some unique exercise of providence God has preserved from corruption every word in the Bible: they say that the various readings are the symbols of profoundest mysteries, and that mighty secrets lie hid in the twenty-eight hiatus which occur, nay, even in the very form of the letters.

Whether they are actuated by folly and anile devotion, or whether by arrogance and malice so that they alone may be held to possess the secrets of God, I know not: this much I do know, that I find in their writings nothing which has the air of a Divine secret, but only childish lucubrations. I have read and known certain Kabbalistic triflers, whose insanity provokes my unceasing as astonishment. That faults have crept in will, I think, be denied by no sensible person who reads the passage about Saul, above quoted (1 Sam. xiii:1) and also 2 Sam. vi:2: "And David arose and went with all the people that were with him from Judah, to bring up from thence the ark of God."

No one can fail to remark that the name of their destination, viz., Kirjath-jearim

18, has been omitted: nor can we deny that 2 Sam. xiii:37, has been tampered with and mutilated. "And Absalom fled, and went to Talmai, the son of Ammihud, king of Geshur. And he mourned for his son every day. So Absalom fled, and went to Geshur, and was there three years." I know that I have remarked other passages of the same kind, but I cannot recall them at the moment.

That the marginal notes which are found continually in the Hebrew Codices are doubtful readings will, I think, be evident to everyone who has noticed that they often arise from the great similarity, of some of the Hebrew letters, such for instance, as the similarity between Kaph and Beth, Jod and Van, Daleth and Reth, &c. For example, the text in 2 Sam. v:24, runs "in the time when thou hearest," and similarly in Judges xxi:22, "And it shall be when their fathers or their brothers come unto us often," the marginal version is "come unto us to complain."

So also many various readings have arisen from the use of the letters named mutes, which are generally not sounded in pronunciation, and are taken promiscuously, one for the other. For example, in Levit. xxv:29, it is written, "The house shall be established which is not in the walled city," but the margin has it, "which is in a walled city."

Though these matters are self-evident, [Endnore 6], it is necessary, to answer the reasonings of certain Pharisees, by which they endeavour to convince us that the marginal notes serve to indicate some mystery, and were added or pointed out by the writers of the sacred books. The first of these reasons, which, in my, opinion, carries little weight, is taken from the practice of reading the Scriptures aloud.

If, it is urged, these notes were added to show various readings which could not be decided upon by posterity, why has custom prevailed that the marginal readings should always be retained? Why has the meaning which is preferred been set down in the margin when it ought to have been incorporated in the text, and not relegated to a side note?

The second reason is more specious, and is taken from the nature of the case. It is admitted that faults have crept into the sacred writings by chance and not by design; but they say that in the five books the word for a girl is, with one exception, written without the letter "he," contrary to all grammatical rules, whereas in the margin it is written correctly according to the universal rule of grammar. Can this have happened by mistake? Is it possible to imagine a clerical error to have been committed every, time the word occurs? Moreover, it would have been easy, to supply the emendation. Hence, when these readings are not accidental or corrections of manifest mistakes, it is supposed that they must have been set down on purpose by the original writers, and have a meaning. However, it is easy to answer such arguments; as to the question of custom having prevailed in the reading of the marginal versions, I will not spare much time for its consideration: I know not the promptings of superstition, and perhaps the practice may have arisen from the idea that both readings were deemed equally good or tolerable, and therefore, lest either should be neglected, one was appointed to be written, and the other to be read. They feared to pronounce judgment in so weighty a matter lest they should mistake the false for the true, and therefore they would give preference to neither, as they must necessarily have done if they had commanded one only to be both read and written. This would be especially the case where the marginal readings were not written down in the sacred books: or the custom may have originated because some things though rightly written down were desired to be read otherwise according to the marginal version, and therefore the general rule was made that the marginal version should be followed in reading the Scriptures. The cause which induced the scribes to expressly prescribe certain passages to be read in the marginal version, I will now touch on, for not all the marginal notes are various readings, but some mark expressions which have passed out of common use, obsolete words and terms which current decency did not allow to be read in a public assembly. The ancient writers, without any evil intention, employed no courtly paraphrase, but called things by their plain names. Afterwards, through the spread of evil thoughts and luxury, words which could be used by the ancients without offence, came to be considered obscene. There was no need for this cause to change the text of Scripture. Still, as a concession to the popular weakness, it became the custom to substitute more decent terms for words denoting sexual intercourse, exereta, &c., and to read them as they were given in the margin.

At any rate, whatever may have been the origin of the practice of reading Scripture according to the marginal version, it was not that the true interpretation is contained therein. For besides that, the Rabbins in the Talmud often differ from the Massoretes, and give other readings which they approve of, as I will shortly show, certain things are found in the margin which appear less warranted by the uses of the Hebrew language. For example, in 2 Samuel xiv:22, we read, "In that the king hath fulfilled the request of his servant," a construction plainly regular, and agreeing with that in chap. xvi. But the margin has it "of thy servant," which does not agree with the person of the verb. So, too, chap. xvi:25 of the same book, we find, "As if one had inquired at the oracle of God," the margin adding "someone" to stand as a nominative to the verb. But the correction is not apparently warranted, for it is a common practice, well known to grammarians in the Hebrew language, to use the third person singular of the active verb impersonally.

The second argument advanced by the Pharisees is easily answered from what has just been said, namely, that the scribes besides the various readings called attention to obsolete words. For there is no doubt that in Hebrew as in other languages, changes of use made many words obsolete and antiquated, and such were found by the later scribes in the sacred books and noted by them with a view to the books being publicly read according to custom. For this reason the word nahgar is always found marked because its gender was originally common, and it had the same meaning as the Latin juvenis (a young person). So also the Hebrew capital was anciently called Jerusalem, not Jerusalaim. As to the pronouns himself and herself, I think that the later scribes changed vau into jod (a very frequent change in Hebrew) when they wished to express the feminine gender, but that the ancients only distinguished the two genders by a change of vowels. I may also remark that the irregular tenses of certain verbs differ in the ancient and modern forms, it being formerly considered a mark of elegance to employ certain letters agreeable to the ear.

In a word, I could easily multiply proofs of this kind if I were not afraid of abusing the patience of the reader. Perhaps I shall be asked how I became acquainted with the fact that all these expressions are obsolete. I reply that I have found them in the most ancient Hebrew writers in the Bible itself, and that they have not been imitated by subsequent authors, and thus they are recognized as antiquated, though the language in which they occur is dead. But perhaps someone may press the question why, if it be true, as I say, that the marginal notes of the Bible generally mark various readings, there are never more than two readings of a passage, that in the text and that in the margin, instead of three or more; and further, how the scribes can have hesitated between two readings, one of which is evidently contrary to grammar, and the other a plain correction.

The answer to these questions also is easy: I will premise that it is almost certain that there once were more various readings than those now recorded. For instance, one finds many in the Talmud which the Massoretes have neglected, and are so different one from the other that even the superstitious editor of the Bomberg Bible confesses that he cannot harmonize them. "We cannot say anything," he writes, "except what we have said above, namely, that the Talmud is generally in contradiction to the Massorete." So that we are nor bound to hold that there never were more than two readings of any passage, yet I am willing to admit, and indeed I believe that more than two readings are never found: and for the following reasons: — (I.) The cause of the differences of reading only admits of two, being generally the similarity of certain letters, so that the question resolved itself into which should be written Beth, or Kaf, Jod or Vau, Daleth or Reth: cases which are constantly occurring, and frequently yielding a fairly good meaning whichever alternative be adopted. Sometimes, too, it is a question whether a syllable be long or short, quantity being determined by the letters called mutes. Moreover, we never asserted that all the marginal versions, without exception, marked various readings; on the contrary, we have stated that many were due to motives of decency or a desire to explain obsolete words. (II.) I am inclined to attribute the fact that more than two readings are never found to the paucity of exemplars, perhaps not more than two or three, found by the scribes. In the treatise of the scribes, chap. vi., mention is made of three only, pretended to have been found in the time of Ezra, in order that the marginal versions might be attributed to him.

However that may be, if the scribes only had three codices we may easily imagine that in a given passage two of them would be in accord, for it would be extraordinary if each one of the three gave a different reading of the same text.

The dearth of copies after the time of Ezra will surprise no one who has read the 1st chapter of Maccabees, or Josephus's "Antiquities," Bk. 12, chap. 5. Nay, it appears wonderful considering the fierce and daily persecution, that even these few should have been preserved. This will, I think, be plain to even a cursory reader of the history of those times.

We have thus discovered the reasons why there are never more than two readings of a passage in the Bible, but this is a long way from supposing that we may therefore conclude that the Bible was purposely written incorrectly in such passages in order to signify some mystery. As to the second argument, that some passages are so faultily written that they are at plain variance with all grammar, and should have been corrected in the text and not in the margin, I attach little weight to it, for I am not concerned to say what religious motive the scribes may have had for acting as they did: possibly they did so from candour, wishing to transmit the few exemplars of the Bible which they had found exactly in their original state, marking the differences they discovered in the margin, not as doubtful readings, but as simple variants. I have myself called them doubtful readings, because it would be generally impossible to say which of the two versions is preferable.

Lastly, besides these doubtful readings the scribes have (by leaving a hiatus in the middle of a paragraph) marked several passages as mutilated. The Massoretes have counted up such instances, and they amount to eight-and-twenty. I do not know whether any mystery is thought to lurk in the number, at any rate the Pharisees religiously preserve a certain amount of empty space.

One of such hiatus occurs (to give an instance) in Gen. iv:8, where it is written, "And Cain said to his brother . . . . and it came to pass while they were in the field, &c.," a space being left in which we should expect to hear what it was that Cain said.

Similarly there are (besides those points we have noticed) eight-and-twenty hiatus left by the scribes. Many of these would not be recognized as mutilated if it were not for the empty space left. But I have said enough on this subject.

11 "With few exceptions." One of these exceptions is found in 2 Kings xviii:20, where we read, "Thou sayest (but they are but vain words)," the second person being used. In Isaiah xxxvi:5, we read "I say (but they are but vain words) I have counsel and strength for war," and in the twenty-second verse of the chapter in Kings it is written, "But if ye say," the plural number being used, whereas Isaiah gives the singular. The text in Isaiah does not contain the words found in 2 Kings xxxii:32. Thus there are several cases of various readings where it is impossible to distinguish the best.

12 "The expressions in the two passages are so varied." For instance we read in 2 Sam. vii:6, "But I have walked in a tent and in a tabernacle." Whereas in 1 Chron. xvii:5, "but have gone from tent to tent and from one tabernacle to another." In 2 Sam. vii:10, we read, "to afflict them," whereas in 1 Chron. vii:9, we find a different expression. I could point out other differences still greater, but a single reading of the chapters in question will suffice to make them manifest to all who are neither blind nor devoid of sense.

13 "This time cannot refer to what immediately precedes." It is plain from the context that this passage must allude to the time when Joseph was sold by his brethren. But this is not all. We may draw the same conclusion from the age of Judah, who was than twenty-two years old at most, taking as basis of calculation his own history just narrated. It follows, indeed, from the last verse of Gen. xxx., that Judah was born in the tenth of the years of Jacob's servitude to Laban, and Joseph in the fourteenth. Now, as we know that Joseph was seventeen years old when sold by his brethren, Judah was then not more than twenty-one. Hence, those writers who assert that Judah's long absence from his father's house took place before Joseph was sold, only seek to delude themselves and to call in question the Scriptural authority which they are anxious to protect.

14 "Dinah was scarcely seven years old when she was violated by Schechem." The opinion held by some that Jacob wandered about eight or ten years between Mesopotamia and Bethel, savours of the ridiculous; if respect for Aben Ezra allows me to say so. For it is clear that Jacob had two reasons for haste: first, the desire to see his old parents; secondly, and chiefly to perform, the vow made when he fled from his brother (Gen. xxviii:10 and xxxi:13, and xxxv:1). We read (Gen. xxxi:3), that God had commanded him to fulfill his vow, and promised him help for returning to his country. If these considerations seem conjectures rather than reasons, I will waive the point and admit that Jacob, more unfortunate than Ulysses, spent eight or ten years or even longer, in this short journey. At any rate it cannot be denied that Benjamin was born in the last year of this wandering, that is by the reckoning of the objectors, when Joseph was sixteen or seventeen years old, for Jacob left Laban seven years after Joseph's birth. Now from the seventeenth year of Joseph's age till the patriarch went into Egypt, not more than twenty-two years elapsed, as we have shown in this chapter. Consequently Benjamin, at the time of the journey to Egypt, was twenty-three or twenty-four at the most. He

would therefore have been a grandfather in the flower of his age (Gen. xlvi:21, cf. Numb. xxvi:38, 40, and 1 Chron. viii;1), for it is certain that Bela, Benjamin's eldest son, had at that time, two sons, Addai and Naa-man. This is just as absurd as the statement that Dinah was violated at the age of seven, not to mention other impossibilities which would result from the truth of the narrative. Thus we see that unskillful endeavours to solve difficulties, only raise fresh ones, and make confusion worse confounded.

15 "Othniel, son of Kenag, was judge for forty years." Rabbi Levi Ben Gerson and others believe that these forty years which the Bible says were passed in freedom, should be counted from the death of Joshua, and consequently include the eight years during which the people were subject to Kushan Rishathaim, while the following eighteen years must be added on to the eighty years of Ehud's and Shamgar's judgeships. In this case it would be necessary to reckon the other years of subjection among those said by the Bible to have been passed in freedom. But the Bible expressly notes the number of years of subjection, and the number of years of freedom, and further declares (Judges ii:18) that the Hebrew state was prosperous during the whole time of the judges. Therefore it is evident that Levi Ben Gerson (certainly a very learned man), and those who follow him, correct rather than interpret the Scriptures.

The same fault is committed by those who assert, that Scripture, by this general calculation of years, only intended to mark the period of the regular administration of the Hebrew state, leaving out the years of anarchy and subjection as periods of misfortune and interregnum. Scripture certainly passes over in silence periods of anarchy, but does not, as they dream, refuse to reckon them or wipe them out of the country's annals. It is clear that Ezra, in 1 Kings vi., wished to reckon absolutely all the years since the flight from Egypt. This is so plain, that no one versed in the Scriptures can doubt it. For, without going back to the precise words of the text, we may see that the genealogy of David given at the end of the book of Ruth, and I Chron. ii., scarcely accounts for so great a number of years. For Nahshon, who was prince of the tribe of Judah (Numb. vii;11), two years after the Exodus, died in the desert, and his son Salmon passed the Jordan with Joshua. Now this Salmon, according to the genealogy, was David's great-grandfather. Deducting, then, from the total of 480 years, four years for Solomon's reign, seventy for David's life, and forty for the time passed in the desert, we find that David was born 366 years after the passage of the Jordan. Hence we must believe that David's father, grandfather, great-grandfather, and great-great-grandfather begat children when they were ninety years old.

16 "Samson was judge for twenty years." Samson was born after the Hebrews had fallen under the dominion of the Philistines.

17 Otherwise, they rather correct than explain Scripture.

18 "Kirjath-jearim." Kirjath-jearim is also called Baale of Judah. Hence Kimchi and others think that the words Baale Judah, which I have translated "the people of Judah," are the name of a town. But this is not so, for the word Baale is in the plural. Moreover, comparing this text in Samuel with I Chron. Xiii:5, we find that David did not rise up and go forth out of Baale, but that he went thither. If the author of the book of Samuel had meant to name the place whence David took the ark, he would, if he spoke Hebrew correctly, have said, "David rose up, and set forth from Baale Judah, and took the ark from thence."

CHAPTER X.

An Examination of the Remaining Books of the Old Testament
According to the Preceding Method.

I NOW PASS on to the remaining books of the Old Testament. Concerning the two books of Chronicles I have nothing particular or important to remark, except that they were certainly written after the time of Ezra, and possibly after the restoration of the Temple by Judas Maccabaeus 19. For in chap. ix. of the first book we find a reckoning of the families who were the first to live in Jerusalem, and in verse 17 the names of the porters, of which two recur in Nehemiah. This shows that the books were certainly compiled after the rebuilding of the city. As to their actual writer, their authority, utility, and doctrine, I come to no conclusion. I have always been astonished that they have been included in the Bible by men who shut out from the canon the books of Wisdom, Tobit, and the others styled apocryphal. I do not aim at disparaging their authority, but as they are universally received I will leave them as they are.

The Psalms were collected and divided into five books in the time of the second temple, for Ps. lxxxviii. was published, according to Philo-Judaeus, while king Jehoiachin was still a prisoner in Babylon; and Ps. lxxxix. when the same king obtained his liberty: I do not think Philo would have made the statement unless either it had been the received opinion in his time, or else had been told him by trustworthy persons.

The Proverbs of Solomon were, I believe, collected at the same time, or at least in the time of King Josiah; for in chap. xxv:1, it is written, "These are also proverbs of Solomon which the men of Hezekiah, king of Judah, copied out." I cannot here pass over in silence the audacity of the Rabbis who wished to exclude from the sacred canon both the Proverbs and Ecclesiastes, and to put them both in the Apocrypha. In fact, they would actually have done so, if they had not lighted on certain passages in which the law of Moses is extolled. It is, indeed, grievous to think that the settling of the sacred canon lay in the hands of such men; however, I congratulate them, in this instance, on their suffering us to see these books in question, though I cannot refrain from doubting whether they have transmitted them in absolute good faith; but I will not now linger on this point.

I pass on, then, to the prophetic books. An examination of these assures me that the prophecies therein contained have been compiled from other books, and are not always set down in the exact order in which they were spoken or written by the prophets, but are only such as were collected here and there, so that they are but fragmentary.

Isaiah began to prophecy in the reign of Uzziah, as the writer himself testifies in the first verse. He not only prophesied at that time, but furthermore wrote the history of that king (see 2 Chron. xxvi:22) in a volume now lost. That which we possess, we have shown to have been taken from the chronicles of the kings of Judah and Israel.

We may add that the Rabbis assert that this prophet prophesied in the reign of Manasseh, by whom he was eventually put to death, and, although this seems to be a myth, it yet shows that they did not think that all Isaiah's prophecies are extant.

The prophecies of Jeremiah, which are related historically are also taken from various chronicles; for not only are they heaped together confusedly, without any account being taken of dates, but also the same story is told in them differently in different passages. For instance, in chap. xxi. we are told that the cause of Jeremiah's arrest was that he had prophesied the destruction of the city to Zedekiah who consulted him. This narrative suddenly passes, in chap xxii., to the prophet's remonstrances to Jehoiakim (Zedekiah's predecessor), and the prediction he made of that king's captivity; then, in chap. xxv., come the revelations granted to the prophet previously, that is in the fourth year of Jehoiakim, and, further on still, the revelations received in the first year of the same reign. The continuator of Jeremiah goes on heaping prophecy upon prophecy without any regard to dates, until at last, in chap. xxxviii. (as if the intervening chapters had been a parenthesis), he takes up the thread dropped in chap. xxi.

In fact, the conjunction with which chap. xxxviii. begins, refers to the 8th, 9th, and 10th verses of chap. xxi. Jeremiah's last arrest is then very differently described, and a totally separate cause is given for his daily retention in the court of the prison.

We may thus clearly see that these portions of the book have been compiled from various sources, and are only from this point of view comprehensible. The prophecies contained in the remaining chapters, where Jeremiah speaks in the first person, seem to be taken from a book written by Baruch, at Jeremiah's dictation. These, however, only comprise (as appears from chap. xxxvi:2) the prophecies revealed to the prophet from the time of Josiah to the fourth year of Jehoiakim, at which period the book begins. The contents of chap. xlv:2, on to chap. li:59, seem taken from the same volume.

That the book of Ezekiel is only a fragment, is clearly indicated by the first verse. For anyone may see that the conjunction with which it begins, refers to something already said, and connects what follows therewith. However, not only this conjunction, but the whole text of the discourse implies other writings. The fact of the present work beginning the thirtieth year shows that the prophet is continuing, not commencing a discourse; and this is confirmed by the writer, who parenthetically states in verse 3, "The word of the Lord came often unto Ezekiel the priest, the son of Buzi, in the land of the Chaldeans," as if to say that the prophecies which he is about to relate are the sequel to revelations formerly received by Ezekiel from God. Furthermore, Josephus, 11 Antiq." x:9, says that Ezekiel prophesied that Zedekiah should not see Babylon, whereas the book we now have not only contains no such statement, but contrariwise asserts in chap. xvii. that he should be taken to Babylon as a captive, 20.

Of Hosea I cannot positively state that he wrote more than is now extant in the book bearing his name, but I am astonished at the smallness of the quantity, we possess, for the sacred writer asserts that the prophet prophesied for more than eighty years.

We may assert, speaking generally, that the compiler of the prophetic books neither collected all the prophets, nor all the writings of those we have; for of the prophets who are said to have prophesied in the reign of Manasseh and of whom general mention is made in 2 Chron. xxxiii:10, 18, we have, evidently, no prophecies extant; neither have we all the prophecies of the twelve who give their names to books. Of Jonah we have only, the prophecy concerning the Ninevites, though he also prophesied to the children of Israel, as we learn in 2 Kings xiv:25.

The book and the personality of Job have caused much controversy. Some think that the book is the work of Moses, and the whole narrative merely allegorical. Such is the opinion of the Rabbins recorded in the Talmud, and they are supported by, Maimonides in his "More Nebuchim." Others believe it to be a true history, and some suppose that Job lived in the time of Jacob, and was married to his daughter Dinah. Aben Ezra, however, as I have already stated, affirms, in his commentaries, that the work is a translation into Hebrew from some other language: I could wish that he could advance more cogent arguments than he does, for we might then conclude that the Gentiles also had sacred books. I myself leave the matter undecided, but I conjecture Job to have been a Gentile, and a man of very stable character, who at first prospered, then was assailed with terrible calamities, and finally, was restored to great happiness. (He is thus named, among others, by Ezekiel, xiv:12.) I take it that the constancy of his mind amid the vicissitudes of his fortune occasioned many men to dispute about God's providence, or at least caused the writer of the book in question to compose his dialogues; for the contents, and also the style, seem to emanate far less from a man wretchedly ill and lying among ashes, than from one reflecting at ease in his study. I should also be inclined to agree with Aben Ezra that the book is a translation, for its poetry seems akin to that of the Gentiles; thus the Father of Gods summons a council, and Momus, here called Satan, criticizes the Divine decrees with the utmost freedom. But these are mere conjectures without any solid foundation.

I pass on to the book of Daniel, which, from chap. viii. onwards, undoubtedly contains the writing of Daniel himself. Whence the first seven chapters are derived I cannot say; we may, however, conjecture that, as they were first written in Chaldean, they are taken from Chaldean chronicles. If this could be proved, it would form a very striking proof of the fact that the sacredness of Scripture depends on our understanding of the doctrines therein signified, and not on the words, the language, and the phrases in which these doctrines are conveyed to us; and it would further show us that books which teach and speak of whatever is highest and best are equally sacred, whatever be the tongue in which they are written, or the nation to which they belong.

We can, however, in this case only remark that the chapters in question were written in Chaldee, and yet are as sacred as the rest of the Bible.

The first book of Ezra is so intimately connected with the book of Daniel that both are plainly recognizable as the work of the same author, writing of Jewish history from the time of the first captivity onwards. I have no hesitation in joining to this the book of Esther, for the conjunction with which it begins can refer to nothing else. It cannot be the same work as that written by Mordecai, for, in chap. ix:20-22, another person relates that Mordecai wrote letters, and tells us their contents; further, that Queen Esther confirmed the days of Purim in their times appointed, and that the decree was written in the book that is (by a Hebraism), in a book known to all then living, which, as Aben Ezra and the rest confess, has now perished. Lastly, for the rest of the acts of Mordecai, the historian refers us to the chronicles of the kings of Persia. Thus there is no doubt that this book was written by the same person as he who recounted the history of Daniel and Ezra, and who wrote Nehemiah, 21, sometimes called the second book of Ezra. We may, then, affirm that all these books are from one hand; but we have no clue whatever to the personality of the author. However, in order to determine whence he, whoever he was, had gained a knowledge of the histories which he had, perchance, in great measure himself written, we may remark that the governors or chiefs of the Jews, after the restoration of the Temple, kept scribes or historiographers, who wrote annals or chronicles of them. The chronicles of the kings are often quoted in the books of Kings, but the chronicles of the chiefs and priests are quoted for the first time in Nehemiah xii:23, and again in 1 Macc. xvi:24. This is undoubtedly the book referred to as containing the decree of Esther and the acts of Mordecai; and which, as we said with Aben Ezra, is now lost. From it were taken the whole contents of these four books, for no other authority is quoted by their writer, or is known to us.

That these books were not written by either Ezra or Nehemiah is plain from Nehemiah xii:9, where the descendants of the high priest, Joshua are traced down to Jaddua, the sixth high priest, who went to meet Alexander the Great, when the Persian empire was almost subdued (Josephus, "Ant." ii. 108), or who, according to Philo-Judaeus, was the sixth and last high priest under the Persians. In the same chapter of Nehemiah, verse 22, this point is clearly brought out: "The Levites in the days of Eliashib, Joiada, and Johanan, and Jaddua, were recorded chief of the fathers: also the priests, to the reign of Darius the Persian" — that is to say, in the chronicles; and, I suppose, no one thinks, 22, that the lives of Nehemiah and Ezra were so prolonged that they outlived fourteen kings of Persia. Cyrus was the first who granted the Jews permission to rebuild their Temple: the period between his time and Darius, fourteenth and last king of Persia, extends over 230 years. I have, therefore, no doubt that these books were written after Judas Maccabaeus had restored the worship in the Temple, for at that time false books of Daniel, Ezra, and Esther were published by evil-disposed persons, who were almost certainly Sadducees, for the writings were never recognized by the Pharisees, so far as I am aware; and, although certain myths in the fourth book of Ezra are repeated in the Talmud, they must not be set down to the Pharisees, for all but the most ignorant admit that they have been added by some trifler: in fact, I think, someone must have made such additions with a view to casting ridicule on all the traditions of the sect.

Perhaps these four books were written out and published at the time I have mentioned with a view to showing the people that the prophecies of Daniel had been fulfilled, and thus kindling their piety, and awakening a hope of future deliverance in the midst of their misfortunes. In spite of their recent origin, the books before us contain many errors, due, I suppose, to the haste with which they were written. Marginal readings, such as I have mentioned in the last chapter, are found here as elsewhere, and in even greater abundance; there are, moreover, certain passages which can only be accounted for by supposing some such cause as hurry.

However, before calling attention to the marginal readings, I will remark that, if the Pharisees are right in supposing them to have been ancient, and the work of the original scribes, we must perforce admit that these scribes (if there were more than one) set them down because they found that the text from which they were copying was inaccurate, and did yet not venture to alter what was written by their predecessors and superiors. I need not again go into the subject at length, and will, therefore, proceed to mention some discrepancies not noticed in the margin.

I. Some error has crept into the text of the second chapter of Ezra, for in verse 64 we are told that the total of all those mentioned in the rest of the chapter amounts to 42,360; but, when we come to add up the several items we get as result only 29,818. There must, therefore, be an error, either in the total, or in the details. The total is probably correct, for it would most likely be well known to all as a noteworthy thing; but with the details, the case would be different. If, then, any error had crept into the total, it would at once have been remarked, and easily corrected. This view is confirmed by Nehemiah vii., where this chapter of Ezra is mentioned, and a total is given in plain correspondence thereto; but the details are altogether different — some are larger, and some less, than those in Ezra, and altogether they amount to 31,089. We may, therefore, conclude that both in Ezra and in Nehemiah the details are erroneously given. The commentators who attempt to harmonize these evident contradictions draw on their imagination, each to the best of his ability; and while professing adoration for each letter and word of Scripture, only succeed in holding up the sacred writers to ridicule, as though they knew not how to write or relate a plain narrative. Such persons effect nothing but to render the clearness of Scripture obscure. If the Bible could everywhere be interpreted after their fashion, there would be no such thing as a rational statement of which the meaning could be relied on. However, there is no need to dwell on the subject; only I am convinced that if any historian were to attempt to imitate the proceedings freely attributed to the writers of the Bible, the commentators would cover him with contempt. If it be blasphemy to assert that there are any errors in Scripture, what name shall we apply to those who foist into it their own fancies, who degrade the sacred writers till they seem to write confused nonsense, and who deny the plainest and most evident meanings? What in the whole Bible can be plainer than the fact that Ezra and his companions, in the second chapter of the book attributed to him, have given in detail the reckoning of all the Hebrews who set out with them for Jerusalem? This is proved by the reckoning being given, not only of those who told their lineage, but also of those who were unable to do so. Is it not equally clear from Nehemiah vii:5, that the writer merely there copies the list given in Ezra? Those, therefore, who explain these pas sages otherwise, deny the plain meaning of Scripture — nay, they deny Scripture itself. They think it pious to reconcile one passage of Scripture with another — a pretty piety, forsooth, which accommodates the clear passages to the obscure, the correct to the faulty, the sound to the corrupt.

Far be it from me to call such commentators blasphemers, if their motives be pure: for to err is human. But I return to my subject.

Besides these errors in numerical details, there are others in the genealogies, in the history, and, I fear also in the prophecies. The prophecy of Jeremiah (chap. xxii.), concerning Jechoniah, evidently does not agree with his history, as given in I Chronicles iii:17-19, and especially with the last words of the chapter, nor do I see how the prophecy, "thou shalt die in peace," can be applied to Zedekiah, whose eyes were dug out after his sons had been slain before him. If prophecies are to be interpreted by their issue, we must make a change of name, and read Jechoniah for Zedekiah, and vice versa This, however, would be too paradoxical a proceeding; so I prefer to leave the matter unexplained, especially as the error, if error there be, must be set down to the historian, and not to any fault in the authorities.

Other difficulties I will not touch upon, as I should only weary the reader, and, moreover, be repeating the remarks of other writers. For R. Selomo, in face of the manifest contradiction in the above-mentioned genealogies, is compelled to break forth into these words (see his commentary on 1 Chron. viii.): "Ezra (whom he supposes to be the author of the book of Chronicles) gives different names and a different genealogy to the sons of Benjamin from those which we find in Genesis, and describes most of the Levites differently from Joshua, because he found original discrepancies." And, again, a little later: "The genealogy of Gibeon and others is described twice in different ways, from different tables of each genealogy, and in writing them down Ezra adopted the version given in the majority of the texts, and when the authority was equal he gave both." Thus granting that these books were compiled from sources originally incorrect and uncertain.

In fact the commentators, in seeking to harmonize difficulties, generally do no more than indicate their causes: for I suppose no sane person supposes that the sacred historians deliberately wrote with the object of appearing to contradict themselves freely. Perhaps I shall be told that I am overthrowing the authority of Scripture, for that, according to me, anyone may suspect it of error in any passage; but, on the contrary, I have shown that my object has been to prevent the clear and uncorrupted passages being accommodated to and corrupted by the faulty ones; neither does the fact that some passages are corrupt warrant us in suspecting all. No book ever was completely free from faults, yet I would ask, who suspects all books to be everywhere faulty? Surely no one, especially when the phraseology is clear and the intention of the author plain.

I have now finished the task I set myself with respect to the books of the Old Testament. We may easily conclude from what has been said, that before the time of the Maccabees there was no canon of sacred books, 23, but that those which we now possess were selected from a multitude of others at the period of the restoration of the Temple by the Pharisees (who also instituted the set form of prayers), who are alone responsible for their acceptance. Those, therefore, who would demonstrate the authority of Holy Scripture, are bound to show the authority of each separate book; it is not enough to prove the Divine origin of a single book in order to infer the Divine origin of the rest. In that case we should have to assume that the council of Pharisees was, in its choice of books, infallible, and this could never be proved. I am led to assert that the Pharisees alone selected the books of the Old Testament, and inserted them in the canon, from the fact that in Daniel ii. is proclaimed the doctrine of the Resurrection, which the Sadducees denied; and, furthermore, the Pharisees plainly assert in the Talmud that they so selected them. For in the treatise of Sabbathus, chapter ii., folio 30, page 2, it is written: R. Jehuda, surnamed Rabbi, reports that the experts wished to conceal the book of Ecclesiastes because they found therein words opposed to the law (that is, to the book of the law of Moses). Why did they not hide it? "Because it begins in accordance with the law, and ends according to the law;" and a little further on we read: "They sought also to conceal the book of Proverbs." And in the first chapter of the same treatise, fol. 13, page 2: "Verily, name one man for good, even he who was called Neghunja, the son of Hezekiah: for, save for him, the book of Ezekiel would been concealed, because it agreed not with the words of the law."

It is thus abundantly clear that men expert in the law summoned a council to decide which books should be received into the canon, and which excluded. If any man, therefore, wishes to be certified as to the authority of all the books, let him call a fresh council, and ask every member his reasons.

The time has now come for examining in the same manner the books in the New Testament; but as I learn that the task has been already performed by men highly skilled in science and languages, and as I do not myself possess a knowledge of Greek sufficiently exact for the task; lastly, as we have lost the originals of those books which were written in Hebrew, I prefer to decline the undertaking. However, I will touch on those points which have most bearing on my subject in the following chapter.

19 "After the restoration of the Temple by Judas Maccaboeus." This conjecture, if such it be, is founded on the genealogy of King Jeconiah, given in 1 Chron. iii., which finishes at the sons of Elioenai, the thirteenth in direct descent from him: whereon we must observe that Jeconiah, before his captivity, had no children; but it is probable that he had two while he was in prison, if we may draw any inference from the names he gave them. As to his grandchildren, it is evident that they were born after his deliverance, if the names be any guide, for his grandson, Pedaiah (a name meaning God hath delivered me), who, according to this chapter, was the father of Zerubbabel, was born in the thirty-seventh or thirty-eighth year of Jeconiah's life, that is thirty-three years before the restoration of liberty to the Jews by Cyrus. Therefore Zerubbabel, to whom Cyrus gave the principality of Judaea, was thirteen or fourteen years old. But we need not carry the inquiry so far: we need only read attentively the chapter of 1 Chron., already quoted, where (v. 17, sqq.) mention is made of all the posterity of Jeconiah, and compare it with the Septuagint version to see clearly that these books were not published, till after Maccabaeus had restored the Temple, the sceptre no longer belonging to the house of Jeconiah.

20 "Zedekiah should be taken to Babylon." No one could then have suspected that the prophecy of Ezekiel contradicted that of Jeremiah, but the suspicion occurs to everyone who reads the narrative of Josephus. The event proved that both prophets were in the right.

21 "And who wrote Nehemiah." That the greater part of the book of Nehemiah was taken from the work composed by the prophet Nehemiah himself, follows from the testimony of its author. (See chap. i.). But it is obvious that the whole of the passage contained between chap. viii. and chap. xii. verse 26, together with the two last verses of chap. xii., which form a sort of parenthesis to Nehemiah's words, were added by the historian himself, who outlived Nehemiah.

22 "I suppose no one thinks" that Ezra was the uncle of the first high priest, named Joshua (see Ezra vii., and 1 Chron. vi:14), and went to Jerusalem from Babylon with Zerubbabel (see Nehemiah xii:1). But it appears that when he saw, that the Jews were in a state of anarchy, he returned to Babylon, as also did others (Nehem. i;2), and remained there till the reign of Artaxerxes, when his requests were granted and he went a second time to Jerusalem. Nehemiah also went to Jerusalem with Zerubbabel in the time of Cyrus (Ezra ii:2 and 63, cf. x:9, and Nehemiah x:1). The version given of the Hebrew word, translated "ambassador," is not supported by any authority, while it is certain that fresh names were given to those Jews who frequented the court. Thus Daniel was named Balteshazzar, and Zerubbabel Sheshbazzar (Dan. i:7). Nehemiah was called Atirsata, while in virtue of his office he was styled governor, or president. (Nehem. v. 24, xii:26.)

23 "Before the time of the Maccabees there was no canon of sacred books." The synagogue styled "the great" did not begin before the subjugation of Asia by the Macedonians. The contention of Maimonides, Rabbi Abraham, Ben-David, and others, that the presidents of this synagogue were Ezra, Daniel, Nehemiah, Haggai, Zechariah, &c., is a pure fiction, resting only on rabbinical tradition. Indeed they assert that the dominion of the Persians only lasted thirty-four years, and this is their chief reason for maintaining that the decrees of the "great synagogue," or synod (rejected by the Sadducees, but accepted by the Pharisees) were ratified by the prophets, who received them from former prophets, and so in direct succession from Moses, who received them from God Himself. Such is the doctrine which the Pharisees maintain with their wonted obstinacy. Enlightened persons, however,

who know the reasons for the convoking of councils, or synods, and are no strangers to the differences between Pharisees and Sadducees, can easily divine the causes which led to the assembling of this great synagogue. It is very certain that no prophet was there present, and that the decrees of the Pharisees, which they style their traditions, derive all their authority from it.

CHAPTER XI.

An Inquiry whether the Apostles wrote their Epistles as Apostles and Prophets, or merely as Teachers; and an explanation of what is meant by an Apostle.

NO READER OF the New Testament can doubt that the Apostles were prophets; but as a prophet does not always speak by revelation, but only, at rare intervals, as we showed at the end of Chap. I., we may fairly inquire whether the Apostles wrote their Epistles as prophets, by revelation and express mandate, as Moses, Jeremiah, and others did, or whether only as private individuals or teachers, especially as Paul, in Corinthians xiv:6, mentions two sorts of preaching.

If we examine the style of the Epistles, we shall find it totally different from that employed by the prophets.

The prophets are continually asserting that they speak by the command of God: "Thus saith the Lord," "The Lord of hosts saith," "The command of the Lord," &c.; and this was their habit not only in assemblies of the prophets, but also in their epistles containing revelations, as appears from the epistle of Elijah to Jehoram, 2 Chron. xxi:12, which begins, "Thus saith the Lord."

In the Apostolic Epistles we find nothing of the sort. Contrariwise, in I Cor. vii:40 Paul speaks according to his own opinion and in many passages we come across doubtful and perplexed phrase; such as, "We think, therefore," Rom. iii:28; "Now I think," 24, Rom. viii:18, and so on. Besides these, other expressions are met with very different from those used by the prophets. For instance, 1 Cor. vii:6, "But I speak this by permission, not by commandment;" "I give my judgment as one that hath obtained mercy of the Lord to be faithful" (1 Cor. vii:25), and so on in many other passages. We must also remark that in the aforesaid chapter the Apostle says that when he states that he has or has not the precept or commandment of God, he does not mean the precept or commandment of God revealed to himself, but only the words uttered by Christ in His Sermon on the Mount. Furthermore, if we examine the manner in which the Apostles give out evangelical doctrine, we shall see that it differs materially from the method adopted by the prophets. The Apostles everywhere reason as if they were arguing rather than prophesying; the prophecies, on the other hand, contain only dogmas and commands. God is therein introduced not as speaking to reason, but as issuing decrees by His absolute fiat. The authority of the prophets does not submit to discussion, for whosoever wishes to find rational ground for his arguments, by that very wish submits them to everyone's private judgment. This Paul, inasmuch as he uses reason, appears to have done, for he says in 1 Cor. x:15, "I speak as to wise men, judge ye what I say." The prophets, as we showed at the end of Chapter I., did not perceive what was revealed by virtue of their natural reason, and though there are certain passages in the Pentateuch which seem to be appeals to induction, they turn out, on nearer examination, to be nothing but peremptory commands. For instance, when Moses says, Deut. xxxi:27, "Behold, while I am yet alive with you, this day ye have been rebellious against the Lord; and how much more after my death," we must by no means conclude that Moses wished to convince the Israelites by reason that they would necessarily fall away from the worship of the Lord after his death; for the argument would have been false, as Scripture itself shows: the Israelites continued faithful during the lives of Joshua and the elders, and afterwards during the time of Samuel, David, and Solomon. Therefore the words of Moses are merely a moral injunction, in which he predicts rhetorically the future backsliding of the people so as to impress it vividly on their imagination. I say that Moses spoke of himself in order to lend likelihood to his prediction, and not as a prophet by revelation, because in verse 21 of the same chapter we are told that God revealed the same thing to Moses in different words, and there was no need to make Moses certain by argument of God's prediction and decree; it was only necessary that it should be vividly impressed on his imagination, and this could not be better accomplished than by imagining the existing contumacy of the people, of which he had had frequent experience, as likely to extend into the future.

All the arguments employed by Moses in the five books are to be understood in a similar manner; they are not drawn from the armoury of reason, but are merely, modes of expression calculated to instil with efficacy, and present vividly to the imagination the commands of God. However, I do not wish absolutely to deny that the prophets ever argued from revelation; I only maintain that the prophets made more legitimate use of argument in proportion as their knowledge approached more nearly to ordinary knowledge, and by this we know that they possessed a knowledge above the ordinary, inasmuch as they proclaimed absolute dogmas, decrees, or judgments. Thus Moses, the chief of the prophets, never used legitimate argument, and, on the other hand, the long deductions and arguments of Paul, such as we find in the Epistle to the Romans, are in nowise written from supernatural revelation.

The modes of expression and discourse adopted by the Apostles in the Epistles, show very clearly that the latter were not written by revelation and Divine command, but merely by the natural powers and judgment of the authors. They consist in brotherly admonitions and courteous expressions such as would never be employed in prophecy, as for instance, Paul's excuse in Romans xv:15, "I have written the more boldly unto you in some sort, my brethren."

We may arrive at the same conclusion from observing that we never read that the Apostles were commanded to write, but only that they went everywhere preaching, and confirmed their words with signs. Their personal presence and signs were absolutely necessary for the conversion and establishment in religion of the Gentiles; as Paul himself expressly states in Rom. i:11, "But I long to see you, that I may impart to you some spiritual gift, to the end that ye may be established."

It may be objected that we might prove in similar fashion that the Apostles did not preach as prophets, for they did not go to particular places, as the prophets did, by the command of God. We read in the Old Testament that Jonah went to Nineveh to preach, and at the same time that he was expressly sent there, and told that he most preach. So also it is related, at great length, of Moses that he went to Egypt as the messenger of God, and was told at the same time what he should say to the children of Israel and to king Pharaoh, and what wonders he should work before them to give credit to his words. Isaiah, Jeremiah, and Ezekiel were expressly commanded to preach to the Israelites. Lastly, the prophets only preached what we are assured by Scripture they had received from God, whereas this is hardly ever said of the Apostles in the New Testament, when they went about to preach. On the contrary, we find passages expressly implying that the Apostles chose the places where they should preach on their own responsibility, for there was a difference amounting to a quarrel between Paul and Barnabas on the subject (Acts xv:37, 38). Often they wished to go to a place, but were prevented, as Paul writes, Rom. i:13, "Oftentimes I purposed to come to you, but was let hitherto;" and in I Cor. xvi:12, "As touching our brother Apollos, I greatly desired him to come unto you with the brethren, but his will was not at all to come at this time: but he will come when he shall have convenient time."

From these expressions and differences of opinion among the Apostles, and also from the fact that Scripture nowhere testifies of them, as of the ancient prophets, that they went by the command of God, one might conclude that they preached as well as wrote in their capacity of teachers, and not as prophets: but the question is easily solved if we observe the difference between the mission of an Apostle and that of an Old Testament prophet. The latter were not called to preach and prophesy to all nations, but to certain specified ones, and therefore an express and peculiar mandate was required for each of them; the Apostles, on the other hand, were called to preach to all men absolutely, and to turn all men to religion. Therefore, whithersoever they went, they were fulfilling Christ's commandment; there was no need to reveal to them beforehand what they should preach, for they were the disciples of Christ to whom their Master Himself said (Matt. X:19, 20): "But, when they deliver you up, take no thought how or what ye shall speak, for it shall be given you in that same hour what ye shall speak." We therefore conclude that the Apostles were only indebted to special revelation in what they orally preached and confirmed by signs (see the beginning of Chap. 11.); that which they taught in speaking or writing without any confirmatory signs and wonders they taught from their natural knowledge. (See I Cor. xiv:6.) We need not be deterred by the fact that all the Epistles begin by citing the imprimatur of the Apostleship, for the Apostles, as I will shortly show, were granted, not only the faculty of prophecy, but also the authority to teach. We may therefore admit that they wrote their Epistles as Apostles, and for this cause every one of them began by citing the Apostolic imprimatur, possibly with a view to the attention of the reader by asserting that they were the persons who had made such mark among the faithful by their preaching, and had shown by many marvelous works that they were teaching true religion and the way of salvation. I observe that what is said in the Epistles with regard to the Apostolic vocation and the Holy Spirit of God which inspired them, has reference to their former preaching, except in those passages where the expressions of the Spirit of God and the Holy Spirit are used to signify a mind pure, upright, and devoted to God. For instance, in 1 Cor. vii:40, Paul says: But she is happier if she so abide, after my judgment, and I think also that I have the Spirit of God." By the Spirit of God the Apostle here refers to his mind, as we may see from the context: his meaning is as follows: "I account blessed a widow who does not wish to marry a second husband; such is my opinion, for I have settled to live unmarried, and I think that I am blessed." There are other similar passages which I need not now quote.

As we have seen that the Apostles wrote their Epistles solely by the light of natural reason, we must inquire how they were enabled to teach by natural knowledge matters outside its scope. However, if we bear in mind what we said in Chap. VII. of this treatise our difficulty will vanish: for although the contents of the Bible entirely surpass our understanding, we may safely discourse of them, provided we assume nothing not told us in Scripture: by the same method the Apostles, from what they saw and heard, and from what was revealed to them, were enabled to form and elicit many conclusions which they would have been able to teach to men had it been permissible.

Further, although religion, as preached by the Apostles, does not come within the sphere of reason, in so far as it consists in the narration of the life of Christ, yet its essence, which is chiefly moral, like the whole of Christ's doctrine, can readily, be apprehended by the natural faculties of all.

Lastly, the Apostles had no lack of supernatural illumination for the purpose of adapting the religion they had attested by signs to the understanding of everyone so that it might be readily received; nor for exhortations on the subject: in fact, the object of the Epistles is to teach and exhort men to lead that manner of life which each of the Apostles judged best for confirming them in religion. We may here repeat our former remark, that the Apostles had received not only the faculty of preaching the history, of Christ as prophets, and confirming it with signs, but also authority for teaching and exhorting according as each thought best. Paul (2 Tim. i:11), "Whereunto I am appointed a preacher, and an apostle, and a teacher of the Gentiles;" and again (I Tim. ii:7), "Whereunto I am ordained a preacher and an apostle (I speak the truth in Christ and lie not), a teacher of the Gentiles in faith and verity." These passages, I say, show clearly the stamp both of the apostleship and the teachership: the authority for admonishing whomsoever and wheresoever he pleased is asserted by Paul in the Epistle to Philemon, v:8: "Wherefore, though I might be much bold in Christ to enjoin thee that which is convenient, yet," &c., where we may remark that if Paul had received from God as a prophet what he wished to enjoin Philemon, and had been bound to speak in his prophetic capacity, he would not have been able to change the command of God into entreaties. We must therefore understand him to refer to the permission to admonish which he had received as a teacher, and not as a prophet. We have not yet made it quite clear that the Apostles might each choose his own way of teaching, but only that by virtue of their Apostleship they were teachers as well as prophets; however, if we call reason to our aid we shall clearly see that an authority to teach implies authority to choose the method. It will nevertheless be, perhaps, more satisfactory to draw all our proofs from Scripture; we are there plainly told that each Apostle chose his particular method (Rom. xv: 20): "Yea, so have I strived to preach the gospel, not where Christ was named, lest I should build upon another man's foundation." If all the Apostles had adopted the same method of teaching, and had all built up the Christian religion on the same foundation, Paul would have had no reason to call the work of a fellow-Apostle "another man's foundation," inasmuch as it would have been identical with his own: his calling it another man's proved that each Apostle built up his religious instruction on different foundations, thus resembling other teachers who have each their own method, and prefer instructing quite ignorant people who have never learnt under another master, whether the subject be science, languages, or even the indisputable truths of mathematics. Furthermore, if we go through the Epistles at all attentively, we shall see that the Apostles, while agreeing about religion itself, are at variance as to the foundations it rests on. Paul, in order to strengthen men's religion, and show them that salvation depends solely on the grace of God, teaches that no one can boast of works, but only of faith, and that no one can be justified by works (Rom. iii:27,28); in fact, he preaches the complete doctrine of predestination. James, on the other hand, states that man is justified by works, and not by faith only (see his Epistle, ii:24), and omitting all the disputations of Paul, confines religion to a very few elements.

Lastly, it is indisputable that from these different ground; for religion selected by the Apostles, many quarrels and schisms distracted the Church, even in the earliest times, and doubtless they will continue so to distract it for ever, or at least till religion is separated from philosophical speculations, and reduced to the few simple doctrines taught by Christ to His disciples; such a task was impossible for the Apostles, because the Gospel was then unknown to mankind, and lest its novelty should offend men's ears it had to be adapted to the disposition of contemporaries (2 Cor. ix:19, 20), and built up on the groundwork most familiar and accepted at the time. Thus none of the Apostles philosophized more than did Paul, who was called to preach to the Gentiles; other Apostles preaching to the Jews, who despised philosophy, similarly, adapted themselves to the temper of their hearers (see Gal. ii. 11), and preached a religion free from all philosophical speculations. How blest would our age be if it could witness a religion freed also from all the trammels of superstition!

24 "Now I think." The translators render the {Greek} word "I infer", and assert that Paul uses it as synonymous with {a Greek word}. But the former word has, in Greek, the same meaning as the Hebrew word rendered to think, to esteem, to judge. And this signification would be in entire agreement with the Syriac translation. This Syriac translation (if it be a translation, which is very doubtful, for we know neither the time of its appearance, nor the translators and Syriac was the vernacular of the Apostles) renders the text before us in a way well explained by Tremellius as "we think, therefore."

CHAPTER XII.

Of the true original of the Divine Law, and wherefore Scripture is called Sacred, and the Word of God. How that, in so far as it contains the Word of God, it has come down to us uncorrupted.

THOSE WHO LOOK upon the Bible as a message sent down by God from Heaven to men, will doubtless cry out that I have committed the sin against the Holy Ghost because I have asserted that the Word of God is faulty, mutilated, tampered with, and inconsistent; that we possess it only in fragments, and that the original of the covenant which God made with the Jews has been lost. However, I have no doubt that a little reflection will cause them to desist from their uproar: for not only reason but the expressed opinions of prophets and apostles openly proclaim that God's eternal Word and covenant, no less than true religion, is Divinely inscribed in human hearts, that is, in the human mind, and that this is the true original of God's covenant, stamped with His own seal, namely, the idea of Himself, as it were, with the image of His Godhood.

Religion was imparted to the early Hebrews as a law written down, because they were at that time in the condition of children, but afterwards Moses (Deut. xxx:6) and Jeremiah (xxxi:33) predicted a time coming when the Lord should write His law in their hearts. Thus only the Jews, and amongst them chiefly the Sadducees, struggled for the law written on tablets; least of all need those who bear it inscribed on their hearts join in the contest. Those, therefore, who reflect, will find nothing in what I have written repugnant either to the Word of God or to true religion and faith, or calculated to weaken either one or the other: contrariwise, they will see that I have strengthened religion, as I showed at the end of Chapter X.; indeed, had it not been so, I should certainly have decided to hold my peace, nay, I would even have asserted as a way out of all difficulties that the Bible contains the most profound hidden mysteries; however, as this doctrine has given rise to gross superstition and other pernicious results spoken of at the beginning of Chapter V., I have thought such a course unnecessary, especially as religion stands in no need of superstitious adornments, but is, on the contrary, deprived by such trappings of some of her splendour.

Still, it will be said, though the law of God is written in the heart, the Bible is none the less the Word of God, and it is no more lawful to say of Scripture than of God's Word that it is mutilated and corrupted. I fear that such objectors are too anxious to be pious, and that they are in danger of turning religion into superstition, and worshipping paper and ink in place of God's Word.

I am certified of thus much: I have said nothing unworthy of Scripture or God's Word, and I have made no assertions which I could not prove by most plain argument to be true. I can, therefore, rest assured that I have advanced nothing which is impious or even savours of impiety.

from what I have said, assume a licence to sin, and without any reason, at I confess that some profane men, to whom religion is a burden, may, the simple dictates of their lusts conclude that Scripture is everywhere faulty and falsified, and that therefore its authority is null; but such men are beyond the reach of help, for nothing, as the pro verb has it, can be said so rightly that it cannot be twisted into wrong. Those who wish to give rein to their lusts are at no loss for an excuse, nor were those men of old who possessed the original Scriptures, the ark of the covenant, nay, the prophets and apostles in person among them, any better than the people of today. Human nature, Jew as well as Gentile, has always been the same, and in every age virtue has been exceedingly rare.

Nevertheless, to remove every scruple, I will here show in what sense the Bible or any inanimate thing should be called sacred and Divine; also wherein the law of God consists, and how it cannot be contained in a certain number of books; and, lastly, I will show that Scripture, in so far as it teaches what is necessary for obedience and salvation, cannot have been corrupted. From these considerations everyone will be able to judge that I have neither said anything against the Word of God nor given any foothold to impiety.

A thing is called sacred and Divine when it is designed for promoting piety, and continues sacred so long as it is religiously used: if the users cease to be pious, the thing ceases to be sacred: if it be turned to base uses, that which was formerly sacred becomes unclean and profane. For instance, a certain spot was named by the patriarch Jacob the house of God, because he worshipped God there revealed to him: by the prophets the same spot was called the house of iniquity (see Amos v:5, and Hosea x:5), because the Israelites were wont, at the instigation of Jeroboam, to sacrifice there to idols. Another example puts the matter in the plainest light. Words gain their meaning solely from their usage, and if they are arranged according to their accepted signification so as to move those who read them to devotion, they will become sacred, and the book so written will be sacred also. But if their usage afterwards dies out so that the words have no meaning, or the book becomes utterly neglected, whether from unworthy motives, or because it is no longer needed, then the words and the book will lose both their use and their sanctity: lastly, if these same words be otherwise arranged, or if their customary meaning becomes perverted into its opposite, then both the words and the book containing them become, instead of sacred, impure and profane.

From this it follows that nothing is in itself absolutely sacred, or profane, and unclean, apart from the mind, but only relatively thereto. Thus much is clear from many passages in the Bible. Jeremiah (to select one case out of many) says (chap. vii:4), that the Jews of his time were wrong in calling Solomon's Temple, the Temple of God, for, as he goes on to say in the same chapter, God's name would only be given to the Temple so long as it was frequented by men who worshipped Him, and defended justice, but that, if it became the resort of murderers, thieves, idolaters, and other wicked persons, it would be turned into a den of malefactors.

Scripture, curiously enough, nowhere tells us what became of the Ark of the Covenant, though there is no doubt that it was destroyed, or burnt together with the Temple; yet there was nothing which the Hebrews considered more sacred, or held in greater reverence. Thus Scripture is sacred, and its words Divine so long as it stirs mankind to devotion towards God: but if it be utterly neglected, as it formerly was by the Jews, it becomes nothing but paper and ink, and is left to be desecrated or corrupted: still, though Scripture be thus corrupted or destroyed, we must not say that the Word of God has suffered in like manner, else we shall be like the Jews, who said that the Temple which would then be the Temple of God had perished in the flames. Jeremiah tells us this in respect to the law, for he thus chides the ungodly of his time, "Wherefore, say you we are masters, and the law of the Lord is with us? Surely it has been given in vain, it is in vain that the pen of the scribes" (has been made) — that is, you say falsely that the Scripture is in your power, and that you possess the law of God; for ye have made it of none effect.

So also, when Moses broke the first tables of the law, he did not by any means cast the Word of God from his hands in anger and shatter it — such an action would be inconceivable, either of Moses or of God's Word — he only broke the tables of stone, which, though they had before been holy from containing the covenant wherewith the Jews had bound themselves in obedience to God, had entirely lost their sanctity when the covenant had been violated by the worship of the calf, and were, therefore, as liable to perish as the ark of the covenant. It is thus scarcely to be wondered at, that the original documents of Moses are no longer extant, nor that the books we possess met with the fate we have described, when we consider that the true original of the Divine covenant, the most sacred object of all, has totally perished.

Let them cease, therefore, who accuse us of impiety, inasmuch as we have said nothing against the Word of God, neither have we corrupted it, but let them keep their anger, if they would wreak it justly, for the ancients whose malice desecrated the Ark, the Temple, and the Law of God, and all that was held sacred, subjecting them to corruption. Furthermore, if, according to the saying of the Apostle in 2 Cor. iii:3, they possessed "the Epistle of Christ, written not with ink, but with the Spirit of the living God, not in tables of stone, but in the fleshy tables of the heart," let them cease to worship the letter, and be so anxious concerning it.

I think I have now sufficiently shown in what respect Scripture should be accounted sacred and Divine; we may now see what should rightly be understood by the expression, the Word of the Lord; debar (the Hebrew original) signifies word, speech, command, and thing. The causes for which a thing is in Hebrew said to be of God, or is referred to Him, have been already detailed in Chap. I., and we can therefrom easily gather what meaning Scripture attaches to the phrases, the word, the speech, the command, or the thing of God. I need not, therefore, repeat what I there said, nor what was shown under the third head in the chapter on miracles. It is enough to mention the repetition for the better understanding of what I am about to say — viz., that the Word of the Lord when it has reference to anyone but God Himself, signifies that Divine law treated of in Chap. IV.; in other words, religion, universal and catholic to the whole human race, as Isaiah describes it (chap. i:10), teaching that the true way of life consists, not in ceremonies, but in charity, and a true heart, and calling it indifferently God's Law and God's Word.

The expression is also used metaphorically for the order of nature and destiny (which, indeed, actually depend and follow from the eternal mandate of the Divine nature), and especially for such parts of such order as were foreseen by the prophets, for the prophets did not perceive future events as the result of natural causes, but as the fiats and decrees of God. Lastly, it is employed for the command of any prophet, in so far as he had perceived it by his peculiar faculty or prophetic gift, and not by the natural light of reason; this use springs chiefly from the usual prophetic conception of God as a legislator, which we remarked in Chap. IV. There are, then, three causes for the Bible's being called the Word of God: because it teaches true religion, of which God is the eternal Founder; because it narrates predictions of future events as though they were decrees of God; because its actual authors generally perceived things not by their ordinary natural faculties, but by a power peculiar to themselves, and introduced these things perceived, as told them by God.

Although Scripture contains much that is merely historical and can be perceived by natural reason, yet its name is acquired from its chief subject matter.

We can thus easily see how God can be said to be the Author of the Bible: it is because of the true religion therein contained, and not because He wished to communicate to men a certain number of books. We can also learn from hence the reason for the division into Old and New Testament. It was made because the prophets who preached religion before Christ, preached it as a national law in virtue of the covenant entered into under Moses; while the Apostles who came after Christ, preached it to all men as a universal religion solely in virtue of Christ's Passion: the cause for the division is not that the two parts are different in doctrine, nor that they were written as originals of the covenant, nor, lastly, that the catholic religion (which is in entire harmony with our nature) was new except in relation to those who had not known it: " it was in the world," as John the Evangelist says, " and the world knew it not."

Thus, even if we had fewer books of the Old and New Testament than we have, we should still not be deprived of the Word of God (which, as we have said, is identical with true religion), even as we do not now hold ourselves to be deprived of it, though we lack many cardinal writings such as the Book of the Law, which was religiously guarded in the Temple as the original of the Covenant, also the Book of Wars, the Book of Chronicles, and many others, from whence the extant Old Testament was taken and compiled. The above conclusion may be supported by many reasons.

I. Because the books of both Testaments were not written by express command at one place for all ages, but are a fortuitous collection of the works of men, writing each as his period and disposition dictated. So much is clearly shown by the call of the prophets who were bade to admonish the ungodly of their time, and also by the Apostolic Epistles.

II. Because it is one thing to understand the meaning of Scripture and the prophets, and quite another thing to understand the meaning of God, or the actual truth. This follows from what we said in Chap. II. We showed, in Chap. VI., that it applied to historic narratives, and to miracles: but it by no means applies to questions concerning true religion and virtue.

III. Because the books of the Old Testament were selected from many, and were collected and sanctioned by a council of the Pharisees, as we showed in Chap. X. The books of the New Testament were also chosen from many by councils which rejected as spurious other books held sacred by many. But these councils, both Pharisee and Christian, were not composed of prophets, but only of learned men and teachers. Still, we must grant that they were guided in their choice by a regard for the Word of God; and they must, therefore, have known what the law of God was.

IV. Because the Apostles wrote not as prophets, but as teachers (see last Chapter), and chose whatever method they thought best adapted for those whom they addressed: and consequently, there are many things in the Epistles (as we showed at the end of the last Chapter) which are not necessary to salvation.

V. Lastly, because there are four Evangelists in the New Testament, and it is scarcely credible that God can have designed to narrate the life of Christ four times over, and to communicate it thus to mankind. For though there are some details related in one Gospel which are not in another, and one often helps us to understand another, we cannot thence conclude that all that is set down is of vital importance to us, and that God chose the four Evangelists in order that the life of

Christ might be better understood; for each one preached his Gospel in a separate locality, each wrote it down as he preached it, in simple language, in order that the history of Christ might be clearly told, not with any view of explaining his fellow-Evangelists.

If there are some passages which can be better, and more easily understood by comparing the various versions, they are the result of chance, and are not numerous: their continuance in obscurity would have impaired neither the clearness of the narrative nor the blessedness of mankind.

We have now shown that Scripture can only be called the Word of God in so far as it affects religion, or the Divine law; we must now point out that, in respect to these questions, it is neither faulty, tampered with, nor corrupt. By faulty, tampered with, and corrupt, I here mean written so incorrectly, that the meaning cannot be arrived at by a study of the language, nor from the authority of Scripture. I will not go to such lengths as to say that the Bible, in so far as it contains the Divine law, has always preserved the same vowel-points, the same letters, or the same words (I leave this to be proved by, the Massoretes and other worshippers of the letter), I only, maintain that the meaning by, which alone an utterance is entitled to be called Divine, has come down to us uncorrupted, even though the original wording may have been more often changed than we suppose. Such alterations, as I have said above, detract nothing from the Divinity of the Bible, for the Bible would have been no less Divine had it been written in different words or a different language. That the Divine law has in this sense come down to us uncorrupted, is an assertion which admits of no dispute. For from the Bible itself we learn, without the smallest difficulty or ambiguity,, that its cardinal precept is: To love God above all things, and one's neighbour as one's self. This cannot be a spurious passage, nor due to a hasty and mistaken scribe, for if the Bible had ever put forth a different doctrine it would have had to change the whole of its teaching, for this is the corner-stone of religion, without which the whole fabric would fall headlong to the ground. The Bible would not be the work we have been examining, but something quite different.

We remain, then, unshaken in our belief that this has always been the doctrine of Scripture, and, consequently, that no error sufficient to vitiate it can have crept in without being instantly, observed by all; nor can anyone have succeeded in tampering with it and escaped the discovery of his malice.

As this corner-stone is intact, we must perforce admit the same of whatever other passages are indisputably dependent on it, and are also fundamental, as, for instance, that a God exists, that He foresees all things, that He is Almighty, that by His decree the good prosper and the wicked come to naught, and, finally, that our salvation depends solely on His grace.

These are doctrines which Scripture plainly teaches throughout, and which it is bound to teach, else all the rest would be empty and baseless; nor can we be less positive about other moral doctrines, which plainly are built upon this universal foundation — for instance, to uphold justice, to aid the weak, to do no murder, to covet no man's goods, &c. Precepts, I repeat, such as these, human malice and the lapse of ages are alike powerless to destroy, for if any part of them perished, its loss would immediately be supplied from the fundamental principle, especially the doctrine of charity, which is everywhere in both Testaments extolled above all others. Moreover, though it be true that there is no conceivable crime so heinous that it has never been committed, still there is no one who would attempt in excuse for his crimes to destroy, the law, or introduce an impious doctrine in the place of what is eternal and salutary; men's nature is so constituted that everyone (be he king or subject) who has committed a base action, tries to deck out his conduct with spurious excuses, till he seems to have done nothing but what is just and right.

We may conclude, therefore, that the whole Divine law, as taught by Scripture, has come down to us uncorrupted. Besides this there are certain facts which we may be sure have been transmitted in good faith. For instance, the main facts of Hebrew history, which were perfectly well known to everyone. The Jewish people were accustomed in former times to chant the ancient history of their nation in psalms. The main facts, also, of Christ's life and passion were immediately spread abroad through the whole Roman empire. It is therefore scarcely credible, unless nearly everybody, consented thereto, which we cannot suppose, that successive generations have handed down the broad outline of the Gospel narrative otherwise than as they received it.

Whatsoever, therefore, is spurious or faulty can only have reference to details — some circumstances in one or the other history or prophecy designed to stir the people to greater devotion; or in some miracle, with a view of confounding philosophers; or, lastly, in speculative matters after they had become mixed up with religion, so that some individual might prop up his own inventions with a pretext of Divine authority. But such matters have little to do with salvation, whether they be corrupted little or much, as I will show in detail in the next chapter, though I think the question sufficiently plain from what I have said already, especially in Chapter II.

CHAPTER XIII.

It is shown that Scripture teaches only very simple Doctrines, such as suffice for Right Conduct.

IN THE SECOND chapter of this treatise we pointed out that the prophets were gifted with extraordinary powers of imagination, but not of understanding; also that God only revealed to them such things as are very simple — not philosophic mysteries, — and that He adapted His communications to their previous opinions. We further showed in Chap. V. that Scripture only transmits and teaches truths which can readily be comprehended by all; not deducing and concatenating its conclusions from definitions and axioms, but narrating quite simply, and confirming its statements, with a view to inspiring belief, by an appeal to experience as exemplified in miracles and history, and setting forth its truths in the style and phraseology which would most appeal to the popular mind (cf. Chap. VI., third division).

Lastly, we demonstrated in Chap. VIII. that the difficulty of understanding Scripture lies in the language only, and not in the abstruseness of the argument.

To these considerations we may add that the Prophets did not preach only to the learned, but to all Jews, without exception, while the Apostles were wont to teach the gospel doctrine in churches where there were public meetings; whence it follows that Scriptural doctrine contains no lofty speculations nor philosophic reasoning, but only very simple matters, such as could be understood by the slowest intelligence.

I am consequently lost in wonder at the ingenuity of those whom I have already mentioned, who detect in the Bible mysteries so profound that they cannot be explained in human language, and who have introduced so many philosophic speculations into religion that the Church seems like an academy, and religion like a science, or rather a dispute.

It is not to be wondered at that men, who boast of possessing supernatural intelligence, should be unwilling to yield the palm of knowledge to philosophers who have only their ordinary, faculties; still I should be surprised if I found them teaching any new speculative doctrine, which was not a commonplace to those Gentile philosophers whom, in spite of all, they stigmatize as blind; for, if one inquires what these mysteries lurking in Scripture may be, one is confronted with nothing but the reflections of Plato or Aristotle, or the like, which it would often be easier for an ignorant man to dream than for the most accomplished scholar to wrest out of the Bible.

However, I do not wish to affirm absolutely that Scripture contains no doctrines in the sphere of philosophy, for in the last chapter I pointed out some of the kind, as fundamental principles; but I go so far as to say that such doctrines are very few and very simple. Their precise nature and definition I will now set forth. The task will be easy, for we know that Scripture does not aim at imparting scientific knowledge, and, therefore, it demands from men nothing but obedience, and censures obstinacy, but not ignorance.

Furthermore, as obedience to God consists solely in love to our neighbour — for whosoever loveth his neighbour, as a means of obeying God, hath, as St. Paul says (Rom. xiii:8), fulfilled the law, — it follows that no knowledge is commended in the Bible save that which is necessary for enabling all men to obey God in the manner stated, and without which they would become rebellious, or without the discipline of obedience.

Other speculative questions, which have no direct bearing on this object, or are concerned with the knowledge of natural events, do not affect Scripture, and should be entirely separated from religion.

Now, though everyone, as we have said, is now quite able to see this truth for himself, I should nevertheless wish, considering that the whole of Religion depends thereon, to explain the entire question more accurately and clearly. To this end I must first prove that the intellectual or accurate knowledge of God is not a gift, bestowed upon all good men like obedience; and, further, that the knowledge of God, required by Him through His prophets from everyone without exception, as needful to be known, is simply a knowledge of His Divine justice and charity. Both these points are easily proved from Scripture. The first plainly follows from Exodus vi:2, where God, in order to show the singular grace bestowed upon Moses, says to him: "And I appeared unto Abraham, unto Isaac, and unto Jacob by the name of El Sadai (A. V. God Almighty); but by my name Jehovah was I not known to them" — for the better understanding of which passage I may remark that El Sadai, in Hebrew, signifies the God who suffices, in that He gives to every man that which suffices for him; and, although Sadai is often used by itself, to signify God, we cannot doubt that the word El (God, {power, might}) is everywhere understood. Furthermore, we must note that Jehovah is the only word found in Scripture with the meaning of the absolute essence of God, without reference to created things. The Jews maintain, for this reason, that this is, strictly speaking, the only name of God; that the rest of the words used are merely titles; and, in truth, the other names of God, whether they be substantives or adjectives, are merely attributive, and belong to Him, in so far as He is conceived of in relation to created things, or manifested through them. Thus El, or Eloah, signifies powerful, as is well known, and only applies to God in respect to His supremacy, as when we call Paul an apostle; the faculties of his power are set forth in an accompanying adjective, as El, great, awful, just, merciful, &c., or else all are understood at once by the use of El in the plural number, with a singular signification, an expression frequently adopted in Scripture.

Now, as God tells Moses that He was not known to the patriarchs by the name of Jehovah, it follows that they were not cognizant of any attribute of God which expresses His absolute essence, but only of His deeds and promises that is, of His power, as manifested in visible things. God does not thus speak to Moses in order to accuse the patriarchs of infidelity, but, on the contrary, as a means of extolling their belief and faith, inasmuch as, though they possessed no extraordinary knowledge of God (such as Moses had), they yet accepted His promises as fixed and certain; whereas Moses, though his thoughts about God were more exalted, nevertheless doubted about the Divine promises, and complained to God that, instead of the promised deliverance, the prospects of the Israelites had darkened.

As the patriarchs did not know the distinctive name of God, and as God mentions the fact to Moses, in praise of their faith and single-heartedness, and in contrast to the extraordinary grace granted to Moses, it follows, as we stated at first, that men are not bound by, decree to have knowledge of the attributes of God, such knowledge being only granted to a few of the faithful: it is hardly worth while to quote further examples from Scripture, for everyone must recognize that knowledge of God is not equal among all good men. Moreover, a man cannot be ordered to be wise any more than he can be ordered to live and exist. Men, women, and children are all alike able to obey by, commandment, but not to be wise. If any tell us that it is not necessary to understand the Divine attributes, but that we must believe them simply, without proof, he is plainly, trifling. For what is invisible and can only, be perceived by the mind, cannot be apprehended by any, other means than proofs; if these are absent the object remains ungrasped; the repetition of what has been heard on such subjects no more indicates or attains to their meaning than the words of a parrot or a puppet speaking without sense or signification.

Before I proceed I ought to explain how it comes that we are often told in Genesis that the patriarchs preached in the name of Jehovah, this being in plain contradiction to the text above quoted. A reference to what was said in Chap. VIII. will readily explain the difficulty. It was there shown that the writer of the Pentateuch did not always speak of things and places by the names they bore in the times of which he was writing, but by the names best known to his contemporaries. God is thus said in the Pentateuch to have been preached by the patriarchs under the name of Jehovah, not because such was the name by which the patriarchs knew Him, but because this name was the one most reverenced by the Jews. This point, I say, must necessarily be noticed, for in Exodus it is expressly stated that God was not known to the patriarchs by this name; and in chap. iii:13, it is said that Moses desired to know the name of God. Now, if this name had been already known it would have been known to Moses. We must therefore draw the conclusion indicated, namely, that the faithful patriarchs did not know this name of God, and that the knowledge of God is bestowed and not commanded by the Deity.

It is now time to pass on to our second point, and show that God through His prophets required from men no other knowledge of Himself than is contained in a knowledge of His justice and charity — that is, of attributes which a certain manner of life will enable men to imitate. Jeremiah states this in so many words (xxii:15, 16): "Did not thy father eat, and drink, and do judgment and justice? and then it was well with him. He judged the cause of the poor and needy; then it was well with him: was not this to know Me? saith the Lord." The words in chap. ix:24 of the same book are equally, clear. "But let him that glorieth glory in this, that he understandeth and knoweth Me, that I am the Lord which exercise loving-kindness, judgment, and righteousness in the earth; for in these things I delight, saith the Lord." The same doctrine maybe gathered from Exod. xxxiv:6, where God revealed to Moses only, those of His attributes which display the Divine justice and charity. Lastly, we may call attention to a passage in John which we shall discuss at more length hereafter; the Apostle explains the nature of God (inasmuch as no one has beheld Him) through charity only, and concludes that he who possesses charity possesses, and in very, truth knows God.

We have thus seen that Moses, Jeremiah, and John sum up in a very short compass the knowledge of God needful for all, and that they state it to consist in exactly what we said, namely, that God is supremely just, and supremely merciful — in other words, the one perfect pattern of the true life. We may add that Scripture nowhere gives an express definition of God, and does not point out any other of His attributes which should be apprehended save these, nor does it in set terms praise any others. Wherefore we may draw the general conclusion that an intellectual knowledge of God, which takes cognizance of His nature in so far as it actually is, and which cannot by any manner of living be imitated by mankind or followed as an example, has no bearing whatever on true rules of conduct, on faith, or on revealed religion; consequently that men may be in complete error on the subject without incurring the charge of sinfulness. We need now no longer wonder that God adapted Himself to the existing opinions and imaginations of the prophets, or that the faithful held different ideas of God, as we showed in Chap. II.; or, again, that the sacred books speak very inaccurately of God, attributing to Him hands, feet, eyes, ears, a mind, and motion from one place to another; or that they ascribe to Him emotions, such as jealousy, mercy, &c., or, lastly, that they describe Him as a Judge in heaven sitting on a royal throne with Christ on His right hand. Such expressions are adapted to the understanding of the multitude, it being the object of the Bible to make men not learned but obedient.

In spite of this the general run of theologians, when they come upon any of these phrases which they cannot rationally harmonize with the Divine nature, maintain that they should be interpreted metaphorically, passages they cannot understand they say should be interpreted literally. But if every expression of this kind in the Bible is necessarily to be interpreted and understood metaphorically, Scripture must have been written, not for the people and the unlearned masses, but chiefly for accomplished experts and philosophers.

If it were indeed a sin to hold piously and simply the ideas about God we have just quoted, the prophets ought to have been strictly on their guard against the use of such expressions, seeing the weak-mindedness of the people, and ought, on the other hand, to have set forth first of all, duly and clearly, those attributes of God which are needful to be understood.

This they have nowhere done; we cannot, therefore, think that opinions taken in themselves without respect to actions are either pious or impious, but must maintain that a man is pious or impious in his beliefs only in so far as he is thereby incited to obedience, or derives from them license to sin and rebel. If a man, by believing what is true, becomes rebellious, his creed is impious; if by believing what is false he becomes obedient, his creed is pious; for the true knowledge of God comes not by commandment, but by Divine gift. God has required nothing from man but a knowledge of His Divine justice and charity, and that not as necessary to scientific accuracy, but to obedience.

CHAPTER XIV.

Definitions of Faith, the Faith, and the Foundations of Faith,
which is once for all separated from Philosophy.

FOR A TRUE knowledge of faith it is above all things necessary to understand that the Bible was adapted to the intelligence, not only of the prophets, but also of the diverse and fickle Jewish multitude. This will be recognized by all who give any thought to the subject, for they will see that a person who accepted promiscuously everything in Scripture as being the universal and absolute teaching of God, without accurately defining what was adapted to the popular intelligence, would find it impossible to escape confounding the opinions of the masses with the Divine doctrines, praising the judgments and comments of man as the teaching of God, and making a wrong use of Scriptural authority. Who, I say, does not perceive that this is the chief reason why so many sectaries teach contradictory opinions as Divine documents, and support their contentions with numerous Scriptural texts, till it has passed in Belgium into a proverb, geen ketter sonder letter — no heretic without a text? The sacred books were not written by one man, nor for the people of a single period, but by many authors of different temperaments, at times extending from first to last over nearly two thousand years, and perhaps much longer. We will not, however, accuse the sectaries of impiety because they have adapted the words of Scripture to their own opinions; it is thus that these words were adapted to the understanding of the masses originally, and everyone is at liberty so to treat them if he sees that he can thus obey God in matters relating to justice and charity with a more full consent: but we do accuse those who will not grant this freedom to their fellows, but who persecute all who differ from them, as God's enemies, however honourable and virtuous be their lives; while, on the other hand, they cherish those who agree with them, however foolish they may be, as God's elect. Such conduct is as wicked and dangerous to the state as any that can be conceived.

In order, therefore, to establish the limits to which individual freedom should extend, and to decide what persons, in spite of the diversity of their opinions, are to be looked upon as the faithful, we must define faith and its essentials. This task I hope to accomplish in the present chapter, and also to separate faith from philosophy, which is the chief aim of the whole treatise.

In order to proceed duly to the demonstration let us recapitulate the chief aim and object of Scripture; this will indicate a standard by which we may define faith.

We have said in a former chapter that the aim and object of Scripture is only to teach obedience. Thus much, I think, no one can question. Who does not see that both Testaments are nothing else but schools for this object, and have neither of them any aim beyond inspiring mankind with a voluntary obedience? For (not to repeat what I said in the last chapter) I will remark that Moses did not seek to convince the Jews by reason, but bound them by a covenant, by oaths, and by conferring benefits; further, he threatened the people with punishment if they should infringe the law, and promised rewards if they should obey it. All these are not means for teaching knowledge, but for inspiring obedience. The doctrine of the Gospels enjoins nothing but simple faith, namely, to believe in God and to honour Him, which is the same thing as to obey him. There is no occasion for me to throw further light on a question so plain by citing Scriptural texts commending obedience, such as may be found in great numbers in both Testaments. Moreover, the Bible teaches very clearly in a great many passages what everyone ought to do in order to obey God; the whole duty is summed up in love to one's neighbour. It cannot, therefore, be denied that he who by God's command loves his neighbour as himself is truly obedient and blessed according to the law, whereas he who hates his neighbour or neglects him is rebellious and obstinate.

Lastly, it is plain to everyone that the Bible was not written and disseminated only, for the learned, but for men of every age and race; wherefore we may, rest assured that we are not bound by Scriptural command to believe anything beyond what is absolutely necessary, for fulfilling its main precept.

This precept, then, is the only standard of the whole Catholic faith, and by it alone all the dogmas needful to be believed should be determined. So much being abundantly manifest, as is also the fact that all other doctrines of the faith can be legitimately deduced therefrom by reason alone, I leave it to every man to decide for himself how it comes to pass that so many divisions have arisen in the Church: can it be from any other cause than those suggested at the beginning of Chap. VIII.? It is these same causes which compel me to explain the method of determining the dogmas of the faith from the foundation we have discovered, for if I neglected to do so, and put the question on a regular basis, I might justly be said to have promised too lavishly, for that anyone might, by my showing, introduce any doctrine he liked into religion, under the pretext that it was a necessary means to obedience: especially would this be the case in questions respecting the Divine attributes.

In order, therefore, to set forth the whole matter methodically, I will begin with a definition of faith, which on the principle above given, should be as follows: —

Faith consists in a knowledge of God, without which obedience to Him would be impossible, and which the mere fact of obedience to Him implies. This definition is so clear, and follows so plainly from what we have already proved, that it needs no explanation. The consequences involved therein I will now briefly show.

(I.) Faith is not salutary in itself, but only in respect to the obedience it implies, or as James puts it in his Epistle, ii:17, "Faith without works is dead" (see the whole of the chapter quoted).

(II.) He who is truly obedient necessarily possesses true and saving faith; for if obedience be granted, faith must be granted also, as the same Apostle expressly says in these words (ii:18), "Show me thy faith without thy works, and I will show thee my faith by my works." So also John, I Ep. iv:7: "Everyone that loveth is born of God, and knoweth God: he that loveth not, knoweth not God; for God is love." From these texts, I repeat, it follows that we can only judge a man faithful or unfaithful by his works. If his works be good, he is faithful, however much his doctrines may differ from those of the rest of the faithful: if his works be evil, though he may verbally conform, he is unfaithful. For obedience implies faith, and faith without works is dead.

John, in the 13th verse of the chapter above quoted, expressly teaches the same doctrine: "Hereby," he says, "know we that we dwell in Him and He in us, because He hath given us of His Spirit," i.e. love. He had said before that God is love, and therefore he concludes (on his own received principles), that whoso possesses love possesses truly the Spirit of God. As no one has beheld God he infers that no one has knowledge or consciousness of God, except from love towards his neighbour, and also that no one can have knowledge of any of God's attributes, except this of love, in so far as we participate therein.

If these arguments are not conclusive, they, at any rate, show the Apostle's meaning, but the words in chap. ii:3, 4, of the same Epistle are much clearer, for they state in so many words our precise contention: "And hereby we do know that we know Him, if we keep His commandments. He that saith, I know Him, and keepeth not His commandments, is a liar, and the truth is not in him."

From all this, I repeat, it follows that they are the true enemies of Christ who persecute honourable and justice-loving men because they differ from them, and do not uphold the same religious dogmas as themselves: for whosoever loves justice and charity we know, by that very fact, to be faithful: whosoever persecutes the faithful, is an enemy to Christ.

Lastly, it follows that faith does not demand that dogmas should be true as that they should be pious — that is, such as will stir up the heart to obey; though there be many such which contain not a shadow of truth, so long as they be held in good faith, otherwise their adherents are disobedient, for how can anyone, desirous of loving justice and obeying God, adore as Divine what he knows to be alien from the Divine nature? However, men may err from simplicity of mind, and Scripture, as we have seen, does not condemn ignorance, but obstinacy. This is the necessary result of our definition of faith, and all its branches should spring from the universal rule above given, and from the evident aim and object of the Bible, unless we choose to mix our own inventions therewith. Thus it is not true doctrines which are expressly required by the Bible, so much as doctrines necessary for obedience, and to confirm in our hearts the love of our neighbour, wherein (to adopt the words of John) we are in God, and God in us.

As, then, each man's faith must be judged pious or impious only in respect of its producing obedience or obstinacy, and not in respect of its truth; and as no one will dispute that men's dispositions are exceedingly varied, that all do not acquiesce in the same things, but are ruled some by one opinion some by another, so that what moves one to devotion moves another to laughter and contempt, it follows that there can be no doctrines in the Catholic, or universal, religion, which can give rise to controversy among good men. Such doctrines might be pious to some and impious to others, whereas they should be judged solely by their fruits.

To the universal religion, then, belong only such dogmas as are absolutely required in order to attain obedience to God, and without which such obedience would be impossible; as for the rest, each man — seeing that he is the best judge of his own character should adopt whatever he thinks best adapted to strengthen his love of justice. If this were so, I think there would be no further occasion for controversies in the Church.

I have now no further fear in enumerating the dogmas of universal faith or the fundamental dogmas of the whole of Scripture, inasmuch as they all tend (as may be seen from what has been said) to this one doctrine, namely, that there exists a God, that is, a Supreme Being, Who loves justice and charity, and Who must be obeyed by whosoever would be saved; that the worship of this Being consists in the practice of justice and love towards one's neighbour, and that they contain nothing beyond the following doctrines: —

I. That God or a Supreme Being exists, sovereignly just and merciful, the Exemplar of the true life; that whosoever is ignorant of or disbelieves in His existence cannot obey Him or know Him as a Judge.

II. That He is One. Nobody will dispute that this doctrine is absolutely necessary for entire devotion, admiration, and love towards God. For devotion, admiration, and love spring from the superiority of one over all else.

III. That He is omnipresent, or that all things are open to Him, for if anything could be supposed to be concealed from Him, or to be unnoticed by, Him, we might doubt or be ignorant of the equity of His judgment as directing all things.

IV. That He has supreme right and dominion over all things, and that He does nothing under compulsion, but by His absolute fiat and grace. All things are bound to obey Him, He is not bound to obey any.

V. That the worship of God consists only in justice and charity, or love towards one's neighbour.

VI. That all those, and those only, who obey God by their manner of life are saved; the rest of mankind, who live under the sway of their pleasures, are lost. If we did not believe this, there would be no reason for obeying God rather than pleasure.

VII. Lastly, that God forgives the sins of those who repent. No one is free from sin, so that without this belief all would despair of salvation, and there would be no reason for believing in the mercy of God. He who firmly believes that God, out of the mercy and grace with which He directs all things, forgives the sins of men, and who feels his love of God kindled thereby, he, I say, does really, know Christ according to the Spirit, and Christ is in him.

No one can deny that all these doctrines are before all things necessary, to be believed, in order that every man, without exception, may be able to obey God according to the bidding of the Law above explained, for if one of these precepts be disregarded obedience is destroyed. But as to what God, or the Exemplar of the true life, may be, whether fire, or spirit, or light, or thought, or what not, this, I say, has nothing to do with faith any more than has the question how He comes to be the Exemplar of the true life, whether it be because He has a just and merciful mind, or because all things exist and act through Him, and consequently that we understand through Him, and through Him see what is truly just and good. Everyone may think on such questions as he likes,

Furthermore, faith is not affected, whether we hold that God is omnipresent essentially or potentially; that He directs all things by absolute fiat, or by the necessity of His nature; that He dictates laws like a prince, or that He sets them forth as eternal truths; that man obeys Him by virtue of free will, or by virtue of the necessity of the Divine decree; lastly, that the reward of the good and the punishment of the wicked is natural or supernatural: these and such like questions have no bearing on faith, except in so far as they are used as means to give us license to sin more, or to obey God less. I will go further, and maintain that every man is bound to adapt these dogmas to his own way of thinking, and to interpret them according as he feels that he can give them his fullest and most unhesitating assent, so that he may the more easily obey God with his whole heart.

Such was the manner, as we have already pointed out, in which the faith was in old time revealed and written, in accordance with the understanding and opinions of the prophets and people of the period; so, in like fashion, every man is bound to adapt it to his own opinions, so that he may accept it without any hesitation or mental repugnance. We have shown that faith does not so much re quire truth as piety, and that it is only quickening and pious through obedience, consequently no one is faithful save by obedience alone. The best faith is not necessarily possessed by him who displays the best reasons, but by him who displays the best fruits of justice and charity. How salutary and necessary this doctrine is for a state, in order that men may dwell together in peace and concord; and how many and how great causes of disturbance and crime are thereby cut off, I leave everyone to judge for himself!

Before we go further, I may remark that we can, by means of what we have just proved, easily answer the objections raised in Chap. I., when we were discussing God's speaking with the Israelites on Mount Sinai. For, though the voice heard by the Israelites could not give those men any philosophical or mathematical certitude of God's existence, it was yet sufficient to thrill them with admiration for God, as they already knew Him, and to stir them up to obedience: and such was the object of the display. God did not wish to teach the Israelites the absolute attributes of His essence (none of which He then revealed), but to break down their hardness of heart, and to draw them to obedience: therefore He did not appeal to them with reasons, but with the sound of trumpets, thunder, and lightnings.

It remains for me to show that between faith or theology, and philosophy, there is no connection, nor affinity. I think no one will dispute the fact who has knowledge of the aim and foundations of the two subjects, for they are as wide apart as the poles.

Philosophy has no end in view save truth: faith, as we have abundantly proved, looks for nothing but obedience and piety. Again, philosophy is based on axioms which must be sought from nature alone: faith is based on history and language, and must be sought for only in Scripture and revelation, as we showed in Chap. VII. Faith, therefore, allows the greatest latitude in philosophic speculation, allowing us without blame to think what we like about anything, and only condemning, as heretics and schismatics, those who teach opinions which tend to produce obstinacy, hatred, strife, and anger; while, on the other hand, only considering as faithful those who persuade us, as far as their reason and faculties will permit, to follow justice and charity.

Lastly, as what we are now setting forth are the most important subjects of my treatise, I would most urgently beg the reader, before I proceed, to read these two chapters with especial attention, and to take the trouble to weigh them well in his mind: let him take for granted that I have not written with a view to introducing novelties, but in order to do away with abuses, such as I hope I may, at some future time, at last see reformed.

CHAPTER XV.

Theology is shown not to be Subservient to Reason, nor Reason to Theology: a Definition of the Reason which enables us to accept the authority of the Bible.

THOSE WHO KNOW not that philosophy and reason are distinct, dispute whether Scripture should be made subservient to reason, or reason to Scripture: that is, whether the meaning of Scripture should be made to agreed with reason; or whether reason should be made to agree with Scripture: the latter position is assumed by the sceptics who deny the certitude of reason, the former by the dogmatists. Both parties are, as I have shown, utterly in the wrong, for either doctrine would require us to tamper with reason or with Scripture.

We have shown that Scripture does not teach philosophy, but merely obedience, and that all it contains has been adapted to the understanding and established opinions of the multitude. Those, therefore, who wish to adapt it to philosophy, must needs ascribe to the prophets many ideas which they never even dreamed of, and give an extremely forced interpretation to their words: those on the other hand, who would make reason and philosophy subservient to theology, will be forced to accept as Divine utterances the prejudices of the ancient Jews, and to fill and confuse their mind therewith. In short, one party will run wild with the aid of reason, and the other will run wild without the aid of reason.

The first among the Pharisees who openly maintained that Scripture should be made to agree with reason, was Maimonides, whose opinion we reviewed, and abundantly refuted in Chap. VIII.: now, although this writer had much authority among his contemporaries, he was deserted on this question by almost all, and the majority went straight over to the opinion of a certain R. Jehuda Alpakhar, who, in his anxiety to avoid the error of Maimonides, fell into another, which was its exact contrary. He held that reason should be made subservient, and entirely give way to Scripture. He thought that a passage should not be interpreted metaphorically, simply because it was repugnant to reason, but only in the cases when it is inconsistent with Scripture itself — that is, with its clear doctrines. Therefore he laid down the universal rule, that whatsoever Scripture teaches dogmatically, and affirms expressly, must on its own sole authority be admitted as absolutely true: that there is no doctrine in the Bible which directly contradicts the general tenor of the whole: but only some which appear to involve a difference, for the phrases of Scripture often seem to imply something contrary to what has been expressly taught. Such phrases, and such phrases only, we may interpret metaphorically.

For instance, Scripture clearly teaches the unity of God (see Deut. vi:4), nor is there any text distinctly asserting a plurality of gods; but in several passages God speaks of Himself, and the prophets speak of Him, in the plural number; such phrases are simply a manner of speaking, and do not mean that there actually are several gods: they are to be explained metaphorically, not because a plurality of gods is repugnant to reason, but because Scripture distinctly asserts that there is only one.

So, again, as Scripture asserts (as Alpakhar thinks) in Deut. iv:15, that God is incorporeal, we are bound, solely by the authority of this text, and not by reason, to believe that God has no body: consequently we must explain metaphorically, on the sole authority of Scripture, all those passages which attribute to God hands, feet, &c., and take them merely as figures of speech. Such is the opinion of

Alpakhar. In so far as he seeks to explain Scripture by Scripture, I praise him, but I marvel that a man gifted with reason should wish to debase that faculty. It is true that Scripture should be explained by Scripture, so long as we are in difficulties about the meaning and intention of the prophets, but when we have elicited the true meaning, we must of necessity make use of our judgment and reason in order to assent thereto. If reason, however, much as she rebels, is to be entirely subjected to Scripture, I ask, are we to effect her submission by her own aid, or without her, and blindly? If the latter, we shall surely act foolishly and injudiciously; if the former, we assent to Scripture under the dominion of reason, and should not assent to it without her. Moreover, I may ask now, is a man to assent to anything against his reason? What is denial if it be not reason's refusal to assent? In short, I am astonished that anyone should wish to subject reason, the greatest of gifts and a light from on high, to the dead letter which may have been corrupted by human malice; that it should be thought no crime to speak with contempt of mind, the true handwriting of God's Word, calling it corrupt, blind, and lost, while it is considered the greatest of crimes to say the same of the letter, which is merely the reflection and image of God's Word. Men think it pious to trust nothing to reason and their own judgment, and impious to doubt the faith of those who have transmitted to us the sacred books. Such conduct is not piety, but mere folly. And, after all, why are they so anxious? What are they afraid of? Do they think that faith and religion cannot be upheld unless — men purposely keep themselves in ignorance, and turn their backs on reason? If this be so, they have but a timid trust in Scripture.

However, be it far from me to say that religion should seek to enslave reason, or reason religion, or that both should not be able to keep their sovereignty in perfect harmony. I will revert to this question presently, for I wish now to discuss Alpakhar's rule.

He requires, as we have stated, that we should accept as true, or reject as false, everything asserted or denied by Scripture, and he further states that Scripture never expressly asserts or denies anything which contradicts its assertions or negations elsewhere. The rashness of such a requirement and statement can escape no one. For (passing over the fact that he does not notice that Scripture consists of different books, written at different times, for different people, by different authors: and also that his requirement is made on his own authority without any corroboration from reason or Scripture) he would be bound to show that all passages which are indirectly contradictory of the rest, can be satisfactorily explained metaphorically through the nature of the language and the context: further, that Scripture has come down to us untampered with. However, we will go into the matter at length.

Firstly, I ask what shall we do if reason prove recalcitrant? Shall we still be bound to affirm whatever Scripture affirms, and to deny whatever Scripture denies? Perhaps it will be answered that Scripture contains nothing repugnant to reason. But I insist!hat it expressly affirms and teaches that God is jealous (namely, in the decalogue itself, and in Exod. xxxiv:14, and in Deut. iv:24, and in many other places), and I assert that such a doctrine is repugnant to reason. It must, I suppose, in spite of all, be accepted as true. If there are any passages in Scripture which imply that God is not jealous, they must be taken metaphorically as meaning nothing of the kind. So, also, Scripture expressly states (Exod. xix:20, &c.) that God came down to Mount Sinai, and it attributes to Him other movements from place to place, nowhere directly stating that God does not so move. Wherefore, we must take the passage literally, and Solomon's words (I Kings viii:27), "But will God dwell on the earth? Behold the heavens and earth cannot contain thee," inasmuch as they do not expressly state that God does not move from place to place, but only imply it, must be explained away till they have no further semblance of denying locomotion to the Deity. So also we must believe that the sky is the habitation and throne of God, for Scripture expressly says so; and similarly many passages expressing the opinions of the prophets or the multitude, which reason and philosophy, but not Scripture, tell us to be false, must be taken as true if we are io follow the guidance of our author, for according to him, reason has nothing to do with the matter. Further, it is untrue that Scripture never contradicts itself directly, but only by implication. For Moses says, in so many words (Deut. iv:24), "The Lord thy God is a consuming fire," and elsewhere expressly denies that God has any likeness to visible things. (Deut. iv. 12.) If it be decided that the latter passage only contradicts the former by implication, and must be adapted thereto, lest it seem to negative it, let us grant that God is a fire; or rather, lest we should seem to have taken leave of our senses, let us pass the matter over and take another example.

Samuel expressly denies that God ever repents, "for he is not a man that he should repent" (I Sam. xv:29). Jeremiah, on the other hand, asserts that God does repent, both of the evil and of the good which He had intended to do (Jer. xviii:8-10). What? Are not these two texts directly contradictory? Which of the two, then, would our author want to explain metaphorically? Both statements are general, and each is the opposite of the other — what one flatly affirms, the other flatly, denies. So, by his own rule, he would be obliged at once to reject them as false, and to accept them as true.

Again, what is the point of one passage, not being contradicted by another directly, but only by implication, if the implication is clear, and the nature and context of the passage preclude metaphorical interpretation? There are many such instances in the Bible, as we saw in Chap. II. (where we pointed out that the prophets held different and contradictory opinions), and also in Chaps. IX. and X., where we drew attention to the contradictions in the historical narratives. There is no need for me to go through them all again, for what I have said sufficiently exposes the absurdities which would follow from an opinion and rule such as we are discussing, and shows the hastiness of its propounder.

We may, therefore, put this theory, as well as that of Maimonides, entirely out of court; and we may, take it for indisputable that theology is not bound to serve reason, nor reason theology, but that each has her own domain.

The sphere of reason is, as we have said, truth and wisdom; the sphere of theology, is piety and obedience. The power of reason does not extend so far as to determine for us that men may be blessed through simple obedience, without understanding. Theology, tells us nothing else, enjoins on us no command save obedience, and has neither the will nor the power to oppose reason: she defines the dogmas of faith (as we pointed out in the last chapter) only in so far as they may be necessary, for obedience, and leaves reason to determine their precise truth: for reason is the light of the mind, and without her all things are dreams and phantoms.

By theology, I here mean, strictly speaking, revelation, in so far as it indicates the object aimed at by Scripture namely, the scheme and manner of obedience, or the true dogmas of piety and faith. This may truly be called the Word of God, which does not consist in a certain number of books (see Chap. XII.). Theology thus understood, if we regard its precepts or rules of life, will be found in accordance with reason; and, if we look to its aim and object, will be seen to be in nowise repugnant thereto, wherefore it is universal to all men.

As for its bearing on Scripture, we have shown in Chap. VII. that the meaning of Scripture should be gathered from its own history, and not from the history of nature in general, which is the basis of philosophy.

We ought not to be hindered if we find that our investigation of the meaning of Scripture thus conducted shows us that it is here and there repugnant to reason; for whatever we may find of this sort in the Bible, which men may be in ignorance of, without injury to their charity, has, we may be sure, no bearing on theology or the Word of God, and may, therefore, without blame, be viewed by every one as he pleases.

To sum up, we may draw the absolute conclusion that the Bible must not be accommodated to reason, nor reason to the Bible.

Now, inasmuch as the basis of theology — the doctrine that man may be saved by obedience alone — cannot be proved by reason whether it be true or false, we may be asked, Why, then, should we believe it? If we do so without the aid of reason, we accept it blindly, and act foolishly and injudiciously; if, on the other hand, we settle that it can be proved by reason, theology becomes a part of philosophy, and inseparable therefrom. But I make answer that I have absolutely established that this basis of theology cannot be investigated by the natural light of reason, or, at any rate, that no one ever has proved it by such means, and, therefore, revelation was necessary. We should, however, make use of our reason, in order to grasp with moral certainty what is revealed — I say, with moral certainty, for we cannot hope to attain greater certainty, than the prophets: yet their certainty was only, moral, as I showed in Chap. II.

Those, therefore, who attempt to set forth the authority of Scripture with mathematical demonstrations are wholly in error: for the authority, of the Bible is dependent on the authority of the prophets, and can be supported by no stronger arguments than those employed in old time by the prophets for convincing the people of their own authority. Our certainty on the same subject can be founded on no other basis than that which served as foundation for the certainty of the prophets.

Now the certainty of the prophets consisted (as we pointed out) in these elements: — (I.) A distinct and vivid imagination. (II.) A sign. (III.) Lastly, and chiefly, a mind turned to what is just and good. It was based on no other reasons than these, and consequently they cannot prove their authority by any other reasons, either to the multitude whom they addressed orally, nor to us whom they address in writing.

The first of these reasons, namely, the vivid imagination, could be valid only for the prophets; therefore, our certainty concerning revelation must, and ought to be, based on the remaining two — namely, the sign and the teaching. Such is the express doctrine of Moses, for (in Deut. xviii.) he bids the people obey the prophet who should give a true sign in the name of the Lord, but if he should predict falsely, even though it were in the name of the Lord, he should be put to death, as should also he who strives to lead away the people from the true religion, though he confirm his authority with signs and portents. We may compare with the above Deut. xiii. Whence it follows that a true prophet could be distinguished from a false one, both by his doctrine and by the miracles he wrought, for Moses declares such an one to be a true prophet, and bids the people trust him without fear of deceit. He condemns as false, and worthy, of death, those who predict anything falsely even in the name of the Lord, or who preach false gods, even though their miracles be real.

The only reason, then, which we have for belief in Scripture or the writings of the prophets, is the doctrine we find therein, and the signs by which it is confirmed. For as we see that the prophets extol charity and justice above all things, and have no other object, we conclude that they did not write from unworthy motives, but because they really thought that men might become blessed through obedience and faith: further, as we see that they confirmed their teaching with signs and wonders, we become persuaded that they did not speak at random, nor run riot in their prophecies. We are further strengthened in our conclusion by the fact that the morality they teach is in evident agreement with reason, for it is no accidental coincidence that the Word of God which we find in the prophets coincides with the Word of God written in our hearts. We may, I say, conclude this from the sacred books as certainly as did the Jews of old from the living voice of the prophets: for we showed in Chap. XII. that Scripture has come down to us intact in respect to its doctrine and main narratives.

Therefore this whole basis of theology and Scripture, though it does not admit of mathematical proof, may yet be accepted with the approval of our judgment. It would be folly to refuse to accept what is confirmed by such ample prophetic testimony, and what has proved such a comfort to those whose reason is comparatively weak, and such a benefit to the state; a doctrine, moreover, which we may believe in without the slightest peril or hurt, and should reject simply because it cannot be mathematically proved: it is as though we should admit nothing as true, or as a wise rule of life, which could ever, in any possible way, be called in question; or as though most of our actions were not full of uncertainty and hazards.

I admit that those who believe that theology and philosophy are mutually contradictory, and that therefore either one or the other must be thrust from its throne — I admit, I say, that such persons are not unreasonable in attempting to put theology on a firm basis, and to demonstrate its truth mathematically. Who, unless he were desperate or mad, would wish to bid an incontinent farewell to reason, or to despise the arts and sciences, or to deny reason's certitude? But, in the meanwhile, we cannot wholly absolve them from blame, inasmuch as they invoke the aid of reason for her own defeat, and attempt infallibly to prove her fallible. While they are trying to prove mathematically the authority and truth of theology, and to take away the authority of natural reason, they are in reality only bringing theology under reason's dominion, and proving that her authority has no weight unless natural reason be at the back of it.

If they boast that they themselves assent because of the inward testimony of the Holy Spirit, and that they only invoke the aid of reason because of unbelievers, in order to convince them, not even so can this meet with our approval, for we can easily show that they have spoken either from emotion or vain-glory. It most clearly follows from the last chapter that the Holy Spirit only gives its testimony in favour of works, called by Paul (in Gal. v:22) the fruits of the Spirit, and is in itself really nothing but the mental acquiescence which follows a good action in our souls. No spirit gives testimony concerning the certitude of matters within the sphere of speculation, save only reason, who is mistress, as we have shown, of the whole realm of truth. If then they assert that they possess this Spirit which makes them certain of truth, they speak falsely, and according to the prejudices of the emotions, or else they are in great dread lest they should be vanquished by philosophers and exposed to public ridicule, and therefore they flee, as it were, to the altar; but their refuge is vain, for what altar will shelter a man who has outraged reason? However, I pass such persons over, for I think I have fulfilled my purpose, and shown how philosophy should be separated from theology, and wherein each consists; that neither should be subservient to the other, but that each should keep her unopposed dominion. Lastly, as occasion offered, I have pointed out the absurdities, the inconveniences, and the evils following from the extraordinary confusion which has hitherto prevailed between the two subjects, owing to their not being properly distinguished and separated. Before I go further I would expressly state (though I have said it before) that I consider the utility and the need for Holy Scripture or Revelation to be very great. For as we cannot perceive by the natural light of reason that simple obedience is the path of salvation 25, and are taught by revelation only that it is so by the special grace of God, which our reason cannot attain, it follows that the Bible has brought a very great consolation to mankind. All are able to obey, whereas there are but very few, compared with the aggregate of humanity, who can acquire the habit of virtue under the unaided guidance of reason. Thus if we had not the testimony of Scripture, we should doubt of the salvation of nearly all men.

25 "That simple obedience is the path of salvation." In other words, it is enough for salvation or blessedness, that we should embrace the Divine decrees as laws or commands; there is no need to conceive them as eternal truths. This can be taught us by Revelation, not Reason, as appears from the demonstrations given in Chapter IV.

CHAPTER XVI.

Of the Foundations of a State; of the Natural and Civil Rights of Individuals; and of the Rights of the Sovereign Power.

HITHERTO OUR CARE has been to separate philosophy from theology, and to show the freedom of thought which such separation insures to both. It is now time to determine the limits to which such freedom of thought and discussion may extend itself in the ideal state. For the due consideration of this question we must examine the foundations of a State, first turning our attention to the natural rights of individuals, and afterwards to religion and the state as a whole.

By the right and ordinance of nature, I merely mean those natural laws wherewith we conceive every individual to be conditioned by nature, so as to live and act in a given way. For instance, fishes are naturally conditioned for swimming, and the greater for devouring the less; therefore fishes enjoy the water, and the greater devour the less by sovereign natural right. For it is certain that nature, taken in the abstract, has sovereign right to do anything, she can; in other words, her right is co-extensive with her power. The power of nature is the power of God, which has sovereign right over all things; and, inasmuch as the power of nature is simply the aggregate of the powers of all her individual components, it follows that every, individual has sovereign right to do all that he can; in other words, the rights of an individual extend to the utmost limits of his power as it has been conditioned. Now it is the sovereign law and right of nature that each individual should endeavour to preserve itself as it is, without regard to anything but itself; therefore this sovereign law and right belongs to every individual, namely, to exist and act according to its natural conditions. We do not here acknowledge any difference between mankind and other individual natural entities, nor between men endowed with reason and those to whom reason is unknown; nor between fools, madmen, and sane men. Whatsoever an individual does by the laws of its nature it has a sovereign right to do, inasmuch as it acts as it was conditioned by nature, and cannot act otherwise. Wherefore among men, so long as they are considered as living under the sway of nature, he who does not yet know reason, or who has not yet acquired the habit of virtue, acts solely according to the laws of his desire with as sovereign a right as he who orders his life entirely by the laws of reason.

That is, as the wise man has sovereign right to do all that reason dictates, or to live according to the laws of reason, so also the ignorant and foolish man has sovereign right to do all that desire dictates, or to live according to the laws of desire. This is identical with the teaching of Paul, who acknowledges that previous to the law — that is, so long as men are considered of as living under the sway of nature, there is no sin.

The natural right of the individual man is thus determined, not by sound reason, but by desire and power. All are not naturally conditioned so as to act according to the laws and rules of reason; nay, on the contrary, all men are born ignorant, and before they can learn the right way of life and acquire the habit of virtue, the greater part of their life, even if they have been well brought up, has passed away. Nevertheless, they are in the meanwhile bound to live and preserve themselves as far as they can by the unaided impulses of desire. Nature has given them no other guide, and has denied them the present power of living according to sound reason; so that they are no more bound to live by the dictates of an enlightened mind, than a cat is bound to live by the laws of the nature of a lion.

Whatsoever, therefore, an individual (considered as under the sway of nature) thinks useful for himself, whether led by sound reason or impelled by the passions, that he has a sovereign right to seek and to take for himself as he best can, whether by force, cunning, entreaty, or any other means; consequently he may regard as an enemy anyone who hinders the accomplishment of his purpose.

It follows from what we have said that the right and ordinance of nature, under which all men are born, and under which they mostly live, only prohibits such things as no one desires, and no one can attain: it does not forbid strife, nor hatred, nor anger, nor deceit, nor, indeed, any of the means suggested by desire.

This we need not wonder at, for nature is not bounded by the laws of human reason, which aims only at man's true benefit and preservation; her limits are infinitely wider, and have reference to the eternal order of nature, wherein man is but a speck; it is by the necessity of this alone that all individuals are conditioned for living and acting in a particular way. If anything, therefore, in nature seems to us ridiculous, absurd, or evil, it is because we only know in part, and are almost entirely ignorant of the order and interdependence of nature as a whole, and also because we want everything to be arranged according to the dictates of our human reason; in reality that which reason considers evil, is not evil in respect to the order and laws of nature as a whole, but only in respect to the laws of our reason.

Nevertheless, no one can doubt that it is much better for us to live according to the laws and assured dictates of reason, for, as we said, they have men's true good for their object. Moreover, everyone wishes to live as far as possible securely beyond the reach of fear, and this would be quite impossible so long as everyone did everything he liked, and reason's claim was lowered to a par with those of hatred and anger; there is no one who is not ill at ease in the midst of enmity, hatred, anger, and deceit, and who does not seek to avoid them as much as he can. When we reflect that men without mutual help, or the aid of reason, must needs live most miserably, as we clearly proved in Chap. V., we shall plainly see that men must necessarily come to an agreement to live together as securely and well as possible if they are to enjoy as a whole the rights which naturally belong to them as individuals, and their life should be no more conditioned by the force and desire of individuals, but by the power and will of the whole body. This end they will be unable to attain if desire be their only guide (for by the laws of desire each man is drawn in a different direction); they must, therefore, most firmly decree and establish that they will be guided in everything by reason (which nobody will dare openly to repudiate lest he should be taken for a madman), and will restrain any desire which is injurious to a man's fellows, that they will do to all as they would be done by, and that they will defend their neighbour's rights as their own.

How such a compact as this should be entered into, how ratified and established, we will now inquire.

Now it is a universal law of human nature that no one ever neglects anything which he judges to be good, except with the hope of gaining a greater good, or from the fear of a greater evil; nor does anyone endure an evil except for the sake of avoiding a greater evil, or gaining a greater good. That is, everyone will, of two goods, choose that which he thinks the greatest; and, of two evils, that which he thinks the least. I say advisedly that which he thinks the greatest or the least, for it does not necessarily follow that he judges right. This law is so deeply implanted in the human mind that it ought to be counted among eternal truths and axioms.

As a necessary consequence of the principle just enunciated, no one can honestly promise to forego the right which he has over all things 26, and in general no one will abide by his promises, unless under the fear of a greater evil, or the hope of a greater good. An example will make the matter clearer. Suppose that a robber forces me to promise that I will give him my goods at his will and pleasure. It is plain (inasmuch as my natural right is, as I have shown, co-extensive with my power) that if I can free myself from this robber by stratagem, by assenting to his demands, I have the natural right to do so, and to pretend to accept his conditions. Or again, suppose I have genuinely promised someone that for the space of twenty days I will not taste food or any nourishment; and suppose I afterwards find that was foolish, and cannot be kept without very great injury to myself; as I am bound by natural law and right to choose the least of two evils, I have complete right to break my compact, and act as if my promise had never been uttered. I say that I should have perfect natural right to do so, whether I was actuated by true and evident reason, or whether I was actuated by mere opinion in thinking I had promised rashly; whether my reasons were true or false, I should be in fear of a greater evil, which, by the ordinance of nature, I should strive to avoid by every means in my power.

We may, therefore, conclude that a compact is only made valid by its utility, without which it becomes null and void. It is, therefore, foolish to ask a man to keep his faith with us for ever, unless we also endeavour that the violation of the compact we enter into shall involve for the violator more harm than good. This consideration should have very great weight in forming a state. However, if all men could be easily led by reason alone, and could recognize what is best and most useful for a state, there would be no one who would not forswear deceit, for everyone would keep most religiously to their compact in their desire for the chief good, namely, the shield and buckler of the commonwealth. However, it is far from being the case that all men can always be easily led by reason alone; everyone is drawn away by his pleasure, while avarice, ambition, envy, hatred, and the like so engross the mind that, reason has no place therein. Hence, though men make — promises with all the appearances of good faith, and agree that they will keep to their engagement, no one can absolutely rely on another man's promise unless there is something behind it. Everyone has by nature a right to act deceitfully. and to break his compacts, unless he be restrained by the hope of some greater good, or the fear of some greater evil.

However, as we have shown that the natural right of the individual is only limited by his power, it is clear that by transferring, either willingly or under compulsion, this power into the hands of another, he in so doing necessarily cedes also a part of his right; and further, that the Sovereign right over all men belongs to him who has sovereign power, wherewith he can compel men by force, or restrain them by threats of the universally feared punishment of death; such sovereign right he will retain only so long as he can maintain his power of enforcing his will; otherwise he will totter on his throne, and no one who is stronger than he will be bound unwillingly to obey him.

In this manner a society can be formed without any violation of natural right, and the covenant can always be strictly kept — that is, if each individual hands over the whole of his power to the body politic, the latter will then possess sovereign natural right over all things; that is, it will have sole and unquestioned dominion, and everyone will be bound to obey, under pain of the severest punishment. A body politic of this kind is called a Democracy, which may be defined as a society which wields all its power as a whole. The sovereign power is not restrained by any laws, but everyone is bound to obey it in all things; such is the state of things implied when men either tacitly or expressly handed over to it all their power of self-defence, or in other words, all their right. For if they had wished to retain any right for themselves, they ought to have taken precautions for its defence and preservation; as they have not done so, and indeed could not have done so without dividing and consequently ruining the state, they placed themselves absolutely at the mercy of the sovereign power; and, therefore, having acted (as we have shown) as reason and necessity demanded, they are obliged to fulfil the commands of the sovereign power, however absurd these may be, else they will be public enemies, and will act against reason, which urges the preservation of the state as a primary duty. For reason bids us choose the least of two evils.

Furthermore, this danger of submitting absolutely to the dominion and will of another, is one which may be incurred with a light heart: for we have shown that sovereigns only possess this right of imposing their will, so long as they have the full power to enforce it: if such power be lost their right to command is lost also, or lapses to those who have assumed it and can keep it. Thus it is very rare for sovereigns to impose thoroughly irrational commands, for they are bound to consult their own interests, and retain their power by consulting the public good and acting according to the dictates of reason, as Seneca says, "violenta imperia nemo continuit diu." No one can long retain a tyrant's sway.

In a democracy, irrational commands are still less to be feared: for it is almost impossible that the majority of a people, especially if it be a large one, should agree in an irrational design: and, moreover, the basis and aim of a democracy is to avoid the desires as irrational, and to bring men as far as possible under the control of reason, so that they may live in peace and harmony: if this basis be removed the whole fabric falls to ruin.

Such being the ends in view for the sovereign power, the duty of subjects is, as I have said, to obey its commands, and to recognize no right save that which it sanctions.

It will, perhaps, be thought that we are turning subjects into slaves: for slaves obey commands and free men live as they like; but this idea is based on a misconception, for the true slave is he who is led away by his pleasures and can neither see what is good for him nor act accordingly: he alone is free who lives with free consent under the entire guidance of reason.

Action in obedience to orders does take away freedom in a certain sense, but it does not, therefore, make a man a slave, all depends on the object of the action. If the object of the action be the good of the state, and not the good of the agent, the latter is a slave and does himself no good: but in a state or kingdom where the weal of the whole people, and not that of the ruler, is the supreme law, obedience to the sovereign power does not make a man a slave, of no use to himself, but a subject. Therefore, that state is the freest whose laws are founded on sound reason, so that every member of it may, if he will, be free 27; that is, live with full consent under the entire guidance of reason.

Children, though they are bound to obey all the commands of their parents, are yet not slaves: for the commands of parents look generally to the children's benefit.

We must, therefore, acknowledge a great difference between a slave, a son, and a subject; their positions may be thus defined. A slave is one who is bound to obey his master's orders, though they are given solely in the master's interest: a son is one who obeys his father's orders, given in his own interest; a subject obeys the orders of the sovereign power, given for the common interest, wherein he is included.

I think I have now shown sufficiently clearly the basis of a democracy: I have especially desired to do so, for I believe it to be of all forms of government the most natural, and the most consonant with individual liberty. In it no one transfers his natural right so absolutely that he has no further voice in affairs, he only hands it over to the majority of a society, whereof he is a unit. Thus all men remain as they were in the state of nature, equals.

This is the only form of government which I have treated of at length, for it is the one most akin to my purpose of showing the benefits of freedom in a state.

I may pass over the fundamental principles of other forms of government, for we may gather from what has been said whence their right arises without going into its origin. The possessor of sovereign power, whether he be one, or many, or the whole body politic, has the sovereign right of imposing any commands he pleases: and he who has either voluntarily, or under compulsion, transferred the right to defend him to another, has, in so doing, renounced his natural right and is therefore bound to obey, in all things, the commands of the sovereign power; and will be bound so to do so long as the king, or nobles, or the people preserve the sovereign power which formed the basis of the original transfer. I need add no more.

The bases and rights of dominion being thus displayed, we shall readily be able to define private civil right, wrong, justice, and injustice, with their relations to the state; and also to determine what constitutes an ally, or an enemy, or the crime of treason.

By private civil right we can only mean the liberty every man possesses to preserve his existence, a liberty limited by the edicts of the sovereign power, and preserved only by its authority: for when a man has transferred to another his right of living as he likes, which was only limited by his power, that is, has transferred his liberty and power of self-defence, he is bound to live as that other dictates, and to trust to him entirely for his defence. Wrong takes place when a citizen, or subject, is forced by another to undergo some loss or pain in contradiction to the authority of the law, or the edict of the sovereign power.

Wrong is conceivable only in an organized community: nor can it ever accrue to subjects from any act of the sovereign, who has the right to do what he likes. It can only arise, therefore, between private persons, who are bound by law and right not to injure one another. Justice consists in the habitual rendering to every man his lawful due: injustice consists in depriving a man, under the pretence of legality, of what the laws, rightly interpreted, would allow him. These last are also called equity and iniquity, because those who administer the laws are bound to show no respect of persons, but to account all men equal, and to defend every man's right equally, neither envying the rich nor despising the poor.

The men of two states become allies, when for the sake of avoiding war, or for some other advantage, they covenant to do each other no hurt, but on the contrary, to assist each other if necessity arises, each retaining his independence. Such a covenant is valid so long as its basis of danger or advantage is in force: no one enters into an engagement, or is bound to stand by his compacts unless there be a hope of some accruing good, or the fear of some evil: if this basis be removed the compact thereby becomes void: this has been abundantly shown by experience. For although different states make treaties not to harm one another, they always take every possible precaution against such treaties being broken by the stronger party, and do not rely on the compact, unless there is a sufficiently obvious object and advantage to both parties in observing it. Otherwise they would fear a breach of faith, nor would there be any wrong done thereby: for who in his proper senses, and aware of the right of the sovereign power, would trust in the promises of one who has the will and the power to do what he likes, and who aims solely at the safety and advantage of his dominion? Moreover, if we consult loyalty and religion, we shall see that no one in possession of power ought to abide by his promises to the injury of his dominion; for he cannot keep such promises without breaking the engagement he made with his subjects, by which both he and they are most solemnly bound. An enemy is one who lives apart from the state, and does not recognize its authority either as a subject or as an ally. It is not hatred which makes a man an enemy, but the rights of the state. The rights of the state are the same in regard to him who does not recognize by any compact the state authority, as they are against him who has done the state an injury: it has the right to force him as best it can, either to submit, or to contract an alliance.

Lastly, treason can only be committed by subjects, who by compact, either tacit or expressed, have transferred all their rights to the state: a subject is said to have committed this crime when he has attempted, for whatever reason, to seize the sovereign power, or to place it in different hands. I say, has attempted, for if punishment were not to overtake him till he had succeeded, it would often come too late, the sovereign rights would have been acquired or transferred already.

I also say, has attempted, for whatever reason, to seize the sovereign power, and I recognize no difference whether such an attempt should be followed by public loss or public gain. Whatever be his reason for acting, the crime is treason, and he is rightly condemned: in war, everyone would admit the justice of his sentence. If a man does not keep to his post, but approaches the enemy without the knowledge of his commander, whatever may be his motive, so long as he acts on his own motion, even if he advances with the design of defeating the enemy, he is rightly put to death, because he has violated his oath, and infringed the rights of his commander. That all citizens are equally bound by these rights in time of peace, is not so generally recognized, but the reasons for obedience are in both cases identical. The state must be preserved and directed by the sole authority of the sovereign, and such authority and right have been accorded by universal consent to him alone: if, therefore, anyone else attempts, without his consent, to execute any public enterprise, even though the state might (as we said) reap benefit therefrom, such person has none the less infringed the sovereigns right, and would be rightly punished for treason.

In order that every scruple may be removed, we may now answer the inquiry, whether our former assertion that everyone who has not the practice of reason, may, in the state of nature, live by sovereign natural right, according to the laws of his desires, is not in direct opposition to the law and right of God as revealed. For as all men absolutely (whether they be less endowed with reason or more) are equally bound by the Divine command to love their neighbour as themselves, it may be said that they cannot, without wrong, do injury to anyone, or live according to their desires.

This objection, so far as the state of nature is concerned, can be easily answered, for the state of nature is, both in nature and in time, prior to religion. No one knows by nature that he owes any obedience to God 28, nor can he attain thereto by any exercise of his reason, but solely by revelation confirmed by signs. Therefore, previous to revelation, no one is bound by a Divine law and right of which he is necessarily in ignorance. The state of nature must by no means be confounded with a state of religion, but must be conceived as without either religion or law, and consequently without sin or wrong: this is how we have described it, and we are confirmed by the authority of Paul. It is not only in respect of ignorance that we conceive the state of nature as prior to, and lacking the Divine revealed law and right; but in respect of freedom also, wherewith all men are born endowed.

If men were naturally bound by the Divine law and right, or if the Divine law and right were a natural necessity, there would have been no need for God to make a covenant with mankind, and to bind them thereto with an oath and agreement.

We must, then, fully grant that the Divine law and right originated at the time when men by express covenant agreed to obey God in all things, and ceded, as it were, their natural freedom, transferring their rights to God in the manner described in speaking of the formation of a state.

However, I will treat of these matters more at length presently.

It may be insisted that sovereigns are as much bound by the Divine law as subjects: whereas we have asserted that they retain their natural rights, and may do whatever they like.

In order to clear up the whole difficulty, which arises rather concerning the natural right than the natural state, I maintain that everyone is bound, in the state of nature, to live according to Divine law, in the same way as he is bound to live according to the dictates of sound reason; namely, inasmuch as it is to his advantage, and necessary for his salvation; but, if he will not so live, he may do otherwise at his own risk. He is thus bound to live according to his own laws, not according to anyone else's, and to recognize no man as a judge, or as a superior in religion. Such, in my opinion, is the position of a sovereign, for he may take advice from his fellow-men, but he is not bound to recognize any as a judge, nor anyone besides himself as an arbitrator on any question of right, unless it be a prophet sent expressly by God and attesting his mission by indisputable signs. Even then he does not recognize a man, but God Himself as His judge.

If a sovereign refuses to obey God as revealed in His law, he does so at his own risk and loss, but without violating any civil or natural right. For the civil right is dependent on his own decree; and natural right is dependent on the laws of nature, which latter are not adapted to religion, whose sole aim is the good of humanity, but to the order of nature — that is, to God's eternal decree unknown to us.

This truth seems to be adumbrated in a somewhat obscurer form by those who maintain that men can sin against God's revelation, but not against the eternal decree by which He has ordained all things.

We may be asked, what should we do if the sovereign commands anything contrary to religion, and the obedience which we have expressly vowed to God? should we obey the Divine law or the human law? I shall treat of this question at length hereafter, and will therefore merely say now, that God should be obeyed before all else, when we have a certain and indisputable revelation of His will: but men are very prone to error on religious subjects, and, according to the diversity of their dispositions, are wont with considerable stir to put forward their own inventions, as experience more than sufficiently attests, so that if no one were bound to obey the state in matters which, in his own opinion concern religion, the rights of the state would be dependent on every man's judgment and passions. No one would consider himself bound to obey laws framed against his faith or superstition; and on this pretext he might assume unbounded license. In this way, the rights of the civil authorities would be utterly set at nought, so that we must conclude that the sovereign power, which alone is bound both by Divine and natural right to preserve and guard the laws of the state, should have supreme authority for making any laws about religion which it thinks fit; all are bound to obey its behests on the subject in accordance with their promise which God bids them to keep.

However, if the sovereign power be heathen, we should either enter into no engagements therewith, and yield up our lives sooner than transfer to it any of our rights; or, if the engagement be made, and our rights transferred, we should (inasmuch as we should have ourselves transferred the right of defending ourselves and our religion) be bound to obey them, and to keep our word: we might even rightly be bound so to do, except in those cases where God, by indisputable revelation, has promised His special aid against tyranny, or given us special exemption from obedience. Thus we see that, of all the Jews in Babylon, there were only three youths who were certain of the help of God, and, therefore, refused to obey Nebuchadnezzar. All the rest, with the sole exception of Daniel, who was beloved by the king, were doubtless compelled by right to obey, perhaps thinking that they had been delivered up by God into the hands of the king, and that the king had obtained and preserved his dominion by God's design. On the other hand, Eleazar, before his country had utterly fallen, wished to give a proof of his constancy to his compatriots, in order that they might follow in his footsteps, and go to any lengths, rather than allow their right and power to be transferred to the Greeks, or brave any torture rather than swear allegiance to the heathen. Instances are occurring every day in confirmation of what I here advance. The rulers of Christian kingdoms do not hesitate, with a view to strengthening their dominion, to make treaties with Turks and heathen, and to give orders to their subjects who settle among such peoples not to assume more freedom, either in things secular or religious, than is set down in the treaty, or allowed by the foreign government. We may see this exemplified in the Dutch treaty with the Japanese, which I have already mentioned.

26 "No one can honestly promise to forego the right which he has over all things." In the state of social life, where general right determines what is good or evil, stratagem is rightly distinguished as of two kinds, good and evil. But in the state of Nature, where every man is his own judge, possessing the absolute right to lay down laws for himself, to interpret them as he pleases, or to abrogate them if he thinks it convenient, it is not conceivable that stratagem should be evil.

27 "Every member of it may, if he will, be free." Whatever be the social state a man finds; himself in, he may be free. For certainly a man is free, in so far as he is led by reason. Now reason (though Hobbes thinks otherwise) is always on the side of peace, which cannot be attained unless the general laws of the state be respected. Therefore the more he is free, the more constantly will he respect the laws of his country, and obey the commands of the sovereign power to which he is subject.

28 "No one knows by nature that he owes any obedience to God." When Paul says that men have in themselves no refuge, he speaks as a man: for in the ninth chapter of the same epistle he expressly teaches that God has mercy on whom He will, and that men are without excuse, only because they are in God's power like clay in the hands of a potter, who out of the same lump makes vessels, some for honour and some for dishonour, not because they have been forewarned. As regards the Divine natural law whereof the chief commandment is, as we have said, to love God, I have called it a law in the same sense, as philosophers style laws those general rules of nature, according to which everything happens. For the love of God is not a state of obedience: it is a virtue which necessarily exists in a man who knows God rightly. Obedience has regard to the will of a ruler, not to necessity and truth. Now as we are ignorant of the nature of God's will, and on the other hand know that everything happens solely by God's power, we cannot, except through revelation, know whether God wishes in any way to be honoured as a sovereign.

Again; we have shown that the Divine rights appear to us in the light of rights or commands, only so long as we are ignorant of their cause: as soon as their cause is known, they cease to be rights, and we embrace them no longer as rights but as eternal truths; in other words, obedience passes into love of God, which emanates from true knowledge as necessarily as light emanates from the sun. Reason then leads us to love God, but cannot lead us to obey Him; for we cannot embrace the commands of God as Divine, while we are in ignorance of their cause, neither can we rationally conceive God as a sovereign laying down laws as a sovereign.

CHAPTER XVII.

It is shown that no one can, or need, transfer all his Rights to the Sovereign Power. Of the Hebrew Republic, as it was during the lifetime of Moses, and after his death, till the foundation of the Monarchy; and of its Excellence. Lastly, of the causes why the Theocratic Republic fell, and why it could hardly have continued without Dissension.

THE THEORY PUT forward in the last chapter, of the universal rights of the sovereign power, and of the natural rights of the individual transferred thereto, though it corresponds in many respects with actual practice, and though practice may be so arranged as to conform to it more and more, must nevertheless always remain in many respects purely ideal. No one can ever so utterly transfer to another his power and, consequently, his rights, as to cease to be a man; nor can there ever be a power so sovereign that it can carry out every possible wish. It will always be vain to order a subject to hate what he believes brings him advantage, or to love what brings him loss, or not to be offended at insults, or not to wish to be free from fear, or a hundred other things of the sort, which necessarily follow from the laws of human nature. So much, I think, is abundantly shown by experience: for men have never so far ceded their power as to cease to be an object of fear to the rulers who received such power and right; and dominions have always been in as much danger from their own subjects as from external enemies. If it were really the case, that men could be deprived of their natural rights so utterly as never to have any further influence on affairs 29, except with the permission of the holders of sovereign right, it would then be possible to maintain with impunity the most violent tyranny, which, I suppose, no one would for an instant admit.

We must, therefore, grant that every man retains some part of his right, in dependence on his own decision, and no one else's.

However, in order correctly to understand the extent of the sovereign's right and power, we must take notice that it does not cover only those actions to which it can compel men by fear, but absolutely every action which it can induce men to perform: for it is the fact of obedience, not the motive for obedience, which makes a man a subject.

Whatever be the cause which leads a man to obey the commands of the sovereign, whether it be fear or hope, or love of his country, or any other emotion — the fact remains that the man takes counsel with himself, and nevertheless acts as his sovereign orders. We must not, therefore, assert that all actions resulting from a man's deliberation with himself are done in obedience to the rights of the individual rather than the sovereign: as a matter of fact, all actions spring from a man's deliberation with himself, whether the determining motive be love or fear of punishment; therefore, either dominion does not exist, and has no rights over its subjects, or else it extends over every instance in which it can prevail on men to decide to obey it. Consequently, every action which a subject performs in accordance with the commands of the sovereign, whether such action springs from love, or fear, or (as is more frequently the case) from hope and fear together, or from reverence. compounded of fear and admiration, or, indeed, any motive whatever, is performed in virtue of his submission to the sovereign, and not in virtue of his own authority.

This point is made still more clear by the fact that obedience does not consist so much in the outward act as in the mental state of the person obeying; so that he is most under the dominion of another who with his whole heart determines to obey another's commands; and consequently the firmest dominion belongs to the sovereign who has most influence over the minds of his subjects; if those who are most feared possessed the firmest dominion, the firmest dominion would belong to the subjects of a tyrant, for they are always greatly feared by their ruler. Furthermore, though it is impossible to govern the mind as completely as the tongue, nevertheless minds are, to a certain extent, under the control of the sovereign, for he can in many ways bring about that the greatest part of his subjects should follow his wishes in their beliefs, their loves, and their hates. Though such emotions do not arise at the express command of the sovereign they often result (as experience shows) from the authority of his power, and from his direction; in other words, in virtue of his right; we may, therefore, without doing violence to our understanding, conceive men who follow the instigation of their sovereign in their beliefs, their loves, their hates, their contempt, and all other emotions whatsoever.

Though the powers of government, as thus conceived, are sufficiently ample, they can never become large enough to execute every possible wish of their possessors. This, I think, I have already shown clearly enough. The method of forming a dominion which should prove lasting I do not, as I have said, intend to discuss, but in order to arrive at the object I have in view, I will touch on the teaching of Divine revelation to Moses in this respect, and we will consider the history and the success of the Jews, gathering therefrom what should be the chief concessions made by sovereigns to their subjects with a view to the security and increase of their dominion.

That the preservation of a state chiefly depends on the subjects' fidelity and constancy in carrying out the orders they receive, is most clearly taught both by reason and experience; how subjects ought to be guided so as best to preserve their fidelity and virtue is not so obvious. All, both rulers and ruled, are men, and prone to follow after their lusts. The fickle disposition of the multitude almost reduces those who have experience of it to despair, for it is governed solely by emotions, not by reason: it rushes headlong into every enterprise, and is easily corrupted either by avarice or luxury: everyone thinks himself omniscient and wishes to fashion all things to his liking, judging a thing to be just or unjust, lawful or unlawful, according as he thinks it will bring him profit or loss: vanity leads him to despise his equals, and refuse their guidance: envy of superior fame or fortune (for such gifts are never equally distributed) leads him to desire and rejoice in his neighbour's downfall. I need not go through the whole list, everyone knows already how much crime. results from disgust at the present — desire for change, headlong anger, and contempt for poverty — and how men's minds are engrossed and kept in turmoil thereby.

To guard against all these evils, and form a dominion where no room is left for deceit; to frame our institutions so that every man, whatever his disposition, may prefer public right to private advantage, this is the task and this the toil. Necessity is often the mother of invention, but she has never yet succeeded in framing a dominion that was in less danger from its own citizens than from open enemies, or whose rulers did not fear the latter less than the former. Witness the state of Rome, invincible by her enemies, but many times conquered and sorely oppressed by her own citizens, especially in the war between Vespasian and Vitellius. (See Tacitus, Hist. bk. iv. for a description of the pitiable state of the city.)

Alexander thought prestige abroad more easy to acquire than prestige at home, and believed that his greatness could be destroyed by his own followers. Fearing such a disaster, he thus addressed his friends: "Keep me safe from internal treachery and domestic plots, and I will front without fear the dangers of battle and of war. Philip was more secure in the battle array than in the theatre: he often escaped from the hands of the enemy, he could not escape from his own subjects. If you think over the deaths of kings, you will count up more who have died by the assassin than by the open foe." (Q. Curtius, chap. vi.)

For the sake of making themselves secure, kings who seized the throne in ancient times used to try to spread the idea that they were descended from the immortal gods, thinking that if their subjects and the rest of mankind did not look on them as equals, but believed them to be gods, they would willingly submit to their rule, and obey their commands. Thus Augustus persuaded the Romans that he was descended from AEneas, who was the son of Venus, and numbered among the gods. "He wished himself to be worshipped in temples, like the gods, with flamens and priests." (Tacitus, Ann. i. 10.)

Alexander wished to be saluted as the son of Jupiter, not from motives of pride but of policy, as he showed by his answer to the invective of Hermolaus: "It is almost laughable," said he, that Hermolaus asked me to contradict Jupiter, by whose oracle I am recognized. Am I responsible for the answers of the gods? It offered me the name of son; acquiescence was by no means foreign to my present designs. Would that the Indians also would believe me to be a god! Wars are carried through by prestige, falsehoods that are believed often gain the force of truth." (Curtius, viii,. Para, 8.) In these few words he cleverly contrives to palm off a fiction on the ignorant, and at the same time hints at the motive for the deception.

Cleon, in his speech persuading the Macedonians to obey their king, adopted a similar device: for after going through the praises of Alexander with admiration, and recalling his merits, he proceeds, "the Persians are not only pious, but prudent in worshipping their kings as gods: for kingship is the shield of public safety," and he ends thus, "I, myself, when the king enters a banquet hall, should prostrate my body on the ground; other men should do the like, especially those who are wise " (Curtius, viii. Para. 66). However, the Macedonians were more prudent — indeed, it is only complete barbarians who can be so openly cajoled, and can suffer themselves to be turned from subjects into slaves without interests of their own. Others, notwithstanding, have been able more easily to spread the belief that kingship is sacred, and plays the part of God on the earth, that it has been instituted by God, not by the suffrage and consent of men; and that it is preserved and guarded by Divine special providence and aid. Similar fictions have been promulgated by monarchs, with the object of strengthening their dominion, but these I will pass over, and in order to arrive at my main purpose, will merely recall and discuss the teaching on the subject of Divine revelation to Moses in ancient times.

We have said in Chap. V. that after the Hebrews came up out of Egypt they were not bound by the law and right of any other nation, but were at liberty to institute any new rites at their pleasure, and to occupy whatever territory they chose. After their liberation from the intolerable bondage of the Egyptians, they were bound by no covenant to any man; and, therefore, every man entered into his natural right, and was free to retain it or to give it up, and transfer it to another. Being, then, in the state of nature, they followed the advice of Moses, in whom they chiefly trusted, and decided to transfer their right to no human being, but only to God;

without further delay they all, with one voice, promised to obey all the commands of the Deity, and to acknowledge no right that He did not proclaim as such by prophetic revelation. This promise, or transference of right to God, was effected in the same manner as we have conceived it to have been in ordinary societies, when men agree to divest themselves of their natural rights. It is, in fact, in virtue of a set covenant, and an oath (see Exod. xxxiv:10), that the Jews freely, and not under compulsion or threats, surrendered their rights and transferred them to God. Moreover, in order that this covenant might be ratified and settled, and might be free from all suspicion of deceit, God did not enter into it till the Jews had had experience of His wonderful power by which alone they had been, or could be, preserved in a state of prosperity (Exod. xix:4, 5). It is because they believed that nothing but God's power could preserve them that they surrendered to God the natural power of self-preservation, which they formerly, perhaps, thought they possessed, and consequently they surrendered at the same time all their natural right.

God alone, therefore, held dominion over the Hebrews, whose state was in virtue of the covenant called God's kingdom, and God was said to be their king; consequently the enemies of the Jews were said to be the enemies of God, and the citizens who tried to seize the dominion were guilty of treason against God; and, lastly, the laws of the state were called the laws and commandments of God. Thus in the Hebrew state the civil and religious authority, each consisting solely of obedience to God, were one and the same. The dogmas of religion were not precepts, but laws and ordinances; piety was regarded as the same as loyalty, impiety as the same as disaffection. Everyone who fell away from religion ceased to be a citizen, and was, on that ground alone, accounted an enemy: those who died for the sake of religion, were held to have died for their country; in fact, between civil and religious law and right there was no distinction whatever. {in Biblical Hebrew, there was no word for what we call Religion." Modern Hebrew has selected a word whose root is "knowledge."} For this reason the government could be called a Theocracy, inasmuch as the citizens were not bound by anything save the revelations of God.

However, this state of things existed rather in theory than in practice, for it will appear from what we are about to say, that the Hebrews, as a matter of fact, retained absolutely in their own hands the right of sovereignty: this is shown by the method and plan by which the government was carried on, as I will now explain.

Inasmuch as the Hebrews did not transfer their rights to any other person but, as in a democracy, all surrendered their rights equally, and cried out with one voice, "Whatsoever God shall speak (no mediator or mouthpiece being named) that will we do," it follows that all were equally bound by the covenant, and that all had an equal right to consult the Deity, to accept and to interpret His laws, so that all had an exactly equal share in the government. Thus at first they all approached God together, so that they might learn His commands, but in this first salutation, they were so thoroughly terrified and so astounded to hear God speaking, that they thought their last hour was at hand: full of fear, therefore, they went afresh to Moses, and said, "Lo, we have heard God speaking in the fire, and there is no cause why we should wish to die: surely this great fire will consume us: if we hear again the voice of God, we shall surely die. Thou, therefore, go near, and hear all the words of our God, and thou (not God) shalt speak with us: all that God shall tell us, that will we hearken to and perform."

They thus clearly abrogated their former covenant, and absolutely transferred to

Moses their right to consult God and interpret His commands: for they do not here promise obedience to all that God shall tell them, but to all that God shall tell Moses (see Deut. v:20 after the Decalogue, and chap. xviii:15, 16). Moses, therefore, remained the sole promulgator and interpreter of the Divine laws, and consequently also the sovereign judge, who could not be arraigned himself, and who acted among the Hebrews the part, of God; in other words, held the sovereign kingship: he alone had the right to consult God, to give the Divine answers to the people, and to see that they were carried out. I say he alone, for if anyone during the life of Moses was desirous of preaching anything in the name of the Lord, he was, even if a true prophet, considered guilty and a usurper of the sovereign right (Numb. xi:28) 30. We may here notice, that though the people had elected Moses, they could not rightfully elect Moses's successor; for having transferred to Moses their right of consulting God, and absolutely promised to regard him as a Divine oracle, they had plainly forfeited the whole of their right, and were bound to accept as chosen by God anyone proclaimed by Moses as his successor. If Moses had so chosen his successor, who like him should wield the sole right of government, possessing the sole right of consulting God, and consequently of making and abrogating laws, of deciding on peace or war, of sending ambassadors, appointing judges — in fact, discharging all the functions of a sovereign, the state would have become simply a monarchy, only differing from other monarchies in the fact, that the latter are, or should be, carried on in accordance with God's decree, unknown even to the monarch, whereas the Hebrew monarch would have been the only person to whom the decree was revealed. A difference which increases, rather than diminishes the monarch's authority. As far as the people in both cases are concerned, each would be equally subject, and equally ignorant of the Divine decree, for each would be dependent on the monarch's words, and would learn from him alone, what was lawful or unlawful: nor would the fact that the people believed that the monarch was only issuing commands in accordance with God's decree revealed to him, make it less in subjection, but rather more. However, Moses elected no such successor, but left the dominion to those who came after him in a condition which could not be called a popular government, nor an aristocracy, nor a monarchy, but a Theocracy. For the right of interpreting laws was vested in one man, while the right and power of administering the state according to the laws thus interpreted, was vested in another man (see Numb. xxvii:21) 31.

In order that the question may be thoroughly understood, I will duly set forth the administration of the whole state.

First, the people were commanded to build a tabernacle, which should be, as it were, the dwelling of God — that is, of the sovereign authority of the state. This tabernacle was to be erected at the cost of the whole people, not of one man, in order that the place where God was consulted might be public property. The Levites were chosen as courtiers and administrators of this royal abode; while Aaron, the brother of Moses, was chosen to be their chief and second, as it were, to God their King, being succeeded in the office by his legitimate sons.

He, as the nearest to God, was the sovereign interpreter of the Divine laws; he communicated the answers of the Divine oracle to the people, and entreated God's favour for them. If, in addition to these privileges, he had possessed the right of ruling, he would have been neither more nor less than an absolute monarch; but, in respect to government, he was only a private citizen: the whole tribe of Levi was so completely divested of governing rights that it did not even take its share with the others in the partition of territory. Moses provided for its support by inspiring the common people with great reverence for it, as the only tribe dedicated to God.

Further, the army, formed from the remaining twelve tribes, was commanded to invade the land of Canaan, to divide it into twelve portions, and to distribute it among the tribes by lot. For this task twelve captains were chosen, one from every tribe, and were, together with Joshua and Eleazar, the high priest, empowered to divide the land into twelve equal parts, and distribute it by lot. Joshua was chosen for the chief command of the army, inasmuch as none but he had the right to consult God in emergencies, not like Moses, alone in his tent, or in the tabernacle, but through the high priest, to whom only the answers of God were revealed. Furthermore, he was empowered to execute, and cause the people to obey God's commands, transmitted through the high priests; to find, and to make use of, means for carrying them out; to choose as many, army captains as he liked; to make whatever choice he thought best; to send ambassadors in his own name; and, in short, to have the entire control of the war. To his office there was no rightful successor — indeed, the post was only filled by the direct order of the Deity, on occasions of public emergency. In ordinary times, all the management of peace and war was vested in the captains of the tribes, as I will shortly point out. Lastly, all men between the ages of twenty and sixty were ordered to bear arms, and form a citizen army, owing allegiance, not to its general-inchief, nor to the high priest, but to Religion and to God. The army, or the hosts, were called the army of God, or the hosts of God. For this reason God was called by the Hebrews the God of Armies; and the ark of the covenant was borne in the midst of the army in important battles, when the safety or destruction of the whole people hung upon the issue, so that the people might, as it were, see their King among them, and put forth all their strength.

From these directions, left by Moses to his successors, we plainly see that he chose administrators, rather than despots, to come after him; for he invested no one with the power of consulting God, where he liked and alone, consequently, no one had the power possessed by himself of ordaining and abrogating laws, of deciding on war or peace, of choosing men to fill offices both religious and secular: all these are the prerogatives of a sovereign. The high priest, indeed, had the right of interpreting laws, and communicating the answers of God, but he could not do so when he liked, as Moses could, but only when he was asked by the general-inchief of the army, the council, or some similar authority. The general-inchief and the council could consult God when they liked, but could only receive His answers through the high priest; so that the utterances of God, as reported by the high priest, were not decrees, as they were when reported by Moses, but only answers; they were accepted by Joshua and the council, and only then had the force of commands and decrees {Like the separation of powers in the United States of America.}

The high priest, both in the case of Aaron and of his son Eleazar, was chosen by Moses; nor had anyone, after Moses' death, a right to elect to the office, which became hereditary . The general-inchief of the army was also chosen by Moses, and assumed his functions in virtue of the commands, not of the high priest, but of Moses: indeed, after the death of Joshua, the high priest did not appoint anyone in his place, and the captains did not consult God afresh about a general-inchief, but each retained Joshua's power in respect to the contingent of his own tribe, and all retained it collectively, in respect to the whole army. There seems to have been no need of a general-inchief, except when they were obliged to unite their forces against a common enemy. This occurred most frequently during the time of Joshua, when they had no fixed dwelling. place, and possessed all things in common. After all the tribes had gained their territories by right of conquest, and had divided their allotted gains, they, became separated, having no longer their possessions in common, so that the need for a single commander ceased, for the different tribes should be considered rather in the light of confederated states than of bodies of fellow-citizens. In respect to their God and their religion, they, were fellow-citizens; but, in respect to the rights which one possessed with regard to another, they were only confederated: they, were, in fact, in much the same position (if one excepts the Temple common to all) as the United States of the Netherlands {or United States of America}. The division of property, held in common is only another phrase for the possession of his share by each of the owners singly, and the surrender by the others of their rights over such share. This is why Moses elected captains of the tribes — namely, that when the dominion was divided, each might take care of his own part; consulting God through the high priest on the affairs of his tribe, ruling over his army, building and fortifying cities, appointing judges, attacking the enemies of his own dominion, and having complete control over all civil and military affairs. He was not bound to acknowledge any superior judge save God 32, or a prophet whom God should expressly send. If he departed from the worship of God, the rest of the tribes did not arraign him as a subject, but attacked him as an enemy. Of this we have examples in Scripture. When Joshua was dead, the children of Israel (not a fresh general-inchief) consulted God; it being decided that the tribe of Judah should be the first to attack its enemies, the tribe in question contracted a single alliance with the tribe of Simeon, for uniting their forces, and attacking their common enemy, the rest of the tribes not being included in the alliance (Judges i:1, 2, 3). Each tribe separately made war against its own enemies, and, according to its pleasure, received them as subjects or allies, though it had been commanded not to spare them on any conditions, but to destroy them utterly. Such disobedience met with reproof from the rest of the tribes, but did not cause the offending tribe to be arraigned: it was not considered a sufficient reason for proclaiming a civil war, or interfering in one another's affairs. But when the tribe of Benjamin offended against the others, and so loosened the bonds of peace that none of the confederated tribes could find refuge within its borders, they attacked it as an enemy, and gaining the victory over it after three battles, put to death both guilty and innocent, according to the laws of war: an act which they subsequently bewailed with tardy repentance.

These examples plainly confirm what we have said concerning the rights of each tribe. Perhaps we shall be asked who elected the successors to the captains of each tribe; on this point I can gather no positive information in Scripture, but I conjecture that as the tribes were divided into families, each headed by its senior member, the senior of all these heads of families succeeded by right to the office of captain, for Moses chose from among these seniors his seventy coadjutors, who formed with himself the supreme council. Those who administered the government after the death of Joshua were called elders, and elder is a very common Hebrew expression in the sense of judge, as I suppose everyone knows; however, it is not very important for us to make up our minds on this point. It is enough to have shown that after the death of Moses no one man wielded all the power of a sovereign; as affairs were not all managed by one man, nor by a single council, nor by the popular vote, but partly by one tribe, partly by the rest in equal shares, it is most evident that the government, after the death of Moses, was neither monarchic, nor aristocratic, nor popular, but, as we have said, Theocratic. The reasons for applying this name are:

I. Because the royal seat of government was the Temple, and in respect to it alone, as we have shown, all the tribes were fellow-citizens,

II. Because all the people owed allegiance to God, their supreme Judge, to whom only they had promised implicit obedience in all things.

III. Because the general-inchief or dictator, when there was need of such, was elected by none save God alone. This was expressly commanded by Moses in the name of God (Deut. xix:15), and witnessed by the actual choice of Gideon, of Samson, and of Samuel; wherefrom we may conclude that the other faithful leaders were chosen in the same manner, though it is not expressly told us.

These preliminaries being stated, it is now time to inquire the effects of forming a dominion on this plan, and to see whether it so effectually kept within bounds both rulers and ruled, that the former were never tyrannical and the latter never rebellious.

Those who administer or possess governing power, always try to surround their high-handed actions with a cloak of legality, and to persuade the people that they act from good motives; this they are easily able to effect when they are the sole interpreters of the law; for it is evident that they are thus able to assume a far greater freedom to carry out their wishes and desires than if the interpretation if the law is vested in someone else, or if the laws were so self-evident that no one could be in doubt as to their meaning. We thus see that the power of evil-doing was greatly curtailed for the Hebrew captains by the fact that the whole interpretation of the law was vested in the Levites (Deut. xxi:5), who, on their part, had no share in the government, and depended for all their support and consideration on a correct interpretation of the laws entrusted to them. Moreover, the whole people was commanded to come together at a certain place every seven years and be instructed in the law by the high-priest; further, each individual was bidden to read the book of the law through and through continually with scrupulous care. (Deut. xxxi:9, 10, and vi:7.) The captains were thus for their own sakes bound to take great care to administer everything according to the laws laid down, and well known to all, if they, wished to be held in high honour by, the people, who would regard them as the administrators of God's dominion, and as God's vicegerents; otherwise they could not have escaped all the virulence of theological hatred. There was another very important check on the unbridled license of the captains, in the fact, that the army was formed from the whole body, of the citizens, between the ages of twenty and sixty, without exception, and that the captains were not able to hire any foreign soldiery. This I say was very, important, for it is well known that princes can oppress their peoples with the single aid of the soldiery in their pay; while there is nothing more formidable to them than the freedom of citizen soldiers, who have established the freedom and glory of their country, by their valour, their toil, and their blood. Thus Alexander, when he was about to make wax on Darius, a second time, after hearing the advice of Parmenio, did not chide him who gave the advice, but Polysperchon, who was standing by. For, as Curtius says (iv. Para. 13), he did not venture to reproach Parmenio again after having shortly, before reproved him too sharply. This freedom of the Macedonians, which he so dreaded, he was not able to subdue till after the number of captives enlisted in the army, surpassed that of his own people: then, but not till then, he gave rein to his anger so long checked by, the independence of his chief fellow-countrymen.

If this independence of citizen soldiers can restrain the princes of ordinary states who are wont to usurp the whole glory of victories, it must have been still more effectual against the Hebrew captains, whose soldiers were fighting, not for the glory of a prince, but for the glory of God, and who did not go forth to battle till the Divine assent had been given.

We must also remember that the Hebrew captains were associated only by the bonds of religion: therefore, if any one of them had transgressed, and begun to violate the Divine right, he might have been treated by the rest as an enemy and lawfully subdued.

An additional check may be found in the fear of a new prophet arising, for if a man of unblemished life could show by certain signs that he was really a prophet, he ipso facto obtained the sovereign right to rule, which was given to him, as to Moses formerly, in the name of God, as revealed to himself alone; not merely through the high priest, as in the case of the captains. There is no doubt that such an one would easily be able to enlist an oppressed people in his cause, and by trifling signs persuade them of anything he wished: on the other hand, if affairs were well ordered, the captain would be able to make provision in time; that the prophet should be submitted to his approval, and be examined whether he were really of unblemished life, and possessed indisputable signs of his mission: also, whether the teaching he proposed to set forth in the name of the Lord agreed with received doctrines, and the general laws of the country; if his credentials were insufficient, or his doctrines new, he could lawfully be put to death, or else received on the captain's sole responsibility and authority.

Again, the captains were not superior to the others in nobility or birth, but only administered the government in virtue of their age and personal qualities. Lastly, neither captains nor army had any reason for preferring war to peace. The army, as we have stated, consisted entirely of citizens, so that affairs were managed by the same persons both in peace and war. The man who was a soldier in the camp was a citizen in the market-place, he who was a leader in the camp was a judge in the law courts, he who was a general in the camp was a ruler in the state. Thus no one could desire war for its own sake, but only for the sake of preserving peace and liberty; possibly the captains avoided change as far as possible, so as not to be obliged to consult the high priest and submit to the indignity of standing in his presence.

So much for the precautions for keeping the captains within bounds. We must now look for the restraints upon the people: these, however, are very clearly indicated in the very groundwork of the social fabric.

Anyone who gives the subject the slightest attention, will see that the state was so ordered as to inspire the most ardent patriotism in the hearts of the citizens, so that the latter would be very hard to persuade to betray their country, and be ready to endure anything rather than submit to a foreign yoke. After they had transferred their right to God, they thought that their kingdom belonged to God, and that they themselves were God's children. Other nations they looked upon as God's enemies, and regarded with intense hatred (which they took to be piety, see Psalm cxxxix:21, 22): nothing would have been more abhorrent to them than swearing allegiance to a foreigner, and promising him obedience: nor could they conceive any greater or more execrable crime than the betrayal of their country, the kingdom of the God whom they adored.

It was considered wicked for anyone to settle outside of the country, inasmuch as the worship of God by which they were bound could not be carried on elsewhere:

their own land alone was considered holy, the rest of the earth unclean and profane.

David, who was forced to live in exile, complained before Saul as follows: "But if they be the children of men who have stirred thee up against me, cursed be they before the Lord; for they have driven me out this day from abiding in the inheritance of the Lord, saying, Go, serve other gods." (I Sam. xxvi:19.) For the same reason no citizen, as we should especially remark, was ever sent into exile: he who sinned was liable to punishment, but not to disgrace.

Thus the love of the Hebrews for their country was not only patriotism, but also piety, and was cherished and nurtured bv daily rites till, like their hatred of other nations, it must have passed into their nature. Their daily worship was not only different from that of other nations (as it might well be, considering that they were a peculiar people and entirely apart from the rest), it was absolutely contrary. Such daily reprobation naturally gave rise to a lasting hatred, deeply implanted in the heart: for of all hatreds none is more deep and tenacious than that which springs from extreme devoutness or piety, and is itself cherished as pious. Nor was a general cause lacking for inflaming such hatred more and more, inasmuch as it was reciprocated; the surrounding nations regarding the Jews with a hatred just as intense.

How great was the effect of all these causes, namely, freedom from man's dominion; devotion to their country; absolute rights over all other men; a hatred not only permitted but pious; a contempt for their fellow-men; the singularity of their customs and religious rites; the effect, I repeat, of all these causes in strengthening the hearts of the Jews to bear all things for their country, with extraordinary constancy and valour, will at once be discerned by reason and attested by experience. Never, so long as the city was standing, could they endure to remain under foreign dominion; and therefore they called Jerusalem "a rebellious city" (Ezra iv:12). Their state after its reestablishment (which was a mere shadow of the first, for the high priests had usurped the rights of the tribal captains) was, with great difficulty, destroyed by the Romans, as Tacitus bears witness (Hist. ii:4):— "Vespasian had closed the war against the Jews, abandoning the siege of Jerusalem as an enterprise difficult and arduous rather from the character of the people and the obstinacy of their superstition, than from the strength left to the besieged for meeting their necessities." But besides these characteristics, which are merely ascribed by an individual opinion, there was one feature peculiar to this state and of great importance in retaining the affections of the citizens, and checking all thoughts of desertion, or abandonment of the country: namely, self-interest, the strength and life of all human action. This was peculiarly engaged in the Hebrew state, for nowhere else did citizens possess their goods so securely, as did the subjects of this community, for the latter possessed as large a share in the land and the fields as did their chiefs, and were owners of their plots of ground in perpetuity; for if any man was compelled by poverty to sell his farm or his pasture, he received it back again intact at the year of jubilee: there were other similar enactments against the possibility of alienating real property.

Again, poverty w as nowhere more endurable than in a country where duty towards one's neighbour, that is, one's fellow-citizen, was practised with the utmost piety, as a means of gaining the favour of God the King. Thus the Hebrew citizens would nowhere be so well off as in their own country; outside its limits they met with nothing but loss and disgrace.

The following considerations were of weight, not only in keeping them at home, but also in preventing civil war and removing causes of strife; no one was bound to serve his equal, but only to serve God, while charity and love towards fellow-citizens was accounted the highest piety; this last feeling was not a little fostered by the general hatred with which they regarded foreign nations and were regarded by them. Furthermore, the strict discipline of obedience in which they were brought up, was a very important factor; for they were bound to carry on all their actions according to the set rules of the law: a man might not plough when he liked, but only at certain times, in certain years, and with one sort of beast at a time; so, too, he might only sow and reap in a certain method and season — in fact, his whole life was one long school of obedience (see Chap. V. on the use of ceremonies); such a habit was thus engendered, that conformity seemed freedom instead of servitude, and men desired what was commanded rather than what was forbidden. This result was not a little aided by the fact that the people were bound, at certain seasons of the year, to give themselves up to rest and rejoicing, not for their own pleasure, but in order that they might worship God cheerfully.

Three times in the year they feasted before the Lord; on the seventh day of every week they were bidden to abstain from all work and to rest; besides these, there were other occasions when innocent rejoicing and feasting were not only allowed but enjoined. I do not think any better means of influencing men's minds could be devised; for there is no more powerful attraction than joy springing from devotion, a mixture of admiration and love. It was not easy to be wearied by constant repetition, for the rites on the various festivals were varied and recurred seldom. We may add the deep reverence for the Temple which all most religiously fostered, on account of the peculiar rites and duties that they were obliged to perform before approaching thither. Even now, Jews cannot read without horror of the crime of Manasseh, who dared to place au idol in the Temple. The laws, scrupulously preserved in the inmost sanctuary, were objects of equal reverence to the people. Popular reports and misconceptions were, therefore, very little to be feared in this quarter, for no one dared decide on sacred matters, but all felt bound to obey, without consulting their reason, all the commands given by the answers of God received in the Temple, and all the laws which God had ordained.

I think I have now explained clearly, though briefly,, the main features of the Hebrew commonwealth. I must now inquire into the causes which led the people so often to fall away from the law, which brought about their frequent subjection, and, finally, the complete destruction of their dominion. Perhaps I shall be told that it sprang from their hardness of heart; but this is childish, for why should this people be more hard of heart than others; was it by nature?

But nature forms individuals, not peoples; the latter are only distinguishable by the difference of their language, their customs, and their laws; while from the two last — i.e., customs and laws, — it may arise that they have a peculiar disposition, a peculiar manner of life, and peculiar prejudices. If, then, the Hebrews were harder of heart than other nations, the fault lay with their laws or customs.

This is certainly true, in the sense that, if God had wished their dominion to be more lasting, He would have given them other rites and laws, and would have instituted a different form of government. We can, therefore, only say that their God was angry with them, not only, as Jeremiah says, from the building of the city, but even from the founding of their laws.

This is borne witness to by Ezekiel xx:25: "Wherefore I gave them also statutes that were not good, and judgments whereby they should not live; and I polluted them in their own gifts, in that they caused to pass through the fire all that openeth the womb; that I might make them desolate, to the end that they might know that I am the Lord."

In order that we may understand these words, and the destruction of the Hebrew commonwealth, we must bear in mind that it had at first been intended to entrust the whole duties of the priesthood to the firstborn, and not to the Levites (see Numb. viii:17). It was only when all the tribes, except the Levites, worshipped the golden calf, that the firstborn were rejected and defiled, and the Levites chosen in their stead (Deut. x:8). When I reflect on this change, I feel disposed to break forth with the words of Tacitus. God's object at that time was not the safety of the Jews, but vengeance. I am greatly astonished that the celestial mind was so inflamed with anger that it ordained laws, which always are supposed to promote the honour, well-being, and security of a people, with the purpose of vengeance, for the sake of punishment; so that the laws do not seem so much laws — that is, the safeguard of the people — as pains and penalties.

The gifts which the people were obliged to bestow on the Levites and priests — the redemption of the firstborn, the poll-tax due to the Levites, the privilege possessed by the latter of the sole performance of sacred rites — all these, I say, were a continual reproach to the people, a continual reminder of their defilement and rejection. Moreover, we may be sure that the Levites were for ever heaping reproaches upon them: for among so many thousands there must have been many importunate dabblers in theology. Hence the people got into the way of watching the acts of the Levites, who were but human; of accusing the whole body of the faults of one member, and continually murmuring.

Besides this, there was the obligation to keep in idleness men hateful to them, and connected by no ties of blood. Especially would this seem grievous when provisions were dear. What wonder, then, if in times of peace, when striking miracles had ceased, and no men of paramount authority were forthcoming, the irritable and greedy temper of the people began to wax cold, and at length to fall away from a worship, which, though Divine, was also humiliating, and even hostile, and to seek after something fresh; or can we be surprised that the captains, who always adopt the popular course, in order to gain the sovereign power for themselves by enlisting the sympathies of the people, and alienating the high priest, should have yielded to their demands, and introduced a new worship? If the state had been formed according to the original intention, the rights and honour of all the tribes would have been equal, and everything would have rested on a firm basis. Who is there who would willingly violate the religious rights of his kindred? What could a man desire more than to support his own brothers and parents, thus fulfilling the duties of religion? Who would not rejoice in being taught by them the interpretation of the laws, and receiving through them the answers of God?

The tribes would thus have been united by a far closer bond, if all alike had possessed the right to the priesthood. All danger would have been obviated, if the choice of the Levites had not been dictated by anger and revenge. But, as we have said, the Hebrews had offended their God, Who, as Ezekiel says, polluted them in their own gifts by rejecting all that openeth the womb, so that He might destroy them.

This passage is also confirmed by their history. As soon as the people in the wilderness began to live in ease and plenty, certain men of no mean birth began to rebel against the choice of the Levites, and to make it a cause for believing that

Moses had not acted by the commands of God, but for his own good pleasure, inasmuch as he had chosen his own tribe before all the rest, and had bestowed the high priesthood in perpetuity on his own brother. They, therefore, stirred up a tumult, and came to him, crying out that all men were equally sacred, and that he had exalted himself above his fellows wrongfully. Moses was not able to pacify them with reasons; but by the intervention of a miracle in proof of the faith, they all perished. A fresh sedition then arose among the whole people, who believed that their champions had not been put to death by the judgment of God, but by the device of Moses. After a great slaughter, or pestilence, the rising subsided from inanition, but in such a manner that all preferred death to life under such conditions.

We should rather say that sedition ceased than that harmony was re-established. This is witnessed by Scripture (Deut. xxxi:21), where God, after predicting to Moses that the people after his death will fall away from the Divine worship, speaks thus: "For I know their imagination which they go about, even now before I have brought them into the land which I sware;" and, a little while after (xxxi:27), Moses says: For I know thy rebellion and thy stiff neck: behold while I am yet alive with you this day, ye have been rebellious against the Lord; and how much more after my death!"

Indeed, it happened according to his words, as we all know. Great changes, extreme license, luxury, and hardness of heart grew up; things went from bad to worse, till at last the people, after being frequently conquered, came to an open rupture with the Divine right, and wished for a mortal king, so that the seat of government might be the Court, instead of the Temple, and that the tribes might remain fellow-citizens in respect to their king, instead of in respect to Divine right and the high priesthood.

A vast material for new seditions was thus produced, eventually resulting in the ruin of the entire state. Kings are above all things jealous of a precarious rule, and can in nowise brook a dominion within their own. The first monarchs, being chosen from the ranks of private citizens, were content with the amount of dignity to which they had risen; but their sons, who obtained the throne by right of inheritance, began gradually to introduce changes, so as to get all the sovereign rights into their own hands. This they were generally unable to accomplish, so long as the right of legislation did not rest with them, but with the high priest, who kept the laws in the sanctuary, and interpreted them to the people. The kings were thus bound to obey the laws as much as were the subjects, and were unable to abrogate them, or to ordain new laws of equal authority; moreover, they were prevented by the Levites from administering the affairs of religion, king and subject being alike unclean. Lastly, the whole safety of their dominion depended on the will of one man, if that man appeared to be a prophet; and of this they had seen an example, namely, how completely Samuel had been able to command Saul, and how easily, because of a single disobedience, he had been able to transfer the right of sovereignty to David. Thus the kings found a dominion within their own, and wielded a precarious sovereignty.

In order to surmount these difficulties, they allowed other temples to be dedicated to the gods, so that there might be no further need of consulting the Levites; they also sought out many who prophesied in the name of God, so that they might have creatures of their own to oppose to the true prophets. However, in spite of all their attempts, they never attained their end. For the prophets, prepared against every emergency, waited for a favourable opportunity, such as the beginning of a new reign, which is always precarious, while the memory of the previous reign remains green. At these times they could easily pronounce by Divine authority that the king was tyrannical, and could produce a champion of distinguished virtue to vindicate the Divine right, and lawfully to claim dominion, or a share in it. Still, not even so could the prophets effect much. They could, indeed, remove a tyrant; but there were reasons which prevented them from doing more than setting up, at great cost of civil bloodshed, another tyrant in his stead. Of discords and civil wars there was no end, for the causes for the violation of Divine right remained always the same, and could only be removed by a complete remodelling of the state.

We have now seen how religion was introduced into the Hebrew commonwealth, and how the dominion might have lasted for ever, if the just wrath of the Lawgiver had allowed it. As this was impossible, it was bound in time to perish. I am now speaking only of the first commonwealth, for the second was a mere shadow of the first, inasmuch as the people were bound by the rights of the Persians to whom they were subject. After the restoration of freedom, the high priests usurped the rights of the secular chiefs, and thus obtained absolute dominion. The priests were inflamed with an intense desire to wield the powers of the sovereignty and the high priesthood at the same time. I have, therefore, no need to speak further of the second commonwealth. Whether the first, in so far as we deem it to have been durable, is capable of imitation, and whether it would be pious to copy it as far as possible, will appear from what fellows. I wish only to draw attention, as a crowning conclusion, to the principle indicated already — namely, that it is evident, from what we have stated in this chapter, that the Divine right, or the right of religion, originates in a compact: without such compact, none but natural rights exist. The Hebrews were not bound by their religion to evince any pious care for other nations not included in the compact, but only for their own fellow-citizens.

29 "If men could lose their natural rights so as to be absolutely unable for the future to oppose the will of the sovereign" Two common soldiers undertook to change the Roman dominion, and did change it. (Tacitus, Hist. i:7.)

30 See Numbers xi. 28. In this passage it is written that two men prophesied in the camp, and that Joshua wished to punish them. This he would not have done, if it had been lawful for anyone to deliver the Divine oracles to the people without the consent of Moses. But Moses thought good to pardon the two men, and rebuked Joshua for exhorting him to use his royal prerogative, at a time when he was so weary of reigning, that he preferred death to holding undivided sway (Numb. xi:14). For he made answer to Joshua, "Enviest thou for my sake? Would God that all the Lord's people were prophets, and that the Lord would put His spirit upon them." That is to say, would God that the right of taking counsel of God were general, and the power were in the hands of the people. Thus Joshua was not mistaken as to the right, but only as to the time for using it, for which he was rebuked by Moses, in the same way as Abishai was rebuked by David for counselling that Shimei, who had undoubtedly been guilty of treason, should be put to death. See 2 Sam. xix:22, 23.

31 See Numbers xxvii:21. The translators of the Bible have rendered incorrectly verses 19 and 23 of this chapter. The passage does not mean that Moses gave precepts or advice to Joshua, but that he made or established him chief of the Hebrews. The phrase is very freguent in Scripture (see Exodus, xviii:23; 1 Sam. xiii:15; Joshua i:9; 1 Sam. xxv:80).

32 "There was no judge over each of the captains save God." The Rabbis and

some Christians equally foolish pretend that the Sanhedrin, called "the great" was instituted by Moses. As a matter of fact, Moses chose seventy colleagues to assist him in governing, because he was not able to bear alone the burden of the whole people; but he never passed any law for forming a college of seventy members; on the contrary he ordered every tribe to appoint for itself, in the cities which God had given it, judges to settle disputes according to the laws which he himself had laid down. In cases where the opinions of the judges differed as to the interpretation of these laws, Moses bade them take counsel of the High Priest (who was the chief interpreter of the law), or of the chief judge, to whom they were then subordinate (who had the right of consulting the High Priest), and to decide the dispute in accordance with the answer obtained. If any subordinate judge should assert, that he was not bound by the decision of the High Priest, received either directly or through the chief of his state, such an one was to be put to death (Deut. xvii:9) by the chief judge, whoever he might be, to whom he was a subordinate. This chief judge would either be Joshua, the supreme captain of the whole people, or one of the tribal chiefs who had been entrusted, after the division of the tribes, with the right of consulting the high priest concerning the affairs of his tribe, of deciding on peace or war, of fortifying towns, of appointing inferior judges, &c. Or, again, it might be the king, in whom all or some of the tribes had vested their rights.I could cite many instances in confirmation of what I here advance. I will confine myself to one, which appears to me the most important of all. When the Shilomitish prophet anointed Jeroboam king, he, in so doing, gave him the right of consulting the high priest, of appointing judges, &c. In fact he endowed him with all the rights over the ten tribes, which Rehoboam retained over the two tribes. Consequently Jeroboam could set up a supreme council in his court with as much right as Jehoshaphat could at Jerusalem (2 Chron. xix:8). For it is plain that neither Jeroboam, who was king by God's command, nor Jeroboam's subjects, were bound by the Law of Moses to accept the judgments of Rehoboam, who was not their king. Still less were they under the jurisdiction of the judge, whom Rehoboam had set up in Jerusalem as subordinate to himself. According, therefore, as the Hebrew dominion was divided, so was a supreme council setup in each division. Those who neglect the variations in the constitution of the Hebrew States, and confuse them all together in one, fall into numerous difficulties.

CHAPTER XVIII.

From the Commonwealth of the Hebrews, and Their History,
Certain Political Doctrines are Deduced.

ALTHOUGH THE COMMONWEALTH of the Hebrews, as we have conceived it, might have lasted for ever, it would be impossible to imitate it at the present day, nor would it be advisable so to do. If a people wished to transfer their rights to God it would be necessary to make an express covenant with Him, and for this would be needed not only the consent of those transferring their rights, but also the consent of God. God, however, has revealed through his Apostles that the covenant of God is no longer written in ink, or on tables of stone, but with the Spirit of God in the fleshy tables of the heart.

Furthermore, such a form of government would only be available for those who desire to have no foreign relations, but to shut themselves up within their own frontiers, and to live apart from the rest of the world; it would be useless to men who must have dealings with other nations; so that the cases where it could be adopted are very few indeed.

Nevertheless, though it could not be copied in its entirety, it possessed many excellent features which might be brought to our notice, and perhaps imitated with advantage. My intention, however, is not to write a treatise on forms of government, so I will pass over most of such points in silence, and will only touch on those which bear upon my purpose.

God's kingdom is not infringed upon by the choice of an earthly ruler endowed with sovereign rights; for after the Hebrews had transferred their rights to God, they conferred the sovereign right of ruling on Moses, investing him with the sole power of instituting and abrogating laws in the name of God, of choosing priests, of judging, of teaching, of punishing — in fact, all the prerogatives of an absolute monarch.

Again, though the priests were the interpreters of the laws, they had no power to judge the citizens, or to excommunicate anyone: this could only be done by the judges and chiefs chosen from among the people. A consideration of the successes and the histories of the Hebrews will bring to light other considerations worthy of note. To wit:

I. That there were no religious sects, till after the high priests, in the second commonwealth, possessed the authority to make decrees, and transact the business of government. In order that such authority might last for ever, the high priests usurped the rights of secular rulers, and at last wished to be styled kings. The reason for this is ready to hand; in the first commonwealth no decrees could bear the name of the high priest, for he had no right to ordain laws, but only to give the answers of God to questions asked by the captains or the councils: he had, therefore, no motive for making changes in the law, but took care, on the contrary, to administer and guard what had already been received and accepted. His only means of preserving his freedom in safety against the will of the captains lay in cherishing the law intact. After the high priests had assumed the power of carrying on the government, and added the rights of secular rulers to those they already possessed, each one began both in things religious and in things secular, to seek for the glorification of his own name, settling everything by sacerdotal authority, and issuing every day, concerning ceremonies, faith, and all else, new decrees which he sought to make as sacred and authoritative as the laws of Moses. Religion thus sank into a degrading superstition, while the true meaning and interpretation of the laws became corrupted. Furthermore, while the high priests were paving their way to the secular rule just after the restoration, they attempted to gain popular favour by assenting to every demand; approving whatever the people did, however impious, and accommodating Scripture to the very depraved current morals. Malachi bears witness to this in no measured terms: he chides the priests of his time as despisers of the name of God, and then goes on with his invective as follows (Mal ii:7, 8): "For the priest's lips should keep knowledge, and they should seek the law at his mouth: for he is the messenger of the Lord of hosts. But ye are departed out of the way; ye have caused many to stumble at the law, ye have corrupted the covenant of Levi, saith the Lord of hosts." He further accuses them of interpreting the laws according to their own pleasure, and paying no respect to God but only to persons. It is certain that the high priests were never so cautious in their conduct as to escape the remark of the more shrewd among the people, for the latter were at length emboldened to assert that no laws ought to be kept save those that were written, and that the decrees which the Pharisees (consisting, as Josephus says in his " Amtiquities," chiefly, of the common people), were deceived into calling the traditions of the fathers, should not be observed at all. However this may be, we can in nowise doubt that flattery of the high priest, the corruption of religion and the laws, and the enormous increase of the extent of the last-named, gave very great and frequent occasion for disputes and altercations impossible to allay. When men begin to quarrel with all the ardour of superstition, and the magistracy to back up one side or the other, they can never come to a compromise, but are bound to split into sects.

II. It is worthy of remark that the prophets, who were in a private station of life, rather irritated than reformed mankind by their freedom of warning, rebuke, and censure; whereas the kings, by their reproofs and punishments, could always produce an effect. The prophets were often intolerable even to pious kings, on account of the authority they assumed for judging whether an action was right or wrong, or for reproving the kings themselves if they dared to transact any business, whether public or private, without prophetic sanction. King Asa who, according to the testimony of Scripture, reigned piously, put the prophet Hanani into a prison-house because he had ventured freely to chide and reprove him for entering into a covenant with the king of Armenia.

Other examples might be cited, tending to prove that religion gained more harm than good by such freedom, not to speak of the further consequence, that if the prophets had retained their rights, great civil wars would have resulted.

III. It is remarkable that during all the period, during which the people held the reins of power, there was only one civil war, and that one was completely extinguished, the conquerors taking such pity on the conquered, that they endeavoured in every way to reinstate them in their former dignity and power. But after that the people, little accustomed to kings, changed its first form of government into a monarchy, civil war raged almost continuously; and battles were so fierce as to exceed all others recorded; in one engagement (taxing our faith to the utmost) five hundred thousand Israelites were slaughtered by the men of Judah, and in another the Israelites slew great numbers of the men of Judah (the figures are not given in Scripture), almost razed to the ground the walls of Jerusalem, and sacked the Temple in their unbridled fury. At length, laden with the spoils of their brethren, satiated with blood, they took hostages, and leaving the king in his well-nigh devastated kingdom, laid down their arms, relying on the weakness rather than the good faith of their foes. A few years after, the men of Judah, with recruited strength, again took the field, but were a second time beaten by the Israelites, and slain to the number of a hundred and twenty thousand, two hundred thousand of their wives and children were led into captivity, and a great booty again seized. Worn out with these and similar battles set forth at length in their histories, the Jews at length fell a prey to their enemies.

Furthermore, if we reckon up the times during which peace prevailed under each form of government, we shall find a great discrepancy. Before the monarchy forty years and more often passed, and once eighty years (an almost unparalleled period), without any war, foreign or civil. After the kings acquired sovereign power, the fighting was no longer for peace and liberty, but for glory; accordingly we find that they all, with the exception of Solomon (whose virtue and wisdom would be better displayed in peace than in war) waged war, and finally a fatal desire for power gained ground, which, in many cases, made the path to the throne a bloody one.

Lastly, the laws, during the rule of the people, remained uncorrupted and were studiously observed. Before the monarchy there were very, few prophets to admonish the people, but after the establishment of kings there were a great number at the same time. Obadiah saved a hundred from death and hid them away, lest they should be slain with the rest. The people, so far as we can see, were never deceived by false prophets till after the power had been vested in kings, whose creatures many of the prophets were. Again, the people, whose heart was generally proud or humble according to its circumstances, easily corrected it-self under misfortune, turned again to God, restored His laws, and so freed itself from all peril; but the kings, whose hearts were always equally puffed up, and who could not be corrected without humiliation, clung pertinaciously to their vices, even till the last overthrow of the city.

We may now clearly see from what I have said: —

I. How hurtful to religion and the state is the concession to ministers of religion of any power of issuing decrees or transacting the business of government: how, on the contrary, far greater stability is afforded, if the said ministers are only allowed to give answers to questions duly put to them, and are, as a rule, obliged to preach and practise the received and accepted doctrines.

II How dangerous it is to refer to Divine right matters merely speculative and subject or liable to dispute. The most tyrannical governments are those which make crimes of opinions, for everyone has an inalienable right over his thoughts — nay, such a state of things leads to the rule of popular passion.

Pontius Pilate made concession to the passion of the Pharisees in consenting to the crucifixion of Christ, whom he knew to be innocent. Again, the Pharisees, in order to shake the position of men richer than themselves, began to set on foot questions of religion, and accused the Sadducees of impiety, and, following their example, the vilest — hypocrites, stirred, as they pretended, by the same holy wrath which they called zeal for the Lord, persecuted men whose unblemished character and distinguished virtue had excited the popular hatred, publicly denounced their opinions, and inflamed the fierce passions of the people against them.

This wanton licence being cloaked with the specious garb of religion could not easily be repressed, especially when the sovereign authorities introduced a sect of which they, were not the head; they were then regarded not as interpreters of Divine right, but as sectarians — that is, as persons recognizing the right of Divine interpretation assumed by the leaders of the sect. The authority of the magistrates thus became of little account in such matters in comparison with the authority of sectarian leaders before whose interpretations kings were obliged to bow.

To avoid such evils in a state, there is no safer way, than to make piety and religion to consist in acts only — that is, in the practice of justice and charity, leaving everyone's judgment in other respects free. But I will speak of this more at length presently.

III. We see how necessary it is, both in the interests of the state and in the interests of religion, to confer on the sovereign power the right of deciding what is lawful or the reverse. If this right of judging actions could not be given to the very prophets of God without great injury, to the state and religion, how much less should it be entrusted to those who can neither foretell the future nor work miracles! But this again I will treat of more fully hereafter.

IV. Lastly,, we see how disastrous it is for a people unaccustomed to kings, and possessing a complete code of laws, to set up a monarchy. Neither can the subjects brook such a sway, nor the royal authority submit to laws and popular rights set up by anyone inferior to itself. Still less can a king be expected to defend such laws, for they were not framed to support his dominion, but the dominion of the people, or some council which formerly ruled, so that in guarding the popular rights the king would seem to be a slave rather than a master. The representative of a new monarchy will employ all his zeal in attempting to frame new laws, so as to wrest the rights of dominion to his own use, and to reduce the people till they find it easier to increase than to curtail the royal prerogative. I must not, however, omit to state that it is no less dangerous to remove a monarch, though he is on all hands admitted to be a tyrant. For his people are accustomed to royal authority and will obey no other, despising and mocking at any less august control.

It is therefore necessary, as the prophets discovered of old, if one king be removed, that he should be replaced by another, who will be a tyrant from necessity rather than choice. For how will he be able to endure the sight of the hands of the citizens reeking with royal blood, and to rejoice in their regicide as a glorious exploit? Was not the deed perpetrated as an example and warning for himself?

If he really wishes to be king, and not to acknowledge the people as the judge of kings and the master of himself, or to wield a precarious sway, he must avenge the death of his predecessor, making an example for his own sake, lest the people should venture to repeat a similar crime. He will not, however, be able easily to avenge the death of the tyrant by the slaughter of citizens unless he defends the cause of tyranny and approves the deeds of his predecessor, thus following in his footsteps.

Hence it comes to pass that peoples have often changed their tyrants, but never removed them or changed the monarchical form of government into any other.

The English people furnish us with a terrible example of this fact. They sought how to depose their monarch under the forms of law, but when he had been removed, they were utterly unable to change the form of government, and after much bloodshed only brought it about, that a new monarch should be hailed under a different name (as though it had been a mere question of names); this new monarch could only consolidate his power by completely destroying the royal stock, putting to death the king's friends, real or supposed, and disturbing with war the peace which might encourage discontent, in order that the populace might be engrossed with novelties and divert its mind from brooding over the slaughter of the king. At last, however, the people reflected that it had accomplished nothing for the good of the country beyond violating the rights of the lawful king and changing everything for the worse. It therefore decided to retrace its steps as soon as possible, and never rested till it had seen a complete restoration of the original state of affairs.

It may perhaps be objected that the Roman people was easily able to remove its tyrants, but I gather from its history a strong confirmation of my contention. Though the Roman people was much more than ordinarily capable of removing their tyrants and changing their form of government, inasmuch as it held in its own hands the power of electing its king and his successor, said being composed of rebels and criminals had not long been used to the royal yoke (out of its six kings it had put to death three), nevertheless it could accomplish nothing beyond electing several tyrants in place of one, who kept it groaning under a continual state of war, both foreign and civil, till at last it changed its government again to a form differing from monarchy, as in England, only in name.

As for the United States of the Netherlands, they have never, as we know, had a king, but only counts, who never attained the full rights of dominion. The States of the Netherlands evidently acted as principals in the settlement made by them at the time of the Earl of Leicester's mission: they always reserved for themselves the authority to keep the counts up to their duties, and the power to preserve this authority and the liberty of the citizens. They had ample means of vindicating their rights if their rulers should prove tyrannical, and could impose such restraints that nothing could be done without their consent and approval.

Thus the rights of sovereign power have always been vested in the States, though the last count endeavoured to usurp them. It is therefore little likely that the States should give them up, especially as they have just restored their original dominion, lately almost lost.

These examples, then, confirm us in our belief, that every dominion should retain its original form, and, indeed, cannot change it without danger of the utter ruin of the whole state. Such are the points I have here thought worthy of remark.

CHAPTER XIX.

It is shown that the Right over matters Spiritual lies wholly with the Sovereign, and that the outward forms of Religion should be in accordance with Public Peace, if we would obey God aright.

WHEN I SAID that the possessors of sovereign power have rights over everything, and that all rights are dependent on their decree, I did not merely mean temporal rights, but also spiritual rights; of the latter, no less than the former, they ought to be the interpreters and the champions. I wish to draw special attention to this point, and to discuss it fully in this chapter, because many persons deny that the right of deciding religious questions belongs to the sovereign power, and refuse to acknowledge it as the interpreter of Divine right. They accordingly assume full licence to accuse and arraign it, nay, even to excommunicate it from the Church, as Ambrosius treated the Emperor Theodosius in old time. However, I will show later on in this chapter that they take this means of dividing the government, and paving the way to their own ascendancy. I wish, however, first to point out that religion acquires its force as law solely from the decrees of the sovereign. God has no special kingdom among men except in so far as He reigns through temporal rulers. Moreover, the rites of religion and the outward observances of piety should be in accordance with the public peace and well-being, and should therefore be determined by the sovereign power alone. I speak here only of the outward observances of piety and the external rites of religion, not of piety, itself, nor of the inward worship of God, nor the means by which the mind is inwardly led to do homage to God in singleness of heart.

Inward worship of God and piety in itself are within the sphere of everyone's private rights, and cannot be alienated (as I showed at the end of Chapter VII.). What I here mean by the kingdom of God is, I think, sufficiently clear from what has been said in Chapter XIV. I there showed that a man best fulfils Gods law who worships Him, according to His command, through acts of justice and charity; it follows, therefore, that wherever justice and charity have the force of law and ordinance, there is God's kingdom.

I recognize no difference between the cases where God teaches and commands the practice of justice and charity through our natural faculties, and those where He makes special revelations; nor is the form of the revelation of importance so long as such practice is revealed and becomes a sovereign and supreme law to men. If, therefore, I show that justice and charity can only acquire the force of right and law through the rights of rulers, I shall be able readily to arrive at the conclusion (seeing that the rights of rulers are in the possession of the sovereign), that religion can only acquire the force of right by means of those who have the right to command, and that God only rules among men through the instrumentality of earthly potentates. It follows from what has been said, that the practice of justice and charity only acquires the force of law through the rights of the sovereign authority; for we showed in Chapter XVI. that in the state of nature reason has no more rights than desire, but that men living either by the laws of the former or the laws of the latter, possess rights co-extensive with their powers.

For this reason we could not conceive sin to exist in the state of nature, nor imagine God as a judge punishing man's transgressions; but we supposed all things to happen according to the general laws of universal nature, there being no difference between pious and impious, between him that was pure (as Solomon says) and him that was impure, because there was no possibility either of justice or charity.

In order that the true doctrines of reason, that is (as we showed in Chapter IV.), the true Divine doctrines might obtain absolutely the force of law and right, it was necessary that each individual should cede his natural right, and transfer it either to society as a whole, or to a certain body of men, or to one man. Then, and not till then, does it first dawn upon us what is justice and what is injustice, what is equity and what is iniquity.

Justice, therefore, and absolutely all the precepts of reason, including love towards one's neighbour, receive the force of laws and ordinances solely through the rights of dominion, that is (as we showed in the same chapter) solely on the decree of those who possess the right to rule. Inasmuch as the kingdom of God consists entirely in rights applied to justice and charity or to true religion, it follows that (as we asserted) the kingdom of God can only exist among men through the means of the sovereign powers; nor does it make any difference whether religion be apprehended by our natural faculties or by revelation: the argument is sound in both cases, inasmuch as religion is one and the same, and is equally revealed by God, whatever be the manner in which it becomes known to men.

Thus, in order that the religion revealed by the prophets might have the force of law among the Jews, it was necessary that every man of them should yield up his natural right, and that all should, with one accord, agree that they would only obey such commands as God should reveal to them through the prophets. Just as we have shown to take place in a democracy, where men with one consent agree to live according to the dictates of reason. Although the Hebrews furthermore transferred their right to God, they were able to do so rather in theory than in practice, for, as a matter of fact (as we pointed out above) they absolutely retained the right of dominion till they transferred it to Moses, who in his turn became absolute king, so that it was only through him that God reigned over the Hebrews. For this reason (namely, that religion only acquires the force of law by means of the sovereign power) Moses was not able to punish those who, before the covenant, and consequently while still in possession of their rights, violated the Sabbath (Exod. xvi:27), but was able to do so after the covenant (Numb. xv:36), because everyone had then yielded up his natural rights, and the ordinance of the Sabbath had received the force of law.

Lastly, for the same reason, after the destruction of the Hebrew dominion, revealed religion ceased to have the force of law; for we cannot doubt that as soon as the Jews transferred their right to the king of Babylon, the kingdom of God and the Divine right forthwith ceased. For the covenant wherewith they promised to obey all the utterances of God was abrogated; God's kingdom, which was based thereupon, also ceased. The Hebrews could no longer abide thereby, inasmuch as their rights no longer belonged to them but to the king of Babylon, whom (as we showed in Chapter XVI.) they were bound to obey in all things. Jeremiah (chap. xxix:7) expressly admonishes them of this fact: "And seek the peace of the city, whither I have caused you to be carried away captives, and pray unto the Lord for it; for in the peace thereof shall ye have peace." Now, they could not seek the peace of the City as having a share in its government, but only as slaves, being, as they were, captives; by obedience in all things, with a view to avoiding seditions, and by observing all the laws of the country, however different from their own. It is thus abundantly evident that religion among the Hebrews only acquired the form of law through the right of the sovereign rule; when that rule was destroyed, it could no longer be received as the law of a particular kingdom, but only as the universal precept of reason. I say of reason, for the universal religion had not yet become known by revelation. We may therefore draw the general conclusion that religion, whether revealed through our natural faculties or through prophets, receives the force of a command solely through the decrees of the holders of sovereign power; and, further, that God has no special kingdom among men, except in so far as He reigns through earthly potentates.

We may now see in a clearer light what was stated in Chapter IV., namely, that all the decrees of God involve eternal truth and necessity, so that we cannot conceive God as a prince or legislator giving laws to mankind. For this reason the Divine precepts, whether revealed through our natural faculties, or through prophets, do not receive immediately from God the force of a command, but only from those, or through the mediation of those, who possess the right of ruling and legislating. It is only through these latter means that God rules among men, and directs human affairs with justice and equity.

This conclusion is supported by experience, for we find traces of Divine justice only in places where just men bear sway; elsewhere the same lot (to repeat, again Solomon's words) befalls the just and the unjust, the pure and the impure: a state of things which causes Divine Providence to be doubted by many who think that God immediately reigns among men, and directs all nature for their benefit.

As, then, both reason and experience tell us that the Divine right is entirely dependent on the decrees of secular rulers, it follows that secular rulers are its proper interpreters. How this is so we shall now see, for it is time to show that the outward observances of religion, and all the external practices of piety should be brought into accordance with the public peace and well-being if we would obey God rightly. When this has been shown we shall easily understand how the sovereign rulers are the proper interpreters of religion and piety.

It is certain that duties towards one's country are the highest that man can fulfil; for, if government be taken away, no good thing can last, all falls into dispute, anger and anarchy reign unchecked amid universal fear. Consequently there can be no duty towards our neighbour which would not become an offence if it involved injury to the whole state, nor can there be any offence against our duty towards our neighbour, or anything but loyalty in what we do for the sake of preserving the state. For instance: it is in the abstract my duty when my neighbour quarrels with me and wishes to take my cloak, to give him my coat also; but if it be thought that such conduct is hurtful to the maintenance of the state, I ought to bring him to trial, even at the risk of his being condemned to death.

For this reason Manlius Torquatus is held up to honour, inasmuch as the public welfare outweighed with him his duty towards his children. This being so, it follows that the public welfare is the sovereign law to which all others, Divine and human, should be made to conform. Now, it is the function of the sovereign only to decide what is necessary for the public welfare and the safety of the state, and to give orders accordingly; therefore it is also the function of the sovereign only to decide the limits of our duty towards our neighbour — in other words, to determine how we should obey God. We can now clearly understand how the sovereign is the interpreter of religion, and further, that no one can obey God rightly, if the practices of his piety do not conform to the public welfare; or, consequently, if he does not implicitly obey all the commands of the sovereign. For as by God's command we are bound to do our duty to all men without exception, and to do no man an injury, we are also bound not to help one man at another's loss, still less at a loss to the whole state. Now, no private citizen can know what is good for the state, except he learn it through the sovereign power, who alone has the right to transact public business: therefore no one can rightly practise piety or obedience to God, unless he obey the sovereign power's commands in all things. This proposition is confirmed by the facts of experience. For if the sovereign adjudge a man to be worthy of death or an enemy, whether he be a citizen or a foreigner, a private individual or a separate ruler, no subject is allowed to give him assistance. So also though the Jews were bidden to love their fellow-citizens as themselves (Levit. xix:17, 18), they were nevertheless bound, if a man offended against the law, to point him out to the judge (Levit. v:1, and Deut. xiii:8, 9), and, if he should be condemned to death, to slay him (Deut. xvii:7).

Further, in order that the Hebrews might preserve the liberty they had gained, and might retain absolute sway over the territory they had conquered, it was necessary, as we showed in Chapter XVII., that their religion should be adapted to their particular government, and that they should separate themselves from the rest of the nations: wherefore it was commanded to them, "Love thy neighbour and hate thine enemy" (Matt. v:43), but after they had lost their dominion and had gone into captivity in Babylon, Jeremiah bid them take thought for the safety of the state into which they had been led captive; and Christ when He saw that they would be spread over the whole world, told them to do their duty by all men without exception; all of which instances show that religion has always been made to conform to the public welfare. Perhaps someone will ask: By what right, then, did the disciples of Christ, being private citizens, preach a new religion? I answer that they did so by the right of the power which they had received from Christ against unclean spirits (see Matt. x:1). I have already stated in Chapter XVI. that all are bound to obey a tyrant, unless they have received from God through undoubted revelation a promise of aid against him; so let no one take example from the Apostles unless he too has the power of working miracles. The point is brought out more clearly by Christ's command to His disciples, "Fear not those who kill the body" (Matt. x:28). If this command were imposed on everyone, governments would be founded in vain, and Solomon's words (Prov. xxiv:21), "My son, fear God and the king," would be impious, which they certainly are not; we must therefore admit that the authority which Christ gave to His disciples was given to them only, and must not be taken as an example for others.

I do not pause to consider the arguments of those who wish to separate secular rights from spiritual rights, placing the former under the control of the sovereign, and the latter under the control of the universal Church; such pretensions are too frivolous to merit refutation. I cannot however, pass over in silence the fact that such persons are woefully deceived when they seek to support their seditious opinions (I ask pardon for the somewhat harsh epithet) by the example of the Jewish high priest, who, in ancient times, had the right of administering the sacred offices. Did not the high priests receive their right by the decree of Moses (who, as I have shown, retained the sole right to rule), and could they not by the same means be deprived of it? Moses himself chose not only Aaron, but also his son Eleazar, and his grandson Phineas, and bestowed on them the right of administering the office of high priest. This right was retained by the high priests afterwards, but none the less were they delegates of Moses — that is, of the sovereign power. Moses, as we have shown, left no successor to his dominion, but so distributed his prerogatives, that those who came after him seemed, as it were, regents who administer the government when a king is absent but not dead.

In the second commonwealth the high priests held their right absolutely, after they had obtained the rights of principality in addition. Wherefore the rights of the high priesthood always depended on the edict of the sovereign, and the high priests did not possess them till they became sovereigns also. Rights in matters spiritual always remained under the control of the kings absolutely (as I will show at the end of this chapter), except in the single particular that they were not allowed to administer in person the sacred duties in the Temple, inasmuch as they were not of the family of Aaron, and were therefore considered unclean, a reservation which would have no force in a Christian community.

We cannot, therefore, doubt that the daily sacred rites (whose performance does not require a particular genealogy but only a special mode of life, and from which the holders of sovereign power are not excluded as unclean) are under the sole control of the sovereign power; no one, save by the authority or concession of such sovereign, has the right or power of administering them, of choosing others to administer them, of defining or strengthening the foundations of the Church and her doctrines; of judging on questions of morality or acts of piety; of receiving anyone into the Church or excommunicating him therefrom, or, lastly, of providing for the poor.

These doctrines are proved to be not only true (as we have already pointed out), but also of primary necessity for the preservation of religion and the state. We all know what weight spiritual right and authority carries in the popular mind: how everyone hangs on the lips, as it were, of those who possess it. We may even say that those who wield such authority have the most complete sway over the popular mind.

Whosoever, therefore, wishes to take this right away from the sovereign power, is desirous of dividing the dominion; from such division, contentions, and strife will necessarily spring up, as they did of old between the Jewish kings and high priests, and will defy all attempts to allay them. Nay, further, he who strives to deprive the sovereign power of such authority, is aiming (as we have said), at gaining dominion for himself. What is left for the sovereign power to decide on, if this right be denied him? Certainly nothing concerning either war or peace, if he has to ask another man's opinion as to whether what he believes to be beneficial would be pious or impious. Everything would depend on the verdict of him who had the right of deciding and judging what was pious or impious, right or wrong.

When such a right was bestowed on the Pope of Rome absolutely, he gradually acquired complete control over the kings, till at last he himself mounted to the summits of dominion; however much monarchs, and especially the German emperors, strove to curtail his authority, were it only by a hairsbreadth, they effected nothing, but on the contrary by their very endeavours largely increased it. That which no monarch could accomplish with fire and sword, ecclesiastics could bring about with a stroke of the pen; whereby we may easily see the force and power at the command of the Church, and also how necessary it is for sovereigns to reserve such prerogatives for themselves.

If we reflect on what was said in the last chapter we shall see that such reservation conduced not a little to the increase of religion and piety; for we observed that the prophets themselves, though gifted with Divine efficacy, being merely private citizens, rather irritated than reformed the people by their freedom of warning, reproof, and denunciation, whereas the kings by warnings and punishments easily bent men to their will. Furthermore, the kings themselves, not possessing the right in question absolutely, very often fell away from religion and took with them nearly the whole people. The same thing has often happened from the same cause in Christian states.

Perhaps I shall be asked, "But if the holders of sovereign power choose to be wicked, who will be the rightful champion of piety? Should the sovereigns still be its interpreters?" "I meet them with the counter-question, "But if ecclesiastics (who are also human, and private citizens, and who ought to mind only their own affairs), or if others whom it is proposed to entrust with spiritual authority, choose to be wicked, should they still be considered as piety's rightful interpreters?" It is quite certain that when sovereigns wish to follow their own pleasure, whether they have control over spiritual matters or not, the whole state, spiritual and secular, will go to ruin, and it will go much faster if private citizens seditiously assume the championship of the Divine rights.

Thus we see that not only is nothing gained by denying such rights to sovereigns, but on the contrary, great evil ensues. For (as happened with the Jewish kings who did not possess such rights absolutely) rulers are thus driven into wickedness, and the injury and loss to the state become certain and inevitable, instead of uncertain and possible. Whether we look to the abstract truth, or the security of states, or the increase of piety, we are compelled to maintain that the Divine right, or the right of control over spiritual matters, depends absolutely on the decree of the sovereign, who is its legitimate interpreter and champion. Therefore the true ministers of God's word are those who teach piety to the people in obedience to the authority of the sovereign rulers by whose decree it has been brought into conformity with the public welfare.

There remains for me to point out the cause for the frequent disputes on the subject of these spiritual rights in Christian states; whereas the Hebrews, so far as I know, never, had any doubts about the matter. It seems monstrous that a question so plain and vitally important should thus have remained undecided, and that the secular rulers could never obtain the prerogative without controversy, nay, nor without great danger of sedition and injury to religion. If no cause for this state of things were forthcoming, I could easily persuade myself that all I have said in this chapter is mere theorizing, or a kind of speculative reasoning which can never be of any practical use. However, when we reflect on the beginnings of Christianity the cause at once becomes manifest. The Christian religion was not taught at first by kings, but by private persons, who, against the wishes of those in power, whose subjects they, were, were for a long time accustomed to hold meetings in secret churches, to institute and perform sacred rites, and on their own authority to settle and decide on their affairs without regard to the state, When, after the lapse of many years, the religion was taken up by the authorities, the ecclesiastics were obliged to teach it to the emperors themselves as they had defined it: wherefore they easily gained recognition as its teachers and interpreters, and the church pastors were looked upon as vicars of God. The ecclesiastics took good care that the Christian kings should not assume their authority, by prohibiting marriage to the chief ministers of religion and to its highest interpreter. They furthermore elected their purpose by multiplying the dogmas of religion to such an extent and so blending them with philosophy that their chief interpreter was bound to be a skilled philosopher and theologian, and to have leisure for a host of idle speculations: conditions which could only be fulfilled by a private individual with much time on his hands.

Among the Hebrews things were very differently arranged: for their Church began at the same time as their dominion, and Moses, their absolute ruler, taught religion to the people, arranged their sacred rites, and chose their spiritual ministers. Thus the royal authority carried very great weight with the people, and the kings kept a firm hold on their spiritual prerogatives.

Although, after the death of Moses, no one held absolute sway, yet the power of deciding both in matters spiritual and matters temporal was in the hands of the secular chief, as I have already pointed out. Further, in order that it might be taught religion and piety, the people was bound to consult the supreme judge no less than the high priest (Deut. xvii:9, 11). Lastly, though the kings had not as much power as Moses, nearly the whole arrangement and choice of the sacred ministry depended on their decision. Thus David arranged the whole service of the Temple (see 1 Chron. xxviii:11, 12, &c.); from all the Levites he chose twenty-four thousand for the sacred psalms; six thousand of these formed the body from which were chosen the judges and proctors, four thousand were porters, and four thousand to play on instruments (see 1 Chron. xxiii:4, 5). He further divided them into companies (of whom he chose the chiefs), so that each in rotation, at the allotted time, might perform the sacred rites. The priests he also divided into as many companies; I will not go through the whole catalogue, but refer the reader to 2 Chron. viii:13, where it is stated, "Then Solomon offered burnt offerings to the Lord . . . . . after a certain rate every day, offering according to the commandments of Moses;" and in verse 14, "And he appointed, according to the order of David his father, the courses of the priests to their service . . . . . . for so had David the man of God commanded." Lastly, the historian bears witness in verse 15: "And they departed not from the commandment of the king unto the priests and Levites concerning any matter, or concerning the treasuries."

From these and other histories of the kings it is abundantly evident, that the whole practice of religion and the sacred ministry depended entirely on the commands of the king.

When I said above that the kings had not the same right as Moses to elect the high priest, to consult God without intermediaries, and to condemn the prophets who prophesied during their reign; I said so simply because the prophets could, in virtue of their mission, choose a new king and give absolution for regicide, not because they could call a king who offended against the law to judgment, or could rightly act against him 33.

Wherefore if there had been no prophets who, in virtue of a special revelation, could give absolution for regicide, the kings would have possessed absolute rights over all matters both spiritual and temporal. Consequently the rulers of modern times, who have no prophets and would not rightly be bound in any case to receive them (for they are not subject to Jewish law), have absolute possession of the spiritual prerogative, although they are not celibates, and they will always retain it, if they will refuse to allow religious dogmas to be unduly multiplied or confounded with philosophy.

33 I must here bespeak special attention for what was said in Chap. XVI. concerning rights.

CHAPTER XX.

That in a Free State Every Man May Think what he Likes, and Say what he Thinks.

IF MEN'S MINDS were as easily controlled as their tongues, every king would sit safely on his throne, and government by compulsion would cease; for every subject would shape his life according to the intentions of his rulers, and would esteem a thing true or false, good or evil, just or unjust, in obedience to their dictates. However, we have shown already (Chapter XVII.) that no man's mind can possibly lie wholly at the disposition of another, for no one can willingly transfer his natural right of free reason and judgment, or be compelled so to do. For this reason government which attempts to control minds is accounted tyrannical, and it is considered an abuse of sovereignty and a usurpation of the rights of subjects, to seek to prescribe what shall be accepted as true, or rejected as false, or what opinions should actuate men in their worship of God. All these questions fall within a man's natural right, which he cannot abdicate even with his own consent.

I admit that the judgment can be biassed in many ways, and to an almost incredible degree, so that while exempt from direct external control it may be so dependent on another man's words, that it may fitly be said to be ruled by him; but although this influence is carried to great lengths, it has never gone so far as to invalidate the statement, that every man's understanding is his own, and that brains are as diverse as palates.

Moses, not by fraud, but by Divine virtue, gained such a hold over the popular judgment that he was accounted superhuman, and believed to speak and act through the inspiration of the Deity; nevertheless, even he could not escape murmurs and evil interpretations. How much less then can other monarchs avoid them! Yet such unlimited power, if it exists at all, must belong to a monarch, and least of all to a democracy, where the whole or a great part of the people wield authority collectively. This is a fact which I think everyone can explain for himself.

However unlimited, therefore, the power of a sovereign may be, however implicitly it is trusted as the exponent of law and religion, it can never prevent men from forming judgments according to their intellect, or being influenced by any given emotion. It is true that it has the right to treat as enemies all men whose opinions do not, on all subjects, entirely coincide with its own; but we are not discussing its strict rights, but its proper course of action. I grant that it has the right to rule in the most violent manner, and to put citizens to death for very trivial causes, but no one supposes it can do this with the approval of sound judgment. Nay, inasmuch as such things cannot be done without extreme peril to itself, we may even deny that it has the absolute power to do them, or, consequently, the absolute right; for the rights of the sovereign are limited by his power.

Since, therefore, no one can abdicate his freedom of judgment and feeling; since every man is by indefeasible natural right the master of his own thoughts, it follows that men thinking in diverse and contradictory fashions, cannot, without disastrous results, be compelled to speak only according to the dictates of the supreme power. Not even the most experienced, to say nothing of the multitude, know how to keep silence. Men's common failing is to confide their plans to others, though there be need for secrecy, so that a government would be most harsh which deprived the individual of his freedom of saying and teaching what he thought; and would be moderate if such freedom were granted. Still we cannot deny that authority may be as much injured by words as by actions; hence, although the freedom we are discussing cannot be entirely denied to subjects, its unlimited concession would be most baneful; we must, therefore, now inquire, how far such freedom can and ought to be conceded without danger to the peace of the state, or the power of the rulers; and this, as I said at the beginning of Chapter XVI., is my principal object.

It follows, plainly, from the explanation given above, of the foundations of a state, that the ultimate aim of government is not to rule, or restrain, by fear, nor to exact obedience, but contrariwise, to free every man from fear, that he may live in all possible security; in other words, to strengthen his natural right to exist and work — without injury to himself or others.

No, the object of government is not to change men from rational beings into beasts or puppets, but to enable them to develope their minds and bodies in security, and to employ their reason unshackled; neither showing hatred, anger, or deceit, nor watched with the eyes of jealousy and injustice. In fact, the true aim of government is liberty.

Now we have seen that in forming a state the power of making laws must either be vested in the body of the citizens, or in a portion of them, or in one man. For, although mens free judgments are very diverse, each one thinking that he alone knows everything, and although complete unanimity of feeling and speech is out of the question, it is impossible to preserve peace, unless individuals abdicate their right of acting entirely on their own judgment. Therefore, the individual justly cedes the right of free action, though not of free reason and judgment; no one can act against the authorities without danger to the state, though his feelings and judgment may be at variance therewith; he may even speak against them, provided that he does so from rational conviction, not from fraud, anger, or hatred, and provided that he does not attempt to introduce any change on his private authority.

For instance, supposing a man shows that a law is repugnant to sound reason, and should therefore be repealed; if he submits his opinion to the judgment of the authorities (who, alone, have the right of making and repealing laws), and meanwhile acts in nowise contrary to that law, he has deserved well of the state, and has behaved as a good citizen should; but if he accuses the authorities of injustice, and stirs up the people against them, or if he seditiously strives to abrogate the law without their consent, he is a mere agitator and rebel.

Thus we see how an individual may declare and teach what he believes, without injury to the authority of his rulers, or to the public peace; namely, by leaving in their hands the entire power of legislation as it affects action, and by doing nothing against their laws, though he be compelled often to act in contradiction to what he believes, and openly feels, to be best.

Such a course can be taken without detriment to justice and dutifulness, nay, it is the one which a just and dutiful man would adopt. We have shown that justice is dependent on the laws of the authorities, so that no one who contravenes their accepted decrees can be just, while the highest regard for duty, as we have pointed out in the preceding chapter, is exercised in maintaining public peace and tranquillity; these could not be preserved if every man were to live as he pleased; therefore it is no less than undutiful for a man to act contrary to his country's laws, for if the practice became universal the ruin of states would necessarily follow.

Hence, so long as a man acts in obedience to the laws of his rulers, he in nowise contravenes his reason, for in obedience to reason he transferred the right of controlling his actions from his own hands to theirs. This doctrine we can confirm from actual custom, for in a conference of great and small powers, schemes are seldom carried unanimously, yet all unite in carrying out what is decided on, whether they voted for or against. But I return to my proposition.

From the fundamental notions of a state, we have discovered how a man may exercise free judgment without detriment to the supreme power: from the same premises we can no less easily determine what opinions would be seditious. Evidently those which by their very nature nullify the compact by which the right of free action was ceded. For instance, a man who holds that the supreme power has no rights over him, or that promises ought not to be kept, or that everyone should live as he pleases, or other doctrines of this nature in direct opposition to the above-mentioned contract, is seditious, not so much from his actual opinions and judgment, as from the deeds which they involve; for he who maintains such theories abrogates the contract which tacitly, or openly, he made with his rulers. Other opinions which do not involve acts violating the contract, such as revenge, anger, and t he like, are not seditious, unless it be in some. corrupt state, where superstitious and ambitious persons, unable to endure men of learning, are so popular with the multitude that their word is more valued than the law.

However, I do not deny that there are some doctrines which, while they are apparently only concerned with abstract truths and falsehoods, are yet propounded and published with unworthy motives. This question we have discussed in Chapter XV., and shown that reason should nevertheless remain unshackled. If we hold to the principle that a man's loyalty to the state should be judged, like his loyalty to God, from his actions only — namely, from his charity towards his neighbours; we cannot doubt that the best government will allow freedom of philosophical speculation no less than of religious belief. I confess that from such freedom inconveniences may sometimes arise, but what question was ever settled so wisely that no abuses could possibly spring therefrom? He who seeks to regulate everything by law, is more likely to arouse vices than to reform them. It is best to grant what cannot be abolished, even though it be in itself harmful. How many evils spring from luxury, envy, avarice, drunkenness, and the like, yet these are tolerated — vices as they are — because they cannot be prevented by legal enactments. How much more then should free thought be granted, seeing that it is in itself a virtue and that it cannot be crushed! Besides, the evil results can easily be checked, as I will show, by the secular authorities, not to mention that such freedom is absolutely necessary for progress in science and the liberal arts: for no man follows such pursuits to advantage unless his judgment be entirely free and unhampered.

But let it be granted that freedom may be crushed, and men be so bound down, that they do not dare to utter a whisper, save at the bidding of their rulers; nevertheless this can never be carried to the pitch of making them think according to authority, so that the necessary consequences would be that men would daily be thinking one thing and saying another, to the corruption of good faith, that mainstay of government, and to the fostering of hateful flattery and perfidy, whence spring stratagems, and the corruption of every good art.

It is far from possible to impose uniformity of speech, for the more rulers strive to curtail freedom of speech, the more obstinately are they resisted; not indeed by the avaricious, the flatterers, and other numskulls, who think supreme salvation consists in filling their stomachs and gloating over their money-bags, but by those whom good education, sound morality, and virtue have rendered more free. Men, as generally constituted, are most prone to resent the branding as criminal of opinions which they believe to be true, and the proscription as wicked of that which inspires them with piety towards God and man; hence they are ready to forswear the laws and conspire against the authorities, thinking it not shameful but honourable to stir up seditions and perpetuate any sort of crime with this end in view. Such being the constitution of human nature, we see that laws directed against opinions affect the generous minded rather than the wicked, and are adapted less for coercing criminals than for irritating the upright; so that they cannot be maintained without great peril to the state.

Moreover, such laws are almost always useless, for those who hold that the opinions proscribed are sound, cannot possibly obey the law; whereas those who already reject them as false, accept the law as a kind of privilege, and make such boast of it, that authority is powerless to repeal it, even if such a course be subsequently desired.

To these considerations may be added what we said in Chapter XVIII. in treating of the history of the Hebrews. And, lastly, how many schisms have arisen in the Church from the attempt of the authorities to decide by law the intricacies of theological controversy! If men were not allured by the hope of getting the law and the authorities on their side, of triumphing over their adversaries in the sight of an applauding multitude, and of acquiring honourable distinctions, they would not strive so maliciously, nor would such fury sway their minds. This is taught not only by reason but by daily examples, for laws of this kind prescribing what every man shall believe and forbidding anyone to speak or write to the contrary, have often been passed, as sops or concessions to the anger of those who cannot tolerate men of enlightenment, and who, by such harsh and crooked enactments, can easily turn the devotion of the masses into fury and direct it against whom they will. How much better would it be to restrain popular anger and fury, instead of passing useless laws, which can only be broken by those who love virtue and the liberal arts, thus paring down the state till it is too small to harbour men of talent. What greater misfortune for a state can be conceived then that honourable men should be sent like criminals into exile, because they hold diverse opinions which they cannot disguise? What, I say, can be more hurtful than that men who have committed no crime or wickedness should, simply because they are enlightened, be treated as enemies and put to death, and that the scaffold, the terror of evil-doers, should become the arena where the highest examples of tolerance and virtue are displayed to the people with all the marks of ignominy that authority can devise?

He that knows himself to be upright does not fear the death of a criminal, and shrinks from no punishment; his mind is not wrung with remorse for any disgraceful deed: he holds that death in a good cause is no punishment, but an honour, and that death for freedom is glory.

What purpose then is served by the death of such men, what example in proclaimed? the cause for which they die is unknown to the idle and the foolish, hateful to the turbulent, loved by the upright. The only lesson we can draw from such scenes is to flatter the persecutor, or else to imitate the victim.

If formal assent is not to be esteemed above conviction, and if governments are to retain a firm hold of authority and not be compelled to yield to agitators, it is imperative that freedom of judgment should be granted, so that men may live together in harmony, however diverse, or even openly contradictory their opinions may be. We cannot doubt that such is the best system of government and open to the fewest objections, since it is the one most in harmony with human nature. In a democracy (the most natural form of government, as we have shown in Chapter XVI.) everyone submits to the control of authority over his actions, but not over his judgment and reason; that is, seeing that all cannot think alike, the voice of the majority has the force of law, subject to repeal if circumstances bring about a change of opinion. In proportion as the power of free judgment is withheld we depart from the natural condition of mankind, and consequently the government becomes more tyrannical.

In order to prove that from such freedom no inconvenience arises, which cannot easily be checked by the exercise of the sovereign power, and that men's actions can easily be kept in bounds, though their opinions be at open variance, it will be well to cite an example. Such an one is not very, far to seek. The city of Amsterdam reaps the fruit of this freedom in its own great prosperity and in the admiration of all other people. For in this most flourishing state, and most splendid city, men of every, nation and religion live together in the greatest harmony, and ask no questions before trusting their goods to a fellow-citizen, save whether he be rich or poor, and whether he generally acts honestly, or the reverse. His religion and sect is considered of no importance: for it has no effect before the judges in gaining or losing a cause, and there is no sect so despised that its followers, provided that they harm no one, pay every man his due, and live uprightly, are deprived of the protection of the magisterial authority.

On the other hand, when the religious controversy between Remonstrants and Counter-Remonstrants began to be taken up by politicians and the States, it grew into a schism, and abundantly showed that laws dealing with religion and seeking to settle its controversies are much more calculated to irritate than to reform, and that they give rise to extreme licence: further, it was seen that schisms do not originate in a love of truth, which is a source of courtesy and gentleness, but rather in an inordinate desire for supremacy, From all these considerations it is clearer than the sun at noonday, that the true schismatics are those who condemn other men's writings, and seditiously stir up the quarrelsome masses against their authors, rather than those authors themselves, who generally write only for the learned, and appeal solely to reason. In fact, the real disturbers of the peace are those who, in a free state, seek to curtail the liberty of judgment which they are unable to tyrannize over.

I have thus shown: —

I. That it is impossible to deprive men of the liberty of saying what they think.

II. That such liberty can be conceded to every man without injury to the rights and authority of the sovereign power, and that every man may retain it without injury to such rights, provided that he does not presume upon it to the extent of introducing any new rights into the state, or acting in any way contrary, to the existing laws.

III. That every man may enjoy this liberty without detriment to the public peace, and that no inconveniences arise therefrom which cannot easily be checked.

IV. That every man may enjoy it without injury to his allegiance.

V. That laws dealing with speculative problems are entirely useless.

VI. Lastly, that not only may such liberty be granted without prejudice to the public peace, to loyalty, and to the rights of rulers, but that it is even necessary, for their preservation. For when people try to take it away, and bring to trial, not only the acts which alone are capable of offending, but also the opinions of mankind, they only succeed in surrounding their victims with an appearance of martyrdom, and raise feelings of pity and revenge rather than of terror. Uprightness and good faith are thus corrupted, flatterers and traitors are encouraged, and sectarians triumph, inasmuch as concessions have been made to their animosity, and they have gained the state sanction for the doctrines of which they are the interpreters. Hence they arrogate to themselves the state authority and rights, and do not scruple to assert that they have been directly chosen by God, and that their laws are Divine, whereas the laws of the state are human, and should therefore yield obedience to the laws of God — in other words, to their own laws. Everyone must see that this is not a state of affairs conducive to public welfare. Wherefore, as we have shown in Chapter XVIII., the safest way for a state is to lay down the rule that religion is comprised solely in the exercise of charity and justice, and that the rights of rulers in sacred, no less than in secular matters, should merely have to do with actions, but that every man should think what he likes and say what he thinks.

I have thus fulfilled the task I set myself in this treatise. It remains only to call attention to the fact that I have written nothing which I do not most willingly submit to the examination and approval of my country's rulers; and that I am willing to retract anything which they shall decide to be repugnant to the laws, or prejudicial to the public good. I know that I am a man, and as a man liable to error, but against error I have taken scrupulous care, and have striven to keep in entire accordance with the laws of my country, with loyalty, and with morality.

POLITICAL TREATISE

PREFACE.

MEN WOULD NEVER be superstitious, if they could govern all their circumstances by set rules, or if they were always favoured by fortune: but being frequently driven into straits where rules are useless, and being often kept fluctuating pitiably between hope and fear by the uncertainty of fortune's greedily coveted favours, they are consequently, for the most part, very prone to credulity. The human mind is readily swayed this way or that in times of doubt, especially when hope and fear are struggling for the mastery, though usually it is boastful, over — confident, and vain.

This as a general fact I suppose everyone knows, though few, I believe, know their own nature; no one can have lived in the world without observing that most people, when in prosperity, are so over-brimming with wisdom (however inexperienced they may be), that they take every offer of advice as a personal insult, whereas in adversity they know not where to turn, but beg and pray for counsel from every passer-by. No plan is then too futile, too absurd, or too fatuous for their adoption; the most frivolous causes will raise them to hope, or plunge them into despair — if anything happens during their fright which reminds them of some past good or ill, they think it portends a happy or unhappy issue, and therefore (though it may have proved abortive a hundred times before) style it a lucky or unlucky omen. Anything which excites their astonishment they believe to be a portent signifying the anger of the gods or of the Supreme Being, and, mistaking superstition for religion, account it impious not to avert the evil with prayer and sacrifice. Signs and wonders of this sort they conjure up perpetually, till one might think Nature as mad as themselves, they interpret her so fantastically.

Thus it is brought prominently before us, that superstition's chief victims are those persons who greedily covet temporal advantages; they it is, who (especially when they are in danger, and cannot help themselves) are wont with Prayers and womanish tears to implore help from God: upbraiding Reason as blind, because she cannot show a sure path to the shadows they pursue, and rejecting human wisdom as vain; but believing the phantoms of imagination, dreams, and other childish absurdities, to be the very oracles of Heaven. As though God had turned away from the wise, and written His decrees, not in the mind of man but in the entrails of beasts, or left them to be proclaimed by the inspiration and instinct of fools, madmen, and birds. Such is the unreason to which terror can drive mankind!

Superstition, then, is engendered, preserved, and fostered by fear. If anyone desire an example, let him take Alexander, who only began superstitiously to seek guidance from seers, when he first learnt to fear fortune in the passes of Sysis (Curtius, v. 4); whereas after he had conquered Darius he consulted prophets no more, till a second time frightened by reverses. When the Scythians were provoking a battle, the Bactrians had deserted, and he himself was lying sick of his wounds, "he once more turned to superstition, the mockery of human wisdom, and bade Aristander, to whom he confided his credulity, inquire the issue of affairs with sacrificed victims." Very numerous examples of a like nature might be cited, clearly showing the fact, that only while under the dominion of fear do men fall a prey to superstition; that all the portents ever invested with the reverence of misguided religion are mere phantoms of dejected and fearful minds; and lastly, that prophets have most power among the people, and are most formidable to rulers, precisely at those times when the state is in most peril. I think this is sufficiently plain to all, and will therefore say no more on the subject.

The origin of superstition above given affords us a clear reason for the fact, that it comes to all men naturally, though some refer its rise to a dim notion of God, universal to mankind, and also tends to show, that it is no less inconsistent and variable than other mental hallucinations and emotional impulses, and further that it can only be maintained by hope, hatred, anger, and deceit; since it springs, not from reason, but solely from the more powerful phases of emotion. Furthermore, we may readily understand how difficult it is, to maintain in the same course men prone to every form of credulity. For, as the mass of mankind remains always at about the same pitch of misery, it never assents long to any one remedy, but is always best pleased by a novelty which has not yet proved illusive.

This element of inconsistency has been the cause of many terrible wars and revolutions; for, as Curtius well says (lib. iv. chap. 10): "The mob has no ruler more potent than superstition," and is easily led, on the plea of religion, at one moment to adore its kings as gods, and anon to execrate and abjure them as humanity's common bane. Immense pains have therefore been taken to counteract this evil by investing religion, whether true or false, with such pomp and ceremony, that it may, rise superior to every shock, and be always observed with studious reverence by the whole people — a system which has been brought to great perfection by the Turks, for they consider even controversy impious, and so clog men's minds with dogmatic formulas, that they leave no room for sound reason, not even enough to doubt with.

But if, in despotic statecraft, the supreme and essential mystery be to hoodwink the subjects, and to mask the fear, which keeps them clown, with the specious garb of religion, so that men may fight as bravely for slavery as for safety, and count it not shame but highest honour to risk their blood and their lives for the vainglory of a tyrant; yet in a free state no more mischievous expedient could be planned or attempted. Wholly repugnant to the general freedom are such devices as enthralling men's minds with prejudices, forcing their judgment, or employing any of the weapons of quasi-religious sedition; indeed, such seditions only spring up, when law enters the domain of speculative thought, and opinions are put on trial and condemned on the same footing as crimes, while those who defend and follow them are sacrificed, not to public safety, but to their opponents' hatred and cruelty. If deeds only could be made the grounds of criminal charges, and words were always allowed to pass free, such seditions would be divested of every semblance of justification, and would be separated from mere controversies by a hard and fast line.

Now, seeing that we have the rare happiness of living in a republic, where everyone's judgment is free and unshackled, where each may worship God as his conscience dictates, and where freedom is esteemed before all things dear and precious, I have believed that I should be undertaking no ungrateful or unprofitable task, in demonstrating that not only can such freedom be granted without prejudice to the public peace, but also, that without such freedom, piety cannot flourish nor the public peace be secure.

Such is the chief conclusion I seek to establish in this treatise; but, in order to reach it, I must first point out the misconceptions which, like scars of our former bondage, still disfigure our notion of religion, and must expose the false views about the civil authority which many have most impudently advocated, endeavouring to turn the mind of the people, still prone to heathen superstition, away from its legitimate rulers, and so bring us again into slavery. As to the order of my treatise I will speak presently, but first I will recount the causes which led me to write.

I have often wondered, that persons who make a boast of professing the Christian religion, namely, love, joy, peace, temperance, and charity to all men, should quarrel with such rancorous animosity, and display daily towards one another such bitter hatred, that this, rather than the virtues they claim, is the readiest criterion of their faith. Matters have long since come to such a pass, that one can only pronounce a man Christian, Turk, Jew, or Heathen, by his general appearance and attire, by his frequenting this or that place of worship, or employing the phraseology of a particular sect — as for manner of life, it is in all cases the same. Inquiry into the cause of this anomaly leads me unhesitatingly to ascribe it to the fact, that the ministries of the Church are regarded by the masses merely as dignities, her offices as posts of emolument — in short, popular religion may be summed up as respect for ecclesiastics. The spread of this misconception inflamed every worthless fellow with an intense desire to enter holy orders, and thus the love of diffusing God's religion degenerated into sordid avarice and ambition. Every church became a theatre, where orators, instead of church teachers, harangued, caring not to instruct the people, but striving to attract admiration, to bring opponents to public scorn, and to preach only novelties and paradoxes, such as would tickle the ears of their congregation. This state of things necessarily stirred up an amount of controversy, envy, and hatred, which no lapse of time could appease; so that we can scarcely wonder that of the old religion nothing survives but its outward forms (even these, in the mouth of the multitude, seem rather adulation than adoration of the Deity), and that faith has become a mere compound of credulity and prejudices — aye, prejudices too, which degrade man from rational being to beast, which completely stifle the power of judgment between true and false, which seem, in fact, carefully fostered for the purpose of extinguishing the last spark of reason! Piety, great God! and religion are become a tissue of ridiculous mysteries; men, who flatly despise reason, who reject and turn away from understanding as naturally corrupt, these, I say, these of all men, are thought, 0 lie most horrible! to possess light from on High. Verily, if they had but one spark of light from on High, they would not insolently rave, but would learn to worship God more wisely, and would be as marked among their fellows for mercy as they now are for malice; if they were concerned for their opponents' souls, instead of for their own reputations, they would no longer fiercely persecute, but rather be filled with pity and compassion.

Furthermore, if any Divine light were in them, it would appear from their doctrine. I grant that they are never tired of professing their wonder at the profound mysteries of Holy Writ; still I cannot discover that they teach anything but speculations of Platonists and Aristotelians, to which (in order to save their credit for Christianity) they have made Holy Writ conform; not content to rave with the Greeks themselves, they want to make the prophets rave also; showing conclusively, that never even in sleep have they caught a glimpse of Scripture's Divine nature. The very vehemence of their admiration for the mysteries plainly attests, that their belief in the Bible is a formal assent rather than a living faith: and the fact is made still more apparent by their laying down beforehand, as a foundation for the study and true interpretation of Scripture, the principle that it is in every passage true and divine. Such a doctrine should be reached only after strict scrutiny and thorough comprehension of the Sacred Books (which would teach it much better, for they stand in need no human factions), and not be set up on the threshold, as it were, of inquiry.

As I pondered over the facts that the light of reason is not only despised, but by many even execrated as a source of impiety, that human commentaries are accepted as divine records, and that credulity is extolled as faith; as I marked the fierce controversies of philosophers raging in Church and State, the source of bitter hatred and dissension, the ready instruments of sedition and other ills innumerable, I determined to examine the Bible afresh in a careful, impartial, and unfettered spirit, making no assumptions concerning it, and attributing to it no doctrines, which I do not find clearly therein set down. With these precautions I constructed a method of Scriptural interpretation, and thus equipped proceeded to inquire — what is prophecy? In what sense did God reveal himself to the prophets, and why were these particular men — chosen by him? Was it on account of the sublimity of their thoughts about the Deity and nature, or was it solely on account of their piety? These questions being answered, I was easily able to conclude, that the authority of the prophets has weight only in matters of morality, and that their speculative doctrines affect us little.

Next I inquired, why the Hebrews were called God's chosen people, and discovering that it was only because God had chosen for them a certain strip of territory, where they might live peaceably and at ease, I learnt that the Law revealed by God to Moses was merely the law of the individual Hebrew state, therefore that it was binding on none but Hebrews, and not even on Hebrews after the downfall of their nation. Further, in order to ascertain, whether it could be concluded from Scripture, that the human understanding standing is naturally corrupt, I inquired whether the Universal Religion, the Divine Law revealed through the Prophets and Apostles to the whole human race, differs from that which is taught by the light of natural reason, whether miracles can take place in violation of the laws of nature, and if so, whether they imply the existence of God more surely and clearly than events, which we understand plainly and distinctly through their immediate natural causes.

Now, as in the whole course of my investigation I found nothing taught expressly by Scripture, which does not agree with our understanding, or which is repugnant thereto, and as I saw that the prophets taught nothing, which is not very simple and easily to be grasped by all, and further, that they clothed their leaching in the style, and confirmed it with the reasons, which would most deeply move the mind of the masses to devotion towards God, I became thoroughly convinced, that the Bible leaves reason absolutely free, that it has nothing in common with philosophy, in fact, that Revelation and Philosophy stand on different footings. In order to set this forth categorically and exhaust the whole question, I point out the way in which the Bible should be interpreted, and show that all of spiritual questions should be sought from it alone, and not from the objects of ordinary knowledge. Thence I pass on to indicate the false notions, which have from the fact that the multitude — ever prone to superstition, and caring more for the shreds of antiquity for eternal truths — pays homage to the Books of the Bible, rather than to the Word of God. I show that the Word of God has not been revealed as a certain number of books, was displayed to the prophets as a simple idea of the mind, namely, obedience to God in singleness of heart, and in the practice of justice and charity; and I further point out, that this doctrine is set forth in Scripture in accordance with the opinions and understandings of those, among whom the Apostles and Prophets preached, to the end that men might receive it willingly, and with their whole heart.

Having thus laid bare the bases of belief, I draw the conclusion that Revelation has obedience for its sole object, therefore, in purpose no less than in foundation and method, stands entirely aloof from ordinary knowledge; each has its separate province, neither can be called the handmaid of the other.

Furthermore, as men's habits of mind differ, so that some more readily embrace one form of faith, some another, for what moves one to pray may move another only to scoff, I conclude, in accordance with what has gone before, that everyone should be free to choose for himself the foundations of his creed, and that faith should be judged only by its fruits; each would then obey God freely with his whole heart, while nothing would be publicly honoured save justice and charity.

Having thus drawn attention to the liberty conceded to everyone by the revealed law of God, I pass on to another part of my subject, and prove that this same liberty can and should be accorded with safety to the state and the magisterial authority — in fact, that it cannot be withheld without great danger to peace and detriment to the community.

In order to establish my point, I start from the natural rights of the individual, which are co-extensive with his desires and power, and from the fact that no one is bound to live as another pleases, but is the guardian of his own liberty. I show that these rights can only be transferred to those whom we depute to defend us, who acquire with the duties of defence the power of ordering our lives, and I thence infer that rulers possess rights only limited by their power, that they are the sole guardians of justice and liberty, and that their subjects should act in all things as they dictate: nevertheless, since no one can so utterly abdicate his own power of self-defence as to cease to be a man, I conclude that no one can be deprived of his natural rights absolutely, but that subjects, either by tacit agreement, or by social contract, retain a certain number, which cannot be taken from them without great danger to the state.

From these considerations I pass on to the Hebrew State, which I describe at some length, in order to trace the manner in which Religion acquired the force of law, and to touch on other noteworthy points. I then prove, that the holders of sovereign power are the depositories and interpreters of religious no less than of civil ordinances, and that they alone have the right to decide what is just or unjust, pious or impious; lastly, I conclude by showing, that they best retain this right and secure safety to their state by allowing every man to think what he likes, and say what he thinks.

Such, Philosophical Reader, are the questions I submit to your notice, counting on your approval, for the subject matter of the whole book and of the several chapters is important and profitable. I would say more, but I do not want my preface to extend to a volume, especially as I know that its leading propositions are to Philosophers but common places. To the rest of mankind I care not to commend my treatise, for I cannot expect that it contains anything to please them: I know how deeply rooted are the prejudices embraced under the name of religion; I am aware that in the mind of the masses superstition is no less deeply rooted than fear; I recognize that their constancy is mere obstinacy, and that they are led to praise or blame by impulse rather than reason. Therefore the multitude, and those of like passions with the multitude, I ask not to read my book; nay, I would rather that they should utterly neglect it, than that they should misinterpret it after their wont. They would gain no good themselves, and might prove a stumbling-block to others, whose philosophy is hampered by the belief that Reason is a mere handmaid to Theology, and whom I seek in this work especially to benefit. But as there will be many who have neither the leisure, nor, perhaps, the inclination to read through all I have written, I feel bound here, as at the end of my treatise, to declare that I have written nothing, which I do not most willingly submit to the examination and judgment of my country's rulers, and that I am ready to retract anything, which they shall decide to be repugnant to the laws or prejudicial to the public good. I know that I am a man and, as a man, liable to error, but against error I have taken scrupulous care, and striven to keep in entire accordance with the laws of my country, with loyalty, and with morality.

CHAPTER I.

Of Prophecy

PROPHECY, OR REVELATION is sure knowledge revealed by God to man. A prophet is one who interprets the revelations of God {insights} to those who are unable to attain to sure knowledge of the matters revealed, and therefore can only apprehend them by simple faith.

The Hebrew word for prophet is "nabi", 1 i.e. speaker or interpreter, but in Scripture its meaning is restricted to interpreter of God, as we may learn from Exodus vii:1, where God says to Moses, "See, I have made thee a god to Pharaoh, and Aaron thy brother shall be thy prophet;" implying that, since in interpreting Moses' words to Pharaoh, Aaron acted the part of a prophet, Moses would be to Pharaoh as a god, or in the attitude of a god.

Prophets I will treat of in the next chapter, and at present consider prophecy.

Now it is evident, from the definition above given, that prophecy really includes ordinary knowledge; for the knowledge which we acquire by our natural faculties depends on knowledge of God and His eternal laws; but ordinary knowledge is common to all men as men, and rests on foundations which all share, whereas the multitude always strains after rarities and exceptions, and thinks little of the gifts of nature; so that, when prophecy is talked of, ordinary knowledge is not supposed to be included. Nevertheless it has as much right as any other to be called Divine, for God's nature, in so far as we share therein, and God's laws, dictate it to us; nor does it suffer from that to which we give the preeminence, except in so far as the latter transcends its limits and cannot be accounted for by natural laws taken in themselves. In respect to the certainty it involves, and the source from which it is derived, i.e. God, ordinary, knowledge is no whit inferior to prophetic, unless indeed we believe, or rather dream, that the prophets had human bodies but superhuman minds, and therefore that their sensations and consciousness were entirely different from our own.

But, although ordinary knowledge is Divine, its professors cannot be called prophets 2, for they teach what the rest of mankind could perceive and apprehend, not merely by simple faith, but as surely and honourably as themselves.

Seeing then that our mind subjectively contains in itself and partakes of the nature of God, and solely from this cause is enabled to form notions explaining natural phenomena and inculcating morality, it follows that we may rightly assert the nature of the human mind (in so far as it is thus conceived) to be a primary cause of Divine revelation. All that we clearly and distinctly understand is dictated to us, as I have just pointed out, by the idea and nature of God; not indeed through words, but in a way far more excellent and agreeing perfectly with the nature of the mind, as all who have enjoyed intellectual certainty will doubtless attest. Here, however, my chief purpose is to speak of matters having reference to Scripture, so these few words on the light of reason will suffice.

I will now pass on to, and treat more fully, the other ways and means by which God makes revelations to mankind, both of that which transcends ordinary knowledge, and of that within its scope; for there is no reason why God should not employ other means to communicate what we know already by the power of reason.

Our conclusions on the subject must be drawn solely from Scripture; for what can we affirm about matters transcending our knowledge except what is told us by the words or writings of prophets? And since there are, so far as I know, no prophets now alive, we have no alternative but to read the books of prophets departed, taking care the while not to reason from metaphor or to ascribe anything to our authors which they do not themselves distinctly state. I must further premise that the Jews never make any mention or account of secondary, or particular causes, but in a spirit of religion, piety, and what is commonly called godliness, refer all things directly to the Deity. For instance if they make money by a transaction, they say God gave it to them; if they desire anything, they say God has disposed their hearts towards it; if they think anything, they say God told them. Hence we must not suppose that everything is prophecy or revelation which is described in Scripture as told by God to anyone, but only such things as are expressly announced as prophecy or revelation, or are plainly pointed to as such by the context.

A perusal of the sacred books will show us that all God's revelations to the prophets were made through words or appearances, or a combination of the two. These words and appearances were of two kinds; 1. — real when external to the mind of the prophet who heard or saw them, 2. — imaginary when the imagination of the prophet was in a state which led him distinctly to suppose that he heard or saw them.

With a real voice God revealed to Moses the laws which He wished to be transmitted to the Hebrews, as we may see from Exodus xxv:22, where God says, "And there I will meet with thee and I will commune with thee from the mercy seat which is between the Cherubim." Some sort of real voice must necessarily have been employed, for Moses found God ready to commune with him at any time. This, as I shall shortly show, is the only instance of a real voice.

We might, perhaps, suppose that the voice with which God called Samuel was real, for in 1 Sam. iii:21, we read, "And the Lord appeared again in Shiloh, for the Lord revealed Himself to Samuel in Shiloh by the word of the Lord;" implying that the appearance of the Lord consisted in His making Himself known to Samuel through a voice; in other words, that Samuel heard the Lord speaking. But we are compelled to distinguish between the prophecies of Moses and those of other prophets, and therefore must decide that this voice was imaginary, a conclusion further supported by the voice's resemblance to the voice of Eli, which Samuel was in the habit of hearing, and therefore might easily imagine; when thrice called by the Lord, Samuel supposed it to have been Eli.

The voice which Abimelech heard was imaginary, for it is written, Gen. xx:6, "And God said unto him in a dream." So that the will of God was manifest to him, not in waking, but only, in sleep, that is, when the imagination is most active and uncontrolled. Some of the Jews believe that the actual words of the Decalogue were not spoken by God, but that the Israelites heard a noise only, without any distinct words, and during its continuance apprehended the Ten Commandments by pure intuition; to this opinion I myself once inclined, seeing that the words of the Decalogue in Exodus are different from the words of the Decalogue in Deuteronomy, for the discrepancy seemed to imply (since God only spoke once) that the Ten Commandments were not intended to convey the actual words of the Lord, but only His meaning. However, unless we would do violence to Scripture, we must certainly admit that the Israelites heard a real voice, for Scripture expressly says, Deut. v:4," God spake with you face to face," i.e. as two men ordinarily interchange ideas through the instrumentality of their two bodies; and therefore it seems more consonant with Holy Writ to suppose that God really did create a voice of some kind with which the Decalogue was revealed. The discrepancy of the two versions is treated of in Chap. VIII.

Yet not even thus is all difficulty removed, for it seems scarcely reasonable to affirm that a created thing, depending on God in the same manner as other created things, would be able to express or explain the nature of God either verbally or really by means of its individual organism: for instance, by declaring in the first person, "I am the Lord your God."

Certainly when anyone says with his mouth, "I understand," we do not attribute the understanding to the mouth, but to the mind of the speaker; yet this is because the mouth is the natural organ of a man speaking, and the hearer, knowing what understanding is, easily comprehends, by a comparison with himself, that the speaker's mind is meant; but if we knew nothing of God beyond the mere name and wished to commune with Him, and be assured of His existence, I fail to see how our wish would be satisfied by the declaration of a created thing (depending on God neither more nor less than ourselves), "I am the Lord." If God contorted the lips of Moses, or, I will not say Moses, but some beast, till they pronounced the words, "I am the Lord," should we apprehend the Lord's existence therefrom?

Scripture seems clearly to point to the belief that God spoke Himself, having descended from heaven to Mount Sinai for the purpose — and not only that the Israelites heard Him speaking, but that their chief men beheld Him (Ex:xxiv.) Further the law of Moses, which might neither be added to nor curtailed, and which was set up as a national standard of right, nowhere prescribed the belief that God is without body, or even without form or figure, but only ordained that the Jews should believe in His existence and worship Him alone: it forbade them to invent or fashion any likeness of the Deity, but this was to insure purity of service; because, never having seen God, they could not by means of images recall the likeness of God, but only the likeness of some created thing which might thus gradually take the place of God as the object of their adoration. Nevertheless, the Bible clearly implies that God has a form, and that Moses when he heard God speaking was permitted to behold it, or at least its hinder parts.

Doubtless some mystery lurks in this question which we will discuss more fully below. For the present I will call attention to the passages in Scripture indicating the means by which God has revealed His laws to man.

Revelation may be through figures only, as in I Chron:xxii., where God displays his anger to David by means of an angel bearing a sword, and also in the story of Balaam.

Maimonides and others do indeed maintain that these and every other instance of angelic apparitions (e.g. to Manoah and to Abraham offering up Isaac) occurred during sleep, for that no one with his eyes open ever could see an angel, but this is mere nonsense. The sole object of such commentators seems to be to extort from Scripture confirmations of Aristotelian quibbles and their own inventions, a proceeding which I regard as the acme of absurdity.

In figures, not real but existing only in the prophet's imagination, God revealed to Joseph his future lordship, and in words and figures He revealed to Joshua that He would fight for the Hebrews, causing to appear an angel, as it were the Captain of the Lord's host, bearing a sword, and by this means communicating verbally. The forsaking of Israel by Providence was portrayed to Isaiah by a vision of the Lord, the thrice Holy, sitting on a very lofty throne, and the Hebrews, stained with the mire of their sins, sunk as it were in uncleanness, and thus as far as possible distant from God. The wretchedness of the people at the time was thus revealed, while future calamities were foretold in words. I could cite from Holy Writ many similar examples, but I think they are sufficiently well known already.

However, we get a still more clear confirmation of our position in Num xii:6,7, as follows: "If there be any prophet among you, I the Lord will make myself known unto him in a vision" (i.e. by appearances and signs, for God says of the prophecy of Moses that it was a vision without signs), "and will speak unto him in a dream " (i.e. not with actual words and an actual voice). "My servant Moses is not so; with him will I speak mouth to mouth, even apparently, and not in dark speeches, and the similitude of the Lord he shall behold," i.e. looking on me as a friend and not afraid, he speaks with me (cf. Ex xxxiii:17).

This makes it indisputable that the other prophets did not hear a real voice, and we gather as much from Deut. xxiv:10: "And there arose not a prophet since in Israel like unto Moses whom the Lord knew face to face," which must mean that the Lord spoke with none other; for not even Moses saw the Lord's face. These are the only media of communication between God and man which I find mentioned in Scripture, and therefore the only ones which may be supposed or invented. We may be able quite to comprehend that God can communicate immediately with man, for without the intervention of bodily means He communicates to our minds His essence; still, a man who can by pure intuition comprehend ideas which are neither contained in nor deducible from the foundations of our natural knowledge, must necessarily possess a mind far superior to those of his fellow men, nor do I believe that any have been so endowed save Christ. To Him the ordinances of God leading men to salvation were revealed directly without words or visions, so that God manifested Himself to the Apostles through the mind of Christ as He formerly did to Moses through the supernatural voice. In this sense the voice of Christ, like the voice which Moses heard, may be called the voice of God, and it may be said that the wisdom of God (,i.e. wisdom more than human) took upon itself in Christ human nature, and that Christ was the way of salvation. I must at this juncture declare that those doctrines which certain churches put forward concerning Christ, I neither affirm nor deny, for I freely confess that I do not understand them. What I have just stated I gather from Scripture, where I never read that God appeared to Christ, or spoke to Christ, but that God was revealed to the Apostles through Christ; that Christ was the Way of Life, and that the old law was given through an angel, and not immediately by God; whence it follows that if Moses spoke with God face to face as a man speaks with his friend (i.e. by means of their two bodies) Christ communed with God mind to mind.

Thus we may conclude that no one except Christ received the revelations of God without the aid of imagination, whether in words or vision. Therefore the power of prophecy implies not a peculiarly perfect mind, but a peculiarly vivid imagination, as I will show more clearly in the next chapter. We will now inquire what is meant in the Bible by the Spirit of God breathed into the prophets, or by the prophets speaking with the Spirit of God; to that end we must determine the exact signification of the Hebrew word ruagh, commonly translated spirit.

The word ruagh literally means a wind, e..q. the south wind, but it is frequently employed in other derivative significations.

It is used as equivalent to,

(1.) Breath: "Neither is there any spirit in his mouth," Ps. cxxxv:17.

(2.) Life, or breathing: "And his spirit returned to him" 1 Sam. xxx:12; i.e. he breathed again.

(3.) Courage and strength: "Neither did there remain any more spirit in any man," Josh. ii:11; "And the spirit entered into me, and made me stand on my feet," Ezek. ii:2.

(4.) Virtue and fitness: "Days should speak, and multitudes of years should teach wisdom; but there is a spirit in man,"Job xxxii:7; i.e. wisdom is not always found among old men for I now discover that it depends on individual virtue and capacity. So, "A man in whom is the Spirit," Numbers xxvii:18.

(5.) Habit of mind: "Because he had another spirit with him," Numbers xiv:24; i.e. another habit of mind. "Behold I will pour out My Spirit unto you," Prov. i:23.

(6.) Will, purpose, desire, impulse: "Whither the spirit was to go, they went," Ezek. 1:12; "That cover with a covering, but not of My Spirit," Is. xxx:1; "For the Lord hath poured out on you the spirit of deep sleep," Is. xxix:10; "Then was their spirit softened," Judges viii:3; "He that ruleth his spirit, is better than he that taketh a city," Prov. xvi:32; "He that hath no ru over his own spirit," Prov. xxv:28; "Your spirit as fire shall devour you," Isaiah xxxiii:l.

From the meaning of disposition we get —

(7.) Passions and faculties. A lofty spirit means pride, a lowly spirit humility, an evil spirit hatred and melancholy. So, too, the expressions spirits of jealousy, fornication, wisdom, counsel, bravery, stand for a jealous, lascivious, wise, prudent, or brave mind (for we Hebrews use substantives in preference to adjectives), or these various qualities.

(8.) The mind itself, or the life: "Yea, they have all one spirit," Eccles. iii:19 "The spirit shall return to God Who gave it."

(9.) The quarters of the world (from the winds which blow thence), or even the side of anything turned towards a particular quarter — Ezek. xxxvii:9; xlii:16, 17, 18, 19, &c.

I have already alluded to the way in which things are referred to God, and said to be of God.

(1.) As belonging to His nature, and being, as it were, part of Him; e.g the power of God, the eyes of God.

(2.) As under His dominion, and depending on His pleasure; thus the heavens are called the heavens of the Lord, as being His chariot and habitation. So Nebuchadnezzar is called the servant of God, Assyria the scourge of God, &c.

(3.) As dedicated to Him, e.g. the Temple of God, a Nazarene of God, the Bread of God.

(4.) As revealed through the prophets and not through our natural faculties. In this sense the Mosaic law is called the law of God.

(5.) As being in the superlative degree. Very high mountains are styled the mountains of God, a very deep sleep, the sleep of God, &c. In this sense we must explain Amos iv:11: "I have overthrown you as the overthrow of the Lord came upon Sodom and Gomorrah," i.e. that memorable overthrow, for since God Himself is the Speaker, the passage cannot well be taken otherwise. The wisdom of Solomon is called the wisdom of God, or extraordinary. The size of the cedars of Lebanon is alluded to in the Psalmist's expression, "the cedars of the Lord."

Similarly, if the Jews were at a loss to understand any phenomenon, or were ignorant of its cause, they referred it to God. Thus a storm was termed the chiding of God, thunder and lightning the arrows of God, for it was thought that God kept the winds confined in caves, His treasuries; thus differing merely in name from the Greek wind-god Eolus. In like manner miracles were called works of God, as being especially marvellous; though in reality, of course, all natural events are the works of God, and take place solely by His power. The Psalmist calls the miracles in Egypt the works of God, because the Hebrews found in them a way of safety which they had not looked for, and therefore especially marvelled at.

As, then, unusual natural phenomena are called works of God, and trees of unusual size are called trees of God, we cannot wonder that very strong and tall men, though impious robbers and whoremongers, are in Genesis called sons of God.

This reference of things wonderful to God was not peculiar to the Jews. Pharaoh, on hearing the interpretation of his dream, exclaimed that the mind of the gods was in Joseph. Nebuchadnezzar told Daniel that he possessed the mind of the holy gods; so also in Latin anything well made is often said to be wrought with Divine hands, which is equivalent to the Hebrew phrase, wrought with the hand of God.

We can now very easily understand and explain those passages of Scripture which speak of the Spirit of God. In some places the expression merely means a very strong, dry, and deadly wind, as in Isaiah xl:7, "The grass withereth, the flower fadeth, because the Spirit of the Lord bloweth upon it." Similarly in Gen. i:2: "The Spirit of the Lord moved over the face of the waters." At other times it is used as equivalent to a high courage, thus the spirit of Gideon and of Samson is called the Spirit of the Lord, as being very bold, and prepared for any emergency. Any unusual virtue or power is called the Spirit or Virtue of the Lord, Ex. xxxi:3: "I will fill him (Bezaleel) with the Spirit of the Lord," i.e., as the Bible itself explains, with talent above man's usual endowment. So Isa. xi:2: "And the Spirit of the Lord shall rest upon him," is explained afterwards in the text to mean the spirit of wisdom and understanding, of counsel and might.

The melancholy of Saul is called the melancholy of the Lord, or a very deep melancholy, the persons who applied the term showing that they understood by it nothing supernatural, in that they sent for a musician to assuage it by harp-playing. Again, the "Spirit of the Lord" is used as equivalent to the mind of man, for instance, Job xxvii:3: "And the Spirit of the Lord in my nostrils," the allusion being to Gen. ii:7: "And God breathed into man's nostrils the breath of life." Ezekiel also, prophesying to the dead, says (xxvii:14), "And I will give to you My Spirit, and ye shall live;" i.e. I will restore you to life. In Job xxxiv:14, we read: "If He gather unto Himself His Spirit and breath;" in Gen. vi:3: "My Spirit shall not always strive with man, for that he also is flesh," i.e. since man acts on the dictates of his body, and not the spirit which I gave him to discern the good, I will let him alone. So, too, Ps. li:12: "Create in me a clean heart, 0 God, and renew a right spirit within me; cast me not away from Thy presence, and take not Thy Holy Spirit from me." It was supposed that sin originated only from the body, and that good impulses come from the mind; therefore the Psalmist invokes the aid of God against the bodily appetites, but prays that the spirit which the Lord, the Holy One, had given him might be renewed. Again, inasmuch as the Bible, in concession to popular ignorance, describes God as having a mind, a heart, emotions — nay, even a body and breath — the expression Spirit of the Lord is used for God's mind, disposition, emotion, strength, or breath. Thus, Isa. xl:13: "Who hath disposed the Spirit of the Lord?" i.e. who, save Himself, hath caused the mind of the Lord to will anything,? and Isa. lxiii:10: "But they rebelled, and vexed the Holy Spirit."

The phrase comes to be used of the law of Moses, which in a sense expounds God's will, Is. lxiii. 11, "Where is He that put His Holy Spirit within him?" meaning, as we clearly gather from the context, the law of Moses. Nehemiah, speaking of the giving of the law, says, i:20, "Thou gavest also thy good Spirit to instruct them." This is referred to in Deut. iv:6, "This is your wisdom and understanding," and in Ps. cxliii:10, "Thy good Spirit will lead me into the land of uprightness." The Spirit of the Lord may mean the breath of the Lord, for breath, no less than a mind, a heart, and a body are attributed to God in Scripture, as in Ps. xxxiii:6. Hence it gets to mean the power, strength, or faculty of God, as in Job xxxiii:4, "The Spirit of the Lord made me," i.e. the power, or, if you prefer, the decree of the Lord. So the Psalmist in poetic language declares, xxxiii:6, "By the word of the Lord were the heavens made, and all the host of them by the breath of His mouth," i.e. by a mandate issued, as it were, in one breath. Also Ps. cxxxix:7, "Wither shall I go from Thy Spirit, or whither shall I flee from Thy presence?" i.e. whither shall I go so as to be beyond Thy power and Thy presence?

Lastly, the Spirit of the Lord is used in Scripture to express the emotions of God, e.g. His kindness and mercy, Micah ii:7, "Is the Spirit [i.e. the mercy] of the Lord straitened? Are these cruelties His doings?" Zech. iv:6, "Not by might or by power, but My Spirit [i.e. mercy], saith the Lord of hosts." The twelfth verse of the seventh chapter of the same prophet must, I think, be interpreted in like manner: "Yea, they made their hearts as an adamant stone, lest they should hear the law, and the words which the Lord of hosts hath sent in His Spirit [i.e. in His mercy] by the former prophets." So also Haggai ii:5: "So My Spirit remaineth among you: fear not."

The passage in Isaiah xlviii:16, "And now the Lord and His Spirit hath sent me," may be taken to refer to God's mercy or His revealed law; for the prophet says, "From the beginning" (i.e. from the time when I first came to you, to preach God's anger and His sentence forth against you) "I spoke not in secret; from the time that it was, there am I," and now I am sent by the mercy of God as a joyful messenger to preach your restoration. Or we may understand him to mean by the revealed law that he had before come to warn them by the command of the law (Levit. xix:17) in the same manner under the same conditions as Moses had warned them, that now, like Moses, he ends by preaching their restoration. But the first explanation seems to me the best.

Returning, then, to the main object of our discussion, we find that the Scriptural phrases, "The Spirit of the Lord was upon a prophet," "The Lord breathed His Spirit into men," "Men were filled with the Spirit of God, with the Holy Spirit," &c., are quite clear to us, and mean that prophets were endowed with a peculiar and extraordinary power, and devoted themselves to piety with especial constancy

3; that thus they perceived the mind or the thought of God, for we have shown that God's Spirit signifies in Hebrew God's mind or thought, and that the law which shows His mind and thought is called His Spirit; hence that the imagination of the prophets, inasmuch as through it were revealed the decrees of God, may equally be called the mind of God, and the prophets be said to have possessed the mind of God. On our minds also the mind of God and His eternal thoughts are impressed; but this being the same for all men is less taken into account, especially by the Hebrews, who claimed a pre-eminence, and despised other men and other men's knowledge.

Lastly, the prophets were said to possess the Spirit of God because men knew not the cause of prophetic knowledge, and in their wonder referred it with other marvels directly to the Deity, styling it Divine knowledge.

We need no longer scruple to affirm that the prophets only perceived God's revelation by the aid of imagination, that is, by words and figures either real or imaginary. We find no other means mentioned in Scripture, and therefore must not invent any. As to the particular law of Nature by which the communications took place, I confess my ignorance. I might, indeed, say as others do, that they took place by the power of God; but this would be mere trifling, and no better than explaining some unique specimen by a transcendental term. Everything takes place by the power of God. Nature herself is the power of God under another name, and our ignorance of the power of God is co-extensive with our ignorance of Nature. It is absolute folly, therefore, to ascribe an event to the power of God when we know not its natural cause, which is the power of God.

However, we are not now inquiring into the causes of prophetic knowledge. We are only attempting, as I have said, to examine the Scriptural documents, and to draw our conclusions from them as from ultimate natural facts; the causes of the documents do not concern us.

As the prophets perceived the revelations of God by the aid of imagination, they could indisputably perceive much that is beyond the boundary of the intellect, for many more ideas can be constructed from words and figures than from the principles and notions on which the whole fabric of reasoned knowledge is reared.

Thus we have a clue to the fact that the prophets perceived nearly everything in parables and allegories, and clothed spiritual truths in bodily forms, for such is the usual method of imagination. We need no longer wonder that Scripture and the prophets speak so strangely and obscurely of God's Spirit or Mind (cf. Numbers xi:17, 1 Kings xxii:21, &c.), that the Lord was seen by Micah as sitting, by Daniel as an old man clothed in white, by Ezekiel as a fire, that the Holy Spirit appeared to those with Christ as a descending dove, to the apostles as fiery tongues, to Paul on his conversion as a great light. All these expressions are plainly in harmony with the current ideas of God and spirits.

Inasmuch as imagination is fleeting and inconstant, we find that the power of prophecy did not remain with a prophet for long, nor manifest itself frequently, but was very rare; manifesting itself only in a few men, and in them not often.

We must necessarily inquire how the prophets became assured of the truth of what they perceived by imagination, and not by sure mental laws; but our investigation must be confined to Scripture, for the subject is one on which we cannot acquire certain knowledge, and which we cannot explain by the immediate causes. Scripture teaching about the assurance of prophets I will treat of in the next chapter.

1 The word nabi is rightly interpreted by Rabbi Salomon Jarchi, but the sense is hardly caught by Aben Ezra, who was not so good a Hebraist. We must also remark that this Hebrew word for prophecy has a universal meaning and embraces all kinds of prophecy. Other terms are more special, and denote this or that sort of prophecy, as I believe is well known to the learned.

2 "Although, ordinary knowledge is Divine, its professors cannot be called prophets." That is, interpreters of God. For he alone is an interpreter of God, who interprets the decrees which God has revealed to him, to others who have not received such revelation, and whose belief, therefore, rests merely on the prophet's authority and the confidence reposed in him. If it were otherwise, and all who listen to prophets became prophets themselves, as all who listen to philosophers become philosophers, a prophet would no longer be the interpreter of Divine decrees, inasmuch as his hearers would know the truth, not on the, authority of the prophet, but by means of actual Divine revelation and inward testimony. Thus the sovereign powers are the interpreters of their own rights of sway, because these are defended only by their authority and supported by their testimony.

3 "Prophets were endowed with a peculiar and extraordinary power." Though some men enjoy gifts which nature has not bestowed on their fellows, they are not said to surpass the bounds of human nature, unless their special qualities are such as cannot be said to be deducible from the definition of human nature. For instance, a giant is a rarity, but still human. The gift of composing poetry extempore is given to very few, yet it is human. The same may, therefore, be said of the faculty possessed by some of imagining things as vividly as though they saw them before them, and this not while asleep, but while awake. But if anyone could be found who possessed other means and other foundations for knowledge, he might be said to transcend the limits of human nature.

CHAPTER II.

Of Prophets.

IT FOLLOWS FROM the last chapter that, as I have said, the prophets were endowed with unusually vivid imaginations, and not with unusually, perfect minds. This conclusion is amply sustained by Scripture, for we are told that Solomon was the wisest of men, but had no special faculty of prophecy. Heman, Calcol, and Dara, though men of great talent, were not prophets, whereas uneducated countrymen, nay, even women, such as Hagar, Abraham's handmaid, were thus gifted. Nor is this contrary to ordinary experience and reason. Men of great imaginative power are less fitted for abstract reasoning, whereas those who excel in intellect and its use keep their imagination more restrained and controlled, holding it in subjection, so to speak, lest it should usurp the place of reason.

Thus to suppose that knowledge of natural and spiritual phenomena can be gained from the prophetic books, is an utter mistake, which I shall endeavour to expose, as I think philosophy, the age, and the question itself demand. I care not for the girdings of superstition, for superstition is the bitter enemy, of all true knowledge and true morality. Yes; it has come to this! Men who openly confess that they can form no idea of God, and only know Him through created things, of which they know not the causes, can unblushingly, accuse philosophers of Atheism. Treating the question methodically, I will show that prophecies varied, not only according to the imagination and physical temperament of the prophet, but also according to his particular opinions; and further that prophecy never rendered the prophet wiser than he was before. But I will first discuss the assurance of truth which the prophets received, for this is akin to the subject-matter of the chapter, and will serve to elucidate somewhat our present point.

Imagination does not, in its own nature, involve any certainty of truth, such as is implied in every clear and distinct idea, but requires some extrinsic reason to assure us of its objective reality: hence prophecy cannot afford certainty, and the prophets were assured of God's revelation by some sign, and not by the fact of revelation, as we may see from Abraham, who, when he had heard the promise of God, demanded a sign, not because he did not believe in God, but because he wished to be sure that it was God Who made the promise. The fact is still more evident in the case of Gideon: "Show me," he says to God, "show me a sign, that I may know that it is Thou that talkest with me." God also says to Moses: "And let this be a sign that I have sent thee." Hezekiah, though he had long known Isaiah to be a prophet, none the less demanded a sign of the cure which he predicted. It is thus quite evident that the prophets always received some sign to certify them of their prophetic imaginings; and for this reason Moses bids the Jews (Deut. xviii.) ask of the prophets a sign, namely, the prediction of some coming event. In this respect, prophetic knowledge is inferior to natural knowledge, which needs no sign, and in itself implies certitude. Moreover, Scripture warrants the statement that the certitude of the prophets was not mathematical, but moral. Moses lays down the punishment of death for the prophet who preaches new gods, even though he confirm his doctrine by signs and wonders (Deut. xiii.); "For," he says, "the Lord also worketh signs and wonders to try His people." And Jesus Christ warns His disciples of the same thing (Matt. xxiv:24). Furthermore, Ezekiel (xiv:9) plainly states that God sometimes deceives men with false revelations; and Micaiah bears like witness in the case of the prophets of Ahab.

Although these instances go to prove that revelation is open to doubt, it nevertheless contains, as we have said, a considerable element of certainty, for God never deceives the good, nor His chosen, but (according to the ancient proverb, and as appears in the history of Abigail and her speech), God uses the good as instruments of goodness, and the wicked as means to execute His wrath. This may be seen from the case of Micaiah above quoted; for although God had determined to deceive Ahab, through prophets, He made use of lying prophets; to the good prophet He revealed the truth, and did not forbid his proclaiming it.

Still the certitude of prophecy, remains, as I have said, merely, moral; for no one can justify himself before God, nor boast that he is an instrument for God's goodness. Scripture itself teaches and shows that God led away David to number the people, though it bears ample witness to David's piety.

The whole question of the certitude of prophecy, was based on these three considerations:

1. That the things revealed were imagined very vividly, affecting the prophets in the same way as things seen when awake;

2. The presence of a sign;

3. Lastly, and chiefly, that the mind of the prophet was given wholly, to what was right and good.

Although Scripture does not always make mention of a sign, we must nevertheless suppose that a sign was always vouchsafed; for Scripture does not always relate every, condition and circumstance (as many, have remarked), but rather takes them for granted. We may, however, admit that no sign was needed when the prophecy declared nothing that was not already contained in the law of Moses, because it was confirmed by that law. For instance, Jeremiah's prophecy, of the destruction of Jerusalem was confirmed by the prophecies of other prophets, and by the threats in the law, and, therefore, it needed no sign; whereas Hananiah, who, contrary to all the prophets, foretold the speedy restoration of the state, stood in need of a sign, or he would have been in doubt as to the truth of his prophecy, until it was confirmed by facts. "The prophet which prophesieth of peace, when the word of the prophet shall come to pass, then shall the prophet be known that the Lord hath truly sent him."

As, then, the certitude afforded to the prophet by signs was not mathematical (i.e. did not necessarily follow from the perception of the thing perceived or seen), but only moral, and as the signs were only given to convince the prophet, it follows that such signs were given according to the opinions and capacity of each prophet, so that a sign which convince one prophet would fall far short of convincing another who was imbued with different opinions. Therefore the signs varied according to the individual prophet.

So also did the revelation vary, as we have stated, according to individual disposition and temperament, and according to the opinions previously held.

It varied according to disposition, in this way: if a prophet was cheerful, victories, peace, and events which make men glad, were revealed to him; in that he was naturally more likely to imagine such things. If, on the contrary, he was melancholy, wars, massacres, and calamities were revealed; and so, according as a prophet was merciful, gentle, quick to anger, or severe, he was more fitted for one kind of revelation than another. It varied according to the temper of imagination in this way: if a prophet was cultivated he perceived the mind of God in a cultivated way, if he was confused he perceived it confusedly. And so with revelations perceived through visions. If a prophet was a countryman he saw visions of oxen, cows, and the like; if he was a soldier, he saw generals and armies; if a courtier, a royal throne, and so on.

Lastly, prophecy varied according to the opinions held by the prophets; for instance, to the Magi, who believed in the follies of astrology, the birth of Christ was revealed through the vision of a star in the East. To the augurs of Nebuchadnezzar the destruction of Jerusalem was revealed through entrails, whereas the king himself inferred it from oracles and the direction of arrows which he shot into the air. To prophets who believed that man acts from free choice and by his own power, God was revealed as standing apart from and ignorant of future human actions. All of which we will illustrate from Scripture.

The first point is proved from the case of Elisha, who, in order to prophecy to Jehoram, asked for a harp, and was unable to perceive the Divine purpose till he had been recreated by its music; then, indeed, he prophesied to Jehoram and to his allies glad tidings, which previously he had been unable to attain to because he was angry with the king, and these who are angry with anyone can imagine evil of him, but not good. The theory that God does not reveal Himself to the angry or the sad, is a mere dream: for God revealed to Moses while angry, the terrible slaughter of the firstborn, and did so without the intervention of a harp. To Cain in his rage, God was revealed, and to Ezekiel, impatient with anger, was revealed the contumacy and wretchedness of the Jews. Jeremiah, miserable and weary of life, prophesied the disasters of the Hebrews, so that Josiah would not consult him, but inquired of a woman, inasmuch as it was more in accordance with womanly nature that God should reveal His mercy thereto. So, Micaiah never prophesied good to Ahab, though other true prophets had done so, but invariably evil. Thus we see that individual prophets were by temperament more fitted for one sort of revelation than another.

The style of the prophecy also varied according to the eloquence of the individual prophet. The prophecies of Ezekiel and Amos are not written in a cultivated style like those of Isaiah and Nahum, but more rudely. Any Hebrew scholar who wishes to inquire into this point more closely, and compares chapters of the different prophets treating of the same subject, will find great dissimilarity of style. Compare, for instance, chap. i. of the courtly Isaiah, verse 11 to verse 20, with chap. v. of the countryman Amos, verses 21-24. Compare also the order and reasoning of the prophecies of Jeremiah, written in Idumaea (chap. xhx.), with the order and reasoning of Obadiah. Compare, lastly, Isa. xl:19, 20, and xliv:8, with Hosea viii:6, and xiii:2. And so on.

A due consideration of these passage will clearly show us that God has no particular style in speaking, but, according to the learning and capacity of the prophet, is cultivated, compressed, severe, untutored, prolix, or obscure.

There was, moreover, a certain variation in the visions vouchsafed to the prophets, and in the symbols by which they expressed them, for Isaiah saw the glory of the Lord departing from the Temple in a different form from that presented to Ezekiel. The Rabbis, indeed, maintain that both visions were really the same, but that Ezekiel, being a countryman, was above measure impressed by it, and therefore set it forth in full detail; but unless there is a trustworthy tradition on the subject, which I do not for a moment believe, this theory is plainly an invention. Isaiah saw seraphim with six wings, Ezekiel beasts with four wings; Isaiah saw God clothed and sitting on a royal throne, Ezekiel saw Him in the likeness of a fire; each doubtless saw God under the form in which he usually imagined Him.

Further, the visions varied in clearness as well as in details; for the revelations of Zechariah were too obscure to be understood by the prophet without explanation, as appears from his narration of them; the visions of Daniel could not be understood by him even after they had been explained, and this obscurity did not arise from the difficulty of the matter revealed (for being merely human affairs, these only transcended human capacity in being future), but solely in the fact that Daniel's imagination was not so capable for prophecy while he was awake as while he was asleep; and this is further evident from the fact that at the very beginning of the vision he was so terrified that he almost despaired of his strength. Thus, on account of the inadequacy of his imagination and his strength, the things revealed were so obscure to him that he could not understand them even after they had been explained. Here we may note that the words heard by Daniel, were, as we have shown above, simply imaginary, so that it is hardly wonderful that in his frightened state he imagined them so confusedly and obscurely that afterwards he could make nothing of them. Those who say that God did not wish to make a clear revelation, do not seem to have read the words of the angel, who expressly says that he came to make the prophet understand what should befall his people in the latter days (Dan. x:14).

The revelation remained obscure because no one was found, at that time, with imagination sufficiently strong to conceive it more clearly. Lastly, the prophets, to whom it was revealed that God would take away Elijah, wished to persuade Elisha that he had been taken somewhere where they would find him; showing sufficiently clearly that they had not understood God's revelation aright.

There is no need to set this out more amply, for nothing is more plain in the Bible than that God endowed some prophets with far greater gifts of prophecy than others. But I will show in greater detail and length, for I consider the point more important, that the prophecies varied according to the opinions previously embraced by the prophets, and that the prophets held diverse and even contrary opinions and prejudices. (I speak, be it understood, solely of matters speculative, for in regard to uprightness and morality the case is widely different.) From thence I shall conclude that prophecy never rendered the prophets more learned, but left them with their former opinions, and that we are, therefore, not at all bound to trust them in matters of intellect.

Everyone has been strangely hasty in affirming that the prophets knew everything within the scope of human intellect; and, although certain passages of Scripture plainly affirm that the prophets were in certain respects ignorant, such persons would rather say that they do not understand the passages than admit that there was anything which the prophets did not know; or else they try to wrest the Scriptural words away from their evident meaning.

If either of these proceedings is allowable we may as well shut our Bibles, for vainly shall we attempt to prove anything from them if their plainest passages may be classed among obscure and impenetrable mysteries, or if we may put any interpretation on them which we fancy. For instance, nothing is more clear in the Bible than that Joshua, and perhaps also the author who wrote his history, thought that the sun revolves round the earth, and that the earth is fixed, and further that the sun for a certain period remained still. Many, who will not admit any movement in the heavenly bodies, explain away the passage till it seems to mean something quite different; others, who have learned to philosophize more correctly, and understand that the earth moves while the sun is still, or at any rate does not revolve round the earth, try with all their might to wrest this meaning from Scripture, though plainly nothing of the sort is intended. Such quibblers excite my wonder! Are we, forsooth, bound to believe that Joshua the Soldier was a learned astronomer? or that a miracle could not be revealed to him, or that the light of the sun could not remain longer than usual above the horizon, without his knowing the cause? To me both alternatives appear ridiculous, and therefore I would rather say, that Joshua was ignorant of the true cause of the lengthened day, and that he and the whole host with him thought that the sun moved round the earth every day, and that on that particular occasion it stood still for a time, thus causing the light to remain longer; and I would say, that they did not conjecture that, from the amount of snow in the air (see Josh. x:11), the refraction may have been greater than usual, or that there may have been some other cause which we will not now inquire into.

So also the sign of the shadow going back was revealed to Isaiah according to his understanding; that is, as proceeding from a going backwards of the sun; for he, too, thought that the sun moves and that the earth is still; of parhelia he perhaps never even dreamed. We may arrive at this conclusion without any, scruple, for the sign could really have come to pass, and have been predicted by Isaiah to the king, without the prophet being aware of the real cause.

With regard to the building of the Temple by Solomon, if it was really dictate by God we must maintain the same doctrine: namely, that all the measurements were revealed according to the opinions and understanding of the king; for as we are not bound to believe that Solomon was a mathematician, we may affirm that he was ignorant of the true ratio between the circumference and the diameter of a circle, and that, like the generality of workmen, he thought that it was as three to one. But if it is allowable to declare that we do not understand the passage, in good sooth I know nothing in the Bible that we can understand; for the process of building is there narrated simply and as a mere matter of history. If, again, it is permitted to pretend that the passage has another meaning, and was written as it is from some reason unknown to us, this is no less than a complete subversal of the Bible; for every absurd and evil invention of human perversity could thus, without detriment to Scriptural authority, be defended and fostered. Our conclusion is in no wise impious, for though Solomon, Isaiah, Joshua, &c. were prophets, they were none the less men, and as such not exempt from human shortcomings.

According to the understanding of Noah it was revealed to him that God as about to destroy the whole human race, for Noah thought that beyond the limits of Palestine the world was not inhabited.

Not only in matters of this kind, but in others more important, the about the Divine attributes, but held quite ordinary notions about God, and to these notions their revelations were adapted, as I will demonstrate by ample Scriptural testimony; from all which one may easily see that they were praised and commended, not so much for the sublimity and eminence of their intellect as for their piety and faithfulness.

Adam, the first man to whom God was revealed, did not know that He is omnipotent and omniscient; for he hid himself from Him, and attempted to make excuses for his fault before God, as though he had had to do with a man; therefore to him also was God revealed according to his understanding — that is, as being unaware of his situation or his sin, for Adam heard, or seemed to hear, the Lord walling, in the garden, calling him and asking him where he was; and then, on seeing his shamefacedness, asking him whether he had eaten of the forbidden fruit. Adam evidently only knew the Deity as the Creator of all things. To Cain also God was revealed, according to his understanding, as ignorant of human affairs, nor was a higher conception of the Deity required for repentance of his sin.

To Laban the Lord revealed Himself as the God of Abraham, because Laban believed that each nation had its own special divinity (see Gen. xxxi:29). Abraham also knew not that God is omnipresent, and has foreknowledge of all things; for when he heard the sentence against the inhabitants of Sodom, he prayed that the Lord should not execute it till He had ascertained whether they all merited such punishment; for he said (see Gen. xviii:24), "Peradventure there be fifty righteous within the city," and in accordance with this belief God was revealed to him; as Abraham imagined, He spake thus: "I will go down now, and see whether they have done altogether according to the cry of it which is come unto Me; and, if not, I will know." Further, the Divine testimony concerning Abraham asserts nothing but that he was obedient, and that he "commanded his household after him that they should keep the way of the Lord" (Gen. xviii:19); it does not state that he held sublime conceptions of the Deity.

Moses, also, was not sufficiently aware that God is omniscient, and directs human actions by His sole decree, for although God Himself says that the Israelites should hearken to Him, Moses still considered the matter doubtful and repeated, "But if they will not believe me, nor hearken unto my voice." To him in like manner God was revealed as taking no part in, and as being ignorant of, future human actions: the Lord gave him two signs and said, "And it shall come to pass that if they will not believe thee, neither hearken to the voice of the first sign, that they will believe the voice of the latter sign; but if not, thou shalt take of the water of the river," &c. Indeed, if any one considers without prejudice the recorded opinions of Moses, he will plainly see that Moses conceived the Deity as a Being Who has always existed, does exist, and always will exist, and for this cause he calls Him by the name Jehovah, which in Hebrew signifies these three phases of existence: as to His nature, Moses only taught that He is merciful, gracious, and exceeding jealous, as appears from many passages in the Pentateuch. Lastly, he believed and taught that this Being was so different from all other beings, that He could not be expressed by the image of any visible thing; also, that He could not be looked upon, and that not so much from inherent impossibility as from human infirmity; further, that by reason of His power He was without equal and unique. Moses admitted, indeed, that there were beings (doubtless by the plan and command of the Lord) who acted as God's vicegerents — that is, beings to whom God had given the right, authority, and power to direct nations, and to provide and care for them; but he taught that this Being Whom they were bound to obey was the highest and Supreme God, or (to use the Hebrew phrase) God of gods, and thus in the song (Exod. xv:11) he exclaims, "Who is like unto Thee, O Lord, among the gods?" and Jethro says (Exod. xviii:11), "Now I know that the Lord is greater than all gods." That is to say, "I am at length compelled to admit to Moses that Jehovah is greater than all gods, and that His power is unrivalled." We must remain in doubt whether Moses thought that these beings who acted as God's vicegerents were created by Him, for he has stated nothing, so far as we know, about their creation and origin. He further taught that this Being had brought the visible world into order from Chaos, and had given Nature her germs, and therefore that He possesses supreme right and power over all things; further, that by reason of this supreme right and power He had chosen for Himself alone the Hebrew nation and a certain strip of territory, and had handed over to the care of other gods substituted by Himself the rest of the nations and territories, and that therefore He was called the God of Israel and the God of Jerusalem, whereas the other gods were called the gods of the Gentiles. For this reason the Jews believed that the strip of territory which God had chosen for Himself, demanded a Divine worship quite apart and different from the worship which obtained elsewhere, and that the Lord would not suffer the worship of other gods adapted to other countries. Thus they thought that the people whom the king of Assyria had brought into Judaea were torn in pieces by lions because they knew not the worship of the National Divinity (2 Kings xvii:25).

Jacob, according to Aben Ezra's opinion, therefore admonished his sons when he wished them to seek out a new country, that they should prepare themselves for a new worship, and lay aside the worship of strange, gods — that is, of the gods of the land where they were (Gen. xxxv:2, 3).

David, in telling Saul that he was compelled by the king's persecution to live away from his country, said that he was driven out from the heritage of the Lord, and sent to worship other gods (1 Sam. xxvi:19). Lastly, he believed that this Being or Deity had His habitation in the heavens (Deut. xxxiii:27), an opinion very common among the Gentiles.

If we now examine the revelations to Moses, we shall find that they were accommodated to these opinions; as he believed that the Divine Nature was subject to the conditions of mercy, graciousness, &c., so God was revealed to him in accordance with his idea and under these attributes (see Exodus xxxiv:6, 7, and the second commandment). Further it is related (Ex. xxxiii:18) that Moses asked of God that he might behold Him, but as Moses (as we have said) had formed no mental image of God, and God (as I have shown) only revealed Himself to the prophets in accordance with the disposition of their imagination, He did not reveal Himself in any form. This, I repeat, was because the imagination of Moses was unsuitable, for other prophets bear witness that they saw the Lord; for instance, Isaiah, Ezekiel, Daniel, &c. For this reason God answered Moses, "Thou canst not see My face;" and inasmuch as Moses believed that God can be looked upon — that is, that no contradiction of the Divine nature is therein involved (for otherwise he would never have preferred his request) — it is added, "For no one shall look on Me and live," thus giving a reason in accordance with Moses' idea, for it is not stated that a contradiction of the Divine nature would be involved, as was really the case, but that the thing would not come to pass because of human infirmity.

When God would reveal to Moses that the Israelites, because they worshipped the calf, were to be placed in the same category as other nations, He said (ch. xxxiii:2, 3), that He would send an angel (that is, a being who should have charge of the Israelites, instead of the Supreme Being), and that He Himself would no longer remain among them; thus leaving Moses no ground for supposing that the Israelites were more beloved by God than the other nations whose guardianship He had entrusted to other beings or angels (vide verse 16).

Lastly, as Moses believed that God dwelt in the heavens, God was revealed to him as coming down from heaven on to a mountain, and in order to talk with the Lord Moses went up the mountain, which he certainly need not have done if he could have conceived of God as omnipresent.

The Israelites knew scarcely anything of God, although He was revealed to them; and this is abundantly evident from their transferring, a few days afterwards, the honour and worship due to Him to a calf, which they believed to be the god who had brought them out of Egypt. In truth, it is hardly likely that men accustomed to the superstitions of Egypt, uncultivated and sunk in most abject slavery, should have held any sound notions about the Deity, or that Moses should have taught them anything beyond a rule of right living; inculcating it not like a philosopher, as the result of freedom, but like a lawgiver compelling them to be moral by legal authority. Thus the rule of right living, the worship and love of God, was to them rather a bondage than the true liberty, the gift and grace of the Deity. Moses bid them love God and keep His law, because they had in the past received benefits from Him (such as the deliverance from slavery in Egypt), and further terrified them with threats if they transgressed His commands, holding out many promises of good if they should observe them; thus treating them as parents treat irrational children. It is, therefore, certain that they knew not the excellence of virtue and the true happiness.

Jonah thought that he was fleeing from the sight of God, which seems to show that he too held that God had entrusted the care of the nations outside Judaea to other substituted powers. No one in the whole of the Old Testament speaks more rationally of God than Solomon, who in fact surpassed all the men of his time in natural ability. Yet he considered himself above the law (esteeming it only to have been given for men without reasonable and intellectual grounds for their actions), and made small account of the laws concerning kings, which are mainly three: nay, he openly violated them (in this he did wrong, and acted in a manner unworthy of a philosopher, by indulging in sensual pleasure), and taught that all Fortune's favours to mankind are vanity, that humanity has no nobler gift than wisdom, and no greater punishment than folly. See Proverbs xvi:22, 23.

But let us return to the prophets whose conflicting opinions we have undertaken to note. The expressed ideas of Ezekiel seemed so diverse from those of Moses to the Rabbis who have left us the extant prophetic books (as is told in the treatise of Sabbathus, i:13, 2), that they had serious thoughts of omitting his prophecy from the canon, and would doubtless have thus excluded it if a certain Hananiah had not undertaken to explain it; a task which (as is there narrated) he with great zeal and labour accomplished. How he did so does not sufficiently appear, whether it was by writing a commentary which has now perished, or by altering Ezekiel's words and audaciously — striking out phrases according to his fancy. However this may be, chapter xviii. certainly does not seem to agree with Exodus xxxiv:7, Jeremiah xxxii:18, &c.

Samuel believed that the Lord never repented of anything He had decreed (1 Sam. xv:29), for when Saul was sorry for his sin, and wished to worship God and ask for forgiveness, Samuel said that the Lord would not go back from his decree.

To Jeremiah, on the other hand, it was revealed that, "If that nation against whom I (the Lord) have pronounced, turn from their evil, I will repent of the evil that I thought to do unto them. If it do evil in my sight, that it obey not my voice, then I will repent of the good wherewith I said I would benefit them" (Jer. xviii:8-10). Joel (ii:13) taught that the Lord repented Him only of evil. Lastly, it is clear from Gen iv: 7 that a man can overcome the temptations of sin, and act righteously; for this doctrine is told to Cain, though, as we learn from Josephus and the Scriptures, he never did so overcome them. And this agrees with the chapter of Jeremiah just cited, for it is there said that the Lord repents of the good or the evil pronounced, if the men in question change their ways and manner of life. But, on the other hand, Paul (Rom.ix:10) teaches as plainly as possible that men have no control over the temptations of the flesh save by the special vocation and grace of God. And when (Rom. iii:5 and vi:19) he attributes righteousness to man, he corrects himself as speaking merely humanly and through the infirmity of the flesh.

We have now more than sufficiently proved our point, that God adapted revelations to the understanding and opinions of the prophets, and that in matters of theory without bearing on charity or morality the prophets could be, and, in fact, were, ignorant, and held conflicting opinions. It therefore follows that we must by no means go to the prophets for knowledge, either of natural or of spiritual phenomena.

We have determined, then, that we are only bound to believe in the prophetic writings, the object and substance of the revelation; with regard to the details, every one may believe or not, as he likes.

For instance, the revelation to Cain only teaches us that God admonished him to lead the true life, for such alone is the object and substance of the revelation, not doctrines concerning free will and philosophy. Hence, though the freedom of the will is clearly implied in the words of the admonition, we are at liberty to hold a contrary opinion, since the words and reasons were adapted to the understanding of Cain.

So, too, the revelation to Micaiah would only teach that God revealed to him the true issue of the battle between Ahab and Aram; and this is all we are bound to believe. Whatever else is contained in the revelation concerning the true and the false Spirit of God, the army of heaven standing on the right hand and on the left, and all the other details, does not affect us at all. Everyone may believe as much of it as his reason allows.

The reasonings by which the Lord displayed His power to Job (if they really were a revelation, and the author of the history is narrating, and not merely, as some suppose, rhetorically adorning his own conceptions), would come under the same category — that is, they were adapted to Job's understanding, for the purpose of convincing him, and are not universal, or for the convincing of all men.

We can come to no different conclusion with respect to the reasonings of Christ, by which He convicted the Pharisees of pride and ignorance, and exhorted His disciples to lead the true life. He adapted them to each man's opinions and principles. For instance, when He said to the Pharisees (Matt. xii:26), "And if Satan cast out devils, his house is divided against itself, how then shall his kingdom stand? "He only wished to convince the Pharisees according, to their own principles, not to teach that there are devils, or any kingdom of devils. So, too, when He said to His disciples (Matt. viii:10), "See that ye despise not one of these little ones, for I say unto you that their angels," &c., He merely desired to warn them against pride and despising any of their fellows, not to insist on the actual reason given, which was simply adopted in order to persuade them more easily.

Lastly, we should say, exactly the same of the apostolic signs and reasonings, but there is no need to go further into the subject. If I were to enumerate all the passages of Scripture addressed only to individuals, or to a particular man's understanding, and which cannot, without great danger to philosophy, be defended as Divine doctrines, I should go far beyond the brevity at which I aim. Let it suffice, then, to have indicated a few instances of general application, and let the curious reader consider others by himself. Although the points we have just raised concerning prophets and prophecy are the only ones which have any direct bearing on the end in view, namely, the separation of Philosophy from Theology, still, as I have touched on the general question, I may here inquire whether the gift of prophecy was peculiar to the Hebrews, or whether it was common to all nations. I must then come to a conclusion about the vocation of the Hebrews, all of which I shall do in the ensuing chapter.

CHAPTER III.

Of the Vocation of the Hebrews, and
Whether the Gift of Prophecy was Peculiar to Them.

EVERY MAN'S TRUE happiness and blessedness consist solely in the enjoyment of what is good, not in the pride that he alone is enjoying it, to the exclusion of others. He who thinks himself the more blessed because he is enjoying benefits which others are not, or because he is more blessed or more fortunate than his fellows, is ignorant of true happiness and blessedness, and the joy which he feels is either childish or envious and malicious. For instance, a man's true happiness consists only in wisdom, and the knowledge of the truth, not at all in the fact that he is wiser than others, or that others lack such knowledge: such considerations do not increase his wisdom or true happiness.

Whoever, therefore, rejoices for such reasons, rejoices in another's misfortune, and is, so far, malicious and bad, knowing neither true happiness nor the peace of the true life.

When Scripture, therefore, in exhorting the Hebrews to obey the law, says that the Lord has chosen them for Himself before other nations (Deut. x:15); that He is near them, but not near others (Deut. iv:7); that to them alone He has given just laws (Deut. iv:8); and, lastly, that He has marked them out before others (Deut. iv:32); it speaks only according to the understanding of its hearers, who, as we have shown in the last chapter, and as Moses also testifies (Deut. ix:6, 7), knew not true blessedness. For in good sooth they would have been no less blessed if God had called all men equally to salvation, nor would God have been less present to them for being equally present to others; their laws, would have been no less just if they had been ordained for all, and they themselves would have been no less wise. The miracles would have shown God's power no less by being wrought for other nations also; lastly, the Hebrews would have been just as much bound to worship God if He had bestowed all these gifts equally on all men.

When God tells Solomon (1 Kings iii:12) that no one shall be as wise as he in time to come, it seems to be only a manner of expressing surpassing wisdom; it is little to be believed that God would have promised Solomon, for his greater happiness, that He would never endow anyone with so much wisdom in time to come; this would in no wise have increased Solomon's intellect, and the wise king would have given equal thanks to the Lord if everyone had been gifted with the same faculties.

Still, though we assert that Moses, in the passages of the Pentateuch just cited, spoke only according to the understanding of the Hebrews, we have no wish to deny that God ordained the Mosaic law for them alone, nor that He spoke to them alone, nor that they witnessed marvels beyond those which happened to any other nation; but we wish to emphasize that Moses desired to admonish the Hebrews in such a manner, and with such reasonings as would appeal most forcibly to their childish understanding, and constrain them to worship the Deity. Further, we wished to show that the Hebrews did not surpass other nations in knowledge, or in piety, but evidently in some attribute different from these; or (to speak like the Scriptures, according to their understanding), that the Hebrews were not chosen by God before others for the sake of the true life and sublime ideas, though they were often thereto admonished, but with some other object. What that object was,

I will duly show.

But before I begin, I wish in a few words to explain what I mean by the guidance of God, by the help of God, external and inward, and, lastly, what I understand by fortune.

By the help of God, I mean the fixed and unchangeable order of nature or the chain of natural events: for I have said before and shown elsewhere that the universal laws of nature, according to which all things exist and are determined, are only another name for the eternal decrees of God, which always involve eternal truth and necessity.

So that to say that everything happens according to natural laws, and to say that everything is ordained by the decree and ordinance of God, is the same thing. Now since the power in nature is identical with the power of God, by which alone all things happen and are determined, it follows that whatsoever man, as a part of nature, provides himself with to aid and preserve his existence, or whatsoever nature affords him without his help, is given to him solely by the Divine power, acting either through human nature or through external circumstance. So whatever human nature can furnish itself with by its own efforts to preserve its existence, may be fitly called the inward aid of God, whereas whatever else accrues to man's profit from outward causes may be called the external aid of God.

We can now easily understand what is meant by the election of God. For since no one can do anything save by the predetermined order of nature, that is by God's eternal ordinance and decree, it follows that no one can choose a plan of life for himself, or accomplish any work save by God's vocation choosing him for the work or the plan of life in question, rather than any other. Lastly, by fortune, I mean the ordinance of God in so far as it directs human life through external and unexpected means. With these preliminaries I return to my purpose of discovering the reason why the Hebrews were said to be elected by God before other nations, and with the demonstration I thus proceed.

All objects of legitimate desire fall, generally speaking, under one of these three categories:

1. The knowledge of things through their primary causes. 2. The government of the passions, or the acquirement of the habit of virtue. 3. Secure and healthy life.

The means which most directly conduce towards the first two of these ends, and which may be considered their proximate and efficient causes are contained in human nature itself, so that their acquisition hinges only on our own power, and on the laws of human nature. It may be concluded that these gifts are not peculiar to any nation, but have always been shared by the whole human race, unless, indeed, we would indulge the dream that nature formerly created men of different kinds. But the means which conduce to security and health are chiefly in external circumstance, and are called the gifts of fortune because they depend chiefly on objective causes of which we are ignorant; for a fool may be almost as liable to happiness or unhappiness as a wise man. Nevertheless, human management and watchfulness can greatly assist towards living in security and warding off the injuries of our fellow-men, and even of beasts. Reason and experience show no more certain means of attaining this object than the formation of a society with fixed laws, the occupation of a strip of territory and the concentration of all forces, as it were, into one body, that is the social body. Now for forming and preserving a society, no ordinary ability and care is required: that society will be most secure, most stable, and least liable to reverses, which is founded and directed by far-seeing and careful men; while, on the other hand, a society constituted by men without trained skill, depends in a great measure on fortune, and is less constant. If, in spite of all, such a society lasts a long time, it is owing to some other directing influence than its own; if it overcomes great perils and its affairs prosper, it will perforce marvel at and adore the guiding Spirit of God (in so far, that is, as God works through hidden means, and not through the nature and mind of man), for everything happens to it unexpectedly and contrary to anticipation, it may even be said and thought to be by miracle. Nations, then, are distinguished from one another in respect to the social organization and the laws under which they live and are governed; the Hebrew nation was not chosen by God in respect to its wisdom nor its tranquillity of mind, but in respect to its social organization and the good fortune with which it obtained supremacy and kept it so many years. This is abundantly clear from Scripture. Even a cursory perusal will show us that the only respects in which the Hebrews surpassed other nations, are in their successful conduct of matters relating to government, and in their surmounting great perils solely by God's external aid; in other ways they were on a par with their fellows, and God was equally gracious to all. For in respect to intellect (as we have shown in the last chapter) they held very ordinary ideas about God and nature, so that they cannot have been God's chosen in this respect; nor were they so chosen in respect of virtue and the true life, for here again they, with the exception of a very few elect, were on an equality with other nations: therefore their choice and vocation consisted only in the temporal happiness and advantages of independent rule. In fact, we do not see that God promised anything beyond this to the patriarchs 4 or their successors; in the law no other reward is offered for obedience than the continual happiness of an independent commonwealth and other goods of this life; while, on the other hand, against contumacy and the breaking of the covenant is threatened the downfall of the commonwealth and great hardships. Nor is this to be wondered at; for the ends of every social organization and commonwealth are (as appears from what we have said, and as we will explain more at length hereafter) security and comfort; a commonwealth can only exist by the laws being binding on all. If all the members of a state wish to disregard the law, by that very fact they dissolve the state and destroy the commonwealth. Thus, the only reward which could be promised to the Hebrews for continued obedience to the law was security 5 and its attendant advantages, while no surer punishment could be threatened for disobedience, than the ruin of the state and the evils which generally follow therefrom, in addition to such further consequences as might accrue to the Jews in particular from the ruin of their especial state. But there is no need here to go into this point at more length. I will only add that the laws of the Old Testament were revealed and ordained to the Jews only, for as God chose them in respect to the special constitution of their society and government, they must, of course, have had special laws. Whether God ordained special laws for other nations also, and revealed Himself to their lawgivers prophetically, that is, under the attributes by which the latter were accustomed to imagine Him, I cannot sufficiently determine. It is evident from Scripture itself that other nations acquired supremacy and particular laws by the external aid of God; witness only the two following passages:

In Genesis xiv:18, 19, 20, it is related that Melchisedek was king of Jerusalem and priest of the Most High God, that in exercise of his priestly functions he blessed Abraham, and that Abraham the beloved of the Lord gave to this priest of God a tithe of all his spoils. This sufficiently shows that before He founded the Israelitish nation God constituted kings and priests in Jerusalem, and ordained for them rites and laws. Whether He did so prophetically is, as I have said, not sufficiently clear; but I am sure of this, that Abraham, whilst he sojourned in the city, lived scrupulously according to these laws, for Abraham had received no special rites from God; and yet it is stated (Gen. xxvi:5), that he observed the worship, the precepts, the statutes, and the laws of God, which must be interpreted to mean the worship, the statutes, the precepts, and the laws of king Melchisedek. Malachi chides the Jews as follows (i:10-11.): "Who is there among you that will shut the doors? [of the Temple]; neither do ye kindle fire on mine altar for nought. I have no pleasure in you, saith the Lord of Hosts. For from the rising of the sun, even until the going down of the same My Name shall be great among the Gentiles; and in every place incense shall be offered in My Name, and a pure offering; for My Name is great among the heathen, saith the Lord of Hosts." These words, which, unless we do violence to them, could only refer to the current period, abundantly testify that the Jews of that time were not more beloved by God than other nations, that God then favoured other nations with more miracles than He vouchsafed to the Jews, who had then partly recovered their empire without miraculous aid; and, lastly, that the Gentiles possessed rites and ceremonies acceptable to God. But I pass over these points lightly: it is enough for my purpose to have shown that the election of the Jews had regard to nothing but temporal physical happiness and freedom, in other words, autonomous government, and to the manner and means by which they obtained it; consequently to the laws in so far as they were necessary to the preservation of that special government; and, lastly, to the manner in which they were revealed. In regard to other matters, wherein man's true happiness consists, they were on a par with the rest of the nations.

When, therefore, it is said in Scripture (Deut. iv:7) that the Lord is not so nigh to any other nation as He is to the Jews, reference is only made to their government, and to the period when so many miracles happened to them, for in respect of intellect and virtue — that is, in respect of blessedness — God was, as we have said already, and are now demonstrating, equally gracious to all. Scripture itself bears testimony to this fact, for the Psalmist says (cxlv:18), "The Lord is near to all them that call upon Him, to all that call upon Him in truth." So in the same Psalm, verse 9, "The Lord is good to all, and His tender mercies are over all His works." In Ps. xxxiii:16, it is clearly stated that God has granted to all men the same intellect, in these words, He fashioneth their hearts alike." The heart was considered by the Hebrews, as I suppose everyone knows, to be the seat of the soul and the intellect.

Lastly, from Job xxxviii:28, it is plain that God had ordained for the whole human race the law to reverence God, to keep from evil doing, or to do well, and that Job, although a Gentile, was of all men most acceptable to God, because he exceeded all in piety and religion. Lastly, from Jonah iv:2, it is very evident that, not only to the Jews but to all men, God was gracious, merciful, long — suffering, and of great goodness, and repented Him of the evil, for Jonah says: "Therefore I determined to flee before unto Tarshish, for I know that Thou art a gracious God, and merciful, slow to anger, and of great kindness," &c., and that, therefore, God would pardon the Ninevites. We conclude, therefore (inasmuch as God is to all men equally gracious, and the Hebrews were only, chosen by him in respect to their social organization and government), that the individual Jew, taken apart from his social organization and government, possessed no gift of God above other men, and that there was no difference between Jew and Gentile. As it is a fact that God is equally gracious, merciful, and the rest, to all men; and as the function of the prophet was to teach men not so much the laws of their country, as true virtue, and to exhort them thereto, it is not to be doubted that all nations possessed prophets, and that the prophetic gift was not peculiar to the Jews. Indeed, history, both profane and sacred, bears witness to the fact. Although, from the sacred histories of the Old Testament, it is not evident that the other nations had as many prophets as the Hebrews, or that any Gentile prophet was expressly sent by God to the nations, this does not affect the question, for the Hebrews were careful to record their own affairs, not those of other nations. It suffices, then, that we find in the Old Testament Gentiles, and uncircumcised, as Noah, Enoch, Abimelech, Balaam, &c., exercising prophetic gifts; further, that Hebrew prophets were sent by God, not only to their own nation but to many others also. Ezekiel prophesied to all the nations then known; Obadiah to none, that we are aware of, save the Idumeans; and Jonah was chiefly the prophet to the Ninevites. Isaiah bewails and predicts the calamities, and hails the restoration not only of the Jews but also of other nations, for he says (chap. xvi:9), "Therefore I will bewail Jazer with weeping;" and in chap. xix. he foretells first the calamities and then the restoration of the Egyptians (see verses 19, 20, 21, 25), saying that God shall send them a Saviour to free them, that the Lord shall be known in Egypt, and, further, that the Egyptians shall worship God with sacrifice and oblation; and, at last, he calls that nation the blessed Egyptian people of God; all of which particulars are specially noteworthy.

Jeremiah is called, not the prophet of the Hebrew nation, but simply the prophet of the nations (see Jer:i.5). He also mournfully foretells the calamities of the nations, and predicts their restoration, for he says (xlviii:31) of the Moabites, "Therefore will I howl for Moab, and I will cryout for all Moab" (verse 36), "and therefore mine heart shall sound for Moab like pipes;" in the end he prophesies their restoration, as also the restoration of the Egyptians, Ammonites, and Elamites. Wherefore it is beyond doubt that other nations also, like the Jews, had their prophets, who prophesied to them.

Although Scripture only, makes mention of one man, Balaam, to whom the future of the Jews and the other nations was revealed, we must not suppose that Balaam prophesied only once, for from the narrative itself it is abundantly clear that he had long previously been famous for prophesy and other Divine gifts. For when Balak bade him to come to him, he said (Num. xxii:6), "For I know that he whom thou blessest is blessed, and he whom thou cursest is cursed." Thus we see that he possessed the gift which God had bestowed on Abraham. Further, as accustomed to prophesy, Balaam bade the messengers wait for him till the will of the Lord was revealed to him. When he prophesied, that is, when he interpreted the true mind of God, he was wont to say this of himself: "He hath said, which heard the words of God and knew the knowledge of the Most High, which saw the vision of the Almighty falling into a trance, but having his eyes open." Further, after he had blessed the Hebrews by the command of God, he began (as was his custom) to prophesy to other nations, and to predict their future; all of which abundantly shows that he had always been a prophet, or had often prophesied, and (as we may also remark here) possessed that which afforded the chief certainty to prophets of the truth of their prophecy, namely, a mind turned wholly to what is right and good, for he did not bless those whom he wished to bless, nor curse those whom he wished to curse, as Balak supposed, but only those whom God wished to be blessed or cursed. Thus he answered Balak: "If Balak should give me his house full of silver and gold, I cannot go beyond the commandment of the Lord to do either good or bad of my own mind; but what the Lord saith, that will I speak." As for God being angry with him in the way, the same happened to Moses when he set out to Egypt by the command of the Lord; and as to his receiving money for prophesying, Samuel did the same (1 Sam. ix:7, 8); if in anyway he sinned, "there is not a just man upon earth that doeth good and sinneth not," Eccles. vii:20. (Vide 2 Epist. Peter ii:15, 16, and Jude 5:11.)

His speeches must certainly have had much weight with God, and His power for cursing must assuredly have been very great from the number of times that we find stated in Scripture, in proof of God's great mercy to the Jews, that God would not hear Balaam, and that He changed the cursing to blessing (see Deut. xxiii:6, Josh. xxiv:10, Neh. xiii:2). Wherefore he was without doubt most acceptable to God, for the speeches and cursings of the wicked move God not at all. As then he was a true prophet, and nevertheless Joshua calls him a soothsayer or augur, it is certain that this title had an honourable signification, and that those whom the Gentiles called augurs and soothsayers were true prophets, while those whom Scripture often accuses and condemns were false soothsayers, who deceived the Gentiles as false prophets deceived the Jews; indeed, this is made evident from other passages in the Bible, whence we conclude that the gift of prophecy was not peculiar to the Jews, but common to all nations. The Pharisees, however, vehemently contend that this Divine gift was peculiar to their nation, and that the other nations foretold the future (what will superstition invent next?) by some unexplained diabolical faculty. The principal passage of Scripture which they cite, by way of confirming their theory with its authority, is Exodus xxxiii:16, where Moses says to God, "For wherein shall it be known here that I and Thy people have found grace in Thy sight? is it not in that Thou goest with us? so shall we be separated, I and Thy people, from all the people that are upon the face of the earth." From this they would infer that Moses asked of God that He should be present to the Jews, and should reveal Himself to them prophetically; further, that He should grant this favour to no other nation. It is surely absurd that Moses should have been jealous of God's presence among the Gentiles, or that he should have dared to ask any such thing. The act is, as Moses knew that the disposition and spirit of his nation was rebellious, he clearly saw that they could not carry out what they had begun without very great miracles and special external aid from God; nay, that without such aid they must necessarily perish: as it was evident that God wished them to be preserved, he asked for this special external aid. Thus he says (Ex. xxxiv:9), "If now I have found grace in Thy sight, 0 Lord, let my Lord, I pray Thee, go among us; for it is a stiffnecked people." The reason, therefore, for his seeking special external aid from God was the stiffneckedness of the people, and it is made still more plain, that he asked for nothing beyond this special external aid by God's answer — for God answered at once (verse 10 of the same chapter)— "Behold, I make a covenant: before all Thy people I will do marvels, such as have not been done in all the earth, nor in any nation." Therefore Moses had in view nothing beyond the special election of the Jews, as I have explained it, and made no other request to God. I confess that in Paul's Epistle to the Romans, I find another text which carries more weight, namely, where Paul seems to teach a different doctrine from that here set down, for he there says (Rom. iii:1): "What advantage then hath the Jew? or what profit is there of circumcision? Much every way: chiefly, because that unto them were committed the oracles of God."

But if we look to the doctrine which Paul especially desired to teach, we shall find nothing repugnant to our present contention; on the contrary, his doctrine is the same as ours, for he says (Rom. iii:29) "that God is the God of the Jews and of the Gentiles, and" (ch. ii:25, 26) "But, if thou be a breaker of the law, thy circumcision is made uncircumcision. Therefore if the uncircumcision keep the righteousness of the law, shall not his uncircumcision be counted for circumcision?" Further, in chap. iv:verse 9, he says that all alike, Jew and Gentile, were under sin, and that without commandment and law there is no sin. Wherefore it is most evident that to all men absolutely was revealed the law under which all lived — namely, the law which has regard only to true virtue, not the law established in respect to, and in the formation of a particular state and adapted to the disposition of a particular people. Lastly, Paul concludes that since God is the God of all nations, that is, is equally gracious to all, and since all men equally live under the law and under sin, so also to all nations did God send His Christ, to free all men equally from the bondage of the law, that they should no more do right by the command of the law, but by the constant determination of their hearts. So that Paul teaches exactly the same as ourselves. When, therefore, he says "To the Jews only were entrusted the oracles of God," we must either understand that to them only were the laws entrusted in writing, while they were given to other nations merely in revelation and conception, or else (as none but Jews would object to the doctrine he desired to advance) that Paul was answering only in accordance with the understanding and current ideas of the Jews, for in respect to teaching things which he had partly seen, partly heard, he was to the Greeks a Greek, and to the Jews a Jew.

It now only remains to us to answer the arguments of those who would persuade themselves that the election of the Jews was not temporal, and merely in respect of their commonwealth, but eternal; for, they say, we see the Jews after the loss of their commonwealth, and after being scattered so many years and separated from all other nations, still surviving, which is without parallel among other peoples, and further the Scriptures seem to teach that God has chosen for Himself the Jews for ever, so that though they have lost their commonwealth, they still nevertheless remain God's elect.

The passages which they think teach most clearly this eternal election, are chiefly:

(1.) Jer. xxxi:36, where the prophet testifies that the seed of Israel shall for ever remain the nation of God, comparing them with the stability of the heavens and nature;

(2.) Ezek. xx:32, where the prophet seems to intend that though the Jews wanted after the help afforded them to turn their backs on the worship of the Lord, that God would nevertheless gather them together again from all the lands in which they were dispersed, and lead them to the wilderness of the peoples — as He had led their fathers to the wilderness of the land of Egypt — and would at length, after purging out from among them the rebels and transgressors, bring them thence to his Holy mountain, where the whole house of Israel should worship Him. Other passages are also cited, especially by the Pharisees, but I think I shall satisfy everyone if I answer these two, and this I shall easily accomplish after showing from Scripture itself that God chose not the Hebrews for ever, but only on the condition under which He had formerly chosen the Canaanites, for these last, as we have shown, had priests who religiously worshipped God, and whom God at length rejected because of their luxury, pride, and corrupt worship.

Moses (Lev. xviii:27) warned the Israelites that they be not polluted with whoredoms, lest the land spue them out as it had spued out the nations who had dwelt there before, and in Deut. viii:19, 20, in the plainest terms He threatens their total ruin, for He says, "I testify against you that ye shall surely perish. As the nations which the Lord destroyeth before your face, so shall ye perish." In like manner many other passages are found in the law which expressly show that God chose the Hebrews neither absolutely nor for ever. If, then, the prophets foretold for them a new covenant of the knowledge of God, love, and grace, such a promise is easily proved to be only made to the elect, for Ezekiel in the chapter which we have just quoted expressly says that God will separate from them the rebellious and transgressors, and Zephaniah (iii:12, 13), says that "God will take away the proud from the midst of them, and leave the poor." Now, inasmuch as their election has regard to true virtue, it is not to be thought that it was promised to the Jews alone to the exclusion of others, but we must evidently believe that the true Gentile prophets (and every nation, as we have shown, possessed such) promised the same to the faithful of their own people, who were thereby comforted. Wherefore this eternal covenant of the knowledge of God and love is universal, as is clear, moreover, from Zeph. iii:10, 11: no difference in this respect can be admitted between Jew and Gentile, nor did the former enjoy any special election beyond that which we have pointed out.

When the prophets, in speaking of this election which regards only true virtue, mixed up much concerning sacrifices and ceremonies, and the rebuilding of the temple and city, they wished by such figurative expressions, after the manner and nature of prophecy, to expound matters spiritual, so as at the same time to show to the Jews, whose prophets they were, the true restoration of the state and of the temple to be expected about the time of Cyrus.

At the present time, therefore, there is absolutely nothing which the Jews can arrogate to themselves beyond other people.

As to their continuance so long after dispersion and the loss of empire, there is nothing marvellous in it, for they so separated themselves from every other nation as to draw down upon themselves universal hate, not only by their outward rites, rites conflicting with those of other nations, but also by the sign of circumcision which they most scrupulously observe.

That they have been preserved in great measure by Gentile hatred, experience demonstrates. When the king of Spain formerly compelled the Jews to embrace the State religion or to go into exile, a large number of Jews accepted Catholicism. Now, as these renegades were admitted to all the native privileges of Spaniards, and deemed worthy of filling all honourable offices, it came to pass that they straightway became so intermingled with the Spaniards as to leave of themselves no relic or remembrance. But exactly the opposite happened to those whom the king of Portugal compelled to become Christians, for they always, though converted, lived apart, inasmuch as they were considered unworthy of any civic honours.

The sign of circumcision is, as I think, so important, that I could persuade myself that it alone would preserve the nation for ever. Nay, I would go so far as to believe that if the foundations of their religion have not emasculated their minds they may even, if occasion offers, so changeable are human affairs, raise up their empire afresh, and that God may a second time elect them.

Of such a possibility we have a very famous example in the Chinese. They, too, have some distinctive mark on their heads which they most scrupulously observe, and by which they keep themselves apart from everyone else, and have thus kept themselves during so many thousand years that they far surpass all other nations in antiquity. They have not always retained empire, but they have recovered it when lost, and doubtless will do so again after the spirit of the Tartars becomes relaxed through the luxury of riches and pride.

Lastly, if any one wishes to maintain that the Jews, from this or from any other cause, have been chosen by God for ever, I will not gainsay him if he will admit that this choice, whether temporary or eternal, has no regard, in so far as it is peculiar to the Jews, to aught but dominion and physical advantages (for by such alone can one nation be distinguished from another), whereas in regard to intellect and true virtue, every nation is on a par with the rest, and God has not in these respects chosen one people rather than another.

4 In Gen. xv. it is written that God promised Abraham to protect him, and to grant him ample rewards. Abraham answered that he could expect nothing which could be of any value to him, as he was childless and well stricken in years.

5 That a keeping of the commandments of the old Testament is not sufficient for eternal life, appears from Mark x:21.

CHAPTER IV.

Of the Divine Law.

THE WORD LAW, taken in the abstract, means that by which an individual, or all things, or as many things as belong to a particular species, act in one and the same fixed and definite manner, which manner depends either on natural necessity or on human decree. A law which depends on natural necessity is one which necessarily follows from the nature, or from the definition of the thing in question; a law which depends on human decree, and which is more correctly called an ordinance, is one which men have laid down for themselves and others in order to live more safely or conveniently, or from some similar reason.

For example, the law that all bodies impinging on lesser bodies, lose as much of their own motion as they communicate to the latter is a universal law of all bodies, and depends on natural necessity. So, too, the law that a man in remembering one thing, straightway remembers another either like it, or which he had perceived simultaneously with it, is a law which necessarily follows from the nature of man. But the law that men must yield, or be compelled to yield, somewhat of their natural right, and that they bind themselves to live in a certain way, depends on human decree. Now, though I freely admit that all things are predetermined by universal natural laws to exist and operate in a given, fixed, and definite manner, I still assert that the laws I have just mentioned depend on human decree.

(1.) Because man, in so far as he is a part of nature, constitutes a part of the power of nature. Whatever, therefore, follows necessarily from the necessity of human nature (that is, from nature herself, in so far as we conceive of her as acting through man) follows, even though it be necessarily, from human power. Hence the sanction of such laws may very well be said to depend on man's decree, for it principally depends on the power of the human mind; so that the human mind in respect to its perception of things as true and false, can readily be conceived as without such laws, but not without necessary law as we have just defined it.

(2.) I have stated that these laws depend on human decree because it is well to define and explain things by their proximate causes. The general consideration of fate and the concatenation of causes would aid us very little in forming and arranging our ideas concerning particular questions. Let us add that as to the actual coordination and concatenation of things, that is how things are ordained and linked together, we are obviously ignorant; therefore, it is more profitable for right living, nay, it is necessary for us to consider things as contingent. So much about law in the abstract.

Now the word law seems to be only applied to natural phenomena by analogy, and is commonly taken to signify a command which men can either obey or neglect, inasmuch as it restrains human nature within certain originally exceeded limits, and therefore lays down no rule beyond human strength. Thus it is expedient to define law more particularly as a plan of life laid down by man for himself or others with a certain object.

However, as the true object of legislation is only perceived by a few, and most men are almost incapable of grasping it, though they live under its conditions, legislators, with a view to exacting general obedience, have wisely put forward another object, very different from that which necessarily follows from the nature of law: they promise to the observers of the law that which the masses chiefly desire, and threaten its violators with that which they chiefly fear: thus endeavouring to restrain the masses, as far as may be, like a horse with a curb; whence it follows that the word law is chiefly applied to the modes of life enjoined on men by the sway of others; hence those who obey the law are said to live under it and to be under compulsion. In truth, a man who renders everyone their due because he fears the gallows, acts under the sway and compulsion of others, and cannot be called just. But a man who does the same from a knowledge of the true reason for laws and their necessity, acts from a firm purpose and of his own accord, and is therefore properly called just. This, I take it, is Paul's meaning when he says, that those who live under the law cannot be justified through the law, for justice, as commonly defined, is the constant and perpetual will to render every man his due. Thus Solomon says (Prov. xxi:15), "It is a joy to the just to do judgment," but the wicked fear.

Law, then, being a plan of living which men have for a certain object laid down for themselves or others, may, as it seems, be divided into human law and Divine law. {But both are opposite sides of the same coin}

By human law I mean a plan of living which serves only to render life and the state secure. By Divine law I mean that which only regards the highest good, in other words, the true knowledge of God and love.

I call this law Divine because of the nature of the highest good, which I will here shortly explain as clearly as I can.

Inasmuch as the intellect is the best part of our being, it is evident that we should make every effort to perfect it as far as possible if we desire to search for what is really profitable to us. For in intellectual perfection the highest good should consist. Now, since all our knowledge, and the certainty which removes every doubt, depend solely on the knowledge of God; — firstly, because without God nothing can exist or be conceived; secondly, because so long as we have no clear and distinct idea of God we may remain in universal doubt — it follows that our highest good and perfection also depend solely on the knowledge of God. Further, since without God nothing can exist or be conceived, it is evident that all natural phenomena involve and express the conception of God as far as their essence and perfection extend, so that we have greater and more perfect knowledge of God in proportion to our knowledge of natural phenomena: conversely (since the knowledge of an effect through its cause is the same thing as the knowledge of a particular property of a cause) the greater our knowledge of natural phenomena, the more perfect is our knowledge of the essence of God (which is the cause of all things). So, then, our highest good not only depends on the knowledge of God, but wholly consists therein; and it further follows that man is perfect or the reverse in proportion to the nature and perfection of the object of his special desire; hence the most perfect and the chief sharer in the highest blessedness is he who prizes above all else, and takes especial delight in, the intellectual knowledge of God, the most perfect Being.

Hither, then, our highest good and our highest blessedness aim — namely, to the knowledge and love of God; therefore the means demanded by this aim of all human actions, that is, by God in so far as the idea of him is in us, may be called the commands of God, because they proceed, as it were, from God Himself, inasmuch as He exists in our minds, and the plan of life which has regard to this aim may be fitly called the law of God.

The nature of the means, and the plan of life which this aim demands, how the foundations of the best states follow its lines, and how men's life is conducted, are questions pertaining to general ethics. Here I only proceed to treat of the Divine law in a particular application.

As the love of God is man's highest happiness and blessedness, and the ultimate end and aim of all human actions, it follows that he alone lives by the Divine law who loves God not from fear of punishment, or from love of any other object, such as sensual pleasure, fame, or the like; but solely because he has knowledge of God, or is convinced that the knowledge and love of God is the highest good. The sum and chief precept, then, of the Divine law is to love God as the highest good, namely, as we have said, not from fear of any pains and penalties, or from the love of any other object in which we desire to take pleasure. The idea of God lays down the rule that God is our highest good — in other words, that the knowledge and love of God is the ultimate aim to which all our actions should be directed. The worldling cannot understand these things, they appear foolishness to him. because he has too meager a knowledge of God, and also because in this highest good he can discover nothing which he can handle or eat, or which affects the fleshly appetites wherein he chiefly delights, for it consists solely in thought and the pure reason. They, on the other hand, who know that they possess no greater gift than intellect and sound reason, will doubtless accept what I have said without question.

We have now explained that wherein the Divine law chiefly consists, and what are human laws, namely, all those which have a different aim unless they have been ratified by revelation, for in this respect also things are referred to God (as we have shown above) and in this sense the law of Moses, although it was not universal, but entirely adapted to the disposition and particular preservation of a single people, may yet be called a law of God or Divine law, inasmuch as we believe that it was ratified by prophetic insight. If we consider the nature of natural Divine law as we have just explained it, we shall see:

I. — That it is universal or common to all men, for we have deduced it from universal human nature.

II. That it does not depend on the truth of any historical narrative whatsoever, for inasmuch as this natural Divine law is comprehended solely by the consideration of human nature, it is plain that we can conceive it as existing as well in Adam as in any other man, as well in a man living among his fellows, as in a man who lives by himself.

The truth of a historical narrative, however assured, cannot give us the knowledge nor consequently the love of God, for love of God springs from knowledge of Him, and knowledge of Him should be derived from general ideas, in themselves certain and known, so that the truth of a historical narrative is very far from being a necessary requisite for our attaining our highest good.

Still, though the truth of histories cannot give us the knowledge and love of God, I do not deny that reading them is very useful with a view to life in the world, for the more we have observed and known of men's customs and circumstances, which are best revealed by their actions, the more warily we shall be able to order our lives among them, and so far as reason dictates to adapt our actions to their dispositions.

III. We see that this natural Divine law does not demand the performance of ceremonies — that is, actions in themselves indifferent, which are called good from the fact of their institution, or actions symbolizing something profitable for salvation, or (if one prefers this definition) actions of which the meaning surpasses human understanding. The natural light of reason does not demand anything which it is itself unable to supply, but only such as it can very clearly show to be good, or a means to our blessedness. Such things as are good simply because they have been commanded or instituted, or as being symbols of something good, are mere shadows which cannot be reckoned among actions that are the offsprings as it were, or fruit of a sound mind and of intellect. There is no need for me to go into this now in more detail.

IV. Lastly, we see that the highest reward of the Divine law is the law itself, namely, to know God and to love Him of our free choice, and with an undivided and fruitful spirit; while its penalty is the absence of these things, and being in bondage to the flesh — that is, having an inconstant and wavering spirit.

These points being noted, I must now inquire:

I. Whether by the natural light of reason we can conceive of God as a law-giver or potentate ordaining laws for men?

II. What is the teaching of Holy Writ concerning this natural light of reason and natural law?

III. With what objects were ceremonies formerly instituted?

IV. Lastly, what is the good gained by knowing the sacred histories and believing them?

Of the first two I will treat in this chapter, of the remaining two in the following one.

Our conclusion about the first is easily deduced from the nature of God's will, which is only distinguished from His understanding in relation to our intellect — that is, the will and the understanding of God are in reality one and the same, and are only distinguished in relation to our thoughts which we form concerning God's understanding. For instance, if we are only looking to the fact that the nature of a triangle is from eternity contained in the Divine nature as an eternal verity, we say that God possesses the idea of a triangle, or that He understands the nature of a triangle; but if afterwards we look to the fact that the nature of a triangle is thus contained in the Divine nature, solely by the necessity of the Divine nature, and not by the necessity of the nature and essence of a triangle — in fact, that the necessity of a triangle's essence and nature, in so far as they are conceived of as eternal verities, depends solely on the necessity of the Divine nature and intellect, we then style God's will or decree, that which before we styled His intellect. Wherefore we make one and the same affirmation concerning God when we say that He has from eternity decreed that three angles of a triangle are equal to two right angles, as when we say that He has understood it.

Hence the affirmations and the negations of God always involve necessity or truth; so that, for example, if God said to Adam that He did not wish him to eat of the tree of knowledge of good and evil, it would have involved a contradiction that Adam should have been able to eat of it, and would therefore have been impossible that he should have so eaten, for the Divine command would have involved an eternal necessity and truth. But since Scripture nevertheless narrates that God did give this command to Adam, and yet that none the less Adam ate of the tree, we must perforce say that God revealed to Adam the evil which would surely follow if he should eat of the tree, but did not disclose that such evil would of necessity come to pass. Thus it was that Adam took the revelation to be not an eternal and necessary truth, but a law — that is, an ordinance followed by gain or loss, not depending necessarily on the nature of the act performed, but solely on the will and absolute power of some potentate, so that the revelation in question was solely in relation to Adam, and solely through his lack of knowledge a law, and God was, as it were, a lawgiver and potentate. From the same cause, namely, from lack of knowledge, the Decalogue in relation to the Hebrews was a law, for since they knew not the existence of God as an eternal truth, they must have taken as a law that which was revealed to them in the Decalogue, namely, that God exists, and that God only should be worshipped. But if God had spoken to them without the intervention of any bodily means, immediately they would have perceived it not as a law, but as an eternal truth.

What we have said about the Israelites and Adam, applies also to all the prophets who wrote laws in God's name — they did not adequately conceive God's decrees as eternal truths. For instance, we must say of Moses that from revelation, from the basis of what was revealed to him, he perceived the method by which the Israelitish nation could best be united in a particular territory, and could form a body politic or state, and further that he perceived the method by which that nation could best be constrained to obedience; but he did not perceive, nor was it revealed to him, that this method was absolutely the best, nor that the obedience of the people in a certain strip of territory would necessarily imply the end he had in view. Wherefore he perceived these things not as eternal truths, but as precepts and ordinances, and he ordained them as laws of God, and thus it came to be that he conceived God as a ruler, a legislator, a king, as merciful, just, &c., whereas such qualities are simply attributes of human nature, and utterly alien from the nature of the Deity. Thus much we may affirm of the prophets who wrote laws in the name of God; but we must not affirm it of Christ, for Christ, although He too seems to have written laws in the name of God, must be taken to have had a clear and adequate perception, for Christ was not so much a prophet as the mouthpiece of God. For God made revelations to mankind through Christ as He had before done through angels — that is, a created voice, visions, &c. It would be as unreasonable to say that God had accommodated his revelations to the opinions of Christ as that He had before accommodated them to the opinions of angels (that is, of a created voice or visions) as matters to be revealed to the prophets, a wholly absurd hypothesis. Moreover, Christ was sent to teach not only the Jews but the whole human race, and therefore it was not enough that His mind should be accommodated to the opinions the Jews alone, but also to the opinion and fundamental teaching common to the whole human race — in other words, to ideas universal and true. Inasmuch as God revealed Himself to Christ, or to Christ's mind immediately, and not as to the prophets through words and symbols, we must needs suppose that Christ perceived truly what was revealed, in other words, He understood it, for a, matter is understood when it is perceived simply by the mind without words or symbols.

Christ, then, perceived (truly and adequately) what was revealed, and if He ever proclaimed such revelations as laws, He did so because of the ignorance and obstinacy of the people, acting in this respect the part of God; inasmuch as He accommodated Himself to the comprehension of the people, and though He spoke somewhat more clearly than the other prophets, yet He taught what was revealed obscurely, and generally through parables, especially when He was speaking to those to whom it was not yet given to understand the kingdom of heaven. (See Matt. xiii:10, &c.) To those to whom it was given to understand the mysteries of heaven, He doubtless taught His doctrines as eternal truths, and did not lay them down as laws, thus freeing the minds of His hearers from the bondage of that law which He further confirmed and established. Paul apparently points to this more than once (e.g. Rom. vii:6, and iii:28), though he never himself seems to wish to speak openly, but, to quote his own words (Rom. iii:6, and vi:19), "merely humanly." This he expressly states when he calls God just, and it was doubtless in concession to human weakness that he attributes mercy, grace, anger, and similar qualities to God, adapting his language to the popular mind, or, as he puts it (1 Cor. iii:1, 2), to carnal men. In Rom. ix:18, he teaches undisguisedly that God's auger and mercy depend not on the actions of men, but on God's own nature or will; further, that no one is justified by the works of the law, but only by faith, which he seems to identify with the full assent of the soul; lastly, that no one is blessed unless he have in him the mind of Christ (Rom. viii:9), whereby he perceives the laws of God as eternal truths. We conclude, therefore, that God is described as a lawgiver or prince, and styled just, merciful, &c., merely in concession to popular understanding, and the imperfection of popular knowledge; that in reality God acts and directs all things simply by the necessity of His nature and perfection, and that His decrees and volitions are eternal truths, and always involve necessity. So much for the first point which I wished to explain and demonstrate.

Passing on to the second point, let us search the sacred pages for their teaching concerning the light of nature and this Divine law. The first doctrine we find in the history of the first man, where it is narrated that God commanded Adam not to eat of the fruit of the tree of the knowledge of good and evil; this seems to mean that God commanded Adam to do and to seek after righteousness because it was good, not because the contrary was evil: that is, to seek the good for its own sake, not from fear of evil. We have seen that he who acts rightly from the true knowledge and love of right, acts with freedom and constancy, whereas he who acts from fear of evil, is under the constraint of evil, and acts in bondage under external control. So that this commandment of God to Adam comprehends the whole Divine natural law, and absolutely agrees with the dictates of the light of nature; nay, it would be easy to explain on this basis the whole history or allegory of the first man. But I prefer to pass over the subject in silence, because, in the first place, I cannot be absolutely certain that my explanation would be in accordance with the intention of the sacred writer; and, secondly, because many do not admit that this history is an allegory, maintaining it to be a simple narrative of facts. It will be better, therefore, to adduce other passages of Scripture, especially such as were written by him, who speaks with all the strength of his natural understanding, in which he surpassed all his contemporaries, and whose sayings are accepted by the people as of equal weight with those of the prophets. I mean Solomon, whose prudence and wisdom are commended in Scripture rather than his piety and gift of prophecy. Life being taken to mean the true life (as is evident from Deut. xxx:19), the fruit of the understanding consists only in the true life, and its absence constitutes punishment. All this absolutely agrees with what was set out in our fourth point concerning natural law. Moreover our position that it is the wellspring of life, and that the intellect alone lays down laws for the wise, is plainly taught by, the sage, for he says (Prov. xiii14): "The law of the wise is a fountain of life " — that is, as we gather from the preceding text, the understanding. In chap. iii:13, he expressly teaches that the understanding renders man blessed and happy, and gives him true peace of mind. "Happy is the man that findeth wisdom, and the man that getteth understanding," for "Wisdom gives length of days, and riches and honour; her ways are ways of pleasantness, and all her paths peace" (xiiii6, 17). According to Solomon, therefore, it is only, the wise who live in peace and equanimity, not like the wicked whose minds drift hither and thither, and (as Isaiah says, chap. lvii:20) "are like the troubled sea, for them there is no peace."

Lastly, we should especially note the passage in chap. ii. of Solomon's proverbs which most clearly confirms our contention: "If thou criest after knowledge, and liftest up thy voice for understanding . . . then shalt thou understand the fear of the Lord, and find the knowledge of God; for the Lord giveth wisdom; out of His mouth cometh knowledge and understanding." These words clearly enunciate, that wisdom or intellect alone teaches us to fear God wisely — that is, to worship Him truly;, that wisdom and knowledge flow from God's mouth, and that God bestows on us this gift; this we have already shown in proving that our understanding and our knowledge depend on, spring from, and are perfected by the idea or knowledge of God, and nothing else. Solomon goes on to say in so many words that this knowledge contains and involves the true principles of ethics and politics: "When wisdom entereth into thy heart, and knowledge is pleasant to thy soul, discretion shall preserve thee, understanding shall keep thee, then shalt thou understand righteousness, and judgment, and equity, yea every good path." All of which is in obvious agreement with natural knowledge: for after we have come to the understanding of things, and have tasted the excellence of knowledge, she teaches us ethics and true virtue.

Thus the happiness and the peace of him who cultivates his natural understanding lies, according to Solomon also, not so much under the dominion of fortune (or God's external aid) as in inward personal virtue (or God's internal aid), for the latter can to a great extent be preserved by vigilance, right action, and thought.

Lastly, we must by no means pass over the passage in Paul's Epistle to the Romans, i:20, in which he says: "For the invisible things of God from the creation of the world are clearly seen, being understood by the things that are made, even His eternal power and Godhead; so that they are without excuse, because, when they knew God, they glorified Him not as God, neither were they thankful." These words clearly show that everyone can by the light of nature clearly understand the goodness and the eternal divinity of God, and can thence know and deduce what they should seek for and what avoid; wherefore the Apostle says that they are without excuse and cannot plead ignorance, as they certainly might if it were a question of supernatural light and the incarnation, passion, and resurrection of Christ. "Wherefore," he goes on to say (ib. 24), "God gave them up to uncleanness through the lusts of their own hearts;" and so on, through the rest of the chapter, he describes the vices of ignorance, and sets them forth as the punishment of ignorance. This obviously agrees with the verse of Solomon, already quoted, "The instruction of fools is folly," so that it is easy to understand why Paul says that the wicked are without excuse. As every man sows so shall he reap: out of evil, evils necessarily spring, unless they be wisely counteracted.

Thus we see that Scripture literally approves of the light of natural reason and the natural Divine law, and I have fulfilled the promises made at the beginning of this chapter.

CHAPTER V.

Of the Ceremonial Law.

IN THE FOREGOING chapter we have shown that the Divine law, which renders men truly blessed, and teaches them the true life, is universal to all men; nay, we have so intimately deduced it from human nature that it must be esteemed innate, and, as it were, ingrained in the human mind.

But with regard to the ceremonial observances which were ordained in the Old Testament for the Hebrews only, and were so adapted to their state that they could for the most part only be observed by the society as a whole and not by each individual, it is evident that they formed no part of the Divine law, and had nothing to do with blessedness and virtue, but had reference only to the election of the Hebrews, that is (as I have shown in Chap. II.), to their temporal bodily happiness and the tranquillity of their kingdom, and that therefore they were only valid while that kingdom lasted. If in the Old Testament they are spoken of as the law of God, it is only because they were founded on revelation, or a basis of revelation. Still as reason, however sound, has little weight with ordinary theologians, I will adduce the authority of Scripture for what I here assert, and will further show, for the sake of greater clearness, why and how these ceremonials served to establish and preserve the Jewish kingdom. Isaiah teaches most plainly that the Divine law in its strict sense signifies that universal law which consists in a true manner of life, and does not signify ceremonial observances. In chapter i:10, the prophet calls on his countrymen to hearken to the Divine law as he delivers it, and first excluding all kinds of sacrifices and all feasts, he at length sums up the law in these few words, "Cease to do evil, learn to do well: seek judgment, relieve the oppressed." Not less striking testimony is given in Psalm xl:7 — 9, where the Psalmist addresses God: "Sacrifice and offering Thou didst not desire; mine ears hast Thou opened; burnt offering and sin-offering hast Thou not required; I delight to do Thy will, 0 my God; yea, Thy law is within my heart." Here the Psalmist reckons as the law of God only that which is inscribed in his heart, and excludes ceremonies therefrom, for the latter are good and inscribed on the heart only from the fact of their institution, and not because of their intrinsic value.

Other passages of Scripture testify to the same truth, but these two will suffice. We may also learn from the Bible that ceremonies are no aid to blessedness, but only have reference to the temporal prosperity of the kingdom; for the rewards promised for their observance are merely temporal advantages and delights, blessedness being reserved for the universal Divine law. In all the five books commonly attributed to Moses nothing is promised, as I have said, beyond temporal benefits, such as honours, fame, victories, riches, enjoyments, and health. Though many moral precepts besides ceremonies are contained in these five books, they appear not as moral doctrines universal to all men, but as commands especially adapted to the understanding and character of the Hebrew people, and as having reference only to the welfare of the kingdom. For instance, Moses does not teach the Jews as a prophet not to kill or to steal, but gives these commandments solely as a lawgiver and judge; he does not reason out the doctrine, but affixes for its non-observance a penalty which may and very properly does vary in different nations. So, too, the command not to commit adultery is given merely with reference to the welfare of the state; for if the moral doctrine had been intended, with reference not only to the welfare of the state, but also to the tranquillity and blessedness of the individual, Moses would have condemned not merely the outward act, but also the mental acquiescence, as is done by Christ, Who taught only universal moral precepts, and for this cause promises a spiritual instead of a temporal reward. Christ, as I have said, was sent into the world, not to preserve the state nor to lay down laws, but solely to teach the universal moral law, so we can easily understand that He wished in nowise to do away with the law of Moses, inasmuch as He introduced no new laws of His own — His sole care was to teach moral doctrines, and distinguish them from the laws of the state; for the Pharisees, in their ignorance, thought that the observance of the state law and the Mosaic law was the sum total of morality; whereas such laws merely had reference to the public welfare, and aimed not so much at instructing the Jews as at keeping them under constraint. But let us return to our subject, and cite other passages of Scripture which set forth temporal benefits as rewards for observing the ceremonial law, and blessedness as reward for the universal law.

None of the prophets puts the point more clearly than Isaiah. (18.) After condemning hypocrisy he commends liberty and charity towards one's self and one's neighbours, and promises as a reward: "Then shall thy light break forth as the morning, and thy health shall spring forth speedily, thy righteousness shall go before thee, and the glory of the Lord shall be thy reward" (chap. lviii:8). Shortly afterwards he commends the Sabbath, and for a due observance of it, promises: "Then shalt thou delight thyself in the Lord, and I will cause thee to ride upon the high places of the earth, and feed thee with the heritage of Jacob thy father: for the mouth of the Lord has spoken it." Thus the prophet for liberty bestowed, and charitable works, promises a healthy mind in a healthy body, and the glory of the Lord even after death; whereas, for ceremonial exactitude, he only promises security of rule, prosperity, and temporal happiness.

In Psalms xv. and xxiv. no mention is made of ceremonies, but only of moral doctrines, inasmuch as there is no question of anything but blessedness, and blessedness is symbolically promised: it is quite certain that the expressions, "the hill of God," and "His tents and the dwellers therein," refer to blessedness and security of soul, not to the actual mount of Jerusalem and the tabernacle of Moses, for these latter were not dwelt in by anyone, and only the sons of Levi ministered there. Further, all those sentences of Solomon to which I referred in the last chapter, for the cultivation of the intellect and wisdom, promise true blessedness, for by wisdom is the fear of God at length understood, and the knowledge of God found.

That the Jews themselves were not bound to practise their ceremonial observances after the destruction of their kingdom is evident from Jeremiah. For when the prophet saw and foretold that the desolation of the city was at hand, he said that God only delights in those who know and understand that He exercises loving-kindness, judgment, and righteousness in the earth, and that such persons only are worthy of praise. (Jer. ix:23.) As though God had said that, after the desolation of the city, He would require nothing special from the Jews beyond the natural law by which all men are bound.

The New Testament also confirms this view, for only moral doctrines are therein taught, and the kingdom of heaven is promised as a reward, whereas ceremonial observances are not touched on by the Apostles, after they began to preach the Gospel to the Gentiles. The Pharisees certainly continued to practise these rites after the destruction of the kingdom, but more with a view of opposing the Christians than of pleasing God: for after the first destruction of the city, when they were led captive to Babylon, not being then, so far as I am aware, split up into sects, they straightway neglected their rites, bid farewell to the Mosaic law, buried their national customs in oblivion as being plainly superfluous, and began to mingle with other nations, as we may abundantly learn from Ezra and Nehemiah. We cannot, therefore, doubt that they were no more bound by the law of Moses, after the destruction of their kingdom, than they had been before it had been begun, while they were still living among other peoples before the exodus from Egypt, and were subject to no special law beyond the natural law, and also, doubtless, the law of the state in which they were living, in so far as it was consonant with the Divine natural law.

As to the fact that the patriarchs offered sacrifices, I think they did so for the purpose of stimulating their piety, for their minds had been accustomed from childhood to the idea of sacrifice, which we know had been universal from the time of Enoch; and thus they found in sacrifice their most powerful incentive. The patriarchs, then, did not sacrifice to God at the bidding of a Divine right, or as taught by the basis of the Divine law, but simply in accordance with the custom of the time; and, if in so doing they followed any ordinance, it was simply the ordinance of the country they were living in, by which (as we have seen before in the case of Melchisedek) they were bound.

I think that I have now given Scriptural authority for my view: it remains to show why and how the ceremonial observances tended to preserve and confirm the Hebrew kingdom; and this I can very briefly do on grounds universally accepted.

The formation of society serves not only for defensive purposes, but is also very useful, and, indeed, absolutely necessary, as rendering possible the division of labour. If men did not render mutual assistance to each other, no one would have either the skill or the time to provide for his own sustenance and preservation: for all men are not equally apt for all work, and no one would be capable of preparing all that he individually stood in need of. Strength and time, I repeat, would fail, if every one had in person to plough, to sow, to reap, to grind corn, to cook, to weave, to stitch, and perform the other numerous functions required to keep life going; to say nothing of the arts and sciences which are also entirely necessary to the perfection and blessedness of human nature. We see that peoples living, in uncivilized barbarism lead a wretched and almost animal life, and even they would not be able to acquire their few rude necessaries without assisting one another to a certain extent.

Now if men were so constituted by nature that they desired nothing but what is designated by true reason, society would obviously have no need of laws: it would be sufficient to inculcate true moral doctrines; and men would freely, without hesitation, act in accordance with their true interests. But human nature is framed in a different fashion: every one, indeed, seeks his own interest, but does not do so in accordance with the dictates of sound reason, for most men's ideas of desirability and usefulness are guided by their fleshly instincts and emotions, which take no thought beyond the present and the immediate object. Therefore, no society can exist without government, and force, and laws to restrain and repress men's desires and immoderate impulses. Still human nature will not submit to absolute repression. Violent governments, as Seneca says, never last long; the moderate governments endure. So long as men act simply from fear they act contrary to their inclinations, taking no thought for the advantages or necessity of their actions, but simply endeavouring to escape punishment or loss of life. They must needs rejoice in any evil which befalls their ruler, even if it should involve themselves; and must long for and bring about such evil by every means in their power. Again, men are especially intolerant of serving and being ruled by their equals. Lastly, it is exceedingly difficult to revoke liberties once granted.

From these considerations it follows, firstly, that authority should either be vested in the hands of the whole state in common, so that everyone should be bound to serve, and yet not be in subjection to his equals; or else, if power be in the hands of a few, or one man, that one man should be something above average humanity, or should strive to get himself accepted as such. Secondly, laws should in every government be so arranged that people should be kept in bounds by the hope of some greatly desired good, rather than by fear, for then everyone will do his duty willingly.

Lastly, as obedience consists in acting at the bidding of external authority, it would have no place in a state where the government is vested in the whole people, and where laws are made by common consent. In such a society the people would remain free, whether the laws were added to or diminished, inasmuch as it would not be done on external authority, but their own free consent. The reverse happens when the sovereign power is vested in one man, for all act at his bidding; and, therefore, unless they had been trained from the first to depend on the words of their ruler, the latter would find it difficult, in case of need, to abrogate liberties once conceded, and impose new laws.

From these universal considerations, let us pass on to the kingdom of the Jews. The Jews when they first came out of Egypt were not bound by any national laws, and were therefore free to ratify any laws they liked, or to make new ones, and were at liberty to set up a government and occupy a territory wherever they chose. However, they, were entirely unfit to frame a wise code of laws and to keep the sovereign power vested in the community; they were all uncultivated and sunk in a wretched slavery, therefore the sovereignty was bound to remain vested in the hands of one man who would rule the rest and keep them under constraint, make laws and interpret them. This sovereignty was easily retained by Moses, because he surpassed the rest in virtue and persuaded the people of the fact, proving it by many testimonies (see Exod. chap. xiv., last verse, and chap. xix:9). He then, by the Divine virtue he possessed, made laws and ordained them for the people, taking the greatest care that they should be obeyed willingly and not through fear, being specially induced to adopt this course by the obstinate nature of the Jews, who would not have submitted to be ruled solely by constraint; and also by the imminence of war, for it is always better to inspire soldiers with a thirst for glory than to terrify them with threats; each man will then strive to distinguish himself by valour and courage, instead of merely trying to escape punishment. Moses, therefore, by his virtue and the Divine command, introduced a religion, so that the people might do their duty from devotion rather than fear. Further, he bound them over by benefits, and prophesied many advantages in the future; nor were his laws very severe, as anyone may see for himself, especially if he remarks the number of circumstances necessary in order to procure the conviction of an accused person.

Lastly, in order that the people which could not govern itself should be entirely dependent on its ruler, he left nothing to the free choice of individuals (who had hitherto been slaves); the people could do nothing but remember the law, and follow the ordinances laid down at the good pleasure of their ruler; they were not allowed to plough, to sow, to reap, nor even to eat; to clothe themselves, to shave, to rejoice, or in fact to do anything whatever as they liked, but were bound to follow the directions given in the law; and not only this, but they were obliged to have marks on their door-posts, on their hands, and between their eyes to admonish them to perpetual obedience.

This, then, was the object of the ceremonial law, that men should do nothing of their own free will, but should always act under external authority, and should continually confess by their actions and thoughts that they were not their own masters, but were entirely under the control of others.

From all these considerations it is clearer than day that ceremonies have nothing to do with a state of blessedness, and that those mentioned in the Old Testament, i.e. the whole Mosaic Law, had reference merely to the government of the Jews, and merely temporal advantages.

As for the Christian rites, such as baptism, the Lord's Supper, festivals, public prayers, and any other observances which are, and always have been, common to all Christendom, if they were instituted by Christ or His Apostles (which is open to doubt), they were instituted as external signs of the universal church, and not as having anything to do with blessedness, or possessing any sanctity in themselves. Therefore, though such ceremonies were not ordained for the sake of upholding a government, they were ordained for the preservation of a society, and accordingly he who lives alone is not bound by them: nay, those who live in a country where the Christian religion is forbidden, are bound to abstain from such rites, and can none the less live in a state of blessedness. We have an example of this in Japan, where the Christian religion is forbidden, and the Dutch who live there are enjoined by their East India Company not to practise any outward rites of religion. I need not cite other examples, though it would be easy to prove my point from the fundamental principles of the New Testament, and to adduce many confirmatory instances; but I pass on the more willingly, as I am anxious to proceed to my next proposition. I will now, therefore, pass on to what I proposed to treat of in the second part of this chapter, namely, what persons are bound to believe in the narratives contained in Scripture, and how far they are so bound. Examining this question by the aid of natural reason, I will proceed as follows.

If anyone wishes to persuade his fellows for or against anything which is not self-evident 6, he must deduce his contention from their admissions, and convince them either by experience or by ratiocination; either by appealing to facts of natural experience, or to self-evident intellectual axioms. Now unless the experience be of such a kind as to be clearly and distinctly understood, though it may convince a man, it will not have the same effect on his mind and disperse the clouds of his doubt so completely as when the doctrine taught is deduced entirely from intellectual axioms — that is, by the mere power of the understanding and logical order, and this is especially the case in spiritual matters which have nothing to do with the senses.

But the deduction of conclusions from general truths . priori, usually requires a long chain of arguments, and, moreover, very great caution, acuteness, and self-restraint — qualities which are not often met with; therefore people prefer to be taught by experience rather than deduce their conclusion from a few axioms, and set them out in logical order. Whence it follows, that if anyone wishes to teach a doctrine to a whole nation (not to speak of the whole human race), and to be understood by all men in every particular, he will seek to support his teaching with experience, and will endeavour to suit his reasonings and the definitions of his doctrines as far as possible to the understanding of the common people, who form the majority of mankind, and he will not set them forth in logical sequence nor adduce the definitions which serve to establish them. Otherwise he writes only for the learned — that is, he will be understood by only a small proportion of the human race.

All Scripture was written primarily for an entire people, and secondarily for the whole human race; therefore its contents must necessarily be adapted as far as possible to the understanding of the masses, and proved only by examples drawn from experience. We will explain ourselves more clearly. The chief speculative doctrines taught in Scripture are the existence of God, or a Being Who made all things, and Who directs and sustains the world with consummate wisdom; furthermore, that God takes the greatest thought for men, or such of them as live piously and honourably, while He punishes, with various penalties, those who do evil, separating them from the good. All this is proved in Scripture entirely through experience-that is, through the narratives there related. No definitions of doctrine are given, but all the sayings and reasonings are adapted to the understanding of the masses. Although experience can give no clear knowledge of these things, nor explain the nature of God, nor how He directs and sustains all things, it can nevertheless teach and enlighten men sufficiently to impress obedience and devotion on their minds.

It is now, I think, sufficiently clear what persons are bound to believe in the Scripture narratives, and in what degree they are so bound, for it evidently follows from what has been said that the knowledge of and belief in them is particularly necessary to the masses whose intellect is not capable of perceiving things clearly and distinctly. Further, he who denies them because he does not believe that God exists or takes thought for men and the world, may be accounted impious; but a man who is ignorant of them, and nevertheless knows by natural reason that God exists, as we have said, and has a true plan of life, is altogether blessed — yes, more blessed than the common herd of believers, because besides true opinions he possesses also a true and distinct conception. Lastly, he who is ignorant of the Scriptures and knows nothing by the light of reason, though he may not be impious or rebellious, is yet less than human and almost brutal, having none of God's gifts.

We must here remark that when we say that the knowledge of the sacred narrative is particularly necessary to the masses, we do not mean the knowledge of absolutely all the narratives in the Bible, but only of the principal ones, those which, taken by themselves, plainly display the doctrine we have just stated, and have most effect over men's minds.

If all the narratives in Scripture were necessary for the proof of this doctrine, and if no conclusion could be drawn without the general consideration of every one of the histories contained in the sacred writings, truly the conclusion and demonstration of such doctrine would overtask the understanding and strength not only of the masses, but of humanity; who is there who could give attention to all the narratives at once, and to all the circumstances, and all the scraps of doctrine to be elicited from such a host of diverse histories? I cannot believe that the men who have left us the Bible as we have it were so abounding in talent that they attempted setting about such a method of demonstration, still less can I suppose that we cannot understand Scriptural doctrine till we have given heed to the quarrels of Isaac, the advice of Achitophel to Absalom, the civil war between Jews and Israelites, and other similar chronicles; nor can I think that it was more difficult to teach such doctrine by means of history to the Jews of early times, the contemporaries of Moses, than it was to the contemporaries of Esdras. But more will be said on this point hereafter, we may now only note that the masses are only bound to know those histories which can most powerfully dispose their mind to obedience and devotion. However, the masses are not sufficiently skilled to draw conclusions from what they read, they take more delight in the actual stories, and in the strange and unlooked-for issues of events than in the doctrines implied; therefore, besides reading these narratives, they are always in need of pastors or church ministers to explain them to their feeble intelligence.

But not to wander from our point, let us conclude with what has been our principal object — namely, that the truth of narratives, be they what they may, has nothing to do with the Divine law, and serves for nothing except in respect of doctrine, the sole element which makes one history better than another. The narratives in the Old and New Testaments surpass profane history, and differ among themselves in merit simply by reason of the salutary doctrines which they inculcate. Therefore, if a man were to read the Scripture narratives believing the whole of them, but were to give no heed to the doctrines they contain, and make no amendment in his life, he might employ himself just as profitably in reading the Koran or the poetic drama, or ordinary chronicles, with the attention usually given to such writings; on the other hand, if a man is absolutely ignorant of the Scriptures, and none the less has right opinions and a true plan of life, he is absolutely blessed and truly possesses in himself the spirit of Christ.

The Jews are of a directly contrary way of thinking, for they hold that true opinions and a true plan of life are of no service in attaining blessedness, if their possessors have arrived at them by the light of reason only, and not like the documents prophetically revealed to Moses. Maimonides ventures openly to make this assertion: "Every man who takes to heart the seven precepts and diligently follows them, is counted with the pious among the nation, and an heir of the world to come; that is to say, if he takes to heart and follows them because God ordained them in the law, and revealed them to us by Moses, because they were of aforetime precepts to the sons of Noah: but he who follows them as led thereto by reason, is not counted as a dweller among the pious or among the wise of the nations." Such are the words Of Maimonides, to which R. Joseph, the son of Shem Job, adds in his book which he calls "Kebod Elohim, or God's Glory," that although Aristotle (whom he considers to have written the best ethics and to be above everyone else) has not omitted anything that concerns true ethics, and which he has adopted in his own book, carefully following the lines laid down, yet this was not able to suffice for his salvation, inasmuch as he embraced his doctrines in accordance with the dictates of reason and not as Divine documents prophetically revealed.

However, that these are mere figments, and are not supported by Scriptural authority will, I think, be sufficiently evident to the attentive reader, so that an examination of the theory will be sufficient for its refutation. It is not my purpose here to refute the assertions of those who assert that the natural light of reason can teach nothing, of any value concerning the true way of salvation. People who lay no claims to reason for themselves, are not able to prove by reason this their assertion; and if they hawk about something superior to reason, it is a mere figment, and far below reason, as their general method of life sufficiently shows. But there is no need to dwell upon such persons. I will merely add that we can only judge of a man by his works. If a man abounds in the fruits of the Spirit, charity, joy, peace, long-suffering, kindness, goodness, faith, gentleness, chastity, against which, as Paul says (Gal. v:22), there is no law, such an one, whether he be taught by reason only or by the Scripture only, has been in very truth taught by God, and is altogether blessed. Thus have I said all that I undertook to say concerning Divine law.

6 We doubt of the existence of God, and consequently of all else, so long as we have no clear and distinct idea of God, but only a confused one. For as he who knows not rightly the nature of a triangle, knows not that its three angles are equal to two right angles, so he who conceives the Divine nature confusedly, does not see that it pertains to the nature of God to exist. Now, to conceive the nature of God clearly and distinctly, it is necessary to pay attention to a certain number of very simple notions, called general notions, and by their help to associate the conceptions which we form of the attributes of the Divine nature. It then, for the first time, becomes clear to us, that God exists necessarily, that He is omnipresent, and that all our conceptions involve in themselves the nature of God and are conceived through it. Lastly, we see that all our adequate ideas are true. Compare on this point the prolegomena to book, "Principles of Descartes's philosophy set forth geometrically."

CHAPTER VI.

Of Miracles.

AS MEN ARE accustomed to call Divine the knowledge which transcends human understanding, so also do they style Divine, or the work of God, anything of which the cause is not generally known: for the masses think that the power and providence of God are most clearly displayed by events that are extraordinary and contrary to the conception they have formed of nature, especially if such events bring them any profit or convenience: they think that the clearest possible proof of God's existence is afforded when nature, as they suppose, breaks her accustomed order, and consequently they believe that those who explain or endeavour to understand phenomena or miracles through their natural causes are doing away with God and His providence. They suppose, forsooth, that God is inactive so long as nature works in her accustomed order, and vice versa, that the power of nature and natural causes are idle so long as God is acting: thus they imagine two powers distinct one from the other, the power of God and the power of nature, though the latter is in a sense determined by God, or (as most people believe now) created by Him. What they mean by either, and what they understand by God and nature they do not know, except that they imagine the power of God to be like that of some royal potentate, and nature's power to consist in force and energy.

The masses then style unusual phenomena, "miracles," and partly from piety, partly for the sake of opposing the students of science, prefer to remain in ignorance of natural causes, and only to hear of those things which they know least, and consequently admire most. In fact, the common people can only adore God, and refer all things to His power by removing natural causes, and conceiving things happening out of their due course, and only admires the power of God when the power of nature is conceived of as in subjection to it.

This idea seems to have taken its rise among the early Jews who saw the Gentiles round them worshipping visible gods such as the sun, the moon, the earth, water, air, &c., and in order to inspire the conviction that such divinities were weak and inconstant, or changeable, told how they themselves were under the sway of an invisible God, and narrated their miracles, trying further to show that the God whom they worshipped arranged the whole of nature for their sole benefit: this idea was so pleasing to humanity that men go on to this day imagining miracles, so that they may believe themselves God's favourites, and the final cause for which God created and directs all things.

What pretension will not people in their folly advance! They have no single sound idea concerning either God or nature, they confound God's decrees with human decrees, they conceive nature as so limited that they believe man to be its chief part! I have spent enough space in setting forth these common ideas and prejudices concerning nature and miracles, but in order to afford a regular demonstration I will show —

I. That nature cannot be contravened, but that she preserves a fixed and immutable order, and at the same time I will explain what is meant by a miracle.

II. That God's nature and existence, and consequently His providence cannot be known from miracles, but that they can all be much better perceived from the fixed and immutable order of nature.

III. That by the decrees and volitions, and consequently the providence of God, Scripture (as I will prove by Scriptural examples) means nothing but nature's order following necessarily from her eternal laws.

IV. Lastly, I will treat of the method of interpreting Scriptural miracles, and the chief points to be noted concerning the narratives of them.

Such are the principal subjects which will be discussed in this chapter, and which will serve, I think, not a little to further the object of this treatise.

Our first point is easily proved from what we showed in Chap. IV. about Divine law — namely, that all that God wishes or determines involves eternal necessity, and truth, for we demonstrated that God's understanding is identical with His will, and that it is the same thing to say that God wills a thing, as to say, that He understands it; hence, as it follows necessarily, from the Divine nature and perfection that God understands a thing as it is, it follows no less necessarily that He wills it as it is. Now, as nothing is necessarily true save only by, Divine decree, it is plain that the universal laws of nature are decrees of God following from the necessity and perfection of the Divine nature. Hence, any event happening in nature which contravened nature's universal laws, would necessarily also contravene the Divine decree, nature, and understanding; or if anyone asserted that God acts in contravention to the laws of nature, he, ipso facto, would be compelled to assert that God acted against His own nature — an evident absurdity. One might easily show from the same premises that the power and efficiency, of nature are in themselves the Divine power and efficiency, and that the Divine power is the very essence of God, but this I gladly pass over for the present.

Nothing, then, comes to pass in nature (N.B. I do not mean here by "nature," merely matter and its modifications, but infinite other things besides matter.) in contravention to her universal laws, nay, everything agrees with them and follows from them, for whatsoever comes to pass, comes to pass by the will and eternal decree of God; that is, as we have just pointed out, whatever comes to pass, comes to pass according to laws and rules which involve eternal necessity and truth; nature, therefore, always observes laws and rules which involve eternal necessity, and truth, although they may not all be known to us, and therefore she keeps a fixed and mutable order. Nor is there any sound reason for limiting the power and efficacy of nature, and asserting that her laws are fit for certain purposes, but not for all; for as the efficacy, and power of nature, are the very, efficacy and power of God, and as the laws and rules of nature are the decrees of God, it is in every way to be believed that the power of nature is infinite, and that her laws are broad enough to embrace everything conceived by, the Divine intellect; the only alternative is to assert that God has created nature so weak, and has ordained for her laws so barren, that He is repeatedly compelled to come afresh to her aid if He wishes that she should be preserved, and that things should happen as He desires: a conclusion, in My opinion, very far removed from reason. Further, as nothing happens in nature which does not follow from her laws, and as her laws embrace everything conceived by the Divine intellect, and lastly, as nature preserves a fixed and immutable order; it most clearly follows that miracles are only intelligible as in relation to human opinions, and merely mean events of which the natural cause cannot be explained by a reference to any ordinary occurrence, either by us, or at any rate, by the writer and narrator of the miracle.

We may, in fact, say that a miracle is an event of which the causes annot be explained by the natural reason through a reference to ascertained workings of nature; but since miracles were wrought according to the understanding of the masses, who are wholly ignorant of the workings of nature, it is certain that the ancients took for a miracle whatever they could not explain by the method adopted by the unlearned in such cases, namely, an appeal to the memory, a recalling of something similar, which is ordinarily regarded without wonder; for most people think they sufficiently understand a thing when they have ceased to wonder at it. The ancients, then, and indeed most men up to the present day, had no other criterion for a miracle; hence we cannot doubt that many things are narrated in Scripture as miracles of which the causes could easily be explained by reference to ascertained workings of nature. We have hinted as much in Chap. II., in speaking of the sun standing still in the time of Joshua, and to say on the subject when we come to treat of the interpretation of miracles later on in this chapter.

It is now time to pass on to the second point, and show that we cannot gain an understanding of God's essence, existence, or providence by means of miracles, but that these truths are much better perceived through the fixed and immutable order of nature. I thus proceed with the demonstration. As God's existence is not self-evident it must necessarily be inferred from ideas so firmly and incontrovertibly true, that no power can be postulated or conceived sufficient to impugn them. They ought certainly so to appear to us when we infer from them God's existence, if we wish to place our conclusion beyond the reach of doubt; for if we could conceive that such ideas could be impugned by any power whatsoever, we should doubt of their truth, we should doubt of our conclusion, namely, of God's existence, and should never be able to be certain of anything. Further, we know that nothing either agrees with or is contrary to nature, unless it agrees with or is contrary to these primary ideas; wherefore if we would conceive that anything could be done in nature by any power whatsoever which would be contrary to the laws of nature, it would also be contrary to our primary ideas, and we should have either to reject it as absurd, or else to cast doubt (as just shown) on our primary ideas, and consequently on the existence of God, and on everything howsoever perceived. Therefore miracles, in the sense of events contrary to the laws of nature, so far from demonstrating to us the existence of God, would, on the contrary, lead us to doubt it, where, otherwise, we might have been absolutely certain of it, as knowing that nature follows a fixed and immutable order.

Let us take miracle as meaning that which cannot be explained through natural causes. This may be interpreted in two senses: either as that which has natural causes, but cannot be examined by the human intellect; or as that which has no cause save God and God's will. But as all things which come to pass through natural causes, come to pass also solely through the will and power of God, it comes to this, that a miracle, whether it has natural causes or not, is a result which cannot be explained by its cause, that is a phenomenon which surpasses human understanding; but from such a phenomenon, and certainly from a result surpassing our understanding, we can gain no knowledge. For whatsoever we understand clearly and distinctly should be plain to us either in itself or by means of something else clearly and distinctly understood; wherefore from a miracle or a phenomenon which we cannot understand, we can gain no knowledge of God's essence, or existence, or indeed anything about God or nature; whereas when we know that all things are ordained and ratified by God, that the operations of nature follow from the essence of God, and that the laws of nature are eternal decrees and volitions of God, we must perforce conclude that our knowledge of God, and of God's will increases in proportion to our knowledge and clear understanding of nature, as we see how she depends on her primal cause, and how she works according to eternal law. Wherefore so far as our understanding goes, those phenomena which we clearly and distinctly understand have much better right to be called works of God, and to be referred to the will of God than those about which we are entirely ignorant, although they appeal powerfully to the imagination, and compel men's admiration.

It is only phenomena that we clearly and distinctly understand, which heighten our knowledge of God, and most clearly indicate His will and decrees. Plainly, they are but triflers who, when they cannot explain a thing, run back to the will of God; this is, truly, a ridiculous way of expressing ignorance. Again, even supposing that some conclusion could be drawn from miracles, we could not possibly infer from them the existence of God: for a miracle being an event under limitations is the expression of a fixed and limited power; therefore we could not possibly infer from an effect of this kind the existence of a cause whose power is infinite, but at the utmost only of a cause whose power is greater than that of the said effect. I say at the utmost, for a phenomenon may be the result of many concurrent causes, and its power may be less than the power of the sum of such causes, but far greater than that of any one of them taken individually. On the other hand, the laws of nature, as we have shown, extend over infinity, and are conceived by us as, after a fashion, eternal, and nature works in accordance with them in a fixed and immutable order; therefore, such laws indicate to us in a certain degree the infinity, the eternity, and the immutability of God.

We may conclude, then, that we cannot gain knowledge of the existence and providence of God by means of miracles, but that we can far better infer them from the fixed and immutable order of nature. By miracle, I here mean an event which surpasses, or is thought to surpass, human comprehension: for in so far as it is supposed to destroy or interrupt the order of nature or her laws, it not only can give us no knowledge of God, but, contrariwise, takes away that which we naturally have, and makes us doubt of God and everything else.

Neither do I recognize any difference between an event against the laws of nature and an event beyond the laws of nature (that is, according to some, an event which does not contravene nature, though she is inadequate to produce or effect it) — for a miracle is wrought in, and not beyond nature, though it may be said in itself to be above nature, and, therefore, must necessarily interrupt the order of nature, which otherwise we conceive of as fixed and unchangeable, according to God's decrees. If, therefore, anything should come to pass in nature which does not follow from her laws, it would also be in contravention to the order which God has established in nature for ever through universal natural laws: it would, therefore, be in contravention to God's nature and laws, and, consequently, belief in it would throw doubt upon everything, and lead to Atheism.

I think I have now sufficiently established my second point, so that we can again conclude that a miracle, whether in contravention to, or beyond, nature, is a mere absurdity; and, therefore, that what is meant in Scripture by a miracle can only be a work of nature, which surpasses, or is believed to surpass, human comprehension. Before passing on to my third point, I will adduce Scriptural authority for my assertion that God cannot be known from miracles. Scripture nowhere states the doctrine openly, but it can readily be inferred from several passages. Firstly, that in which Moses commands (Deut. xiii.) that a false prophet should be put to death, even though he work miracles: "If there arise a prophet among you, and giveth thee a sign or wonder, and the sign or wonder come to pass, saying, Let us go after other gods . . . thou shalt not hearken unto the voice of that prophet; for the Lord your God proveth you, and that prophet shall be put to death." From this it clearly follows that miracles could be wrought even by false prophets; and that, unless men are honestly endowed with the true knowledge and love of God, they may be as easily led by miracles to follow false gods as to follow the true God; for these words are added: "For the Lord your God tempts you, that He may know whether you love Him with all your heart and with all your mind."

Further, the Israelites, from all their miracles, were unable to form a sound conception of God, as their experience testified: for when they had persuaded themselves that Moses had departed from among them, they petitioned Aaron to give them visible gods; and the idea of God they had formed as the result of all their miracles was — a calf!

Asaph, though he had heard of so many miracles, yet doubted of the providence of God, and would have turned himself from the true way, if he had not at last come to understand true blessedness. (See Ps. lxxxiii.) Solomon, too, at a time when the Jewish nation was at the height of its prosperity, suspects that all things happen by chance. (See Eccles. iii:19, 20, 21; and chap. ix:2, 3, &c.)

Lastly, nearly all the prophets found it very hard to reconcile the order of nature and human affairs with the conception they had formed of God's providence, whereas philosophers who endeavour to understand things by clear conceptions of them, rather than by miracles, have always found the task extremely easy — at least, such of them as place true happiness solely in virtue and peace of mind, and who aim at obeying nature, rather than being obeyed by her. Such persons rest assured that God directs nature according to the requirements of universal laws, not according to the requirements of the particular laws of human nature, and trial, therefore, God's scheme comprehends, not only the human race, but the whole of nature.

It is plain, then, from Scripture itself, that miracles can give no knowledge of God, nor clearly teach us the providence of God. As to the frequent statements in Scripture, that God wrought miracles to make Himself plain to man — as in Exodus x:2, where He deceived the Egyptians, and gave signs of Himself, that the Israelites might know that He was God — it does not, therefore, follow that miracles really taught this truth, but only that the Jews held opinions which laid them easily open to conviction by miracles. We have shown in Chap. II. that the reasons assigned by the prophets, or those which are formed from revelation, are not assigned in accordance with ideas universal and common to all, but in accordance with the accepted doctrines, however absurd, and with the opinions of those to whom the revelation was given, or those whom the Holy Spirit wished to convince.

This we have illustrated by many Scriptural instances, and can further cite Paul, who to the Greeks was a Greek, and to the Jews a Jew. But although these miracles could convince the Egyptians and Jews from their standpoint, they could not give a true idea and knowledge of God, but only cause them to admit that there was a Deity more powerful than anything known to them, and that this Deity took special care of the Jews, who had just then an unexpectedly happy issue of all their affairs. They could not teach them that God cares equally for all, for this can be taught only by philosophy: the Jews, and all who took their knowledge of God's providence from the dissimilarity of human conditions of life and the inequalities of fortune, persuaded themselves that God loved the Jews above all men, though they did not surpass their fellows in true human perfection.

I now go on to my third point, and show from Scripture that the decrees and mandates of God, and consequently His providence, are merely the order of nature — that is, when Scripture describes an event as accomplished by God or God's will, we must understand merely that it was in accordance with the law and order of nature, not, as most people believe, that nature had for a season ceased to act, or that her order was temporarily interrupted. But Scripture does not directly teach matters unconnected with its doctrine, wherefore it has no care to explain things by their natural causes, nor to expound matters merely speculative. Wherefore our conclusion must be gathered by inference from those Scriptural narratives which happen to be written more at length and circumstantially than usual. Of these I will cite a few.

In the first book of Samuel, ix:15, 16, it is related that God revealed to Samuel that He would send Saul to him, yet God did not send Saul to Samuel as people are wont to send one man to another. His "sending" was merely the ordinary course of nature. Saul was looking for the asses he had lost, and was meditating a return home without them, when, at the suggestion of his servant, he went to the prophet Samuel, to learn from him where he might find them. From no part of the narrative does it appear that Saul had any command from God to visit Samuel beyond this natural motive.

In Psalm cv. 24 it is said that God changed the hearts of the Egyptians, so that they hated the Israelites. This was evidently a natural change, as appears from Exodus, chap.i., where we find no slight reason for the Egyptians reducing the Israelites to slavery.

In Genesis ix:13, God tells Noah that He will set His bow in the cloud; this action of God's is but another way of expressing the refraction and reflection which the rays of the sun are subjected to in drops of water.

In Psalm cxlvii:18, the natural action and warmth of the wind, by which hoar frost and snow are melted, are styled the word of the Lord, and in verse 15 wind and cold are called the commandment and word of God.

In Psalm civ:4, wind and fire are called the angels and ministers of God, and various other passages of the same sort are found in Scripture, clearly showing that the decree, commandment, fiat, and word of God are merely expressions for the action and order of nature.

Thus it is plain that all the events narrated in Scripture came to pass naturally, and are referred directly to God because Scripture, as we have shown, does not aim at explaining things by their natural causes, but only at narrating what appeals to the popular imagination, and doing so in the manner best calculated to excite wonder, and consequently to impress the minds of the masses with devotion. If, therefore, events are found in the Bible which we cannot refer to their causes, nay, which seem entirely to contradict the order of nature, we must not come to a stand, but assuredly believe that whatever did really happen happened naturally. This view is confirmed by the fact that in the case of every miracle there were many attendant circumstances, though these were not always related, especially where the narrative was of a poetic character.

The circumstances of the miracles clearly show, I maintain, that natural causes were needed. For instance, in order to infect the Egyptians with blains, it was necessary that Moses should scatter ashes in the air (Exod. ix: 10); the locusts also came upon the land of Egypt by a command of God in accordance with nature, namely, by an east wind blowing for a whole day and night; and they departed by a very strong west wind (Exod. x:14, 19). By a similar Divine mandate the sea opened a way for the Jews (Exo. xiv:21), namely, by an east wind which blew very strongly all night.

So, too, when Elisha would revive the boy who was believed to be dead, he was obliged to bend over him several times until the flesh of the child waxed warm, and at last he opened his eyes (2 Kings iv:34, 35).

Again, in John's Gospel (chap. ix.) certain acts are mentioned as performed by Christ preparatory to healing the blind man, and there are numerous other instances showing that something further than the absolute fiat of God is required for working a miracle.

Wherefore we may believe that, although the circumstances attending miracles are not related always or in full detail, yet a miracle was never performed without them.

This is confirmed by Exodus xiv:27, where it is simply stated that "Moses stretched forth his hand, and the waters of the sea returned to their strength in the morning," no mention being made of a wind; but in the song of Moses (Exod. xv:10) we read, "Thou didst blow with Thy wind (i.e. with a very strong wind), and the sea covered them." Thus the attendant circumstance is omitted in the history, and the miracle is thereby enhanced.

But perhaps someone will insist that we find many things in Scripture which seem in nowise explicable by natural causes, as for instance, that the sins of men and their prayers can be the cause of rain and of the earth's fertility, or that faith can heal the blind, and so on. But I think I have already made sufficient answer: I have shown that Scripture does not explain things by their secondary causes, but only narrates them in the order and the style which has most power to move men, and especially uneducated men, to devotion; and therefore it speaks inaccurately of God and of events, seeing that its object is not to convince the reason, but to attract and lay hold of the imagination. If the Bible were to describe the destruction of an empire in the style of political historians, the masses would remain unstirred, whereas the contrary is the case when it adopts the method of poetic description, and refers all things immediately to God. When, therefore, the Bible says that the earth is barren because of men's sins, or that the blind were healed by faith, we ought to take no more notice than when it says that God is angry at men's sins, that He is sad, that He repents of the good He has promised and done; or that on seeing a sign he remembers something He had promised, and other similar expressions, which are either thrown out poetically or related according to the opinion and prejudices of the writer.

We may, then, be absolutely certain that every event which is truly described in Scripture necessarily happened, like everything else, according to natural laws; and if anything is there set down which can be proved in set terms to contravene the order of nature, or not to be deducible therefrom, we must believe it to have been foisted into the sacred writings by irreligious hands; for whatsoever is contrary to nature is also contrary to reason, and whatsoever is contrary to reason is absurd, and, ipso facto, to be rejected.

There remain some points concerning the interpretation of miracles to be noted, or rather to be recapitulated, for most of them have been already stated. These I proceed to discuss in the fourth division of my subject, and I am led to do so lest anyone should, by wrongly interpreting a miracle, rashly suspect that he has found something in Scripture contrary to human reason.

It is very rare for men to relate an event simply as it happened, without adding any element of their own judgment. When they see or hear anything new, they are, unless strictly on their guard, so occupied with their own preconceived opinions that they perceive something quite different from the plain facts seen or heard, especially if such facts surpass the comprehension of the beholder or hearer, and, most of all, if he is interested in their happening in a given way.

Thus men relate in chronicles and histories their own opinions rather than actual events, so that one and the same event is so differently related by two men of different opinions, that it seems like two separate occurrences; and, further, it is very easy from historical chronicles to gather the personal opinions of the historian.

I could cite many instances in proof of this from the writings both of natural philosophers and historians, but I will content myself with one only from Scripture, and leave the reader to judge of the rest.

In the time of Joshua the Hebrews held the ordinary opinion that the sun moves with a daily motion, and that the earth remains at rest; to this preconceived opinion they adapted the miracle which occurred during their battle with the five kings. They did not simply relate that that day was longer than usual, but asserted that the sun and moon stood still, or ceased from their motion — a statement which would be of great service to them at that time in convincing and proving by experience to the Gentiles, who worshipped the sun, that the sun was under the control of another deity who could compel it to change its daily course. Thus, partly through religious motives, partly through preconceived opinions, they conceived of and related the occurrence as something quite different from what really happened.

Thus in order to interpret the Scriptural miracles and understand from the narration of them how they really happened, it is necessary to know the opinions of those who first related them, and have recorded them for us in writing, and to distinguish such opinions from the actual impression made upon their senses, otherwise we shall confound opinions and judgments with the actual miracle as it really occurred: nay, further, we shall confound actual events with symbolical and imaginary ones. For many things are narrated in Scripture as real, and were believed to be real, which were in fact only symbolical and imaginary. As, for instance, that God came down from heaven (Exod. xix:28, Deut. v:28), and that Mount Sinai smoked because God descended upon it surrounded with fire; or, again that Elijah ascended into heaven in a chariot of fire, with horses of fire; all these things were assuredly merely symbols adapted to the opinions of those who have handed them down to us as they were represented to them, namely, as real. All who have any education know that God has no right hand nor left; that He is not moved nor at rest, nor in a particular place, but that He is absolutely infinite and contains in Himself all perfections.

These things, I repeat, are known to whoever judges of things by the perception of pure reason, and not according as his imagination is affected by his outward senses. Following the example of the masses who imagine a bodily Deity, holding a royal court with a throne on the convexity of heaven, above the stars, which are believed to be not very, far off from the earth.

To these and similar opinions very many narrations in Scripture are adapted, and should not, therefore, be mistaken by philosophers for realities.

Lastly, in order to understand, in the case of miracles, what actually took place, we ought to be familiar with Jewish phrases and metaphors; anyone who did not make sufficient allowance for these, would be continually seeing miracles in Scripture where nothing of the kind is intended by the writer; he would thus miss the knowledge not only of what actually happened, but also of the mind of the writers of the sacred text. For instance, Zechariah speaking of some future war says (chap. xiv;7): "It shall be one day which shall be known to the Lord, not day, nor night; but at even time it shall be light." In these words he seems to predict a great miracle, yet he only means that the battle will be doubtful the whole day, that the issue will be known only to God, but that in the evening they will gain the victory: the prophets frequently used to predict victories and defeats of the nations in similar phrases. Thus Isaiah, describing the destruction of Babylon, says (chap. xiii.): "The stars of heaven, and the constellations thereof, shall not give their light; the sun shall be darkened in his going forth, and the moon shall not cause her light to shine." Now I suppose no one imagines that at the destruction of Babylon these phenomena actually occurred any more than that which the prophet adds, "For I will make the heavens to tremble, and remove the earth out of her place."

So, too, Isaiah in foretelling to the Jews that they would return from Babylon to Jerusalem in safety, and would not suffer from thirst on their journey, says: "And they thirsted not when He led them through the deserts; He caused the waters to flow out of the rocks for them; He clave the rocks, and the waters gushed out." These words merely mean that the Jews, like other people, found springs in the desert, at which they quenched their thirst; for when the Jews returned to Jerusalem with the consent of Cyrus, it is admitted that no similar miracles befell them.

In this way many occurrences in the Bible are to be regarded merely as Jewish expressions. There is no need for me to go through them in detail; but I will call attention generally to the fact that the Jews employed such phrases not only rhetorically, but also, and indeed chiefly, from devotional motives. Such is the reason for the substitution of "bless God" for "curse God" in 1 Kings xxi:10, and Job ii:9, and for all things being referred to God, whence it appears that the Bible seems to relate nothing but miracles, even when speaking of the most ordinary occurrences, as in the examples given above.

Hence we must believe that when the Bible says that the Lord hardened Pharaoh's heart, it only means that Pharaoh was obstinate; when it says that God opened the windows of heaven, it only means that it rained very hard, and so on. When we reflect on these peculiarities, and also on the fact that most things are related very shortly, with very little details and almost in abridgments, we shall see that there is hardly anything in Scripture which can be proved contrary to natural reason, while, on the other hand, many things which before seemed obscure, will after a little consideration be understood and easily explained.

I think I have now very clearly explained all that I proposed to explain, but before I finish this chapter I would call attention to the fact that I have adopted a different method in speaking of miracles to that which I employed in treating of prophecy. Of prophecy I have asserted nothing which could not be inferred from promises revealed in Scripture, whereas in this chapter I have deduced my conclusions solely from the principles ascertained by the natural light of reason. I have proceeded in this way advisedly, for prophecy, in that it surpasses human knowledge, is a purely theological question; therefore, I knew that I could not make any assertions about it, nor learn wherein it consists, except through deductions from premises that have been revealed; therefore I was compelled to collate the history of prophecy, and to draw therefrom certain conclusions which would teach me, in so far as such teaching is possible, the nature and properties of the gift. But in the case of miracles, as our inquiry is a question purely philosophical (namely, whether anything can happen which contravenes or does not follow from the laws of nature), I was not under any such necessity: I therefore thought it wiser to unravel the difficulty through premises ascertained and thoroughly known by could also easily have solved the problem merely from the doctrines and fundamental principles of Scripture: in order that everyone may acknowledge this, I will briefly show how it could be done.

Scripture makes the general assertion in several passages that nature's course is fixed and unchangeable. In Ps. cxlviii:6, for instance, and Jer. xxxi:35. The wise man also, in Eccles. i:10, distinctly teaches that "there is nothing new under the sun," and in verses 11, 12, illustrating the same idea, he adds that although something occasionally happens which seems new, it is not really new, but "hath been already of old time, which was before us, whereof there is no remembrance, neither shall there be any remembrance of things that are to come with those that come after." Again in chap. iii:11, he says, "God hath made everything beautiful in his time," and immediately afterwards adds, "I know that whatsoever God doeth, it shall be for ever; nothing can be put to it, nor anything taken from it."

Now all these texts teach most distinctly that nature preserves a fixed and unchangeable order, and that God in all ages, known and unknown, has been the same; further, that the laws of nature are so perfect, that nothing can be added thereto nor taken therefrom; and, lastly, that miracles only appear as something new because of man's ignorance.

Such is the express teaching of Scripture: nowhere does Scripture assert that anything happens which contradicts, or cannot follow from the laws of nature; and, therefore, we should not attribute to it such a doctrine.

To these considerations we must add, that miracles require causes and attendant circumstances, and that they follow, not from some mysterious royal power which the masses attribute to God, but from the Divine rule and decree, that is (as we have shown from Scripture itself) from the laws and order of nature; lastly, that miracles can be wrought even by false prophets, as is proved from Deut. xiii. and Matt. xxiv:24.

The conclusion, then, that is most plainly put before us is, that miracles were natural occurrences, and must therefore be so explained as to appear neither new (in the words of Solomon) nor contrary to nature, but, as far as possible, in complete agreement with ordinary events. This can easily be done by anyone, now that I have set forth the rules drawn from Scripture. Nevertheless, though I maintain that Scripture teaches this doctrine, I do not assert that it teaches it as a truth necessary to salvation, but only that the prophets were in agreement with ourselves on the point; therefore everyone is free to think on the subject as he likes, according as he thinks it best for himself, and most likely to conduce to the worship of God and to singlehearted religion.

This is also the opinion of Josephus, for at the conclusion of the second book of his "Antiquities," he writes: Let no man think this story incredible of the sea's dividing to save these people, for we find it in ancient records that this hath been seen before, whether by God's extraordinary will or by the course of nature it is indifferent. The same thing happened one time to the Macedonians, under the command of Alexander, when for want of another passage the Pamphylian Sea divided to make them way; God's Providence making use of Alexander at that time as His instrument for destroying the Persian Empire. This is attested by all the historians who have pretended to write the Life of that Prince. But people are at liberty to think what they please."

Such are the words of Josephus, and such is his opinion on faith in miracles.

CHAPTER VII.

Of the Interpretation of Scripture

WHEN PEOPLE DECLARE, as all are ready, to do, that the Bible is the Word of God teaching man true blessedness and the way of salvation, they evidently do not mean what they, say; for the masses take no pains at all to live according to Scripture, and we see most people endeavouring to hawk about their own commentaries as the word of God, and giving their best efforts, under the guise of religion, to compelling others to think as they do: we generally see, I say, theologians anxious to learn how to wring their inventions and sayings out of the sacred text, and to fortify, them with Divine authority. Such persons never display, less scruple or more zeal than when they, are interpreting Scripture or the mind of the Holy Ghost; if we ever see them perturbed, it is not that they fear to attribute some error to the Holy Spirit, and to stray from the right path, but that they are afraid to be convicted of error by, others, and thus to overthrow and bring into contempt their own authority. But if men really believed what they verbally testify of Scripture, they would adopt quite a different plan of life: their minds would not be agitated by so many contentions, nor so many hatreds, and they would cease to be excited by such a blind and rash passion for interpreting the sacred writings, and excogitating novelties in religion. On the contrary, they would not dare to adopt, as the teaching of Scripture, anything which they could not plainly deduce therefrom: lastly, those sacrilegious persons who have dared, in several passages, to interpolate the Bible, would have shrunk from so great a crime, and would have stayed their sacrilegious hands.

Ambition and unscrupulousness have waxed so powerful, that religion is thought to consist, not so much in respecting the writings of the Holy Ghost, as in defending human commentaries, so that religion is no longer identified with charity, but with spreading discord and propagating insensate hatred disguised under the name of zeal for the Lord, and eager ardour.

To these evils we must add superstition, which teaches men to despise reason and nature, and only to admire and venerate that which is repugnant to both: whence it is not wonderful that for the sake of increasing the admiration and veneration felt for Scripture, men strive to explain it so as to make it appear to contradict, as far as possible, both one and the other: thus they dream that most profound mysteries lie hid in the Bible, and weary themselves out in the investigation of these absurdities, to the neglect of what is useful. Every result of their diseased imagination they attribute to the Holy Ghost, and strive to defend with the utmost zeal and passion; for it is an observed fact that men employ their reason to defend conclusions arrived at by reason, but conclusions arrived at by the passions are defended by the passions.

If we would separate ourselves from the crowd and escape from theological prejudices, instead of rashly accepting human commentaries for Divine documents, we must consider the true method of interpreting Scripture and dwell upon it at some length: for if we remain in ignorance of this we cannot know, certainly, what the Bible and the Holy Spirit wish to teach.

I may sum up the matter by saying that the method of interpreting Scripture does not widely differ from the method of interpreting nature — in fact, it is almost the same. For as the interpretation of nature consists in the examination of the history of nature, and therefrom deducing definitions of natural phenomena on certain fixed axioms, so Scriptural interpretation proceeds by the examination of Scripture, and inferring the intention of its authors as a legitimate conclusion from its fundamental principles. By working in this manner everyone will always advance without danger of error — that is, if they admit no principles for interpreting Scripture, and discussing its contents save such as they find in Scripture itself — and will be able with equal security to discuss what surpasses our understanding, and what is known by the natural light of reason.

In order to make clear that such a method is not only correct, but is also the only one advisable, and that it agrees with that employed in interpreting nature, I must remark that Scripture very often treats of matters which cannot be deduced from principles known to reason: for it is chiefly made up of narratives and revelation: the narratives generally contain miracles — that is, as we have shown in the last chapter, relations of extraordinary natural occurrences adapted to the opinions and judgment of the historians who recorded them: the revelations also were adapted to the opinions of the prophets, as we showed in Chap. II., and in themselves surpassed human comprehension. Therefore the knowledge of all these — that is, of nearly the whole contents of Scripture, must be sought from Scripture alone, even as the knowledge of nature is sought from nature. As for the moral doctrines which are also contained in the Bible, they may be demonstrated from received axioms, but we cannot prove in the same manner that Scripture intended to teach them, this can only be learned from Scripture itself.

If we would bear unprejudiced witness to the Divine origin of Scripture, we must prove solely on its own authority that it teaches true moral doctrines, for by such means alone can its Divine origin be demonstrated: we have shown that the certitude of the prophets depended chiefly on their having minds turned towards what is just and good, therefore we ought to have proof of their possessing this quality before we repose faith in them. From miracles God's divinity cannot be proved, as I have already shown, and need not now repeat, for miracles could be wrought by false prophets. Wherefore the Divine origin of Scripture must consist solely in its teaching true virtue. But we must come to our conclusion simply on Scriptural grounds, for if we were unable to do so we could not, unless strongly prejudiced accept the Bible and bear witness to its Divine origin.

Our knowledge of Scripture must then be looked for in Scripture only.

Lastly, Scripture does not give us definition of things any more than nature does: therefore, such definitions must be sought in the latter case from the diverse workings of nature; in the former case, from the various narratives about the given subject which occur in the Bible.

The universal rule, then, in interpreting Scripture is to accept nothing as an authoritative Scriptural statement which we do not perceive very clearly when we examine it in the light of its history. What I mean by its history, and what should be the chief points elucidated, I will now explain.

The history of a Scriptural statement comprises —

I. The nature and properties of the language in which the books of the Bible were written, and in which their authors were, accustomed to speak. We shall thus be able to investigate every expression by comparison with common conversational usages.

Now all the writers both of the Old Testament and the New were Hebrews: therefore, a knowledge of the Hebrew language is before all things necessary, not only for the comprehension of the Old Testament, which was written in that tongue, but also of the New: for although the latter was published in other languages, yet its characteristics are Hebrew.

II. An analysis of each book and arrangement of its contents under heads; so that we may have at hand the various texts which treat of a given subject. Lastly, a note of all the passages which are ambiguous or obscure, or which seem mutually contradictory.

I call passages clear or obscure according as their meaning is inferred easily or with difficulty in relation to the context, not according as their truth is perceived easily or the reverse by reason. We are at work not on the truth of passages, but solely on their meaning. We must take especial care, when we are in search of the meaning of a text, not to be led away by our reason in so far as it is founded on principles of natural knowledge (to say nothing of prejudices): in order not to confound the meaning of a passage with its truth, we must examine it solely by means of the signification of the words, or by a reason acknowledging no foundation but Scripture.

I will illustrate my meaning by an example. The words of Moses, "God is a fire" and "God is jealous," are perfectly clear so long as we regard merely the signification of the words, and I therefore reckon them

among the clear passages, though in relation to reason and truth they are most obscure: still, although the literal meaning is repugnant to the natural light of reason, nevertheless, if it cannot be clearly overruled on grounds and principles derived from its Scriptural "history," it, that is, the literal meaning, must be the one retained: and contrariwise if these passages literally interpreted are found to clash with principles derived from Scripture, though such literal interpretation were in absolute harmony with reason, they must be interpreted in a different manner, i.e. metaphorically.

If we would know whether Moses believed God to be a fire or not, we must on no account decide the question on grounds of the reasonableness or the reverse of such an opinion, but must judge solely by the other opinions of Moses which are on record.

In the present instance, as Moses says in several other passages that God has no likeness to any visible thing, whether in heaven or in earth, or in the water, either all such passages must be taken metaphorically, or else the one before us must be so explained. However, as we should depart as little as possible from the literal sense, we must first ask whether this text, God is a fire, admits of any but the literal meaning — that is, whether the word fire ever means anything besides ordinary natural fire. If no such second meaning can be found, the text must be taken literally, however repugnant to reason it may be: and all the other passages, though in complete accordance with reason, must be brought into harmony with it. If the verbal expressions would not admit of being thus harmonized, we should have to set them down as irreconcilable, and suspend our judgment concerning them. However, as we find the name fire applied to anger and jealousy (see Job xxxi:12) we can thus easily reconcile the words of Moses, and legitimately conclude that the two propositions God is a fire, and God is jealous, are in meaning identical.

Further, as Moses clearly teaches that God is jealous, and nowhere states that God is without passions or emotions, we must evidently infer that Moses held this doctrine himself, or at any rate, that he wished to teach it, nor must we refrain because such a belief seems contrary to reason: for as we have shown, we cannot wrest the meaning of texts to suit the dictates of our reason, or our preconceived opinions. The whole knowledge of the Bible must be sought solely from itself.

III. Lastly, such a history should relate the environment of all the prophetic books extant; that is, the life, the conduct, and the studies of the author of each book, who he was, what was the occasion, and the epoch of his writing, whom did he write for, and in what language. Further, it should inquire into the fate of each book: how it was first received, into whose hands it fell, how many different versions there were of it, by whose advice was it received into the Bible, and, lastly, how all the books now universally accepted as sacred, were united into a single whole.

All such information should, as I have said, be contained in the "history" of Scripture. For, in order to know what statements are set forth as laws, and what as moral precepts, it is important to be acquainted with the life, the conduct, and the pursuits of their author: moreover, it becomes easier to explain a man's writings in proportion as we have more intimate knowledge of his genius and temperament.

Further, that we may not confound precepts which are eternal with those which served only a temporary purpose, or were only meant for a few, we should know what was the occasion, the time, the age, in which each book was written, and to what nation it was addressed.Lastly, we should have knowledge on the other points I have mentioned, in order to be sure, in addition to the authenticity of the work, that it has not been tampered with by sacrilegious hands, or whether errors can have crept in, and, if so, whether they have been corrected by men sufficiently skilled and worthy of credence. All these things should be known, that we may not be led away by blind impulse to accept whatever is thrust on our notice, instead of only that which is sure and indisputable.

Now when we are in possession of this history of Scripture, and have finally decided that we assert nothing as prophetic doctrine which does not directly follow from such history, or which is not clearly deducible from it, then, I say, it will be time to gird ourselves for the task of investigating the mind of the prophets and of the Holy Spirit. But in this further arguing, also, we shall require a method very like that employed in interpreting nature from her history. As in the examination of natural phenomena we try first to investigate what is most universal and common to all nature — such, for instance, as motion and rest, and their laws and rules, which nature always observes, and through which she continually works — and then we proceed to what is less universal; so, too, in the history of Scripture, we seek first for that which is most universal, and serves for the basis and foundation of all Scripture, a doctrine, in fact, that is commended by all the prophets as eternal and most profitable to all men. For example, that God is one, and that He is omnipotent, that He alone should be worshipped, that He has a care for all men, and that He especially loves those who adore Him and love their neighbour as themselves, &c. These and similar doctrines, I repeat, Scripture everywhere so clearly and expressly teaches, that no one was ever in doubt of its meaning concerning them.

The nature of God, His manner of regarding and providing for things, and similar doctrines, Scripture nowhere teaches professedly, and as eternal doctrine; on the contrary, we have shown that the prophets themselves did not agree on the subject;

therefore, we must not lay down any doctrine as Scriptural on such subjects, though it may appear perfectly clear on rational grounds.

From a proper knowledge of this universal doctrine of Scripture, we must then proceed to other doctrines less universal, but which, nevertheless, have regard to the general conduct of life, and flow from the universal doctrine like rivulets from a source; such are all particular external manifestations of true virtue, which need a given occasion for their exercise; whatever is obscure or ambiguous on such points in Scripture must be explained and defined by its universal doctrine; with regard to contradictory instances, we must observe the occasion and the time in which they were written. For instance, when Christ says, "Blessed are they that mourn, for they shall be comforted" we do not know, from the actual passage, what sort of mourners are meant; as, however, Christ afterwards teaches that we should have care for nothing, save only for the kingdom of God and His righteousness, which is commended as the highest good (see Matt. vi;33), it follows that by mourners He only meant those who mourn for the kingdom of God and righteousness neglected by man: for this would be the only cause of mourning to those who love nothing but the Divine kingdom and justice, and who evidently despise the gifts of fortune. So, too, when Christ says: "But if a man strike you on the right cheek, turn to him the left also," and the words which follow.

If He had given such a command, as a lawgiver, to judges, He would thereby have abrogated the law of Moses, but this He expressly says He did not do (Matt. v:17). Wherefore we must consider who was the speaker, what was the occasion, and to whom were the words addressed. Now Christ said that He did not ordain laws as a legislator, but inculcated precepts as a teacher: inasmuch as He did not aim at correcting outward actions so much as the frame of mind. Further, these words were spoken to men who were oppressed, who lived in a corrupt commonwealth on the brink of ruin, where justice was utterly neglected. The very doctrine inculcated here by Christ just before the destruction of the city was also taught by Jeremiah before the first destruction of Jerusalem, that is, in similar circumstances, as we see from Lamentations iii:25-30.

Now as such teaching was only set forth by the prophets in times of oppression, and was even then never laid down as a law; and as, on the other hand, Moses (who did not write in times of oppression, but — mark this — strove to found a well-ordered commonwealth), while condemning envy and hatred of one's neighbour, yet ordained that an eye should be given for an eye, it follows most clearly from these purely Scriptural grounds that this precept of Christ and Jeremiah concerning submission to injuries was only valid in places where justice is neglected, and in a time of oppression, but does not hold good in a well-ordered state.

In a well-ordered state where justice is administered every one is bound, if he would be accounted just, to demand penalties before the judge (see Lev:1), not for the sake of vengeance (Lev. xix:17, 18), but in order to defend justice and his country's laws, and to prevent the wicked rejoicing in their wickedness. All this is plainly in accordance with reason. I might cite many other examples in the same manner, but I think the foregoing are sufficient to explain my meaning and the utility of this method, and this is all my present purpose. Hitherto we have only shown how to investigate those passages of Scripture which treat of practical conduct, and which, therefore, are more easily examined, for on such subjects there was never really any controversy among the writers of the Bible.

The purely speculative passages cannot be so easily, traced to their real meaning:

the way becomes narrower, for as the prophets differed in matters speculative among themselves, and the narratives are in great measure adapted to the prejudices of each age, we must not, on any, account infer the intention of one prophet from clearer passages in the writings of another; nor must we so explain his meaning, unless it is perfectly plain that the two prophets were at one in the matter.

How we are to arrive at the intention of the prophets in such cases I will briefly explain. Here, too, we must begin from the most universal proposition, inquiring first from the most clear Scriptural statements what is the nature of prophecy or revelation, and wherein does it consist; then we must proceed to miracles, and so on to whatever is most general till we come to the opinions of a particular prophet, and, at last, to the meaning of a particular revelation, prophecy, history, or miracle. We have already pointed out that great caution is necessary not to confound the mind of a prophet or historian with the mind of the Holy Spirit and the truth of the matter; therefore I need not dwell further on the subject. I would, however, here remark concerning the meaning of revelation, that the present method only teaches us what the prophets really saw or heard, not what they desired to signify or represent by symbols. The latter may be guessed at but cannot be inferred with certainty from Scriptural premises.

We have thus shown the plan for interpreting Scripture, and have, at the same time, demonstrated that it is the one and surest way of investigating its true meaning. I am willing indeed to admit that those persons (if any such there be) would be more absolutely certainly right, who have received either a trustworthy tradition or an assurance from the prophets themselves, such as is claimed by the Pharisees; or who have a pontiff gifted with infallibility in the interpretation of Scripture, such as the Roman Catholics boast. But as we can never be perfectly sure, either of such a tradition or of the authority of the pontiff, we cannot found any certain conclusion on either: the one is denied by the oldest sect of Christians, the other by the oldest sect of Jews. Indeed, if we consider the series of years (to mention no other point) accepted by the Pharisees from their Rabbis, during which time they say they have handed down the tradition from Moses, we shall find that it is not correct, as I show elsewhere. Therefore such a tradition should be received with extreme suspicion; and although, according to our method, we are bound to consider as uncorrupted the tradition of the Jews, namely, the meaning of the Hebrew words which we received from them, we may accept the latter while retaining our doubts about the former.

No one has ever been able to change the meaning of a word in ordinary use, though many have changed the meaning of a particular sentence. Such a proceeding would be most difficult; for whoever attempted to change the meaning of a word, would be compelled, at the same time, to explain all the authors who employed it, each according to his temperament and intention, or else, with consummate cunning, to falsify them.

Further, the masses and the learned alike preserve language, but it is only the learned who preserve the meaning of particular sentences and books: thus, we may easily imagine that the learned having a very rare book in their power, might change or corrupt the meaning of a sentence in it, but they could not alter the signification of the words; moreover, if anyone wanted to change the meaning of a common word he would not be able to keep up the change among posterity, or in common parlance or writing.

For these and such-like reasons we may readily conclude that it would never enter into the mind of anyone to corrupt a language, though the intention of a writer may often have been falsified by changing his phrases or interpreting them amiss. As then our method (based on the principle that the knowledge of Scripture must be sought from itself alone) is the sole true one, we must evidently renounce any knowledge which it cannot furnish for the complete understanding of Scripture. I will now point out its difficulties and shortcomings, which prevent our gaining a complete and assured knowledge of the Sacred Text.

Its first great difficulty consists in its requiring a thorough knowledge of the Hebrew language. Where is such knowledge to be obtained? The men of old who employed the Hebrew tongue have left none of the principles and bases of their language to posterity; we have from them absolutely nothing in the way of dictionary, grammar, or rhetoric.

Now the Hebrew nation has lost all its grace and beauty (as one would expect after the defeats and persecutions it has gone through), and has only retained certain fragments of its language and of a few books. Nearly all the names of fruits, birds, and fishes, and many other words have perished in the wear and tear of time. Further, the meaning of many nouns and verbs which occur in the Bible are either utterly lost, or are subjects of dispute. And not only are these gone, but we are lacking in a knowledge of Hebrew phraseology. The devouring tooth of time has destroyed turns of expression peculiar to the Hebrews, so that we know them no more.

Therefore we cannot investigate as we would all the meanings of a sentence by the uses of the language; and there are many phrases of which the meaning is most obscure or altogether inexplicable, though the component words are perfectly plain.

To this impossibility of tracing the history of the Hebrew language must be added its particular nature and composition: these give rise to so many ambiguities that it is impossible to find a method which would enable us to gain a certain knowledge of all the statements in Scripture 7. In addition to the sources of ambiguities common to all languages, there are many peculiar to Hebrew. These, I think, it worth while to mention.

Firstly, an ambiguity often arises in the Bible from our mistaking one letter for another similar one. The Hebrews divide the letters of the alphabet into five classes, according to the five organs of the month employed in pronouncing them, namely, the lips, the tongue, the teeth, the palate, and the throat. For instance, Alpha, Ghet, Hgain, He, are called gutturals, and are barely distinguishable, by any sign that we know, one from the other. El, which signifies to, is often taken for hgal, which signifies above, and vice versa. Hence sentences are often rendered rather ambiguous or meaningless.

A second difficulty arises from the multiplied meaning of conjunctions and adverbs. For instance, vau serves promiscuously for a particle of union or of separation, meaning, and, but, because, however, then: ki, has seven or eight meanings, namely, wherefore, although, if, when, inasmuch as, because, a burning, &c., and so on with almost all particles.

The third very fertile source of doubt is the fact that Hebrew verbs in the indicative mood lack the present, the past imperfect, the pluperfect, the future perfect, and other tenses most frequently employed in other languages; in the imperative and infinitive moods they are wanting in all except the present, and a subjunctive mood does not exist. Now, although all these defects in moods and tenses may be supplied by certain fundamental rules of the language with ease and even elegance, the ancient writers evidently neglected such rules altogether, and employed indifferently future for present and past, and vice versa past for future, and also indicative for imperative and subjunctive, with the result of considerable confusion.

Besides these sources of ambiguity there are two others, one very important. Firstly, there are in Hebrew no vowels; secondly, the sentences are not separated by any marks elucidating the meaning or separating the clauses. Though the want of these two has generally been supplied by points and accents, such substitutes cannot be accepted by us, inasmuch as they were invented and designed by men of an after age whose authority should carry no weight. The ancients wrote without points (that is, without vowels and accents), as is abundantly testified; their descendants added what was lacking, according to their own ideas of Scriptural interpretation; wherefore the existing accents and points are simply current interpretations, and are no more authoritative than any other commentaries.

Those who are ignorant of this fact cannot justify the author of the Epistle to the Hebrews for interpreting (chap. xi;21) Genesis (xlvii:31) very differently from the version given in our Hebrew text as at present pointed, as though the Apostle had been obliged to learn the meaning of Scripture from those who added the points. In my opinion the latter are clearly wrong. In order that everyone may judge for himself, and also see how the discrepancy arose simply from the want of vowels, I will give both interpretations. Those who pointed our version read, "And Israel bent himself over, or (changing Hqain into Aleph, a similar letter) towards, the head of the bed." The author of the Epistle reads, "And Israel bent himself over the head of his staff," substituting mate for mita, from which it only differs in respect of vowels. Now as in this narrative it is Jacob's age only that is in question, and not his illness, which is not touched on till the next chapter, it seems more likely that the historian intended to say that Jacob bent over the head of his staff (a thing commonly used by men of advanced age for their support) than that he bowed himself at the head of his bed, especially as for the former reading no substitution of letters is required. In this example I have desired not only to reconcile the passage in the Epistle with the passage in Genesis, but also and chiefly to illustrate how little trust should be placed in the points and accents which are found in our present Bible, and so to prove that he who would be without bias in interpreting Scripture should hesitate about accepting them, and inquire afresh for himself. Such being the nature and structure of the Hebrew language, one may easily understand that many difficulties are likely to arise, and that no possible method could solve all of them. It is useless to hope for a way out of our difficulties in the comparison of various parallel passages (we have shown that the only method of discovering the true sense of a passage out of many alternative ones is to see what are the usages of the language), for this comparison of parallel passages can only accidentally throw light on a difficult point, seeing that the prophets never wrote with the express object of explaining their own phrases or those of other people, and also because we cannot infer the meaning of one prophet or apostle by the meaning of another, unless on a purely practical question, not when the matter is speculative, or if a miracle, or history is being narrated. I might illustrate my point with instances, for there are many inexplicable phrases in Scripture, but I would rather pass on to consider the difficulties and imperfections of the method under discussion.

A further difficulty attends the method, from the fact that it requires the history of all that has happened to every book in the Bible; such a history we are often quite unable to furnish. Of the authors, or (if the expression be preferred), the writers of many of the books, we are either in complete ignorance, or at any rate in doubt, as I will point out at length. Further, we do not know either the occasions or the epochs when these books of unknown authorship were written; we cannot say into what hands they fell, nor how the numerous varying versions originated; nor, lastly, whether there were not other versions, now lost. I have briefly shown that such knowledge is necessary, but I passed over certain considerations which I will now draw attention to.

If we read a book which contains incredible or impossible narratives, or is written in a very obscure style, and if we know nothing of its author, nor of the time or occasion of its being written, we shall vainly endeavour to gain any certain knowledge of its true meaning. For being in ignorance on these points we cannot possibly know the aim or intended aim of the author; if we are fully informed, we so order our thoughts as not to be in any way prejudiced either in ascribing to the author or him for whom the author wrote either more or less than his meaning, and we only take into consideration what the author may have had in his mind, or what the time and occasion demanded. I think this must be tolerably evident to all.

It often happens that in different books we read histories in themselves similar, but which we judge very differently, according to the opinions we have formed of the authors. I remember once to have read in some book that a man named Orlando Furioso used to drive a kind of winged monster through the air, fly over any countries he liked, kill unaided vast numbers of men and giants, and such like fancies, which from the point of view of reason are obviously absurd. A very similar story I read in Ovid of Perseus, and also in the books of Judges and Kings of Samson, who alone and unarmed killed thousands of men, and of Elijah, who flew through the air, said at last went up to heaven in a chariot of fire, with horses of fire. All these stories are obviously alike, but we judge them very differently. The first only sought to amuse, the second had a political object, the third a religious object. We gather this simply from the opinions we had previously formed of the authors. Thus it is evidently necessary to know something of the authors of writings which are obscure or unintelligible, if we would interpret their meaning; and for the same reason, in order to choose the proper reading from among a great variety, we ought to have information as to the versions in which the differences are found, and as to the possibility of other readings having been discovered by persons of greater authority.

A further difficulty attends this method in the case of some of the books of Scripture, namely, that they are no longer extant in their original language. The Gospel according to Matthew, and certainly the Epistle to the Hebrews, were written, it is thought, in Hebrew, though they no longer exist in that form. Aben Ezra affirms in his commentaries that the book of Job was translated into Hebrew out of another language, and that its obscurity arises from this fact. I say nothing of the apocryphal books, for their authority stands on very inferior ground.

The foregoing difficulties in this method of interpreting Scripture from its own history, I conceive to be so great that I do not hesitate to say that the true meaning of Scripture is in many places inexplicable, or at best mere subject for guesswork; but I must again point out, on the other hand, that such difficulties only arise when we endeavour to follow the meaning of a prophet in matters which cannot be perceived, but only imagined, not in things, whereof the understanding can give a clear idea, and which are conceivable through themselves:, 8, matters which by their nature are easily perceived cannot be expressed so obscurely as to be unintelligible; as the proverb says, "a word is enough to the wise." Euclid, who only wrote of matters very simple and easily understood, can easily be comprehended by anyone in any language; we can follow his intention perfectly, and be certain of his true meaning, without having a thorough knowledge of the language in which he wrote; in fact, a quite rudimentary acquaintance is sufficient. We need make no researches concerning the life, the pursuits, or the habits of the author; nor need we inquire in what language, nor when he wrote, nor the vicissitudes of his book, nor its various readings, nor how, nor by whose advice it has been received.

What we here say of Euclid might equally be said of any book which treats of things by their nature perceptible: thus we conclude that we can easily follow the intention of Scripture in moral questions, from the history we possess of it, and we can be sure of its true meaning.

The precepts of true piety are expressed in very ordinary language, and are equally simple and easily understood. Further, as true salvation and blessedness consist in a true assent of the soul — and we truly assent only to what we clearly understand — it is most plain that we can follow with certainty the intention of Scripture in matters relating to salvation and necessary to blessedness; therefore, we need not be much troubled about what remains: such matters, inasmuch as we generally cannot grasp them with our reason and understanding, are more curious than profitable.

I think I have now set forth the true method of Scriptural interpretation, and have sufficiently explained my own opinion thereon. Besides, I do not doubt that everyone will see that such a method only requires the aid of natural reason. The nature and efficacy of the natural reason consists in deducing and proving the unknown from the known, or in carrying premises to their legitimate conclusions; and these are the very processes which our method desiderates. Though we must admit that it does not suffice to explain everything in the Bible, such imperfection does not spring from its own nature, but from the fact that the path which it teaches us, as the true one, has never been tended or trodden by men, and has thus, by the lapse of time, become very difficult, and almost impassable, as, indeed, I have shown in the difficulties I draw attention to.

There only remains to examine the opinions of those who differ from me. The first which comes under our notice is, that the light of nature has no power to interpret Scripture, but that a supernatural faculty is required for the task. What is meant by this supernatural faculty I will leave to its propounders to explain. Personally, I can only suppose that they have adopted a very obscure way of stating their complete uncertainty about the true meaning of Scripture. If we look at their interpretations, they contain nothing supernatural, at least nothing but the merest conjectures.

Let them be placed side by side with the interpretations of those who frankly confess that they have no faculty beyond their natural ones; we shall see that the two are just alike — both human, both long pondered over, both laboriously invented. To say that the natural reason is insufficient for such results is plainly untrue, firstly, for the reasons above stated, namely, that the difficulty of interpreting Scripture arises from no defect in human reason, but simply from the carelessness (not to say malice) of men who neglected the history of the Bible while there were still materials for inquiry; secondly, from the fact (admitted, I think, by all) that the supernatural faculty is a Divine gift granted only to the faithful. But the prophets and apostles did not preach to the faithful only, but chiefly to the unfaithful and wicked. Such persons, therefore, were able to understand the intention of the prophets and apostles, otherwise the prophets and apostles would have seemed to be preaching to little boys and infants, not to men endowed with reason. Moses, too, would have given his laws in vain, if they could only be comprehended by the faithful, who need no law. Indeed, those who demand supernatural faculties for comprehending the meaning of the prophets and apostles seem truly lacking in natural faculties, so that we should hardly suppose such persons the possessors of a Divine supernatural gift.

The opinion of Maimonides was widely different. He asserted that each passage in Scripture admits of various, nay, contrary, meanings; but that we could never be certain of any particular one till we knew that the passage, as we interpreted it, contained nothing contrary or repugnant to reason. If the literal meaning clashes with reason, though the passage seems in itself perfectly clear, it must be interpreted in some metaphorical sense. This doctrine he lays down very plainly in chap. xxv. part ii. of his book, "More Nebuchim," for he says: "Know that we shrink not from affirming that the world hath existed from eternity, because of what Scripture saith concerning the world's creation. For the texts which teach that the world was created are not more in number than those which teach that God hath a body; neither are the approaches in this matter of the world's creation closed, or even made hard to us: so that we should not be able to explain what is written, as we did when we showed that God hath no body, nay, peradventure, we could explain and make fast the doctrine of the world's eternity more easily than we did away with the doctrines that God hath a beatified body. Yet two things hinder me from doing as I have said, and believing that the world is eternal. As it hath been clearly shown that God hath not a body, we must perforce explain all those passages whereof the literal sense agreeth not with the demonstration, for sure it is that they can be so explained. But the eternity of the world hath not been so demonstrated, therefore it is not necessary to do violence to Scripture in support of some common opinion, whereof we might, at the bidding of reason, embrace the contrary."

Such are the words of Maimonides, and they are evidently sufficient to establish our point: for if he had been convinced by reason that the world is eternal, he would not have hesitated to twist and explain away the words of Scripture till he made them appear to teach this doctrine. He would have felt quite sure that Scripture, though everywhere plainly denying the eternity of the world, really intends to teach it. So that, however clear the meaning of Scripture may be, he would not feel certain of having grasped it, so long as he remained doubtful of the truth of what, was written. For we are in doubt whether a thing is in conformity with reason, or contrary thereto, so long as we are uncertain of its truth, and, consequently, we cannot be sure whether the literal meaning of a passage be true or false.

If such a theory as this were sound, I would certainly grant that some faculty beyond the natural reason is required for interpreting Scripture. For nearly all things that we find in Scripture cannot be inferred from known principles of the natural reason, and, therefore, we should be unable to come to any conclusion about their truth, or about the real meaning and intention of Scripture, but should stand in need of some further assistance.

Further, the truth of this theory would involve that the masses, having generally no comprehension of, nor leisure for, detailed proofs, would be reduced to receiving all their knowledge of Scripture on the authority and testimony of philosophers, and, consequently, would be compelled to suppose that the interpretations given by philosophers were infallible.

Truly this would be a new form of ecclesiastical authority, and a new sort of priests or pontiffs, more likely to excite men's ridicule than their veneration. Certainly our method demands a knowledge of Hebrew for which the masses have no leisure; but no such objection as the foregoing can be brought against us. For the ordinary Jews or Gentiles, to whom the prophets and apostles preached and wrote, understood the language, and, consequently, the intention of the prophet or apostle addressing them; but they did not grasp the intrinsic reason of what was preached, which, according to Maimonides, would be necessary for an understanding of it.

There is nothing, then, in our method which renders it necessary that the masses should follow the testimony of commentators, for I point to a set of unlearned people who understood the language of the prophets and apostles; whereas Maimonides could not point to any such who could arrive at the prophetic or apostolic meaning through their knowledge of the causes of things.

As to the multitude of our own time, we have shown that whatsoever is necessary to salvation, though its reasons may be unknown, can easily be understood in any language, because it is thoroughly ordinary and usual; it is in such understanding as this that the masses acquiesce, not in the testimony of commentators; with regard to other questions, the ignorant and the learned fare alike.

But let us return to the opinion of Maimonides, and examine it more closely. In the first place, he supposes that the prophets were in entire agreement one with another, and that they were consummate philosophers and theologians; for he would have them to have based their conclusions on the absolute truth. Further, he supposes that the sense of Scripture cannot be made plain from Scripture itself, for the truth of things is not made plain therein (in that it does not prove any thing, nor teach the matters of which it speaks through their definitions and first causes), therefore, according to Maimonides, the true sense of Scripture cannot be made plain from itself, and must not be there sought.

The falsity of such a doctrine is shown in this very chapter, for we have shown both by reason and examples that the meaning of Scripture is only made plain through Scripture itself, and even in questions deducible from ordinary knowledge should be looked for from no other source.

Lastly, such a theory supposes that we may explain the words of Scripture according to our preconceived opinions, twisting them about, and reversing or completely changing the literal sense, however plain it may be. Such licence is utterly opposed to the teaching of this and the preceding chapters, and, moreover, will be evident to everyone as rash and excessive.

But if we grant all this licence, what can it effect after all? Absolutely nothing. Those things which cannot be demonstrated, and which make up the greater part of Scripture, cannot be examined by reason, and cannot therefore be explained or interpreted by this rule; whereas, on the contrary, by following our own method, we can explain many questions of this nature, and discuss them on a sure basis, as we have already shown, by reason and example. Those matters which are by their nature comprehensible we can easily explain, as has been pointed out, simply by means of the context.

Therefore, the method of Maimonides is clearly useless: to which we may add, that it does away with all the certainty which the masses acquire by candid reading, or which is gained by any other persons in any other way. In conclusion, then, we dismiss Maimonides' theory as harmful, useless, and absurd.

As to the tradition of the Pharisees, we have already shown that it is not consistent, while the authority of the popes of Rome stands in need of more credible evidence; the latter, indeed, I reject simply on this ground, for if the popes could point out to us the meaning of Scripture as surely as did the high priests of the Jews, I should not be deterred by the fact that there have been heretic and impious Roman pontiffs; for among the Hebrew high-priests of old there were also heretics and impious men who gained the high — priesthood by improper means, but who, nevertheless, had Scriptural sanction for their supreme power of interpreting the law. (See Deut. xvii:11, 12, and xxxiii:10, also Malachi ii:8.)

However, as the popes can show no such sanction, their authority remains open to very grave doubt, nor should anyone be deceived by the example of the Jewish high-priests and think that the Catholic religion also stands in need of a pontiff; he should bear in mind that the laws of Moses being also the ordinary laws of the country, necessarily required some public authority to insure their observance; for, if everyone were free to interpret the laws of his country as he pleased, no state could stand, but would for that very reason be dissolved at once, and public rights would become private rights.

With religion the case is widely different. Inasmuch as it consists not so much in outward actions as in simplicity and truth of character, it stands outside the sphere of law and public authority. Simplicity and truth of character are not produced by the constraint of laws, nor by the authority of the state, no one the whole world over can be forced or legislated into a state of blessedness; the means required for such a consummation are faithful and brotherly admonition, sound education, and, above all, free use of the individual judgment.

Therefore, as the supreme right of free thinking, even on religion, is in every man's power, and as it is inconceivable that such power could be alienated, it is also in every man's power to wield the supreme right and authority of free judgment in this behalf, and to explain and interpret religion for himself. The only reason for vesting the supreme authority in the interpretation of law, and judgment on public affairs in the hands of the magistrates, is that it concerns questions of public right. Similarly the supreme authority in explaining religion, and in passing judgment thereon, is lodged with the individual because it concerns questions of individual right. So far, then, from the authority of the Hebrew high-priests telling in confirmation of the authority of the Roman pontiffs to interpret religion, it would rather tend to establish individual freedom of judgment. Thus in this way also, we have shown that our method of interpreting Scripture is the best. For as the highest power of Scriptural interpretation belongs to every man, the rule for such interpretation should be nothing but the natural light of reason which is common to all — not any supernatural light nor any external authority; moreover, such a rule ought not to be so difficult that it can only be applied by very skilful philosophers, but should be adapted to the natural and ordinary faculties and capacity of mankind. And such I have shown our method to be, for such difficulties as it has arise from men's carelessness, and are no part of its nature.

7 "It is impossible to find a method which would enable us to gain a certain knowledge of all the statements in Scripture." I mean impossible for us who have

not the habitual use of the language, and have lost the precise meaning of its phraseology.

8 "Not in things whereof the understanding can gain a clear and distinct idea, and which are conceivable through themselves." By things conceivable I mean not only those which are rigidly proved, but also those whereof we are morally certain, and are wont to hear without wonder, though they are incapable of proof. Everyone can see the truth of Euclid's propositions before they are proved. So also the histories of things both future and past which do not surpass human credence, laws, institutions, manners, I call conceivable and clear, though they cannot be proved mathematically. But hieroglyphics and histories which seem to pass the bounds of belief I call inconceivable; yet even among these last there are many which our method enables us to investigate, and to discover the meaning of their narrator.

CHAPTER VIII.

Of the Authorship of the Pentateuch and
the Other Historical Books of the Old Testament

IN THE FORMER chapter we treated of the foundations and principles of Scriptural knowledge, and showed that it consists solely in a trustworthy history of the sacred writings; such a history, in spite of its indispensability, the ancients neglected, or at any rate, whatever they may have written or handed down has perished in the lapse of time, consequently the groundwork for such an investigation is to a great extent, cut from under us. This might be put up with if succeeding generations had confined themselves within the limits of truth, and had handed down conscientiously what few particulars they had received or discovered without any additions from their own brains: as it is, the history of the Bible is not so much imperfect as untrustworthy: the foundations are not only too scanty for building upon, but are also unsound. It is part of my purpose to remedy these defects, and to remove common theological prejudices. But I fear that I am attempting my task too late, for men have arrived at the pitch of not suffering contradiction, but defending obstinately whatever they have adopted under the name of religion. So widely have these prejudices taken possession of men's minds, that very few, comparatively speaking, will listen to reason. However, I will make the attempt, and spare no efforts, for there is no positive reason for despairing of success.

In order to treat the subject methodically, I will begin with the received opinions concerning the true authors of the sacred books, and in the first place, speak of the author of the Pentateuch, who is almost universally supposed to have been Moses. The Pharisees are so firmly convinced of his identity, that they account as a heretic anyone who differs from them on the subject. Wherefore, Aben Ezra, a man of enlightened intelligence, and no small learning, who was the first, so far as I know, to treat of this opinion, dared not express his meaning openly, but confined himself to dark hints which I shall not scruple to elucidate, thus throwing, full light on the subject.

The words of Aben Ezra which occur in his commentary on Deuteronomy are as follows: "Beyond Jordan, &c . . . If so be that thou understandest the mystery of the twelve . . . moreover Moses wrote the law . . . The Canaanite was then in the land . . . . it shall be revealed on the mount of God . . . . then also behold his bed, his iron bed, then shalt thou know the truth." In these few words he hints, and also shows that it was not Moses who wrote the Pentateuch, but someone who lived long after him, and further, that the book which Moses wrote was something different from any now extant.

To prove this, I say, he draws attention to the facts:

I. That the preface to Deuteronomy could not have been written by Moses, inasmuch as he ad never crossed the Jordan.

II. That the whole book of Moses was written at full length on the circumference of a single altar (Deut. xxvii, and Josh. viii:37), which altar, according to the Rabbis, consisted of only twelve stones: therefore the book of Moses must have been of far less extent than the Pentateuch. This is what our author means, I think, by the mystery of the twelve, unless he is referring to the twelve curses contained in the chapter of Deuteronomy above cited, which he thought could not have been contained in the law, because Moses bade the Levites read them after the recital of the law, and so bind the people to its observance. Or again, he may have had in his mind the last chapter of Deuteronomy which treats of the death of Moses, and which contains twelve verses. But there is no need to dwell further on these and similar conjectures.

III. That in Deut. xxxi:9, the expression occurs, "and Moses wrote the law:" words that cannot be ascribed to Moses, but must be those of some other writer narrating the deeds and writings of Moses.

IV. That in Genesis xii:6, the historian, after narrating that Abraham journeyed through the and of Canaan, adds, "and the Canaanite was then in the land," thus clearly excluding the time at which he wrote. So that this passage must have been written after the death of Moses, when the Canaanites had been driven out, and no longer possessed the land.

Aben Ezra, in his commentary on the passage, alludes to the difficulty as follows:— "And the Canaanite was then in the land: it appears that Canaan, the grandson of Noah, took from another the land which bears his name; if this be not the true meaning, there lurks some mystery in the passage, and let him who understands it keep silence." That is, if Canaan invaded those regions, the sense will be, the Canaanite was then in the land, in contradistinction to the time when it had been held by another: but if, as follows from Gen. chap. x. Canaan was the first to inhabit the land, the text must mean to exclude the time present, that is the time at which it was written; therefore it cannot be the work of Moses, in whose time the Canaanites still possessed those territories: this is the mystery concerning which silence is recommended.

V. That in Genesis xxii:14 Mount Moriah is called the mount of God, 9, a name which it did not acquire till after the building of the Temple; the choice of the mountain was not made in the time of Moses, for Moses does not point out any spot as chosen by God; on the contrary, he foretells that God will at some future time choose a spot to which this name will be given.

VI. Lastly, that in Deut. chap. iii., in the passage relating to Og, king of Bashan, these words are inserted: "For only Og king of Bashan remained of the remnant of giants: behold, his bedstead was a bedstead of iron: is it not in Rabbath of the children of Ammon? nine cubits was the length thereof, and four cubits the breadth of it, after the cubit of a man." This parenthesis most plainly shows that its writer lived long after Moses; for this mode of speaking is only employed by one treating of things long past, and pointing to relics for the sake of gaining credence: moreover, this bed was almost certainly first discovered by David, who conquered the city of Rabbath (2 Sam. xii:30.) Again, the historian a little further on inserts after the words of Moses, "Jair, the son of Manasseh, took all the country of Argob unto the coasts of Geshuri and Maachathi; and called them after his own name, Bashan-havoth-jair, unto this day." This passage, I say, is inserted to explain the words of Moses which precede it. "And the rest of Gilead, and all Bashan, being the kingdom of Og, gave I unto the half tribe of Manasseh; all the region of Argob, with all Bashan, which is called the land of the giants." The Hebrews in the time of the writer indisputably knew what territories belonged to the tribe of Judah, but did not know them under the name of the jurisdiction of Argob, or the land of the giants. Therefore the writer is compelled to explain what these places were which were anciently so styled, and at the same time to point out why they were at the time of his writing known by the name of Jair, who was of the tribe of Manasseh, not of Judah. We have thus made clear the meaning of Aben Ezra and also the passages of the Pentateuch which he cites in proof of his contention. However, Aben Ezra does not call attention to every instance, or even the chief ones; there remain many of greater importance, which may be cited. Namely (I.), that the writer of the books in question not only speaks of Moses in the third person, but also bears witness to many details concerning him; for instance, "Moses talked with God;" "The Lord spoke with Moses face to face; " "Moses was the meekest of men" (Numb. xii:3); "Moses was wrath with the captains of the host; "Moses, the man of God, "Moses, the servant of the Lord, died;" "There was never a prophet in Israel like unto Moses," &c. On the other hand, in Deuteronomy, where the law which Moses had expounded to the people and written is set forth, Moses speaks and declares what he has done in the first person: "God spake with me " (Deut. ii:1, 17, &c.), "I prayed to the Lord," &c. Except at the end of the book, when the historian, after relating the words of Moses, begins again to speak in the third person, and to tell how Moses handed over the law which he had expounded to the people in writing, again admonishing them, and further, how Moses ended his life. All these details, the manner of narration, the testimony, and the context of the whole story lead to the plain conclusion that these books were written by another, and not by Moses in person.

III. We must also remark that the history relates not only the manner of Moses' death and burial, and the thirty days' mourning of the Hebrews, but further compares him with all the prophets who came after him, and states that he surpassed them all. "There was never a prophet in Israel like unto Moses, whom the Lord knew face to face." Such testimony cannot have been given of Moses by, himself, nor by any who immediately succeeded him, but it must come from someone who lived centuries afterwards, especially, as the historian speaks of past times. "There was never a prophet," &c. And of the place of burial, "No one knows it to this day."

III. We must note that some places are not styled by the names they bore during Moses' lifetime, but by others which they obtained subsequently. For instance, Abraham is said to have pursued his enemies even unto Dan, a name not bestowed on the city till long after the death of Joshua (Gen. xiv;14, Judges xviii;29).

IV. The narrative is prolonged after the death of Moses, for in Exodus xvi:34 we read that "the children of Israel did eat manna forty years until they came to a land inhabited, until they came unto the borders of the land of Canaan." In other words, until the time alluded to in Joshua vi:12.

So, too, in Genesis xxxvi:31 it is stated, "These are the kings that reigned in Edom before there reigned any king over the children of Israel." The historian, doubtless, here relates the kings of Idumaea before that territory was conquered by David 10 and garrisoned, as we read in 2 Sam. viii:14. From what has been said, it is thus clearer than the sun at noonday that the Pentateuch was not written by Moses, but by someone who lived long after Moses. Let us now turn our attention to the books which Moses actually did write, and which are cited in the Pentateuch; thus, also, shall we see that they were different from the Pentateuch. Firstly, it appears from Exodus xvii:14 that Moses, by the command of God, wrote an account of the war against Amalek. The book in which he did so is not named in the chapter just quoted, but in Numb. xxi:12 a book is referred to under the title of the wars of God, and doubtless this war against Amalek and the castrametations said in Numb. xxxiii:2 to have been written by Moses are therein described. We hear also in Exod. xxiv:4 of another book called the Book of the Covenant, which Moses read before the Israelites when they first made a covenant with God. But this book or this writing contained very little, namely, the laws or commandments of God which we find in Exodus xx:22 to the end of chap. xxiv., and this no one will deny who reads the aforesaid chapter rationally and impartially. It is there stated that as soon as Moses had learnt the feeling of the people on the subject of making a covenant with God, he immediately wrote down God's laws and utterances, and in the morning, after some ceremonies had been performed, read out the conditions of the covenant to an assembly of the whole people. When these had been gone through, and doubtless understood by all, the whole people gave their assent.

Now from the shortness of the time taken in its perusal and also from its nature as a compact, this document evidently contained nothing more than that which we have just described. Further, it is clear that Moses explained all the laws which he had received in the fortieth year after the exodus from Egypt; also that he bound over the people a second time to observe them, and that finally he committed them to writing (Deut. i:5; xxix:14; xxxi:9), in a book which contained these laws explained, and the new covenant, and this book was therefore called the book of the law of God: the same which was afterwards added to by Joshua when he set forth the fresh covenant with which he bound over the people and which he entered into with God (Josh. xxiv:25, 26).

Now, as we have extent no book containing this covenant of Moses and also the covenant of Joshua, we must perforce conclude that it has perished, unless, indeed, we adopt the wild conjecture of the Chaldean paraphrast Jonathan, and twist about the words of Scripture to our heart's content. This commentator, in the face of our present difficulty, preferred corrupting the sacred text to confessing his own ignorance. The passage in the book of Joshua which runs, "and Joshua wrote these words in the book of the law of God," he changes into "and Joshua wrote these words and kept them with the book of the law of God." What is to be done with persons who will only see what pleases them? What is such a proceeding if it is not denying Scripture, and inventing another Bible out of our own heads? We may therefore conclude that the book of the law of God which Moses wrote was not the Pentateuch, but something quite different, which the author of the Pentateuch duly inserted into his book. So much is abundantly plain both from what I have said and from what I am about to add. For in the passage of Deuteronomy above quoted, where it is related that Moses wrote the book of the law, the historian adds that he handed it over to the priests and bade them read it out at a stated time to the whole people. This shows that the work was of much less length than the Pentateuch, inasmuch as it could be read through at one sitting so as to be understood by all; further, we must not omit to notice that out of all the books which Moses wrote, this one book of the second covenant and the song (which latter he wrote afterwards so that all the people might learn it), was the only one which he caused to be religiously guarded and preserved. In the first covenant he had only bound over those who were present, but in the second covenant he bound over all their descendants also (Dent. xxix:14), and therefore ordered this covenant with future ages to be religiously preserved, together with the Song, which was especially addressed to posterity: as, then, we have no proof that Moses wrote any book save this of the covenant, and as he committed no other to the care of posterity; and, lastly, as there are many passages in the Pentateuch which Moses could not have written, it follows that the belief that Moses was the author of the Pentateuch is ungrounded and even irrational. Someone will perhaps ask whether Moses did not also write down other laws when they were first revealed to him — in other words, whether, during the course of forty years, he did not write down any of the laws which he promulgated, save only those few which I have stated to be contained in the book of the first covenant. To this I would answer, that although it seems reasonable to suppose that Moses wrote down the laws at the time when he wished to communicate them to the people, yet we are not warranted to take it as proved, for I have shown above that we must make no assertions in such matters which we do not gather from Scripture, or which do not flow as legitimate consequences from its fundamental principles. We must not accept whatever is reasonably probable. However even reason in this case would not force such a conclusion upon us: for it may be that the assembly of elders wrote down the decrees of Moses and communicated them to the people, and the historian collected them, and duly set them forth in his narrative of the life of Moses. So much for the five books of Moses: it is now time for us to turn to the other sacred writings.

The book of Joshua may be proved not to be an autograph by reasons similar to those we have just employed: for it must be some other than Joshua who testifies that the fame of Joshua was spread over the whole world; that he omitted nothing of what Moses had taught (Josh. vi:27; viii. last verse; xi:15); that he grew old and summoned an assembly of the whole people, and finally that he departed this life. Furthermore, events are related which took place after Joshua's death. For instance, that the Israelites worshipped God, after his death, so long as there were any old men alive who remembered him; and in chap. xvi:10, we read that "Ephraim and Manasseh did not drive out the Canaanites which dwelt in Gezer, but the Canaanite dwelt in the land of Ephraim unto this day, and was tributary to him." This is the same statement as that in Judges, chap. i., and the phrase "unto this day" shows that the writer was speaking of ancient times. With these texts we may compare the last verse of chap. xv., concerning the sons of Judah, and also the history of Caleb in the same chap. v:14. Further, the building of an altar beyond Jordan by the two tribes and a half, chap. xxii:10, sqq., seems to have taken place after the death of Joshua, for in the whole narrative his name is never mentioned, but the people alone held council as to waging war, sent out legates, waited for their return, and finally approved of their answer.

Lastly, from chap. x:14, it is clear that the book was written many generations after the death of Joshua, for it bears witness, there was never any, day like unto, that day, either before or after, that the Lord hearkened to the voice of a man," &c. If, therefore, Joshua wrote any book at all, it was that which is quoted in the work now before us, chap. x:13.

With regard to the book of Judges, I suppose no rational person persuades himself that it was written by the actual Judges. For the conclusion of the whole history contained in chap. ii. clearly shows that it is all the work — of a single historian. Further, inasmuch as the writer frequently tells us that there was then no king in Israel, it is evident that the book was written after the establishment of the monarchy.

The books of Samuel need not detain us long, inasmuch as the narrative in them is continued long after Samuel's death; but I should like to draw attention to the fact that it was written many generations after Samuel's death. For in book i. chap. ix:9, the historian remarks in a, parenthesis, "Beforetime, in Israel, when a man went to inquire of God, thus he spake: Come, and let us go to the seer; for he that is now called a prophet was beforetime called a seer."

Lastly, the books of Kings, as we gather from internal evidence, were compiled from the books of King Solomon (I Kings xi:41), from the chronicles of the kings of Judah (1 Kings xiv:19, 29), and the chronicles of the kings of Israel.

We may, therefore, conclude that all the books we have considered hitherto are compilations, and that the events therein are recorded as having happened in old time. Now, if we turn our attention to the connection and argument of all these books, we shall easily see that they were all written by a single historian, who wished to relate the antiquities of the Jews from their first beginning down to the first destruction of the city. The way in which the several books are connected one with the other is alone enough to show us that they form the narrative of one and the same writer. For as soon as he has related the life of Moses, the historian thus passes on to the story of Joshua: "And it came to pass after that Moses the servant of the Lord was dead, that God spake unto Joshua," &c., so in the same way, after the death of Joshua was concluded, he passes with identically the same transition and connection to the history of the Judges: "And it came to pass after that Joshua was dead, that the children of Israel sought from God," &c. To the book of Judges he adds the story of Ruth, as a sort of appendix, in these words: "Now it came to pass in the days that the judges ruled, that there was a famine in the land."

The first book of Samuel is introduced with a similar phrase; and so is the second book of Samuel. Then, before the history of David is concluded, the historian passes in the same way to the first book of Kings, and, after David's death, to the Second book of Kings.

The putting together, and the order of the narratives, show that they are all the work of one man, writing with a create aim; for the historian begins with relating the first origin of the Hebrew nation, and then sets forth in order the times and the occasions in which Moses put forth his laws, and made his predictions. He then proceeds to relate how the Israelites invaded the promised land in accordance with Moses' prophecy (Deut. vii.); and how, when the land was subdued, they turned their backs on their laws, and thereby incurred many misfortunes (Deut. xxxi:16, 17). He tells how they wished to elect rulers, and how, according as these rulers observed the law, the people flourished or suffered (Deut. xxviii:36); finally, how destruction came upon the nation, even as Moses had foretold. In regard to other matters, which do not serve to confirm the law, the writer either passes over them in silence, or refers the reader to other books for information. All that is set down in the books we have conduces to the sole object of setting forth the words and laws of Moses, and proving them by subsequent events. When we put together these three considerations, namely, the unity of the subject of all the books, the connection between them, and the fact that they are compilations made many generations after the events they relate had taken place, we come to the conclusion, as I have just stated, that they are all the work of a single historian. Who this historian was, it is not so easy to show; but I suspect that he was Ezra, and there are several strong reasons for adopting this hypothesis.

The historian whom we already know to be but one individual brings his history down to the liberation of Jehoiakim, and adds that he himself sat at the king's table all his life — that is, at the table either of Jehoiakim, or of the son of Nebuchadnezzar, for the sense of the passage is ambiguous: hence it follows that he did not live before the time of Ezra. But Scripture does not testify of any except of Ezra (Ezra vii:10), that he "prepared his heart to seek the law of the Lord, and to set it forth, and further that he was a ready scribe in the law of Moses." Therefore, I can not find anyone, save Ezra, to whom to attribute the sacred books.

Further, from this testimony concerning Ezra, we see that he prepared his heart, not only to seek the law of the Lord, but also to set it forth; and, in Nehemiah viii:8, we read that "they read in the book of the law of God distinctly, and gave the sense, and caused them to understand the reading."

As, then, in Deuteronomy, we find not only the book of the law of Moses, or the greater part of it, but also many things inserted for its better explanation, I conjecture that this Deuteronomy is the book of the law of God, written, set forth, and explained by Ezra, which is referred to in the text above quoted. Two examples of the way matters were inserted parenthetically in the text of Deuteronomy, with a view to its fuller explanation, we have already given, in speaking of Aben Ezra's opinion. Many others are found in the course of the work: for instance, in chap. ii:12: "The Horims dwelt also in Seir beforetime; but the children of Esau succeeded them, when they had destroyed them from before them, and dwelt in their stead; as Israel did unto the land of his possession, which the Lord gave unto them." This explains verses 3 and 4 of the same chapter, where it is stated that Mount Seir, which had come to the children of Esau for a possession, did not fall into their hands uninhabited; but that they invaded it, and turned out and destroyed the Horims, who formerly dwelt therein, even as the children of Israel had done unto the Canaanites after the death of Moses.

So, also, verses 6, 7, 8, 9, of the tenth chapter are inserted parenthetically among the words of Moses. Everyone must see that verse 8, which begins, "At that time the Lord separated the tribe of Levi," necessarily refers to verse 5, and not to the death of Aaron, which is only mentioned here by Ezra because Moses, in telling of the golden calf worshipped by the people, stated that he had prayed for Aaron.

He then explains that at the time at which Moses spoke, God had chosen for Himself the tribe of Levi in order that He may point out the reason for their election, and for the fact of their not sharing in the inheritance; after this digression, he resumes the thread of Moses' speech. To these parentheses we must add the preface to the book, and all the passages in which Moses is spoken of in the third person, besides many which we cannot now distinguish, though, doubtless, they would have been plainly recognized by the writer's contemporaries.

If, I say, we were in possession of the book of the law as Moses wrote it, I do not doubt that we should find a great difference in the words of the precepts, the order in which they are given, and the reasons by which they are supported.

A comparison of the decalogue in Deuteronomy with the decalogue in Exodus, where its history is explicitly set forth, will be sufficient to show us a wide discrepancy in all these three particulars, for the fourth commandment is given not only in a different form, but at much greater length, while the reason for its observance differs wholly from that stated in Exodus. Again, the order in which the tenth commandment is explained differs in the two versions. I think that the differences here as elsewhere are the work of Ezra, who explained the law of God to his contemporaries, and who wrote this book of the law of God, before anything else; this I gather from the fact that it contains the laws of the country, of which the people stood in most need, and also because it is not joined to the book which precedes it by any connecting phrase, but begins with the independent statement, "these are the words of Moses." After this task was completed, I think Ezra set himself to give a complete account of the history of the Hebrew nation from the creation of the world to the entire destruction of the city, and in this account he inserted the book of Deuteronomy, and, possibly, he called the first five books by the name of Moses, because his life is chiefly contained therein, and forms their principal subject; for the same reason he called the sixth Joshua, the seventh Judges, the eighth Ruth, the ninth, and perhaps the tenth, Samuel, and, lastly, the eleventh and twelfth Kings. Whether Ezra put the finishing touches to this work and finished it as he intended, we will discuss in the next chapter.

9 "Mount Moriah is called the mount of God." That is by the historian, not by Abraham, for he says that the place now called "In the mount of the Lord it shall be revealed," was called by Abraham, "the Lord shall provide."

10 "Before that territory [Idumoea] was conquered by David." From this time to the reign of Jehoram when they again separated from the Jewish kingdom (2 Kings viii:20), the Idumaeans had no king, princes appointed by the Jews supplied the place of kings (1 Kings xxii:48), in fact the prince of Idumaea is called a king (2 Kings iii:9).

It may be doubted whether the last of the Idumaean kings had begun to reign before the accession of Saul, or whether Scripture in this chapter of Genesis wished to enumerate only such kings as were independent. It is evidently mere trifling to wish to enrol among Hebrew kings the name of Moses, who set up a dominion entirely different from a monarchy.

CHAPTER IX.

Other questions concerning the same Books: namely, whether they were
completely finished by Ezra, and, further, whether the Marginal notes which are
found in the Hebrew texts were various readings.

HOW GREATLY THE inquiry we have just made concerning the real writer of the
twelve books aids us in attaining a complete understanding of them, may be easily
gathered solely from the passages which we have adduced in confirmation of our
opinion, and which would be most obscure without it. But besides the question of
the writer, there are other points to notice which common superstition forbids the
multitude to apprehend. Of these the chief is, that Ezra (whom I will take to be the
author of the aforesaid books until some more likely person be suggested) did not
put the finishing touches to the narrative contained therein, but merely collected
the histories from various writers, and sometimes simply set them down, leaving
their examination and arrangement to posterity.

The cause (if it were not untimely death) which prevented him from completing
his work in all its portions, I cannot conjecture, but the fact remains most clear,
although we have lost the writings of the ancient Hebrew historians, and can only
judge from the few fragments which are still extant. For the history of Hezekiah
(2 Kings xviii:17), as written in the vision of Isaiah, is related as it is found in the
chronicles of the kings of Judah. We read the same story, told with few exceptions,
11, in the same words, in the book of Isaiah which was contained in the chronicles
of the kings of Judah (2 Chron. xxxii:32). From this we must conclude that there
were various versions of this narrative of Isaiah's, unless, indeed, anyone would
dream that in this, too, there lurks a mystery. Further, the last chapter of 2 Kings
27-30 is repeated in the last chapter of Jeremiah, v.31-34.

Again, we find 2 Sam. vii. repeated in I Chron. xvii., but the expressions in the
two passages are so curiously varied 12, that we can very easily see that these two
chapters were taken from two different versions of the history of Nathan.

Lastly, the genealogy of the kings of Idumaea contained in Genesis xxxvi:31, is
repeated in the same words in 1 Chron. i., though we know that the author of the
latter work took his materials from other historians, not from the twelve books
we have ascribed to Ezra. We may therefore be sure that if we still possessed the
writings of the historians, the matter would be made clear; however, as we have
lost them, we can only examine the writings still extant, and from their order and
connection, their various repetitions, and, lastly, the contradictions in dates which
they contain, judge of the rest.

These, then, or the chief of them, we will now go through. First, in the story of
Judah and Tamar (Gen. xxxviii.) the historian thus begins: "And it came to pass at
that time that Judah went down from his brethren." This time cannot refer to what
immediately precedes 13, but must necessarily refer to something else, for from
the time when Joseph was sold into Egypt to the time when the patriarch Jacob,
with all his family, set out thither, cannot be reckoned as more than twenty-two
years, for Joseph, when he was sold by his brethren, was seventeen years old, and
when he was summoned by Pharaoh from prison was thirty; if to this we add the
seven years of plenty and two of famine, the total amounts to twenty-two years.
Now, in so short a period, no one can suppose that so many things happened as are
described; that Judah had three children, one after the other, from one wife, whom

he married at the beginning of the period; that the eldest of these, when he was old enough, married Tamar, and that after he died his next brother succeeded to her; that, after all this, Judah, without knowing it, had intercourse with his daughter-inlaw, and that she bore him twins, and, finally, that the eldest of these twins became a father within the aforesaid period. As all these events cannot have taken place within the period mentioned in Genesis, the reference must necessarily be to something treated of in another book: and Ezra in this instance simply related the story, and inserted it without examination among his other writings.

However, not only this chapter but the whole narrative of Joseph and Jacob is collected and set forth from various histories, inasmuch as it is quite inconsistent with itself. For in Gen. xlvii. we are told that Jacob, when he came at Joseph's bidding to salute Pharaoh, was 130 years old. If from this we deduct the twenty-two years which he passed sorrowing for the absence of Joseph and the seventeen years forming Joseph's age when he was sold, and, lastly, the seven years for which Jacob served for Rachel, we find that he was very advanced in life, namely, eighty four, when he took Leah to wife, whereas Dinah was scarcely seven years old when she was violated by Shechem, 14. Simeon and Levi were aged respectively eleven and twelve when they spoiled the city and slew all the males therein with the sword.

There is no need that I should go through the whole Pentateuch. If anyone pays attention to the way in which all the histories and precepts in these five books are set down promiscuously and without order, with no regard for dates; and further, how the same story is often repeated, sometimes in a different version, he will easily, I say, discern that all the materials were promiscuously collected and heaped together, in order that they might at some subsequent time be more readily examined and reduced to order. Not only these five books, but also the narratives contained in the remaining seven, going down to the destruction of the city, are compiled in the same way. For who does not see that in Judges ii:6 a new historian is being quoted, who had also written of the deeds of Joshua, and that his words are simply copied? For after our historian has stated in the last chapter of the book of Joshua that Joshua died and was buried, and has promised, in the first chapter of Judges, to relate what happened after his death, in what way, if he wished to continue the thread of his history, could he connect the statement here made about Joshua with what had gone before?

So, too, 1 Sam. 17, 18, are taken from another historian, who assigns a cause for David's first frequenting Saul's court very different from that given in chap. xvi. of the same book. For he did not think that David came to Saul in consequence of the advice of Saul's servants, as is narrated in chap. xvi., but that being sent by chance to the camp by his father on a message to his brothers, he was for the first time remarked by Saul on the occasion of his victory, over Goliath the Philistine, and was retained at his court.

I suspect the same thing has taken place in chap. xxvi. of the same book, for the historian there seems to repeat the narrative given in chap. xxiv. according to another man's version. But I pass over this, and go on to the computation of dates.

In I Kings, chap. vi., it is said that Solomon built the Temple in the four hundred and eightieth year after the exodus from Egypt; but from the historians themselves we get a much longer period, for:

	Years
Moses governed the people in the desert	40
Joshua, who lived 110 years, did not, according to Josephus and others' opinion rule more than	26
Cusban Rishathaim held the people in subjection	8
Othniel, son of Kenag, was judge for 15	40
Eglon, King of Moab, governed the people	18
Ehucl and Shamgar were judges	80
Jachin, King of Canaan, held the people in subjection	20
The people was at peace subsequently for	40
It was under subjection to Median	7
It obtained freedom under Gideon for	40
It fell under the rule of Abimelech	3

Tola, son of Puah, was judge	23
Jair was judge	22
The people was in subjection to the Philistines and Ammonites	18
Jephthah was judge	6
Ibzan, the Bethlehemite, was judge	7
Elon, the Zabulonite	10
Abclon, the Pirathonite	8
The people was again subject to the Philistines	40
Samson was judge 16	20
Eli was judge	40
The people again fell into subjection to the Philistines, till they were delivered by Samuel	20
David reigned	40
Solomon reigned before he built the temple	4

All these periods added together make a total of 580 years. But to these must be added the years during which the Hebrew republic flourished after the death of Joshua, until it was conquered by Cushan Rishathaim, which I take to be very numerous, for I cannot bring myself to believe that immediately after the death of Joshua all those who had witnessed his miracles died simultaneously, nor that their successors at one stroke bid farewell to their laws, and plunged from the highest virtue into the depth of wickedness and obstinacy.

Nor, lastly, that Cushan Rishathaim subdued them on the instant; each one of these circumstances requires almost a generation, and there is no doubt that Judges ii:7, 9, 10, comprehends a great many years which it passes over in silence. We must also add the years during which Samuel was judge, the number of which is not stated in Scripture, and also the years during which Saul reigned, which are not clearly shown from his history. It is, indeed, stated in 1 Sam. xiii:1, that he reigned two years, but the text in that passage is mutilated, and the records of his reign lead us to suppose a longer period. That the text is mutilated I suppose no one will doubt who has ever advanced so far as the threshold of the Hebrew language, for it runs as follows: "Saul was in his — year, when he began to reign, and he reigned two years over Israel." Who, I say, does not see that the number of the years of Saul's age when he began to reign has been omitted? That the record of the reign presupposes a greater number of years is equally beyond doubt, for in the same book, chap. xxvii:7, it is stated that David sojourned among the Philistines, to whom he had fled on account of Saul, a year and four months; thus the rest of the reign must have been comprised in a space of eight months, which I think no one will credit. Josephus, at the end of the sixth book of his antiquities, thus corrects the text: Saul reigned eighteen years while Samuel was alive, and two years after his death. However, all the narrative in chap. Xiii. is in complete disagreement with what goes before. At the end of chap. vii. it is narrated that the Philistines were so crushed by the Hebrews that they did not venture, during Samuel's life, to invade the borders of Israel; but in chap. xiii. we are told that the Hebrews were invaded during the life of Samuel by the Philistines, and reduced by them to such a state of wretchedness and poverty that they were deprived not only of weapons with which to defend themselves, but also of the means of making more. I should be at pains enough if I were to try and harmonize all the narratives contained in this first book of Samuel so that they should seem to be all written and arranged by a single historian. But I return to my object. The years, then, during which Saul reigned must be added to the above computation; and, lastly, I have not counted the years of the Hebrew anarchy, for I cannot from Scripture gather their number. I cannot, I say, be certain as to the period occupied by the events related in Judges chap. xvii. on till the end of the book.

It is thus abundantly evident that we cannot arrive at a true computation of years from the histories, and, further, that the histories are inconsistent themselves on the subject. We are compelled to confess that these histories were compiled from various writers without previous arrangement and examination. Not less discrepancy is found between the dates given in the Chronicles of the Kings of Judah, and those in the Chronicles of the Kings of Israel; in the latter, it is stated that Jehoram, the son of Ahab, began to reign in the second year of the reign of Jehoram, the son of Jehoshaphat (2 Kings i:17), but in the former we read that Jehoram, the son of Jehoshaphat, began to reign in the fifth year of Jehoram, the son of Ahab (2 Kings viii:16). Anyone who compares the narratives in Chronicles with the narratives in the books of Kings, will find many similar discrepancies. These there is no need for me to examine here, and still less am I called upon to treat of the commentaries of those who endeavour to harmonize them. The Rabbis evidently let their fancy run wild. Such commentators as I have, read, dream, invent, and as a last resort, play fast and loose with the language. For instance, when it is said in 2 Chronicles, that Ahab was forty-two years old when he began to reign, they pretend that these years are computed from the reign of Omri, not from the birth of Ahab. If this can be shown to be the real meaning of the writer of the book of Chronicles, all I can say is, that he did not know how to state a fact. The commentators make many other assertions of this kind, which if true, would prove that the ancient Hebrews were ignorant both of their own language, and of the way to relate a plain narrative. I should in such case recognize no rule or reason in interpreting Scripture, but it would be permissible to hypothesize to one's heart's content.

If anyone thinks that I am speaking too generally, and without sufficient warrant, I would ask him to set himself to showing us some fixed plan in these histories which might be followed without blame by other writers of chronicles, and in his efforts at harmonizing and interpretation, so strictly to observe and explain the phrases and expressions, the order and the connections, that we may be able to imitate these also in our writings 17. If he succeeds, I will at once give him my hand, and he shall be to me as great Apollo; for I confess that after long endeavours I have been unable to discover anything of the kind. I may add that I set down nothing here which I have not long reflected upon, and that, though I was imbued from my boyhood up with the ordinary opinions about the Scriptures, I have been unable to withstand the force of what I have urged.

However, there is no need to detain the reader with this question, and drive him to attempt an impossible task; I merely mentioned the fact in order to throw light on my intention.

I now pass on to other points concerning the treatment of these books. For we must remark, in addition to what has been shown, that these books were not guarded by posterity with such care that no faults crept in. The ancient scribes draw attention to many doubtful readings, and some mutilated passages, but not to all that exist: whether the faults are of sufficient importance to greatly embarrass the reader I will not now discuss. I am inclined to think that they are of minor moment to those, at any rate, who read the Scriptures with enlightenment: and I can positively, affirm that I have not noticed any fault or various reading in doctrinal passages sufficient to render them obscure or doubtful.

There are some people, however, who will not admit that there is any corruption, even in other passages, but maintain that by some unique exercise of providence God has preserved from corruption every word in the Bible: they say that the various readings are the symbols of profoundest mysteries, and that mighty secrets lie hid in the twenty-eight hiatus which occur, nay, even in the very form of the letters.

Whether they are actuated by folly and anile devotion, or whether by arrogance and malice so that they alone may be held to possess the secrets of God, I know not: this much I do know, that I find in their writings nothing which has the air of a Divine secret, but only childish lucubrations. I have read and known certain Kabbalistic triflers, whose insanity provokes my unceasing as astonishment. That faults have crept in will, I think, be denied by no sensible person who reads the passage about Saul, above quoted (1 Sam. xiii:1) and also 2 Sam. vi:2: "And David arose and went with all the people that were with him from Judah, to bring up from thence the ark of God."

No one can fail to remark that the name of their destination, viz., Kirjath-jearim 18, has been omitted: nor can we deny that 2 Sam. xiii:37, has been tampered with and mutilated. "And Absalom fled, and went to Talmai, the son of Ammihud, king of Geshur. And he mourned for his son every day. So Absalom fled, and went to Geshur, and was there three years." I know that I have remarked other passages of the same kind, but I cannot recall them at the moment.

That the marginal notes which are found continually in the Hebrew Codices are doubtful readings will, I think, be evident to everyone who has noticed that they often arise from the great similarity, of some of the Hebrew letters, such for instance, as the similarity between Kaph and Beth, Jod and Van, Daleth and Reth, &c. For example, the text in 2 Sam. v:24, runs "in the time when thou hearest," and similarly in Judges xxi:22, "And it shall be when their fathers or their brothers come unto us often," the marginal version is "come unto us to complain."

So also many various readings have arisen from the use of the letters named mutes, which are generally not sounded in pronunciation, and are taken promiscuously, one for the other. For example, in Levit. xxv:29, it is written, "The house shall be established which is not in the walled city," but the margin has it, "which is in a walled city."

Though these matters are self-evident, [Endnore 6], it is necessary, to answer the reasonings of certain Pharisees, by which they endeavour to convince us that the marginal notes serve to indicate some mystery, and were added or pointed out by the writers of the sacred books. The first of these reasons, which, in my, opinion, carries little weight, is taken from the practice of reading the Scriptures aloud.

If, it is urged, these notes were added to show various readings which could not be decided upon by posterity, why has custom prevailed that the marginal readings should always be retained? Why has the meaning which is preferred been set down in the margin when it ought to have been incorporated in the text, and not relegated to a side note?

The second reason is more specious, and is taken from the nature of the case. It is admitted that faults have crept into the sacred writings by chance and not by design; but they say that in the five books the word for a girl is, with one exception, written without the letter "he," contrary to all grammatical rules, whereas in the margin it is written correctly according to the universal rule of grammar. Can this have happened by mistake? Is it possible to imagine a clerical error to have been committed every, time the word occurs? Moreover, it would have been easy, to supply the emendation. Hence, when these readings are not accidental or corrections of manifest mistakes, it is supposed that they must have been set down on purpose by the original writers, and have a meaning. However, it is easy to answer such arguments; as to the question of custom having prevailed in the reading of the marginal versions, I will not spare much time for its consideration: I know not the promptings of superstition, and perhaps the practice may have arisen from the idea that both readings were deemed equally good or tolerable, and therefore, lest either should be neglected, one was appointed to be written, and the other to be read. They feared to pronounce judgment in so weighty a matter lest they should mistake the false for the true, and therefore they would give preference to neither, as they must necessarily have done if they had commanded one only to be both read and written. This would be especially the case where the marginal readings were not written down in the sacred books: or the custom may have originated because some things though rightly written down were desired to be read otherwise according to the marginal version, and therefore the general rule was made that the marginal version should be followed in reading the Scriptures. The cause which induced the scribes to expressly prescribe certain passages to be read in the marginal version, I will now touch on, for not all the marginal notes are various readings, but some mark expressions which have passed out of common use, obsolete words and terms which current decency did not allow to be read in a public assembly. The ancient writers, without any evil intention, employed no courtly paraphrase, but called things by their plain names. Afterwards, through the spread of evil thoughts and luxury, words which could be used by the ancients without offence, came to be considered obscene. There was no need for this cause to change the text of Scripture. Still, as a concession to the popular weakness, it became the custom to substitute more decent terms for words denoting sexual intercourse, exereta, &c., and to read them as they were given in the margin.

At any rate, whatever may have been the origin of the practice of reading Scripture according to the marginal version, it was not that the true interpretation is contained therein. For besides that, the Rabbins in the Talmud often differ from the Massoretes, and give other readings which they approve of, as I will shortly show, certain things are found in the margin which appear less warranted by the uses of the Hebrew language. For example, in 2 Samuel xiv:22, we read, "In that the king hath fulfilled the request of his servant," a construction plainly regular, and agreeing with that in chap. xvi. But the margin has it "of thy servant," which does not agree with the person of the verb. So, too, chap. xvi:25 of the same book, we find, "As if one had inquired at the oracle of God," the margin adding "someone" to stand as a nominative to the verb. But the correction is not apparently warranted, for it is a common practice, well known to grammarians in the Hebrew language, to use the third person singular of the active verb impersonally.

The second argument advanced by the Pharisees is easily answered from what has just been said, namely, that the scribes besides the various readings called attention to obsolete words. For there is no doubt that in Hebrew as in other languages, changes of use made many words obsolete and antiquated, and such were found by the later scribes in the sacred books and noted by them with a view to the books being publicly read according to custom. For this reason the word nahgar is always found marked because its gender was originally common, and it had the same meaning as the Latin juvenis (a young person). So also the Hebrew capital was anciently called Jerusalem, not Jerusalaim. As to the pronouns himself and herself, I think that the later scribes changed vau into jod (a very frequent change in Hebrew) when they wished to express the feminine gender, but that the ancients only distinguished the two genders by a change of vowels. I may also remark that the irregular tenses of certain verbs differ in the ancient and modern forms, it being formerly considered a mark of elegance to employ certain letters agreeable to the ear.

In a word, I could easily multiply proofs of this kind if I were not afraid of abusing the patience of the reader. Perhaps I shall be asked how I became acquainted with the fact that all these expressions are obsolete. I reply that I have found them in the most ancient Hebrew writers in the Bible itself, and that they have not been imitated by subsequent authors, and thus they are recognized as antiquated, though the language in which they occur is dead. But perhaps someone may press the question why, if it be true, as I say, that the marginal notes of the Bible generally mark various readings, there are never more than two readings of a passage, that in the text and that in the margin, instead of three or more; and further, how the scribes can have hesitated between two readings, one of which is evidently contrary to grammar, and the other a plain correction.

The answer to these questions also is easy: I will premise that it is almost certain that there once were more various readings than those now recorded. For instance, one finds many in the Talmud which the Massoretes have neglected, and are so different one from the other that even the superstitious editor of the Bomberg Bible confesses that he cannot harmonize them. "We cannot say anything," he writes, "except what we have said above, namely, that the Talmud is generally in contradiction to the Massorete." So that we are nor bound to hold that there never were more than two readings of any passage, yet I am willing to admit, and indeed I believe that more than two readings are never found: and for the following reasons: — (I.) The cause of the differences of reading only admits of two, being generally the similarity of certain letters, so that the question resolved itself into which should be written Beth, or Kaf, Jod or Vau, Daleth or Reth: cases which are constantly occurring, and frequently yielding a fairly good meaning whichever alternative be adopted. Sometimes, too, it is a question whether a syllable be long or short, quantity being determined by the letters called mutes. Moreover, we never asserted that all the marginal versions, without exception, marked various readings; on the contrary, we have stated that many were due to motives of decency or a desire to explain obsolete words. (II.) I am inclined to attribute the fact that more than two readings are never found to the paucity of exemplars, perhaps not more than two or three, found by the scribes. In the treatise of the scribes, chap. vi., mention is made of three only, pretended to have been found in the time of Ezra, in order that the marginal versions might be attributed to him.

However that may be, if the scribes only had three codices we may easily imagine that in a given passage two of them would be in accord, for it would be extraordinary if each one of the three gave a different reading of the same text.

The dearth of copies after the time of Ezra will surprise no one who has read the 1st chapter of Maccabees, or Josephus's "Antiquities," Bk. 12, chap. 5. Nay, it appears wonderful considering the fierce and daily persecution, that even these few should have been preserved. This will, I think, be plain to even a cursory reader of the history of those times.

We have thus discovered the reasons why there are never more than two readings of a passage in the Bible, but this is a long way from supposing that we may therefore conclude that the Bible was purposely written incorrectly in such passages in order to signify some mystery. As to the second argument, that some passages are so faultily written that they are at plain variance with all grammar, and should have been corrected in the text and not in the margin, I attach little weight to it, for I am not concerned to say what religious motive the scribes may have had for acting as they did: possibly they did so from candour, wishing to transmit the few exemplars of the Bible which they had found exactly in their original state, marking the differences they discovered in the margin, not as doubtful readings, but as simple variants. I have myself called them doubtful readings, because it would be generally impossible to say which of the two versions is preferable.

Lastly, besides these doubtful readings the scribes have (by leaving a hiatus in the middle of a paragraph) marked several passages as mutilated. The Massoretes have counted up such instances, and they amount to eight-and-twenty. I do not know whether any mystery is thought to lurk in the number, at any rate the Pharisees religiously preserve a certain amount of empty space.

One of such hiatus occurs (to give an instance) in Gen. iv:8, where it is written, "And Cain said to his brother . . . . and it came to pass while they were in the field, &c.," a space being left in which we should expect to hear what it was that Cain said.

Similarly there are (besides those points we have noticed) eight-and-twenty hiatus left by the scribes. Many of these would not be recognized as mutilated if it were not for the empty space left. But I have said enough on this subject.

11 "With few exceptions." One of these exceptions is found in 2 Kings xviii:20, where we read, "Thou sayest (but they are but vain words)," the second person being used. In Isaiah xxxvi:5, we read "I say (but they are but vain words) I have counsel and strength for war," and in the twenty-second verse of the chapter in Kings it is written, "But if ye say," the plural number being used, whereas Isaiah gives the singular. The text in Isaiah does not contain the words found in 2 Kings xxxii:32. Thus there are several cases of various readings where it is impossible to distinguish the best.

12 "The expressions in the two passages are so varied." For instance we read in 2 Sam. vii:6, "But I have walked in a tent and in a tabernacle." Whereas in 1 Chron. xvii:5, "but have gone from tent to tent and from one tabernacle to another." In 2 Sam. vii:10, we read, "to afflict them," whereas in 1 Chron. vii:9, we find a different expression. I could point out other differences still greater, but a single reading of the chapters in question will suffice to make them manifest to all who are neither blind nor devoid of sense.

13 "This time cannot refer to what immediately precedes." It is plain from the context that this passage must allude to the time when Joseph was sold by his brethren. But this is not all. We may draw the same conclusion from the age of Judah, who was than twenty-two years old at most, taking as basis of calculation his own history just narrated. It follows, indeed, from the last verse of Gen. xxx., that Judah was born in the tenth of the years of Jacob's servitude to Laban, and Joseph in the fourteenth. Now, as we know that Joseph was seventeen years old when sold by his brethren, Judah was then not more than twenty-one. Hence, those writers who assert that Judah's long absence from his father's house took place before Joseph was sold, only seek to delude themselves and to call in question the Scriptural authority which they are anxious to protect.

14 "Dinah was scarcely seven years old when she was violated by Schechem." The opinion held by some that Jacob wandered about eight or ten years between Mesopotamia and Bethel, savours of the ridiculous; if respect for Aben Ezra, allows me to say so. For it is clear that Jacob had two reasons for haste: first, the desire to see his old parents; secondly, and chiefly to perform, the vow made when he fled from his brother (Gen. xxviii:10 and xxxi:13, and xxxv:1). We read (Gen. xxxi:3), that God had commanded him to fulfill his vow, and promised him help for returning to his country. If these considerations seem conjectures rather than reasons, I will waive the point and admit that Jacob, more unfortunate than Ulysses, spent eight or ten years or even longer, in this short journey. At any rate it cannot be denied that Benjamin was born in the last year of this wandering, that is by the reckoning of the objectors, when Joseph was sixteen or seventeen years old, for Jacob left Laban seven years after Joseph's birth. Now from the seventeenth year of Joseph's age till the patriarch went into Egypt, not more than twenty-two years elapsed, as we have shown in this chapter. Consequently Benjamin, at the time of the journey to Egypt, was twenty-three or twenty-four at the most. He would therefore have been a grandfather in the flower of his age (Gen. xlvi:21, cf. Numb. xxvi:38, 40, and 1 Chron. viii;1), for it is certain that Bela, Benjamin's eldest son, had at that time, two sons, Addai and Naa-man. This is just as absurd as the statement that Dinah was violated at the age of seven, not to mention other impossibilities which would result from the truth of the narrative. Thus we see

that unskillful endeavours to solve difficulties, only raise fresh ones, and make confusion worse confounded.

15 "Othniel, son of Kenag, was judge for forty years." Rabbi Levi Ben Gerson and others believe that these forty years which the Bible says were passed in freedom, should be counted from the death of Joshua, and consequently include the eight years during which the people were subject to Kushan Rishathaim, while the following eighteen years must be added on to the eighty years of Ehud's and Shamgar's judgeships. In this case it would be necessary to reckon the other years of subjection among those said by the Bible to have been passed in freedom. But the Bible expressly notes the number of years of subjection, and the number of years of freedom, and further declares (Judges ii:18) that the Hebrew state was prosperous during the whole time of the judges. Therefore it is evident that Levi Ben Gerson (certainly a very learned man), and those who follow him, correct rather than interpret the Scriptures.

The same fault is committed by those who assert, that Scripture, by this general calculation of years, only intended to mark the period of the regular administration of the Hebrew state, leaving out the years of anarchy and subjection as periods of misfortune and interregnum. Scripture certainly passes over in silence periods of anarchy, but does not, as they dream, refuse to reckon them or wipe them out of the country's annals. It is clear that Ezra, in 1 Kings vi., wished to reckon absolutely all the years since the flight from Egypt. This is so plain, that no one versed in the Scriptures can doubt it. For, without going back to the precise words of the text, we may see that the genealogy of David given at the end of the book of Ruth, and I Chron. ii., scarcely accounts for so great a number of years. For Nahshon, who was prince of the tribe of Judah (Numb. vii;11), two years after the Exodus, died in the desert, and his son Salmon passed the Jordan with Joshua. Now this Salmon, according to the genealogy, was David's great-grandfather. Deducting, then, from the total of 480 years, four years for Solomon's reign, seventy for David's life, and forty for the time passed in the desert, we find that David was born 366 years after the passage of the Jordan. Hence we must believe that David's father, grandfather, great-grandfather, and great-great-grandfather begat children when they were ninety years old.

16 "Samson was judge for twenty years." Samson was born after the Hebrews had fallen under the dominion of the Philistines.

17 Otherwise, they rather correct than explain Scripture.

18 "Kirjath-jearim." Kirjath-jearim is also called Baale of Judah. Hence Kimchi and others think that the words Baale Judah, which I have translated "the people of Judah," are the name of a town. But this is not so, for the word Baale is in the plural. Moreover, comparing this text in Samuel with I Chron. Xiii:5, we find that David did not rise up and go forth out of Baale, but that he went thither. If the author of the book of Samuel had meant to name the place whence David took the ark, he would, if he spoke Hebrew correctly, have said, "David rose up, and set forth from Baale Judah, and took the ark from thence."

CHAPTER X.

An Examination of the Remaining Books of the Old Testament
According to the Preceding Method.

I NOW PASS on to the remaining books of the Old Testament. Concerning the two books of Chronicles I have nothing particular or important to remark, except that they were certainly written after the time of Ezra, and possibly after the restoration of the Temple by Judas Maccabaeus 19. For in chap. ix. of the first book we find a reckoning of the families who were the first to live in Jerusalem, and in verse 17 the names of the porters, of which two recur in Nehemiah. This shows that the books were certainly compiled after the rebuilding of the city. As to their actual writer, their authority, utility, and doctrine, I come to no conclusion. I have always been astonished that they have been included in the Bible by men who shut out from the canon the books of Wisdom, Tobit, and the others styled apocryphal. I do not aim at disparaging their authority, but as they are universally received I will leave them as they are.

The Psalms were collected and divided into five books in the time of the second temple, for Ps. lxxxviii. was published, according to Philo-Judaeus, while king Jehoiachin was still a prisoner in Babylon; and Ps. lxxxix. when the same king obtained his liberty: I do not think Philo would have made the statement unless either it had been the received opinion in his time, or else had been told him by trustworthy persons.

The Proverbs of Solomon were, I believe, collected at the same time, or at least in the time of King Josiah; for in chap. xxv:1, it is written, "These are also proverbs of Solomon which the men of Hezekiah, king of Judah, copied out." I cannot here pass over in silence the audacity of the Rabbis who wished to exclude from the sacred canon both the Proverbs and Ecclesiastes, and to put them both in the Apocrypha. In fact, they would actually have done so, if they had not lighted on certain passages in which the law of Moses is extolled. It is, indeed, grievous to think that the settling of the sacred canon lay in the hands of such men; however, I congratulate them, in this instance, on their suffering us to see these books in question, though I cannot refrain from doubting whether they have transmitted them in absolute good faith; but I will not now linger on this point.

I pass on, then, to the prophetic books. An examination of these assures me that the prophecies therein contained have been compiled from other books, and are not always set down in the exact order in which they were spoken or written by the prophets, but are only such as were collected here and there, so that they are but fragmentary.

Isaiah began to prophecy in the reign of Uzziah, as the writer himself testifies in the first verse. He not only prophesied at that time, but furthermore wrote the history of that king (see 2 Chron. xxvi:22) in a volume now lost. That which we possess, we have shown to have been taken from the chronicles of the kings of Judah and Israel.

We may add that the Rabbis assert that this prophet prophesied in the reign of Manasseh, by whom he was eventually put to death, and, although this seems to be a myth, it yet shows that they did not think that all Isaiah's prophecies are extant.

The prophecies of Jeremiah, which are related historically are also taken from various chronicles; for not only are they heaped together confusedly, without any account being taken of dates, but also the same story is told in them differently in different passages. For instance, in chap. xxi. we are told that the cause of Jeremiah's arrest was that he had prophesied the destruction of the city to Zedekiah who consulted him. This narrative suddenly passes, in chap xxii., to the prophet's remonstrances to Jehoiakim (Zedekiah's predecessor), and the prediction he made of that king's captivity; then, in chap. xxv., come the revelations granted to the prophet previously, that is in the fourth year of Jehoiakim, and, further on still, the revelations received in the first year of the same reign. The continuator of Jeremiah goes on heaping prophecy upon prophecy without any regard to dates, until at last, in chap. xxxviii. (as if the intervening chapters had been a parenthesis), he takes up the thread dropped in chap. xxi.

In fact, the conjunction with which chap. xxxviii. begins, refers to the 8th, 9th, and 10th verses of chap. xxi. Jeremiah's last arrest is then very differently described, and a totally separate cause is given for his daily retention in the court of the prison.

We may thus clearly see that these portions of the book have been compiled from various sources, and are only from this point of view comprehensible. The prophecies contained in the remaining chapters, where Jeremiah speaks in the first person, seem to be taken from a book written by Baruch, at Jeremiah's dictation. These, however, only comprise (as appears from chap. xxxvi:2) the prophecies revealed to the prophet from the time of Josiah to the fourth year of Jehoiakim, at which period the book begins. The contents of chap. xlv:2, on to chap. li:59, seem taken from the same volume.

That the book of Ezekiel is only a fragment, is clearly indicated by the first verse. For anyone may see that the conjunction with which it begins, refers to something already said, and connects what follows therewith. However, not only this conjunction, but the whole text of the discourse implies other writings. The fact of the present work beginning the thirtieth year shows that the prophet is continuing, not commencing a discourse; and this is confirmed by the writer, who parenthetically states in verse 3, "The word of the Lord came often unto Ezekiel the priest, the son of Buzi, in the land of the Chaldeans," as if to say that the prophecies which he is about to relate are the sequel to revelations formerly received by Ezekiel from God. Furthermore, Josephus, 11 Antiq." x:9, says that Ezekiel prophesied that Zedekiah should not see Babylon, whereas the book we now have not only contains no such statement, but contrariwise asserts in chap. xvii. that he should be taken to Babylon as a captive, 20.

Of Hosea I cannot positively state that he wrote more than is now extant in the book bearing his name, but I am astonished at the smallness of the quantity, we possess, for the sacred writer asserts that the prophet prophesied for more than eighty years.

We may assert, speaking generally, that the compiler of the prophetic books neither collected all the prophets, nor all the writings of those we have; for of the prophets who are said to have prophesied in the reign of Manasseh and of whom general mention is made in 2 Chron. xxxiii:10, 18, we have, evidently, no prophecies extant; neither have we all the prophecies of the twelve who give their names to books. Of Jonah we have only, the prophecy concerning the Ninevites, though he also prophesied to the children of Israel, as we learn in 2 Kings xiv:25.

The book and the personality of Job have caused much controversy. Some think that the book is the work of Moses, and the whole narrative merely allegorical. Such is the opinion of the Rabbins recorded in the Talmud, and they are supported by, Maimonides in his "More Nebuchim." Others believe it to be a true history, and some suppose that Job lived in the time of Jacob, and was married to his daughter Dinah. Aben Ezra, however, as I have already stated, affirms, in his commentaries, that the work is a translation into Hebrew from some other language: I could wish that he could advance more cogent arguments than he does, for we might then conclude that the Gentiles also had sacred books. I myself leave the matter undecided, but I conjecture Job to have been a Gentile, and a man of very stable character, who at first prospered, then was assailed with terrible calamities, and finally, was restored to great happiness. (He is thus named, among others, by Ezekiel, xiv:12.) I take it that the constancy of his mind amid the vicissitudes of his fortune occasioned many men to dispute about God's providence, or at least caused the writer of the book in question to compose his dialogues; for the contents, and also the style, seem to emanate far less from a man wretchedly ill and lying among ashes, than from one reflecting at ease in his study. I should also be inclined to agree with Aben Ezra that the book is a translation, for its poetry seems akin to that of the Gentiles; thus the Father of Gods summons a council, and Momus, here called Satan, criticizes the Divine decrees with the utmost freedom. But these are mere conjectures without any solid foundation.

I pass on to the book of Daniel, which, from chap. viii. onwards, undoubtedly contains the writing of Daniel himself. Whence the first seven chapters are derived I cannot say; we may, however, conjecture that, as they were first written in Chaldean, they are taken from Chaldean chronicles. If this could be proved, it would form a very striking proof of the fact that the sacredness of Scripture depends on our understanding of the doctrines therein signified, and not on the words, the language, and the phrases in which these doctrines are conveyed to us; and it would further show us that books which teach and speak of whatever is highest and best are equally sacred, whatever be the tongue in which they are written, or the nation to which they belong.

We can, however, in this case only remark that the chapters in question were written in Chaldee, and yet are as sacred as the rest of the Bible.

The first book of Ezra is so intimately connected with the book of Daniel that both are plainly recognizable as the work of the same author, writing of Jewish history from the time of the first captivity onwards. I have no hesitation in joining to this the book of Esther, for the conjunction with which it begins can refer to nothing else. It cannot be the same work as that written by Mordecai, for, in chap. ix:20-22, another person relates that Mordecai wrote letters, and tells us their contents; further, that Queen Esther confirmed the days of Purim in their times appointed, and that the decree was written in the book that is (by a Hebraism), in a book known to all then living, which, as Aben Ezra and the rest confess, has now perished. Lastly, for the rest of the acts of Mordecai, the historian refers us to the chronicles of the kings of Persia. Thus there is no doubt that this book was written by the same person as he who recounted the history of Daniel and Ezra, and who wrote Nehemiah, 21, sometimes called the second book of Ezra. We may, then, affirm that all these books are from one hand; but we have no clue whatever to the personality of the author. However, in order to determine whence he, whoever he was, had gained a knowledge of the histories which he had, perchance, in great measure himself written, we may remark that the governors or chiefs of the Jews, after the restoration of the Temple, kept scribes or historiographers, who wrote annals or chronicles of them. The chronicles of the kings are often quoted in the books of Kings, but the chronicles of the chiefs and priests are quoted for the first time in Nehemiah xii:23, and again in 1 Macc. xvi:24. This is undoubtedly the book referred to as containing the decree of Esther and the acts of Mordecai; and which, as we said with Aben Ezra, is now lost. From it were taken the whole contents of these four books, for no other authority is quoted by their writer, or is known to us.

That these books were not written by either Ezra or Nehemiah is plain from Nehemiah xii:9, where the descendants of the high priest, Joshua are traced down to Jaddua, the sixth high priest, who went to meet Alexander the Great, when the Persian empire was almost subdued (Josephus, "Ant." ii. 108), or who, according to Philo-Judaeus, was the sixth and last high priest under the Persians. In the same chapter of Nehemiah, verse 22, this point is clearly brought out: "The Levites in the days of Eliashib, Joiada, and Johanan, and Jaddua, were recorded chief of the fathers: also the priests, to the reign of Darius the Persian" — that is to say, in the chronicles; and, I suppose, no one thinks, 22, that the lives of Nehemiah and Ezra were so prolonged that they outlived fourteen kings of Persia. Cyrus was the first who granted the Jews permission to rebuild their Temple: the period between his time and Darius, fourteenth and last king of Persia, extends over 230 years. I have, therefore, no doubt that these books were written after Judas Maccabaeus had restored the worship in the Temple, for at that time false books of Daniel, Ezra, and Esther were published by evil-disposed persons, who were almost certainly Sadducees, for the writings were never recognized by the Pharisees, so far as I am aware; and, although certain myths in the fourth book of Ezra are repeated in the Talmud, they must not be set down to the Pharisees, for all but the most ignorant admit that they have been added by some trifler: in fact, I think, someone must have made such additions with a view to casting ridicule on all the traditions of the sect.

Perhaps these four books were written out and published at the time I have mentioned with a view to showing the people that the prophecies of Daniel had been fulfilled, and thus kindling their piety, and awakening a hope of future deliverance in the midst of their misfortunes. In spite of their recent origin, the books before us contain many errors, due, I suppose, to the haste with which they were written. Marginal readings, such as I have mentioned in the last chapter, are found here as elsewhere, and in even greater abundance; there are, moreover, certain passages which can only be accounted for by supposing some such cause as hurry.

However, before calling attention to the marginal readings, I will remark that, if the Pharisees are right in supposing them to have been ancient, and the work of the original scribes, we must perforce admit that these scribes (if there were more than one) set them down because they found that the text from which they were copying was inaccurate, and did yet not venture to alter what was written by their predecessors and superiors. I need not again go into the subject at length, and will, therefore, proceed to mention some discrepancies not noticed in the margin.

I. Some error has crept into the text of the second chapter of Ezra, for in verse 64 we are told that the total of all those mentioned in the rest of the chapter amounts to 42,360; but, when we come to add up the several items we get as result only 29,818. There must, therefore, be an error, either in the total, or in the details. The total is probably correct, for it would most likely be well known to all as a noteworthy thing; but with the details, the case would be different. If, then, any error had crept into the total, it would at once have been remarked, and easily corrected. This view is confirmed by Nehemiah vii., where this chapter of Ezra is mentioned, and a total is given in plain correspondence thereto; but the details are altogether different — some are larger, and some less, than those in Ezra, and altogether they amount to 31,089. We may, therefore, conclude that both in Ezra and in Nehemiah the details are erroneously given. The commentators who attempt to harmonize these evident contradictions draw on their imagination, each to the best of his ability; and while professing adoration for each letter and word of Scripture, only succeed in holding up the sacred writers to ridicule, as though they knew not how to write or relate a plain narrative. Such persons effect nothing but to render the clearness of Scripture obscure. If the Bible could everywhere be interpreted after their fashion, there would be no such thing as a rational statement of which the meaning could be relied on. However, there is no need to dwell on the subject; only I am convinced that if any historian were to attempt to imitate the proceedings freely attributed to the writers of the Bible, the commentators would cover him with contempt. If it be blasphemy to assert that there are any errors in Scripture, what name shall we apply to those who foist into it their own fancies, who degrade the sacred writers till they seem to write confused nonsense, and who deny the plainest and most evident meanings? What in the whole Bible can be plainer than the fact that Ezra and his companions, in the second chapter of the book attributed to him, have given in detail the reckoning of all the Hebrews who set out with them for Jerusalem? This is proved by the reckoning being given, not only of those who told their lineage, but also of those who were unable to do so. Is it not equally clear from Nehemiah vii:5, that the writer merely there copies the list given in Ezra? Those, therefore, who explain these pas sages otherwise, deny the plain meaning of Scripture — nay, they deny Scripture itself. They think it pious to reconcile one passage of Scripture with another — a pretty piety, forsooth, which accommodates the clear passages to the obscure, the correct to the faulty, the sound to the corrupt.

Far be it from me to call such commentators blasphemers, if their motives be pure: for to err is human. But I return to my subject.

Besides these errors in numerical details, there are others in the genealogies, in the history, and, I fear also in the prophecies. The prophecy of Jeremiah (chap. xxii.), concerning Jechoniah, evidently does not agree with his history, as given in I Chronicles iii:17-19, and especially with the last words of the chapter, nor do I see how the prophecy, "thou shalt die in peace," can be applied to Zedekiah, whose eyes were dug out after his sons had been slain before him. If prophecies are to be interpreted by their issue, we must make a change of name, and read Jechoniah for Zedekiah, and vice versa This, however, would be too paradoxical a proceeding; so I prefer to leave the matter unexplained, especially as the error, if error there be, must be set down to the historian, and not to any fault in the authorities.

Other difficulties I will not touch upon, as I should only weary the reader, and, moreover, be repeating the remarks of other writers. For R. Selomo, in face of the manifest contradiction in the above-mentioned genealogies, is compelled to break forth into these words (see his commentary on 1 Chron. viii.): "Ezra (whom he supposes to be the author of the book of Chronicles) gives different names and a different genealogy to the sons of Benjamin from those which we find in Genesis, and describes most of the Levites differently from Joshua, because he found original discrepancies." And, again, a little later: "The genealogy of Gibeon and others is described twice in different ways, from different tables of each genealogy, and in writing them down Ezra adopted the version given in the majority of the texts, and when the authority was equal he gave both." Thus granting that these books were compiled from sources originally incorrect and uncertain.

In fact the commentators, in seeking to harmonize difficulties, generally do no more than indicate their causes: for I suppose no sane person supposes that the sacred historians deliberately wrote with the object of appearing to contradict themselves freely. Perhaps I shall be told that I am overthrowing the authority of Scripture, for that, according to me, anyone may suspect it of error in any passage; but, on the contrary, I have shown that my object has been to prevent the clear and uncorrupted passages being accommodated to and corrupted by the faulty ones; neither does the fact that some passages are corrupt warrant us in suspecting all. No book ever was completely free from faults, yet I would ask, who suspects all books to be everywhere faulty? Surely no one, especially when the phraseology is clear and the intention of the author plain.

I have now finished the task I set myself with respect to the books of the Old Testament. We may easily conclude from what has been said, that before the time of the Maccabees there was no canon of sacred books, 23, but that those which we now possess were selected from a multitude of others at the period of the restoration of the Temple by the Pharisees (who also instituted the set form of prayers), who are alone responsible for their acceptance. Those, therefore, who would demonstrate the authority of Holy Scripture, are bound to show the authority of each separate book; it is not enough to prove the Divine origin of a single book in order to infer the Divine origin of the rest. In that case we should have to assume that the council of Pharisees was, in its choice of books, infallible, and this could never be proved. I am led to assert that the Pharisees alone selected the books of the Old Testament, and inserted them in the canon, from the fact that in Daniel ii. is proclaimed the doctrine of the Resurrection, which the Sadducees denied; and, furthermore, the Pharisees plainly assert in the Talmud that they so selected them. For in the treatise of Sabbathus, chapter ii., folio 30, page 2, it is written: R. Jehuda, surnamed Rabbi, reports that the experts wished to conceal the book of Ecclesiastes because they found therein words opposed to the law (that is, to the book of the law of Moses). Why did they not hide it? "Because it begins in accordance with the law, and ends according to the law;" and a little further on we read: "They sought also to conceal the book of Proverbs." And in the first chapter of the same treatise, fol. 13, page 2: "Verily, name one man for good, even he who was called Neghunja, the son of Hezekiah: for, save for him, the book of Ezekiel would been concealed, because it agreed not with the words of the law."

It is thus abundantly clear that men expert in the law summoned a council to decide which books should be received into the canon, and which excluded. If any man, therefore, wishes to be certified as to the authority of all the books, let him call a fresh council, and ask every member his reasons.

The time has now come for examining in the same manner the books in the New Testament; but as I learn that the task has been already performed by men highly skilled in science and languages, and as I do not myself possess a knowledge of Greek sufficiently exact for the task; lastly, as we have lost the originals of those books which were written in Hebrew, I prefer to decline the undertaking. However, I will touch on those points which have most bearing on my subject in the following chapter.

19 "After the restoration of the Temple by Judas Maccaboeus." This conjecture, if such it be, is founded on the genealogy of King Jeconiah, given in 1 Chron. iii., which finishes at the sons of Elioenai, the thirteenth in direct descent from him: whereon we must observe that Jeconiah, before his captivity, had no children; but it is probable that he had two while he was in prison, if we may draw any inference from the names he gave them. As to his grandchildren, it is evident that they were born after his deliverance, if the names be any guide, for his grandson, Pedaiah (a name meaning God hath delivered me), who, according to this chapter, was the father of Zerubbabel, was born in the thirty-seventh or thirty-eighth year of Jeconiah's life, that is thirty-three years before the restoration of liberty to the Jews by Cyrus. Therefore Zerubbabel, to whom Cyrus gave the principality of Judaea, was thirteen or fourteen years old. But we need not carry the inquiry so far: we need only read attentively the chapter of 1 Chron., already quoted, where (v. 17, sqq.) mention is made of all the posterity of Jeconiah, and compare it with the Septuagint version to see clearly that these books were not published, till after Maccabaeus had restored the Temple, the sceptre no longer belonging to the house of Jeconiah.

20 "Zedekiah should be taken to Babylon." No one could then have suspected that the prophecy of Ezekiel contradicted that of Jeremiah, but the suspicion occurs to everyone who reads the narrative of Josephus. The event proved that both prophets were in the right.

21 "And who wrote Nehemiah." That the greater part of the book of Nehemiah was taken from the work composed by the prophet Nehemiah himself, follows from the testimony of its author. (See chap. i.). But it is obvious that the whole of the passage contained between chap. viii. and chap. xii. verse 26, together with the two last verses of chap. xii., which form a sort of parenthesis to Nehemiah's words, were added by the historian himself, who outlived Nehemiah.

22 "I suppose no one thinks" that Ezra was the uncle of the first high priest, named Joshua (see Ezra vii., and 1 Chron. vi:14), and went to Jerusalem from Babylon with Zerubbabel (see Nehemiah xii:1). But it appears that when he saw, that the Jews were in a state of anarchy, he returned to Babylon, as also did others (Nehem. i;2), and remained there till the reign of Artaxerxes, when his requests were granted and he went a second time to Jerusalem. Nehemiah also went to Jerusalem with Zerubbabel in the time of Cyrus (Ezra ii:2 and 63, cf. x:9, and Nehemiah x:1). The version given of the Hebrew word, translated "ambassador," is not supported by any authority, while it is certain that fresh names were given to those Jews who frequented the court. Thus Daniel was named Balteshazzar, and Zerubbabel Sheshbazzar (Dan. i:7). Nehemiah was called Atirsata, while in virtue of his office he was styled governor, or president. (Nehem. v. 24, xii:26.)

23 "Before the time of the Maccabees there was no canon of sacred books." The synagogue styled "the great" did not begin before the subjugation of Asia by the Macedonians. The contention of Maimonides, Rabbi Abraham, Ben-David, and others, that the presidents of this synagogue were Ezra, Daniel, Nehemiah, Haggai, Zechariah, &c., is a pure fiction, resting only on rabbinical tradition. Indeed they assert that the dominion of the Persians only lasted thirty-four years, and this is their chief reason for maintaining that the decrees of the "great synagogue," or synod (rejected by the Sadducees, but accepted by the Pharisees) were ratified by the prophets, who received them from former prophets, and so in direct succession from Moses, who received them from God Himself. Such is the doctrine which the Pharisees maintain with their wonted obstinacy. Enlightened persons, however,

who know the reasons for the convoking of councils, or synods, and are no strangers to the differences between Pharisees and Sadducees, can easily divine the causes which led to the assembling of this great synagogue. It is very certain that no prophet was there present, and that the decrees of the Pharisees, which they style their traditions, derive all their authority from it.

CHAPTER XI.

An Inquiry whether the Apostles wrote their Epistles as Apostles and Prophets, or merely as Teachers; and an explanation of what is meant by an Apostle.

NO READER OF the New Testament can doubt that the Apostles were prophets; but as a prophet does not always speak by revelation, but only, at rare intervals, as we showed at the end of Chap. I., we may fairly inquire whether the Apostles wrote their Epistles as prophets, by revelation and express mandate, as Moses, Jeremiah, and others did, or whether only as private individuals or teachers, especially as Paul, in Corinthians xiv:6, mentions two sorts of preaching.

If we examine the style of the Epistles, we shall find it totally different from that employed by the prophets.

The prophets are continually asserting that they speak by the command of God: "Thus saith the Lord," "The Lord of hosts saith," "The command of the Lord," &c.; and this was their habit not only in assemblies of the prophets, but also in their epistles containing revelations, as appears from the epistle of Elijah to Jehoram, 2 Chron. xxi:12, which begins, "Thus saith the Lord."

In the Apostolic Epistles we find nothing of the sort. Contrariwise, in I Cor. vii:40 Paul speaks according to his own opinion and in many passages we come across doubtful and perplexed phrase; such as, "We think, therefore," Rom. iii:28; "Now I think," 24, Rom. viii:18, and so on. Besides these, other expressions are met with very different from those used by the prophets. For instance, 1 Cor. vii:6, "But I speak this by permission, not by commandment;" "I give my judgment as one that hath obtained mercy of the Lord to be faithful" (1 Cor. vii:25), and so on in many other passages. We must also remark that in the aforesaid chapter the Apostle says that when he states that he has or has not the precept or commandment of God, he does not mean the precept or commandment of God revealed to himself, but only the words uttered by Christ in His Sermon on the Mount. Furthermore, if we examine the manner in which the Apostles give out evangelical doctrine, we shall see that it differs materially from the method adopted by the prophets. The Apostles everywhere reason as if they were arguing rather than prophesying; the prophecies, on the other hand, contain only dogmas and commands. God is therein introduced not as speaking to reason, but as issuing decrees by His absolute fiat. The authority of the prophets does not submit to discussion, for whosoever wishes to find rational ground for his arguments, by that very wish submits them to everyone's private judgment. This Paul, inasmuch as he uses reason, appears to have done, for he says in 1 Cor. x:15, "I speak as to wise men, judge ye what I say." The prophets, as we showed at the end of Chapter I., did not perceive what was revealed by virtue of their natural reason, and though there are certain passages in the Pentateuch which seem to be appeals to induction, they turn out, on nearer examination, to be nothing but peremptory commands. For instance, when Moses says, Deut. xxxi:27, "Behold, while I am yet alive with you, this day ye have been rebellious against the Lord; and how much more after my death," we must by no means conclude that Moses wished to convince the Israelites by reason that they would necessarily fall away from the worship of the Lord after his death; for the argument would have been false, as Scripture itself shows: the Israelites continued faithful during the lives of Joshua and the elders, and afterwards during the time of Samuel, David, and Solomon. Therefore the words of Moses are merely a moral injunction, in which he predicts rhetorically the future backsliding of the people so as to impress it vividly on their imagination. I say that Moses spoke of himself in order to lend likelihood to his prediction, and not as a prophet by revelation, because in verse 21 of the same chapter we are told that God revealed the same thing to Moses in different words, and there was no need to make Moses certain by argument of God's prediction and decree; it was only necessary that it should be vividly impressed on his imagination, and this could not be better accomplished than by imagining the existing contumacy of the people, of which he had had frequent experience, as likely to extend into the future.

All the arguments employed by Moses in the five books are to be understood in a similar manner; they are not drawn from the armoury of reason, but are merely, modes of expression calculated to instil with efficacy, and present vividly to the imagination the commands of God. However, I do not wish absolutely to deny that the prophets ever argued from revelation; I only maintain that the prophets made more legitimate use of argument in proportion as their knowledge approached more nearly to ordinary knowledge, and by this we know that they possessed a knowledge above the ordinary, inasmuch as they proclaimed absolute dogmas, decrees, or judgments. Thus Moses, the chief of the prophets, never used legitimate argument, and, on the other hand, the long deductions and arguments of Paul, such as we find in the Epistle to the Romans, are in nowise written from supernatural revelation.

The modes of expression and discourse adopted by the Apostles in the Epistles, show very clearly that the latter were not written by revelation and Divine command, but merely by the natural powers and judgment of the authors. They consist in brotherly admonitions and courteous expressions such as would never be employed in prophecy, as for instance, Paul's excuse in Romans xv:15, "I have written the more boldly unto you in some sort, my brethren."

We may arrive at the same conclusion from observing that we never read that the Apostles were commanded to write, but only that they went everywhere preaching, and confirmed their words with signs. Their personal presence and signs were absolutely necessary for the conversion and establishment in religion of the Gentiles; as Paul himself expressly states in Rom. i:11, "But I long to see you, that I may impart to you some spiritual gift, to the end that ye may be established."

It may be objected that we might prove in similar fashion that the Apostles did not preach as prophets, for they did not go to particular places, as the prophets did, by the command of God. We read in the Old Testament that Jonah went to Nineveh to preach, and at the same time that he was expressly sent there, and told that he most preach. So also it is related, at great length, of Moses that he went to Egypt as the messenger of God, and was told at the same time what he should say to the children of Israel and to king Pharaoh, and what wonders he should work before them to give credit to his words. Isaiah, Jeremiah, and Ezekiel were expressly commanded to preach to the Israelites. Lastly, the prophets only preached what we are assured by Scripture they had received from God, whereas this is hardly ever said of the Apostles in the New Testament, when they went about to preach. On the contrary, we find passages expressly implying that the Apostles chose the places where they should preach on their own responsibility, for there was a difference amounting to a quarrel between Paul and Barnabas on the subject (Acts xv:37, 38). Often they wished to go to a place, but were prevented, as Paul writes, Rom. i:13, "Oftentimes I purposed to come to you, but was let hitherto;" and in I Cor. xvi:12, "As touching our brother Apollos, I greatly desired him to come unto you with the brethren, but his will was not at all to come at this time: but he will come when he shall have convenient time."

From these expressions and differences of opinion among the Apostles, and also from the fact that Scripture nowhere testifies of them, as of the ancient prophets, that they went by the command of God, one might conclude that they preached as well as wrote in their capacity of teachers, and not as prophets: but the question is easily solved if we observe the difference between the mission of an Apostle and that of an Old Testament prophet. The latter were not called to preach and prophesy to all nations, but to certain specified ones, and therefore an express and peculiar mandate was required for each of them; the Apostles, on the other hand, were called to preach to all men absolutely, and to turn all men to religion. Therefore, whithersoever they went, they were fulfilling Christ's commandment; there was no need to reveal to them beforehand what they should preach, for they were the disciples of Christ to whom their Master Himself said (Matt. X:19, 20): "But, when they deliver you up, take no thought how or what ye shall speak, for it shall be given you in that same hour what ye shall speak." We therefore conclude that the Apostles were only indebted to special revelation in what they orally preached and confirmed by signs (see the beginning of Chap. 11.); that which they taught in speaking or writing without any confirmatory signs and wonders they taught from their natural knowledge. (See I Cor. xiv:6.) We need not be deterred by the fact that all the Epistles begin by citing the imprimatur of the Apostleship, for the Apostles, as I will shortly show, were granted, not only the faculty of prophecy, but also the authority to teach. We may therefore admit that they wrote their Epistles as Apostles, and for this cause every one of them began by citing the Apostolic imprimatur, possibly with a view to the attention of the reader by asserting that they were the persons who had made such mark among the faithful by their preaching, and had shown bv many marvelous works that they were teaching true religion and the way of salvation. I observe that what is said in the Epistles with regard to the Apostolic vocation and the Holy Spirit of God which inspired them, has reference to their former preaching, except in those passages where the expressions of the Spirit of God and the Holy Spirit are used to signify a mind pure, upright, and devoted to God. For instance, in 1 Cor. vii:40, Paul says: But she is happier if she so abide, after my judgment, and I think also that I have the Spirit of God." By the Spirit of God the Apostle here refers to his mind, as we may see from the context: his meaning is as follows: "I account blessed a widow who does not wish to marry a second husband; such is my opinion, for I have settled to live unmarried, and I think that I am blessed." There are other similar passages which I need not now quote.

As we have seen that the Apostles wrote their Epistles solely by the light of natural reason, we must inquire how they were enabled to teach by natural knowledge matters outside its scope. However, if we bear in mind what we said in Chap. VII. of this treatise our difficulty will vanish: for although the contents of the Bible entirely surpass our understanding, we may safely discourse of them, provided we assume nothing not told us in Scripture: by the same method the Apostles, from what they saw and heard, and from what was revealed to them, were enabled to form and elicit many conclusions which they would have been able to teach to men had it been permissible.

Further, although religion, as preached by the Apostles, does not come within the sphere of reason, in so far as it consists in the narration of the life of Christ, yet its essence, which is chiefly moral, like the whole of Christ's doctrine, can readily, be apprehended by the natural faculties of all.

Lastly, the Apostles had no lack of supernatural illumination for the purpose of adapting the religion they had attested by signs to the understanding of everyone so that it might be readily received; nor for exhortations on the subject: in fact, the object of the Epistles is to teach and exhort men to lead that manner of life which each of the Apostles judged best for confirming them in religion. We may here repeat our former remark, that the Apostles had received not only the faculty of preaching the history, of Christ as prophets, and confirming it with signs, but also authority for teaching and exhorting according as each thought best. Paul (2 Tim. i:11), "Whereunto I am appointed a preacher, and an apostle, and a teacher of the Gentiles;" and again (I Tim. ii:7), "Whereunto I am ordained a preacher and an apostle (I speak the truth in Christ and lie not), a teacher of the Gentiles in faith and verity." These passages, I say, show clearly the stamp both of the apostleship and the teachership: the authority for admonishing whomsoever and wheresoever he pleased is asserted by Paul in the Epistle to Philemon, v:8: "Wherefore, though I might be much bold in Christ to enjoin thee that which is convenient, yet," &c., where we may remark that if Paul had received from God as a prophet what he wished to enjoin Philemon, and had been bound to speak in his prophetic capacity, he would not have been able to change the command of God into entreaties. We must therefore understand him to refer to the permission to admonish which he had received as a teacher, and not as a prophet. We have not yet made it quite clear that the Apostles might each choose his own way of teaching, but only that by virtue of their Apostleship they were teachers as well as prophets; however, if we call reason to our aid we shall clearly see that an authority to teach implies authority to choose the method. It will nevertheless be, perhaps, more satisfactory to draw all our proofs from Scripture; we are there plainly told that each Apostle chose his particular method (Rom. xv: 20): "Yea, so have I strived to preach the gospel, not where Christ was named, lest I should build upon another man's foundation." If all the Apostles had adopted the same method of teaching, and had all built up the Christian religion on the same foundation, Paul would have had no reason to call the work of a fellow-Apostle "another man's foundation," inasmuch as it would have been identical with his own: his calling it another man's proved that each Apostle built up his religious instruction on different foundations, thus resembling other teachers who have each their own method, and prefer instructing quite ignorant people who have never learnt under another master, whether the subject be science, languages, or even the indisputable truths of mathematics. Furthermore, if we go through the Epistles at all attentively, we shall see that the Apostles, while agreeing about religion itself, are at variance as to the foundations it rests on. Paul, in order to strengthen men's religion, and show them that salvation depends solely on the grace of God, teaches that no one can boast of works, but only of faith, and that no one can be justified by works (Rom. iii:27,28); in fact, he preaches the complete doctrine of predestination. James, on the other hand, states that man is justified by works, and not by faith only (see his Epistle, ii:24), and omitting all the disputations of Paul, confines religion to a very few elements.

Lastly, it is indisputable that from these different ground; for religion selected by the Apostles, many quarrels and schisms distracted the Church, even in the earliest times, and doubtless they will continue so to distract it for ever, or at least till religion is separated from philosophical speculations, and reduced to the few simple doctrines taught by Christ to His disciples; such a task was impossible for the Apostles, because the Gospel was then unknown to mankind, and lest its novelty should offend men's ears it had to be adapted to the disposition of contemporaries (2 Cor. ix:19, 20), and built up on the groundwork most familiar and accepted at the time. Thus none of the Apostles philosophized more than did

Paul, who was called to preach to the Gentiles; other Apostles preaching to the Jews, who despised philosophy, similarly, adapted themselves to the temper of their hearers (see Gal. ii. 11), and preached a religion free from all philosophical speculations. How blest would our age be if it could witness a religion freed also from all the trammels of superstition!

24 "Now I think." The translators render the {Greek} word "I infer", and assert that Paul uses it as synonymous with {a Greek word}. But the former word has, in Greek, the same meaning as the Hebrew word rendered to think, to esteem, to judge. And this signification would be in entire agreement with the Syriac translation. This Syriac translation (if it be a translation, which is very doubtful, for we know neither the time of its appearance, nor the translators and Syriac was the vernacular of the Apostles) renders the text before us in a way well explained by Tremellius as "we think, therefore."

CHAPTER XII.

Of the true original of the Divine Law, and wherefore Scripture is called Sacred, and the Word of God. How that, in so far as it contains the Word of God, it has come down to us uncorrupted.

THOSE WHO LOOK upon the Bible as a message sent down by God from Heaven to men, will doubtless cry out that I have committed the sin against the Holy Ghost because I have asserted that the Word of God is faulty, mutilated, tampered with, and inconsistent; that we possess it only in fragments, and that the original of the covenant which God made with the Jews has been lost. However, I have no doubt that a little reflection will cause them to desist from their uproar: for not only reason but the expressed opinions of prophets and apostles openly proclaim that God's eternal Word and covenant, no less than true religion, is Divinely inscribed in human hearts, that is, in the human mind, and that this is the true original of God's covenant, stamped with His own seal, namely, the idea of Himself, as it were, with the image of His Godhood.

Religion was imparted to the early Hebrews as a law written down, because they were at that time in the condition of children, but afterwards Moses (Deut. xxx:6) and Jeremiah (xxxi:33) predicted a time coming when the Lord should write His law in their hearts. Thus only the Jews, and amongst them chiefly the Sadducees, struggled for the law written on tablets; least of all need those who bear it inscribed on their hearts join in the contest. Those, therefore, who reflect, will find nothing in what I have written repugnant either to the Word of God or to true religion and faith, or calculated to weaken either one or the other: contrariwise, they will see that I have strengthened religion, as I showed at the end of Chapter X.; indeed, had it not been so, I should certainly have decided to hold my peace, nay, I would even have asserted as a way out of all difficulties that the Bible contains the most profound hidden mysteries; however, as this doctrine has given rise to gross superstition and other pernicious results spoken of at the beginning of Chapter V., I have thought such a course unnecessary, especially as religion stands in no need of superstitious adornments, but is, on the contrary, deprived by such trappings of some of her splendour.

Still, it will be said, though the law of God is written in the heart, the Bible is none the less the Word of God, and it is no more lawful to say of Scripture than of God's Word that it is mutilated and corrupted. I fear that such objectors are too anxious to be pious, and that they are in danger of turning religion into superstition, and worshipping paper and ink in place of God's Word.

I am certified of thus much: I have said nothing unworthy of Scripture or God's Word, and I have made no assertions which I could not prove by most plain argument to be true. I can, therefore, rest assured that I have advanced nothing which is impious or even savours of impiety.

from what I have said, assume a licence to sin, and without any reason, at I confess that some profane men, to whom religion is a burden, may, the simple dictates of their lusts conclude that Scripture is everywhere faulty and falsified, and that therefore its authority is null; but such men are beyond the reach of help, for nothing, as the pro verb has it, can be said so rightly that it cannot be twisted into wrong. Those who wish to give rein to their lusts are at no loss for an excuse, nor were those men of old who possessed the original Scriptures, the ark of the covenant, nay, the prophets and apostles in person among them, any better than the people of today. Human nature, Jew as well as Gentile, has always been the same, and in every age virtue has been exceedingly rare.

Nevertheless, to remove every scruple, I will here show in what sense the Bible or any inanimate thing should be called sacred and Divine; also wherein the law of God consists, and how it cannot be contained in a certain number of books; and, lastly, I will show that Scripture, in so far as it teaches what is necessary for obedience and salvation, cannot have been corrupted. From these considerations everyone will be able to judge that I have neither said anything against the Word of God nor given any foothold to impiety.

A thing is called sacred and Divine when it is designed for promoting piety, and continues sacred so long as it is religiously used: if the users cease to be pious, the thing ceases to be sacred: if it be turned to base uses, that which was formerly sacred becomes unclean and profane. For instance, a certain spot was named by the patriarch Jacob the house of God, because he worshipped God there revealed to him: by the prophets the same spot was called the house of iniquity (see Amos v:5, and Hosea x:5), because the Israelites were wont, at the instigation of Jeroboam, to sacrifice there to idols. Another example puts the matter in the plainest light. Words gain their meaning solely from their usage, and if they are arranged according to their accepted signification so as to move those who read them to devotion, they will become sacred, and the book so written will be sacred also. But if their usage afterwards dies out so that the words have no meaning, or the book becomes utterly neglected, whether from unworthy motives, or because it is no longer needed, then the words and the book will lose both their use and their sanctity: lastly, if these same words be otherwise arranged, or if their customary meaning becomes perverted into its opposite, then both the words and the book containing them become, instead of sacred, impure and profane.

From this it follows that nothing is in itself absolutely sacred, or profane, and unclean, apart from the mind, but only relatively thereto. Thus much is clear from many passages in the Bible. Jeremiah (to select one case out of many) says (chap. vii:4), that the Jews of his time were wrong in calling Solomon's Temple, the Temple of God, for, as he goes on to say in the same chapter, God's name would only be given to the Temple so long as it was frequented by men who worshipped Him, and defended justice, but that, if it became the resort of murderers, thieves, idolaters, and other wicked persons, it would be turned into a den of malefactors.

Scripture, curiously enough, nowhere tells us what became of the Ark of the Covenant, though there is no doubt that it was destroyed, or burnt together with the Temple; yet there was nothing which the Hebrews considered more sacred, or held in greater reverence. Thus Scripture is sacred, and its words Divine so long as it stirs mankind to devotion towards God: but if it be utterly neglected, as it formerly was by the Jews, it becomes nothing but paper and ink, and is left to be desecrated or corrupted: still, though Scripture be thus corrupted or destroyed, we must not say that the Word of God has suffered in like manner, else we shall be like the Jews, who said that the Temple which would then be the Temple of God had perished in the flames. Jeremiah tells us this in respect to the law, for he thus chides the ungodly of his time, "Wherefore, say you we are masters, and the law of the Lord is with us? Surely it has been given in vain, it is in vain that the pen of the scribes" (has been made) — that is, you say falsely that the Scripture is in your power, and that you possess the law of God; for ye have made it of none effect.

So also, when Moses broke the first tables of the law, he did not by any means cast the Word of God from his hands in anger and shatter it — such an action would be inconceivable, either of Moses or of God's Word — he only broke the tables of stone, which, though they had before been holy from containing the covenant wherewith the Jews had bound themselves in obedience to God, had entirely lost their sanctity when the covenant had been violated by the worship of the calf, and were, therefore, as liable to perish as the ark of the covenant. It is thus scarcely to be wondered at, that the original documents of Moses are no longer extant, nor that the books we possess met with the fate we have described, when we consider that the true original of the Divine covenant, the most sacred object of all, has totally perished.

Let them cease, therefore, who accuse us of impiety, inasmuch as we have said nothing against the Word of God, neither have we corrupted it, but let them keep their anger, if they would wreak it justly, for the ancients whose malice desecrated the Ark, the Temple, and the Law of God, and all that was held sacred, subjecting them to corruption. Furthermore, if, according to the saying of the Apostle in 2 Cor. iii:3, they possessed "the Epistle of Christ, written not with ink, but with the Spirit of the living God, not in tables of stone, but in the fleshy tables of the heart," let them cease to worship the letter, and be so anxious concerning it.

I think I have now sufficiently shown in what respect Scripture should be accounted sacred and Divine; we may now see what should rightly be understood by the expression, the Word of the Lord; debar (the Hebrew original) signifies word, speech, command, and thing. The causes for which a thing is in Hebrew said to be of God, or is referred to Him, have been already detailed in Chap. I., and we can therefrom easily gather what meaning Scripture attaches to the phrases, the word, the speech, the command, or the thing of God. I need not, therefore, repeat what I there said, nor what was shown under the third head in the chapter on miracles. It is enough to mention the repetition for the better understanding of what I am about to say — viz., that the Word of the Lord when it has reference to anyone but God Himself, signifies that Divine law treated of in Chap. IV.; in other words, religion, universal and catholic to the whole human race, as Isaiah describes it (chap. i:10), teaching that the true way of life consists, not in ceremonies, but in charity, and a true heart, and calling it indifferently God's Law and God's Word.

The expression is also used metaphorically for the order of nature and destiny (which, indeed, actually depend and follow from the eternal mandate of the Divine nature), and especially for such parts of such order as were foreseen by the prophets, for the prophets did not perceive future events as the result of natural causes, but as the fiats and decrees of God. Lastly, it is employed for the command of any prophet, in so far as he had perceived it by his peculiar faculty or prophetic gift, and not by the natural light of reason; this use springs chiefly from the usual prophetic conception of God as a legislator, which we remarked in Chap. IV. There are, then, three causes for the Bible's being called the Word of God: because it teaches true religion, of which God is the eternal Founder; because it narrates predictions of future events as though they were decrees of God; because its actual authors generally perceived things not by their ordinary natural faculties, but by a power peculiar to themselves, and introduced these things perceived, as told them by God.

Although Scripture contains much that is merely historical and can be perceived by natural reason, yet its name is acquired from its chief subject matter.

We can thus easily see how God can be said to be the Author of the Bible: it is because of the true religion therein contained, and not because He wished to communicate to men a certain number of books. We can also learn from hence the reason for the division into Old and New Testament. It was made because the prophets who preached religion before Christ, preached it as a national law in virtue of the covenant entered into under Moses; while the Apostles who came after Christ, preached it to all men as a universal religion solely in virtue of Christ's Passion: the cause for the division is not that the two parts are different in doctrine, nor that they were written as originals of the covenant, nor, lastly, that the catholic religion (which is in entire harmony with our nature) was new except in relation to those who had not known it: " it was in the world," as John the Evangelist says, " and the world knew it not."

Thus, even if we had fewer books of the Old and New Testament than we have, we should still not be deprived of the Word of God (which, as we have said, is identical with true religion), even as we do not now hold ourselves to be deprived of it, though we lack many cardinal writings such as the Book of the Law, which was religiously guarded in the Temple as the original of the Covenant, also the Book of Wars, the Book of Chronicles, and many others, from whence the extant Old Testament was taken and compiled. The above conclusion may be supported by many reasons.

I. Because the books of both Testaments were not written by express command at one place for all ages, but are a fortuitous collection of the works of men, writing each as his period and disposition dictated. So much is clearly shown by the call of the prophets who were bade to admonish the ungodly of their time, and also by the Apostolic Epistles.

II. Because it is one thing to understand the meaning of Scripture and the prophets, and quite another thing to understand the meaning of God, or the actual truth. This follows from what we said in Chap. II. We showed, in Chap. VI., that it applied to historic narratives, and to miracles: but it by no means applies to questions concerning true religion and virtue.

III. Because the books of the Old Testament were selected from many, and were collected and sanctioned by a council of the Pharisees, as we showed in Chap. X. The books of the New Testament were also chosen from many by councils which rejected as spurious other books held sacred by many. But these councils, both Pharisee and Christian, were not composed of prophets, but only of learned men and teachers. Still, we must grant that they were guided in their choice by a regard for the Word of God; and they must, therefore, have known what the law of God was.

IV. Because the Apostles wrote not as prophets, but as teachers (see last Chapter), and chose whatever method they thought best adapted for those whom they addressed: and consequently, there are many things in the Epistles (as we showed at the end of the last Chapter) which are not necessary to salvation.

V. Lastly, because there are four Evangelists in the New Testament, and it is scarcely credible that God can have designed to narrate the life of Christ four times over, and to communicate it thus to mankind. For though there are some details related in one Gospel which are not in another, and one often helps us to understand another, we cannot thence conclude that all that is set down is of vital importance to us, and that God chose the four Evangelists in order that the life of

Christ might be better understood; for each one preached his Gospel in a separate locality, each wrote it down as he preached it, in simple language, in order that the history of Christ might be clearly told, not with any view of explaining his fellow-Evangelists.

If there are some passages which can be better, and more easily understood by comparing the various versions, they are the result of chance, and are not numerous: their continuance in obscurity would have impaired neither the clearness of the narrative nor the blessedness of mankind.

We have now shown that Scripture can only be called the Word of God in so far as it affects religion, or the Divine law; we must now point out that, in respect to these questions, it is neither faulty, tampered with, nor corrupt. By faulty, tampered with, and corrupt, I here mean written so incorrectly, that the meaning cannot be arrived at by a study of the language, nor from the authority of Scripture. I will not go to such lengths as to say that the Bible, in so far as it contains the Divine law, has always preserved the same vowel-points, the same letters, or the same words (I leave this to be proved by, the Massoretes and other worshippers of the letter), I only, maintain that the meaning by, which alone an utterance is entitled to be called Divine, has come down to us uncorrupted, even though the original wording may have been more often changed than we suppose. Such alterations, as I have said above, detract nothing from the Divinity of the Bible, for the Bible would have been no less Divine had it been written in different words or a different language. That the Divine law has in this sense come down to us uncorrupted, is an assertion which admits of no dispute. For from the Bible itself we learn, without the smallest difficulty or ambiguity,, that its cardinal precept is: To love God above all things, and one's neighbour as one's self. This cannot be a spurious passage, nor due to a hasty and mistaken scribe, for if the Bible had ever put forth a different doctrine it would have had to change the whole of its teaching, for this is the corner-stone of religion, without which the whole fabric would fall headlong to the ground. The Bible would not be the work we have been examining, but something quite different.

We remain, then, unshaken in our belief that this has always been the doctrine of Scripture, and, consequently, that no error sufficient to vitiate it can have crept in without being instantly, observed by all; nor can anyone have succeeded in tampering with it and escaped the discovery of his malice.

As this corner-stone is intact, we must perforce admit the same of whatever other passages are indisputably dependent on it, and are also fundamental, as, for instance, that a God exists, that He foresees all things, that He is Almighty, that by His decree the good prosper and the wicked come to naught, and, finally, that our salvation depends solely on His grace.

These are doctrines which Scripture plainly teaches throughout, and which it is bound to teach, else all the rest would be empty and baseless; nor can we be less positive about other moral doctrines, which plainly are built upon this universal foundation — for instance, to uphold justice, to aid the weak, to do no murder, to covet no man's goods, &c. Precepts, I repeat, such as these, human malice and the lapse of ages are alike powerless to destroy, for if any part of them perished, its loss would immediately be supplied from the fundamental principle, especially the doctrine of charity, which is everywhere in both Testaments extolled above all others. Moreover, though it be true that there is no conceivable crime so heinous that it has never been committed, still there is no one who would attempt in excuse for his crimes to destroy, the law, or introduce an impious doctrine in the place of what is eternal and salutary; men's nature is so constituted that everyone (be he king or subject) who has committed a base action, tries to deck out his conduct with spurious excuses, till he seems to have done nothing but what is just and right.

We may conclude, therefore, that the whole Divine law, as taught by Scripture, has come down to us uncorrupted. Besides this there are certain facts which we may be sure have been transmitted in good faith. For instance, the main facts of Hebrew history, which were perfectly well known to everyone. The Jewish people were accustomed in former times to chant the ancient history of their nation in psalms. The main facts, also, of Christ's life and passion were immediately spread abroad through the whole Roman empire. It is therefore scarcely credible, unless nearly everybody, consented thereto, which we cannot suppose, that successive generations have handed down the broad outline of the Gospel narrative otherwise than as they received it.

Whatsoever, therefore, is spurious or faulty can only have reference to details — some circumstances in one or the other history or prophecy designed to stir the people to greater devotion; or in some miracle, with a view of confounding philosophers; or, lastly, in speculative matters after they had become mixed up with religion, so that some individual might prop up his own inventions with a pretext of Divine authority. But such matters have little to do with salvation, whether they be corrupted little or much, as I will show in detail in the next chapter, though I think the question sufficiently plain from what I have said already, especially in Chapter II.

CHAPTER XIII.

It is shown that Scripture teaches only very simple Doctrines,
such as suffice for Right Conduct.

IN THE SECOND chapter of this treatise we pointed out that the prophets were
gifted with extraordinary powers of imagination, but not of understanding; also
that God only revealed to them such things as are very simple — not philosophic
mysteries, — and that He adapted His communications to their previous opinions.
We further showed in Chap. V. that Scripture only transmits and teaches truths
which can readily be comprehended by all; not deducing and concatenating
its conclusions from definitions and axioms, but narrating quite simply, and
confirming its statements, with a view to inspiring belief, by an appeal to
experience as exemplified in miracles and history, and setting forth its truths in
the style and phraseology which would most appeal to the popular mind (cf. Chap.
VI., third division).

Lastly, we demonstrated in Chap. VIII. that the difficulty of understanding
Scripture lies in the language only, and not in the abstruseness of the argument.

To these considerations we may add that the Prophets did not preach only to
the learned, but to all Jews, without exception, while the Apostles were wont to
teach the gospel doctrine in churches where there were public meetings; whence
it follows that Scriptural doctrine contains no lofty speculations nor philosophic
reasoning, but only very simple matters, such as could be understood by the
slowest intelligence.

I am consequently lost in wonder at the ingenuity of those whom I have already
mentioned, who detect in the Bible mysteries so profound that they cannot be
explained in human language, and who have introduced so many philosophic
speculations into religion that the Church seems like an academy, and religion like
a science, or rather a dispute.

It is not to be wondered at that men, who boast of possessing supernatural
intelligence, should be unwilling to yield the palm of knowledge to philosophers
who have only their ordinary, faculties; still I should be surprised if I found them
teaching any new speculative doctrine, which was not a commonplace to those
Gentile philosophers whom, in spite of all, they stigmatize as blind; for, if one
inquires what these mysteries lurking in Scripture may be, one is confronted with
nothing but the reflections of Plato or Aristotle, or the like, which it would often
be easier for an ignorant man to dream than for the most accomplished scholar to
wrest out of the Bible.

However, I do not wish to affirm absolutely that Scripture contains no doctrines
in the sphere of philosophy, for in the last chapter I pointed out some of the kind,
as fundamental principles; but I go so far as to say that such doctrines are very
few and very simple. Their precise nature and definition I will now set forth. The
task will be easy, for we know that Scripture does not aim at imparting scientific
knowledge, and, therefore, it demands from men nothing but obedience, and
censures obstinacy, but not ignorance.

Furthermore, as obedience to God consists solely in love to our neighbour — for
whosoever loveth his neighbour, as a means of obeying God, hath, as St. Paul says
(Rom. xiii:8), fulfilled the law, — it follows that no knowledge is commended

in the Bible save that which is necessary for enabling all men to obey God in the manner stated, and without which they would become rebellious, or without the discipline of obedience.

Other speculative questions, which have no direct bearing on this object, or are concerned with the knowledge of natural events, do not affect Scripture, and should be entirely separated from religion.

Now, though everyone, as we have said, is now quite able to see this truth for himself, I should nevertheless wish, considering that the whole of Religion depends thereon, to explain the entire question more accurately and clearly. To this end I must first prove that the intellectual or accurate knowledge of God is not a gift, bestowed upon all good men like obedience; and, further, that the knowledge of God, required by Him through His prophets from everyone without exception, as needful to be known, is simply a knowledge of His Divine justice and charity. Both these points are easily proved from Scripture. The first plainly follows from Exodus vi:2, where God, in order to show the singular grace bestowed upon Moses, says to him: "And I appeared unto Abraham, unto Isaac, and unto Jacob by the name of El Sadai (A. V. God Almighty); but by my name Jehovah was I not known to them" — for the better understanding of which passage I may remark that El Sadai, in Hebrew, signifies the God who suffices, in that He gives to every man that which suffices for him; and, although Sadai is often used by itself, to signify God, we cannot doubt that the word El (God, {power, might}) is everywhere understood. Furthermore, we must note that Jehovah is the only word found in Scripture with the meaning of the absolute essence of God, without reference to created things. The Jews maintain, for this reason, that this is, strictly speaking, the only name of God; that the rest of the words used are merely titles; and, in truth, the other names of God, whether they be substantives or adjectives, are merely attributive, and belong to Him, in so far as He is conceived of in relation to created things, or manifested through them. Thus El, or Eloah, signifies powerful, as is well known, and only applies to God in respect to His supremacy, as when we call Paul an apostle; the faculties of his power are set forth in an accompanying adjective, as El, great, awful, just, merciful, &c., or else all are understood at once by the use of El in the plural number, with a singular signification, an expression frequently adopted in Scripture.

Now, as God tells Moses that He was not known to the patriarchs by the name of Jehovah, it follows that they were not cognizant of any attribute of God which expresses His absolute essence, but only of His deeds and promises that is, of His power, as manifested in visible things. God does not thus speak to Moses in order to accuse the patriarchs of infidelity, but, on the contrary, as a means of extolling their belief and faith, inasmuch as, though they possessed no extraordinary knowledge of God (such as Moses had), they yet accepted His promises as fixed and certain; whereas Moses, though his thoughts about God were more exalted, nevertheless doubted about the Divine promises, and complained to God that, instead of the promised deliverance, the prospects of the Israelites had darkened.

As the patriarchs did not know the distinctive name of God, and as God mentions the fact to Moses, in praise of their faith and single-heartedness, and in contrast to the extraordinary grace granted to Moses, it follows, as we stated at first, that men are not bound by, decree to have knowledge of the attributes of God, such knowledge being only granted to a few of the faithful: it is hardly worth while to quote further examples from Scripture, for everyone must recognize that knowledge of God is not equal among all good men. Moreover, a man cannot be ordered to be wise any more than he can be ordered to live and exist. Men, women, and children are all alike able to obey by, commandment, but not to be wise. If any tell us that it is not necessary to understand the Divine attributes, but that we must believe them simply, without proof, he is plainly, trifling. For what is invisible and can only, be perceived by the mind, cannot be apprehended by any, other means than proofs; if these are absent the object remains ungrasped; the repetition of what has been heard on such subjects no more indicates or attains to their meaning than the words of a parrot or a puppet speaking without sense or signification.

Before I proceed I ought to explain how it comes that we are often told in Genesis that the patriarchs preached in the name of Jehovah, this being in plain contradiction to the text above quoted. A reference to what was said in Chap. VIII. will readily explain the difficulty. It was there shown that the writer of the Pentateuch did not always speak of things and places by the names they bore in the times of which he was writing, but by the names best known to his contemporaries. God is thus said in the Pentateuch to have been preached by the patriarchs under the name of Jehovah, not because such was the name by which the patriarchs knew Him, but because this name was the one most reverenced by the Jews. This point, I say, must necessarily be noticed, for in Exodus it is expressly stated that God was not known to the patriarchs by this name; and in chap. iii:13, it is said that Moses desired to know the name of God. Now, if this name had been already known it would have been known to Moses. We must therefore draw the conclusion indicated, namely, that the faithful patriarchs did not know this name of God, and that the knowledge of God is bestowed and not commanded by the Deity.

It is now time to pass on to our second point, and show that God through His prophets required from men no other knowledge of Himself than is contained in a knowledge of His justice and charity — that is, of attributes which a certain manner of life will enable men to imitate. Jeremiah states this in so many words (xxii:15, 16): "Did not thy father eat, and drink, and do judgment and justice? and then it was well with him. He judged the cause of the poor and needy; then it was well with him: was not this to know Me? saith the Lord." The words in chap. ix:24 of the same book are equally, clear. "But let him that glorieth glory in this, that he understandeth and knoweth Me, that I am the Lord which exercise loving-kindness, judgment, and righteousness in the earth; for in these things I delight, saith the Lord." The same doctrine maybe gathered from Exod. xxxiv:6, where God revealed to Moses only, those of His attributes which display the Divine justice and charity. Lastly, we may call attention to a passage in John which we shall discuss at more length hereafter; the Apostle explains the nature of God (inasmuch as no one has beheld Him) through charity only, and concludes that he who possesses charity possesses, and in very, truth knows God.

We have thus seen that Moses, Jeremiah, and John sum up in a very short compass the knowledge of God needful for all, and that they state it to consist in exactly what we said, namely, that God is supremely just, and supremely merciful — in other words, the one perfect pattern of the true life. We may add that Scripture nowhere gives an express definition of God, and does not point out any other of His attributes which should be apprehended save these, nor does it in set terms praise any others. Wherefore we may draw the general conclusion that an intellectual knowledge of God, which takes cognizance of His nature in so far as it actually is, and which cannot by any manner of living be imitated by mankind or followed as an example, has no bearing whatever on true rules of conduct, on faith, or on revealed religion; consequently that men may be in complete error on the subject without incurring the charge of sinfulness. We need now no longer wonder that God adapted Himself to the existing opinions and imaginations of the prophets, or that the faithful held different ideas of God, as we showed in Chap. II.; or, again, that the sacred books speak very inaccurately of God, attributing to Him hands, feet, eyes, ears, a mind, and motion from one place to another; or that they ascribe to Him emotions, such as jealousy, mercy, &c., or, lastly, that they describe Him as a Judge in heaven sitting on a royal throne with Christ on His right hand. Such expressions are adapted to the understanding of the multitude, it being the object of the Bible to make men not learned but obedient.

In spite of this the general run of theologians, when they come upon any of these phrases which they cannot rationally harmonize with the Divine nature, maintain that they should be interpreted metaphorically, passages they cannot understand they say should be interpreted literally. But if every expression of this kind in the Bible is necessarily to be interpreted and understood metaphorically, Scripture must have been written, not for the people and the unlearned masses, but chiefly for accomplished experts and philosophers.

If it were indeed a sin to hold piously and simply the ideas about God we have just quoted, the prophets ought to have been strictly on their guard against the use of such expressions, seeing the weak-mindedness of the people, and ought, on the other hand, to have set forth first of all, duly and clearly, those attributes of God which are needful to be understood.

This they have nowhere done; we cannot, therefore, think that opinions taken in themselves without respect to actions are either pious or impious, but must maintain that a man is pious or impious in his beliefs only in so far as he is thereby incited to obedience, or derives from them license to sin and rebel. If a man, by believing what is true, becomes rebellious, his creed is impious; if by believing what is false he becomes obedient, his creed is pious; for the true knowledge of God comes not by commandment, but by Divine gift. God has required nothing from man but a knowledge of His Divine justice and charity, and that not as necessary to scientific accuracy, but to obedience.

CHAPTER XIV.

Definitions of Faith, the Faith, and the Foundations of Faith,
which is once for all separated from Philosophy.

FOR A TRUE knowledge of faith it is above all things necessary to understand that the Bible was adapted to the intelligence, not only of the prophets, but also of the diverse and fickle Jewish multitude. This will be recognized by all who give any thought to the subject, for they will see that a person who accepted promiscuously everything in Scripture as being the universal and absolute teaching of God, without accurately defining what was adapted to the popular intelligence, would find it impossible to escape confounding the opinions of the masses with the Divine doctrines, praising the judgments and comments of man as the teaching of God, and making a wrong use of Scriptural authority. Who, I say, does not perceive that this is the chief reason why so many sectaries teach contradictory opinions as Divine documents, and support their contentions with numerous Scriptural texts, till it has passed in Belgium into a proverb, geen ketter sonder letter — no heretic without a text? The sacred books were not written by one man, nor for the people of a single period, but by many authors of different temperaments, at times extending from first to last over nearly two thousand years, and perhaps much longer. We will not, however, accuse the sectaries of impiety because they have adapted the words of Scripture to their own opinions; it is thus that these words were adapted to the understanding of the masses originally, and everyone is at liberty so to treat them if he sees that he can thus obey God in matters relating to justice and charity with a more full consent: but we do accuse those who will not grant this freedom to their fellows, but who persecute all who differ from them, as God's enemies, however honourable and virtuous be their lives; while, on the other hand, they cherish those who agree with them, however foolish they may be, as God's elect. Such conduct is as wicked and dangerous to the state as any that can be conceived.

In order, therefore, to establish the limits to which individual freedom should extend, and to decide what persons, in spite of the diversity of their opinions, are to be looked upon as the faithful, we must define faith and its essentials. This task I hope to accomplish in the present chapter, and also to separate faith from philosophy, which is the chief aim of the whole treatise.

In order to proceed duly to the demonstration let us recapitulate the chief aim and object of Scripture; this will indicate a standard by which we may define faith.

We have said in a former chapter that the aim and object of Scripture is only to teach obedience. Thus much, I think, no one can question. Who does not see that both Testaments are nothing else but schools for this object, and have neither of them any aim beyond inspiring mankind with a voluntary obedience? For (not to repeat what I said in the last chapter) I will remark that Moses did not seek to convince the Jews by reason, but bound them by a covenant, by oaths, and by conferring benefits; further, he threatened the people with punishment if they should infringe the law, and promised rewards if they should obey it. All these are not means for teaching knowledge, but for inspiring obedience. The doctrine of the Gospels enjoins nothing but simple faith, namely, to believe in God and to honour Him, which is the same thing as to obey him. There is no occasion for me to throw further light on a question so plain by citing Scriptural texts commending obedience, such as may be found in great numbers in both Testaments. Moreover, the Bible teaches very clearly in a great many passages what everyone ought to do in order to obey God; the whole duty is summed up in love to one's neighbour. It cannot, therefore, be denied that he who by God's command loves his neighbour as himself is truly obedient and blessed according to the law, whereas he who hates his neighbour or neglects him is rebellious and obstinate.

Lastly, it is plain to everyone that the Bible was not written and disseminated only, for the learned, but for men of every age and race; wherefore we may, rest assured that we are not bound by Scriptural command to believe anything beyond what is absolutely necessary, for fulfilling its main precept.

This precept, then, is the only standard of the whole Catholic faith, and by it alone all the dogmas needful to be believed should be determined. So much being abundantly manifest, as is also the fact that all other doctrines of the faith can be legitimately deduced therefrom by reason alone, I leave it to every man to decide for himself how it comes to pass that so many divisions have arisen in the Church: can it be from any other cause than those suggested at the beginning of Chap. VIII.? It is these same causes which compel me to explain the method of determining the dogmas of the faith from the foundation we have discovered, for if I neglected to do so, and put the question on a regular basis, I might justly be said to have promised too lavishly, for that anyone might, by my showing, introduce any doctrine he liked into religion, under the pretext that it was a necessary means to obedience: especially would this be the case in questions respecting the Divine attributes.

In order, therefore, to set forth the whole matter methodically, I will begin with a definition of faith, which on the principle above given, should be as follows: —

Faith consists in a knowledge of God, without which obedience to Him would be impossible, and which the mere fact of obedience to Him implies. This definition is so clear, and follows so plainly from what we have already proved, that it needs no explanation. The consequences involved therein I will now briefly show.

(I.) Faith is not salutary in itself, but only in respect to the obedience it implies, or as James puts it in his Epistle, ii:17, "Faith without works is dead" (see the whole of the chapter quoted).

(II.) He who is truly obedient necessarily possesses true and saving faith; for if obedience be granted, faith must be granted also, as the same Apostle expressly says in these words (ii:18), "Show me thy faith without thy works, and I will show thee my faith by my works." So also John, I Ep. iv:7: "Everyone that loveth is born of God, and knoweth God: he that loveth not, knoweth not God; for God is love." From these texts, I repeat, it follows that we can only judge a man faithful or unfaithful by his works. If his works be good, he is faithful, however much his doctrines may differ from those of the rest of the faithful: if his works be evil, though he may verbally conform, he is unfaithful. For obedience implies faith, and faith without works is dead.

John, in the 13th verse of the chapter above quoted, expressly teaches the same doctrine: "Hereby," he says, "know we that we dwell in Him and He in us, because He hath given us of His Spirit," i.e. love. He had said before that God is love, and therefore he concludes (on his own received principles), that whoso possesses love possesses truly the Spirit of God. As no one has beheld God he infers that no one has knowledge or consciousness of God, except from love towards his neighbour, and also that no one can have knowledge of any of God's attributes, except this of love, in so far as we participate therein.

If these arguments are not conclusive, they, at any rate, show the Apostle's meaning, but the words in chap. ii:3, 4, of the same Epistle are much clearer, for they state in so many words our precise contention: "And hereby we do know that we know Him, if we keep His commandments. He that saith, I know Him, and keepeth not His commandments, is a liar, and the truth is not in him."

From all this, I repeat, it follows that they are the true enemies of Christ who persecute honourable and justice-loving men because they differ from them, and do not uphold the same religious dogmas as themselves: for whosoever loves justice and charity we know, by that very fact, to be faithful: whosoever persecutes the faithful, is an enemy to Christ.

Lastly, it follows that faith does not demand that dogmas should be true as that they should be pious — that is, such as will stir up the heart to obey; though there be many such which contain not a shadow of truth, so long as they be held in good faith, otherwise their adherents are disobedient, for how can anyone, desirous of loving justice and obeying God, adore as Divine what he knows to be alien from the Divine nature? However, men may err from simplicity of mind, and Scripture, as we have seen, does not condemn ignorance, but obstinacy. This is the necessary result of our definition of faith, and all its branches should spring from the universal rule above given, and from the evident aim and object of the Bible, unless we choose to mix our own inventions therewith. Thus it is not true doctrines which are expressly required by the Bible, so much as doctrines necessary for obedience, and to confirm in our hearts the love of our neighbour, wherein (to adopt the words of John) we are in God, and God in us.

As, then, each man's faith must be judged pious or impious only in respect of its producing obedience or obstinacy, and not in respect of its truth; and as no one will dispute that men's dispositions are exceedingly varied, that all do not acquiesce in the same things, but are ruled some by one opinion some by another, so that what moves one to devotion moves another to laughter and contempt, it follows that there can be no doctrines in the Catholic, or universal, religion, which can give rise to controversy among good men. Such doctrines might be pious to some and impious to others, whereas they should be judged solely by their fruits.

To the universal religion, then, belong only such dogmas as are absolutely required in order to attain obedience to God, and without which such obedience would be impossible; as for the rest, each man — seeing that he is the best judge of his own character should adopt whatever he thinks best adapted to strengthen his love of justice. If this were so, I think there would be no further occasion for controversies in the Church.

I have now no further fear in enumerating the dogmas of universal faith or the fundamental dogmas of the whole of Scripture, inasmuch as they all tend (as may be seen from what has been said) to this one doctrine, namely, that there exists a God, that is, a Supreme Being, Who loves justice and charity, and Who must be obeyed by whosoever would be saved; that the worship of this Being consists in the practice of justice and love towards one's neighbour, and that they contain nothing beyond the following doctrines: —

I. That God or a Supreme Being exists, sovereignly just and merciful, the Exemplar of the true life; that whosoever is ignorant of or disbelieves in His existence cannot obey Him or know Him as a Judge.

II. That He is One. Nobody will dispute that this doctrine is absolutely necessary for entire devotion, admiration, and love towards God. For devotion, admiration, and love spring from the superiority of one over all else.

III. That He is omnipresent, or that all things are open to Him, for if anything could be supposed to be concealed from Him, or to be unnoticed by, Him, we might doubt or be ignorant of the equity of His judgment as directing all things.

IV. That He has supreme right and dominion over all things, and that He does nothing under compulsion, but by His absolute fiat and grace. All things are bound to obey Him, He is not bound to obey any.

V. That the worship of God consists only in justice and charity, or love towards one's neighbour.

VI. That all those, and those only, who obey God by their manner of life are saved; the rest of mankind, who live under the sway of their pleasures, are lost. If we did not believe this, there would be no reason for obeying God rather than pleasure.

VII. Lastly, that God forgives the sins of those who repent. No one is free from sin, so that without this belief all would despair of salvation, and there would be no reason for believing in the mercy of God. He who firmly believes that God, out of the mercy and grace with which He directs all things, forgives the sins of men, and who feels his love of God kindled thereby, he, I say, does really, know Christ according to the Spirit, and Christ is in him.

No one can deny that all these doctrines are before all things necessary, to be believed, in order that every man, without exception, may be able to obey God according to the bidding of the Law above explained, for if one of these precepts be disregarded obedience is destroyed. But as to what God, or the Exemplar of the true life, may be, whether fire, or spirit, or light, or thought, or what not, this, I say, has nothing to do with faith any more than has the question how He comes to be the Exemplar of the true life, whether it be because He has a just and merciful mind, or because all things exist and act through Him, and consequently that we understand through Him, and through Him see what is truly just and good. Everyone may think on such questions as he likes,

Furthermore, faith is not affected, whether we hold that God is omnipresent essentially or potentially; that He directs all things by absolute fiat, or by the necessity of His nature; that He dictates laws like a prince, or that He sets them forth as eternal truths; that man obeys Him by virtue of free will, or by virtue of the necessity of the Divine decree; lastly, that the reward of the good and the punishment of the wicked is natural or supernatural: these and such like questions have no bearing on faith, except in so far as they are used as means to give us license to sin more, or to obey God less. I will go further, and maintain that every man is bound to adapt these dogmas to his own way of thinking, and to interpret them according as he feels that he can give them his fullest and most unhesitating assent, so that he may the more easily obey God with his whole heart.

Such was the manner, as we have already pointed out, in which the faith was in old time revealed and written, in accordance with the understanding and opinions of the prophets and people of the period; so, in like fashion, every man is bound to adapt it to his own opinions, so that he may accept it without any hesitation or mental repugnance. We have shown that faith does not so much re quire truth as piety, and that it is only quickening and pious through obedience, consequently no one is faithful save by obedience alone. The best faith is not necessarily possessed by him who displays the best reasons, but by him who displays the best fruits of justice and charity. How salutary and necessary this doctrine is for a state, in order that men may dwell together in peace and concord; and how many and how great causes of disturbance and crime are thereby cut off, I leave everyone to judge for himself!

Before we go further, I may remark that we can, by means of what we have just proved, easily answer the objections raised in Chap. I., when we were discussing God's speaking with the Israelites on Mount Sinai. For, though the voice heard by the Israelites could not give those men any philosophical or mathematical certitude of God's existence, it was yet sufficient to thrill them with admiration for God, as they already knew Him, and to stir them up to obedience: and such was the object of the display. God did not wish to teach the Israelites the absolute attributes of His essence (none of which He then revealed), but to break down their hardness of heart, and to draw them to obedience: therefore He did not appeal to them with reasons, but with the sound of trumpets, thunder, and lightnings.

It remains for me to show that between faith or theology, and philosophy, there is no connection, nor affinity. I think no one will dispute the fact who has knowledge of the aim and foundations of the two subjects, for they are as wide apart as the poles.

Philosophy has no end in view save truth: faith, as we have abundantly proved, looks for nothing but obedience and piety. Again, philosophy is based on axioms which must be sought from nature alone: faith is based on history and language, and must be sought for only in Scripture and revelation, as we showed in Chap. VII. Faith, therefore, allows the greatest latitude in philosophic speculation, allowing us without blame to think what we like about anything, and only condemning, as heretics and schismatics, those who teach opinions which tend to produce obstinacy, hatred, strife, and anger; while, on the other hand, only considering as faithful those who persuade us, as far as their reason and faculties will permit, to follow justice and charity.

Lastly, as what we are now setting forth are the most important subjects of my treatise, I would most urgently beg the reader, before I proceed, to read these two chapters with especial attention, and to take the trouble to weigh them well in his mind: let him take for granted that I have not written with a view to introducing novelties, but in order to do away with abuses, such as I hope I may, at some future time, at last see reformed.

CHAPTER XV.

Theology is shown not to be Subservient to Reason, nor Reason to Theology: a Definition of the Reason which enables us to accept the authority of the Bible.

THOSE WHO KNOW not that philosophy and reason are distinct, dispute whether Scripture should be made subservient to reason, or reason to Scripture: that is, whether the meaning of Scripture should be made to agreed with reason; or whether reason should be made to agree with Scripture: the latter position is assumed by the sceptics who deny the certitude of reason, the former by the dogmatists. Both parties are, as I have shown, utterly in the wrong, for either doctrine would require us to tamper with reason or with Scripture.

We have shown that Scripture does not teach philosophy, but merely obedience, and that all it contains has been adapted to the understanding and established opinions of the multitude. Those, therefore, who wish to adapt it to philosophy, must needs ascribe to the prophets many ideas which they never even dreamed of, and give an extremely forced interpretation to their words: those on the other hand, who would make reason and philosophy subservient to theology, will be forced to accept as Divine utterances the prejudices of the ancient Jews, and to fill and confuse their mind therewith. In short, one party will run wild with the aid of reason, and the other will run wild without the aid of reason.

The first among the Pharisees who openly maintained that Scripture should be made to agree with reason, was Maimonides, whose opinion we reviewed, and abundantly refuted in Chap. VIII.: now, although this writer had much authority among his contemporaries, he was deserted on this question by almost all, and the majority went straight over to the opinion of a certain R. Jehuda Alpakhar, who, in his anxiety to avoid the error of Maimonides, fell into another, which was its exact contrary. He held that reason should be made subservient, and entirely give way to Scripture. He thought that a passage should not be interpreted metaphorically, simply because it was repugnant to reason, but only in the cases when it is inconsistent with Scripture itself — that is, with its clear doctrines. Therefore he laid down the universal rule, that whatsoever Scripture teaches dogmatically, and affirms expressly, must on its own sole authority be admitted as absolutely true: that there is no doctrine in the Bible which directly contradicts the general tenour of the whole: but only some which appear to involve a difference, for the phrases of Scripture often seem to imply something contrary to what has been expressly taught. Such phrases, and such phrases only, we may interpret metaphorically.

For instance, Scripture clearly teaches the unity of God (see Deut. vi:4), nor is there any text distinctly asserting a plurality of gods; but in several passages God speaks of Himself, and the prophets speak of Him, in the plural number; such phrases are simply a manner of speaking, and do not mean that there actually are several gods: they are to be explained metaphorically, not because a plurality of gods is repugnant to reason, but because Scripture distinctly asserts that there is only one.

So, again, as Scripture asserts (as Alpakhar thinks) in Deut. iv:15, that God is incorporeal, we are bound, solely by the authority of this text, and not by reason, to believe that God has no body: consequently we must explain metaphorically, on the sole authority of Scripture, all those passages which attribute to God hands, feet, &c., and take them merely as figures of speech. Such is the opinion of

Alpakhar. In so far as he seeks to explain Scripture by Scripture, I praise him, but I marvel that a man gifted with reason should wish to debase that faculty. It is true that Scripture should be explained by Scripture, so long as we are in difficulties about the meaning and intention of the prophets, but when we have elicited the true meaning, we must of necessity make use of our judgment and reason in order to assent thereto. If reason, however, much as she rebels, is to be entirely subjected to Scripture, I ask, are we to effect her submission by her own aid, or without her, and blindly? If the latter, we shall surely act foolishly and injudiciously; if the former, we assent to Scripture under the dominion of reason, and should not assent to it without her. Moreover, I may ask now, is a man to assent to anything against his reason? What is denial if it be not reason's refusal to assent? In short, I am astonished that anyone should wish to subject reason, the greatest of gifts and a light from on high, to the dead letter which may have been corrupted by human malice; that it should be thought no crime to speak with contempt of mind, the true handwriting of God's Word, calling it corrupt, blind, and lost, while it is considered the greatest of crimes to say the same of the letter, which is merely the reflection and image of God's Word. Men think it pious to trust nothing to reason and their own judgment, and impious to doubt the faith of those who have transmitted to us the sacred books. Such conduct is not piety, but mere folly. And, after all, why are they so anxious? What are they afraid of? Do they think that faith and religion cannot be upheld unless — men purposely keep themselves in ignorance, and turn their backs on reason? If this be so, they have but a timid trust in Scripture.

However, be it far from me to say that religion should seek to enslave reason, or reason religion, or that both should not be able to keep their sovereignity in perfect harmony. I will revert to this question presently, for I wish now to discuss Alpakhar's rule.

He requires, as we have stated, that we should accept as true, or reject as false, everything asserted or denied by Scripture, and he further states that Scripture never expressly asserts or denies anything which contradicts its assertions or negations elsewhere. The rashness of such a requirement and statement can escape no one. For (passing over the fact that he does not notice that Scripture consists of different books, written at different times, for different people, by different authors: and also that his requirement is made on his own authority without any corroboration from reason or Scripture) he would be bound to show that all passages which are indirectly contradictory of the rest, can be satisfactorily explained metaphorically through the nature of the language and the context: further, that Scripture has come down to us untampered with. However, we will go into the matter at length.

Firstly, I ask what shall we do if reason prove recalcitrant? Shall we still be bound to affirm whatever Scripture affirms, and to deny whatever Scripture denies? Perhaps it will be answered that Scripture contains nothing repugnant to reason. But I insist!hat it expressly affirms and teaches that God is jealous (namely, in the decalogue itself, and in Exod. xxxiv:14, and in Deut. iv:24, and in many other places), and I assert that such a doctrine is repugnant to reason. It must, I suppose, in spite of all, be accepted as true. If there are any passages in Scripture which imply that God is not jealous, they must be taken metaphorically as meaning nothing of the kind. So, also, Scripture expressly states (Exod. xix:20, &c.) that God came down to Mount Sinai, and it attributes to Him other movements from place to place, nowhere directly stating that God does not so move. Wherefore, we must take the passage literally, and Solomon's words (I Kings viii:27), "But will God dwell on the earth? Behold the heavens and earth cannot contain thee," inasmuch as they do not expressly state that God does not move from place to place, but only imply it, must be explained away till they have no further semblance of denying locomotion to the Deity. So also we must believe that the sky is the habitation and throne of God, for Scripture expressly says so; and similarly many passages expressing the opinions of the prophets or the multitude, which reason and philosophy, but not Scripture, tell us to be false, must be taken as true if we are io follow the guidance of our author, for according to him, reason has nothing to do with the matter. Further, it is untrue that Scripture never contradicts itself directly, but only by implication. For Moses says, in so many words (Deut. iv:24), "The Lord thy God is a consuming fire," and elsewhere expressly denies that God has any likeness to visible things. (Deut. iv. 12.) If it be decided that the latter passage only contradicts the former by implication, and must be adapted thereto, lest it seem to negative it, let us grant that God is a fire; or rather, lest we should seem to have taken leave of our senses, let us pass the matter over and take another example.

Samuel expressly denies that God ever repents, "for he is not a man that he should repent" (I Sam. xv:29). Jeremiah, on the other hand, asserts that God does repent, both of the evil and of the good which He had intended to do (Jer. xviii:8-10). What? Are not these two texts directly contradictory? Which of the two, then, would our author want to explain metaphorically? Both statements are general, and each is the opposite of the other — what one flatly affirms, the other flatly, denies. So, by his own rule, he would be obliged at once to reject them as false, and to accept them as true.

Again, what is the point of one passage, not being contradicted by another directly, but only by implication, if the implication is clear, and the nature and context of the passage preclude metaphorical interpretation? There are many such instances in the Bible, as we saw in Chap. II. (where we pointed out that the prophets held different and contradictory opinions), and also in Chaps. IX. and X., where we drew attention to the contradictions in the historical narratives. There is no need for me to go through them all again, for what I have said sufficiently exposes the absurdities which would follow from an opinion and rule such as we are discussing, and shows the hastiness of its propounder.

We may, therefore, put this theory, as well as that of Maimonides, entirely out of court; and we may, take it for indisputable that theology is not bound to serve reason, nor reason theology, but that each has her own domain.

The sphere of reason is, as we have said, truth and wisdom; the sphere of theology, is piety and obedience. The power of reason does not extend so far as to determine for us that men may be blessed through simple obedience, without understanding. Theology, tells us nothing else, enjoins on us no command save obedience, and has neither the will nor the power to oppose reason: she defines the dogmas of faith (as we pointed out in the last chapter) only in so far as they may be necessary, for obedience, and leaves reason to determine their precise truth: for reason is the light of the mind, and without her all things are dreams and phantoms.

By theology, I here mean, strictly speaking, revelation, in so far as it indicates the object aimed at by Scripture namely, the scheme and manner of obedience, or the true dogmas of piety and faith. This may truly be called the Word of God, which does not consist in a certain number of books (see Chap. XII.). Theology thus understood, if we regard its precepts or rules of life, will be found in accordance with reason; and, if we look to its aim and object, will be seen to be in nowise repugnant thereto, wherefore it is universal to all men.

As for its bearing on Scripture, we have shown in Chap. VII. that the meaning of Scripture should be gathered from its own history, and not from the history of nature in general, which is the basis of philosophy.

We ought not to be hindered if we find that our investigation of the meaning of Scripture thus conducted shows us that it is here and there repugnant to reason; for whatever we may find of this sort in the Bible, which men may be in ignorance of, without injury to their charity, has, we may be sure, no bearing on theology or the Word of God, and may, therefore, without blame, be viewed by every one as he pleases.

To sum up, we may draw the absolute conclusion that the Bible must not be accommodated to reason, nor reason to the Bible.

Now, inasmuch as the basis of theology — the doctrine that man may be saved by obedience alone — cannot be proved by reason whether it be true or false, we may be asked, Why, then, should we believe it? If we do so without the aid of reason, we accept it blindly, and act foolishly and injudiciously; if, on the other hand, we settle that it can be proved by reason, theology becomes a part of philosophy, and inseparable therefrom. But I make answer that I have absolutely established that this basis of theology cannot be investigated by the natural light of reason, or, at any rate, that no one ever has proved it by such means, and, therefore, revelation was necessary. We should, however, make use of our reason, in order to grasp with moral certainty what is revealed — I say, with moral certainty, for we cannot hope to attain greater certainty, than the prophets: yet their certainty was only, moral, as I showed in Chap. II.

Those, therefore, who attempt to set forth the authority of Scripture with mathematical demonstrations are wholly in error: for the authority, of the Bible is dependent on the authority of the prophets, and can be supported by no stronger arguments than those employed in old time by the prophets for convincing the people of their own authority. Our certainty on the same subject can be founded on no other basis than that which served as foundation for the certainty of the prophets.

Now the certainty of the prophets consisted (as we pointed out) in these elements: — (I.) A distinct and vivid imagination. (II.) A sign. (III.) Lastly, and chiefly, a mind turned to what is just and good. It was based on no other reasons than these, and consequently they cannot prove their authority by any other reasons, either to the multitude whom they addressed orally, nor to us whom they address in writing.

The first of these reasons, namely, the vivid imagination, could be valid only for the prophets; therefore, our certainty concerning revelation must, and ought to be, based on the remaining two — namely, the sign and the teaching. Such is the express doctrine of Moses, for (in Deut. xviii.) he bids the people obey the prophet who should give a true sign in the name of the Lord, but if he should predict falsely, even though it were in the name of the Lord, he should be put to death, as should also he who strives to lead away the people from the true religion, though he confirm his authority with signs and portents. We may compare with the above Deut. xiii. Whence it follows that a true prophet could be distinguished from a false one, both by his doctrine and by the miracles he wrought, for Moses declares such an one to be a true prophet, and bids the people trust him without fear of deceit. He condemns as false, and worthy, of death, those who predict anything falsely even in the name of the Lord, or who preach false gods, even though their miracles be real.

The only reason, then, which we have for belief in Scripture or the writings of the prophets, is the doctrine we find therein, and the signs by which it is confirmed. For as we see that the prophets extol charity and justice above all things, and have no other object, we conclude that they did not write from unworthy motives, but because they really thought that men might become blessed through obedience and faith: further, as we see that they confirmed their teaching with signs and wonders, we become persuaded that they did not speak at random, nor run riot in their prophecies. We are further strengthened in our conclusion by the fact that the morality they teach is in evident agreement with reason, for it is no accidental coincidence that the Word of God which we find in the prophets coincides with the Word of God written in our hearts. We may, I say, conclude this from the sacred books as certainly as did the Jews of old from the living voice of the prophets: for we showed in Chap. XII. that Scripture has come down to us intact in respect to its doctrine and main narratives.

Therefore this whole basis of theology and Scripture, though it does not admit of mathematical proof, may yet be accepted with the approval of our judgment. It would be folly to refuse to accept what is confirmed by such ample prophetic testimony, and what has proved such a comfort to those whose reason is comparatively weak, and such a benefit to the state; a doctrine, moreover, which we may believe in without the slightest peril or hurt, and should reject simply because it cannot be mathematically proved: it is as though we should admit nothing as true, or as a wise rule of life, which could ever, in any possible way, be called in question; or as though most of our actions were not full of uncertainty and hazards.

I admit that those who believe that theology and philosophy are mutually contradictory, and that therefore either one or the other must be thrust from its throne — I admit, I say, that such persons are not unreasonable in attempting to put theology on a firm basis, and to demonstrate its truth mathematically. Who, unless he were desperate or mad, would wish to bid an incontinent farewell to reason, or to despise the arts and sciences, or to deny reason's certitude? But, in the meanwhile, we cannot wholly absolve them from blame, inasmuch as they invoke the aid of reason for her own defeat, and attempt infallibly to prove her fallible. While they are trying to prove mathematically the authority and truth of theology, and to take away the authority of natural reason, they are in reality only bringing theology under reason's dominion, and proving that her authority has no weight unless natural reason be at the back of it.

If they boast that they themselves assent because of the inward testimony of the Holy Spirit, and that they only invoke the aid of reason because of unbelievers, in order to convince them, not even so can this meet with our approval, for we can easily show that they have spoken either from emotion or vain-glory. It most clearly follows from the last chapter that the Holy Spirit only gives its testimony in favour of works, called by Paul (in Gal. v:22) the fruits of the Spirit, and is in itself really nothing but the mental acquiescence which follows a good action in our souls. No spirit gives testimony concerning the certitude of matters within the sphere of speculation, save only reason, who is mistress, as we have shown, of the whole realm of truth. If then they assert that they possess this Spirit which makes them certain of truth, they speak falsely, and according to the prejudices of the emotions, or else they are in great dread lest they should be vanquished by philosophers and exposed to public ridicule, and therefore they flee, as it were, to the altar; but their refuge is vain, for what altar will shelter a man who has outraged reason? However, I pass such persons over, for I think I have fulfilled my purpose, and shown how philosophy should be separated from theology, and wherein each consists; that neither should be subservient to the other, but that each should keep her unopposed dominion. Lastly, as occasion offered, I have pointed out the absurdities, the inconveniences, and the evils following from the extraordinary confusion which has hitherto prevailed between the two subjects, owing to their not being properly distinguished and separated. Before I go further I would expressly state (though I have said it before) that I consider the utility and the need for Holy Scripture or Revelation to be very great. For as we cannot perceive by the natural light of reason that simple obedience is the path of salvation 25, and are taught by revelation only that it is so by the special grace of God, which our reason cannot attain, it follows that the Bible has brought a very great consolation to mankind. All are able to obey, whereas there are but very few, compared with the aggregate of humanity, who can acquire the habit of virtue under the unaided guidance of reason. Thus if we had not the testimony of Scripture, we should doubt of the salvation of nearly all men.

25 "That simple obedience is the path of salvation." In other words, it is enough for salvation or blessedness, that we should embrace the Divine decrees as laws or commands; there is no need to conceive them as eternal truths. This can be taught us by Revelation, not Reason, as appears from the demonstrations given in Chapter IV.

CHAPTER XVI.

Of the Foundations of a State; of the Natural and Civil Rights of Individuals; and of the Rights of the Sovereign Power.

HITHERTO OUR CARE has been to separate philosophy from theology, and to show the freedom of thought which such separation insures to both. It is now time to determine the limits to which such freedom of thought and discussion may extend itself in the ideal state. For the due consideration of this question we must examine the foundations of a State, first turning our attention to the natural rights of individuals, and afterwards to religion and the state as a whole.

By the right and ordinance of nature, I merely mean those natural laws wherewith we conceive every individual to be conditioned by nature, so as to live and act in a given way. For instance, fishes are naturally conditioned for swimming, and the greater for devouring the less; therefore fishes enjoy the water, and the greater devour the less by sovereign natural right. For it is certain that nature, taken in the abstract, has sovereign right to do anything, she can; in other words, her right is co-extensive with her power. The power of nature is the power of God, which has sovereign right over all things; and, inasmuch as the power of nature is simply the aggregate of the powers of all her individual components, it follows that every, individual has sovereign right to do all that he can; in other words, the rights of an individual extend to the utmost limits of his power as it has been conditioned. Now it is the sovereign law and right of nature that each individual should endeavour to preserve itself as it is, without regard to anything but itself; therefore this sovereign law and right belongs to every individual, namely, to exist and act according to its natural conditions. We do not here acknowledge any difference between mankind and other individual natural entities, nor between men endowed with reason and those to whom reason is unknown; nor between fools, madmen, and sane men. Whatsoever an individual does by the laws of its nature it has a sovereign right to do, inasmuch as it acts as it was conditioned by nature, and cannot act otherwise. Wherefore among men, so long as they are considered as living under the sway of nature, he who does not yet know reason, or who has not yet acquired the habit of virtue, acts solely according to the laws of his desire with as sovereign a right as he who orders his life entirely by the laws of reason.

That is, as the wise man has sovereign right to do all that reason dictates, or to live according to the laws of reason, so also the ignorant and foolish man has sovereign right to do all that desire dictates, or to live according to the laws of desire. This is identical with the teaching of Paul, who acknowledges that previous to the law — that is, so long as men are considered of as living under the sway of nature, there is no sin.

The natural right of the individual man is thus determined, not by sound reason, but by desire and power. All are not naturally conditioned so as to act according to the laws and rules of reason; nay, on the contrary, all men are born ignorant, and before they can learn the right way of life and acquire the habit of virtue, the greater part of their life, even if they have been well brought up, has passed away. Nevertheless, they are in the meanwhile bound to live and preserve themselves as far as they can by the unaided impulses of desire. Nature has given them no other guide, and has denied them the present power of living according to sound reason; so that they are no more bound to live by the dictates of an enlightened mind, than a cat is bound to live by the laws of the nature of a lion.

Whatsoever, therefore, an individual (considered as under the sway of nature) thinks useful for himself, whether led by sound reason or impelled by the passions, that he has a sovereign right to seek and to take for himself as he best can, whether by force, cunning, entreaty, or any other means; consequently he may regard as an enemy anyone who hinders the accomplishment of his purpose.

It follows from what we have said that the right and ordinance of nature, under which all men are born, and under which they mostly live, only prohibits such things as no one desires, and no one can attain: it does not forbid strife, nor hatred, nor anger, nor deceit, nor, indeed, any of the means suggested by desire.

This we need not wonder at, for nature is not bounded by the laws of human reason, which aims only at man's true benefit and preservation; her limits are infinitely wider, and have reference to the eternal order of nature, wherein man is but a speck; it is by the necessity of this alone that all individuals are conditioned for living and acting in a particular way. If anything, therefore, in nature seems to us ridiculous, absurd, or evil, it is because we only know in part, and are almost entirely ignorant of the order and interdependence of nature as a whole, and also because we want everything to be arranged according to the dictates of our human reason; in reality that which reason considers evil, is not evil in respect to the order and laws of nature as a whole, but only in respect to the laws of our reason.

Nevertheless, no one can doubt that it is much better for us to live according to the laws and assured dictates of reason, for, as we said, they have men's true good for their object. Moreover, everyone wishes to live as far as possible securely beyond the reach of fear, and this would be quite impossible so long as everyone did everything he liked, and reason's claim was lowered to a par with those of hatred and anger; there is no one who is not ill at ease in the midst of enmity, hatred, anger, and deceit, and who does not seek to avoid them as much as he can. When we reflect that men without mutual help, or the aid of reason, must needs live most miserably, as we clearly proved in Chap. V., we shall plainly see that men must necessarily come to an agreement to live together as securely and well as possible if they are to enjoy as a whole the rights which naturally belong to them as individuals, and their life should be no more conditioned by the force and desire of individuals, but by the power and will of the whole body. This end they will be unable to attain if desire be their only guide (for by the laws of desire each man is drawn in a different direction); they must, therefore, most firmly decree and establish that they will be guided in everything by reason (which nobody will dare openly to repudiate lest he should be taken for a madman), and will restrain any desire which is injurious to a man's fellows, that they will do to all as they would be done by, and that they will defend their neighbour's rights as their own.

How such a compact as this should be entered into, how ratified and established, we will now inquire.

Now it is a universal law of human nature that no one ever neglects anything which he judges to be good, except with the hope of gaining a greater good, or from the fear of a greater evil; nor does anyone endure an evil except for the sake of avoiding a greater evil, or gaining a greater good. That is, everyone will, of two goods, choose that which he thinks the greatest; and, of two evils, that which he thinks the least. I say advisedly that which he thinks the greatest or the least, for it does not necessarily follow that he judges right. This law is so deeply implanted in the human mind that it ought to be counted among eternal truths and axioms.

As a necessary consequence of the principle just enunciated, no one can honestly promise to forego the right which he has over all things 26, and in general no one will abide by his promises, unless under the fear of a greater evil, or the hope of a greater good. An example will make the matter clearer. Suppose that a robber forces me to promise that I will give him my goods at his will and pleasure. It is plain (inasmuch as my natural right is, as I have shown, co-extensive with my power) that if I can free myself from this robber by stratagem, by assenting to his demands, I have the natural right to do so, and to pretend to accept his conditions. Or again, suppose I have genuinely promised someone that for the space of twenty days I will not taste food or any nourishment; and suppose I afterwards find that was foolish, and cannot be kept without very great injury to myself; as I am bound by natural law and right to choose the least of two evils, I have complete right to break my compact, and act as if my promise had never been uttered. I say that I should have perfect natural right to do so, whether I was actuated by true and evident reason, or whether I was actuated by mere opinion in thinking I had promised rashly; whether my reasons were true or false, I should be in fear of a greater evil, which, by the ordinance of nature, I should strive to avoid by every means in my power.

We may, therefore, conclude that a compact is only made valid by its utility, without which it becomes null and void. It is, therefore, foolish to ask a man to keep his faith with us for ever, unless we also endeavour that the violation of the compact we enter into shall involve for the violator more harm than good. This consideration should have very great weight in forming a state. However, if all men could be easily led by reason alone, and could recognize what is best and most useful for a state, there would be no one who would not forswear deceit, for everyone would keep most religiously to their compact in their desire for the chief good, namely, the shield and buckler of the commonwealth. However, it is far from being the case that all men can always be easily led by reason alone; everyone is drawn away by his pleasure, while avarice, ambition, envy, hatred, and the like so engross the mind that, reason has no place therein. Hence, though men make — promises with all the appearances of good faith, and agree that they will keep to their engagement, no one can absolutely rely on another man's promise unless there is something behind it. Everyone has by nature a right to act deceitfully. and to break his compacts, unless he be restrained by the hope of some greater good, or the fear of some greater evil.

However, as we have shown that the natural right of the individual is only limited by his power, it is clear that by transferring, either willingly or under compulsion, this power into the hands of another, he in so doing necessarily cedes also a part of his right; and further, that the Sovereign right over all men belongs to him who has sovereign power, wherewith he can compel men by force, or restrain them by threats of the universally feared punishment of death; such sovereign right he will retain only so long as he can maintain his power of enforcing his will; otherwise he will totter on his throne, and no one who is stronger than he will be bound unwillingly to obey him.

In this manner a society can be formed without any violation of natural right, and the covenant can always be strictly kept — that is, if each individual hands over the whole of his power to the body politic, the latter will then possess sovereign natural right over all things; that is, it will have sole and unquestioned dominion, and everyone will be bound to obey, under pain of the severest punishment. A body politic of this kind is called a Democracy, which may be defined as a society which wields all its power as a whole. The sovereign power is not restrained by any laws, but everyone is bound to obey it in all things; such is the state of things implied when men either tacitly or expressly handed over to it all their power of self-defence, or in other words, all their right. For if they had wished to retain any right for themselves, they ought to have taken precautions for its defence and preservation; as they have not done so, and indeed could not have done so without dividing and consequently ruining the state, they placed themselves absolutely at the mercy of the sovereign power; and, therefore, having acted (as we have shown) as reason and necessity demanded, they are obliged to fulfil the commands of the sovereign power, however absurd these may be, else they will be public enemies, and will act against reason, which urges the preservation of the state as a primary duty. For reason bids us choose the least of two evils.

Furthermore, this danger of submitting absolutely to the dominion and will of another, is one which may be incurred with a light heart: for we have shown that sovereigns only possess this right of imposing their will, so long as they have the full power to enforce it: if such power be lost their right to command is lost also, or lapses to those who have assumed it and can keep it. Thus it is very rare for sovereigns to impose thoroughly irrational commands, for they are bound to consult their own interests, and retain their power by consulting the public good and acting according to the dictates of reason, as Seneca says, "violenta imperia nemo continuit diu." No one can long retain a tyrant's sway.

In a democracy, irrational commands are still less to be feared: for it is almost impossible that the majority of a people, especially if it be a large one, should agree in an irrational design: and, moreover, the basis and aim of a democracy is to avoid the desires as irrational, and to bring men as far as possible under the control of reason, so that they may live in peace and harmony: if this basis be removed the whole fabric falls to ruin.

Such being the ends in view for the sovereign power, the duty of subjects is, as I have said, to obey its commands, and to recognize no right save that which it sanctions.

It will, perhaps, be thought that we are turning subjects into slaves: for slaves obey commands and free men live as they like; but this idea is based on a misconception, for the true slave is he who is led away by his pleasures and can neither see what is good for him nor act accordingly: he alone is free who lives with free consent under the entire guidance of reason.

Action in obedience to orders does take away freedom in a certain sense, but it does not, therefore, make a man a slave, all depends on the object of the action. If the object of the action be the good of the state, and not the good of the agent, the latter is a slave and does himself no good: but in a state or kingdom where the weal of the whole people, and not that of the ruler, is the supreme law, obedience to the sovereign power does not make a man a slave, of no use to himself, but a subject. Therefore, that state is the freest whose laws are founded on sound reason, so that every member of it may, if he will, be free 27; that is, live with full consent under the entire guidance of reason.

Children, though they are bound to obey all the commands of their parents, are yet not slaves: for the commands of parents look generally to the children's benefit.

We must, therefore, acknowledge a great difference between a slave, a son, and a subject; their positions may be thus defined. A slave is one who is bound to obey his master's orders, though they are given solely in the master's interest: a son is one who obeys his father's orders, given in his own interest; a subject obeys the orders of the sovereign power, given for the common interest, wherein he is included.

I think I have now shown sufficiently clearly the basis of a democracy: I have especially desired to do so, for I believe it to be of all forms of government the most natural, and the most consonant with individual liberty. In it no one transfers his natural right so absolutely that he has no further voice in affairs, he only hands it over to the majority of a society, whereof he is a unit. Thus all men remain as they were in the state of nature, equals.

This is the only form of government which I have treated of at length, for it is the one most akin to my purpose of showing the benefits of freedom in a state.

I may pass over the fundamental principles of other forms of government, for we may gather from what has been said whence their right arises without going into its origin. The possessor of sovereign power, whether he be one, or many, or the whole body politic, has the sovereign right of imposing any commands he pleases: and he who has either voluntarily, or under compulsion, transferred the right to defend him to another, has, in so doing, renounced his natural right and is therefore bound to obey, in all things, the commands of the sovereign power; and will be bound so to do so long as the king, or nobles, or the people preserve the sovereign power which formed the basis of the original transfer. I need add no more.

The bases and rights of dominion being thus displayed, we shall readily be able to define private civil right, wrong, justice, and injustice, with their relations to the state; and also to determine what constitutes an ally, or an enemy, or the crime of treason.

By private civil right we can only mean the liberty every man possesses to preserve his existence, a liberty limited by the edicts of the sovereign power, and preserved only by its authority: for when a man has transferred to another his right of living as he likes, which was only limited by his power, that is, has transferred his liberty and power of self-defence, he is bound to live as that other dictates, and to trust to him entirely for his defence. Wrong takes place when a citizen, or subject, is forced by another to undergo some loss or pain in contradiction to the authority of the law, or the edict of the sovereign power.

Wrong is conceivable only in an organized community: nor can it ever accrue to subjects from any act of the sovereign, who has the right to do what he likes. It can only arise, therefore, between private persons, who are bound by law and right not to injure one another. Justice consists in the habitual rendering to every man his lawful due: injustice consists in depriving a man, under the pretence of legality, of what the laws, rightly interpreted, would allow him. These last are also called equity and iniquity, because those who administer the laws are bound to show no respect of persons, but to account all men equal, and to defend every man's right equally, neither envying the rich nor despising the poor.

The men of two states become allies, when for the sake of avoiding war, or for some other advantage, they covenant to do each other no hurt, but on the contrary, to assist each other if necessity arises, each retaining his independence. Such a covenant is valid so long as its basis of danger or advantage is in force: no one enters into an engagement, or is bound to stand by his compacts unless there be a hope of some accruing good, or the fear of some evil: if this basis be removed the compact thereby becomes void: this has been abundantly shown by experience. For although different states make treaties not to harm one another, they always take every possible precaution against such treaties being broken by the stronger party, and do not rely on the compact, unless there is a sufficiently obvious object and advantage to both parties in observing it. Otherwise they would fear a breach of faith, nor would there be any wrong done thereby: for who in his proper senses, and aware of the right of the sovereign power, would trust in the promises of one who has the will and the power to do what he likes, and who aims solely at the safety and advantage of his dominion? Moreover, if we consult loyalty and religion, we shall see that no one in possession of power ought to abide by his promises to the injury of his dominion; for he cannot keep such promises without breaking the engagement he made with his subjects, by which both he and they are most solemnly bound. An enemy is one who lives apart from the state, and does not recognize its authority either as a subject or as an ally. It is not hatred which makes a man an enemy, but the rights of the state. The rights of the state are the same in regard to him who does not recognize by any compact the state authority, as they are against him who has done the state an injury: it has the right to force him as best it can, either to submit, or to contract an alliance.

Lastly, treason can only be committed by subjects, who by compact, either tacit or expressed, have transferred all their rights to the state: a subject is said to have committed this crime when he has attempted, for whatever reason, to seize the sovereign power, or to place it in different hands. I say, has attempted, for if punishment were not to overtake him till he had succeeded, it would often come too late, the sovereign rights would have been acquired or transferred already.

I also say, has attempted, for whatever reason, to seize the sovereign power, and I recognize no difference whether such an attempt should be followed by public loss or public gain. Whatever be his reason for acting, the crime is treason, and he is rightly condemned: in war, everyone would admit the justice of his sentence. If a man does not keep to his post, but approaches the enemy without the knowledge of his commander, whatever may be his motive, so long as he acts on his own motion, even if he advances with the design of defeating the enemy, he is rightly put to death, because he has violated his oath, and infringed the rights of his commander. That all citizens are equally bound by these rights in time of peace, is not so generally recognized, but the reasons for obedience are in both cases identical. The state must be preserved and directed by the sole authority of the sovereign, and such authority and right have been accorded by universal consent to him alone: if, therefore, anyone else attempts, without his consent, to execute any public enterprise, even though the state might (as we said) reap benefit therefrom, such person has none the less infringed the sovereigns right, and would be rightly punished for treason.

In order that every scruple may be removed, we may now answer the inquiry, whether our former assertion that everyone who has not the practice of reason, may, in the state of nature, live by sovereign natural right, according to the laws of his desires, is not in direct opposition to the law and right of God as revealed. For as all men absolutely (whether they be less endowed with reason or more) are equally bound by the Divine command to love their neighbour as themselves, it may be said that they cannot, without wrong, do injury to anyone, or live according to their desires.

This objection, so far as the state of nature is concerned, can be easily answered, for the state of nature is, both in nature and in time, prior to religion. No one knows by nature that he owes any obedience to God 28, nor can he attain thereto by any exercise of his reason, but solely by revelation confirmed by signs. Therefore, previous to revelation, no one is bound by a Divine law and right of which he is necessarily in ignorance. The state of nature must by no means be confounded with a state of religion, but must be conceived as without either religion or law, and consequently without sin or wrong: this is how we have described it, and we are confirmed by the authority of Paul. It is not only in respect of ignorance that we conceive the state of nature as prior to, and lacking the Divine revealed law and right; but in respect of freedom also, wherewith all men are born endowed.

If men were naturally bound by the Divine law and right, or if the Divine law and right were a natural necessity, there would have been no need for God to make a covenant with mankind, and to bind them thereto with an oath and agreement.

We must, then, fully grant that the Divine law and right originated at the time when men by express covenant agreed to obey God in all things, and ceded, as it were, their natural freedom, transferring their rights to God in the manner described in speaking of the formation of a state.

However, I will treat of these matters more at length presently.

It may be insisted that sovereigns are as much bound by the Divine law as subjects: whereas we have asserted that they retain their natural rights, and may do whatever they like.

In order to clear up the whole difficulty, which arises rather concerning the natural right than the natural state, I maintain that everyone is bound, in the state of nature, to live according to Divine law, in the same way as he is bound to live according to the dictates of sound reason; namely, inasmuch as it is to his advantage, and necessary for his salvation; but, if he will not so live, he may do otherwise at his own risk. He is thus bound to live according to his own laws, not according to anyone else's, and to recognize no man as a judge, or as a superior in religion. Such, in my opinion, is the position of a sovereign, for he may take advice from his fellow-men, but he is not bound to recognize any as a judge, nor anyone besides himself as an arbitrator on any question of right, unless it be a prophet sent expressly by God and attesting his mission by indisputable signs. Even then he does not recognize a man, but God Himself as His judge.

If a sovereign refuses to obey God as revealed in His law, he does so at his own risk and loss, but without violating any civil or natural right. For the civil right is dependent on his own decree; and natural right is dependent on the laws of nature, which latter are not adapted to religion, whose sole aim is the good of humanity, but to the order of nature — that is, to God's eternal decree unknown to us.

This truth seems to be adumbrated in a somewhat obscurer form by those who maintain that men can sin against God's revelation, but not against the eternal decree by which He has ordained all things.

We may be asked, what should we do if the sovereign commands anything contrary to religion, and the obedience which we have expressly vowed to God? should we obey the Divine law or the human law? I shall treat of this question at length hereafter, and will therefore merely say now, that God should be obeyed before all else, when we have a certain and indisputable revelation of His will: but men are very prone to error on religious subjects, and, according to the diversity of their dispositions, are wont with considerable stir to put forward their own inventions, as experience more than sufficiently attests, so that if no one were bound to obey the state in matters which, in his own opinion concern religion, the rights of the state would be dependent on every man's judgment and passions. No one would consider himself bound to obey laws framed against his faith or superstition; and on this pretext he might assume unbounded license. In this way, the rights of the civil authorities would be utterly set at nought, so that we must conclude that the sovereign power, which alone is bound both by Divine and natural right to preserve and guard the laws of the state, should have supreme authority for making any laws about religion which it thinks fit; all are bound to obey its behests on the subject in accordance with their promise which God bids them to keep.

However, if the sovereign power be heathen, we should either enter into no engagements therewith, and yield up our lives sooner than transfer to it any of our rights; or, if the engagement be made, and our rights transferred, we should (inasmuch as we should have ourselves transferred the right of defending ourselves and our religion) be bound to obey them, and to keep our word: we might even rightly be bound so to do, except in those cases where God, by indisputable revelation, has promised His special aid against tyranny, or given us special exemption from obedience. Thus we see that, of all the Jews in Babylon, there were only three youths who were certain of the help of God, and, therefore, refused to obey Nebuchadnezzar. All the rest, with the sole exception of Daniel, who was beloved by the king, were doubtless compelled by right to obey, perhaps thinking that they had been delivered up by God into the hands of the king, and that the king had obtained and preserved his dominion by God's design. On the other hand, Eleazar, before his country had utterly fallen, wished to give a proof of his constancy to his compatriots, in order that they might follow in his footsteps, and go to any lengths, rather than allow their right and power to be transferred to the Greeks, or brave any torture rather than swear allegiance to the heathen. Instances are occurring every day in confirmation of what I here advance. The rulers of Christian kingdoms do not hesitate, with a view to strengthening their dominion, to make treaties with Turks and heathen, and to give orders to their subjects who settle among such peoples not to assume more freedom, either in things secular or religious, than is set down in the treaty, or allowed by the foreign government. We may see this exemplified in the Dutch treaty with the Japanese, which I have already mentioned.

26 "No one can honestly promise to forego the right which he has over all things." In the state of social life, where general right determines what is good or evil, stratagem is rightly distinguished as of two kinds, good and evil. But in the state of Nature, where every man is his own judge, possessing the absolute right to lay down laws for himself, to interpret them as he pleases, or to abrogate them if he thinks it convenient, it is not conceivable that stratagem should be evil.

27 "Every member of it may, if he will, be free." Whatever be the social state a man finds; himself in, he may be free. For certainly a man is free, in so far as he is led by reason. Now reason (though Hobbes thinks otherwise) is always on the side of peace, which cannot be attained unless the general laws of the state be respected. Therefore the more he is free, the more constantly will he respect the laws of his country, and obey the commands of the sovereign power to which he is subject.

28 "No one knows by nature that he owes any obedience to God." When Paul says that men have in themselves no refuge, he speaks as a man: for in the ninth chapter of the same epistle he expressly teaches that God has mercy on whom He will, and that men are without excuse, only because they are in God's power like clay in the hands of a potter, who out of the same lump makes vessels, some for honour and some for dishonour, not because they have been forewarned. As regards the Divine natural law whereof the chief commandment is, as we have said, to love God, I have called it a law in the same sense, as philosophers style laws those general rules of nature, according to which everything happens. For the love of God is not a state of obedience: it is a virtue which necessarily exists in a man who knows God rightly. Obedience has regard to the will of a ruler, not to necessity and truth. Now as we are ignorant of the nature of God's will, and on the other hand know that everything happens solely by God's power, we cannot, except through revelation, know whether God wishes in any way to be honoured as a sovereign.

Again; we have shown that the Divine rights appear to us in the light of rights or commands, only so long as we are ignorant of their cause: as soon as their cause is known, they cease to be rights, and we embrace them no longer as rights but as eternal truths; in other words, obedience passes into love of God, which emanates from true knowledge as necessarily as light emanates from the sun. Reason then leads us to love God, but cannot lead us to obey Him; for we cannot embrace the commands of God as Divine, while we are in ignorance of their cause, neither can we rationally conceive God as a sovereign laying down laws as a sovereign.

CHAPTER XVII.

It is shown that no one can, or need, transfer all his Rights to the Sovereign Power. Of the Hebrew Republic, as it was during the lifetime of Moses, and after his death, till the foundation of the Monarchy; and of its Excellence. Lastly, of the causes why the Theocratic Republic fell, and why it could hardly have continued without Dissension.

THE THEORY PUT forward in the last chapter, of the universal rights of the sovereign power, and of the natural rights of the individual transferred thereto, though it corresponds in many respects with actual practice, and though practice may be so arranged as to conform to it more and more, must nevertheless always remain in many respects purely ideal. No one can ever so utterly transfer to another his power and, consequently, his rights, as to cease to be a man; nor can there ever be a power so sovereign that it can carry out every possible wish. It will always be vain to order a subject to hate what he believes brings him advantage, or to love what brings him loss, or not to be offended at insults, or not to wish to be free from fear, or a hundred other things of the sort, which necessarily follow from the laws of human nature. So much, I think, is abundantly shown by experience: for men have never so far ceded their power as to cease to be an object of fear to the rulers who received such power and right; and dominions have always been in as much danger from their own subjects as from external enemies. If it were really the case, that men could be deprived of their natural rights so utterly as never to have any further influence on affairs 29, except with the permission of the holders of sovereign right, it would then be possible to maintain with impunity the most violent tyranny, which, I suppose, no one would for an instant admit.

We must, therefore, grant that every man retains some part of his right, in dependence on his own decision, and no one else's.

However, in order correctly to understand the extent of the sovereign's right and power, we must take notice that it does not cover only those actions to which it can compel men by fear, but absolutely every action which it can induce men to perform: for it is the fact of obedience, not the motive for obedience, which makes a man a subject.

Whatever be the cause which leads a man to obey the commands of the sovereign, whether it be fear or hope, or love of his country, or any other emotion — the fact remains that the man takes counsel with himself, and nevertheless acts as his sovereign orders. We must not, therefore, assert that all actions resulting from a man's deliberation with himself are done in obedience to the rights of the individual rather than the sovereign: as a matter of fact, all actions spring from a man's deliberation with himself, whether the determining motive be love or fear of punishment; therefore, either dominion does not exist, and has no rights over its subjects, or else it extends over every instance in which it can prevail on men to decide to obey it. Consequently, every action which a subject performs in accordance with the commands of the sovereign, whether such action springs from love, or fear, or (as is more frequently the case) from hope and fear together, or from reverence. compounded of fear and admiration, or, indeed, any motive whatever, is performed in virtue of his submission to the sovereign, and not in virtue of his own authority.

This point is made still more clear by the fact that obedience does not consist so much in the outward act as in the mental state of the person obeying; so that he is most under the dominion of another who with his whole heart determines to obey another's commands; and consequently the firmest dominion belongs to the sovereign who has most influence over the minds of his subjects; if those who are most feared possessed the firmest dominion, the firmest dominion would belong to the subjects of a tyrant, for they are always greatly feared by their ruler. Furthermore, though it is impossible to govern the mind as completely as the tongue, nevertheless minds are, to a certain extent, under the control of the sovereign, for he can in many ways bring about that the greatest part of his subjects should follow his wishes in their beliefs, their loves, and their hates. Though such emotions do not arise at the express command of the sovereign they often result (as experience shows) from the authority of his power, and from his direction; in other words, in virtue of his right; we may, therefore, without doing violence to our understanding, conceive men who follow the instigation of their sovereign in their beliefs, their loves, their hates, their contempt, and all other emotions whatsoever.

Though the powers of government, as thus conceived, are sufficiently ample, they can never become large enough to execute every possible wish of their possessors. This, I think, I have already shown clearly enough. The method of forming a dominion which should prove lasting I do not, as I have said, intend to discuss, but in order to arrive at the object I have in view, I will touch on the teaching of Divine revelation to Moses in this respect, and we will consider the history and the success of the Jews, gathering therefrom what should be the chief concessions made by sovereigns to their subjects with a view to the security and increase of their dominion.

That the preservation of a state chiefly depends on the subjects' fidelity and constancy in carrying out the orders they receive, is most clearly taught both by reason and experience; how subjects ought to be guided so as best to preserve their fidelity and virtue is not so obvious. All, both rulers and ruled, are men, and prone to follow after their lusts. The fickle disposition of the multitude almost reduces those who have experience of it to despair, for it is governed solely by emotions, not by reason: it rushes headlong into every enterprise, and is easily corrupted either by avarice or luxury: everyone thinks himself omniscient and wishes to fashion all things to his liking, judging a thing to be just or unjust, lawful or unlawful, according as he thinks it will bring him profit or loss: vanity leads him to despise his equals, and refuse their guidance: envy of superior fame or fortune (for such gifts are never equally distributed) leads him to desire and rejoice in his neighbour's downfall. I need not go through the whole list, everyone knows already how much crime. results from disgust at the present — desire for change, headlong anger, and contempt for poverty — and how men's minds are engrossed and kept in turmoil thereby.

To guard against all these evils, and form a dominion where no room is left for deceit; to frame our institutions so that every man, whatever his disposition, may prefer public right to private advantage, this is the task and this the toil. Necessity is often the mother of invention, but she has never yet succeeded in framing a dominion that was in less danger from its own citizens than from open enemies, or whose rulers did not fear the latter less than the former. Witness the state of Rome, invincible by her enemies, but many times conquered and sorely oppressed by her own citizens, especially in the war between Vespasian and Vitellius. (See Tacitus, Hist. bk. iv. for a description of the pitiable state of the city.)

Alexander thought prestige abroad more easy to acquire than prestige at home, and believed that his greatness could be destroyed by his own followers. Fearing such a disaster, he thus addressed his friends: "Keep me safe from internal treachery and domestic plots, and I will front without fear the dangers of battle and of war. Philip was more secure in the battle array than in the theatre: he often escaped from the hands of the enemy, he could not escape from his own subjects. If you think over the deaths of kings, you will count up more who have died by the assassin than by the open foe." (Q. Curtius, chap. vi.)

For the sake of making themselves secure, kings who seized the throne in ancient times used to try to spread the idea that they were descended from the immortal gods, thinking that if their subjects and the rest of mankind did not look on them as equals, but believed them to be gods, they would willingly submit to their rule, and obey their commands. Thus Augustus persuaded the Romans that he was descended from AEneas, who was the son of Venus, and numbered among the gods. "He wished himself to be worshipped in temples, like the gods, with flamens and priests." (Tacitus, Ann. i. 10.)

Alexander wished to be saluted as the son of Jupiter, not from motives of pride but of policy, as he showed by his answer to the invective of Hermolaus: "It is almost laughable," said he, that Hermolaus asked me to contradict Jupiter, by whose oracle I am recognized. Am I responsible for the answers of the gods? It offered me the name of son; acquiescence was by no means foreign to my present designs. Would that the Indians also would believe me to be a god! Wars are carried through by prestige, falsehoods that are believed often gain the force of truth." (Curtius, viii,. Para, 8.) In these few words he cleverly contrives to palm off a fiction on the ignorant, and at the same time hints at the motive for the deception.

Cleon, in his speech persuading the Macedonians to obey their king, adopted a similar device: for after going through the praises of Alexander with admiration, and recalling his merits, he proceeds, "the Persians are not only pious, but prudent in worshipping their kings as gods: for kingship is the shield of public safety," and he ends thus, "I, myself, when the king enters a banquet hall, should prostrate my body on the ground; other men should do the like, especially those who are wise " (Curtius, viii. Para. 66). However, the Macedonians were more prudent — indeed, it is only complete barbarians who can be so openly cajoled, and can suffer themselves to be turned from subjects into slaves without interests of their own. Others, notwithstanding, have been able more easily to spread the belief that kingship is sacred, and plays the part of God on the earth, that it has been instituted by God, not by the suffrage and consent of men; and that it is preserved and guarded by Divine special providence and aid. Similar fictions have been promulgated by monarchs, with the object of strengthening their dominion, but these I will pass over, and in order to arrive at my main purpose, will merely recall and discuss the teaching on the subject of Divine revelation to Moses in ancient times.

We have said in Chap. V. that after the Hebrews came up out of Egypt they were not bound by the law and right of any other nation, but were at liberty to institute any new rites at their pleasure, and to occupy whatever territory they chose. After their liberation from the intolerable bondage of the Egyptians, they were bound by no covenant to any man; and, therefore, every man entered into his natural right, and was free to retain it or to give it up, and transfer it to another. Being, then, in the state of nature, they followed the advice of Moses, in whom they chiefly trusted, and decided to transfer their right to no human being, but only to God;

without further delay they all, with one voice, promised to obey all the commands of the Deity, and to acknowledge no right that He did not proclaim as such by prophetic revelation. This promise, or transference of right to God, was effected in the same manner as we have conceived it to have been in ordinary societies, when men agree to divest themselves of their natural rights. It is, in fact, in virtue of a set covenant, and an oath (see Exod. xxxiv:10), that the Jews freely, and not under compulsion or threats, surrendered their rights and transferred them to God. Moreover, in order that this covenant might be ratified and settled, and might be free from all suspicion of deceit, God did not enter into it till the Jews had had experience of His wonderful power by which alone they had been, or could be, preserved in a state of prosperity (Exod. xix:4, 5). It is because they believed that nothing but God's power could preserve them that they surrendered to God the natural power of self-preservation, which they formerly, perhaps, thought they possessed, and consequently they surrendered at the same time all their natural right.

God alone, therefore, held dominion over the Hebrews, whose state was in virtue of the covenant called God's kingdom, and God was said to be their king; consequently the enemies of the Jews were said to be the enemies of God, and the citizens who tried to seize the dominion were guilty of treason against God; and, lastly, the laws of the state were called the laws and commandments of God. Thus in the Hebrew state the civil and religious authority, each consisting solely of obedience to God, were one and the same. The dogmas of religion were not precepts, but laws and ordinances; piety was regarded as the same as loyalty, impiety as the same as disaffection. Everyone who fell away from religion ceased to be a citizen, and was, on that ground alone, accounted an enemy: those who died for the sake of religion, were held to have died for their country; in fact, between civil and religious law and right there was no distinction whatever. {in Biblical Hebrew, there was no word for what we call Religion." Modern Hebrew has selected a word whose root is "knowledge."} For this reason the government could be called a Theocracy, inasmuch as the citizens were not bound by anything save the revelations of God.

However, this state of things existed rather in theory than in practice, for it will appear from what we are about to say, that the Hebrews, as a matter of fact, retained absolutely in their own hands the right of sovereignty: this is shown by the method and plan by which the government was carried on, as I will now explain.

Inasmuch as the Hebrews did not transfer their rights to any other person but, as in a democracy, all surrendered their rights equally, and cried out with one voice, "Whatsoever God shall speak (no mediator or mouthpiece being named) that will we do," it follows that all were equally bound by the covenant, and that all had an equal right to consult the Deity, to accept and to interpret His laws, so that all had an exactly equal share in the government. Thus at first they all approached God together, so that they might learn His commands, but in this first salutation, they were so thoroughly terrified and so astounded to hear God speaking, that they thought their last hour was at hand: full of fear, therefore, they went afresh to Moses, and said, "Lo, we have heard God speaking in the fire, and there is no cause why we should wish to die: surely this great fire will consume us: if we hear again the voice of God, we shall surely die. Thou, therefore, go near, and hear all the words of our God, and thou (not God) shalt speak with us: all that God shall tell us, that will we hearken to and perform."

They thus clearly abrogated their former covenant, and absolutely transferred to

Moses their right to consult God and interpret His commands: for they do not here promise obedience to all that God shall tell them, but to all that God shall tell Moses (see Deut. v:20 after the Decalogue, and chap. xviii:15, 16). Moses, therefore, remained the sole promulgator and interpreter of the Divine laws, and consequently also the sovereign judge, who could not be arraigned himself, and who acted among the Hebrews the part, of God; in other words, held the sovereign kingship: he alone had the right to consult God, to give the Divine answers to the people, and to see that they were carried out. I say he alone, for if anyone during the life of Moses was desirous of preaching anything in the name of the Lord, he was, even if a true prophet, considered guilty and a usurper of the sovereign right (Numb. xi:28) 30. We may here notice, that though the people had elected Moses, they could not rightfully elect Moses's successor; for having transferred to Moses their right of consulting God, and absolutely promised to regard him as a Divine oracle, they had plainly forfeited the whole of their right, and were bound to accept as chosen by God anyone proclaimed by Moses as his successor. If Moses had so chosen his successor, who like him should wield the sole right of government, possessing the sole right of consulting God, and consequently of making and abrogating laws, of deciding on peace or war, of sending ambassadors, appointing judges — in fact, discharging all the functions of a sovereign, the state would have become simply a monarchy, only differing from other monarchies in the fact, that the latter are, or should be, carried on in accordance with God's decree, unknown even to the monarch, whereas the Hebrew monarch would have been the only person to whom the decree was revealed. A difference which increases, rather than diminishes the monarch's authority. As far as the people in both cases are concerned, each would be equally subject, and equally ignorant of the Divine decree, for each would be dependent on the monarch's words, and would learn from him alone, what was lawful or unlawful: nor would the fact that the people believed that the monarch was only issuing commands in accordance with God's decree revealed to him, make it less in subjection, but rather more. However, Moses elected no such successor, but left the dominion to those who came after him in a condition which could not be called a popular government, nor an aristocracy, nor a monarchy, but a Theocracy. For the right of interpreting laws was vested in one man, while the right and power of administering the state according to the laws thus interpreted, was vested in another man (see Numb. xxvii:21) 31.

In order that the question may be thoroughly understood, I will duly set forth the administration of the whole state.

First, the people were commanded to build a tabernacle, which should be, as it were, the dwelling of God — that is, of the sovereign authority of the state. This tabernacle was to be erected at the cost of the whole people, not of one man, in order that the place where God was consulted might be public property. The Levites were chosen as courtiers and administrators of this royal abode; while Aaron, the brother of Moses, was chosen to be their chief and second, as it were, to God their King, being succeeded in the office by his legitimate sons.

He, as the nearest to God, was the sovereign interpreter of the Divine laws; he communicated the answers of the Divine oracle to the people, and entreated God's favour for them. If, in addition to these privileges, he had possessed the right of ruling, he would have been neither more nor less than an absolute monarch; but, in respect to government, he was only a private citizen: the whole tribe of Levi was so completely divested of governing rights that it did not even take its share with the others in the partition of territory. Moses provided for its support by inspiring the common people with great reverence for it, as the only tribe dedicated to God.

Further, the army, formed from the remaining twelve tribes, was commanded to invade the land of Canaan, to divide it into twelve portions, and to distribute it among the tribes by lot. For this task twelve captains were chosen, one from every tribe, and were, together with Joshua and Eleazar, the high priest, empowered to divide the land into twelve equal parts, and distribute it by lot. Joshua was chosen for the chief command of the army, inasmuch as none but he had the right to consult God in emergencies, not like Moses, alone in his tent, or in the tabernacle, but through the high priest, to whom only the answers of God were revealed. Furthermore, he was empowered to execute, and cause the people to obey God's commands, transmitted through the high priests; to find, and to make use of, means for carrying them out; to choose as many, army captains as he liked; to make whatever choice he thought best; to send ambassadors in his own name; and, in short, to have the entire control of the war. To his office there was no rightful successor — indeed, the post was only filled by the direct order of the Deity, on occasions of public emergency. In ordinary times, all the management of peace and war was vested in the captains of the tribes, as I will shortly point out. Lastly, all men between the ages of twenty and sixty were ordered to bear arms, and form a citizen army, owing allegiance, not to its general-inchief, nor to the high priest, but to Religion and to God. The army, or the hosts, were called the army of God, or the hosts of God. For this reason God was called by the Hebrews the God of Armies; and the ark of the covenant was borne in the midst of the army in important battles, when the safety or destruction of the whole people hung upon the issue, so that the people might, as it were, see their King among them, and put forth all their strength.

From these directions, left by Moses to his successors, we plainly see that he chose administrators, rather than despots, to come after him; for he invested no one with the power of consulting God, where he liked and alone, consequently, no one had the power possessed by himself of ordaining and abrogating laws, of deciding on war or peace, of choosing men to fill offices both religious and secular: all these are the prerogatives of a sovereign. The high priest, indeed, had the right of interpreting laws, and communicating the answers of God, but he could not do so when he liked, as Moses could, but only when he was asked by the general-inchief of the army, the council, or some similar authority. The general-inchief and the council could consult God when they liked, but could only receive His answers through the high priest; so that the utterances of God, as reported by the high priest, were not decrees, as they were when reported by Moses, but only answers; they were accepted by Joshua and the council, and only then had the force of commands and decrees {Like the separation of powers in the United States of America.}

The high priest, both in the case of Aaron and of his son Eleazar, was chosen by Moses; nor had anyone, after Moses' death, a right to elect to the office, which became hereditary . The general-inchief of the army was also chosen by Moses, and assumed his functions in virtue of the commands, not of the high priest, but of Moses: indeed, after the death of Joshua, the high priest did not appoint anyone in his place, and the captains did not consult God afresh about a general-inchief, but each retained Joshua's power in respect to the contingent of his own tribe, and all retained it collectively, in respect to the whole army. There seems to have been no need of a general-inchief, except when they were obliged to unite their forces against a common enemy. This occurred most frequently during the time of Joshua, when they had no fixed dwelling. place, and possessed all things in common. After all the tribes had gained their territories by right of conquest, and had divided their allotted gains, they, became separated, having no longer their possessions in common, so that the need for a single commander ceased, for the different tribes should be considered rather in the light of confederated states than of bodies of fellow-citizens. In respect to their God and their religion, they, were fellow-citizens; but, in respect to the rights which one possessed with regard to another, they were only confederated: they, were, in fact, in much the same position (if one excepts the Temple common to all) as the United States of the Netherlands {or United States of America}. The division of property, held in common is only another phrase for the possession of his share by each of the owners singly, and the surrender by the others of their rights over such share. This is why Moses elected captains of the tribes — namely, that when the dominion was divided, each might take care of his own part; consulting God through the high priest on the affairs of his tribe, ruling over his army, building and fortifying cities, appointing judges, attacking the enemies of his own dominion, and having complete control over all civil and military affairs. He was not bound to acknowledge any superior judge save God 32, or a prophet whom God should expressly send. If he departed from the worship of God, the rest of the tribes did not arraign him as a subject, but attacked him as an enemy. Of this we have examples in Scripture. When Joshua was dead, the children of Israel (not a fresh general-inchief) consulted God; it being decided that the tribe of Judah should be the first to attack its enemies, the tribe in question contracted a single alliance with the tribe of Simeon, for uniting their forces, and attacking their common enemy, the rest of the tribes not being included in the alliance (Judges i:1, 2, 3). Each tribe separately made war against its own enemies, and, according to its pleasure, received them as subjects or allies, though it had been commanded not to spare them on any conditions, but to destroy them utterly. Such disobedience met with reproof from the rest of the tribes, but did not cause the offending tribe to be arraigned: it was not considered a sufficient reason for proclaiming a civil war, or interfering in one another's affairs. But when the tribe of Benjamin offended against the others, and so loosened the bonds of peace that none of the confederated tribes could find refuge within its borders, they attacked it as an enemy, and gaining the victory over it after three battles, put to death both guilty and innocent, according to the laws of war: an act which they subsequently bewailed with tardy repentance.

These examples plainly confirm what we have said concerning the rights of each tribe. Perhaps we shall be asked who elected the successors to the captains of each tribe; on this point I can gather no positive information in Scripture, but I conjecture that as the tribes were divided into families, each headed by its senior member, the senior of all these heads of families succeeded by right to the office of captain, for Moses chose from among these seniors his seventy coadjutors, who formed with himself the supreme council. Those who administered the government after the death of Joshua were called elders, and elder is a very common Hebrew expression in the sense of judge, as I suppose everyone knows; however, it is not very important for us to make up our minds on this point. It is enough to have shown that after the death of Moses no one man wielded all the power of a sovereign; as affairs were not all managed by one man, nor by a single council, nor by the popular vote, but partly by one tribe, partly by the rest in equal shares, it is most evident that the government, after the death of Moses, was neither monarchic, nor aristocratic, nor popular, but, as we have said, Theocratic. The reasons for applying this name are:

I. Because the royal seat of government was the Temple, and in respect to it alone, as we have shown, all the tribes were fellow-citizens,

II. Because all the people owed allegiance to God, their supreme Judge, to whom only they had promised implicit obedience in all things.

III. Because the general-inchief or dictator, when there was need of such, was elected by none save God alone. This was expressly commanded by Moses in the name of God (Deut. xix:15), and witnessed by the actual choice of Gideon, of Samson, and of Samuel; wherefrom we may conclude that the other faithful leaders were chosen in the same manner, though it is not expressly told us.

These preliminaries being stated, it is now time to inquire the effects of forming a dominion on this plan, and to see whether it so effectually kept within bounds both rulers and ruled, that the former were never tyrannical and the latter never rebellious.

Those who administer or possess governing power, always try to surround their high-handed actions with a cloak of legality, and to persuade the people that they act from good motives; this they are easily able to effect when they are the sole interpreters of the law; for it is evident that they are thus able to assume a far greater freedom to carry out their wishes and desires than if the interpretation if the law is vested in someone else, or if the laws were so self-evident that no one could be in doubt as to their meaning. We thus see that the power of evil-doing was greatly curtailed for the Hebrew captains by the fact that the whole interpretation of the law was vested in the Levites (Deut. xxi:5), who, on their part, had no share in the government, and depended for all their support and consideration on a correct interpretation of the laws entrusted to them. Moreover, the whole people was commanded to come together at a certain place every seven years and be instructed in the law by the high-priest; further, each individual was bidden to read the book of the law through and through continually with scrupulous care. (Deut. xxxi:9, 10, and vi:7.) The captains were thus for their own sakes bound to take great care to administer everything according to the laws laid down, and well known to all, if they, wished to be held in high honour by, the people, who would regard them as the administrators of God's dominion, and as God's vicegerents; otherwise they could not have escaped all the virulence of theological hatred. There was another very important check on the unbridled license of the captains, in the fact, that the army was formed from the whole body, of the citizens, between the ages of twenty and sixty, without exception, and that the captains were not able to hire any foreign soldiery. This I say was very, important, for it is well known that princes can oppress their peoples with the single aid of the soldiery in their pay; while there is nothing more formidable to them than the freedom of citizen soldiers, who have established the freedom and glory of their country, by their valour, their toil, and their blood. Thus Alexander, when he was about to make wax on Darius, a second time, after hearing the advice of Parmenio, did not chide him who gave the advice, but Polysperchon, who was standing by. For, as Curtius says (iv. Para. 13), he did not venture to reproach Parmenio again after having shortly, before reproved him too sharply. This freedom of the Macedonians, which he so dreaded, he was not able to subdue till after the number of captives enlisted in the army, surpassed that of his own people: then, but not till then, he gave rein to his anger so long checked by, the independence of his chief fellow-countrymen.

If this independence of citizen soldiers can restrain the princes of ordinary states who are wont to usurp the whole glory of victories, it must have been still more effectual against the Hebrew captains, whose soldiers were fighting, not for the glory of a prince, but for the glory of God, and who did not go forth to battle till the Divine assent had been given.

We must also remember that the Hebrew captains were associated only by the bonds of religion: therefore, if any one of them had transgressed, and begun to violate the Divine right, he might have been treated by the rest as an enemy and lawfully subdued.

An additional check may be found in the fear of a new prophet arising, for if a man of unblemished life could show by certain signs that he was really a prophet, he ipso facto obtained the sovereign right to rule, which was given to him, as to Moses formerly, in the name of God, as revealed to himself alone; not merely through the high priest, as in the case of the captains. There is no doubt that such an one would easily be able to enlist an oppressed people in his cause, and by trifling signs persuade them of anything he wished: on the other hand, if affairs were well ordered, the captain would be able to make provision in time; that the prophet should be submitted to his approval, and be examined whether he were really of unblemished life, and possessed indisputable signs of his mission: also, whether the teaching he proposed to set forth in the name of the Lord agreed with received doctrines, and the general laws of the country; if his credentials were insufficient, or his doctrines new, he could lawfully be put to death, or else received on the captain's sole responsibility and authority.

Again, the captains were not superior to the others in nobility or birth, but only administered the government in virtue of their age and personal qualities. Lastly, neither captains nor army had any reason for preferring war to peace. The army, as we have stated, consisted entirely of citizens, so that affairs were managed by the same persons both in peace and war. The man who was a soldier in the camp was a citizen in the market-place, he who was a leader in the camp was a judge in the law courts, he who was a general in the camp was a ruler in the state. Thus no one could desire war for its own sake, but only for the sake of preserving peace and liberty; possibly the captains avoided change as far as possible, so as not to be obliged to consult the high priest and submit to the indignity of standing in his presence.

So much for the precautions for keeping the captains within bounds. We must now look for the restraints upon the people: these, however, are very clearly indicated in the very groundwork of the social fabric.

Anyone who gives the subject the slightest attention, will see that the state was so ordered as to inspire the most ardent patriotism in the hearts of the citizens, so that the latter would be very hard to persuade to betray their country, and be ready to endure anything rather than submit to a foreign yoke. After they had transferred their right to God, they thought that their kingdom belonged to God, and that they themselves were God's children. Other nations they looked upon as God's enemies, and regarded with intense hatred (which they took to be piety, see Psalm cxxxix:21, 22): nothing would have been more abhorrent to them than swearing allegiance to a foreigner, and promising him obedience: nor could they conceive any greater or more execrable crime than the betrayal of their country, the kingdom of the God whom they adored.

It was considered wicked for anyone to settle outside of the country, inasmuch as the worship of God by which they were bound could not be carried on elsewhere:

their own land alone was considered holy, the rest of the earth unclean and profane.

David, who was forced to live in exile, complained before Saul as follows: "But if they be the children of men who have stirred thee up against me, cursed be they before the Lord; for they have driven me out this day from abiding in the inheritance of the Lord, saying, Go, serve other gods." (I Sam. xxvi:19.) For the same reason no citizen, as we should especially remark, was ever sent into exile: he who sinned was liable to punishment, but not to disgrace.

Thus the love of the Hebrews for their country was not only patriotism, but also piety, and was cherished and nurtured bv daily rites till, like their hatred of other nations, it must have passed into their nature. Their daily worship was not only different from that of other nations (as it might well be, considering that they were a peculiar people and entirely apart from the rest), it was absolutely contrary. Such daily reprobation naturally gave rise to a lasting hatred, deeply implanted in the heart: for of all hatreds none is more deep and tenacious than that which springs from extreme devoutness or piety, and is itself cherished as pious. Nor was a general cause lacking for inflaming such hatred more and more, inasmuch as it was reciprocated; the surrounding nations regarding the Jews with a hatred just as intense.

How great was the effect of all these causes, namely, freedom from man's dominion; devotion to their country; absolute rights over all other men; a hatred not only permitted but pious; a contempt for their fellow-men; the singularity of their customs and religious rites; the effect, I repeat, of all these causes in strengthening the hearts of the Jews to bear all things for their country, with extraordinary constancy and valour, will at once be discerned by reason and attested by experience. Never, so long as the city was standing, could they endure to remain under foreign dominion; and therefore they called Jerusalem "a rebellious city" (Ezra iv:12). Their state after its reestablishment (which was a mere shadow of the first, for the high priests had usurped the rights of the tribal captains) was, with great difficulty, destroyed by the Romans, as Tacitus bears witness (Hist. ii:4):— "Vespasian had closed the war against the Jews, abandoning the siege of Jerusalem as an enterprise difficult and arduous rather from the character of the people and the obstinacy of their superstition, than from the strength left to the besieged for meeting their necessities." But besides these characteristics, which are merely ascribed by an individual opinion, there was one feature peculiar to this state and of great importance in retaining the affections of the citizens, and checking all thoughts of desertion, or abandonment of the country: namely, self-interest, the strength and life of all human action. This was peculiarly engaged in the Hebrew state, for nowhere else did citizens possess their goods so securely, as did the subjects of this community, for the latter possessed as large a share in the land and the fields as did their chiefs, and were owners of their plots of ground in perpetuity; for if any man was compelled by poverty to sell his farm or his pasture, he received it back again intact at the year of jubilee: there were other similar enactments against the possibility of alienating real property.

Again, poverty w as nowhere more endurable than in a country where duty towards one's neighbour, that is, one's fellow-citizen, was practised with the utmost piety, as a means of gaining the favour of God the King. Thus the Hebrew citizens would nowhere be so well off as in their own country; outside its limits they met with nothing but loss and disgrace.

The following considerations were of weight, not only in keeping them at home, but also in preventing civil war and removing causes of strife; no one was bound to serve his equal, but only to serve God, while charity and love towards fellow-citizens was accounted the highest piety; this last feeling was not a little fostered by the general hatred with which they regarded foreign nations and were regarded by them. Furthermore, the strict discipline of obedience in which they were brought up, was a very important factor; for they were bound to carry on all their actions according to the set rules of the law: a man might not plough when he liked, but only at certain times, in certain years, and with one sort of beast at a time; so, too, he might only sow and reap in a certain method and season — in fact, his whole life was one long school of obedience (see Chap. V. on the use of ceremonies); such a habit was thus engendered, that conformity seemed freedom instead of servitude, and men desired what was commanded rather than what was forbidden. This result was not a little aided by the fact that the people were bound, at certain seasons of the year, to give themselves up to rest and rejoicing, not for their own pleasure, but in order that they might worship God cheerfully.

Three times in the year they feasted before the Lord; on the seventh day of every week they were bidden to abstain from all work and to rest; besides these, there were other occasions when innocent rejoicing and feasting were not only allowed but enjoined. I do not think any better means of influencing men's minds could be devised; for there is no more powerful attraction than joy springing from devotion, a mixture of admiration and love. It was not easy to be wearied by constant repetition, for the rites on the various festivals were varied and recurred seldom. We may add the deep reverence for the Temple which all most religiously fostered, on account of the peculiar rites and duties that they were obliged to perform before approaching thither. Even now, Jews cannot read without horror of the crime of Manasseh, who dared to place au idol in the Temple. The laws, scrupulously preserved in the inmost sanctuary, were objects of equal reverence to the people. Popular reports and misconceptions were, therefore, very little to be feared in this quarter, for no one dared decide on sacred matters, but all felt bound to obey, without consulting their reason, all the commands given by the answers of God received in the Temple, and all the laws which God had ordained.

I think I have now explained clearly, though briefly,, the main features of the Hebrew commonwealth. I must now inquire into the causes which led the people so often to fall away from the law, which brought about their frequent subjection, and, finally, the complete destruction of their dominion. Perhaps I shall be told that it sprang from their hardness of heart; but this is childish, for why should this people be more hard of heart than others; was it by nature?

But nature forms individuals, not peoples; the latter are only distinguishable by the difference of their language, their customs, and their laws; while from the two last — i.e., customs and laws, — it may arise that they have a peculiar disposition, a peculiar manner of life, and peculiar prejudices. If, then, the Hebrews were harder of heart than other nations, the fault lay with their laws or customs.

This is certainly true, in the sense that, if God had wished their dominion to be more lasting, He would have given them other rites and laws, and would have instituted a different form of government. We can, therefore, only say that their God was angry with them, not only, as Jeremiah says, from the building of the city, but even from the founding of their laws.

This is borne witness to by Ezekiel xx:25: "Wherefore I gave them also statutes that were not good, and judgments whereby they should not live; and I polluted them in their own gifts, in that they caused to pass through the fire all that openeth the womb; that I might make them desolate, to the end that they might know that I am the Lord."

In order that we may understand these words, and the destruction of the Hebrew commonwealth, we must bear in mind that it had at first been intended to entrust the whole duties of the priesthood to the firstborn, and not to the Levites (see Numb. viii:17). It was only when all the tribes, except the Levites, worshipped the golden calf, that the firstborn were rejected and defiled, and the Levites chosen in their stead (Deut. x:8). When I reflect on this change, I feel disposed to break forth with the words of Tacitus. God's object at that time was not the safety of the Jews, but vengeance. I am greatly astonished that the celestial mind was so inflamed with anger that it ordained laws, which always are supposed to promote the honour, well-being, and security of a people, with the purpose of vengeance, for the sake of punishment; so that the laws do not seem so much laws — that is, the safeguard of the people — as pains and penalties.

The gifts which the people were obliged to bestow on the Levites and priests — the redemption of the firstborn, the poll-tax due to the Levites, the privilege possessed by the latter of the sole performance of sacred rites — all these, I say, were a continual reproach to the people, a continual reminder of their defilement and rejection. Moreover, we may be sure that the Levites were for ever heaping reproaches upon them: for among so many thousands there must have been many importunate dabblers in theology. Hence the people got into the way of watching the acts of the Levites, who were but human; of accusing the whole body of the faults of one member, and continually murmuring.

Besides this, there was the obligation to keep in idleness men hateful to them, and connected by no ties of blood. Especially would this seem grievous when provisions were dear. What wonder, then, if in times of peace, when striking miracles had ceased, and no men of paramount authority were forthcoming, the irritable and greedy temper of the people began to wax cold, and at length to fall away from a worship, which, though Divine, was also humiliating, and even hostile, and to seek after something fresh; or can we be surprised that the captains, who always adopt the popular course, in order to gain the sovereign power for themselves by enlisting the sympathies of the people, and alienating the high priest, should have yielded to their demands, and introduced a new worship? If the state had been formed according to the original intention, the rights and honour of all the tribes would have been equal, and everything would have rested on a firm basis. Who is there who would willingly violate the religious rights of his kindred? What could a man desire more than to support his own brothers and parents, thus fulfilling the duties of religion? Who would not rejoice in being taught by them the interpretation of the laws, and receiving through them the answers of God?

The tribes would thus have been united by a far closer bond, if all alike had possessed the right to the priesthood. All danger would have been obviated, if the choice of the Levites had not been dictated by anger and revenge. But, as we have said, the Hebrews had offended their God, Who, as Ezekiel says, polluted them in their own gifts by rejecting all that openeth the womb, so that He might destroy them.

This passage is also confirmed by their history. As soon as the people in the wilderness began to live in ease and plenty, certain men of no mean birth began to rebel against the choice of the Levites, and to make it a cause for believing that

Moses had not acted by the commands of God, but for his own good pleasure, inasmuch as he had chosen his own tribe before all the rest, and had bestowed the high priesthood in perpetuity on his own brother. They, therefore, stirred up a tumult, and came to him, crying out that all men were equally sacred, and that he had exalted himself above his fellows wrongfully. Moses was not able to pacify them with reasons; but by the intervention of a miracle in proof of the faith, they all perished. A fresh sedition then arose among the whole people, who believed that their champions had not been put to death by the judgment of God, but by the device of Moses. After a great slaughter, or pestilence, the rising subsided from inanition, but in such a manner that all preferred death to life under such conditions.

We should rather say that sedition ceased than that harmony was re-established. This is witnessed by Scripture (Deut. xxxi:21), where God, after predicting to Moses that the people after his death will fall away from the Divine worship, speaks thus: "For I know their imagination which they go about, even now before I have brought them into the land which I sware;" and, a little while after (xxxi:27), Moses says: For I know thy rebellion and thy stiff neck: behold while I am yet alive with you this day, ye have been rebellious against the Lord; and how much more after my death!"

Indeed, it happened according to his words, as we all know. Great changes, extreme license, luxury, and hardness of heart grew up; things went from bad to worse, till at last the people, after being frequently conquered, came to an open rupture with the Divine right, and wished for a mortal king, so that the seat of government might be the Court, instead of the Temple, and that the tribes might remain fellow-citizens in respect to their king, instead of in respect to Divine right and the high priesthood.

A vast material for new seditions was thus produced, eventually resulting in the ruin of the entire state. Kings are above all things jealous of a precarious rule, and can in nowise brook a dominion within their own. The first monarchs, being chosen from the ranks of private citizens, were content with the amount of dignity to which they had risen; but their sons, who obtained the throne by right of inheritance, began gradually to introduce changes, so as to get all the sovereign rights into their own hands. This they were generally unable to accomplish, so long as the right of legislation did not rest with them, but with the high priest, who kept the laws in the sanctuary, and interpreted them to the people. The kings were thus bound to obey the laws as much as were the subjects, and were unable to abrogate them, or to ordain new laws of equal authority; moreover, they were prevented by the Levites from administering the affairs of religion, king and subject being alike unclean. Lastly, the whole safety of their dominion depended on the will of one man, if that man appeared to be a prophet; and of this they had seen an example, namely, how completely Samuel had been able to command Saul, and how easily, because of a single disobedience, he had been able to transfer the right of sovereignty to David. Thus the kings found a dominion within their own, and wielded a precarious sovereignty.

In order to surmount these difficulties, they allowed other temples to be dedicated to the gods, so that there might be no further need of consulting the Levites; they also sought out many who prophesied in the name of God, so that they might have creatures of their own to oppose to the true prophets. However, in spite of all their attempts, they never attained their end. For the prophets, prepared against every emergency, waited for a favourable opportunity, such as the beginning of a new reign, which is always precarious, while the memory of the previous reign remains green. At these times they could easily pronounce by Divine authority that the king was tyrannical, and could produce a champion of distinguished virtue to vindicate the Divine right, and lawfully to claim dominion, or a share in it. Still, not even so could the prophets effect much. They could, indeed, remove a tyrant; but there were reasons which prevented them from doing more than setting up, at great cost of civil bloodshed, another tyrant in his stead. Of discords and civil wars there was no end, for the causes for the violation of Divine right remained always the same, and could only be removed by a complete remodelling of the state.

We have now seen how religion was introduced into the Hebrew commonwealth, and how the dominion might have lasted for ever, if the just wrath of the Lawgiver had allowed it. As this was impossible, it was bound in time to perish. I am now speaking only of the first commonwealth, for the second was a mere shadow of the first, inasmuch as the people were bound by the rights of the Persians to whom they were subject. After the restoration of freedom, the high priests usurped the rights of the secular chiefs, and thus obtained absolute dominion. The priests were inflamed with an intense desire to wield the powers of the sovereignty and the high priesthood at the same time. I have, therefore, no need to speak further of the second commonwealth. Whether the first, in so far as we deem it to have been durable, is capable of imitation, and whether it would be pious to copy it as far as possible, will appear from what fellows. I wish only to draw attention, as a crowning conclusion, to the principle indicated already — namely, that it is evident, from what we have stated in this chapter, that the Divine right, or the right of religion, originates in a compact: without such compact, none but natural rights exist. The Hebrews were not bound by their religion to evince any pious care for other nations not included in the compact, but only for their own fellow-citizens.

29 "If men could lose their natural rights so as to be absolutely unable for the future to oppose the will of the sovereign" Two common soldiers undertook to change the Roman dominion, and did change it. (Tacitus, Hist. i:7.)

30 See Numbers xi. 28. In this passage it is written that two men prophesied in the camp, and that Joshua wished to punish them. This he would not have done, if it had been lawful for anyone to deliver the Divine oracles to the people without the consent of Moses. But Moses thought good to pardon the two men, and rebuked Joshua for exhorting him to use his royal prerogative, at a time when he was so weary of reigning, that he preferred death to holding undivided sway (Numb. xi:14). For he made answer to Joshua, "Enviest thou for my sake? Would God that all the Lord's people were prophets, and that the Lord would put His spirit upon them." That is to say, would God that the right of taking counsel of God were general, and the power were in the hands of the people. Thus Joshua was not mistaken as to the right, but only as to the time for using it, for which he was rebuked by Moses, in the same way as Abishai was rebuked by David for counselling that Shimei, who had undoubtedly been guilty of treason, should be put to death. See 2 Sam. xix:22, 23.

31 See Numbers xxvii:21. The translators of the Bible have rendered incorrectly verses 19 and 23 of this chapter. The passage does not mean that Moses gave precepts or advice to Joshua, but that he made or established him chief of the Hebrews. The phrase is very freguent in Scripture (see Exodus, xviii:23; 1 Sam. xiii:15; Joshua i:9; 1 Sam. xxv:80).

32 "There was no judge over each of the captains save God." The Rabbis and

some Christians equally foolish pretend that the Sanhedrin, called "the great" was instituted by Moses. As a matter of fact, Moses chose seventy colleagues to assist him in governing, because he was not able to bear alone the burden of the whole people; but he never passed any law for forming a college of seventy members; on the contrary he ordered every tribe to appoint for itself, in the cities which God had given it, judges to settle disputes according to the laws which he himself had laid down. In cases where the opinions of the judges differed as to the interpretation of these laws, Moses bade them take counsel of the High Priest (who was the chief interpreter of the law), or of the chief judge, to whom they were then subordinate (who had the right of consulting the High Priest), and to decide the dispute in accordance with the answer obtained. If any subordinate judge should assert, that he was not bound by the decision of the High Priest, received either directly or through the chief of his state, such an one was to be put to death (Deut. xvii:9) by the chief judge, whoever he might be, to whom he was a subordinate. This chief judge would either be Joshua, the supreme captain of the whole people, or one of the tribal chiefs who had been entrusted, after the division of the tribes, with the right of consulting the high priest concerning the affairs of his tribe, of deciding on peace or war, of fortifying towns, of appointing inferior judges, &c. Or, again, it might be the king, in whom all or some of the tribes had vested their rights.I could cite many instances in confirmation of what I here advance. I will confine myself to one, which appears to me the most important of all. When the Shilomitish prophet anointed Jeroboam king, he, in so doing, gave him the right of consulting the high priest, of appointing judges, &c. In fact he endowed him with all the rights over the ten tribes, which Rehoboam retained over the two tribes. Consequently Jeroboam could set up a supreme council in his court with as much right as Jehoshaphat could at Jerusalem (2 Chron. xix:8). For it is plain that neither Jeroboam, who was king by God's command, nor Jeroboam's subjects, were bound by the Law of Moses to accept the judgments of Rehoboam, who was not their king. Still less were they under the jurisdiction of the judge, whom Rehoboam had set up in Jerusalem as subordinate to himself. According, therefore, as the Hebrew dominion was divided, so was a supreme council setup in each division. Those who neglect the variations in the constitution of the Hebrew States, and confuse them all together in one, fall into numerous difficulties.

CHAPTER XVIII.

From the Commonwealth of the Hebrews, and Their History, Certain Political Doctrines are Deduced.

ALTHOUGH THE COMMONWEALTH of the Hebrews, as we have conceived it, might have lasted for ever, it would be impossible to imitate it at the present day, nor would it be advisable so to do. If a people wished to transfer their rights to God it would be necessary to make an express covenant with Him, and for this would be needed not only the consent of those transferring their rights, but also the consent of God. God, however, has revealed through his Apostles that the covenant of God is no longer written in ink, or on tables of stone, but with the Spirit of God in the fleshy tables of the heart.

Furthermore, such a form of government would only be available for those who desire to have no foreign relations, but to shut themselves up within their own frontiers, and to live apart from the rest of the world; it would be useless to men who must have dealings with other nations; so that the cases where it could be adopted are very few indeed.

Nevertheless, though it could not be copied in its entirety, it possessed many excellent features which might be brought to our notice, and perhaps imitated with advantage. My intention, however, is not to write a treatise on forms of government, so I will pass over most of such points in silence, and will only touch on those which bear upon my purpose.

God's kingdom is not infringed upon by the choice of an earthly ruler endowed with sovereign rights; for after the Hebrews had transferred their rights to God, they conferred the sovereign right of ruling on Moses, investing him with the sole power of instituting and abrogating laws in the name of God, of choosing priests, of judging, of teaching, of punishing — in fact, all the prerogatives of an absolute monarch.

Again, though the priests were the interpreters of the laws, they had no power to judge the citizens, or to excommunicate anyone: this could only be done by the judges and chiefs chosen from among the people. A consideration of the successes and the histories of the Hebrews will bring to light other considerations worthy of note. To wit:

I. That there were no religious sects, till after the high priests, in the second commonwealth, possessed the authority to make decrees, and transact the business of government. In order that such authority might last for ever, the high priests usurped the rights of secular rulers, and at last wished to be styled kings. The reason for this is ready to hand; in the first commonwealth no decrees could bear the name of the high priest, for he had no right to ordain laws, but only to give the answers of God to questions asked by the captains or the councils: he had, therefore, no motive for making changes in the law, but took care, on the contrary, to administer and guard what had already been received and accepted. His only means of preserving his freedom in safety against the will of the captains lay in cherishing the law intact. After the high priests had assumed the power of carrying on the government, and added the rights of secular rulers to those they already possessed, each one began both in things religious and in things secular, to seek for the glorification of his own name, settling everything by sacerdotal authority, and issuing every day, concerning ceremonies, faith, and all else, new decrees which he sought to make as sacred and authoritative as the laws of Moses. Religion thus sank into a degrading superstition, while the true meaning and interpretation of the laws became corrupted. Furthermore, while the high priests were paving their way to the secular rule just after the restoration, they attempted to gain popular favour by assenting to every demand; approving whatever the people did, however impious, and accommodating Scripture to the very depraved current morals. Malachi bears witness to this in no measured terms: he chides the priests of his time as despisers of the name of God, and then goes on with his invective as follows (Mal ii:7, 8): "For the priest's lips should keep knowledge, and they should seek the law at his mouth: for he is the messenger of the Lord of hosts. But ye are departed out of the way; ye have caused many to stumble at the law, ye have corrupted the covenant of Levi, saith the Lord of hosts." He further accuses them of interpreting the laws according to their own pleasure, and paying no respect to God but only to persons. It is certain that the high priests were never so cautious in their conduct as to escape the remark of the more shrewd among the people, for the latter were at length emboldened to assert that no laws ought to be kept save those that were written, and that the decrees which the Pharisees (consisting, as Josephus says in his " Amtiquities," chiefly, of the common people), were deceived into calling the traditions of the fathers, should not be observed at all. However this may be, we can in nowise doubt that flattery of the high priest, the corruption of religion and the laws, and the enormous increase of the extent of the last-named, gave very great and frequent occasion for disputes and altercations impossible to allay. When men begin to quarrel with all the ardour of superstition, and the magistracy to back up one side or the other, they can never come to a compromise, but are bound to split into sects.

II. It is worthy of remark that the prophets, who were in a private station of life, rather irritated than reformed mankind by their freedom of warning, rebuke, and censure; whereas the kings, by their reproofs and punishments, could always produce an effect. The prophets were often intolerable even to pious kings, on account of the authority they assumed for judging whether an action was right or wrong, or for reproving the kings themselves if they dared to transact any business, whether public or private, without prophetic sanction. King Asa who, according to the testimony of Scripture, reigned piously, put the prophet Hanani into a prison-house because he had ventured freely to chide and reprove him for entering into a covenant with the king of Armenia.

Other examples might be cited, tending to prove that religion gained more harm than good by such freedom, not to speak of the further consequence, that if the prophets had retained their rights, great civil wars would have resulted.

III. It is remarkable that during all the period, during which the people held the reins of power, there was only one civil war, and that one was completely extinguished, the conquerors taking such pity on the conquered, that they endeavoured in every way to reinstate them in their former dignity and power. But after that the people, little accustomed to kings, changed its first form of government into a monarchy, civil war raged almost continuously; and battles were so fierce as to exceed all others recorded; in one engagement (taxing our faith to the utmost) five hundred thousand Israelites were slaughtered by the men of Judah, and in another the Israelites slew great numbers of the men of Judah (the figures are not given in Scripture), almost razed to the ground the walls of Jerusalem, and sacked the Temple in their unbridled fury. At length, laden with the spoils of their brethren, satiated with blood, they took hostages, and leaving the king in his well-nigh devastated kingdom, laid down their arms, relying on the weakness rather than the good faith of their foes. A few years after, the men of Judah, with recruited strength, again took the field, but were a second time beaten by the Israelites, and slain to the number of a hundred and twenty thousand, two hundred thousand of their wives and children were led into captivity, and a great booty again seized. Worn out with these and similar battles set forth at length in their histories, the Jews at length fell a prey to their enemies.

Furthermore, if we reckon up the times during which peace prevailed under each form of government, we shall find a great discrepancy. Before the monarchy forty years and more often passed, and once eighty years (an almost unparalleled period), without any war, foreign or civil. After the kings acquired sovereign power, the fighting was no longer for peace and liberty, but for glory; accordingly we find that they all, with the exception of Solomon (whose virtue and wisdom would be better displayed in peace than in war) waged war, and finally a fatal desire for power gained ground, which, in many cases, made the path to the throne a bloody one.

Lastly, the laws, during the rule of the people, remained uncorrupted and were studiously observed. Before the monarchy there were very, few prophets to admonish the people, but after the establishment of kings there were a great number at the same time. Obadiah saved a hundred from death and hid them away, lest they should be slain with the rest. The people, so far as we can see, were never deceived by false prophets till after the power had been vested in kings, whose creatures many of the prophets were. Again, the people, whose heart was generally proud or humble according to its circumstances, easily corrected it-self under misfortune, turned again to God, restored His laws, and so freed itself from all peril; but the kings, whose hearts were always equally puffed up, and who could not be corrected without humiliation, clung pertinaciously to their vices, even till the last overthrow of the city.

We may now clearly see from what I have said: —

I. How hurtful to religion and the state is the concession to ministers of religion of any power of issuing decrees or transacting the business of government: how, on the contrary, far greater stability is afforded, if the said ministers are only allowed to give answers to questions duly put to them, and are, as a rule, obliged to preach and practise the received and accepted doctrines.

II How dangerous it is to refer to Divine right matters merely speculative and subject or liable to dispute. The most tyrannical governments are those which make crimes of opinions, for everyone has an inalienable right over his thoughts — nay, such a state of things leads to the rule of popular passion.

Pontius Pilate made concession to the passion of the Pharisees in consenting to the crucifixion of Christ, whom he knew to be innocent. Again, the Pharisees, in order to shake the position of men richer than themselves, began to set on foot questions of religion, and accused the Sadducees of impiety, and, following their example, the vilest — hypocrites, stirred, as they pretended, by the same holy wrath which they called zeal for the Lord, persecuted men whose unblemished character and distinguished virtue had excited the popular hatred, publicly denounced their opinions, and inflamed the fierce passions of the people against them.

This wanton licence being cloaked with the specious garb of religion could not easily be repressed, especially when the sovereign authorities introduced a sect of which they, were not the head; they were then regarded not as interpreters of Divine right, but as sectarians — that is, as persons recognizing the right of Divine interpretation assumed by the leaders of the sect. The authority of the magistrates thus became of little account in such matters in comparison with the authority of sectarian leaders before whose interpretations kings were obliged to bow.

To avoid such evils in a state, there is no safer way, than to make piety and religion to consist in acts only — that is, in the practice of justice and charity, leaving everyone's judgment in other respects free. But I will speak of this more at length presently.

III. We see how necessary it is, both in the interests of the state and in the interests of religion, to confer on the sovereign power the right of deciding what is lawful or the reverse. If this right of judging actions could not be given to the very prophets of God without great injury, to the state and religion, how much less should it be entrusted to those who can neither foretell the future nor work miracles! But this again I will treat of more fully hereafter.

IV. Lastly,, we see how disastrous it is for a people unaccustomed to kings, and possessing a complete code of laws, to set up a monarchy. Neither can the subjects brook such a sway, nor the royal authority submit to laws and popular rights set up by anyone inferior to itself. Still less can a king be expected to defend such laws, for they were not framed to support his dominion, but the dominion of the people, or some council which formerly ruled, so that in guarding the popular rights the king would seem to be a slave rather than a master. The representative of a new monarchy will employ all his zeal in attempting to frame new laws, so as to wrest the rights of dominion to his own use, and to reduce the people till they find it easier to increase than to curtail the royal prerogative. I must not, however, omit to state that it is no less dangerous to remove a monarch, though he is on all hands admitted to be a tyrant. For his people are accustomed to royal authority and will obey no other, despising and mocking at any less august control.

It is therefore necessary, as the prophets discovered of old, if one king be removed, that he should be replaced by another, who will be a tyrant from necessity rather than choice. For how will he be able to endure the sight of the hands of the citizens reeking with royal blood, and to rejoice in their regicide as a glorious exploit? Was not the deed perpetrated as an example and warning for himself?

If he really wishes to be king, and not to acknowledge the people as the judge of kings and the master of himself, or to wield a precarious sway, he must avenge the death of his predecessor, making an example for his own sake, lest the people should venture to repeat a similar crime. He will not, however, be able easily to avenge the death of the tyrant by the slaughter of citizens unless he defends the cause of tyranny and approves the deeds of his predecessor, thus following in his footsteps.

Hence it comes to pass that peoples have often changed their tyrants, but never removed them or changed the monarchical form of government into any other.

The English people furnish us with a terrible example of this fact. They sought how to depose their monarch under the forms of law, but when he had been removed, they were utterly unable to change the form of government, and after much bloodshed only brought it about, that a new monarch should be hailed under a different name (as though it had been a mere question of names); this new monarch could only consolidate his power by completely destroying the royal stock, putting to death the king's friends, real or supposed, and disturbing with war the peace which might encourage discontent, in order that the populace might be engrossed with novelties and divert its mind from brooding over the slaughter of the king. At last, however, the people reflected that it had accomplished nothing for the good of the country beyond violating the rights of the lawful king and changing everything for the worse. It therefore decided to retrace its steps as soon as possible, and never rested till it had seen a complete restoration of the original state of affairs.

It may perhaps be objected that the Roman people was easily able to remove its tyrants, but I gather from its history a strong confirmation of my contention. Though the Roman people was much more than ordinarily capable of removing their tyrants and changing their form of government, inasmuch as it held in its own hands the power of electing its king and his successor, said being composed of rebels and criminals had not long been used to the royal yoke (out of its six kings it had put to death three), nevertheless it could accomplish nothing beyond electing several tyrants in place of one, who kept it groaning under a continual state of war, both foreign and civil, till at last it changed its government again to a form differing from monarchy, as in England, only in name.

As for the United States of the Netherlands, they have never, as we know, had a king, but only counts, who never attained the full rights of dominion. The States of the Netherlands evidently acted as principals in the settlement made by them at the time of the Earl of Leicester's mission: they always reserved for themselves the authority to keep the counts up to their duties, and the power to preserve this authority and the liberty of the citizens. They had ample means of vindicating their rights if their rulers should prove tyrannical, and could impose such restraints that nothing could be done without their consent and approval.

Thus the rights of sovereign power have always been vested in the States, though the last count endeavoured to usurp them. It is therefore little likely that the States should give them up, especially as they have just restored their original dominion, lately almost lost.

These examples, then, confirm us in our belief, that every dominion should retain its original form, and, indeed, cannot change it without danger of the utter ruin of the whole state. Such are the points I have here thought worthy of remark.

CHAPTER XIX.

It is shown that the Right over matters Spiritual lies wholly with the Sovereign, and that the outward forms of Religion should be in accordance with Public Peace, if we would obey God aright.

WHEN I SAID that the possessors of sovereign power have rights over everything, and that all rights are dependent on their decree, I did not merely mean temporal rights, but also spiritual rights; of the latter, no less than the former, they ought to be the interpreters and the champions. I wish to draw special attention to this point, and to discuss it fully in this chapter, because many persons deny that the right of deciding religious questions belongs to the sovereign power, and refuse to acknowledge it as the interpreter of Divine right. They accordingly assume full licence to accuse and arraign it, nay, even to excommunicate it from the Church, as Ambrosius treated the Emperor Theodosius in old time. However, I will show later on in this chapter that they take this means of dividing the government, and paving the way to their own ascendancy. I wish, however, first to point out that religion acquires its force as law solely from the decrees of the sovereign. God has no special kingdom among men except in so far as He reigns through temporal rulers. Moreover, the rites of religion and the outward observances of piety should be in accordance with the public peace and well-being, and should therefore be determined by the sovereign power alone. I speak here only of the outward observances of piety and the external rites of religion, not of piety, itself, nor of the inward worship of God, nor the means by which the mind is inwardly led to do homage to God in singleness of heart.

Inward worship of God and piety in itself are within the sphere of everyone's private rights, and cannot be alienated (as I showed at the end of Chapter VII.). What I here mean by the kingdom of God is, I think, sufficiently clear from what has been said in Chapter XIV. I there showed that a man best fulfils Gods law who worships Him, according to His command, through acts of justice and charity; it follows, therefore, that wherever justice and charity have the force of law and ordinance, there is God's kingdom.

I recognize no difference between the cases where God teaches and commands the practice of justice and charity through our natural faculties, and those where He makes special revelations; nor is the form of the revelation of importance so long as such practice is revealed and becomes a sovereign and supreme law to men. If, therefore, I show that justice and charity can only acquire the force of right and law through the rights of rulers, I shall be able readily to arrive at the conclusion (seeing that the rights of rulers are in the possession of the sovereign), that religion can only acquire the force of right by means of those who have the right to command, and that God only rules among men through the instrumentality of earthly potentates. It follows from what has been said, that the practice of justice and charity only acquires the force of law through the rights of the sovereign authority; for we showed in Chapter XVI. that in the state of nature reason has no more rights than desire, but that men living either by the laws of the former or the laws of the latter, possess rights co-extensive with their powers.

For this reason we could not conceive sin to exist in the state of nature, nor imagine God as a judge punishing man's transgressions; but we supposed all things to happen according to the general laws of universal nature, there being no difference between pious and impious, between him that was pure (as Solomon says) and him that was impure, because there was no possibility either of justice or charity.

In order that the true doctrines of reason, that is (as we showed in Chapter IV.), the true Divine doctrines might obtain absolutely the force of law and right, it was necessary that each individual should cede his natural right, and transfer it either to society as a whole, or to a certain body of men, or to one man. Then, and not till then, does it first dawn upon us what is justice and what is injustice, what is equity and what is iniquity.

Justice, therefore, and absolutely all the precepts of reason, including love towards one's neighbour, receive the force of laws and ordinances solely through the rights of dominion, that is (as we showed in the same chapter) solely on the decree of those who possess the right to rule. Inasmuch as the kingdom of God consists entirely in rights applied to justice and charity or to true religion, it follows that (as we asserted) the kingdom of God can only exist among men through the means of the sovereign powers; nor does it make any difference whether religion be apprehended by our natural faculties or by revelation: the argument is sound in both cases, inasmuch as religion is one and the same, and is equally revealed by God, whatever be the manner in which it becomes known to men.

Thus, in order that the religion revealed by the prophets might have the force of law among the Jews, it was necessary that every man of them should yield up his natural right, and that all should, with one accord, agree that they would only obey such commands as God should reveal to them through the prophets. Just as we have shown to take place in a democracy, where men with one consent agree to live according to the dictates of reason. Although the Hebrews furthermore transferred their right to God, they were able to do so rather in theory than in practice, for, as a matter of fact (as we pointed out above) they absolutely retained the right of dominion till they transferred it to Moses, who in his turn became absolute king, so that it was only through him that God reigned over the Hebrews. For this reason (namely, that religion only acquires the force of law by means of the sovereign power) Moses was not able to punish those who, before the covenant, and consequently while still in possession of their rights, violated the Sabbath (Exod. xvi:27), but was able to do so after the covenant (Numb. xv:36), because everyone had then yielded up his natural rights, and the ordinance of the Sabbath had received the force of law.

Lastly, for the same reason, after the destruction of the Hebrew dominion, revealed religion ceased to have the force of law; for we cannot doubt that as soon as the Jews transferred their right to the king of Babylon, the kingdom of God and the Divine right forthwith ceased. For the covenant wherewith they promised to obey all the utterances of God was abrogated; God's kingdom, which was based thereupon, also ceased. The Hebrews could no longer abide thereby, inasmuch as their rights no longer belonged to them but to the king of Babylon, whom (as we showed in Chapter XVI.) they were bound to obey in all things. Jeremiah (chap. xxix:7) expressly admonishes them of this fact: "And seek the peace of the city, whither I have caused you to be carried away captives, and pray unto the Lord for it; for in the peace thereof shall ye have peace." Now, they could not seek the peace of the City as having a share in its government, but only as slaves, being, as they were, captives; by obedience in all things, with a view to avoiding seditions, and by observing all the laws of the country, however different from their own. It is thus abundantly evident that religion among the Hebrews only acquired the form of law through the right of the sovereign rule; when that rule was destroyed, it could no longer be received as the law of a particular kingdom, but only as the universal precept of reason. I say of reason, for the universal religion had not yet become known by revelation. We may therefore draw the general conclusion that religion, whether revealed through our natural faculties or through prophets, receives the force of a command solely through the decrees of the holders of sovereign power; and, further, that God has no special kingdom among men, except in so far as He reigns through earthly potentates.

We may now see in a clearer light what was stated in Chapter IV., namely, that all the decrees of God involve eternal truth and necessity, so that we cannot conceive God as a prince or legislator giving laws to mankind. For this reason the Divine precepts, whether revealed through our natural faculties, or through prophets, do not receive immediately from God the force of a command, but only from those, or through the mediation of those, who possess the right of ruling and legislating. It is only through these latter means that God rules among men, and directs human affairs with justice and equity.

This conclusion is supported by experience, for we find traces of Divine justice only in places where just men bear sway; elsewhere the same lot (to repeat, again Solomon's words) befalls the just and the unjust, the pure and the impure: a state of things which causes Divine Providence to be doubted by many who think that God immediately reigns among men, and directs all nature for their benefit.

As, then, both reason and experience tell us that the Divine right is entirely dependent on the decrees of secular rulers, it follows that secular rulers are its proper interpreters. How this is so we shall now see, for it is time to show that the outward observances of religion, and all the external practices of piety should be brought into accordance with the public peace and well-being if we would obey God rightly. When this has been shown we shall easily understand how the sovereign rulers are the proper interpreters of religion and piety.

It is certain that duties towards one's country are the highest that man can fulfil; for, if government be taken away, no good thing can last, all falls into dispute, anger and anarchy reign unchecked amid universal fear. Consequently there can be no duty towards our neighbour which would not become an offence if it involved injury to the whole state, nor can there be any offence against our duty towards our neighbour, or anything but loyalty in what we do for the sake of preserving the state. For instance: it is in the abstract my duty when my neighbour quarrels with me and wishes to take my cloak, to give him my coat also; but if it be thought that such conduct is hurtful to the maintenance of the state, I ought to bring him to trial, even at the risk of his being condemned to death.

For this reason Manlius Torquatus is held up to honour, inasmuch as the public welfare outweighed with him his duty towards his children. This being so, it follows that the public welfare is the sovereign law to which all others, Divine and human, should be made to conform. Now, it is the function of the sovereign only to decide what is necessary for the public welfare and the safety of the state, and to give orders accordingly; therefore it is also the function of the sovereign only to decide the limits of our duty towards our neighbour — in other words, to determine how we should obey God. We can now clearly understand how the sovereign is the interpreter of religion, and further, that no one can obey God rightly, if the practices of his piety do not conform to the public welfare; or, consequently, if he does not implicitly obey all the commands of the sovereign. For as by God's command we are bound to do our duty to all men without exception, and to do no man an injury, we are also bound not to help one man at another's loss, still less at a loss to the whole state. Now, no private citizen can know what is good for the state, except he learn it through the sovereign power, who alone has the right to transact public business: therefore no one can rightly practise piety or obedience to God, unless he obey the sovereign power's commands in all things. This proposition is confirmed by the facts of experience. For if the sovereign adjudge a man to be worthy of death or an enemy, whether he be a citizen or a foreigner, a private individual or a separate ruler, no subject is allowed to give him assistance. So also though the Jews were bidden to love their fellow-citizens as themselves (Levit. xix:17, 18), they were nevertheless bound, if a man offended against the law, to point him out to the judge (Levit. v:1, and Deut. xiii:8, 9), and, if he should be condemned to death, to slay him (Deut. xvii:7).

Further, in order that the Hebrews might preserve the liberty they had gained, and might retain absolute sway over the territory they had conquered, it was necessary, as we showed in Chapter XVII., that their religion should be adapted to their particular government, and that they should separate themselves from the rest of the nations: wherefore it was commanded to them, "Love thy neighbour and hate thine enemy" (Matt. v:43), but after they had lost their dominion and had gone into captivity in Babylon, Jeremiah bid them take thought for the safety of the state into which they had been led captive; and Christ when He saw that they would be spread over the whole world, told them to do their duty by all men without exception; all of which instances show that religion has always been made to conform to the public welfare. Perhaps someone will ask: By what right, then, did the disciples of Christ, being private citizens, preach a new religion? I answer that they did so by the right of the power which they had received from Christ against unclean spirits (see Matt. x:1). I have already stated in Chapter XVI. that all are bound to obey a tyrant, unless they have received from God through undoubted revelation a promise of aid against him; so let no one take example from the Apostles unless he too has the power of working miracles. The point is brought out more clearly by Christ's command to His disciples, "Fear not those who kill the body" (Matt. x:28). If this command were imposed on everyone, governments would be founded in vain, and Solomon's words (Prov. xxiv:21), "My son, fear God and the king," would be impious, which they certainly are not; we must therefore admit that the authority which Christ gave to His disciples was given to them only, and must not be taken as an example for others.

I do not pause to consider the arguments of those who wish to separate secular rights from spiritual rights, placing the former under the control of the sovereign, and the latter under the control of the universal Church; such pretensions are too frivolous to merit refutation. I cannot however, pass over in silence the fact that such persons are woefully deceived when they seek to support their seditious opinions (I ask pardon for the somewhat harsh epithet) by the example of the Jewish high priest, who, in ancient times, had the right of administering the sacred offices. Did not the high priests receive their right by the decree of Moses (who, as I have shown, retained the sole right to rule), and could they not by the same means be deprived of it? Moses himself chose not only Aaron, but also his son Eleazar, and his grandson Phineas, and bestowed on them the right of administering the office of high priest. This right was retained by the high priests afterwards, but none the less were they delegates of Moses — that is, of the sovereign power. Moses, as we have shown, left no successor to his dominion, but so distributed his prerogatives, that those who came after him seemed, as it were, regents who administer the government when a king is absent but not dead.

In the second commonwealth the high priests held their right absolutely, after they had obtained the rights of principality in addition. Wherefore the rights of the high priesthood always depended on the edict of the sovereign, and the high priests did not possess them till they became sovereigns also. Rights in matters spiritual always remained under the control of the kings absolutely (as I will show at the end of this chapter), except in the single particular that they were not allowed to administer in person the sacred duties in the Temple, inasmuch as they were not of the family of Aaron, and were therefore considered unclean, a reservation which would have no force in a Christian community.

We cannot, therefore, doubt that the daily sacred rites (whose performance does not require a particular genealogy but only a special mode of life, and from which the holders of sovereign power are not excluded as unclean) are under the sole control of the sovereign power; no one, save by the authority or concession of such sovereign, has the right or power of administering them, of choosing others to administer them, of defining or strengthening the foundations of the Church and her doctrines; of judging on questions of morality or acts of piety; of receiving anyone into the Church or excommunicating him therefrom, or, lastly, of providing for the poor.

These doctrines are proved to be not only true (as we have already pointed out), but also of primary necessity for the preservation of religion and the state. We all know what weight spiritual right and authority carries in the popular mind: how everyone hangs on the lips, as it were, of those who possess it. We may even say that those who wield such authority have the most complete sway over the popular mind.

Whosoever, therefore, wishes to take this right away from the sovereign power, is desirous of dividing the dominion; from such division, contentions, and strife will necessarily spring up, as they did of old between the Jewish kings and high priests, and will defy all attempts to allay them. Nay, further, he who strives to deprive the sovereign power of such authority, is aiming (as we have said), at gaining dominion for himself. What is left for the sovereign power to decide on, if this right be denied him? Certainly nothing concerning either war or peace, if he has to ask another man's opinion as to whether what he believes to be beneficial would be pious or impious. Everything would depend on the verdict of him who had the right of deciding and judging what was pious or impious, right or wrong.

When such a right was bestowed on the Pope of Rome absolutely, he gradually acquired complete control over the kings, till at last he himself mounted to the summits of dominion; however much monarchs, and especially the German emperors, strove to curtail his authority, were it only by a hairsbreadth, they effected nothing, but on the contrary by their very endeavours largely increased it. That which no monarch could accomplish with fire and sword, ecclesiastics could bring about with a stroke of the pen; whereby we may easily see the force and power at the command of the Church, and also how necessary it is for sovereigns to reserve such prerogatives for themselves.

If we reflect on what was said in the last chapter we shall see that such reservation conduced not a little to the increase of religion and piety; for we observed that the prophets themselves, though gifted with Divine efficacy, being merely private citizens, rather irritated than reformed the people by their freedom of warning, reproof, and denunciation, whereas the kings by warnings and punishments easily bent men to their will. Furthermore, the kings themselves, not possessing the right in question absolutely, very often fell away from religion and took with them nearly the whole people. The same thing has often happened from the same cause in Christian states.

Perhaps I shall be asked, "But if the holders of sovereign power choose to be wicked, who will be the rightful champion of piety? Should the sovereigns still be its interpreters? "I meet them with the counter-question, "But if ecclesiastics (who are also human, and private citizens, and who ought to mind only their own affairs), or if others whom it is proposed to entrust with spiritual authority, choose to be wicked, should they still be considered as piety's rightful interpreters?" It is quite certain that when sovereigns wish to follow their own pleasure, whether they have control over spiritual matters or not, the whole state, spiritual and secular, will go to ruin, and it will go much faster if private citizens seditiously assume the championship of the Divine rights.

Thus we see that not only is nothing gained by denying such rights to sovereigns, but on the contrary, great evil ensues. For (as happened with the Jewish kings who did not possess such rights absolutely) rulers are thus driven into wickedness, and the injury and loss to the state become certain and inevitable, instead of uncertain and possible. Whether we look to the abstract truth, or the security of states, or the increase of piety, we are compelled to maintain that the Divine right, or the right of control over spiritual matters, depends absolutely on the decree of the sovereign, who is its legitimate interpreter and champion. Therefore the true ministers of God's word are those who teach piety to the people in obedience to the authority of the sovereign rulers by whose decree it has been brought into conformity with the public welfare.

There remains for me to point out the cause for the frequent disputes on the subject of these spiritual rights in Christian states; whereas the Hebrews, so far as I know, never, had any doubts about the matter. It seems monstrous that a question so plain and vitally important should thus have remained undecided, and that the secular rulers could never obtain the prerogative without controversy, nay, nor without great danger of sedition and injury to religion. If no cause for this state of things were forthcoming, I could easily persuade myself that all I have said in this chapter is mere theorizing, or akind of speculative reasoning which can never be of any practical use. However, when we reflect on the beginnings of Christianity the cause at once becomes manifest. The Christian religion was not taught at first by kings, but by private persons, who, against the wishes of those in power, whose subjects they, were, were for a long time accustomed to hold meetings in secret churches, to institute and perform sacred rites, and on their own authority to settle and decide on their affairs without regard to the state, When, after the lapse of many years, the religion was taken up by the authorities, the ecclesiastics were obliged to teach it to the emperors themselves as they had defined it: wherefore they easily gained recognition as its teachers and interpreters, and the church pastors were looked upon as vicars of God. The ecclesiastics took good care that the Christian kings should not assume their authority, by prohibiting marriage to the chief ministers of religion and to its highest interpreter. They furthermore elected their purpose by multiplying the dogmas of religion to such an extent and so blending them with philosophy that their chief interpreter was bound to be a skilled philosopher and theologian, and to have leisure for a host of idle speculations: conditions which could only be fulfilled by a private individual with much time on his hands.

Among the Hebrews things were very differently arranged: for their Church began at the same time as their dominion, and Moses, their absolute ruler, taught religion to the people, arranged their sacred rites, and chose their spiritual ministers. Thus the royal authority carried very great weight with the people, and the kings kept a firm hold on their spiritual prerogatives.

Although, after the death of Moses, no one held absolute sway, yet the power of deciding both in matters spiritual and matters temporal was in the hands of the secular chief, as I have already pointed out. Further, in order that it might be taught religion and piety, the people was bound to consult the supreme judge no less than the high priest (Deut. xvii:9, 11). Lastly, though the kings had not as much power as Moses, nearly the whole arrangement and choice of the sacred ministry depended on their decision. Thus David arranged the whole service of the Temple (see 1 Chron. xxviii:11, 12, &c.); from all the Levites he chose twenty-four thousand for the sacred psalms; six thousand of these formed the body from which were chosen the judges and proctors, four thousand were porters, and four thousand to play on instruments (see 1 Chron. xxiii:4, 5). He further divided them into companies (of whom he chose the chiefs), so that each in rotation, at the allotted time, might perform the sacred rites. The priests he also divided into as many companies; I will not go through the whole catalogue, but refer the reader to 2 Chron. viii:13, where it is stated, "Then Solomon offered burnt offerings to the Lord . . . . . after a certain rate every day, offering according to the commandments of Moses;" and in verse 14, "And he appointed, according to the order of David his father, the courses of the priests to their service . . . . . . for so had David the man of God commanded." Lastly, the historian bears witness in verse 15: "And they departed not from the commandment of the king unto the priests and Levites concerning any matter, or concerning the treasuries."

From these and other histories of the kings it is abundantly evident, that the whole practice of religion and the sacred ministry depended entirely on the commands of the king.

When I said above that the kings had not the same right as Moses to elect the high priest, to consult God without intermediaries, and to condemn the prophets who prophesied during their reign; I said so simply because the prophets could, in virtue of their mission, choose a new king and give absolution for regicide, not because they could call a king who offended against the law to judgment, or could rightly act against him 33.

Wherefore if there had been no prophets who, in virtue of a special revelation, could give absolution for regicide, the kings would have possessed absolute rights over all matters both spiritual and temporal. Consequently the rulers of modern times, who have no prophets and would not rightly be bound in any case to receive them (for they are not subject to Jewish law), have absolute possession of the spiritual prerogative, although they are not celibates, and they will always retain it, if they will refuse to allow religious dogmas to be unduly multiplied or confounded with philosophy.

33 I must here bespeak special attention for what was said in Chap. XVI. concerning rights.

CHAPTER XX.

That in a Free State Every Man May Think what he Likes, and Say what he Thinks.

IF MEN'S MINDS were as easily controlled as their tongues, every king would sit safely on his throne, and government by compulsion would cease; for every subject would shape his life according to the intentions of his rulers, and would esteem a thing true or false, good or evil, just or unjust, in obedience to their dictates. However, we have shown already (Chapter XVII.) that no man's mind can possibly lie wholly at the disposition of another, for no one can willingly transfer his natural right of free reason and judgment, or be compelled so to do. For this reason government which attempts to control minds is accounted tyrannical, and it is considered an abuse of sovereignty and a usurpation of the rights of subjects, to seek to prescribe what shall be accepted as true, or rejected as false, or what opinions should actuate men in their worship of God. All these questions fall within a man's natural right, which he cannot abdicate even with his own consent.

I admit that the judgment can be biassed in many ways, and to an almost incredible degree, so that while exempt from direct external control it may be so dependent on another man's words, that it may fitly be said to be ruled by him; but although this influence is carried to great lengths, it has never gone so far as to invalidate the statement, that every man's understanding is his own, and that brains are as diverse as palates.

Moses, not by fraud, but by Divine virtue, gained such a hold over the popular judgment that he was accounted superhuman, and believed to speak and act through the inspiration of the Deity; nevertheless, even he could not escape murmurs and evil interpretations. How much less then can other monarchs avoid them! Yet such unlimited power, if it exists at all, must belong to a monarch, and least of all to a democracy, where the whole or a great part of the people wield authority collectively. This is a fact which I think everyone can explain for himself.

However unlimited, therefore, the power of a sovereign may be, however implicitly it is trusted as the exponent of law and religion, it can never prevent men from forming judgments according to their intellect, or being influenced by any given emotion. It is true that it has the right to treat as enemies all men whose opinions do not, on all subjects, entirely coincide with its own; but we are not discussing its strict rights, but its proper course of action. I grant that it has the right to rule in the most violent manner, and to put citizens to death for very trivial causes, but no one supposes it can do this with the approval of sound judgment. Nay, inasmuch as such things cannot be done without extreme peril to itself, we may even deny that it has the absolute power to do them, or, consequently, the absolute right; for the rights of the sovereign are limited by his power.

Since, therefore, no one can abdicate his freedom of judgment and feeling; since every man is by indefeasible natural right the master of his own thoughts, it follows that men thinking in diverse and contradictory fashions, cannot, without disastrous results, be compelled to speak only according to the dictates of the supreme power. Not even the most experienced, to say nothing of the multitude, know how to keep silence. Men's common failing is to confide their plans to others, though there be need for secrecy, so that a government would be most harsh which deprived the individual of his freedom of saying and teaching what he thought; and would be moderate if such freedom were granted. Still we cannot deny that authority may be as much injured by words as by actions; hence, although the freedom we are discussing cannot be entirely denied to subjects, its unlimited concession would be most baneful; we must, therefore, now inquire, how far such freedom can and ought to be conceded without danger to the peace of the state, or the power of the rulers; and this, as I said at the beginning of Chapter XVI., is my principal object. It follows, plainly, from the explanation given above, of the foundations of a state, that the ultimate aim of government is not to rule, or restrain, by fear, nor to exact obedience, but contrariwise, to free every man from fear, that he may live in all possible security; in other words, to strengthen his natural right to exist and work — without injury to himself or others.

No, the object of government is not to change men from rational beings into beasts or puppets, but to enable them to develope their minds and bodies in security, and to employ their reason unshackled; neither showing hatred, anger, or deceit, nor watched with the eyes of jealousy and injustice. In fact, the true aim of government is liberty.

Now we have seen that in forming a state the power of making laws must either be vested in the body of the citizens, or in a portion of them, or in one man. For, although mens free judgments are very diverse, each one thinking that he alone knows everything, and although complete unanimity of feeling and speech is out of the question, it is impossible to preserve peace, unless individuals abdicate their right of acting entirely on their own judgment. Therefore, the individual justly cedes the right of free action, though not of free reason and judgment; no one can act against the authorities without danger to the state, though his feelings and judgment may be at variance therewith; he may even speak against them, provided that he does so from rational conviction, not from fraud, anger, or hatred, and provided that he does not attempt to introduce any change on his private authority.

For instance, supposing a man shows that a law is repugnant to sound reason, and should therefore be repealed; if he submits his opinion to the judgment of the authorities (who, alone, have the right of making and repealing laws), and meanwhile acts in nowise contrary to that law, he has deserved well of the state, and has behaved as a good citizen should; but if he accuses the authorities of injustice, and stirs up the people against them, or if he seditiously strives to abrogate the law without their consent, he is a mere agitator and rebel.

Thus we see how an individual may declare and teach what he believes, without injury to the authority of his rulers, or to the public peace; namely, by leaving in their hands the entire power of legislation as it affects action, and by doing nothing against their laws, though he be compelled often to act in contradiction to what he believes, and openly feels, to be best.

Such a course can be taken without detriment to justice and dutifulness, nay, it is the one which a just and dutiful man would adopt. We have shown that justice is dependent on the laws of the authorities, so that no one who contravenes their accepted decrees can be just, while the highest regard for duty, as we have pointed out in the preceding chapter, is exercised in maintaining public peace and tranquillity; these could not be preserved if every man were to live as he pleased; therefore it is no less than undutiful for a man to act contrary to his country's laws, for if the practice became universal the ruin of states would necessarily follow.

Hence, so long as a man acts in obedience to the laws of his rulers, he in nowise contravenes his reason, for in obedience to reason he transferred the right of controlling his actions from his own hands to theirs. This doctrine we can confirm from actual custom, for in a conference of great and small powers, schemes are seldom carried unanimously, yet all unite in carrying out what is decided on, whether they voted for or against. But I return to my proposition.

From the fundamental notions of a state, we have discovered how a man may exercise free judgment without detriment to the supreme power: from the same premises we can no less easily determine what opinions would be seditious. Evidently those which by their very nature nullify the compact by which the right of free action was ceded. For instance, a man who holds that the supreme power has no rights over him, or that promises ought not to be kept, or that everyone should live as he pleases, or other doctrines of this nature in direct opposition to the above-mentioned contract, is seditious, not so much from his actual opinions and judgment, as from the deeds which they involve; for he who maintains such theories abrogates the contract which tacitly, or openly, he made with his rulers. Other opinions which do not involve acts violating the contract, such as revenge, anger, and t he like, are not seditious, unless it be in some. corrupt state, where superstitious and ambitious persons, unable to endure men of learning, are so popular with the multitude that their word is more valued than the law.

However, I do not deny that there are some doctrines which, while they are apparently only concerned with abstract truths and falsehoods, are yet propounded and published with unworthy motives. This question we have discussed in Chapter XV., and shown that reason should nevertheless remain unshackled. If we hold to the principle that a man's loyalty to the state should be judged, like his loyalty to God, from his actions only — namely, from his charity towards his neighbours; we cannot doubt that the best government will allow freedom of philosophical speculation no less than of religious belief. I confess that from such freedom inconveniences may sometimes arise, but what question was ever settled so wisely that no abuses could possibly spring therefrom? He who seeks to regulate everything by law, is more likely to arouse vices than to reform them. It is best to grant what cannot be abolished, even though it be in itself harmful. How many evils spring from luxury, envy, avarice, drunkenness, and the like, yet these are tolerated — vices as they are — because they cannot be prevented by legal enactments. How much more then should free thought be granted, seeing that it is in itself a virtue and that it cannot be crushed! Besides, the evil results can easily be checked, as I will show, by the secular authorities, not to mention that such freedom is absolutely necessary for progress in science and the liberal arts: for no man follows such pursuits to advantage unless his judgment be entirely free and unhampered.

But let it be granted that freedom may be crushed, and men be so bound down, that they do not dare to utter a whisper, save at the bidding of their rulers; nevertheless this can never be carried to the pitch of making them think according to authority, so that the necessary consequences would be that men would daily be thinking one thing and saying another, to the corruption of good faith, that mainstay of government, and to the fostering of hateful flattery and perfidy, whence spring stratagems, and the corruption of every good art.

It is far from possible to impose uniformity of speech, for the more rulers strive to curtail freedom of speech, the more obstinately are they resisted; not indeed by the avaricious, the flatterers, and other numskulls, who think supreme salvation consists in filling their stomachs and gloating over their money-bags, but by those whom good education, sound morality, and virtue have rendered more free. Men, as generally constituted, are most prone to resent the branding as criminal of opinions which they believe to be true, and the proscription as wicked of that which inspires them with piety towards God and man; hence they are ready to forswear the laws and conspire against the authorities, thinking it not shameful but honourable to stir up seditions and perpetuate any sort of crime with this end in view. Such being the constitution of human nature, we see that laws directed against opinions affect the generous minded rather than the wicked, and are adapted less for coercing criminals than for irritating the upright; so that they cannot be maintained without great peril to the state.

Moreover, such laws are almost always useless, for those who hold that the opinions proscribed are sound, cannot possibly obey the law; whereas those who already reject them as false, accept the law as a kind of privilege, and make such boast of it, that authority is powerless to repeal it, even if such a course be subsequently desired.

To these considerations may be added what we said in Chapter XVIII. in treating of the history of the Hebrews. And, lastly, how many schisms have arisen in the Church from the attempt of the authorities to decide by law the intricacies of theological controversy! If men were not allured by the hope of getting the law and the authorities on their side, of triumphing over their adversaries in the sight of an applauding multitude, and of acquiring honourable distinctions, they would not strive so maliciously, nor would such fury sway their minds. This is taught not only by reason but by daily examples, for laws of this kind prescribing what every man shall believe and forbidding anyone to speak or write to the contrary, have often been passed, as sops or concessions to the anger of those who cannot tolerate men of enlightenment, and who, by such harsh and crooked enactments, can easily turn the devotion of the masses into fury and direct it against whom they will. How much better would it be to restrain popular anger and fury, instead of passing useless laws, which can only be broken by those who love virtue and the liberal arts, thus paring down the state till it is too small to harbour men of talent. What greater misfortune for a state can be conceived then that honourable men should be sent like criminals into exile, because they hold diverse opinions which they cannot disguise? What, I say, can be more hurtful than that men who have committed no crime or wickedness should, simply because they are enlightened, be treated as enemies and put to death, and that the scaffold, the terror of evil-doers, should become the arena where the highest examples of tolerance and virtue are displayed to the people with all the marks of ignominy that authority can devise?

He that knows himself to be upright does not fear the death of a criminal, and shrinks from no punishment; his mind is not wrung with remorse for any disgraceful deed: he holds that death in a good cause is no punishment, but an honour, and that death for freedom is glory.

What purpose then is served by the death of such men, what example in proclaimed? the cause for which they die is unknown to the idle and the foolish, hateful to the turbulent, loved by the upright. The only lesson we can draw from such scenes is to flatter the persecutor, or else to imitate the victim.

If formal assent is not to be esteemed above conviction, and if governments are to retain a firm hold of authority and not be compelled to yield to agitators, it is imperative that freedom of judgment should be granted, so that men may live together in harmony, however diverse, or even openly contradictory their opinions may be. We cannot doubt that such is the best system of government and open to the fewest objections, since it is the one most in harmony with human nature. In a democracy (the most natural form of government, as we have shown in Chapter XVI.) everyone submits to the control of authority over his actions, but not over his judgment and reason; that is, seeing that all cannot think alike, the voice of the majority has the force of law, subject to repeal if circumstances bring about a change of opinion. In proportion as the power of free judgment is withheld we depart from the natural condition of mankind, and consequently the government becomes more tyrannical.

In order to prove that from such freedom no inconvenience arises, which cannot easily be checked by the exercise of the sovereign power, and that men's actions can easily be kept in bounds, though their opinions are at open variance, it will be well to cite an example. Such an one is not very, far to seek. The city of Amsterdam reaps the fruit of this freedom in its own great prosperity and in the admiration of all other people. For in this most flourishing state, and most splendid city, men of every, nation and religion live together in the greatest harmony, and ask no questions before trusting their goods to a fellow-citizen, save whether he be rich or poor, and whether he generally acts honestly, or the reverse. His religion and sect is considered of no importance: for it has no effect before the judges in gaining or losing a cause, and there is no sect so despised that its followers, provided that they harm no one, pay every man his due, and live uprightly, are deprived of the protection of the magisterial authority.

On the other hand, when the religious controversy between Remonstrants and Counter-Remonstrants began to be taken up by politicians and the States, it grew into a schism, and abundantly showed that laws dealing with religion and seeking to settle its controversies are much more calculated to irritate than to reform, and that they give rise to extreme licence: further, it was seen that schisms do not originate in a love of truth, which is a source of courtesy and gentleness, but rather in an inordinate desire for supremacy, From all these considerations it is clearer than the sun at noonday, that the true schismatics are those who condemn other men's writings, and seditiously stir up the quarrelsome masses against their authors, rather than those authors themselves, who generally write only for the learned, and appeal solely to reason. In fact, the real disturbers of the peace are those who, in a free state, seek to curtail the liberty of judgment which they are unable to tyrannize over.

I have thus shown: —

I. That it is impossible to deprive men of the liberty of saying what they think.

II. That such liberty can be conceded to every man without injury to the rights and authority of the sovereign power, and that every man may retain it without injury to such rights, provided that he does not presume upon it to the extent of introducing any new rights into the state, or acting in any way contrary, to the existing laws.

III. That every man may enjoy this liberty without detriment to the public peace, and that no inconveniences arise therefrom which cannot easily be checked.

IV. That every man may enjoy it without injury to his allegiance.

V. That laws dealing with speculative problems are entirely useless.

VI. Lastly, that not only may such liberty be granted without prejudice to the public peace, to loyalty, and to the rights of rulers, but that it is even necessary, for their preservation. For when people try to take it away, and bring to trial, not only the acts which alone are capable of offending, but also the opinions of mankind, they only succeed in surrounding their victims with an appearance of martyrdom, and raise feelings of pity and revenge rather than of terror. Uprightness and good faith are thus corrupted, flatterers and traitors are encouraged, and sectarians triumph, inasmuch as concessions have been made to their animosity, and they have gained the state sanction for the doctrines of which they are the interpreters. Hence they arrogate to themselves the state authority and rights, and do not scruple to assert that they have been directly chosen by God, and that their laws are Divine, whereas the laws of the state are human, and should therefore yield obedience to the laws of God — in other words, to their own laws. Everyone must see that this is not a state of affairs conducive to public welfare. Wherefore, as we have shown in Chapter XVIII., the safest way for a state is to lay down the rule that religion is comprised solely in the exercise of charity and justice, and that the rights of rulers in sacred, no less than in secular matters, should merely have to do with actions, but that every man should think what he likes and say what he thinks.

I have thus fulfilled the task I set myself in this treatise. It remains only to call attention to the fact that I have written nothing which I do not most willingly submit to the examination and approval of my country's rulers; and that I am willing to retract anything which they shall decide to be repugnant to the laws, or prejudicial to the public good. I know that I am a man, and as a man liable to error, but against error I have taken scrupulous care, and have striven to keep in entire accordance with the laws of my country, with loyalty, and with morality.

ETHICS

PART I. CONCERNING GOD.

DEFINITIONS.

I. BY THAT which is self — caused, I mean that of which the essence involves existence, or that of which the nature is only conceivable as existent.

II. A thing is called finite after its kind, when it can be limited by another thing of the same nature; for instance, a body is called finite because we always conceive another greater body. So, also, a thought is limited by another thought, but a body is not limited by thought, nor a thought by body.

III. By substance, I mean that which is in itself, and is conceived through itself: in other words, that of which a conception can be formed independently of any other conception.

IV. By attribute, I mean that which the intellect perceives as constituting the essence of substance.

V. By mode, I mean the modifications1 of substance, or that which exists in, and is conceived through, something other than itself.

1 "Affectiones"

VI. By God, I mean a being absolutely infinite — that is, a substance consisting in infinite attributes, of which each expresses eternal and infinite essentiality.

Explanation — I say absolutely infinite, not infinite after its kind: for, of a thing infinite only after its kind, infinite attributes may be denied; but that which is absolutely infinite, contains in its essence whatever expresses reality, and involves no negation.

VII. That thing is called free, which exists solely by the necessity of its own nature, and of which the action is determined by itself alone. On the other hand, that thing is necessary, or rather constrained, which is determined by something external to itself to a fixed and definite method of existence or action.

VIII. By eternity, I mean existence itself, in so far as it is conceived necessarily to follow solely from the definition of that which is eternal.

Explanation — Existence of this kind is conceived as an eternal truth, like the essence of a thing, and, therefore, cannot be explained by means of continuance or time, though continuance may be conceived without a beginning or end.

AXIOMS.

I. EVERYTHING WHICH exists, exists either in itself or in something else.

II. That which cannot be conceived through anything else must be conceived through itself.

III. From a given definite cause an effect necessarily follows; and, on the other hand, if no definite cause be granted, it is impossible that an effect can follow.

IV. The knowledge of an effect depends on and involves the knowledge of a cause.

V. Things which have nothing in common cannot be understood, the one by means of the other; the conception of one does not involve the conception of the other.

VI. A true idea must correspond with its ideate or object.

VII. If a thing can be conceived as non — existing, its essence does not involve existence.

PROPOSITIONS.

PROP. I. SUBSTANCE is by nature prior to its modifications.

Proof. — This is clear from Deff. iii. and v.

PROP. II. Two substances, whose attributes are different, have nothing in common.

Proof. — Also evident from Def. iii. For each must exist in itself, and be conceived through itself; in other words, the conception of one does not imply the conception of the other.

PROP. III. Things which have nothing in common cannot be one the cause of the other.

Proof. — If they have nothing in common, it follows that one cannot be apprehended by means of the other (Ax. v.), and, therefore, one cannot be the cause of the other (Ax. iv.). Q.E.D.

PROP. IV. Two or more distinct things are distinguished one from the other, either by the difference of the attributes of the substances, or by the difference of their modifications.

Proof. — Everything which exists, exists either in itself or in something else (Ax. i.), — that is (by Deff. iii. and v.), nothing is granted in addition to the understanding, except substance and its modifications. Nothing is, therefore, given besides the understanding, by which several things may be distinguished one from the other, except the substances, or, in other words (see Ax. iv.), their attributes and modifications. Q.E.D.

PROP. V. There cannot exist in the universe two or more substances having the same nature or attribute.

Proof. — If several distinct substances be granted, they must be distinguished one from the other, either by the difference of their attributes, or by the difference of their modifications (Prop. iv.). If only by the difference of their attributes, it will be granted that there cannot be more than one with an identical attribute. If by the difference of their modifications — as substance is naturally prior to its modifications (Prop. i.), — it follows that setting the modifications aside, and considering substance in itself, that is truly, (Deff. iii. and vi.), there cannot be conceived one substance different from another, — that is (by Prop. iv.), there cannot be granted several substances, but one substance only. Q.E.D.

PROP. VI. One substance cannot be produced by another substance.

Proof. — It is impossible that there should be in the universe two substances with an identical attribute, i.e. which have anything common to them both (Prop. ii.), and, therefore (Prop. iii.), one cannot be the cause of the other, neither can one be produced by the other. Q.E.D.

Corollary. — Hence it follows that a substance cannot be produced by anything external to itself. For in the universe nothing is granted, save substances and their modifications (as appears from Ax. i. and Deff. iii. and v.). Now (by the last Prop.) substance cannot be produced by another substance, therefore it cannot be produced by anything external to itself. Q.E.D. This is shown still more readily by the absurdity of the contradictory. For, if substance be produced by an external cause, the knowledge of it would depend on the knowledge of its cause (Ax. iv.), and (by Def. iii.) it would itself not be substance.

PROP. VII. Existence belongs to the nature of substances.

Proof. — Substance cannot be produced by anything external (Corollary, Prop vi.), it must, therefore, be its own cause — that is, its essence necessarily involves existence, or existence belongs to its nature.

PROP. VIII. Every substance is necessarily infinite.

Proof. — There can only be one substance with an identical attribute, and existence follows from its nature (Prop. vii.); its nature, therefore, involves existence, either as finite or infinite. It does not exist as finite, for (by Def. ii.) it would then be limited by something else of the same kind, which would also necessarily exist (Prop. vii.); and there would be two substances with an identical attribute, which is absurd (Prop. v.). It therefore exists as infinite. Q.E.D.

Note I. — As finite existence involves a partial negation, and infinite existence is the absolute affirmation of the given nature, it follows (solely from Prop. vii.) that every substance is necessarily infinite.

Note II. — No doubt it will be difficult for those who think about things loosely, and have not been accustomed to know them by their primary causes, to comprehend the demonstration of Prop. vii.: for such persons make no distinction between the modifications of substances and the substances themselves, and are ignorant of the manner in which things are produced; hence they may attribute to substances the beginning which they observe in natural objects. Those who are ignorant of true causes, make complete confusion — think that trees might talk just as well as men — that men might be formed from stones as well as from seed; and imagine that any form might be changed into any other. So, also, those who confuse the two natures, divine and human, readily attribute human passions to the deity, especially so long as they do not know how passions originate in the mind. But, if people would consider the nature of substance, they would have no doubt about the truth of Prop. vii. In fact, this proposition would be a universal axiom, and accounted a truism. For, by substance, would be understood that which is in itself, and is conceived through itself — that is, something of which the conception requires not the conception of anything else; whereas modifications exist in something external to themselves, and a conception of them is formed by means of a conception of the thing in which they exist. Therefore, we may have true ideas of non — existent modifications; for, although they may have no actual existence apart from the conceiving intellect, yet their essence is so involved in something external to themselves that they may through it be conceived. Whereas the only truth substances can have, external to the intellect, must consist in their existence, because they are conceived through themselves. Therefore, for a person to say that he has a clear and distinct — that is, a true — idea of a substance, but that he is not sure whether such substance exists, would be the same as if he said that he had a true idea, but was not sure whether or no it was false (a little consideration will make this plain); or if anyone affirmed that substance is created, it would be the same as saying that a false idea was true — in short, the height of absurdity. It must, then, necessarily be admitted that the existence of substance as its essence is an eternal truth. And we can hence conclude by another process of reasoning — that there is but one such substance. I think that this may profitably be done at once; and, in order to proceed regularly with the demonstration, we must premise: ——

1. The true definition of a thing neither involves nor expresses anything beyond the nature of the thing defined. From this it follows that ——

2. No definition implies or expresses a certain number of individuals, inasmuch as it expresses nothing beyond the nature of the thing defined. For instance, the definition of a triangle expresses nothing beyond the actual nature of a triangle: it does not imply any fixed number of triangles.

3. There is necessarily for each individual existent thing a cause why it should exist.

4. This cause of existence must either be contained in the nature and definition of the thing defined, or must be postulated apart from such definition.

It therefore follows that, if a given number of individual things exist in nature, there must be some cause for the existence of exactly that number, neither more nor less. For example, if twenty men exist in the universe (for simplicity's sake, I will suppose them existing simultaneously, and to have had no predecessors), and we want to account for the existence of these twenty men, it will not be enough to show the cause of human existence in general; we must also show why there are exactly twenty men, neither more nor less: for a cause must be assigned for the existence of each individual. Now this cause cannot be contained in the actual nature of man, for the true definition of man does not involve any consideration of the number twenty. Consequently, the cause for the existence of these twenty men, and, consequently, of each of them, must necessarily be sought externally to each individual. Hence we may lay down the absolute rule, that everything which may consist of several individuals must have an external cause. And, as it has been shown already that existence appertains to the nature of substance, existence must necessarily be included in its definition; and from its definition alone existence must be deducible. But from its definition (as we have shown, notes ii., iii.), we cannot infer the existence of several substances; therefore it follows that there is only one substance of the same nature. Q.E.D.

PROP. IX. The more reality or being a thing has, the greater the number of its attributes (Def. iv.).

PROP. X. Each particular attribute of the one substance must be conceived through itself.

Proof. — An attribute is that which the intellect perceives of substance, as constituting its essence (Def. iv.), and, therefore, must be conceived through itself (Def. iii.). Q.E.D.

Note — It is thus evident that, though two attributes are, in fact, conceived as distinct — that is, one without the help of the other — yet we cannot, therefore, conclude that they constitute two entities, or two different substances. For it is the nature of substance that each of its attributes is conceived through itself, inasmuch as all the attributes it has have always existed simultaneously in it, and none could be produced by any other; but each expresses the reality or being of substance. It is, then, far from an absurdity to ascribe several attributes to one substance: for nothing in nature is more clear than that each and every entity must be conceived under some attribute, and that its reality or being is in proportion to the number of its attributes expressing necessity or eternity and infinity. Consequently it is abundantly clear, that an absolutely infinite being must necessarily be defined as consisting in infinite attributes, each of which expresses a certain eternal and infinite essence.

If anyone now ask, by what sign shall he be able to distinguish different substances, let him read the following propositions, which show that there is but one substance in the universe, and that it is absolutely infinite, wherefore such a sign would be sought in vain.

PROP. XI. God, or substance, consisting of infinite attributes, of which each expresses eternal and infinite essentiality, necessarily exists.

Proof. — If this be denied, conceive, if possible, that God does not exist: then his essence does not involve existence. But this (Prop. vii.) is absurd. Therefore God necessarily exists.

Another proof. — Of everything whatsoever a cause or reason must be assigned, either for its existence, or for its non — existence — e.g. if a triangle exist, a reason or cause must be granted for its existence; if, on the contrary, it does not exist, a cause must also be granted, which prevents it from existing, or annuls its existence. This reason or cause must either be contained in the nature of the thing in question, or be external to it. For instance, the reason for the non — existence of a square circle is indicated in its nature, namely, because it would involve a contradiction. On the other hand, the existence of substance follows also solely from its nature, inasmuch as its nature involves existence. (See Prop. vii.)

But the reason for the existence of a triangle or a circle does not follow from the nature of those figures, but from the order of universal nature in extension. From the latter it must follow, either that a triangle necessarily exists, or that it is impossible that it should exist. So much is self — evident. It follows therefrom that a thing necessarily exists, if no cause or reason be granted which prevents its existence.

If, then, no cause or reason can be given, which prevents the existence of God, or which destroys his existence, we must certainly conclude that he necessarily does exist. If such a reason or cause should be given, it must either be drawn from the very nature of God, or be external to him — that is, drawn from another substance of another nature. For if it were of the same nature, God, by that very fact, would be admitted to exist. But substance of another nature could have nothing in common with God (by Prop. ii.), and therefore would be unable either to cause or to destroy his existence.

As, then, a reason or cause which would annul the divine existence cannot be drawn from anything external to the divine nature, such cause must perforce, if God does not exist, be drawn from God's own nature, which would involve a contradiction. To make such an affirmation about a being absolutely infinite and supremely perfect is absurd; therefore, neither in the nature of God, nor externally to his nature, can a cause or reason be assigned which would annul his existence. Therefore, God necessarily exists. Q.E.D.

Another proof. — The potentiality of non — existence is a negation of power, and contrariwise the potentiality of existence is a power, as is obvious. If, then, that which necessarily exists is nothing but finite beings, such finite beings are more powerful than a being absolutely infinite, which is obviously absurd; therefore, either nothing exists, or else a being absolutely infinite necessarily exists also. Now we exist either in ourselves, or in something else which necessarily exists (see Axiom. i. and Prop. vii.). Therefore a being absolutely infinite — in other words, God (Def. vi.) — necessarily exists. Q.E.D.

Note. — In this last proof, I have purposely shown God's existence à posteriori, so that the proof might be more easily followed, not because, from the same premises, God's existence does not follow à priori. For, as the potentiality of existence is a power, it follows that, in proportion as reality increases in the nature of a thing, so also will it increase its strength for existence. Therefore a being absolutely infinite, such as God, has from himself an absolutely infinite power of existence, and hence he does absolutely exist. Perhaps there will be many who will be unable to see the force of this proof, inasmuch as they are accustomed only to consider those things which flow from external causes. Of such things, they see that those which quickly come to pass — that is, quickly come into existence — quickly also disappear; whereas they regard as more difficult of accomplishment — that is, not so easily brought into existence — those things which they conceive as more complicated.

However, to do away with this misconception, I need not here show the measure of truth in the proverb, "What comes quickly, goes quickly," nor discuss whether, from the point of view of universal nature, all things are equally easy, or otherwise: I need only remark that I am not here speaking of things, which come to pass through causes external to themselves, but only of substances which (by Prop. vi.) cannot be produced by any external cause. Things which are produced by external causes, whether they consist of many parts or few, owe whatsoever perfection or reality they possess solely to the efficacy of their external cause; and therefore their existence solely from the perfection of their external cause, not from their own. Contrariwise, whatsoever perfection is possessed by substance is due to no external cause; wherefore the existence of substance must arise solely from its own nature, which is nothing else but its essence. Thus, the perfection of a thing does not annul its existence, but, on the contrary, asserts it. Imperfection, on the other hand, does annul it; therefore we cannot be more certain of the existence of anything, than of the existence of a being absolutely infinite or perfect — that is, of God. For inasmuch as his essence excludes all imperfection, and involves absolute perfection, all cause for doubt concerning his existence is done away, and the utmost certainty on the question is given. This, I think, will be evident to every moderately attentive reader.

PROP. XII. No attribute of substance can be conceived from which it would follow that substance can be divided.

Proof. — The parts into which substance as thus conceived would be divided either will retain the nature of substance, or they will not. If the former, then (by Prop. viii.) each part will necessarily be infinite, and (by Prop. vi.) self — caused, and (by Prop. v.) will perforce consist of a different attribute, so that, in that case, several substances could be formed out of one substance, which (by Prop. vi.) is absurd. Moreover, the parts (by Prop. ii.) would have nothing in common with their whole, and the whole (by Def. iv. and Prop. x.) could both exist and be conceived without its parts, which everyone will admit to be absurd. If we adopt the second alternative — namely, that the parts will not retain the nature of substance — then, if the whole substance were divided into equal parts, it would lose the nature of substance, and would cease to exist, which (by Prop. vii.) is absurd.

PROP. XIII. Substance absolutely infinite is indivisible.

Proof. — If it could be divided, the parts into which it was divided would either retain the nature of absolutely infinite substance, or they would not. If the former, we should have several substances of the same nature, which (by Prop. v.) is absurd. If the latter, then (by Prop. vii.) substance absolutely infinite could cease to exist, which (by Prop. xi.) is also absurd.

Corollary. — It follows, that no substance, and consequently no extended substance, in so far as it is substance, is divisible.

Note. — The indivisibility of substance may be more easily understood as follows. The nature of substance can only be conceived as infinite, and by a part of substance, nothing else can be understood than finite substance, which (by Prop. viii) involves a manifest contradiction.

PROP. XIV. Besides God no substance can be granted or conceived.

Proof. — As God is a being absolutely infinite, of whom no attribute that expresses the essence of substance can be denied (by Def. vi.), and he necessarily exists (by Prop. xi.); if any substance besides God were granted, it would have to be explained by some attribute of God, and thus two substances with the same attribute would exist, which (by Prop. v.) is absurd; therefore, besides God no substance can be granted, or, consequently, be conceived. If it could be conceived, it would necessarily have to be conceived as existent; but this (by the first part of this proof) is absurd. Therefore, besides God no substance can be granted or conceived. Q.E.D.

Corollary I. — Clearly, therefore: 1. God is one, that is (by Def. vi.) only one substance can be granted in the universe, and that substance is absolutely infinite, as we have already indicated (in the note to Prop. x.).

Corollary II. — It follows: 2. That extension and thought are either attributes of God or (by Ax. i.) accidents (affections) of the attributes of God.

PROP. XV. Whatsoever is, is in God, and without God nothing can be, or be conceived.

Proof. — Besides God, no substance is granted or can be conceived (by Prop. xiv.), that is (by Def. iii.) nothing which is in itself and is conceived through itself. But modes (by Def. v.) can neither be, nor be conceived without substance; wherefore they can only be in the divine nature, and can only through it be conceived. But substances and modes form the sum total of existence (by Ax. i.), therefore, without God nothing can be, or be conceived. Q.E.D.

Note. — Some assert that God, like a man, consists of body and mind, and is susceptible of passions. How far such persons have strayed from the truth is sufficiently evident from what has been said. But these I pass over. For all who have in anywise reflected on the divine nature deny that God has a body. Of this they find excellent proof in the fact that we understand by body a definite quantity, so long, so broad, so deep, bounded by a certain shape, and it is the height of absurdity to predicate such a thing of God, a being absolutely infinite.

But meanwhile by other reasons with which they try to prove their point, they show that they think corporeal or extended substance wholly apart from the divine nature, and say it was created by God. Wherefrom the divine nature can have been created, they are wholly ignorant; thus they clearly show, that they do not know the meaning of their own words. I myself have proved sufficiently clearly, at any rate in my own judgment (Coroll. Prop. vi, and note 2, Prop. viii.), that no substance can be produced or created by anything other than itself. Further, I showed (in Prop. xiv.), that besides God no substance can be granted or conceived. Hence we drew the conclusion that extended substance is one of the infinite attributes of God. However, in order to explain more fully, I will refute the arguments of my adversaries, which all start from the following points: ——

Extended substance, in so far as it is substance, consists, as they think, in parts, wherefore they deny that it can be infinite, or consequently, that it can appertain to God. This they illustrate with many examples, of which I will take one or two. If extended substance, they say, is infinite, let it be conceived to be divided into two parts; each part will then be either finite or infinite. If the former, then infinite substance is composed of two finite parts, which is absurd. If the latter, then one infinite will be twice as large as another infinite, which is also absurd.

Further, if an infinite line be measured out in foot lengths, it will consist of an infinite number of such parts; it would equally consist of an infinite number of parts, if each part measured only an inch: therefore, one infinity would be twelve times as great as the other.

Lastly, if from a single point there be conceived to be drawn two diverging lines which at first are at a definite distance apart, but are produced to infinity, it is certain that the distance between the two lines will be continually increased, until at length it changes from definite to indefinable. As these absurdities follow, it is said, from considering quantity as infinite, the conclusion is drawn, that extended substance must necessarily be finite, and, consequently, cannot appertain to the nature of God.

The second argument is also drawn from God's supreme perfection. God, it is said, inasmuch as he is a supremely perfect being, cannot be passive; but extended substance, insofar as it is divisible, is passive. It follows, therefore, that extended substance does not appertain to the essence of God.

Such are the arguments I find on the subject in writers, who by them try to prove that extended substance is unworthy of the divine nature, and cannot possibly appertain thereto. However, I think an attentive reader will see that I have already answered their propositions; for all their arguments are founded on the hypothesis that extended substance is composed of parts, and such a hypothesis I have shown (Prop. xii., and Coroll. Prop. xiii.) to be absurd. Moreover, anyone who reflects will see that all these absurdities (if absurdities they be, which I am not now discussing), from which it is sought to extract the conclusion that extended substance is finite, do not at all follow from the notion of an infinite quantity, but merely from the notion that an infinite quantity is measurable, and composed of finite parts therefore, the only fair conclusion to be drawn is that: infinite quantity is not measurable, and cannot be composed of finite parts. This is exactly what we have already proved (in Prop. xii.). Wherefore the weapon which they aimed at us has in reality recoiled upon themselves. If, from this absurdity of theirs, they persist in drawing the conclusion that extended substance must be finite, they will in good sooth be acting like a man who asserts that circles have the properties of squares, and, finding himself thereby landed in absurdities, proceeds to deny that circles have any center, from which all lines drawn to the circumference are equal. For, taking extended substance, which can only be conceived as infinite, one, and indivisible (Props. viii., v., xii.) they assert, in order to prove that it is finite, that it is composed of finite parts, and that it can be multiplied and divided.

So, also, others, after asserting that a line is composed of points, can produce many arguments to prove that a line cannot be infinitely divided. Assuredly it is not less absurd to assert that extended substance is made up of bodies or parts, than it would be to assert that a solid is made up of surfaces, a surface of lines, and a line of points. This must be admitted by all who know clear reason to be infallible, and most of all by those who deny the possibility of a vacuum. For if extended substance could be so divided that its parts were really separate, why should not one part admit of being destroyed, the others remaining joined together as before? And why should all be so fitted into one another as to leave no vacuum? Surely in the case of things, which are really distinct one from the other, one can exist without the other, and can remain in its original condition. As, then, there does not exist a vacuum in nature (of which anon), but all parts are bound to come together to prevent it, it follows from this that the parts cannot really be distinguished, and that extended substance in so far as it is substance cannot be divided.

If anyone asks me the further question, Why are we naturally so prone to divide quantity? I answer, that quantity is conceived by us in two ways; in the abstract and superficially, as we imagine it; or as substance, as we conceive it solely by the intellect. If, then, we regard quantity as it is represented in our imagination, which we often and more easily do, we shall find that it is finite, divisible, and compounded of parts; but if we regard it as it is represented in our intellect, and conceive it as substance, which it is very difficult to do, we shall then, as I have sufficiently proved, find that it is infinite, one, and indivisible. This will be plain enough to all who make a distinction between the intellect and the imagination, especially if it be remembered, that matter is everywhere the same, that its parts are not distinguishable, except in so far as we conceive matter as diversely modified, whence its parts are distinguished, not really, but modally. For instance, water, in so far as it is water, we conceive to be divided, and its parts to be separated one from the other; but not in so far as it is extended substance; from this point of view it is neither separated nor divisible. Further, water, in so far as it is water, is produced and corrupted; but, in so far as it is substance, it is neither produced nor corrupted.

I think I have now answered the second argument; it is, in fact, founded on the same assumption as the first — namely, that matter, in so far as it is substance, is divisible, and composed of parts. Even if it were so, I do not know why it should be considered unworthy of the divine nature, inasmuch as besides God (by Prop. xiv.) no substance can be granted, wherefrom it could receive its modifications. All things, I repeat, are in God, and all things which come to pass, come to pass solely through the laws of the infinite nature of God, and follow (as I will shortly show) from the necessity of his essence. Wherefore it can in nowise be said, that God is passive in respect to anything other than himself, or that extended substance is unworthy of the Divine nature, even if it be supposed divisible, so long as it is granted to be infinite and eternal. But enough of this for the present.

PROP. XVI. From the necessity of the divine nature must follow an infinite number of things in infinite ways — that is, all things which can fall within the sphere of infinite intellect.

Proof. — This proposition will be clear to everyone, who remembers that from the given definition of any thing the intellect infers several properties, which really necessarily follow therefrom (that is, from the actual essence of the thing defined); and it infers more properties in proportion as the definition of the thing expresses more reality, that is, in proportion as the essence of the thing defined involves more reality. Now, as the divine nature has absolutely infinite attributes (by Def. vi.), of which each expresses infinite essence after its kind, it follows that from the necessity of its nature an infinite number of things (that is, everything which can fall within the sphere of an infinite intellect) must necessarily follow. Q.E.D.

Corollary I. — Hence it follows, that God is the efficient cause of all that can fall within the sphere of an infinite intellect.

Corollary II. — It also follows that God is a cause in himself, and not through an accident of his nature.

Corollary III. — It follows, thirdly, that God is the absolutely first cause.

PROP. XVII. God acts solely by the laws of his own nature, and is not constrained by anyone.·

Proof. — We have just shown (in Prop. xvi.), that solely from the necessity of the divine nature, or, what is the same thing, solely from the laws of his nature, an infinite number of things absolutely follow in an infinite number of ways; and we proved (in Prop. xv.), that without God nothing can be nor be conceived but that all things are in God. Wherefore nothing can exist; outside himself, whereby he can be conditioned or constrained to act. Wherefore God acts solely by the laws of his own nature, and is not constrained by anyone. Q.E.D.

Corollary I. — It follows: 1. That there can be no cause which, either extrinsically or intrinsically, besides the perfection of his own nature, moves God to act.

Corollary II. — It follows: 2. That God is the sole free cause. For God alone exists by the sole necessity of his nature (by Prop. xi. and Prop. xiv., Coroll. i.), and acts by the sole necessity of his own nature, wherefore God is (by Def. vii.) the sole free cause. Q.E.D.

Note. — Others think that God is a free cause, because he can, as they think, bring it about, that those things which we have said follow from his nature — that is, which are in his power, should not come to pass, or should not be produced by him. But this is the same as if they said, that God could bring it about, that it should follow from the nature of a triangle that its three interior angles should not be equal to two right angles; or that from a given cause no effect should follow, which is absurd.

Moreover, I will show below, without the aid of this proposition, that neither intellect nor will appertain to God's nature. I know that there are many who think that they can show, that supreme intellect and free will do appertain to God's nature; for they say they know of nothing more perfect, which they can attribute to God, than that which is the highest perfection in ourselves. Further, although they conceive God as actually supremely intelligent, they yet do not believe that he can bring into existence everything which he actually understands, for they think that they would thus destroy God's power. If, they contend, God had created everything which is in his intellect, he would not be able to create anything more, and this, they think, would clash with God's omnipotence; therefore, they prefer to asset that God is indifferent to all things, and that he creates nothing except that which he has decided, by some absolute exercise of will, to create. However, I think I have shown sufficiently clearly (by Prop. xvi.), that from God's supreme power, or infinite nature, an infinite number of things — that is, all things have necessarily flowed forth in an infinite number of ways, or always flow from the same necessity; in the same way as from the nature of a triangle it follows from eternity and for eternity, that its three interior angles are equal to two right angles. Wherefore the omnipotence of God has been displayed from all eternity, and will for all eternity remain in the same state of activity. This manner of treating the question attributes to God an omnipotence, in my opinion, far more perfect. For, otherwise, we are compelled to confess that God understands an infinite number of creatable things, which he will never be able to create, for, if he created all that he understands, he would, according to this showing, exhaust his omnipotence, and render himself imperfect. Wherefore, in order to establish that God is perfect, we should be reduced to establishing at the same time, that he cannot bring to pass everything over which his power extends; this seems to be a hypothesis most absurd, and most repugnant to God's omnipotence.

Further (to say a word here concerning the intellect and the will which we attribute to God), if intellect and will appertain to the eternal essence of God, we must take these words in some significance quite different from those they usually bear. For intellect and will, which should constitute the essence of God, would perforce be as far apart as the poles from the human intellect and will, in fact, would have nothing in common with them but the name; there would be about as much correspondence between the two as there is between the Dog, the heavenly constellation, and a dog, an animal that barks. This I will prove as follows. If intellect belongs to the divine nature, it cannot be in nature, as ours is generally thought to be, posterior to, or simultaneous with the things understood, inasmuch as God is prior to all things by reason of his causality (Prop. xvi., Coroll. i.). On the contrary, the truth and formal essence of things is as it is, because it exists by representation as such in the intellect of God. Wherefore the intellect of God, in so far as it is conceived to constitute God's essence, is, in reality, the cause of things, both of their essence and of their existence. This seems to have been recognized by those who have asserted, that God's intellect, God's will, and God's power, are one and the same. As, therefore, God's intellect is the sole cause of things, namely, both of their essence and existence, it must necessarily differ from them in respect to its essence, and in respect to its existence. For a cause differs from a thing it causes, precisely in the quality which the latter gains from the former.

For example, a man is the cause of another man's existence, but not of his essence (for the latter is an eternal truth), and, therefore, the two men may be entirely similar in essence, but must be different in existence; and hence if the existence of one of them cease, the existence of the other will not necessarily cease also; but if the essence of one could be destroyed, and be made false, the essence of the other would be destroyed also. Wherefore, a thing which is the cause both of the essence and of the existence of a given effect, must differ from such effect both in respect to its essence, and also in respect to its existence. Now the intellect of God is the cause both of the essence and the existence of our intellect; therefore, the intellect of God in so far as it is conceived to constitute the divine essence, differs from our intellect both in respect to essence and in respect to existence, nor can it in anywise agree therewith save in name, as we said before. The reasoning would be identical in the case of the will, as anyone can easily see.

PROP. XVIII. God is the indwelling and not the transient cause of all things.

Proof. — All things which are, are in God, and must be conceived through God (by Prop. xv.), therefore (by Prop. xvi., Coroll. i.) God is the cause of those things which are in him. This is our first point. Further, besides God there can be no substance (by Prop. xiv.), that is nothing in itself external to God. This is our second point. God, therefore, is the indwelling and not the transient cause of all things. Q.E.D.

PROP. XIX. God, and all the attributes of God, are eternal.

Proof. — God (by Def. vi.) is substance, which (by Prop. xi.) necessarily exists, that is (by Prop. vii.) existence appertains to its nature, or (what is the same thing) follows from its definition; therefore, God is eternal (by Def. viii.). Further, by the attributes of God we must understand that which (by Def. iv.) expresses the essence of the divine substance — in other words, that which appertains to substance: that, I say, should be involved in the attributes of substance. Now eternity appertains to the nature of substance (as I have already shown in Prop. vii.); therefore, eternity must appertain to each of the attributes, and thus all are eternal. Q.E.D.

Note. — This proposition is also evident from the manner in which (in Prop. xi.) I demonstrated the existence of God; it is evident, I repeat, from that proof, that the existence of God, like his essence, is an eternal truth. Further (in Prop. xix. of my "Principles of the Cartesian Philosophy"), I have proved the eternity of God, in another manner, which I need not here repeat.

PROP. XX. The existence of God and his essence are one and the same.

Proof. — God (by the last Prop.) and all his attributes are eternal, that is (by Def. viii.) each of his attributes expresses existence. Therefore the same attributes of God which explain his eternal essence, explain at the same time his eternal existence — in other words, that which constitutes God's essence constitutes at the same time his existence. Wherefore God's existence and God's essence are one and the same. Q.E.D.

Coroll. I. — Hence it follows that God's existence, like his essence, is an eternal truth.

Coroll. II — Secondly, it follows that God, and all the attributes of God, are unchangeable. For if they could be changed in respect to existence, they must also be able to be changed in respect to essence — that is, obviously, be changed from true to false, which is absurd.

PROP. XXI. All things which follow from the absolute nature of any attribute of God must always exist and be infinite, or, in other words, are eternal and infinite through the said attribute.

Proof. — Conceive, if it be possible (supposing the proposition to be denied), that something in some attribute of God can follow from the absolute nature of the said attribute, and that at the same time it is finite, and has a conditioned existence or duration; for instance, the idea of God expressed in the attribute thought. Now thought, in so far as it is supposed to be an attribute of God, is necessarily (by Prop. xi.) in its nature infinite. But, in so far as it possesses the idea of God, it is supposed finite. It cannot, however, be conceived as finite, unless it be limited by thought (by Def. ii.); but it is not limited by thought itself, in so far as it has constituted the idea of God (for so far it is supposed to be finite); therefore, it is limited by thought, in so far as it has not constituted the idea of God, which nevertheless (by Prop. xi.) must necessarily exist.

We have now granted, therefore, thought not constituting the idea of God, and, accordingly, the idea of God does not naturally follow from its nature in so far as it is absolute thought (for it is conceived as constituting, and also as not constituting, the idea of God), which is against our hypothesis. Wherefore, if the idea of God expressed in the attribute thought, or, indeed, anything else in any attribute of God (for we may take any example, as the proof is of universal application) follows from the necessity of the absolute nature of the said attribute, the said thing must necessarily be infinite, which was our first point.

Furthermore, a thing which thus follows from the necessity of the nature of any attribute cannot have a limited duration. For if it can, suppose a thing, which follows from the necessity of the nature of some attribute, to exist in some attribute of God, for instance, the idea of God expressed in the attribute thought, and let it be supposed at some time not to have existed, or to be about not to exist.

Now thought being an attribute of God, must necessarily exist unchanged (by Prop. xi., and Prop. xx., Coroll. ii.); and beyond the limits of the duration of the idea of God (supposing the latter at some time not to have existed, or not to be going to exist) thought would perforce have existed without the idea of God, which is contrary to our hypothesis, for we supposed that, thought being given, the idea of God necessarily flowed therefrom. Therefore the idea of God expressed in thought, or anything which necessarily follows from the absolute nature of some attribute of God, cannot have a limited duration, but through the said attribute is eternal, which is our second point. Bear in mind that the same proposition may be affirmed of anything, which in any attribute necessarily follows from God's absolute nature.

PROP. XXII. Whatsoever follows from any attribute of God, in so far as it is modified by a modification, which exists necessarily and as infinite, through the said attribute, must also exist necessarily and as infinite.

Proof. — The proof of this proposition is similar to that of the preceding one.

PROP. XXIII. Every mode, which exists both necessarily and as infinite, must necessarily follow either from the absolute nature of some attribute of God, or from an attribute modified by a modification which exists necessarily, and as infinite.

Proof. — A mode exists in something else, through which it must be conceived (Def. v.), that is (Prop. xv.), it exists solely in God, and solely through God can be conceived. If therefore a mode is conceived as necessarily existing and infinite, it must necessarily be inferred or perceived through some attribute of God, in so far as such attribute is conceived as expressing the infinity and necessity of existence, in other words (Def. viii.) eternity; that is, in so far as it is considered absolutely. A mode, therefore, which necessarily exists as infinite, must follow from the absolute nature of some attribute of God, either immediately (Prop. xxi.) or through the means of some modification, which follows from the absolute nature of the said attribute; that is (by Prop. xxii.), which exists necessarily and as infinite.

PROP. XXIV. The essence of things produced by God does not involve existence.

Proof. — This proposition is evident from Def. i. For that of which the nature (considered in itself) involves existence is self — caused, and exists by the sole necessity of its own nature.

Corollary. — Hence it follows that God is not only the cause of things coming into existence, but also of their continuing in existence, that is, in scholastic phraseology, God is cause of the being of things (essendi rerum). For whether things exist, or do not exist, whenever we contemplate their essence, we see that it involves neither existence nor duration; consequently, it cannot be the cause of either the one or the other. God must be the sole cause, inasmuch as to him alone does existence appertain. (Prop. xiv. Coroll. i.) Q.E.D.

PROP. XXV. God is the efficient cause not only of the existence of things, but also of their essence.

Proof. — If this be denied, then God is not the cause of the essence of things; and therefore the essence of things can (by Ax. iv.) be conceived without God. This (by Prop. xv.) is absurd. Therefore, God is the cause of the essence of things. Q.E.D.

Note. — This proposition follows more clearly from Prop. xvi. For it is evident thereby that, given the divine nature, the essence of things must be inferred from it, no less than their existence — in a word, God must be called the cause of all things, in the same sense as he is called the cause of himself. This will be made still clearer by the following corollary.

Corollary. — Individual things are nothing but modifications of the attributes of God, or modes by which the attributes of God are expressed in a fixed and definite manner. The proof appears from Prop. xv. and Def. v.

PROP. XXVI. A thing which is conditioned to act in a particular manner, has necessarily been thus conditioned by God; and that which has not been conditioned by God cannot condition itself to act.

Proof. — That by which things are said to be conditioned to act in a particular manner is necessarily something positive (this is obvious); therefore both of its essence and of its existence God by the necessity of his nature is the efficient cause (Props. xxv. and xvi.); this is our first point. Our second point is plainly to be inferred therefrom. For if a thing, which has not been conditioned by God, could condition itself, the first part of our proof would be false, and this, as we have shown is absurd.

PROP. XXVII. A thing, which has been conditioned by God to act in a particular way, cannot render itself unconditioned.

Proof. — This proposition is evident from the third axiom.

PROP. XXVIII. Every individual thing, or everything which is finite and has a conditioned existence, cannot exist or be conditioned to act, unless it be conditioned for existence and action by a cause other than itself, which also is finite, and has a conditioned existence; and likewise this cause cannot in its turn exist, or be conditioned to act, unless it be conditioned for existence and action by another cause, which also is finite, and has a conditioned existence, and so on to infinity.

Proof. — Whatsoever is conditioned to exist and act, has been thus conditioned by God (by Prop. xxvi. and Prop. xxiv., Coroll.).

But that which is finite, and has a conditioned existence, cannot be produced by the absolute nature of any attribute of God; for whatsoever follows from the absolute nature of any attribute of God is infinite and eternal (by Prop. xxi.). It must, therefore, follow from some attribute of God, in so far as the said attribute is considered as in some way modified; for substance and modes make up the sum total of existence (by Ax. i. and Def. iii., v.), while modes are merely modifications of the attributes of God. But from God, or from any of his attributes, in so far as the latter is modified by a modification infinite and eternal, a conditioned thing cannot follow. Wherefore it must follow from, or be conditioned for, existence and action by God or one of his attributes, in so far as the latter are modified by some modification which is finite, and has a conditioned existence. This is our first point. Again, this cause or this modification (for the reason by which we established the first part of this proof) must in its turn be conditioned by another cause, which also is finite, and has a conditioned existence, and, again, this last by another (for the same reason); and so on (for the same reason) to infinity. Q.E.D.

Note. — As certain things must be produced immediately by God, namely those things which necessarily follow from his absolute nature, through the means of these primary attributes, which, nevertheless, can neither exist nor be conceived without God, it follows: — 1. That God is absolutely the proximate cause of those things immediately produced by him. I say absolutely, not after his kind, as is usually stated. For the effects of God cannot either exist or be conceived without a cause (Prop. xv. and Prop. xxiv. Coroll.). 2. That God cannot properly be styled the remote cause of individual things, except for the sake of distinguishing these from what he immediately produces, or rather from what follows from his absolute nature. For, by a remote cause, we understand a cause which is in no way conjoined to the effect. But all things which are, are in God, and so depend on God, that without him they can neither be nor be conceived.

PROP. XXIX. Nothing in the universe is contingent, but all things are conditioned to exist and operate in a particular manner by the necessity of the divine nature.

Proof. — Whatsoever is, is in God (Prop. xv.). But God cannot be called a thing contingent. For (by Prop. xi.) he exists necessarily, and not contingently. Further, the modes of the divine nature follow therefrom necessarily, and not contingently (Prop. xvi.); and they thus follow, whether we consider the divine nature absolutely, or whether we consider it as in any way conditioned to act (Prop. xxvii.). Further, God is not only the cause of these modes, in so far as they simply exist (by Prop. xxiv, Coroll.), but also in so far as they are considered as conditioned for operating in a particular manner (Prop. xxvi.). If they be not conditioned by God (Prop. xxvi.), it is impossible, and not contingent, that they should condition themselves; contrariwise, if they be conditioned by God, it is impossible, and not contingent, that they should render themselves unconditioned. Wherefore all things are conditioned by the necessity of the divine nature, not only to exist, but also to exist and operate in a particular manner, and there is nothing that is contingent. Q.E.D.

Note. — Before going any further, I wish here to explain, what we should understand by nature viewed as active (natura naturans), and nature viewed as passive (natura naturata). I say to explain, or rather call attention to it, for I think that, from what has been said, it is sufficiently clear, that by nature viewed as active we should understand that which is in itself, and is conceived through itself, or those attributes of substance, which express eternal and infinite essence, in other words (Prop. xiv., Coroll. i., and Prop. xvii., Coroll. ii) God, in so far as he is considered as a free cause.

By nature viewed as passive I understand all that which follows from the necessity of the nature of God, or of any of the attributes of God, that is, all the modes of the attributes of God, in so far as they are considered as things which are in God, and which without God cannot exist or be conceived.

PROP. XXX. Intellect, in function (actu) finite, or in function infinite, must comprehend the attributes of God and the modifications of God, and nothing else.

Proof. — A true idea must agree with its object (Ax. vi.); in other words (obviously), that which is contained in the intellect in representation must necessarily be granted in nature. But in nature (by Prop. xiv., Coroll. i.) there is no substance save God, nor any modifications save those (Prop. xv.) which are in God, and cannot without God either be or be conceived. Therefore the intellect, in function finite, or in function infinite, must comprehend the attributes of God and the modifications of God, and nothing else. Q.E.D.

PROP. XXXI. The intellect in function, whether finite or infinite, as will, desire, love, &c., should be referred to passive nature and not to active nature.

Proof. — By the intellect we do not (obviously) mean absolute thought, but only a certain mode of thinking, differing from other modes, such as love, desire, &c., and therefore (Def. v.) requiring to be conceived through absolute thought. It must (by Prop. xv. and Def. vi.), through some attribute of God which expresses the eternal and infinite essence of thought, be so conceived, that without such attribute it could neither be nor be conceived. It must therefore be referred to nature passive rather than to nature active, as must also the other modes of thinking. Q.E.D.

Note. — I do not here, by speaking of intellect in function, admit that there is such a thing as intellect in potentiality: but, wishing to avoid all confusion, I desire to speak only of what is most clearly perceived by us, namely, of the very act of understanding, than which nothing is more clearly perceived. For we cannot perceive anything without adding to our knowledge of the act of understanding.

PROP. XXXII. Will cannot be called a free cause, but only a necessary cause.

Proof. — Will is only a particular mode of thinking, like intellect; therefore (by Prop. xxviii.) no volition can exist, nor be conditioned to act, unless it be conditioned by some cause other than itself, which cause is conditioned by a third cause, and so on to infinity. But if will be supposed infinite, it must also be conditioned to exist and act by God, not by virtue of his being substance absolutely infinite, but by virtue of his possessing an attribute which expresses the infinite and eternal essence of thought (by Prop. xxiii.). Thus, however it be conceived, whether as finite or infinite, it requires a cause by which it should be conditioned to exist and act. Thus (Def. vii.) it cannot be called a free cause, but only a necessary or constrained cause. Q.E.D.

Coroll. I. — Hence it follows, first, that God does not act according to freedom of the will.

Coroll. II. — It follows, secondly, that will and intellect stand in the same relation to the nature of God as do motion, and rest, and absolutely all natural phenomena, which must be conditioned by God (Prop. xxix.) to exist and act in a particular manner. For will, like the rest, stands in need of a cause, by which it is conditioned to exist and act in a particular manner. And although, when will or intellect be granted, an infinite number of results may follow, yet God cannot on that account be said to act from freedom of the will, any more than the infinite number of results from motion and rest would justify us in saying that motion and rest act by free will. Wherefore will no more appertains to God than does anything else in nature, but stands in the same relation to him as motion, rest, and the like, which we have shown to follow from the necessity of the divine nature, and to be conditioned by it to exist and act in a particular manner.

PROP. XXXIII. Things could not have been brought into being by God in any manner or in any order different from that which has in fact obtained.

Proof — All things necessarily follow from the nature of God (Prop. xvi.), and by the nature of God are conditioned to exist and act in a particular way (Prop. xxix.). If things, therefore, could have been of a different nature, or have been conditioned to act in a different way, so that the order of nature would have been different, God's nature would also have been able to be different from what it now is; and therefore (by Prop. xi.) that different nature also would have perforce existed, and consequently there would have been able to be two or more Gods. This (by Prop. xiv., Coroll. i.) is absurd. Therefore things could not have been brought into being by God in any other manner, &c. Q.E.D.

Note I. — As I have thus shown, more clearly than the sun at noonday, that there is nothing to justify us in calling things contingent, I wish to explain briefly what meaning we shall attach to the word contingent; but I will first explain the words necessary and impossible.

A thing is called necessary either in respect to its essence or in respect to its cause; for the existence of a thing necessarily follows, either from its essence and definition, or from a given efficient cause. For similar reasons a thing is said to be impossible; namely, inasmuch as its essence or definition involves a contradiction, or because no external cause is granted, which is conditioned to produce such an effect; but a thing can in no respect be called contingent, save in relation to the imperfection of our knowledge.

A thing of which we do not know whether the essence does or does not involve a contradiction, or of which, knowing that it does not involve a contradiction, we are still in doubt concerning the existence, because the order of causes escapes us, — such a thing, I say, cannot appear to us either necessary or impossible. Wherefore we call it contingent or possible.

Note II. — It clearly follows from what we have said, that things have been brought into being by God in the highest perfection, inasmuch as they have necessarily followed from a most perfect nature. Nor does this prove any imperfection in God, for it has compelled us to affirm his perfection. From its contrary proposition, we should clearly gather (as I have just shown), that God is not supremely perfect, for if things had been brought into being in any other way, we should have to assign to God a nature different from that, which we are bound to attribute to him from the consideration of an absolutely perfect being.

I do not doubt, that many will scout this idea as absurd, and will refuse to give their minds up to contemplating it, simply because they are accustomed to assign to God a freedom very different from that which we (Def. vii.) have deduced. They assign to him, in short, absolute free will. However, I am also convinced that if such persons reflect on the matter, and duly weigh in their minds our series of propositions, they will reject such freedom as they now attribute to God, not only as nugatory, but also as a great impediment to organized knowledge. There is no need for me to repeat what I have said in the note to Prop. xvii. But, for the sake of my opponents, I will show further, that although it be granted that will pertains to the essence of God, it nevertheless follows from his perfection, that things could not have been by him created other than they are, or in a different order; this is easily proved, if we reflect on what our opponents themselves concede, namely, that it depends solely on the decree and will of God, that each thing is what it is. If it were otherwise, God would not be the cause of all things. Further, that all the decrees of God have been ratified from all eternity by God himself. If it were otherwise, God would be convicted of imperfection or change. But in eternity there is no such thing as when, before, or after; hence it follows solely from the perfection of God, that God never can decree, or never could have decreed anything but what is; that God did not exist before his decrees, and would not exist without them. But, it is said, supposing that God had made a different universe, or had ordained other decrees from all eternity concerning nature and her order, we could not therefore conclude any imperfection in God. But persons who say this must admit that God can change his decrees. For if God had ordained any decrees concerning nature and her order, different from those which he has ordained — in other words, if he had willed and conceived something different concerning nature — he would perforce have had a different intellect from that which he has, and also a different will. But if it were allowable to assign to God a different intellect and a different will, without any change in his essence or his perfection, what would there be to prevent him changing the decrees which he has made concerning created things, and nevertheless remaining perfect? For his intellect and will concerning things created and their order are the same, in respect to his essence and perfection, however they be conceived.

Further, all the philosophers whom I have read admit that God's intellect is entirely actual, and not at all potential; as they also admit that God's intellect, and God's will, and God's essence are identical, it follows that, if God had had a different actual intellect and a different will, his essence would also have been different; and thus, as I concluded at first, if things had been brought into being by God in a different way from that which has obtained, God's intellect and will, that is (as is admitted) his essence would perforce have been different, which is absurd.

As these things could not have been brought into being by God in any but the actual way and order which has obtained; and as the truth of this proposition follows from the supreme perfection of God; we can have no sound reason for persuading ourselves to believe that God did not wish to create all the things which were in his intellect, and to create them in the same perfection as he had understood them.

But, it will be said, there is in things no perfection nor imperfection; that which is in them, and which causes them to be called perfect or imperfect, good or bad, depends solely on the will of God. If God had so willed, he might have brought it about that what is now perfection should be extreme imperfection, and vice versâ. What is such an assertion, but an open declaration that God, who necessarily understands that which he wishes, might bring it about by his will, that he should understand things differently from the way in which he does understand them? This (as we have just shown) is the height of absurdity. Wherefore, I may turn the argument against its employers, as follows: — All things depend on the power of God. In order that things should be different from what they are, God's will would necessarily have to be different. But God's will cannot be different (as we have just most clearly demonstrated) from God's perfection. Therefore neither can things be different. I confess, that the theory which subjects all things to the will of an indifferent deity, and asserts that they are all dependent on his fiat, is less far from the truth than the theory of those, who maintain that God acts in all things with a view of promoting what is good. For these latter persons seem to set up something beyond God, which does not depend on God, but which God in acting looks to as an exemplar, or which he aims at as a definite goal. This is only another name for subjecting God to the dominion of destiny, an utter absurdity in respect to God, whom we have shown to be the first and only free cause of the essence of all things and also of their existence. I need, therefore, spend no time in refuting such wild theories.

PROP. XXXIV. God's power is identical with his essence.

Proof. — From the sole necessity of the essence of God it follows that God is the cause of himself (Prop. xi.) and of all things (Prop. xvi. and Coroll.). Wherefore the power of God, by which he and all things are and act, is identical with his essence. Q.E.D.

PROP. XXXV. Whatsoever we conceive to be in the power of God, necessarily exists.

Proof. — Whatsoever is in God's power, must (by the last Prop.) be comprehended in his essence in such a manner, that it necessarily follows therefrom, and therefore necessarily exists. Q.E.D.

PROP. XXXVI. There is no cause from whose nature some effect does not follow.

Proof. — Whatsoever exists expresses God's nature or essence in a given conditioned manner (by Prop. xxv., Coroll.); that is, (by Prop. xxxiv.), whatsoever exists, expresses in a given conditioned manner God's power, which is the cause of all things, therefore an effect must (by Prop. xvi.) necessarily follow. Q.E.D.

APPENDIX:

IN THE FOREGOING I have explained the nature and properties of God. I have shown that he necessarily exists, that he is one: that he is, and acts solely by the necessity of his own nature; that he is the free cause of all things, and how he is so; that all things are in God, and so depend on him, that without him they could neither exist nor be conceived; lastly, that all things are predetermined by God, not through his free will or absolute fiat, but from the very nature of God or infinite power. I have further, where occasion afforded, taken care to remove the prejudices, which might impede the comprehension of my demonstrations. Yet there still remain misconceptions not a few, which might and may prove very grave hindrances to the understanding of the concatenation of things, as I have explained it above. I have therefore thought it worth while to bring these misconceptions before the bar of reason.

All such opinions spring from the notion commonly entertained, that all things in nature act as men themselves act, namely, with an end in view. It is accepted as certain, that God himself directs all things to a definite goal (for it is said that God made all things for man, and man that he might worship him). I will, therefore, consider this opinion, asking first, why it obtains general credence, and why all men are naturally so prone to adopt it? secondly, I will point out its falsity; and, lastly, I will show how it has given rise to prejudices about good and bad, right and wrong, praise and blame, order and confusion, beauty and ugliness, and the like. However, this is not the place to deduce these misconceptions from the nature of the human mind: it will be sufficient here, if I assume as a starting point, what ought to be universally admitted, namely, that all men are born ignorant of the causes of things, that all have the desire to seek for what is useful to them, and that they are conscious of such desire. Herefrom it follows, first, that men think themselves free inasmuch as they are conscious of their volitions and desires, and never even dream, in their ignorance, of the causes which have disposed them so to wish and desire. Secondly, that men do all things for an end, namely, for that which is useful to them, and which they seek. Thus it comes to pass that they only look for a knowledge of the final causes of events, and when these are learned, they are content, as having no cause for further doubt. If they cannot learn such causes from external sources, they are compelled to turn to considering themselves, and reflecting what end would have induced them personally to bring about the given event, and thus they necessarily judge other natures by their own. Further, as they find in themselves and outside themselves many means which assist them not a little in the search for what is useful, for instance, eyes for seeing, teeth for chewing, herbs and animals for yielding food, the sun for giving light, the sea for breeding fish, &c., they come to look on the whole of nature as a means for obtaining such conveniences. Now as they are aware, that they found these conveniences and did not make them, they think they have cause for believing, that some other being has made them for their use. As they look upon things as means, they cannot believe them to be self — created; but, judging from the means which they are accustomed to prepare for themselves, they are bound to believe in some ruler or rulers of the universe endowed with human freedom, who have arranged and adapted everything for human use. They are bound to estimate the nature of such rulers (having no information on the subject) in accordance with their own nature, and therefore they assert that the gods ordained everything for the use of man, in order to bind man to themselves and obtain from him the highest honor. Hence also it follows, that everyone thought out for himself, according to his abilities, a different way of worshipping God, so that God might love him more than his fellows, and direct the whole course of nature for the satisfaction of his blind cupidity and insatiable avarice. Thus the prejudice developed into superstition, and took deep root in the human mind; and for this reason everyone strove most zealously to understand and explain the final causes of things; but in their endeavor to show that nature does nothing in vain, i.e. nothing which is useless to man, they only seem to have demonstrated that nature, the gods, and men are all mad together. Consider, I pray you, the result: among the many helps of nature they were bound to find some hindrances, such as storms, earthquakes, diseases, &c.: so they declared that such things happen, because the gods are angry at some wrong done to them by men, or at some fault committed in their worship. Experience day by day protested and showed by infinite examples, that good and evil fortunes fall to the lot of pious and impious alike; still they would not abandon their inveterate prejudice, for it was more easy for them to class such contradictions among other unknown things of whose use they were ignorant, and thus to retain their actual and innate condition of ignorance, than to destroy the whole fabric of their reasoning and start afresh. They therefore laid down as an axiom, that God's judgments far transcend human understanding. Such a doctrine might well have sufficed to conceal the truth from the human race for all eternity, if mathematics had not furnished another standard of verity in considering solely the essence and properties of figures without regard to their final causes. There are other reasons (which I need not mention here) besides mathematics, which might have caused men's minds to be directed to these general prejudices, and have led them to the knowledge of the truth.

I have now sufficiently explained my first point. There is no need to show at length, that nature has no particular goal in view, and that final causes are mere human figments. This, I think, is already evident enough, both from the causes and foundations on which I have shown such prejudice to be based, and also from Prop. xvi., and the Corollary of Prop. xxxii., and, in fact, all those propositions in which I have shown, that everything in nature proceeds from a sort of necessity, and with the utmost perfection. However, I will add a few remarks, in order to overthrow this doctrine of a final cause utterly. That which is really a cause it considers as an effect, and vice versâ: it makes that which is by nature first to be last, and that which is highest and most perfect to be most imperfect. Passing over the questions of cause and priority as self — evident, it is plain from Props. xxi., xxii., xxiii. that the effect is most perfect which is produced immediately by God; the effect which requires for its production several intermediate causes is, in that respect, more imperfect. But if those things which were made immediately by God were made to enable him to attain his end, then the things which come after, for the sake of which the first were made, are necessarily the most excellent of all.

Further, this doctrine does away with the perfection of God: for, if God acts for an object, he necessarily desires something which he lacks. Certainly, theologians and metaphysicians draw a distinction between the object of want and the object of assimilation; still they confess that God made all things for the sake of himself, not for the sake of creation. They are unable to point to anything prior to creation, except God himself, as an object for which God should act, and are therefore driven to admit (as they clearly must), that God lacked those things for whose attainment he created means, and further that he desired them.

We must not omit to notice that the followers of this doctrine, anxious to display their talent in assigning final causes, have imported a new method of argument in proof of their theory — namely, a reduction, not to the impossible, but to ignorance;

thus showing that they have no other method of exhibiting their doctrine. For example, if a stone falls from a roof on to someone's head, and kills him, they will demonstrate by their new method, that the stone fell in order to kill the man; for, if it had not by God's will fallen with that object, how could so many circumstances (and there are often many concurrent circumstances) have all happened together by chance? Perhaps you will answer that the event is due to the facts that the wind was blowing, and the man was walking that way. "But why," they will insist, "was the wind blowing, and why was the man at that very time walking that way?" If you again answer, that the wind had then sprung up because the sea had begun to be agitated the day before, the weather being previously calm, and that the man had been invited by a friend, they will again insist: "But why was the sea agitated, and why was the man invited at that time?" So they will pursue their questions from cause to cause, till at last you take refuge in the will of God — in other words, the sanctuary of ignorance. So, again, when they survey the frame of the human body, they are amazed; and being ignorant of the causes of so great a work of art, conclude that it has been fashioned, not mechanically, but by divine and supernatural skill, and has been so put together that one part shall not hurt another.

Hence anyone who seeks for the true causes of miracles, and strives to understand natural phenomena as an intelligent being, and not to gaze at them like a fool, is set down and denounced as an impious heretic by those, whom the masses adore as the interpreters of nature and the gods. Such persons know that, with the removal of ignorance, the wonder which forms their only available means for proving and preserving their authority would vanish also. But I now quit this subject, and pass on to my third point.

After men persuaded themselves, that everything which is created is created for their sake, they were bound to consider as the chief quality in everything that which is most useful to themselves, and to account those things the best of all which have the most beneficial effect on mankind. Further, they were bound to form abstract notions for the explanation of the nature of things, such as goodness, badness, order, confusion, warmth, cold, beauty, deformity, and so on; and from the belief that they are free agents arose the further notions of praise and blame, sin and merit.

I will speak of these latter hereafter, when I treat of human nature; the former I will briefly explain here.

Everything which conduces to health and the worship of God they have called good, everything which hinders these objects they have styled bad; and inasmuch as those who do not understand the nature of things do not verify phenomena in any way, but merely imagine them after a fashion, and mistake their imagination for understanding, such persons firmly believe that there is an order in things, being really ignorant both of things and their own nature. When phenomena are of such a kind, that the impression they make on our senses requires little effort of imagination, and can consequently be easily remembered, we say that they are well — ordered; if the contrary, that they are ill — ordered or confused. Further, as things which are easily imagined are more pleasing to us, men prefer order to confusion — as though there were any order in nature, except in relation to our imagination — and say that God has created all things in order; thus, without knowing it, attributing imagination to God, unless, indeed, they would have it that God foresaw human imagination, and arranged everything, so that it should be most easily imagined. If this be their theory, they would not, perhaps, be daunted by the fact that we find an infinite number of phenomena, far surpassing our imagination, and very many others which confound its weakness. But enough has been said on this subject. The other abstract notions are nothing but modes of imagining, in which the imagination is differently affected: though they are considered by the ignorant as the chief attributes of things, inasmuch as they believe that everything was created for the sake of themselves; and, according as they are affected by it, style it good or bad, healthy or rotten and corrupt. For instance, if the motion which objects we see communicate to our nerves be conducive to health, the objects causing it are styled beautiful; if a contrary motion be excited, they are styled ugly.

Things which are perceived through our sense of smell are styled fragrant or fetid; if through our taste, sweet or bitter, full — flavored or insipid; if through our touch, hard or soft, rough or smooth, &c.

Whatsoever affects our ears is said to give rise to noise, sound, or harmony. In this last case, there are men lunatic enough to believe, that even God himself takes pleasure in harmony; and philosophers are not lacking who have persuaded themselves, that the motion of the heavenly bodies gives rise to harmony — all of which instances sufficiently show that everyone judges of things according to the state of his brain, or rather mistakes for things the forms of his imagination. We need no longer wonder that there have arisen all the controversies we have witnessed, and finally skepticism: for, although human bodies in many respects agree, yet in very many others they differ; so that what seems good to one seems bad to another; what seems well ordered to one seems confused to another; what is pleasing to one displeases another, and so on. I need not further enumerate, because this is not the place to treat the subject at length, and also because the fact is sufficiently well known. It is commonly said: "So many men, so many minds; everyone is wise in his own way; brains differ as completely as palates." All of which proverbs show, that men judge of things according to their mental disposition, and rather imagine than understand: for, if they understood phenomena, they would, as mathematicians attest, be convinced, if not attracted, by what I have urged.

We have now perceived, that all the explanations commonly given of nature are mere modes of imagining, and do not indicate the true nature of anything, but only the constitution of the imagination; and, although they have names, as though they were entities, existing externally to the imagination, I call them entities imaginary rather than real; and, therefore, all arguments against us drawn from such abstractions are easily rebutted.

Many argue in this way. If all things follow from a necessity of the absolutely perfect nature of God, why are there so many imperfections in nature? such, for instance, as things corrupt to the point of putridity, loathsome deformity, confusion, evil, sin, &c. But these reasoners are, as I have said, easily confuted, for the perfection of things is to be reckoned only from their own nature and power; things are not more or less perfect, according as they delight or offend human senses, or according as they are serviceable or repugnant to mankind. To those who ask why God did not so create all men, that they should be governed only by reason, I give no answer but this: because matter was not lacking to him for the creation of every degree of perfection from highest to lowest; or, more strictly, because the laws of his nature are so vast, as to suffice for the production of everything conceivable by an infinite intelligence, as I have shown in Prop. xvi.

Such are the misconceptions I have undertaken to note; if there are any more of the same sort, everyone may easily dissipate them for himself with the aid of a little reflection.

PART II. ON THE NATURE AND ORIGIN OF THE MIND

PREFACE

I NOW PASS on to explaining the results, which must necessarily follow from the essence of God, or of the eternal and infinite being; not, indeed, all of them (for we proved in Part i., Prop. xvi., that an infinite number must follow in an infinite number of ways), but only those which are able to lead us, as it were by the hand, to the knowledge of the human mind and its highest blessedness.

DEFINITIONS

DEFINITION I. BY body I mean a mode which expresses in a certain determinate manner the essence of God, in so far as he is considered as an extended thing. (See Pt. i., Prop. xxv., Coroll.)

DEFINITION II. I consider as belonging to the essence of a thing that, which being given, the thing is necessarily given also, and, which being removed, the thing is necessarily removed also; in other words, that without which the thing, and which itself without the thing, can neither be nor be conceived.

DEFINITION III. By idea, I mean the mental conception which is formed by the mind as a thinking thing.

Explanation. — I say conception rather than perception, because the word perception seems to imply that the mind is passive in respect to the object; whereas conception seems to express an activity of the mind.

DEFINITION IV. By an adequate idea, I mean an idea which, in so far as it is considered in itself, without relation to the object, has all the properties or intrinsic marks of a true idea.

Explanation. — I say intrinsic, in order to exclude that mark which is extrinsic, namely, the agreement between the idea and its object (ideatum).

DEFINITION V. Duration is the indefinite continuance of existing.

Explanation. — I say indefinite, because it cannot be determined through the existence itself of the existing thing, or by its efficient cause, which necessarily gives the existence of the thing, but does not take it away.

DEFINITION VI. Reality and perfection I use as synonymous terms.

DEFINITION VII. By particular things, I mean things which are finite and have a conditioned existence; but if several individual things concur in one action, so as to be all simultaneously the effect of one cause, I consider them all, so far, as one particular thing.

AXIOMS

I. THE ESSENCE of man does not involve necessary existence, that is, it may, in the order of nature, come to pass that this or that man does or does not exist.

II. Man thinks.

III. Modes of thinking, such as love, desire, or any other of the passions, do not take place, unless there be in the same individual an idea of the thing loved, desired, &c. But the idea can exist without the presence of any other mode of thinking.

IV. We perceive that a certain body is affected in many ways.

V. We feel and perceive no particular things, save bodies and modes of thought.

N.B. The Postulates are given after the conclusion of Prop. xiii.

PROPOSITIONS

PROP. I. THOUGHT is an attribute of God, or God is a thinking thing.

Proof. — Particular thoughts, or this and that thought, are modes which, in a certain conditioned manner, express the nature of God (Pt. i., Prop. xxv., Coroll.). God therefore possesses the attribute (Pt. i., Def. v.) of which the concept is involved in all particular thoughts, which latter are conceived thereby. Thought, therefore, is one of the infinite attributes of God, which express God's eternal and infinite essence (Pt. i., Def. vi.). In other words, God is a thinking thing. Q.E.D.

Note. — This proposition is also evident from the fact, that we are able to conceive an infinite thinking being. For, in proportion as a thinking being is conceived as thinking more thoughts, so is it conceived as containing more reality or perfection. Therefore a being, which can think an infinite number of things in an infinite number of ways, is, necessarily, in respect of thinking, infinite. As, therefore, from the consideration of thought alone, we conceive an infinite being, thought is necessarily (Pt. i., Deff. iv. and vi.) one of the infinite attributes of God, as we were desirous of showing.

PROP. II. Extension is an attribute of God, or God is an extended thing.

Proof. — The proof of this proposition is similar to that of the last.

PROP. III. In God there is necessarily the idea not only of his essence, but also of all things which necessarily follow from his essence.

Proof. — God (by the first Prop. of this Part) can think an infinite number of things in infinite ways, or (what is the same thing, by Prop. xvi., Part i.) can form the idea of his essence, and of all things which necessarily follow therefrom. Now all that is in the power of God necessarily is (Pt. i., Prop. xxxv.). Therefore, such an idea as we are considering necessarily is, and in God alone. Q.E.D. (Part i., Prop. xv.)

Note. — The multitude understand by the power of God the free will of God, and the right over all things that exist, which latter are accordingly generally considered as contingent. For it is said that God has the power to destroy all things, and to reduce them to nothing. Further, the power of God is very often likened to the power of kings. But this doctrine we have refuted (Pt. i., Prop. xxxii., Corolls. i. and ii.), and we have shown (Part i., Prop. xvi.) that God acts by the same necessity, as that by which he understands himself; in other words, as it follows from the necessity of the divine nature (as all admit), that God understands himself, so also does it follow by the same necessity, that God performs infinite acts in infinite ways. We further showed (Part i., Prop. xxxiv.), that God's power is identical with God's essence in action; therefore it is as impossible for us to conceive God as not acting, as to conceive him as non — existent. If we might pursue the subject further, I could point out, that the power which is commonly attributed to God is not only human (as showing that God is conceived by the multitude as a man, or in the likeness of a man), but involves a negation of power. However, I am unwilling to go over the same ground so often. I would only beg the reader again and again, to turn over frequently in his mind what I have said in Part I from Prop. xvi. to the end. No one will be able to follow my meaning, unless he is scrupulously careful not to confound the power of God with the human power and right of kings.

PROP. IV. The idea of God, from which an infinite number of things follow in infinite ways, can only be one.

Proof. — Infinite intellect comprehends nothing save the attributes of God and his modifications (Part i., Prop. xxx.). Now God is one (Part i., Prop. xiv., Coroll.). Therefore the idea of God, wherefrom an infinite number of things follow in infinite ways, can only be one. Q.E.D.

PROP. V. The actual being of ideas owns God as its cause, only in so far as he is considered as a thinking thing, not in so far as he is unfolded in any other attribute; that is, the ideas both of the attributes of God and of particular things do not own as their efficient cause their objects (ideata) or the things perceived, but God himself in so far as he is a thinking thing.

Proof. — This proposition is evident from Prop. iii. of this Part. We there drew the conclusion, that God can form the idea of his essence, and of all things which follow necessarily therefrom, solely because he is a thinking thing, and not because he is the object of his own idea. Wherefore the actual being of ideas owns for cause God, in so far as he is a thinking thing. It may be differently proved as follows: the actual being of ideas is (obviously) a mode of thought, that is (Part i., Prop. xxv., Coroll.) a mode which expresses in a certain manner the nature of God, in so far as he is a thinking thing, and therefore (Part i., Prop. x.) involves the conception of no other attribute of God, and consequently (by Part i., Ax. iv.) is not the effect of any attribute save thought. Therefore the actual being of ideas owns God as its cause, in so far as he is considered as a thinking thing, &c. Q.E.D.

PROP. VI. The modes of any given attribute are caused by God, in so far as he is considered through the attribute of which they are modes, and not in so far as he is considered through any other attribute.

Proof. — Each attribute is conceived through itself, without any other (Part i., Prop. x.); wherefore the modes of each attribute involve the conception of that attribute, but not of any other. Thus (Part i., Ax. iv.) they are caused by God, only in so far as he is considered through the attribute whose modes they are, and not in so far as he is considered through any other. Q.E.D.

Corollary. — Hence the actual being of things, which are not modes of thought, does not follow from the divine nature, because that nature has prior knowledge of the things. Things represented in ideas follow, and are derived from their particular attribute, in the same manner, and with the same necessity as ideas follow (according to what we have shown) from the attribute of thought.

PROP. VII. The order and connection of ideas is the same as the order and connection of things.

Proof. — This proposition is evident from Part i., Ax. iv. For the idea of everything that is caused depends on a knowledge of the cause, whereof it is an effect.

Corollary. — Hence God's power of thinking is equal to his realized power of action — that is, whatsoever follows from the infinite nature of God in the world of extension (formaliter), follows without exception in the same order and connection from the idea of God in the world of thought (objective).

Note. — Before going any further, I wish to recall to mind what has been pointed out above — namely, that whatsoever can be perceived by the infinite intellect as constituting the essence of substance, belongs altogether only to one substance: consequently, substance thinking and substance extended are one and the same substance, comprehended now through one attribute, now through the other. So, also, a mode of extension and the idea of that mode are one and the same thing, though expressed in two ways. This truth seems to have been dimly recognized by those Jews who maintained that God, God's intellect, and the things understood by God are identical. For instance, a circle existing in nature, and the idea of a circle existing, which is also in God, are one and the same thing displayed through different attributes. Thus, whether we conceive nature under the attribute of extension, or under the attribute of thought, or under any other attribute, we shall find the same order, or one and the same chain of causes — that is, the same things following in either case.

I said that God is the cause of an idea — for instance, of the idea of a circle, — in so far as he is a thinking thing; and of a circle, in so far as he is an extended thing, simply because the actual being of the idea of a circle can only be perceived as a proximate cause through another mode of thinking, and that again through another, and so on to infinity; so that, so long as we consider things as modes of thinking, we must explain the order of the whole of nature, or the whole chain of causes, through the attribute of thought only. And, in so far as we consider things as modes of extension, we must explain the order of the whole of nature through the attributes of extension only; and so on, in the case of the other attributes. Wherefore of things as they are in themselves God is really the cause, inasmuch as he consists of infinite attributes. I cannot for the present explain my meaning more clearly.

PROP. VIII. The ideas of particular things, or of modes, that do not exist, must be comprehended in the infinite idea of God, in the same way as the formal essences of particular things or modes are contained in the attributes of God.

Proof. — This proposition is evident from the last; it is understood more clearly from the preceding note.

Corollary. — Hence, so long as particular things do not exist, except in so far as they are comprehended in the attributes of God, their representations in thought or ideas do not exist, except in so far as the infinite idea of God exists; and when particular things are said to exist, not only in so far as they are involved in the attributes of God, but also in so far as they are said to continue, their ideas will also involve existence, through which they are said to continue.

Note. — If anyone desires an example to throw more light on this question, I shall,

I fear, not be able to give him any, which adequately explains the thing of which I here speak, inasmuch as it is unique; however, I will endeavour to illustrate it as far as possible. The nature of a circle is such that if any number of straight lines intersect within it, the rectangles formed by their segments will be equal to one another; thus, infinite equal rectangles are contained in a circle. Yet none of these rectangles can be said to exist, except in so far as the circle exists; nor can the idea of any of these rectangles be said to exist, except in so far as they are comprehended in the idea of the circle. Let us grant that, from this infinite number of rectangles, two only exist. The ideas of these two not only exist, in so far as they are contained in the idea of the circle, but also as they involve the existence of those rectangles; wherefore they are distinguished from the remaining ideas of the remaining rectangles.

PROP. IX. The idea of an individual thing actually existing is caused by God, not in so far as he is infinite, but in so far as he is considered as affected by another idea of a thing actually existing, of which he is the cause, in so far as he is affected by a third idea, and so on to infinity.

Proof. — The idea of an individual thing actually existing is an individual mode of thinking, and is distinct from other modes (by the Corollary and note to Prop. viii. of this part); thus (by Prop. vi. of this part) it is caused by God, in so far only as he is a thinking thing. But not (by Prop. xxviii. of Part i.) in so far as he is a thing thinking absolutely, only in so far as he is considered as affected by another mode of thinking; and he is the cause of this latter, as being affected by a third, and so on to infinity. Now, the order and connection of ideas is (by Prop. vii. of this book) the same as the order and connection of causes. Therefore of a given individual idea another individual idea, or God, in so far as he is considered as modified by that idea, is the cause; and of this second idea God is the cause, in so far as he is affected by another idea, and so on to infinity. Q.E.D.

Corollary. — Whatsoever takes place in the individual object of any idea, the knowledge thereof is in God, in so far only as he has the idea of the object.

Proof. — Whatsoever takes place in the object of any idea, its idea is in God (by Prop. iii. of this part), not in so far as he is infinite, but in so far as he is considered as affected by another idea of an individual thing (by the last Prop.); but (by Prop. vii. of this part) the order and connection of ideas is the same as the order and connection of things. The knowledge, therefore, of that which takes place in any individual object will be in God, in so far only as he has the idea of that object. Q.E.D.

PROP. X. The being of substance does not appertain to the essence of man — in other words, substance does not constitute the actual being2 of man.

2 "Forma"

Proof. — The being of substance involves necessary existence (Part i., Prop. vii.). If, therefore, the being of substance appertains to the essence of man, substance being granted, man would necessarily be granted also (II. Def. ii.), and, consequently, man would necessarily exist, which is absurd (II. Ax. i.). Therefore, &c. Q.E.D.

Note. — This proposition may also be proved from I.v., in which it is shown that there cannot be two substances of the same nature; for as there may be many men, the being of substance is not that which constitutes the actual being of man. Again, the proposition is evident from the other properties of substance — namely, that substance is in its nature infinite, immutable, indivisible, &c., as anyone may see for himself.

Corollary. — Hence it follows, that the essence of man is constituted by certain modifications of the attributes of God. For (by the last Prop.) the being of substance does not belong to the essence of man. That essence therefore (by i. 15) is something which is in God, and which without God can neither be nor be conceived, whether it be a modification (i. 25. Coroll.), or a mode which expresses God's nature in a certain conditioned manner.

Note. — Everyone must surely admit, that nothing can be or be conceived without God. All men agree that God is the one and only cause of all things, both of their essence and of their existence; that is, God is not only the cause of things in respect to their being made (secundum fieri), but also in respect to their being (secundum esse).

At the same time many assert, that that, without which a thing cannot be nor be conceived, belongs to the essence of that thing; wherefore they believe that either the nature of God appertains to the essence of created things, or else that created things can be or be conceived without God; or else, as is more probably the case, they hold inconsistent doctrines. I think the cause for such confusion is mainly, that they do not keep to the proper order of philosophic thinking. The nature of God, which should be reflected on first, inasmuch as it is prior both in the order of knowledge and the order of nature, they have taken to be last in the order of knowledge, and have put into the first place what they call the objects of sensation; hence, while they are considering natural phenomena, they give no attention at all to the divine nature, and, when afterwards they apply their mind to the study of the divine nature, they are quite unable to bear in mind the first hypotheses, with which they have overlaid the knowledge of natural phenomena, inasmuch as such hypotheses are no help towards understanding the divine nature. So that it is hardly to be wondered at, that these persons contradict themselves freely.

However, I pass over this point. My intention her was only to give a reason for not saying, that that, without which a thing cannot be or be conceived, belongs to the essence of that thing: individual things cannot be or be conceived without God, yet God does not appertain to their essence. I said that "I considered as belonging to the essence of a thing that, which being given, the thing is necessarily given also, and which being removed, the thing is necessarily removed also; or that without which the thing, and which itself without the thing can neither be nor be conceived." (II. Def. ii.)

PROP. XI. The first element, which constitutes the actual being of the human mind, is the idea of some particular thing actually existing.

Proof. — The essence of man (by the Coroll. of the last Prop.) is constituted by certain modes of the attributes of God, namely (by II. Ax. ii.), by the modes of thinking, of all which (by II. Ax. iii.) the idea is prior in nature, and, when the idea is given, the other modes (namely, those of which the idea is prior in nature) must be in the same individual (by the same Axiom). Therefore an idea is the first element constituting the human mind. But not the idea of a non — existent thing, for then (II. viii. Coroll.) the idea itself cannot be said to exist; it must therefore be the idea of something actually existing. But not of an infinite thing. For an infinite thing (I. xxi., xxii.), must always necessarily exist; this would (by II. Ax. i.) involve an absurdity. Therefore the first element, which constitutes the actual being of the human mind, is the idea of something actually existing. Q.E.D.

Corollary. — Hence it follows, that the human mind is part of the infinite intellect of God; thus when we say, that the human mind perceives this or that, we make the assertion, that God has this or that idea, not in so far as he is infinite, but in so far as he is displayed through the nature of the human mind, or in so far as he constitutes the essence of the human mind; and when we say that God has this or that idea, not only in so far as he constitutes the essence of the human mind, but also in so far as he, simultaneously with the human mind, has the further idea of another thing, we assert that the human mind perceives a thing in part or inadequately.

Note. — Here, I doubt not, readers will come to a stand, and will call to mind many things which will cause them to hesitate; I therefore beg them to accompany me slowly, step by step, and not to pronounce on my statements, till they have read to the end.

PROP. XII. Whatsoever comes to pass in the object of the idea, which constitutes the human mind, must be perceived by the human mind, or there will necessarily be an idea in the human mind of the said occurrence. That is, if the object of the idea constituting the human mind be a body, nothing can take place in that body without being perceived by the mind.

Proof. — Whatsoever comes to pass in the object of any idea, the knowledge thereof is necessarily in God (II. ix. Coroll.), in so far as he is considered as affected by the idea of the said object, that is (II. xi.), in so far as he constitutes the mind of anything. Therefore, whatsoever takes place in the object constituting the idea of the human mind, the knowledge thereof is necessarily in God, in so far as he constitutes the essence of the human mind; that is (by II. xi. Coroll.) the knowledge of the said thing will necessarily be in the mind, in other words the mind perceives it.

Note. — This proposition is also evident, and is more clearly to be understood from II. vii., which see.

PROP. XIII. The object of the idea constituting the human mind is the body, in other words a certain mode of extension which actually exists, and nothing else.

Proof. — If indeed the body were not the object of the human mind, the ideas of the modifications of the body would not be in God (II. ix. Coroll.) in virtue of his constituting our mind, but in virtue of his constituting the mind of something else; that is (II. xi. Coroll.) the ideas of the modifications of the body would not be in our mind: now (by II. Ax. iv.) we do possess the idea of the modifications of the body. Therefore the object of the idea constituting the human mind is the body, and the body as it actually exists (II. xi.). Further, if there were any other object of the idea constituting the mind besides body, then, as nothing can exist from which some effect does not follow (I. xxxvi.) there would necessarily have to be in our mind an idea, which would be the effect of that other object (II. xi.); but (I. Ax. v.) there is no such idea. Wherefore the object of our mind is the body as it exists, and nothing else. Q.E.D.

Note. — We thus comprehend, not only that the human mind is united to the body, but also the nature of the union between mind and body. However, no one will be able to grasp this adequately or distinctly, unless he first has adequate knowledge of the nature of our body. The propositions we have advanced hitherto have been entirely general, applying not more to men than to other individual things, all of which, though in different degrees, are animated.3 For of everything there is necessarily an idea in God, of which God is the cause, in the same way as there is an idea of the human body; thus whatever we have asserted of the idea of the human body must necessarily also be asserted of the idea of everything else. Still, on the other hand, we cannot deny that ideas, like objects, differ one from the other, one being more excellent than another and containing more reality, just as the object of one idea is more excellent than the object of another idea, and contains more reality.

3 "Animata"

Wherefore, in order to determine, wherein the human mind differs from other things, and wherein it surpasses them, it is necessary for us to know the nature of its object, that is, of the human body. What this nature is, I am not able here to explain, nor is it necessary for the proof of what I advance, that I should do so. I will only say generally, that in proportion as any given body is more fitted than others for doing many actions or receiving many impressions at once, so also is the mind, of which it is the object, more fitted than others for forming many simultaneous perceptions; and the more the actions of the body depend on itself alone, and the fewer other bodies concur with it in action, the more fitted is the mind of which it is the object for distinct comprehension. We may thus recognize the superiority of one mind over others, and may further see the cause, why we have only a very confused knowledge of our body, and also many kindred questions, which I will, in the following propositions, deduce from what has been advanced. Wherefore I have thought it worth while to explain and prove more strictly my present statements. In order to do so, I must premise a few propositions concerning the nature of bodies.

AXIOM I. All bodies are either in motion or at rest.

AXIOM II. Every body is moved sometimes more slowly, sometimes more quickly.

LEMMA I. Bodies are distinguished from one another in respect of motion and rest, quickness and slowness, and not in respect of substance.

Proof. — The first part of this proposition is, I take it, self — evident. That bodies are not distinguished in respect of substance, is plain both from I. v. and I. viii. It is brought out still more clearly from I. xv, note.

LEMMA II. All bodies agree in certain respects.

Proof. — All bodies agree in the fact, that they involve the conception of one and the same attribute (II., Def. i.). Further, in the fact that they may be moved less or more quickly, and may be absolutely in motion or at rest.

LEMMA III. A body in motion or at rest must be determined to motion or rest by another body, which other body has been determined to motion or rest by a third body, and that third again by a fourth, and so on to infinity.

Proof. — Bodies are individual things (II., Def. i.), which (Lemma I.) are distinguished one from the other in respect to motion and rest; thus (I. xxviii.) each must necessarily be determined to motion or rest by another individual thing, namely (II. vi.), by another body, which other body is also (Ax. i.) in motion or at rest. And this body again can only have been set in motion or caused to rest by being determined by a third body to motion or rest. This third body again by a fourth, and so on to infinity. Q.E.D.

Corollary. — Hence it follows, that a body in motion keeps in motion, until it is determined to a state of rest by some other body; and a body at rest remains so, until it is determined to a state of motion by some other body. This is indeed self — evident. For when I suppose, for instance, that a given body, A, is at rest, and do not take into consideration other bodies in motion, I cannot affirm anything concerning the body A, except that it is at rest. If it afterwards comes to pass that A is in motion, this cannot have resulted from its having been at rest, for no other consequence could have been involved than its remaining at rest. If, on the other hand, A be given in motion, we shall, so long as we only consider A, be unable to affirm anything concerning it, except that it is in motion. If A is subsequently found to be at rest, this rest cannot be the result of A's previous motion, for such motion can only have led to continued motion; the state of rest therefore must have resulted from something, which was not in A, namely, from an external cause determining A to a state of rest.

Axiom I. — All modes, wherein one body is affected by another body, follow simultaneously from the nature of the body affected and the body affecting; so that one and the same body may be moved in different modes, according to the difference in the nature of the bodies moving it; on the other hand, different bodies may be moved in different modes by one and the same body.

Axiom II. — When a body in motion impinges on another body at rest, which it is unable to move, it recoils, in order to continue its motion, and the angle made by the line of motion in the recoil and the plane of the body at rest, whereon the moving body has impinged, will be equal to the angle formed by the line of motion of incidence and the same plane.

So far we have been speaking only of the most simple bodies, which are only distinguished one from the other by motion and rest, quickness and slowness. We now pass on to compound bodies.

Definition. — When any given bodies of the same or different magnitude are compelled by other bodies to remain in contact, or if they be moved at the same or different rates of speed, so that their mutual movements should preserve among themselves a certain fixed relation, we say that such bodies are in union, and that together they compose one body or individual, which is distinguished from other bodies by the fact of this union.

Axiom III. — In proportion as the parts of an individual, or a compound body, are in contact over a greater or less superficies, they will with greater or less difficulty admit of being moved from their position; consequently the individual will, with greater or less difficulty, be brought to assume another form. Those bodies, whose parts are in contact over large superficies, are called hard; those, whose parts are in contact over small superficies, are called soft; those, whose parts are in motion among one another, are called fluid.

LEMMA IV. If from a body or individual, compounded of several bodies, certain bodies be separated, and if, at the same time, an equal number of other bodies of the same nature take their place, the individual will preserve its nature as before, without any change in its actuality (forma).

Proof. — Bodies (Lemma i.) are not distinguished in respect of substance: that which constitutes the actuality (formam) of an individual consists (by the last Def.) in a union of bodies; but this union, although there is a continual change of bodies, will (by our hypothesis) be maintained; the individual, therefore, will retain its nature as before, both in respect of substance and in respect of mode. Q.E.D.

LEMMA V. If the parts composing an individual become greater or less, but in such proportion, that they all preserve the same mutual relations of motion and rest, the individual will still preserve its original nature, and its actuality will not be changed.

Proof. — The same as for the last Lemma.

LEMMA VI. If certain bodies composing an individual be compelled to change the motion, which they have in one direction, for motion in another direction, but in such a manner, that they be able to continue their motions and their mutual communication in the same relations as before, the individual will retain its own nature without any change of its actuality.

Proof. — This proposition is self — evident, for the individual is supposed to retain all that, which, in its definition, we spoke of as its actual being.

LEMMA VII. Furthermore, the individual thus composed preserves its nature, whether it be, as a whole, in motion or at rest, whether it be moved in this or that direction; so long as each part retains its motion, and preserves its communication with other parts as before.

Proof. — This proposition is evident from the definition of an individual prefixed to Lemma iv.

Note. — We thus see, how a composite individual may be affected in many different ways, and preserve its nature notwithstanding. Thus far we have conceived an individual as composed of bodies only distinguished one from the other in respect of motion and rest, speed and slowness; that is, of bodies of the most simple character. If, however, we now conceive another individual composed of several individuals of diverse natures, we shall find that the number of ways in which it can be affected, without losing its nature, will be greatly multiplied. Each of its parts would consist of several bodies, and therefore (by Lemma vi.) each part would admit, without change to its nature, of quicker or slower motion, and would consequently be able to transmit its motions more quickly or more slowly to the remaining parts. If we further conceive a third kind of individuals composed of individuals of this second kind, we shall find that they may be affected in a still greater number of ways without changing their actuality. We may easily proceed thus to infinity, and conceive the whole of nature as one individual, whose parts, that is, all bodies, vary in infinite ways, without any change in the individual as a whole. I should feel bound to explain and demonstrate this point at more length, if I were writing a special treatise on body. But I have already said that such is not my object; I have only touched on the question, because it enables me to prove easily that which I have in view.

POSTULATES

I. THE HUMAN body is composed of a number of individual parts, of diverse nature, each one of which is in itself extremely complex.

II. Of the individual parts composing the human body some are fluid, some soft, some hard.

III. The individual parts composing the human body, and consequently the human body itself, are affected in a variety of ways by external bodies.

IV. The human body stands in need for its preservation of a number of other bodies, by which it is continually, so to speak, regenerated.

V. When the fluid part of the human body is determined by an external body to impinge often on another soft part, it changes the surface of the latter, and, as it were, leaves the impression thereupon of the external body which impels it.

VI. The human body can move external bodies, and arrange them in a variety of ways.

PROP. XIV. The human mind is capable of perceiving a great number of things, and is so in proportion as its body is capable of receiving a great number of impressions.

Proof. — The human body (by Post. iii. and vi.) is affected in very many ways by external bodies, and is capable in very many ways of affecting external bodies. But (II. xii.) the human mind must perceive all that takes place in the human body; the human mind is, therefore, capable of perceiving a great number of things, and is so in proportion, &c. Q.E.D.

PROP. XV. The idea, which constitutes the actual being of the human mind, is not simple, but compounded of a great number of ideas.

Proof. — The idea constituting the actual being of the human mind is the idea of the body (II. xiii.), which (Post. i.) is composed of a great number of complex individual parts. But there is necessarily in God the idea of each individual part whereof the body is composed (II. viii. Coroll.); therefore (II. vii.), the idea of the human body is composed of these numerous ideas of its component parts. Q.E.D.

PROP. XVI. The idea of every mode, in which the human body is affected by external bodies, must involve the nature of the human body, and also the nature of the external body.

Proof. — All the modes, in which any given body is affected, follow from the nature of the body affected, and also from the nature of the affecting body (by Ax. i., after the Coroll. of Lemma iii.), wherefore their idea also necessarily (by I. Ax. iv.) involves the nature of both bodies; therefore, the idea of every mode, in which the human body is affected by external bodies, involves the nature of the human body and of the external body. Q.E.D.

Corollary I. — Hence it follows, first, that the human mind perceives the nature of a variety of bodies, together with the nature of its own.

Corollary II. — It follows, secondly, that the ideas, which we have of external bodies, indicate rather the constitution of our own body than the nature of external bodies. I have amply illustrated this in the Appendix to Part I.

PROP. XVII. If the human body is affected in a manner which involves the nature of any external body, the human mind will regard the said external body as actually existing, or as present to itself, until the human body be affected in such a way, as to exclude the existence or the presence of the said external body.

Proof. — This proposition is self — evident, for so long as the human body continues to be thus affected, so long will the human mind (II. xii.) regard this modification of the body — that is (by the last Prop.), it will have the idea of the mode as actually existing, and this idea involves the nature of the external body. In other words, it will have the idea which does not exclude, but postulates the existence or presence of the nature of the external body; therefore the mind (by II. xvi., Coroll. i.) will regard the external body as actually existing, until it is affected, &c. Q.E.D.

Corollary. — The mind is able to regard as present external bodies, by which the human body has once been affected, even though they be no longer in existence or present.

Proof. — When external bodies determine the fluid parts of the human body, so that they often impinge on the softer parts, they change the surface of the last named (Post. v.); hence (Ax. ii., after the Coroll. of Lemma iii.) they are refracted therefrom in a different manner from that which they followed before such change; and, further, when afterwards they impinge on the new surfaces by their own spontaneous movement, they will be refracted in the same manner, as though they had been impelled towards those surfaces by external bodies; consequently, they will, while they continue to be thus refracted, affect the human body in the same manner, whereof the mind (II. xii.) will again take cognizance — that is (II. xvii.), the mind will again regard the external body as present, and will do so, as often as the fluid parts of the human body impinge on the aforesaid surfaces by their own spontaneous motion. Wherefore, although the external bodies, by which the human body has once been affected, be no longer in existence, the mind will nevertheless regard them as present, as often as this action of the body is repeated. Q.E.D.

Note. — We thus see how it comes about, as is often the case, that we regard as present many things which are not. It is possible that the same result may be brought about by other causes; but I think it suffices for me here to have indicated one possible explanation, just as well as if I had pointed out the true cause. Indeed, I do not think I am very far from the truth, for all my assumptions are based on postulates, which rest, almost without exception, on experience, that cannot be controverted by those who have shown, as we have, that the human body, as we feel it, exists (Coroll. after II. xiii.). Furthermore (II. vii. Coroll., II. xvi. Coroll. ii.), we clearly understand what is the difference between the idea, say, of Peter, which constitutes the essence of Peter's mind, and the idea of the said Peter, which is in another man, say, Paul. The former directly answers to the essence of Peter's own body, and only implies existence so long as Peter exists; the latter indicates rather the disposition of Paul's body than the nature of Peter, and, therefore, while this disposition of Paul's body lasts, Paul's mind will regard Peter as present to itself, even though he no longer exists. Further, to retain the usual phraseology, the modifications of the human body, of which the ideas represent external bodies as present to us, we will call the images of things, though they do not recall the figure of things. When the mind regards bodies in this fashion, we say that it imagines. I will here draw attention to the fact, in order to indicate where error lies, that the imaginations of the mind, looked at in themselves, do not contain error. The mind does not err in the mere act of imagining, but only in so far as it is regarded as being without the idea, which excludes the existence of such things as it imagines to be present to it. If the mind, while imagining non — existent things as present to it, is at the same time conscious that they do not really exist, this power of imagination must be set down to the efficacy of its nature, and not to a fault, especially if this faculty of imagination depend solely on its own nature — that is (I. Def. vii.), if this faculty of imagination be free.

PROP. XVIII. If the human body has once been affected by two or more bodies at the same time, when the mind afterwards imagines any of them, it will straightway remember the others also.

Proof. — The mind (II. xvii. Coroll.) imagines any given body, because the human body is affected and disposed by the impressions from an external body, in the same manner as it is affected when certain of its parts are acted on by the said external body; but (by our hypothesis) the body was then so disposed, that the mind imagined two bodies at once; therefore, it will also in the second case imagine two bodies at once, and the mind, when it imagines one, will straightway remember the other. Q.E.D.

Note. — We now clearly see what Memory is. It is simply a certain association of ideas involving the nature of things outside the human body, which association arises in the mind according to the order and association of the modifications (affectiones) of the human body. I say, first, it is an association of those ideas only, which involve the nature of things outside the human body: not of ideas which answer to the nature of the said things: ideas of the modifications of the human body are, strictly speaking (II. xvi.), those which involve the nature both of the human body and of external bodies. I say, secondly, that this association arises according to the order and association of the modifications of the human body, in order to distinguish it from that association of ideas, which arises from the order of the intellect, whereby the mind perceives things through their primary causes, and which is in all men the same. And hence we can further clearly understand, why the mind from the thought of one thing, should straightway arrive at the thought of another thing, which has no similarity with the first; for instance, from the thought of the word pomum (an apple), a Roman would straightway arrive at the thought of the fruit apple, which has no similitude with the articulate sound in question, nor anything in common with it, except that the body of the man has often been affected by these two things; that is, that the man has often heard the word pomum, while he was looking at the fruit; similarly every man will go on from one thought to another, according as his habit has ordered the images of things in his body. For a soldier, for instance, when he sees the tracks of a horse in sand, will at once pass from the thought of a horse to the thought of a horseman, and thence to the thought of war, &c.; while a countryman will proceed from the thought of a horse to the thought of a plough, a field, &c. Thus every man will follow this or that train of thought, according as he has been in the habit of conjoining and associating the mental images of things in this or that manner.

PROP. XIX. The human mind has no knowledge of the body, and does not know it to exist, save through the ideas of the modifications whereby the body is affected.

Proof. — The human mind is the very idea or knowledge of the human body (II. xiii.), which (II. ix.) is in God, in so far as he is regarded as affected by another idea of a particular thing actually existing: or, inasmuch as (Post. iv.) the human body stands in need of very many bodies whereby it is, as it were, continually regenerated; and the order and connection of ideas is the same as the order and connection of causes (II. vii.); this idea will therefore be in God, in so far as he is regarded as affected by the ideas of very many particular things. Thus God has the idea of the human body, or knows the human body, in so far as he is affected by very many other ideas, and not in so far as he constitutes the nature of the human mind; that is (by II. xi. Coroll.), the human mind does not know the human body. But the ideas of the modifications of body are in God, in so far as he constitutes the nature of the human mind, or the human mind perceives those modifications (II. xii.), and consequently (II. xvi.) the human body itself, and as actually existing; therefore the mind perceives thus far only the human body. Q.E.D.

PROP. XX. The idea or knowledge of the human mind is also in God, following in God in the same manner, and being referred to God in the same manner, as the idea or knowledge of the human body.

Proof. — Thought is an attribute of God (II. i.); therefore (II. iii.) there must necessarily be in God the idea both of thought itself and of all its modifications, consequently also of the human mind (II. xi.). Further, this idea or knowledge of the mind does not follow from God, in so far as he is infinite, but in so far as he is affected by another idea of an individual thing (II. ix.). But (II. vii.) the order and connection of ideas is the same as the order and connection of causes; therefore this idea or knowledge of the mind is in God and is referred to God, in the same manner as the idea or knowledge of the body. Q.E.D.

PROP. XXI. This idea of the mind is united to the mind in the same way as the mind is united to the body.

Proof. — That the mind is united to the body we have shown from the fact, that the body is the object of the mind (II. xii. and xiii.); and so for the same reason the idea of the mind must be united with its object, that is, with the mind in the same manner as the mind is united to the body. Q.E.D.

Note. — This proposition is comprehended much more clearly from what we have said in the note to II. vii. We there showed that the idea of body and body, that is, mind and body (II. xiii.), are one and the same individual conceived now under the attribute of thought, now under the attribute of extension; wherefore the idea of the mind and the mind itself are one and the same thing, which is conceived under one and the same attribute, namely, thought. The idea of the mind, I repeat, and the mind itself are in God by the same necessity and follow from him from the same power of thinking. Strictly speaking, the idea of the mind, that is, the idea of an idea, is nothing but the distinctive quality (forma) of the idea in so far as it is conceived as a mode of thought without reference to the object; if a man knows anything, he, by that very fact, knows that he knows it, and at the same time knows that he knows that he knows it, and so on to infinity. But I will treat of this hereafter.

PROP. XXII. The human mind perceives not only the modifications of the body, but also the ideas of such modifications.

Proof. — The ideas of the ideas of modifications follow in God in the same manner, and are referred to God in the same manner, as the ideas of the said modifications. This is proved in the same way as II. xx. But the ideas of the modifications of the body are in the human mind (II. xii.), that is, in God, in so far as he constitutes the essence of the human mind; therefore the ideas of these ideas will be in God, in so far as he has the knowledge or idea of the human mind, that is (II. xxi.), they will be in the human mind itself, which therefore perceives not only the modifications of the body, but also the ideas of such modifications. Q.E.D.

PROP. XXIII. The mind does not know itself, except in so far as it perceives the ideas of the modifications of the body.

Proof. — The idea or knowledge of the mind (II. xx.) follows in God in the same manner, and is referred to God in the same manner, as the idea or knowledge of the body. But since (II. xix.) the human mind does not know the human body itself, that is (II. xi. Coroll.), since the knowledge of the human body is not referred to God, in so far as he constitutes the nature of the human mind; therefore, neither is the knowledge of the mind referred to God, in so far as he constitutes the essence of the human mind; therefore (by the same Coroll. II. xi.), the human mind thus far has no knowledge of itself. Further the ideas of the modifications, whereby the body is affected, involve the nature of the human body itself (II. xvi.), that is (II. xiii.), they agree with the nature of the mind; wherefore the knowledge of these ideas necessarily involves knowledge of the mind; but (by the last Prop.) the knowledge of these ideas is in the human mind itself; wherefore the human mind thus far only has knowledge of itself. Q.E.D.

PROP. XXIV. The human mind does not involve an adequate knowledge of the parts composing the human body.

Proof. — The parts composing the human body do not belong to the essence of that body, except in so far as they communicate their motions to one another in a certain fixed relation (Def. after Lemma iii.), not in so far as they can be regarded as individuals without relation to the human body. The parts of the human body are highly complex individuals (Post. i.), whose parts (Lemma iv.) can be separated from the human body without in any way destroying the nature and distinctive quality of the latter, and they can communicate their motions (Ax. i., after Lemma iii.) to other bodies in another relation; therefore (II. iii.) the idea or knowledge of each part will be in God, inasmuch (II. ix.) as he is regarded as affected by another idea of a particular thing, which particular thing is prior in the order of nature to the aforesaid part (II. vii.). We may affirm the same thing of each part of each individual composing the human body; therefore, the knowledge of each part composing the human body is in God, in so far as he is affected by very many ideas of things, and not in so far as he has the idea of the human body only, in other words, the idea which constitutes the nature of the human mind (II. xiii); therefore (II. xi. Coroll.), the human mind does not involve an adequate knowledge of the human body. Q.E.D.

PROP. XXV. The idea of each modification of the human body does not involve an adequate knowledge of the external body.

Proof. — We have shown that the idea of a modification of the human body involves the nature of an external body, in so far as that external body conditions the human body in a given manner. But, in so far as the external body is an individual, which has no reference to the human body, the knowledge or idea thereof is in God (II. ix.), in so far as God is regarded as affected by the idea of a further thing, which (II.

vii.) is naturally prior to the said external body. Wherefore an adequate knowledge of the external body is not in God, in so far as he has the idea of the modification of the human body; in other words, the idea of the modification of the human body does not involve an adequate knowledge of the external body. Q.E.D.

PROP. XXVI. The human mind does not perceive any external body as actually existing, except through the ideas of the modifications of its own body.

Proof. — If the human body is in no way affected by a given external body, then (II. vii.) neither is the idea of the human body, in other words, the human mind, affected in any way by the idea of the existence of the said external body, nor does it in any manner perceive its existence. But, in so far as the human body is affected in any way by a given external body, thus far (II. xvi. and Coroll.) it perceives that external body. Q.E.D.

Corollary. — In so far as the human mind imagines an external body, it has not an adequate knowledge thereof.

Proof. — When the human mind regards external bodies through the ideas of the modifications of its own body, we say that it imagines (see II. xvii. note); now the mind can only imagine external bodies as actually existing. Therefore (by II. xxv.), in so far as the mind imagines external bodies, it has not an adequate knowledge of them. Q.E.D.

PROP. XXVII. The idea of each modification of the human body does not involve an adequate knowledge of the human body itself.

Proof. — Every idea of a modification of the human body involves the nature of the human body, in so far as the human body is regarded as affected in a given manner (II. xvi.). But, inasmuch as the human body is an individual which may be affected in many other ways, the idea of the said modification, &c. Q.E.D.

PROP. XXVIII. The ideas of the modifications of the human body, in so far as they have reference only to the human mind, are not clear and distinct, but confused.

Proof. — The ideas of the modifications of the human body involve the nature both of the human body and of external bodies (II. xvi.); they must involve the nature not only of the human body but also of its parts; for the modifications are modes (Post. iii.), whereby the parts of the human body, and, consequently, the human body as a whole are affected. But (by II. xxiv., xxv.) the adequate knowledge of external bodies, as also of the parts composing the human body, is not in God, in so far as he is regarded as affected by the human mind, but in so far as he is regarded as affected by other ideas. These ideas of modifications, in so far as they are referred to the human mind alone, are as consequences without premisses, in other words, confused ideas. Q.E.D.

Note. — The idea which constitutes the nature of the human mind is, in the same manner, proved not to be, when considered in itself alone, clear and distinct; as also is the case with the idea of the human mind, and the ideas of the ideas of the modifications of the human body, in so far as they are referred to the mind only, as everyone may easily see.

PROP. XXIX. The idea of the idea of each modification of the human body does not involve an adequate knowledge of the human mind.

Proof. — The idea of a modification of the human body (II. xxvii.) does not involve an adequate knowledge of the said body, in other words, does not adequately express its nature; that is (II. xiii.) it does not agree with the nature of the mind adequately; therefore (I. Ax. vi) the idea of this idea does not adequately express the nature of the human mind, or does not involve an adequate knowledge thereof.

Corollary. — Hence it follows that the human mind, when it perceives things after the common order of nature, has not an adequate but only a confused and fragmentary knowledge of itself, of its own body, and of external bodies. For the mind does not know itself, except in so far as it perceives the ideas of the modifications of body (II. xxiii.). It only perceives its own body (II. xix.) through the ideas of the modifications, and only perceives external bodies through the same means; thus, in so far as it has such ideas of modification, it has not an adequate knowledge of itself (II. xxix.), nor of its own body (II. xxvii.), nor of external bodies (II. xxv.), but only a fragmentary and confused knowledge thereof (II. xxviii. and note). Q.E.D.

Note. — I say expressly, that the mind has not an adequate but only a confused knowledge of itself, its own body, and of external bodies, whenever it perceives things after the common order of nature; that is, whenever it is determined from without, namely, by the fortuitous play of circumstance, to regard this or that; not at such times as it is determined from within, that is, by the fact of regarding several things at once, to understand their points of agreement, difference, and contrast. Whenever it is determined in anywise from within, it regards things clearly and distinctly, as I will show below.

PROP. XXX. We can only have a very inadequate knowledge of the duration of our body.

Proof. — The duration of our body does not depend on its essence (II. Ax. i.), nor on the absolute nature of God (I. xxi.). But (I. xxviii.) it is conditioned to exist and operate by causes, which in their turn are conditioned to exist and operate in a fixed and definite relation by other causes, these last again being conditioned by others, and so on to infinity. The duration of our body therefore depends on the common order of nature, or the constitution of things. Now, however a thing may be constituted, the adequate knowledge of that thing is in God, in so far as he has the ideas of all things, and not in so far as he has the idea of the human body only. (II. ix. Coroll.) Wherefore the knowledge of the duration of our body is in God very inadequate, in so far as he is only regarded as constituting the nature of the human mind; that is (II. xi. Coroll.), this knowledge is very inadequate to our mind. Q.E.D.

PROP. XXXI. We can only have a very inadequate knowledge of the duration of particular things external to ourselves.

Proof. — Every particular thing, like the human body, must be conditioned by another particular thing to exist and operate in a fixed and definite relation; this other particular thing must likewise be conditioned by a third, and so on to infinity. (I. xxviii.) As we have shown in the foregoing proposition, from this common property of particular things, we have only a very inadequate knowledge of the duration of our body; we must draw a similar conclusion with regard to the duration of particular things, namely, that we can only have a very inadequate knowledge of the duration thereof. Q.E.D.

Corollary. — Hence it follows that all particular things are contingent and perishable. For we can have no adequate idea of their duration (by the last Prop.), and this is what we must understand by the contingency and perishableness of things. (I. xxxiii., Note i.) For (I. xxix.), except in this sense, nothing is contingent.

PROP. XXXII. All ideas, in so far as they are referred to God, are true.

Proof. — All ideas which are in God agree in every respect with their objects (II. vii. Coroll.), therefore (I. Ax. vi.) they are all true. Q.E.D.

PROP. XXXIII. There is nothing positive in ideas, which causes them to be called false.

Proof. — If this be denied, conceive, if possible, a positive mode of thinking, which should constitute the distinctive quality of falsehood. Such a mode of thinking cannot be in God (II. xxxii.); external to God it cannot be or be conceived (I. xv.). Therefore there is nothing positive in ideas which causes them to be called false. Q.E.D.

PROP. XXXIV. Every idea, which in us is absolute or adequate and perfect, is true.

Proof. — When we say that an idea in us is adequate and perfect, we say, in other words (II. xi. Coroll.), that the idea is adequate and perfect in God, in so far as he constitutes the essence of our mind; consequently (II. xxxii.), we say that such an idea is true. Q.E.D.

PROP. XXXV. Falsity consists in the privation of knowledge, which inadequate, fragmentary, or confused ideas involve.

Proof. — There is nothing positive in ideas, which causes them to be called false (II. xxxiii.); but falsity cannot consist in simple privation (for minds, not bodies, are said to err and to be mistaken), neither can it consist in absolute ignorance, for ignorance and error are not identical; wherefore it consists in the privation of knowledge, which inadequate, fragmentary, or confused ideas involve. Q.E.D.

Note. — In the note to II. xvii. I explained how error consists in the privation of knowledge, but in order to throw more light on the subject I will give an example. For instance, men are mistaken in thinking themselves free; their opinion is made up of consciousness of their own actions, and ignorance of the causes by which they are conditioned. Their idea of freedom, therefore, is simply their ignorance of any cause for their actions. As for their saying that human actions depend on the will, this is a mere phrase without any idea to correspond thereto. What the will is, and how it moves the body, they none of them know; those who boast of such knowledge, and feign dwellings and habitations for the soul, are wont to provoke either laughter or disgust. So, again, when we look at the sun, we imagine that it is distant from us about two hundred feet; this error does not lie solely in this fancy, but in the fact that, while we thus imagine, we do not know the sun's true distance or the cause of the fancy. For although we afterwards learn, that the sun is distant from us more than six hundred of the earth's diameters, we none the less shall fancy it to be near; for we do not imagine the sun as near us, because we are ignorant of its true distance, but because the modification of our body involves the essence of the sun, in so far as our said body is affected thereby.

PROP. XXXVI. Inadequate and confused ideas follow by the same necessity, as adequate or clear and distinct ideas.

Proof. — All ideas are in God (I. xv.), and in so far as they are referred to God are true (II. xxxii.) and (II. vii. Coroll.) adequate; therefore there are no ideas confused or inadequate, except in respect to a particular mind (cf. II. xxiv. and xxviii.); therefore all ideas, whether adequate or inadequate, follow by the same necessity (II. vi.). Q.E.D.

PROP. XXXVII. That which is common to all (cf. Lemma II., above), and which is equally in a part and in the whole, does not constitute the essence of any particular thing.

Proof. — If this be denied, conceive, if possible, that it constitutes the essence of some particular thing; for instance, the essence of B. Then (II. Def. ii.) it cannot without B either exist or be conceived; but this is against our hypothesis. Therefore it does not appertain to B's essence, nor does it constitute the essence of any particular thing. Q.E.D.

PROP. XXXVIII. Those things, which are common to all, and which are equally in a part and in the whole, cannot be conceived except adequately.

Proof. — Let A be something, which is common to all bodies, and which is equally present in the part of any given body and in the whole. I say A cannot be conceived except adequately. For the idea thereof in God will necessarily be adequate (II. vii. Coroll.), both in so far as God has the idea of the human body, and also in so far as he has the idea of the modifications of the human body, which (II. xvi., xxv., xxvii.) involve in part the nature of the human body and the nature of external bodies; that is (II. xii., xiii.), the idea in God will necessarily be adequate, both in so far as he constitutes the human mind, and in so far as he has the ideas, which are in the human mind. Therefore the mind (II. xi. Coroll.) necessarily perceives A adequately, and has this adequate perception, both in so far as it perceives itself, and in so far as it perceives its own or any external body, nor can A be conceived in any other manner. Q.E.D.

Corollary — Hence it follows that there are certain ideas or notions common to all men; for (by Lemma ii.) all bodies agree in certain respects, which (by the foregoing Prop.) must be adequately or clearly and distinctly perceived by all.

PROP. XXXIX. That, which is common to and a property of the human body and such other bodies as are wont to affect the human body, and which is present equally in each part of either, or in the whole, will be represented by an adequate idea in the mind.

Proof. — If A be that, which is common to and a property of the human body and external bodies, and equally present in the human body and in the said external bodies, in each part of each external body and in the whole, there will be an adequate idea of A in God (II. vii. Coroll.), both in so far as he has the idea of the human body, and in so far as he has the ideas of the given external bodies. Let it now be granted, that the human body is affected by an external body through that, which it has in common therewith, namely, A; the idea of this modification will involve the property A (II. xvi.), and therefore (II. vii. Coroll.) the idea of this modification, in so far as it involves the property A, will be adequate in God, in so far as God is affected by the idea of the human body; that is (II. xiii.), in so far as he constitutes the nature of the human mind; therefore (II. xi. Coroll.) this idea is also adequate in the human mind. Q.E.D.

Corollary. — Hence it follows that the mind is fitted to perceive adequately more things, in proportion as its body has more in common with other bodies.

PROP. XL. Whatsoever ideas in the mind follow from ideas which are therein adequate, are also themselves adequate.

Proof. — This proposition is self — evident. For when we say that an idea in the human mind follows from ideas which are therein adequate, we say, in other words (II. xi. Coroll.), that an idea is in the divine intellect, whereof God is the cause, not in so far as he is infinite, nor in so far as he is affected by the ideas of very many particular things, but only in so far as he constitutes the essence of the human mind.

Note I. — I have thus set forth the cause of those notions, which are common to all men, and which form the basis of our ratiocination. But there are other causes of certain axioms or notions, which it would be to the purpose to set forth by this method of ours; for it would thus appear what notions are more useful than others, and what notions have scarcely any use at all. Furthermore, we should see what notions are common to all men, and what notions are only clear and distinct to those who are unshackled by prejudice, and we should detect those which are ill — founded. Again we should discern whence the notions called secondary derived their origin, and consequently the axioms on which they are founded, and other points of interest connected with these questions. But I have decided to pass over the subject here, partly because I have set it aside for another treatise, partly because I am afraid of wearying the reader by too great prolixity. Nevertheless, in order not to omit anything necessary to be known, I will briefly set down the causes, whence are derived the terms styled transcendental, such as Being, Thing, Something. These terms arose from the fact, that the human body, being limited, is only capable of distinctly forming a certain number of images (what an image is I explained in the II. xvii. note) within itself at the same time; if this number be exceeded, the images will begin to be confused; if this number of images, of which the body is capable of forming distinctly within itself, be largely exceeded, all will become entirely confused one with another. This being so, it is evident (from II. Prop. xvii. Coroll., and xviii.) that the human mind can distinctly imagine as many things simultaneously, as its body can form images simultaneously. When the images become quite confused in the body, the mind also imagines all bodies confusedly without any distinction, and will comprehend them, as it were, under one attribute, namely, under the attribute of Being, Thing, &c. The same conclusion can be drawn from the fact that images are not always equally vivid, and from other analogous causes, which there is no need to explain here; for the purpose which we have in view it is sufficient for us to consider one only. All may be reduced to this, that these terms represent ideas in the highest degree confused. From similar causes arise those notions, which we call general, such as man, horse, dog, &c. They arise, to wit, from the fact that so many images, for instance, of men, are formed simultaneously in the human mind, that the powers of imagination break down, not indeed utterly, but to the extent of the mind losing count of small differences between individuals (e.g. colour, size, &c.) and their definite number, and only distinctly imagining that, in which all the individuals, in so far as the body is affected by them, agree; for that is the point, in which each of the said individuals chiefly affected the body; this the mind expresses by the name man, and this it predicates of an infinite number of particular individuals.

For, as we have said, it is unable to imagine the definite number of individuals. We must, however, bear in mind, that these general notions are not formed by all men in the same way, but vary in each individual according as the point varies, whereby the body has been most often affected and which the mind most easily imagines or remembers. For instance, those who have most often regarded with admiration the stature of man, will by the name of man understand an animal of erect stature; those who have been accustomed to regard some other attribute, will form a different general image of man, for instance, that man is a laughing animal, a two — footed animal without feathers, a rational animal, and thus, in other cases, everyone will form general images of things according to the habit of his body.

It is thus not to be wondered at, that among philosophers, who seek to explain things in nature merely by the images formed of them, so many controversies should have arisen.

Note II. — From all that has been said above it is clear, that we, in many cases, perceive and form our general notions: — (1.) From particular things represented to our intellect fragmentarily, confusedly, and without order through our senses (II. xxix. Coroll.); I have settled to call such perceptions by the name of knowledge from the mere suggestions of experience.4

4 A Baconian phrase. Nov. Org. Aph. 100. [Pollock, p. 126, n.]

(2.) From symbols, e.g., from the fact of having read or heard certain words we remember things and form certain ideas concerning them, similar to those through which we imagine things (II. xviii. note). I shall call both these ways of regarding things knowledge of the first kind, opinion, or imagination. (3.) From the fact that we have notions common to all men, and adequate ideas of the properties of things (II. xxxviii. Coroll., xxxix. and Coroll. and xl.); this I call reason and knowledge of the second kind. Besides these two kinds of knowledge, there is, as I will hereafter show, a third kind of knowledge, which we will call intuition. This kind of knowledge proceeds from an adequate idea of the absolute essence of certain attributes of God to the adequate knowledge of the essence of things. I will illustrate all three kinds of knowledge by a single example. Three numbers are given for finding a fourth, which shall be to the third as the second is to the first. Tradesmen without hesitation multiply the second by the third, and divide the product by the first; either because they have not forgotten the rule which they received from a master without any proof, or because they have often made trial of it with simple numbers, or by virtue of the proof of the nineteenth proposition of the seventh book of Euclid, namely, in virtue of the general property of proportionals.

But with very simple numbers there is no need of this. For instance, one, two, three, being given, everyone can see that the fourth proportional is six; and this is much clearer, because we infer the fourth number from an intuitive grasping of the ratio, which the first bears to the second.

PROP. XLI. Knowledge of the first kind is the only source of falsity, knowledge of the second and third kinds is necessarily true.

Proof. — To knowledge of the first kind we have (in the foregoing note) assigned all those ideas, which are inadequate and confused; therefore this kind of knowledge is the only source of falsity (II. xxxv.). Furthermore, we assigned to the second and third kinds of knowledge those ideas which are adequate; therefore these kinds are necessarily true (II. xxxiv.). Q.E.D.

PROP. XLII. Knowledge of the second and third kinds, not knowledge of the first kind, teaches us to distinguish the true from the false.

Proof. — This proposition is self — evident. He, who knows how to distinguish between true and false, must have an adequate idea of true and false. That is (II. xl., note ii.), he must know the true and the false by the second or third kind of knowledge.

PROP. XLIII. He, who has a true idea, simultaneously knows that he has a true idea, and cannot doubt of the truth of the thing perceived.

Proof. — A true idea in us is an idea which is adequate in God, in so far as he is displayed through the nature of the human mind (II. xi. Coroll.). Let us suppose that there is in God, in so far as he is displayed through the human mind, an adequate idea, A. The idea of this idea must also necessarily be in God, and be referred to him in the same way as the idea A (by II. xx., whereof the proof is of universal application). But the idea A is supposed to be referred to God, in so far as he is displayed through the human mind; therefore, the idea of the idea A must be referred to God in the same manner; that is (by II. xi. Coroll.), the adequate idea of the idea A will be in the mind, which has the adequate idea A; therefore he, who has an adequate idea or knows a thing truly (II. xxxiv.), must at the same time have an adequate idea or true knowledge of his knowledge; that is, obviously, he must be assured. Q.E.D.

Note. — I explained in the note to II. xxi. what is meant by the idea of an idea; but we may remark that the foregoing proposition is in itself sufficiently plain. No one, who has a true idea, is ignorant that a true idea involves the highest certainty. For to have a true idea is only another expression for knowing a thing perfectly, or as well as possible. No one, indeed, can doubt of this, unless he thinks that an idea is something lifeless, like a picture on a panel, and not a mode of thinking — namely, the very act of understanding. And who, I ask, can know that he understands anything, unless he do first understand it? In other words, who can know that he is sure of a thing, unless he be first sure of that thing? Further, what can there be more clear, and more certain, than a true idea as a standard of truth? Even as light displays both itself and darkness, so is truth a standard both of itself and of falsity.

I think I have thus sufficiently answered these questions — namely, if a true idea is distinguished from a false idea, only in so far as it is said to agree with its object, a true idea has no more reality or perfection than a false idea (since the two are only distinguished by an extrinsic mark); consequently, neither will a man who has a true idea have any advantage over him who has only false ideas. Further, how comes it that men have false ideas? Lastly, how can anyone be sure, that he has ideas which agree with their objects? These questions, I repeat, I have, in my opinion, sufficiently answered. The difference between a true idea and a false idea is plain: from what was said in II. xxxv., the former is related to the latter as being is to not — being. The causes of falsity I have set forth very clearly in II. xix. and II. xxxv. with the note. From what is there stated, the difference between a man who has true ideas, and a man who has only false ideas, is made apparent. As for the last question — as to how a man can be sure that he has ideas that agree with their objects, I have just pointed out, with abundant clearness, that his knowledge arises from the simple fact, that he has an idea which corresponds with its object — in other words, that truth is its own standard. We may add that our mind, in so far as it perceives things truly, is part of the infinite intellect of God (II. xi.

Coroll.); therefore, the clear and distinct ideas of the mind are as necessarily true as the ideas of God.

PROP. XLIV. It is not in the nature of reason to regard things as contingent, but as necessary.

Proof. — It is in the nature of reason to perceive things truly (II. xli.), namely (I. Ax. vi.), as they are in themselves — that is (I. xxix.), not as contingent, but as necessary. Q.E.D.

Corollary I. — Hence it follows, that it is only through our imagination that we consider things, whether in respect to the future or the past, as contingent.

Note. — How this way of looking at things arises, I will briefly explain. We have shown above (II. xvii. and Coroll.) that the mind always regards things as present to itself, even though they be not in existence, until some causes arise which exclude their existence and presence. Further (II. xviii.), we showed that, if the human body has once been affected by two external bodies simultaneously, the mind, when it afterwards imagines one of the said external bodies, will straightway remember the other — that is, it will regard both as present to itself, unless there arise causes which exclude their existence and presence. Further, no one doubts that we imagine time, from the fact that we imagine bodies to be moved some more slowly than others, some more quickly, some at equal speed. Thus, let us suppose that a child yesterday saw Peter for the first time in the morning, Paul at noon, and Simon in the evening; then, that today he again sees Peter in the morning. It is evident, from II. Prop. xviii., that, as soon as he sees the morning light, he will imagine that the sun will traverse the same parts of the sky, as it did when he saw it on the preceding day; in other words, he will imagine a complete day, and, together with his imagination of the morning, he will imagine Peter; with noon, he will imagine Paul; and with evening, he will imagine Simon — that is, he will imagine the existence of Paul and Simon in relation to a future time; on the other hand, if he sees Simon in the evening, he will refer Peter and Paul to a past time, by imagining them simultaneously with the imagination of a past time. If it should at any time happen, that on some other evening the child should see James instead of Simon, he will, on the following morning, associate with his imagination of evening sometimes Simon, sometimes James, not both together: for the child is supposed to have seen, at evening, one or other of them, not both together. His imagination will therefore waver; and, with the imagination of future evenings, he will associate first one, then the other — that is, he will imagine them in the future, neither of them as certain, but both as contingent. This wavering of the imagination will be the same, if the imagination be concerned with things which we thus contemplate, standing in relation to time past or time present: consequently, we may imagine things as contingent, whether they be referred to time present, past, or future.

Corollary II. — It is in the nature of reason to perceive things under a certain form of eternity (sub quâdam æternitatis specie).

Proof. — It is in the nature of reason to regard things, not as contingent, but as necessary (II. xliv.). Reason perceives this necessity of things (II. xli.) truly — that is (I. Ax. vi.), as it is in itself. But (I. xvi.) this necessity of things is the very necessity of the eternal nature of God; therefore, it is in the nature of reason to regard things under this form of eternity. We may add that the bases of reason are the notions (II. xxxviii.), which answer to things common to all, and which (II.

xxxvii.) do not answer to the essence of any particular thing: which must therefore be conceived without any relation to time, under a certain form of eternity.

PROP. XLV. Every idea of every body, or of every particular thing actually existing, necessarily involves the eternal and infinite essence of God.

Proof. — The idea of a particular thing actually existing necessarily involves both the existence and the essence of the said thing (II. viii.). Now particular things cannot be conceived without God (I. xv.); but, inasmuch as (II. vi.) they have God for their cause, in so far as he is regarded under the attribute of which the things in question are modes, their ideas must necessarily involve (I. Ax. iv.) the conception of the attributes of those ideas — that is (I. vi.), the eternal and infinite essence of God. Q.E.D.

Note. — By existence I do not here mean duration — that is, existence in so far as it is conceived abstractedly, and as a certain form of quantity. I am speaking of the very nature of existence, which is assigned to particular things, because they follow in infinite numbers and in infinite ways from the eternal necessity of God's nature (I. xvi.). I am speaking, I repeat, of the very existence of particular things, in so far as they are in God. For although each particular thing be conditioned by another particular thing to exist in a given way, yet the force whereby each particular thing perseveres in existing follows from the eternal necessity of God's nature (cf. I. xxiv. Coroll.).

PROP. XLVI. The knowledge of the eternal and infinite essence of God which every idea involves is adequate and perfect.

Proof. — The proof of the last proposition is universal; and whether a thing be considered as a part or a whole, the idea thereof, whether of the whole or of a part (by the last Prop.), will involve God's eternal and infinite essence. Wherefore, that, which gives knowledge of the eternal and infinite essence of God, is common to all, and is equally in the part and in the whole; therefore (II. xxxviii.) this knowledge will be adequate. Q.E.D.

PROP. XLVII. The human mind has an adequate knowledge of the eternal and infinite essence of God.

Proof. — The human mind has ideas (II. xxii.), from which (II. xxiii.) it perceives itself and its own body (II. xix.) and external bodies (II. xvi. Coroll. i. and II. xvii.) as actually existing; therefore (II. xlv. and xlvi.) it has an adequate knowledge of the eternal and infinite essence of God. Q.E.D.

Note. — Hence we see, that the infinite essence and the eternity of God are known to all. Now as all things are in God, and are conceived through God, we can from this knowledge infer many things, which we may adequately know, and we may form that third kind of knowledge of which we spoke in the note to II. xl., and of the excellence and use of which we shall have occasion to speak in Part V. Men have not so clear a knowledge of God as they have of general notions, because they are unable to imagine God as they do bodies, and also because they have associated the name God with images of things that they are in the habit of seeing, as indeed they can hardly avoid doing, being, as they are, men, and continually affected by external bodies. Many errors, in truth, can be traced to this head, namely, that we do not apply names to things rightly. For instance, when a man says that the lines drawn from the centre of a circle to its circumference are not equal, he then, at all events, assuredly attaches a meaning to the word circle different from that assigned by mathematicians. So again, when men make mistakes in calculation, they have one set of figures in their mind, and another on the paper. If we could see into their minds, they do not make a mistake; they seem to do so, because we think, that they have the same numbers in their mind as they have on the paper. If this were not so, we should not believe them to be in error, any more than I thought that a man was in error, whom I lately heard exclaiming that his entrance hall had flown into a neighbour's hen, for his meaning seemed to me sufficiently clear. Very many controversies have arisen from the fact, that men do not rightly explain their meaning, or do not rightly interpret the meaning of others. For, as a matter of fact, as they flatly contradict themselves, they assume now one side, now another, of the argument, so as to oppose the opinions, which they consider mistaken and absurd in their opponents.

PROP. XLVIII. In the mind there is no absolute or free will; but the mind is determined to wish this or that by a cause, which has also been determined by another cause, and this last by another cause, and so on to infinity.

Proof. — The mind is a fixed and definite mode of thought (II. xi.), therefore it cannot be the free cause of its actions (I. xvii. Coroll. ii.); in other words, it cannot have an absolute faculty of positive or negative volition; but (by I. xxviii.) it must be determined by a cause, which has also been determined by another cause, and this last by another, &c. Q.E.D.

Note. — In the same way it is proved, that there is in the mind no absolute faculty of understanding, desiring, loving, &c. Whence it follows, that these and similar faculties are either entirely fictitious, or are merely abstract and general terms, such as we are accustomed to put together from particular things. Thus the intellect and the will stand in the same relation to this or that idea, or this or that volition, as "lapidity" to this or that stone, or as "man" to Peter and Paul. The cause which leads men to consider themselves free has been set forth in the Appendix to Part I. But, before I proceed further, I would here remark that, by the will to affirm and decide, I mean the faculty, not the desire. I mean, I repeat, the faculty, whereby the mind affirms or denies what is true or false, not the desire, wherewith the mind wishes for or turns away from any given thing. After we have proved, that these faculties of ours are general notions, which cannot be distinguished from the particular instances on which they are based, we must inquire whether volitions themselves are anything besides the ideas of things. We must inquire, I say, whether there is in the mind any affirmation or negation beyond that, which the idea, in so far as it is an idea, involves. On which subject see the following proposition, and II. Def. iii., lest the idea of pictures should suggest itself. For by ideas I do not mean images such as are formed at the back of the eye, or in the midst of the brain, but the conceptions of thought.

PROP. XLIX. There is in the mind no volition or affirmation and negation, save that which an idea, inasmuch as it is an idea, involves.

Proof. — There is in the mind no absolute faculty of positive or negative volition, but only particular volitions, namely, this or that affirmation, and this or that negation. Now let us conceive a particular volition, namely, the mode of thinking whereby the mind affirms, that the three interior angles of a triangle are equal to two right angles. This affirmation involves the conception or idea of a triangle, that is, without the idea of a triangle it cannot be conceived. It is the same thing to say, that the concept A must involve the concept B, as it is to say, that A cannot be conceived without B. Further, this affirmation cannot be made (II. Ax. iii.) without the idea of a triangle. Therefore, this affirmation can neither be nor be conceived, without the idea of a triangle. Again, this idea of a triangle must involve this same affirmation, namely, that its three interior angles are equal to two right angles. Wherefore, and vice versâ, this idea of a triangle can neither be nor be conceived without this affirmation, therefore, this affirmation belongs to the essence of the idea of a triangle, and is nothing besides. What we have said of this volition (inasmuch as we have selected it at random) may be said of any other volition, namely, that it is nothing but an idea. Q.E.D.

Corollary. — Will and understanding are one and the same.

Proof. — Will and understanding are nothing beyond the individual volitions and ideas (II. xlviii. and note). But a particular volition and a particular idea are one and the same (by the foregoing Prop.); therefore, will and understanding are one and the same. Q.E.D.

Note. — We have thus removed the cause which is commonly assigned for error. For we have shown above, that falsity consists solely in the privation of knowledge involved in ideas which are fragmentary and confused. Wherefore, a false idea, inasmuch as it is false, does not involve certainty. When we say, then, that a man acquiesces in what is false, and that he has no doubts on the subject, we do not say that he is certain, but only that he does not doubt, or that he acquiesces in what is false, inasmuch as there are no reasons, which should cause his imagination to waver (see II. xliv. note). Thus, although the man be assumed to acquiesce in what is false, we shall never say that he is certain. For by certainty we mean something positive (II. xliii. and note), not merely the absence of doubt.

However, in order that the foregoing proposition may be fully explained, I will draw attention to a few additional points, and I will furthermore answer the objections which may be advanced against our doctrine. Lastly, in order to remove every scruple, I have thought it worth while to point out some of the advantages, which follow therefrom. I say "some," for they will be better appreciated from what we shall set forth in the fifth part.

I begin, then, with the first point, and warn my readers to make an accurate distinction between an idea, or conception of the mind, and the images of things which we imagine. It is further necessary that they should distinguish between idea and words, whereby we signify things. These three — namely, images, words, and ideas — are by many persons either entirely confused together, or not distinguished with sufficient accuracy or care, and hence people are generally in ignorance, how absolutely necessary is a knowledge of this doctrine of the will, both for philosophic purposes and for the wise ordering of life. Those who think that ideas consist in images which are formed in us by contact with external bodies, persuade themselves that the ideas of those things, whereof we can form no mental picture, are not ideas, but only figments, which we invent by the free decree of our will; they thus regard ideas as though they were inanimate pictures on a panel, and, filled with this misconception, do not see that an idea, inasmuch as it is an idea, involves an affirmation or negation. Again, those who confuse words with ideas, or with the affirmation which an idea involves, think that they can wish something contrary to what they feel, affirm, or deny. This misconception will easily be laid aside by one, who reflects on the nature of knowledge, and seeing that it in no wise involves the conception of extension, will therefore clearly understand, that an idea (being a mode of thinking) does not consist in the image of anything, nor in words. The essence of words and images is put together by bodily motions, which in no wise involve the conception of thought.

These few words on this subject will suffice: I will therefore pass on to consider the objections, which may be raised against our doctrine. Of these, the first is advanced by those, who think that the will has a wider scope than the understanding, and that therefore it is different therefrom. The reason for their holding the belief, that the will has wider scope than the understanding, is that they assert, that they have no need of an increase in their faculty of assent, that is of affirmation or negation, in order to assent to an infinity of things which we do not perceive, but that they have need of an increase in their faculty of understanding. The will is thus distinguished from the intellect, the latter being finite and the former infinite. Secondly, it may be objected that experience seems to teach us especially clearly, that we are able to suspend our judgment before assenting to things which we perceive; this is confirmed by the fact that no one is said to be deceived, in so far as he perceives anything, but only in so far as he assents or dissents.

For instance, he who feigns a winged horse, does not therefore admit that a winged horse exists; that is, he is not deceived, unless he admits in addition that a winged horse does exist. Nothing therefore seems to be taught more clearly by experience, than that the will or faculty of assent is free and different from the faculty of understanding. Thirdly, it may be objected that one affirmation does not apparently contain more reality than another; in other words, that we do not seem to need for affirming, that what is true is true, any greater power than for affirming, that what is false is true. We have, however, seen that one idea has more reality or perfection than another, for as objects are some more excellent than others, so also are the ideas of them some more excellent than others; this also seems to point to a difference between the understanding and the will. Fourthly, it may be objected, if man does not act from free will, what will happen if the incentives to action are equally balanced, as in the case of Buridan's ass? Will he perish of hunger and thirst? If I say that he would, I shall seem to have in my thoughts an ass or the statue of a man rather than an actual man. If I say that he would not, he would then determine his own action, and would consequently possess the faculty of going and doing whatever he liked. Other objections might also be raised, but, as I am not bound to put in evidence everything that anyone may dream, I will only set myself to the task of refuting those I have mentioned, and that as briefly as possible.

To the first objection I answer, that I admit that the will has a wider scope than the understanding, if by the understanding be meant only clear and distinct ideas; but I deny that the will has a wider scope than the perceptions, and the faculty of forming conceptions; nor do I see why the faculty of volition should be called infinite, any more than the faculty of feeling: for, as we are able by the same faculty of volition to affirm an infinite number of things (one after the other, for we cannot affirm an infinite number simultaneously), so also can we, by the same faculty of feeling, feel or perceive (in succession) an infinite number of bodies. If it be said that there is an infinite number of things which we cannot perceive, I answer, that we cannot attain to such things by any thinking, nor, consequently, by any faculty of volition. But, it may still be urged, if God wished to bring it about that we should perceive them, he would be obliged to endow us with a greater faculty of perception, but not a greater faculty of volition than we have already. This is the same as to say that, if God wished to bring it about that we should understand an infinite number of other entities, it would be necessary for him to give us a greater understanding, but not a more universal idea of entity than that which we have already, in order to grasp such infinite entities. We have shown that will is a universal entity or idea, whereby we explain all particular volitions — in other words, that which is common to all such volitions.

As, then, our opponents maintain that this idea, common or universal to all volitions, is a faculty, it is little to be wondered at that they assert, that such a faculty extends itself into the infinite, beyond the limits of the understanding: for what is universal is predicated alike of one, of many, and of an infinite number of individuals.

To the second objection I reply by denying, that we have a free power of suspending our judgment: for, when we say that anyone suspends his judgment, we merely mean that he sees, that he does not perceive the matter in question adequately. Suspension of judgment is, therefore, strictly speaking, a perception, and not free will. In order to illustrate the point, let us suppose a boy imagining a horse, and perceive nothing else. Inasmuch as this imagination involves the existence of the horse (II. xvii. Coroll.), and the boy does not perceive anything which would exclude the existence of the horse, he will necessarily regard the horse as present: he will not be able to doubt of its existence, although he be not certain thereof. We have daily experience of such a state of things in dreams; and I do not suppose that there is anyone, who would maintain that, while he is dreaming, he has the free power of suspending his judgment concerning the things in his dream, and bringing it about that he should not dream those things, which he dreams that he sees; yet it happens, notwithstanding, that even in dreams we suspend our judgment, namely, when we dream that we are dreaming.

Further, I grant that no one can be deceived, so far as actual perception extends — that is, I grant that the mind's imaginations, regarded in themselves, do not involve error (II. xvii. note); but I deny, that a man does not, in the act of perception, make any affirmation. For what is the perception of a winged horse, save affirming that a horse has wings? If the mind could perceive nothing else but the winged horse, it would regard the same as present to itself: it would have no reasons for doubting its existence, nor any faculty of dissent, unless the imagination of a winged horse be joined to an idea which precludes the existence of the said horse, or unless the mind perceives that the idea which it possess of a winged horse is inadequate, in which case it will either necessarily deny the existence of such a horse, or will necessarily be in doubt on the subject.

I think that I have anticipated my answer to the third objection, namely, that the will is something universal which is predicated of all ideas, and that it only signifies that which is common to all ideas, namely, an affirmation, whose adequate essence must, therefore, in so far as it is thus conceived in the abstract, be in every idea, and be, in this respect alone, the same in all, not in so far as it is considered as constituting the idea's essence: for, in this respect, particular affirmations differ one from the other, as much as do ideas. For instance, the affirmation which involves the idea of a circle, differs from that which involves the idea of a triangle, as much as the idea of a circle differs from the idea of a triangle.

Further, I absolutely deny, that we are in need of an equal power of thinking, to affirm that that which is true is true, and to affirm that that which is false is true. These two affirmations, if we regard the mind, are in the same relation to one another as being and not — being; for there is nothing positive in ideas, which constitutes the actual reality of falsehood (II. xxxv. note, and xlvii. note).

We must therefore conclude, that we are easily deceived, when we confuse universals with singulars, and the entities of reason and abstractions with realities. As for the fourth objection, I am quite ready to admit, that a man placed in the equilibrium described (namely, as perceiving nothing but hunger and thirst, a certain food and a certain drink, each equally distant from him) would die of hunger and thirst. If I am asked, whether such an one should not rather be considered an ass than a man; I answer, that I do not know, neither do I know how a man should be considered, who hangs himself, or how we should consider children, fools, madmen, &c.

It remains to point out the advantages of a knowledge of this doctrine as bearing on conduct, and this may be easily gathered from what has been said. The doctrine is good,

1. Inasmuch as it teaches us to act solely according to the decree of God, and to be partakers in the Divine nature, and so much the more, as we perform more perfect actions and more and more understand God. Such a doctrine not only completely tranquilizes our spirit, but also shows us where our highest happiness or blessedness is, namely, solely in the knowledge of God, whereby we are led to act only as love and piety shall bid us. We may thus clearly understand, how far astray from a true estimate of virtue are those who expect to be decorated by God with high rewards for their virtue, and their best actions, as for having endured the direst slavery; as if virtue and the service of God were not in itself happiness and perfect freedom.

2. Inasmuch as it teaches us, how we ought to conduct ourselves with respect to the gifts of fortune, or matters which are not in our power, and do not follow from our nature. For it shows us, that we should await and endure fortune's smiles or frowns with an equal mind, seeing that all things follow from the eternal decree of God by the same necessity, as it follows from the essence of a triangle, that the three angles are equal to two right angles.

3. This doctrine raises social life, inasmuch as it teaches us to hate no man, neither to despise, to deride, to envy, or to be angry with any. Further, as it tells us that each should be content with his own, and helpful to his neighbour, not from any womanish pity, favour, or superstition, but solely by the guidance of reason, according as the time and occasion demand, as I will show in Part III.

4. Lastly, this doctrine confers no small advantage on the commonwealth; for it teaches how citizens should be governed and led, not so as to become slaves, but so that they may freely do whatsoever things are best.

I have thus fulfilled the promise made at the beginning of this note, and I thus bring the second part of my treatise to a close. I think I have therein explained the nature and properties of the human mind at sufficient length, and, considering the difficulty of the subject, with sufficient clearness. I have laid a foundation, whereon may be raised many excellent conclusions of the highest utility and most necessary to be known, as will, in what follows, be partly made plain.

PART III. ON THE ORIGIN AND NATURE OF THE EMOTIONS

MOST WRITERS ON the emotions and on human conduct seem to be treating rather of matters outside nature than of natural phenomena following nature's general laws. They appear to conceive man to be situated in nature as a kingdom within a kingdom: for they believe that he disturbs rather than follows nature's order, that he has absolute control over his actions, and that he is determined solely by himself. They attribute human infirmities and fickleness, not to the power of nature in general, but to some mysterious flaw in the nature of man, which accordingly they bemoan, deride, despise, or, as usually happens, abuse: he, who succeeds in hitting off the weakness of the human mind more eloquently or more acutely than his fellows, is looked upon as a seer. Still there has been no lack of very excellent men (to whose toil and industry I confess myself much indebted), who have written many noteworthy things concerning the right way of life, and have given much sage advice to mankind. But no one, so far as I know, has defined the nature and strength of the emotions, and the power of the mind against them for their restraint.

I do not forget, that the illustrious Descartes, though he believed, that the mind has absolute power over its actions, strove to explain human emotions by their primary causes, and, at the same time, to point out a way, by which the mind might attain to absolute dominion over them. However, in my opinion, he accomplishes nothing beyond a display of the acuteness of his own great intellect, as I will show in the proper place. For the present I wish to revert to those, who would rather abuse or deride human emotions than understand them. Such persons will, doubtless think it strange that I should attempt to treat of human vice and folly geometrically, and should wish to set forth with rigid reasoning those matters which they cry out against as repugnant to reason, frivolous, absurd, and dreadful. However, such is my plan. Nothing comes to pass in nature, which can be set down to a flaw therein; for nature is always the same, and everywhere one and the same in her efficacy and power of action; that is, nature's laws and ordinances, whereby all things come to pass and change from one form to another, are everywhere and always the same; so that there should be one and the same method of understanding the nature of all things whatsoever, namely, through nature's universal laws and rules. Thus the passions of hatred, anger, envy, and so on, considered in themselves, follow from this same necessity and efficacy of nature; they answer to certain definite causes, through which they are understood, and possess certain properties as worthy of being known as the properties of anything else, whereof the contemplation in itself affords us delight. I shall, therefore, treat of the nature and strength of the emotions according to the same method, as I employed heretofore in my investigations concerning God and the mind. I shall consider human actions and desires in exactly the same manner, as though I were concerned with lines, planes, and solids.

DEFINITIONS

I. BY AN adequate cause, I mean a cause through which its effect can be clearly and distinctly perceived. By an inadequate or partial cause, I mean a cause through which, by itself, its effect cannot be understood.

II. I say that we act when anything takes place, either within us or externally to us, whereof we are the adequate cause; that is (by the foregoing definition) when through our nature something takes place within us or externally to us, which can through our nature alone be clearly and distinctly understood. On the other hand, I say that we are passive as regards something when that something takes place within us, or follows from our nature externally, we being only the partial cause.

III. By emotion I mean the modifications of the body, whereby the active power of the said body is increased or diminished, aided or constrained, and also the ideas of such modifications.

N.B. If we can be the adequate cause of any of these modifications, I then call the emotion an activity, otherwise I call it a passion, or state wherein the mind is passive.

POSTULATES

I. THE HUMAN body can be affected in many ways, whereby its power of activity is increased or diminished, and also in other ways which do not render its power of activity either greater or less.

N.B. This postulate or axiom rests on Postulate i. and Lemmas v. and vii., which see after II. xiii.

II. The human body can undergo many changes, and, nevertheless, retain the impressions or traces of objects (cf. II. Post. v.), and, consequently, the same images of things (see note II. xvii.).

PROP. I. Our mind is in certain cases active, and in certain cases passive. In so far as it has adequate ideas it is necessarily active, and in so far as it has inadequate ideas, it is necessarily passive.

Proof. — In every human mind there are some adequate ideas, and some ideas that are fragmentary and confused (II. xl. note). Those ideas which are adequate in the mind are adequate also in God, inasmuch as he constitutes the essence of the mind (II. xl. Coroll.), and those which are inadequate in the mind are likewise (by the same Coroll.) adequate in God, not inasmuch as he contains in himself the essence of the given mind alone, but as he, at the same time, contains the minds of other things. Again, from any given idea some effect must necessarily follow (I. 36); of this effect God is the adequate cause (III. Def. i.), not inasmuch as he is infinite, but inasmuch as he is conceived as affected by the given idea (II. ix.). But of that effect whereof God is the cause, inasmuch as he is affected by an idea which is adequate in a given mind, of that effect, I repeat, the mind in question is the adequate cause (II. xi. Coroll.). Therefore our mind, in so far as it has adequate ideas (III. Def. ii.), is in certain cases necessarily active; this was our first point. Again, whatsoever necessarily follows from the idea which is adequate in God, not by virtue of his possessing in himself the mind of one man only, but by virtue of his containing, together with the mind of that one man, the minds of other things also, of such an effect (II. xi. Coroll.) the mind of the given man is not an adequate, but only a partial cause; thus (III. Def. ii.) the mind, inasmuch as it has inadequate ideas, is in certain cases necessarily passive; this was our second point. Therefore our mind, &c. Q.E.D.

Corollary. — Hence it follows that the mind is more or less liable to be acted upon, in proportion as it possesses inadequate ideas, and, contrariwise, is more or less active in proportion as it possesses adequate ideas.

PROP. II. Body cannot determine mind to think, neither can mind determine body to motion or rest or any state different from these, if such there be.

Proof. — All modes of thinking have for their cause God, by virtue of his being a thinking thing, and not by virtue of his being displayed under any other attribute (II. vi.). That, therefore, which determines the mind to thought is a mode of thought, and not a mode of extension; that is (II. Def. i.), it is not body. This was our first point. Again, the motion and rest of a body must arise from another body, which has also been determined to a state of motion or rest by a third body, and absolutely everything which takes place in a body must spring from God, in so far as he is regarded as affected by some mode of extension, and not by some mode of thought (II. vi.); that is, it cannot spring from the mind, which is a mode of thought. This was our second point. Therefore body cannot determine mind, &c. Q.E.D.

Note. — This is made more clear by what was said in the note to II. vii., namely, that mind and body are one and the same thing, conceived first under the attribute of thought, secondly, under the attribute of extension. Thus it follows that the order or concatenation of things is identical, whether nature be conceived under the one attribute or the other; consequently the order of states of activity and passivity in our body is simultaneous in nature with the order of states of activity and passivity in the mind. The same conclusion is evident from the manner in which we proved II. xii.

Nevertheless, though such is the case, and though there be no further room for doubt, I can scarcely believe, until the fact is proved by experience, that men can be induced to consider the question calmly and fairly, so firmly are they convinced that it is merely at the bidding of the mind, that the body is set in motion or at rest, or performs a variety of actions depending solely on the mind's will or the exercise of thought. However, no one has hitherto laid down the limits to the powers of the body, that is, no one has as yet been taught by experience what the body can accomplish solely by the laws of nature, in so far as she is regarded as extension. No one hitherto has gained such an accurate knowledge of the bodily mechanism, that he can explain all its functions; nor need I call attention to the fact that many actions are observed in the lower animals, which far transcend human sagacity, and that somnambulists do many things in their sleep, which they would not venture to do when awake: these instances are enough to show, that the body can by the sole laws of its nature do many things which the mind wonders at.

Again, no one knows how or by what means the mind moves the body, nor how many various degrees of motion it can impart to the body, nor how quickly it can move it. Thus, when men say that this or that physical action has its origin in the mind, which latter has dominion over the body, they are using words without meaning, or are confessing in specious phraseology that they are ignorant of the cause of the said action, and do not wonder at it.

But, they will say, whether we know or do not know the means whereby the mind acts on the body, we have, at any rate, experience of the fact that unless the human mind is in a fit state to think, the body remains inert. Moreover, we have experience, that the mind alone can determine whether we speak or are silent, and a variety of similar states which, accordingly, we say depend on the mind's decree. But, as to the first point, I ask such objectors, whether experience does not also teach, that if the body be inactive the mind is simultaneously unfitted for thinking? For when the body is at rest in sleep, the mind simultaneously is in a state of torpor also, and has no power of thinking, such as it possesses when the body is awake. Again, I think everyone's experience will confirm the statement, that the mind is not at all times equally fit for thinking on a given subject, but according as the body is more or less fitted for being stimulated by the image of this or that object, so also is the mind more or less fitted for contemplating the said object.

But, it will be urged, it is impossible that solely from the laws of nature considered as extended substance, we should be able to deduce the causes of buildings, pictures, and things of that kind, which are produced only by human art; nor would the human body, unless it were determined and led by the mind, be capable of building a single temple. However, I have just pointed out that the objectors cannot fix the limits of the body's power, or say what can be concluded from a consideration of its sole nature, whereas they have experience of many things being accomplished solely by the laws of nature, which they would never have believed possible except under the direction of mind: such are the actions performed by somnambulists while asleep, and wondered at by their performers when awake. I would further call attention to the mechanism of the human body, which far surpasses in complexity all that has been put together by human art, not to repeat what I have already shown, namely, that from nature, under whatever attribute she be considered, infinite results follow. As for the second objection, I submit that the world would be much happier, if men were as fully able to keep silence as they are to speak. Experience abundantly shows that men can govern anything more easily than their tongues, and restrain anything more easily than their appetites; when it comes about that many believe, that we are only free in respect to objects which we moderately desire, because our desire for such can easily be controlled by the thought of something else frequently remembered, but that we are by no means free in respect to what we seek with violent emotion, for our desire cannot then be allayed with the remembrance of anything else. However, unless such persons had proved by experience that we do many things which we afterwards repent of, and again that we often, when assailed by contrary emotions, see the better and follow the worse, there would be nothing to prevent their believing that we are free in all things. Thus an infant believes that of its own free will it desires milk, an angry child believes that it freely desires vengeance, a timid child believes that it freely desires to run away; further, a drunken man believes that he utters from the free decision of his mind words which, when he is sober, he would willingly have withheld: thus, too, a delirious man, a garrulous woman, a child, and others of like complexion, believe that they speak from the free decision of their mind, when they are in reality unable to restrain their impulse to talk. Experience teaches us no less clearly than reason, that men believe themselves to be free, simply because they are conscious of their actions, and unconscious of the causes whereby those actions are determined; and, further, it is plain that the dictates of the mind are but another name for the appetites, and therefore vary according to the varying state of the body. Everyone shapes his actions according to his emotion, those who are assailed by conflicting emotions know not what they wish; those who are not attacked by any emotion are readily swayed this way or that. All these considerations clearly show that a mental decision and a bodily appetite, or determined state, are simultaneous, or rather are one and the same thing, which we call decision, when it is regarded under and explained through the attribute of thought, and a conditioned state, when it is regarded under the attribute of extension, and deduced from the laws of motion and rest. This will appear yet more plainly in the sequel. For the present I wish to call attention to another point, namely, that we cannot act by the decision of the mind, unless we have a remembrance of having done so. For instance, we cannot say a word without remembering that we have done so. Again, it is not within the free power of the mind to remember or forget a thing at will. Therefore the freedom of the mind must in any case be limited to the power of uttering or not uttering something which it remembers. But when we dream that we speak, we believe that we speak from a free decision of the mind, yet we do not speak, or, if we do, it is by a spontaneous motion of the body. Again, we dream that we are concealing something, and we seem to act from the same decision of the mind as that, whereby we keep silence when awake concerning something we know. Lastly, we dream that from the free decision of our mind we do something, which we should not dare to do when awake.

Now I should like to know whether there be in the mind two sorts of decisions, one sort illusive, and the other sort free? If our folly does not carry us so far as this, we must necessarily admit, that the decision of the mind, which is believed to be free, is not distinguishable from the imagination or memory, and is nothing more than the affirmation, which an idea, by virtue of being an idea, necessarily involves (II. xlix.). Wherefore these decisions of the mind arise in the mind by the same necessity, as the ideas of things actually existing. Therefore those who believe, that they speak or keep silence or act in any way from the free decision of their mind, do but dream with their eyes open.

PROP. III. The activities of the mind arise solely from adequate ideas; the passive states of the mind depend solely on inadequate ideas.

Proof. — The first element, which constitutes the essence of the mind, is nothing else but the idea of the actually existent body (II. xi. and xiii.), which (II. xv.) is compounded of many other ideas, whereof some are adequate and some inadequate (II. xxix. Coroll., II. xxxviii. Coroll.). Whatsoever therefore follows from the nature of mind, and has mind for its proximate cause, through which it must be understood, must necessarily follow either from an adequate or from an inadequate idea. But in so far as the mind (III. i.) has inadequate ideas, it is necessarily passive: wherefore the activities of the mind follow solely from adequate ideas, and accordingly the mind is only passive in so far as it has inadequate ideas. Q.E.D.

Note. — Thus we see, that passive states are not attributed to the mind, except in so far as it contains something involving negation, or in so far as it is regarded as a part of nature, which cannot be clearly and distinctly perceived through itself without other parts: I could thus show, that passive states are attributed to individual things in the same way that they are attributed to the mind, and that they cannot otherwise be perceived, but my purpose is solely to treat of the human mind.

PROP. IV. Nothing can be destroyed, except by a cause external to itself.

Proof. — This proposition is self — evident, for the definition of anything affirms the essence of that thing, but does not negative it; in other words, it postulates the essence of the thing, but does not take it away. So long therefore as we regard only the thing itself, without taking into account external causes, we shall not be able to find in it anything which could destroy it. Q.E.D.

PROP. V. Things are naturally contrary, that is, cannot exist in the same object, in so far as one is capable of destroying the other.

Proof. — If they could agree together or co — exist in the same object, there would then be in the said object something which could destroy it; but this, by the foregoing proposition, is absurd, therefore things, &c. Q.E.D.

PROP. VI. Everything, in so far as it is in itself, endeavours to persist in its own being.

Proof. — Individual things are modes whereby the attributes of God are expressed in a given determinate manner (I. xxv. Coroll.); that is, (I. xxxiv.), they are things which express in a given determinate manner the power of God, whereby God is and acts; now no thing contains in itself anything whereby it can be destroyed, or which can take away its existence (III. iv.); but contrariwise it is opposed to all that could take away its existence (III. v.). Therefore, in so far as it can, and in so far as it is in itself, it endeavours to persist in its own being. Q.E.D.

PROP. VII. The endeavour, wherewith everything endeavours to persist in its own being, is nothing else but the actual essence of the thing in question.

Proof. — From the given essence of any thing certain consequences necessarily follow (I. xxxvi.), nor have things any power save such as necessarily follows from their nature as determined (I. xxix.); wherefore the power of any given thing, or the endeavour whereby, either alone or with other things, it acts, or endeavours to act, that is (III. vi.), the power or endeavour, wherewith it endeavours to persist in its own being, is nothing else but the given or actual essence of the thing in question. Q.E.D.

PROP. VIII. The endeavour, whereby a thing endeavours to persist in its own being, involves no finite time, but an indefinite time.

Proof. — If it involved a limited time, which should determine the duration of the thing, it would then follow solely from that power whereby the thing exists, that the thing could not exist beyond the limits of that time, but that it must be destroyed; but this (III. iv.) is absurd. Wherefore the endeavour wherewith a thing exists involves no definite time; but, contrariwise, since (III. iv.) it will by the same power whereby it already exists always continue to exist, unless it be destroyed by some external cause, this endeavour involves an indefinite time.

PROP. IX. The mind, both in so far as it has clear and distinct ideas, and also in so far as it has confused ideas, endeavours to persist in its being for an indefinite period, and of this endeavour it is conscious.

Proof. — The essence of the mind is constituted by adequate and inadequate ideas (III. iii.), therefore (III. vii.), both in so far as it possesses the former, and in so far as it possesses the latter, it endeavours to persist in its own being, and that for an indefinite time (III. viii.). Now as the mind (II. xxiii.) is necessarily conscious of itself through the ideas of the modifications of the body, the mind is therefore (III. vii.) conscious of its own endeavour.

Note. — This endeavour, when referred solely to the mind, is called will, when referred to the mind and body in conjunction it is called appetite; it is, in fact, nothing else but man's essence, from the nature of which necessarily follow all those results which tend to its preservation; and which man has thus been determined to perform.

Further, between appetite and desire there is no difference, except that the term desire is generally applied to men, in so far as they are conscious of their appetite, and may accordingly be thus defined: Desire is appetite with consciousness thereof. It is thus plain from what has been said, that in no case do we strive for, wish for, long for, or desire anything, because we deem it to be good, but on the other hand we deem a thing to be good, because we strive for it, wish for it, long for it, or desire it.

PROP. X. An idea, which excludes the existence of our body, cannot be postulated in our mind, but is contrary thereto.

Proof. — Whatsoever can destroy our body, cannot be postulated therein (III. v.). Therefore neither can the idea of such a thing occur in God, in so far as he has the idea of our body (II. ix. Coroll.); that is (II. xi., xiii.), the idea of that thing cannot be postulated as in our mind, but contrariwise, since (II. xi., xiii.) the first element, that constitutes the essence of the mind, is the idea of the human body as actually existing, it follows that the first and chief endeavour of our mind is the endeavour to affirm the existence of our body: thus, an idea, which negatives the existence of our body, is contrary to our mind, &c. Q.E.D.

PROP. XI. Whatsoever increases or diminishes, helps or hinders the power of activity in our body, the idea thereof increases or diminishes, helps or hinders the power of thought in our mind.

Proof. — This proposition is evident from II. vii. or from II. xiv.

Note. — Thus we see, that the mind can undergo many changes, and can pass sometimes to a state of greater perfection, sometimes to a state of lesser perfection. These passive states of transition explain to us the emotions of pleasure and pain. By pleasure therefore in the following propositions I shall signify a passive state wherein the mind passes to a greater perfection. By pain I shall signify a passive state wherein the mind passes to a lesser perfection. Further, the emotion of pleasure in reference to the body and mind together I shall call stimulation (titillatio) or merriment (hilaritas), the emotion of pain in the same relation I shall call suffering or melancholy. But we must bear in mind, that stimulation and suffering are attributed to man, when one part of his nature is more affected than the rest, merriment and melancholy, when all parts are alike affected. What I mean by desire I have explained in the note to Prop. ix. of this part; beyond these three I recognize no other primary emotion; I will show as I proceed, that all other emotions arise from these three. But, before I go further, I should like here to explain at greater length Prop. x of this part, in order that we may clearly understand how one idea is contrary to another. In the note to II. xvii. we showed that the idea, which constitutes the essence of mind, involves the existence of body, so long as the body itself exists. Again, it follows from what we pointed out in the Corollary to II. viii., that the present existence of our mind depends solely on the fact, that the mind involves the actual existence of the body. Lastly, we showed (II. xvii., xviii. and note) that the power of the mind, whereby it imagines and remembers things, also depends on the fact, that it involves the actual existence of the body. Whence it follows, that the present existence of the mind and its power of imagining are removed, as soon as the mind ceases to affirm the present existence of the body. Now the cause, why the mind ceases to affirm this existence of the body, cannot be the mind itself (III. iv.), nor again the fact that the body ceases to exist. For (by II. vi.) the cause, why the mind affirms the existence of the body, is not that the body began to exist; therefore, for the same reason, it does not cease to affirm the existence of the body, because the body ceases to exist; but (II. xvii.) this result follows from another idea, which excludes the present existence of our body and, consequently, of our mind, and which is therefore contrary to the idea constituting the essence of our mind.

PROP. XII. The mind, as far as it can, endeavours to conceive those things, which increase or help the power of activity in the body.

Proof. — So long as the human body is affected in a mode, which involves the nature of any external body, the human mind will regard that external body as present (II. xvii.), and consequently (II. vii.), so long as the human mind regards an external body as present, that is (II. xvii. note), conceives it, the human body is affected in a mode, which involves the nature of the said external body; thus so long as the mind conceives things, which increase or help the power of activity in our body, the body is affected in modes which increase or help its power of activity (III. Post. i.); consequently (III. xi.) the mind's power of thinking is for that period increased or helped. Thus (III. vi., ix.) the mind, as far as it can, endeavours to imagine such things. Q.E.D.

PROP. XIII. When the mind conceives things which diminish or hinder the body's power of activity, it endeavours, as far as possible, to remember things which exclude the existence of the first — named things.

Proof. — So long as the mind conceives anything of the kind alluded to, the power of the mind and body is diminished or constrained (cf. III. xii. Proof); nevertheless it will continue to conceive it, until the mind conceives something else, which excludes the present existence thereof (II. xvii.); that is (as I have just shown), the power of the mind and of the body is diminished, or constrained, until the mind conceives something else, which excludes the existence of the former thing conceived: therefore the mind (III. ix.), as far as it can, will endeavour to conceive or remember the latter. Q.E.D.

Corollary. — Hence it follows that the mind shrinks from conceiving those things, which diminish or constrain the power of itself and of the body.

Note. — From what has been said we may clearly understand the nature of Love and Hate. Love is nothing else but pleasure accompanied by the idea of an external cause: Hate is nothing else but pain accompanied by the idea of an external cause. We further see, that he who loves necessarily endeavours to have, and to keep present to him, the object of his love; while he who hates endeavours to remove and destroy the object of his hatred. But I will treat of these matters at more length hereafter.

PROP. XIV. If the mind has once been affected by two emotions at the same time, it will, whenever it is afterwards affected by one of these two, be also affected by the other.

Proof. — If the human body has once been affected by two bodies at once, whenever afterwards the mind conceives one of them, it will straightway remember the other also (II. xviii.). But the mind's conceptions indicate rather the emotions of our body than the nature of external bodies (II. xvi. Coroll. ii.); therefore, if the body, and consequently the mind (III. Def. iii.) has been once affected by two emotions at the same time, it will, whenever it is afterwards affected by one of the two, be also affected by the other.

PROP. XV. Anything can, accidentally, be the cause of pleasure, pain, or desire.

Proof. — Let it be granted that the mind is simultaneously affected by two emotions, of which one neither increases nor diminishes its power of activity, and the other does either increase or diminish the said power (III. Post. i.). From the foregoing proposition it is evident that, whenever the mind is afterwards affected by the former, through its true cause, which (by hypothesis) neither increases nor diminishes its power of action, it will be at the same time affected by the latter, which does increase or diminish its power of activity, that is (III. xi. note) it will be affected with pleasure or pain. Thus the former of the two emotions will, not through itself, but accidentally, be the cause of pleasure or pain. In the same way also it can be easily shown, that a thing may be accidentally the cause of desire. Q.E.D.

Corollary. — Simply from the fact that we have regarded a thing with the emotion of pleasure or pain, though that thing be not the efficient cause of the emotion, we can either love or hate it.

Proof. — For from this fact alone it arises (III. xiv.), that the mind afterwards conceiving the said thing is affected with the emotion of pleasure or pain, that is (III. xi. note), according as the power of the mind and body may be increased or diminished, &c.; and consequently (III. xii.), according as the mind may desire or shrink from the conception of it (III. xiii. Coroll.), in other words (III. xiii. note), according as it may love or hate the same. Q.E.D.

Note. — Hence we understand how it may happen, that we love or hate a thing without any cause for our emotion being known to us; merely, as a phrase is, from sympathy or antipathy. We should refer to the same category those objects, which affect us pleasurably or painfully, simply because they resemble other objects which affect us in the same way. This I will show in the next Prop. I am aware that certain authors, who were the first to introduce these terms "sympathy" and "antipathy," wished to signify thereby some occult qualities in things; nevertheless I think we may be permitted to use the same terms to indicate known or manifest qualities.

PROP. XVI. Simply from the fact that we conceive, that a given object has some point of resemblance with another object which is wont to affect the mind pleasurably or painfully, although the point of resemblance be not the efficient cause of the said emotions, we shall still regard the first — named object with love or hate.

Proof. — The point of resemblance was in the object (by hypothesis), when we regarded it with pleasure or pain, thus (III. xiv.), when the mind is affected by the image thereof, it will straightway be affected by one or the other emotion, and consequently the thing, which we perceive to have the same point of resemblance, will be accidentally (III. xv.) a cause of pleasure or pain. Thus (by the foregoing Corollary), although the point in which the two objects resemble one another be not the efficient cause of the emotion, we shall still regard the first — named object with love or hate. Q.E.D.

PROP. XVII. If we conceive that a thing, which is wont to affect us painfully, has any point of resemblance with another thing which is wont to affect us with an equally strong emotion of pleasure, we shall hate the first — named thing, and at the same time we shall love it.

Proof. — The given thing is (by hypothesis) in itself a cause of pain, and (III. xiii. note), in so far as we imagine it with this emotion, we shall hate it: further, inasmuch as we conceive that it has some point of resemblance to something else, which is wont to affect us with an equally strong emotion of pleasure, we shall with an equally strong impulse of pleasure love it (III. xvi.); thus we shall both hate and love the same thing. Q.E.D.

Note. — This disposition of the mind, which arises from two contrary emotions, is called vacillation; it stands to the emotions in the same relation as doubt does to the imagination (II. xliv. note); vacillation and doubt do not differ one from the other, except as greater differs from less. But we must bear in mind that I have deduced this vacillation from causes, which give rise through themselves to one of the emotions, and to the other accidentally. I have done this, in order that they might be more easily deduced from what went before; but I do not deny that vacillation of the disposition generally arises from an object, which is the efficient cause of both emotions. The human body is composed (II. Post. i.) of a variety of individual parts of different nature, and may therefore (Ax.i. after Lemma iii. after II. xiii.) be affected in a variety of different ways by one and the same body; and contrariwise, as one and the same thing can be affected in many ways, it can also in many different ways affect one and the same part of the body. Hence we can easily conceive, that one and the same object may be the cause of many and conflicting emotions.

PROP. XVIII. A man is as much affected pleasurably or painfully by the image of a thing past or future as by the image of a thing present.

Proof. — So long as a man is affected by the image of anything, he will regard that thing as present, even though it be non — existent (II. xvii. and Coroll.), he will not conceive it as past or future, except in so far as its image is joined to the image of time past or future (II. xliv. note). Wherefore the image of a thing, regarded in itself alone, is identical, whether it be referred to time past, time future, or time present; that is (II. xvi. Coroll.), the disposition or emotion of the body is identical, whether the image be of a thing past, future, or present. Thus the emotion of pleasure or pain is the same, whether the image be of a thing past or future. Q.E.D.

Note I. — I call a thing past or future, according as we either have been or shall be affected thereby. For instance, according as we have seen it, or are about to see it, according as it has recreated us, or will recreate us, according as it has harmed us, or will harm us. For, as we thus conceive it, we affirm its existence; that is, the body is affected by no emotion which excludes the existence of the thing, and therefore (II. xvii.) the body is affected by the image of the thing, in the same way as if the thing were actually present. However, as it generally happens that those, who have had many experiences, vacillate, so long as they regard a thing as future or past, and are usually in doubt about its issue (II. xliv. note); it follows that the emotions which arise from similar images of things are not so constant, but are generally disturbed by the images of other things, until men become assured of the issue.

Note II. — From what has just been said, we understand what is meant by the terms Hope, Fear, Confidence, Despair, Joy, and Disappointment.5 Hope is nothing else but an inconstant pleasure, arising from the image of something future or past, whereof we do not yet know the issue. Fear, on the other hand, is an inconstant pain also arising from the image of something concerning which we are in doubt. If the element of doubt be removed from these emotions, hope becomes Confidence and fear becomes Despair. In other words, Pleasure or Pain arising from the image of something concerning which we have hoped or feared. Again, Joy is Pleasure arising from the image of something past whereof we have doubted the issue. Disappointment is the Pain opposed to Joy.

5 Conscientiæ morsus — thus rendered by Mr. Pollock.

PROP. XIX. He who conceives that the object of his love is destroyed will feel pain; if he conceives that it is preserved he will feel pleasure.

Proof. — The mind, as far as possible, endeavours to conceive those things which increase or help the body's power of activity (III. xii.); in other words (III. xii. note), those things which it loves. But conception is helped by those things which postulate the existence of a thing, and contrariwise is hindered by those which exclude the existence of a thing (II. xvii.); therefore the images of things, which postulate the existence of an object of love, help the mind's endeavour to conceive the object of love, in other words (III. xi. note), affect the mind pleasurably; contrariwise those things, which exclude the existence of an object of love, hinder the aforesaid mental endeavour; in other words, affect the mind painfully. He, therefore, who conceives that the object of his love is destroyed will feel pain, &c. Q.E.D.

PROP. XX. He who conceives that the object of his hate is destroyed will also feel pleasure.

Proof. — The mind (III. xiii.) endeavours to conceive those things, which exclude the existence of things whereby the body's power of activity is diminished or constrained; that is (III. xiii. note), it endeavours to conceive such things as exclude the existence of what it hates; therefore the image of a thing, which excludes the existence of what the mind hates, helps the aforesaid mental effort, in other words (III. xi. note), affects the mind pleasurably. Thus he who conceives that the object of his hate is destroyed will feel pleasure. Q.E.D.

PROP. XXI. He who conceives, that the object of his love is affected pleasurably or painfully, will himself be affected pleasurably or painfully; and the one or the other emotion will be greater or less in the lover according as it is greater or less in the thing loved.

Proof. — The images of things (as we showed in III. xix.) which postulate the existence of the object of love, help the mind's endeavour to conceive the said object. But pleasure postulates the existence of something feeling pleasure, so much the more in proportion as the emotion of pleasure is greater; for it is (III. xi. note) a transition to a greater perfection; therefore the image of pleasure in the object of love helps the mental endeavour of the lover; that is, it affects the lover pleasurably, and so much the more, in proportion as this emotion may have been greater in the object of love. This was our first point. Further, in so far as a thing is affected with pain, it is to that extent destroyed, the extent being in proportion to the amount of pain (III. xi. note); therefore (III. xix.) he who conceives, that the object of his love is affected painfully, will himself be affected painfully, in proportion as the said emotion is greater or less in the object of love. Q.E.D.

PROP. XXII. If we conceive that anything pleasurably affects some object of our love, we shall be affected with love towards that thing. Contrariwise, if we conceive that it affects an object of our love painfully, we shall be affected with hatred towards it.

Proof. — He, who affects pleasurably or painfully the object of our love, affects us also pleasurably or painfully — that is, if we conceive the loved object as affected with the said pleasure or pain (III. xxi.). But this pleasure or pain is postulated to come to us accompanied by the idea of an external cause; therefore (III. xiii. note), if we conceive that anyone affects an object of our love pleasurably or painfully, we shall be affected with love or hatred towards him. Q.E.D.

Note. — Prop. xxi. explains to us the nature of Pity, which we may define as pain arising from another's hurt. What term we can use for pleasure arising from another's gain, I know not.

We will call the love towards him who confers a benefit on another, Approval; and the hatred towards him who injures another, we will call Indignation. We must further remark, that we not only feel pity for a thing which we have loved (as shown in III. xxi.), but also for a thing which we have hitherto regarded without emotion, provided that we deem that it resembles ourselves (as I will show presently). Thus, we bestow approval on one who has benefited anything resembling ourselves, and, contrariwise, are indignant with him who has done it an injury.

PROP. XXIII. He who conceives, that an object of his hatred is painfully affected, will feel pleasure. Contrariwise, if he thinks that the said object is pleasurably affected, he will feel pain. Each of these emotions will be greater or less, according as its contrary is greater or less in the object of hatred.

Proof. — In so far as an object of hatred is painfully affected, it is destroyed, to an extent proportioned to the strength of the pain (III. xi. note). Therefore, he (III. xx.) who conceives, that some object of his hatred is painfully affected, will feel pleasure, to an extent proportioned to the amount of pain he conceives in the object of his hatred. This was our first point. Again, pleasure postulates the existence of the pleasurably affected thing (III. xi. note), in proportion as the pleasure is greater or less. If anyone imagines that an object of his hatred is pleasurably affected, this conception (III. xiii.) will hinder his own endeavour to persist; in other words (III. xi. note), he who hates will be painfully affected. Q.E.D.

Note. — This pleasure can scarcely be felt unalloyed, and without any mental conflict. For (as I am about to show in Prop. xxvii.), in so far as a man conceives that something similar to himself is affected by pain, he will himself be affected in like manner; and he will have the contrary emotion in contrary circumstances. But here we are regarding hatred only.

PROP. XXIV. If we conceive that anyone pleasurably affects an object of our hate, we shall feel hatred towards him also. If we conceive that he painfully affects that said object, we shall feel love towards him.

Proof. — This proposition is proved in the same way as III. xxii., which see.

Note. — These and similar emotions of hatred are attributable to envy, which, accordingly, is nothing else but hatred, in so far as it is regarded as disposing a man to rejoice in another's hurt, and to grieve at another's advantage.

PROP. XXV. We endeavour to affirm, concerning ourselves, and concerning what we love, everything that we can conceive to affect pleasurably ourselves, or the loved object. Contrariwise, we endeavour to negative everything, which we conceive to affect painfully ourselves or the loved object.

Proof. — That, which we conceive to affect an object of our love pleasurably or painfully, affects us also pleasurably or painfully (III. xxi.). But the mind (III. xii.) endeavours, as far as possible, to conceive those things which affect us pleasurably; in other words (II. xvii. and Coroll.), it endeavours to regard them as present. And, contrariwise (III. xiii.), it endeavours to exclude the existence of such things as affect us painfully; therefore, we endeavour to affirm concerning ourselves, and concerning the loved object, whatever we conceive to affect ourselves, or the love object pleasurably. Q.E.D.

PROP. XXVI. We endeavour to affirm, concerning that which we hate, everything which we conceive to affect it painfully; and, contrariwise, we endeavour to deny, concerning it, everything which we conceive to affect it pleasurably.

Proof. — This proposition follows from III. xxiii., as the foregoing proposition followed from III. xxi.

Note. — Thus we see that it may readily happen, that a man may easily think too highly of himself, or a loved object, and, contrariwise, too meanly of a hated object. This feeling is called pride, in reference to the man who thinks too highly of himself, and is a species of madness, wherein a man dreams with his eyes open, thinking that he can accomplish all things that fall within the scope of his conception, and thereupon accounting them real, and exulting in them, so long as he is unable to conceive anything which excludes their existence, and determines his own power of action. Pride, therefore, is pleasure springing from a man thinking too highly of himself. Again, the pleasure which arises from a man thinking too highly of another is called over — esteem. Whereas the pleasure which arises from thinking too little of a man is called disdain.

PROP. XXVII. By the very fact that we conceive a thing, which is like ourselves, and which we have not regarded with any emotion, to be affected with any emotion, we are ourselves affected with a like emotion (affectus).

Proof. — The images of things are modifications of the human body, whereof the ideas represent external bodies as present to us (II. xvii.); in other words (II. x.), whereof the ideas involve the nature of our body, and, at the same time, the nature of the external bodies as present. If, therefore, the nature of the external body be similar to the nature of our body, then the idea which we form of the external body will involve a modification of our own body similar to the modification of the external body. Consequently, if we conceive anyone similar to ourselves as affected by any emotion, this conception will express a modification of our body similar to that emotion. Thus, from the fact of conceiving a thing like ourselves to be affected with any emotion, we are ourselves affected with a like emotion. If, however, we hate the said thing like ourselves, we shall, to that extent, be affected by a contrary, and not similar, emotion. Q.E.D.

Note I. — This imitation of emotions, when it is referred to pain, is called compassion (cf. III. xxii. note); when it is referred to desire, it is called emulation, which is nothing else but the desire of anything, engendered in us by the fact that we conceive that others have the like desire.

Corollary I. — If we conceive that anyone, whom we have hitherto regarded with no emotion, pleasurably affects something similar to ourselves, we shall be affected with love towards him. If, on the other hand, we conceive that he painfully affects the same, we shall be affected with hatred towards him.

Proof. — This is proved from the last proposition in the same manner as III. xxii. is proved from III. xxi.

Corollary II. — We cannot hate a thing which we pity, because its misery affects us painfully.

Proof. — If we could hate it for this reason, we should rejoice in its pain, which is contrary to the hypothesis.

Corollary III. — We seek to free from misery, as far as we can, a thing which we pity.

Proof. — That, which painfully affects the object of our pity, affects us also with similar pain (by the foregoing proposition); therefore, we shall endeavour to recall everything which removes its existence, or which destroys it (cf. III. xiii.); in other words (III. ix. note), we shall desire to destroy it, or we shall be determined for its destruction; thus, we shall endeavour to free from misery a thing which we pity. Q.E.D.

Note II. — This will or appetite for doing good, which arises from pity of the thing whereon we would confer a benefit, is called benevolence, and is nothing else but desire arising from compassion. Concerning love or hate towards him who has done good or harm to something, which we conceive to be like ourselves, see III. xxii. note.

PROP. XXVIII. We endeavour to bring about whatsoever we conceive to conduce to pleasure; but we endeavour to remove or destroy whatsoever we conceive to be truly repugnant thereto, or to conduce to pain.

Proof. — We endeavour, as far as possible, to conceive that which we imagine to conduce to pleasure (III. xii.); in other words (II. xvii.) we shall endeavour to conceive it as far as possible as present or actually existing. But the endeavour of the mind, or the mind's power of thought, is equal to, and simultaneous with, the endeavour of the body, or the body's power of action. (This is clear from II. vii. Coroll. and II. xi. Coroll.). Therefore we make an absolute endeavour for its existence, in other words (which by III. ix. note, come to the same thing) we desire and strive for it; this was our first point. Again, if we conceive that something, which we believed to be the cause of pain, that is (III. xiii. note), which we hate, is destroyed, we shall rejoice (III. xx.). We shall, therefore (by the first part of this proof), endeavour to destroy the same, or (III. xiii.) to remove it from us, so that we may not regard it as present; this was our second point. Wherefore whatsoever conduces to pleasure, &c. Q.E.D.

PROP. XXIX. We shall also endeavour to do whatsoever we conceive men6 to regard with pleasure, and contrariwise we shall shrink from doing that which we conceive men to shrink from.

6 By "men" in this and the following propositions, I mean men whom we regard without any particular emotion.

Proof. — From the fact of imagining, that men love or hate anything, we shall love or hate the same thing (III. xxvii.). That is (III. xiii. note), from this mere fact we shall feel pleasure or pain at the thing's presence. And so we shall endeavour to do whatsoever we conceive men to love or regard with pleasure, etc. Q.E.D.

Note. — This endeavour to do a thing or leave it undone, solely in order to please men, we call ambition, especially when we so eagerly endeavour to please the vulgar, that we do or omit certain things to our own or another's hurt: in other cases it is generally called kindliness. Furthermore I give the name of praise to the pleasure, with which we conceive the action of another, whereby he has endeavoured to please us; but of blame to the pain wherewith we feel aversion to his action.

PROP. XXX. If anyone has done something which he conceives as affecting other men pleasurably, he will be affected by pleasure, accompanied by the idea of himself as cause; in other words, he will regard himself with pleasure. On the other hand, if he has done anything which he conceives as affecting others painfully, he will regard himself with pain.

Proof. — He who conceives, that he affects others with pleasure or pain, will, by that very fact, himself be affected with pleasure or pain (III. xxvii.), but, as a man (II. xix. and xxiii.) is conscious of himself through the modifications whereby he is determined to action, it follows that he who conceives, that he affects others pleasurably, will be affected with pleasure accompanied by the idea of himself as cause; in other words, he will regard himself with pleasure. And so mutatis mutandis in the case of pain. Q.E.D.

Note. — As love (III. xiii.) is pleasure accompanied by the idea of an external cause, and hatred is pain accompanied by the idea of an external cause; the pleasure and pain in question will be a species of love and hatred. But, as the terms love and hatred are used in reference to external objects, we will employ other names for the emotions now under discussion: pleasure accompanied by the idea of an external cause7 we will style Honour, and the emotion contrary thereto we will style Shame: I mean in such cases as where pleasure or pain arises from a man's belief, that he is being praised or blamed: otherwise pleasure accompanied by the idea of an external cause8 is called self — complacency, and its contrary pain is called repentance. Again, as it may happen (II. xvii. Coroll.) that the pleasure, wherewith a man conceives that he affects others, may exist solely in his own imagination, and as (III. xxv.) everyone endeavours to conceive concerning himself that which he conceives will affect him with pleasure, it may easily come to pass that a vain man may be proud and may imagine that he is pleasing to all, when in reality he may be an annoyance to all.

7 So Van Vloten and Bruder. The Dutch version and Camerer read, "an internal cause." "Honor" = Gloria.

8 See previous endnote.

PROP. XXXI. If we conceive that anyone loves, desires, or hates anything which we ourselves love, desire, or hate, we shall thereupon regard the thing in question with more steadfast love, &c. On the contrary, if we think that anyone shrinks from something that we love, we shall undergo vacillations of soul.

Proof. — From the mere fact of conceiving that anyone loves anything we shall ourselves love that thing (III. xxvii.): but we are assumed to love it already; there is, therefore, a new cause of love, whereby our former emotion is fostered; hence we shall thereupon love it more steadfastly. Again, from the mere fact of conceiving that anyone shrinks from anything, we shall ourselves shrink from that thing (III. xxvii.). If we assume that we at the same time love it, we shall then simultaneously love it and shrink from it; in other words, we shall be subject to vacillation (III. xvii. note). Q.E.D.

Corollary. — From the foregoing, and also from III. xxviii. it follows that everyone endeavours, as far as possible, to cause others to love what he himself loves, and to hate what he himself hates: as the poet says: "As lovers let us share every hope and every fear: ironhearted were he who should love what the other leaves."9

9 Ovid, "Amores," II. xix. 4,5. Spinoza transposes the verses.

"Speremus pariter, pariter metuamus amantes;

Ferreus est, si quis, quod sinit alter, amat."

Note. — This endeavour to bring it about, that our own likes and dislikes should meet with universal approval, is really ambition (see III. xxix. note); wherefore we see that everyone by nature desires (appetere), that the rest of mankind should live according to his own individual disposition: when such a desire is equally present in all, everyone stands in everyone else's way, and in wishing to be loved or praised by all, all become mutually hateful.

PROP. XXXII. If we conceive that anyone takes delight in something, which only one person can possess, we shall endeavour to bring it about that the man in question shall not gain possession thereof.

Proof. — From the mere fact of our conceiving that another person takes delight in a thing (III. xxvii. and Coroll.) we shall ourselves love that thing and desire to take delight therein. But we assumed that the pleasure in question would be prevented by another's delight in its object; we shall, therefore, endeavour to prevent his possession thereof (III. xxviii.). Q.E.D.

Note. — We thus see that man's nature is generally so constituted, that he takes pity on those who fare ill, and envies those who fare well with an amount of hatred proportioned to his own love for the goods in their possession. Further, we see that from the same property of human nature, whence it follows that men are merciful, it follows also that they are envious and ambitious. Lastly, if we make appeal to Experience, we shall find that she entirely confirms what we have said; more especially if we turn our attention to the first years of our life. We find that children, whose body is continually, as it were, in equilibrium, laugh or cry simply because they see others laughing or crying; moreover, they desire forthwith to imitate whatever they see others doing, and to possess themselves of whatever they conceive as delighting others: inasmuch as the images of things are, as we have said, modifications of the human body, or modes wherein the human body is affected and disposed by external causes to act in this or that manner.

PROP. XXXIII. When we love a thing similar to ourselves we endeavour, as far as we can, to bring about that it should love us in return.

Proof. — That which we love we endeavour, as far as we can, to conceive in preference to anything else (III. xii.). If the thing be similar to ourselves, we shall endeavour to affect it pleasurably in preference to anything else (III. xxix.). In other words, we shall endeavour, as far as we can, to bring it about, that the thing should be affected with pleasure accompanied by the idea of ourselves, that is (III. xiii. note), that it should love us in return. Q.E.D.

PROP. XXXIV. The greater the emotion with which we conceive a loved object to be affected towards us, the greater will be our complacency.

Proof. — We endeavour (III. xxxiii.), as far as we can, to bring about, that what we love should love us in return: in other words, that what we love should be affected with pleasure accompanied by the idea of ourself as cause. Therefore, in proportion as the loved object is more pleasurably affected because of us, our endeavour will be assisted. — that is (III. xi. and note) the greater will be our pleasure. But when we take pleasure in the fact, that we pleasurably affect something similar to ourselves, we regard ourselves with pleasure (III. 30); therefore the greater the emotion with which we conceive a loved object to be affected, &c. Q.E.D.

PROP. XXXV. If anyone conceives, that an object of his love joins itself to another with closer bonds of friendship than he himself has attained to, he will be affected with hatred towards the loved object and with envy towards his rival.

Proof. — In proportion as a man thinks, that a loved object is well affected towards him, will be the strength of his self — approval (by the last Prop.), that is (III. xxx. note), of his pleasure; he will, therefore (III. xxviii.), endeavour, as far as he can, to imagine the loved object as most closely bound to him: this endeavour or desire will be increased, if he thinks that someone else has a similar desire (III. xxxi.). But this endeavour or desire is assumed to be checked by the image of the loved object in conjunction with the image of him whom the loved object has joined to itself; therefore (III. xi. note) he will for that reason be affected with pain, accompanied by the idea of the loved object as a cause in conjunction with the image of his rival; that is, he will be (III. xiii.) affected with hatred towards the loved object and also towards his rival (III. xv. Coroll.), which latter he will envy as enjoying the beloved object. Q.E.D.

Note. — This hatred towards an object of love joined with envy is called Jealousy, which accordingly is nothing else but a wavering of the disposition arising from combined love and hatred, accompanied by the idea of some rival who is envied. Further, this hatred towards the object of love will be greater, in proportion to the pleasure which the jealous man had been wont to derive from the reciprocated love of the said object; and also in proportion to the feelings he had previously entertained towards his rival. If he had hated him, he will forthwith hate the object of his love, because he conceives it is pleasurably affected by one whom he himself hates: and also because he is compelled to associate the image of his loved one with the image of him whom he hates. This condition generally comes into play in the case of love for a woman: for he who thinks, that a woman whom he loves prostitutes herself to another, will feel pain, not only because his own desire is restrained, but also because, being compelled to associate the image of her he loves with the parts of shame and the excreta of another, he therefore shrinks from her.

We must add, that a jealous man is not greeted by his beloved with the same joyful countenance as before, and this also gives him pain as a lover, as I will now show.

PROP. XXXVI. He who remembers a thing, in which he has once taken delight, desires to possess it under the same circumstances as when he first took delight therein.

Proof. — Everything, which a man has seen in conjunction with the object of his love, will be to him accidentally a cause of pleasure (III. xv.); he will, therefore, desire to possess it, in conjunction with that wherein he has taken delight; in other words, he will desire to possess the object of his love under the same circumstances as when he first took delight therein. Q.E.D.

Corollary. — A lover will, therefore, feel pain if one of the aforesaid attendant circumstances be missing.

Proof. — For, in so far as he finds some circumstance to be missing, he conceives something which excludes its existence. As he is assumed to be desirous for love's sake of that thing or circumstance (by the last Prop.), he will, in so far as he conceives it to be missing, feel pain (III. xix.). Q.E.D.

Note. — This pain, in so far as it has reference to the absence of the object of love, is called Regret.

PROP. XXXVII. Desire arising through pain or pleasure, hatred or love, is greater in proportion as the emotion is greater.

Proof. — Pain diminishes or constrains a man's power of activity (III. xi. note), in other words (III. vii.), diminishes or constrains the effort, wherewith he endeavours to persist in his own being; therefore (III. v.) it is contrary to the said endeavour: thus all the endeavours of a man affected by pain are directed to removing that pain. But (by the definition of pain), in proportion as the pain is greater, so also is it necessarily opposed to a greater part of man's power of activity; therefore the greater the pain, the greater the power of activity employed to remove it; that is, the greater will be the desire or appetite in endeavouring to remove it. Again, since pleasure (III. xi. note) increases or aids a man's power of activity, it may easily be shown in like manner, that a man affected by pleasure has no desire further than to preserve it, and his desire will be in proportion to the magnitude of the pleasure.

Lastly, since hatred and love are themselves emotions of pain and pleasure, it follows in like manner that the endeavour, appetite, or desire, which arises through hatred or love, will be greater in proportion to the hatred or love. Q.E.D.

PROP. XXXVIII. If a man has begun to hate an object of his love, so that love is thoroughly destroyed, he will, causes being equal, regard it with more hatred than if he had never loved it, and his hatred will be in proportion to the strength of his former love.

Proof. — If a man begins to hate that which he had loved, more of his appetites are put under restraint than if he had never loved it. For love is a pleasure (III. xiii.

note) which a man endeavours as far as he can to render permanent (III. xxviii.); he does so by regarding the object of his love as present, and by affecting it as far as he can pleasurably; this endeavour is greater in proportion as the love is greater, and so also is the endeavour to bring about that the beloved should return his affection (III. xxxiii.). Now these endeavours are constrained by hatred towards the object of love (III. xiii. Coroll. and III. xxiii.); wherefore the lover (III. xi. note) will for this cause also be affected with pain, the more so in proportion as his love has been greater; that is, in addition to the pain caused by hatred, there is a pain caused by the fact that he has loved the object; wherefore the lover will regard the beloved with greater pain, or in other words, will hate it more than if he had never loved it, and with the more intensity in proportion as his former love was greater. Q.E.D.

PROP. XXXIX. He who hates anyone will endeavour to do him an injury, unless he fears that a greater injury will thereby accrue to himself; on the other hand, he who loves anyone will, by the same law, seek to benefit him.

Proof. — To hate a man is (III. xiii. note) to conceive him as a cause of pain; therefore he who hates a man will endeavour to remove or destroy him. But if anything more painful, or, in other words, a greater evil, should accrue to the hater thereby — and if the hater thinks he can avoid such evil by not carrying out the injury, which he planned against the object of his hate — he will desire to abstain from inflicting that injury (III. xxviii.), and the strength of his endeavour (III. xxxvii.) will be greater than his former endeavour to do injury, and will therefore prevail over it, as we asserted. The second part of this proof proceeds in the same manner. Wherefore he who hates another, etc. Q.E.D.

Note. — By good I here mean every kind of pleasure, and all that conduces thereto, especially that which satisfies our longings, whatsoever they may be. By evil, I mean every kind of pain, especially that which frustrates our longings. For I have shown (III. ix. note) that we in no case desire a thing because we deem it good, but, contrariwise, we deem a thing good because we desire it: consequently we deem evil that which we shrink from; everyone, therefore, according to his particular emotions, judges or estimates what is good, what is bad, what is better, what is worse, lastly, what is best, and what is worst. Thus a miser thinks that abundance of money is the best, and want of money the worst; an ambitious man desires nothing so much as glory, and fears nothing so much as shame. To an envious man nothing is more delightful than another's misfortune, and nothing more painful than another's success. So every man, according to his emotions, judges a thing to be good or bad, useful or useless. The emotion, which induces a man to turn from that which he wishes, or to wish for that which he turns from, is called timidity, which may accordingly be defined as the fear whereby a man is induced to avoid an evil which he regards as future by encountering a lesser evil (III. xxviii.). But if the evil which he fears be shame, timidity becomes bashfulness. Lastly, if the desire to avoid a future evil be checked by the fear of another evil, so that the man knows not which to choose, fear becomes consternation, especially if both the evils feared be very great.

PROP. XL. He, who conceives himself to be hated by another, and believes that he has given him no cause for hatred, will hate that other in return.

Proof. — He who conceives another as affected with hatred, will thereupon be affected himself with hatred (III. xxvii.), that is, with pain, accompanied by the idea of an external cause. But, by the hypothesis, he conceives no cause for this pain except him who is his enemy; therefore, from conceiving that he is hated by some one, he will be affected with pain, accompanied by the idea of his enemy; in other words, he will hate his enemy in return. Q.E.D.

Note. — He who thinks that he has given just cause for hatred will (III. xxx. and note) be affected with shame; but this case (III. xxv.) rarely happens. This reciprocation of hatred may also arise from the hatred, which follows an endeavour to injure the object of our hate (III. xxxix.). He therefore who conceives that he is hated by another will conceive his enemy as the cause of some evil or pain; thus he will be affected with pain or fear, accompanied by the idea of his enemy as cause; in other words, he will be affected with hatred towards his enemy, as I said above.

Corollary I. — He who conceives, that one whom he loves hates him, will be a prey to conflicting hatred and love. For, in so far as he conceives that he is an object of hatred, he is determined to hate his enemy in return. But, by the hypothesis, he nevertheless loves him: wherefore he will be a prey to conflicting hatred and love.

Corollary II. — If a man conceives that one, whom he has hitherto regarded without emotion, has done him any injury from motives of hatred, he will forthwith seek to repay the injury in kind.

Proof. — He who conceives, that another hates him, will (by the last proposition) hate his enemy in return, and (III. xxvi.) will endeavour to recall everything which can affect him painfully; he will moreover endeavour to do him an injury (III. xxxix.). Now the first thing of this sort which he conceives is the injury done to himself; he will, therefore, forthwith endeavour to repay it in kind. Q.E.D.

Note. — The endeavour to injure one whom we hate is called Anger; the endeavour to repay in kind injury done to ourselves is called Revenge.

PROP. XLI. If anyone conceives that he is loved by another, and believes that he has given no cause for such love, he will love that other in return. (Cf. III. xv. Coroll., and III. xvi.)

Proof. — This proposition is proved in the same way as the preceding one. See also the note appended thereto.

Note. — If he believes that he has given just cause for the love, he will take pride therein (III. xxx. and note); this is what most often happens (III. xxv.), and we said that its contrary took place whenever a man conceives himself to be hated by another. (See note to preceding proposition.) This reciprocal love, and consequently the desire of benefiting him who loves us (III. xxxix.), and who endeavours to benefit us, is called gratitude or thankfulness. It thus appears that men are much more prone to take vengeance than to return benefits.

Corollary. — He who imagines that he is loved by one whom he hates, will be a prey to conflicting hatred and love. This is proved in the same way as the first corollary of the preceding proposition.

Note. — If hatred be the prevailing emotion, he will endeavour to injure him who loves him; this emotion is called cruelty, especially if the victim be believed to have given no ordinary cause for hatred.

PROP. XLII. He who has conferred a benefit on anyone from motives of love or honour will feel pain, if he sees that the benefit is received without gratitude.

Proof. — When a man loves something similar to himself, he endeavours, as far as he can, to bring it about that he should be loved thereby in return (III. xxxiii.). Therefore he who has conferred a benefit confers it in obedience to the desire, which he feels of being loved in return; that is (III. xxxiv.) from the hope of honour or (III. xxx. note) pleasure; hence he will endeavour, as far as he can, to conceive this cause of honour, or to regard it as actually existing. But, by the hypothesis, he conceives something else, which excludes the existence of the said cause of honour: wherefore he will thereat feel pain (III. xix.). Q.E.D.

PROP. XLIII. Hatred is increased by being reciprocated, and can on the other hand be destroyed by love.

Proof. — He who conceives, that an object of his hatred hates him in return, will thereupon feel a new hatred, while the former hatred (by hypothesis) still remains (III. xl.). But if, on the other hand, he conceives that the object of hate loves him, he will to this extent (III. xxxviii.) regard himself with pleasure, and (III. xxix.) will endeavour to please the cause of his emotion. In other words, he will endeavour not to hate him (III. xli.), and not to affect him painfully; this endeavour (III. xxxvii.) will be greater or less in proportion to the emotion from which it arises. Therefore, if it be greater than that which arises from hatred, and through which the man endeavours to affect painfully the thing which he hates, it will get the better of it and banish the hatred from his mind. Q.E.D.

PROP. XLIV. Hatred which is completely vanquished by love passes into love: and love is thereupon greater than if hatred had not preceded it.

Proof. — The proof proceeds in the same way as Prop. xxxviii. of this Part: for he who begins to love a thing, which he was wont to hate or regard with pain, from the very fact of loving feels pleasure. To this pleasure involved in love is added the pleasure arising from aid given to the endeavour to remove the pain involved in hatred (III. xxxvii.), accompanied by the idea of the former object of hatred as cause.

Note. — Though this be so, no one will endeavour to hate anything, or to be affected with pain, for the sake of enjoying this greater pleasure; that is, no one will desire that he should be injured, in the hope of recovering from the injury, nor long to be ill for the sake of getting well. For everyone will always endeavour to persist in his being, and to ward off pain as far as he can. If the contrary is conceivable, namely, that a man should desire to hate someone, in order that he might love him the more thereafter, he will always desire to hate him. For the strength of love is in proportion to the strength of the hatred, wherefore the man would desire, that the hatred be continually increased more and more, and, for a similar reason, he would desire to become more and more ill, in order that he might take a greater pleasure in being restored to health: in such a case he would always endeavour to be ill, which (III. vi.) is absurd.

PROP. XLV. If a man conceives, that anyone similar to himself hates anything also similar to himself, which he loves, he will hate that person.

Proof. — The beloved object feels reciprocal hatred towards him who hates it (III. xl.); therefore the lover, in conceiving that anyone hates the beloved object, conceives the beloved thing as affected by hatred, in other words (III. xiii.), by pain; consequently he is himself affected by pain accompanied by the idea of the hater of the beloved thing as cause; that is, he will hate him who hates anything which he himself loves (III. xiii. note). Q.E.D.

PROP. XLVI. If a man has been affected pleasurably or painfully by anyone, of a class or nation different from his own, and if the pleasure or pain has been accompanied by the idea of the said stranger as cause, under the general category of the class or nation: the man will feel love or hatred, not only to the individual stranger, but also to the whole class or nation whereto he belongs.

Proof. — This is evident from III. xvi.

PROP. XLVII. Joy arising from the fact, that anything we hate is destroyed, or suffers other injury, is never unaccompanied by a certain pain in us.

Proof. — This is evident from III. xxvii. For in so far as we conceive a thing similar to ourselves to be affected with pain, we ourselves feel pain.

Note. — This proposition can also be proved from the Corollary to II. xvii. Whenever we remember anything, even if it does not actually exist, we regard it only as present, and the body is affected in the same manner; wherefore, in so far as the remembrance of the thing is strong, a man is determined to regard it with pain; this determination, while the image of the thing in question lasts, is indeed checked by the remembrance of other things excluding the existence of the aforesaid thing, but is not destroyed: hence, a man only feels pleasure in so far as the said determination is checked: for this reason the joy arising from the injury done to what we hate is repeated, every time we remember that object of hatred. For, as we have said, when the image of the thing in question, is aroused, inasmuch as it involves the thing's existence, it determines the man to regard the thing with the same pain as he was wont to do, when it actually did exist. However, since he has joined to the image of the thing other images, which exclude its existence, this determination to pain is forthwith checked, and the man rejoices afresh as often as the repetition takes place. This is the cause of men's pleasure in recalling past evils, and delight in narrating dangers from which they have escaped. For when men conceive a danger, they conceive it as still future, and are determined to fear it; this determination is checked afresh by the idea of freedom, which became associated with the idea of the danger when they escaped therefrom: this renders them secure afresh: therefore they rejoice afresh.

PROP. XLVIII. Love or hatred towards, for instance, Peter is destroyed, if the pleasure involved in the former, or the pain involved in the latter emotion, be associated with the idea of another cause: and will be diminished in proportion as we conceive Peter not to have been the sole cause of either emotion.

Proof. — This Prop. is evident from the mere definition of love and hatred (III. xiii. note). For pleasure is called love towards Peter, and pain is called hatred towards Peter, simply in so far as Peter is regarded as the cause of one emotion or the other. When this condition of causality is either wholly or partly removed, the emotion towards Peter also wholly or in part vanishes. Q.E.D.

PROP. XLIX. Love or hatred towards a thing, which we conceive to be free, must, other conditions being similar, be greater than if it were felt towards a thing acting by necessity.

Proof. — A thing which we conceive as free must (I. Def. vii.) be perceived through itself without anything else. If, therefore, we conceive it as the cause of pleasure or pain, we shall therefore (III. xiii. note) love it or hate it, and shall do so with the utmost love or hatred that can arise from the given emotion. But if the thing which causes the emotion be conceived as acting by necessity, we shall then (by the same Def. vii. Part I.) conceive it not as the sole cause, but as one of the causes of the emotion, and therefore our love or hatred towards it will be less. Q.E.D.

Note. — Hence it follows, that men, thinking themselves to be free, feel more love or hatred towards one another than towards anything else: to this consideration we must add the imitation of emotions treated of in III. xxvii., xxxiv., xl. and xliii.

PROP. L. Anything whatever can be, accidentally, a cause of hope or fear.

Proof. — This proposition is proved in the same way as III. xv., which see, together with the note to III. xviii.

Note. — Things which are accidentally the causes of hope or fear are called good or evil omens. Now, in so far as such omens are the cause of hope or fear, they are (by the definitions of hope and fear given in III. xviii. note) the causes also of pleasure and pain; consequently we, to this extent, regard them with love or hatred, and endeavour either to invoke them as means towards that which we hope for, or to remove them as obstacles, or causes of that which we fear. It follows, further, from III. xxv., that we are naturally so constituted as to believe readily in that which we hope for, and with difficulty in that which we fear; moreover, we are apt to estimate such objects above or below their true value. Hence there have arisen superstitions, whereby men are everywhere assailed. However, I do not think it worth while to point out here the vacillations springing from hope and fear; it follows from the definition of these emotions, that there can be no hope without fear, and no fear without hope, as I will duly explain in the proper place. Further, in so far as we hope for or fear anything, we regard it with love or hatred; thus everyone can apply by himself to hope and fear what we have said concerning love and hatred.

PROP. LI. Different men may be differently affected by the same object, and the same man may be differently affected at different times by the same object.

Proof. — The human body is affected by external bodies in a variety of ways (II. Post. iii.). Two men may therefore be differently affected at the same time, and therefore (by Ax. i. after Lemma iii. after II. xiii.) may be differently affected by one and the same object. Further (by the same Post.) the human body can be affected sometimes in one way, sometimes in another; consequently (by the same Axiom) it may be differently affected at different times by one and the same object. Q.E.D.

Note. — We thus see that it is possible, that what one man loves another may hate, and that what one man fears another may not fear; or, again, that one and the same man may love what he once hated, or may be bold where he once was timid, and so on. Again, as everyone judges according to his emotions what is good, what bad, what better, and what worse (III. xxxix. note), it follows that men's judgments may vary no less than their emotions10, hence when we compare some with others, we distinguish them solely by the diversity of their emotions, and style some intrepid, others timid, others by some other epithet. For instance,

I shall call a man intrepid, if he despises an evil which I am accustomed to fear; if I further take into consideration, that, in his desire to injure his enemies and to benefit those whom he loves, he is not restrained by the fear of an evil which is sufficient to restrain me, I shall call him daring. Again, a man will appear timid to me, if he fears an evil which I am accustomed to despise; and if I further take into consideration that his desire is restrained by the fear of an evil, which is not sufficient to restrain me, I shall say that he is cowardly; and in like manner will everyone pass judgment.

10 This is possible, though the human mind is part of the divine intellect, as I have shown in II. xiii. note.

Lastly, from this inconstancy in the nature of human judgment, inasmuch as a man often judges things solely by his emotions, and inasmuch as the things which he believes cause pleasure or pain, and therefore endeavours to promote or prevent, are often purely imaginary, not to speak of the uncertainty of things alluded to in III. xxviii.; we may readily conceive that a man may be at one time affected with pleasure, and at another with pain, accompanied by the idea of himself as cause. Thus we can easily understand what are Repentance and Self — complacency. Repentance is pain, accompanied by the idea of one's self as cause; Self — complacency is pleasure, accompanied by the idea of one's self as cause, and these emotions are most intense because men believe themselves to be free (III. xlix.).

PROP. LII. An object which we have formerly seen in conjunction with others, and which we do not conceive to have any property that is not common to many, will not be regarded by us for so long, as an object which we conceive to have some property peculiar to itself.

Proof. — As soon as we conceive an object which we have seen in conjunction with others, we at once remember those others (II. xviii. and note), and thus we pass forthwith from the contemplation of one object to the contemplation of another object. And this is the case with the object, which we conceive to have no property that is not common to many. For we thereupon assume that we are regarding therein nothing, which we have not before seen in conjunction with other objects. But when we suppose that we conceive an object something special, which we have never seen before, we must needs say that the mind, while regarding that object, has in itself nothing which it can fall to regarding instead thereof; therefore it is determined to the contemplation of that object only. Therefore an object, &c. Q.E.D.

Note. — This mental modification, or imagination of a particular thing, in so far as it is alone in the mind, is called Wonder; but if it be excited by an object of fear, it is called Consternation, because wonder at an evil keeps a man so engrossed in the simple contemplation thereof, that he has no power to think of anything else whereby he might avoid the evil. If, however, the object of wonder be a man's prudence, industry, or anything of that sort, inasmuch as the said man, is thereby regarded as far surpassing ourselves, wonder is called Veneration; otherwise, if a man's anger, envy, &c., be what we wonder at, the emotion is called Horror. Again, if it be the prudence, industry, or what not, of a man we love, that we wonder at, our love will on this account be the greater (III. xii.), and when joined to wonder or veneration is called Devotion. We may in like manner conceive hatred, hope, confidence, and the other emotions, as associated with wonder; and we should thus be able to deduce more emotions than those which have obtained names in ordinary speech. Whence it is evident, that the names of the emotions have been applied in accordance rather with their ordinary manifestations than with an accurate knowledge of their nature.

To wonder is opposed Contempt, which generally arises from the fact that, because we see someone wondering at, loving, or fearing something, or because something, at first sight, appears to be like things, which we ourselves wonder at, love, fear, &c., we are, in consequence (III. xv. Coroll. and III. xxvii.), determined to wonder at, love, or fear that thing. But if from the presence, or more accurate contemplation of the said thing, we are compelled to deny concerning it all that can be the cause of wonder, love, fear, &c., the mind then, by the presence of the thing, remains determined to think rather of those qualities which are not in it, than of those which are in it; whereas, on the other hand, the presence of the object would cause it more particularly to regard that which is therein. As devotion springs from wonder at a thing which we love, so does Derision spring from contempt of a thing which we hate or fear, and Scorn from contempt of folly, as veneration from wonder at prudence. Lastly, we can conceive the emotions of love, hope, honour, &c., in association with contempt, and can thence deduce other emotions, which are not distinguished one from another by any recognized name.

PROP. LIII. When the mind regards itself and its own power of activity, it feels pleasure: and that pleasure is greater in proportion to the distinctness wherewith it conceives itself and its own power of activity.

Proof. — A man does not know himself except through the modifications of his body, and the ideas thereof (II. xix. and xxiii.). When, therefore, the mind is able to contemplate itself, it is thereby assumed to pass to a greater perfection, or (III. xi. note) to feel pleasure; and the pleasure will be greater in proportion to the distinctness, wherewith it is able to conceive itself and its own power of activity. Q.E.D.

Corollary. — This pleasure is fostered more and more, in proportion as a man conceives himself to be praised by others. For the more he conceives himself as praised by others, the more he will imagine them to be affected with pleasure, accompanied by the idea of himself (III. xxix. note); thus he is (III. xxvii.) himself affected with greater pleasure, accompanied by the idea of himself. Q.E.D.

PROP. LIV. The mind endeavours to conceive only such things as assert its power of activity.

Proof. — The endeavour or power of the mind is the actual essence thereof (III. vii.); but the essence of the mind obviously only affirms that which the mind is and can do; not that which it neither is nor can do; therefore the mind endeavours to conceive only such things as assert or affirm its power of activity. Q.E.D.

PROP. LV. When the mind contemplates its own weakness, it feels pain thereat.

Proof. — The essence of the mind only affirms that which the mind is, or can do; in other words, it is the mind's nature to conceive only such things as assert its power of activity (last Prop.). Thus, when we say that the mind contemplates its own weakness, we are merely saying that while the mind is attempting to conceive something which asserts its power of activity, it is checked in its endeavour —— in other words (III. xi. note), it feels pain. Q.E.D.

Corollary. — This pain is more and more fostered, if a man conceives that he is blamed by others; this may be proved in the same way as the corollary to III. liii.

Note. — This pain, accompanied by the idea of our own weakness, is called humility; the pleasure, which springs from the contemplation of ourselves, is called self — love or self — complacency. And inasmuch as this feeling is renewed as often as a man contemplates his own virtues, or his own power of activity, it follows that everyone is fond of narrating his own exploits, and displaying the force both of his body and mind, and also that, for this reason, men are troublesome to one another. Again, it follows that men are naturally envious (III. xxiv. note, and III. xxxii. note), rejoicing in the shortcomings of their equals, and feeling pain at their virtues. For whenever a man conceives his own actions, he is affected with pleasure (III. liii.), in proportion as his actions display more perfection, and he conceives them more distinctly — that is (II. xl. note), in proportion as he can distinguish them from others, and regard them as something special. Therefore, a man will take most pleasure in contemplating himself, when he contemplates some quality which he denies to others. But, if that which he affirms of himself be attributable to the idea of man or animals in general, he will not be so greatly pleased: he will, on the contrary, feel pain, if he conceives that his own actions fall short when compared with those of others. This pain (III. xxviii.) he will endeavour to remove, by putting a wrong construction on the actions of his equals, or by, as far as he can, embellishing his own.

It is thus apparent that men are naturally prone to hatred and envy, which latter is fostered by their education. For parents are accustomed to incite their children to virtue solely by the spur of honour and envy. But, perhaps, some will scruple to assent to what I have said, because we not seldom admire men's virtues, and venerate their possessors. In order to remove such doubts, I append the following corollary.

Corollary. — No one envies the virtue of anyone who is not his equal.

Proof. — Envy is a species of hatred (III. xxiv. note) or (III. xiii. note) pain, that is (III. xi. note), a modification whereby a man's power of activity, or endeavour towards activity, is checked. But a man does not endeavour or desire to do anything, which cannot follow from his nature as it is given; therefore a man will not desire any power of activity or virtue (which is the same thing) to be attributed to him, that is appropriate to another's nature and foreign to his own; hence his desire cannot be checked, nor he himself pained by the contemplation of virtue in some one unlike himself, consequently he cannot envy such an one. But he can envy his equal, who is assumed to have the same nature as himself. Q.E.D.

Note. — When, therefore, as we said in the note to III. lii., we venerate a man, through wonder at his prudence, fortitude, &c., we do so, because we conceive those qualities to be peculiar to him, and not as common to our nature; we, therefore, no more envy their possessor, than we envy trees for being tall, or lions for being courageous.

PROP. LVI. There are as many kinds of pleasure, of pain, of desire, and of every emotion compounded of these, such as vacillations of spirit, or derived from these, such as love, hatred, hope, fear, &c., as there are kinds of objects whereby we are affected.

Proof. — Pleasure and pain, and consequently the emotions compounded thereof, or derived therefrom, are passions, or passive states (III. xi. note); now we are necessarily passive (III. i.), in so far as we have inadequate ideas; and only in so far as we have such ideas are we passive (III. iii.); that is, we are only necessarily passive (II. xl. note), in so far as we conceive, or (II. xvii. and note) in so far as we are affected by an emotion, which involves the nature of our own body, and the nature of an external body. Wherefore the nature of every passive state must necessarily be so explained, that the nature of the object whereby we are affected be expressed. Namely, the pleasure, which arises from, say, the object A, involves the nature of that object A, and the pleasure, which arises from the object B, involves the nature of the object B; wherefore these two pleasurable emotions are by nature different, inasmuch as the causes whence they arise are by nature different. So again the emotion of pain, which arises from one object, is by nature different from the pain arising from another object, and, similarly, in the case of love, hatred, hope, fear, vacillation, &c.

Thus, there are necessarily as many kinds of pleasure, pain, love, hatred, &c., as there are kinds of objects whereby we are affected. Now desire is each man's essence or nature, in so far as it is conceived as determined to a particular action by any given modification of itself (III. ix. note); therefore, according as a man is affected through external causes by this or that kind of pleasure, pain, love, hatred, &c., in other words, according as his nature is disposed in this or that manner, so will his desire be of one kind or another, and the nature of one desire must necessarily differ from the nature of another desire, as widely as the emotions differ, wherefrom each desire arose. Thus there are as many kinds of desire, as there are kinds of pleasure, pain, love, &c., consequently (by what has been shown) there are as many kinds of desire, as there are kinds of objects whereby we are affected. Q.E.D.

Note. — Among the kinds of emotions, which, by the last proposition, must be very numerous, the chief are luxury, drunkenness, lust, avarice, and ambition, being merely species of love or desire, displaying the nature of those emotions in a manner varying according to the object, with which they are concerned. For by luxury, drunkenness, lust, avarice, ambition, &c., we simply mean the immoderate love of feasting, drinking, venery, riches, and fame. Furthermore, these emotions, in so far as we distinguish them from others merely by the objects wherewith they are concerned, have no contraries. For temperance, sobriety, and chastity, which we are wont to oppose to luxury, drunkenness, and lust, are not emotions or passive states, but indicate a power of the mind which moderates the last — named emotions. However, I cannot here explain the remaining kinds of emotions (seeing that they are as numerous as the kinds of objects), nor, if I could, would it be necessary. It is sufficient for our purpose, namely, to determine the strength of the emotions, and the mind's power over them, to have a general definition of each emotion. It is sufficient, I repeat, to understand the general properties of the emotions and the mind, to enable us to determine the quality and extent of the mind's power in moderating and checking the emotions. Thus, though there is a great difference between various emotions of love, hatred, or desire, for instance between love felt towards children, and love felt towards a wife, there is no need for us to take cognizance of such differences, or to track out further the nature and origin of the emotions.

PROP. LVII. Any emotion of a given individual differs from the emotion of another individual, only in so far as the essence of the one individual differs from the essence of the other.

Proof. — This proposition is evident from Ax. i. (which see after Lemma iii. Prop.

xiii., Part II.). Nevertheless, we will prove it from the nature of the three primary emotions.

All emotions are attributable to desire, pleasure, or pain, as their definitions above given show. But desire is each man's nature or essence (III. ix. note); therefore desire in one individual differs from desire in another individual, only in so far as the nature or essence of the one differs from the nature or essence of the other. Again, pleasure and pain are passive states or passions, whereby every man's power or endeavour to persist in his being is increased or diminished, helped or hindered (III. xi. and note). But by the endeavour to persist in its being, in so far as it is attributable to mind and body in conjunction, we mean appetite and desire (III. ix. note); therefore pleasure and pain are identical with desire or appetite, in so far as by external causes they are increased or diminished, helped or hindered, in other words, they are every man's nature; wherefore the pleasure and pain felt by one man differ from the pleasure and pain felt by another man, only in so far as the nature or essence of the one man differs from the essence of the other; consequently, any emotion of one individual only differs, &c. Q.E.D.

Note. — Hence it follows, that the emotions of the animals which are called irrational (for after learning the origin of mind we cannot doubt that brutes feel) only differ from man's emotions, to the extent that brute nature differs from human nature. Horse and man are alike carried away by the desire of procreation; but the desire of the former is equine, the desire of the latter is human. So also the lusts and appetites of insects, fishes, and birds must needs vary according to the several natures. Thus, although each individual lives content and rejoices in that nature belonging to him wherein he has his being, yet the life, wherein each is content and rejoices, is nothing else but the idea, or soul, of the said individual, and hence the joy of one only differs in nature from the joy of another, to the extent that the essence of one differs from the essence of another. Lastly, it follows from the foregoing proposition, that there is no small difference between the joy which actuates, say, a drunkard, and the joy possessed by a philosopher, as I just mention here by the way. Thus far I have treated of the emotions attributable to man, in so far as he is passive. It remains to add a few words on those attributable to him in so far as he is active.

PROP. LVIII. Besides pleasure and desire, which are passivities or passions, there are other emotions derived from pleasure and desire, which are attributable to us in so far as we are active.

Proof. — When the mind conceives itself and its power of activity, it feels pleasure (III. liii.): now the mind necessarily contemplates itself, when it conceives a true or adequate idea (II. xliii.). But the mind does conceive certain adequate ideas (II. xl. note 2.). Therefore it feels pleasure in so far as it conceives adequate ideas; that is, in so far as it is active (III. i.). Again, the mind, both in so far as it has clear and distinct ideas, and in so far as it has confused ideas, endeavours to persist in its own being (III. ix.); but by such an endeavour we mean desire (by the note to the same Prop.); therefore, desire is also attributable to us, in so far as we understand, or (III. i.) in so far as we are active. Q.E.D.

PROP. LIX. Among all the emotions attributable to the mind as active, there are none which cannot be referred to pleasure or desire.

Proof. — All emotions can be referred to desire, pleasure, or pain, as their definitions, already given, show. Now by pain we mean that the mind's power of thinking is diminished or checked (III. xi. and note); therefore, in so far as the mind feels pain, its power of understanding, that is, of activity, is diminished or checked (III. i.); therefore, no painful emotions can be attributed to the mind in virtue of its being active, but only emotions of pleasure and desire, which (by the last Prop.) are attributable to the mind in that condition. Q.E.D.

Note. — All actions following from emotion, which are attributable to the mind in virtue of its understanding, I set down to strength of character (fortitudo), which I divide into courage (animositas) and highmindedness (generositas). By courage I mean the desire whereby every man strives to preserve his own being in accordance solely with the dictates of reason. By highmindedness I mean the desire whereby every man endeavours, solely under the dictates of reason, to aid other men and to unite them to himself in friendship. Those actions, therefore, which have regard solely to the good of the agent I set down to courage, those which aim at the good of others I set down to highmindedness. Thus temperance, sobriety, and presence of mind in danger, &c., are varieties of courage; courtesy, mercy, &c., are varieties of highmindedness.

I think I have thus explained, and displayed through their primary causes the principal emotions and vacillations of spirit, which arise from the combination of the three primary emotions, to wit, desire, pleasure, and pain. It is evident from what I have said, that we are in many ways driven about by external causes, and that like waves of the sea driven by contrary winds we toss to and fro unwitting of the issue and of our fate. But I have said, that I have only set forth the chief conflicting emotions, not all that might be given. For, by proceeding in the same way as above, we can easily show that love is united to repentance, scorn, shame, &c. I think everyone will agree from what has been said, that the emotions may be compounded one with another in so many ways, and so many variations may arise therefrom, as to exceed all possibility of computation. However, for my purpose, it is enough to have enumerated the most important; to reckon up the rest which I have omitted would be more curious than profitable. It remains to remark concerning love, that it very often happens that while we are enjoying a thing which we longed for, the body, from the act of enjoyment, acquires a new disposition, whereby it is determined in another way, other images of things are aroused in it, and the mind begins to conceive and desire something fresh. For example, when we conceive something which generally delights us with its flavour, we desire to enjoy, that is, to eat it. But whilst we are thus enjoying it, the stomach is filled and the body is otherwise disposed. If, therefore, when the body is thus otherwise disposed, the image of the food which is present be stimulated, and consequently the endeavour or desire to eat it be stimulated also, the new disposition of the body will feel repugnance to the desire or attempt, and consequently the presence of the food which we formerly longed for will become odious. This revulsion of feeling is called satiety or weariness. For the rest, I have neglected the outward modifications of the body observable in emotions, such, for instance, as trembling, pallor, sobbing, laughter, &c., for these are attributable to the body only, without any reference to the mind. Lastly, the definitions of the emotions require to be supplemented in a few points; I will therefore repeat them, interpolating such observations as I think should here and there be added.

DEFINITIONS OF THE EMOTIONS

I. DESIRE IS the actual essence of man, in so far as it is conceived, as determined to a particular activity by some given modification of itself.

Explanation. — We have said above, in the note to Prop. ix. of this part, that desire is appetite, with consciousness thereof; further, that appetite is the essence of man, in so far as it is determined to act in a way tending to promote its own persistence. But, in the same note, I also remarked that, strictly speaking, I recognize no distinction between appetite and desire. For whether a man be conscious of his appetite or not, it remains one and the same appetite. Thus, in order to avoid the appearance of tautology, I have refrained from explaining desire by appetite; but I have take care to define it in such a manner, as to comprehend, under one head, all those endeavours of human nature, which we distinguish by the terms appetite, will, desire, or impulse. I might, indeed, have said, that desire is the essence of man, in so far as it is conceived as determined to a particular activity; but from such a definition (cf. II. xxiii.) it would not follow that the mind can be conscious of its desire or appetite. Therefore, in order to imply the cause of such consciousness, it was necessary to add, in so far as it is determined by some given modification, &c. For, by a modification of man's essence, we understand every disposition of the said essence, whether such disposition be innate, or whether it be conceived solely under the attribute of thought, or solely under the attribute of extension, or whether, lastly, it be referred simultaneously to both these attributes. By the term desire, then, I here mean all man's endeavours, impulses, appetites, and volitions, which vary according to each man's disposition, and are, therefore, not seldom opposed one to another, according as a man is drawn in different directions, and knows not where to turn.

II. Pleasure is the transition of a man from a less to a greater perfection.

III. Pain is the transition of a man from a greater to a less perfection.

Explanation — I say transition: for pleasure is not perfection itself. For, if man were born with the perfection to which he passes, he would possess the same, without the emotion of pleasure. This appears more clearly from the consideration of the contrary emotion, pain. No one can deny, that pain consists in the transition to a less perfection, and not in the less perfection itself: for a man cannot be pained, in so far as he partakes of perfection of any degree. Neither can we say, that pain consists in the absence of a greater perfection. For absence is nothing, whereas the emotion of pain is an activity; wherefore this activity can only be the activity of transition from a greater to a less perfection — in other words, it is an activity whereby a man's power of action is lessened or constrained (cf. III. xi. note). I pass over the definitions of merriment, stimulation, melancholy, and grief, because these terms are generally used in reference to the body, and are merely kinds of pleasure or pain.

IV. Wonder is the conception (imaginatio) of anything, wherein the mind comes to a stand, because the particular concept in question has no connection with other concepts (cf. III. lii. and note).

Explanation — In the note to II. xviii. we showed the reason, why the mind, from the contemplation of one thing, straightway falls to the contemplation of another thing, namely, because the images of the two things are so associated and arranged, that one follows the other. This state of association is impossible, if the image of the thing be new; the mind will then be at a stand in the contemplation thereof, until it is determined by other causes to think of something else.

Thus the conception of a new object, considered in itself, is of the same nature as other conceptions; hence, I do not include wonder among the emotions, nor do

I see why I should so include it, inasmuch as this distraction of the mind arises from no positive cause drawing away the mind from other objects, but merely from the absence of a cause, which should determine the mind to pass from the contemplation of one object to the contemplation of another.

I, therefore, recognize only three primitive or primary emotions (as I said in the note to III. xi.), namely, pleasure, pain, and desire. I have spoken of wonder simply because it is customary to speak of certain emotions springing from the three primitive ones by different names, when they are referred to the objects of our wonder. I am led by the same motive to add a definition of contempt.

V. Contempt is the conception of anything which touches the mind so little, that its presence leads the mind to imagine those qualities which are not in it rather than such as are in it (cf. III. lii. note).

The definitions of veneration and scorn I here pass over, for I am not aware that any emotions are named after them.

VI. Love is pleasure, accompanied by the idea of an external cause.

Explanation — This definition explains sufficiently clearly the essence of love; the definition given by those authors who say that love is the lover's wish to unite himself to the loved object expresses a property, but not the essence of love; and, as such authors have not sufficiently discerned love's essence, they have been unable to acquire a true conception of its properties, accordingly their definition is on all hands admitted to be very obscure. It must, however, be noted, that when I say that it is a property of love, that the lover should wish to unite himself to the beloved object, I do not here mean by wish consent, or conclusion, or a free decision of the mind (for I have shown such, in II. xlviii., to be fictitious); neither do I mean a desire of being united to the loved object when it is absent, or of continuing in its presence when it is at hand; for love can be conceived without either of these desires; but by wish I mean the contentment, which is in the lover, on account of the presence of the beloved object, whereby the pleasure of the lover is strengthened, or at least maintained.

VII. Hatred is pain, accompanied by the idea of an external cause.

Explanation — These observations are easily grasped after what has been said in the explanation of the preceding definition (cf. also III. xiii. note).

VIII. Inclination is pleasure, accompanied by the idea of something which is accidentally a cause of pleasure.

IX. Aversion is pain, accompanied by the idea of something which is accidentally the cause of pain (cf. III. xv. note).

X. Devotion is love towards one whom we admire.

Explanation — Wonder (admiratio) arises (as we have shown, III. lii.) from the novelty of a thing. If, therefore, it happens that the object of our wonder is often conceived by us, we shall cease to wonder at it; thus we see, that the emotion of devotion readily degenerates into simple love.

XI. Derision is pleasure arising from our conceiving the presence of a quality, which we despise, in an object which we hate.

Explanation — In so far as we despise a thing which we hate, we deny existence thereof (III. lii. note), and to that extent rejoice (III. xx.). But since we assume that man hates that which he derides, it follows that the pleasure in question is not without alloy (cf. III. xlvii. note).

XII. Hope is an inconstant pleasure, arising from the idea of something past or future, whereof we to a certain extent doubt the issue.

XIII. Fear is an inconstant pain arising from the idea of something past or future, whereof we to a certain extent doubt the issue (cf. III. xviii. note).

Explanation — From these definitions it follows, that there is no hope unmingled with fear, and no fear unmingled with hope. For he, who depends on hope and doubts concerning the issue of anything, is assumed to conceive something, which excludes the existence of the said thing in the future; therefore he, to this extent, feels pain (cf. III. xix.); consequently, while dependent on hope, he fears for the issue. Contrariwise he, who fears, in other words doubts, concerning the issue of something which he hates, also conceives something which excludes the existence of the thing in question; to this extent he feels pleasure, and consequently to this extent he hopes that it will turn out as he desires (III. xx.).

XIV. Confidence is pleasure arising from the idea of something past or future, wherefrom all cause of doubt has been removed.

XV. Despair is pain arising from the idea of something past or future, wherefrom all cause of doubt has been removed.

Explanation — Thus confidence springs from hope, and despair from fear, when all cause for doubt as to the issue of an event has been removed: this comes to pass, because man conceives something past or future as present and regards it as such, or else because he conceives other things, which exclude the existence of the causes of his doubt. For, although we can never be absolutely certain of the issue of any particular event (II. xxxi. Coroll.), it may nevertheless happen that we feel no doubt concerning it. For we have shown, that to feel no doubt concerning a thing is not the same as to be quite certain of it (II. xlix. note). Thus it may happen that we are affected by the same emotion of pleasure or pain concerning a thing past or future, as concerning the conception of a thing present; this I have already shown in III. xviii., to which, with its note, I refer the reader.

XVI. Joy is pleasure accompanied by the idea of something past, which has had an issue beyond our hope.

XVII. Disappointment is pain accompanied by the idea of something past, which has had an issue contrary to our hope.

XVIII. Pity is pain accompanied by the idea of evil, which has befallen someone else whom we conceive to be like ourselves (cf. III. xxii. note, and III. xxvii. note).

Explanation — Between pity and sympathy (misericordia) there seems to be no difference, unless perhaps that the former term is used in reference to a particular action, and the latter in reference to a disposition.

XIX. Approval is love towards one who has done good to another.

XX. Indignation is hatred towards one who has done evil to another.

Explanation — I am aware that these terms are employed in senses somewhat different from those usually assigned. But my purpose is to explain, not the meaning of words, but the nature of things. I therefore make use of such terms, as may convey my meaning without any violent departure from their ordinary signification. One statement of my method will suffice. As for the cause of the above — named emotions see III. xxvii. Coroll. i., and III. xxii. note.

XXI. Partiality is thinking too highly of anyone because of the love we bear him.

XXII. Disparagement is thinking too meanly of anyone because we hate him.

Explanation — Thus partiality is an effect of love, and disparagement an effect of hatred: so that partiality may also be defined as love, in so far as it induces a man to think too highly of a beloved object. Contrariwise, disparagement may be defined as hatred, in so far as it induces a man to think too meanly of a hated object. Cf. III. xxvi. note.

XXIII. Envy is hatred, in so far as it induces a man to be pained by another's good fortune, and to rejoice in another's evil fortune.

Explanation — Envy is generally opposed to sympathy, which, by doing some violence to the meaning of the word, may therefore be thus defined:

XXIV. Sympathy (misericordia) is love, in so far as it induces a man to feel pleasure at another's good fortune, and pain at another's evil fortune.

Explanation — Concerning envy see the notes to III. xxiv. and xxxii. These emotions also arise from pleasure or pain accompanied by the idea of something external, as cause either in itself or accidentally. I now pass on to other emotions, which are accompanied by the idea of something within as a cause.

XXV. Self — approval is pleasure arising from a man's contemplation of himself and his own power of action.

XXVI. Humility is pain arising from a man's contemplation of his own weakness of body or mind.

Explanation — Self — complacency is opposed to humility, in so far as we thereby mean pleasure arising from a contemplation of our own power of action; but, in so far as we mean thereby pleasure accompanied by the idea of any action which we believe we have performed by the free decision of our mind, it is opposed to repentance, which we may thus define:

XXVII. Repentance is pain accompanied by the idea of some action, which we believe we have performed by the free decision of our mind.

Explanation — The causes of these emotions we have set forth in III. li. note, and in III. liii., liv., lv. and note. Concerning the free decision of the mind see II. xxxv. note. This is perhaps the place to call attention to the fact, that it is nothing wonderful that all those actions, which are commonly called wrong, are followed by pain, and all those, which are called right, are followed by pleasure. We can easily gather from what has been said, that this depends in great measure on education. Parents, by reprobating the former class of actions, and by frequently chiding their children because of them, and also by persuading to and praising the latter class, have brought it about, that the former should be associated with pain and the latter with pleasure. This is confirmed by experience. For custom and religion are not the same among all men, but that which some consider sacred others consider profane, and what some consider honourable others consider disgraceful. According as each man has been educated, he feels repentance for a given action or glories therein.

XXVIII. Pride is thinking too highly of one's self from self — love.

Explanation — Thus pride is different from partiality, for the latter term is used in reference to an external object, but pride is used of a man thinking too highly of himself. However, as partiality is the effect of love, so is pride the effect or property of self — love, which may therefore be thus defined, love of self or self — approval, in so far as it leads a man to think too highly of himself. To this emotion there is no contrary. For no one thinks too meanly of himself because of self — hatred; I say that no one thinks too meanly of himself, in so far as he conceives that he is incapable of doing this or that. For whatsoever a man imagines that he is incapable of doing, he imagines this of necessity, and by that notion he is so disposed, that he really cannot do that which he conceives that he cannot do. For, so long as he conceives that he cannot do it, so long is he not determined to do it, and consequently so long is it impossible for him to do it. However, if we consider such matters as only depend on opinion, we shall find it conceivable that a man may think too meanly of himself; for it may happen, that a man, sorrowfully regarding his own weakness, should imagine that he is despised by all men, while the rest of the world are thinking of nothing less than of despising him. Again, a man may think too meanly of himself, if he deny of himself in the present something in relation to a future time of which he is uncertain. As, for instance, if he should say that he is unable to form any clear conceptions, or that he can desire and do nothing but what is wicked and base, &c. We may also say, that a man thinks too meanly of himself, when we see him from excessive fear of shame refusing to do things which others, his equals, venture. We can, therefore, set down as a contrary to pride an emotion which I will call self — abasement, for as from self — complacency springs pride, so from humility springs self — abasement, which I will accordingly thus define:

XXIX. Self — abasement is thinking too meanly of one's self by reason of pain.

Explanation — We are nevertheless generally accustomed to oppose pride to humility, but in that case we pay more attention to the effect of either emotion than to its nature. We are wont to call proud the man who boasts too much (III. xxx. note), who talks of nothing but his own virtues and other people's faults, who wishes to be first; and lastly who goes through life with a style and pomp suitable to those far above him in station. On the other hand, we call humble the man who too often blushes, who confesses his faults, who sets forth other men's virtues, and who, lastly, walks with bent head and is negligent of his attire. However, these emotions, humility and self — abasement, are extremely rare. For human nature, considered in itself, strives against them as much as it can (see III. xiii., liv.); hence those, who are believed to be most self — abased and humble, are generally in reality the most ambitious and envious.

XXX. Honour11 is pleasure accompanied by the idea of some action of our own, which we believe to be praised by others.

11 Gloria.

XXXI. Shame is pain accompanied by the idea of some action of our own, which we believe to be blamed by others.

Explanation — On this subject see the note to III. xxx. But we should here remark the difference which exists between shame and modesty. Shame is the pain following the deed whereof we are ashamed. Modesty is the fear or dread of shame, which restrains a man from committing a base action. Modesty is usually opposed to shamelessness, but the latter is not an emotion, as I will duly show; however, the names of the emotions (as I have remarked already) have regard rather to their exercise than to their nature.

I have now fulfilled the task of explaining the emotions arising from pleasure and pain. I therefore proceed to treat of those which I refer to desire.

XXXII. Regret is the desire or appetite to possess something, kept alive by the remembrance of the said thing, and at the same time constrained by the remembrance of other things which exclude the existence of it.

Explanation — When we remember a thing, we are by that very fact, as I have already said more than once, disposed to contemplate it with the same emotion as if it were something present; but this disposition or endeavour, while we are awake, is generally checked by the images of things which exclude the existence of that which we remember. Thus when we remember something which affected us with a certain pleasure, we by that very fact endeavour to regard it with the same emotion of pleasure as though it were present, but this endeavour is at once checked by the remembrance of things which exclude the existence of the thing in question. Wherefore regret is, strictly speaking, a pain opposed to that of pleasure, which arises from the absence of something we hate (cf. III. xlvii. note). But, as the name regret seems to refer to desire, I set this emotion down, among the emotions springing from desire.

XXXIII. Emulation is the desire of something, engendered in us by our conception that others have the same desire.

Explanation — He who runs away, because he sees others running away, or he who fears, because he sees others in fear; or again, he who, on seeing that another man has burnt his hand, draws towards him his own hand, and moves his body as though his own were burnt; such an one can be said to imitate another's emotion, but not to emulate him; not because the causes of emulation and imitation are different, but because it has become customary to speak of emulation only in him, who imitates that which we deem to be honourable, useful, or pleasant. As to the cause of emulation, cf. III. xxvii. and note. The reason why this emotion is generally coupled with envy may be seen from III. xxxii. and note.

XXXIV. Thankfulness or Gratitude is the desire or zeal springing from love, whereby we endeavour to benefit him, who with similar feelings of love has conferred a benefit on us. Cf. III. xxxix. note and xl.

XXXV. Benevolence is the desire of benefiting one whom we pity. Cf. III. xxvii. note.

XXXVI. Anger is the desire, whereby through hatred we are induced to injure one whom we hate, III. xxxix.

XXXVII. Revenge is the desire whereby we are induced, through mutual hatred, to injure one who, with similar feelings, has injured us. (See III. xl. Coroll. ii and note.)

XXXVIII. Cruelty or savageness is the desire, whereby a man is impelled to injure one whom we love or pity.

Explanation — To cruelty is opposed clemency, which is not a passive state of the mind, but a power whereby man restrains his anger and revenge.

XXXIX. Timidity is the desire to avoid a greater evil, which we dread, by undergoing a lesser evil. Cf. III. xxxix. note.

XL. Daring is the desire, whereby a man is set on to do something dangerous which his equals fear to attempt.

XLI. Cowardice is attributed to one, whose desire is checked by the fear of some danger which his equals dare to encounter.

Explanation — Cowardice is, therefore, nothing else but the fear of some evil, which most men are wont not to fear; hence I do not reckon it among the emotions springing from desire. Nevertheless, I have chosen to explain it here, because, in so far as we look to the desire, it is truly opposed to the emotion of daring.

XLII. Consternation is attributed to one, whose desire of avoiding evil is checked by amazement at the evil which he fears.

Explanation — Consternation is, therefore, a species of cowardice. But, inasmuch as consternation arises from a double fear, it may be more conveniently defined as a fear which keeps a man so bewildered and wavering, that he is not able to remove the evil. I say bewildered, in so far as we understand his desire of removing the evil to be constrained by his amazement. I say wavering, in so far as we understand the said desire to be constrained by the fear of another evil, which equally torments him: whence it comes to pass that he knows not, which he may avert of the two. On this subject, see III. xxxix. note, and III. lii. note. Concerning cowardice and daring, see III. li. note.

XLIII. Courtesy, or deference (Humanitas seu modestia), is the desire of acting in a way that should please men, and refraining from that which should displease them.

XLIV. Ambition is the immoderate desire of power.

Explanation — Ambition is the desire, whereby all the emotions (cf. III. xxvii. and xxxi.) are fostered and strengthened; therefore this emotion can with difficulty be overcome. For, so long as a man is bound by any desire, he is at the same time necessarily bound by this. "The best men," says Cicero, "are especially led by honour. Even philosophers, when they write a book contemning honour, sign their names thereto," and so on.

XLV. Luxury is excessive desire, or even love of living sumptuously.

XLVI. Intemperance is the excessive desire and love of drinking.

XLVII. Avarice is the excessive desire and love of riches.

XLVIII. Lust is desire and love in the matter of sexual intercourse.

Explanation — Whether this desire be excessive or not, it is still called lust. These last five emotions (as I have shown in III. lvi.) have on contraries. For deference is a species of ambition. Cf. III. xxix. note.

Again, I have already pointed out, that temperance, sobriety, and chastity indicate rather a power than a passivity of the mind. It may, nevertheless, happen, that an avaricious, an ambitious, or a timid man may abstain from excess in eating, drinking, or sexual indulgence, yet avarice, ambition, and fear are not contraries to luxury, drunkenness, and debauchery. For an avaricious man often is glad to gorge himself with food and drink at another man's expense. An ambitious man will restrain himself in nothing, so long as he thinks his indulgences are secret; and if he lives among drunkards and debauchees, he will, from the mere fact of being ambitious, be more prone to those vices. Lastly, a timid man does that which he would not. For though an avaricious man should, for the sake of avoiding death, cast his riches into the sea, he will none the less remain avaricious; so, also, if a lustful man is downcast, because he cannot follow his bent, he does not, on the ground of abstention, cease to be lustful. In fact, these emotions are not so much concerned with the actual feasting, drinking, &c., as with the appetite and love of such. Nothing, therefore, can be opposed to these emotions, but high — mindedness and valour, whereof I will speak presently.

The definitions of jealousy and other waverings of the mind I pass over in silence, first, because they arise from the compounding of the emotions already described; secondly, because many of them have no distinctive names, which shows that it is sufficient for practical purposes to have merely a general knowledge of them. However, it is established from the definitions of the emotions, which we have set forth, that they all spring from desire, pleasure, or pain, or, rather, that there is nothing besides these three; wherefore each is wont to be called by a variety of names in accordance with its various relations and extrinsic tokens. If we now direct our attention to these primitive emotions, and to what has been said concerning the nature of the mind, we shall be able thus to define the emotions, in so far as they are referred to the mind only.

GENERAL DEFINITION
OF THE EMOTIONS

EMOTION, WHICH IS called a passivity of the soul, is a confused idea, whereby the mind affirms concerning its body, or any part thereof, a force for existence (existendi vis) greater or less than before, and by the presence of which the mind is determined to think of one thing rather than another.

Explanation — I say, first, that emotion or passion of the soul is a confused idea. For we have shown that the mind is only passive, in so far as it has inadequate or confused ideas. (III. iii.) I say, further, whereby the mind affirms concerning its body or any part thereof a force for existence greater than before. For all the ideas of bodies, which we possess, denote rather the actual disposition of our own body (II. xvi. Coroll. ii.) than the nature of an external body. But the idea which constitutes the reality of an emotion must denote or express the disposition of the body, or of some part thereof, because its power of action or force for existence is increased or diminished, helped or hindered. But it must be noted that, when I say a greater or less force for existence than before, I do not mean that the mind compares the present with the past disposition of the body, but that the idea which constitutes the reality of an emotion affirms something of the body, which, in fact, involves more or less of reality than before.

And inasmuch as the essence of mind consists in the fact (II. xi., xiii.), that it affirms the actual existence of its own body, and inasmuch as we understand by perfection the very essence of a thing, it follows that the mind passes to greater or less perfection, when it happens to affirm concerning its own body, or any part thereof, something involving more or less reality than before.

When, therefore, I said above that the power of the mind is increased or diminished, I merely meant that the mind had formed of its own body, or of some part thereof, an idea involving more or less of reality, than it had already affirmed concerning its own body. For the excellence of ideas, and the actual power of thinking are measured by the excellence of the object. Lastly, I have added by the presence of which the mind is determined to think of one thing rather than another, so that, besides the nature of pleasure and pain, which the first part of the definition explains, I might also express the nature of desire.

PART IV. OF HUMAN BONDAGE, OR THE STRENGTH OF THE EMOTIONS

PREFACE

HUMAN INFIRMITY IN moderating and checking the emotions I name bondage: for, when a man is a prey to his emotions, he is not his own master, but lies at the mercy of fortune: so much so, that he is often compelled, while seeing that which is better for him, to follow that which is worse. Why this is so, and what is good or evil in the emotions, I propose to show in this part of my treatise. But, before I begin, it would be well to make a few prefatory observations on perfection and imperfection, good and evil.

When a man has purposed to make a given thing, and has brought it to perfection, his work will be pronounced perfect, not only by himself, but by everyone who rightly knows, or thinks that he knows, the intention and aim of its author. For instance, suppose anyone sees a work (which I assume to be not yet completed), and knows that the aim of the author of that work is to build a house, he will call the work imperfect; he will, on the other hand, call it perfect, as soon as he sees that it is carried through to the end, which its author had purposed for it. But if a man sees a work, the like whereof he has never seen before, and if he knows not the intention of the artificer, he plainly cannot know, whether that work be perfect or imperfect. Such seems to be the primary meaning of these terms.

But, after men began to form general ideas, to think out types of houses, buildings, towers, &c., and to prefer certain types to others, it came about, that each man called perfect that which he saw agree with the general idea he had formed of the thing in question, and called imperfect that which he saw agree less with his own preconceived type, even though it had evidently been completed in accordance with the idea of its artificer. This seems to be the only reason for calling natural phenomena, which, indeed, are not made with human hands, perfect or imperfect: for men are wont to form general ideas of things natural, no less than of things artificial, and such ideas they hold as types, believing that Nature (who they think does nothing without an object) has them in view, and has set them as types before herself. Therefore, when they behold something in Nature, which does not wholly conform to the preconceived type which they have formed of the thing in question, they say that Nature has fallen short or has blundered, and has left her work incomplete. Thus we see that men are wont to style natural phenomena perfect or imperfect rather from their own prejudices, than from true knowledge of what they pronounce upon.

Now we showed in the Appendix to Part I., that Nature does not work with an end in view. For the eternal and infinite Being, which we call God or Nature, acts by the same necessity as that whereby it exists. For we have shown, that by the same necessity of its nature, whereby it exists, it likewise works (I. xvi.). The reason or cause why God or Nature exists, and the reason why he acts, are one and the same. Therefore, as he does not exist for the sake of an end, so neither does he act for the sake of an end; of his existence and of his action there is neither origin nor end. Wherefore, a cause which is called final is nothing else but human desire, in so far as it is considered as the origin or cause of anything. For example, when we say that to be inhabited is the final cause of this or that house, we mean nothing more than that a man, conceiving the conveniences of household life, had a desire to build a house. Wherefore, the being inhabited, in so far as it is regarded as a final cause, is nothing else but this particular desire, which is really the efficient cause; it is regarded as the primary cause, because men are generally ignorant of the causes of their desires. They are, as I have often said already, conscious of their own actions and appetites, but ignorant of the causes whereby they are determined to any particular desire. Therefore, the common saying that Nature sometimes falls short, or blunders, and produces things which are imperfect, I set down among the glosses treated of in the Appendix to Part I. Perfection and imperfection, then, are in reality merely modes of thinking, or notions which we form from a comparison among one another of individuals of the same species; hence I said above (II. Def. vi.), that by reality and perfection I mean the same thing. For we are wont to refer all the individual things in nature to one genus, which is called the highest genus, namely, to the category of Being, whereto absolutely all individuals in nature belong. Thus, in so far as we refer the individuals in nature to this category, and comparing them one with another, find that some possess more of being or reality than others, we, to this extent, say that some are more perfect than others. Again, in so far as we attribute to them anything implying negation — as term, end, infirmity, etc., we, to this extent, call them imperfect, because they do not affect our mind so much as the things which we call perfect, not because they have any intrinsic deficiency, or because Nature has blundered. For nothing lies within the scope of a thing's nature, save that which follows from the necessity of the nature of its efficient cause, and whatsoever follows from the necessity of the nature of its efficient cause necessarily comes to pass.

As for the terms good and bad, they indicate no positive quality in things regarded in themselves, but are merely modes of thinking, or notions which we form from the comparison of things one with another. Thus one and the same thing can be at the same time good, bad, and indifferent. For instance, music is good for him that is melancholy, bad for him that mourns; for him that is deaf, it is neither good nor bad.

Nevertheless, though this be so, the terms should still be retained. For, inasmuch as we desire to form an idea of man as a type of human nature which we may hold in view, it will be useful for us to retain the terms in question, in the sense I have indicated.

In what follows, then, I shall mean by, "good" that, which we certainly know to be a means of approaching more nearly to the type of human nature, which we have set before ourselves; by "bad," that which we certainly know to be a hindrance to us in approaching the said type. Again, we shall that men are more perfect, or more imperfect, in proportion as they approach more or less nearly to the said type. For it must be specially remarked that, when I say that a man passes from a lesser to a greater perfection, or vice versâ, I do not mean that he is changed from one essence or reality to another; for instance, a horse would be as completely destroyed by being changed into a man, as by being changed into an insect. What I mean is, that we conceive the thing's power of action, in so far as this is understood by its nature, to be increased or diminished. Lastly, by perfection in general I shall, as I have said, mean reality — in other words, each thing's essence, in so far as it exists, and operates in a particular manner, and without paying any regard to its duration. For no given thing can be said to be more perfect, because it has passed a longer time in existence. The duration of things cannot be determined by their essence, for the essence of things involves no fixed and definite period of existence; but everything, whether it be more perfect or less perfect, will always be able to persist in existence with the same force wherewith it began to exist; wherefore, in this respect, all things are equal.

DEFINITIONS.

I. BY GOOD I mean that which we certainly know to be useful to us.

II. By evil I mean that which we certainly know to be a hindrance to us in the attainment of any good.

(Concerning these terms see the foregoing preface towards the end.)

III. Particular things I call contingent in so far as, while regarding their essence only, we find nothing therein, which necessarily asserts their existence or excludes it.

IV. Particular things I call possible in so far as, while regarding the causes whereby they must be produced, we know not, whether such causes be determined for producing them.

(In I. xxxiii. note. i., I drew no distinction between possible and contingent, because there was in that place no need to distinguish them accurately.)

V. By conflicting emotions I mean those which draw a man in different directions, though they are of the same kind, such as luxury and avarice, which are both species of love, and are contraries, not by nature, but by accident.

VI. What I mean by emotion felt towards a thing, future, present, and past, I explained in III. xviii., notes. i. and ii., which see.

(But I should here also remark, that we can only distinctly conceive distance of space or time up to a certain definite limit; that is, all objects distant from us more than two hundred feet, or whose distance from the place where we are exceeds that which we can distinctly conceive, seem to be an equal distance from us, and all in the same plane; so also objects, whose time of existing is conceived as removed from the present by a longer interval than we can distinctly conceive, seem to be all equally distant from the present, and are set down, as it were, to the same moment of time.)

VII. By an end, for the sake of which we do something, I mean a desire.

VIII. By virtue (virtus) and power I mean the same thing; that is (III. vii), virtue, in so far as it is referred to man, is a man's nature or essence, in so far as it has the power of effecting what can only be understood by the laws of that nature.

AXIOM.

THERE IS NO individual thing in nature, than which there is not another more powerful and strong. Whatsoever thing be given, there is something stronger whereby it can be destroyed.

PROPOSITIONS.

PROP. I. NO positive quality possessed by a false idea is removed by the presence of what is true, in virtue of its being true.

Proof. — Falsity consists solely in the privation of knowledge which inadequate ideas involve (II. xxxv.), nor have they any positive quality on account of which they are called false (II. xxxiii.); contrariwise, in so far as they are referred to God, they are true (II. xxxii.). Wherefore, if the positive quality possessed by a false idea were removed by the presence of what is true, in virtue of its being true, a true idea would then be removed by itself, which (IV. iii.) is absurd. Therefore, no positive quality possessed by a false idea, &c. Q.E.D.

Note. — This proposition is more clearly understood from II. xvi. Coroll. ii. For imagination is an idea, which indicates rather the present disposition of the human body than the nature of the external body; not indeed distinctly, but confusedly; whence it comes to pass, that the mind is said to err. For instance, when we look at the sun, we conceive that it is distant from us about two hundred feet; in this judgment we err, so long as we are in ignorance of its true distance; when its true distance is known, the error is removed, but not the imagination; or, in other words, the idea of the sun, which only explains tho nature of that luminary, in so far as the body is affected thereby: wherefore, though we know the real distance, we shall still nevertheless imagine the sun to be near us. For, as we said in II. xxxv. note, we do not imagine the sun to be so near us, because we are ignorant of its true distance, but because the mind conceives the magnitude of the sun to the extent that the body is affected thereby. Thus, when the rays of the sun falling on the surface of water are reflected into our eyes, we imagine the sun as if it were in the water, though we are aware of its real position; and similarly other imaginations, wherein the mind is deceived, whether they indicate the natural disposition of the body, or that its power of activity is increased or diminished, are not contrary to the truth, and do not vanish at its presence. It happens indeed that, when we mistakenly fear an evil, the fear vanishes when we hear the true tidings; but the contrary also happens, namely, that we fear an evil which will certainly come, and our fear vanishes when we hear false tidings; thus imaginations do not vanish at the presence of the truth, in virtue of its being true, but because other imaginations, stronger than the first, supervene and exclude the present existence of that which we imagined, as I have shown in II. xvii.

PROP. II. We are only passive, in so far as we are apart of Nature, which cannot be conceived by itself without other parts.

Proof. — We are said to be passive, when something arises in us, whereof we are only a partial cause (III. Def. ii.), that is (III. Def. i.), something which cannot be deduced solely from the laws of our nature. We are passive therefore, in so far as we are a part of Nature, which cannot be conceived by itself without other parts. Q.E.D.

PROP. III. The force whereby a man persists in existing is limited, and is infinitely surpassed by the power of external causes.

Proof. — This is evident from the axiom of this part. For, when man is given, there is something else — say A — more powerful; when A is given, there is something else — say B — more powerful than A, and so on to infinity; thus the power of man is limited by the power of some other thing, and is infinitely surpassed by the power of external causes. Q.E.D.

PROP. IV. It is impossible, that man should not be a part of Nature, or that he should be capable of undergoing no changes, save such as can be understood through his nature only as their adequate cause.

Proof. — The power, whereby each particular thing, and consequently man, preserves his being, is the power of God or of Nature (I. xxiv. Coroll.); not in so far as it is infinite, but in so far as it can be explained by the actual human essence (III. vii.). Thus the power of man, in so far as it is explained through his own actual essence, is a part of the infinite power of God or Nature, in other words, of the essence thereof (I. xxxiv.). This was our first point. Again, if it were possible, that man should undergo no changes save such as can be understood solely through the nature of man, it would follow that he would not be able to die, but would always necessarily exist; this would be the necessary consequence of a cause whose power was either finite or infinite; namely, either of man's power only, inasmuch as he would be capable of removing from himself all changes which could spring from external causes; or of the infinite power of Nature, whereby all individual things would be so ordered, that man should be incapable of undergoing any changes save such as tended towards his own preservation. But the first alternative is absurd (by the last Prop., the proof of which is universal, and can be applied to all individual things). Therefore, if it be possible, that man should not be capable of undergoing any changes, save such as can be explained solely through his own nature, and consequently that he must always (as we have shown) necessarily exist; such a result must follow from the infinite power of God, and consequently (I. xvi.) from the necessity of the divine nature, in so far as it is regarded as affected by the idea of any given man, the whole order of nature as conceived under the attributes of extension and thought must be deducible. It would therefore follow (I. xxi.) that man is infinite, which (by the first part of this proof) is absurd. It is, therefore, impossible, that man should not undergo any changes save those whereof he is the adequate cause. Q.E.D.

Corollary. — Hence it follows, that man is necessarily always a prey to his passions, that he follows and obeys the general order of nature, and that he accommodates himself thereto, as much as the nature of things demands.

PROP. V. The power and increase of every passion, and its persistence in existing are not defined by the power, whereby we ourselves endeavour to persist in existing, but by the power of an external cause compared with our own.

Proof. — The essence of a passion cannot be explained through our essence alone (III. Deff. i. and ii.), that is (III. vii.), the power of a passion cannot be defined by the power, whereby we ourselves endeavour to persist in existing, but (as is shown in II. xvi.) must necessarily be defined by the power of an external cause compared with our own. Q.E.D.

PROP. VI. The force of any passion or emotion can overcome the rest of a man's activities or power, so that the emotion becomes obstinately fixed to him.

Proof. — The force and increase of any passion and its persistence in existing are defined by the power of an external cause compared with our own (by the foregoing Prop.); therefore (IV. iii.) it can overcome a man's power, &e. Q.E.D.

PROP. VII. An emotion can only be controlled or destroyed by another emotion contrary thereto, and with more power for controlling emotion.

Proof. — Emotion, in so far as it is referred to the mind, is an idea, whereby the mind affirms of its body a greater or less force of existence than before (cf. the general Definition of the Emotions at the end of Part III.). When, therefore, the mind is assailed by any emotion, the body is at the same time affected with a modification whereby its power of activity is increased or diminished. Now this modification of the body (IV. v.) receives from its cause the force for persistence in its being; which force can only be checked or destroyed by a bodily cause (II. vi.), in virtue of the body being affected with a modification contrary to (III. v.) and stronger than itself (IV. Ax.); wherefore (II. xii.) the mind is affected by the idea of a modification contrary to, and stronger than the former modification, in other words, (by the general definition of the emotions) the mind will be affected by an emotion contrary to and stronger than the former emotion, which will exclude or destroy the existence of the former emotion; thus an emotion cannot be destroyed nor controlled except by a contrary and stronger emotion. Q.E.D.

Corollary. — An emotion, in so far as it is referred to the mind, can only be controlled or destroyed through an idea of a modification of the body contrary to, and stronger than, that which we are undergoing. For the emotion which we undergo can only be checked or destroyed by an emotion contrary to, and stronger than, itself, in other words, (by the general Definition of the Emotions) only by an idea of a modification of the body contrary to, and stronger than, the modification which we undergo.

PROP. VIII. The knowledge of good and evil is nothing else but the emotions of pleasure or pain, in so far as we are conscious thereof.

Proof. — We call a thing good or evil, when it is of service or the reverse in preserving our being (IV. Deff. i. and ii.), that is (III. vii.), when it increases or diminishes, helps or hinders, our power of activity. Thus, in so far as we perceive that a thing affects us with pleasure or pain, we call it good or evil; wherefore the knowledge of good and evil is nothing else but the idea of the pleasure or pain, which necessarily follows from that pleasurable or painful emotion (II. xxii.). But this idea is united to the emotion in the same way as mind is united to body (II. xxi.); that is, there is no real distinction between this idea and the emotion or idea of the modification of the body, save in conception only. Therefore the knowledge of good and evil is nothing else but the emotion, in so far as we are conscious thereof. Q.E.D.

PROP. IX. An emotion, whereof we conceive the cause to be with us at the present time, is stronger than if we did not conceive the cause to be with us.

Proof. — Imagination or conception is the idea, by which the mind regards a thing as present (II. xvii. note), but which indicates the disposition of the mind rather than the nature of the external thing (II. xvi. Coroll. ii.). An emotion is therefore a conception, in so far as it indicates the disposition of the body. But a conception (by II. xvii.) is stronger, so long as we conceive nothing which excludes the present existence of the external object; wherefore an emotion is also stronger or more intense, when we conceive the cause to be with us at the present time, than when we do not conceive the cause to be with us. Q.E.D.

Note. — When I said above in III. xviii. that we are affected by the image of what is past or future with the same emotion as if the thing conceived were present, I expressly stated, that this is only true in so far as we look solely to the image of the thing in question itself; for the thing's nature is unchanged, whether we have conceived it or not; I did not deny that the image becomes weaker, when we regard as present to us other things which exclude the present existence of the future object: I did not expressly call attention to the fact, because I purposed to treat of the strength of the emotions in this part of my work.

Corollary. — The image of something past or future, that is, of a thing which we regard as in relation to time past or time future, to the exclusion of time present, is, when other conditions are equal, weaker than the image of something present; consequently an emotion felt towards what is past or future is less intense, other conditions being equal, than an emotion felt towards something present.

PROP. X. Towards something future, which we conceive as close at hand, we are affected more intensely, than if we conceive that its time for existence is separated from the present by a longer interval; so too by the remembrance of what we conceive to have not long passed away we are affected more intensely, than if we conceive that it has long passed away.

Proof. — In so far as we conceive a thing as close at hand, or not long passed away, we conceive that which excludes the presence of the object less, than if its period of future existence were more distant from the present, or if it had long passed away (this is obvious) therefore (by the foregoing Prop.) we are, so far, more intensely affected towards it. Q.E.D.

Corollary. — From the remarks made in Def. vi. of this part it follows that, if objects are separated from the present by a longer period than we can define in conception, though their dates of occurrence be widely separated one from the other, they all affect us equally faintly.

PROP. XI. An emotion towards that which we conceive as necessary is, when other conditions are equal, more intense than an emotion towards that which possible, or contingent, or non — necessary.

Proof. — In so far as we conceive a thing to be necessary, we, to that extent, affirm its existence; on the other hand we deny a thing's existence, in so far as we conceive it not to be necessary (I. xxxiii. note. i.); wherefore (IV. ix.) an emotion towards that which is necessary is, other conditions being equal, more intense than an emotion that which is non — necessary. Q.E.D.

PROP. XII. An emotion towards a thing, which we know not to exist at the present time, and which we conceive as possible, is more intense, other conditions being equal, than an emotion towards a thing contingent.

Proof. — In so far as we conceive a thing as contingent, we are affected by the conception of some further thing, which would assert the existence of the former (IV. Def. iii.); but, on the other hand, we (by hypothesis) conceive certain things, which exclude its present existence. But, in so far as we conceive a thing to be possible in the future, we there by conceive things which assert its existence (IV. iv.), that is (III. xviii.), things which promote hope or fear: wherefore an emotion towards something possible is more vehement. Q.E.D.

Corollary. — An emotion towards a thing, which we know not to exist in the present, and which we conceive as contingent, is far fainter, than if we conceive the thing to be present with us.

Proof. — Emotion towards a thing, which we conceive to exist, is more intense than it would be, if we conceived the thing as future (IV. ix. Coroll.), and is much more vehement, than if the future time be conceived as far distant from the present (IV. x.). Therefore an emotion towards a thing, whose period of existence we conceive to be far distant from the present, is far fainter, than if we conceive the thing as present; it is, nevertheless, more intense, than if we conceived the thing as contingent, wherefore an emotion towards a thing, which we regard as contingent, will be far fainter, than if we conceived the thing to be present with us. Q.E.D.

PROP. XIII. Emotion towards a thing contingent, which we know not to exist in the present, is, other conditions being equal, fainter than an emotion towards a thing past.

Proof. — In so far as we conceive a thing as contingent, we are not affected by the image of any other thing, which asserts the existence of the said thing (IV. Def. iii.), but, on the other hand (by hypothesis), we conceive certain things excluding its present existence. But, in so far as we conceive it in relation to time past, we are assumed to conceive something, which recalls the thing to memory, or excites the image thereof (II. xviii. and note), which is so far the same as regarding it as present (II. xvii. Coroll.). Therefore (IV. ix.) an emotion towards a thing contingent, which we know does not exist in the present, is fainter, other conditions being equal, than an emotion towards a thing past. Q.E.D.

PROP. XIV. A true knowledge of good and evil cannot check any emotion by virtue of being true, but only in so far as it is considered as an emotion.

Proof. — An emotion is an idea, whereby the mind affirms of its body a greater or less force of existing than before (by the general Definition of the Emotions); therefore it has no positive quality, which can be destroyed by the presence of what is true; consequently the knowledge of good and evil cannot, by virtue of being true, restrain any emotion. But, in so far as such knowledge is an emotion (IV. viii.) if it have more strength for restraining emotion, it will to that extent be able to restrain the given emotion. Q.E.D.

PROP. XV. Desire arising from the knowledge of good and bad can be quenched or checked by many of the other desires arising from the emotions whereby we are assailed.

Proof. — From the true knowledge of good and evil, in so far as it is an emotion, necessarily arises desire (Def. of the Emotions, i.), the strength of which is proportioned to the strength of the emotion wherefrom it arises (III. xxxvii.). But, inasmuch as this desire arises (by hypothesis) from the fact of our truly understanding anything, it follows that it is also present with us, in so far as we are active (III. i.), and must therefore be understood through our essence only (III. Def. ii.); consequently (III. vii.) its force and increase can be defined solely by human power. Again, the desires arising from the emotions whereby we are assailed are stronger, in proportion as the said emotions are more vehement; wherefore their force and increase must be defined solely by the power of external causes, which, when compared with our own power, indefinitely surpass it (IV. iii.); hence the desires arising from like emotions may be more vehement, than the desire which arises from a true knowledge of good and evil, and may, consequently, control or quench it. Q.E.D.

PROP. XVI. Desire arising from the knowledge of good and evil, in so far as such knowledge regards what is future, may be more easily controlled or quenched, than the desire for what is agreeable at the present moment.

Proof. — Emotion towards a thing, which we conceive as future, is fainter than emotion towards a thing that is present (IV. ix. Coroll.). But desire, which arises from the true knowledge of good and evil, though it be concerned with things which are good at the moment, can be quenched or controlled by any headstrong desire (by the last Prop., the proof whereof is of universal application). Wherefore desire arising from such knowledge, when concerned with the future, can be more easily controlled or quenched, &c. Q.E.D.

PROP. XVII. Desire arising from the true knowledge of good and evil, in so far as such knowledge is concerned with what is contingent, can be controlled far more easily still, than desire for things that are present.

Proof. — This Prop. is proved in the same way as the last Prop. from IV. xii. Coroll.

Note. — I think I have now shown the reason, why men are moved by opinion more readily than by true reason, why it is that the true knowledge of good and evil stirs up conflicts in the soul, and often yields to every kind of passion. This state of things gave rise to the exclamation of the poet:12 — — "The better path I gaze at and approve, The worse — I follow."

12 Ov. Met. vii.20, "Video meliora proboque, Deteriora sequor."

Ecclesiastes seems to have had the same thought in his mind, when he says, "He who increaseth knowledge increaseth sorrow." I have not written the above with the object of drawing the conclusion, that ignorance is more excellent than knowledge, or that a wise man is on a par with a fool in controlling his emotions, but because it is necessary to know the power and the infirmity of our nature, before we can determine what reason can do in restraining the emotions, and what is beyond her power. I have said, that in the present part I shall merely treat of human infirmity. The power of reason over the emotions I have settled to treat separately.

PROP. XVIII. Desire arising from pleasure is, other conditions being equal, stronger than desire arising from pain.

Proof. — Desire is the essence of a man (Def. of the Emotions, i.), that is, the endeavour whereby a man endeavours to persist in his own being. Wherefore desire arising from pleasure is, by the fact of pleasure being felt, increased or helped; on the contrary, desire arising from pain is, by the fact of pain being felt, diminished or hindered; hence the force of desire arising from pleasure must be defined by human power together with the power of an external cause, whereas desire arising from pain must be defined by human power only. Thus the former is the stronger of the two. Q.E.D.

Note. — In these few remarks I have explained the causes of human infirmity and inconstancy, and shown why men do not abide by the precepts of reason. It now remains for me to show what course is marked out for us by reason, which of the emotions are in harmony with the rules of human reason, and which of them are contrary thereto. But, before I begin to prove my Propositions in detailed geometrical fashion, it is advisable to sketch them briefly in advance, so that everyone may more readily grasp my meaning.

As reason makes no demands contrary to nature, it demands, that every man should love himself, should seek that which is useful to him — I mean, that which is really useful to him, should desire everything which really brings man to greater perfection, and should, each for himself, endeavour as far as he can to preserve his own being. This is as necessarily true, as that a whole is greater than its part. (Cf. III. iv.)

Again, as virtue is nothing else but action in accordance with the laws of one's own nature (IV. Def. viii.), and as no one endeavours to preserve his own being, except in accordance with the laws of his own nature, it follows, first, that the foundation of virtue is the endeavour to preserve one's own being, and that happiness consists in man's power of preserving his own being; secondly, that virtue is to be desired for its own sake, and that there is nothing more excellent or more useful to us, for the sake of which we should desire it; thirdly and lastly, that suicides are weak — minded, and are overcome by external causes repugnant to their nature. Further, it follows from Postulate iv., Part II., that we can never arrive at doing without all external things for the preservation of our being or living, so as to have no relations with things which are outside ourselves. Again, if we consider our mind, we see that our intellect would be more imperfect, if mind were alone, and could understand nothing besides itself. There are, then, many things outside ourselves, which are useful to us, and are, therefore, to be desired. Of such none can be discerned more excellent, than those which are in entire agreement with our nature. For if, for example, two individuals of entirely the same nature are united, they form a combination twice as powerful as either of them singly.

Therefore, to man there is nothing more useful than man — nothing, I repeat, more excellent for preserving their being can be wished for by men, than that all should so in all points agree, that the minds and bodies of all should form, as it were, one single mind and one single body, and that all should, with one consent, as far as they are able, endeavour to preserve their being, and all with one consent seek what is useful to them all. Hence, men who are governed by reason — that is, who seek what is useful to them in accordance with reason, desire for themselves nothing, which they do not also desire for the rest of mankind, and, consequently, are just, faithful, and honourable in their conduct.

Such are the dictates of reason, which I purposed thus briefly to indicate, before beginning to prove them in greater detail. I have taken this course, in order, if possible, to gain the attention of those who believe, that the principle that every man is bound to seek what is useful for himself is the foundation of impiety, rather than of piety and virtue.

Therefore, after briefly showing that the contrary is the case, I go on to prove it by the same method, as that whereby I have hitherto proceeded.

PROP. XIX. Every man, by the laws of his nature, necessarily desires or shrinks from that which he deems to be good or bad.

Proof. — The knowledge of good and evil is (IV. viii.) the emotion of pleasure or pain, in so far as we are conscious thereof; therefore, every man necessarily desires what he thinks good, and shrinks from what he thinks bad. Now this appetite is nothing else but man's nature or essence (Cf. the Definition of Appetite, III. ix.

note, and Def. of the Emotions, i.). Therefore, every man, solely by the laws of his nature, desires the one, and shrinks from the other, &c. Q.E.D.

PROP. XX. The more every man endeavours, and is able to seek what is useful to him — in other words, to preserve his own being — the more is he endowed with virtue; on the contrary, in proportion as a man neglects to seek what is useful to him, that is, to preserve his own being, he is wanting in power.

Proof. — Virtue is human power, which is defined solely by man's essence (IV. Def. viii.), that is, which is defined solely by the endeavour made by man to persist in his own being. Wherefore, the more a man endeavours, and is able to preserve his own being, the more is he endowed with virtue, and, consequently (III. iv. and vi.), in so far as a man neglects to preserve his own being, he is wanting in power. Q.E.D.

Note. — No one, therefore, neglects seeking his own good, or preserving his own being, unless he be overcome by causes external and foreign to his nature. No one, I say, from the necessity of his own nature, or otherwise than under compulsion from external causes, shrinks from food, or kills himself: which latter may be done in a variety of ways. A man, for instance, kills himself under the compulsion of another man, who twists round his right hand, wherewith he happened to have taken up a sword, and forces him to turn the blade against his own heart; or, again, he may be compelled, like Seneca, by a tyrant's command, to open his own veins — that is, to escape a greater evil by incurring, a lesser; or, lastly, latent external causes may so disorder his imagination, and so affect his body, that it may assume a nature contrary to its former one, and whereof the idea cannot exist in the mind (III. x.) But that a man, from the necessity of his own nature, should endeavour to become non — existent, is as impossible as that something should be made out of nothing, as everyone will see for himself, after a little reflection.

PROP. XXI. No one can desire to be blessed, to act rightly, and to live rightly, without at the same time wishing to be, act, and to live — in other words, to actually exist.

Proof. — The proof of this proposition, or rather the proposition itself, is self — evident, and is also plain from the definition of desire. For the desire of living, acting, &c., blessedly or rightly, is (Def. of the Emotions, i.) the essence of man — that is (III. vii.), the endeavour made by everyone to preserve his own being. Therefore, no one can desire, &c. Q.E.D.

PROP. XXII. No virtue can be conceived as prior to this endeavour to preserve one's own being.

Proof. — The effort for self — preservation is the essence of a thing (III. vii.); therefore, if any virtue could be conceived as prior thereto, the essence of a thing would have to be conceived as prior to itself, which is obviously absurd. Therefore no virtue, &c. Q.E.D.

Corollary. — The effort for self — preservation is the first and only foundation of virtue. For prior to this principle nothing can be conceived, and without it no virtue can be conceived.

PROP. XXIII. Man, in so far as he is determined to a particular action because he has inadequate ideas, cannot be absolutely said to act in obedience to virtue; he can only be so described, in so far as he is determined for the action because he understands.

Proof. — In so far as a man is determined to an action through having inadequate ideas, he is passive (III. i.), that is (III. Deff. i., and iii.), he does something, which cannot be perceived solely through his essence, that is (by IV. Def. viii.), which does not follow from his virtue. But, in so far as he is determined for an action because he understands, he is active; that is, he does something, which is perceived through his essence alone, or which adequately follows from his virtue. Q.E.D.

PROP. XXIV. To act absolutely in obedience to virtue is in us the same thing as to act, to live, or to preserve one's being (these three terms are identical in meaning) in accordance with the dictates of reason on the basis of seeking what is useful to one's self.

Proof. — To act absolutely in obedience to virtue is nothing else but to act according to the laws of one's own nature. But we only act, in so far as we understand (III. iii.): therefore to act in obedience to virtue is in us nothing else but to act, to live, or to preserve one's being in obedience to reason, and that on the basis of seeking what is useful for us (IV. xxii. Coroll.). Q.E.D.

PROP. XXV. No one wishes to preserve his being for the sake of anything else.

Proof. — The endeavour, wherewith everything endeavours to persist in its being, is defined solely by the essence of the thing itself (III. vii.); from this alone, and not from the essence of anything else, it necessarily follows (III. vi.) that everyone endeavours to preserve his being. Moreover, this proposition is plain from IV. xxii. Coroll., for if a man should endeavour to preserve his being for the sake of anything else, the last — named thing would obviously be the basis of virtue, which, by the foregoing corollary, is absurd. Therefore no one, &c. Q.E.D.

PROP. XXVI. Whatsoever we endeavour in obedience to reason is nothing further than to understand; neither does the mind, in so far as it makes use of reason, judge anything to be useful to it, save such things as are conducive to understanding.

Proof. — The effort for self — preservation is nothing else but the essence of the thing in question (III. vii.), which, in so far as it exists such as it is, is conceived to have force for continuing in existence (III. vi.) and doing such things as necessarily follow from its given nature (see the Def. of Appetite, III. ix. note). But the essence of reason is nought else but our mind, in so far as it clearly and distinctly understands (see the definition in II. xl. note. ii.); therefore (II. xl.) whatsoever we endeavour in obedience to reason is nothing else but to understand. Again, since this effort of the mind wherewith the mind endeavours, in so far as it reasons, to preserve its own being is nothing else but understanding; this effort at understanding is (IV. xxii. Coroll.) the first and single basis of virtue, nor shall we endeavour to understand things for the sake of any ulterior object (IV. xxv.); on the other hand, the mind, in so far as it reasons, will not be able to conceive any good for itself, save such things as are conducive to understanding.

PROP. XXVII. We know nothing to be certainly good or evil, save such things as really conduce to understanding, or such as are able to hinder us from understanding.

Proof. — The mind, in so far as it reasons, desires nothing beyond understanding, and judges nothing to be useful to itself, save such things as conduce to understanding (by the foregoing Prop.). But the mind (II. xli., xliii. and note) cannot possess certainty concerning anything, except in so far as it has adequate ideas, or (what by II. xl. note, is the same thing) in so far as it reasons. Therefore we know nothing to be good or evil save such things as really conduce, &c. Q.E.D.

PROP. XXVIII. The mind's highest good is the knowledge of God, and the mind's highest virtue is to know God.

Proof. — The mind is not capable of understanding anything higher than God, that is (I. Def. vi.), than a Being absolutely infinite, and without which (I. xv.) nothing can either be or be conceived; therefore (IV. xxvi. and xxvii.), the mind's highest utility or (IV. Def. i.) good is the knowledge of God. Again, the mind is active, only in so far as it understands, and only to the same extent can it be said absolutely to act virtuously. The mind's absolute virtue is therefore to understand. Now, as we have already shown, the highest that the mind can understand is God; therefore the highest virtue of the mind is to understand or to know God. Q.E.D.

PROP. XXIX. No individual thing, which is entirely different from our own nature, can help or check our power of activity, and absolutely nothing can do us good or harm, unless it has something in common with our nature.

Proof. — The power of every individual thing, and consequently the power of man, whereby he exists and operates, can only be determined by an individual thing (I. xxviii.), whose nature (II. vi.) must be understood through the same nature as that, through which human nature is conceived. Therefore our power of activity, however it be conceived, can be determined and consequently helped or hindered by the power of any other individual thing, which has something in common with us, but not by the power of anything, of which the nature is entirely different from our own; and since we call good or evil that which is the cause of pleasure or pain (IV. viii.), that is (III. xi. note), which increases or diminishes, helps or hinders, our power of activity; therefore, that which is entirely different from our nature can neither be to us good nor bad. Q.E.D.

PROP. XXX. A thing cannot be bad for us through the quality which it has in common with our nature, but it is bad for us in so far as it is contrary to our nature.

Proof. — We call a thing bad when it is the cause of pain (IV. viii.), that is (by the Def., which see in III. xi. note), when it diminishes or checks our power of action. Therefore, if anything were bad for us through that quality which it has in common with our nature, it would be able itself to diminish or check that which it has in common with our nature, which (III. iv.) is absurd. Wherefore nothing can be bad for us through that quality which it has in common with us, but, on the other hand, in so far as it is bad for us, that is (as we have just shown), in so far as it can diminish or check our power of action, it is contrary to our nature. Q.E.D.

PROP. XXXI. In so far as a thing is in harmony with our nature, it is necessarily good.

Proof. — In so far as a thing is in harmony with our nature, it cannot be bad for it. It will therefore necessarily be either good or indifferent. If it be assumed that it be neither good nor bad, nothing will follow from its nature (IV. Def. i.), which tends to the preservation of our nature, that is (by the hypothesis), which tends to the preservation of the thing itself; but this (III. vi.) is absurd; therefore, in so far as a thing is in harmony with our nature, it is necessarily good. Q.E.D.

Corollary. — Hence it follows, that, in proportion as a thing is in harmony with our nature, so is it more useful or better for us, and vice versâ, in proportion as a thing is more useful for us, so is it more in harmony with our nature. For, in so far as it is not in harmony with our nature, it will necessarily be different therefrom or contrary thereto. If different, it can neither be good nor bad (IV. xxix.); if contrary, it will be contrary to that which is in harmony with our nature, that is, contrary to what is good — in short, bad. Nothing, therefore, can be good, except in so far as it is in harmony with our nature; and hence a thing is useful, in proportion as it is in harmony with our nature, and vice versâ. Q.E.D.

PROP. XXXII. In so far as men are a prey to passion, they cannot, in that respect, be said to be naturally in harmony.

Proof. — Things, which are said to be in harmony naturally, are understood to agree in power (III. vii.), not in want of power or negation, and consequently not in passion (III. iii. note); wherefore men, in so far as they are a prey to their passions, cannot be said to be naturally in harmony. Q.E.D.

Note. — This is also self — evident; for, if we say that white and black only agree in the fact that neither is red, we absolutely affirm that the do not agree in any respect. So, if we say that a man and a stone only agree in the fact that both are finite — wanting in power, not existing by the necessity of their own nature, or, lastly, indefinitely surpassed by the power of external causes — we should certainly affirm that a man and a stone are in no respect alike; therefore, things which agree only in negation, or in qualities which neither possess, really agree in no respect.

PROP. XXXIII. Men can differ in nature, in so far as they are assailed by those emotions, which are passions, or passive states; and to this extent one and the same man is variable and inconstant.

Proof. — The nature or essence of the emotions cannot be explained solely through our essence or nature (III. Deff. i., ii.), but it must be defined by the power, that is (III. vii.), by the nature of external causes in comparison with our own; hence it follows, that there are as many kinds of each emotion as there are external objects whereby we are affected (III. lvi.), and that men may be differently affected by one and the same object (III. li.), and to this extent differ in nature; lastly, that one and the same man may be differently affected towards the same object, and may therefore be variable and inconstant. Q.E.D.

PROP. XXXIV. In so far as men are assailed by emotions which are passions, they can be contrary one to another.

Proof. — A man, for instance Peter, can be the cause of Paul's feeling pain, because he (Peter) possesses something similar to that which Paul hates (III. xvi.), or because Peter has sole possession of a thing which Paul also loves (III. xxxii. and note), or for other causes (of which the chief are enumerated in III. lv. note); it may therefore happen that Paul should hate Peter (Def. of Emotions, vii.), consequently it may easily happen also, that Peter should hate Paul in return, and that each should endeavour to do the other an injury, (III. xxxix.), that is (IV. xxx.), that they should be contrary one to another. But the emotion of pain is always a passion or passive state (III. lix.); hence men, in so far as they are assailed by emotions which are passions, can be contrary one to another. Q.E.D.

Note. — I said that Paul may hate Peter, because he conceives that Peter possesses something which he (Paul) also loves; from this it seems, at first sight, to follow, that these two men, through both loving the same thing, and, consequently, through agreement of their respective natures, stand in one another's way; if this were so, Props. xxx. and xxxi. of this part would be untrue. But if we give the matter our unbiased attention, we shall see that the discrepancy vanishes. For the two men are not in one another's way in virtue of the agreement of their natures, that is, through both loving the same thing, but in virtue of one differing from the other. For, in so far as each loves the same thing, the love of each is fostered thereby (III. xxxi.), that is (Def. of the Emotions, vi.) the pleasure of each is fostered thereby. Wherefore it is far from being the case, that they are at variance through both loving the same thing, and through the agreement in their natures. The cause for their opposition lies, as I have said, solely in the fact that they are assumed to differ. For we assume that Peter has the idea of the loved object as already in his possession, while Paul has the idea of the loved object as lost. Hence the one man will be affected with pleasure, the other will be affected with pain, and thus they will be at variance one with another. We can easily show in like manner, that all other causes of hatred depend solely on differences, and not on the agreement between men's natures.

PROP. XXXV. In so far only as men live in obedience to reason, do they always necessarily agree in nature.

Proof. — In so far as men are assailed by emotions that are passions, they can be different in nature (IV. xxxiii.), and at variance one with another. But men are only said to be active, in so far as they act in obedience to reason (III. iii.); therefore, what so ever follows from human nature in so far as it is defined by reason must (III. Def. ii.) be understood solely through human nature as its proximate cause. But, since every man by the laws of his nature desires that which he deems good, and endeavours to remove that which he deems bad (IV. xix.); and further, since that which we, in accordance with reason, deem good or bad, necessarily is good or bad (II. xli.); it follows that men, in so far as they live in obedience to reason, necessarily do only such things as are necessarily good for human nature, and consequently for each individual man (IV. xxxi. Coroll.); in other words, such things as are in harmony with each man's nature. Therefore, men in so far as they live in obedience to reason, necessarily live always in harmony one with another. Q.E.D.

Corollary I. — There is no individual thing in nature, which is more useful to man, than a man who lives in obedience to reason. For that thing is to man most useful, which is most in harmony with his nature (IV. xxxi. Coroll.); that is, obviously, man. But man acts absolutely according to the laws of his nature, when he lives in obedience to reason (III. Def. ii.), and to this extent only is always necessarily in harmony with the nature of another man (by the last Prop.); wherefore among individual things nothing is more useful to man, than a man who lives in obedience to reason. Q.E.D.

Corollary II. — As every man seeks most that which is useful to him, so are men most useful one to another. For the more a man seeks what is useful to him and endeavours to preserve himself, the more is he endowed with virtue (IV. xx.), or, what is the same thing (IV. Def. viii.), the more is he endowed with power to act according to the laws of his own nature, that is to live in obedience to reason. But men are most in natural harmony, when they live in obedience to reason (by the last Prop.); therefore (by the foregoing Coroll.) men will be most useful one to another, when each seeks most that which is useful to him. Q.E.D.

Note. — What we have just shown is attested by experience so conspicuously, that it is in the mouth of nearly everyone: "Man is to man a God." Yet it rarely happens that men live in obedience to reason, for things are so ordered among them, that they are generally envious and troublesome one to another. Nevertheless they are scarcely able to lead a solitary life, so that the definition of man as a social animal has met with general assent; in fact, men do derive from social life much more convenience than injury. Let satirists then laugh their fill at human affairs, let theologians rail, and let misanthropes praise to their utmost the life of untutored rusticity, let them heap contempt on men and praises on beasts; when all is said, they will find that men can provide for their wants much more easily by mutual help, and that only by uniting their forces can they escape from the dangers that on every side beset them: not to say how much more excellent and worthy of our knowledge it is, to study the actions of men than the actions of beasts. But I will treat of this more at length elsewhere.

PROP. XXXVI. The highest good of those who follow virtue is common to all, and therefore all can equally rejoice therein.

Proof. — To act virtuously is to act in obedience with reason (IV. xxiv.), and whatsoever we endeavour to do in obedience to reason is to understand (IV. xxvi.); therefore (IV. xxviii.) the highest good for those who follow after virtue is to know God; that is (II. xlvii. and note) a good which is common to all and can be possessed by all men equally, in so far as they are of the same nature. Q.E.D.

Note. — Someone may ask how it would be, if the highest good of those who follow after virtue were not common to all? Would it not then follow, as above (IV. xxxiv.), that men living in obedience to reason, that is (IV. xxxv.), men in so far as they agree in nature, would be at variance one with another? To such an inquiry, I make answer, that it follows not accidentally but from the very nature of reason, that main's highest good is common to all, inasmuch as it is deduced from the very essence of man, in so far as defined by reason; and that a man could neither be, nor be conceived without the power of taking pleasure in this highest good. For it belongs to the essence of the human mind (II. xlvii.), to have an adequate knowledge of the eternal and infinite essence of God.

PROP. XXXVII. The good which every man, who follows after virtue, desires for himself he will also desire for other men, and so much the more, in proportion as he has a greater knowledge of God.

Proof. — Men, in so far as they live in obedience to reason, are most useful to their fellow men (IV. xxxv; Coroll. i.); therefore (IV. xix.), we shall in obedience to reason necessarily endeavour to bring about that men should live in obedience to reason. But the good which every man, in so far as he is guided by reason, or, in other words, follows after virtue, desires for himself, is to understand (IV. xxvi.); wherefore the good, which each follower of virtue seeks for himself, he will desire also for others. Again, desire, in so far as it is referred to the mind, is the very essence of the mind (Def. of the Emotions, i.); now the essence of the mind consists in knowledge (II. xi.), which involves the knowledge of God (II. xlvii.), and without it (I. xv.), can neither be, nor be conceived; therefore, in proportion as the mind's essence involves a greater knowledge of God, so also will be greater the desire of the follower of virtue, that other men should possess that which he seeks as good for himself. Q.E.D.

Another Proof. — The good, which a man desires for himself and loves, he will love more constantly, if he sees that others love it also (III. xxxi.); he will therefore endeavour that others should love it also; and as the good in question is common to all, and therefore all can rejoice therein, he will endeavour, for the same reason, to bring about that all should rejoice therein, and this he will do the more (III. xxxvii.), in proportion as his own enjoyment of the good is greater.

Note I. — He who, guided by emotion only, endeavours to cause others to love what he loves himself, and to make the rest of the world live according to his own fancy, acts solely by impulse, and is, therefore, hateful, especially, to those who take delight in something different, and accordingly study and, by similar impulse, endeavour, to make men live in accordance with what pleases themselves. Again, as the highest good sought by men under the guidance of emotion is often such, that it can only be possessed by a single individual, it follows that those who love it are not consistent in their intentions, but, while they delight to sing its praises, fear to be believed. But he, who endeavours to lead men by reason, does not act by impulse but courteously and kindly, and his intention is always consistent. Again, whatsoever we desire and do, whereof we are the cause in so far as we possess the idea of God, or know God, I set down to Religion. The desire of well — doing, which is engendered by a life according to reason, I call piety. Further, the desire, whereby a man living according to reason is bound to associate others with himself in friendship, I call honour13; by honourable I mean that which is praised by men living according to reason, and by base I mean that which is repugnant to the gaining of friendship. I have also shown in addition what are the foundations of a state; and the difference between true virtue and infirmity may be readily gathered from what I have said; namely, that true virtue is nothing else but living in accordance with reason; while infirmity is nothing else but man's allowing himself to be led by things which are external to himself, and to be by them determined to act in a manner demanded by the general disposition of things rather than by his own nature considered solely in itself.

13 Honestas

Such are the matters which I engaged to prove in Prop. xviii. of this Part, whereby it is plain that the law against the slaughtering of animals is founded rather on vain superstition and womanish pity than on sound reason. The rational quest of what is useful to us further teaches us the necessity of associating ourselves with our fellow men, but not with beasts, or things, whose nature is different from our own; we have the same rights in respect to them as they have in respect to us. Nay, as everyone's right is defined by his virtue, or power, men have far greater rights over beasts than beasts have over men. Still I do not deny that beasts feel: what I deny is, that we may not consult our own advantage and use them as we please, treating them in the way which best suits us; for their nature is not like ours, and their emotions are naturally different from human emotions (III. lvii. note). It remains for me to explain what I mean by just and unjust, sin and merit. On these points see the following note.

Note II. — In the Appendix to Part I. I undertook to explain praise and blame, merit and sin, justice and injustice.

Concerning praise and blame I have spoken in III. xxix. note: the time has now come to treat of the remaining terms. But I must first say a few words concerning man in the state of nature and in society.

Every man exists by sovereign natural right, and, consequently, by sovereign natural right performs those actions which follow from the necessity of his own nature; therefore by sovereign natural right every man judges what is good and what is bad, takes care of his own advantage according to his own disposition (IV. xix. and IV. xx.), avenges the wrongs done to him (III. xl. Coroll. ii.), and endeavours to preserve that which he loves and to destroy that which he hates (III. xxviii.). Now, if men lived under the guidance of reason, everyone would remain in possession of this his right, without any injury being done to his neighbour (IV. xxxv. Coroll. i.). But seeing that they are a prey to their emotions, which far surpass human power or virtue (IV. vi.), they are often drawn in different directions, and being at variance one with another (IV. xxxiii. xxxiv.), stand in need of mutual help (IV. xxxv. note). Wherefore, in order that men may live together in harmony, and may aid one another, it is necessary that they should forego their natural right, and, for the sake of security, refrain from all actions which can injure their fellow — men. The way in which this end can be obtained, so that men who are necessarily a prey to their emotions (IV. iv. Coroll.), inconstant, and diverse, should be able to render each other mutually secure, and feel mutual trust, is evident from IV. vii. and III. xxxix. It is there shown, that an emotion can only be restrained by an emotion stronger than, and contrary to itself, and that men avoid inflicting injury through fear of incurring a greater injury themselves.

On this law society can be established, so long as it keeps in its own hand the right, possessed by everyone, of avenging injury, and pronouncing on good and evil; and provided it also possesses the power to lay down a general rule of conduct, and to pass laws sanctioned, not by reason, which is powerless in restraining emotion, but by threats (IV. xvii. note). Such a society established with laws and the power of preserving itself is called a State, while those who live under its protection are called citizens. We may readily understand that there is in the state of nature nothing, which by universal consent is pronounced good or bad; for in the state of nature everyone thinks solely of his own advantage, and according to his disposition, with reference only to his individual advantage, decides what is good or bad, being bound by no law to anyone besides himself.

In the state of nature, therefore, sin is inconceivable; it can only exist in a state, where good and evil are pronounced on by common consent, and where everyone is bound to obey the State authority. Sin, then, is nothing else but disobedience, which is therefore punished by the right of the State only. Obedience, on the other hand, is set down as merit, inasmuch as a man is thought worthy of merit, if he takes delight in the advantages which a State provides.

Again, in the state of nature, no one is by common consent master of anything, nor is there anything in nature, which can be said to belong to one man rather than another: all things are common to all. Hence, in the state of nature, we can conceive no wish to render to every man his own, or to deprive a man of that which belongs to him; in other words, there is nothing in the state of nature answering to justice and injustice. Such ideas are only possible in a social state, when it is decreed by common consent what belongs to one man and what to another.

From all these considerations it is evident, that justice and injustice, sin and merit, are extrinsic ideas, and not attributes which display the nature of the mind. But I have said enough.

PROP. XXXVIII. Whatsoever disposes the human body, so as to render it capable of being affected in an increased number of ways, or of affecting external bodies in an increased number of ways, is useful to man; and is so, in proportion as the body is thereby rendered more capable of being affected or affecting other bodies in an increased number of ways; contrariwise, whatsoever renders the body less capable in this respect is hurtful to man.

Proof. — Whatsoever thus increases the capabilities of the body increases also the mind's capability of perception (II. xiv.); therefore, whatsoever thus disposes the body and thus renders it capable, is necessarily good or useful (IV. xxvi. xxvii.); and is so in proportion to the extent to which it can render the body capable; contrariwise (II. xiv., IV. xxvi. xxvii.), it is hurtful, if it renders the body in this respect less capable. Q.E.D.

PROP. XXXIX. Whatsoever brings about the preservation of the proportion of motion and rest, which the parts of the human body mutually possess, is good; contrariwise, whatsoever causes a change in such proportion is bad.

Proof. — The human body needs many other bodies for its preservation (II. Post. iv.). But that which constitutes the specific reality (forma) of a human body is, that its parts communicate their several motions one to another in a certain fixed proportion (Def. before Lemma iv. after II. xiii.). Therefore, whatsoever brings about the preservation of the proportion between motion and rest, which the parts of the human body mutually possess, preserves the specific reality of the human body, and consequently renders the human body capable of being affected in many ways and of affecting external bodies in many ways; consequently it is good (by the last Prop.). Again, whatsoever brings about a change in the aforesaid proportion causes the human body to assume another specific character, in other words (see Preface to this Part towards the end, though the point is indeed self — evident), to be destroyed, and consequently totally incapable of being affected in an increased numbers of ways; therefore it is bad. Q.E.D.

Note. — The extent to which such causes can injure or be of service to the mind will be explained in the Fifth Part. But I would here remark that I consider that a body undergoes death, when the proportion of motion and rest which obtained mutually among its several parts is changed. For I do not venture to deny that a human body, while keeping the circulation of the blood and other properties, wherein the life of a body is thought to consist, may none the less be changed into another nature totally different from its own. There is no reason, which compels me to maintain that a body does not die, unless it becomes a corpse; nay, experience would seem to point to the opposite conclusion. It sometimes happens, that a man undergoes such changes, that I should hardly call him the same. As I have heard tell of a certain Spanish poet, who had been seized with sickness, and though he recovered therefrom yet remained so oblivious of his past life, that he would not believe the plays and tragedies he had written to be his own: indeed, he might have been taken for a grown — up child, if he had also forgotten his native tongue. If this instance seems incredible, what shall we say of infants? A man of ripe age deems their nature so unlike his own, that he can only be persuaded that he too has been an infant by the analogy of other men. However, I prefer to leave such questions undiscussed, lest I should give ground to the superstitious for raising new issues.

PROP. XL. Whatsoever conduces to man's social life, or causes men to live together in harmony, is useful, whereas whatsoever brings discord into a State is bad.

Proof. — For whatsoever causes men to live together in harmony also causes them to live according to reason (IV. xxxv.), and is therefore (IV. xxvi. xxvii.) good, and (for the same reason) whatsoever brings about discord is bad. Q.E.D.

PROP. XLI. Pleasure in itself is not bad but good: contrariwise, pain in itself is bad.

Proof. — Pleasure (III. xi. and note) is emotion, whereby the body's power of activity is increased or helped; pain is emotion, whereby the body's power of activity is diminished or checked; therefore (IV. xxxviii.) pleasure in itself is good, &c. Q.E.D.

PROP. XLII. Mirth cannot be excessive, but is always good; contrariwise, Melancholy is always bad.

Proof. — Mirth (see its Def. in III. xi. note) is pleasure, which, in so far as it is referred to the body, consists in all parts of the body being affected equally: that is (III. xi.), the body's power of activity is increased or aided in such a manner, that the several parts maintain their former proportion of motion and rest; therefore Mirth is always good (IV. xxxix.), and cannot be excessive. But Melancholy (see its Def. in the same note to III. xi.) is pain, which, in so far as it is referred to the body, consists in the absolute decrease or hindrance of the body's power of activity; therefore (IV. xxxviii.) it is always bad. Q.E.D.

PROP. XLIII. Stimulation may be excessive and bad; on the other hand, grief may be good, in so far as stimulation or pleasure is bad.

Proof. — Localized pleasure or stimulation (titillatio) is pleasure, which, in so far as it is referred to the body, consists in one or some of its parts being affected more than the rest (see its Definition, III. xi. note); the power of this emotion may be sufficient to overcome other actions of the body (IV. vi.), and may remain obstinately fixed therein, thus rendering it incapable of being affected in a variety of other ways: therefore (IV. xxxviii.) it may be bad. Again, grief, which is pain, cannot as such be good (IV. xli.). But, as its force and increase is defined by the power of an external cause compared with our own (IV. v.), we can conceive infinite degrees and modes of strength in this emotion (IV. iii.); we can, therefore, conceive it as capable of restraining stimulation, and preventing its becoming excessive, and hindering the body's capabilities; thus, to this extent, it will be good. Q.E.D.

PROP. XLIV. Love and desire may be excessive.

Proof. — Love is pleasure, accompanied by the idea of an external cause (Def. of Emotions, vi.); therefore stimulation, accompanied by the idea of an external cause is love (III. xi. note); hence love maybe excessive. Again, the strength of desire varies in proportion to the emotion from which it arises (III. xxxvii.). Now emotion may overcome all the rest of men's actions (IV. vi.); so, therefore, can desire, which arises from the same emotion, overcome all other desires, and become excessive, as we showed in the last proposition concerning stimulation.

Note. — Mirth, which I have stated to be good, can be conceived more easily than it can be observed. For the emotions, whereby we are daily assailed, are generally referred to some part of the body which is affected more than the rest; hence the emotions are generally excessive, and so fix the mind in the contemplation of one object, that it is unable to think of others; and although men, as a rule, are a prey to many emotions — and very few are found who are always assailed by one and the same — yet there are cases, where one and the same emotion remains obstinately fixed. We sometimes see men so absorbed in one object, that, although it be not present, they think they have it before them; when this is the case with a man who is not asleep, we say he is delirious or mad; nor are those persons who are inflamed with love, and who dream all night and all day about nothing but their mistress, or some woman, considered as less mad, for they are made objects of ridicule. But when a miser thinks of nothing but gain or money, or when an ambitious man thinks of nothing but glory, they are not reckoned to be mad, because they are generally harmful, and are thought worthy of being hated. But, in reality, Avarice, Ambition, Lust, &c., are species of madness, though they may not be reckoned among diseases.

PROP. XLV. Hatred can never be good.

Proof. — When we hate a man, we endeavour to destroy him (III. xxxix.), that is (IV. xxxvii.), we endeavour to do something that is bad. Therefore, &c. Q.E.D.

N.B. Here, and in what follows, I mean by hatred only hatred towards men.

Corollary I. — Envy, derision, contempt, anger, revenge, and other emotions attributable to hatred, or arising therefrom, are bad; this is evident from III. xxxix. and IV. xxxvii.

Corollary II. — Whatsoever we desire from motives of hatred is base, and in a State unjust. This also is evident from III. xxxix., and from the definitions of baseness and injustice in IV. xxxvii. note.

Note. — Between derision (which I have in Coroll. I. stated to be bad) and laughter I recognize a great difference. For laughter, as also jocularity, is merely pleasure; therefore, so long as it be not excessive, it is in itself good (IV. xli.). Assuredly nothing forbids man to enjoy himself, save grim and gloomy superstition. For why is it more lawful to satiate one's hunger and thirst than to drive away one's melancholy? I reason, and have convinced myself as follows: No deity, nor anyone else, save the envious, takes pleasure in my infirmity and discomfort, nor sets down to my virtue the tears, sobs, fear, and the like, which axe signs of infirmity of spirit; on the contrary, the greater the pleasure wherewith we are affected, the greater the perfection whereto we pass; in other words, the more must we necessarily partake of the divine nature. Therefore, to make use of what comes in our way, and to enjoy it as much as possible (not to the point of satiety, for that would not be enjoyment) is the part of a wise man. I say it is the part of a wise man to refresh and recreate himself with moderate and pleasant food and drink, and also with perfumes, with the soft beauty of growing plants, with dress, with music, with many sports, with theatres, and the like, such as every man may make use of without injury to his neighbour. For the human body is composed of very numerous parts, of diverse nature, which continually stand in need of fresh and varied nourishment, so that the whole body may be equally capable of performing all the actions, which follow from the necessity of its own nature; and, consequently, so that the mind may also be equally capable of understanding many things simultaneously. This way of life, then, agrees best with our principles, and also with general practice; therefore, if there be any question of another plan, the plan we have mentioned is the best, and in every way to be commended. There is no need for me to set forth the matter more clearly or in more detail.

PROP. XLVI. He, who lives under the guidance of reason, endeavours, as far as possible, to render back love, or kindness, for other men's hatred, anger, contempt, &c., towards him.

Proof. — All emotions of hatred are bad (IV. xlv. Coroll. i.); therefore he who lives under the guidance of reason will endeavour, as far as possible, to avoid being assailed by such emotions (IV. xix.); consequently, he will also endeavour to prevent others being so assailed (IV. xxxvii.). But hatred is increased by being reciprocated, and can be quenched by love (III. xliii.), so that hatred may pass into love (III. xliv.); therefore he who lives under the guidance of reason will endeavour to repay hatred with love, that is, with kindness. Q.E.D.

Note. — He who chooses to avenge wrongs with hatred is assuredly wretched. But he, who strives to conquer hatred with love, fights his battle in joy and confidence; he withstands many as easily as one, and has very little need of fortune's aid. Those whom he vanquishes yield joyfully, not through failure, but through increase in their powers; all these consequences follow so plainly from the mere definitions of love and understanding, that I have no need to prove them in detail.

PROP. XLVII. Emotions of hope and fear cannot be in themselves good.

Proof. — Emotions of hope and fear cannot exist without pain. For fear is pain (Def. of the Emotions, xiii.), and hope (Def. of the Emotions, Explanation xii. and xiii.) cannot exist without fear; therefore (IV. xli.) these emotions cannot be good in themselves, but only in so far as they can restrain excessive pleasure (IV. xliii.). Q.E.D.

Note. — We may add, that these emotions show defective knowledge and an absence of power in the mind; for the same reason confidence, despair, joy, and disappointment are signs of a want of mental power. For although confidence and joy are pleasurable emotions, they nevertheless imply a preceding pain, namely, hope and fear. Wherefore the more we endeavour to be guided by reason, the less do we depend on hope; we endeavour to free ourselves from fear, and, as far as we can, to dominate fortune, directing our actions by the sure counsels of wisdom.

PROP. XLVIII. The emotions of over — esteem and disparagement are always bad.

Proof. — These emotions (see Def. of the Emotions, xxi. xxii.) are repugnant to reason; and are therefore (IV. xxvi. xxvii.) bad. Q.E.D.

PROP. XLIX. Over — esteem is apt to render its object proud.

Proof. — If we see that any one rates us too highly, for love's sake, we are apt to become elated (III. xli.), or to be pleasurably affected (Def. of the Emotions, xxx.); the good which we hear of ourselves we readily believe (III. xxv.); and therefore, for love's sake, rate ourselves too highly; in other words, we are apt to become proud. Q.E.D.

PROP. L. Pity, in a man who lives under the guidance of reason, is in itself bad and useless.

Proof. — Pity (Def. of the Emotions, xviii.) is a pain, and therefore (IV. xli.) is in itself bad. The good effect which follows, namely, our endeavour to free the object of our pity from misery, is an action which we desire to do solely at the dictation of reason (IV. xxxvii.); only at the dictation of reason are we able to perform any action, which we know for certain to be good (IV. xxvii.); thus, in a man who lives under the guidance of reason, pity in itself is useless and bad. Q.E.D.

Note. — He who rightly realizes, that all things follow from the necessity of the divine nature, and come to pass in accordance with the eternal laws and rules of nature, will not find anything worthy of hatred, derision, or contempt, nor will he bestow pity on anything, but to the utmost extent of human virtue he will endeavour to do well, as the saying is, and to rejoice. We may add, that he, who is easily touched with compassion, and is moved by another's sorrow or tears, often does something which he afterwards regrets; partly because we can never be sure that an action caused by emotion is good, partly because we are easily deceived by false tears. I am in this place expressly speaking of a man living under the guidance of reason. He who is moved to help others neither by reason nor by compassion, is rightly styled inhuman, for (III. xxvii.) he seems unlike a man.

PROP. LI. Approval is not repugnant to reason, but can agree therewith and arise therefrom.

Proof. — Approval is love towards one who has done good to another (Def. of the Emotions, xix.); therefore it may be referred to the mind, in so far as the latter is active (III. lix.), that is (III. iii.), in so far as it understands; therefore, it is in agreement with reason, &c. Q.E.D.

Another Proof. — He, who lives under the guidance of reason, desires for others the good which he seeks for himself (IV. xxxvii.); wherefore from seeing someone doing good to his fellow his own endeavour to do good is aided; in other words, he will feel pleasure (III. xi. note) accompanied by the idea of the benefactor. Therefore he approves of him. Q.E.D.

Note. — Indignation as we defined it (Def. of the Emotions, xx.) is necessarily evil (IV. xlv.); we may, however, remark that, when the sovereign power for the sake of preserving peace punishes a citizen who has injured another, it should not be said to be indignant with the criminal, for it is not incited by hatred to ruin him, it is led by a sense of duty to punish him.

PROP. LII. Self — approval may arise from reason, and that which arises from reason is the highest possible.

Proof. — Self — approval is pleasure arising from a man's contemplation of himself and his own power of action (Def. of the Emotions, xxv.). But a man's true power of action or virtue is reason herself (III. iii.), as the said man clearly and distinctly contemplates her (II. xl. xliii.); therefore self — approval arises from reason. Again, when a man is contemplating himself, he only perceived clearly and distinctly or adequately, such things as follow from his power of action (III. Def. ii.), that is (III. iii.), from his power of understanding; therefore in such contemplation alone does the highest possible self — approval arise. Q.E.D.

Note. — Self — approval is in reality the highest object for which we can hope. For (as we showed in IV. xxv.) no one endeavours to preserve his being for the sake of any ulterior object, and, as this approval is more and more fostered and strengthened by praise (III. liii. Coroll.), and on the contrary (III. lv. Coroll.) is more and more disturbed by blame, fame becomes the most powerful of incitements to action, and life under disgrace is almost unendurable.

PROP. LIII. Humility is not a virtue, or does not arise from reason.

Proof. — Humility is pain arising from a man's contemplation of his own infirmities (Def. of the Emotions, xxvi.). But, in so far as a man knows himself by true reason, he is assumed to understand his essence, that is, his power (III. vii.). Wherefore, if a man in self — contemplation perceives any infirmity in himself, it is not by virtue of his understanding himself, but (III. lv.) by virtue of his power of activity being checked. But, if we assume that a man perceives his own infirmity by virtue of understanding something stronger than himself, by the knowledge of which he determines his own power of activity, this is the same as saying that we conceive that a man understands himself distinctly (IV. xxvi.), because14 his power of activity is aided. Wherefore humility, or the pain which arises from a man's contemplation of his own infirmity, does not arise from the contemplation or reason, and is not a virtue but a passion. Q.E.D.

14 Land reads: "Quod ipsius agendi potentia juvatur" — which I have translated above. He suggests as alternative readings to 'quod', 'quo' (= whereby) and 'quodque' (= and that).

PROP. LIV. Repentance is not a virtue, or does not arise from reason; but he who repents of an action is doubly wretched or infirm.

Proof. — The first part of this proposition is proved like the foregoing one. The second part is proved from the mere definition of the emotion in question (Def. of the Emotions, xxvii.). For the man allows himself to be overcome, first, by evil desires; secondly, by pain.

Note. — As men seldom live under the guidance of reason, these two emotions, namely, Humility and Repentance, as also Hope and Fear, bring more good than harm; hence, as we must sin, we had better sin in that direction. For, if all men who are a prey to emotion were all equally proud, they would shrink from nothing, and would fear nothing; how then could they be joined and linked together in bonds of union? The crowd plays the tyrant, when it is not in fear; hence we need not wonder that the prophets, who consulted the good, not of a few, but of all, so strenuously commended Humility, Repentance, and Reverence. Indeed those who are a prey to these emotions may be led much more easily than others to live under the guidance of reason, that is, to become free and to enjoy the life of the blessed.

PROP. LV. Extreme pride or dejection indicates extreme ignorance of self.

Proof. — This is evident from Def. of the Emotions, xxviii. and xxix.

PROP. LVI. Extreme pride or dejection indicates extreme infirmity of spirit.

Proof. — The first foundation of virtue is self — preservation (IV. xxii. Coroll.) under the guidance of reason (IV. xxiv.). He, therefore, who is ignorant of himself, is ignorant of the foundation of all virtues, and consequently of all virtues. Again, to act virtuously is merely to act under the guidance of reason (IV. xxiv.): now he, that acts under the guidance of reason, must necessarily know that he so acts (II. xliii.). Therefore he who is in extreme ignorance of himself, and consequently of all virtues, acts least in obedience to virtue; in other words (IV. Def. viii.), is most infirm of spirit. Thus extreme pride or dejection indicates extreme infirmity of spirit. Q.E.D.

Corollary. — Hence it most clearly follows, that the proud and the dejected specially fall a prey to the emotions.

Note. — Yet dejection can be more easily corrected than pride; for the latter being a pleasurable emotion, and the former a painful emotion, the pleasurable is stronger than the painful (IV. xviii.).

PROP. LVII. The proud man delights in the company of flatterers and parasites, but hates the company of the high — minded.

Proof. — Pride is pleasure arising from a man's over estimation of himself (Def. of the Emotions, xxviii. and vi.); this estimation the proud man will endeavour to foster by all the means in his power (III. xiii. note); he will therefore delight in the company of flatterers and parasites (whose character is too well known to need definition here), and will avoid the company of high — minded men, who value him according to his deserts. Q.E.D.

Note. — It would be too long a task to enumerate here all the evil results of pride, inasmuch as the proud are a prey to all the emotions, though to none of them less than to love and pity. I cannot, however, pass over in silence the fact, that a man may be called proud from his underestimation of other people; and, therefore, pride in this sense may be defined as pleasure arising from the false opinion, whereby a man may consider himself superior to his fellows. The dejection, which is the opposite quality to this sort of pride, may be defined as pain arising from the false opinion, whereby a man may think himself inferior to his fellows. Such being the ease, we can easily see that a proud man is necessarily envious (III. xli. note), and only takes pleasure in the company, who fool his weak mind to the top of his bent, and make him insane instead of merely foolish.

Though dejection is the emotion contrary to pride, yet is the dejected man very near akin to the proud man. For, inasmuch as his pain arises from a comparison between his own infirmity and other men's power or virtue, it will be removed, or, in other words, he will feel pleasure, if his imagination be occupied in contemplating other men's faults; whence arises the proverb, "The unhappy are comforted by finding fellow — sufferers." Contrariwise, he will be the more pained in proportion as he thinks himself inferior to others; hence none are so prone to envy as the dejected, they are specially keen in observing men's actions, with a view to fault — finding rather than correction, in order to reserve their praises for dejection, and to glory therein, though all the time with a dejected air. These effects follow as necessarily from the said emotion, as it follows from the nature of a triangle, that the three angles are equal to two right angles. I have already said that I call these and similar emotions bad, solely in respect to what is useful to man. The laws of nature have regard to nature's general order, whereof man is but a part. I mention this, in passing, lest any should think that I have wished to set forth the faults and irrational deeds of men rather than the nature and properties of things. For, as I said in the preface to the third Part, I regard human emotions and their properties as on the same footing with other natural phenomena. Assuredly human emotions indicate the power and ingenuity, of nature, if not of human nature, quite as fully as other things which we admire, and which we delight to contemplate. But I pass on to note those qualities in the emotions, which bring advantage to man, or inflict injury upon him.

PROP. LVIII. Honour (gloria) is not repugnant to reason, but may arise therefrom.

Proof. — This is evident from Def. of the Emotions, xxx., and also from the definition of an honourable man (IV. xxxvii. note. i.).

Note — Empty honour, as it is styled, is self — approval, fostered only by the good opinion of the populace; when this good opinion ceases there ceases also the self — approval, in other words, the highest object of each man's love (IV. lii. note); consequently, he whose honour is rooted in popular approval must, day by day, anxiously strive, act, and scheme in order to retain his reputation. For the populace is variable and inconstant, so that, if a reputation be not kept up, it quickly withers away. Everyone wishes to catch popular applause for himself, and readily represses the fame of others. The object of the strife being estimated as the greatest of all goods, each combatant is seized with a fierce desire to put down his rivals in every possible way, till he who at last comes out victorious is more proud of having done harm to others than of having done good to himself. This sort of honour, then, is really empty, being nothing.

The points to note concerning shame may easily be inferred from what was said on the subject of mercy and repentance. I will only add that shame, like compassion, though not a virtue, is yet good, in so far as it shows, that the feeler of shame is really imbued with the desire to live honourably; in the same way as suffering is good, as showing that the injured part is not mortified. Therefore, though a man who feels shame is sorrowful, he is yet more perfect than he, who is shameless, and has no desire to live honourably.

Such are the points which I undertook to remark upon concerning the emotions of pleasure and pain; as for the desires, they are good or bad according as they spring from good or evil emotions. But all, in so far as they are engendered in us by emotions wherein the mind is passive, are blind (as is evident from what was said in IV. xliv. note), and would be useless, if men could easily, be induced to live by the guidance of reason only, as I will now briefly, show.

PROP. LIX. To all the actions, whereto we are determined by emotion wherein the mind is passive; we can be determined without emotion by reason.

Proof. — To act rationally, is nothing else (III. iii. and Def. ii.) but to perform those actions, which follow from the necessity, of our nature considered in itself alone. But pain is bad, in so far as it diminishes or checks the power of action (IV. xli.); wherefore we cannot by pain be determined to any action, which we should be unable to perform under the guidance of reason. Again, pleasure is bad only in so far as it hinders a man's capability for action (IV. xli. xliii.); therefore to this extent we could not be determined by it to any action, which we could not perform under the guidance of reason. Lastly, pleasure, in so far as it is good, is in harmony with reason (for it consists in the fact that a man's capability for action is increased or aided); nor is the mind passive therein, except in so far as a man's power of action is not increased to the extent of affording him an adequate conception of himself and his actions (III. iii., and note).

Wherefore, if a man who is pleasurably affected be brought to such a state of perfection, that he gains an adequate conception of himself and his own actions, he will be equally, nay more, capable of those actions, to which he is determined by emotion wherein the mind is passive. But all emotions are attributable to pleasure, to pain, or to desire (Def. of the Emotions, iv. explanation); and desire (Def. of the

Emotions, i.) is nothing else but the attempt to act; therefore, to all actions, &c. Q.E.D.

Another Proof. — A given action is called bad, in so far as it arises from one being affected by hatred or any evil emotion. But no action, considered in itself alone, is either good or bad (as we pointed out in the preface to Pt. IV.), one and the same action being sometimes good, sometimes bad; wherefore to the action which is sometimes bad, or arises from some evil emotion, we may be led by reason (IV. xix.). Q.E.D.

Note. — An example will put this point in a clearer light. The action of striking, in so far as it is considered physically, and in so far as we merely look to the fact that a man raises his arm, clenches his fist, and moves his whole arm violently downwards, is a virtue or excellence which is conceived as proper to the structure of the human body. If, then, a man, moved by anger or hatred, is led to clench his fist or to move his arm, this result takes place (as we showed in Pt. II.), because one and the same action can be associated with various mental images of things; therefore we may be determined to the performance of one and the same action by confused ideas, or by clear and distinct ideas. Hence it is evident that every desire which springs from emotion, wherein the mind is passive, would become useless, if men could be guided by reason. Let us now see why desire which arises from emotion, wherein the mind is passive, is called by us blind.

PROP. LX. Desire arising from a pleasure or pain, that is not attributable to the whole body, but only to one or certain parts thereof, is without utility in respect to a man as a whole.

Proof. — Let it be assumed, for instance, that A, a part of a body, is so strengthened by some external cause, that it prevails over the remaining parts (IV. vi.). This part will not endeavour to do away with its own powers, in order that the other parts of the body may perform its office; for this it would be necessary for it to have a force or power of doing away with its own powers, which (III. vi.) is absurd. The said part, and, consequently, the mind also, will endeavour to preserve its condition. Wherefore desire arising from a pleasure of the kind aforesaid has no utility in reference to a man as a whole. If it be assumed, on the other hand, that the part, A, be checked so that the remaining parts prevail, it may be proved in the same manner that desire arising from pain has no utility in respect to a man as a whole. Q.E.D.

Note. — As pleasure is generally (IV. xliv. note) attributed to one part of the body, we generally desire to preserve our being with out taking into consideration our health as a whole: to which it may be added, that the desires which have most hold over us (IV. ix.) take account of the present and not of the future.

PROP. LXI. Desire which springs from reason cannot be excessive.

Proof. — Desire (Def. of the Emotions, i.) considered absolutely is the actual essence of man, in so far as it is conceived as in any way determined to a particular activity by some given modification of itself. Hence desire, which arises from reason, that is (III. iii.), which is engendered in us in so far as we act, is the actual essence or nature of man, in so far as it is conceived as determined to such activities as are adequately conceived through man's essence only (III. Def. ii.). Now, if such desire could be excessive, human nature considered in itself alone would be able to exceed itself, or would be able to do more than it can, a manifest contradiction. Therefore, such desire cannot be excessive. Q.E.D.

PROP. LXII. In so far as the mind conceives a thing under the dictates of reason, it is affected equally, whether the idea be of a thing future, past, or present.

Proof. — Whatsoever the mind conceives under the guidance of reason, it conceives under the form of eternity or necessity (II. xliv. Coroll. ii.), and is therefore affected with the same certitude (II. xliii. and note). Wherefore, whether the thing be present, past, or future, the mind conceives it under the same necessity and is affected with the same certitude; and whether the idea be of something present, past, or future, it will in all cases be equally true (II. xli.); that is, it will always possess the same properties of an adequate idea (II. Def. iv.); therefore, in so far as the mind conceives things under the dictates of reason, it is affected in the same manner, whether the idea be of a thing future, past, or present. Q.E.D.

Note. — If we could possess an adequate knowledge of the duration of things, and could determine by reason their periods of existence, we should contemplate things future with the same emotion as things present; and the mind would desire as though it were present the good which it conceived as future; consequently it would necessarily neglect a lesser good in the present for the sake of a greater good in the future, and would in no wise desire that which is good in the present but a source of evil in the future, as we shall presently show. However, we can have but a very inadequate knowledge of the duration of things (II. xxxi.); and the periods of their existence (II. xliv. note.) we can only determine by imagination, which is not so powerfully affected by the future as by the present. Hence such true knowledge of good and evil as we possess is merely abstract or general, and the judgment which we pass on the order of things and the connection of causes, with a view to determining what is good or bad for us in the present, is rather imaginary than real. Therefore it is nothing wonderful, if the desire arising from such knowledge of good and evil, in so far as it looks on into the future, be more readily checked than the desire of things which are agreeable at the present time. (Cf. IV. xvi.)

PROP. LXIII. He who is led by fear, and does good in order to escape evil, is not led by reason.

Proof. — All the emotions which are attributable to the mind as active, or in other words to reason, are emotions of pleasure and desire (III. lix.); therefore, he who is led by fear, and does good in order to escape evil, is not led by reason.

Note. — Superstitions persons, who know better how to rail at vice than how to teach virtue, and who strive not to guide men by reason, but so to restrain them that they would rather escape evil than love virtue, have no other aim but to make others as wretched as themselves; wherefore it is nothing wonderful, if they be generally troublesome and odious to their fellow — men.

Corollary. — Under desire which springs from reason, we seek good directly, and shun evil indirectly.

Proof. — Desire which springs from reason can only spring from a pleasurable emotion, wherein the mind is not passive (III. lix.), in other words, from a pleasure which cannot be excessive (IV. lxi.), and not from pain; wherefore this desire springs from the knowledge of good, not of evil (IV. viii.); hence under the guidance of reason we seek good directly and only by implication shun evil.

Q.E.D.

Note. — This Corollary may be illustrated by the example of a sick and a healthy man. The sick man through fear of death eats what he naturally shrinks from, but the healthy man takes pleasure in his food, and thus gets a better enjoyment out of life, than if he were in fear of death, and desired directly to avoid it. So a judge, who condemns a criminal to death, not from hatred or anger but from love of the public well — being, is guided solely by reason.

PROP. LXIV. The knowledge of evil is an inadequate knowledge.

Proof. — The knowledge of evil (IV. viii.) is pain, in so far as we are conscious thereof. Now pain is the transition to a lesser perfection (Def. of the Emotions, iii.) and therefore cannot be understood through man's nature (III. vi., and vii.); therefore it is a passive state (III. Def. ii.) which (III. iii.) depends on inadequate ideas; consequently the knowledge thereof (II. xxix.), namely, the knowledge of evil, is inadequate. Q.E.D.

Corollary. — Hence it follows that, if the human mind possessed only adequate ideas, it would form no conception of evil.

PROP. LXV. Under the guidance of reason we should pursue the greater of two goods and the lesser of two evils.

Proof. — A good which prevents our enjoyment of a greater good is in reality an evil; for we apply the terms good and bad to things, in so far as we compare them one with another (see preface to this Part); therefore, evil is in reality a lesser good; hence under the guidance of reason we seek or pursue only the greater good and the lesser evil. Q.E.D.

Corollary. — We may, under the guidance of reason, pursue the lesser evil as though it were the greater good, and we may shun the lesser good, which would be the cause of the greater evil. For the evil, which is here called the lesser, is really good, and the lesser good is really evil, wherefore we may seek the former and shun the latter. Q.E.D.

PROP. LXVI. We may, under the guidance of reason, seek a greater good in the future in preference to a lesser good in the present, and we may seek a lesser evil in the present in preference to a greater evil in the future.15

15 "Maltim praesens minus prae majori futuro." (Van Vloten). Bruder reads: "Malum praesens minus, quod causa est faturi alicujus mali." The last word of the latter is an obvious misprint, and is corrected by the Dutch translator into "majoris boni." (Pollock, p. 268, note.)

Proof. — If the mind could have an adequate knowledge of things future, it would be affected towards what is future in the same way as towards what is present (IV. lxii.); wherefore, looking merely to reason, as in this proposition we are assumed to do, there is no difference, whether the greater good or evil be assumed as present, or assumed as future; hence (IV. lxv.) we may seek a greater good in the future in preference to a lesser good in the present, &c. Q.E.D.

Corollary. — We may, under the guidance of reason, seek a lesser evil in the present, because it is the cause of a greater good in the future, and we may shun a lesser good in the present, because it is the cause of a greater evil in the future. This Corollary is related to the foregoing Proposition as the Corollary to IV. lxv. is related to the said IV. lxv.

Note. — If these statements be compared with what we have pointed out concerning the strength of the emotions in this Part up to Prop. xviii., we shall readily see the difference between a man, who is led solely by emotion or opinion, and a man, who is led by reason. The former, whether will or no, performs actions whereof he is utterly ignorant; the latter is his own master and only performs such actions, as he knows are of primary importance in life, and therefore chiefly desires; wherefore I call the former a slave, and the latter a free man, concerning whose disposition and manner of life it will be well to make a few observations.

PROP. LXVII. A free man thinks of death least of all things; and his wisdom is a meditation not of death but of life.

Proof. — A free man is one who lives under the guidance of reason, who is not led by fear (IV. lxiii.), but who directly desires that which is good (IV. lxiii. Coroll.), in other words (IV. xxiv.), who strives to act, to live, and to preserve his being on the basis of seeking his own true advantage; wherefore such an one thinks of nothing less than of death, but his wisdom is a meditation of life. Q.E.D.

PROP. LXVIII. If men were born free, they would, so long as they remained free, form no conception of good and evil.

Proof. — I call free him who is led solely by reason; he, therefore, who is born free, and who remains free, has only adequate ideas; therefore (IV. lxiv. Coroll.) he has no conception of evil, or consequently (good and evil being correlative) of good. Q.E.D.

Note. — It is evident, from IV. iv., that the hypothesis of this Proposition is false and inconceivable, except in so far as we look solely to the nature of man, or rather to God; not in so far as the latter is infinite, but only in so far as he is the cause of man's existence.

This, and other matters which we have already proved, seem to have been signifieded by Moses in the history of the first man. For in that narrative no other power of God is conceived, save that whereby he created man, that is the power wherewith he provided solely for man's advantage; it is stated that God forbade man, being free, to eat of the tree of the knowledge of good and evil, and that, as soon as man should have eaten of it, he would straightway fear death rather than desire to live. Further, it is written that when man had found a wife, who was in entire harmony with his nature, he knew that there could be nothing in nature which could be more useful to him; but that after he believed the beasts to be like himself, he straightway began to imitate their emotions (III. xxvii.), and to lose his freedom; this freedom was afterwards recovered by the patriarchs, led by the spirit of Christ; that is, by the idea of God, whereon alone it depends, that man may be free, and desire for others the good which he desires for himself, as we have shown above (IV. xxxvii.).

PROP. LXIX. The virtue of a free man is seen to be as great, when it declines dangers, as when it overcomes them.

Proof. — Emotion can only be checked or removed by an emotion contrary to itself, and possessing more power in restraining emotion (IV. vii.). But blind daring and fear are emotions, which can be conceived as equally great (IV. v. and iii.): hence, no less virtue or firmness is required in checking daring than in checking fear (III. lix. note); in other words (Def. of the Emotions, xl. and xli.), the free man shows as much virtue, when he declines dangers, as when he strives to overcome them. Q.E.D.

Corollary. — The free man is as courageous in timely retreat as in combat; or, a free man shows equal courage or presence of mind, whether he elect to give battle or to retreat.

Note. — What courage (animositas) is, and what I mean thereby, I explained in III. lix. note. By danger I mean everything, which can give rise to any evil, such as pain, hatred, discord, &c.

PROP. LXX. The free man, who lives among the ignorant, strives, as far as he can, to avoid receiving favours from them.

Proof. — Everyone judges what is good according to his disposition (III. xxxix. note); wherefore an ignorant man, who has conferred a benefit on another, puts his own estimate upon it, and, if it appears to be estimated less highly by the receiver, will feel pain (III. xlii.). But the free man only desires to join other men to him in friendship (IV. xxxvii.), not repaying their benefits with others reckoned as of like value, but guiding himself and others by the free decision of reason, and doing only such things as he knows to be of primary importance. Therefore the free man, lest he should become hateful to the ignorant, or follow their desires rather than reason, will endeavour, as far as he can, to avoid receiving their favours.

Note. — I say, as far as he can. For though men be ignorant, yet are they men, and in cases of necessity could afford us human aid, the most excellent of all things: therefore it is often necessary to accept favours from them, and consequently to repay such favours in kind; we must, therefore, exercise caution in declining favours, lest we should have the appearance of despising those who bestow them, or of being, from avaricious motives, unwilling to requite them, and so give ground for offence by the very fact of striving to avoid it. Thus, in declining favours, we must look to the requirements of utility and courtesy.

PROP. LXXI. Only free men are thoroughly grateful one to another.

Proof. — Only free men are thoroughly useful one to another, and associated among themselves by the closest necessity of friendship (IV. xxxv., and Coroll. i.), only such men endeavour, with mutual zeal of love, to confer benefits on each other (IV. xxxvii.), and, therefore, only they are thoroughly grateful one to another. Q.E.D.

Note. — The goodwill, which men who are led by blind desire have for one another, is generally a bargaining or enticement, rather than pure goodwill. Moreover, ingratitude is not an emotion. Yet it is base, inasmuch as it generally shows, that a man is affected by excessive hatred, anger, pride, avarice, &c. He who, by reason of his folly, knows not how to return benefits, is not ungrateful, much less he who is not gained over by the gifts of a courtesan to serve her lust, or by a thief to conceal his thefts, or by any similar persons. Contrariwise, such an one shows a constant mind, inasmuch as he cannot by any gifts be corrupted, to his own or the general hurt.

PROP. LXXII. The free man never acts fraudulently, but always in good faith.

Proof. — If it be asked: What should a man's conduct be in a case where he could by breaking faith free himself from the danger of present death? Would not his plan of self — preservation completely persuade him to deceive? This may be answered by pointing out that, if reason persuaded him to act thus, it would persuade all men to act in a similar manner, in which case reason would persuade men not to agree in good faith to unite their forces, or to have laws in common, that is, not to have any general laws, which is absurd.

PROP. LXXIII. The man, who is guided by reason, is more free in a State, where he lives under a general system of law, than in solitude, where he is independent.

Proof. — The man, who is guided by reason, does not obey through fear (IV. lxiii.): but, in so far as he endeavours to preserve his being according to the dictates of reason, that is (IV. lxvi. note), in so far as he endeavours to live in freedom, he desires to order his life according to the general good (IV. xxxvii.), and, consequently (as we showed in IV. xxxvii. note. ii.), to live according to the laws of his country. Therefore the free man, in order to enjoy greater freedom, desires to possess the general rights of citizenship. Q.E.D.

Note. — These and similar observations, which we have made on man's true freedom, may be referred to strength, that is, to courage and nobility of character (III. lix. note). I do not think it worth while to prove separately all the properties of strength; much less need I show, that he that is strong hates no man, is angry with no man, envies no man, is indignant with no man, despises no man, and least of all things is proud. These propositions, and all that relate to the true way of life and religion, are easily proved from IV. xxxvii. and IV. xlvi.; namely, that hatred should be overcome with love, and that every man should desire for others the good which he seeks for himself. We may also repeat what we drew attention to in the note to IV. l., and in other places; namely, that the strong man has ever first in his thoughts, that all things follow from the necessity of the divine nature; so that whatsoever he deems to be hurtful and evil, and whatsoever, accordingly, seems to him impious, horrible, unjust, and base, assumes that appearance owing to his own disordered, fragmentary, and confused view of the universe. Wherefore he strives before all things to conceive things as they really are, and to remove the hindrances to true knowledge, such as are hatred, anger, envy, derision, pride, and similar emotions, which I have mentioned above. Thus he endeavours, as we said before, as far as in him lies, to do good, and to go on his way rejoicing. How far human virtue is capable of attaining to such a condition, and what its powers may be, I will prove in the following Part.

APPENDIX.

WHAT HAVE SAID in this Part concerning the right way of life has not been arranged, so as to admit of being seen at one view, but has been set forth piece — meal, according as I thought each Proposition could most readily be deduced from what preceded it. I propose, therefore, to rearrange my remarks and to bring them under leading heads.

I. All our endeavours or desires so follow from the necessity of our nature, that they can be understood either through it alone, as their proximate cause, or by virtue of our being a part of nature, which cannot be adequately conceived through itself without other individuals.

II. Desires, which follow from our nature in such a manner, that they can be understood through it alone, are those which are referred to the mind, in so far as the latter is conceived to consist of adequate ideas: the remaining desires are only referred to the mind, in so far as it conceives things inadequately, and their force and increase are generally defined not by the power of man, but by the power of things external to us: wherefore the former are rightly called actions, the latter passions, for the former always indicate our power, the latter, on the other hand, show our infirmity and fragmentary knowledge.

III. Our actions, that is, those desires which are defined by man's power or reason, are always good. The rest may be either good or bad.

IV. Thus in life it is before all things useful to perfect the understanding, or reason, as far as we can, and in this alone man's highest happiness or blessedness consists, indeed blessedness is nothing else but the contentment of spirit, which arises from the intuitive knowledge of God: now, to perfect the understanding is nothing else but to understand God, God's attributes, and the actions which follow from the necessity of his nature. Wherefore of a man, who is led by reason, the ultimate aim or highest desire, whereby he seeks to govern all his fellows, is that whereby he is brought to the adequate conception of himself and of all things within the scope of his intelligence.

V. Therefore, without intelligence there is not rational life: and things are only good, in so far as they aid man in his enjoyment of the intellectual life, which is defined by intelligence. Contrariwise, whatsoever things hinder man's perfecting of his reason, and capability to enjoy the rational life, are alone called evil.

VI. As all things whereof man is the efficient cause are necessarily good, no evil can befall man except through external causes; namely, by virtue of man being a part of universal nature, whose laws human nature is compelled to obey, and to conform to in almost infinite ways.

VII. It is impossible, that man should not be a part of nature, or that he should not follow her general order; but if he be thrown among individuals whose nature is in harmony with his own, his power of action will thereby be aided and fostered, whereas, if he be thrown among such as are but very little in harmony with his nature, he will hardly be able to accommodate himself to them without undergoing a great change himself.

VIII. Whatsoever in nature we deem to be evil, or to be capable of injuring our faculty for existing and enjoying the rational life, we may endeavour to remove in whatever way seems safest to us; on the other hand, whatsoever we deem to be good or useful for preserving our being, and enabling us to enjoy the rational life, we may appropriate to our use and employ as we think best. Everyone without exception may, by sovereign right of nature, do whatsoever he thinks will advance his own interest.

IX. Nothing can be in more harmony with the nature of any given thing than other individuals of the same species; therefore (cf. vii.) for man in the preservation of his being and the enjoyment of the rational life there is nothing more useful than his fellow — man who is led by reason. Further, as we know not anything among individual things which is more excellent than a man led by reason, no man can better display the power of his skill and disposition, than in so training men, that they come at last to live under the dominion of their own reason.

X. In so far as men are influenced by envy or any kind of hatred, one towards another, they are at variance, and are therefore to be feared in proportion, as they are more powerful than their fellows.

XI. Yet minds are not conquered by force, but by love and high — mindedness.

XII. It is before all things useful to men to associate their ways of life, to bind themselves together with such bonds as they think most fitted to gather them all into unity, and generally to do whatsoever serves to strengthen friendship.

XIII. But for this there is need of skill and watchfulness. For men are diverse (seeing that those who live under the guidance of reason are few), yet are they generally envious and more prone to revenge than to sympathy. No small force of character is therefore required to take everyone as he is, and to restrain one's self from imitating the emotions of others. But those who carp at mankind, and are more skilled in railing at vice than in instilling virtue, and who break rather than strengthen men's dispositions, are hurtful both to themselves and others. Thus many from too great impatience of spirit, or from misguided religious zeal, have preferred to live among brutes rather than among men; as boys or youths, who cannot peaceably endure the chidings of their parents, will enlist as soldiers and choose the hardships of war and the despotic discipline in preference to the comforts of home and the admonitions of their father: suffering any burden to be put upon them, so long as they may spite their parents.

XIV. Therefore, although men are generally governed in everything by their own lusts, yet their association in common brings many more advantages than drawbacks. Wherefore it is better to bear patiently the wrongs they may do us, and to strive to promote whatsoever serves to bring about harmony and friendship.

XV. Those things, which beget harmony, are such as are attributable to justice, equity, and honourable living. For men brook ill not only what is unjust or iniquitous, but also what is reckoned disgraceful, or that a man should slight the received customs of their society. For winning love those qualities are especially necessary which have regard to religion and piety (cf. IV. xxxvii. notes. i. ii.; xlvi. note; and lxxiii. note).

XVI. Further, harmony is often the result of fear: but such harmony is insecure. Further, fear arises from infirmity of spirit, and moreover belongs not to the exercise of reason: the same is true of compassion, though this latter seems to bear a certain resemblance to piety.

XVII. Men are also gained over by liberality, especially such as have not the means to buy what is necessary to sustain life. However, to give aid to every poor man is far beyond the power and the advantage of any private person. For the riches of any private person are wholly inadequate to meet such a call. Again, an individual man's resources of character are too limited for him to be able to make all men his friends. Hence providing for the poor is a duty, which falls on the State as a whole, and has regard only to the general advantage.

XVIII. In accepting favours, and in returning gratitude our duty must be wholly different (cf. IV. lxx. note; lxxi. note).

XIX. Again, meretricious love, that is, the lust of generation arising from bodily beauty, and generally every sort of love, which owns anything save freedom of soul as its cause, readily passes into hate; unless indeed, what is worse, it is a species of madness; and then it promotes discord rather than harmony (cf. III. xxxi. Coroll.).

XX. As concerning marriage, it is certain that this is in harmony with reason, if the desire for physical union be not engendered solely by bodily beauty, but also by the desire to beget children and to train them up wisely; and moreover, if the love of both, to wit, of the man and of the woman, is not caused by bodily beauty only, but also by freedom of soul.

XXI. Furthermore, flattery begets harmony; but only by means of the vile offence of slavishness or treachery. None are more readily taken with flattery than the proud, who wish to be first, but are not.

XXII. There is in abasement a spurious appearance of piety and religion. Although abasement is the opposite to pride, yet is he that abases himself most akin to the proud (IV. lvii. note).

XXIII. Shame also brings about harmony, but only in such matters as cannot be hid. Further, as shame is a species of pain, it does not concern the exercise of reason.

XXIV. The remaining emotions of pain towards men are directly opposed to justice, equity, honour, piety, and religion; and, although indignation seems to bear a certain resemblance to equity, yet is life but lawless, where every man may pass judgment on another's deeds, and vindicate his own or other men's rights.

XXV. Correctness of conduct (modestia), that is, the desire of pleasing men which is determined by reason, is attributable to piety (as we said in IV. xxxvii. note. i.). But, if it spring from emotion, it is ambition, or the desire whereby, men, under the false cloak of piety, generally stir up discords and seditions. For he who desires to aid his fellows either in word or in deed, so that they may together enjoy the highest good, he, I say, will before all things strive to win them over with love: not to draw them into admiration, so that a system may be called after his name, nor to give any cause for envy. Further, in his conversation he will shrink from talking of men's faults, and will be careful to speak but sparingly of human infirmity: but he will dwell at length on human virtue or power, and the way whereby it may be perfected. Thus will men be stirred not by fear, nor by aversion, but only by the emotion of joy, to endeavour, so far as in them lies, to live in obedience to reason.

XXVI. Besides men, we know of no particular thing in nature in whose mind we may rejoice, and whom we can associate with ourselves in friendship or any sort of fellowship; therefore, whatsoever there be in nature besides man, a regard for our advantage does not call on us to preserve, but to preserve or destroy according to its various capabilities, and to adapt to our use as best we may.

XXVII. The advantage which we derive from things external to us, besides the experience and knowledge which we acquire from observing them, and from recombining their elements in different forms, is principally the preservation of the body; from this point of view, those things are most useful which can so feed and nourish the body, that all its parts may rightly fulfil their functions. For, in proportion as the body is capable of being affected in a greater variety of ways, and of affecting external bodies in a great number of ways, so much the more is the mind capable of thinking (IV. xxxviii., xxxix.). But there seem to be very few things of this kind in nature; wherefore for the due nourishment of the body we must use many foods of diverse nature. For the human body is composed of very many parts of different nature, which stand in continual need of varied nourishment, so that the whole body may be equally capable of doing everything that can follow from its own nature, and consequently that the mind also may be equally capable of forming many perceptions.

XXVIII. Now for providing these nourishments the strength of each individual would hardly suffice, if men did not lend one another mutual aid. But money has furnished us with a token for everything: hence it is with the notion of money, that the mind of the multitude is chiefly engrossed: nay, it can hardly conceive any kind of pleasure, which is not accompanied with the idea of money as cause.

XXIX. This result is the fault only of those, who seek money, not from poverty or to supply their necessary wants, but because they have learned the arts of gain, wherewith they bring themselves to great splendour. Certainly they nourish their bodies, according to custom, but scantily, believing that they lose as much of their wealth as they spend on the preservation of their body. But they who know the true use of money, and who fix the measure of wealth solely with regard to their actual needs, live content with little.

XXX. As, therefore, those things are good which assist the various parts of the body, and enable them to perform their functions; and as pleasure consists in an increase of, or aid to, man's power, in so far as he is composed of mind and body; it follows that all those things which bring pleasure are good. But seeing that things do not work with the object of giving us pleasure, and that their power of action is not tempered to suit our advantage, and, lastly, that pleasure is generally referred to one part of the body more than to the other parts; therefore most emotions of pleasure (unless reason and watchfulness be at hand), and consequently the desires arising therefrom, may become excessive. Moreover we may add that emotion leads us to pay most regard to what is agreeable in the present, nor can we estimate what is future with emotions equally vivid. (IV. xliv. note, and lx. note.)

XXXI. Superstition, on the other hand, seems to account as good all that brings pain, and as bad all that brings pleasure. However, as we said above (IV. xlv. note), none but the envious take delight in my infirmity and trouble. For the greater the pleasure whereby we are affected, the greater is the perfection whereto we pass, and consequently the more do we partake of the divine nature: no pleasure can ever be evil, which is regulated by a true regard for our advantage. But contrariwise he, who is led by fear and does good only to avoid evil, is not guided by reason.

XXXII. But human power is extremely limited, and is infinitely surpassed by the power of external causes; we have not, therefore, an absolute power of shaping to our use those things which are without us. Nevertheless, we shall bear with an equal mind all that happens to us in contravention to the claims of our own advantage, so long as we are conscious, that we have done our duty, and that the power which we possess is not sufficient to enable us to protect ourselves completely; remembering that we are a part of universal nature, and that we follow her order. If we have a clear and distinct understanding of this, that part of our nature which is defined by intelligence, in other words the better part of ourselves, will assuredly acquiesce in what befalls us, and in such acquiescence will endeavour to persist. For, in so far as we are intelligent beings, we cannot desire anything save that which is necessary, nor yield absolute acquiescence to anything, save to that which is true: wherefore, in so far as we have a right understanding of these things, the endeavour of the better part of ourselves is in harmony with the order of nature as a whole.

PART V. OF THE POWER OF THE UNDERSTANDING, OR OF HUMAN FREEDOM

PREFACE

AT LENGTH I pass to the remaining portion of my Ethics, which is concerned with the way leading to freedom. I shall therefore treat therein of the power of the reason, showing how far the reason can control the emotions, and what is the nature of Mental Freedom or Blessedness; we shall then be able to see, how much more powerful the wise man is than the ignorant. It is no part of my design to point out the method and means whereby the understanding may be perfected, nor to show the skill whereby the body may be so tended, as to be capable of the due performance of its functions. The latter question lies in the province of Medicine, the former in the province of Logic. Here, therefore, I repeat, I shall treat only of the power of the mind, or of reason; and I shall mainly show the extent and nature of its dominion over the emotions, for their control and moderation. That we do not possess absolute dominion over them, I have already shown. Yet the Stoics have thought, that the emotions depended absolutely on our will, and that we could absolutely govern them. But these philosophers were compelled, by the protest of experience, not from their own principles, to confess, that no slight practice and zeal is needed to control and moderate them: and this someone endeavoured to illustrate by the example (if I remember rightly) of two dogs, the one a house — dog and the other a hunting — dog. For by long training it could be brought about, that the house — dog should become accustomed to hunt, and the hunting — dog to cease from running after hares. To this opinion Descartes not a little inclines. For he maintained, that the soul or mind is specially united to a particular part of the brain, namely, to that part called the pineal gland, by the aid of which the mind is enabled to feel all the movements which are set going in the body, and also external objects, and which the mind by a simple act of volition can put in motion in various ways. He asserted, that this gland is so suspended in the midst of the brain, that it could be moved by the slightest motion of the animal spirits: further, that this gland is suspended in the midst of the brain in as many different manners, as the animal spirits can impinge thereon; and, again, that as many different marks are impressed on the said gland, as there are different external objects which impel the animal spirits towards it; whence it follows, that if the will of the soul suspends the gland in a position, wherein it has already been suspended once before by the animal spirits driven in one way or another, the gland in its turn reacts on the said spirits, driving and determining them to the condition wherein they were, when repulsed before by a similar position of the gland. He further asserted, that every act of mental volition is united in nature to a certain given motion of the gland. For instance, whenever anyone desires to look at a remote object, the act of volition causes the pupil of the eye to dilate, whereas, if the person in question had only thought of the dilatation of the pupil, the mere wish to dilate it would not have brought about the result, inasmuch as the motion of the gland, which serves to impel the animal spirits towards the optic nerve in a way which would dilate or contract the pupil, is not associated in nature with the wish to dilate or contract the pupil, but with the wish to look at remote or very near objects. Lastly, he maintained that, although every motion of the aforesaid gland seems to have been united by nature to one particular thought out of the whole number of our thoughts from the very beginning of our life, yet it can nevertheless become through habituation associated with other thoughts; this he endeavours to prove in the Passions de l'âme, I.50. He thence concludes, that there is no soul so weak, that it cannot, under proper direction, acquire absolute power over its passions. For passions as defined by him are "perceptions, or feelings, or disturbances of the soul, which are referred to the soul as species, and which (mark the expression) are produced, preserved, and strengthened through some movement of the spirits." (Passions de l'âme, I.27). But, seeing that we can join any motion of the gland, or consequently of the spirits, to any volition, the determination of the will depends entirely on our own powers; if, therefore, we determine our will with sure and firm decisions in the direction to which we wish our actions to tend, and associate the motions of the passions which we wish to acquire with the said decisions, we shall acquire an absolute dominion over our passions. Such is the doctrine of this illustrious philosopher (in so far as I gather it from his own words); it is one which, had it been less ingenious, I could hardly believe to have proceeded from so great a man. Indeed, I am lost in wonder, that a philosopher, who had stoutly asserted, that he would draw no conclusions which do not follow from self — evident premises, and would affirm nothing which he did not clearly and distinctly perceive, and who had so often taken to task the scholastics for wishing to explain obscurities through occult qualities, could maintain a hypothesis, beside which occult qualities are commonplace. What does he understand, I ask, by the union of the mind and the body? What clear and distinct conception has he got of thought in most intimate union with a certain particle of extended matter? Truly I should like him to explain this union through its proximate cause. But he had so distinct a conception of mind being distinct from body, that he could not assign any particular cause of the union between the two, or of the mind itself, but was obliged to have recourse to the cause of the whole universe, that is to God. Further, I should much like to know, what degree of motion the mind can impart to this pineal gland, and with what force can it hold it suspended? For I am in ignorance, whether this gland can be agitated more slowly or more quickly by the mind than by the animal spirits, and whether the motions of the passions, which we have closely united with firm decisions, cannot be again disjoined therefrom by physical causes; in which case it would follow that, although the mind firmly intended to face a given danger, and had united to this decision the motions of boldness, yet at the sight of the danger the gland might become suspended in a way, which would preclude the mind thinking of anything except running away. In truth, as there is no common standard of volition and motion, so is there no comparison possible between the powers of the mind and the power or strength of the body; consequently the strength of one cannot in any wise be determined by the strength of the other. We may also add, that there is no gland discoverable in the midst of the brain, so placed that it can thus easily be set in motion in so many ways, and also that all the nerves are not prolonged so far as the cavities of the brain. Lastly, I omit all the assertions which he makes concerning the will and its freedom, inasmuch as I have abundantly proved that his premises are false. Therefore, since the power of the mind, as I have shown above, is defined by the understanding only, we shall determine solely by the knowledge of the mind the remedies against the emotions, which I believe all have had experience of, but do not accurately observe or distinctly see, and from the same basis we shall deduce all those conclusions, which have regard to the mind's blessedness.

AXIOMS.

I. IF TWO contrary actions be started in the same subject, a change must necessarily take place, either in both, or in one of the two, and continue until they cease to be contrary.

II. The power of an effect is defined by the power of its cause, in so far as its essence is explained or defined by the essence of its cause.

(This axiom is evident from III. vii.)

PROPOSITIONS.

PROP. I. EVEN as thoughts and the ideas of things are arranged and associated in the mind, so are the modifications of body or the images of things precisely in the same way arranged and associated in the body.

Proof. — The order and connection of ideas is the same (II. vii.) as the order and connection of things, and vice versâ the order and connection of things is the same (II. vi. Coroll. and vii.) as the order and connection of ideas. Wherefore, even as the order and connection of ideas in the mind takes place according to the order and association of modifications of the body (II. xviii.), so vice versâ (III. ii.) the order and connection of modifications of the body takes place in accordance with the manner, in which thoughts and the ideas of things are arranged and associated in the mind. Q.E.D.

PROP. II. If we remove a disturbance of the spirit, or emotion, from the thought of an external cause, and unite it to other thoughts, then will the love or hatred towards that external cause, and also the vacillations of spirit which arise from these emotions, be destroyed.

Proof. — That, which constitutes the reality of love or hatred, is pleasure or pain, accompanied by the idea of an external cause (Def. of the Emotions, vi. vii.); wherefore, when this cause is removed, the reality of love or hatred is removed with it; therefore these emotions and those which arise therefrom are destroyed. Q.E.D.

PROP. III. An emotion, which is a passion, ceases to be a passion, as soon as we form a clear and distinct idea thereof.

Proof. — An emotion, which is a passion, is a confused idea (by the general Def. of the Emotions). If, therefore, we form a clear and distinct idea of a given emotion, that idea will only be distinguished from the emotion, in so far as it is referred to the mind only, by reason (II. xxi., and note); therefore (III. iii.), the emotion will cease to be a passion. Q.E.D.

Corollary — An emotion therefore becomes more under our control, and the mind is less passive in respect to it, in proportion as it is more known to us.

PROP. IV. There is no modification of the body, whereof we cannot form some clear and distinct conception.

Proof. — Properties which are common to all things can only be conceived adequately (II. xxxviii.); therefore (II. xii. and Lemma ii. after II. xiii.) there is no modification of the body, whereof we cannot form some clear and distinct conception. Q.E.D.

Corollary. — Hence it follows that there is no emotion, whereof we cannot form some clear and distinct conception. For an emotion is the idea of a modification of the body (by the general Def. of the Emotions), and must therefore (by the preceding Prop.) involve some clear and distinct conception.

Note. — Seeing that there is nothing which is not followed by an effect (I. xxxvi.), and that we clearly and distinctly understand whatever follows from an idea, which in us is adequate (II. xl.), it follows that everyone has the power of clearly and distinctly understanding himself and his emotions, if not absolutely, at any rate in part, and consequently of bringing it about, that he should become less subject to them. To attain this result, therefore, we must chiefly direct our efforts to acquiring, as far as possible, a clear and distinct knowledge of every emotion, in order that the mind may thus, through emotion, be determined to think of those things which it clearly and distinctly perceives, and wherein it fully acquiesces: and thus that the emotion itself may be separated from the thought of an external cause, and may be associated with true thoughts; whence it will come to pass, not only that love, hatred, &c. will be destroyed (V. ii.), but also that the appetites or desires, which are wont to arise from such emotion, will become incapable of being excessive (IV. lxi.). For it must be especially remarked, that the appetite through which a man is said to be active, and that through which he is said to be passive is one and the same. For instance, we have shown that human nature is so constituted, that everyone desires his fellow — men to live after his own fashion (III. xxxi. note); in a man, who is not guided by reason, this appetite is a passion which is called ambition, and does not greatly differ from pride; whereas in a man, who lives by the dictates of reason, it is an activity or virtue which is called piety (IV. xxxvii. note. i. and second proof). In like manner all appetites or desires are only passions, in so far as they spring from inadequate ideas; the same results are accredited to virtue, when they are aroused or generated by adequate ideas. For all desires, whereby we are determined to any given action, may arise as much from adequate as from inadequate ideas (IV. lix.). Than this remedy for the emotions (to return to the point from which I started), which consists in a true knowledge thereof, nothing more excellent, being within our power, can be devised. For the mind has no other power save that of thinking and of forming adequate ideas, as we have shown above (III. iii.).

PROP. V. An emotion towards a thing, which we conceive simply, and not as necessary, or as contingent, or as possible, is, other conditions being equal, greater than any other emotion.

Proof. — An emotion towards a thing, which we conceive to be free, is greater than one towards what we conceive to be necessary (III. xlix.), and, consequently, still greater than one towards what we conceive as possible, or contingent (IV. xi.). But to conceive a thing as free can be nothing else than to conceive it simply, while we are in ignorance of the causes whereby it has been determined to action (II. xxxv. note); therefore, an emotion towards a thing which we conceive simply is, other conditions being equal, greater than one, which we feel towards what is necessary, possible, or contingent, and, consequently, it is the greatest of all. Q.E.D.

PROP. VI. The mind has greater power over the emotions and is less subject thereto, in so far as it understands all things as necessary.

Proof. — The mind understands all things to be necessary (I. xxix.) and to be determined to existence and operation by an infinite chain of causes; therefore (by the foregoing Proposition), it thus far brings it about, that it is less subject to the emotions arising therefrom, and (III. xlviii.) feels less emotion towards the things themselves. Q.E.D.

Note. — The more this knowledge, that things are necessary, is applied to particular things, which we conceive more distinctly and vividly, the greater is the power of the mind over the emotions, as experience also testifies. For we see, that the pain arising from the loss of any good is mitigated, as soon as the man who has lost it perceives, that it could not by any means have been preserved. So also we see that no one pities an infant, because it cannot speak, walk, or reason, or lastly, because it passes so many years, as it were, in unconsciousness. Whereas, if most people were born full — grown and only one here and there as an infant, everyone would pity the infants; because infancy would not then be looked on as a state natural and necessary, but as a fault or delinquency in Nature; and we may note several other instances of the same sort.

PROP. VII. Emotions which are aroused or spring from reason, if we take account of time, are stronger than those, which are attributable to particular objects that we regard as absent.

Proof. — We do not regard a thing as absent, by reason of the emotion wherewith we conceive it, but by reason of the body, being affected by another emotion excluding the existence of the said thing (II. xvii.). Wherefore, the emotion, which is referred to the thing which we regard as absent, is not of a nature to overcome the rest of a man's activities and power (IV. vi.), but is, on the contrary, of a nature to be in some sort controlled by the emotions, which exclude the existence of its external cause (IV. ix.). But an emotion which springs from reason is necessarily referred to the common properties of things (see the def. of reason in II. xl. note. ii.), which we always regard as present (for there can be nothing to exclude their present existence), and which we always conceive in the same manner (II. xxxviii.). Wherefore an emotion of this kind always remains the same; and consequently (V. Ax. i.) emotions, which are contrary thereto and are not kept going by their external causes, will be obliged to adapt themselves to it more and more, until they are no longer contrary to it; to this extent the emotion which springs from reason is more powerful. Q.E.D.

PROP. VIII. An emotion is stronger in proportion to the number of simultaneous concurrent causes whereby it is aroused.

Proof. — Many simultaneous causes are more powerful than a few (III. vii.): therefore (IV. v.), in proportion to the increased number of simultaneous causes whereby it is aroused, an emotion becomes stronger. Q.E.D.

Note — This proposition is also evident from V. Ax. ii.

PROP. IX. An emotion, which is attributable to many and diverse causes which the mind regards as simultaneous with the emotion itself, is less hurtful, and we are less subject thereto and less affected towards each of its causes, than if it were a different and equally powerful emotion attributable to fewer causes or to a single cause.

Proof. — An emotion is only bad or hurtful, in so far as it hinders the mind from being able to think (IV. xxvi. xxvii.); therefore, an emotion, whereby the mind is determined to the contemplation of several things at once, is less hurtful than another equally powerful emotion, which so engrosses the mind in the single contemplation of a few objects or of one, that it is unable to think of anything else; this was our first point. Again, as the mind's essence, in other words, its power (III. vii.), consists solely in thought (II. xi.), the mind is less passive in respect to an emotion, which causes it to think of several things at once, than in regard to an equally strong emotion, which keeps it engrossed in the contemplation of a few or of a single object: this was our second point. Lastly, this emotion (III. xlviii.), in so far as it is attributable to several causes, is less powerful in regard to each of them. Q.E.D.

PROP. X. So long as we are not assailed by emotions contrary to our nature, we have the power of arranging and associating the modifications of our body according to the intellectual order.

Proof. — The emotions, which are contrary to our nature, that is (IV. xxx.), which are bad, are bad in so far as they impede the mind from understanding (IV. xxvii.). So long, therefore, as we are not assailed by emotions contrary to our nature, the mind's power, whereby it endeavours to understand things (IV. xxvi.), is not impeded, and therefore it is able to form clear and distinct ideas and to deduce them one from another (II. xl. note. ii. and II. xlvii. note); consequently we have in such cases the power of arranging and associating the modifications of the body according to the intellectual order. Q.E.D.

Note. — By this power of rightly arranging and associating the bodily modifications we can guard ourselves from being easily affected by evil emotions. For (V. vii.) a greater force is needed for controlling the emotions, when they are arranged and associated according to the intellectual order, than when they, are uncertain and unsettled. The best we can do, therefore, so long as we do not possess a perfect knowledge of our emotions, is to frame a system of right conduct, or fixed practical precepts, to commit it to memory, and to apply it forthwith16 to the particular circumstances which now and again meet us in life, so that our imagination may become fully imbued therewith, and that it may be always ready to our hand. For instance, we have laid down among the rules of life (IV. xlvi. and note), that hatred should be overcome with love or high — mindedness, and not required with hatred in return. Now, that this precept of reason may be always ready to our hand in time of need, we should often think over and reflect upon the wrongs generally committed by men, and in what manner and way they may be best warded off by high — mindedness: we shall thus associate the idea of wrong with the idea of this precept, which accordingly will always be ready for use when a wrong is done to us (II. xviii.). If we keep also in readiness the notion of our true advantage, and of the good which follows from mutual friendships, and common fellowships; further, if we remember that complete acquiescence is the result of the right way of life (IV. lii.), and that men, no less than everything else, act by the necessity of their nature: in such case I say the wrong, or the hatred, which commonly arises therefrom, will engross a very small part of our imagination and will be easily overcome; or, if the anger which springs from a grievous wrong be not overcome easily, it will nevertheless be overcome, though not without a spiritual conflict, far sooner than if we had not thus reflected on the subject beforehand. As is indeed evident from V. vi. vii. viii. We should, in the same way, reflect on courage as a means of overcoming fear; the ordinary dangers of life should frequently be brought to mind and imagined, together with the means whereby through readiness of resource and strength of mind we can avoid and overcome them. But we must note, that in arranging our thoughts and conceptions we should always bear in mind that which is good in every individual thing (IV. lxiii. Coroll. and III. lix.), in order that we may always be determined to action by an emotion of pleasure. For instance, if a man sees that he is too keen in the pursuit of honour, let him think over its right use, the end for which it should be pursued, and the means whereby he may attain it. Let him not think of its misuse, and its emptiness, and the fickleness of mankind, and the like, whereof no man thinks except through a morbidness of disposition; with thoughts like these do the most ambitious most torment themselves, when they despair of gaining the distinctions they hanker after, and in thus giving vent to their anger would fain appear wise. Wherefore it is certain that those, who cry out the loudest against the misuse of honour and the vanity of the world, are those who most greedily covet it. This is not peculiar to the ambitious, but is common to all who are ill — used by fortune, and who are infirm in spirit. For a poor man also, who is miserly, will talk incessantly of the misuse of wealth and of the vices of the rich; whereby he merely torments himself, and shows the world that he is intolerant, not only of his own poverty, but also of other people's riches. So, again, those who have been ill received by a woman they love think of nothing but the inconstancy, treachery, and other stock faults of the fair sex; all of which they consign to oblivion, directly they are again taken into favour by their sweetheart. Thus he who would govern his emotions and appetite solely by the love of freedom strives, as far as he can, to gain a knowledge of the virtues and their causes, and to fill his spirit with the joy which arises from the true knowledge of them: he will in no wise desire to dwell on men's faults, or to carp at his fellows, or to revel in a false show of freedom. Whosoever will diligently observe and practise these precepts (which indeed are not difficult) will verily, in a short space of time, be able, for the most part, to direct his actions according to the commandments of reason.

16 Continuo. Rendered "constantly" by Mr. Pollock on the ground that the classical meaning of the word does not suit the context.

PROP. XI. In proportion as a mental image is referred to more objects, so is it more frequent, or more often vivid, and occupies the mind more.

Proof. — In proportion as a mental image or an emotion is referred to more objects, so are there more causes whereby it can be aroused and fostered, all of which (by hypothesis) the mind contemplates simultaneously in association with the given emotion; therefore the emotion is more frequent, or is more often in full vigour, and (V. viii.) occupies the mind more. Q.E.D.

PROP. XII. The mental images of things are more easily associated with the images referred to things which we clearly and distinctly understand, than with others.

Proof. — Things, which we clearly and distinctly understand, are either the common properties of things or deductions therefrom (see definition of Reason, II. xl. note ii.), and are consequently (by the last Prop.) more often aroused in us. Wherefore it may more readily happen, that we should contemplate other things in conjunction with these than in conjunction with something else, and consequently (II. xviii.) that the images of the said things should be more often associated with the images of these than with the images of something else. Q.E.D.

PROP. XIII. A mental image is more often vivid, in proportion as it is associated with a greater number of other images.

Proof. — In proportion as an image is associated with a greater number of other images, so (II. xviii.) are there more causes whereby it can be aroused. Q.E.D.

PROP. XIV. The mind can bring it about, that all bodily modifications or images of things may be referred to the idea of God.

Proof. — There is no modification of the body, whereof the mind may not form some clear and distinct conception (V. iv.); wherefore it can bring it about, that they should all be referred to the idea of God (I. xv.). Q.E.D.

PROP. XV. He who clearly and distinctly understands himself and his emotions loves God, and so much the more in proportion as he more understands himself and his emotions.

Proof. — He who clearly and distinctly understands himself and his emotions feels pleasure (III. liii.), and this pleasure is (by the last Prop.) accompanied by the idea of God; therefore (Def. of the Emotions, vi.) such an one loves God, and (for the same reason) so much the more in proportion as he more understands himself and his emotions. Q.E.D.

PROP. XVI. This love towards God must hold the chief place in the mind.

Proof. — For this love is associated with all the modifications of the body (V. xiv.) and is fostered by them all (V. xv.); therefore (V. xi.), it must hold the chief place in the mind. Q.E.D.

PROP. XVII. God is without passions, neither is he affected by any emotion of pleasure or pain.

Proof. — All ideas, in so far as they are referred to God, are true (II. xxxii.), that is (II. Def. iv.) adequate; and therefore (by the general Def. of the Emotions) God is without passions. Again, God cannot pass either to a greater or to a lesser perfection (I. xx. Coroll. ii.); therefore (by Def. of the Emotions, ii. iii.) he is not affected by any emotion of pleasure or pain.

Corollary. — Strictly speaking, God does not love or hate anyone. For God (by the foregoing Prop.) is not affected by any emotion of pleasure or pain, consequently (Def. of the Emotions, vi. vii.) he does not love or hate anyone.

PROP. XVIII. No one can hate God.

Proof. — The idea of God which is in us is adequate and perfect (II. xlvi. xlvii.); wherefore, in so far as we contemplate God, we are active (III. iii.); consequently (III. lix.) there can be no pain accompanied by the idea of God, in other words (Def. of the Emotions, vii.), no one can hate God. Q.E.D.

Corollary. — Love towards God cannot be turned into hate.

Note. — It may be objected that, as we understand God as the cause of all things, we by that very fact regard God as the cause of pain. But I make answer, that, in so far as we understand the causes of pain, it to that extent (V. iii.) ceases to be a passion, that is, it ceases to be pain (III. lix.); therefore, in so far as we understand

God to be the cause of pain, we to that extent feel pleasure.

PROP. XIX. He, who loves God, cannot endeavour that God should love him in return.

Proof. — For, if a man should so endeavour, he would desire (V. xvii. Coroll.) that God, whom he loves, should not be God, and consequently he would desire to feel pain (III. xix.); which is absurd (III. xxviii.). Therefore, he who loves God, &c. Q.E.D.

PROP. XX. This love towards God cannot be stained by the emotion of envy or jealousy: contrariwise, it is the more fostered, in proportion as we conceive a greater number of men to be joined to God by the same bond of love.

Proof. — This love towards God is the highest good which we can seek for under the guidance of reason (IV. xxviii.), it is common to all men (IV. xxxvi.), and we desire that all should rejoice therein (IV. xxxvii.); therefore (Def. of the Emotions, xxiii.), it cannot be stained by the emotion envy, nor by the emotion of jealousy (V. xviii. see definition of Jealousy, III. xxxv. note); but, contrariwise, it must needs be the more fostered, in proportion as we conceive a greater number of men to rejoice therein. Q.E.D.

Note. — We can in the same way show, that there is no emotion directly contrary to this love, whereby this love can be destroyed; therefore we may conclude, that this love towards God is the most constant of all the emotions, and that, in so far as it is referred to the body, it cannot be destroyed, unless the body be destroyed also. As to its nature, in so far as it is referred to the mind only, we shall presently inquire.

I have now gone through all the remedies against the emotions, or all that the mind, considered in itself alone, can do against them. Whence it appears that the mind's power over the emotions consists: ——

I. In the actual knowledge of the emotions (V. iv. note).

II. In the fact that it separates the emotions from the thought of an external cause, which we conceive confusedly (V. ii. and V. iv. note).

III. In the fact, that, in respect to time, the emotions referred to things, which we distinctly understand, surpass those referred to what we conceive in a confused and fragmentary manner (V. vii.).

IV. In the number of causes whereby those modifications17 are fostered, which have regard to the common properties of things or to God (V. ix. xi.).

17 Affectiones. Camerer reads affectus —— emotions.

V. Lastly, in the order wherein the mind can arrange and associate, one with another, its own emotions (V. x. note and xii. xiii. xiv.).

But, in order that this power of the mind over the emotions may be better understood, it should be specially observed that the emotions are called by us strong, when we compare the emotion of one man with the emotion of another, and see that one man is more troubled than another by the same emotion; or when we are comparing the various emotions of the same man one with another, and find that he is more affected or stirred by one emotion than by another. For the strength of every emotion is defined by a comparison of our own power with the power of an external cause. Now the power of the mind is defined by knowledge only, and its infirmity or passion is defined by the privation of knowledge only: it therefore follows, that that mind is most passive, whose greatest part is made up of inadequate ideas, so that it may be characterized more readily by its passive states than by its activities: on the other hand, that mind is most active, whose greatest part is made up of adequate ideas, so that, although it may contain as many inadequate ideas as the former mind, it may yet be more easily characterized by ideas attributable to human virtue, than by ideas which tell of human infirmity. Again, it must be observed, that spiritual unhealthiness and misfortunes can generally be traced to excessive love for something which is subject to many variations, and which we can never become masters of. For no one is solicitous or anxious about anything, unless he loves it; neither do wrongs, suspicions, enmities, &c. arise, except in regard to things whereof no one can be really master.

We may thus readily conceive the power which clear and distinct knowledge, and especially that third kind of knowledge (II. xlvii. note), founded on the actual knowledge of God, possesses over the emotions: if it does not absolutely destroy them, in so far as they are passions (V. iii. and iv. note); at any rate, it causes them to occupy a very small part of the mind (V. xiv.). Further, it begets a love towards a thing immutable and eternal (V. xv.), whereof we may really enter into possession (II. xlv.); neither can it be defiled with those faults which are inherent in ordinary love; but it may grow from strength to strength, and may engross the greater part of the mind, and deeply penetrate it.

And now I have finished with all that concerns this present life: for, as I said in the beginning of this note, I have briefly described all the remedies against the emotions. And this everyone may readily have seen for himself, if he has attended to what is advanced in the present note, and also to the definitions of the mind and its emotions, and, lastly, to Propositions i. and iii. of Part III. It is now, therefore, time to pass on to those matters, which appertain to the duration of the mind, without relation to the body.

PROP. XXI. The mind can only imagine anything, or remember what is past, while the body endures.

Proof. — The mind does not express the actual existence of its body, nor does it imagine the modifications of the body as actual, except while the body endures (II. viii. Coroll.); and, consequently (II. xxvi.), it does not imagine any body as actually existing, except while its own body endures. Thus it cannot imagine anything (for definition of Imagination, see II. xvii. note), or remember things past, except while the body endures (see definition of Memory, II. xviii. note). Q.E.D.

PROP. XXII. Nevertheless in God there is necessarily an idea, which expresses the essence of this or that human body under the form of eternity.

Proof. — God is the cause, not only of the existence of this or that human body, but also of its essence (I. xxv.). This essence, therefore, must necessarily be conceived through the very essence of God (I. Ax. iv.), and be thus conceived by a certain eternal necessity (I. xvi.); and this conception must necessarily exist in God (II. iii.). Q.E.D.

PROP. XXIII. The human mind cannot be absolutely destroyed with the body, but there remains of it something which is eternal.

Proof. — There is necessarily in God a concept or idea, which expresses the essence of the human body (last Prop.), which, therefore, is necessarily something appertaining to the essence of the human mind (II. xiii.). But we have not assigned to the human mind any duration, definable by time, except in so far as it expresses the actual existence of the body, which is explained through duration, and may be defined by time — that is (II. viii. Coroll.), we do not assign to it duration, except while the body endures. Yet, as there is something, notwithstanding, which is conceived by a certain eternal necessity through the very essence of God (last Prop.); this something, which appertains to the essence of the mind, will necessarily be eternal. Q.E.D.

Note. — This idea, which expresses the essence of the body under the form of eternity, is, as we have said, a certain mode of thinking, which belongs to the essence of the mind, and is necessarily eternal. Yet it is not possible that we should remember that we existed before our body, for our body can bear no trace of such existence, neither can eternity be defined in terms of time, or have any relation to time. But, notwithstanding, we feel and know that we are eternal. For the mind feels those things that it conceives by understanding, no less than those things that it remembers. For the eyes of the mind, whereby it sees and observes things, are none other than proofs. Thus, although we do not remember that we existed before the body, yet we feel that our mind, in so far as it involves the essence of the body, under the form of eternity, is eternal, and that thus its existence cannot be defined in terms of time, or explained through duration. Thus our mind can only be said to endure, and its existence can only be defined by a fixed time, in so far as it involves the actual existence of the body. Thus far only has it the power of determining the existence of things by time, and conceiving them under the category of duration.

PROP. XXIV. The more we understand particular things, the more do we understand God.

Proof. — This is evident from I. xxv. Coroll.

PROP. XXV. The highest endeavour of the mind, and the highest virtue is to understand things by the third kind of knowledge.

Proof. — The third kind of knowledge proceeds from an adequate idea of certain attributes of God to an adequate knowledge of the essence of things (see its definition II. xl. note. ii.); and, in proportion as we understand things more in this way, we better understand God (by the last Prop.); therefore (IV. xxviii.) the highest virtue of the mind, that is (IV. Def. viii.) the power, or nature, or (III. vii.) highest endeavour of the mind, is to understand things by the third kind of knowledge. Q.E.D.

PROP. XXVI. In proportion as the mind is more capable of understanding things by the third kind of knowledge, it desires more to understand things by that kind.

Proof — This is evident. For, in so far as we conceive the mind to be capable of conceiving things by this kind of knowledge, we, to that extent, conceive it as determined thus to conceive things; and consequently (Def. of the Emotions, i.), the mind desires so to do, in proportion as it is more capable thereof. Q.E.D.

PROP. XXVII. From this third kind of knowledge arises the highest possible mental acquiescence.

Proof. — The highest virtue of the mind is to know God (IV. xxviii.), or to understand things by the third kind of knowledge (V. xxv.), and this virtue is greater in proportion as the mind knows things more by the said kind of knowledge (V. xxiv.): consequently, he who knows things by this kind of knowledge passes to the summit of human perfection, and is therefore (Def. of the Emotions, ii.) affected by the highest pleasure, such pleasure being accompanied by the idea of himself and his own virtue; thus (Def. of the Emotions, xxv.), from this kind of knowledge arises the highest possible acquiescence. Q.E.D.

PROP. XXVIII. The endeavour or desire to know things by the third kind of knowledge cannot arise from the first, but from the second kind of knowledge.

Proof. — This proposition is self — evident. For whatsoever we understand clearly and distinctly, we understand either through itself, or through that which is conceived through itself; that is, ideas which are clear and distinct in us, or which are referred to the third kind of knowledge (II. xl. note. ii.) cannot follow from ideas that are fragmentary and confused, and are referred to knowledge of the first kind, but must follow from adequate ideas, or ideas of the second and third kind of knowledge; therefore (Def. of the Emotions, i.), the desire of knowing things by the third kind of knowledge cannot arise from the first, but from the second kind. Q.E.D.

PROP. XXIX. Whatsoever the mind understands under the form of eternity, it does not understand by virtue of conceiving the present actual existence of the body, but by virtue of conceiving the essence of the body under the form of eternity.

Proof. — In so far as the mind conceives the present existence of its body, it to that extent conceives duration which can be determined by time, and to that extent only has it the power of conceiving things in relation to time (V. xxi. II. xxvi.). But eternity cannot be explained in terms of duration (I. Def. viii. and explanation). Therefore to this extent the mind has not the power of conceiving things under the form of eternity, but it possesses such power, because it is of the nature of reason to conceive things under the form of eternity (II. xliv. Coroll. ii.), and also because it is of the nature of the mind to conceive the essence of the body under the form of eternity (V. xxiii.), for besides these two there is nothing which belongs to the essence of mind (II. xiii.). Therefore this power of conceiving things under the form of eternity only belongs to the mind in virtue of the mind's conceiving the essence of the body under the form of eternity. Q.E.D.

Note. — Things are conceived by us as actual in two ways; either as existing in relation to a given time and place, or as contained in God and following from the necessity of the divine nature. Whatsoever we conceive in this second way as true or real, we conceive under the form of eternity, and their ideas involve the eternal and infinite essence of God, as we showed in II. xlv. and note, which see.

PROP. XXX. Our mind, in so far as it knows itself and the body under the form of eternity, has to that extent necessarily a knowledge of God, and knows that it is in God, and is conceived through God.

Proof. — Eternity is the very essence of God, in so far as this involves necessary existence (I. Def. viii.). Therefore to conceive things under the form of eternity, is to conceive things in so far as they are conceived through the essence of God as real entities, or in so far as they involve existence through the essence of God; wherefore our mind, in so far as it conceives itself and the body under the form of eternity, has to that extent necessarily a knowledge of God, and knows, &c. Q.E.D.

PROP. XXXI. The third kind of knowledge depends on the mind, as its formal cause, in so far as the mind itself is eternal.

Proof. — The mind does not conceive anything under the form of eternity, except in so far as it conceives its own body under the form of eternity (V. xxix.); that is, except in so far as it is eternal (V. xxi. xxiii.); therefore (by the last Prop.), in so far as it is eternal, it possesses the knowledge of God, which knowledge is necessarily adequate (II. xlvi.); hence the mind, in so far as it is eternal, is capable of knowing everything which can follow from this given knowledge of God (II. xl.), in other words, of knowing things by the third kind of knowledge (see Def. in II. xl. note. ii.), whereof accordingly the mind (III. Def. i.), in so far as it is eternal, is the adequate or formal cause of such knowledge. Q.E.D.

Note. — In proportion, therefore, as a man is more potent in this kind of knowledge, he will be more completely conscious of himself and of God; in other words, he will be more perfect and blessed, as will appear more clearly in the sequel. But we must here observe that, although we are already certain that the mind is eternal, in so far as it conceives things under the form of eternity, yet, in order that what we wish to show may be more readily explained and better understood, we will consider the mind itself, as though it had just begun to exist and to understand things under the form of eternity, as indeed we have done hitherto; this we may do without any danger of error, so long as we are careful not to draw any conclusion, unless our premisses are plain.

PROP. XXXII. Whatsoever we understand by the third kind of knowledge, we take delight in, and our delight is accompanied by the idea of God as cause.

Proof. — From this kind of knowledge arises the highest possible mental acquiescence, that is (Def of the Emotions, xxv.), pleasure, and this acquiescence is accompanied by the idea of the mind itself (V. xxvii.), and consequently (V. xxx.) the idea also of God as cause. Q.E.D.

Corollary. — From the third kind of knowledge necessarily arises the intellectual love of God. From this kind of knowledge arises pleasure accompanied by the idea of God as cause, that is (Def. of the Emotions, vi.), the love of God; not in so far as we imagine him as present (V. xxix.), but in so far as we understand him to be eternal; this is what I call the intellectual love of God.

PROP. XXXIII. The intellectual love of God, which arises from the third kind of knowledge, is eternal.

Proof. — The third kind of knowledge is eternal (V. xxxi. I. Ax. iii.); therefore (by the same Axiom) the love which arises therefrom is also necessarily eternal. Q.E.D.

Note. — Although this love towards God has (by the foregoing Prop.) no beginning, it yet possesses all the perfections of love, just as though it had arisen as we feigned in the Coroll. of the last Prop. Nor is there here any difference, except that the mind possesses as eternal those same perfections which we feigned to accrue to it, and they are accompanied by the idea of God as eternal cause. If pleasure consists in the transition to a greater perfection, assuredly blessedness must consist in the mind being endowed with perfection itself.

PROP. XXXIV. The mind is, only while the body endures, subject to those emotions which are attributable to passions.

Proof. — Imagination is the idea wherewith the mind contemplates a thing as present (II. xvii. note); yet this idea indicates rather the present disposition of the human body than the nature of the external thing (II. xvi. Coroll. ii.). Therefore emotion (see general Def. of Emotions) is imagination, in so far as it indicates the present disposition of the body; therefore (V. xxi.) the mind is, only while the body endures, subject to emotions which are attributable to passions. Q.E.D.

Corollary. — Hence it follows that no love save intellectual love is eternal.

Note. — If we look to men's general opinion, we shall see that they are indeed conscious of the eternity of their mind, but that they confuse eternity with duration, and ascribe it to the imagination or the memory which they believe to remain after death.

PROP. XXXV. God loves himself with an infinite intellectual love.

Proof. — God is absolutely infinite (I. Def. vi.), that is (II. Def. vi.), the nature of God rejoices in infinite perfection; and such rejoicing is (II. iii.) accompanied by the idea of himself, that is (I. xi. and Def. i.), the idea of his own cause: now this is what we have (in V. xxxii. Coroll.) described as intellectual love.

PROP. XXXVI. The intellectual love of the mind towards God is that very love of God whereby God loves himself, not in so far as he is infinite, but in so far as he can be explained through the essence of the human mind regarded under the form of eternity; in other words, the intellectual love of the mind towards God is part of the infinite love wherewith God loves himself.

Proof. — This love of the mind must be referred to the activities of the mind (V. xxxii. Coroll. and III. iii.); it is itself, indeed, an activity whereby the mind regards itself accompanied by the idea of God as cause (V. xxxii. and Coroll.); that is (I. xxv. Coroll. and II. xi. Coroll.), an activity whereby God, in so far as he can be explained through the human mind, regards himself accompanied by the idea of himself; therefore (by the last Prop.), this love of the mind is part of the infinite love wherewith God loves himself. Q.E.D.

Corollary. — Hence it follows that God, in so far as he loves himself, loves man, and, consequently, that the love of God towards men, and the intellectual love of the mind towards God are identical.

Note. — From what has been said we clearly understand, wherein our salvation, or blessedness, or freedom, consists: namely, in the constant and eternal love towards God, or in God's love towards men. This love or blessedness is, in the Bible, called Glory, and not undeservedly. For whether this love be referred to God or to the mind, it may rightly be called acquiescence of spirit, which (Def. of the Emotions, xxv. xxx.) is not really distinguished from glory. In so far as it is referred to God, it is (V. xxxv.) pleasure, if we may still use that term, accompanied by the idea of itself, and, in so far as it is referred to the mind, it is the same (V. xxvii.).

Again, since the essence of our mind consists solely in knowledge, whereof the beginning and the foundation is God (I. xv., and II. xlvii. note), it becomes clear to us, in what manner and way our mind, as to its essence and existence, follows from the divine nature and constantly depends on God. I have thought it worth while here to call attention to this, in order to show by this example how the knowledge of particular things, which I have called intuitive or of the third kind (II. xl. note. ii.), is potent, and more powerful than the universal knowledge, which I have styled knowledge of the second kind. For, although in Part I. I showed in general terms, that all things (and consequently, also, the human mind) depend as to their essence and existence on God, yet that demonstration, though legitimate and placed beyond the chances of doubt, does not affect our mind so much, as when the same conclusion is derived from the actual essence of some particular thing, which we say depends on God.

PROP. XXXVII. There is nothing in nature, which is contrary to this intellectual love, or which can take it away.

Proof. — This intellectual love follows necessarily from the nature of the mind, in so far as the latter is regarded through the nature of God as an eternal truth (V. xxxiii. and xxix.). If, therefore, there should be anything which would be contrary to this love, that thing would be contrary to that which is true; consequently, that, which should be able to take away this love, would cause that which is true to be false; an obvious absurdity. Therefore there is nothing in nature which, &c. Q.E.D.

Note. — The Axiom of Part IV. has reference to particular things, in so far as they are regarded in relation to a given time and place: of this, I think, no one can doubt.

PROP. XXXVIII. In proportion as the mind understands more things by the second and third kind of knowledge, it is less subject to those emotions which are evil, and stands in less fear of death.

Proof. — The mind's essence consists in knowledge (II. xi.); therefore, in proportion as the mind understands more things by the second and third kinds of knowledge, the greater will be the part of it that endures (V. xxix. and xxiii.), and, consequently (by the last Prop.), the greater will be the part that is not touched by the emotions, which are contrary to our nature, or in other words, evil (IV. xxx.). Thus, in proportion as the mind understands more things by the second and third kinds of knowledge, the greater will be the part of it, that remains unimpaired, and, consequently, less subject to emotions, &c. Q.E.D.

Note. — Hence we understand that point which I touched on in IV. xxxix. note, and which I promised to explain in this Part; namely, that death becomes less hurtful, in proportion as the mind's clear and distinct knowledge is greater, and, consequently, in proportion as the mind loves God more. Again, since from the third kind of knowledge arises the highest possible acquiescence (V. xxvii.), it follows that the human mind can attain to being of such a nature, that the part thereof which we have shown to perish with the body (V. xxi.) should be of little importance when compared with the part which endures. But I will soon treat of the subject at greater length.

PROP. XXXIX. He, who possesses a body capable of the greatest number of activities, possesses a mind whereof the greatest part is eternal.

Proof. — He, who possesses a body capable of the greatest number of activities, is least agitated by those emotions which are evil (IV. xxxviii.) — that is (IV. xxx.), by those emotions which are contrary to our nature; therefore (V. x.), he possesses the power of arranging and associating the modifications of the body according to the intellectual order, and, consequently, of bringing it about, that all the modifications of the body should be referred to the idea of God; whence it will come to pass that (V. xv.) he will be affected with love towards God, which (V. xvi.) must occupy or constitute the chief part of the mind; therefore (V. xxxiii.), such a man will possess a mind whereof the chief part is eternal. Q.E.D.

Note. — Since human bodies are capable of the greatest number of activities, there is no doubt but that they may be of such a nature, that they may be referred to minds possessing a great knowledge of themselves and of God, and whereof the greatest or chief part is eternal, and, therefore, that they should scarcely fear death. But, in order that this may be understood more clearly, we must here call to mind, that we live in a state of perpetual variation, and, according as we are changed for the better or the worse, we are called happy or unhappy.

For he, who, from being an infant or a child, becomes a corpse, is called unhappy; whereas it is set down to happiness, if we have been able to live through the whole period of life with a sound mind in a sound body. And, in reality, he, who, as in the case of an infant or a child, has a body capable of very few activities, and depending, for the most part, on external causes, has a mind which, considered in itself alone, is scarcely conscious of itself, or of God, or of things; whereas, he, who has a body capable of very many activities, has a mind which, considered in itself alone, is highly conscious of itself, of God, and of things. In this life, therefore, we primarily endeavour to bring it about, that the body of a child, in so far as its nature allows and conduces thereto, may be changed into something else capable of very many activities, and referable to a mind which is highly conscious of itself, of God, and of things; and we desire so to change it, that what is referred to its imagination and memory may become insignificant, in comparison with its intellect, as I have already said in the note to the last Proposition.

PROP. XL. In proportion as each thing possesses more of perfection, so is it more active, and less passive; and, vice versâ, in proportion as it is more active, so is it more perfect.

Proof. — In proportion as each thing is more perfect, it possesses more of reality (II. Def. vi.), and, consequently (III. iii. and note), it is to that extent more active and less passive. This demonstration may be reversed, and thus prove that, in proportion as a thing is more active, so is it more perfect. Q.E.D.

Corollary. — Hence it follows that the part of the mind which endures, be it great or small, is more perfect than the rest. For the eternal part of the mind (V. xxiii. xxix.) is the understanding, through which alone we are said to act (III. iii.); the part which we have shown to perish is the imagination (V. xxi.), through which only we are said to be passive (III. iii. and general Def. of the Emotions); therefore, the former, be it great or small, is more perfect than the latter. Q.E.D.

Note. — Such are the doctrines which I had purposed to set forth concerning the mind, in so far as it is regarded without relation to the body; whence, as also from I. xxi. and other places, it is plain that our mind, in so far as it understands, is an eternal mode of thinking, which is determined by another eternal mode of thinking, and this other by a third, and so on to infinity; so that all taken together at once constitute the eternal and infinite intellect of God.

PROP. XLI. Even if we did not know that our mind is eternal, we should still consider as of primary importance piety and religion, and generally all things which, in Part IV., we showed to be attributable to courage and high — mindedness.

Proof. — The first and only foundation of virtue, or the rule of right living is (IV. xxii. Coroll. and xxiv.) seeking one's own true interest. Now, while we determined what reason prescribes as useful, we took no account of the mind's eternity, which has only become known to us in this Fifth Part. Although we were ignorant at that time that the mind is eternal, we nevertheless stated that the qualities attributable to courage and high — mindedness are of primary importance. Therefore, even if we were still ignorant of this doctrine, we should yet put the aforesaid precepts of reason in the first place. Q.E.D.

Note. — The general belief of the multitude seems to be different. Most people seem to believe that they are free, in so far as they may obey their lusts, and that they cede their rights, in so far as they are bound to live according to the commandments of the divine law. They therefore believe that piety, religion, and, generally, all things attributable to firmness of mind, are burdens, which, after death, they hope to lay aside, and to receive the reward for their bondage, that is, for their piety and religion; it is not only by this hope, but also, and chiefly, by the fear of being horribly punished after death, that they are induced to live according to the divine commandments, so far as their feeble and infirm spirit will carry them.

If men had not this hope and this fear, but believed that the mind perishes with the body, and that no hope of prolonged life remains for the wretches who are broken down with the burden of piety, they would return to their own inclinations, controlling everything in accordance with their lusts, and desiring to obey fortune rather than themselves. Such a course appears to me not less absurd than if a man, because he does not believe that he can by wholesome food sustain his body for ever, should wish to cram himself with poisons and deadly fare; or if, because he sees that the mind is not eternal or immortal, he should prefer to be out of his mind altogether, and to live without the use of reason; these ideas are so absurd as to be scarcely worth refuting.

PROP. XLII. Blessedness is not the reward of virtue, but virtue itself; neither do we rejoice therein, because we control our lusts, but, contrariwise, because we rejoice therein, we are able to control our lusts.

Proof. — Blessedness consists in love towards God (V. xxxvi and note), which love springs from the third kind of knowledge (V. xxxii. Coroll.); therefore this love (III. iii. lix.) must be referred to the mind, in so far as the latter is active; therefore (IV. Def. viii.) it is virtue itself. This was our first point. Again, in proportion as the mind rejoices more in this divine love or blessedness, so does it the more understand (V. xxxii.); that is (V. iii. Coroll.), so much the more power has it over the emotions, and (V. xxxviii.) so much the less is it subject to those emotions which are evil; therefore, in proportion as the mind rejoices in this divine love or blessedness, so has it the power of controlling lusts. And, since human power in controlling the emotions consists solely in the understanding, it follows that no one rejoices in blessedness, because he has controlled his lusts, but, contrariwise, his power of controlling his lusts arises from this blessedness itself. Q.E.D.

Note. — I have thus completed all I wished to set forth touching the mind's power over the emotions and the mind's freedom. Whence it appears, how potent is the wise man, and how much he surpasses the ignorant man, who is driven only by his lusts. For the ignorant man is not only distracted in various ways by external causes without ever gaining the true acquiescence of his spirit, but moreover lives, as it were unwitting of himself, and of God, and of things, and as soon as he ceases to suffer, ceases also to be.

Whereas the wise man, in so far as he is regarded as such, is scarcely at all disturbed in spirit, but, being conscious of himself, and of God, and of things, by a certain eternal necessity, never ceases to be, but always possesses true acquiescence of his spirit.

If the way which I have pointed out as leading to this result seems exceedingly hard, it may nevertheless be discovered. Needs must it be hard, since it is so seldom found. How would it be possible, if salvation were ready to our hand, and could without great labour be found, that it should be by almost all men neglected? But all things excellent are as difficult as they are rare.

SELECTED LETTERS OF BARUCH SPINOZA

LETTER I. HENRY OLDENBURG TO B. DE SPINOZA.

[OLDENBURG, AFTER COMPLIMENTING Spinoza, asks him to enter into a philosophical correspondence.]

ILLUSTRIOUS Sir, and most worthy Friend, —

So painful to me was the separation from you the other day after our meeting in your retreat at Rhijnsburg, that it is my first endeavour, now that I am returned to England, to renew, as far as is possible by correspondence, my intercourse with you. Solid learning, conjoined with courtesy and refinement of manners (wherewith both nature and art have most amply endowed you), carries with it such charms as to command the love of every honourable and liberally-educated man. Let us then, most excellent sir, join hands in sincere friendship, and let us foster the feeling with every zealous endeavour and kind office in our power. Whatever my poor means can furnish I beg you to look on as your own. Allow me in return to claim a share in the riches of your talents, as I may do without inflicting any loss on yourself.

We conversed at Rhijnsburg of God, of extension, of infinite thought, of the differences and agreements between these, of the nature of the connection between the human soul and body, and further, of the principles of the Cartesian and Baconian philosophies.

But, as we then spoke of these great questions merely cursorily and by the way, and as my mind has been not a little tormented with them since, I will appeal to the rights of our newly cemented friendship, and most affectionately beg you to give me at somewhat greater length your opinion on the subjects I have mentioned. On two points especially I ask for enlightenment, if I may presume so far; first: In what do you place the true distinction between thought and matter? secondly: What do you consider to be the chief defects in the Cartesian and Baconian philosophies, and how do you think they might best be removed, and something more sound substituted? The more freely you write to me on these and similar subjects, the more closely will you tie the bonds of our friendship, and the stricter will be the obligation laid on me to repay you, as far as possible, with similar services.

There is at present in the press a collection of physiological discourses written by an Englishman of noble family and distinguished learning. They treat of the nature and elasticity of the air, as proved by forty-three experiments; also of its fluidity, solidity, and other analogous matters. As soon as the work is published, I shall make a point of sending it to you by any friend who may be crossing the sea. Meanwhile, farewell, and remember your friend, who is

Yours, in all affection and zeal,

Henry Oldenburg.

London,

16/26 Aug., 1661.

Benedict de Spinoza

Henry Oldenburg

LETTER II. SPINOZA TO OLDENBURG.

[ANSWER TO LETTER I. Spinoza defines "God," and "attribute," and sends definitions, axioms, and first four propositions of Book I. of Ethics. Some errors of Bacon and Descartes discussed.]

Illustrious Sir, —

How pleasant your friendship is to me, you may yourself judge, if your modesty will allow you to reflect on the abundance of your own excellences. Indeed the thought of these makes me seem not a little bold in entering into such a compact, the more so when I consider that between friends all things, and especially things spiritual, ought to be in common. However, this must lie at the charge of your modesty and kindness rather than of myself. You have been willing to lower yourself through the former and to fill me with the abundance of the latter, till I am no longer afraid to accept the close friendship, which you hold out to me, and which you deign to ask of me in return; no effort on my part shall be spared to render it lasting.

As for my mental endowments, such as they are, I would willingly allow you to share them, even though I knew it would be to my own great hindrance. But this is not meant as an excuse for denying to you what you ask by the rights of friendship. I will therefore endeavour to explain my opinions on the topics you touched on; though I scarcely hope, unless your kindness intervene, that I shall thus draw the bonds of our friendship closer.

I will then begin by speaking briefly of God, Whom I define as a Being consisting in infinite attributes, whereof each is infinite or supremely perfect after its kind. You must observe that by attribute I mean everything, which is conceived through itself and in itself, so that the conception of it does not involve the conception of anything else. For instance, extension is conceived through itself and in itself, but motion is not. The latter is conceived through something else, for the conception of it implies extension.

That the definition above given of God is true appears from the fact, that by God we mean a Being supremely perfect and absolutely infinite. That such a Being exists may easily be proved from the definition; but as this is not the place for such proof, I will pass it over. What I am bound here to prove, in order to satisfy the first inquiry of my distinguished questioner, are the following consequences; first, that in the universe there cannot exist two substances without their differing utterly in essence; secondly, that substance cannot be produced or created — existence pertains to its actual essence; thirdly, that all substance must be infinite or supremely perfect after its kind.

When these points have been demonstrated, my distinguished questioner will readily perceive my drift, if he reflects at the same time on the definition of God. In order to prove them clearly and briefly, I can think of nothing better than to submit them to the bar of your judgment proved in the geometrical method. I therefore enclose them separately and await your verdict upon them.

Again, you ask me what errors I detect in the Cartesian and Baconian philosophies. It is not my custom to expose the errors of others, nevertheless I will yield to your request. The first and the greatest error is, that these philosophers have strayed so far from the knowledge of the first cause and origin of all things; the second is, that they did not know the true nature of the human mind; the third, that they never grasped the true cause of error. The necessity for correct knowledge on these three points can only be ignored by persons completely devoid of learning and training.

That they have wandered astray from the knowledge of the first cause, and of the human mind, may easily be gathered from the truth of the three propositions given above; I therefore devote myself entirely to the demonstration of the third error. Of Bacon I shall say very little, for he speaks very confusedly on the point, and works out scarcely any proofs: he simply narrates. In the first place he assumes, that the human intellect is liable to err, not only through the fallibility of the senses, but also solely through its own nature, and that it frames its conceptions in accordance with the analogy of its own nature, not with the analogy of the universe, so that it is like a mirror receiving rays from external objects unequally, and mingling its own nature with the nature of things, &c.

Secondly, that the human intellect is, by reason of its own nature, prone to abstractions; such things as are in flux it feigns to be constant, &c.

Thirdly, that the human intellect continually augments, and is unable to come to a stand or to rest content. The other causes which he assigns may all be reduced to the one Cartesian principle, that the human will is free and more extensive than the intellect, or, as Verulam himself more confusedly puts it, that "the understanding is not a dry light, but receives infusion from the will." (We may here observe that Verulam often employs "intellect" as synonymous with mind, differing in this respect from Descartes). This cause, then, leaving aside the others as unimportant, I shall show to be false; indeed its falsity would be evident to its supporters, if they would consider, that will in general differs from this or that particular volition in the same way as whiteness differs from this or that white object, or humanity from this or that man. It is, therefore, as impossible to conceive, that will is the cause of a given volition, as to conceive that humanity is the cause of Peter and Paul.

Hence, as will is merely an entity of the reason, and cannot be called the cause of particular volitions, and as some cause is needed for the existence of such volitions, these latter cannot be called free, but are necessarily such as they are determined by their causes; lastly, according to Descartes, errors are themselves particular volitions; hence it necessarily follows that errors, or, in other words, particular volitions, are not free, but are determined by external causes, and in nowise by the will. This is what I undertook to prove.

Henry Oldenburg

27 Sept., 1661

London

Benedict de Spinoza

LETTER III. OLDENBURG TO SPINOZA.

[OLDENBURG PROPOUNDS SEVERAL questions concerning God and His existence, thought, and the axioms of Eth. I. He also informs Spinoza of a philosophical society, and promises to send Boyle's book.]

Most excellent Friend, —

Your learned letter has been delivered to me, and read with great pleasure.

I highly approve of your geometrical method of proof, but I must set it down to my dulness, that I cannot follow with readiness what you set forth with such accuracy. Suffer me, then, I beg, to expose the slowness of my understanding, while I put the following questions, and beg of you to answer them.

First. Do you clearly and indisputably understand solely from the definition you have given of God, that such a Being exists? For my part, when I reflect that definitions contain only the conceptions formed by our minds, and that our mind forms many conceptions of things which do not exist, and is very fertile in multiplying and amplifying what it has conceived, I do not yet see, that from the conception I have of God I can infer God's existence. I am able by a mental combination of all the perfections I perceive in men, in animals, in vegetables, in minerals, &c., to conceive and to form an idea of some single substance uniting in itself all such excellences; indeed my mind is able to multiply and augment such excellences indefinitely; it may thus figure forth for itself a most perfect and excellent Being, but there would be no reason thence to conclude that such a Being actually exists.

Secondly. I wish to ask, whether you think it unquestionable, that body cannot be limited by thought, or thought by body; seeing that it still remains undecided, what thought is, whether it be a physical motion or a spiritual act quite distinct from body?

Thirdly. Do you reckon the axioms, which you have sent to me, as indemonstrable principles known by the light of nature and needing no proof? Perhaps the first is of this nature, but I do not see how the other three can be placed in a like category. The second assumes that nothing exists in the universe save substances and accidents, but many persons would say that time and place cannot be classed either as one or the other. Your third axiom, that things having different attributes have no quality in common, is so far from being clear to me, that its contrary seems to be shown in the whole universe. All things known to us agree in certain respects and differ in others. Lastly, your fourth axiom, that when things have no quality in common, one cannot be produced by another, is not so plain to my groping intelligence as to stand in need of no further illumination. God has nothing actually in common with created things, yet nearly all of us believe Him to be their cause.

As you see that in my opinion your axioms are not established beyond all the assaults of doubt, you will readily gather that the propositions you have based upon them do not appear to me absolutely firm. The more I reflect upon them, the more are doubts suggested to my mind concerning them.

As to the first, I submit that two men are two substances with the same attribute, inasmuch as both are rational; whence I infer that there can be two substances with the same attribute.

As to the second, I opine that, as nothing can be its own cause, it is hardly within the scope of our intellect to pronounce on the truth of the proposition, that substance cannot be produced even by any other substance. Such a proposition asserts all substances to be self-caused, and all and each to be independent of one another, thus making so many gods, and therefore denying the first cause of all things. This, I willingly confess, I cannot understand, unless you will be kind enough to explain your theory on this sublime subject somewhat more fully and simply, informing me what may be the origin and mode of production of substances, and the mutual interdependence and subordination of things. I most strenuously beg and conjure you by that friendship which we have entered into, to answer me freely and faithfully on these points; you may rest assured, that everything which you think fit to communicate to me will remain untampered with and safe, for I will never allow anything to become public through me to your hurt or disadvantage. In our philosophical society we proceed diligently as far as opportunity offers with our experiments and observations, lingering over the compilation of the history of mechanic arts, with the idea that the forms and qualities of things can best be explained from mechanical principles, and that all natural effects can be produced through motion, shape, and consistency, without reference to inexplicable forms or occult qualities, which are but the refuge of ignorance.

I will send the book I promised, whenever the Dutch Ambassadors send (as they frequently do) a messenger to the Hague, or whenever some other friend whom I can trust goes your way. I beg you to excuse my prolixity and freedom, and simply ask you to take in good part, as one friend from another, the straightforward and unpolished reply I have sent to your letter, believing me to be without deceit or affectation,

Yours most faithfully,

Henry Oldenburg.

London,

27 Sept., 1661.

Benedict de Spinoza

Henry Oldenburg

LETTER IV. SPINOZA TO OLDENBURG.

[SPINOZA ANSWERS SOME of Oldenburg's questions and doubts, but has not time to reply to all, as he is just setting out for Amsterdam.]

Illustrious Sir, —

As I was starting for Amsterdam, where I intend staying for a week or two, I received your most welcome letter, and noted the objections you raise to the three propositions I sent you. Not having time to reply fully, I will confine myself to these three.

To the first I answer, that not from every definition does the existence of the thing defined follow, but only (as I showed in a note appended to the three propositions) from the definition or idea of an attribute, that is (as I explained fully in the definition given of God) of a thing conceived through and in itself. The reason for this distinction was pointed out, if I mistake not, in the above-mentioned note sufficiently clearly at any rate for a philosopher, who is assumed to be aware of the difference between a fiction and a clear and distinct idea, and also of the truth of the axiom that every definition or clear and distinct idea is true. When this has been duly noted, I do not see what more is required for the solution of your first question.

I therefore proceed to the solution of the second, wherein you seem to admit that, if thought does not belong to the nature of extension, then extension will not be limited by thought; your doubt only involves the example given. But observe, I beg, if we say that extension is not limited by extension but by thought, is not this the same as saying that extension is not infinite absolutely, but only as far as extension is concerned, in other words, infinite after its kind? But you say: perhaps thought is a corporeal action: be it so, though I by no means grant it: you, at any rate, will not deny that extension, in so far as it is extension, is not thought, and this is all that is required for explaining my definition and proving the third proposition.

Thirdly. You proceed to object, that my axioms ought not to be ranked as universal notions. I will not dispute this point with you; but you further hesitate as to their truth, seeming to desire to show that their contrary is more probable. Consider, I beg, the definition which I gave of substance and attribute, for on that they all depend. When I say that I mean by substance that which is conceived through and in itself; and that I mean by modification or accident that, which is in something else, and is conceived through that wherein it is, evidently it follows that substance is by nature prior to its accidents. For without the former the latter can neither be nor be conceived. Secondly, it follows that, besides substances and accidents, nothing exists really or externally to the intellect. For everything is conceived either through itself or through something else, and the conception of it either involves or does not involve the conception of something else. Thirdly, it follows that things which possess different attributes have nothing in common. For by attribute I have explained that I mean something, of which the conception does not involve the conception of anything else. Fourthly and lastly, it follows that, if two things have nothing in common, one cannot be the cause of the other. For, as there would be nothing in common between the effect and the cause, the whole effect would spring from nothing. As for your contention that God has nothing actually in common with created things, I have maintained the exact opposite in my definition. I said that God is a Being consisting of infinite attributes, whereof each one is infinite or supremely perfect after its kind. With regard to what you say concerning my first proposition, I beg you, my friend, to bear in mind, that men are not created but born, and that their bodies already exist before birth, though under different forms. You draw the conclusion, wherein I fully concur, that, if one particle of matter be annihilated, the whole of extension would forthwith vanish. My second proposition does not make many gods but only one, to wit, a Being consisting of infinite attributes, &c.

Henry Oldenburg

Benedict de Spinoza

LETTER V. OLDENBURG TO SPINOZA.

[OLDENBURG SENDS BOYLE'S book, and laments that Spinoza has not been able to answer all his doubts.]

Most Respected Friend, —

Please accept herewith the book I promised you, and write me in answer your opinion on it, especially on the remarks about nitre, and about fluidity, and solidity. I owe you the warmest thanks for your learned second letter, which I received to-day, but I greatly grieve that your journey to Amsterdam prevented you from answering all my doubts. I beg you will supply the omission, as soon as you have leisure. You have much enlightened me in your last letter, but have not yet dispelled all my darkness; this result will, I believe, be happily accomplished, when you send me clear and distinct information concerning the first origin of things. Hitherto I have been somewhat in doubt as to the cause from which, and the manner in which things took their origin; also, as to what is the nature of their connection with the first cause, if such there be. All that I hear or read on the subject seems inconclusive. Do you then, my very learned master, act, as it were, as my torch-bearer in the matter. You will have no reason to doubt my confidence and gratitude. Such is the earnest petition of

Yours most faithfully,

Henry Oldenburg.

Benedict de Spinoza

Henry Oldenburg

LETTER VI. SPINOZA TO OLDENBURG.

[CONTAINING DETAILED CRITICISMS by Spinoza of Robert Boyle's book.]

Omitted.

LETTER VII. OLDENBURG TO SPINOZA.

[AFTER THANKING SPINOZA, in the name of himself and Boyle, Oldenburg mentions the foundation of the Royal Society, and begs his correspondent to publish his theological and philosophical works.]

* * * * *

The body of philosophers which I formerly mentioned to you has now, by the king's grace, been constituted as a Royal Society, and furnished with a public charter, whereby distinguished privileges are conferred upon it, and an excellent prospect afforded of endowing it with the necessary revenues.

I would by all means advise you not to begrudge to the learned those works in philosophy and theology, which you have composed with the talent that distinguishes you. Publish them, I beg, whatever be the verdict of petty theologians. Your country is free; the course of philosophy should there be free also. Your own prudence will, doubtless, suggest to you, that your ideas and opinions should be put forth as quietly as possible. For the rest, commit the issue to fortune. Come, then, good sir, cast away all fear of exciting against you the pigmies of our time. Long enough have we sacrificed to ignorance and pedantry. Let us spread the sails of true knowledge, and explore the recesses of nature more thoroughly than heretofore. Your meditations can, I take it, be printed in your country with impunity; nor need any scandal among the learned be dreaded because of them. If these be your patrons and supporters (and I warrant me you will find them so), why should you dread the carpings of ignorance? I will not let you go, my honoured friend, till I have gained my request; nor will I ever, so far as in me lies, allow thoughts of such importance as yours to rest in eternal silence. I earnestly beg you to communicate to me, as soon as you conveniently can, your decision in the matter. Perhaps events will occur here not unworthy of your knowledge. The Society I have mentioned will now proceed more strenuously on its course, and, if peace continues on our shores, will possibly illustrate the republic of letters with some extraordinary achievement. Farewell, excellent sir, and believe me,

Your most zealous and friendly,

Henry Oldenburg.

3 April, 1663

London

LETTER VIII. OLDENBURG TO SPINOZA.

[AFTER FURTHER REPLYING to Spinoza's criticisms on Boyle's book, Oldenburg again exhorts his correspondent to publish.]

* * * * *

I now proceed to the question which has arisen between us. First, permit me to ask you whether you have finished the important little work, in which you treat "of the origin of things and their dependence on the first cause, and of the improvement of our understanding." Truly, my dear sir, I believe nothing more pleasing or acceptable to men of true learning and discrimination could possibly be published than such a treatise. This is what a man of your talent and disposition should look to, far more than the gratification of theologians of our time and fashion. The latter have less regard for truth than for their own convenience. I, therefore, conjure you, by the bond of our friendship, by every duty of increasing and proclaiming the truth, not to begrudge us, or withhold from us your writings on these subjects. If anything of greater importance than I can foresee prevents you from publishing the work, I earnestly charge you to give me a summary of it by letter.

Another book is soon to be published by the learned Boyle, which I will send you as an exchange. I will add papers, which will acquaint you with the whole constitution of our Royal Society, whereof I, with twenty others, am on the Council, and, with one other, am Secretary. I have no time to discourse of any further subjects. All the confidence which honest intentions can inspire, all the readiness to serve, which the smallness of my powers will permit, I pledge to you, and am heartily,

Dear sir, yours wholly,

H. Oldenburg.

London,

3 April, 1663.

LETTER IX. SPINOZA TO OLDENBURG.

[SPINOZA INFORMS OLDENBURG that he has removed to Rhijnsburg, and has spent some time at Amsterdam for the purpose of publishing the "Principles of Cartesian Philosophy." He then replies to Boyle's objections.]

Distinguished Sir, —

I have at length received your long wished for letter, and am at liberty to answer it. But, before I do so, I will briefly tell you, what has prevented my replying before. When I removed my household goods here in April, I set out for Amsterdam. While there certain friends asked me to impart to them a treatise containing, in brief, the second part of the principles of Descartes treated geometrically, together with some of the chief points treated of in metaphysics, which I had formerly dictated to a youth, to whom I did not wish to teach my own opinions openly. They further requested me, at the first opportunity, to compose a similar treatise on the first part. Wishing to oblige my friends, I at once set myself to the task, which I finished in a fortnight, and handed over to them. They then asked for leave to print it, which I readily granted on the condition that one of them should, under my supervision, clothe it in more elegant phraseology, and add a little preface warning readers that I do not acknowledge all the opinions there set forth as my own, inasmuch as I hold the exact contrary to much that is there written, illustrating the fact by one or two examples. All this the friend who took charge of the treatise promised to do, and this is the cause for my prolonged stay in Amsterdam. Since I returned to this village, I have hardly been able to call my time my own, because of the friends who have been kind enough to visit me. At last, my dear friend, a moment has come, when I can relate these occurrences to you, and inform you why I allow this treatise to see the light. It may be that on this occasion some of those, who hold the foremost positions in my country, will be found desirous of seeing the rest of my writings, which I acknowledge as my own; they will thus take care that I am enabled to publish them without any danger of infringing the laws of the land. If this be as I think, I shall doubtless publish at once; if things fall out otherwise, I would rather be silent than obtrude my opinions on men, in defiance of my country, and thus render them hostile to me. I therefore hope, my friend, that you will not chafe at having to wait a short time longer; you shall then receive from me either the treatise printed, or the summary of it which you ask for. If meanwhile you would like to have one or two copies of the work now in the press, I will satisfy your wish, as soon as I know of it and of means to send the book conveniently.

[The rest of the letter is taken up with criticisms on Boyle's book.]

LETTERS X-XIV.

[Contain further correspondence concerning Boyle's book, and kindred subjects.]

LETTER XIII.A. OLDENBURG TO SPINOZA.

[THE PLACE OF this letter is between Letters XIII. and XIV. It was written apparently in September, 1665. It mentions the plague, which was then at its height, the war, and the labours of the Royal Society, and especially of Boyle. Then comes the passage here given. The letter terminates with references to the comets, and to Huyghens.]

* * * * *

I see that you are engaged not so much in philosophy as in theology, if I may say so. That is, you are recording your thoughts about angels, prophecy, and miracles, but you are doing this, perhaps, in a philosophical manner; however that may be, I am certain that the work is worthy of you, and that I am most anxious to have it. Since these most difficult times prevent free intercourse, I beg at least that you will not disdain to signify to me in your next letter your design and aim in this writing of yours.

Here we are daily expecting news of a second naval battle, unless indeed your fleet has retired into port. Virtue, the nature of which you hint is being discussed among your friends, belongs to wild beasts not to men. For if men acted according to the guidance of reason, they would not so tear one another in pieces, as they evidently do. But what is the good of my complaining? Vices will exist while men do; but yet they are not continuous, but compensated by the interposition of better things.

* * * * *

LETTER XV. SPINOZA TO OLDENBURG.

[SPINOZA WRITES TO his friend concerning the reasons which lead us to believe, that "every part of nature agrees with the whole, and is associated with all other parts." He also makes a few remarks about Huyghens.]

Distinguished Sir, —

For the encouragement to pursue my speculations given me by yourself and the distinguished R. Boyle, I return you my best thanks. I proceed as far as my slender abilities will allow me, with full confidence in your aid and kindness. When you ask me my opinion on the question raised concerning our knowledge of the means, whereby each part of nature agrees with its whole, and the manner in which it is associated with the remaining parts, I presume you are asking for the reasons which induce us to believe, that each part of nature agrees with its whole, and is associated with the remaining parts. For as to the means whereby the parts are really associated, and each part agrees with its whole, I told you in my former letter that I am in ignorance. To answer such a question, we should have to know the whole of nature and its several parts. I will therefore endeavour to show the reason, which led me to make the statement; but I will premise that I do not attribute to nature either beauty or deformity, order or confusion. Only in relation to our imagination can things be called beautiful or deformed, ordered or confused.

By the association of parts, then, I merely mean that the laws or nature of one part adapt themselves to the laws or nature of another part, so as to cause the least possible inconsistency. As to the whole and the parts, I mean that a given number of things are parts of a whole, in so far as the nature of each of them is adapted to the nature of the rest, so that they all, as far as possible, agree together. On the other hand, in so far as they do not agree, each of them forms, in our mind, a separate idea, and is to that extent considered as a whole, not as a part. For instance, when the parts of lymph, chyle, &c., combine, according to the proportion of the figure and size of each, so as to evidently unite, and form one fluid, the chyle, lymph, &c., considered under this aspect, are part of the blood; but, in so far as we consider the particles of lymph as differing in figure and size from the particles of chyle, we shall consider each of the two as a whole, not as a part.

Let us imagine, with your permission, a little worm, living in the blood, able to distinguish by sight the particles of blood, lymph, &c., and to reflect on the manner in which each particle, on meeting with another particle, either is repulsed, or communicates a portion of its own motion. This little worm would live in the blood, in the same way as we live in a part of the universe, and would consider each particle of blood, not as a part, but as a whole. He would be unable to determine, how all the parts are modified by the general nature of blood, and are compelled by it to adapt themselves, so as to stand in a fixed relation to one another. For, if we imagine that there are no causes external to the blood, which could communicate fresh movements to it, nor any space beyond the blood, nor any bodies whereto the particles of blood could communicate their motion, it is certain that the blood would always remain in the same state, and its particles would undergo no modifications, save those which may be conceived as arising from the relations of motion existing between the lymph, the chyle, &c. The blood would then always have to be considered as a whole, not as a part. But, as there exist, as a matter of fact, very many causes which modify, in a given manner, the nature of the blood, and are, in turn, modified thereby, it follows that other motions and other relations arise in the blood, springing not from the mutual relations of its parts only, but from the mutual relations between the blood as a whole and external causes. Thus the blood comes to be regarded as a part, not as a whole. So much for the whole and the part.

All natural bodies can and ought to be considered in the same way as we have here considered the blood, for all bodies are surrounded by others, and are mutually determined to exist and operate in a fixed and definite proportion, while the relations between motion and rest in the sum total of them, that is, in the whole universe, remain unchanged. Hence it follows that each body, in so far as it exists as modified in a particular manner, must be considered as a part of the whole universe, as agreeing with the whole, and associated with the remaining parts. As the nature of the universe is not limited, like the nature of blood, but is absolutely infinite, its parts are by this nature of infinite power infinitely modified, and compelled to undergo infinite variations. But, in respect to substance, I conceive that each part has a more close union with its whole. For, as I said in my first letter (addressed to you while I was still at Rhijnsburg), substance being infinite in its nature, it follows, as I endeavoured to show, that each part belongs to the nature of substance, and, without it, can neither be nor be conceived.

You see, therefore, how and why I think that the human body is a part of nature. As regards the human mind, I believe that it also is a part of nature; for I maintain that there exists in nature an infinite power of thinking, which, in so far as it is infinite, contains subjectively the whole of nature, and its thoughts proceed in the same manner as nature — that is, in the sphere of ideas. Further, I take the human mind to be identical with this said power, not in so far as it is infinite, and perceives the whole of nature, but in so far as it is finite, and perceives only the human body; in this manner, I maintain that the human mind is a part of an infinite understanding.

But to explain, and accurately prove, all these and kindred questions, would take too long; and I do not think you expect as much of me at present. I am afraid that I may have mistaken your meaning, and given an answer to a different question from that which you asked. Please inform me on this point.

You write in your last letter, that I hinted that nearly all the Cartesian laws of motion are false. What I said was, if I remember rightly, that Huyghens thinks so; I myself do not impeach any of the laws except the sixth, concerning which I think Huyghens is also in error. I asked you at the same time to communicate to me the experiment made according to that hypothesis in your Royal Society; as you have not replied, I infer that you are not at liberty to do so. The above-mentioned Huyghens is entirely occupied in polishing lenses. He has fitted up for the purpose a handsome workshop, in which he can also construct moulds. What will be the result I know not, nor, to speak the truth, do I greatly care. Experience has sufficiently taught me, that the free hand is better and more sure than any machine for polishing spherical moulds. I can tell you nothing certain as yet about the success of the clocks or the date of Huyghens' journey to France.

Henry Oldenburg

8 Dec., 1665

London

LETTER XVI. OLDENBURG TO SPINOZA.

[AFTER SOME REMARKS on Spinoza's last letter, and an account of experiments at the Royal Society and at Oxford, Oldenburg mentions a report about the return of the Jews to Palestine].

* * * * *

But I pass on to politics. Everyone here is talking of a report that the Jews, after remaining scattered for more than two thousand years, are about to return to their country. Few here believe in it, but many desire it. Please tell your friend what you hear and think on the matter. For my part, unless the news is confirmed from trustworthy sources at Constantinople, which is the place chiefly concerned, I shall not believe it. I should like to know, what the Jews of Amsterdam have heard about the matter, and how they are affected by such important tidings which, if true, would assuredly seem to harbinger the end of the world. * * * Believe me to be

Yours most zealously,

Henry Oldenburg

London,

8 Dec., 1665.

P.S. I will shortly (d.v.) tell you the opinion of our philosophers on the recent comets.

Henry Oldenburg

8 June, 1675

London

Benedict de Spinoza

LETTER XVII. OLDENBURG TO SPINOZA.

[OLDENBURG THANKS SPINOZA for the Tractatus Theoligico-Politicus despatched but not received, and modifies an adverse verdict expressed in a former letter (now lost).]

I was unwilling to let pass the convenient opportunity offered me by the journey to Holland of the learned Dr. Bourgeois, an adherent of the Reformed religion, for expressing my thanks a few weeks ago for your treatise forwarded to me, but not yet arrived. But I am doubtful whether my letter was duly delivered. I indicated in them my opinion on the treatise; but on deeper and more careful inspection I now think that my verdict was hasty. Certain arguments seemed to me to be urged at the expense of religion, as measured by the standard supplied by the common run of theologians and the received formulas of creeds which are evidently biassed. But a closer consideration of the whole subject convinced me, that you are far from attempting any injury to true religion and sound philosophy, but, on the contrary, strive to exalt and establish the true object of the Christian religion and the divine loftiness of fruitful philosophy.

Now that I believe that this is your fixed purpose, I would most earnestly beg you to have the kindness to write frequently and explain the nature of what you are now preparing and considering with this object to your old and sincere friend, who is all eager for the happy issue of so lofty a design. I sacredly promise you, that I will not divulge a syllable to anyone, if you enjoin silence; I will only endeavour gently to prepare the minds of good and wise men for the reception of those truths, which you will some day bring before a wider public, and I will try to dispel the prejudices, which have been conceived against your doctrines. Unless I am quite mistaken, you have an insight deeper than common into the nature and powers of the human mind, and its union with the human body. I earnestly beg you to favour me with your reflections on this subject. Farewell, most excellent Sir, and favour the devoted admirer of your teaching and virtue,

Henry Oldenburg.

London,

8 June, 1675.

Henry Oldenburg

LETTER XVIII. OLDENBURG TO SPINOZA.

[OLDENBURG REJOICES AT the renewal of correspondence, and alludes to the five books of the Ethics which Spinoza (in a letter now lost) had announced his intention of publishing.]

Our correspondence being thus happily renewed, I should be unwilling to fall short of a friend's duty in the exchange of letters. I understand from your answer delivered to me on July 5, that you intend to publish your treatise in five parts. Allow me, I beg, to warn you by the sincerity of your affection for me, not to insert any passages which may seem to discourage the practice of religion and virtue; especially as nothing is more sought after in this degenerate and evil age than doctrines of the kind, which seem to give countenance to rampant vice.

However, I will not object to receiving a few copies of the said treatise. I will only ask you that, when the time arrives, they may be entrusted to a Dutch merchant living in London, who will see that they are forwarded to me. There is no need to mention, that books of the kind in question have been sent to me: if they arrive safely to my keeping, I do not doubt that I can conveniently dispose of some copies to my friends here and there, and can obtain a just price for them. Farewell, and when you have leisure write to

Yours most zealously,

Henry Oldenburg.

London,

22 July, 1675.

Benedict de Spinoza

Henry Oldenburg

LETTER XIX. SPINOZA TO OLDENBURG.

[SPINOZA RELATES HIS journey to Amsterdam for the purpose of publishing his Ethics; he was deterred by the dissuasions of theologians and Cartesians. He hopes that Oldenburg will inform him of some of the objections to the Tractatus Theologico-Politicus, made by learned men, so that they may be answered in notes.]

Distinguished and Illustrious Sir, —

When I received your letter of the 22nd July, I had set out to Amsterdam for the purpose of publishing the book I had mentioned to you. While I was negotiating, a rumour gained currency that I had in the press a book concerning God, wherein I endeavoured to show that there is no God. This report was believed by many. Hence certain theologians, perhaps the authors of the rumour, took occasion to complain of me before the prince and the magistrates; moreover, the stupid Cartesians, being suspected of favouring me, endeavoured to remove the aspersion by abusing everywhere my opinions and writings, a course which they still pursue. When I became aware of this through trustworthy men, who also assured me that the theologians were everywhere lying in wait for me, I determined to put off publishing till I saw how things were going, and I proposed to inform you of my intentions. But matters seem to get worse and worse, and I am still uncertain what to do. Meanwhile I do not like to delay any longer answering your letter. I will first thank you heartily for your friendly warning, which I should be glad to have further explained, so that I may know, which are the doctrines which seem to you to be aimed against the practice of religion and virtue. If principles agree with reason, they are, I take it, also most serviceable to virtue. Further, if it be not troubling you too much I beg you to point out the passages in the Tractatus Theologico-Politicus which are objected to by the learned, for I want to illustrate that treatise with notes, and to remove if possible the prejudices conceived against it. Farewell.

Henry Oldenburg

15 Nov., 1675

London

Benedict de Spinoza

LETTER XX. OLDENBURG TO SPINOZA.

AS I SEE from your last letter, the book you propose to publish is in peril. It is impossible not to approve your purpose of illustrating and softening down those passages in the Tractatus Theologico-Politicus, which have given pain to its readers. First I would call attention to the ambiguities in your treatment of God and Nature: a great many people think you have confused the one with the other. Again, you seem to many to take away the authority and value of miracles, whereby alone, as nearly all Christians believe, the certainty of the divine revelation can be established.

Again, people say that you conceal your opinion concerning Jesus Christ, the Redeemer of the world, the only Mediator for mankind, and concerning His incarnation and redemption: they would like you to give a clear explanation of what you think on these three subjects. If you do this and thus give satisfaction to prudent and rational Christians, I think your affairs are safe. Farewell.

London,

15 Nov., 1675.

P.S. — Send me a line, I beg, to inform me whether this note has reached you safely.

Benedict de Spinoza

Henry Oldenburg

LETTER XXI. SPINOZA TO OLDENBURG.

DISTINGUISHED SIR, —

I received on Saturday last your very short letter dated 15th Nov. In it you merely indicate the points in the theological treatise, which have given pain to readers, whereas I had hoped to learn from it, what were the opinions which militated against the practice of religious virtue, and which you formerly mentioned. However, I will speak on the three subjects on which you desire me to disclose my sentiments, and tell you, first, that my opinion concerning God differs widely from that which is ordinarily defended by modern Christians. For I hold that God is of all things the cause immanent, as the phrase is, not transient. I say that all things are in God and move in God, thus agreeing with Paul, and, perhaps, with all the ancient philosophers, though the phraseology may be different; I will even venture to affirm that I agree with all the ancient Hebrews, in so far as one may judge from their traditions, though these are in many ways corrupted. The supposition of some, that I endeavour to prove in the Tractatus Theologico-Politicus the unity of God and Nature (meaning by the latter a certain mass or corporeal matter), is wholly erroneous.

As regards miracles, I am of opinion that the revelation of God can only be established by the wisdom of the doctrine, not by miracles, or in other words by ignorance. This I have shown at sufficient length in Chapter VI. concerning miracles. I will here only add, that I make this chief distinction between religion and superstition, that the latter is founded on ignorance, the former on knowledge; this, I take it, is the reason why Christians are distinguished from the rest of the world, not by faith, nor by charity, nor by the other fruits of the Holy Spirit, but solely by their opinions, inasmuch as they defend their cause, like everyone else, by miracles, that is by ignorance, which is the source of all malice; thus they turn a faith, which may be true, into superstition. Lastly, in order to disclose my opinions on the third point, I will tell you that I do not think it necessary for salvation to know Christ according to the flesh: but with regard to the Eternal Son of God, that is the Eternal Wisdom of God, which has manifested itself in all things and especially in the human mind, and above all in Christ Jesus, the case is far otherwise. For without this no one can come to a state of blessedness, inasmuch as it alone teaches, what is true or false, good or evil. And, inasmuch as this wisdom was made especially manifest through Jesus Christ, as I have said, His disciples preached it, in so far as it was revealed to them through Him, and thus showed that they could rejoice in that spirit of Christ more than the rest of mankind. The doctrines added by certain churches, such as that God took upon Himself human nature, I have expressly said that I do not understand; in fact, to speak the truth, they seem to me no less absurd than would a statement, that a circle had taken upon itself the nature of a square. This I think will be sufficient explanation of my opinions concerning the three points mentioned. Whether it will be satisfactory to Christians you will know better than I. Farewell.

Henry Oldenburg

16 Dec., 1675

London

Benedict de Spinoza

LETTER XXII. OLDENBURG TO SPINOZA.

[OLDENBURG WISHES TO be enlightened concerning the doctrine of fatalism, of which Spinoza has been accused. He discourses on man's limited intelligence and on the incarnation of the Son of God.]

As you seem to accuse me of excessive brevity, I will this time avoid the charge by excessive prolixity. You expected, I see, that I should set forth those opinions in your writings, which seem to discourage the practice of religious virtue in your readers. I will indicate the matter which especially pains them. You appear to set up a fatalistic necessity for all things and actions; if such is conceded and asserted, people aver, that the sinews of all laws, of virtue, and of religion, are severed, and that all rewards and punishment are vain. Whatsoever can compel, or involves necessity, is held also to excuse; therefore no one, they think, can be without excuse in the sight of God. If we are driven by fate, and all things follow a fixed and inevitable path laid down by the hard hand of necessity, they do not see where punishment can come in. What wedge can be brought for the untying of this knot, it is very difficult to say. I should much like to know and learn what help you can supply in the matter.

As to the opinions which you have kindly disclosed to me on the three points I mentioned, the following inquiries suggest themselves. First, In what sense do you take miracles and ignorance to be synonymous and equivalent terms, as you appear to think in your last letter?

The bringing back of Lazarus from the dead, and the resurrection from death of Jesus Christ seem to surpass all the power of created nature, and to fall within the scope of divine power only; it would not be a sign of culpable ignorance, that it was necessary to exceed the limits of finite intelligence confined within certain bounds. But perhaps you do not think it in harmony with the created mind and science, to acknowledge in the uncreated mind and supreme Deity a science and power capable of fathoming, and bringing to pass events, whose reason and manner can neither be brought home nor explained to us poor human pigmies? "We are men;" it appears, that we must "think everything human akin to ourselves."

Again, when you say that you cannot understand that God really took upon Himself human nature, it becomes allowable to ask you, how you understand the texts in the Gospel and the Epistle to the Hebrews, whereof the first says, "The Word was made flesh," and the other, "For verily he took not on him the nature of angels; but he took on him the seed of Abraham." Moreover, the whole tenor of the Gospel infers, as I think, that the only begotten Son of God, the Word (who both was God and was with God), showed Himself in human nature, and by His passion and death offered up the sacrifice for our sins, the price of the atonement. What you have to say concerning this without impugning the truth of the Gospel and the Christian religion, which I think you approve of, I would gladly learn.

I had meant to write more, but am interrupted by friends on a visit, to whom I cannot refuse the duties of courtesy. But what I have already put on paper is enough, and will perhaps weary you in your philosophizing. Farewell, therefore, and believe me to be ever an admirer of your learning and knowledge.

London,

16 Dec., 1675.

Benedict de Spinoza

Henry Oldenburg

LETTER XXIII. SPINOZA TO OLDENBURG.

[SPINOZA EXPOUNDS TO Oldenburg his views on fate and necessity, discriminates between miracles and ignorance, takes the resurrection of Christ as spiritual, and deprecates attributing to the sacred writers Western modes of speech.]

Distinguished Sir, —

At last I see, what it was that you begged me not to publish. However, as it forms the chief foundation of everything in the treatise which I intended to bring out, I should like briefly to explain here, in what sense I assert that a fatal necessity presides over all things and actions. God I in no wise subject to fate: I conceive that all things follow with inevitable necessity from the nature of God, in the same way as everyone conceives that it follows from God's nature that God understands Himself. This latter consequence all admit to follow necessarily from the divine nature, yet no one conceives that God is under the compulsion of any fate, but that He understands Himself quite freely, though necessarily.

Further, this inevitable necessity in things does away neither with divine nor human laws. The principles of morality, whether they receive from God Himself the form of laws or institutions, or whether they do not, are still divine and salutary; whether we receive the good, which flows from virtue and the divine love, as from God in the capacity of a judge, or as from the necessity of the divine nature, it will in either case be equally desirable; on the other hand, the evils following from wicked actions and passions are not less to be feared because they are necessary consequences. Lastly, in our actions, whether they be necessary or contingent, we are led by hope and fear.

Men are only without excuse before God, because they are in God's power, as clay is in the hands of the potter, who from the same lump makes vessels, some to honour, some to dishonour. If you will reflect a little on this, you will, I doubt not, easily be able to reply to any objections which may be urged against my opinion, as many of my friends have already done.

I have taken miracles and ignorance as equivalent terms, because those, who endeavour to establish God's existence and the truth of religion by means of miracles, seek to prove the obscure by what is more obscure and completely unknown, thus introducing a new sort of argument, the reduction, not to the impossible, as the phrase is, but to ignorance. But, if I mistake not, I have sufficiently explained my opinion on miracles in the Theologico-Political treatise. I will only add here, that if you will reflect on the facts; that Christ did not appear to the council, nor to Pilate, nor to any unbeliever, but only to the faithful,; also that God has neither right hand nor left, but is by His essence not in a particular spot, but everywhere; that matter is everywhere the same; that God does not manifest himself in the imaginary space supposed to be outside the world; and lastly, that the frame of the human body is kept within due limits solely by the weight of the air; you will readily see that this apparition of Christ is not unlike that wherewith God appeared to Abraham, when the latter saw men whom he invited to dine with him. But, you will say, all the Apostles thoroughly believed, that Christ rose from the dead and really ascended to heaven: I do not deny it. Abraham, too, believed that God had dined with him, and all the Israelites believed that God descended, surrounded with fire, from heaven to Mount Sinai, and there spoke directly with them; whereas, these apparitions or revelations, and many others like them, were adapted to the understanding and opinions of those men, to whom God wished thereby to reveal His will. I therefore conclude, that the resurrection of Christ from the dead was in reality spiritual, and that to the faithful alone, according to their understanding, it was revealed that Christ was endowed with eternity, and had risen from the dead (using dead in the sense in which Christ said, "let the dead bury their dead"), giving by His life and death a matchless example of holiness. Moreover, He to this extent raises his disciples from the dead, in so far as they follow the example of His own life and death. It would not be difficult to explain the whole Gospel doctrine on this hypothesis. Nay, 1 Cor. ch. xv. cannot be explained on any other, nor can Paul's arguments be understood: if we follow the common interpretation, they appear weak and can easily be refuted: not to mention the fact, that Christians interpret spiritually all those doctrines which the Jews accepted literally. I join with you in acknowledging human weakness. But on the other hand, I venture to ask you whether we "human pigmies" possess sufficient knowledge of nature to be able to lay down the limits of its force and power, or to say that a given thing surpasses that power? No one could go so far without arrogance. We may, therefore, without presumption explain miracles as far as possible by natural causes. When we cannot explain them, nor even prove their impossibility, we may well suspend our judgment about them, and establish religion, as I have said, solely by the wisdom of its doctrines. You think that the texts in John's Gospel and in Hebrews are inconsistent with what I advance, because you measure oriental phrases by the standards of European speech; though John wrote his gospel in Greek, he wrote it as a Hebrew. However this may be, do you believe, when Scripture says that God manifested Himself in a cloud, or that He dwelt in the tabernacle or the temple, that God actually assumed the nature of a cloud, a tabernacle, or a temple? Yet the utmost that Christ says of Himself is, that He is the Temple of God, because, as I said before, God had specially manifested Himself in Christ. John, wishing to express the same truth more forcibly, said that "the Word was made flesh." But I have said enough on the subject.

Henry Oldenburg

14 Jan., 1676

London

Benedict de Spinoza

LETTER XXIV. OLDENBURG TO SPINOZA.

[OLDENBURG RETURNS TO the questions of universal necessity, of miracles, and of the literal and allegorical interpretation of Scripture.]

εὖ πράττειν.

You hit the point exactly, in perceiving the cause why I did not wish the doctrine of the fatalistic necessity of all things to be promulgated, lest the practice of virtue should thereby be aspersed, and rewards and punishments become ineffectual. The suggestions in your last letter hardly seem sufficient to settle the matter, or to quiet the human mind. For if we men are, in all our actions, moral as well as natural, under the power of God, like clay in the hands of the potter, with what face can any of us be accused of doing this or that, seing that it was impossible for him to do otherwise? Should we not be able to cast all responsibility on God? Your inflexible fate, and your irresistible power, compel us to act in a given manner, nor can we possibly act otherwise. Why, then, and by what right do you deliver us up to terrible punishments, which we can in no way avoid, since you direct and carry on all things through supreme necessity, according to your good will and pleasure? When you say that men are only inexcusable before God, because they are in the power of God, I should reverse the argument, and say, with more show of reason, that men are evidently excusable, since they are in the power of God. Everyone may plead, "Thy power cannot be escaped from, O God; therefore, since I could not act otherwise, I may justly be excused."

Again, in taking miracles and ignorance as equivalent terms, you seem to bring within the same limits the power of God and the knowledge of the ablest men; for God is, according to you, unable to do or produce anything, for which men cannot assign a reason, if they employ all the strength of their faculties.

Again, the history of Christ's passion, death, burial, and resurrection seems to be depicted in such lively and genuine colours, that I venture to appeal to your conscience, whether you can believe them to be allegorical, rather than literal, while preserving your faith in the narrative? The circumstances so clearly stated by the Evangelists seem to urge strongly on our minds, that the history should be understood literally. I have ventured to touch briefly on these points, and I earnestly beg you to pardon me, and answer me as a friend with your usual candour. Mr. Boyle sends you his kind regards. I will, another time, tell you what the Royal Society is doing. Farewell, and preserve me in your affection.

London,

14 Jan., 1676.

Benedict de Spinoza

7 Feb., 1676

Henry Oldenburg

ETTER XXV. WRITTEN

7 FEB., 1676.

Spinoza to Oldenburg.

[Spinoza again treats of fatalism. He repeats that he accepts Christ's passion, death, and burial literally, but His resurrection spiritually.]

Distinguished Sir, —

When I said in my former letter that we are inexcusable, because we are in the power of God, like clay in the hands of the potter, I meant to be understood in the sense, that no one can bring a complaint against God for having given him a weak nature, or infirm spirit. A circle might as well complain to God of not being endowed with the properties of a sphere, or a child who is tortured, say, with stone, for not being given a healthy body, as a man of feeble spirit, because God has denied to him fortitude, and the true knowledge and love of the Deity, or because he is endowed with so weak a nature, that he cannot check or moderate his desires. For the nature of each thing is only competent to do that which follows necessarily from its given cause. That every man cannot be brave, and that we can no more command for ourselves a healthy body than a healthy mind, nobody can deny, without giving the lie to experience, as well as to reason. "But," you urge, "if men sin by nature, they are excusable;" but you do not state the conclusion you draw, whether that God cannot be angry with them, or that they are worthy of blessedness — that is, of the knowledge and love of God. If you say the former, I fully admit that God cannot be angry, and that all things are done in accordance with His will; but I deny that all men ought, therefore, to be blessed — men may be excusable, and, nevertheless, be without blessedness and afflicted in many ways. A horse is excusable, for being a horse and not a man; but, nevertheless, he must needs be a horse and not a man. He who goes mad from the bite of a dog is excusable, yet he is rightly suffocated. Lastly, he who cannot govern his desires, and keep them in check with the fear of the laws, though his weakness may be excusable, yet he cannot enjoy with contentment the knowledge and love of God, but necessarily perishes. I do not think it necessary here to remind you, that Scripture, when it says that God is angry with sinners, and that He is a Judge who takes cognizance of human actions, passes sentence on them, and judges them, is speaking humanly, and in a way adapted to the received opinion of the masses, inasmuch as its purpose is not to teach philosophy, nor to render men wise, but to make them obedient.

How, by taking miracles and ignorance as equivalent terms, I reduce God's power and man's knowledge within the same limits, I am unable to discern.

For the rest, I accept Christ's passion, death, and burial literally, as you do, but His resurrection I understand allegorically. I admit, that it is related by the Evangelists in such detail, that we cannot deny that they themselves believed Christ's body to have risen from the dead and ascended to heaven, in order to sit at the right hand of God, or that they believed that Christ might have been seen by unbelievers, if they had happened to be at hand, in the places where He appeared to His disciples; but in these matters they might, without injury to Gospel teaching, have been deceived, as was the case with other prophets mentioned in my last letter. But Paul, to whom Christ afterwards appeared, rejoices, that he knew Christ not after the flesh, but after the spirit. Farewell, honourable Sir, and believe me yours in all affection and zeal.

Henry Oldenburg

11 Feb., 1676

London

Benedict de Spinoza

LETTER XXV.A. OLDENBURG TO SPINOZA.

[OLDENBURG ADDUCES CERTAIN further objections against Spinoza's doctrine of necessity and miracles, and exposes the inconsistency of a partial allegorization of Scripture.]

To the most illustrious Master Benedict de Spinoza Henry Oldenburg sends greetings.

In your last letter, written to me on the 7th of February, there are some points which seem to deserve criticism. You say that a man cannot complain, because God has denied him the true knowledge of Himself, and strength sufficient to avoid sins; forasmuch as to the nature of everything nothing is competent, except that which follows necessarily from its cause. But I say, that inasmuch as God, the Creator of men, formed them after His own image, which seems to imply in its concept wisdom, goodness, and power, it appears quite to follow, that it is more within the sphere of man's power to have a sound mind than to have a sound body. For physical soundness of body follows from mechanical causes, but soundness of mind depends on purpose and design. You add, that men may be inexcusable, and yet suffer pain in many ways. This seems hard at first sight, and what you add by way of proof, namely, that a dog mad from having been bitten is indeed to be excused, but yet is rightly killed, does not seem to settle the question. For the killing of such a dog would argue cruelty, were it not necessary in order to preserve other dogs and animals, and indeed men, from a maddening bite of the same kind.

But if God implanted in man a sound mind, as He is able to do, there would be no contagion of vices to be feared. And, surely, it seems very cruel, that God should devote men to eternal, or at least terrible temporary, torments, for sins which by them could be no wise avoided. Moreover, the tenour of all Holy Scripture seems to suppose and imply, that men can abstain from sins. For it abounds in denunciations and promises, in declarations of rewards and punishments, all of which seem to militate against the necessity of sinning, and infer the possibility of avoiding punishment. And if this were denied, it would have to be said, that the human mind acts no less mechanically than the human body.

Next, when you proceed to take miracles and ignorance to be equivalent, you seem to rely on this foundation, that the creature can and should have perfect insight into the power and wisdom of the Creator: and that the fact is quite otherwise, I have hitherto been firmly persuaded.

Lastly, where you affirm that Christ's passion, death, and burial are to be taken literally, but His resurrection allegorically, you rely, as far as I can see, on no proof at all. Christ's resurrection seems to be delivered in the Gospel as literally as the rest. And on this article of the resurrection the whole Christian religion and its truth rest, and with its removal Christ's mission and heavenly doctrine collapse. It cannot escape you, how Christ, after He was raised from the dead, laboured to convince His disciples of the truth of the Resurrection properly so called. To want to turn all these things into allegories is the same thing, as if one were to busy one's self in plucking up the whole truth of the Gospel history.

These few points I wished again to submit in the interest of my liberty of philosophizing, which I earnestly beg you not to take amiss.

Written in

London,

11 Feb., 1676.

I will communicate with you shortly on the present studies and experiments of the Royal Society, if God grant me life and health.

Simon de Vries

24 Feb., 1663

Amsterdam

Benedict de Spinoza

LETTER XXVI. SIMON DE VRIES TO SPINOZA.

[SIMON DE VRIES, a diligent student of Spinoza's writings and philosophy, describes a club formed for the study of Spinoza's MS. containing some of the matter afterwards worked into the Ethics, and asks questions about the difficulties felt by members of the club.]

Most Honourable Friend, —

I have for a long time wished to be present with you; but the weather and the hard winter have not been propitious to me. I sometimes complain of my lot, in that we are separated from each other by so long a distance. Happy, yes most happy is the fellow-lodger, abiding under the same roof with you, who can talk with you on the best of subjects, at dinner, at supper, and during your walks. However, though I am far apart from you in body, you have been very frequently present to my mind, especially in your writings, while I read and turn them over. But as they are not all clear to the members of our club, for which reason we have begun a fresh series of meetings, and as I would not have you think me unmindful of you, I have applied my mind to writing this letter.

As regards our club, the following is its order. One of us (that is everyone by turn) reads through and, as far as he understands it, expounds and also demonstrates the whole of your work, according to the sequence and order of your propositions. Then, if it happens that on any point we cannot satisfy one another, we have resolved to make a note of it and write to you, so that, if possible, it may be made clearer to us, and that we may be able under your guidance to defend the truth against those who are superstitiously religious, and against the Christians, and to withstand the attack of the whole world. Well then, since, when we first read through and expounded them, the definitions did not all seem clear to us, we differed about the nature of definition. Next in your absence we consulted as our authority a celebrated mathematician, named Borel: for he makes mention of the nature of definition, axiom, and postulate, and adduces the opinions of others on the subject. But his opinion is as follows: "Definitions are cited in a demonstration as premises. Wherefore it is necessary, that they should be accurately known; otherwise scientific or accurate knowledge cannot be attained by their means." And elsewhere he says: "The primary and most known construction or passive quality of a given subject should not be chosen rashly, but with the greatest care; if the construction or passive quality be an impossibility, no scientific definition can be obtained. For instance, if anyone were to say, let two two straight lines enclosing a space be called figurals, the definition would be of non-existences and impossible: hence ignorance rather than knowledge would be deduced therefrom. Again, if the construction or passive quality be possible and true, but unknown or doubtful to us, the definition will not be good. For conclusions arising from what is unknown or doubtful are themselves uncertain or doubtful; they therefore bring about conjecture or opinion, but not certain knowledge.

Jacquet seems to dissent from this opinion, for he thinks that one may proceed from a false premiss directly to a true conclusion, as you are aware. Clavius, however, whose opinion he quotes, thinks as follows: "Definitions," he says, "are artificial phrases, nor is there any need in reasoning that a thing should be defined in a particular way; but it is sufficient that a thing defined should never be said to agree with another thing, until it has been shown that its definition also agrees therewith."

Thus, according to Borel, the definition of a given thing should consist as regards its construction or passive quality in something thoroughly known to us and true. Clavius, on the other hand, holds that it is a matter of indifference, whether the construction or passive quality be well known and true, or the reverse; so long as we do not assert, that our definition agrees with anything, before it has been proved.

I should prefer Borel's opinion to that of Clavius. I know not which you would assent to, if to either. As these difficulties have occurred to me with regard to the nature of definition, which is reckoned among the cardinal points of demonstration, and as I cannot free my mind from them, I greatly desire, and earnestly beg you, when you have leisure and opportunity, to be kind enough to send me your opinion on the matter, and at the same time to tell me the distinction between axioms and definitions. Borel says that the difference is merely nominal, but I believe you decide otherwise.

Further, we cannot make up our minds about the third definition. I adduced to illustrate it, what my master said to me at the Hague, to wit, that a thing may be regarded in two ways, either as it is in itself, or as it is in relation to something else; as in the case of the intellect, for that can be regarded either under the head of thought, or as consisting in ideas. But we do not see the point of the distinction thus drawn. For it seems to us, that, if we rightly conceive thought, we must range it under the head of ideas; as, if all ideas were removed from it, we should destroy thought. As we find the illustration of the matter not sufficiently clear, the matter itself remains somewhat obscure, and we need further explanation.

Lastly, in the third note to the eighth proposition, the beginning runs thus:— "Hence it is plain that, although two attributes really distinct be conceived, that is, one without the aid of the other, we cannot therefore infer, that they constitute two entities or two different substances. For it belongs to the nature of substance, that each of its attributes should be conceived through itself, though all the attributes it possesses exist simultaneously in it." Here our master seems to assume, that the nature of substance is so constituted, that it may have several attributes. But this doctrine has not yet been proved, unless you refer to the sixth definition, of absolutely infinite substance or God. Otherwise, if it be asserted that each substance has only one attribute, and I have two ideas of two attributes, I may rightly infer that, where there are two different attributes, there are also different substances. On this point also we beg you to give a further explanation. Besides I thank you very much for your writings communicated to me by P. Balling, which have greatly delighted me, especially your note on Proposition XIX. If I can do you any service here in anything that is within my power, I am at your dispesal. You have but to let me know. I have begun a course of anatomy, and am nearly half through with it; when it is finished, I shall begin a course of chemistry, and thus under your guidance I shall go through the whole of medicine. I leave off, and await your answer. Accept the greeting of

Your most devoted

S. J. de Vries.

Amsterdam,

24 Feb., 1663.

Benedict de Spinoza

Simon de Vries

LETTER XXVII. SPINOZA
TO SIMON DE VRIES.

[SPINOZA DEPRECATES HIS correspondent's jealousy of Albert Burgh; and answers that distinction must be made between different kinds of definitions. He explains his opinions more precisely.]

Respected Friend, —

I have received your long wished-for letter, for which, and for your affection towards me, I heartily thank you. Your long absence has been no less grievous to me than to you; yet in the meantime I rejoice that my trifling studies are of profit to you and our friends. For thus while you are away, I in my absence speak to you. You need not envy my fellow-lodger. There is no one who is more displeasing to me, nor against whom I have been more anxiously on my guard; and therefore I would have you and all my acquaintance warned not to communicate my opinions to him, except when he has come to maturer years. So far he is too childish and inconstant, and is fonder of novelty than of truth. But I hope, that in a few years he will amend these childish faults. Indeed I am almost sure of it, as far as I can judge from his nature. And so his temperament bids me like him.

As for the questions propounded in your club, which is wisely enough ordered, I see that your difficulties arise from not distinguishing between kinds of definition: that is, between a definition serving to explain a thing, of which the essence only is sought and in question, and a definition which is put forward only for purposes of inquiry. The former having a definite object ought to be true, the latter need not. For instance, if someone asks me for a description of Solomon's temple, I am bound to give him a true description, unless I want to talk nonsense with him. But if I have constructed, in my mind, a temple which I desire to build, and infer from the description of it that I must buy such and such a site and so many thousand stones and other materials, will any sane person tell me that I have drawn a wrong conclusion because my definition is possibly untrue? or will anyone ask me to prove my definition? Such a person would simply be telling me, that I had not conceived that which I had conceived, or be requiring me to prove, that I had conceived that which I had conceived; in fact, evidently trifling. Hence a definition either explains a thing, in so far as it is external to the intellect, in which case it ought to be true and only to differ from a proposition or an axiom in being concerned merely with the essences of things, or the modifications of things, whereas the latter has a wider scope and extends also to eternal truths. Or else it explains a thing, as it is conceived or can be conceived by us; and then it differs from an axiom or proposition, inasmuch as it only requires to be conceived absolutely, and not like an axiom as true. Hence a bad definition is one which is not conceived. To explain my meaning, I will take Borel's example — a man saying that two straight lines enclosing a space shall be called "figurals." If the man means by a straight line the same as the rest of the world means by a curved line, his definition is good (for by the definition would be meant some such figure as (), or the like); so long as he does not afterwards mean a square or other kind of figure. But, if he attaches the ordinary meaning to the words straight line, the thing is evidently inconceivable, and therefore there is no definition. These considerations are plainly confused by Borel, to whose opinion you incline. I give another example, the one you cite at the end of your letter. If I say that each substance has only one attribute, this is an unsupported statement and needs proof. But, if I say that I mean by substance that which consists in only one attribute, the definition will be good, so long as entities consisting of several attributes are afterwards styled by some name other than substance. When you say that I do not prove, that substance (or being) may have several attributes, you do not perhaps pay attention to the proofs given. I adduced two: — First, "that nothing is plainer to us, than that every being may be conceived by us under some attribute, and that the more reality or essence a given being has, the more attributes may be attributed to it. Hence a being absolutely infinite must be defined, &c." Secondly, and I think this is the stronger proof of the two, "the more attributes I assign to any being, the more am I compelled to assign to it existence;" in other words, the more I conceive it as true. The contrary would evidently result, if I were feigning a chimera or some such being.

Your remark, that you cannot conceive thought except as consisting in ideas, because, when ideas are removed, thought is annihilated, springs, I think, from the fact that while you, a thinking thing, do as you say, you abstract all your thoughts and conceptions. It is no marvel that, when you have abstracted all your thoughts and conceptions, you have nothing left for thinking with. On the general subject I think I have shown sufficiently clearly and plainly, that the intellect, although infinite, belongs to nature regarded as passive rather than nature regarded as active (ad naturam naturatam, non vero ad naturam naturantem).

However, I do not see how this helps towards understanding the third definition, nor what difficulty the latter presents. It runs, if I mistake not, as follows: "By substance I mean that, which is in itself and is conceived through itself; that is, of which the conception does not involve the conception of anything else. By attribute I mean the same thing, except that it is called attribute with respect to the understanding, which attributes to substance the particular nature aforesaid." This definition, I repeat, explains with sufficient clearness what I wish to signify by substance or attribute. You desire, though there is no need, that I should illustrate by an example, how one and the same thing can be stamped with two names. In order not to seem miserly, I will give you two. First, I say that by Israel is meant the third patriarch; I mean the same by Jacob, the name Jacob being given, because the patriarch in question had caught hold of the heel of his brother. Secondly, by a colourless surface I mean a surface, which reflects all rays of light without altering them. I mean the same by a white surface, with this difference, that a surface is called white in reference to a man looking at it, &c.

Benedict de Spinoza

Simon de Vries

LETTER XXVIII. SPINOZA TO SIMON DE VRIES.

[SPINOZA, IN ANSWER to a letter from De Vries now lost, speaks of the experience necessary for proving a definition, and also of eternal truths.]

Respected Friend, —

You ask me if we have need of experience, in order to know whether the definition of a given attribute is true. To this I answer, that we never need experience, except in cases when the existence of the thing cannot be inferred from its definition, as, for instance, the existence of modes (which cannot be inferred from their definition); experience is not needed, when the existence of the things in question is not distinguished from their essence, and is therefore inferred from their definition. This can never be taught us by any experience, for experience does not teach us any essences of things; the utmost it can do is to set our mind thinking about definite essences only. Wherefore, when the existence of attributes does not differ from their essence, no experience is capable of attaining it for us.

To your further question, whether things and their modifications are eternal truths, I answer: Certainly. If you ask me, why I do not call them eternal truths, I answer, in order to distinguish them, in accordance with general usage, from those propositions, which do not make manifest any particular thing or modification of a thing; for example, nothing comes from nothing. These and such like propositions are, I repeat, called eternal truths simply, the meaning merely being, that they have no standpoint external to the mind, &c.

Benedict de Spinoza

20 April, 1663

Rhijnsburg

Lewis Meyer

LETTER XXIX. SPINOZA TO L. M. (LEWIS MEYER).

DEAREST FRIEND, —

I have received two letters from you, one dated Jan. 11, delivered to me by our friend, N. N., the other dated March 26, sent by some unknown friend to Leyden. They were both most welcome to me, especially as I gathered from them, that all goes well with you, and that you are often mindful of me. I also owe and repay you the warmest thanks for the courtesy and consideration, with which you have always been kind enough to treat me: I hope you will believe, that I am in no less degree devoted to you, as, when occasion offers, I will always endeavour to prove, as far as my poor powers will admit. As a first proof, I will do my best to answer the questions you ask in your letters. You request me to tell you, what I think about the infinite; I will most readily do so.

Everyone regards the question of the infinite as most difficult, if not insoluble, through not making a distinction between that which must be infinite from its very nature, or in virtue of its definition, and that which has no limits, not in virtue of its essence, but in virtue of its cause; and also through not distinguishing between that which is called infinite, because it has no limits, and that, of which the parts cannot be equalled or expressed by any number, though the greatest and least magnitude of the whole may be known; and, lastly, through not distinguishing between that, which can be understood but not imagined, and that which can also be imagined. If these distinctions, I repeat, had been attended to, inquirers would not have been overwhelmed with such a vast crowd of difficulties. They would then clearly have understood, what kind of infinite is indivisible and possesses no parts; and what kind, on the other hand, may be divided without involving a contradiction in terms. They would further have understood, what kind of infinite may, without solecism, be conceived greater than another infinite, and what kind cannot be so conceived. All this will plainly appear from what I am about to say.

However, I will first briefly explain the terms substance, mode, eternity, and duration.

The points to be noted concerning substance are these: First, that existence appertains to its essence; in other words, that solely from its essence and definition its existence follows. This, if I remember rightly, I have already proved to you by word of mouth, without the aid of any other propositions. Secondly, as a consequence of the above, that substance is not manifold, but single: there cannot be two of the same nature. Thirdly, every substance must be conceived as infinite.

The modifications of substance I call modes. Their definition, in so far as it is not identical with that of substance, cannot involve any existence. Hence, though they exist, we can conceive them as non-existent. From this it follows, that, when we are regarding only the essence of modes, and not the order of the whole of nature, we cannot conclude from their present existence, that they will exist or not exist in the future, or that they have existed or not existed in the past; whence it is abundantly clear, that we conceive the existence of substance as entirely different from the existence of modes. From this difference arises the distinction between eternity and duration. Duration is only applicable to the existence of modes; eternity is applicable to the existence of substance, that is, the infinite faculty of existence or being (infinitum existendi sive (invitâ Latinitate) essendi fruitionem).

From what has been said it is quite clear that, when, as is most often the case, we are regarding only the essence of modes and not the order of nature, we may freely limit the existence and duration of modes without destroying the conception we have formed of them; we may conceive them as greater or less, or may divide them into parts. Eternity and substance, being only conceivable as infinite, cannot be thus treated without our conception of them being destroyed. Wherefore it is mere foolishness, or even insanity, to say that extended substance is made up of parts or bodies really distinct from one another. It is as though one should attempt by the aggregation and addition of many circles to make up a square, or a triangle, or something of totally different essence. Wherefore the whole heap of arguments, by which philosophers commonly endeavour to show that extended substance is finite, falls to the ground by its own weight. For all such persons suppose, that corporeal substance is made up of parts. In the same way, others, who have persuaded themselves that a line is made up of points, have been able to discover many arguments to show that a line is not infinitely divisible. If you ask, why we are by nature so prone to attempt to divide extended substance, I answer, that quantity is conceived by us in two ways, namely, by abstraction or superficially, as we imagine it by the aid of the senses, or as substance, which can only be accomplished through the understanding. So that, if we regard quantity as it exists in the imagination (and this is the more frequent and easy method), it will be found to be divisible, finite, composed of parts, and manifold. But, if we regard it as it is in the understanding, and the thing be conceived as it is in itself (which is very difficult), it will then, as I have sufficiently shown you before, be found to be infinite, indivisible, and single.

Again, from the fact that we can limit duration and quantity at our pleasure, when we conceive the latter abstractedly as apart from substance, and separate the former from the manner whereby it flows from things eternal, there arise time and measure; time for the purpose of limiting duration, measure for the purpose of limiting quantity, so that we may, as far as is possible, the more readily imagine them. Further, inasmuch as we separate the modifications of substance from substance itself, and reduce them to classes, so that we may, as far as is possible, the more readily imagine them, there arises number, whereby we limit them. Whence it is clearly to be seen, that measure, time, and number, are merely modes of thinking, or, rather, of imagining. It is not to be wondered at, therefore, that all, who have endeavoured to understand the course of nature by means of such notions, and without fully understanding even them, have entangled themselves so wondrously, that they have at last only been able to extricate themselves by breaking through every rule and admitting absurdities even of the grossest kind. For there are many things which cannot be conceived through the imagination but only through the understanding, for instance, substance, eternity, and the like; thus, if anyone tries to explain such things by means of conceptions which are mere aids to the imagination, he is simply assisting his imagination to run away with him. Nor can even the modes of substance ever be rightly understood, if we confuse them with entities of the kind mentioned, mere aids of the reason or imagination. In so doing we separate them from substance, and the mode of their derivation from eternity, without which they can never be rightly understood. To make the matter yet more clear, take the following example: when a man conceives of duration abstractedly, and, confusing it with time, begins to divide it into parts, he will never be able to understand how an hour, for instance, can elapse. For in order that an hour should elapse, it is necessary that its half should elapse first, and afterwards half of the remainder, and again half of the half of the remainder, and if you go on thus to infinity, subtracting the half of the residue, you will never be able to arrive at the end of the hour. Wherefore many, who are not accustomed to distinguish abstractions from realities, have ventured to assert that duration is made up of instants, and so in wishing to avoid Charybdis have fallen into Scylla. It is the same thing to make up duration out of instants, as it is to make number simply by adding up noughts.

Further, as it is evident from what has been said, that neither number, nor measure, nor time, being mere aids to the imagination, can be infinite (for, otherwise, number would not be number, nor measure measure, nor time time); it is hence abundantly evident, why many who confuse these three abstractions with realities, through being ignorant of the true nature of things, have actually denied the infinite.

The wretchedness of their reasoning may be judged by mathematicians, who have never allowed themselves to be delayed a moment by arguments of this sort, in the case of things which they clearly and distinctly perceive. For not only have they come across many things, which cannot be expressed by number (thus showing the inadequacy of number for determining all things); but also they have found many things, which cannot be equalled by any number, but surpass every possible number. But they infer hence, that such things surpass enumeration, not because of the multitude of their component parts, but because their nature cannot, without manifest contradiction, be expressed in terms of number. As, for instance, in the case of two circles, non-concentric, whereof one encloses the other, no number can express the inequalities of distance which exist between the two circles, nor all the variations which matter in motion in the intervening space may undergo. This conclusion is not based on the excessive size of the intervening space. However small a portion of it we take, the inequalities of this small portion will surpass all numerical expression. Nor, again, is the conclusion based on the fact, as in other cases, that we do not know the maximum and the minimum of the said space. It springs simply from the fact, that the nature of the space between two non-concentric circles cannot be expressed in number. Therefore, he who would assign a numerical equivalent for the inequalities in question, would be bound, at the same time, to bring about that a circle should not be a circle.

The same result would take place — to return to my subject — if one were to wish to determine all the motions undergone by matter up to the present, by reducing them and their duration to a certain number and time. This would be the same as an attempt to deprive corporeal substance, which we cannot conceive except as existent, of its modifications, and to bring about that it should not possess the nature which it does possess. All this I could clearly demonstrate here, together with many other points touched on in this letter, but I deem it superfluous.

From all that has been said, it is abundantly evident that certain things are in their nature infinite, and can by no means be conceived as finite; whereas there are other things, infinite in virtue of the cause from which they are derived, which can, when conceived abstractedly, be divided into parts, and regarded as finite. Lastly, there are some which are called infinite or, if you prefer, indefinite, because they cannot be expressed in number, which may yet be conceived as greater or less. It does not follow that such are equal, because they are alike incapable of numerical expression. This is plain enough, from the example given, and many others.

Lastly, I have put briefly before you the causes of error and confusion, which have arisen concerning the question of the infinite. I have, if I mistake not, so explained them that no question concerning the infinite remains untreated, or cannot readily be solved from what I have said; wherefore, I do not think it worth while to detain you longer on the matter.

But I should like it first to be observed here, that the later Peripatetics have, I think, misunderstood the proof given by the ancients who sought to demonstrate the existence of God. This, as I find it in a certain Jew named Rabbi Ghasdai, runs as follows:— "If there be an infinite series of causes, all things which are, are caused. But nothing which is caused can exist necessarily in virtue of its own nature. Therefore there is nothing in nature, to whose essence existence necessarily belongs. But this is absurd. Therefore the premise is absurd also." Hence the force of the argument lies not in the impossibility of an actual infinite or an infinite series of causes; but only in the absurdity of the assumption that things, which do not necessarily exist by nature, are not conditioned for existence by a thing, which does by its own nature necessarily exist.

I would now pass on, for time presses, to your second letter: but I shall be able more conveniently to reply to its contents, when you are kind enough to pay me a visit. I therefore beg that you will come as soon as possible; the time for travelling is at hand. Enough. Farewell, and keep in remembrance Yours, &c.

Rhijnsburg,

20 April, 1663.

Benedict de Spinoza

Aug. 3, 1663

Voorberg

Lewis Meyer

LETTER XXIX.A. SPINOZA
TO LEWIS MEYER.

DEAR FRIEND, —

The preface you sent me by our friend De Vries, I now send back to you by the same hand. Some few things, as you will see, I have marked in the margin; but yet a few remain, which I have judged it better to mention to you by letter. First, where on page 4 you give the reader to know on what occasion I composed the first part; I would have you likewise explain there, or where you please, that I composed it within a fortnight. For when this is explained none will suppose the exposition to be so clear as that it cannot be bettered, and so they will not stick at obscurities in this and that phrase on which they may chance to stumble. Secondly, I would have you explain, that when I prove many points otherwise than they be proved by Descartes, 'tis not to amend Descartes, but the better to preserve my order, and not to multiply axioms overmuch: and that for this same reason I prove many things which by Descartes are barely alleged without any proof, and must needs add other matters which Descartes let alone. Lastly, I will earnestly beseech you, as my especial friend, to let be everything you have written towards the end against that creature, and wholly strike it out. And though many reasons determine me to this request, I will give but one. I would fain have all men readily believe that these matters are published for the common profit of the world, and that your sole motive in bringing out the book is the love of spreading the truth; and that it is accordingly all your study to make the work acceptable to all, to bid men, with all courtesy to the pursuit of genuine philosophy, and to consult their common advantage. Which every man will be ready to think when he sees that no one is attacked, nor anything advanced where any man can find the least offence. Notwithstanding, if afterwards the person you know of, or any other, be minded to display his ill will, then you may portray his life and character, and gain applause by it. So I ask that you will not refuse to be patient thus far, and suffer yourself to be entreated, and believe me wholly bounden to you, and

Yours with all affection,

B. de Spinoza.

Voorberg,

Aug. 3, 1663.

Our friend De Vries had promised to take this with him; but seeing he knows not when he will return to you, I send it by another hand.

Along with this I send you part of the scholium to Prop. xxvii. Part II. where page 75 begins, that you may hand it to the printer to be reprinted. The matter I send you must of necessity be reprinted, and fourteen or fifteen lines added, which may easily be inserted.

Benedict de Spinoza

20 July, 1664

Voorburg

Peter Balling

LETTER XXX. SPINOZA
TO PETER BALLING.

[CONCERNING OMENS AND phantoms. The mind may have a confused presentiment of the future.]

Beloved Friend, —

Your last letter, written, if I mistake not, on the 26th of last month, has duly reached me. It caused me no small sorrow and solicitude, though the feeling sensibly diminished when I reflected on the good sense and fortitude, with which you have known how to despise the evils of fortune, or rather of opinion, at a time when they most bitterly assailed you. Yet my anxiety increases daily; I therefore beg and implore you by the claims of our friendship, that you will rouse yourself to write me a long letter. With regard to Omens, of which you make mention in telling me that, while your child was still healthy and strong, you heard groans like those he uttered when he was ill and shortly afterwards died, I should judge that these were not real groans, but only the effect of your imagination; for you say that, when you got up and composed yourself to listen, you did not hear them so clearly either as before or as afterwards, when you had fallen asleep again. This, I think, shows that the groans were purely due to the imagination, which, when it was unfettered and free, could imagine groans more forcibly and vividly than when you sat up in order to listen in a particular direction. I think I can both illustrate and confirm what I say by another occurrence, which befell me at Rhijnsburg last winter. When one morning, after the day had dawned, I woke up from a very unpleasant dream, the images, which had presented themselves to me in sleep, remained before my eyes just as vividly as though the things had been real, especially the image of a certain black and leprous Brazilian whom I had never seen before. This image disappeared for the most part when, in order to divert my thoughts, I cast my eyes on a book, or something else. But, as soon as I lifted my eyes again without fixing my attention on any particular object, the same image of this same negro appeared with the same vividness again and again, until the head of it gradually vanished. I say that the same thing, which occurred with regard to my inward sense of sight, occurred with your hearing; but as the causes were very different, your case was an omen and mine was not. The matter may be clearly grasped by means of what I am about to say. The effects of the imagination arise either from bodily or mental causes. I will proceed to prove this, in order not to be too long, solely from experience. We know that fevers and other bodily ailments are the causes of delirium, and that persons of stubborn disposition imagine nothing but quarrels, brawls, slaughterings, and the like. We also see that the imagination is to a certain extent determined by the character of the disposition, for, as we know by experience, it follows in the tracks of the understanding in every respect, and arranges its images and words, just as the understanding arranges its demonstrations and connects one with another; so that we are hardly at all able to say, what will not serve the imagination as a basis for some image or other. This being so, I say that no effects of imagination springing from physical causes can ever be omens of future events; inasmuch as their causes do not involve any future events. But the effects of imagination, or images originating in the mental disposition, may be omens of some future event; inasmuch as the mind may have a confused presentiment of the future. It may, therefore, imagine a future event as forcibly and vividly, as though it were present; for instance a father (to take an example resembling your own) loves his child so much, that he and the beloved child are, as it were, one and the same. And since (like that which I demonstrated on another occasion) there must necessarily exist in thought the idea of the essence of the child's states and their results, and since the father, through his union with his child, is a part of the said child, the soul of the father must necessarily participate in the ideal essence of the child and his states, and in their results, as I have shown at greater length elsewhere.

Again, as the soul of the father participates ideally in the consequences of his child's essence, he may (as I have said) sometimes imagine some of the said consequences as vividly as if they were present with him, provided that the following conditions are fulfilled: — I. If the occurrence in his son's career be remarkable. II. If it be capable of being readily imagined. III. If the time of its happening be not too remote. IV. If his body be sound, in respect not only of health but of freedom from every care or business which could outwardly trouble the senses. It may also assist the result, if we think of something which generally stimulates similar ideas. For instance, if while we are talking with this or that man we hear groans, it will generally happen that, when we think of the man again, the groans heard when we spoke with him will recur to our mind. This, dear friend, is my opinion on the question you ask me. I have, I confess, been very brief, but I have furnished you with material for writing to me on the first opportunity, &c.

Voorburg,

20 July, 1664.

William de Blyenbergh

12 Dec., 1664

Dordrecht

Benedict de Spinoza

LETTER XXXI. WILLIAM DE BLYENBERGH TO SPINOZA.

UNKNOWN FRIEND AND Sir, —

I have already read several times with attention your treatise and its appendix recently published. I should narrate to others more becomingly than to yourself the extreme solidity I found in it, and the pleasure with which I perused it. But I am unable to conceal my feeelings from you, because the more frequently I study the work with attention, the more it pleases me, and I am constantly observing something which I had not before remarked. However, I will not too loudly extol its author, lest I should seem in this letter to be a flatterer. I am aware that the gods grant all things to labour. Not to detain you too long with wondering who I may be, and how it comes to pass that one unknown to you takes the great liberty of writing to you, I will tell you that he is a man who is impelled by his longing for pure and unadulterated truth, and desires during this brief and frail life to fix his feet in the ways of science, so far as our human faculties will allow; one who in the pursuit of truth has no goal before his eyes save truth herself; one who by his science seeks to obtain as the result of truth neither honour nor riches, but simple truth and tranquillity; one who, out of the whole circle of truths and sciences, takes delight in none more than in metaphysics, if not in all branches at any rate in some; one who places the whole delight of his life in the fact, that he can pass in the study of them his hours of ease and leisure. But no one, I rest assured, is so blessed as yourself, no one has carried his studies so far, and therefore no one has arrived at the pitch of perfection which, as I see from your work, you have attained. To add a last word, the present writer is one with whom you may gain a closer acquaintance, if you choose to attach him to you by enlightening and interpenetrating, as it were, his halting meditations.

But I return to your treatise. While I found in it many things which tickled my palate vastly, some of them proved difficult to digest. Perhaps a stranger ought not to report to you his objections, the more so as I know not whether they will meet with your approval. This is the reason for my making these prefatory remarks, and asking you, if you can find leisure in the winter evenings, and, at the same time, will be willing to answer the difficulties which I still find in your book, and to forward me the result, always under the condition that it does not interrupt any occupation of greater importance or pleasure; for I desire nothing more earnestly than to see the promise made in your book fulfilled by a more detailed exposition of your opinions. I should have communicated to you by word of mouth what I now commit to paper; but my ignorance of your address, the infectious disease, and my duties here, prevented me. I must defer the pleasure for the present.

However, in order that this letter may not be quite empty, and in the hope that it will not be displeasing to you, I will ask you one question. You say in various passages in the "Principia," and in the "Metaphysical Reflections," either as your own opinion, or as explaining the philosophy of Descartes, that creation and preservation are identical (which is, indeed, so evident to those who have considered the question as to be a primary notion); secondly, that God has not only created substances, but also motions in substances — in other words, that God, by a continuous act of creation preserves, not only substances in their normal state, but also the motion and the endeavours of substances. God, for instance, not only brings about by His immediate will and working (whatever be the term employed), that the soul should last and continue in its normal state; but He is also the cause of His will determining, in some way, the movement of the soul — in other words, as God, by a continuous act of creation, brings about that things should remain in existence, so is He also the cause of the movements and endeavours existing in things. In fact, save God, there is no cause of motion. It therefore follows that God is not only the cause of the substance of mind, but also of every endeavour or motion of mind, which we call volition, as you frequently say. From this statement it seems to follow necessarily, either that there is no evil in the motion or volition of the mind, or else that God directly brings about that evil. For that which we call evil comes to pass through the soul, and, consequently, through the immediate influence and concurrence of God. For instance, the soul of Adam wishes to eat of the forbidden fruit. It follows from what has been said above, not only that Adam forms his wish through the influence of God, but also, as will presently be shown, that through that influence he forms it in that particular manner. Hence, either the act forbidden to Adam is not evil, inasmuch as God Himself not only caused the wish, but also the manner of it, or else God directly brought about that which we call evil. Neither you nor Descartes seem to have solved this difficulty by saying that evil is a negative conception, and that, as such, God cannot bring it about. Whence, we may ask, came the wish to eat the forbidden fruit, or the wish of devils to be equal with God? For since (as you justly observe) the will is not something different from the mind, but is only an endeavour or movement of the mind, the concurrence of God is as necessary to it as to the mind itself. Now the concurrence of God, as I gather from your writings, is merely the determining of a thing in a particular manner through the will of God. It follows that God concurs no less in an evil wish, in so far as it is evil, than in a good wish in so far as it is good, in other words, He determines it. For the will of God being the absolute cause of all that exists, either in substance or in effort, seems to be also the primary cause of an evil wish, in so far as it is evil. Again, no exercise of volition takes place in us, that God has not known from all eternity. If we say that God does not know of a particular exercise of volition, we attribute to Him imperfection. But how could God gain knowledge of it except from His decrees? Therefore His decrees are the cause of our volitions, and hence it seems also to follow that either an evil wish is not evil, or else that God is the direct cause of the evil, and brings it about. There is no room here for the theological distinction between an act and the evil inherent in that act. For God decrees the mode of the act, no less than the act, that is, God not only decreed that Adam should eat, but also that he should necessarily eat contrary to the command given. Thus it seems on all sides to follow, either that Adam's eating contrary to the command was not an evil, or else that God Himself brought it to pass.

These, illustrious Sir, are the questions in your treatise, which I am unable, at present, to elucidate. Either alternative seems to me difficult of acceptance. However, I await a satisfactory answer from your keen judgment and learning, hoping to show you hereafter how deeply indebted I shall be to you. Be assured, illustrious Sir, that I put these questions from no other motive than the desire for truth. I am a man of leisure, not tied to any profession, gaining my living by honest trade, and devoting my spare time to questions of this sort. I humbly hope that my difficulties will not be displeasing to you. If you are minded to send an answer, as I most ardently hope, write to, &c.

William de Blyenbergh.

Dordrecht,

12 Dec., 1664.

Benedict de Spinoza

Jan. 5, 1665

Amsterdam

William de Blyenbergh

LETTER XXXII. SPINOZA TO BLYENBERGH.

(SPINOZA ANSWERS WITH his usual courtesy the question propounded by Blyenbergh.)

Unknown Friend, —

I received, at Schiedam, on the 26th of December, your letter dated the 12th of December, enclosed in another written on the 24th of the same month. I gather from it your fervent love of truth, and your making it the aim of all your studies. This compelled me, though by no means otherwise unwilling, not only to grant your petition by answering all the questions you have sent, or may in future send, to the best of my ability, but also to impart to you everything in my power, which can conduce to further knowledge and sincere friendship. So far as in me lies, I value, above all other things out of my own control, the joining hands of friendship with men who are sincere lovers of truth. I believe that nothing in the world, of things outside our own control, brings more peace than the possibility of affectionate intercourse with such men; it is just as impossible that the love we bear them can be disturbed (inasmuch as it is founded on the desire each feels for the knowledge of truth), as that truth once perceived should not be assented to. It is, moreover, the highest and most pleasing source of happiness derivable from things not under our own control. Nothing save truth has power closely to unite different feelings and dispositions. I say nothing of the very great advantages which it brings, lest I should detain you too long on a subject which, doubtless, you know already. I have said thus much, in order to show you better how gladly I shall embrace this and any future opportunity of serving you.

In order to make the best of the present opportunity, I will at once proceed to answer your question. This seems to turn on the point "that it seems to be clear, not only from God's providence, which is identical with His will, but also from God's co-operation and continuous creation of things, either that there are no such things as sin or evil, or that God directly brings sin and evil to pass." You do not, however, explain what you mean by evil. As far as one may judge from the example you give in the predetermined act of volition of Adam, you seem to mean by evil the actual exercise of volition, in so far as it is conceived as predetermined in a particular way, or in so far as it is repugnant to the command of God. Hence you conclude (and I agree with you if this be what you mean) that it is absurd to adopt either alternative, either that God brings to pass anything contrary to His own will, or that what is contrary to God's will can be good.

For my own part, I cannot admit that sin and evil have any positive existence, far less that anything can exist, or come to pass, contrary to the will of God. On the contrary, not only do I assert that sin has no positive existence, I also maintain that only in speaking improperly, or humanly, can we say that we sin against God, as in the expression that men offend God.

As to the first point, we know that whatsoever is, when considered in itself without regard to anything else, possesses perfection, extending in each thing as far as the limits of that thing's essence: for essence is nothing else. I take for an illustration the design or determined will of Adam to eat the forbidden fruit. This design or determined will, considered in itself alone, includes perfection in so far as it expresses reality; hence it may be inferred that we can only conceive imperfection in things, when they are viewed in relation to other things possessing more reality: thus in Adam's decision, so long as we view it by itself and do not compare it with other things more perfect or exhibiting a more perfect state, we can find no imperfection: nay it may be compared with an infinity of other things far less perfect in this respect than itself, such as stones, stocks, &c. This, as a matter of fact, everyone grants. For we all admire in animals qualities which we regard with dislike and aversion in men, such as the pugnacity of bees, the jealousy of doves, &c.; these in human beings are despised, but are nevertheless considered to enhance the value of animals. This being so, it follows that sin, which indicates nothing save imperfection, cannot consist in anything that expresses reality, as we see in the case of Adam's decision and its execution.

Again, we cannot say that Adam's will is at variance with the law of God, and that it is evil because it is displeasing to God; for besides the fact that grave imperfection would be imputed to God, if we say that anything happens contrary to His will, or that He desires anything which He does not obtain, or that His nature resembled that of His creatures in having sympathy with some things more than others; such an occurrence would be at complete variance with the nature of the divine will.

The will of God is identical with His intellect, hence the former can no more be contravened than the latter; in other words, anything which should come to pass against His will must be of a nature to be contrary to His intellect, such, for instance, as a round square. Hence the will or decision of Adam regarded in itself was neither evil nor, properly speaking, against the will of God: it follows that God may — or rather, for the reason you call attention to, must — be its cause; not in so far as it was evil, for the evil in it consisted in the loss of the previous state of being which it entailed on Adam, and it is certain that loss has no positive existence, and is only so spoken of in respect to our and not God's understanding. The difficulty arises from the fact, that we give one and the same definition to all the individuals of a genus, as for instance all who have the outward appearance of men: we accordingly assume all things which are expressed by the same definition to be equally capable of attaining the highest perfection possible for the genus; when we find an individual whose actions are at variance with such perfection, we suppose him to be deprived of it, and to fall short of his nature. We should hardly act in this way, if we did not hark back to the definition and ascribe to the individual a nature in accordance with it. But as God does not know things through abstraction, or form general definitions of the kind above mentioned, and as things have no more reality than the divine understanding and power have put into them and actually endowed them with, it clearly follows that a state of privation can only be spoken of in relation to our intellect, not in relation to God.

Thus, as it seems to me, the difficulty is completely solved. However, in order to make the way still plainer, and remove every doubt, I deem it necessary to answer the two following difficulties: — First, why Holy Scripture says that God wishes for the conversion of the wicked, and also why God forbade Adam to eat of the fruit when He had ordained the contrary? Secondly, that it seems to follow from what I have said, that the wicked by their pride, avarice, and deeds of desperation, worship God in no less degree than the good do by their nobleness, patience, love, &c., inasmuch as both execute God's will.

In answer to the first question, I observe that Scripture, being chiefly fitted for and beneficial to the multitude, speaks popularly after the fashion of men. For the multitude are incapable of grasping sublime conceptions. Hence I am persuaded that all matters, which God revealed to the prophets as necessary to salvation, are set down in the form of laws. With this understanding, the prophets invented whole parables, and represented God as a king and a law-giver, because He had revealed the means of salvation and perdition, and was their cause; the means which were simply causes they styled laws and wrote them down as such; salvation and perdition, which are simply effects necessarily resulting from the aforesaid means, they described as reward and punishment; framing their doctrines more in accordance with such parables than with actual truth. They constantly speak of God as resembling a man, as sometimes angry, sometimes merciful, now desiring what is future, now jealous and suspicious, even as deceived by the devil; so that philosophers and all who are above the law, that is, who follow after virtue, not in obedience to law, but through love, because it is the most excellent of all things, must not be hindered by such expressions.

Thus the command given to Adam consisted solely in this, that God revealed to Adam, that eating of the fruit brought about death; as He reveals to us, through our natural faculties, that poison is deadly. If you ask, for what object did He make this revelation, I answer, in order to render Adam to that extent more perfect in knowledge. Hence, to ask God why He had not bestowed on Adam a more perfect will, is just as absurd as to ask, why the circle has not been endowed with all the properties of a sphere. This follows clearly from what has been said, and I have also proved it in my Principles of Cartesian Philosophy, I. 15.

As to the second difficulty, it is true that the wicked execute after their manner the will of God: but they cannot, therefore, be in any respect compared with the good. The more perfection a thing has, the more does it participate in the deity, and the more does it express perfection. Thus, as the good have incomparably more perfection than the bad, their virtue cannot be likened to the virtue of the wicked, inasmuch as the wicked lack the love of God, which proceeds from the knowledge of God, and by which alone we are, according to our human understanding, called the servants of God. The wicked, knowing not God, are but as instruments in the hand of the workman, serving unconsciously, and perishing in the using; the good, on the other hand, serve consciously, and in serving become more perfect.

This, Sir, is all I can now contribute to answering your question, and I have no higher wish than that it may satisfy you. But in case you still find any difficulty, I beg you to let me know of that also, to see if I may be able to remove it. You have nothing to fear on your side, but so long as you are not satisfied, I like nothing better than to be informed of your reasons, so that finally the truth may appear. I could have wished to write in the tongue in which I have been brought up. I should, perhaps, have been able to express my thoughts better. But be pleased to take it as it is, amend the mistakes yourself, and believe me,

Your sincere friend and servant.

Long Orchard, near

Amsterdam,

Jan. 5, 1665.

William de Blyenbergh

16 Jan., 1665

Dordrecht

Benedict de Spinoza

LETTER XXXIII. BLYENBERGH TO SPINOZA.

(A SUMMARY ONLY of this letter is here given. — Tr.)

I have two rules in my philosophic inquiries: i. Conformity to reason; ii. Conformity to scripture. I consider the second the most important. Examining your letter by the first, I observe that your identification of God's creative power with His preservative power seems to involve, either that evil does not exist, or else that God brings about evil. If evil be only a term relative to our imperfect knowledge, how do you explain the state of a man who falls from a state of grace into sin? If evil be a negation, how can we have the power to sin? If God causes an evil act, he must cause the evil as well as the act. You say that every man can only act, as he, in fact, does act. This removes all distinction between the good and the wicked. Both, according to you, are perfect. You remove all the sanctions of virtue and reduce us to automata. Your doctrine, that strictly speaking we cannot sin against God, is a hard saying.

[The rest of the letter is taken up with an examination of Spinoza's arguments in respect to their conformity to Scripture.]

Dordrecht,

16 Jan., 1665.

Benedict de Spinoza

28 Jan., 1665

Voorberg

William de Blyenbergh

LETTER XXXIV. SPINOZA TO BLYENBERGH.

[SPINOZA COMPLAINS THAT Blyenbergh has misunderstood him: he sets forth his true meaning.]

Voorburg,

28 Jan., 1665.

Friend and Sir, —

When I read your first letter, I thought that our opinions almost coincided. But from the second, which was delivered to me on the 21st of this month, I see that the matter stands far otherwise, for I perceive that we disagree, not only in remote inferences from first principles, but also in first principles themselves; so that I can hardly think that we can derive any mutual instruction from further correspondence. I see that no proof, though it be by the laws of proof most sound, has any weight with you, unless it agrees with the explanation, which either you yourself, or other theologians known to you, attribute to Holy Scripture. However, if you are convinced that God speaks more clearly and effectually through Holy Scripture than through the natural understanding, which He also has bestowed upon us, and with His divine wisdom keeps continually stable and uncorrupted, you have valid reasons for making your understanding bow before the opinions which you attribute to Holy Scripture; I myself could adopt no different course. For my own part, as I confess plainly, and without circumlocution, that I do not understand the Scriptures, though I have spent some years upon them, and also as I feel that when I have obtained a firm proof, I cannot fall into a state of doubt concerning it, I acquiesce entirely in what is commended to me by my understanding, without any suspicion that I am being deceived in the matter, or that Holy Scripture, though I do not search, could gainsay it: for "truth is not at variance with truth," as I have already clearly shown in my appendix to The Principles of Cartesian Philosophy (I cannot give the precise reference, for I have not the book with me here in the country). But if in any instance I found that a result obtained through my natural understanding was false, I should reckon myself fortunate, for I enjoy life, and try to spend it not in sorrow and sighing, but in peace, joy, and cheerfulness, ascending from time to time a step higher. Meanwhile I know (and this knowledge gives me the highest contentment and peace of mind), that all things come to pass by the power and unchangeable decree of a Being supremely perfect.

To return to your letter, I owe you many and sincere thanks for having confided to me your philosophical opinions; but for the doctrines, which you attribute to me, and seek to infer from my letter, I return you no thanks at all. What ground, I should like to know, has my letter afforded you for ascribing to me the opinions; that men are like beasts, that they die and perish after the manner of beasts, that our actions are displeasing to God, &c.? Perhaps we are most of all at variance on this third point. You think, as far as I can judge, that God takes pleasure in our actions, as though He were a man, who has attained his object, when things fall out as he desired. For my part, have I not said plainly enough, that the good worship God, that in continually serving Him they become more perfect, and that they love God? Is this, I ask, likening them to beasts, or saying that they perish like beasts, or that their actions are displeasing to God? If you had read my letter with more attention, you would have clearly perceived, that our whole dissension lies in the following alternative: — Either the perfections which the good receive are imparted to them by God in His capacity of God, that is absolutely without any human qualities being ascribed to Him — this is what I believe; or else such perfections are imparted by God as a judge, which is what you maintain. For this reason you defend the wicked, saying that they carry out God's decrees as far as in them lies, and therefore serve God no less than the good. But if my doctrine be accepted, this consequence by no means follows; I do not bring in the idea of God as a judge, and, therefore, I estimate an action by its intrinsic merits, not by the powers of its performer; the recompense which follows the action follows from it as necessarily as from the nature of a triangle it follows, that the three angles are equal to two right angles. This may be understood by everyone, who reflects on the fact, that our highest blessedness consists in love towards God, and that such love flows naturally from the knowledge of God, which is so strenuously enjoined on us. The question may very easily be proved in general terms, if we take notice of the nature of God's decrees, as explained in my appendix. However, I confess that all those, who confuse the divine nature with human nature, are gravely hindered from understanding it.

I had intended to end my letter at this point, lest I should prove troublesome to you in these questions, the discussion of which (as I discover from the extremely pious postscript added to your letter) serves you as a pastime and a jest, but for no serious use. However, that I may not summarily deny your request, I will proceed to explain further the words privation and negation, and briefly point out what is necessary for the elucidation of my former letter.

I say then, first, that privation is not the act of depriving, but simply and merely a state of want, which is in itself nothing: it is a mere entity of the reason, a mode of thought framed in comparing one thing with another. We say, for example, that a blind man is deprived of sight, because we readily imagine him as seeing, or else because we compare him with others who can see, or compare his present condition with his past condition when he could see; when we regard the man in this way, comparing his nature either with the nature of others or with his own past nature, we affirm that sight belongs to his nature, and therefore assert that he has been deprived of it. But when we are considering the nature and decree of God, we cannot affirm privation of sight in the case of the aforesaid man any more than in the case of a stone; for at the actual time sight lies no more within the scope of the man than of the stone; since there belongs to man and forms part of his nature only that which is granted to him by the understanding and will of God. Hence it follows that God is no more the cause of a blind man not seeing, than he is of a stone not seeing. Not seeing is a pure negation. So also, when we consider the case of a man who is led by lustful desires, we compare his present desires with those which exist in the good, or which existed in himself at some other time; we then assert that he is deprived of the better desires, because we conceive that virtuous desires lie within the scope of his nature. This we cannot do, if we consider the nature and decree of God. For, from this point of view, virtuous desires lie at that time no more within the scope of the nature of the lustful man, than within the scope of the nature of the devil or a stone. Hence, from the latter standpoint the virtuous desire is not a privation but a negation.

Thus privation is nothing else than denying of a thing something, which we think belongs to its nature; negation is denying of a thing something, which we do not think belongs to its nature.

We may now see, how Adam's desire for earthly things was evil from our standpoint, but not from God's. Although God knew both the present and the past state of Adam, He did not, therefore, regard Adam as deprived of his past state, that is, He did not regard Adam's past state as within the scope of Adam's present nature. Otherwise God would have apprehended something contrary to His own will, that is, contrary to His own understanding. If you quite grasp my meaning here and at the same time remember, that I do not grant to the mind the same freedom as Descartes does — L[ewis] M[eyer] bears witness to this in his preface to my book — you will perceive, that there is not the smallest contradiction in what I have said. But I see that I should have done far better to have answered you in my first letter with the words of Descartes, to the effect that we cannot know how our freedom and its consequences agree with the foreknowledge and freedom of God (see several passages in my appendix), that, therefore, we can discover no contradiction between creation by God and our freedom, because we cannot understand how God created the universe, nor (what is the same thing) how He preserves it. I thought that you had read the preface, and that by not giving you my real opinions in reply, I should sin against those duties of friendship which I cordially offered you. But this is of no consequence.

Still, as I see that you have not hitherto thoroughly grasped Descartes' meaning, I will call your attention to the two following points. First, that neither Descartes nor I have ever said, that it appertains to our nature to confine the will within the limits of the understanding; we have only said, that God has endowed us with a determined understanding and an undetermined will, so that we know not the object for which He has created us. Further, that an undetermined or perfect will of this kind not only makes us more perfect, but also, as I will presently show you, is extremely necessary for us.

Secondly: that our freedom is not placed in a certain contingency nor in a certain indifference, but in the method of affirmation or denial; so that, in proportion as we are less indifferent in affirmation or denial, so are we more free. For instance, if the nature of God be Known to us, it follows as necessarily from our nature to affirm that God exists, as from the nature of a triangle it follows, that the three angles are equal to two right angles; we are never more free, than when we affirm a thing in this way. As this necessity is nothing else but the decree of God (as I have clearly shown in my appendix), we may hence, after a fashion, understand how we act freely and are the cause of our action, though all the time we are acting necessarily and according to the decree of God. This, I repeat, we may, after a fashion, understand, whenever we affirm something, which we clearly and distinctly perceive, but when we assert something which we do not clearly and distinctly understand, in other words, when we allow our will to pass beyond the limits of our understanding, we no longer perceive the necessity nor the decree of God, we can only see our freedom, which is always involved in our will; in which respect only our actions are called good or evil. If we then try to reconcile our freedom with God's decree and continuous creation, we confuse that which we clearly and distinctly understand with that which we do not perceive, and, therefore, our attempt is vain. It is, therefore, sufficient for us to know that we are free, and that we can be so notwithstanding God's decree, and further that we are the cause of evil, because an act can only be called evil in relation to our freedom. I have said thus much for Descartes in order to show that, in the question we are considering, his words exhibit no contradiction.

I will now turn to what concerns myself, and will first briefly call attention to the advantage arising from my opinion, inasmuch as, according to it, our understanding offers our mind and body to God freed from all superstition. Nor do I deny that prayer is extremely useful to us. For my understanding is too small to determine all the means, whereby God leads men to the love of Himself, that is, to salvation. So far is my opinion from being hurtful, that it offers to those, who are not taken up with prejudices and childish superstitions, the only means for arriving at the highest stage of blessedness.

When you say that, by making men so dependent on God, I reduce them to the likeness of the elements, plants or stones, you sufficiently show that you have thoroughly misunderstood my meaning, and have confused things which regard the understanding with things which regard the imagination. If by your intellect only you had perceived what dependence on God means, you certainly would not think that things, in so far as they depend on God, are dead, corporeal, and imperfect (who ever dared to speak so meanly of the Supremely Perfect Being?); on the contrary, you would understand that for the very reason that they depend on God they are perfect; so that this dependence and necessary operation may best be understood as God's decree, by considering, not stocks and plants, but the most reasonable and perfect creatures. This sufficiently appears from my second observation on the meaning of Descartes, which you ought to have looked to.

I cannot refrain from expressing my extreme astonishment at your remarking, that if God does not punish wrongdoing (that is, as a judge does, with a punishment not intrinsically connected with the offence, for our whole difference lies in this), what reason prevents me from rushing headlong into every kind of wickedness? Assuredly he, who is only kept from vice by the fear of punishment (which I do not think of you), is in no wise acted on by love, and by no means embraces virtue. For my own part, I avoid or endeavour to avoid vice, because it is at direct variance with my proper nature and would lead me astray from the knowledge and love of God.

Again, if you had reflected a little on human nature and the nature of God's decree (as explained in my appendix), and perceived, and known by this time, how a consequence should be deduced from its premises, before a conclusion is arrived at; you would not so rashly have stated that my opinion makes us like stocks, &c.: nor would you have ascribed to me the many absurdities you conjure up.

As to the two points which you say, before passing on to your second rule, that you cannot understand; I answer, that the first may be solved through Descartes, who says that in observing your own nature you feel that you can suspend your judgment. If you say that you do not feel, that you have at present sufficient force to keep your judgment suspended, this would appear to Descartes to be the same as saying that we cannot at present see, that so long as we exist we shall always be thinking things, or retain the nature of thinking things; in fact it would imply a contradiction.

As to your second difficulty, I say with Descartes, that if we cannot extend our will beyond the bounds of our extremely limited understanding, we shall be most wretched — it will not be in our power to eat even a crust of bread, or to walk a step, or to go on living, for all things are uncertain and full of peril.

I now pass on to your second rule, and assert that I believe, though I do not ascribe to Scripture that sort of truth which you think you find in it, I nevertheless assign to it as great if not greater authority than you do. I am far more careful than others not to ascribe to Scripture any childish and absurd doctrines, a precaution which demands either a thorough acquaintance with philosophy or the possession of divine revelations. Hence I pay very little attention to the glosses put upon Scripture by ordinary theologians, especially those of the kind who always interpret Scripture according to the literal and outward meaning: I have never, except among the Socinians, found any theologian stupid enough to ignore that Holy Scripture very often speaks in human fashion of God and expresses its meaning in parables; as for the contradiction which you vainly (in my opinion) endeavour to show, I think you attach to the word parable a meaning different from that usually given. For who ever heard, that a man, who expressed his opinions in parables, had therefore taken leave of his senses? When Micaiah said to King Ahab, that he had seen God sitting on a throne, with the armies of heaven standing on the right hand and the left, and that God asked His angels which of them would deceive Ahab, this was assuredly a parable employed by the prophet on that occasion (which was not fitted for the inculcation of sublime theological doctrines), as sufficiently setting forth the message he had to deliver in the name of God. We cannot say that he had in anywise taken leave of his senses. So also the other prophets of God made manifest God's commands to the people in this fashion as being the best adapted, though not expressly enjoined by God, for leading the people to the primary object of Scripture, which, as Christ Himself says, is to bid men love God above all things, and their neighbour as themselves. Sublime speculations have, in my opinion, no bearing on Scripture. As far as I am concerned I have never learnt or been able to learn any of God's eternal attributes from Holy Scripture.

As to your fifth argument (that the prophets thus made manifest the word of God, since truth is not at variance with truth), it merely amounts, for those who understand the method of proof, to asking me to prove, that Scripture, as it is, is the true revealed word of God. The mathematical proof of this proposition could only be attained by divine revelation. I, therefore, expressed myself as follows: "I believe, but I do not mathematically know, that all things revealed by God to the prophets," &c. Inasmuch as I firmly believe but do not mathematically know, that the prophets were the most trusted counsellors and faithful ambassadors of God. So that in all I have written there is no contradiction, though several such may be found among holders of the opposite opinion.

The rest of your letter (to wit the passage where you say, "Lastly, the supremely perfect Being knew beforehand," &c; and again, your objections to the illustration from poison, and lastly, the whole of what you say of the appendix and what follows) seems to me beside the question.

As regards Lewis Meyer's preface, the points which were still left to be proved by Descartes before establishing his demonstration of free will, are certainly there set forth; it is added that I hold a contrary opinion, my reasons for doing so being given. I shall, perhaps, in due time give further explanations. For the present I have no such intention.

I have never thought about the work on Descartes, nor given any further heed to it, since it has been translated into Dutch. I have my reasons, though it would be tedious to enumerate them here. So nothing remains for me but to subscribe myself, &c.

William de Blyenbergh

19 Feb., 1665

Dordrecht

Benedict de Spinoza

LETTER XXXV. BLYENBERGH
TO SPINOZA.

[THIS LETTER (EXTENDING over five pages) is only given here in brief summary.]

The tone of your last letter is very different from that of your first. If our essence is equivalent to our state at a given time, we are as perfect when sinning as when virtuous: God would wish for vice as much as virtue. Both the virtuous and the vicious execute God's will — What is the difference between them? You say some actions are more perfect than others; wherein does this perfection consist? If a mind existed so framed, that vice was in agreement with its proper nature, why should such a mind prefer good to evil? If God makes us all that we are, how can we "go astray"? Can rational substances depend on God in any way except lifelessly? What is the difference between a rational being's dependence on God, and an irrational being's? If we have no free will, are not our actions God's actions, and our will God's will? I could ask several more questions, but do not venture.

P.S. In my hurry I forgot to insert this question: Whether we cannot by foresight avert what would otherwise happen to us?

Dordrecht,

19 Feb., 1665.

Benedict de Spinoza

13th March, 1665

Voorburg

William de Blyenbergh

LETTER XXXVI. SPINOZA TO BLYENBERGH.

[SPINOZA REPLIES, THAT there is a difference between the theological and the philosophical way of speaking of God and things divine. He proceeds to discuss Blyenbergh's questions. (Voorburg, 13th March, 1665.)]

Friend and Sir, —

I have received two letters from you this week; the second, dated 9th March, only served to inform me of the first written on February 19th, and sent to me at Schiedam. In the former I see that you complain of my saying, that "demonstration carried no weight with you," as though I had spoken of my own arguments, which had failed to convince you. Such was far from my intention. I was referring to your own words, which ran as follows:— "And if after long investigation it comes to pass, that my natural knowledge appears either to be at variance with the word (of Scripture), or not sufficiently well, &c.; the word has so great authority with me, that I would rather doubt of the conceptions, which I think I clearly perceive," &c. You see I merely repeat in brief your own phrase, so that I cannot think you have any cause for anger against me, especially as I merely quoted in order to show the great difference between our standpoints.

Again, as you wrote at the end of your letter that your only hope and wish is to continue in faith and hope, and that all else, which we may become convinced of through our natural faculties, is indifferent to you; I reflected, as I still continue to do, that my letters could be of no use to you, and that I should best consult my own interests by ceasing to neglect my pursuits (which I am compelled while writing to you to interrupt) for the sake of things which could bring no possible benefit. Nor is this contrary to the spirit of my former letter, for in that I looked upon you as simply a philosopher, who (like not a few who call themselves Christians) possesses no touchstone of truth save his natural understanding, and not as a theologian. However, you have taught me to know better, and have also shown me that the foundation, on which I was minded to build up our friendship, has not, as I imagined, been laid.

As for the rest, such are the general accompaniments of controversy, so that I would not on that account transgress the limits of courtesy: I will, therefore, pass over in your second letter, and in this, these and similar expressions, as though they had never been observed. So much for your taking offence; to show you that I have given you no just cause, and, also, that I am quite willing to brook contradiction. I now turn a second time to answering your objections.

I maintain, in the first place, that God is absolutely and really the cause of all things which have essence, whatsoever they may be. If you can demonstrate that evil, error, crime, &c., have any positive existence, which expresses essence, I will fully grant you that God is the cause of crime, evil, error, &c. I believe myself to have sufficiently shown, that that which constitutes the reality of evil, error, crime, &c., does not consist in anything, which expresses essence, and therefore we cannot say that God is its cause. For instance, Nero's matricide, in so far as it comprehended anything positive, was not a crime; the same outward act was perpetrated, and the same matricidal intention was entertained by Orestes; who, nevertheless, is not blamed — at any rate, not so much as Nero. Wherein, then, did Nero's crime consist? In nothing else, but that by his deed he showed himself to be ungrateful, unmerciful, and disobedient. Certainly none of these qualities express aught of essence, therefore God was not the cause of them, though He was the cause of Nero's act and intention.

Further, I would have you observe, that, while we speak philosophically, we ought not to employ theological phrases. For, since theology frequently, and not unwisely, represents God as a perfect man, it is often expedient in theology to say, that God desires a given thing, that He is angry at the actions of the wicked, and delights in those of the good. But in philosophy, when we clearly perceive that the attributes which make men perfect can as ill be ascribed and assigned to God, as the attributes which go to make perfect the elephant and the ass can be ascribed to man; here I say these and similar phrases have no place, nor can we employ them without causing extreme confusion in our conceptions. Hence, in the language of philosophy, it cannot be said that God desires anything of any man, or that anything is displeasing or pleasing to Him: all these are human qualities and have no place in God.

I would have it observed, that although the actions of the good (that is of those who have a clear idea of God, whereby all their actions and their thoughts are determined) and of the wicked (that is of those who do not possess the idea of God, but only the ideas of earthly things, whereby their actions and thoughts are determined), and, in fact, of all things that are, necessarily flow from God's eternal laws and decrees; yet they do not differ from one another in degree only, but also in essence. A mouse no less than an angel, and sorrow no less than joy depend on God; yet a mouse is not a kind of angel, neither is sorrow a kind of joy. I think I have thus answered your objections, if I rightly understand them, for I sometimes doubt, whether the conclusions which you deduce are not foreign to the proposition you are undertaking to prove.

However, this will appear more clearly, if I answer the questions you proposed on these principles. First, Whether murder is as acceptable to God as alms-giving? Secondly, Whether stealing is as good in relation to God as honesty? Thirdly and lastly, Whether if there be a mind so framed, that it would agree with, rather than be repugnant to its proper nature, to give way to lust, and to commit crimes, whether, I repeat, there can be any reason given, why such a mind should do good and eschew evil?

To your first question, I answer, that I do not know, speaking as a philosopher, what you mean by the words "acceptable to God." If you ask, whether God does not hate the wicked, and love the good? whether God does not regard the former with dislike, and the latter with favour? I answer, No. If the meaning of your question is: Are murderers and almsgivers equally good and perfect? my answer is again in the negative. To your second question, I reply: If, by "good in relation to God," you mean that the honest man confers a favour on God, and the thief does Him an injury, I answer that neither the honest man nor the thief can cause God any pleasure or displeasure. If you mean to ask, whether the actions of each, in so far as they possess reality, and are caused by God, are equally perfect? I reply that, if we merely regard the actions and the manner of their execution, both may be equally perfect. If you, therefore, inquire whether the thief and the honest man are equally perfect and blessed? I answer, No. For, by an honest man, I mean one who always desires, that everyone should possess that which is his. This desire, as I prove in my Ethics (as yet unpublished), necessarily derives its origin in the pious from the clear knowledge which they possess, of God and of themselves. As a thief has no desire of the kind, he is necessarily without the knowledge of God and of himself — in other words, without the chief element of our blessedness. If you further ask, What causes you to perform a given action, which I call virtuous, rather than another? I reply, that I cannot know which method, out of the infinite methods at His disposal, God employs to determine you to the said action. It may be, that God has impressed you with a clear idea of Himself, so that you forget the world for love of Him, and love your fellow-men as yourself; it is plain that such a disposition is at variance with those dispositions which are called bad, and, therefore, could not co-exist with them in the same man.

However, this is not the place to expound all the foundations of my Ethics, or to prove all that I have advanced; I am now only concerned in answering your questions, and defending myself against them.

Lastly, as to your third question, it assumes a contradiction, and seems to me to be, as though one asked: If it agreed better with a man's nature that he should hang himself, could any reasons be given for his not hanging himself? Can such a nature possibly exist? If so, I maintain (whether I do or do not grant free will), that such an one, if he sees that he can live more conveniently on the gallows than sitting at his own table, would act most foolishly, if he did not hang himself. So anyone who clearly saw that, by committing crimes, he would enjoy a really more perfect and better life and existence, than he could attain by the practice of virtue, would be foolish if he did not act on his convictions. For, with such a perverse human nature as his, crime would become virtue.

As to the other question, which you add in your postscript, seeing that one might ask a hundred such in an hour, without arriving at a conclusion about any, and seeing that you yourself do not press for an answer, I will send none.

I will now only subscribe myself, &c.

William de Blyenbergh

27th March, 1665

Dordrecht

Benedict de Spinoza

LETTER XXXVII. BLYENBERGH
TO SPINOZA.

[BLYENBERGH, WHO HAD been to see Spinoza, asks the latter to send him a report of their conversation, and to answer five fresh questions. (Dordrecht, 27th March, 1665.)]

Omitted.

Benedict de Spinoza

3rd June, 1665

Voorburg

William de Blyenbergh

LETTER XXXVIII. SPINOZA
TO BLYENBERGH.

[SPINOZA DECLINES FURTHER correspondence with Blyenbergh, but says he will give explanations of certain points by word of mouth. (Voorburg, 3rd June, 1665.)]

Friend and Sir, —

When your letter, dated 27th March, was delivered to me, I was just starting for Amsterdam. I, therefore, after reading half of it, left it at home, to be answered on my return: for I thought it dealt only with questions raised in our first controversy. However, a second perusal showed me, that it embraced a far wider subject, and not only asked me for a proof of what, in my preface to "Principles of Cartesian Philosophy," I wrote (with the object of merely stating, without proving or urging my opinion), but also requested me to impart a great portion of my Ethics, which, as everyone knows, ought to be based on physics and metaphysics. For this reason, I have been unable to allow myself to satisfy your demands. I wished to await an opportunity for begging you, in a most friendly way, by word of mouth, to withdraw your request, for giving you my reasons for refusal, and for showing that your inquiries do not promote the solution of our first controversy, but, on the contrary, are for the most part entirely dependent on its previous settlement. So far are they not essential to the understanding of my doctrine concerning necessity, that they cannot be apprehended, unless the latter question is understood first. However, before such an opportunity offered, a second letter reached me this week, appearing to convey a certain sense of displeasure at my delay. Necessity, therefore, has compelled me to write you these few words, to acquaint you more fully with my proposal and decision. I hope that, when the facts of the case are before you, you will, of your own accord, desist from your request, and will still remain kindly disposed towards me. I, for my part, will, in all things, according to my power, prove myself your, &c.

Benedict de Spinoza

7 Jan., 1666

Voorburg

Christian Huyghens

LETTER XXXIX. SPINOZA TO CHRISTIAN HUYGHENS.

(TREATING OF THE Unity of God.)

Distinguished Sir, —

The demonstration of the unity of God, on the ground that His nature involves necessary existence, which you asked for, and I took note of, I have been prevented by various business from sending to you before. In order to accomplish my purpose, I will premise —

That the true definition of anything includes nothing except the simple nature of the thing defined. From this it follows —

That no definition can involve or express a multitude or a given number of individuals, inasmuch as it involves and expresses nothing except the nature of the thing as it is in itself. For instance, the definition of a triangle includes nothing beyond the simple nature of a triangle; it does not include any given number of triangles. In like manner, the definition of the mind as a thinking thing, or the definition of God as a perfect Being, includes nothing beyond the natures of the mind and of God, not a given number of minds or gods.

That for everything that exists there must necessarily be a positive cause, through which it exists.

This cause may be situate either in the nature and definition of the thing itself (to wit, because existence belongs to its nature or necessarily includes it), or externally to the thing.

From these premises it follows, that if any given number of individuals exists in nature, there must be one or more causes, which have been able to produce exactly that number of individuals, neither more nor less. If, for instance, there existed in nature twenty men (in order to avoid all confusion, I will assume that these all exist together as primary entities), it is not enough to investigate the cause of human nature in general, in order to account for the existence of these twenty; we must also inquire into the reason, why there exist exactly twenty men, neither more nor less. For (by our third hypothesis) for each man a reason and a cause must be forthcoming, why he should exist. But this cause (by our second and third hypotheses) cannot be contained in the nature of man himself; for the true definition of man does not involve the number of twenty men. Hence (by our fourth hypothesis) the cause for the existence of these twenty men, and consequently for the existence of each of them, must exist externally to them. We may thus absolutely conclude, that all things, which are conceived to exist in the plural number, must necessarily be produced by external causes and not by the force of their own nature. But since (by our second hypothesis) necessary existence appertains to the nature of God, His true definition must necessarily include necessary existence: therefore from His true definition His necessary existence must be inferred. But from His true definition (as I have already demonstrated from our second and third hypotheses) the necessary existence of many gods cannot be inferred. Therefore there only follows the existence of a single God. Which was to be proved.

This, distinguished Sir, has now seemed to me the best method for demonstrating the proposition. I have also proved it differently by means of the distinction between essence and existence; but bearing in mind the object you mentioned to me, I have preferred to send you the demonstration given above. I hope it will satisfy you, and I will await your reply, meanwhile remaining, &c.

Voorburg,

7 Jan., 1666.

Benedict de Spinoza

10 April, 1666

Voorburg

Christian Huyghens

LETTER XL. SPINOZA TO CHRISTIAN HUYGHENS.

FURTHER ARGUMENTS FOR the unity of God.

Distinguished Sir, —

In your last letter, written on March 30th, you have excellently elucidated the point, which was somewhat obscure to me in your letter of February 10th. As I now know your opinion, I will set forth the state of the question as you conceive it; whether there be only a single Being who subsists by his own sufficiency or force? I not only affirm this to be so, but also undertake to prove it from the fact, that the nature of such a Being necessarily involves existence; perhaps it may also be readily proved from the understanding of God (as I set forth, "Principles of Cartesian Philosophy," I. Prop. i.), or from others of His attributes. Before treating of the subject I will briefly show, as preliminaries, what properties must be possessed by a Being including necessary existence. To wit: —

It must be eternal. For if a definite duration be assigned to it, it would beyond that definite duration be conceived as non-existent, or as not involving necessary existence, which would be contrary to its definition.

It must be simple, not made up of parts. For parts must in nature and knowledge be prior to the whole they compose: this could not be the case with regard to that which is eternal.

It cannot be conceived as determinate, but only as infinite. For, if the nature of the said Being were determinate, and conceived as determinate, that nature would beyond the said limits be conceived as non-existent, which again is contrary to its definition.

It is indivisible. For if it were divisible, it could be divided into parts, either of the same or of different nature. If the latter, it could be destroyed and so not exist, which is contrary to its definition; if the former, each part would in itself include necessary existence, and thus one part could exist without others, and consequently be conceived as so existing. Hence the nature of the Being would be comprehended as finite, which, by what has been said, is contrary to its definition. Thus we see that, in attempting to ascribe to such a Being any imperfection, we straightway fall into contradictions. For, whether the imperfection which we wish to assign to the said Being be situate in any defect, or in limitations possessed by its nature, or in any change which it might, through deficiency of power, undergo from external causes, we are always brought back to the contradiction, that a nature which involves necessary existence, does not exist, or does not necessarily exist. I conclude, therefore —

That everything, which includes necessary existence, cannot have in itself any imperfection, but must express pure perfection.

Further, since only from perfection can it come about, that any Being should exist by its own sufficiency and force, it follows that, if we assume a Being to exist by its own nature, but not to express all perfections, we must further suppose that another Being exists, which does comprehend in itself all perfections. For, if the less powerful Being exists by its own sufficiency, how much more must the more powerful so exist?

Lastly, to deal with the question, I affirm that there can only be a single Being, of which the existence belongs to its nature; such a Being which possesses in itself all perfections I will call God. If there be any Being to whose nature existence belongs, such a Being can contain in itself no imperfection, but must (by my fifth premiss) express every perfection; therefore, the nature of such a Being seems to belong to God (whose existence we are bound to affirm by Premiss VI.), inasmuch as He has in Himself all perfections and no imperfections. Nor can it exist externally to God. For if, externally to God, there existed one and the same nature involving necessary existence, such nature would be twofold; but this, by what we have just shown, is absurd. Therefore there is nothing save God, but there is a single God, that involves necessary existence, which was to be proved.

Such, distinguished Sir, are the arguments I can now produce for demonstrating this question. I hope I may also demonstrate to you, that I am, &c.

Voorburg,

10 April, 1666

Benedict de Spinoza

May, 1666

Voorburg

Christian Huyghens

LETTER XLI. SPINOZA TO CHRISTIAN HUYGHENS.

[FURTHER DISCUSSION CONCERNING the unity of God. Spinoza asks for advice about polishing lenses. (Voorburg, May, 1666.)]

Distinguished Sir, —

I have been by one means or another prevented from answering sooner your letter, dated 19th May. As I gather that you suspend your judgment with regard to most of the demonstration I sent you (owing, I believe, to the obscurity you find in it), I will here endeavour to explain its meaning more clearly.

First I enumerated four properties, which a Being existing by its own sufficiency or force must possess. These four, and others like them, I reduced in my fifth observation to one. Further, in order to deduce all things necessary for the demonstration from a single premiss, I endeavoured in my sixth observation to demonstrate the existence of God from the given hypothesis; whence, lastly, taking (as you know) nothing beyond the ordinary meaning of the terms, I drew the desired conclusion.

Such, in brief, was my purpose and such my aim. I will now explain the meaning of each step singly, and will first start with the aforesaid four properties.

In the first you find no difficulty, nor is it anything but, as in the case of the second, an axiom. By simple I merely mean not compound, or not made up of parts differing in nature or other parts agreeing in nature. This demonstration is assuredly universal.

The sense of my third observation (that if the Being be thought, it cannot be conceived as limited by thought, but only as infinite, and similarly, if it be extension, it cannot be conceived as limited by extension) you have excellently perceived, though you say you do not perceive the conclusion; this last is based on the fact, that a contradiction is involved in conceiving under the category of non-existence anything, whose definition includes or (what is the same thing) affirms existence. And since determination implies nothing positive, but only a limitation of the existence of the nature conceived as determinate, it follows that that, of which the definition affirms existence, cannot be conceived as determinate. For instance, if the term extension included necessary existence, it would be alike impossible to conceive extension without existence and existence without extension. If this were established, it would be impossible to conceive determinate extension. For, if it be conceived as determinate, it must be determined by its own nature, that is by extension, and this extension, whereby it is determined, must be conceived under the category of non-existence, which by the hypothesis is obviously a contradiction. In my fourth observation, I merely wished to show, that such a Being could neither be divided into parts of the same nature or parts of a different nature, whether those of a different nature involved necessary existence or not. If, I said, we adopt the second view, the Being would be destroyed; for destruction is merely the resolution of a thing into parts so that none of them expresses the nature of the whole; if we adopt the first view, we should be in contradiction with the first three properties.

In my fifth observation, I merely asserted, that perfection consists in being, and imperfection in the privation of being. I say the privation; for although extension denies of itself thought, this argues no imperfection in it. It would be an imperfection in it, if it were in any degree deprived of extension, as it would be, if it were determinate; or again, if it lacked duration, position, &c.

My sixth observation you accept absolutely, and yet you say, that your whole difficulty remains (inasmuch as there may be, you think, several self-existent entities of different nature; as for instance thought and extension are different and perhaps subsist by their own sufficiency). I am, therefore, forced to believe, that you attribute to my observation a meaning quite different from the one intended by me. I think I can discern your interpretation of it; however, in order to save time, I will merely set forth my own meaning. I say then, as regards my sixth observation, that if we assert that anything, which is indeterminate and perfect only after its kind, exists by its own sufficiency, we must also grant the existence of a Being indeterminate and perfect absolutely; such a Being I will call God. If, for example, we wish to assert that extension or thought (which are each perfect after their kind, that is, in a given sphere of being) exists by its own sufficiency, we must grant also the existence of God, who is absolutely perfect, that is of a Being absolutely indeterminate. I would here direct attention to what I have just said with regard to the term imperfection; namely, that it signifies that a thing is deficient in some quality, which, nevertheless, belongs to its nature. For instance, extension can only be called imperfect in respect of duration, position, or quantity: that is, as not enduring longer, as not retaining its position, or as not being greater. It can never be called imperfect, because it does not think, inasmuch as its nature requires nothing of the kind, but consists solely in extension, that is in a certain sphere of being. Only in respect to its own sphere can it be called determinate or indeterminate, perfect or imperfect. Now, since the nature of God is not confined to a certain sphere of being, but exists in being, which is absolutely indeterminate, so His nature also demands everything which perfectly expresses being; otherwise His nature would be determinate and deficient.

This being so, it follows that there can be only one Being, namely God, who exists by His own force. If, for the sake of an illustration, we assert, that extension involves existence; it is, therefore, necessary that it should be eternal and indeterminate, and express absolutely no imperfection, but perfection. Hence extension will appertain to God, or will be something which in some fashion expresses the nature of God, since God is a Being, who not only in a certain respect but absolutely is in essence indeterminate and omnipotent. What we have here said by way of illustration regarding extension must be asserted of all that we ascribe a similar existence to. I, therefore, conclude as in my former letter, that there is nothing external to God, but that God alone exists by His own sufficiency. I think I have said enough to show the meaning of my former letter; however, of this you will be the best judge. * * * * *

(The rest of the letter is occupied with details about the polishing of lenses.)

Benedict de Spinoza

May or June, 1665

John Bresser

LETTER XLI.A. SPINOZA TO * * * * *
(MAY OR JUNE, 1665).

[SPINOZA URGES HIS correspondent to be diligent in studying philosophy, promises to send part of the Ethics, and adds some personal details.]

Dear Friend, —

I do not know whether you have quite forgotten me; but there are many circumstances which lead me to suspect it. First, when I was setting out on my journey, I wished to bid you good-bye; and, after your own invitation, thinking I should certainly find you at home, heard that you had gone to the Hague. I return to Voorburg, nothing doubting but that you would at least have visited me in passing; but you, forsooth, without greeting your friend, went back home. Three weeks have I waited, without getting sight of a letter from you. If you wish this opinion of mine to be changed, you may easily change it by writing; and you can, at the same time, point out a means of entering into a correspondence, as we once talked of doing at your house.

Meanwhile, I should like to ask you, nay I do beg and entreat you, by our friendship, to apply yourself to some serious work with real study, and to devote the chief part of your life to the cultivation of your understanding and your soul. Now, while there is time, and before you complain of having let time and, indeed, your own self slip by. Further, in order to set our correspondence on foot, and to give you courage to write to me more freely, I would have you know that I have long thought, and, indeed, been almost certain, that you are somewhat too diffident of your own abilities, and that you are afraid of advancing some question or proposal unworthy of a man of learning. It does not become me to praise you, and expatiate on your talents to your face; but, if you are afraid that I shall show your letters to others, who will laugh at you, I give you my word of honour, that I will religiously keep them, and will show them to no mortal without your leave. On these conditions, you may enter on a correspondence, unless you doubt of my good faith, which I do not in the least believe. I want to hear your opinion on this in your first letter; and you may, at the same time, send me the conserve of red roses, though I am now much better.

After my journey, I was once bled; but the fever did not cease, though I was somewhat more active than before the bleeding, owing, I think, to the change of air; but I was two or three times laid up with a tertian. This, however, by good diet, I have at length driven away, and sent about its business. Where it has gone, I know not; but I am taking care it does not return here.

As regards the third part of my philosophy, I will shortly send it you, if you wish to be its transmitter, or to our friend De Vries; and, although I had settled not to send any of it, till it was finished, yet, as it takes longer than I thought, I am unwilling to keep you waiting. I will send up to the eightieth proposition, or thereabouts.

Of English affairs I hear a good deal, but nothing for certain. The people continue to be apprehensive, and can see no reason, why the fleet should not be despatched; but the matter does not yet seem to be set on foot. I am afraid our rulers want to be overwise and prudent; but the event will show what they intend, and what they will attempt. May the gods turn it all to good. I want to know, what our people think, where you are, and what they know for certain; but, above all things, I want you to believe me, &c.

Benedict de Spinoza

10 June, 1666

Voorburg

John Bredenburg

LETTER XLII. SPINOZA TO I. B.

[CONCERNING THE BEST method, by which we may safely arrive at the knowledge of things.]

Most learned Sir and dearest Friend, —

I have not been able hitherto to answer your last letter, received some time back. I have been so hindered by various occupations and calls on my time, that I am hardly yet free from them. However, as I have a few spare moments, I do not want to fall short of my duty, but take this first opportunity of heartily thanking you for your affection and kindness towards me, which you have often displayed in your actions, and now also abundantly prove by your letter.

I pass on to your question, which runs as follows: "Is there, or can there be, any method by which we may, without hindrance, arrive at the knowledge of the most excellent things? or are our minds, like our bodies, subject to the vicissitudes of circumstance, so that our thoughts are governed rather by fortune than by skill?" I think I shall satisfy you, if I show that there must necessarily be a method, whereby we are able to direct our clear and distinct perceptions, and that our mind is not, like our body, subject to the vicissitudes of circumstance.

This conclusion may be based simply on the consideration that one clear and distinct perception, or several such together, can be absolutely the cause of another clear and distinct perception. Now, all the clear and distinct perceptions, which we form, can only arise from other clear and distinct perceptions, which are in us; nor do they acknowledge any cause external to us. Hence it follows that the clear and distinct perceptions, which we form, depend solely on our nature, and on its certain and fixed laws; in other words, on our absolute power, not on fortune — that is, not on causes which, although also acting by certain and fixed laws, are yet unknown to us, and alien to our nature and power. As regards other perceptions, I confess that they depend chiefly on fortune. Hence clearly appears, what the true method ought to be like, and what it ought chiefly to consist in — namely, solely in the knowledge of the pure understanding, and its nature and laws. In order that such knowledge may be acquired, it is before all things necessary to distinguish between the understanding and the imagination, or between ideas which are true and the rest, such as the fictitious, the false, the doubtful, and absolutely all which depend solely on the memory. For the understanding of these matters, as far as the method requires, there is no need to know the nature of the mind through its first cause; it is sufficient to put together a short history of the mind, or of perceptions, in the manner taught by Verulam.

I think that in these few words I have explained and demonstrated the true method, and have, at the same time, pointed out the way of acquiring it. It only remains to remind you, that all these questions demand assiduous study, and great firmness of disposition and purpose. In order to fulfil these conditions, it is of prime necessity to follow a fixed mode and plan of living, and to set before one some definite aim. But enough of this for the present, &c.

Voorburg,
10 June, 1666.
Benedict de Spinoza
Oct. 1, 1666
Voorburg
v. M.

LETTER XLIII. SPINOZA TO I. V. M.

[SPINOZA SOLVES FOR his friend an arithmetical problem connected with games of chance. (Voorburg, Oct. 1, 1666.)]

Omitted.

Benedict de Spinoza

Jarig Jellis

LETTERS XLIV., XLV., XLVI. (XXXIX., XL., XLI.)

SPINOZA TO I. I.

XLIV.

[REMARKS ON DESCARTES' treatise on Optics.]

XLV.

[Remarks on some alchemistic experiments, on the third and fourth meditations of Descartes, and on Optics.]

XLVI.

[Remarks on Hydrostatics.]

Benedict de Spinoza

17 Feb., 1671

The Hague

Jarig Jellis

LETTER XLVII. SPINOZA TO I. I.

[SPINOZA BEGS HIS friend to stop the printing of the Dutch version of the Tractatus Theologico-Politicus. Some remarks on a pernicious pamphlet, "Homo Politicus," and on Thales of Miletus.]

Most courteous Sir, —

When Professor N. N. visited me the other day, he told me that my Theologico-Political Treatise has been translated into Dutch, and that someone, whose name he did not know, was about printing it. With regard to this, I earnestly beg you to inquire carefully into the business, and, if possible, stop the printing. This is the request not only of myself, but of many of my friends and acquaintances, who would be sorry to see the book placed under an interdict, as it undoubtedly would be, if published in Dutch. I do not doubt, but that you will do this service to me and the cause.

One of my friends sent me a short time since a pamphlet called "Homo Politicus," of which I had heard much. I have read it, and find it to be the most pernicious work which men could devise or invent. Rank and riches are the author's highest good; he adapts his doctrine accordingly, and shows the means to acquire them; to wit, by inwardly rejecting all religion, and outwardly professing whatever best serves his own advancement, also by keeping faith with no one, except in so far as he himself is profited thereby. For the rest, to feign, to make promises and break them, to lie, to swear falsely, and many such like practices call forth his highest praises. When I had finished reading the book, I debated whether I should write a pamphlet indirectly aimed against its author, wherein I should treat of the highest good and show the troubled and wretched condition of those who are covetous of rank and riches; finally proving by very plain reasoning and many examples, that the insatiable desire for rank and riches must bring and has brought ruin to states.

How much better and more excellent than the doctrines of the aforesaid writer are the reflections of Thales of Miletus, appears from the following. All the goods of friends, he says, are in common; wise men are the friends of the gods, and all things belong to the gods; therefore all things belong to the wise. Thus in a single sentence, this wisest of men accounts himself most rich, rather by nobly despising riches than by sordidly seeking them. In other passages he shows that the wise lack riches, not from necessity, but from choice. For when his friends reproached him with his poverty he answered, "Do you wish me to show you, that I could acquire what I deem unworthy of my labour, but you so diligently seek?" On their answering in the affirmative, he hired every oil-press in the whole of Greece (for being a distinguished astrologer he knew that the olive harvest would be as abundant as in previous years it had been scanty), and sub-let at his own price what he had hired for a very small sum, thus acquiring in a single year a large fortune, which he bestowed liberally as he had gained it industriously, &c.

The Hague,
17 Feb., 1671.
Lambert de Velthuysen
January 24th, 1671
Utrecht
Isaac Orobio

Benedict de Spinoza

LETTER XLVIII.

WRITTEN BY A physician, Lambert de Velthuysen, to Isaac Orobio, and forwarded by the latter to Spinoza. It contains a detailed attack on the Tractatus Theologico-Politicus. Its tenor may be sufficiently seen from Spinoza's reply. (Written at Utrecht, January 24th, 1671.) Velthuysen afterwards became more friendly to Spinoza, as appears from Letter LXXV.

Benedict de Spinoza

1671

The Hague

Isaac Orobio

LETTER XLIX. SPINOZA TO ISAAC OROBIO.

[A DEFENCE OF the Tractatus Theologico-Politicus. (The Hague, 1671.)]

Most Learned Sir, —

You doubtless wonder why I have kept you so long waiting. I could hardly bring myself to reply to the pamphlet of that person, which you thought fit to send me; indeed I only do so now because of my promise. However, in order as far as possible to humour my feelings, I will fulfil my engagement in as few words as I can, and will briefly show how perversely he has interpreted my meaning; whether through malice or through ignorance I cannot readily say. But to the matter in hand.

First he says, "that it is of little moment to know what nation I belong to, or what sort of life I lead." Truly, if he had known, he would not so easily have persuaded himself that I teach Atheism. For Atheists are wont greedily to covet rank and riches, which I have always despised, as all who know me are aware. Again, in order to smooth his path to the object he has in view, he says that, "I am possessed of no mean talents," so that he may, forsooth, more easily convince his readers, that I have knowingly and cunningly with evil intent argued for the cause of the deists, in order to discredit it. This contention sufficiently shows that he has not understood my reasons. For who could be so cunning and clever, as to be able to advance under false pretences so many and such good reasons for a doctrine which he did not believe in? Who will pass for an honest writer in the eyes of a man, that thinks one may argue as soundly for fiction as for truth? But after all I am not astonished. Descartes was formerly served in the same way by Voët, and the most honourable writers are constantly thus treated.

He goes on to say, "In order to shun the reproach of superstition, he seems to me to have thrown off all religion." What this writer means by religion and what by superstition, I know not. But I would ask, whether a man throws off all religion, who maintains that God must be acknowledged as the highest good, and must, as such, be loved with a free mind? or, again, that the reward of virtue is virtue itself, while the punishment of folly and weakness is folly itself? or, lastly, that every man ought to love his neighbour, and to obey the commands of the supreme power? Such doctrines I have not only expressly stated, but have also demonstrated them by very solid reasoning. However, I think I see the mud wherein this person sticks. He finds nothing in virtue and the understanding in themselves to please him, but would prefer to live in accordance with his passions, if it were not for the single obstacle that he fears punishment. He abstains from evil actions, and obeys the divine commands like a slave, with unwillingness and hesitation, expecting as the reward of his bondage to be recompensed by God with gifts far more pleasing than divine love, and greater in proportion to his dislike to goodness and consequent unwillingness to practise it. Hence it comes to pass, that he believes that all, who are not restrained by this fear, lead a life of licence and throw off all religion. But this I pass over, and proceed to the deduction, whereby he wishes to show, that "with covert and disguised arguments I teach atheism." The foundation of his reasoning is, that he thinks I take away freedom from God, and subject Him to fate. This is flatly false. For I have maintained, that all things follow by inevitable necessity from the nature of God, in the same way as all maintain that it follows from the nature of God, that He understands Himself: no one denies that this latter consequence follows necessarily from the divine nature, yet no one conceives that God is constrained by any fate; they believe that He understands Himself with entire freedom, though necessarily. I find nothing here, that cannot be perceived by everyone; if, nevertheless, my adversary thinks that these arguments are advanced with evil intent, what does he think of his own Descartes, who asserted that nothing is done by us, which has not been pre-ordained by God, nay, that we are newly created as it were by God every moment, though none the less we act according to our own free will? This, as Descartes himself confesses, no one can understand.

Further, this inevitable necessity in things destroys neither divine laws nor human. For moral principles, whether they have received from God the form of laws or not, are nevertheless divine and salutary. Whether we accept the good, which follows from virtue and the divine love, as given us by God as a judge, or as emanating from the necessity of the divine nature, it is not in either case more or less to be desired; nor are the evils which follow from evil actions less to be feared, because they follow necessarily: finally, whether we act under necessity or freedom, we are in either case led by hope and fear. Wherefore the assertion is false, "that I maintain that there is no room left for precepts and commands." Or as he goes on to say, "that there is no expectation of reward or punishment, since all things are ascribed to fate, and are said to flow with inevitable necessity from God."

I do not here inquire, why it is the same, or almost the same to say that all things necessarily flow from God, as to say that God is universal; but I would have you observe the insinuation which he not less maliciously subjoins, "that I wish that men should practise virtue, not because of the precepts and law of God, or through hope of reward and fear of punishment, but," &c. Such a sentiment you will assuredly not find anywhere in my treatise: on the contrary, I have expressly stated in Chap. IV., that the sum of the divine law (which, as I have said in Chap. II., has been divinely inscribed on our hearts), and its chief precept is, to love God as the highest good: not, indeed, from the fear of any punishment, for love cannot spring from fear; nor for the love of anything which we desire for our own delight, for then we should love not God, but the object of our desire.

I have shown in the same chapter, that God revealed this law to the prophets, so that, whether it received from God the form of a command, or whether we conceive it to be like God's other decrees, which involve eternal necessity and truth, it will in either case remain God's decree and a salutary principle. Whether I love God in freedom, or whether I love Him from the necessity of the divine decree, I shall nevertheless love God, and shall be in a state of salvation. Wherefore, I can now declare here, that this person is one of that sort, of whom I have said at the end of my preface, that I would rather that they utterly neglected my book, than that by misinterpreting it after their wont, they should become hostile, and hinder others without benefiting themselves.

Though I think I have said enough to prove what I intended, I have yet thought it worth while to add a few observations — namely, that this person falsely thinks, that I have in view the axiom of theologians, which draws a distinction between the words of a prophet when propounding doctrine, and the same prophet when narrating an event. If by such an axiom he means that which in Chap. XV. I attributed to a certain R. Jehuda Alpakhar, how could he think that I agree with it, when in that very chapter I reject it as false? If he does not mean this, I confess I am as yet in ignorance as to what he does mean, and, therefore, could not have had it in view.

Again, I cannot see why he says, that all will adopt my opinions, who deny that reason and philosophy should be the interpreters of Scripture; I have refuted the doctrine of such persons, together with that of Maimonides.

It would take too long to review all the indications he gives of not having judged me altogether calmly. I therefore pass on to his conclusion, where he says, "that I have no arguments left to prove, that Mahomet was not a true prophet." This he endeavours to show from my opinions, whereas from them it clearly follows, that Mahomet was an impostor, inasmuch as he utterly forbids that freedom, which the Catholic religion revealed by our natural faculties and by the prophets grants, and which I have shown should be granted in its completeness. Even if this were not so, am I, I should like to know, bound to show that any prophet is false? Surely the burden lies with the prophets, to prove that they are true. But if he retorts, that Mahomet also taught the divine law, and gave certain signs of his mission, as the rest of the prophets did, there is surely no reason why he should deny, that Mahomet also was a true prophet.

As regards the Turks and other non-Christian nations; if they worship God by the practice of justice and charity towards their neighbour, I believe that they have the spirit of Christ, and are in a state of salvation, whatever they may ignorantly hold with regard to Mahomet and oracles.

Thus you see, my friend, how far this man has strayed from the truth; nevertheless, I grant that he has inflicted the greatest injury, not on me but on himself, inasmuch as he has not been ashamed to declare, that "under disguised and covert arguments I teach atheism."

I do not think, that you will find any expressions I have used against this man too severe. However, if there be any of the kind which offend you, I beg you to correct them, as you shall think fit. I have no disposition to irritate him, whoever he may be, and to raise up by my labours enemies against myself; as this is often the result of disputes like the present, I could scarcely prevail on myself to reply — nor should I have prevailed, if I had not promised. Farewell. I commit to your prudence this letter, and myself, who am, &c.

Benedict de Spinoza

2 June, 1674

The Hague

Jarig Jellis

LETTER L. SPINOZA TO JARIG JELLIS.

[OF THE DIFFERENCE between the political theories of Hobbes and Spinoza, of the Unity of God, of the notion of figure, of the book of a Utrecht professor against the Tractatus Theologico-Politicus.]

Most courteous Sir, —

As regards political theories, the difference which you inquire about between Hobbes and myself, consists in this, that I always preserve natural right intact, and only allot to the chief magistrates in every state a right over their subjects commensurate with the excess of their power over the power of the subjects. This is what always takes place in the state of nature.

Again, with regard to the demonstration which I establish in the appendix to my geometric exposition of Cartesian principles, namely, that God can only with great impropriety be called one or single, I answer that a thing can only be called one or single in respect of existence, not in respect of essence. For we do not conceive things under the category of numbers, unless they have first been reduced to a common genus. For example, he who holds in his hand a penny and a crown piece will not think of the twofold number, unless he can call both the penny and the crown piece by one and the same name, to wit, coins or pieces of money. In the latter case he can say that he holds two coins or pieces of money, inasmuch as he calls the crown as well as the penny, a coin, or piece of money. Hence, it is evident that a thing cannot be called one or single, unless there be afterwards another thing conceived, which (as has been said) agrees with it. Now, since the existence of God is His essence, and of His essence we can form no general idea, it is certain, that he who calls God one or single has no true idea of God, and speaks of Him very improperly.

As to the doctrine that figure is negation and not anything positive, it is plain that the whole of matter considered indefinitely can have no figure, and that figure can only exist in finite and determinate bodies. For he who says, that he perceives a figure, merely indicates thereby, that he conceives a determinate thing, and how it is determinate. This determination, therefore, does not appertain to the thing according to its being, but, on the contrary, is its non-being. As then figure is nothing else than determination, and determination is negation, figure, as has been said, can be nothing but negation.

The book, which a Utrecht professor wrote against mine, and which was published after his death, I saw lying in a bookseller's window. From the little I then read of it, I judged it unworthy of perusal, still less of reply. I, therefore, left the book, and its author. With an inward smile I reflected, that the most ignorant are ever the most audacious and the most ready to rush into print. The Christians seem to me to expose their wares for sale like hucksters, who always show first that which is worst. The devil is said to be very cunning, but to my thinking the tricks of these people are in cunning far beyond his. Farewell.

The Hague,

2 June, 1674.

Godfrey Leibnitz

5 Oct., 1671

Frankfort

Benedict de Spinoza

LETTER LI. GODFREY LEIBNITZ TO SPINOZA.

DISTINGUISHED SIR, —

Among your other merits spread abroad by fame, I understand that you have remarkable skill in optics. I have, therefore, wished to forward my essay, such as it is, to you, as I am not likely to find a better critic in this branch of learning. The paper, which I send you, and which I have styled "a note on advanced optics," has been published with the view of more conveniently making known my ideas to my friends and the curious in such matters. I hear that * * * * * is very clever in the same subject, doubtless he is well known to you. If you could obtain for me his opinion and kind attention, you would greatly increase my obligation to you. The paper explains itself.

I believe you have already received the "Prodromo" of Francis Lana the Jesuit, written in Italian. Some remarkable observations on optics are contained in it. John Oltius too, a young Swiss very learned in these matters, has published "Physico-Mechanical Reflections concerning Vision;" in which he announces a machine for the polishing all kinds of glasses, very simple and of universal applicability, and also declares that he has discovered a means of collecting all the rays coming from different points of an object, so as to obtain an equal number of corresponding points, but only under conditions of a given distance and form of object.

My proposal is, not that the rays from all points should be collected and re-arranged (this is with any object or distance impossible at the present stage of our knowledge); the result I aim at is the equal collection of rays from points outside the optic axis and in the optic axis, so that the apertures of glasses could be made of any size desired without impairing the distinctness of vision. But this must stand according to your skilled verdict. Farewell, and believe me, distinguished Sir, your obedient servant,

Godfrey Leibnitz,

J. U. D., Councillor of the Elector of Mainz.

Frankfort,

5 Oct., 1671

(new style).

Benedict de Spinoza

9 Nov., 1671

The Hague

Godfrey Leibnitz

LETTER LII. SPINOZA TO LEIBNITZ.

[ANSWER TO THE foregoing letter].

Most learned and distinguished Sir, —

I have read the paper you were kind enough to send me, and return you many thanks for the communication. I regret that I have not been able quite to follow your meaning, though you explain it sufficiently clearly, whether you think that there is any cause for making the apertures of the glasses small, except that the rays coming from a single point are not collected accurately at another single point, but in a small area which we generally call the mechanical point, and that this small area is greater or less in proportion to the size of the aperture. Further, I ask whether the lenses which you call "pandochæ" correct this fault, so that the mechanical point or small area, on which the rays coming from a single point are after refraction collected, always preserves the same proportional size, whether the aperture be small or large. If so, one may enlarge the aperture as much as one likes, and consequently these lenses will be far superior to those of any other shape known to me; if not, I hardly see why you praise them so greatly beyond common lenses. For circular lenses have everywhere the same axis; therefore, when we employ them, we must regard all the points of an object as placed in the optic axis; although all the points of the object be not at the same distance, the difference arising thence will not be perceptible, when the objects are very remote; because then the rays coming from a single point would, as they enter the glass, be regarded as parallel. I think your lenses might be of service in obtaining a more distinct representation of all the objects, when we wish to include several objects in one view, as we do, when we employ very large convex circular lenses. However, I would rather suspend my judgment about all these details, till you have more clearly explained your meaning, as I heartily beg you to do. I have, as you requested, sent the other copy of your paper to Mr. * * * *. He answers, that he has at present no time to study it, but he hopes to have leisure in a week or two.

I have not yet seen the "Prodromo" of Francis Lana, nor the "Physico-Mechanical Reflections" of John Oltius. What I more regret is, that your "Physical Hypothesis" has not yet come to my hands, nor is there a copy for sale here at the Hague. The gift, therefore, which you so liberally promise me will be most acceptable to me; if I can be of use to you in any other matter, you will always find me most ready. I hope you will not think it too irksome to reply to this short note.

Distinguished Sir,

Yours sincerely,

B. de Spinoza.

The Hague,

9 Nov., 1671.

P.S. Mr. Diemerbroech does not live here. I am, therefore, forced to entrust this to an ordinary letter-carrier. I doubt not that you know someone at the Hague, who would take charge of our letters; I should like to hear of such a person, that our correspondence might be more conveniently and securely taken care of. If the "Tractatus Theologico-Politicus" has not yet come to your hands, I will, unless you have any objection, send you a copy. Farewell.

Lewis Fabritius

16 Feb., 1673

Heidelberg

Benedict de Spinoza

LETTER LIII. FABRITIUS TO SPINOZA.

[FABRITIUS, UNDER THE order and in the name of the Elector Palatine, offers Spinoza the post of Professor of Philosophy at Heidelberg, under very liberal conditions.]

Most renowned Sir, —

His Most Serene Highness the Elector Palatine, my most gracious master, commands me to write to you, who are, as yet, unknown to me, but most favourably regarded by his Most Serene Highness, and to inquire of you, whether you are willing to accept an ordinary professorship of Philosophy in his illustrious university. An annual salary would be paid to you, equal to that enjoyed at present by the ordinary professors. You will hardly find elsewhere a prince more favourable to distinguished talents, among which he reckons yourself. You will have the most ample freedom in philosophical teaching, which the prince is confident you will not misuse, to disturb the religion publicly established. I cannot refrain from seconding the prince's injunction. I therefore most earnestly beg you to reply as soon as possible, and to address your answer either under cover to the Most Serene Elector's resident at the Hague, Mr. Grotius, or to Mr. Gilles Van der Hele, so that it may come in the packet of letters usually sent to the court, or else to avail yourself of some other convenient opportunity for transmitting it. I will only add, that if you come here, you will live pleasantly a life worthy of a philosopher, unless events turn out quite contrary to our expectation and hope. So farewell.

I remain, illustrious Sir,

Your devoted admirer,

Lewis Fabritius.

Professor of the Academy of Heidelberg, and Councillor of the Elector Palatine.

Heidelberg,

16 Feb., 1673.

Benedict de Spinoza

The Hague

30 March, 1673

Lewis Fabritius

LETTER LIV. SPINOZA TO FABRITIUS.

[SPINOZA THANKS THE Elector for his kind offer, but, owing to his unwillingness to teach in public, and other causes, humbly begs to be allowed time to consider it.]

Distinguished Sir, —

If I had ever desired to take a professorship in any faculty, I could not have wished for any other than that which is offered to me, through you, by His Most Serene Highness the Elector Palatine, especially because of that freedom in philosophical teaching, which the most gracious prince is kind enough to grant, not to speak of the desire which I have long entertained, to live under the rule of a prince, whom all men admire for his wisdom.

But since it has never been my wish to teach in public, I have been unable to induce myself to accept this splendid opportunity, though I have long deliberated about it. I think, in the first place, that I should abandon philosophical research if I consented to find time for teaching young students. I think, in the second place, that I do not know the limits, within which the freedom of my philosophical teaching would be confined, if I am to avoid all appearance of disturbing the publicly established religion. Religious quarrels do not arise so much from ardent zeal for religion, as from men's various dispositions and love of contradiction, which causes them to habitually distort and condemn everything, however rightly it may have been said. I have experienced these results in my private and secluded station, how much more should I have to fear them after my elevation to this post of honour.

Thus you see, distinguished Sir, that I am not holding back in the hope of getting something better, but through my love of quietness, which I think I can in some measure secure, if I keep away from lecturing in public. I therefore most earnestly entreat you to beg of the Most Serene Elector, that I may be allowed to consider further about this matter, and I also ask you to conciliate the favour of the most gracious prince to his most devoted admirer, thus increasing the obligations of your sincere friend,

B. de. S.

The Hague,

30 March, 1673.

Hugo Boxel

14 Sept., 1674

Benedict de Spinoza

LETTER LV. HUGO BOXEL TO SPINOZA.

[A FRIEND ASKS Spinoza's opinion about Ghosts.]

Distinguished Sir, —

My reason for writing to you is, that I want to know your opinion about apparitions and ghosts or spectres; if you admit their existence, what do you think about them, and how long does their life last? For some hold them to be mortal, others immortal. As I am doubtful whether you admit their existence, I will proceed no further.

Meanwhile, it is certain, that the ancients believed in them. The theologians and philosophers of to-day are hitherto agreed as to the existence of some creatures of the kind, though they may not agree as to the nature of their essence. Some assert that they are composed of very thin and subtle matter, others that they are spiritual. But, as I was saying before, we are quite at cross purposes, inasmuch as I am doubtful whether you would grant their existence; though, as you must be aware, so many instances and stories of them are found throughout antiquity, that it would really be difficult either to deny or to doubt them. It is clear that, even if you confess that they exist, you do not believe that some of them are the souls of the dead, as the defenders of the Romish faith would have it. I will here end, and will say nothing about war and rumours, inasmuch as our lot is cast in an age, &c. Farewell.

14 Sept., 1674.

Benedict de Spinoza

Sept., 1674

The Hague

Hugo Boxel

LETTER LVI. SPINOZA TO HUGO BOXEL.

[SPINOZA ANSWERS THAT he does not know what ghosts are, and can gain no information from antiquity. (The Hague, Sept., 1674.)]

Dear Sir, —

Your letter, which I received yesterday, was most welcome to me, both because I wanted to hear news of you, and also because it shows that you have not utterly forgotten me. Although some might think it a bad omen, that ghosts are the cause of your writing to me, I, on the contrary, can discern a deeper meaning in the circumstance; I see that not only truths, but also things trifling and imaginary may be of use to me.

However, let us defer the question, whether ghosts are delusions and imaginary, for I see that not only denial of them, but even doubt about them seems very singular to you, as to one who has been convinced by the numerous histories related by men of to-day and the ancients. The great esteem and honour, in which I have always held and still hold you, does not suffer me to contradict you, still less to humour you. The middle course, which I shall adopt, is to beg you to be kind enough to select from the numerous stories which you have read, one or two of those least open to doubt, and most clearly demonstrating the existence of ghosts. For, to confess the truth, I have never read a trustworthy author, who clearly showed that there are such things. Up to the present time I do not know what they are, and no one has ever been able to tell me. Yet it is evident, that in the case of a thing so clearly shown by experience we ought to know what it is; otherwise we shall have great difficulty in gathering from histories that ghosts exist. We only gather that something exists of nature unknown. If philosophers choose to call things which we do not know "ghosts," I shall not deny the existence of such, for there are an infinity of things, which I cannot make out.

Pray tell me, my dear Sir, before I explain myself further in the matter, What are these ghosts or spectres? Are they children, or fools, or madmen? For all that I have heard of them seems more adapted to the silly than the wise, or, to say the best we can of it, resembles the pastimes of children or of fools. Before I end, I would submit to you one consideration, namely, that the desire which most men have to narrate things, not as they really happened, but as they wished them to happen, can be illustrated from the stories of ghosts and spectres more easily than from any others. The principal reason for this is, I believe, that such stories are only attested by the narrators, and thus a fabricator can add or suppress circumstances, as seems most convenient to him, without fear of anyone being able to contradict him. He composes them to suit special circumstances, in order to justify the fear he feels of dreams and phantoms, or else to confirm his courage, his credit, or his opinion. There are other reasons, which lead me to doubt, if not the actual stories, at least some of the narrated circumstances; and which have a close bearing on the conclusion we are endeavouring to derive from the aforesaid stories. I will here stop, until I have learnt from you what those stories are, which have so completely convinced you, that you regard all doubt about them as absurd, &c.

Hugo Boxel

21 Sept., 1674

Benedict de Spinoza

LETTER LVII. HUGO BOXEL TO SPINOZA.

MOST SAGACIOUS SIR, —

You have sent me just the answer I expected to receive, from a friend holding an opinion adverse to my own. But no matter. Friends may always disagree on indifferent subjects without injury to their friendship.

You ask me, before you gave an opinion as to what these spectres or spirits are, to tell you whether they are children, fools, or madmen, and you add that everything you have heard of them seems to have proceeded rather from the insane than the sane. It is a true proverb, which says that a preconceived opinion hinders the pursuit of truth.

I, then, believe that ghosts exist for the following reasons: first, because it appertains to the beauty and perfection of the universe, that they should; secondly, because it is probable that the Creator created them, as being more like Himself than are embodied creatures; thirdly, because as body exists without soul, soul exists without body; fourthly and lastly, because in the upper air, region, or space, I believe there is no obscure body without inhabitants of its own; consequently, that the measureless space between us and the stars is not empty, but thronged with spiritual inhabitants. Perhaps the highest and most remote are true spirits, whereas the lowest in the lowest region of the air are creatures of very thin and subtle substance, and also invisible. Thus I think there are spirits of all sorts, but, perhaps, none of the female sex.

This reasoning will in no wise convince those, who rashly believe that the world has been created by chance. Daily experience, if these reasons be dismissed, shows that there are spectres, and many stories, both new and old, are current about them. Such may be found in Plutarch's book "De viris illustribus," and in his other works; in Suetonius's "Lives of the Cæsars," also in Wierus's and Lavater's books about ghosts, where the subject is fully treated and illustrated from writers of all kinds. Cardano, celebrated for his learning, also speaks of them in his books "De Subtilitate," "De Varietate," and in his "Life;" showing, by experience, that they have appeared to himself, his relations and friends. Melancthon, a wise man and a lover of truth, testifies to his experience of them, as also do many others. A certain burgomaster, learned and wise, who is still living, once told me that he heard by night the noise of working in his mother's brew-house, going on just as it does while beer is being brewed in the day; this he attested as having occurred frequently. The same sort of thing has happened to me, and will never fade from my memory; hence I am convinced by the above-mentioned experiences and reasons, that there are ghosts.

As for evil spirits, who torture wretched men in this life and the next, and who work spells, I believe the stories of them to be fables. In treatises about spirits you will find a host of details. Besides those I have cited, you may refer to Pliny the younger, bk. vii., the letter to Sura; Suetonius, "Life of Julius Cæsar," ch. xxxii.; Valerius Maximus, I. viii. § § 7, 8; and Alexander ab Alexandro, "Dies Geniales." I am sure these books are accessible to you. I say nothing of monks and priests, for they relate so many tales of souls and evil spirits, or as I should rather say of spectres, that the reader becomes wearied with their abundance. Thyræus, a Jesuit, in the book about the apparition of spirits, also treats of the question. But these last-named discourse on such subjects merely for the sake of gain, and to prove that purgatory is not so bad as is supposed, thus treating the question as a mine, from which they dig up plenteous store of gold and silver. But the same cannot be said of the writers mentioned previously, and other moderns, who merit greater credit from their absence of bias.

As an answer to the passage in your letter, where you speak of fools and madmen, I subjoin this sentence from the learned Lavater, who ends with it his first book on ghosts or spectres. "He who is bold enough to gainsay so many witnesses, both ancient and modern, seems to me unworthy of credit. For as it is a mark of frivolity to lend incontinent credence to everyone who says he has seen a ghost; so, on the other hand, rashly and flatly to contradict so many trustworthy historians, Fathers, and other persons placed in authority would argue a remarkable shamelessness."

21 Sept., 1674

Benedict de Spinoza

Hugo Boxel

LETTER LVIII. SPINOZA
TO HUGO BOXEL.

[SPINOZA TREATS OF the necessary creation of the world — he refutes his friend's arguments and quotations.]

Dear Sir, —

I will rely on what you said in your letter of the 21st of last month, that friends may disagree on indifferent questions, without injury to their friendship, and will frankly tell you my opinion on the reasons and stories, whereon you base your conclusion, that there are ghosts of every kind, but perhaps none of the female sex. The reason for my not replying sooner is that the books you quoted are not at hand, in fact I have not found any except Pliny and Suetonius. However, these two have saved me the trouble of consulting any other, for I am persuaded that they all talk in the same strain and hanker after extraordinary tales, which rouse men's astonishment and compel their wonder. I confess that I am not a little amazed, not at the stories, but at those who narrate them. I wonder, that men of talent and judgment should so employ their readiness of speech, and abuse it in endeavouring to convince us of such trifles.

However, let us dismiss the writers, and turn to the question itself. In the first place, we will reason a little about your conclusion. Let us see whether I, who deny that there are spectres or spirits, am on that account less able to understand the authors, who have written on the subject; or whether you, who assert that such beings exist, do not give to the aforesaid writers more credit than they deserve. The distinction you drew, in admitting without hesitation spirits of the male sex, but doubting whether any female spirits exist, seems to me more like a fancy than a genuine doubt. If it were really your opinion, it would resemble the common imagination, that God is masculine, not feminine. I wonder that those, who have seen naked ghosts, have not cast their eyes on those parts of the person, which would remove all doubt; perhaps they were timid, or did not know of this distinction. You would say that this is ridicule, not reasoning: and hence I see, that your reasons appear to you so strong and well founded, that no one can (at least in your judgment) contradict them, unless he be some perverse fellow, who thinks the world has been made by chance. This impels me, before going into your reasons, to set forth briefly my opinion on the question, whether the world was made by chance. But I answer, that as it is clear that chance and necessity are two contraries, so is it also clear, that he, who asserts the world to be a necessary effect of the divine nature, must utterly deny that the world has been made by chance; whereas, he who affirms, that God need not have made the world, confirms, though in different language, the doctrine that it has been made by chance; inasmuch as he maintains that it proceeds from a wish, which might never have been formed. However, as this opinion and theory is on the face of it absurd, it is commonly very unanimously admitted, that God's will is eternal, and has never been indifferent; hence it must necessarily be also admitted, you will observe, that the world is a necessary effect of the divine nature. Let them call it will, understanding, or any name they like, they come at last to the same conclusion, that under different names they are expressing one and the same thing. If you ask them, whether the divine will does not differ from the human, they answer, that the former has nothing in common with the latter except its name; especially as they generally admit that God's will, understanding, intellect, essence, and nature are all identical; so I, myself, lest I should confound the divine nature with the human, do not assign to God human attributes, such as will, understanding, attention, hearing, &c. I therefore say, as I have said already, that the world is a necessary effect of the divine nature, and that it has not been made by chance. I think this is enough to persuade you, that the opinion of those (if such there be), who say that the world has been made by chance, is entirely contrary to mine; and, relying on this hypothesis, I proceed to examine those reasons which lead you to infer the existence of all kinds of ghosts. I should like to say of these reasons generally, that they seem rather conjectures than reasons, and I can with difficulty believe, that you take them for guiding reasons. However, be they conjectures or be they reasons, let us see whether we can take them for foundations.

Your first reason is, that the existence of ghosts is needful for the beauty and perfection of the universe. Beauty, my dear Sir, is not so much a quality of the object beheld, as an effect in him who beholds it. If our sight were longer or shorter, or if our constitution were different, what now appears beautiful to us would seem misshapen, and what we now think misshapen we should regard as beautiful. The most beautiful hand seen through the microscope will appear horrible. Some things are beautiful at a distance, but ugly near; thus things regarded in themselves, and in relation to God, are neither ugly nor beautiful. Therefore, he who says that God has created the world, so that it might be beautiful, is bound to adopt one of the two alternatives, either that God created the world for the sake of men's pleasure and eyesight, or else that He created men's pleasure and eyesight for the sake of the world. Now, whether we adopt the former or the latter of these views, how God could have furthered His object by the creation of ghosts, I cannot see. Perfection and imperfection are names, which do not differ much from the names beauty and ugliness. I only ask, therefore (not to be tedious), which would contribute most to the perfect adornment of the world, ghosts, or a quantity of monsters, such as centaurs, hydras, harpies, satyrs, gryphons, arguses, and other similar inventions? Truly the world would be handsomely bedecked, if God had adorned and embellished it, in obedience to our fancy, with beings, which anyone may readily imagine and dream of, but no one can understand.

Your second reason is, that because spirits express God's image more than embodied creatures, it is probable that He has created them. I frankly confess, that I am as yet in ignorance, how spirits more than other creatures express God. This I know, that between finite and infinite there is no comparison; so that the difference between God and the greatest and most excellent created thing is no less than the difference between God and the least created thing. This argument, therefore, is beside the mark. If I had as clear an idea of ghosts, as I have of a triangle or a circle, I should not in the least hesitate to affirm that they had been created by God; but as the idea I possess of them is just like the ideas, which my imagination forms of harpies, gryphons, hydras, &c., I cannot consider them as anything but dreams, which differ from God as totally, as that which is not differs from that which is.

Your third reason (that as body exists without soul, so soul should exist without body) seems to me equally absurd. Pray tell me, if it is not also likely, that memory, hearing, sight, &c., exist without bodies, because bodies exist without memory, hearing, sight, &c., or that a sphere exists without a circle, because a circle exists without a sphere?

Your fourth, and last reason, is the same as your first, and I refer you to my answer given above. I will only observe here, that I do not know which are the highest or which the lowest places, which you conceive as existing in infinite matter, unless you take the earth as the centre of the universe. For if the sun or Saturn be the centre of the universe, the sun, or Saturn, not the earth, will be the lowest.

Thus, passing by this argument and what remains, I conclude, that these and similar reasons will convince no one of the existence of all kinds of ghosts and spectres, unless it be those persons, who shut their ears to the understanding, and allow themselves to be led away by superstition. This last is so hostile to right reason, that she lends willing credence to old wives' tales for the sake of discrediting philosophers.

As regards the stories, I have already said in my first letter, that I do not deny them altogether, but only the conclusion drawn from them. To this I may add, that I do not believe them so thoroughly, as not to doubt many of the details, which are generally added rather for ornament than for bringing out the truth of the story or the conclusion drawn from it. I had hoped, that out of so many stories you would at least have produced one or two, which could hardly be questioned, and which would clearly show that ghosts or spectres exist. The case you relate of the burgomaster, who wanted to infer their existence, because he heard spectral brewers working in his mother's brewhouse by night, and making the same noises as he was accustomed to hear by day, seems to me laughable. In like manner it would be tedious here to examine all the stories of people, who have written on these trifles. To be brief, I cite the instance of Julius Cæsar, who, as Suetonius testifies, laughed at such things and yet was happy, if we may trust what Suetonius says in the 59th chapter of his life of that leader. And so should all, who reflect on the human imagination, and the effects of the emotions, laugh at such notions; whatever Lavater and others, who have gone dreaming with him in the matter, may produce to the contrary.

Hugo Boxel

Benedict de Spinoza

LETTER LIX. HUGO
BOXEL TO SPINOZA.

[A CONTINUATION OF the arguments in favour of ghosts, which may be summarized as follows: — I say a thing is done by chance, when it has not been the subject of will on the part of the doer; not when it might never have happened. — Necessity and freedom, not necessity and chance, are contraries. — If we do not in some sense attribute human qualities to God, what meaning can we attach to the term? — You ask for absolute proof of the existence of spirits; such proof is not obtainable for many things, which are yet firmly believed. — Some things are more beautiful intrinsically than others. — As God is a spirit, spirits resemble Him more than embodied creatures do. — A ghost cannot be conceived as clearly as a triangle: can you say that your own idea of God is as clear as your idea of a triangle? — As a circle exists without a sphere, so a sphere exists without a circle. — We call things higher or lower in proportion to their distance from the earth. — All the Stoics, Pythagoreans, and Platonists, Empedocles, Maximus Tyrius, Apuleius, and others, bear witness to ghosts; and no modern denies them. It is presumption to sneer at such a body of testimony. Cæsar did not ridicule ghosts, but omens, and if he had listened to Spurina he would not have been murdered.]

Benedict de Spinoza

1674

The Hague

Hugo Boxel

LETTER LX. SPINOZA TO HUGO BOXEL.

[SPINOZA AGAIN ANSWERS the argument in favour of ghosts. (The Hague, 1674).]

Dear Sir, —

I hasten to answer your letter, received yesterday, for if I delay my reply, I may have to put it off longer than I should like. The state of your health would have made me anxious, if I did not understand that you are better. I hope you are by this time quite well again.

The difficulties experienced by two people following different principles, and trying to agree on a matter, which depends on many other questions, might be shown from this discussion alone, if there were no reason to prove it by. Pray tell me, whether you have seen or read any philosophers, who hold that the world has been made by chance, taking chance in your sense, namely, that God had some design in making the world, and yet has not kept to the plan he had formed. I do not know, that such an idea has ever entered anyone's mind. I am likewise at a loss for the reasons, with which you want to make me believe, that chance and necessity are not contraries. As soon as I affirm that the three angles of a triangle are equal to two right angles necessarily, I deny that they are thus equal by chance. As soon as I affirm that heat is a necessary effect of fire, I deny that it is a chance effect. To say, that necessary and free are two contrary terms, seems to me no less absurd and repugnant to reason. For no one can deny, that God freely knows Himself and all else, yet all with one voice grant that God knows Himself necessarily. Hence, as it seems to me, you draw no distinction between constraint or force and necessity. Man's wishes to live, to love, &c., are not under constraint, but nevertheless are necessary; much more is it necessary, that God wishes to be, to know, and to act. If you will also reflect, that indifference is only another name for ignorance or doubt, and that a will always constant and determined in all things is a necessary property of the understanding, you will see that my words are in complete harmony with truth. If we affirm, that God might have been able not to wish a given event, or not to understand it, we attribute to God two different freedoms, one necessary, the other indifferent; consequently we shall conceive God's will as different from His essence and understanding, and shall thus fall from one absurdity into another.

The attention, which I asked for in my former letter, has not seemed to you necessary. This has been the reason why you have not directed your thoughts to the main issue, and have neglected a point which is very important.

Further, when you say that if I deny, that the operations of seeing, hearing, attending, wishing, &c., can be ascribed to God, or that they exist in Him in any eminent fashion, you do not know what sort of God mine is; I suspect that you believe there is no greater perfection than such as can be explained by the aforesaid attributes. I am not astonished; for I believe that, if a triangle could speak, it would say, in like manner, that God is eminently triangular, while a circle would say that the divine nature is eminently circular. Thus each would ascribe to God its own attributes, would assume itself to be like God, and look on everything else as ill-shaped.

The briefness of a letter and want of time do not allow me to enter into my opinion on the divine nature, or the questions you have propounded. Besides, suggesting difficulties is not the same as producing reasons. That we do many things in the world from conjecture is true, but that our reflections are based on conjecture is false. In practical life we are compelled to follow what is most probable; in speculative thought we are compelled to follow truth. A man would perish of hunger and thirst, if he refused to eat or drink, till he had obtained positive proof that food and drink would be good for him. But in philosophic reflection this is not so. On the contrary, we must take care not to admit as true anything, which is only probable. For when one falsity has been let in, infinite others follow.

Again, we cannot infer that because sciences of things divine and human are full of controversies and quarrels, therefore their whole subject-matter is uncertain; for there have been many persons so enamoured of contradiction, as to turn into ridicule geometrical axioms. Sextus Empiricus and other sceptics, whom you quote, declare, that it is false to say that a whole is greater than its part, and pass similar judgments on other axioms.

However, as I pass over and grant that in default of proof we must be content with probabilities, I say that a probable proof ought to be such that, though we may doubt about it, we cannot maintain its contrary; for that which can be contradicted resembles not truth but falsehood. For instance, if I say that Peter is alive, because I saw him yesterday in good health, this is a probability, in so far as no one can maintain the contrary; but if anyone says that he saw Peter yesterday in a swoon, and that he believed Peter to have departed this life to-day, he will make my statement seem false. That your conjecture about ghosts and spectres seems false, and not even probable, I have shown so clearly, that I can find nothing worthy of answer in your reply.

To your question, whether I have of God as clear an idea as I have of a triangle, I reply in the affirmative. But if you ask me, whether I have as clear a mental image of God as I have of a triangle, I reply in the negative. For we are not able to imagine God, though we can understand Him. You must also here observe, that I do not assert that I thoroughly know God, but that I understand some of His attributes, not all nor the greater part, and it is evident that my ignorance of very many does not hinder the knowledge I have of some. When I learned Euclid's Elements, I understood that the three angles of a triangle are equal to two right angles, and this property of a triangle I perceived clearly, though I might be ignorant of many others.

As regards spectres or ghosts, I have hitherto heard attributed to them no intelligible property: they seem like phantoms, which no one can understand. When you say that spectres, or ghosts, in these lower regions (I adopt your phraseology, though I know not why matter below should be inferior to matter above) consist in a very thin rarefied and subtle substance, you seem to me to be speaking of spiders' webs, air, or vapours. To say, that they are invisible, seems to me to be equivalent to saying that they do not exist, not to stating their nature; unless, perhaps, you wish to indicate, that they render themselves visible or invisible at will, and that the imagination, in these as in other impossibilities, will find a difficulty.

The authority of Plato, Aristotle, and Socrates, does not carry much weight with me. I should have been astonished, if you had brought forward Epicurus, Democritus, Lucretius, or any of the atomists, or upholders of the atomic theory. It is no wonder that persons, who have invented occult qualities, intentional species, substantial forms, and a thousand other trifles, should have also devised spectres and ghosts, and given credence to old wives' tales, in order to take away the reputation of

Democritus, whom they were so jealous of, that they burnt all the books which he had published amid so much eulogy. If you are inclined to believe such witnesses, what reason have you for denying the miracles of the Blessed Virgin, and all the Saints? These have been described by so many famous philosophers, theologians, and historians, that I could produce at least a hundred such authorities for every one of the former. But I have gone further, my dear Sir, than I intended: I do not desire to cause any further annoyance by doctrines which I know you will not grant. For the principles which you follow are far different from my own.

Van Volten

8th October, 1674

Benedict de Spinoza

LETTER LXI. * * * * TO SPINOZA.

[PHILOSOPHERS OFTEN DIFFER through using words in different senses. Thus in the question of free will Descartes means by free, constrained by no cause. You mean by the same, undetermined in a particular way by a cause. The question of free will is threefold: — I. Have we any power whatever over things external to us? II. Have we absolute power over the intentional movements of our own body? III. Have we free use of our reason? Both Descartes and yourself are right according to the terms employed by each (8th October, 1674).]

Benedict de Spinoza

October, 1674

The Hague

G. H. Schaller

LETTER LXII. SPINOZA TO * * * * * (THE HAGUE, OCTOBER, 1674).

[SPINOZA GIVES HIS opinions on liberty and necessity.]

Sir, —

Our friend, J. R. has sent me the letter which you have been kind enough to write to me, and also the judgment of your friend as to the opinions of Descartes and myself regarding free will. Both enclosures were very welcome to me. Though I am, at present, much occupied with other matters, not to mention my delicate health, your singular courtesy, or, to name the chief motive, your love of truth, impels me to satisfy your inquiries, as far as my poor abilities will permit. What your friend wishes to imply by his remark before he appeals to experience, I know not. What he adds, that when one of two disputants affirms something which the other denies, both may be right, is true, if he means that the two, though using the same terms, are thinking of different things. I once sent several examples of this to our friend J. R., and am now writing to tell him to communicate them to you.

I, therefore, pass on to that definition of liberty, which he says is my own; but I know not whence he has taken it. I say that a thing is free, which exists and acts solely by the necessity of its own nature. Thus also God understands Himself and all things freely, because it follows solely from the necessity of His nature, that He should understand all things. You see I do not place freedom in free decision, but in free necessity. However, let us descend to created things, which are all determined by external causes to exist and operate in a given determinate manner. In order that this may be clearly understood, let us conceive a very simple thing. For instance, a stone receives from the impulsion of an external cause, a certain quantity of motion, by virtue of which it continues to move after the impulsion given by the external cause has ceased. The permanence of the stone's motion is constrained, not necessary, because it must be defined by the impulsion of an external cause. What is true of the stone is true of any individual, however complicated its nature, or varied its functions, inasmuch as every individual thing is necessarily determined by some external cause to exist and operate in a fixed and determinate manner.

Further conceive, I beg, that a stone, while continuing in motion, should be capable of thinking and knowing, that it is endeavouring, as far as it can, to continue to move. Such a stone, being conscious merely of its own endeavour and not at all indifferent, would believe itself to be completely free, and would think that it continued in motion solely because of its own wish. This is that human freedom, which all boast that they possess, and which consists solely in the fact, that men are conscious of their own desire, but are ignorant of the causes whereby that desire has been determined. Thus an infant believes that it desires milk freely; an angry child thinks he wishes freely for vengeance, a timid child thinks he wishes freely to run away. Again, a drunken man thinks, that from the free decision of his mind he speaks words, which afterwards, when sober, he would like to have left unsaid. So the delirious, the garrulous, and others of the same sort think that they act from the free decision of their mind, not that they are carried away by impulse. As this misconception is innate in all men, it is not easily conquered. For, although experience abundantly shows, that men can do anything rather than check their desires, and that very often, when a prey to conflicting emotions, they see the better course and follow the worse, they yet believe themselves to be free; because in some cases their desire for a thing is slight, and can easily be overruled by the recollection of something else, which is frequently present in the mind.

I have thus, if I mistake not, sufficiently explained my opinion regarding free and constrained necessity, and also regarding so-called human freedom: from what I have said you will easily be able to reply to your friend's objections. For when he says, with Descartes, that he who is constrained by no external cause is free, if by being constrained he means acting against one's will, I grant that we are in some cases quite unrestrained, and in this respect possess free will. But if by constrained he means acting necessarily, although not against one's will (as I have explained above), I deny that we are in any instance free.

But your friend, on the contrary, asserts that we may employ our reason absolutely, that is, in complete freedom; and is, I think, a little too confident on the point. For who, he says, could deny, without contradicting his own consciousness, that I can think with my thoughts, that I wish or do not wish to write? I should like to know what consciousness he is talking of, over and above that which I have illustrated by the example of the stone.

As a matter of fact I, without, I hope, contradicting my consciousness, that is my reason and experience, and without cherishing ignorance and misconception, deny that I can by any absolute power of thought think, that I wish or do not wish to write. I appeal to the consciousness, which he has doubtless experienced, that in dreams he has not the power of thinking that he wishes, or does not wish to write; and that, when he dreams that he wishes to write, he has not the power not to dream that he wishes to write. I think he must also have experienced, that the mind is not always equally capable of thinking of the same object, but according as the body is more capable for the image of this or that object being excited in it, so is the mind more capable of thinking of the same object.

When he further adds, that the causes for his applying his mind to writing have led him, but not constrained him to write, he merely means (if he will look at the question impartially), that his disposition was then in a state, in which it could be easily acted on by causes, which would have been powerless under other circumstances, as for instance when he was under a violent emotion. That is, causes, which at other times would not have constrained him, have constrained him in this case, not to write against his will but necessarily to wish to write.

As for his statement, that if we were constrained by external causes, no one could acquire the habit of virtue, I know not what is his authority for saying, that firmness and constancy of disposition cannot arise from predestined necessity, but only from free will.

What he finally adds, that if this were granted, all wickedness would be excusable, I meet with the question, What then? Wicked men are not less to be feared, and are not less harmful, when they are wicked from necessity. However, on this point I would ask you to refer to my Principles of Cartesian Philosophy, Part II., chap. viii.

In a word, I should like your friend, who makes these objections, to tell me, how he reconciles the human virtue, which he says arises from the free decision of the mind, with God's pre-ordainment of the universe. If, with Descartes, he confesses his inability to do so, he is endeavouring to direct against me the weapon which has already pierced himself. But in vain. For if you examine my opinion attentively, you will see that it is quite consistent, &c.

E. W. von Tschirnhausen

5 Jan., 1675

Benedict de Spinoza

LETTER LXIII. * * * * TO SPINOZA.

[THE WRITER EXHORTS Spinoza to publish the treatises on Ethics and on the Improvement of the Understanding. — Remarks on the definition of motion. On the difference between a true and an adequate idea.]

Most excellent Sir, —

When shall we have your method of rightly directing the reason in the acquisition of unknown truths, and your general treatise on physics? I know you have already proceeded far with them. The first has already come to my knowledge, and the second I have become aware of from the Lemmas added to the second part of the Ethics; whereby many difficulties in physics are readily solved. If time and opportunity permit, I humbly beg from you a true definition of motion and its explanation; also to know how, seeing that extension in so far as it is conceived in itself is indivisible, immutable, &c., we can infer à priori, that there can arise so many varieties of it, and consequently the existence of figure in the particles of any given body, which are, nevertheless, in every body various, and distinct from the figures of the parts, which compose the reality of any other body. You have already, by word of mouth, pointed out to me a method, which you employ in the search for truths as yet unknown. I find this method to be very excellent, and at the same time very easy, in so far as I have formed an opinion on it, and I can assert that from this single discovery I have made great progress in mathematics. I wish therefore, that you would give me a true definition of an adequate, a true, a false, a fictitious, and a doubtful idea. I have been in search of the difference between a true and an adequate idea. Hitherto, however, I can ascertain nothing except after inquiring into a thing, and forming a certain concept or idea of it. I then (in order to elicit whether this true idea is also an adequate idea of its object) inquire, what is the cause of this idea or concept; when this is ascertained, I again ask, What is the cause of this prior concept? and so I go on always inquiring for the causes of the causes of ideas, until I find a cause of such a kind, that I can not find any cause for it, except that among all the ideas which I can command this alone exists. If, for instance, we inquire the true origin of our errors, Descartes will answer, that it consists in our giving assent to things not yet clearly perceived. But supposing this to be the true idea of the thing, I nevertheless shall not yet be able to determine all things necessary to be known concerning it, unless I have also an adequate idea of the thing in question; in order to obtain such, therefore, I inquire into the cause of this concept, how it happens that we give assent to things not clearly understood — and I answer, that it arises from defective knowledge. But here I cannot inquire further, and ask what is the cause, that we are ignorant of certain things; hence I see that I have detected an adequate idea of the origin of our errors. Here meanwhile I ask you, whether, seeing that many things expressed in infinite modes have an adequate idea of themselves, and that from every adequate idea all that can be known of its object can be inferred, though more readily from some ideas than others, whether, I say, this may be the means of knowing which idea is to be preferred? For instance, one adequate idea of a circle consists in the equality of its radii; another adequate idea consists in the infinite right angles equal to one another, made by the intersection of two lines, &c., and thus we have infinite expressions, each giving the adequate nature of a circle, Now, though all the properties of a circle may be inferred from every one of them, they may be deduced much more easily from some than from others. So also he, who considers lines applied to curves, will be able to draw many conclusions as to the measurement of curves, but will do so more readily from the consideration of tangents, &c. Thus I have wished to indicate how far I have progressed in this study; I await perfection in it, or, if I am wrong on any point, correction; also the definition I asked for. Farewell.

5 Jan., 1675.

Benedict de Spinoza

Jan., 1675

The Hague

E. W. von Tschirnhausen

LETTER LXIV. SPINOZA TO * * * * *.

[THE DIFFERENCE BETWEEN a true and an adequate idea is merely extrinsic, &c. The Hague, Jan., 1675.]

Honoured Sir. —

Between a true and an adequate idea, I recognize no difference, except that the epithet true only has regard to the agreement between the idea and its object, whereas the epithet adequate has regard to the nature of the idea in itself; so that in reality there is no difference between a true and an adequate idea beyond this extrinsic relation. However, in order that I may know, from which idea out of many all the properties of its object may be deduced, I pay attention to one point only, namely, that the idea or definition should express the efficient cause of its object. For instance, in inquiring into the properties of a circle, I ask, whether from the idea of a circle, that it consists of infinite right angles, I can deduce all its properties. I ask, I repeat, whether this idea involves the efficient cause of a circle. If it does not, I look for another, namely, that a circle is the space described by a line, of which one point is fixed, and the other movable. As this definition explains the efficient cause, I know that I can deduce from it all the properties of a circle. So, also, when I define God as a supremely perfect Being, then, since that definition does not express the efficient cause (I mean the efficient cause internal as well as external) I shall not be able to infer therefrom all the properties of God; as I can, when I define God as a Being, &c. (see Ethics, I. Def. vi.). As for your other inquiries, namely, that concerning motion, and those pertaining to method, my observations on them are not yet written out in due order, so I will reserve them for another occasion.

As regards your remark, that he "who considers lines applied to curves makes many deductions with regard to the measurement of curves, but does so with greater facility from the consideration of tangents," &c., I think that from the consideration of tangents many deductions will be made with more difficulty, than from the consideration of lines applied in succession; and I assert absolutely, that from certain properties of any particular thing (whatever idea be given) some things may be discovered more readily, others with more difficulty, though all are concerned with the nature of the thing. I think it need only be observed, that an idea should be sought for of such a kind, that all properties may be inferred, as has been said above. He, who is about to deduce all the properties of a particular thing, knows that the ultimate properties will necessarily be the most difficult to discover, &c.

G. H. Schaller

25 July, 1675

Amsterdam

Benedict de Spinoza

LETTER LXV. G. H. SCHALLER TO SPINOZA.

[SCHALLER ASKS FOR answers to four questions of his friend Tschirnhausen on the attributes of God, and mentions that Tschirnhausen has removed the unfavourable opinion of Spinoza lately conceived by Boyle and Oldenburg.]

Most distinguished and excellent Sir, —

I should blush for my silence, which has lasted so long, and has laid me open to the charge of ingratitude for your kindness extended to me beyond my merits, if I did not reflect that your generous courtesy inclines rather to excuse than to accuse, and also know that you devote your leisure, for the common good of your friends, to serious studies, which it would be harmful and injurious to disturb without due cause. For this reason I have been silent, and have meanwhile been content to hear from friends of your good health: I send you this letter to inform you, that our noble friend von Tschirnhausen is enjoying the same in England, and has three times in the letters he has sent me bidden me convey his kindest regards to the master, again bidding me request from you the solution of the following questions, and forward to him your hoped-for answer: would the master be pleased to convince him by positive proof, not by a reduction to the impossible, that we cannot know any attributes of God, save thought and extension? Further, whether it follows that creatures constituted under other attributes can form no idea of extension? If so, it would follow that there must be as many worlds as there are attributes of God. For instance, there would be as much room for extension in worlds affected by other attributes, as there actually exists of extension in our world. But as we perceive nothing save thought besides extension, so creatures in the other world would perceive nothing besides the attributes of that world and thought.

Secondly, as the understanding of God differs from our understanding as much in essence as in existence, it has, therefore, nothing in common with it; therefore (by Ethics, I. iii.) God's understanding cannot be the cause of our own.

Thirdly (in Ethics, I. x. note) you say, that nothing in nature is clearer than that every entity must be conceived under some attribute (this I thoroughly understand), and that the more it has of reality or being, the more attributes appertain to it. It seems to follow from this, that there are entities possessing three, four, or more attributes (though we gather from what has been demonstrated that every being consists only of two attributes, namely, a certain attribute of God and the idea of that attribute).

Fourthly, I should like to have examples of those things which are immediately produced by God, and those which are produced through the means of some infinite modification. Thought and extension seem to be of the former kind; understanding in thought and motion in extension seem to be of the latter.

And these are the points which our said friend von Tschirnhausen joins with me in wishing to have explained by your excellence, if perchance your spare time allows it. He further relates, that Mr. Boyle and Oldenburg had formed a strange idea of your personal character, but that he has not only removed it, but also given reasons, which have not only led them back to a most worthy and favourable opinion thereof, but also made them value most highly the Theologico-Political Treatise. Of this I have not ventured to inform you, because of your health. Be assured that I am, and live,

Most noble sir,

for every good office your most devoted servant,

G. H. Schaller.

Amsterdam,

25 July, 1675.

Mr. à Gent and J. Rieuwerts dutifully greet you.

Benedict de Spinoza

29 July, 1675

The Hague

E. W. von Tschirnhausen

LETTER LXVI. SPINOZA TO * * * * *.

SPINOZA ANSWERS BY references to the first three books of the Ethics.]

Dear Sir, —

I am glad that you have at last had occasion to refresh me with one of your letters, always most welcome to me. I heartily beg that you will frequently repeat the favour, &c.

I proceed to consider your doubts: to the first I answer, that the human mind can only acquire knowledge of those things which the idea of a body actually existing involves, or of what can be inferred from such an idea. For the power of anything is defined solely by its essence (Ethics, III. vii.); the essence of the mind (Ethics, II. xiii.) consists solely in this, that it is the idea of body actually existing; therefore the mind's power of understanding only extends to things, which this idea of body contains in itself, or which follow therefrom. Now this idea of body does not involve or express any of God's attributes, save extension and thought. For its object (ideatum), namely, body (by Ethics, II. vi.), has God for its cause, in so far as He is regarded under the attribute of extension, and not in so far as He is regarded under any other; therefore (Ethics, I. ax. vi.) this idea of the body involves the knowledge of God, only in so far as He is regarded under the attribute of extension. Further, this idea, in so far as it is a mode of thinking, has also (by the same proposition) God for its cause, in so far as He is regarded as a thinking thing, and not in so far as He is regarded under any other attribute. Hence (by the same axiom) the idea of this idea involves the knowledge of God, in so far as He is regarded under the attribute of thought, and not in so far as He is regarded under any attribute. It is therefore plain, that the human mind, or the idea of the human body neither involves nor expresses any attributes of God save these two. Now from these two attributes, or their modifications, no other attribute of God can (Ethics, I. x.) be inferred or conceived. I therefore conclude, that the human mind cannot attain knowledge of any attribute of God besides these, which is the proposition you inquire about. With regard to your question, whether there must be as many worlds as there are attributes, I refer you to Ethics II. vii. note.

Moreover this proposition might be proved more readily by a reduction to the absurd; I am accustomed, when the proposition is negative, to employ this mode of demonstration as more in character. However, as the question you ask is positive, I make use of the positive method, and ask, whether one thing can be produced from another, from which it differs both in essence and existence; for things which differ to this extent seem to have nothing in common. But since all particular things, except those which are produced from things similar to themselves, differ from their causes both in essence and existence, I see here no reason for doubt.

The sense in which I mean that God is the efficient cause of things, no less of their essence than of their existence, I think has been sufficiently explained in Ethics I. xxv. note and corollary. The axiom in the note to Ethics I. x., as I hinted at the end of the said note, is based on the idea which we have of a Being absolutely infinite, not on the fact, that there are or may be beings possessing three, four, or more attributes.

Lastly, the examples you ask for of the first kind are, in thought, absolutely infinite understanding; in extension, motion and rest; an example of the second kind is the sum of the whole extended universe (facies totius universi), which, though it varies in infinite modes, yet remains always the same. Cf. Ethics II. note to Lemma vii. before Prop. xiv.

Thus, most excellent Sir, I have answered, as I think, the objections of yourself and your friend. If you think any uncertainty remains, I hope you will not neglect to tell me, so that I may, if possible, remove it.

The Hague,

29 July, 1675.

E. W. von Tschirnhausen

12 Aug., 1675

London

Benedict de Spinoza

LETTER LXVII. * * * * TO SPINOZA.

[A FRESH INQUIRY as to whether there are two or more attributes of God.]

Distinguished Sir, —

I should like a demonstration of what you say: namely, that the soul cannot perceive any attributes of God, except extension and thought. Though this might appear evident to me, it seems possible that the contrary might be deduced from Ethics II. vii. note; perhaps because I do not rightly grasp the meaning of that passage. I have therefore resolved, distinguished Sir, to show you how I make the deduction, earnestly begging you to aid me with your usual courtesy, wherever I do not rightly represent your meaning. I reason as follows: — Though I gather that the universe is one, it is not less clear from the passage referred to, that it is expressed in infinite modes, and therefore that every individual thing is expressed in infinite modes. Hence it seems to follow, that the modification constituting my mind, and the modification constituting my body, though one and the same modification, is yet expressed in infinite ways — first, through thought; secondly, through extension; thirdly, through some attribute of God unknown to me, and so on to infinity, seeing that there are in God infinite attributes, and the order and connection of the modifications seem to be the same in all. Hence arises the question: Why the mind, which represents a certain modification, the same modification being expressed not only in extension, but in infinite other ways, — why, I repeat, does the mind perceive that modification only as expressed through extension, to wit, the human body, and not as expressed through any other attributes? Time does not allow me to pursue the subject further; perhaps my difficulties will be removed by further reflection.

London,

12 Aug., 1675.

Benedict de Spinoza

18 August, 1675

The Hague

E. W. von Tschirnhausen

LETTER LXVIII. SPINOZA TO * * * * *.

[IN THIS FRAGMENT of a letter Spinoza refers his friend to Ethics, I. x. and II. vii. note.]

Distinguished Sir, — . . . But in answer to your objection I say, that although each particular thing be expressed in infinite ways in the infinite understanding of God, yet those infinite ideas, whereby it is expressed, cannot constitute one and the same mind of a particular thing, but infinite minds; seeing that each of these infinite ideas has no connection with the rest, as I have explained in the same note to Ethics, II. vii., and as is also evident from I. x. If you will reflect on these passages a little, you will see that all difficulty vanishes, &c.

The Hague,

18 August, 1675.

G. H. Schaller

14 Nov., 1675

Amsterdam

Benedict de Spinoza

LETTER LXVIII.
A. G. H. SCHALLER TO SPINOZA.

[SCHALLER RELATES TO Spinoza Tschirnhausen's doings in France, and letter to him, and makes known to Spinoza the answers contained in that letter to Spinoza's objections in Letter LXVIII. and the request of Leibnitz to see Spinoza's unpublished writings.]

Amsterdam,

14 Nov., 1675.

Most learned and excellent Master, my most venerable Patron, —

I hope that you duly received my letter with— 's method, and likewise, that you are up to the present time in good health, as I am.

But for three months I had no letter from our friend von Tschirnhausen, whence I formed sad conjectures that he had made a fatal journey, when he left England for France. Now that I have received a letter, in my fulness of joy I felt bound, according to his request, to communicate it to the Master, and to let you know, with his most dutiful greeting, that he has arrived safely in Paris, and found there Mr. Huygens, as we had told him, and consequently has in every way sought to please him, and is thus highly esteemed by him. He mentioned, that the Master had recommended to him Huygens's conversation, and made very much of him personally. This greatly pleased Huygens; so he answered that he likewise greatly esteemed you personally, and he has now received from you a copy of the Theologico-Political Treatise, which is esteemed by many there, and it is eagerly inquired, whether there are extant any more of the same writer's works. To this Mr. von Tschirnhausen replied that he knew of none but the Demonstrations in the first and second parts of the Cartesian Principles. But he mentioned nothing about the Master, but what I have said, and so he hopes that he has not displeased you herein.

* * * * *

To the objection that you last made he replies, that those few words which I wrote at the Master's dictation, explained to him your meaning more thoroughly, and that he has favourably entertained the said reasonings (for by these two methods they best admit of explanation). But two reasons have obliged him to continue in the opinion implied in his recent objection. Of these the first is, that otherwise there appears to be a contradiction between the fifth and seventh propositions of the second book. For in the former of these it is laid down, that the objects of ideas are the efficient causes of the ideas, which yet seems to be refuted by the quotation, in the proof of the latter, of the fourth axiom of Part I. "Or, as I rather think, I do not make the right application of this axiom according to the author's intention, which I would most willingly be told by him, if his leisure permits it. The second cause which prevented me from following the explanation he gives was, that thereby the attribute of thought is pronounced to extend much more widely than other attributes. But since every one of the attributes contributes to make up the essence of God, I do not quite see how this fact does not contradict the opinion just stated. I will say just this more, that if I may judge the minds of others by my own, there will be great difficulty in understanding the seventh and eighth propositions of Book II., and this for no other reason than that the author has been pleased (doubtless because they seemed so plain to him) to accompany the demonstrations annexed to them with such short and laconic explanations."

He further mentions, that he has found at Paris a man called Leibnitz, remarkably learned, and most skilled in various sciences, as also free from the vulgar prejudices of theology. With him he has formed an intimate acquaintance, founded on the fact that Leibnitz labours with him to pursue the perfection of the intellect, and, in fact, reckons nothing better or more useful. Von Tschirnhausen says, that he is most practised in ethics, and speaks without any stimulus of the passions by the sole dictate of reason. He adds, that he is most skilled in physics, and also in metaphysical studies concerning God and the soul. Finally, he concludes that he is most worthy of having communicated to him the Master's writings, if you will first give your permission, for he believes that the author will thence gain a great advantage, as he promises to show at length, if the Master be so pleased. But if not, do not doubt, in the least, that he will honourably keep them concealed as he has promised, as in fact he has not made the slightest mention of them. Leibnitz also highly values the Theologico-Political Treatise, on the subject of which he once wrote the Master a letter, if he is not mistaken. And therefore I would beg my Master, that, unless there is some reason against him, you will not refuse your permission in accordance with your gracious kindness, but will, if possible, open your mind to me, as soon as may be, for after receiving your answers I shall be able to reply to our friend von Tschirnhausen, which I would gladly do on Tuesday evening, unless important hindrances cause my Master to delay.

Mr. Bresser, on his return from Cleves, has sent here a large quantity of the beer of that country; I suggested to him that he should make a present to the Master of half a tun, which he promised to do, and added a most friendly greeting.

Finally, excuse my unpractised style and hurried writing, and give me your orders, that I may have a real occasion of proving myself, most excellent Sir,

Your most ready servant,

G. H. Schaller.

Benedict de Spinoza

18 Nov., 1675

The Hague

G. H. Schaller

LETTER LXVIII.B.
SPINOZA TO SCHALLER.

[SPINOZA ANSWERS ALL the points in Schaller's letter, and hesitates to entrust his writings to Leibnitz.]

Most experienced Sir, and valued Friend, —

I was much pleased to learn from your letter, received to-day, that you are well, and that our friend von Tschirnhausen has happily accomplished his journey to France. In the conversation which he had about me with Mr. Huygens, he behaved, at least in my opinion, very judiciously; and besides, I am very glad that he has found so convenient an opportunity for the purpose which he intended. But what it is he has found in the fourth axiom of Part I. that seems to contradict Proposition v. of Part II. I do not see. For in that proposition it is affirmed, that the essence of every idea has for its cause God, in so far as He is considered as a thinking thing; but in that axiom, that the knowledge or idea of a cause depends on the knowledge or idea of an effect. But, to tell the truth, I do not quite follow, in this matter, the meaning of your letter, and suspect that either in it, or in his copy of the book, there is a slip of the pen. For you write, that it is affirmed in Proposition v. that the objects of ideas are the efficient causes of the ideas, whereas this is exactly what is expressly denied in that proposition, and I now think that this is the cause of the whole confusion. Accordingly it would be useless for me at present to try to write at greater length on this subject, but I must wait, till you explain to me his mind more clearly, and till I know whether he has a correct copy. I believe that I have an epistolary acquaintance with the Leibnitz he mentions. But why he, who was a counsellor at Frankfort, has gone to France, I do not know. As far as I could conjecture from his letters, he seemed to me a man of liberal mind, and versed in every science. But yet I think it imprudent so soon to entrust my writings to him. I should like first to know what is his business in France, and the judgment of our friend von Tschirnhausen, when he has been longer in his company, and knows his character more intimately. However, greet that friend of ours in my name, and let him command me what he pleases, if in anything I can be of service to him, and he will find me most ready to obey him in everything.

I congratulate my most worthy friend Mr. Bresser on his arrival or return, and also thank him heartily for the promised beer, and will requite him, too, in any way that I can. Lastly, I have not yet tried to find out your relation's method, nor do I think that I shall be able to apply my mind to trying it. For the more I think over the thing in itself, the more I am persuaded that you have not made gold, but had not sufficiently eliminated that which was hidden in the antimony. But more of this another time: at present I am prevented by want of leisure. In the meanwhile, if in anything I can assist you, you will always find me, most excellent Sir, your friend and devoted servant,

B. de Spinoza.

The Hague,

18 Nov., 1675.

E. W. von Tschirnhausen

2 May, 1676

Benedict de Spinoza

LETTER LXIX. * * * * TO SPINOZA.

[THE WRITER ASKS for explanations of some passages in the letter about the infinite .]

Distinguished Sir, —

In the first place I can with great difficulty conceive, how it can be proved, à priori, that bodies exist having motion and figure, seeing that, in extension considered absolutely in itself, nothing of the kind is met with. Secondly, I should like to learn from you, how this passage in your letter on the infinite is to be understood:— "They do not hence infer that such things elude number by the multitude of their component parts." For, as a matter of fact, all mathematicians seem to me always to demonstrate, with regard to such infinities, that the number of the parts is so great, as to elude all expression in terms of number. And in the example you give of the two circles, you do not appear to prove this statement, which was yet what you had undertaken to do. For in this second passage you only show, that they do not draw this conclusion from "the excessive size of the intervening space," or from the fact that "we do not know the maximum and the minimum of the said space;" but you do not demonstrate, as you intended, that the conclusion is not based on the multitude of parts, &c.

2 May, 1676.

Benedict de Spinoza

5 May, 1676

The Hague

E. W. von Tschirnhausen

LETTER LXX. SPINOZA TO * * * * *

[SPINOZA EXPLAINS HIS view of the infinite.]

Distinguished Sir, —

My statement concerning the infinite, that an infinity of parts cannot be inferred from a multitude of parts, is plain when we consider that, if such a conclusion could be drawn from a multitude of parts, we should not be able to imagine a greater multitude of parts; the first-named multitude, whatever it was, would have to be the greater, which is contrary to fact. For in the whole space between two non-concentric circles we conceive a greater multitude of parts than in half that space, yet the number of parts in the half, as in the whole of the space, exceeds any assignable number. Again, from extension, as Descartes conceives it, to wit, a quiescent mass, it is not only difficult, as you say, but absolutely impossible to prove the existence of bodies. For matter at rest, as it is in itself, will continue at rest, and will only be determined to motion by some more powerful external cause; for this reason I have not hesitated on a former occasion to affirm, that the Cartesian principles of natural things are useless, not to say absurd.

The Hague,

5 May, 1676.

E. W. von Tschirnhausen

23 June, 1676

Paris

Benedict de Spinoza

LETTER LXXI. * * * * TO SPINOZA.

[HOW CAN THE variety of the universe be shown à priori from the Spinozistic conception of extension?]

Most learned Sir, —

I wish you would gratify me in this matter by pointing out how, from the conception of extension, as you give it, the variety of the universe can be shown à priori. You recall the opinion of Descartes, wherein he asserts, that this variety can only be deduced from extension, by supposing that, when motion was started by God, it caused this effect in extension. Now it appears to me, that he does not deduce the existence of bodies from matter at rest, unless, perhaps, you count as nothing the assumption of God as a motive power; you have not shown how such an effect must, à priori, necessarily follow from the nature of God. A difficulty which Descartes professed himself unable to solve as being beyond human understanding. I therefore ask you the question, knowing that you have other thoughts on the matter, unless perhaps there be some weighty cause for your unwillingness hitherto to disclose your opinion. If this, as I suppose, be not expedient, give me some hint of your meaning. You may rest assured, that whether you speak openly with me, or whether you employ reserve, my regard for you will remain unchanged.

My special reasons for making the requests are as follows: — I have always observed in mathematics, that from a given thing considered in itself, that is, from the definition of a given thing, we can only deduce a single property; if, however, we require to find several properties, we are obliged to place the thing defined in relation to other things. Then from the conjunction of the definitions of these things new properties result. For instance, if I regard the circumference of a circle by itself, I can only infer that it is everywhere alike or uniform, in which property it differs essentially from all other curves; I shall never be able to infer any other properties. But if I place it in relation with other things, such as the radii drawn from the centre, two intersecting lines, or many others, I shall be able hence to deduce many properties; this seems to be in opposition to Prop. xvi. of your Ethics, almost the principal proposition of the first book of your treatise. For it is there assumed as known, that from the given definition of anything several properties can be deduced. This seems to me impossible, unless we bring the thing defined into relation with other things; and further, I am for this reason unable to see, how from any attribute regarded singly, for instance, infinite extension, a variety of bodies can result; if you think that this conclusion cannot be drawn from one attribute considered by itself, but from all taken together, I should like to be instructed by you on the point, and shown how it should be conceived. — Farewell, &c.

Paris,

23 June, 1676.

Benedict de Spinoza

15 July, 1676

The Hague

E. W. von Tschirnhausen

LETTER LXXII. SPINOZA TO * * * *

[SPINOZA GIVES THE required explanation. Mentions the treatise of Huet, &c.]

Distinguished Sir, —

With regard to your question as to whether the variety of the universe can be deduced à priori from the conception of extension only, I believe I have shown clearly enough already that it cannot; and that, therefore, matter has been ill-defined by Descartes as extension; it must necessarily be explained through an attribute, which expresses eternal and infinite essence. But perhaps, some day, if my life be prolonged, I may discuss the subject with you more clearly. For hitherto I have not been able to put any of these matters into due order.

As to what you add; namely, that from the definition of a given thing considered in itself we can only deduce a single property, this is, perhaps, true in the case of very simple things (among which I count figures), but not in realities. For, from the fact alone, that I define God as a Being to whose essence belongs existence, I infer several of His properties; namely, that He necessarily exists, that He is One, unchangeable, infinite, &c. I could adduce several other examples, which, for the present, I pass over.

In conclusion, I ask you to inquire, whether Huet's treatise (against the "Tractatus Theologico-Politicus") about which I wrote to you before, has yet been published, and whether you could send me a copy. Also, whether you yet know, what are the new discoveries about refraction. And so farewell, dear Sir, and continue to regard yours, &c.

The Hague,

15 July, 1676.

Albert Burgh

Sept. 3, 1675

Florence

Benedict de Spinoza

LETTER LXXIII.
ALBERT BURGH TO SPINOZA.

[ALBERT BURGH ANNOUNCES his reception into the Romish Church, and exhorts Spinoza to follow his example.]

I promised to write to you on leaving my country, if anything noteworthy occurred on the journey. I take the opportunity which offers of an event of the utmost importance, to redeem my engagement, by informing you that I have, by God's infinite mercy, been received into the Catholic Church and made a member of the same. You may learn the particulars of the step from a letter which I have sent to the distinguished and accomplished Professor Craanen of Leyden. I will here subjoin a few remarks for your special benefit.

Even as formerly I admired you for the subtlety and keenness of your natural gifts, so now do I bewail and deplore you; inasmuch as being by nature most talented, and adorned by God with extraordinary gifts; being a lover, nay a coveter of the truth, you yet allow yourself to be ensnared and deceived by that most wretched and most proud of beings, the prince of evil spirits. As for all your philosophy, what is it but a mere illusion and chimera? Yet to it you entrust not only your peace of mind in this life, but the salvation of your soul for eternity. See on what a wretched foundation all your doctrines rest. You assume that you have at length discovered the true philosophy. How do you know that your philosophy is the best of all that ever have been taught in the world, are now being taught, or ever shall be taught? Passing over what may be devised in the future, have you examined all the philosophies, ancient as well as modern, which are taught here, and in India, and everywhere throughout the whole world? Even if you have duly examined them, how do you know that you have chosen the best? You will say: "My philosophy is in harmony with right reason; other philosophies are not." But all other philosophers except your own followers disagree with you, and with equal right say of their philosophy what you say of yours, accusing you, as you do them, of falsity and error. It is, therefore, plain, that before the truth of your philosophy can come to light, reasons must be advanced, which are not common to other philosophies, but apply solely to your own; or else you must admit that your philosophy is as uncertain and nugatory as the rest.

However, restricting myself for the present to that book of yours with an impious title, and mingling your philosophy with your theology, as in reality you mingle them yourself, though with diabolic cunning you endeavour to maintain, that each is separate from the other, and has different principles, I thus proceed.

Perhaps you will say: "Others have not read Holy Scripture so often as I have; and it is from Holy Scripture, the acknowledgment of which distinguishes Christians from the rest of the world, that I prove my doctrines. But how? By comparing the clear passages with the more obscure I explain Holy Scripture, and out of my interpretations I frame dogmas, or else confirm those which are already concocted in my brain." But, I adjure you, reflect seriously on what you say. How do you know, that you have made a right application of your method, or again that your method is sufficient for the interpretation of Scripture, and that you are thus interpreting Scripture aright, especially as the Catholics say, and most truly, that the universal Word of God is not handed down to us in writing, hence that Holy Scripture cannot be explained through itself, I will not say by one man, but by the Church herself, who is the sole authorized interpreter? The Apostolic traditions must likewise be consulted, as is proved by the testimony of Holy Scripture and the Holy Fathers, and as reason and experience suggest. Thus, as your first principles are most false and lead to destruction, what will become of all your doctrine, built up and supported on so rotten a foundation?

Wherefore, if you believe in Christ crucified, acknowledge your pestilent heresy, reflect on the perverseness of your nature, and be reconciled with the Church.

How do your proofs differ from those of all heretics, who ever have left, are now leaving, or shall in future leave God's Church? All, like yourself, make use of the same principle, to wit, Holy Scripture taken by itself, for the concoction and establishment of their doctrines.

Do not flatter yourself with the thought, that neither the Calvinists, it may be, nor the so-called Reformed Church, nor the Lutherans, nor the Mennonites, nor the Socinians, &c., can refute your doctrines. All these, as I have said, are as wretched as yourself, and like you are dwelling in the shadow of death.

If you do not believe in Christ, you are more wretched than I can express. Yet the remedy is easy. Turn away from your sins, and consider the deadly arrogance of your wretched and insane reasoning. You do not believe in Christ. Why? You will say: "Because the teaching and the life of Christ, and also the Christian teaching concerning Christ are not at all in harmony with my teaching." But again, I say, then you dare to think yourself greater than all those who have ever risen up in the State or Church of God, patriarchs, prophets, apostles, martyrs, doctors, confessors, and holy virgins innumerable, yea, in your blasphemy, than Christ himself. Do you alone surpass all these in doctrine, in manner of life, in every respect? Will you, wretched pigmy, vile worm of the earth, yea, ashes, food of worms, will you in your unspeakable blasphemy, dare to put yourself before the incarnate, infinite wisdom of the Eternal Father? Will you, alone, consider yourself wiser and greater than all those, who from the beginning of the world have been in the Church of God, and have believed, or believe still, that Christ would come or has already come? On what do you base this rash, insane, deplorable, and inexcusable arrogance?

* * * * *

If you cannot pronounce on what I have just been enumerating (divining rods, alchemy, &c.), why, wretched man, are you so puffed up with diabolical pride, as to pass rash judgment on the awful mysteries of Christ's life and passion, which the Catholics themselves in their teaching declare to be incomprehensible? Why do you commit the further insanity of silly and futile carping at the numberless miracles and signs, which have been wrought through the virtue of Almighty God by the apostles and disciples of Christ, and afterwards by so many thousand saints, in testimony to, and confirmation of the truth of the Catholic faith; yea, which are being wrought in our own time in cases without number throughout the world, by God's almighty goodness and mercy? If you cannot gainsay these, and surely you cannot, why stand aloof any longer? Join hands of fellowship, and repent from your sins: put on humility, and be born again.

[Albert Burgh requests Spinoza to consider: (i.) The large number of believers in the Romish faith. (ii.) The uninterrupted succession of the Church. (iii.) The fact that a few unlearned men converted the world to Christianity. (iv.) The antiquity, the immutability, the infallibility, the incorruption, the unity, and the vast extent of the Catholic Religion; also the fact, that secession from it involves damnation, and that it will itself endure as long as the world. (v.) The admirable organization of the Romish Church. (vi.) The superior morality of Catholics. (vii.) The frequent cases of recantation of opinions among heretics. (viii.) The miserable life led by atheists, whatever their outward demeanour may be.] * * * *

I have written this letter to you with intentions truly Christian; first, in order to show the love I bear to you, though you are a heathen; secondly, in order to beg you not to persist in converting others.

I therefore will thus conclude: God is willing to snatch your soul from eternal damnation, if you will allow Him. Do not doubt that the Master, who has called you so often through others, is now calling you for the last time through me, who having obtained grace from the ineffable mercy of God Himself, beg the same for you with my whole heart. Do not deny me. For if you do not now give ear to God who calls you, the wrath of the Lord will be kindled against you, and there is a danger of your being abandoned by His infinite mercy, and becoming a wretched victim of the Divine Justice which consumes all things in wrath. Such a fate may Almighty God avert for the greater glory of His name, and for the salvation of your soul, also for a salutary example for the imitation of your most unfortunate and idolatrous followers, through our Lord and Saviour Jesus Christ, Who with the Eternal Father liveth and reigneth in the Unity of the Holy Spirit, God for all Eternity. Amen.

Florence, III. Non. Sept. CIOIOCLXXV. (Sept. 3, 1675.)

Benedict de Spinoza

1675

The Hague

Albert Burgh

LETTER LXXIV.
SPINOZA TO ALBERT BURGH.

[SPINOZA LAMENTS THE step taken by his pupil, and answers his arguments. The Hague, end of 1675.]

That, which I could scarcely believe when told me by others, I learn at last from your own letter; not only have you been made a member of the Romish Church, but you are become a very keen champion of the same, and have already learned wantonly to insult and rail against your opponents.

At first I resolved to leave your letter unanswered, thinking that time and experience will assuredly be of more avail than reasoning, to restore you to yourself and your friends; not to mention other arguments, which won your approval formerly, when we were discussing the case of Steno, in whose steps you are now following. But some of my friends, who like myself had formed great hopes from your superior talents, strenuously urge me not to fail in the offices of a friend, but to consider what you lately were, rather than what you are, with other arguments of the like nature. I have thus been induced to write you this short reply, which I earnestly beg you will think worthy of calm perusal.

I will not imitate those adversaries of Romanism, who would set forth the vices of priests and popes with a view to kindling your aversion. Such considerations are often put forward from evil and unworthy motives, and tend rather to irritate than to instruct. I will even admit, that more men of learning and of blameless life are found in the Romish Church than in any other Christian body; for, as it contains more members, so will every type of character be more largely represented in it. You cannot possibly deny, unless you have lost your memory as well as your reason, that in every Church there are thoroughly honourable men, who worship God with justice and charity. We have known many such among the Lutherans, the Reformed Church, the Mennonites, and the Enthusiasts. Not to go further, you knew your own relations, who in the time of the Duke of Alva suffered every kind of torture bravely and willingly for the sake of their religion. In fact, you must admit, that personal holiness is not peculiar to the Romish Church, but common to all Churches.

As it is by this, that we know "that we dwell in God and He in us" (1 Ep. John, iv. 13), it follows, that what distinguishes the Romish Church from others must be something entirely superfluous, and therefore founded solely on superstition. For, as John says, justice and charity are the one sure sign of the true Catholic faith, and the true fruits of the Holy Spirit. Wherever they are found, there in truth is Christ; wherever they are absent, Christ is absent also. For only by the Spirit of Christ can we be led to the love of justice and charity. Had you been willing to reflect on these points, you would not have ruined yourself, nor have brought deep affliction on your relations, who are now sorrowfully bewailing your evil case.

But I return to your letter, which you begin, by lamenting that I allow myself to be ensnared by the prince of evil spirits. Pray take heart, and recollect yourself. When you had the use of your faculties, you were wont, if I mistake not, to worship an Infinite God, by Whose efficacy all things absolutely come to pass and are preserved; now you dream of a prince, God's enemy, who against God's will ensnares and deceives very many men (rarely good ones, to be sure), whom God thereupon hands over to this master of wickedness to be tortured eternally. The

Divine justice therefore allows the devil to deceive men and remain unpunished; but it by no means allows to remain unpunished the men, who have been by that self-same devil miserably deceived and ensnared.

These absurdities might so far be tolerated, if you worshipped a God infinite and eternal; not one whom Chastillon, in the town which the Dutch call Tienen, gave with impunity to horses to be eaten. And, poor wretch, you bewail me? My philosophy, which you never beheld, you style a chimera? O youth deprived of understanding, who has bewitched you into believing, that the Supreme and Eternal is eaten by you, and held in your intestines?

Yet you seem to wish to employ reason, and ask me, "How I know that my philosophy is the best among all that have ever been taught in the world, or are being taught, or ever will be taught?" a question which I might with much greater right ask you; for I do not presume that I have found the best philosophy, I know that I understand the true philosophy. If you ask in what way I know it, I answer: In the same way as you know that the three angles of a triangle are equal to two right angles: that this is sufficient, will be denied by no one whose brain is sound, and who does not go dreaming of evil spirits inspiring us with false ideas like the true. For the truth is the index of itself and of what is false.

But you, who presume that you have at last found the best religion, or rather the best men, on whom you have pinned your credulity, you, "who know that they are the best among all who have taught, do now teach, or shall in future teach other religions. Have you examined all religions, ancient as well as modern, taught here and in India and everywhere throughout the world? And, if you have duly examined them, how do you know that you have chosen the best" since you can give no reason for the faith that is in you? But you will say, that you acquiesce in the inward testimony of the Spirit of God, while the rest of mankind are ensnared and deceived by the prince of evil spirits. But all those outside the pale of the Romish Church can with equal right proclaim of their own creed what you proclaim of yours.

As to what you add of the common consent of myriads of men and the uninterrupted ecclesiastical succession, this is the very catch-word of the Pharisees. They with no less confidence than the devotees of Rome bring forward their myriad witnesses, who as pertinaciously as the Roman witnesses repeat what they have heard, as though it were their personal experience. Further, they carry back their line to Adam. They boast with equal arrogance, that their Church has continued to this day unmoved and unimpaired in spite of the hatred of Christians and heathen. They more than any other sect are supported by antiquity. They exclaim with one voice, that they have received their traditions from God Himself, and that they alone preserve the Word of God both written and unwritten. That all heresies have issued from them, and that they have remained constant through thousands of years under no constraint of temporal dominion, but by the sole efficacy of their superstition, no one can deny. The miracles they tell of would tire a thousand tongues. But their chief boast is, that they count a far greater number of martyrs than any other nation, a number which is daily increased by those who suffer with singular constancy for the faith they profess; nor is their boasting false. I myself knew among others of a certain Judah called the faithful, who in the midst of the flames, when he was already thought to be dead, lifted his voice to sing the hymn beginning, "To Thee, O God, I offer up my soul," and so singing perished.

The organization of the Roman Church, which you so greatly praise, I confess to be politic, and to many lucrative. I should believe that there was no other more convenient for deceiving the people and keeping men's minds in check, if it were not for the organization of the Mahometan Church, which far surpasses it. For from the time when this superstition arose, there has been no schism in its church.

If, therefore, you had rightly judged, you would have seen that only your third point tells in favour of the Christians, namely, that unlearned and common men should have been able to convert nearly the whole world to a belief in Christ. But this reason militates not only for the Romish Church, but for all those who profess the name of Christ.

But assume that all the reasons you bring forward tell in favour solely of the Romish Church. Do you think that you can thereby prove mathematically the authority of that Church? As the case is far otherwise, why do you wish me to believe that my demonstrations are inspired by the prince of evil spirits, while your own are inspired by God, especially as I see, and as your letter clearly shows, that you have been led to become a devotee of this Church not by your love of God, but by your fear of hell, the single cause of superstition? Is this your humility, that you trust nothing to yourself, but everything to others, who are condemned by many of their fellow men? Do you set it down to pride and arrogance, that I employ reason and acquiesce in this true Word of God, which is in the mind and can never be depraved or corrupted? Cast away this deadly superstition, acknowledge the reason which God has given you, and follow that, unless you would be numbered with the brutes. Cease, I say, to call ridiculous errors mysteries, and do not basely confound those things which are unknown to us, or have not yet been discovered, with what is proved to be absurd, like the horrible secrets of this Church of yours, which, in proportion as they are repugnant to right reason, you believe to transcend the understanding.

But the fundamental principle of the "Tractatus Theologico-Politicus," that Scripture should only be expounded through Scripture, which you so wantonly without any reason proclaim to be false, is not merely assumed, but categorically proved to be true or sound; especially in chapter vii., where also the opinions of adversaries are confuted; see also what is proved at the end of chapter xv. If you will reflect on these things, and also examine the history of the Church (of which I see you are completely ignorant), in order to see how false, in many respects, is Papal tradition, and by what course of events and with what cunning the Pope of Rome six hundred years after Christ obtained supremacy over the Church, I do not doubt that you will eventually return to your senses. That this result may come to pass I, for your sake, heartily wish. Farewell, &c.

Benedict de Spinoza

Utrecht

Lambert van Velthuysen

LETTER LXXV. SPINOZA TO LAMBERT VAN VELTHUYSEN (DOCTOR OF MEDICINE AT UTRECHT.)

[OF THE PROPOSED annotation of the "Tractatus Theologico-Politicus."

Most excellent and distinguished Sir, —

I wonder at our friend Neustadt having said, that I am meditating the refutation of the various writings circulated against my book, and that among the works for me to refute he places your MS. For I certainly have never entertained the intention of refuting any of my adversaries: they all seem to me utterly unworthy of being answered. I do not remember to have said to Mr. Neustadt anything more, than that I proposed to illustrate some of the obscurer passages in the treatise with notes, and that I should add to these your MS., and my answer, if your consent could be gained, on which last point I begged him to speak to you, adding, that if you refused permission on the ground, that some of the observations in my answer were too harshly put, you should be given full power to modify or expunge them. In the meanwhile, I am by no means angry with Mr. Neustadt, but I wanted to put the matter before you as it stands, that if your permission be not granted, I might show you that I have no wish to publish your MS. against your will. Though I think it might be issued without endangering your reputation, if it appears without your name, I will take no steps in the matter, unless you give me leave. But, to tell the truth, you would do me a far greater kindness, if you would put in writing the arguments with which you think you can impugn my treatise, and add them to your MS. I most earnestly beg you to do this. For there is no one whose arguments I would more willingly consider; knowing, as I do, that you are bound solely by your zeal for truth, and that your mind is singularly candid, I therefore beg you again and again, not to shrink from undertaking this task, and to believe me, Yours most obediently,

B. de Spinoza.